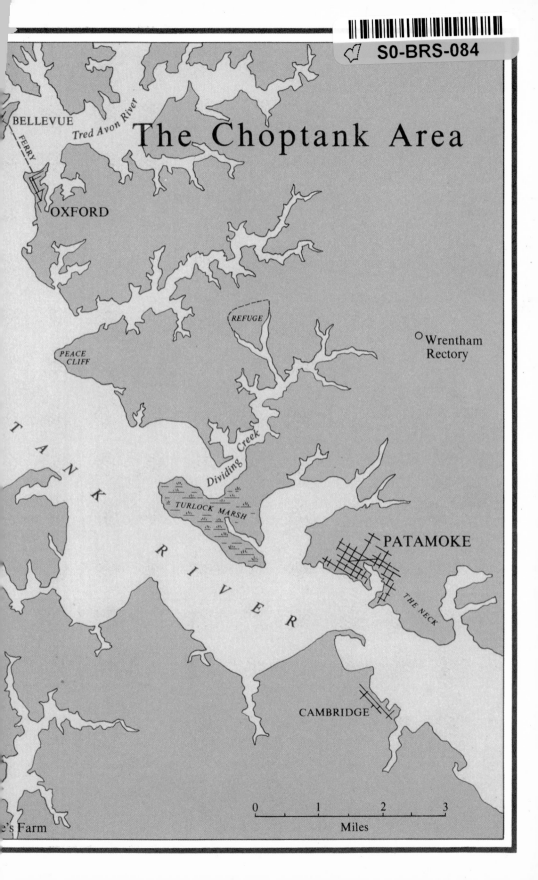

The Choptank Area

BELLEVUE

Tred Avon River

FERRY

OXFORD

REFUGE

○ Wrentham
Rectory

PEACE
CLIFF

TANK

Dividing Creek

TURLOCK MARSH

R I V E R

PATAMOKE

THE NECK

CAMBRIDGE

0   1   2   3

Miles

e's Farm

CHESAPEAKE

CHESAPEAKE

James A. Michener

 Random House *New York*

Library of Congress Cataloging in Publication Data

I. Eastern Shore, Md.—History—Fiction. I. Title.
PZ3.M583Ch   [PS3525.I19]   813'.5'4   78–2892
ISBN 0–394–50079–2
ISBN 0–394–50202–7 lim. ed.
ISBN 0–394–50312–0 deluxe ed.

Manufactured in the United States of America

Designed by Carole Lowenstein

Acknowledgments

I first sailed upon the Chesapeake in 1927 and was a frequent passenger thereafter. From my earliest days on the bay I considered writing about it, but always postponed beginning until such time as I could live along its shores for some extended period. This opportunity came in 1975, when I lived near a small but historic fishing village for two years. During that time I met and worked with the many learned people whose ideas infuse this novel, and I should like here to give them the thanks they so richly earned.

The Chesapeake Bay: Walter Robinson of Swarthmore first took me boating and instilled in me his love of the area. Judge William O'Donnell of Phoenixville allowed me to crew his *Prince of Donegal* scores of times, and Larry Therien helped me to explore. Pearce Coady took me on his *Cleopatra's Barge* to parts of the bay.

The Choptank River: Lawrence McCormick and Richard Springs took me on small-boat excursions to the headwaters of the river. Edward J. Piszek arranged for helicopter explorations at low level. Judge O'Donnell sailed me to all parts of the river, as did Joseph A. Robinson.

Skipjacks: Three captains helped enormously. G.S. Pope, now retired, told me of the old days. Josef Liener instructed me as we sailed the *Rosie Parks,* and Eddie Farley took me out for long hours of oyster dredging on his *Stanley Norman.* I was also allowed to inspect various old boats as they stood on blocks.

Oysters: George Krantz of the University of Maryland's Center for Estuarine Studies shared with me his research findings, and Robert Inglis kept me informed as to his progress in growing oysters in the creek which formed his front yard. Levin Harrison told me casually of the rough old days.

Geese: Ron Vavra, twin brother of the man who provided the photographs for my book *Iberia,* introduced me to the basic research on the Canada goose, and dozens of hunters helped me understand its habits. William H. Julian, Manager of the Blackwater National Wild Life Refuge, showed me his 60,000 geese and was unfailingly helpful.

Herons and ospreys: After I had done a good deal of field work on these enchanting water birds, I had the good luck to meet up with Jan Reese, a leading expert on both species, and he gave me advanced instruction on aspects I had not contemplated.

Big guns: Dr. Harry Walsh, the principal authority, showed me his collection, talked of the old days, and helped me to understand the functioning and mystique of these one-man cannons.

Trees: Stark McLaughlin, Project Forester, State of Maryland, gave much useful advice concerning various aspects of tree growth and culture.

Choptank life: Captain Bill Benson, of the nation's oldest ferry route, provided invaluable reminiscences. Ambassador Philip Crowe was most helpful in telling of recent developments. And Alyce Stocklin, a friend of many years, was hilarious as a constant commentator. H. Robins Hollyday was generous both with his time and his store of old photographs, and Peter Black was helpful in diverse ways.

Black history: Dickson Preston generously shared with me his remarkable discoveries relating to Frederick Douglass; these lend authority to my treatment of slavery in the area. He also read the complete manuscript and made valuable suggestions on historical details. My friend Dorothy Pittman convened some of her black neighbors to talk with me, particularly James Thomas and LeRoy Nichols. Judge William B. Yates provided sober and ecumenical reflections on the days of trouble.

Although for dramatic reasons the action of this novel takes place on the northern shore of the Choptank, much of my most effective research was conducted on the south bank, for which I have a special affection, and I am deeply indebted to the experts of that region. Bayly Orem, of a distinguished Dorchester family, met me on a dove shoot and took it upon himself to introduce me to his neighbors who might prove helpful:

Boat building: James Richardson, famous for his reconstructions of historic boats, was constantly instructive, as were his sons-in-law, Tom Howell and James D. Brighton.

Turkling: State Senator Frederick C. Malkus, the region's premier turtle trapper, took me turkling, as that sport is called.

Gigging: Richard Drescher, one of Maryland's principal athletes, took me night frogging in the marshes of south Dorchester.

Little Choptank: Dale Price allowed me to inspect his place on the Little Choptank, the site occupied by Herman Cline's slave farm prior to the Civil War.

Indians: Judge William B. Yates told me of the Choptank Indians and other matters.

Marshland: Elmer Mowbray allowed me to accompany him on explorations of his privately owned marsh. He is an expert on estuarine life, and I am indebted to him.

Fishing: David Orem and Jay Alban taught me about fishing and the intricacies of nature in the bay area.

Research: Everyone at the Chesapeake Bay Maritime Museum, St. Michaels, was most helpful; the director, R.J. Holt, was especially so. The library in Easton, Maryland, has a distinguished collection of research materials; its director Elizabeth Carroll saw to it that I had assistance, and Mary Starin, custodian of the Maryland Room, was indefatigable in finding books, as she is with all who work in the library. Robert H. Burgess, of the Mariners' Museum in Norfolk, helped with both his books and his counsel.

Studies: Details of early activity were checked against *Tobacco Coast. A Maritime History of the Chesapeake Bay in the Colonial Period* by Arthur Pierce Middleton. The nature of commercial life on an Eastern Shore plantation during the Revolutionary War came from various sources, the most revealing being *In Pursuit of Profit* by Edward C. Papenfuse, which deals with a group of commercial families on the western shore. The significance of the naval battle fought at the mouth of the Chesapeake in September 1781 is not sufficiently appreciated. My account is based on recent research, particularly *Decision at the Chesapeake* by Harold A. Larrabee, which deserves wide attention from those interested in this period.

But my constant assistants were the citizens of the Choptank area. Scores of them talked with me at social gatherings or during investigative meetings held during one of the coldest winters the Eastern Shore has ever experienced and one of the hottest summers. They were provocative, perceptive, amusing . . . and often hopeful that I would quit my project and go elsewhere, lest my writing awaken the rest of the world as to what a sequestered paradise they were enjoying on the Eastern Shore.

Contents

This book is a novel, and to construe it as anything else would be an error. The characters are imaginary; the Steeds, Turlocks, Paxmores, Caters and Caveneys were invented by the author and were based on no real persons. The principal locales—Devon Island, Peace Cliff, the Turlock marshes and the town of Patamoke—are so completely imaginary that they have been located on land that does not even exist. The Refuge is on a creek that does not exist, and in south-central Africa there is no Xanga River or community of people with that name.

Details of the Choptank River are, however, correct insofar as possible, and there has been no invention here. English settlement of the Choptank came somewhat later than depicted, but it did occur at a spot only twenty-three miles to the north.

CHESAPEAKE

Voyage One: 1583

FOR SOME TIME NOW THEY HAD BEEN SUSPICIOUS of him. Spies had monitored his movements, reporting to the priests, and in the tribal councils his advice against going to war with those beyond the bend had been ignored. Even more predictive, the family of the girl he had chosen to replace his dead wife had refused to accept the three lengths of roanoke he had offered as her purchase price.

Reluctantly he was coming to the conclusion that he must leave this tribe which had done everything but outlaw him publicly. As a child he had watched what happened to men declared outcasts, and he had no desire to experience what they had suffered: the isolation, the scorn, the bitter loneliness.

So now, as he fished along the great river or hunted in the meadows or merely sat in contemplation, always alone, he felt he must go. But how? And where?

The trouble had started that day when he voiced his apprehension over a raid proposed by the high chief. For more than a year now relations with tribes beyond the northern bend had been amicable, and during this interval the river had known prosperity, with more than normal trade passing north and south. But the Susquehannocks of the middle section had never in Pentaquod's life been easy in times of peace; they felt intuitively that they should be on the warpath, proving their manhood. So it was within tradition for the high chief to devise justifications for sending his warriors forth: if they triumphed, their victory would redound on him; and if they lost, he would claim that he was merely protecting the boundaries of the tribe.

Pentaquod had argued, 'Those of the northern bend have respected their promises. They have not stolen our beaver nor trespassed on our gardens. To fight them now, with no reason, would be infamous, and our warriors would go into battle knowing that the gods could not be with them.'

His logic was rejected not only by the council of chiefs but also by the common warriors, who felt that for a Susquehannock to pass more than a year in peace would be disgraceful. If their great river had proved an excellent place to live, it must be because their tribe had always fought to protect it, and an old warrior predicted, 'Pentaquod, when the day comes that we are afraid to fight, we lose the river.'

He persisted in talking against a meaningless war, and since any who spoke for peace in the lands along this river would always be charged with treason, his opponents started the rumor that he had been con- taminated by the enemy and served as their spokesman. It was recalled that his wife had died young, which increased the likelihood that the gods rejected his arguments.

To charge him with cowardice was confusing, for he was one of the tallest Susquehannocks in a generation, and they were a tribe of giants. Towering above young men his age, he looked with steady gaze from his great, broad face, darker in color than normal, sure sign of a warrior. This contradiction perplexed children who listened to the accusations against him, and they began to mimic his diffident walk as he moved alone about the edges of the village; soon they would be taunting him openly.

It was one of these children who drove him to his decision. The little boy had been aping him behind his back, causing much merriment among onlookers, when Pentaquod suddenly turned and seized him, demanding to know why he was behaving so, and the child blurted out, 'My father says the council is meeting to punish you.' And when Penta- quod looked about the village he realized that the elders were missing, and he knew that the boy was speaking truth.

It took him only a few moments to reach that decision. The council would not act hastily; it never did. There would have to be long speeches, condemning him, but if this child's father had actually used the word *punish,* a much more serious penalty than outlawing might be in store. His enemies had grown so outspoken that some might even demand death; if they convinced themselves that he was indeed a spy for the northern tribes, this would be logical.

So without returning to his wigwam, where his mother and father would be sitting in the sun, and without any attempt to recover his weapons, for this would excite those designated to watch him, he moved quietly away from the long building in which the council was meeting and toward the bank of the river. He did not, however, approach the canoes, for he knew that this would evoke alarm. Instead he kept his back to them as if watching the village, but from time to time he turned his head to follow the flight of some bird and in this manner was able to estimate the situation on the river.

The war canoe had everything in readiness for instant departure, but it was built of oak and was far too cumbersome for one man to handle. The plan he had in mind could succeed only if he could utilize a canoe light enough for him to portage, and one such stood close at hand; it looked trim and handsome, but he had helped build it and knew its limitations: it had never won a race. Others were tempting, but he rejected them as either too slow or too heavy.

There was, however, one small, swift canoe which he had helped build for one of the hunting chiefs; it had been made of rare white pine from the north, and once during construction, when the fires burning away the insides grew too strong, he had lifted the canoe by himself and plunged it into the river, where the fires were quenched. The chief to whom it belonged had painted it yellow; its sides were stout and it had been fitted with oaken struts. It had been well pointed at the bow and had done well in races. Best of all, it was always armed for hunting and fishing, and so perched beside the river that one man, with a sturdy shove, could launch it.

'The yellow,' he muttered to himself, and left the river area and returned to the heart of the village, walking casually toward the council hall, where he observed with satisfaction that the spies assigned to guard him were withdrawing so as to watch him more stealthily. This was essential to his plan, for he could not outfight them; they were four and valiant, but he could outrun them, for he was swift.

So when he had teased them into moving as far from the river as practical, he turned suddenly and leaped with deerlike speed back toward the river. When he reached the bank he did not rush immediately to the canoe of his choice; instead he dashed along to the war canoe, taking all the paddles. Next he jumped to any lesser canoe showing paddles, and collected them too. Only then did he turn to his target.

With a cry that echoed through the village, he tossed the armful of paddles into the yellow canoe, gave its stern a mighty shove, then chased it into the muddy waters of the river, climbed aboard and started paddling vigorously downriver.

In spite of the fact that his life depended upon the alacrity of his escape, he could not refrain from looking back at his village. There were the wigwams built low to the ground; there was the home in which his parents would just now be hearing the news of his wild action; and there was the long wigwam from which the high chiefs were already running to man the war canoe in which they must overtake the criminal. He could not take his eyes off the old men as they came to the river and saw that they were powerless to pursue him. His last view of his community showed a village in uproar, with stately chiefs running back and forth waving their arms and, he suspected, shouting at their underlings. He burst into laughter.

But now he was alone on the river, and to survive he must exercise every skill he had mastered in his twenty-five years. He would have to pass two Susquehannock villages to the south, and since they were subservient to his, he had to suppose that they would intercept him and hold him for questioning. Furthermore, the men from his tribe would shortly find other paddles with which to activate their canoes, and pursuit would be inevitable. Indeed, he suspected that already runners had been sent overland to alert the southern allies, so that his chances of final escape were not great.

But he was not without tactics of his own, and as soon as his stout strokes brought him near the first village, he chose a daring gambit. The runners can't have reached here yet, he reasoned, so I have one chance. He paddled boldly up to the shore, bellowing in a loud and agitated voice, 'Friends! Have you seen a man and a woman go by in a canoe?'

They came to the foreshore of the western bank to call back, 'We saw no one.'

'My wife!' Pentaquod shouted, and the people began to laugh, because around the world there is nothing funnier than a wronged husband trying to recapture his runaway wife.

'Which way did they go?' he bawled.

'Into the cornfield!' they taunted, and for as long as he remained in sight, paddling desperately downriver, they stood on the shore, laughing at the grotesque figure he made, a husband paddling to overtake his wife and her lover.

It was dusk when he approached the second village, on the eastern bank this time, and he doubted that he could work the same stratagem again, for the runners would have offered rewards for his capture. This time he slipped among the trees on the western shore and waited till deep night had fallen. He knew that on this day the half-moon would not illuminate the river till near midnight, but he also knew that after the moon did rise well in the heavens, no passage of the river would be possible.

So when the village fires had subsided and the watchmen had been placed, he allowed his canoe to drift down the western bank, ever so slowly, ever so silently, moving within the deep protection of the trees that lined the shore. When the canoe reached a position directly opposite the sleeping village, the spot at which detection would be most likely, he scarcely breathed, and to his relief his passage made no sound, alerted no watchman. At dawn he was paddling furiously down the middle of the river, taking advantage of whatever current was then moving.

When the summer sun rose and he began to feel its oppressive heat, he wisely pulled into the mouth of a stream debouching from the west, and there, under the protection of overhanging trees, he slept most of the day. At dusk he was back on the river, hungry and with tired muscles, but he paddled incessantly with those deep, rhythmic strokes which kept the canoe moving purposefully forward.

It was toward morning of the third night, when he had had only two small fish to eat in three days, that he came to those falls which his people called Conowingo, and here he faced the test which would determine the success of his escape. When he approached the white and leaping water he intended to drag his canoe ashore and portage it a long distance downhill, but as he paddled away from the middle of the river to the safety of the shore, he spotted a course of unbroken, swiftly moving water which twisted and curved over rocks, and in the flash of a paddle he elected to trust his fortunes in the river rather than on the shore.

He did so for a good reason: If I portage my canoe, the others may catch up. But if I go down this water, none will dare follow, and I shall be days ahead of them.

As if conducting a ritual, he threw overboard all but two of the paddles he had been carrying, dropping them into the swift waters one by one, to track their passage through the falls. 'They follow the dark smooth water!' he cried. Then he lashed to the struts all hunting gear and one of his remaining paddles, against the chance that the one he was using might be swept away, and with the reassuring knowledge that he risked no more in going forward than he would in turning back, he drove his canoe into the turbulence.

'Hi-ya! Hi-ya!' he shouted as he felt the waters take command, pulling the canoe forward with frightening speed.

It was a stormy ride, with rocks visible on either side and white water piling into the log. His paddle, even when he used it with unaccustomed strength, accomplished little except to keep him preoccupied. At several points he felt sure that he must lose his canoe, and perhaps his life, too, but in the end the sturdy log bounced and chafed its way through the perilous rocks and the roaring water.

When the passage was concluded he was exhausted, and that day slept soundly under the trees. Cool water came down a rivulet, and when he rose he drank copiously. Also, he found a field of strawberries on which he gorged, and with the gear he had saved he caught two more small fish. Reassured in mind and replenished in sinew, he resumed his night paddling down the great river, and next morning decided not to sleep through the day, for ahead lay the vast body of water which he had heard of as a child and which was now his target.

'It lies to the south,' the old seer of his village had said, 'the river of rivers in which the fish of fish abound. To paddle down it would take even the god of rivers many days, and its shores are cut with a hundred places to hide. On this river of rivers a storm lasts for nine days, and fish are so big, one can feed a village. But it is beautiful. It is so beautiful that if you are good and make your arrows straight and tend the yams, you may one day see it. I have never seen it, but it's down there and maybe you will be the fortunate one.'

And there it was, the Chesapeake! In Pentaquod's language the name meant: *the great river in which fish with hard shell coverings abound,* and each village along the Susquehanna possessed precious lengths of roanoke made from these white shells gathered from the Chesapeake. With enough roanoke a man could purchase even a chieftain's daughter.

The Chesapeake! The name was familiar to all children, for on this great water strange things occurred. This was the magical place where the waters became even wider than those of the Susquehanna, where storms of enormous magnitude churned up waves of frightening power. This was the river of rivers, where the fish wore precious shells.

Pentaquod leaned forward with his paddle across his knees, content to allow his yellow canoe to drift quietly into the bay, and with each length that the log moved forward, he saw some new revelation: the immensity of this water, the way the fish jumped as if they were eager to be caught and tasted, the constant movement of birds back and forth, the majestic trees lining the shore, and over all, the arching sky more blue than any he had seen before.

For the whole day he drifted south in wonder, now close to one shore, now venturing out into the terrifying yet consoling middle. It was even bigger than the old seer had been able to convey; it was more beautiful than a lifetime along an inland river would have intimated. From the moment he saw this magnificent body of water he lost all regret at having left his village on the river, for he had exchanged that collection of wattled wigwams for a greater majesty.

He spent two days on the bay, enchanted each hour with some new brilliance: he loved the movement of the fish and the feeding of the birds, the way the sun rose enormous and red from the waters, or went to sleep in flashes of gold.

'Oh, what a universe!' he cried when his joy was greatest. To express this thought he used a Susquehannock word meaning: *all that is seen on earth and unseen in the heavens,* and he never doubted that this word had been invented so that a man like him could describe this new world which he had been allowed to enter.

It had been his intention from the first moment he fled his village to find this legendary bay and take shelter in some likely haven on its western shore, for in his youth the shells his people had treasured had been brought to them by a stalwart tribe of people called the Potomacs, and he remembered that they lived along some river to the west. They were a warlike tribe, and in the years when they did not come in peace to trade, they came in war canoes to ravage. He would seek to join these

Potomacs, reasoning that since he was much taller than most men and broader of shoulder, he would be welcomed.

But now as he drifted down this peaceful body of water, so different from the constricted river he had known, so infinitely grander, he realized that he had no desire to join those warlike Potomacs, among whom he would be forced to serve as warrior. He was surfeited with fighting and with the old men who encouraged it. He wanted refuge in some tribe more placid than the ones he had known along the Susquehanna, more peaceful than the shell-trading Potomacs. So he refrained from paddling to the western shore.

As a child he had been told that along the eastern shore of the bay lived other tribes of lesser breed who accomplished nothing in arms; they were not even brave enough to venture north in trade. Occasionally bands of Susquehannocks had penetrated south to fight them, finding them ridiculously easy to subdue.

'It's hardly fair to call them enemies,' a warrior from beyond the bend had reported to Pentaquod's village. 'They have few arrows and small canoes. Not many surplus shells for making roanoke, and no desirable women. Believe me, they aren't Potomacs. Those Potomacs know how to fight.'

Each disparagement of the eastern tribes that Pentaquod could now remember made them more attractive. If they were unlike the Susquehannocks, that was good; if they differed from the Potomacs, that was better. And now, as if to exemplify this judgment, there appeared on the eastern shore the opening of a broad and congenial river, guarded by a low island burdened with magnificent trees. The river was spacious, inviting, peaceful and glowing with birds.

And so, in the middle of the Chesapeake, Pentaquod, the Susquehannock who was tired of war, turned his log canoe not to the turbulent western shore, as he had intended, but to the quieter eastern shore, and that simple choice made all the difference.

The River

WHEN PENTAQUOD STEERED TOWARD THE EAST-
ern river he was confronted by the tree-covered island he had seen from
a distance, for it dominated the entrance. Poised between two headlands,
one reaching down from the north, the other up from the south, it served
as a welcoming sentinel and seemed to proclaim: All who enter this river
find joy.

The island was low-lying, but its stately trees rose so high and so
unevenly that they created an impression of elevation. Oak, maple,
sweetgum, chestnut, birch, towering pines and iridescent holly grew so
thickly that the earth itself could scarcely be seen, and it was these trees
which protected Pentaquod after he dragged his canoe ashore and collapsed from lack of food and sleep.

When he awoke he became aware of one of earth's most pleasing
sensations: he was lying on a bed of pine needles, soft and aromatic, and
when he looked upward he could not see the sky, for the pines grew so
straight and tall that their branches formed a canopy which sunlight
could not penetrate. The covering gave him confidence, and before he
resumed his sleep he muttered, 'This is a good place, this place of trees.'

He was awakened by a sound he could not immediately identify. It was
warlike and terrifying, coming at him from a spot directly overhead. It
echoed ominously: *Kraannk, kraannk, kraannk!*'

In fear he leaped to his feet, but as he stood there under the tall trees,
preparing to defend himself, he burst into laughter at his foolishness, for
when he listened to the cry again, he remembered where he had heard
it. *Kraannk, kraannk!*' It was Fishing-long-legs, one of the most ingratiating birds of the rivers and marshlands.

There it stood, knee-deep in water: tall, thin, awkward, many hands high, with extremely long legs and rumpled white head. Its most prominent feature was a long yellowish bill, which it kept pointed downward at the water. Infrequently, when Pentaquod was young, this voracious fisherman had visited the Susquehanna to feed, wading tiptoe among the reeds, and often Pentaquod, while playing, had tried to imitate its movements.

Now Pentaquod stood silent, watching the bird with affection as it stalked slowly, clumsily along the muddy shore, and out into the water until its bony knees were submerged. Then, with a dart of its long neck so swift that Pentaquod could not follow, it speared its sharp beak into the water and caught a fish. Raising its head, it tossed the fish in the air, catching it as it descended. With a gulp, it swallowed the fish, and Pentaquod could see the progress of the meal as it slowly passed down the extended gullet. For some time he stayed in the shadows, watching as the bird caught fish after fish. He must have made some sound, for the bird turned suddenly toward him, ran a few ungainly steps along the shore, then rose in slow, extended, lovely flight. *'Kraannk, kraannk!'* it cried as it passed overhead.

Knowing that there would be ample food, if he could but catch it, Pentaquod pulled his canoe farther inland, hiding it among the oaks and maples which lined the shore, for he knew that he must explore this island quickly. And as he moved among the trees and came to a meadow, he heard the comforting cry so familiar in his days along the great river: 'Bob-white! Bob-white!' Now the call came from his left, then from a clump of grass to his right and sometimes from a spot almost under his feet, but always it was as clear and distinct as if an uncle who could whistle had been standing at his side. 'Bob-white!' It was the call of the quail, that sly bird with the brown-and-white head. Of all the birds that flew, this was the best eating, and if this island held a multitude, Pentaquod could not only survive on his fish but eat like a chieftain with his quail.

With extreme caution he started inland, noticing everything, aware that his life might depend upon the carefulness of his observation. With every step he found only reassurance and never a sign of danger: nut trees laden with midsummer shells not yet ripe; droppings of rabbits, and the signs that foxes lived here, and the location of brambled berry bushes, and the woody nests of eagles, and the honeysuckle twisting among the lower branches of the cedar trees.

It was an island rich in signs and promises. On such an island a man with intelligence could live well, if he worked many hours each day, but in spite of its favorable omens Pentaquod was not ready to commit himself to it, for he could not tell whether it was populated by other people, or what its temperament might be in a storm.

He kept probing, and satisfied himself that it was more extensive west to east than it was north to south. A deep bay cutting in from the east almost met a stream in the south, nearly severing the island; the eastern portion of this division was markedly richer than the western. He walked beneath majestic oaks until he reached the eastern tip, and there he stood, dumbfounded, for wherever he looked he saw a grand expanse of water forming itself into bays and creeks and coves and even small rivers for as far as he could see. And along the shores of these varied waters rose land of the most inviting nature: at times broad fields, at other times gently rising land covered with trees even taller than those on the island, and everywhere the impression of opulence, and quietness, and gentle living.

It was the most congenial place he had ever seen. He judged that in a storm this sleeping body of water might have the capacity for considerable turbulence, and he was certain that before he could possess any part of this wonderland he would have to contend with its present owners, who might be just as cantankerous as the Susquehannocks, but of one thing he was certain: along this splendid river he wished to spend the rest of his life.

He had no sooner come to this decision than a snorting kind of sound attracted his attention, and he turned to look behind him, among the trees, and there stood a huge-eyed doe with two brown-speckled fawns. The three deer halted in rigid attention, staring at this stranger. Then the inquisitive doe cocked her head, and this almost undetectable action released the fawns, and they began to move cautiously toward Pentaquod, little deer on unsteady legs exploring their new world.

When they had moved quite close to Pentaquod their suspicious mother gave a cough, and the babies leaped sideways, ran in distracted circles, then stopped. Seeing that nothing harmful had happened, they moved back toward Pentaquod, lifting their spindly legs in delightful awkwardness, probing with their great eyes.

'Heh!' Pentaquod whispered. The fawns stared at him, and one moved closer.

'Heh!' The foremost fawn cocked its little head, waited, then resumed its approach. When it had come so close that Pentaquod could have reached out and touched it, the doe gave a warning snort, leaped aside, raised her white tail and darted back into the woods. The trailing fawn did likewise, but the one closest to Pentaquod became confused, or stubborn, and did not follow the others to safety. It simply stood there, staring at this stranger, and after a moment the mother returned in a series of fine leaps, swept past the inquisitive fawn and lured it into the trees.

Fish and quail and deer! Pentaquod thought. And if one finds seed, maize and probably pumpkins. Turkeys too, if I guess right. And not many people, judging so far. This is the right place.

He returned to his canoe, caught some fish for supper, made a small fire and with a large handful of blackberries to accent the smoking fish, fed well. He slept well, too, except that long before dawn he heard in the sky overhead the cry he would always associate with his first exploration of this river: '*Kraannk, kraannk!*' It was Fishing-long-legs coming back to patrol the shore.

In the days that followed, Pentaquod explored every corner of the island and concluded that whereas others might know of it, they certainly did not think enough of it to build their homes here, for he could find no sign of habitation. And so far as he could ascertain, not even the meadows that appeared at curious intervals among the trees had ever grown corn or squash, and on none of the headlands facing the island could he detect any indication of either homes or cultivated fields.

This did not disturb him. If land as congenial as this existed upriver, there would be no reason for people to settle near the mouth; it would be much safer inland. Storms coming off the bay would be diminished and distances across water shortened. Perhaps the land would be richer, too, and there might be other advantages which he could not envisage. But on one point he was satisfied: life here would be good.

For the time being he quit his speculations, accepting the boon he had been granted. He built himself a small, well-hidden wigwam inland from the northern shore, using bent saplings for the frame and abundant river grasses for the roof. He found it so easy to catch fish that he did not even have to go after them in his canoe: the large brown-speckled ones with the blunt snouts swam up to him determined to be caught, and whereas he had been unable yet to trap any of the numerous bob-whites, he had shot one deer, which would feed him for some time. A fox strolled by one afternoon, and one night a skunk made things odorous.

He rather liked the smell of skunk, if it didn't come too close. It reminded him of the woods which he had trailed as a boy, of cold autumn nights, and the snugness of winter. It was the smell of nature, heavy and pervasive: it assured him that life in all its complexity was thriving. He had rarely seen a skunk, and he saw none now, but he was pleased that they shared the island with him.

It was his friend Fishing-long-legs who introduced him to one of the strangest experiences of the eastern shore. The blue-feathered bird with the long beak had flown in one evening with its accustomed croaking cry and was now probing the shallow waters along the shore, ignoring the man to whom it had become accustomed. Suddenly it shot its fierce bill deep into the water and came up with a struggling something Pentaquod had not seen before.

It was larger than a man's hand, seemed to have numerous legs that squirmed in the fading sunlight and was brown-green in color. The bird was obviously pleased with its catch, for it threw it in the air, severed it with one snap of its beak, gulped down one half, allowing the other to fall into the water. The swallowed portion was so big and with so many protruding legs that it required time and effort to maneuver it down the long gullet, but once this was accomplished, the bird retrieved and ate the other half. Having enjoyed a feast of this kind, it did not bother with mere fish. With a short run it rose in the air, uttered its mournful croaking and soared away.

Pentaquod went to where the fish had feasted, searching for clues. There were none. The bird had eaten everything. Next day he went there with his fishing line, but caught nothing. However, some days later he watched as Fishing-long-legs caught another of these morsels, enjoying it even more than before, and Pentaquod crept close to see if he could determine what it was that the bird was eating. He discovered nothing he had not seen before: bigger than a man's hand, many legs, brown-green in color, so soft that it could easily be bitten in half.

He was determined to solve this mystery, and the first clue came one day while he walked along the southern shore of his island: washed up on the beach and obviously dead lay a creature much like the one the bird had been catching. It was the right size; it had many feet, or what passed for feet; and it was brown-green, with touches of blue underneath. But there the similarity stopped, for this dead animal was encased in a shell so hard that no bird could eat it. Also, its two front legs had formidable jaws with serrated, heavy teeth which could, if the animal were alive, inflict substantial harm.

How could the bird cut this shell in half? Pentaquod asked himself, and then, an even more perplexing question: And how could he swallow it if he did? He tapped the hard substance and knew there was no possible way for that bird to swallow that shell.

For ten days he tried to catch one of these strange creatures on his line and failed, and yet twice in that period he saw Fishing-long-legs catch one, cut it in half and force the food down its long neck. In frustration, he realized that this was a mystery he was not destined to solve.

He did, however, discover two facts about his home that disturbed him. The more he explored the two deep cuts which came close to bisecting the island, the more he realized that some day the two arms must meet, cutting the island in half, and if this could be done, why might there not evolve other cuts to fragment it further?

His second discovery came as the consequence of a sudden and devastating storm. The midpoint of summer had passed and life on the island had been a growing joy; this was really an almost ideal place to live, and he supposed that later on, when he had traveled upriver to establish contact with whatever tribes occupied the area, he would become a member of their unit. But for the time being he was content with his solitary paradise.

It had been a hot day, with heavy moist air, and in the late afternoon a bank of towering clouds gathered in the southwest, on the opposite side of the bay. With a swiftness that he had never witnessed in the north this congregation of blackness started rushing eastward, and even though the sun remained shining over Pentaquod's head, it was obvious that a storm of some magnitude must soon break.

Still the sun shone; still the sky remained clear. Deer moved deeper into the forest and shore birds retreated to their nests, although the only sign of danger was that galloping cloud bank approaching the bay.

Pentaquod watched its arrival. It struck the distant western shore with enormous fury, turning what had been placid water into turbulent, crested waves leaping and tossing white spume into the air. The clouds moved so swiftly that they required only moments to cross the bay, their progress marked by the wildly leaping waves.

With the storm came an immense amount of rain, falling in sheets slanting eastward. For it to speed over the last portion of the bay took only a fragment of time, and then the storm was striking Pentaquod, descending on him in a fury he had not witnessed before. Great jagged flashes of lightning tore through the sky, followed almost instantly by shattering claps of thunder; there was no echo, for the world was drowned in rain. Winds of extraordinary power ripped along the surface of the bay, lashing it into waves of pounding force.

But Pentaquod was not afraid of the storm, and next morning, when it had passed and he surveyed his island, he did not find the damage excessive. He had seen storms before, rather violent ones which swept down the river valley of his home, and although this one had been swifter and more thunderous, it was merely an exaggeration of what he had long known. The trees knocked down were larger than any he had seen go down in the north, and that was about it. If storms on the island were no worse than this, he could abide them.

What was it, then, that disturbed him, causing him to wonder about his new home? After his cursory inspection of the island, and after satisfying himself that his yellow canoe had survived, he behaved like any prudent husbandman and started checking the general situation, desiring to see if any animals had been killed or streams diverted, and as he came to a spot on the northwestern tip of the island, he noticed that the storm, and more particularly the pounding waves, had carried away a substantial portion of the shore. Tall pines and oaks which had marked this point had been undercut and now lay sprawled in the water side by side, like the bodies of dead warriors after battle.

Wherever he went along the western shore he saw this same loss of land. The tragedy of the storm was not that it had knocked down a few trees, for more would grow, and not that it had killed a few fish, for others would breed, but that it had eaten away a substantial edge of the island, and this was a permanent loss. Pentaquod, looking at the destruction, decided that he would abandon this island, congenial though it was, and look farther inland.

Accordingly, he crossed the now-calm river, paddling until he reached the base of a tall cliff which had attracted him from that first day on which he had surveyed the river. It lay due east of the island, and formed a headland with deep water west and north. It guarded the entrance to a fine small creek, but it was the sheer southern exposure which gave the cliff its dignity; taller than five men and topped with oaks and locusts, its sandy composition was so light that it shone for great distances, forming a beacon at the edge of the river. Pentaquod, seeing the crumbling nature of its face, suspected that it, too, might be falling from the action of waves, but when he brought his canoe to its base he was gratified to see that it had not been touched by the recent storm; he judged that it was never menaced because its placement kept it clear of eroding currents.

There was no sensible way to land at the base of the cliff: where would one beach a canoe or hide it? How would one climb to the plateau above? At the eastern end of the cliff's river face there was low land, and it was most inviting, but it was exposed, and Pentaquod avoided it. Paddling into the small creek, he inspected the forbidding slope of the northern face and rejected it, too, but some distance up the creek he found low land, safe and well-wooded, with a score of likely anchorages. Choosing one, he pulled his canoe far inland, hiding it beneath a cluster of maples, and began the stiff climb to the top of the headland.

What a memorable place he discovered: a small plot of flat, open land near the edge of the cliff surrounded by tall and stately oaks and pines. In every direction save east he could see extensively, and his eyes leaped from one spectacular view to another: to the north a bewildering maze of headlands and bays, each its own exemplification of beauty; to the south a new definition of vast loneliness, for there lay the marshes, refuges for innumerable birds and fish and small animals; the noble view lay to the west where the island glowed in sunlight, with the blue waters of the bay beyond. From this headland Pentaquod could see across the bay to the mysterious lands where the Potomacs ruled, but if he looked downward instead of out, he saw on all sides his river, peaceful and reassuring.

On this headland, speculating as to what prudent steps he must take next, Pentaquod spent some of the quietest weeks of his life. The loneliness of the first days of his flight had now vanished, and he was at ease with his decision to quit the Susquehannocks. The spaciousness of his surroundings infected him, and he began to think in slower, less frantic terms. The natural fear that he might be unable to survive in a strange world dissolved, and he discovered in himself a courage much more profound than that required to flee downriver past strange villages; this was a mature courage capable of sustaining him in a confrontation with an entire world. Sometimes he would sit beneath the oak tree under whose protection he had built his small wigwam and simply survey his universe: the fascinating arms of water to the north, the vast marshes to the south, the western shore of the bay where the warlike tribes paraded, and he would think: This is the favored land. This is the richness.

One morning as he worked on his canoe down by the creek he heard a sound which caused him to catch his breath with joy: *'Kraannk, kraannk!'* It was one of the ugliest sounds in nature, as awkward and ungainly as the creature that uttered it, but to Pentaquod it meant the return of a friend, and he rushed to the water's edge to welcome Fishing-long-legs as that inelegant bird landed in a crash and a clutter, throwing mud and water as it dug its feet in to stop.

'Bird! Bird!' he called joyously as the fisher landed. His cry startled the bird, who ran a few additional steps and took off again, flapping its huge blue wings and soaring slowly, spaciously into the sky. 'Come back!' Pentaquod pleaded, but it was gone.

He stayed by the small stream all that day, irritated with himself for having frightened the bird, and toward dusk he was rewarded with another utterance of that sweet, raucous cry. *'Kraannk, kraannk!'* the long-legged creature shouted as it wheeled in for a new try at the fishing grounds. This time Pentaquod did not speak; in fact, he remained quite motionless so that the feeding bird would not be aware of him, and after a while it came probing close to where he stood.

Suddenly the bird looked up, saw him and at the same time saw in the waters below the choicest morsel in the bay. With a swift dart of its beak the small head dived, caught its prey and raised its head exultantly, throwing the catch in the air, then snapping it in two.

'What is that bird eating?' Pentaquod cried aloud petulantly as he watched one of the many-footed halves disappear down its gullet. Ignoring the man, the bird reached into the waters to retrieve the second half, and this, too, it sent down its very long neck. Pentaquod could watch the progress of the mysterious meal, eaten with such relish, and determined to catch a fish for himself.

Unfortunately, he had no concept of what he was trying to catch and so did not succeed. He did, however, find scores of trees with ripening nuts and new kinds of berries and different succulent fish in the river and haunts of deer that seemed so plentiful that no man need ever go hungry.

But now, as autumn approached with an occasional cold day warning of winter, he began to ponder seriously the matter of establishing contact with whatever tribes inhabited this area. All he knew of them were the legends of his youth: Below us at the end of our river is a larger river, much larger. On the west are the Potomacs, mighty in battle, but on the east there is no one of consequence.

If they live on rivers like this, Pentaquod thought, they are of consequence. Then he reflected on what this meant; they were certainly not of any importance to the Susquehannocks, for they had neither trade goods to be envied nor war canoes to fear. No doubt the Potomacs, who had both, had the same low opinion of the easterners. But what did the easterners think of themselves? What did Pentaquod, living gently as an easterner, think of himself? *It is so much easier here.*

He was now convinced that somewhere along this bountiful river tribes were living, and it seemed obligatory that he find them before winter, so with some reluctance he decided to abandon this highly satisfactory home on the cliff and move closer to where his future partners must be hiding. Accordingly, he mended rough spots on his canoe, dragged it into the creek, climbed in and started paddling eastward until he came to a huge, sprawling marsh whose tall grasses rose a uniform fifteen hands above the water.

At the sound of his paddle hundreds of birds arose, and he judged that fish must be plentiful, too. As he moved along the marsh he found it a warm, soggy, gently swaying place, stretching endlessly and writhing with new forms of life. When he had traversed a long segment he found to his satisfaction that a small, well-concealed creek led into the middle of the rushes: An excellent place for protection. And when he had penetrated the wandering cove, invisible from the main body of the river, he found its northern shore composed of fast land well-wooded and of good quality.

A wigwam here would be protected by the marsh, he reasoned, and when it was constructed he felt a sense of security which he had not known before: Even if I find no others, I can live here.

But on the third night, when he was congratulating himself as the fire burned low, he heard a buzzing, and knew, from his childhood days, that mosquitoes had moved in. But never before had he experienced any like these: they came in phalanxes and attacked with the vigor of hunting dogs. One alone could do more damage than twenty along the Susquehanna, and they drove him nearly mad with their incessant onslaughts. In fact, they stung him so furiously that he had to plunge into the creek to drown them, but when he emerged their brothers were waiting.

In the aching dawn, when he surveyed his lumpy arms and felt the sting-spots on his face, he wondered if he could remain in such a place, but on subsequent nights he discovered that if he kept a smudge-fire going, and closed down all the openings of his wigwam, and smeared his face with rancid fish grease, and hid every inch of his body beneath cloth or grass, he could survive. It wasn't pleasant, and he sweated like an animal, but he did survive, and it occurred to him that when the Great Power, Manitou, finished laying down this river, perfect in all details, He had added the mosquito to remind man that no paradise comes free: there are always mosquitoes. And bigger ones than these could not exist.

During the day he fished and hunted, noting where the beaver were and the bear; also, he tentatively probed inland, seeking any signs of human occupation, but he found none. Fishing-long-legs came to visit almost daily, and little green herons and brilliant cardinals and kingfishers from their muddy nests, and hundreds of quail making the autumn afternoons ring with their whistling cries. This was a much more compact world than either the island or the cliff; its horizon was limited to the distance a stone could be tossed, but it was snug and secure, and one afternoon Pentaquod decided: If I must live alone, this won't be so bad . . . especially when cold drives away the mosquitoes.

And then one morning, while he was still abed on his paillasse of pine needles, he heard a wild cacophony, a rumble which seemed to move the earth yet came from the sky, and he rushed out to see descending toward his marsh a veritable cloud of huge birds, all of them crying in loud voices, *'Onk-or, onk-or!'* And in that first moment of seeing the geese he comprehended them totally: jet-black head and neck, snow-white underchin, beautiful cream body with brown top, black tail, raucous, lovable, fat and constantly shouting to each other, *'Onk-or!'*

He had hoped that these powerful birds would land on his waters, but they flew past, arguing loudly, and then more came, and more, and more; they were so numerous he had no system of numbers to count them. But finally one especially noisy group of about seventy wheeled in the air, flew low over his head and landed with riotous splashing in his marsh or with grinding feet upon his land. Close at hand they seemed too big to be called birds; they were more like flying bear cubs loaded with edible meat.

The arrival of this bountiful food was so mysterious that he became afraid. As a boy he had watched when ducks stopped by the Susquehannock; they stayed only for a few days before flying on, and he assumed that these huge creatures would do the same. Each morning he expected them to leave, and each night they remained, foraging in the fields and marshes along the river, always crying, *'Onk-or!'* Every eight or nine days he trapped one and gorged himself on the tasty meat, afraid that this might be his last feast, but always the great birds stayed.

They were with him through the autumn; on some days when they flew off at dawn to feed on new fields, their wings would darken the sky, their honking cries would deafen. Once at the edge of the marsh Pentaquod tried to estimate how thick the cloud was as the birds flew overhead, and he supposed that at each spot as many as three hundred were flying—one above the other until the sun could not be seen.

And in the afternoon when the birds returned they would congregate on the north bank of the river, so that the sun, moving through the southern sky, could warm them, and the muddy banks would be black with birds from the shoreline to where the trees started. Again Pentaquod tried to count how many rows of birds lined the shore at a given spot: starting at the water's edge there would be more than fifty, one after the other, reaching back to the first trees.

It was a richness he could not comprehend. These great noisy birds were infinite. At first he thought that he should kill several, smoke their meat and feed off them through the winter. But what if the birds stayed on, standing there on the shore in endless rows, waiting to be taken? There would be no need to conserve. One would simply catch them, one after another, as need commanded.

And the birds did stay, as rich a food resource as the great bay provided, for along with the larger birds came a bewildering variety of smaller ducks of the kind that Pentaquod had seen once or twice in sparing numbers along his native river. Here they came in waves, shy small creatures unbelievably tasty when caught and cooked.

Once, when many big and little birds settled along the edges of his marsh, Pentaquod sat with his hands over his face in prayer. The birds, preparing for sleep, were making a violent chatter, and he listened to the noise as if it had been sweet music: Great Power, thank You for sending them to feed us through the winter . . .

And as soon as he had uttered the word us he realized how lonely he was, how bereft. And next morning he determined to quit this haven among the marshes and find the people who had to be living somewhere along this fortunate river.

He had paddled only a short distance to the east when he spied a small bay opening into the northern shore. It looked as if it might hide a village, though how one could have existed so close at hand without his noticing was confusing; when he probed into the bay he saw that it opened into several smaller arms, and at the head of one he found what he had been seeking: the remnants of a village.

Pilings had been driven into the shore and to them canoes had once been attached; there were also platforms on which oval wigwams of some size had once stood. The foreshore had been cleared as well as two fields in back, and as he explored the area gingerly, without getting out of his canoe, he found that all along the edges of the bay were other signs of occupation. Returning to the larger site, he beached his canoe, tied it to one of the pilings and walked ashore.

He stayed for many days, gratified to see that the large noisy geese came to the bay at night, and in this time he was able to explore enough of the countryside east of the abandoned town to know that he had come at last upon the occupied portion of the river. Where the people were now he could not say, but all signs indicated that they must have been there recently and moved away of their own volition. There was no indication of battle, and with the food available, there could have been no cause for starvation. Indeed, as he stood on the remnants of the village, he could not know that even though he had already discovered the deer and the abundant fish and now the large birds, he had failed to find the two sources of food supply for which this region would be famous.

The apparent abandonment was the more perplexing in that when Pentaquod inspected the site closely he became convinced of its suitability. It had fresh water, protection, a convenient relationship with the river, many tall trees and a hinterland suitable for either hunting or the cultivation of corn. There was, however, one ominous feature he could not explain, and in the end he reasoned that this might represent the sinister force which had caused the evacuation.

But what was it? A pile, large at the base and almost as high as a man's head, of a kind of shell he had not seen before: somewhat smaller than a hand and much thinner, composed of a hard gray substance on the outside, a shimmering white on the inside. It had no smell, a solidity that mystified him, and one sharp edge. This led him to believe that perhaps the pile had been assembled for use in war; the individual shells might be thrown at the enemy, but when he tried hurling them at a tree, the edges were so sharp he cut his forefinger and concluded that the pile was merely one more mystery of the new river.

And then one afternoon as he sat idly in the deserted village he heard a subdued but persistent noise coming from the east, and at first he thought it must be some animal, but it was so varied and purposeful that he knew it had to be associated with people: A war party victorious and inattentive.

But then the noise grew much louder, with sounds that could be made only by children, and incredulously he muttered, 'It can't be a whole village . . . making such noise as it approaches a dangerous spot.' A band of Susquehannocks moving through the forest would have made so little sound that even the most attentive enemy scouts would not hear. Noisy behavior like this was unbelievable.

He was so bewildered that he moved out to intercept the strangers, darting carefully from one tree to the next as he had been taught. When he was safely located so that he could watch both the forest and the river, he waited while the approaching noises increased.

And then he saw a sight which was even stranger than the sound. Down the trail, ignoring possible danger, came the happy, carefree population of the empty village. Women straggled along; children shouted raucously; and all were led by a white-haired old man wearing upon his chest a disk of polished copper signifying that he was the werowance.

Never before had Pentaquod seen a tribe so poorly led, so pathetically disciplined. Nor had he ever seen people so small.

'They're all children!' he whispered. 'They can't be grown people!' But they were, and this discovery determined what he would do, but even as he reached this decision he was alarmed at its daring: when the frolicking tribe was almost upon him he leaped boldly onto the path, holding up his right hand. The old werowance stopped as commanded; those behind kept coming on; some children screamed; and the warriors knew not what to do. In the confusion Pentaquod cried in a loud voice, 'I am Pentaquod, the Susquehannock!'

The werowance did not hear well, and the little that did come through he did not comprehend. Turning to those behind, he asked what the frightening stranger had said, but they had not understood either. 'Where's Scar-chin?' the trembling werowance pleaded, and when that emaciated warrior was located, his chin cleft years before by the toma-hawk of a Susquehannock, he was pushed forward to ask in the tongue Pentaquod had used, 'Are you a Susquehannock?'

Pentaquod nodded, and the interpreter reported this intelligence to the werowance, who said, 'Ask if he means war.'

'Do you come seeking war?'

'No.' An audible sigh of relief came from the entire band, but then the werowance frowned and said, 'Tell him we have nothing to trade,' and when this was interpreted, Pentaquod said, 'I, too, have nothing.' Again there came the sigh of relief, after which the werowance asked in some perplexity, 'Then why is he here?' and when this was spoken in Sus-quehannock, Pentaquod replied simply, 'I am a fugitive. I come seeking refuge.'

When this startling information was circulated, the little people ut-tered whispers of compassion and said that perhaps he might wish to stay with them, for they needed men, and he was greater than any they had known. They jabbered that once or twice in each generation gangs of Susquehannocks, tall like him, had strayed onto this river, always to plunder or take slaves. Scar-chin had been captured on such a raid and had lived among the warlike northerners for seven years, an adventure of which he never ceased talking, and now he was assigned to walk with the newcomer as the tribe returned to their riverside home for the winter.

'Yes, it's ours,' he said. 'We call it Patamoke. I'm sure the name has a meaning, but I forget what it is. Yes, we leave it every summer to live in the woods close to the great water.'

'The great water is over there,' Pentaquod corrected, pointing toward the bay.

'There is a greater over there,' Scar-chin explained, pointing east. Such information Pentaquod did not believe, but he thought it best not to argue with this excitable little man.

Pentaquod led them to the rude wigwam he had constructed, and the children in the party ran to it, using it as part of a game, laughing at the inept way the sides fitted against the roof. Some of the women gathered about the sleeping place, too, ridiculing its unfamiliar patterns, unaware of rudeness in such behavior, and when Pentaquod moved to protect his few belongings from the children, the women sided with him and called to the boys and girls to leave the stranger's things alone. Then they smiled up at the tall man, their eyes sparkling.

The returning villagers had lingered only briefly, for the werowance now spoke to them in soft tones, whereupon the character of the motley crowd changed abruptly and they scurried back to their home. The warriors went into the woods and began cutting trees, while the women and children attended to the smoothing out of the stone platforms on which the winter's lodgings would be built. When these things were done, the entire tribe moved to the shore and began picking the grasses from which the sides of the wigwams would be woven. Pentaquod was impressed with the orderly way in which the tribe worked; they appeared to be much better builders than the Susquehannocks.

When the preliminary tasks were finished, and the materials laid in strategic spots so that building could progress on the morrow, they rested, and Pentaquod had a chance to talk in more detail with Scar-chin, who told him of his long captivity among the Susquehannocks, and of how much he admired that warrior tribe, and of how the Susquehannock women had made fun of him for being so small and skinny.

'What is your tribe called?' Pentaquod asked.

'We are one small part of the Nanticokes. The great werowances live to the south. We have only a lesser werowance, as you've seen.'

'Have you a name?'

Scar-chin shrugged his shoulders, as if the mystery of names was reserved for shamans or those who cast medicine. He did, however, venture the information that frequently the powerful Nanticokes to the south invaded the village to steal whatever the local people had acquired.

'Are they so much braver?'

'No, more of them.'

'Do you fight back? In battle?'

Scar-chin laughed. 'We're not Susquehannocks. When the Nanticokes come, we run into the woods. We leave enough behind so they won't want to pursue us, and when they've taken what they want, they leave, and then we come back.'

Such behavior was so extraordinary that Pentaquod could think of no sensible comment. He sat tapping his fingers together, and as he did so he spied the pile of white shells. 'Don't you use them against the Nanticokes?'

'Use what?'

'Those . . . well, those shells?'

'Those!' Scar-chin stared at the shells, then broke into laughter. He summoned a group of tribesmen and shared the hilarious joke with them —'He thinks we throw them at the Nanticokes!' And all his listeners began to laugh, and some of the children started skimming the white shells into the river.

Pentaquod, taking no offense asked, 'What are they?'

'You don't know?' Scar-chin asked in amazement. From one of the teasing children he took a shell, held it at chest level and imitated a man eating from it, whereupon one of the women ran to the shore, dived into the cold water, and within a few moments reappeared, holding in her hand a dripping object constructed of two of the shells bound together.

Running to Pentaquod, her hair dripping about her shoulders, she extended her two hands, presenting him with the river-born object. He took it, was impressed by its roughness and heaviness. 'What is it?' he asked Scar-chin.

'He doesn't know what it is!' the interpreter shouted, pleased with his new-found importance as the only one in the town who could speak with this Susquehannock.

'He doesn't know what it is!' the children echoed gleefully, and everyone watched as the tall man from the north wrestled with the connected shells.

Finally the young woman who had brought him the present took it back, reached for a sharp-pointed stick and deftly split open the shell. One half she threw away. The other she handed gravely to Pentaquod, indicating that he should eat.

Trained on venison and rabbit and fish, he looked at the strange object in his hand. In no way could he relate it to food such as he had known: it was watery, and slippery, and had no bones, and there was no sensible way to attack it.

The girl solved his problem. Taking the laden shell from his nervous hand, she lifted it to his lips, told him to open his mouth, and with a delicate twist of her fingers popped the food in. For an instant he was aware of a fine, salty taste and a pleasing sensation. Then the food, whatever it was, disappeared, leaving on his face a most bewildered look. With an easy throwing motion, the girl tossed the empty shell onto the mound.

'We call them kawshek,' Scar-chin explained. 'More sleeping in the river than you could count. All winter we feed on kawshek.'

Pentaquod contemplated this: in addition to the abundance of food he had discovered by himself, there was this additional supply hidden in the river. It was inconceivable, and as he sat perplexed, trying to unravel the mystery of oysters, he thought of his friend Fishing-long-legs, and he queried Scar-chin. 'What is it he catches on the bottom, cuts in two and swallows with such difficulty?'

'Fish.'

'I know fish. This is no fish. Shaped like a hand, with many legs.'

As soon as Pentaquod uttered these words a benign smile spread over the scarred face of his interpreter, who said nothing. Obviously he was recalling moments of past happiness, after which he summoned the girl who had caught the oysters. 'He doesn't know crabs, either,' he whispered.

The girl smiled and with her right hand gave an imitation of a crab wriggling its many feet. Then a look of compassion filled her eyes; to be ignorant of the oyster was amusing, but to be unacquainted with the crab was pathetic.

'What is crab?' Pentaquod asked, and Scar-chin replied, 'When Manitou, the Great Power, finished populating the river with everything our village required—pine trees for canoes, deer to feed us in summer, geese and oysters for winter—He saw that we were grateful and well disposed. So in His grace He created one thing more, to stand as a token of His eternal concern. He made the crab and hid him in our salty waters.'

Women in the crowd asked what he had said so far, then prompted him to add details that interested them: 'A crab provides little food, so he is not easy to eat. But the little he does offer is the best food under the sky. To eat crab you must work, which makes you appreciate him more. He is the blessing, the remembrance. And no man or woman ever ate enough.'

Pentaquod listened with growing respect as Scar-chin reported on this delicacy, and when the oration ended he asked tentatively, 'Could I taste some?'

'They come only in summer.'

'Didn't you dry any?'

This question, when interpreted, brought laughter, which ended when the girl moved forward to indicate that the meat of the crab was so delicate it had to be eaten immediately; her fine fingers danced as she portrayed this.

Again Pentaquod fell to rumination, confused by this barrage of strange information. 'But if the crab has the hard shell that I found on the island . . .' He hesitated as the girl nodded, then knocked her knuckles together to prove how hard the shell was.

'Aha!' Pentaquod demanded, grabbing her by the wrist. 'If the shell is so hard, how is it that Fishing-long-legs can cut it in half with his beak?'

When Scar-chin explained that the Susquehannock used that name for the great blue heron, and that he was referring to the manner in which the heron caught crabs, tossed them in the air and cut them in half, the girl's expression became even more compassionate.

'It's the soft crab,' she explained.

'The what?'

'In the summer we catch crabs that have no shell . . .'

This was totally incomprehensible, and Pentaquod shook his head, but the girl continued, 'They have no shell, and we roast them over the fire, and they are the best.'

Pentaquod could make absolutely nothing of this, and he was about to drop the whole discussion when a boy of about nine summers moved beside the girl and by a series of swift gestures of hand-to-mouth indicated that he himself could eat four or five of the no-shell crabs. This seemed preposterous and Pentaquod turned away, but the daring boy tugged on his arm and repeated the pantomime: he could indeed eat five no-shells.

When the crowd dispersed to arrange ramshackle sleeping quarters for the night, Pentaquod retreated from the shore to his own wigwam, but before he fell asleep he found Scar-chin standing in the rude doorway. 'Stay with us,' the little man said. Pentaquod made no reply. 'The werowance is old now, and sad.' No comment. 'The girl who caught the oyster for you, she is his granddaughter, and whenever he sees her it causes pain.' This was impenetrable, but the little man continued, 'Her father, the werowance's son who should be in command now, died of the fever and the girl reminds him of this loss.'

Pentaquod saw no reason to respond to any of this, so in the darkness the little interpreter remained in the doorway, content to watch the shadowy form of the tall Susquehannock who had made this day so memorable. At last, when night surrounded the village, the former slave of the Susquehannocks slipped away.

In the ensuing weeks the villagers rebuilt their wigwams and instructed Pentaquod in their language, a much simpler one than his. In all ways this tribe lived on a less complicated level than the Susquehannocks: their werowance had little power and their possessions were fewer. Their medicine man was not so formidable as the mysterious shamans of the north, and for him to try to enforce decisions of life and death would have been laughable; he was a good-luck charm and nothing more.

The little old werowance was named Orapak; he was past sixty and must soon die, but was allowed to retain his office because there was none to challenge him. He was a wise old man, and gentle too, and for many years he had kept his tribe out of serious trouble. 'When the Nanticokes come north to fight us, we flee farther north,' he explained. 'And when the Susquehannocks come south to fight us, we flee to the south.'

'Doesn't that take you into Nanticoke country?'

'No, because when we flee south, we go into the marshes, and the Nanticokes wouldn't dare follow us.' He hesitated. 'Mosquitoes, you know.'

'I know. Last summer I lived in the marsh.'

'Brave man,' the werowance said. Then he asked, 'Why did you think we leave our village each summer?'

'What good do mosquitoes do?' Pentaquod asked, whereupon the old man raised his eyes to heaven and replied, 'On that first day Scar-chin here told you of how Manitou gave this river everything, and then one thing more, the crab. Well, when that was done He said, "Now I will keep men from becoming arrogant," and He threw in the mosquito.'

'Why?'

'To remind us that He can do anything He pleases, and we have to like it.'

Pentaquod decided that now was the time to raise the question of his membership in the tribe. 'The river is excellent. I enjoyed it when I lived here alone.'

The werowance studied this declaration, then blew out his cheeks, signifying that he appreciated the gravity of what had been said. The Susquehannock was pointing out that he had acquired possession of the place after the villagers had deserted it. He was intimating ownership, even though many warriors were available to contest it. Orapak realized how powerful this stranger was; quite likely he could defeat any of the warriors who up to now had defeated nobody. Warily he said, 'It would be good if you stayed with us,' adding hastily, 'in the wigwam that's already yours.'

'I would like that,' Pentaquod replied, and no more was said about his citizenship. He continued to occupy his wigwam, which women showed him how to finish properly, and he began paying court to Navitan, the werowance's granddaughter. At seventeen she had been eyeing some of the young warriors during the summer encampment, but nothing much had happened and she now showed herself receptive to the moves the tall Susquehannock was making.

They were married before the first snow. The old women were delighted that their Navitan had caught herself such a daring man, and the shaman who performed the ceremony gave it as his opinion that Manitou Himself had sent Pentaquod to protect this village.

In the division of labor common to tribes along the Chesapeake, Pentaquod specialized in cutting tall trees, shaping them and burning out their interior so that canoes could be built. He also became the expert in hunting geese, those remarkable fowl that he had known simply as big birds: from oak and pine he carved eighteen rude likenesses of the geese, coloring them with earthen paints discovered by the tribe, and these he placed at strategic spots related to wind and shore, luring the birds so close that he rarely missed with his strong bow. But the killing of a goose always bothered him; for although he loved the taste of the roasted flesh, he did not like to see the stately birds destroyed.

It was at the end of winter when the sad night came. Navitan had been scraping the reef for oysters when she saw a flock of geese in a cornfield acting strangely. The males were running at one another, and the yearlings were restless, gathering twigs as if to build nests they knew they did not need. Uneasy chatter murmured through the flock, when suddenly an old gander, much heavier than the rest, ran awkwardly a few steps, flapped his great wings and soared into the air.

In an instant that whole field of geese flew aloft, circled a few times, then set out resolutely for the north. From other fields which Navitan could not see, other flocks rose into the air, and soon the sky was dark with great black-and-gray geese flying north. 'Oh!' she cried, alerting the village. 'They're leaving!'

No one required to be told who was leaving. The geese, those notable birds on whom the tribe had feasted for generation after generation, were quitting the river. In nine days there would not be a goose visible anywhere, and to see them flying north, to hear them honking as they repaired to the distant ice-bound fields on which they would raise their young, was a moment of such sadness that many of the older men and women wept, for the great geese had been their calendars and the counting of their years.

Now the werowance appeared, white and stiff-legged, with his face to the sky, and after he had cast his blessing on the geese, the shaman uttered the timeless prayer:

> 'Great Power, You who watch over us and establish the seasons, guard the geese as they leave us. Watch over them as they fly to distant areas. Find them grain for their long flight and keep them from storms. They are our need, our protection from hunger, our sentinels at night, our companions through the winter, our source of food and warmth, our tenants on the land, our watchmen in the sky, the guardians of our streams, the chatterers at the coming and going. Great Power, protect them while they are gone from us, and in due season bring them back to this river, which is their home and ours.'

No child made a sound, for this was the most sacred moment of the year. If the mysteries were not properly cast, the geese might fail to return, and the winter when that occurred would be terrible indeed.

Some moons after the geese had gone, crabs moved in to take their place as the principal source of food, and now Pentaquod discovered what the villagers meant when they claimed that Manitou, the Great Power, looked after them especially. It was a day in late spring when Navitan led him to her canoe, handing him a basketful of fish heads and bear gristle to tote along. The concoction smelled offensive, but Navitan assured him this was what the crabs preferred, and he wondered how the loose and almost rotting stuff could be attached to the curved hooks used in fishing.

To his surprise, his wife had no hooks. 'What kind of fishing is this?' he asked, and she smiled without offering an explanation. But once he had paddled her to the spot she had selected, she produced long strands of twisted fiber and deer gut, and to these she tied fish heads and chunks of gristly bear meat, throwing the lines aft.

Pentaquod looked for the telltale signs which indicated that a fish had bitten the lure, but there was no such movement and he concluded that Navitan was not going to catch any crabs, but after a while, when there was no visible reason for her doing so, she began to pull in one of her lines with her left hand, holding in her right a long pole to which was attached a loosely woven wicker basket. As the line slowly left the water, Pentaquod saw that the first fish head was about to appear, but what he did not see was that attached to it was a crab, cutting at the meat with his powerful claws and oblivious of the fact that it was being pulled almost out of the water.

When the crab was visible to Navitan, she deftly swept her basket into the water and under the startled crab, lifting it as it tried to fall away, and plopping it, all legs wiggling and claws snapping, into the canoe.

Pentaquod was stunned by the performance, and when his wife continued to haul in her line, catching crab after crab, he realized that here was a brand of fishing totally unlike any in which he had ever participated. 'Why don't they swim away from the bait?' he asked. 'Can't they see you're going to catch them?'

'They like us to eat them,' Navitan said. 'Manitou sends them to us for that purpose.'

Pentaquod gingerly touched one and found the shell extremely hard, but he could not examine it closely, for the fierce claws snapped at him. He was even more perplexed when Navitan carried her two dozen crabs to camp and pitched them into a pot of boiling water, for within moments they turned bright red. She then instructed him in how to pick meat from the carcasses, and when she had a clay bowl filled she told him to stop, for she knew that picking crab was a tedious and demanding job: a dozen crabs produced only a handful of meat.

But when she took this meat, as her mother had taught her, and mixed it with herbs and vegetables and corn meal, and formed it into small cakes and fried them in sizzling bear fat, she produced one of the finest dishes this river would ever know. 'Cakes of crab,' she called them, and Pentaquod found them subtle and delicious.

'There is better,' Navitan assured him, and when he doubted, she told him to wait until the crabs began to shed, and one day she brought him four that had newly cast their shells, and these she fried directly in hot bear grease, without first boiling or picking them.

'Do I eat legs and all?' Pentaquod asked, and she goaded him into trying them; when he had finished the four he declared them succulent beyond belief.

'Now you are one of us,' Navitan said.

While Pentaquod was initiating himself into such pleasant customs he made a discovery which disturbed him: he found that what Scar-chin had reported was true. This tribe never defended itself from enemies, and when the Susquehannocks intruded from the north, or the Nanticokes from the south, no attempt was made to protect the village. The villagers seemed not to care what happened; they mounted no sentries, sent no patrols to check the frontiers, engaged in no self-defense maneuvers. He was not surprised, therefore, when children ran in one morning to report, 'Here come the Nanticokes again!'

No one panicked. Everyone placed essential goods in deerskin pouches, hid supplies of food in the nearby forest, and fled. The werowance marched at the front of his people, as gallantly as if heading for battle, and took them deep into the fragmented, river-cut area northwest of their village. They had learned from frequent experience that the Nanticokes were reluctant to follow them into that chopped-up area, so they marched with a certain confidence that after a decent interval, during which the invaders would steal everything left behind and then retreat singing victory songs, they could return to their homes and resume life as it had been.

Pentaquod was staggered by this attitude. When the children first reported the invasion he had wanted to storm out to engage the enemy, teach them a lesson and drive them back to the southern regions, but the old werowance would have none of this, nor did any of his people wish to face the sturdier men from the south.

'What do we lose, doing it this way?' one of the women asked Pentaquod as they fled to the land of the broken rivers.

'We lose my wigwam,' he said in some anger.

'A wigwam we can build in a day. The dried fish? Who cares. The salted duck they won't find. We stowed it among the oaks.'

When the tribe had hidden for seven days, it was deemed likely that the Nanticokes had done their damage and retreated, but to confirm this, scouts had to be sent back to ensure that they had really gone. No volunteers offered to do the spying, so Pentaquod, speaking for Scar-chin, said, 'We'll go.' The interpreter, who had been captured once, wanted nothing to do with such a venture, but Pentaquod insisted, and since going in the company of this brave Susquehannock would lend distinction to the little man, he reluctantly agreed.

No spy in the long history of the region ever moved with more circumspection than Scar-chin as he entered the territory occupied by the invaders. Indeed, he was so painfully careful not to snap a twig that Pentaquod realized the little fellow's crafty plan: he would move so slowly that the Nanticokes would have two extra days to clear out. When he and Pentaquod did finally reach the village site, the enemy would be practically back in their own villages.

But Pentaquod would have none of this, and was determined to press forward to see what kind of people the Nanticokes were. But he was simply unable to budge his fellow spy; no amount of scorn, no appeal to Scar-chin's manhood prevailed. The little man refused to move forward ahead of the prudent schedule he had set himself, and in the end he attached himself to a locust tree and could not be budged, so Pentaquod moved alone to the river.

From a vantage point he observed the tag end of the Nanticokes as they rummaged one last time through the captured village, collecting final souvenirs of their raid. While the main body rambled east along the river, chanting a victory song which told of how they had subdued the fiercely resisting village, four laggards remained behind, wrestling with some captured article too big for them to handle. Pentaquod, watching them with amusement, could not resist making an arrogant gesture, even though he knew it was foolish and risky.

Leaping from behind a tree, he uttered his wildest war cry, brandished his spear and lunged at the four startled Nanticokes. They were terrified by this apparition, five hands taller than they and much broader of shoulder, and they fled. But one kept his senses long enough to shout to those ahead, 'The Susquehannocks!' and terror ensued.

The entire foraging party fell into panic, abandoning whatever they had stolen, and with great clatter stormed and thrashed their way in undignified retreat. So definitive were the sounds of defeat that even Scar-chin was lured from his hiding place in time to see his friend Pentaquod brandishing his spear and chasing an entire Nanticoke army through the woods. It had never occurred to Scar-chin that one resolute man might be the equal of four surprised Nanticokes or forty frightened ones, but when he saw the retreating feathers of the southern braves he realized that he had witnessed a miracle, and he began fashioning the ballad that would immortalize the victory of Pentaquod:

> 'Fearless he strode among the robbers,
> Strong he faced the innumerable enemy,
> Thoughtless of danger he engaged them,
> Throwing the bodies up and over,
> Smashing the heads and twisting the legs

Till the exhausted foe screamed and trembled,
Beseeching mercy, kissing his hands in fear . . .

It was an epic, a portrait in the most exalted woodland tradition, and as
Pentaquod casually surveyed the trivial damage done his village and his
wigwam, he listened with amusement to the chant. It reminded him of
the war songs he had heard as a boy, when the Susquehannocks returned
from their forays against the tribes to the south; those songs had depicted
events of unbelievable heroism, and he had believed them:

Now the bravest of the brave Susquehannocks,
Cherodah and Mataloak and Wissikan and Nantiquod
Creep through the forest, spy out the fortress
And leap with violent bravery upon the foe . . .

And it now dawned upon Pentaquod that the village his ancestors had
attacked with such bravery was this village; the enemies they had subdued were ones they had never faced, for the foe had been hiding in
faraway marshes. There had been no battle save in the minds of ancient
poets who knew that when braves march forth to battle, it is obligatory
that there be victory songs.

And yet, even though he knew the fraudulence of such behavior, when
the villagers timidly returned and saw to their delight that this time their
goods had not been carried off, they began to chant Scar-chin's composition and to believe it. With appealing modesty Pentaquod stood silent,
allowing Scar-chin to lead the applause. If the village had been saved,
Pentaquod reasoned, it was because of my actions, and I will accept the
credit. It was that night when the older men began thinking of him as
a possible werowance.

But when word next reached the tribe that Susquehannocks were
moving south, even though Pentaquod assured the villagers that he knew
certain tricks which might fend them off—provided he could find nine
brave men who would not run away—the old werowance brusquely
countermanded his proposal. 'The only sensible thing to do is run into
the marshes. We have been doing this for many years, and in all that time
we have enjoyed a good life, with plenty of food and enough marsh grass
to weave again the sides of our burned wigwams. Let the enemy have his
triumph, if he needs it. Our security is in the marshes.'

The strange aspect of this policy was that it in no way diminished the
self-respect of the villagers, and it certainly did not diminish Pentaquod;
he had proved his valor against the Nanticokes, and Scar-chin had
composed the epic. Pentaquod was a true hero, and he did not have to
repeat his heroics endlessly to retain his reputation. As he fled with the
others into the safety of the southern marshes, every man believed that

if Pentaquod had wanted to oppose the Susquehannocks, he could have done so. Instead he preferred safeguarding his pregnant wife, and this, deemed the villagers, was much more sensible.

As they crossed the river, and hid their canoes, and straggled through the rushes that lined the southern shore, Pentaquod heard two tribal tales that fascinated him, and he kept asking the older men numerous questions: 'You say that to the east, where you go in summer, there is a river much greater than the ones I know?' 'The water is much saltier?' 'The birds are different and no man has ever seen the opposite shore?' 'And it is there, all the time, and a canoe cannot cross it?' 'What do you mean, waves coming to the shore so high they knock down a man?'

He was so excited by their descriptions, and so willing to believe because all agreed, that he wanted to set out immediately to see this marvelous thing, but the werowance said, 'We will be going there in the summer, to escape the mosquitoes.' So he waited.

The other story was incredible, much weightier than the tale of the big river, for it contained disturbing implications. He first caught rumor of it from Scar-chin, who said casually, 'Maybe when the Great Canoe returns, it will chastise the Susquehannocks.'

'What Great Canoe?'

'The one that came many winters ago.'

'It came where?'

'Near the island.'

'How big was it?'

'I didn't see it, but Orapak did, and so did Ponasque.'

He had gone immediately to Ponasque, a very old man now, to ask directly, 'Did you see the Great Canoe?'

'I did,' the old man said as they huddled in the marshes.

'How big was it?'

'Twenty canoes, forty, piled one on the other. It rose high in the air.'

'How many paddlers?'

'None.'

This was the most ominous statement Pentaquod had ever heard, a Great Canoe moving without paddles. He contemplated this for some time, then asked the old man, 'You saw this thing, yourself, not some great story recited at night?'

'I saw it, beyond the island.'

'What did you think of it?'

The old man's eyes grew misty as he recalled that stupendous day when his world changed. 'We were very afraid. All of us, even Orapak. We could not explain what we had seen, but we had seen it. The fear has never left us, but as the years pass we have managed to forget.' He indicated that he was not happy to have a stranger to the tribe revive those distant fears and he would say no more.

By prudent questioning, Pentaquod satisfied himself that all members of the tribe believed that the Great Canoe had indeed come to the mouth of the river, that it was huge in size, that it moved without paddles. One old woman added to the story: 'It was white on top, brown at the bottom.'

Pentaquod carried the disquieting news with him as they penetrated deeper into the swamp, and when they reached relatively solid ground on which they could camp, he went to the werowance and asked bluntly, 'What did you think, Orapak, when you saw the Great Canoe?'

The old man sucked in his breath, then sat down beneath an oak. He reflected on what he should reply to this penetrating question, knowing that it cut to the heart of his tribe's existence, then said slowly, 'I cannot come into the marshes again. I find it too exhausting and know that my time for death is at hand. You must be the next werowance.'

'I did not ask about that, Orapak.'

'But this is the significant answer to what you did ask.'

Of this Pentaquod could make no sense, but the old leader continued, 'When we gathered on the shore that day to see the Great Canoe as it moved slowly north, all of us saw the same thing. You are probably aware of that from the questions you've been asking.'

Pentaquod nodded. He was convinced that this tribal memory was no mere chant composed by some imaginative ancestor like Scar-chin. Satisfied on this point, the old man went on, 'When the others had seen the Canoe, and assured themselves that it was real, they returned home, but my grandfather, the werowance then, took my father and me along the shore, and we were hiding in the forest when the Canoe came close, and we saw that it contained men much like us and yet much different.'

'How?'

'Their skins were white. Their bodies were of some different substance, for the sun glistened when it struck.'

That was all the old man knew, and since none of the others had told him of these startling facts, he realized that this was privileged knowledge, to be possessed only by the succession of werowances. In sharing this sacred knowledge of the glistening bodies, Orapak was passing along to Pentaquod the burden of leadership. He did not need to warn that no mention must be made of what the Great Canoe actually contained, for it was clear that one day it must return, bringing the enigma of men with white skins and bodies that reflected sunlight.

'They will come back, won't they?' Pentaquod asked.

'They will.'

'When?'

'Every day of my life I have risen from my bed with one question: Is this the day they will return? Now that burden is yours. You will never place your head upon the sleeping reeds without wondering: Will they come tomorrow?'

They buried the canny old werowance, a craven who had lost his village a score of times but never a man in battle, deep in the swamps away from the river he had loved. From his tired, worn body they removed the copper disk symbolic of leadership, proffering it to Pentaquod, but he refused, for such disks of authority were not part of the Susquehannock ritual. Instead he planted three tall turkey feathers in his hair, so that he towered even more conspicuously over his little charges, and Scar-chin recited his epic of how the new werowance had once defeated the Nanticokes single-handed. And so this tribe became the next in that strange procession of nations who choose as their leader someone who is not even a member of their tribe.

The first test of Pentaquod's leadership came when the Nanticokes marched north on their traditional raid. The women assumed that the tribe would flee north in the accustomed manner, but some of the younger warriors, infected by Scar-chin's epic, believed they should stand and fight. 'With Pentaquod to plan the battle,' they argued, 'we could repel the invaders and end our annual shame.'

The idea was tempting to Pentaquod the man, but in his capacity as werowance, on whom the safety of the tribe depended, he had to think more cautiously. He could not casually sacrifice any men, for his was a trivial group, small and frightened and inconsequential. A sore defeat might demoralize them, leaving no base for continued existence. Furthermore, he had achieved his memorable victory over the four Nanticoke warriors by surprise, and he was not at all sure this could be repeated. He told the young warriors, 'Let us scout the Nanticokes to see how they approach this time.'

So he and two of the most excitable young fighters crept into the woods, went far upstream and swam across the river onto alien land. There they hid until the noisy Nanticokes came into sight, and as Pentaquod had suspected, this time they did not move without sentinels and forerunners. There would be no surprising this expedition, for it was prepared.

The enthusiasm of the young warriors dampened. In some consternation they scurried back to inform the others, 'They are marching as a well-prepared army. We had better go the rivers.' And with a very willing Pentaquod in the lead, they fled.

When they returned to their village, it was Pentaquod who surveyed the damage; it was not great but it was humiliating, and he vowed: They will not do this again.

That summer he did not allow his people to abandon their land because of the mosquitoes. 'We will stay here and fortify it. We will lay subtle traps along the approaches, and all men will learn some skill at arms. Anyone who complains of the mosquitoes will get no crab meat.'

It was a trying summer. The mosquitoes were terrible; at dusk hundreds would land on any exposed arm or face, and people stayed close to smudge pots when the sun went down. They smeared themselves with bear grease, slept with blankets about their heads and rose weary from the sticky heat which had kept them sweating through the darkness. But they were inspired by the vision held before them by their tall young werowance: 'When the Nanticokes come this year, what a surprise they will get at this tree!' By testing his young men repeatedly, he satisfied himself that they would stand firm and execute their surprise.

He used every military idea developed by the Susquehannocks and invented others appropriate to the situation, and when the mosquitoes disappeared in early autumn they left behind a village prepared to defend itself.

The young men actually hungered for the Nanticokes to arrive, but some untoward event in the south delayed the customary expedition, and the fledgling warriors chafed. Pentaquod, knowing that he must keep their enthusiasm high, divided his tribe into portions, one marching against the other, and thus they perfected their strategies. And then one cool day at the start of winter, when geese lined the river, scouts ran in with the long-awaited news: 'The Nanticokes are coming.'

The southerners came with their accustomed noise and self-assurance, with only casual scouts in the forefront; following Pentaquod's surprising assault on them, they had been attentive to details, but now they were, as he had predicted to his troops, careless once more. They came through the woods like revelers; they forded the river like people swimming for pleasure; they straggled down the right bank of the river as if attending a celebration.

And then they came to Pentaquod's carefully disposed troops. From behind trees arrows were launched, and men appeared with spears, while ahead the ground gave way, projecting the forward troops into pits, and strange sounds echoed through the forest, and even women appeared, beating sticks. Confusion and pain captured the Nanticokes, and in the end all they could do was flee, leaving behind more than twenty prisoners. Never had they known such a debacle.

The little villagers, finding themselves with an unprecedented victory and also a score of captives, did not know what to do with either. Unaccustomed to war other than the retreats it caused, they had no concept of what one did with prisoners, and when Pentaquod explained that in the north his Susquehannocks followed three courses of action, they listened attentively. 'The wounded we kill. The strong we turn into slaves. The swift we send back to their people with insulting messages.'

The villagers nodded approval of these suggestions, completely unaware of what they entailed, but their werowance continued, 'However,
we wounded no one, so there are none to kill.' Most of them saw the
common sense of this judgment, and indeed applauded it because they
had no taste for killing. 'We do not need slaves, because there is no work
for them to do, and if we made work, we would also have to make meals
for them.' This, too, was irrefutable. 'And I do not think we ought to
send insulting messages to the Nanticokes. We want them for our
friends, not our enemies.'

To some, this was a surprising verdict. Many, especially those who had
not participated in the battle, desired to humiliate their enemy and had
devised clever ways for doing so; they were disgusted that Pentaquod
should preach conciliation, but he received support from a strange quarter.

Two young warriors who had stood behind the first tree where the
traps were sprung confessed that they had been terrified, and that if even
one thing had gone wrong, they would have been surrounded and killed.
'It is much better for the Nanticokes to come as friends,' they reasoned.
'Let us feast the prisoners and talk with them and send them south with
our respect.'

As soon as the words were spoken Pentaquod cried, 'Let us do just
that!' and his counsel prevailed, and the feast was held with goose and
deer and yams and baked fish and pumpkin sweetened with the juice of
cornstalks, and tobacco was smoked in long pipes which passed from
hand to hand. One of the Nanticokes of good family said at the conclusion, 'We will inform our people that we are no longer enemies,' and the
sun rose before the new friends parted.

This dramatic change of affairs created a feeling of profound excitement in the village, and talk became heady. 'Never again will we desert
our village to the Nanticokes. We have proved that we can fight better
than those fools. One of these days we'll march south to their villages,
and they'll see what a change has occurred.'

Pentaquod took no notice of this bombast; he recognized it as the
boastfulness which Susquehannock warriors had engaged in when he was
a boy, but when he heard his people tell one another that the entire
system of the world was altered by their victory, he became worried. And
when they boasted that next time the Susquehannocks marched down
from the north there would be war, he called a halt.

'The Susquehannocks are not Nanticokes,' he warned. 'Not one of our
tricks would fool them, because they are Susquehannock tricks, and they
use them against their enemies.' He harangued them for an extended
period, and then a happy metaphor came to him. Lowering his voice and
leaning forward to face his enthusiastic warriors, he told them, 'Among

the Susquehannocks, I was a small man.' His height was so great as he said this, his torso so much broader than theirs, that they could only gasp.

'What shall we do when they come again?' they asked, subdued.

'We shall cross the river, hide our canoes and go into the swamps,' he said, and into the swamps he led them.

In the decade that followed—1586–1595 by western calendar—Pentaquod became the best werowance his people had ever known. He was a tall, courageous, kindly man serving among a small, frightened people. When his tribe went east to the Great Waters, he led the way and carried his share of the burdens, and on the rare occasions when they had to flee into the southern marshes, his ability to absorb such ignominy without losing good spirits inspired them.

They no longer had to hide in the northern rivers, because he had arranged lasting peace with the Nanticokes, and the two tribes now traded instead of fighting: dried deer meat to the Nanticokes, bright shells for roanoke to the villagers. There were even exchanges of visits, which were salutary, for the returning villagers boasted with perverse pride, 'Our mosquitoes are twice as fierce as theirs.'

Pentaquod and Navitan had a son to inherit the title, and then another, and all things prospered. He led his people east to the supreme river and watched as its salty waves came higher than his head to thunder upon the shore in shattering power. As he stood transfixed one day an illumination came to him: If the Great Canoe we await is able to move across this river of such tremendous power, it must be of vast size and the men who steer it must be even greater than the Susquehannocks. And he looked upon the ocean with dismay and wonderment.

There were other mysteries. At far-spread intervals on some starless night a child would cry, 'The light is there!' and in the forest across the river would come a single glimmer, and move about as if controlled by demons, and come to rest, glowing ominously through the dark passage of night. In the village parents hushed their children, and no one spoke of it. Through the long darkness the little people remained at water's edge, staring obsessively, wondering who or what could be moving on the southern shore, but there was never a satisfactory explanation, merely that flickering light emanating from some unknown source. Toward dawn it would vanish and not reappear for many years.

A greater mystery concerned the bay. It lay only a short distance to the west, but rarely did a villager see it and never did they venture upon it. In all their generations of living beside water, they had not discovered the sail, nor the fact that men could move across rivers and bays without paddling; to them the bay was alien. Its abundance of fish and crabs and oysters was proscribed, and all they knew of this great river of rivers was that it was the route by which the fierce Potomacs attacked. They were content to leave this splendid body of water to their enemies, and never did they know the grandeur of sunset on broad waters or the rising of a sudden storm.

It was believed by the villagers that on those nights when portentous affairs impended, Fishing-long-legs would come to the river as the stars were beginning to fade, uttering mournful *kraannks* to warn of imminent wonders. Then the people would huddle in the darkness, listening with terror to the sounds that echoed from the trees bending over the water.

On one such night in 1596, when distant nations were preparing to invade the bay, blue herons flew in great numbers from the swamps, scattering over the landscape before dawn to search the estuaries for swift-moving fish. Their cries filled the night, but if they distressed those men and women of evil conscience and with something to fear, they caused no apprehension in Pentaquod, because he knew that they had flocked to signal the birth of his third child, and before sunrise he heard the reassuring cry.

'A girl!' the midwife reported as she ran from the birthing hut.

'I am content,' Pentaquod replied gravely, but he was far more than that. He had always wanted a daughter who would comfort him when he retired from war, and at last he had one. As soon as it was respectable for him to visit the birthing hut, he stooped low, passed beneath the pine boughs and chains of acorns to take the hands of his wife. 'I am content,' he said and he was permitted to see the new child, so small that it was hard to believe she was his offspring. Holding his two forefingers apart, he indicated to his happy wife how really minute this child was, not at all like her two brothers at that age. He laughed, then lifted the tiny thing and held it against his cheek.

'Her name shall be Tciblento,' he said, and she became the most precious thing in his life, the joy of his later years. He taught her the lore of the river: where the geese clustered, and how to watch beavers at work, and the right striplings to cut for a wigwam, and how to burn out the heart of a tree in order to make a canoe. She learned to dive for oysters and fish for crabs, and with his urging she became an excellent cook.

But it was the grace of her movements that delighted him; she was as deft in dodging among trees as a fawn. The soft color of her skin was like a deer's, too, and she was never more beautiful than when she appeared suddenly from behind some tree as they were working in the forest—unexpected, bright of eye, quick of gesture.

Once as he worked among the trees, seeking pines from which canoes could be burned, he found her sleeping on a bed of needles, her hair thrown carelessly across her breast. Tears came into his eyes and he whispered, 'Tciblento, Tciblento, why were you born into the days of change?' He could foresee that in her lifetime the Great Canoe would return, imposing fearful difficulties as she endeavored to adjust to the new world it would bring. As he watched, a blue heron landed, uttering its mournful *kraannk,* and without waking she twisted an end of hair.

Herons did not cry at random; they sent warnings. And he remembered that on the night of her birth the Choptanks had been warned.

It must be understood that this small tribe did not refer to itself as the Choptanks; that name would come much later and from strangers. No congregation so inconsequential would presume to appropriate a name. It was proper for others to do so, like the powerful Susquehannocks *(from the smooth-flowing stream)* or the crafty Nanticokes *(those who ply the tidewaters)* or the brutal Potomacs who ruled across the bay *(those who live where the goods are brought in).* But Pentaquod's little group of inept fishermen referred to themselves as We, or Us, or, sometimes, The People. By the world they would be remembered as Choptanks.

Nor did they call their river by that name; indeed, they had no concept of it as an entity, with a distant beginning and a termination in the bay. They were content to know their little stretch of it and would have been astonished to learn that they commanded an entire water system which would one day be known by their name.

Nameless little people living upon a nameless river, they were destined to endow their somnolent region with one of the world's most tantalizing titles: Choptank. The word must have had a meaning at some point; if so, it has been forgotten. A very old woman once said that it meant *where the water flows back strongly,* but she could explain nothing.

Pentaquod's two sons were now developing into responsible young adults, and Tciblento was an eight-year-old marvel, not so tall as her brothers but much quicker in mastering the lessons her father taught. She had begun to wear her long black hair in braids and had a saucy way of cocking her head when listening to elders. Her father delighted in his children, and it was partly because of wanting to be with them more that he summoned the tribe for his farewell oration:

'Your food supplies have never been more secure, and your village is no longer ravaged by Nanticokes. Never has your river known a happier time, with crabs for all in the summer and beaver pelts in winter to keep you warm. I have served with you long enough. The time is at hand when you must select one of your own people as werowance.'

Uneasiness followed this announcement, for the little people realized that without his towering guidance they might revert to the old days of fear and flight. The Nanticokes would learn that he was no longer leading the tribe and might conclude that continuing the peace was not in their interest, but the tall Susquehannock was insistent. Then he gave his reasons:

> 'Whenever, in the old days, we fled to the northern rivers I watched one spot where two waters meet, and I have always wanted to live there with Navitan and the children. When I first came to your river I lived on the island where Fishing-long-legs instructed me, and then on the cliff where I saw how beautiful this land can be, and in the marsh where Onk-or the goose came to see me, and then in this mysterious village where no people lived. I am a man who likes to live apart, and I feel a deep urge to build my wigwam between the two waters.'

'Who will be our werowance?' they asked, and he told them that they should select a young man who could serve them for two generations, and when they protested that they had never chosen their leader before, he allowed his eyes to wander over the frightened crowd. They came to rest on Matapank, who had stood beside him in battle, and when the villagers realized that Pentaquod had indicated his choice, they shouted, 'Matapank!' and were gratified.

Pentaquod believed that once he announced his decision to leave, he should do so in a hurry, for if he lingered, he would detract from the importance of the new werowance. Accordingly, he gave Matapank an intensive series of instructions, until that somber day when he joined him in a canoe and paddled downriver past the island to the margin of the bay. There, as the canoe drifted idly, he handed over the hidden burden of leadership. 'You've heard of the time when the Great Canoe came into these waters.' The new werowance nodded. 'What you haven't heard is that when it moved along the shore Orapak, who was a boy then, and his grandfather, who was the werowance, crept behind trees and spied upon the people in the canoe.'

Matapank pursed his lips; he knew the traditions of his tribe, but of such an adventure he had not heard. 'What did they see?'

'The people in the canoe had fair skins, not like us, and they had different bodies.'

'In what way?'

'They glistened. When the sun struck their bodies, they glistened.' Pentaquod allowed this information to sink in, then added, 'And the Great Canoe moved without paddlers.'

This was frightening. Values beyond comprehension were involved, and the young leader could make nothing of them. Then Pentaquod added his last intelligence: 'One day that canoe will return, and we shall be dealing with people entirely different . . . white skins . . . glistening bodies.'

Matapank had been eager to take on the responsibilities of leadership, but these new factors evoked apprehension. 'When they come, will you help me?'

'They may not come in my lifetime,' Pentaquod said.

'I think they will,' the young man replied.

'Why?'

'Long ago I dreamed that I would be the werowance. It happened. And at the same time I dreamed that others came to the river, neither Nanticokes nor Susquehannocks. And they will come.'

Pentaquod liked this response. The leader of a tribe should be one who has visions of the future, who can adjust his thinking to developments which he knows to be inevitable. In his case he had known from the start that peace with the Nanticokes was possible, and his every act as werowance had led in that direction. He had also known that his pitiful little tribe could never defeat the Susquehannocks, and he had kept them from making that fatal effort.

'You are ready to lead,' he told Matapank as they allowed the canoe to drift, and when they reached shore he handed the new leader a cherished talisman, which he had kept hidden for this moment: the copper disk long worn by the werowance of this tribe. Then he promised, 'If the strange ones return while I am alive, I will help.'

That day he and his family left the village. Putting aside his three turkey feathers, he led his family to a pair of sturdy canoes, one burned from oak, one from pine, and together they paddled west past the marshes and around the white cliffs into a beautiful small river. When they had penetrated for some distance, they came to a secondary stream leading inland, and when they had gone up this short way it bifurcated, forming within its arms the small peninsula he had noticed long ago.

Tree-covered, it projected south, to be warmed by the sun in winter. There were no marshes in which mosquitoes could breed, but enough deep salt water to produce oysters and crabs. In the forest there would be deer, and on all the waters geese. It was as fine a setting as the Choptank provided, a refuge with visible security and never-ending beauty. From the point on which Pentaquod and his sons erected their three wigwams the family could look down a broad perspective of the stream to the river and the distant pine trees lining the invisible Choptank.

Here Pentaquod spent the two happiest years of his life, 1605 and 1606 in the western calendar. He was older now and slightly stooped; his great broad face was deeply etched from years of leadership, and his hair was white. But he felt young, for his oldest son had left the refuge one summer's day to paddle back to the village, and when he returned he brought with him the sister of Matapank, the werowance, and soon Pentaquod had a grandson, longer and sturdier than the usual Choptank baby. 'He's to be a fine hunter!' Pentaquod predicted, and before the child could crawl the grandfather was making arrows for him.

But in the next year a canoe came rushing up the creek, and even before it reached land the breathless paddlers shouted in a mixture of confusion and fear, 'Pentaquod! The Great Canoe has come!'

He was forty-nine that year of 1607, a man who had earned repose, but when this long-anticipated information reverberated through the forest, he did what he had always known he must eventually do: he put on his turkey feathers, told his family to pack and ordered them to follow as soon as possible. Almost eagerly, like a young buck bursting into a new meadow, his antlers ready, he jumped into the messengers' canoe and headed back to the village. It was as if he had consciously retired from leadership two years before in order to husband his strength and purify his understandings for the profound tests that lay ahead; he was prepared.

But as the canoe left the small stream to enter the river which would take him to his new responsibilities, he looked back with sorrow and longing at the peninsula which he had transformed. He would not see it again, and he knew this, for with the arrival of the Great Canoe not only would his paradise be lost, but that of all the Choptanks.

Voyage Two: 1608

ON A COLD, BLUSTERY DAY IN MID-DECEMBER 1606 Captain John Smith, a short, choleric, opinionated little man with a beard and a fiery temper, assembled seven daring gentlemen on a dock in the Blackwall section of London and addressed them in crisp terms: 'I have brought you to inspect the vessels in which we shall conquer Virginia.' And he showed them the three small ships that would carry them to the New World, calling off their names: '*Susan Constant,* one hundred tons. *Godspeed,* forty tons. The little pinnace *Discovery,* twenty tons. And down here, at the end, the object of our meeting this day.'

And he showed them, riding on the Thames at the foot of the dock, a small double-ended, single-masted open shallop twenty-three feet long with eight ominous oars. 'You, Edmund Steed, jump in,' Smith commanded, and a fair young man of twenty-five, dressed in the clothes of a scholar, obeyed. Soon all seven were aboard manning their oars while Captain Smith, barely five feet tall, stood approvingly on the dock, watching the little craft adjust to the weight.

'Sturdy vessel!' he cried, snapping his words as if issuing a command. Then, drawing himself to maximum height, he saluted the boat.

He was twenty-six that winter—difficult, vain, unbearably ambitious. He had, by his account, already survived dangers that would have destroyed an ordinary man: mercenary in the most brutal years of the German wars, heroic defender of Christianity when the Muhammadans invaded Hungary, captured slave immured in a Turkish dungeon, foot-traveler to Muscovy and Madrid. And now he surveyed his fleet on the eve of his finest adventure: the establishment of a new colony, the subjugation of a new world.

'We're off!' he shouted as he jumped into the shallop. Grabbing the eighth oar, he began rowing with an energy that shamed the others, and soon they were moving briskly down the Thames. When they passed the three larger ships Smith yelled, 'Mister Steed, have you handled sail?'

'That I have not, sir,' the scholar replied, at which Smith bellowed, 'Then stand clear as Mister Momford runs it up.' And a gentleman who had knowledge of boats manipulated the sheets so that a fore-and-aft sail climbed the mast. With it in place, the shallop moved so smartly that rowing was no longer required.

'Ship the oars!' Smith ordered, but since the gentlemen were unfamiliar with this command, confusion resulted. 'Bring in the oars!' Smith roared, and they were shipped, as he had wanted.

When the brief trip was completed, with the shallop safely in dock, Smith surprised his crew by ordering them to haul the little craft ashore, after which he handed Steed and Momford buckets of paint and brushes, instructing them to number every board used in construction of the boat. 'Each is to have its proper number, at four different spots, indicating its relation to every other board that touches it.'

When this curious task was completed he summoned carpenters, who dismantled the boat, knocking out nails and wooden wedges until only piles of timber lay on the dock. These he ordered tied in lots and carried aboard the *Susan Constant,* where they were stowed below decks, and when all was secure, Smith led Steed to the edge of the hold in which they could see the bundled spars.

'An idea of mine,' he said. 'Conceived while imprisoned in a Turkish harem,' and once more he saluted the boat which would play so crucial a role in establishing the Virginia Colony.

Because of his arrogance and vile temper, Captain Smith fared poorly in Jamestown. Thrown in jail for attempted mutiny, captured by Indians, near death at the hands of Powhatan, and actually led to the gibbet to be hanged for insubordination, he was saved by a last-minute revelation. Cocksure and prescient, he survived travail, gave the colony the iron leadership it required, and found time to pursue his major preoccupation: the exploration of the Chesapeake. 'This is a noble sea,' he told his men at night, after the day's work ended. 'Calm and hospitable, majestic in size. Its potential cannot be imagined.'

He had already mounted two preliminary explorations and was encouraged by what he had found: broad rivers, innumerable harbors, a plenitude of fish and crabs, and meadows yearning to be cultivated. But his two preconceived targets had eluded him: he had not found a passage to India, he had not uncovered the gold and silver which were known to exist somewhere along the shores of the Chesapeake.

'Infuriating,' he growled one July day in 1608. 'Three years ago I heard the facts for myself. The leaders of the expedition were busy securing permissions in London, so a noble lord and I attended a play, very little substance and I was about to leave, for I do not waste my time idly. But destiny tugged my sleeve and kept me . . . for a purpose. An actor in this play strode to the edge of the stage and orated directly at me, none other. He spoke of Virginia and told me what I should find here. Silver more common than copper. Kitchen pans and bedroom pots made of pure gold. Rubies and diamonds in the streets. Children gathering pearls along the streams. The riches are here, if only we can find them.'

On Saturday, August 9, he outlined his plan: 'The gold lies, I am convinced, in towns hidden along the eastern shore of the bay, and there we shall explore most carefully. The passage to India probably starts from the northern tip, so after we have found our gold we shall probe north to identify the passage, then return to Jamestown with our profit.'

The men agreed that this was prudent strategy, and on Sunday all sixteen—seven gentlemen, eight sailors and Captain Smith—attended church, where long prayers were uttered, and on the morning of August 11 he marched his crew to the banks of the James, where he addressed them in solemn tones: 'We shall be gone thirty days, and at the end you will wish it had been ninety.' He then ordered his fifteen hands into the reassembled shallop, directed them to take up their oars, and stood like Alexander the Great in the bow of the boat, looking for new horizons.

Among the gentleman rowers Edmund Steed, who had not participated in Smith's two earlier explorations, had been selected for a particular purpose. Smith had not been entirely pleased with the narrative reports of his first journeys; they had been geographically accurate but had paid insufficient attention to his moral and heroic qualities. This time he was determined that his accomplishments be presented with proper flourishes.

Steed came from an ancient Devon family and was a graduate of Oxford. He wrote well, was familiar with classical allusions and showed a proper respect for the captain. Both on the *Susan Constant* and ashore at Jamestown he attracted attention, and Smith now assured him, 'I seek only an accurate account of what occurs during our exploration. Strict attention to where we sail and special detail when we move ashore.' He paused as Mister Momford prepared to break out the sail, then added confidentially, 'And it would be prudent if you paid attention to the words and heroic deeds of the commander.'

Steed understood. He had always been properly attentive whenever Smith entertained his companions with reports of his adventures in Hungary . . . his painful months undergoing Turkish tortures . . . his romantic escapes in Muscovy . . . his daring in Spain. Steed sometimes marveled that a man only a year older than himself should have experienced so much, and he might have been tempted to brand the little warrior a liar except for the fact that Smith always spoke with an inherent veracity. His tales sounded true, and he quickly convinced the impartial listener that he had really been to the places whose names rolled off his tongue, for he gave the temperature, and how the city lay in relation to its river, and what his captors wore and which specific weapons were carried by the enemies he had slain in hand-to-hand combat.

Steed's belief in his commander stemmed from an incident which had occurred during the long voyage from England, when Smith told in one brief afternoon of wild adventure in four different lands, ending with Spain, and Steed had thought: I'll wager he never touched foot in Spain, the braggart. But then the little captain, as if alerted to the fact that an unbeliever lurked among his hearers, closed with a remarkable evocation:

> 'And of all the cities I was to see in my travels, the one I remember most fondly is the dusty town that lies at the mouth of the great river leading to Sevilla in Spain. Sanlúcar de Barrameda is its name, and it holds the left bank of Wady-al-Quivir, as they call it. It's a small and sun-baked town, with many grazing fields nearby and vast swamps filled with birds. It's favorably regarded by sailors for the delicious pale wine its vintners make, for there is a square near the center of Sanlúcar where the wine-men sell their goods, accompanied by a salty little fish they call the anchoovy. I tasted the fish but not the wine.'

The words rang like a bell at dusk, and Steed abandoned any doubts he may have had. Smith might not have been prisoner in a Turkish harem, and he probably did not kill three adversaries during a horseback tournament with lances, but that he had visited a dusty Spanish town at the mouth of a river, no one could deny.

As Jamestown disappeared behind a bend, Steed took careful note of the shallop lest he omit significant details: no decking, no refuge from storms, barrels of bread already turning sour, a batch of dried meats, some with worms, and a large supply of fishing lines. 'There'll be plenty of fish,' Smith assured the rowers, and when Mister Momford got the frayed sail aloft, Steed took note that it had been mended twice. Such deficiencies he intended to report, for their existence would make the captain's ultimate discovery of gold and the passage even more impressive.

If the gentlemen and the sailors felt any apprehension about exploring with such inadequate gear, their captain did not. His buoyancy was remarkable, and when the shallop responded nicely to the wind he cried, 'Fairly launched! It's to be a famous journey!' Steed wrote down these remarks and others on the folded sheets he carried in a canvas bag, and that night he transcribed them into a proper journal, which Captain Smith reached for as soon as it was completed.

He did not like what he saw. He did not like it at all. The geographical facts were accurate enough, but he was chagrined that he should have misjudged Steed's talents by such a margin, and with the forthrightness which characterized him, he broached the subject. 'Mister Steed, at the beginning of our historic journey you have me saying, "We shall be gone thirty days, and at the end you will wish it had been ninety." That's a poor speech for the launching of a great adventure.'

'It's what you said, sir.'

'I know. But our time onshore was brief. You must take that into consideration.' And he grabbed the pen from his scribe and sat for some time beneath the swaying lantern, composing a more appropriate opening address:

> As the day was far advanced and time precious, Captain Smith gathered his sturdy crew beside the shallop and told them, 'Men, we set forth this day on a journey of exploration which will dazzle the courts of Europe. In Virginia we shall find gold and silver. It may be we shall uncover the hidden passage to the treasures of India and China. We shall garner the aromatic spices of the islands. We shall penetrate to where no Englishmen have gone before, and we shall return with jewels and rare cloths to gladden the heart of any monarch. We make this voyage to further the Glory of God, to carry His Word to lands which know it not, and to bring everlasting greatness to our beloved King James, late of Scotland but now of all Britain.

With a flourish Captain Smith shoved the paper back to his scribe, who held it near the lantern, his blond features betraying the astonishment he felt as he read the captain's corrections.

'You never said those things, Captain.'

'I was thinking them,' Smith snapped. 'Had there been time, I'd have said them.'

Steed was about to protest when he looked into the shadows and saw the bearded face of his little commander. It was like iron edged with oak, and he realized that Smith would have made just such a speech had the occasion permitted, and he sensed that it was not what a soldier said, but what he intended, which provided motivation. John Smith lived intimately with possibilities that other men could not even imagine, and in his dreaming he forced them to become reality. Edmund Steed and Thomas Momford might be in a leaky shallop with poor food and no protection, exploring a land-locked bay; Smith was already through the northwest passage and far into the Pacific, riding a caravel.

On the seventh day of the journey Steed caught a glimpse of the real John Smith and of the island that would command his own attention for the rest of his life. They had been picking their way fruitlessly up the eastern shore, dropping into one disappointing river after another, making desultory contact with Indians who had never seen iron, let alone gold or silver, and Steed had written:

> Wicomico and Nanticoke, we explored these rivers for miles, trusting to find some city of richness where the chamber pots were made of gold, but we found instead only the meanest Indian villages populated by savages with knowledge of nothing. Our heroic captain never lost heart and distinguished himself by trading cleverly for potatoes and lengths of roanoke to be used against the tribes near Jamestown. It was while conducting such trades with the Nanticokes that he cleverly learned of a river next north called the Choptank, whose capital city called Patamoke is known to have much gold.

So the shallop sailed north with its cadre of excited explorers, and when a great broad river was sighted, Smith cried, 'This is our Choptank! Here is Patamoke, city of gold!' But as the little boat breasted the southern headland protecting the river, Edmund Steed saw his island: delicate in outline, secured within the river, perfected by a crown of trees. 'Captain Smith,' he called, 'have you ever seen a fairer island?' and the little warrior studied the land from several angles and said, 'Too low for a fort.'

It required about four hours for the slow-moving shallop to approach and pass the island, and during all that time Steed leaned on one of the sheer strakes and stared. He saw numerous indentations at which they could have landed, had Captain Smith been so inclined, and trees of noble height and even a small river leading into the heart of the island. When he spotted a large meadow crying for cattle, he thought: This is the best of England transported across the sea. I shall name it Devon.

That evening the shallop anchored well into the Choptank, under the protection of a white cliff, and while one assignment of men tried to catch fish for supper a party of Indians appeared in two canoes, announcing in sign language that their werowance desired the leader of the strangers to accompany them to their capital city, where they would be welcomed. Night fell as the Englishmen debated whether or not their captain should risk such a journey, and many opinions were offered, for the invitation posed difficult problems, as Steed reported:

> In the darkness we could not see the waiting Indians nor have any indication of their intentions, but they could see us, for our mast was outlined against the sky. Thomas Momford pointed out that Cap-

tain Smith had twice been lured into traps like this and had, indeed, been captive of Powhatan, leading chief on the western shore. This remembrance encouraged Captain Smith to relate that occurrence. 'Powhatan ordered two blocks of stone to be brought in, and I was stretched across them, and a brave stood above me with his warclub ready to strike out my brains, when a miracle took place and I was saved.'

Steed had heard this story five times now; he was convinced that Smith thought the affair had happened that way, but he was far from sure it had. And then, toward dawn, Smith made his decision:

He told us simply, 'I must go to the City of Patamoke, for it is there we shall find the gold.' No argument would dissuade him, and when light broke he nominated Chirurgeon Ragnall and Edmund Steed to accompany him. As we climbed into the waiting canoe Thomas Momford cried, 'Take care, Captain!' and Smith replied, 'A captain must never fear to meet a captain.'

The short trip from the cliff to the city was one of intense excitement, for Captain Smith could smell gold, and in his anticipation he told Steed, 'If they meet us in great procession, I will go first and you march behind with Ragnall in proper form to impress them with our military bearing.' Steed took notes of what happened:

After passing a huge marsh filled with birds and waving brushes, we approached our long-desired goal, the City of Patamoke, headquarters of the powerful Choptanks who control this river, and our hearts beat fast. Captain Smith, always protecting himself from unexpected attack, leaned forward in the canoe to catch a first sight of the settlement, and when he saw only a circle of wigwams, a mound of oyster shells and nothing more he looked at his companions blankly.

Ashore we faced a new confusion. We identified the werowance immediately, because of the copper disk he wore upon his chest. His name was Matapank, and he impressed us little, for since he lacked both dignity and authority, he was reluctant to make decisions. He was accompanied, however, by a gigantic white-haired Indian wearing three turkey feathers in his hair, and this man, whose name was Pintakood, appeared to be the real werowance.

No gold, no silver, no pearls, no rubies, no emeralds. Even the copper of the disk had been traded for. The Indians were small and lacking in dignity, except the one man Pintakood, whose daughter of some twelve years stayed with him, as handsome as he.

Captain Smith, sorely disappointed with this pitiful village, felt that he must at least go through the motions of an exploration, so he produced from his canvas bag an assortment of attractive items: glass beads from Venice, an iron hatchet, eighteen lengths of highly colored cloth, and for the werowance a final present which captivated all the Indians.

It was a small ivory object, hinged at one side with a metal lid, which, when raised, disclosed a polished glass, covering something unbelievable: a needle, thin and delicate, resting on a pivot so that no matter how the ivory case was turned, this dancing needle found its way back to one constant position.

What could this be? The young werowance took it in his hands, moved it in circles and watched as the needle danced home to its assigned position. He was bewildered.

Those about him were more impressed by the fact that they could see the needle—clearly they could see it—but the invisible glass prevented them from touching it, and this, too, was a miracle. The lesser Choptanks wanted to pass the gift from hand to hand, but the werowance would not surrender it.

Then Smith spoke. Knowing not a word of their language, he used a minimum of gestures to indicate the sky, the darkness of night and the stars which formed the Dipper in the constellation Ursa Major. His gestures were incomprehensible to the young werowance, but the giant with the turkey feathers studied closely, then suddenly reached for a stick and drew in the dust the seven stars of the Big Dipper.

'Yes!' Smith shouted, pointing to the heavens. And with his forefinger he indicated how the constellation pointed to the North Star, but this was unnecessary, for the giant already knew. With his own gestures he indicated that the needle sought north, and Smith nodded.

A feast was held at noon, with bear meat and cakes of crab, after which Captain Smith dispatched Chirurgeon Ragnall back to the shallop with news that all was well; he and Steed would spend the night with the werowance. Ragnall protested that the captain might be falling into yet another trap, but Smith ignored him, and that night, as the summer stars appeared, Steed sat with the daughter of the tall man with the turkey feathers. Her name, he deduced after she had pronounced it for him numerous times, was something like Tsiblinti, and she fed him an exciting mixture of corn and beans which she called succotash, if he had the word right.

When they returned to the shallop he faced the exacting task of describing this adventure. He wanted to be accurate and to report the placid quality of this Indian village, yet he knew that he must also display Captain Smith in heroic posture, and this was difficult. When the commander read the narrative he could not hide his displeasure.

'You want to name the island Devon? And so it shall be, but would it not be wiser to show in the record that this was my decision, not yours?'

'I merely proposed it, sir. Confirmation is left to you.'

'Confirmed, but I would prefer the record to show that the suggestion came from me, too.'

'It will be noted.'

Then Smith frowned and pointed to the real trouble. 'You spend too few words on our departure. You must recall, for you were involved, what a risky business we undertook. It is no mean task for three men to go unarmed into the heart of hostile Indian territory.'

Steed was about to say that he had never seen people less hostile, Indian or not, but he deemed it wiser to keep his silence. Passing the pages over to the captain, he held the lantern so that Smith could edit them, and after a while he was handed this:

We were now entering the most considerable river on the eastern shore, the river of the Choptanks, at whose mouth stands a most beautiful low island with fair meadows and goodly tall trees. We saw fresh waters running through the woods and all men were ravished at the sight thereof. It minded us of the fair lands of Devon and Captain Smith named the island in their honor. After we had passed this island and proceeded a goodly distance up the Choptank we were accosted by a group of fierce and hostile Indians, and the Captain appreciated at once that our safety depended upon how we dealt with these savages, who could have killed our little band supposing they had wished. He therefore adopted the bold strata- gem of demanding that they lead him to their werowance, who was indicated to be at some remove in the capital city of Patamoke. Several men protested the danger of such a journey on his part, pointing out that the savages would outnumber us hundreds to one and could kill us without risk. But Captain Smith was determined to meet the werowance and to conclude a treaty with him for the food we needed, so he assembled his men and told them, 'The wise Machiavel in his instruction to princes has properly said that men, iron, money and bread be the necessities of war, but of these four the first two be of most importance, because men and iron can find money and bread, but bread and money never find men and iron.'

Thereafter he stepped boldly forth with Chirurgeon Ragnall and Mister Steed as companions, and cried to the Indians, 'Take me to Patamoke!' We climbed into the enemy's canoe and went to meet the werowance of the Choptanks. He was a confusing man named Matapank, of little consequence, but in devious manner he masked the real leader, one Pintakood, no brighter than he. The pair were much disposed to harm us, but Captain Smith spoke to them with signs and gave them a compass encased in ivory, which much amused them, especially that they could see the needle through the glass but not touch it. They were incapable of understanding what this strange device was, but our Captain explained to them what the heavens were and the roundness of the earth, and how the planets danced and the sun did chase the night around the world continually.

When Steed read this dumbfounding report he did not know where to begin. It was all true, and at the same time totally false. He skipped the part about the naming of Devon Island; Captain Smith commanded, and until he confirmed a name, it had not been given. He was also willing to ignore Smith's claims that the Indians had been hostile; to one so often the victim of Indian guile they might have seemed so. And he was even content to have the giant warrior with the three turkey feathers appear stupid, because the others were. He thought, with some accuracy: Smith hated the clever Choptank because the Indian was so very tall and he so very short. He wanted him to be stupid.

But it did gall the Oxford student to have Smith quoting Machiavelli to inspire his men. 'I heard no Machiavel,' he said cautiously.

'The Indians were pressing, and I had not the time.'

Steed made no response, and Smith continued, 'If a captain leads his men into strange waters against a strange enemy, it is wise for him to think of Machiavel.' At this, Steed stared at the bottom boards, barely discernible in the darkness, but Smith was not content with acquiescence; he required positive acceptance. With a firm thumb he raised the younger man's face until stars gleamed upon it and their eyes were level. 'Tell me, Mister Steed, why would I have got into the canoe almost alone, and ventured into the enemy camp? Men and iron obtain food. It is never the other way around.'

In the dark night the two men glared at each other, with Steed determined to resist the blandishments of his captain. Smith, sensing this, lifted the young man's head higher and said, 'I insist that you make one more change in the part I have not yet improved.'

'Is this a command?'

'It is. In your account of our departure with the Indians, I want you to write that you volunteered, most gallantly.'

'But you commanded me to go.'

'If I had not, you would have volunteered, because you, like me, are a man of iron.'

Steed made no reply, and Smith moved forward in the shallop, but soon he was back with another emendation. 'Mister Steed, at the moment when I meet the Indian with the turkey feathers, must you emphasize the fact that he is so tall and I so short?' This time Steed said, 'My description was ungracious, and I will gladly change it.'

Still Smith was not through. Much later he awakened Steed with this suggestion: 'I think you should add that Captain Smith was so struck by the giant size of the Indian general that he felt sure the man could not be a Choptank but was probably a Susquehannock.'

Steed could not get back to sleep, and while the shallop rode easily on the waters of Choptank River he alternated between looking at the silhouette of the island he had named—soft and gentle in the night—and the dozing figure of his commander. Smith was an enigma, willing to make any alteration in the personal record of the trip, yet insanely determined to be accurate whenever geography was involved. At the entrance to every river he took repeated bearings. Constantly he consulted his compass, asking others to check him. He never entered into the log the height of a tree or the distance to shore without finding confirmation in the estimates of others, and with mapping he was meticulous. If he described the dress of a Choptank, he did so accurately.

He was restless in his sleep, and toward dawn came back to tell Steed, 'I think you can write that we shall not find gold or silver. That dream was vain.' He spoke these words with such obvious sorrow that Steed shared his heartache, but with the breaking of the sun the little commander was all energy as he shouted to the men, 'Well, to the westward passage.' And he sped the shallop north to his next disappointment.

He was a severe leader. One evening, as he assembled his company at the mouth of the Susquehanna, he whispered to Steed, 'I want you to write with special care what I do and say this night.' He then ordered the gentlemen to stand in one group, the sailors in another, and from the latter he commanded Robert Small to stand forth. When the man had done so he said harshly, 'Lift your right arm,' and when the arm was aloft, Smith stood on the fallen trunk of a tree and with a large goblet poured down the man's arm a large draft of cold water. 'Refill the goblet,' he told Steed, and when this was done he ordered the sailor to raise his left arm, whereupon he emptied the water down that sleeve.

'Tell the assembly what you did to warrant this punishment,' Smith snapped.

'I used an oath, sir.'

'You spoke God's name in anger?'

'I did, sir. I had caught a large fish and he escaped.'

'Return to ranks, Small.' The little captain then wheeled to address the entire company. 'If I demand that you conduct yourselves carefully, I have done the same. I have never drunk spirits, nor diced, nor gamed, nor smoked, nor uttered an oath, nor dallied with women, nor in any way diminished myself. I am a soldier, and I hold myself always to be one. If you sail with me, you do not dice or drink or utter oaths.'

That night, when the writing had been completed to Smith's satisfaction, he asked Steed, 'Do you propose becoming a soldier, too?'

'I have not the stomach for it, sir.'

'Some don't. What do you intend?'

'Devon Island is much in my mind. I think to settle there when this trip is done.'

'You have no patent. No permission.'

'It would be well, Captain, if the men at Jamestown thought less about patents and permissions.'

To a military man this was an unpalatable doctrine. A soldier identified his king or general, then served him; patents and proper orders and permissions were the lifeblood of the profession. But he could not expect Steed to understand; in this young scholar there was something devious, something hidden that Smith had not yet probed, and he was not surprised at the stated plans.

The passage to India was not found. The upper end of the bay petered out in a succession of flats and marshes on which the shallop repeatedly grounded, and on the fifth time that sailors swam out with the anchor so that the boat could be kedged, Captain Smith snapped, 'Mister Steed, tonight you can write that the passage does not exist . . . not for us.' Never again would he speak of that lost dream.

The exploration ended curiously. As the shallop drifted homeward down the western shore, Steed kept a fishing line astern, and of a sudden it was taken by a fish so large that he could not pull it in, and as he played the creature, Captain Smith reached into the water to help and was struck furiously in the wrist by the tail of a massive stingray.

Brushing the fish away, he looked at his arm and watched it begin to swell. Within moments it became immense—larger than his thigh—and the fingers began to turn purple. The pain was intense, so hurtful that he had to bite upon a piece of wood, and at the end of ninety minutes, when the arm grew darker in color and the pain unbearable, the little captain said to Steed and the surgeon, 'I am about to die. Dig me a grave from which I can see the bay.' And a group of sailors dug a grave and Smith marched to it, sitting himself at one end with his feet dangling inside.

As he sat there, saying nothing, contemplating the end of his adventures, the pain began to subside and the dreadful purple coloring left his arm, and when it became apparent that he would not die, nor lose the arm, he recovered his spirits and asked, 'Did we land the fish?'

'We did,' Steed said.

'Good. I will eat it for my supper.' It was fried and he ate it.

In the closing hours of this disappointing voyage Steed had to acknowledge that he had developed a positive affection for his captain. Smith stood a good four inches shorter than he and weighed fifteen pounds less, but he was pure energy, pure dedication to soldiering, and if he constructed entries to make himself seem braver than he had been, this was not ordinary falsification, because if events had demanded heroism, he would have provided it. Steed thought: Smith's trouble is with words. He demands that they convey what might have been.

The last river they visited was the York, and even though the weary sailors were approaching home, they complained bitterly of the food, the rain from which they had no protection, the insects. 'Thunderation!' Smith exploded. 'I could build a new Jerusalem on this bay if only I could find seventeen men unafraid of mosquitoes.'

Disconsolately he walked with Steed along the riverbank until they were hot and weary; then he fell onto a pile of drying leaves and confessed the failure of his grand designs. 'I sought brocaded cloths and found Indians wearing matted bark. I sought gold and was rewarded with marshy weeds. This bay has riches, but I was not destined to find them.'

As he spoke his hand restlessly stroked the leaves upon which he sat —tobacco, brought down the York by Indians for shipment to London. In years to come, bundles and bales and whole shiploads of this weed would move down the rivers of Virginia and Maryland, producing more gold and brocade than even Captain Smith had dreamed of.

The Island

TO UNDERSTAND HOW EDMUND STEED, GENTLE-
man, happened to accompany Captain John Smith on his exploration of
the Chesapeake in 1608, it is necessary to go back more than a hundred
years.

As the fifteenth century ended, every soul in England was Catholic,
which was understandable, since there were no other Christian religions
in existence at that time and it was debated whether the few Jews in the
realm had souls. King Henry VII, having wrested his throne from the
infamous Richard III, ruled with the blessing of the Pope, to whom he
willingly accorded both spiritual and temporal allegiance. After years of
disturbance the country was at peace, the great monasteries housed
clerics of power, and good Englishmen were content to be good Catholics. Martin Luther, who would later challenge this happy somnolence,
was then fifteen years old and studying with enthusiasm to be a Catholic
priest.

Englishmen had been happy, therefore, when in 1489 King Henry
announced the formal engagement of his three-year-old son Arthur to
the four-year-old Catherine of Spain, daughter of Ferdinand and Isa-
bella, the most Catholic of majesties. This promised union of insignificant England with powerful Spain was a joyous occasion promising
many benefits to the smaller island kingdom.

Twelve years later, when Catherine actually landed in England, she
was seen to be a kindly, quiet, well-bred princess who promised to bring
love and loyalty to the throne. Young Arthur was enchanted by his first
sight of her, and married her gladly in October 1501, with representatives
of the Pope lending official approval to this happy union of two Catholic
kingdoms. It was an auspicious start to the new century.

Unfortunately, Arthur, heir to the throne of England, proved sickly, and in March 1502 he died. His widow, to the disappointment of all, was not pregnant.

This left King Henry VII with a nice dynastic problem: if he allowed Princess Catherine to escape England and return to Spain, he would forfeit whatever advantages might have accrued to a Spanish wedding; but there was no practical excuse for keeping her as a kind of hostage in London to ensure the good behavior of the Spanish monarchs.

Clever advisors, of which England seemed always to have an abundant supply, pointed out that the king had one justifiable way of preventing Catherine from slipping back to Spain: 'Marry her to dead Arthur's brother.' It was a capital idea, except that Henry, the brother, was only eleven years old, six years younger than his proposed bride.

And besides, no sooner had this diplomatic marriage been proposed than thoughtful clerics dismissed it, for it was contrary to church law. Thundered one divine, 'Leviticus twenty, verse twenty-one clarifies the matter for all time,' and he quoted the monitory verse in his own rude translation into English:

'No man shall marry his brother's widow. It is forbidden. To do so shames his brother's good name, and the couple shall remain childless.'

Nations had found through sad experience that family life could not be secure if brothers felt free to steal each other's wives. Royalty in particular had learned that younger brothers must understand from the start that they would not profit from the deaths of their older brothers. For the Widow Catherine to marry the brother of her dead husband would be immoral, illegal and contrary to church custom.

But the dynastic pressures continued. King Henry was an old man now, all of forty-five, and never in the best of health. He must take any steps necessary to secure the future of his hard-won crown, and the surest way to accomplish this would be to preserve and reinforce the alliance with Spain. Catherine must be kept in England.

So he sought out lesser divines who had not hastily committed themselves when the marriage had first been proposed, and sure enough, when these scholars searched the Bible they uncovered that fortunate passage at Deuteronomy 25:5 which contradicted Leviticus and not only permitted a man to marry his brother's widow, but actually commanded him to do so.

'If two brothers dwell together and one of them shall die childless, the widow of the dead man must not marry a stranger. Her dead husband's brother shall take her as his wife, and have children by her, and perform all the duties of a husband.'

There could hardly be a more concise instruction than that, or one which covered England's dynastic problem better, and when King Henry heard this injunction read aloud he clapped his hands and ordered an engagement to be arranged for his eleven-year-old son.

The king did not live long enough to see his heir happily married; he died on April 21, 1509, and out of respect for his memory—for he had been a sturdy king—young Henry, against his own best judgment, went ahead with his marriage to a woman six years his elder. The wedding took place a few weeks after the old king's burial and had happy consequences, except in the matter of providing an heir to the throne. Catherine was fertile enough, and seemed to be constantly pregnant: she bore child after child—boys among them—but they all died. One sickly daughter, Mary, did survive, but it was not a daughter that Henry sought.

In 1533 King Henry belatedly convinced himself that his marriage to this aging Spanish paragon had from the start been illegal and immoral. In the end he returned to Leviticus, abandoning Deuteronomy. With increasing rage he stormed among the Catholic clergy, demanding that they find scholars who would support him in his contention that Catherine had never been properly married to him and was therefore technically divorced. He found such scholars, of course, but not of high standing, and the Pope in Rome refused to acquiesce in their findings on various sensible grounds: that whereas the marriage might have been initially suspect, it had been performed; it had been consummated, as the child Mary proved; and it had endured for nearly a quarter of a century. Divorce was denied.

Now, King Henry was as staunch a Catholic as the kings of Europe provided; eleven years earlier he had written with his own hand and circulated widely a pamphlet refuting the renegade Martin Luther and reconfirming the leadership of the Pope. In gratitude for this advocacy, the Pope had officially proclaimed Henry 'Defender of the Faith,' a cherished title which all future sovereigns of England would hold. Since Henry had proved himself a veritable right hand of the Pope, he could not easily reject the pontiff because of one unpalatable decision; moreover, Henry honestly accepted the doctrines of the church and would have been appalled if anyone had accused him of lacking in enthusiasm for Catholicism. The upshot was that Henry could not divorce Catherine, which meant that he could not marry the toothsome young court attendant on whom his fancy had fallen, Mistress Anne Boleyn.

What to do? One cynic in London whispered, 'The Pope's bull has tied up the King's balls,' and later, when the issue had been resolved, this witticism would be remembered. The charge against this jokester would first be *lèse-majesté*, later blasphemy, and finally treason, for which he would be strangled in the Tower. For one clever phrase he died.

Now the rumor began to circulate that Anne Boleyn was pregnant, with what everyone hoped would be a son, so a speedy resolution of the conflict with the Pope became imperative, lest the future king be born a bastard. The impasse was resolved rather cleverly: King Henry stated that whereas England and all Englishmen remained as Catholic as ever, acknowledging as before the Pope's spiritual supremacy, they rejected his temporal leadership. Henceforth there would be a Catholic church in various parts of Europe presided over by the Pope, and there would be another in England, equally Catholic but governed in all managerial matters by King Henry.

In a blaze of religious fervor he divorced Catherine the Spaniard and married Anne the lusty English girl. This caused such turmoil throughout Europe that he was goaded into proving he really was head of the local church, and he did this by a most practical maneuver. It occurred to him one night as he lay with Anne Boleyn that the Pope controlled more than one third the land of England; cathedrals, monasteries, churches, nunneries all owned vast estates and the peasants who worked them. With one simple edict Henry expropriated all those holdings, closed down the monasteries, denuded the cathedrals of their lands and, as he said, 'kicked the monks and friars and nuns into the village streets, forcing them to earn an honest living.' Then in his canny way he devised the most brilliant stratagem of all: he did not keep the new possessions for himself, nor did he deliver them to powerful dukes and earls who might later combine against him; he handed them instead to those stalwart men of the middle class who had supported him in his fight against the Pope. In this way he converted one third of England into his bounden supporters, and it was during this transfer that the ancestors of Edmund Steed entered the picture.

In the County of Devon, southeast of London, in the little town of Bishop's Nympton, halfway between Dartmoor and Exmoor, there had lived for several hundred years a distinguished and stubborn local family named Steed. They had been farmers of some wealth; the fathers had served as justices of the peace and the sons had gone off to Oxford. Both sons and daughters had married conservatively, and no scandal had ever touched the family, which, if it had produced no barons or earls, did produce a steady supply of men on whom the kings could rely.

Such a man was Devon Steed, forty-nine years old when his king, Henry, sought to divorce the Spanish queen. When the debate was most acrimonious, the king sought support from rural gentlemen of good reputation, and Cardinal Wolsey himself, the one who constantly connived to become Pope, asked Steed to rally assistance in his district.

Such a request posed a serious moral problem for Steed: he was a devout Catholic, he loved the Pope, he tithed, he led his family to the local chapel every Wednesday and Sunday, and he personally provided the priest's living. To side with a king against the Pope in an argument over the two contrasting verses in the Bible was a most grievous responsibility, and for some weeks he refrained, wrestling with his conscience over that passage in Leviticus which specifically forbade the kind of marriage Henry had been forced into with Catherine.

Could it be that the Pope was ignoring the Bible? Devon Steed would never concede that. But was it not possible that King Henry was right in claiming that he had had no legitimate male children because the curse of God was upon him, due to his incestuous marriage? Did not Leviticus warn that such a marriage would have no children?

For some days he stood on this precarious ledge, inclining now toward the Pope, now toward Henry. The dilemma was resolved ingeniously: Cardinal Wolsey sent a personal emissary, young Hugh Latimer, related to the Steeds and godfather of Devon's son Latimer, all the way to Bishop's Nympton with an argument that could not be refuted: 'Cousin Steed, are you not aware that our king has already fathered no less than six sons, illegitimately of course, but sons nevertheless. The barrenness cannot be his fault. You know Henry Fitzroy, he who was made Duke of Richmond at the age of six. He's Henry's son, and so are five others of less degree. If he can shed himself of the Spanish clod and marry lively young Anne, we'll have a future king, and England will be protected.' Latimer, an austere man, winked and added, 'You know, I suppose, that Mistress Anne is heavy with child right now, a son the midwives assure us, so we must act promptly.'

Satisfied as to the facts, Devon Steed led the western counties in their support of the divorce; he backed the king against the Pope. He neither solicited nor expected anything in return for having obeyed his conscience, but when the dissolution of the monasteries took place, and great estates were distributed to loyal supporters, especially those of the middle class like the Steeds, Hugh Latimer saw to it that his Cousin Devon was placed on the list of eligibles.

When agents came to inquire which of the eight hundred monasteries he would prefer, he replied in some innocence, 'Glastonbury. It's nearby and I've always admired the buildings Richard Bere erected there when he was abbot.'

The agent coughed and said, 'Glastonbury's so big it's been reserved.'

'I am sorry,' Steed apologized. 'What did the king have in mind for me?'

'He rather likes to have the new recipients move out of their established localities. Conflicting loyalties, you know. There's a splendid monastery at Queen's Wenlock over in Berks.'

'I know it!' Steed said with enthusiasm. He had stopped there once on his way to Oxford and remembered the place with affection: low towers, a modest cloister, innumerable chimneys, and four noble Gothic arches enclosing the gates at which the poor assembled to receive their charity.

'Fifteen hundred acres accompany the monastery buildings,' the agent said, 'and two villages populated with sturdy farmers. You will own the entire as Sir Devon Steed.'

He assumed the knighthood in 1537 as Sir Devon; he had five Christian names and none of them was Devon. That was a nickname given him at Oxford, and it had become accepted; now as Sir Devon he moved his family to his new estate. The first thing he did upon arrival at the old monastery, built in 1387 by Good Queen Anne of Bohemia, wife of King Richard II, was to hold prayers in the former chapel, and as he knelt on those ancient and sacred stones he reconfirmed his abiding faith in Catholicism and the spiritual supremacy of the Pope.

Nothing changed much, actually. England remained Catholic. King Henry, vastly disappointed when Anne Boleyn gave him another daughter and no son, shortly thereafter had her head chopped off, and again Sir Devon supported him, as did his counterparts in the other 799 expropriated monasteries: they called Boleyn 'the Whore of the Howards,' and were glad to see her disposed of.

Ugly gossip circulated when certain court circles, always scheming to protect the line of inheritance to the throne, proposed that little Princess Mary, daughter of Henry's first wife Catherine, be married to the Duke of Richmond, her own half brother. Those who broached the subject to Steed argued, 'Don't you see? This would unite all strands which might have a just claim. The position of the couple would be impregnable, and when they produced a son he would be king in every sense of the word.'

'If they produced a son,' Steed snapped, 'he would have two heads.'

Fortunately, King Henry, always a moral man, was revolted at the idea of his daughter's marrying her illegitimate half brother, and he rejected it. When he heard that Sir Devon Steed at Queen's Wenlock had rejected the proposal on the same grounds, he felt additional warmth for the new knight and added to his acreage.

As long as King Henry lived, Sir Devon experienced no religious pangs. Both he and the king remained devout Catholics, and when the latter ordered two heretical Lutherans burned at the stake, Sir Devon applauded. 'We want no schismatics here,' he told his son Latimer.

He died three months after his king, thus escaping the chaos into which England fell when the boy, Edward VI, reigned briefly. Sir Latimer Steed, who inherited the title and the considerable estate which went with it, was even more devotedly attached to Catholicism and the Pope than his father had been, and he was appalled at the crass manner in which the young king's advisors sought to convert England into a Protestant country. Sir Latimer fulminated against it, and he allowed to all who visited the former monastery that 'the honest men of England will never embrace the heresies of Geneva.' He was much relieved when Edward, always sickly, as if God had cursed his father for having had six wives and beheading two of them, died.

Now Mary, thirty-seven years old and tested in the furnace of Tudor wrangling, assassination and piety, approached the throne, determined to put everything right. It was a glorious day for good Catholics like Sir Latimer when she accepted the crown, and it was not long before the heretical leaders who had tried to lure England away from Rome paid the penalty for their treason. One after another went to the stake, and Sir Latimer, praying in the chapel which his father had stolen from the church, gave his benediction to the fires—'It's the only way to keep England pure.'

The first sign he received that things were going strangely came on October 19, 1555, when his son Fairleigh rushed in from London with shocking news: 'Hugh Latimer was burned at the stake.'

It was unbelievable. The Steeds had known the Latimers for more than a hundred years, and they had watched with shared pride as young Hugh progressed up the various rungs of the church. When Cardinal Wolsey missed being elected Pope, it had not been too much to hope that Latimer might succeed, and now he had perished at the stake. What dreadful miscalculation had caused such injustice?

It could not be said of young Fairleigh that he was a devout Catholic; he was much more. He loved the church; as a child playing in the vast rooms of the former monastery, now circumspectly called the grange, he gained a vision of what a sovereign church should be, and at Oxford he had led the young men who set bonfires at the accession of Queen Mary, for in her cleansing arrival he saw the salvation of the church. He understood that harsh steps must be taken before England could be brought back into its proper channels, and he applauded her force of character.

'She had to destroy him, Father,' he explained. 'Hugh Latimer preached the most pernicious doctrine, and if he had gone unchecked, he would have seduced England into Protestantism. He was no better then Calvin.'

And so the son led the father through the troubled but glorious days of Queen Mary's reign. When Mary took King Philip of Spain as her husband, young Fairleigh explained everything and quieted his father's fears that this might mean a Spanish ascendancy. 'Not ever! Spain and England will become united under the leadership of the Pope. There will be an end to fratricidal strife, and together Spain and England will put down the heresy in Germany and the Low Countries.'

They were heady days, these days of reconstruction, and Queen's Wenlock was often filled with Oxford students arguing about the characteristics of the England that was to come. Certain fanatics had proposed that the stolen monasteries be returned to the church, but Queen Mary, depending upon the solid families that now occupied them, would have none of that. Sir Latimer applauded her decision, as did the Oxford students, most of whom came from families that had profited from the expropriation.

And then Mary died. The throne passed to her half sister, Elizabeth the Protestant, the bastard daughter of Anne Boleyn, that Whore of the Howards. Sir Latimer, reflecting on the disaster, told Fairleigh, 'That line is bad altogether. It was no accident that the two queens Henry had to behead were both Howards. Full cousins they were, and whores both of them.' He paused to look at the ancient rafters of his knightly hall, and said, 'So now we have as queen the illegitimate daughter of a whore. Times will be bad, Fairleigh, and we shall all have to know where we stand.'

For good Catholics the times were worse than he had foreseen: the saintly Pope, Pius V, issued a bull which excommunicated Elizabeth as a heretic and advised the Catholics of England that they no longer owed her allegiance. She retaliated by condemning to death anyone who circulated the bull on English soil.

The battle was joined; step by step, harsh measures were promulgated against these devout people like young Fairleigh Steed who loved both the church of Rome and the land of England. Any Catholic caught attending a Mass: £ 70 fine, a horrendous sum in those days. Any Catholic who refused to attend Protestant church: £ 20 fine each year levied against each member of the family, young or old. Any English man or woman who endeavored to convert good Protestants into Catholics: death by hanging. And any believers, such as the Steeds, who attempted to cling to the religion they had always followed: endless harassment, persecution and the risk of death if they harbored a secret priest.

Queen Elizabeth could never comprehend the obstinate behavior of people like the Steeds. Her new religion preserved almost all the characteristics of the old: the Mass, transubstantiation, the high altar, baptism, rigorous attention to confession, nothing but fish to be eaten on Wednesday, and a celibate clergy dressed in customary vestments. It was Elizabeth's belief that a non-contentious person could worship according to the new ritual and never be aware that it was not Catholic. Furthermore, she outlawed with extreme severity any manifestations of Calvinistic Protestantism, and gleefully executed those Lutherans who sought to promulgate the pernicious teachings of Geneva.

All that Elizabeth demanded of her subjects was that they forswear Rome and acknowledge her as governor of the church as it functioned in England. The harsh law of 1581 explained all in its title: *To Retain the Queen Majesty's Subjects in Due Obedience.* Spiritual obedience to a human sovereign the Steeds refused to concede. They became surreptitious Catholics, secret adherents to the ancient faith, daring protectors of itinerant priests who labored in peril to keep that faith alive.

Queen's Wenlock, once one of the notable smaller monasteries of England, became in the 1570s a center of the Catholic missionary spirit. Old Sir Latimer said that he would be damned before he would permit a Whore of the Howards to advise him in spiritual matters. Lady Steed cautioned him to mind his tongue lest he be hanged, and reminded him that it was not one of the Whores of the Howards who was doing this to England but the illegitimate daughter of one of the whores.

It was young Fairleigh, now twenty-five and down from Oxford, who felt the pressure of the age most keenly. He revered the old ways and believed that he could adhere to them without being treasonous to the new queen, even though he despised her. He was both a Catholic and an Englishman, and it ought to be possible to be a faithful, loyal citizen of both worlds. As to the preposterous charge of the Protestants that to be a Catholic meant automatically that one was eager to take up arms for the Pope and against England, he had never heard such nonsense. There were more than 160,000 practicing Catholics in England and only a handful of traitors among them.

But things kept happening that weakened his position. Fanatics with no knowledge of England were captured while trying to engineer a Spanish invasion to put King Philip back on the throne he had once shared with Mary. Other fools, seeking to inspire an uprising in favor of that other Mary, the Catholic Queen of Scots, were caught with letters on their persons spelling out details. Crazed people, torn apart by religious conflicts they could not comprehend, tried to assassinate the queen, as madmen in all countries endeavor to kill their appointed leaders.

All this led to suspicion and hatred; good Englishmen who should have known better came to believe without question that the Pope intended to invade their land with Spanish help and reconvert them to old-style Catholicism. It was against this prejudice that the Steeds now had to operate.

They bore unwavering testimony, all members of the family, that being a Catholic did not entail heresy. Even the slightest invitation that might look suspicious, they not only rejected but spoke against. The one forbidden thing they would not surrender was correspondence with the courageous priests.

'These priests, ordained of God, are our spiritual guides,' Sir Latimer proclaimed to any who would hear. The old bumbler was becoming a most stalwart man; in the ordinary course of events that had prevailed in England for centuries he would have been the village squire, dispensing a hit-or-miss kind of justice, refusing to sentence even the worst criminal to death, and husbanding his estates so that each generation should be a few acres better off than the preceding. It was by the accident of King Henry's divorce that he had inherited a knighthood, and although he was pleased with the buildings and estates which accompanied it, he was not really at ease in his minor castle. He would have been much more comfortable tending the hogs back in Devon. Certainly he was in no way prepared to enter religious debate. All he knew was that the Steeds had always obeyed the Pope and they intended to keep on doing so.

It was understandable, therefore, that when devout English priests, ordained at the émigré English seminary at Douai across the Channel in the Spanish Netherlands, were filtered surreptitiously into England to protect the faith, they should carry with them unwritten instructions to seek out the Steeds at Queen's Wenlock, and this they did. By Elizabethan definition such priests were treasonous—they sought not the salvation of souls but the fomenting of revolution—and anyone who harbored them did so at risk of life. The Steeds took that risk.

It would be dusk when the wandering priests converged at some agreed-upon meeting spot in the countryside west of London. They would maintain a furtiveness lest the paid spies of Walsingham and Burleigh, who circulated about the countryside, detect them. As night fell they would move swiftly to the four vaulted doors of the old monastery and knock rapidly. A light would shine. One door would creak open a few inches. The priests would announce themselves, pronounce the password given them by Catholics in London, and enter swiftly as the door clanged shut.

Inside, Sir Latimer would pour the drinks and ask what was happening at Douai. The translation of the Bible into English acceptable to Catholics was proceeding. New priests were being ordained regularly, and those with fortitude were being spirited into England. Four of the most recent arrivals had already been hanged, but other would-be martyrs were on the way.

And what of the new Pope? The young priests said that he was about to take a step which would assist them mightily in their work. He would announce that the bull of his predecessor commanding all good Catholics to oppose Queen Elizabeth would be placed in some kind of suspension so that Catholics could obey the queen in all things temporal.

'Damned clever of the Pope!' Sir Latimer cried. 'That absolves us of heresy.'

'It does indeed,' the priests agreed.

But courts subservient to the queen saw the papal move as subterfuge, and the hanging of priests continued.

In the summer of 1580 there came to the grange a fugitive priest so luminous that he seemed to carry with him visible proof of his sanctity and his coming martyrdom. He was Edmund Campion, forty years old that summer, one of the brightest students Oxford had ever known, a distinguished scholar at the Catholic seminary in Douai, and one of the most skilled argumentators among the Jesuits at Rome. He was a philosopher, a historian, an author of pamphlets and a superb theologian. Among his friends, Protestants and Catholics alike, he was known as the marvel of his age, and fourteen years earlier Queen Elizabeth herself, enchanted by an oration he delivered before her when she visited Oxford, had said, 'For this young man, unlimited preferment waits.'

He had chosen instead the thorny road of missionary priest, and on the day when he slipped ashore at Dover he knew that his fame was such that he must be spotted by Walsingham's spies and burned as a martyr. Secure in this knowledge and satisfied with his fate, he moved courageously through the countryside, holding prayer meetings and ignoring the likelihood that Protestant informers were tracking him.

He arrived at Queen's Wenlock one Friday and told Sir Latimer, of whom he had heard valorous reports, that he wished to conduct Mass for Catholics in the area, and these were hastily assembled, each man and woman knowing that death would be the consequence of betrayal. When they streamed into the grange, this saving remnant of an older faith, they found awaiting them tough old Sir Latimer, bushy eyebrows in a furrow, and the serene face of Edmund Campion.

He chose as his text a passage from St. Paul's journeys and compared the work Paul had done with what the fugitive priests were doing. 'Pagan Rome sought Paul no less avidly than Protestant Walsingham seeks me. In the end, Paul triumphed, and so shall we.' His preaching consisted of simple yet powerful examples of what the furtive graduates of Douai had accomplished in keeping alive in England the sacred flames of Catholicism. 'The glory of our Church is their martyrdom. The fires of their burned bodies inflame our holy spirit.'

He spoke like one possessed, but he did not rant, nor did he ever point to himself as an exemplar. He simply reported what Catholics were attaining in these decisive times. When he finished he performed the ceremony of the Mass, blessing the wine and sanctifying the wafers which had been prepared for this holy feast. As he placed on each tongue the body of Christ he said, 'Peace shall be with us.'

Perhaps it was the tragic events that happened later which led persons who attended this Mass to claim in years to come that it had been a holy moment, but all so testified: 'The future stood revealed, and about the blessed head of Edmund Campion we saw the halo of martyrdom.' In any case, Father Campion left Queen's Wenlock in a state of exaltation, as if his days of testing were already at hand.

Sir Latimer and his son Fairleigh accompanied Campion to his next preaching, at a grange near Faringdon, in Bucks, and from there to Oxford itself, where young Steed introduced the daring priest to numerous undergraduates committed to Catholicism. With these young minds he discussed the future of the church in England and the nature of individual vocation. After his final Mass he intended heading for Norfolk, where the heavy incidence of Catholics would render him relatively safe, but at the last minute he was prevailed upon to return to Faringdon to preach again to large numbers of the faithful who had not been privileged to hear him on his earlier visit to Queen's Wenlock.

Acceding to the supplications so urgently pressed upon him, he retraced his steps to Sir Latimer's home, where Protestant spies awaited. It was they who had engineered the clamant invitation and it was they who conducted him a prisoner back to London and a cell in the Tower.

He was lodged in Little Ease, the famous crib too low for standing, too cramped for sleeping, and there he was held in crouching solitary confinement without adequate food for four days. He was then racked three separate times until his joints spread apart, and in his extremity he confirmed what Burleigh and Walsingham already knew, that he had been protected by Sir Latimer Steed of the grange at Queen's Wenlock.

The old knight was promptly arrested and thrown like his priest into Little Ease, from which he emerged a shattered man, bumbling and speaking in fragmentary sentences. But as his body deteriorated, his spiritual force increased, and no matter what the hideous jailers and the rack-masters did to him, he bore one simple testimony: that he was loyal to England and faithful to his Church. The interrogators screamed at him, charged him with ingratitude, reminded him that he was a creature of whatever king or queen possessed the throne at the moment, and thus obligated to swear fealty to whichever form of religion that monarch professed.

Such an idea was repugnant, and he rejected it scornfully, so in late November 1581 he and Father Campion were dragged into Westminster Hall, in whose fine and lofty chambers the leaders of law and clergy met to pass judgment on treasonous heretics. Fairleigh Steed was allowed to attend the trial, along with many Protestants who cheered every point scored against the convicts.

The trial was a sham. No witness could be found to prove that Father Campion had ever preached treason, whereas eleven came forward to testify that he had specifically told everyone at the grange that their civil duty was to pay respect to Elizabeth and her laws. As for Sir Latimer, the whole testimony of his life was that of loyalty to the crown. Fairleigh, listening as closely as he could to all that was said, could not imagine any verdict but innocent, and he sat in numbed horror when the judges, responsible and decent men of the realm, read out their sentence:

'You must go to the place from whence you came, there to remain until you shall be drawn through the open City of London upon hurdles to the place of execution, and there be hanged. But you shall be let down while still alive, and your privy parts shall be cut off, and your entrails taken out and burnt in your sight, and then your bodies shall be divided into four parts to be disposed of at Her Gracious Majesty's pleasure. And God have mercy on your souls.'

Ten days later the sentence was carried out in meticulous detail, and Fairleigh Steed forced himself to watch as his father and this sainted priest were jerked about horribly, cut down, butchered and forced to watch as their bodies were torn apart. Neither the old man nor the young uttered a cry, and Fairleigh was convinced that when their spirits departed they entered heaven to take their place in the bosom of Abraham.

A week later Sir Fairleigh's wife gave birth to a son, whom a new priest from Douai christened Edmund.

Sir Latimer Steed's head was stuck on a pike and exhibited for nine weeks at Tyburn, during which time his family at Queen's Wenlock tried to formulate a plan for continued existence. Curiously, in view of the savage death meted out to the old knight, the family's lands were not confiscated; Sir Latimer's descendants suffered no attainder, because the monarchs of England generally allowed the treason of a parent to end there, in hopes that the children might learn from their elders' mistakes, and reform.

The Steeds made two decisions: they would in all things be loyal to England, and they would continue to hear Mass. Young Edmund spent the first six years of his life being indoctrinated into these twin principles; when he thought of his father he visualized a quiet gentleman who tended the affairs of his huge holdings and then prayed resolutely with whatever priest happened to pass by, for he was determined to hold on to his Catholic heritage. Edmund patterned himself after his father, and throughout England in these quiet years from 1581 through 1587 this type of sensible truce prevailed.

But in 1588 King Philip of Spain, seeking to regain the English throne he had once occupied as Mary's husband, blasted all reasonable hopes held by families like the Steeds. He sent his conquering Armada up the Channel to invade England, destroy Protestantism and forcibly lead the captured land back to Rome. Stupid Englishmen, especially those who had lived abroad in exile, made stupid statements about the restoration of the Pope, and within the island other misguided idiots believed that as soon as Spanish troops set foot on English soil, Catholics of the realm would rise up to greet them and aid in the subjugation of their homeland.

From that summer day on which Drake and Hawkins and Howard routed the Spanish galleons off Plymouth and sent them to their graves in storms off the Hebrides, the fate of ordinary Catholics like the Steeds was sealed. The general populace knew them to be treasonous, the whole lot of them, and it was further believed that only a miracle had enabled the English to defend themselves against papal invasion and the restoration of the burnings which Queen Mary had sponsored during her brief and bloody reign.

The ostracism fell most heavily on young Edmund. At school he was a child who kept apart, and at Oxford one to be avoided. He could never hold public office; nor serve as a justice of the peace, like his forebears; nor testify in certain kinds of trials; nor marry into the good families; nor serve as an officer in either navy or army. He had to pay special taxes, and worst of all, was held in contempt by the countryside. The hearing of Mass became more difficult, for in the wake of the Armada fugitive priests were hunted down with extra severity. As the sixteenth century closed, a young Catholic could exist in England, but that was about all.

But in 1602, as Edmund reached his majority, Queen Elizabeth sickened, and in 1603 she died—bald, bewigged and uglier than sin. As prayers were being said for the salvation of her grand and murderous soul, Sir Fairleigh Steed assembled his family in the great hall at Queen's Wenlock, where a fugitive priest read a Mass for the departed queen, asking the Steed family to forgive her for the wrongs she had done them. When all in the room had pledged allegiance to their new king, James VI of Scotland and I of England, a fervent prayer was uttered by Sir Fairleigh, asking that God make the new monarch more understanding than the old.

Nothing changed. Catholics continued to be excluded from government, and one of Edmund's professors told him, 'You should have been a don at Oxford, were you not a Catholic.' It was in this confusion that Edmund came down from the university with an immoral proposal which shocked his father: 'I'm going to embrace the new faith.' Sir Fairleigh gasped, whereupon Edmund added, 'Publicly. If this nation continues to place infirmities upon Catholics, I deem it permissible for me to deceive the nation. When I return to Oxford, I shall take the Oath of Conformity. From that day forth I shall be a public Protestant.'

'And inwardly?'

'As good a Catholic as ever. When you hold Mass, I shall attend.'

'Edmund, you undertake a grievous task.'

'I have no desire to have my guts torn out.'

'No man does, but sometimes it happens.'

'It won't happen to me. I'll play their filthy game.'

'Young men often think,' Sir Fairleigh said, 'that they can play any game, if only they keep their hearts pure.'

'I intend trying,' Edmund said, and on the first anniversary of King James' ascension he rode to Oxford and in public ceremony announced that he was forswearing Catholicism, affirming that he no longer owed any spiritual allegiance to either Pope or priests. He allowed a chaplain to administer the Oath of Conformity, and from that moment became an ostensible Protestant, to the delight of friends who had always wished him well. In fact, his conversion gave so much pleasure that he was offered preferments as an inducement to other Catholics to follow suit, and his professors reopened discussion of a post at the university.

In this manner Edmund Steed was lured back into the mainstream of English life. He worked for the government in London and was invited by his associates to their places in the country, where he met old gentlemen who in their youth had known Sir Devon, and one such man in Bucks told Edmund frankly that he hoped the time would come when Steed would join their family, seeing they had such a plethora of daughters.

But whenever he returned to the handsome old grange at Queen's Wenlock, and the doors were closed, and night fell, and the fugitive priests from Douai materialized, he resumed his Catholic identity, trembling when the sacred host touched his tongue.

It was during such a visit, when the Mass had been especially significant, that he took his father out into the timeless orchards which had been planted personally by Good Queen Anne in 1387, and there under the gnarled trees told him, 'Father, the burden is too great. I can't dissemble. My soul is being torn apart.'

'I supposed it would be,' the wise old man said. 'What do you propose?'

'A company's being formed to establish a new settlement in America. I shall subscribe.'

'I understand,' Sir Fairleigh said. He did not press him on how he would survive in a distant land without the consoling reassurances of this grange and these memories, for he was certain that Edmund had weighed his losses. What was important was that his son get back on solid footing, the kind the Steeds had always preferred. 'I suppose you'll quit the Protestant masquerade?'

'As soon as possible.'

'Why not now?'

'Because I must first get to America. The company won't welcome Catholics.'

'Don't delay too long, Edmund. Dissembling corrodes.'

'I intend placing myself in a position where it's no longer necessary.'

The old knight did not want to see his youngest son quit England, and especially he did not want him to end his association with the grange, for the strength of the Steeds had always been their reliance on the land: the furrows and the hunting and the birth of lambs. He knew how desperately Edmund would long for these pastures and orchards when he pined in a savage land, but if leaving would help clarify his soul, he must leave.

'I won't see you again, Father.'

'You sail so soon?'

'Within the month, they say.'

They neither embraced nor shook hands; excessive display was not the way of the Steeds, but when he said farewell in the vaulted doorway built so many years ago, the old man shivered. 'These have not been good years for Catholics,' he said. 'Of late I've been seeing Sir Latimer's head on that pike. That's the end of all of us, I'm afraid.' They looked at each other and parted.

Few of mankind's memorable adventures started more poorly than the English settlement of Virginia. During the last days of December 1606 the company to which Edmund Steed had subscribed piled 105 courageous emigrants onto the three small ships and set sail for the New World, expecting to make landfall within five weeks.

Off the coast, but still in sight of England, they were becalmed for six agonizing weeks. The wind would not rise and there was nothing the infuriated captains could do; ominously, the leaders of the expedition watched the would-be settlers consume much of the food intended to see them through the first months of the experiment. It was not until May 14 that the ships unloaded at a swampy island in the James River, grandiloquently named Jamestown, as if it were an operating city.

Lack of food, miasmal land, confusion in leadership, hostility from Indians and rampaging epidemics beset the newcomers, so that when the dreadful summer ended, only thirty-eight of the original group still lived. That these could survive the winter seemed doubtful.

The behavior of the Indians who populated the western shore of the Chesapeake bewildered the settlers: for six weeks the redskins would be amiable, bringing to the stockade food which saved the lives of the remnant; for the next six weeks they would kill any settler who stepped outside. It was difficult for the Englishmen to accept such irrational behavior, and most came to fear and hate the Indian.

Edmund Steed did neither. His contact with red men led him to believe that they were much like other humans, capable of trust and desirable as neighbors. He felt at ease traveling amongst them, so that when Captain Smith launched his serious exploration of the Chesapeake, seeking the gold and silver known to exist there, it was natural for Steed to participate, and his contacts with the peaceful Indians of the eastern shore confirmed his attitudes.

But in November 1608 he accompanied Smith on an expedition up the James River which had horrifying results. It was an exploration to ascertain what kind of land lay beyond the confluence of the Chickahominy, and after the little band left their canoes, Steed marched at the rear with the carpenter George Landon, and his easy experiences with the Choptanks lulled him into carelessness. Farther and farther the two stragglers fell behind, and when they were totally detached, a band of howling savages overwhelmed them. A hideous orgy followed, with warriors jabbing pointed sticks at their faces, stopping just short of the eyes. Then, as Steed would later report:

> The women of the tribe descended upon us, pushed the braves their brothers away, and lashed us to stakes set into the ground. With much dancing and glee they attended to Landon first, using sharp oyster shells to cut off all his fingers, one knuckle at a time. While he was screaming so loud that he drowned out the exulting cries of the women, they knelt down and sawed away his toes in the same protracted manner. This done, they started at his scalp, and moving slowly downward, ripped off his living skin. While he was still alive they piled brush about his stake and set it afire. When their dancing ended they came at me with their shells, but Captain Smith and his men had doubled back to find us and came upon the scene in time to save me.

Later, a group of heavily laden supply ships arrived from London under the leadership of Captain John Ratcliffe, who had served as captain aboard the tiny pinnace *Discovery* during the original voyage of 1607 and who had later held the presidency of the council. Since he was well informed on affairs in Virginia, he was sent with a body of soldiers to negotiate with Chief Powhatan for more land, but that insidious Indian lured the Englishmen with promises, set upon them nefariously and slew most. They kept Ratcliffe, Steed and one other alive for special tortures, and once again the Oxford student was rescued to report the horrible incident:

> With our dead lying about us, we were tied naked to stakes, before which hot fires were set, and when we were toasted near to death women attacked poor Ratcliffe and with shells scraped away all the flesh on his left arm up to the shoulder, tossing the bits into the fire. They did the same with his right arm and then his right leg, where-upon he died.

When such evidence was endlessly repeated, Edmund Steed lost all trust in Indians. He came to see them as crafty, cruel, lazy and uncivilized, and it was a prudent white man who anticipated their perfidy. Now when trading parties ascended the James to deal with Powhatan, Steed remained apart, between two soldiers, ready to discharge his musket straight at the heart of any savage who threatened a treacherous move.

As his faith in Indians diminished, his trust in Captain Smith grew. He saw him as the only savior of the colony, a man of petty foibles and ramrod rectitude. When the little captain announced that he must quit the colony to ensure a more faithful chain of supplies from London, swearing vociferously that he was not abandoning the settlers but would return, Steed foresaw that once safe in England he would become caught up in a hundred fascinating schemes involving dukes and foreign princes and wars in Muscovy.

'I shall not see you again, Captain,' Steed said mournfully as Smith stood on the dock, surrounded by packets of arrows he was taking back to England for display.

'You'll survive. Remember, you're one of the men of iron.'

'I meant . . . you'll not return.'

'Me! This bay is blood to me. It courses through my veins.' He said much more, and in the end drew himself to maximum height, saluted the little colony he had kept alive, and was seen no more in Virginia.

On the day he sailed down the river, the testing time began, those starving weeks and months of autumn 1609 and winter 1610. When Smith left, the expanding colony contained 507 members; six terrible months later only 61 remained. Of this foodless, heatless catastrophe Steed reported to the managers in London:

> All who might lead are dead. The doctor and the carpenters and all who worked to keep the town functioning, they are dead. Even as I write the room is cluttered with bodies, for we no longer have any to bury them. We have neither a bean nor a biscuit, and I shudder to inform you that some, beyond the point of desperation, have taken to digging up the bodies of those already dead and endeavouring to eat them, and from doing this, some have gone mad and cast themselves into the river and died. And if we who are able to move seek to leave the fort to find food, the lurking Indians slay us.

It was a time of such gnawing horror that those few who survived sought ever after to erase it from their memory, and yet it was the foundation of fact on which the great colony of Virginia was erected.

On May 23, 1610, when the spring breezes made starvation even more monstrous, a man who had crawled to the river to die set up a howling, and when Steed went to him he saw that the man was pointing downstream where two rescue ships hove into view, and when they moved to shore Steed saw that their names were *Patience* and *Deliverance*.

It was during the following spring, in 1611, when the colony was stabilized, that Steed decided to quit Jamestown and start a new life on that hospitable island he had scouted with Captain Smith three summers earlier. During all the trials which beset him in Virginia, he had kept alive his vision of that island with the tall trees and abundant fish, and even when it seemed that the Indian women must hack him to pieces, or that starvation would evaporate him before the day ended, he could visualize that island and imagine himself living quietly there.

He could even recall the Indians he and Captain Smith had met along the river, especially the giant chief, and he wanted desperately to believe that they were different from the mercurial and untrustworthy tribes under Powhatan. He had no evidence to support this hope, but he had seen those gentle Choptank Indians, and it was not unreasonable to hope that they were different.

The driving force which impelled him to leave Jamestown was one which his ancestors would have understood: Sir Devon with his simplistic sense of right and wrong; bumbling, stumbling Sir Latimer willing to be torn apart for his faith; hesitant Sir Fairleigh trying to be both a good Catholic and a loyal Englishman—they would have comprehended when he said, 'I am strangled with duplicity. I must live where I can stand forth as an honest Catholic.'

Jamestown was far too preoccupied with mere survival to worry much about the forms of religion; it was not flamboyantly anti-Catholic, but that was because the leaders of the settlement could not imagine that any of their flock were Catholic. With them it was always 'Good Queen Bess for whom Virginia was named' and 'Faithful King James, a reliable man even though his mother was that Catholic whore, Mary of Scotland.' It was known, of course, that Steed's grandfather, Sir Latimer, had been drawn and quartered for his treasonous adherence to Rome, but it was also known that young Steed had abjured that poisonous faith; besides, on various occasions he had proved his valor, and that counted.

Edmund Steed could have continued his masquerade as a false Protestant, and his offspring, when he had them, could certainly have been counted among the first families of Virginia, but the tricky doubleness of his position—Protestant by day, Catholic by night—was more than he could sustain. He was indeed sick of dissembling and determined to put an end to it. For a Catholic, there was no future in the Virginia settlement, so he would go elsewhere.

He was not forthright in offering his reasons for moving to the eastern shore. 'I want to go where the oystering is better,' he said lamely. 'Trade with the Indians who live across the bay could be profitable to Virginia.' One after another he paraded his spurious reasons, and in the end the governors of the colony granted him permission—'It will be to our advantage to have an outpost firmly located on the eastern shore.'

So in May 1611 he rose each day before dawn to hack out the planks required for the boat he had in mind. Samuel Dwight, a ship's carpenter on one of the rescue ships, gave Steed some rule-of-thumb advice.

'For these shallow waters make her flat-bottomed. Also, it's easier for them as doesn't know to build a keel. One mast is all a man alone can handle, and it a short one. Pointed bow for probing, transom stern for stability. And leeboards to hold her into the wind.'

'What are leeboards?' Steed inquired.

'When you've finished putting her together, I'll instruct you.'

It took Steed four weeks, with spasmodic help from Mr. Dwight, to build his small craft. It was only fifteen feet long, but it was sturdy, and if the uneven finishing of the planks allowed water to flow in at a rate that would soon sink her, stout caulking would cure that. It was launched on the last day of June, and when it swayed on the placid waters of the James, Steed asked his carpenter, 'What type of boat is it?' and the newcomer replied, 'Bateau,' and he demonstrated how the leeboards must be attached.

They were two stout oval slabs of wood, fastened outboard at amidships by pivots, one to the starboard, the other to port. By convenient ropes they could be lowered into the water or lifted out, and their purpose was to counteract the normal sideways drift of a boat under sail. They were, in short, a clever, practical substitute for a fixed keel, and they worked. Like two misplaced fins of a fish, they dominated the appearance of the bateau, but Carpenter Dwight said of them approvingly, 'You'll find them valuable in the bay. Remember, when the wind is pushing you sideways on the starboard tack, put down your port leeboard. And when it pushes you from port, put down your starboard.' Steed said he thought he could manage the low, heavy bateau.

Into it he piled the goods he had collected from those unfortunates who had died during the starving time, with special attention to axes, knives, gunpowder and nails. He left Jamestown with one barrel of dried foods, an extra pair of heavy trousers and three woolen shirts. He had no medicine, no small tools, no needles for sewing, and only two knives, three forks, four spoons and a pair of guns. Yet he had not the slightest doubt that he could occupy his island, and tame it, and make it an industrious part of the empire. On June 12, 1611, he set forth, and because there was no wind, he rowed all that day down the James. His fancy leeboards were of no use, but his hands were well blistered.

However, on June 13 a tidy breeze came down the James and into it he hoisted his sail. Since the wind came from directly behind, he still had no use for his leeboards, but on the third day, as he approached the bay itself, a brisk wind swept down from the northwest, and he put his bateau on a port tack so that it would head up the bay, against the wind, and now he dropped his starboard leeboard and felt it catch the water and brace him against sideward drifting.

'Carpenter Dwight knew what he was doing!' he exulted as the wind drove him forward, and all that day he lay at ease admiring the bateau he had built.

Now the waters of the bay became familiar and he was able to tick off the rivers of the western shore—York, Rappahannock, Potomac—and when he reached the Patuxent he knew it was time to start swinging eastward to strike the entrance to the Choptank and the island he sought.

It was the longest day of the year when he approached the western end of the island, and he decided not to go ashore that night, because he could not foretell what mood the once-peaceful Choptank Indians might be in. Of one thing he was certain: he would rather be here than anywhere else in the world. This would be his empire; here he would live according to the principles of his fathers. When long-delayed night closed in, and the outlines of the island became increasingly dim, so that in the end it existed only in his mind, he uttered a prayer: 'Divine Leader Who has brought me here, permit me safe conduct onto my island and allow me to live here in Thy ways.'

He could not sleep. All night he sat in his bateau staring in the direction of land, and toward four, when dawn began to brighten and his island rose from the mists like a sanctuary preserved, he shouted joyously and steered his boat around the north shore and into that safe creek he had noted three years before. As he sailed its deep clear waters and saw the massive trees lining the banks like courtiers arranged to welcome a returning king, he nodded gravely and announced, 'This is the island of Devon, proprietary of the Steeds, and so it shall remain forever.'

He anchored at the head of the creek and waded ashore. After scouting the area for likely spots, he found a rise containing only a few trees, with open space enough to build a hut from which he would be able to watch the river and his boat. With the good luck that comes to countrymen who have a feeling for land, he had stumbled upon the choicest spot for building, and as the days progressed and he cleared the brush, he was satisfied that he had chosen well.

He worked from dawn till dusk, day after day, catching fish and crabs for his food and spotting the berry patches and nut trees for future use. Deer came to watch. Raccoons were plentiful and three blue herons patrolled his shore, catching so many fish that he felt certain he could do the same.

With all this food, he reflected, why did we starve in Jamestown? But as soon as he posed the question he knew the answer: Because the Virginia Indians were hostile and would not allow us to hunt or fish. And he wondered how long his muskets and bullets would defend him if the Choptank Indians turned hostile.

With so much work to do, he could not brood upon this possibility, but he did refrain from wasting ammunition. With his ax he went to the woods and began chopping down the small trees he would need for his hut, and when the outline was formed, he cut branches and wove them between the poles, as he had seen Indians do, but the result was rough and rain entered almost unimpeded. But then he brought rushes from the river and tangled them among the branches, and when he compacted them, like a woman tightening threads upon a loom, he had a satisfactory wall.

He was then free to explore his island, and found it a fascinating place. Utilizing various tricks of measurement, he calculated that it ran about two and a quarter miles east and west, one and a half north and south, for a total of something more than two thousand acres. It was cut nearly in the middle by the intruding river and a deep bay leading up from the south, and the two halves were sufficiently different to accommodate two varied styles of husbandry: sheep to the west, corn to the east. He had no premonition of what the real treasure of this land was going to be.

He had occupied his island for more than four weeks without seeing any Indians, or signs of any. No canoes had appeared on the river, nor had any fires been set. He tried to recall how far to the east he and Captain Smith had gone before they encountered the village of Pata-moke, but his memory was vague.

Where can the Indians be? he thought one morning as he surveyed the empty river; he could not know they had moved eastward to escape mosquitoes.

And then toward the end of September, while he felled trees on the eastern point of the island, he saw three canoes edging gingerly out from the white cliffs opposite. They were not war canoes, so they could not have come seeking war; they seemed, in fact, timorous, for when they reached a spot about a half mile from the island they stopped. There they stayed all day, making no further gesture, even though they must have seen Steed. Finally they retired.

They repeated this for two days, and on the third Steed made signals and lured them closer, and when they were less than a hundred yards from shore, so that their faces were becoming distinct, a short thin man shouted in a language Steed could not understand. The canoes milled about, guided by what must have been conflicting suggestions, and on the spur of the moment Steed dropped his ax, walked to the edge of the water and held up his hands, empty.

The canoes moved closer, until the faces became so individualized that he could see one of the men had a cleft chin. No one spoke. Steed continued to hold his hands open and pointed to the emptiness behind him, indicating that he was alone. The Indians stared at him stolidly, remained in position for perhaps half an hour, then smartly withdrew, paddling upstream to their village.

On the fourth day this procedure was repeated, and Steed suspected that the man with the cleft chin wanted to come ashore but was re-strained by the men in his canoe.

On the fifth day Steed kept about his work, watching the canoes out of the corner of his eye, but again no moves were taken by the Indians, and well before dusk they retired. He judged that on the morrow something definite would happen, and he prepared his axes and his guns. That evening, as the sun left the sky and a darkness deeper than usual enveloped the island, he recalled the scenes of torture he had witnessed, and the destructive fighting on the western shore, and he prayed: 'God, let my Indians come in peace.'

He could not sleep. His hut seemed unbearably close and he left it to sit on a log, staring into the darkness and wondering what he might be forced to do in the coming day, and when the pale streaks of early dawn lighted the east he decided that he would stay in his hut, like a proper chief, and wait for the Indians to come to him. Day brightened and nothing happened. Forenoon brought buzzing insects and an inquisitive deer, but no visitors. High noon arrived, bringing with it a stillness that quieted even the rustling of the tallest trees, and then when the sun had begun its descent he saw four canoes come into his river, and in the lead position in the lead canoe sat the immensely tall Indian with the three turkey feathers, whom he and Captain Smith had met.

As the canoes approached his undefended bateau his heart beat with hammers; if the Indians wished, they could sink the boat and leave him powerless. They passed it by and came to the rock landing he had fashioned. The man with the cleft chin jumped out first, and led the way for the chief, who seemed even larger as he came on this crucial visit.

When the giant was about to reach the hut, Steed rose, extended both hands, palms up to prove that they were empty. The Indian studied them, extended his own, and looked for a place to sit. Steed beckoned him inside, and for more than an hour they talked. Neither knew a word of the other's speech, but they spoke of deer, which were plentiful, and of oysters, which were good when dried, and of the woven wall Steed had built. The Indian considered it commendable and showed his followers that he could not penetrate its close weaving with his finger. They were unusually interested in his tools, and he showed them the axes with their sharp edges. He took down one of his guns and laboriously explained its loading and preparation. Having done this, he led the tall Indian outside and waited till some doves flew by; taking extra precautions and holding his breath so as to steady the gun, he fired. A dove fell not far from the chief, who sent the man with the cleft chin to fetch it.

'How did such a thing happen?' he asked in pantomime, and Steed explained. But remarkable as the gun was, it was the bateau that tantalized the giant chief and he asked if he might inspect it. The visit had proceeded so amicably that Steed was ready to believe that these Indians were exactly as they had been before: they were not infected by the wars of the Potomacs. So he took the tall chief to where the bateau was moored, and four of the Indians climbed aboard. They wanted to know how the sail, which lay in the bottom of the boat, operated, and what the oval leeboards were; they were perplexed by the length of the oars, but always they came back to the sail. Then began a mysterious operation, repeated many times: the chief touched the sail, then touched Steed's face, and the Englishman could make nothing of the gestures. But finally it dawned upon him that what the Indian was comparing was the whiteness of the sail and the face.

'Yes,' Steed said. 'A sail is always white.' And he hauled it up the mast and showed the Indians how to lift the anchor, and when a breeze came the boat and its five passengers moved down the creek.

Seeing their chieftain being spirited away alarmed the Indians on shore and they launched a great clatter, which the chief silenced with a gesture. He then studied the sail's whiteness, and Steed saw that he was weeping from some deep and powerful remembrance.

When Steed was satisfied that friendly relations were possible, he indicated that he wanted to pay the tribe for the land he was occupying, so a formal procession was arranged—the bateau carrying Steed and the tall chieftain, followed by the four canoes—and it went upriver to the village of Patamoke, where the young werowance was informed of all that had occurred on the island. A deed was drawn up, dated 10 October 1611, and signed by Steed, who showed the werowance how to make his mark. The tall chief did likewise, as did the little fellow with the cleft chin. When this was completed he handed the werowance one ax, one hatchet, such cloth as he could spare and seven nails. He had traded a fair portion of his worldly wealth for an island the Indians not only did not need, but had never used.

And when the paper was folded, and the long clay pipes were smoked, he did more. By sign language he promised them that when trade was established he would give them additional gifts, and he insisted upon this because the pact had brought him slightly more than four thousand acres, half on the island, half on the facing shore, and some of it the choicest land along the river. By this treaty, his immediate problems of existence were also relieved, for he received an unlimited supply of vegetables, and he could sleep at night untroubled.

But what galvanized his imagination was something he saw as he was about to leave: in the corner of the long house lay a bundle of beaver pelts, and when he asked where they had come from, the werowance pointed generally to the south, indicating that in the marshy lands across the river there was an endless supply of beaver.

Then Steed knew what he must do: he must convince the Indians to bring him many pelts against future trading privileges; he would deliver the furs to Jamestown, where ships from England would barter for them.

The result would be a constant flow of axes, cloth, guns and nails, with a generous profit to him on all transactions. His ancestors in England, dating back to the thirteenth century, would have been mortified to think that Steed was about to engage in trade—that was forbidden a gentleman—but Edmund rationalized that none of them had tried to settle virgin acreage. He would make himself the best trader in the colony.

But like Captain Smith on the banks of the York, he failed to spot the commodity which would form the true basis of his wealth. As he stowed the beaver pelts in his bateau he did not notice that in an opposite corner of the long house the werowance had another treasure, a pile of the best tobacco leaves. The English gentlemen who emigrated to the New World did not learn rapidly; they were amazingly delinquent in acquiring the skills that mattered, like fertilizing corn with dead fish or living off oysters when meat was unavailable, but when they did finally learn something, they clung to it desperately and made it better: Edmund Steed had learned how to accumulate beaver pelts.

But there was one question the Choptanks did not answer for him, the one that would perplex every European settlement in the New World: where would the men who fought the wilderness find women? Each nation solved this vital problem according to its traditions. In Canada the French forerunners were already taking Indian brides. In Mexico to the south, where a flourishing civilization had developed, Spaniards had adopted two solutions: some married Aztecs, some sent home for childhood acquaintances. In Brazil the Portuguese, finding jungle Indians incompatible, chose black women who had been imported as slaves from Africa. And in Virginia the stiff-lipped Englishmen did nothing until such time as shiploads of properly assembled London women could be delivered by artful ships' captains, who sold the ladies off for payment of their passage money, plus an undisclosed profit.

Edmund Steed, now thirty-two, would never have thought of taking into his hut an Indian girl. An English gentleman married an English gentlewoman, preferably of one's own county and religion, and if none came along, the gentleman might wait till he was thirty-five or even forty. Steed thought that when he delivered his beaver pelts to Jamestown it would be about time to consider buying a bride, but until then he was content to live alone.

Not really content, not really alone. The tall chief, having observed his loneliness, waited for a day when he and Steed bargained in broken words for a pile of pelts, and when a trade was concluded and the lesser Indians had left, he uttered a low call. From behind reeds at the end of the wigwam a seventeen-year-old girl appeared, wearing soft brown deerskin and cockleshells in her hair. Steed recognized her as the child he had seen on that first trip to the Choptank, and he even recalled her name, Tciblento, although at their first meeting he had misspelled it.

'She is to accompany you to the island,' the white-haired chief said. 'She has been saved for this moment.'

The beautiful girl kept her gaze downcast and would not look at her father's guest, but her eagerness to visit the island was apparent. Steed blushed and rejected the offer with prolonged attention to protocol: he was honored; she was lovely; the chief's friendship meant everything. And something in the way he spoke conveyed to the waiting girl the fact that he was rejecting her, and her slim shoulders drooped like the petals of a flower left in the sun.

Her father would not accept this decision; in agitated words he explained that his two sons were married to Choptank maidens, but that he had always hoped Tciblento might mate with a Susquehannock worthy of her. But this had not happened. He ended with his eyes close to Steed's, pleading with him to accept this child, and when the Oxford man indicated by manner, if not by words, that never could he marry an Indian, the old man said, 'I bided my time and trusted that when the Great Canoe came . . .'

'What is the Great Canoe?' Steed asked.

'It came a long time ago, and we knew it would return. We waited.' He formed a sail with his fingers.

'You mean our ship?'

'Yes, we knew you were coming.' He would say no more, but he did persist in the matter of his daughter. 'She is a good girl. She cooks, traps beaver, knows where the oysters and crabs are.'

Steed was embarrassed. For a chief to be peddling his daughter was undignified, and for an Englishman to accept would be repugnant. Firmly he said, 'No. She cannot come.' The girl did not weep or run away; she stared at Steed with her great dark eyes as if to say, 'Sir, what an error you make.'

Pentaquod, his self-respect shattered by what was happening, felt that he must show the Englishman the character of a Susquehannock warrior. Summoning the man with the cleft chin, he ordered him to designate two Choptank men to accompany Steed back to the island and there to make their homes, helping him in all things. Each of the men brought a woman and built a wigwam, so that Devon was properly settled.

But this was no solution for Steed—he still lacked a wife, and when the time approached in 1614 for him to load his bateau with beaver pelts and return to Jamestown, he felt a growing sense of excitement. He thought: One of the ships coming to trade would surely bring a cargo of women. Perhaps he would find one whose passage money he could pay. But a moment's reflection warned him that if any women had arrived, they would have been picked off by the local settlers; his chances of finding a wife would not be good. He therefore drafted a letter to his father, not even knowing if Sir Fairleigh was still alive:

Dearest Father,

I am settled into a resplendent island, rich in all things, and I am
on my way to building an estate of which you would be proud. But
I am surrounded only by savages and I most urgently need a wife.
Will you enquire of your friends in Berks whether there be a woman
of Catholic upbringing and good family who knows her letters who
would consent to join me in this enterprise? And if so, please arrange
her passage to Jamestown, where I will reimburse the captain of the
ship she takes.

Edmund

Folding the letter neatly, he tucked it among the beaver pelts, cast off
the bateau, and with his two Indian braves as crew set out for Jamestown.

It was a long and peaceful sail, during which he was able for the first
time to savor the Chesapeake and see it for the glorious body of water
it was, without the pressure of exploration or flight. He lay back with
the tiller tucked under one knee, his only obligation being to advise the
Indians when he wished to come about; they loved this operation when
the boom swung, and the sail filled from the opposite quarter, and the
leeboards were shifted. It was a game which never palled, this trick of
sailing into the wind, making it do what you commanded. Sometimes
they asked Steed to allow them to supervise the maneuver, and one of
them would take the tiller, and watch the wind and the sail, and cry in
a loud voice, 'Prepare to come about! Hard alee!' and the other would
swing the boom and work the lines. Then both would smile.

So long as the course remained down the Chesapeake, Steed felt no
unusual emotion, but once the boat breasted the headland of the James
and started tacking upriver, he became tense, for here some of the great
days of his life had been spent: his defense of Captain Smith when the
mob had wanted to hang him; his escape from the murderous Indians
who had flayed his partner; his magical survival of the starving time,
when eighteen of his closest associates had perished; and most memorable of all, the sense of having helped launch a little colony in a new land.

It wasn't so small a colony now; large ships were arriving from England with all the trading goods the early colonists had longed for, and
where once there had been only men protecting themselves within a
stockade, there were now women joining them to build families which
occupied separate homes.

As his bateau pulled up to the wharf, now a sturdy affair projecting
well into the river, Steed was captivated by the sight of the women; he
had seen no Englishwomen for many years and had almost forgotten the
grace with which they moved, the fall of their heavy skirts and the way
they tied bits of cloth about their throats. They were like magic to him,

a reminder of all he had surrendered in fleeing to his island, and he was filled with that hungriness which would determine all he would do on this trip.

There was a ship in the river, the *Victorious* out of Bristol, and its captain, Henry Hackett, was excited when he saw the bundles of beaver pelts. 'I'll take all of them you bring, Steed,' he growled. 'And what's that aft, sassafras root? I'll take all of it, too.' It was much prized for distillations and the making of infusions to lower fevers. But Hackett's chief delight were the two small tubs in which Steed had stored his salted sturgeon eggs.

'Caviar!' the captain shouted. 'I'd take twenty tubs. Fish eggs is in great demand in London. They turn rancid quick but they're worth the risk.'

In return for this strange collection of goods, Captain Hackett offered Steed a choice of axes, saws, nails, dried beans, salted pork, a compass, folds of writing paper, ink and a dozen books bound in leather. He chose only after the most careful calculations, as he had done when a boy being offered lollies at the grange, and when he was through, the captain said, 'You should have been here to choose two weeks ago.'

'What extra had you then?'

'Brides.'

'Women? English women?'

'And a few Dutch. With your credit you could have bought yourself a beauty.'

'Will you be bringing more?'

'That I will.'

'Will you deliver my letter, then, to my father?' He rummaged among the beaver pelts and produced the carefully composed message, and when he handed it to the captain he explained, 'I'm asking my father to pick me out a bride and send her here in your ship.'

'You pay her passage, I'll deliver her to the gates of hell.'

'I'll pay in stacks of pelts,' Steed said in quivering excitement. 'When will you return?'

'November, likely, if we get passable winds.'

'I hope you do,' Steed said fervently. 'I do hope the winds are good.'

When trading was completed, and the bateau loaded, he invited his two Indian helpers to climb aboard the English ship and see for themselves how mighty it was. In slow, grave movements the two little Choptanks went from item to item of the ship's goods, never touching, never speaking, but when they came to the remnants of brightly colored cloth, their greed became uncontrollable, and each man grabbed an armful.

'Halloo!' a sailor protested. 'You can't just walk off with that there.' In sign language he explained that they must bring him something in trade, and in signs they indicated they had nothing. 'Then get something,' he said, and they rushed to the railing and looked down at Steed, crying in Choptank, 'Master, we must have the cloth!' When he asked why, they said, 'As presents for our wives,' and without reflection he tossed them one of his axes, and they carried it to the sailors, who gave them the cloth they desired. And as they climbed down into the bateau, happy and chattering, with gifts in their arms, Steed realized that among all the goods he had purchased, there was not one intended for a woman, and he was desolate.

To the surprise of the Indians he did not weigh anchor. Reluctant to depart, he went ashore, to sup at the home of a man he had befriended during the starving time; this man had purchased a wife three years before from one of the earlier shiploads, and now had two children and a third on the way. Steed could not keep from staring, for he thought this woman the most wonderful he had ever seen. She moved and smiled with such grace. Back in England she would not have been considered even pretty; his mother had been a true beauty and he knew the difference, but this woman had a primitive grandeur which no mere prettiness could equal. She was, he thought, much like a statue he had seen at Oxford, solid and clean and perfectly fitted to its surroundings, and although the topic had not been introduced, he blurted out, 'Have any of the women who came in the ship with you become widows?'

She did not laugh. 'No,' she said evenly, 'we were all married within two days, and we are married still.'

No more was said, and soon a stern-faced bailiff came to the house to advise Steed that sailors on the English ship had given one of his Indians whiskey and the fellow had become obstreperous. Steed hurried away to find the Indian, red-faced, sweating and out of control. He had insisted upon leaping into the river to touch the sides of the ship, and twice he had been hauled out practically dead, but was determined to try again.

'Asquas!' Steed shouted. 'Lie down!'

The little swimmer looked at Steed with unsteady eyes, recognized him as in command, and collapsed in the bottom of the bateau, where he lay motionless through the long night. Steed, aware that he should quit Jamestown the next day, remained aboard but could not sleep. He stood most of the night at the sheer strakes, staring at the rude collection of huts which represented the civilized world. He could visualize himself returning to it again and again. 'Oh God!' he cried suddenly. 'I wish it was November.'

In the morning he reported to the governors of Jamestown, advising them that he was returning to his island. He gave them a full account of the Indian tribes in that region, and of the trading goods that he would be delivering on future trips. They inquired of him the difference between the western shore of the Chesapeake and the eastern, and he replied, 'In all respects the western is more vigorous. Your Indians are warlike and your land excitable, your rivers are significant and your trees taller. One day Jamestown will be a new Jerusalem, and Virginia a nation of its own. On the eastern shore things are more subdued. There is neither war nor excitement and we will never have a Jerusalem there, nor a London neither. Our Indians are small and avoid war. We have no great riches, and our mosquitoes are twice the size of yours and three times more ferocious.' He hesitated, then added, 'On your western shore drums beat, but on the eastern shore we hear only the echoes.' About this time the custom arose of referring to the Eastern Shore with capital letters, as if it were a special place; this tribute was never paid the western shore.

As he left the building in which the magistrates had interrogated him, he heard a commotion at the far end of the village and suspected that his Choptanks might be drunk again, but the noise came from a striking, well-developed blond young woman who was engaging in a public brawl with her husband, much older than she.

He was endeavoring to quieten her, but she kept shouting, 'I'll not stay!' And she pushed him away. In her determination to escape whatever threat he posed, she ran down the dusty path that served as the village street, flouncing her petticoats and generating a tumult.

When she neared the council building at whose door Steed was standing, she turned back to address the populace: 'He drags me miles upriver to a filthy stable surrounded by murderous Indians. I'll none of it.'

In lusty cries she appealed to the crowd for support, but a woman in a red kerchief, herself lately arrived from England, shouted back like a fishwife, 'Go back, you slut. Be a decent wife.'

'I'll not go back,' she screamed, pushing her husband away. 'He lied to me. No farm. No boat of his own. Nothing but Indians.'

The woman with the kerchief cried, 'It's no heaven for none of us. But it's better than what you knew.'

'It's not!' the angry wife screamed. 'In London, I lived in a proper house, not a grassy hut.'

'You lived in jail,' the other replied, and a fight might have ensued except that the runaway noticed Steed in the doorway, watching her with curious intensity. Since he appeared to be headed for the bateau riding at the dock, she seized upon him.

'Are you Steed, from the island?' she asked boldly.

'I am.'

'And that's your boat, isn't it?'

'It is.'

'Oh, take me with you,' she begged. 'Take me!' and she clung to him with such a show of anguish that he could not shake her loose, even though her husband was coming forward to claim her.

'Come home, Meg,' her husband pleaded. He made a pathetic figure, a short, squarish countryman who must have worked hard in some rural English county and harder here in Virginia. He wore thick, patched homespun trousers, a rough wool shirt and shoes that some inept cobbler had hacked from a stretch of cowhide. He was in his thirties, the type of rural worker Steed had long known and liked.

'I'm Simon Janney,' he said. 'She's mine and you must give her back.'

'Of course I must,' Steed said. 'By no device is she mine. And she is yours.'

'I'm not!' the woman shouted, moving in front of Steed to confront the man Edmund had assumed to be her husband. 'We're not married yet, nor ever shall be.'

'She's not your wife?' Steed asked, poking his head around from behind her bobbing curls.

'I paid for her passage,' Janney said.

'And he took me to his pigsty. He can have his money back.'

'How?' the woman in the red kerchief demanded.

In desperation the fugitive left Steed, threw her arms wide in a beseeching gesture and asked the crowd, 'Will no one pay my passage?'

A shocked silence greeted this extraordinary proposal, then Steed said, 'I will.'

He was standing close to Simon Janney when he said this and he heard the countryman gasp. 'You mustn't, Mr. Steed. She's to be my wife.' He spoke stolidly, as if trying to protect a valuable ewe.

'Never!' she shouted.

'Friend Steed,' the other woman bellowed, 'don't meddle with that one. Maria from the ship can tell you about her.'

The blonde whipped about to confront her accuser, and the swift movement of her ample body conveyed an excitement Steed had not experienced before; she was like some powerful goddess turning to protect herself. 'Bring Maria here,' she said with menacing softness, 'and I'll attend her.' She reached for Steed's hand, drawing him close to her, and he, feeling for the first time the sexually powerful body of a woman pressing against his, clasped her hand. And by that action he committed himself.

'Friend Janney,' he said persuasively, 'let her go. She'll never be yours.'

'She must,' the stubborn little farmer said. His square red face, unshaved for three days, betrayed the torment he was feeling, and Steed felt sorry for him. But then Janney mumbled like a peasant, 'I paid for her.'

'I'll repay you, and more. I need a wife on my island.'

This simple statement of need echoed through the crowd, and all who had waited for the bride ships understood, but his confession had its greatest effect on the woman. Dropping his hand, she gently slipped her arm about his waist, and he felt dizzy and stammered, 'We'll be married this day.'

'Oh no!' she cried, withdrawing her arm. 'I'm to see the island first. No more pigsties for me.'

'Don't meddle with her, Steed!' warned the other woman again.

'I can't pay you now,' Steed explained to Janney, 'but when I next bring my goods, you shall be paid first.'

'He paid seven pounds,' the blonde said.

'Then I shall give him eight.'

'But she's to be my wife,' Janney repeated. He was like a stunted oak damaged by careless plows but still deeply rooted in earth.

'She will never be,' Steed said, and he led Meg Shipton to his bateau.

The couple arrived at Devon in June 1614, he thirty-two years old, she twenty-five. At the moment of disembarking he had never yet kissed any woman but his mother; he had been too busy defining his relationship to God in England and to Indians in Virginia; but she had been at the job of kissing men for some fourteen years, and during this crossing of the bay she had developed a deep curiosity as to what it might be like when she finally plopped Mister Steed into bed.

She was delayed, however, when he required her to survey the land to which he was bringing her: the flourishing fields, the trees, the birds. 'Are there Indians?' she asked apprehensively, and he pointed to the two who were tying the bateau to shore.

'And their wives will be here to help you,' he assured her, pointing to the smaller wigwams near his own. 'They're gentle folk,' he began expansively. Then suddenly he lost his bravado and clutched her hands. 'My home's a pigsty too. I need you, Meg.'

She squeezed his fingers. He was so courteous that she could believe what the others had said in Jamestown: that he was from Oxford, dismissed by his noble family because of some petty quarrel. He had been very brave during the starving time, they told her, and had twice escaped murder by the Indians. But there was some mystery about him, else why would he seek an island? Looking at his eagerness to please and sensing his gentleness, she almost fell in love with him, but instinct warned her against such folly. First she must inspect this island, and determine what he intended doing with it, and whether he had the funds to open new fields and build a real house. She acknowledged an obligation to repay him for her passage money, but she would do this in her own practiced way. Indeed, she was eager to begin.

But when they reached his wigwam, a shabby affair of saplings and woven grass, she was prevented from entering by the arrival of the two Indian wives bringing baskets of vegetables and wriggling crabs. They proposed instructing her in how to cook Indian dishes, an art in which she had no interest whatever, and after several hours were wasted in domestic trivialities she snapped, 'Let's clear them out and jump into bed.'

The words intimidated Steed, for he had been conjuring up a much different approach to their first bedding, one which contained copious samples of the poetry he had acquired at Oxford, but since most of it was in Latin, it could hardly have been of much practical use. The Indians were dismissed and now the potential husband and wife were alone.

'It's a fearful place, this,' she said, poking her finger at the grassy wall, 'but it's no pigsty.' Deftly she slipped out of her clothes, and then, seeing that he had made no move to do likewise, said chidingly, 'Come, get on with it,' and she pulled him onto the straw bedding; from long practice she knew how to handle such a lover.

But when morning came she leaped from the rude bed in terror. 'Good God, what's that?'

It was the blue heron uttering his hideous yet reassuring cry. 'The Indians call him Fishing-long-legs,' he whispered, laughing gently at her fright. His night with her had been an experience of great joy, and he reached for one of her long, handsome legs to pull her down beside him again.

'We've work to do,' she reprimanded, and the next sixteen months were a revelation. Meg Shipton, raised in squalid London quarters, took to the island as if she had been reared on farms. She sweated to help plow the fields on which the wealth of this enterprise depended and grew greasy-black from tending the fires that burned away the bark of tall trees that had to be cleared from new fields. She grew skillful in collecting crabs and oysters, and came to enjoy the two Indian women who taught her tricks like making hominy: 'Mistress, you place corn in hot water mixed with wood ashes. The lye eats away the yellow covering, leaving only the white insides. So delicious fried in venison drippings.'

And yet, for all her voluntary work and the eagerness with which she helped Steed build a real house, she was somehow reserved in her relations with him; they had wild delights beneath the covers, but he sensed that she held him in some kind of contempt. They talked freely, but she always seemed to be laughing at him, and he gained the impression that she was being compatible only because she owed him a debt. Often he caught her looking at him quizzically, and he tried to determine in what way he had failed her, but whenever he came close to touching upon this subject, she drew back and smiled at him indulgently. But in spite of her obvious reserve about him, she never disciplined him in bed: he had agreed to buy her and she was his.

At the end of the first year Meg informed Steed that she was pregnant, and this galvanized him into insisting on various kinds of action: 'We've got to cross the bay. You can't have a baby till you're married.' She replied, 'It looks as if that's what I'm doing.' And she was doing it rather well, too, with the help of advice she was receiving from the women Pentaquod had sent from the village.

It was now that Steed began a frenzy of building, not a house and not a barn. For some days Meg couldn't decipher what it was, but then Chief Pentaquod appeared on the island with four helpers who cut and planked oak trees while Steed served as architect. Finally the building was done, a solid, low structure with a rude signboard over the door on which Steed had printed:

> Surely the Lord lives in this place. This is none other than the house of God. This is the gateway to heaven. Genesis XXVIII.

When Meg asked what this signified, Steed took her inside and placed her on one of the benches Pentaquod had made. 'These are solemn times,' he said. 'The birth of a baby. The start of a new family.'

'The baby's no problem,' she said, slapping her expanding belly.

Steed ignored the jest. Grasping her reverently by both hands, he announced solemnly, 'I'm a Catholic. This is to be our chapel.'

Meg stared at him, then burst into laughter. 'A bloody Papist!' Shoving his hands away, she rose from the bench and moved to the door, where she broke into uncontrolled giggles, not mocking him or his chapel, but rather, ridiculing herself.

'A Papist!' she repeated. Then she came back to him, kissed him on the forehead and said, 'It's jolly. And what a surprise those farts in Jamestown will get when they hear about it.' Her words offended Steed, and he drew back, but she continued her lively laughter. 'I think it's wonderful, Edmund. And you've got yourself a fine chapel.' But then she broke into laughter again, unable to control herself. 'Meg Shipton, wedded to a Papist!' She left the chapel, still chuckling, and refused to set foot in it again.

She was having trouble with Pentaquod, too. Never having known a father, she had at first found this white-haired old man reassuring. She liked his stately mannerisms and his stories of how the Indians had lived before the white man came: 'Turtles! Two or three times a year one would swim into our river. Delicious.' He owned a gun now, which he fired ceremoniously once a month, hitting nothing, and a heavy ax which he wielded with startling power, felling the trees used in building the chapel. And when he found an oak of proper size, he directed Steed and the two Indian helpers in burning out the center and making a canoe so massive that it required four men to handle it. 'For the baby,' he told Meg.

She wanted to like this old chief but suspected that he did not approve of her. As Steed's woman she merited his deference and he protected her as he would any pregnant woman, but consistently he rejected her rather blatant efforts to win him as a friend, and in the end she told Steed petulantly, 'Get him out of here,' and Pentaquod was sent back to the village.

With the Indian gone, she became surprisingly tender, conceding one day, 'It's been rather good here, Steed. When you take your beaver pelts to Jamestown, you might as well pay Janney his eight pounds . . . if you think I'm still worth it.'

'You are!' he cried enthusiastically.

'Maybe I'll even go with you . . . get married proper.'

The child was born on March 3, 1616, the first white infant on the Eastern Shore, a robust boy in whom the Indian women took delight. Meg allowed them to tend him pretty much as they wished, laughing heartily when they tossed him into the salty creek to see if he would float. 'Good sign when a boy floats,' they assured her. 'With a girl it don't matter.' His first playthings were a deer's antler and a bear's claw; his first attempted sound was the *kraannk* of the heron.

In August, Edmund Steed packed his bateau with cords of trade goods and lashed the new canoe astern to house the overflow. When the last pail of caviar was stowed, Steed called to Meg, 'We're ready for the sail.' On the first day in Jamestown he would pay for her, and on the second make her his wife. As she came down the path to the wharf, wearing a dress made from cloth woven on the island, carrying the baby easily on her hip, she was fair and buxom and laughing, and Steed knew a greater happiness than he had ever before experienced: this strange, secretive, passionate woman he had stumbled upon was a treasure, precisely the kind required to build an empire.

And then, just as they were about to leave, a pinnace sailed into the mouth of the creek, dropped its canvas and moved slowly to the wharf. In the bow stood a determined Simon Janney, impatient to leap ashore, and Steed had to assume that he had come to fight for Meg, whose passage money had not yet been repaid and who was theoretically still his property.

In the moment before the pinnace landed, Steed had to decide what he would do, the extent of his love for Meg. His two years with her had satisfied him that not in all Virginia could he find a better wife; there could be no equal to the way she had worked in the fields, no mother happier with her son, and even if she did frequently refuse Steed entrance to her inner thoughts, she had been exciting and satisfying. Meg Shipton was worth holding on to, and he would fight Janney to keep her.

As soon as the pinnace touched, the sturdy little farmer leaped ashore and rushed right at Steed, who resolutely presented his fists. No blows fell, because when the countryman reached Steed he extended his arms and cried, 'Steed, great news!'

Steed dropped his hands and asked, 'What?'

'I can take Meg home. You owe me nothing.'

'Meg has a child,' Steed said, pointing to where the handsome woman stood with the baby.

'No matter!' Janney cried in great excitement. 'She . . .'

He never finished the sentence, for at the rear of the pinnace appeared a woman, dressed in a cape which in spite of the August heat she held close to her throat. She was tall, slender, dark of hair and with hands that were extremely white. She moved hesitantly, picking her way over bundles cluttering the deck, and with the help of sailors climbed carefully onto the wharf, where she adjusted her cape. But once ashore, all hesitancy vanished. Walking firmly, she came up the wharf, passed the two men and went directly to where Meg stood with the baby.

'You must be Meg,' she said softly, extending a long, thin hand. 'And this I presume is your daughter.'

'Son,' Meg said suspiciously.

'You can go back to Jamestown, Meg,' the visitor said. 'I'm the new mistress of the island.'

'She is!' Janney cried happily. 'Your father sent her, Steed.'

Now the tall woman turned slowly to face the man whose invitation had brought her to this remote island, and she came to him with the same resolution she had shown in tackling Meg. Extending her hand once more, she said, 'Edmund Steed, I bring you greetings from your father. I am Martha Keene of High Wycombe in Bucks.'

Steed could manage nothing, not even a stammering welcome, but Simon Janney moved forward, ready to handle any eventuality—except the strange one that now developed. 'She's a fine woman, Edmund,' he said rapidly. 'Everyone on shipboard respected her.'

'Mr. Janney has my boxes in the pinnace,' the newcomer said, and when they were handed ashore, lending finality to her arrival, Janney said, 'Now Meg can come home with me.'

'That I will never do,' Meg said. With exaggerated gestures she handed the baby to Martha Keene, saying, 'You can have the little bastard, and the big one too.' She looked at Steed and sniffed. 'They're both yours, Mistress Keene. I've been ready to get out of here for some time.'

'Meg!' Steed cried.

'Boat's loaded. Let's be off!' And she flounced toward the shore, with Simon Janney attempting to stop her, to grab her, to do anything to get her into his pinnace.

'I'm to take you back,' he pleaded softly. 'The fees are paid.'

She had had enough. Planting her feet resolutely on the wharf, her arms akimbo, she surveyed Janney and Steed contemptuously and cried, 'Damn you both. You paid this and you paid that and you offered to buy. I'm not for sale. I came here and worked my hands red to build this island. I'd have done the same for you, Janney, if you'd given me a decent house. But now all talk of buying and selling is ended. Shove your fees up your arse and to hell with both of you.'

Steed was too shocked to make a response, but Janney asked in a whisper, 'Where will you go, Meg?'

'To Jamestown. To someone who appreciates a wife for what she is.' To Steed's surprise, she reserved her greatest bitterness for him. Regarding him scornfully, she railed, 'Trap your beavers and build your chapels and be damned to you.'

Steed gasped. He had never suspected she harbored such bitterness, and in the fire of her rejection she seemed even more desirable than when she had passively accepted him because of her gratitude for his offering her a refuge.

It was Martha Keene who best comprehended what was happening. With the stateliness inherent in a large family accustomed to English county living, she pursued Meg down the wharf, holding the baby, and asked quietly, 'Are you in good mind . . . to leave your child?'

'Take the Papist bastard and be damned. He'll amount to nothing, and if I should feel need of another, I can catch one.'

Mistress Keene offered a response that would be long remembered in the Choptank: she took Meg's hand, brought it to her lips and kissed it. 'You will have better days,' she said quietly. 'And thank you for the child. What's his name?'

'Ralph,' Meg said, and to everyone's surprise she climbed down not into Janney's pinnace nor into Steed's bateau but into the stout oak canoe. 'This is my boat,' she said grandly. 'We're off to Jamestown.'

No appeal from Janney could dislodge her from her perch among the beaver pelts, and Steed, shocked by her disclosures, made no effort to lure her into his bateau. From her canoe Meg fired a parting shot. To Mistress Keene she shouted, 'You'll be insisting upon a proper marriage, I should think. Join me and we'll find a priest somewheres.'

It had been Martha Keene's intention to sail back with Steed for a ceremony, but Meg's insulting behavior forestalled this. Taking Steed far from the wharf, but keeping the baby in her arms, she confided, 'Your father chose me because I'm Catholic. My family has suffered as deeply as yours, and to me the faith is precious.' She spoke crisply and with authority, as if she had read books and in them learned of Sir Latimer's martyrdom. She was only twenty-two that summer, but aged in wisdom. 'Your father foresaw difficulties and so did mine. They agreed that if they arose, I might wait with you on the island until such time as a priest arrived.'

'It could be years.'

'I know.'

'And you will be my wife till the priest comes?'

'I will.'

He led her to the log chapel, where, after pausing to read the inscription from Genesis, she knelt to give thanks for her safe arrival. When she rose, Steed took her by the hands and said, 'You must understand. I could not have built this island, nor this chapel—'

'Without Meg,' she interrupted. 'I do understand, but now it's we who live here.'

She kissed him, then smiled as she heard Meg bellowing from her canoe, ordering the boats to sail for Jamestown. She accompanied Steed to the wharf, watched as he boarded the bateau and hoisted sail. She stood there firm-chinned, holding the baby as the three craft stood out for the Choptank.

Three weeks later, when Steed's bateau headed back into Devon Creek, he experienced a welter of confusions. His trading trip to Jamestown had been an unprecedented success—he was returning not only with more trade goods than he had expected but also with several Spanish coins, since he had not been required to pay Simon Janney eight pounds for Meg Shipton. But mixed with his elation was uneasiness over the fact that when his boat landed at Devon he would be alone with the stranger who was now his wife.

He knew nothing of her except that she had been chosen by his father, that she came from the neighboring county of Bucks and that she was Catholic. In the brief moments he had spoken with her she had seemed quite austere, but she may have felt the same about him; in her favor she had adjusted with remarkable ease to the extraordinary behavior of Meg Shipton and had accepted the baby without apparent qualms. One further thing: at least three fellow passengers from Captain Hackett's *Victorious* had sought Steed out to assure him that in Martha Keene he was catching himself a wonderful woman: 'She was most helpful on seasick days, and she a lady.'

Asquas and the other Indians had seen the Devon bateau approaching, and they were waiting on the wharf as it lowered its sails, but Martha Keene was not, so as the boat maneuvered into position one of the women went to fetch her. This was not necessary; Martha was tardy only because she had been attending the baby; now, carrying it as if she were a madonna, she came from the hut to greet her returning husband.

Steed would never forget this moment. He had been directing the Indians how to unload and bore in his arms a heavy bundle of cloth, its tag ends blowing in the breeze, when he saw her picking her way carefully down the path and onto the wharf. She moved with studied grace, as if entering a church, and carried the child as if it were her own. Her pale face was rimmed by a black cloth tied about her head, but her eyes and lips joined in a smile of welcome that seemed to Steed the warmest human expression he had ever seen.

Dropping the bundled cloth, he leaped ashore and ran to her, embracing her and kissing her in front of the startled Indians. 'I am so glad you're here,' he mumbled.

'This is my home,' she said.

But Steed would always be a special kind of Catholic, a poetic traditionalist: five thousand years of Celtic poetry onto which had been grafted a thousand years of Saxon prudence. He could never rest easily with Martha Keene until they had been married ritually, and when in December he discussed it with her, he found that she, too, was experiencing a heavy burden of sin. They tried to ease their conscience by embellishing the chapel, the first such Catholic structure in Virginia, with a rude crucifix which he carved and a purple cloth which she wove and stained, as if this would impart sanction. But as the new year dawned, she asked abruptly, 'Would the werowance marry us . . . in his fashion?'

That very day they sailed upstream to Patamoke, and as soon as Pentaquod saw the new woman, so austere and formal, he said in Choptank, 'Steed, this one is much better.'

'We want the werowance to marry us.'

'You never bothered before.'

'I was afraid she'd run away.'

'I, too,' the old chief said, and as he spoke his eyes wandered to Tciblento, who had been listening to the conversation, and he wondered why it was that this man had been unable to find in his daughter the wife he needed. A most perplexing matter, for in his first glimpse of Meg Shipton he had known that Steed must not marry her; she was swift and darting like the black duck and no man could catch her. The new one would be strong and stable, like Onk-or the goose, a good wife but lacking in fire. And all the time there stood Tciblento, the finest woman this river had produced, or ever would produce, and he had found no way to convince Steed of this truth. It was indeed perplexing, as if the Englishman had a film over his eyes which prevented him from seeing the excellence of an Indian.

Nevertheless, Pentaquod arranged a stately wedding, beneath tall oak trees inland from the river, and all members of the tribe assembled in tribute to a man they had grown to trust. The shaman chanted blessings and midwives predicted that the union would be fruitful. Crabs and fish and beaver pelts were laid before the gods, who, properly propitiated, could be trusted to give their protection to this marriage. Four children from the tribe brought flowers for Mistress Keene to stand upon and four boys handed Steed a long pipe and an arrow tipped with eagle feathers.

Then Pentaquod spoke in words that Martha could not understand. He referred to himself and Steed as two strangers who had come to this tribe, and who had found happiness and good lives along this river. He pointed out that both he and Steed had taken alien women to be their brides and that often such things worked well, as had been proved in his case. He then said that when a man goes to a new place, and takes a new bride, he associates himself forever with the fortunes of that place, and is obligated to defend it in war and guide it in peace. Steed had proved that he was the good neighbor. The Indians working on Devon Island had assured him that Steed's wife would be a good neighbor, too, and he blessed them both for coming to this river.

Steed had tears in his eyes when the old man finished, and so did Tciblento, who appreciated with terrible intensity the appropriateness of what her father had said. While the werowance was conducting the ceremony she had tried, desperately she tried, to keep her dark eyes away from Steed, but in the end she could not. Looking at him with a longing that consumed her, she asked that question which has no answer: Why? Why?

When the bateau delivered the couple back to the island, Martha said, 'The little Indian girl with the braids . . . the one with the dark eyes . . . she's in love with you, Edmund.'

'Tciblento? She's Pentaquod's daughter.'

'Why didn't you marry her . . . to begin with?'

'An Indian!'

Martha never mentioned the matter again, but later, when Tciblento offered to visit the island to help instruct her in Indian ways, she politely refused, and sometimes whole months would pass without the Steeds' seeing Tciblento, but one day in 1619 Pentaquod himself came to Devon to inform the settlers that his daughter was to be married, and he would be pleased if they would attend the ceremony. They did, and Martha saw that the Indian girl, now twenty-three and beautiful in her dress of deerskin adorned with beaver and porcupine quills, stood close to tears throughout the ritual. It was Martha's judgment that the young brave she was marrying amounted to little and she doubted that he would ever inherit the title of werowance.

In these years the Steeds paid Pentaquod and the Choptanks substantial sums for any new land they occupied. They now owned 2,160 acres on Devon Island, the exact extent having been calculated by Martha, with the aid of careful measurements made by her husband. Only a few were under cultivation, but they also had title to another 2,488 acres on the mainland. None of this had yet been cleared; it was Steed's intention to burn down the trees as soon as he had trained enough Indians to tend the fields, from which he would send increasing boatloads of corn to Jamestown.

It was in 1626 that Steed's fortunes took a radical turn, after which the clearing of additional acres became an urgent necessity. In December of that year he had guided his bateau back to Jamestown with a heavy cargo of corn, beaver, sassafras and caviar, and as he was unloading onto a two-masted ship from London, he found that a crude river boat from somewhere up the James was unloading on the opposite side of the trader. It was Simon Janney, and the cargo he was hefting about with the aid of ropes was new to Steed.

'What are those great bales?' he asked.

'The stinking weed,' Janney replied.

'Tobacco? Is there profit in tobacco?'

'The surest,' Janney said.

'Where's your farm?'

'Far upstream.'

A silence, then, 'Is Meg with you?'

'Never.'

More silence, then, 'What happened to her?'

Janney did not care to answer this. 'If you have cleared land, Steed, you should consider tobacco. Difficult to grow but easy to sell.'

'I spend my acres on corn.'

'Switch to tobacco, You'll never regret.'

'And where's Meg?'

Janney kicked at one of the bales, then confessed, 'Two hours after she climbed out of her canoe at Jamestown she met a man looking for a wife. Before nightfall he had paid me her transit money and as soon as proper he married her. She lives in one of the new houses on the riverbank.'

Steed saw her once. She carried a parasol and wore a large straw hat edged with gold ribbon, her blond hair peeking out provocatively to glisten in the sun. She walked with a light step and seemed to be smiling to herself, even before she spotted her former husband, as Steed insisted upon calling himself. When she saw that it was Steed of Devon beside the road, she nodded gravely, smiled slightly, as if unable to control her inward laughter, and passed on. Her husband, men at the wharf told Steed, was a man of growing importance in the colony.

But it was Simon Janney who made the lasting impression during this 1626 trip, for when both Steed's boat and his own were unloaded he led the islander to a tavern, where they talked seriously for a long time. 'If you have good land at the ready, Edmund, you should plant tobacco instantly. I have more seed than I need, and I'd be prepared to bring it to Devon to get you started, providing you'd share profits with me.'

'You said difficult to grow. How difficult?'

'Many pitfalls. You must watch the land it doesn't grow musty. Nor get too much heat. And it's best if you have a shed for drying, but even if you do, you must turn the leaves.'

They spent that night discussing the cultivation of this delicate plant, and toward morning Janney convinced Steed to take the gamble. 'I'd not bother you, Steed, if I had land of my own available, but the Indians are fractious. My wife and I have not been able to clear—'

'What wife?'

'Captain Hackett brought her over. One hundred and thirty-seven of them. All disposed of within two days. Mine's scrawny but she can work.'

Mrs. Janney had been a serving girl in London, made pregnant by the master, who fell sobbing in his wife's arms with the lament: 'She tempted me, that one.' She had been hauled into court by the clergy and condemned for a harlot; when her child was stillborn everyone involved deemed it best that she be sent to Virginia, so her mistress paid her passage with Captain Hackett.

He, of course, conveniently forgot that her passage had been paid and offered her for sale upon arrival, a gaunt, gawky thing, meriting her husband's description of *scrawny*. She had excited no bidding in the early stages of the auction, for she was certainly not a prime prospect, but this did not deter Hackett. 'Someone's bound to want you,' he kept assuring her. 'Women are at a premium . . . any women.' And even when she and two other ungainly scarecrows stood alone at the end of the line, the captain was still confident that he would uncover some ill-favored planter who would need her.

Simon Janney was that man. Once bitterly disappointed in this game, he haggled with Hackett over price, and when a bargain was reached he took her west. This time he encountered no problem in holding his woman; for her, he represented a final haven.

Steed remained longer in Jamestown than he had intended, because Janney insisted that he sail far up the James to inspect the tobacco fields, and when they landed at the rickety wharf and he saw the foul conditions in which Janney lived, he appreciated Meg's decision to run away.

'This is Bess,' Janney said as Steed entered his hovel. He saw an emaciated woman in a torn dress. Her teeth were bad and her hair unkempt. But when she and her husband took him out to inspect their fields he found all things neat and trimmed, and he understood their strategy: fields first. 'These are handsome acres, Simon,' he said. 'Do they yield good tobacco?'

'They do. And if I could trust the Indians to help, I'd clear those beyond the trees.'

'Help may be a long time coming,' Steed said, thinking of how peaceful the Choptanks were and how dangerous the Potomacs.

'There's talk of bringing in more blacks from Africa,' Janney said. 'But even then us little planters would be at the far end of the barrel. We'd see none of them.'

'You must have help to clear this country,' Steed agreed. He then watched as Janney unriddled the mysteries of growing tobacco, the cultivation of the fields, the processing of the leaf. Steed had never smoked tobacco and was most doubtful that the fad would be permanent, but when he was told of the earnings Janney had made on his small fields, his cupidity was aroused. 'Could I do the same on my big ones?' he asked.

'Better! I studied your fields when I went to fetch Meg.' This mournful recollection slowed his enthusiasm, so on a more subdued level he argued, 'Steed, with your fields and your Indians you could treble what I earn.'

They reached an agreement whereby Janney would collect as much tobacco seed as possible, then follow Steed to Devon, where he would show the Indians how to grow what he called 'the stinking weed.' When he arrived, Steed and his wife talked Pentaquod into lending them six additional Choptanks to till the fields and tend the delicate plants. They also built along the shore a pair of long sheds for drying the leaf, and Janney taught them how to construct oaken hogsheads. A substantial industry developed on Devon, and when the crop was harvested and cured, the great hogsheads were rolled down to the wharf where Captain Hackett docked his *Victorious.*

Custom already required that Virginians, as colonists, send their precious tobacco only to the mother country, and only in English ships. This meant that Captain Hackett and his storm-racked *Victorious* exercised a monopoly which paid the colonists meagerly and the factors in London well. Even so, when shiploads of trade goods began pouring back into Devon, delighting the Indians along the Choptank, Steed realized that he was on his way to building a fortune.

He was goaded to even greater profits by Janney, who pointed out that since Steed could use Indians, he really must develop the copious lands he owned on the north bank. So in 1631 Steed assembled a work force of himself, Janney and seven new Indians to clear massive fields across the channel, the agreement being as before: Janney would return to Jamestown once the fields were prepared and come back with tobacco seed, sharing in whatever profits were realized.

All through the winter and spring, fires smoked the sky as Indians knelt about the trunks of towering oaks and loblolly pine, girdling them and forcing them to die. On fields where the trunks had been earlier burned, ropes were attached to upper branches, now dead, and the forest sentinels were pulled down. Then Steed and Janney would wait for a rainy day, when danger of fire spreading out of control was at a minimum, and on such days they would light vast conflagrations to burn away the fallen trees, for which they could devise no use. For weeks the sky over the Choptank would be black with smoke and the men even blacker with soot.

'We're making our fortunes!' Janney exulted. 'And when we've finished here, we'll transport these Indians across the bay and burn off some new forests I've spotted along the Rappahannock.'

'Would you leave your farm on the James?'

'For me it's been an unfortunate river.'

'Why not come here? Take up land along the Choptank?'

'Oh no!' Janney said without hesitation. 'The center of life will always be over there.' And no argument could persuade him to quit the western shore, where the great fortunes would be gathered, the lasting reputations forged.

Captain John Smith had become a garrulous old man who bored his London cronies with rambling tales of Hungary and Virginia. It was not until many years after his flight from the colony and the death of the Indian princess Pocahontas that he revealed that when Chief Powhatan had spared him from the chopping block, it was only because the lovely princess had thrown herself across his, Smith's, prostrate body. 'She loved me,' he confided, 'desperately she loved me.'

'Then why did she marry Rolfe and not you?' asked a man who had known Pocahontas when she visited the English court.

'Marry!' Smith snorted. 'An English captain dally with an Indian maid? Let alone marry her! That's for lesser men like young Rolfe.'

He was dismayed when travelers from Virginia informed him that Edmund Steed, with whom he had served at Jamestown, had finally disclosed his true colors and stood forth as a Catholic. 'A Papist?' he repeated several times, shaking his head incredulously.

Then his mind cleared and he remembered his adventures with this gallant young man. 'He came close to death, that one. They were cutting the flesh off poor Ratcliffe, inch by inch, and the poor fellow died. No regrets from me. He'd voted at Nevis to have me hanged, but I stormed back in time to save young Steed.' It hadn't happened that way. Smith had been long gone before Ratcliffe died.

'I was with him in the sickness, too. Steed, that is, not Ratcliffe. In one tent seven of us dead with the flux, except that I fought back. Steed shared his last food with me.'

There had been other adventures, but Smith could not recall them now. 'I remember I had to correct his writing. Careless about details. And I must confess I was always suspicious of him. Devious, I called him once. Not clear, like a decent Englishman. A Papist, eh? I knew he was hiding something.'

In succeeding months Smith spoke often of Steed and cited his subversive Catholicism as an example of why King Charles should not confer favors on the Catholic Lords Baltimore. 'The idea of granting them a colony in Virginia! Shameful! Papists will take over the continent. Devious, they are. Steed's grandfather, you know, had to be hanged and quartered by Good Queen Bess. All devious.'

Before the year was out he was dead, lamenting the dark changes engineered by the two kings, James and Charles. One of his last judgments was that things had been much better handled by Elizabeth.

Pentaquod had foreseen that when the white man came to the Choptank, all traditions of Indian life would be in jeopardy, and he had willingly come out of retirement to help his tribe make the transition. What he had not foreseen were the curious ways in which the impact would manifest itself.

He had not expected any white man to be as congenial as the one who settled on Devon Island, nor to have in common with him those problems encountered by all men: trouble with women, the constant fight for food, difficulty in rearing children, safeguarding whatever gains had been made. On three different occasions Indian messengers from across the bay had come to the Choptanks, hoping to lead them in rebellion against the whites: on a specified day Pentaquod would murder all of them on Devon, then storm across the bay to slaughter and burn along the James and the Rappahannock. Each time he had replied, 'Steed is a friend more to be trusted than most of our own.' Not only had he refused to kill Steed, he had sent extra Choptanks to guard the island against Potomac efforts. So when hideous massacres scarred the western shore, nothing happened on the eastern. Relationships with Steed were better than could have been expected.

On the other hand, he had been mortally hurt when the quiet Englishman rejected Tciblento; Pentaquod had known why and he suspected that his daughter did, too. Indians were inferior, and any contact between the races must be kept to the level of work and trade. The old man was appalled at the eagerness with which his people grabbed for whatever geegaws white traders dangled before them. Here was the danger, Pentaquod saw: that the values of his people might be destroyed. For the present they were content to keep on fishing and hunting beaver and digging sassafras and tending their corn, but the day would come when the old pursuits would be abandoned, and on that day the Choptanks would begin to diminish.

He was meticulous in not interfering with the prerogatives of the young werowance. He had come back to serve as senior counsel, and in spite of great pressures to resume the leadership, he restricted himself to that role. He did so from deep conviction: the younger men must learn how to work with whites if they hoped to bring their people through these perilous times. Therefore, when Captain Smith first appeared at Patamoke, Pentaquod had kept to the background so that the werowance might have experience in estimating the newcomers' intentions, and in all dealings with Steed, Pentaquod effaced himself. When the deeds to

Devon Island had to be signed, it was the werowance who made the first mark.

The old man did retain his three turkey feathers, and as he moved among the Choptanks they knew that he was their leader, and it was to him that they looked whenever crisis neared. Now they came to him, perplexed.

'Each day new fires rage,' they protested. 'They consume all the trees between the rivers where we used to hide.'

So Pentaquod got into his canoe and paddled downriver to talk with Steed. 'Is it necessary to burn the ancient trees?'

'It is.'

'With such desolation?' And he pointed to deer fleeing the flames and a bewildered beaver clinging to his lodge as fire approached.

'We must have more fields for tobacco,' Steed explained.

'We grow all the tobacco we can smoke,' Pentaquod said, pointing to the trivial clearings in which the women of his tribe had cultivated the weed.

'Enough for you, but not enough for London.'

'Must we burn our forests for London?' the old man asked.

Steed found it difficult to clarify the intricacies of transocean trading, to explain that it was not only obligatory but morally imperative to burn forests in Virginia so that tobacco might be burned in London. Pentaquod could not understand.

Three times he returned to protest this abuse of the Choptank forests, and on the last visit Simon Janney grew impatient. Knowing no Choptank words, he would not allow the old man to waste precious time. Shoving him aside, he growled, 'Be gone, old man! We've work to do.'

Pentaquod returned to his canoe, defeated. Heavily he plied his paddle, and when he reached the village he informed the werowance that soon something must be done to halt these hungry fires. The two leaders talked a long time, neither willing to face up to the inevitable: fight or flee. And when a silent impasse had been reached, two young members of the tribe ran in with harsh news: 'Pentaquod! They have set fires which will burn your refuge!'

Together the two leaders paddled down past the marsh and up the small river to the forked creek where Pentaquod once lived, and as they approached they saw vast fires creeping in from many sides, erasing the field Navitan had cultivated for yams, burning away the spot where Tciblento had been born, destroying the trees in which his sons had kept their bear cubs. As the two Indians watched, the crackling grew stronger, until it seemed as if the creek itself might boil, and then all was gone: the trees, the small wharf, the memories of Tciblento playing by the house. Transfixed, Pentaquod refused to believe that men would destroy everything for tobacco leaves, but they had.

'We must go back,' Pentaquod told the werowance, and that night they made their decision: it was impossible to live side-by-side with the white man, so messengers bearing firm orders were dispatched in secrecy, and next morning when Steed and Janney prepared to set new fires they found no Indians to help them. Steed assumed that they must have slept the night at Devon with their friends, but when he sailed his small boat home he found that not only were the field crew missing, but the island Indians as well, including their wives. 'Canoes came for them last night,' Martha reported. 'Took everything with them. I doubt they'll be coming back.'

'Impossible! Where'd they go?'

'To their village, I judge.'

Without waiting to collect Janney, he sailed as speedily as he could to Patamoke, and there his Indians were, sitting disconsolately before the long hut. 'What are you doing here?' he demanded, but none would speak. When he repeated his question, one of the wives gestured toward the door of the hut. 'Did they make you leave us?' Steed shouted.

His loud voice alerted the werowance, who appeared at the doorway, hesitant and unwilling to face the white man. In a moment Pentaquod appeared, leaning on the shoulder of Tciblento. Together the three Indians approached Steed, and on the face of each showed the respect they held for this honest Englishman. It was a moment that would never be forgotten by any participant, for this was the day when parting became inevitable.

'What are you doing to me?' Steed asked the werowance.

The young man remained silent. Pentaquod nudged him, but still he was afraid to speak. It was the old man who responded: 'What have you done to us? Burned our pines. Cut down our tallest oaks. Driven deer from their homes and beaver from their lodges. Singed the feathers of birds and torn down the places where our children played. Steed, you have destroyed the paradise we shared with you.'

Steed fell back before this torrent of accusation, then said persuasively, 'Pentaquod, dear and trusted friend, you do not understand. If we burn the fields, we grow more tobacco. If we grow more tobacco, Captain Hackett's ship will come more often. And when it does, you and your people can have guns for hunting.'

'Before you came we earned our meat without guns.'

'But you can have mirrors, too, and compasses like the one Captain Smith gave you. Remember?'

'I have always known where north was,' the old man said.

Then, in tones of bitter sadness, he informed Steed that henceforth no Choptanks would work for him, and no pleas from the Englishman reversed this harsh decision. In the midst of the great sweep to clear the fields, Steed's entire labor force was retracted; not even one woman was permitted to help Martha and her three children. When Janney learned of the decision he proposed that they sail to Jamestown, conscript an army and burn the village unless the Indians returned to work, but Steed ridiculed such folly.

Instead he and Janney stayed overnight at Patamoke, and in the morning sought a formal consultation with the werowance and Pentaquod. It was granted, and once more the white-haired old man appeared leaning upon his beautiful daughter. The realization that old ties were about to be shattered saddened the former leader, and he spoke gently to his friend. 'What is it, Steed?'

'Pentaquod, ally of many years, why do you harm us?'

'There is no way that you and we can share this river.'

'But we can! Your children and mine play together, speak the same tongue, love the same animals.'

'No, Steed. In all things we grow apart. The time for separation is upon us.'

'No need. When Captain Hackett's ship comes you can have all the things we have.'

'We do not want your things. They bring us only trouble.'

When this was translated for Janney he wanted Steed to tell the old fool that if the Indians refused to work, they'd find out what real trouble was—even war. Such words Steed refused to translate, but Tciblento had learned enough English to advise her father as to what the other Englishman had said.

'War?' Pentaquod repeated. 'You speak of war? Do you know what happened across the bay when war came? Countless dead and hatred forever. Have you subdued the Potomacs or driven the Piscataways from your rivers, Janney? Steed and I have striven to see that such war does not scar our friendship, nor will it while I live.'

Steed ignored this line of argument and did not translate for Janney, who sat glaring at the old man. What Steed focused on was labor. 'Pentaquod, if you send your men to work for us, we'll pay them . . . well.'

'And what will they buy with the roanoke?'

'What they wish.' And he spread his hands to indicate the largesse of Europe.

Pentaquod brushed aside this irrelevant logic and reminded Steed: 'When you and your wife needed our help to build a home on your island, we worked for you. And when you wanted to clear fields to grow food, we helped again. I even told my people to instruct you in all skills you needed. Did not my own daughter Tciblento offer to instruct your wives?'

Steed looked at the Indian girl, dressed in deerskin ornamented with fringes of mink and a necklace of beaver teeth, and for the first time realized what an amazingly beautiful woman she had become. His vision was cleared, perhaps, by the realization that after this fateful day there would be no more meetings. He became aware that he was blushing and that his eyes held on to hers for a shameful period, but he was incapable of looking away. Then he shook his head as if to awaken, and conceded, 'Tciblento was most helpful.'

Sadly the old man announced, 'Steed, on this day we leave our village. You will see us no more.'

'No!' Steed pleaded.

'During many moons I have told my people that you and we could share the river, but I was wrong. You will always want to burn more, destroy more. We shall leave you to your fires.'

Janney asked, 'What's he threatening now?'

'They're leaving,' Steed said.

'Good!' Janney said with sudden approval. 'Help them along. Kick them out.'

'What do you mean?' Steed asked, but before the tough little country-man could explain, Pentaquod took Steed aside to ask a question which had perplexed him for years. 'Dear friend,' he said, 'many summers ago when the Great Canoe came into the bay, our people watched it care-fully. They saw the white sails, but they also saw that the men had skins that glistened. What was this, Steed?'

The Englishman pondered the question but could find no reasonable explanation, so Pentaquod repeated the problem, indicating himself on the deck of the ancient ship, with sun glinting from his body. 'Oh!' Steed exclaimed. 'It must have been a Spanish ship. Armor!' And he explained how a man encased in armor would glisten in sunlight, and then Penta-quod broached the matter that truly disturbed him. 'In later days, when I am gone, the Choptanks will return to this village. Will you watch over Tciblento?'

Steed did not reply. Tears so filled the old man's eyes that no further words were necessary. They embraced, returned to the long hut, and separated for the last time. Tciblento stood on the riverbank as they started their sail homeward, a radiant woman, not waving goodbye, not tearful, just standing there in fading light aware that never again in this life would she see the fair Englishman.

When the bateau reached the marsh Janney said excitedly, 'We're lucky to be rid of the lazy swine.'

'But what are we going to do for help?'

'Ships bring many an indentured lad to Jamestown.'

'Can we afford them?'

'Secret is, buy them cheap, work them to the bone. And when their seven years are up, kiss them goodbye.' He sucked on a tooth, then added, 'But better times are coming. They've begun to bring whole shiploads of slaves from Africa. Captain Hackett offers them for sale.'

'Same question. Can we afford them?'

'Look, Steed. You can't afford not to have them. You buy a slave once, he's yours for life. He and his children. Best bargain ever offered.'

But it was not as simple as Janney had proposed. Slaves did not arrive by shipload, and those that did straggle in as part of a cargo were kept in Virginia; they were too valuable to be wasted on uncertain fields across the bay. So as the Indians departed, their place was taken by white men from the dregs of London, but the bulk of the work was done by Steed and his wife. Theirs was the only plantation on the Eastern Shore, a daring, lonely outpost where the proprietors worked fifteen and sixteen hours a day, the unremitting toil always required if a home or a nation was to be built.

Steed personally supervised each step in raising tobacco, from hoarding the precious seed—ten thousand did not fill a teaspoon—to topping the young plants, an operation which prevented useless leaves from proliferating high on the stalk and ensured a few big rich leaves at workable height; it had to be performed during the hottest days of July and August, when heat shimmered on still waters. Then Steed moved among his plants, nipping off tops by catching them between his right thumbnail and forefinger; in time his right hand grew larger and stronger than his left, his right thumbnail huge and dark and thick.

One morning at breakfast Martha Keene—she would not adopt the name Steed before she was properly married—noticed the discoloration on Edmund's thumb and surprised him by leaning across the table and kissing it—'The badge of our real nobility.'

At that time in distant England, Edmund's older brother held the baronetcy and was known as Sir Philip Steed, but in the New World a new nobility was being born, of which the Steeds of Devon would be one of the founding families.

When Martha Keene had volunteered to emigrate to Virginia, she performed an act of courage oft repeated, rarely appreciated; but when she moved on to the isolation of Dover Island, it was sheer heroism.

How did she survive? Precariously. There was no doctor and only the slightest medication: calomel for indigestion, sassafras tea for fever. Constipation was a constant fear, for it could lead to more serious ills, so every family had its favorite purge; the ague was also a torment. Teeth were a special problem, and each locality owned one pair of forceps, worn and rusty, for the yanking away of rotting molars, plus some strong-armed man with good eyesight who did the job; two men held the patient by the shoulders, another lay across his knees, and the forceps would go to work, twisting and pulling until something shattered.

Mothers watched with anguish as their children contracted an endless chain of diseases, sitting awake through fevered nights and grieving as the little ones were buried beneath loblolly pines. However, if the children survived this deadly assault, they developed an immunity that was striking; often they would live from eighteen through forty-eight with scarce an illness, rocklike people who could resist cold and hunger and poor nutrition, but by then they were elders and at fifty they were usually dead. Women especially died young, and it was not unusual for one husband to bury two wives before he left a young widow to survive him for twenty years.

The house to which Martha came had been much improved by its former occupant, the lively Meg Shipton, but it was still little more than a primitive hut. It was superbly sited: as you left the Chesapeake your shallop moved due east through the channel north of the island, then turned south to enter the broad estuary leading to Devon Creek. A mile up that deep body of water brought you to a wharf projecting out from the northern shore, and above the wharf, on a small plateau of fine level land overlooking vast distances, stood the house. It had been built in stages, first a shack, then a separate kitchen located to the east so that the sun reached it at dawn, then a second floor with bedrooms fearfully cold in winter, and finally some connected sheds and storage areas.

Meager furniture slapped together from local wood, sparse utensils carved from oak, a few knives and forks with spoons of wood, those were the things Martha had to work with. She had one iron kettle, suspended by a hook over an open fire, and a kind of iron-and-clay oven in which she performed miracles. A low fire was kept burning day and night, fueled by immense piles of wood outside the door. The place had few blankets but many animal skins, which in some ways were better, for they showed little soiling, and no sheets. Clothing was precious, a man's trousers lasting for twelve or fifteen years of constant use, a woman's dress surviving innumerable alterations and additions. Adornments were few, and those which a husband did bring were rarely worn though deeply cherished.

The house had two peculiarities, one which infuriated Martha, one which provided foolish contentment. Since there was little glass in Jamestown and none in Devon, the Steeds had covered their windows with oiled paper, itself a precious commodity, and a score of times Martha, contemplating windows which allowed light but not vision, would catch herself complaining, 'I do wish we had glass that someone could see through,' and each time a ship left their wharf for Bristol she begged, 'Can't they bring back some Holland glass?' What pleased her were the heavy pewter dishes; they had a solid quality, and to see them piled neatly in their pine cupboard was an experience she treasured. 'I value them more than silver,' she told her husband, and as she washed them, she exulted: They are mine.

Labor was specialized, for with the arrival of slaves at Jamestown it became practical for plantation managers there to cultivate particular skills among them. Slave women who could sew were taken indoors; men who could make shoes were valued; and especially treasured were those blacks who could convert oak trees into staves, and staves into hogsheads for shipping tobacco. Poor Steed, without access to slaves, had to master all the mechanical arts himself, then teach them to new servants as they reached Devon. It was a thankless task; he would spend two years instructing some clumsy lad how to shape a barrel, then enjoy only four years of profitable work from the young man, because the seventh year was largely wasted: the servant spent most of that time trying to locate land of his own on which to start a farm. Steed became the master teacher of the Eastern Shore, and Devon the university through which the Choptank would be civilized.

A peculiar feature of life on Devon was that money did not exist. Sometimes the Steeds would go three years without seeing a coin, and when they did, it was apt to be of either Spanish or French origin. English pounds and shillings were incredibly scarce, a planned design on the part of the government in London and the king's officers in the colonies. 'As long as we control the flow of coins,' they reasoned, 'we shall be in command.' So the plantations were strangled for lack of exchange; no Steed boy ever had a penny to spend, for there were no pennies, no place to spend them and nothing to spend them on.

In self-defense the colonists invented their own specie: roanoke was universally accepted; tobacco could be legally used to pay any debt; and taxes were specifically levied in hogsheads of the weed. The total wealth of the Steeds, which was becoming impressive, was represented in tobacco, either in the fields, or in the drying sheds, or in hogsheads awaiting shipment, or in transit across the Atlantic, or in some warehouse in London. Slips of paper, often tattered, represented their savings.

They looked to London for everything good. How precious a packet of needles was, how Martha grieved if she lost even one. Nails were like gold; one servant did nothing all year long but carve wooden nails, becoming so skillful that his fine products were exchanged widely throughout Virginia. Books came from London, and cloth, and utensils, and furniture, and every other thing that made a remote island tolerable. The Steeds still loved England, and when cross-ocean ships came into the creek the entire family crowded the wharf to find what good things had arrived from home, and often the letters brought tears, not from loss but from terrible homesickness.

The wharf was interesting. To it and from it moved the lifeblood of the plantation, and its survival became a paramount concern. Tall cedar trees were sought, heavy at the base, tapering as they rose. These were cut, trimmed and hauled to the water's edge. There heavy crossbars six feet long were nailed and lashed to a pole, whose thin end was then driven as far into the mud as the strength of two men determined. Then two additional men swung from the ends of the crossbar and worried the cedar pole into the river bottom. Finally, when it was well settled, two other men climbed a stand and with heavy blows of sledge hammers drove the piling home. It was to twenty-six such pilings that the wharf was attached, and it became so solid that even large ships could tie up to it with security.

Learning was a constant concern. Martha taught the three boys arithmetic and Latin, knowing that no young man could be considered educated unless proficient in that splendid tongue. Edmund felt it his responsibility to teach them history and Greek, but sometimes, after working so hard in the fields, he would fall asleep as the lessons progressed, and Ralph would nudge him and he would mumble, 'Get on with your Greek. Do you want to be savages?' Each morning at five Edmund prepared himself for the day by reading books he had brought from Oxford—Thuycidides and Josephus in Greek, Seneca and Cicero in Latin—and from these authors, along with Plutarch, whom he loved, he gained insight as to how men and nations should behave.

Finally there was the chapel, that unpretentious building with the wooden crucifix. Here the Steeds met for prayer and the reaffirmation of their faith. They believed that God supervised their lives and marked it in their favor when they were kind to servants; but whenever the family left this place of prayer Martha lingered at the door, looked back at the altar and thought: One day I shall be married here.

The problem of Steed's religion no longer troubled the leaders of Virginia; he was known to be a difficult type, adhering to the faith for which his grandfather had been hanged, and certain books containing woodcuts of Sir Latimer being quartered for being a treasonous Papist circulated in the colony, but most Virginians seemed quite content to have him off to one side, across the bay and out of sight. Trouble arose in late 1633 when his son Ralph, now seventeen, felt that it was time to marry and start his own farm in the fields opposite Devon. Accordingly, he sailed down the Chesapeake, put into Jamestown, and asked permission to marry the daughter of a Virginia planter; relatives pointed out that the boy was Papist, son of an avowed Catholic father and a mother specially imported from England, but others argued, and with right, that young Ralph was hardly the son of the Catholic wife but of Meg Shipton, who was as fine a Protestant as the colony provided, she being the wife of the leading factor in the region. That left Ralph only half Catholic, but that was enough to prevent a marriage.

The boy was desolated by this rebuff and retired to Devon in such low spirits that his father and mother halted what they had been doing to counsel with him. 'Our family adheres to the one true faith,' Edmund said. 'My grandfather died for it. My father suffered grave disqualifications. And I fled preferment in England so that I could raise my own chapel in Virginia. This is a heritage so precious that the loss of any girl, no matter how—'

'Penny's not any girl,' the boy countered.

'She's lovely,' Martha conceded, 'and now she's engaged to another, and what can be done about it but forget her and go back to work?'

'I'll never forget her,' Ralph said.

'Nor should you,' Edmund said quickly, adding when his wife scowled, 'I mean in the sense of remembering her as a fine young lady. But she's gone, Ralph, and you've discovered what it means to be Catholic.'

The boy must have been tempted to shout, 'I don't want to be Catholic!' but instead he folded his hands in his lap and lowered his head. 'I always intended being a good Catholic,' he said. 'I think I should like to be a priest.'

'Now, Ralph!' his mother began, but Edmund halted whatever protest she was about to make: 'Have you a sincere calling?' He proposed that they go to the chapel, and when they were inside, with bluebottles buzzing against the thick glass imported from Holland, he asked his son if he had ever heard of the Blessed Edmund Campion, and for some hours he spoke of that luminous spirit. He recalled the folklore of the subterranean Catholic movement in England, and especially of how he himself had for a brief period denied the church until that moment when he wakened near strangled with remorse. It was under such circumstances that he had decided to come to a new world where he could practice his love of God in the ways God Himself had decreed.

Ralph's parents were dedicated to the belief that only one church could represent the will of God, and for proof they cited those solemn words which sealed the matter for sensible people. Taking down the heavy Bible that Edmund had imported from England, the new one translated by the scholars of King James, they opened it to the page on which Jesus Himself launched the one true religion:

> And I say also unto thee, That thou art Peter, and upon this rock I will build my church; and the gates of hell shall not prevail against it.

> And I will give unto thee the keys of the kingdom of heaven: and whatsoever thou shalt bind on earth shall be bound in heaven: and whatsoever thou shalt loose on earth shall be loosed in heaven.

'It was this truth that sustained our family,' Edmund said, 'just as it sustained Campion and will sustain you.' He told Ralph that if he was experiencing a true call to the church, no summons could be more profound, and that if he wanted to become a priest, he must dedicate his life now to that high purpose.

'How?' the boy asked.

'In Virginia it's impossible,' Steed said, excited by the possibility that the Steeds of Devon might produce a priest. 'What we'll do, Ralph, is ship you to London with Captain Hackett, and from there you must make your way to Rome and the seminary for Englishmen.' In an ecstasy he grasped his son's hands and suggested that all kneel and pray. 'You are treading in the path of martyrs.'

The plan proved impractical. Captain Hackett, disoriented by the huge profits to be made in the slave trade, announced on his next arrival at Jamestown, when Ralph was there to take passage, that he would probably never go back to England. 'I'm heading straight for Luanda.'

'Where's that?' Edmund asked, impatient to get his son to Rome.

'Portugal. A shipping point in Africa.'

This made no sense, and Steed demanded an explanation, so Hackett spelled out the facts: 'Luanda's a miserable town owned by Portugal in Africa. Arabians collect slaves in the jungle and drive them in chains to Luanda for easy shipment. We load the *Victorious* there and you have slaves here.'

But as it turned out, it was not so simple as that. He did sail directly to Luanda, and he did cram untold numbers of blacks into the fetid holds of his ship, but three days out, or perhaps four, the ship foundered and was lost, along with Hackett and all the slaves chained to the bulwarks.

The two Steeds returned to Devon, where Martha consoled them. She insisted that if God had prevented their contract with Captain Hackett, it must have been for a specific purpose, but she had barely said these words when a pinnace put into Devon Creek with startling news that would transform the history of the Steeds. The pinnace came not from Jamestown but from a point across the bay near the entrance to the Potomac River, and it carried, of all things, a Catholic priest named Father Whitson. The intelligence he brought could scarcely be comprehended.

'This island is no longer a part of Virginia,' he said, his own excitement and joy jumbling his words. 'The king has ordained that a Catholic colony be established in his New World. You now belong to the Palatinate of Maryland.'

These developments were so radical that he required many minutes to unravel them. He spoke of George Calvert, Lord Baltimore, who had converted to Catholicism late in life but who had been allowed to serve King James as counselor. He had tried to establish an earlier colony in far New England, but it had perished of cold, and now King Charles, whom many suspected of being a secret Catholic, had granted him a new domain north of Virginia to be named after Queen Mary.

Father Whitson had a score of other revelations to share, but before he could do so, Edmund Steed said, 'Father, could we repair to our chapel to hear Mass?'

'Chapel?'

Steed led the way to the rough building, and when Father Whitson saw it he could not speak. Kneeling before the quotation from Genesis, he said a prayer; he had been tested in the fires of Douai and Rome and had survived the mortal dangers of the surreptitious Mass in England, but this visible proof of persistent faith confounded him. When he rose he whispered, 'Even in the wilderness.'

After he had spread a cloth upon the altar and taken the ritual implements from their canvas bag he started the ceremony, and Edmund felt his throat choke as the noble Latin words—the same as at any Mass throughout the world—were repeated once more and in such God-granted surroundings. Then came the sweet mysteries of the blood and body, and as the wafer touched his tongue Edmund knew that he had returned to the arms of his church. Father Whitson, looking into the faces of this kneeling family, felt a depth of emotion he had rarely experienced, even at those midnight Masses in the granges of rural England, but there was more.

As he was about to pack his gear Martha Keene genuflected before him and whispered, 'Father, you must baptize our children,' and when this was done, she said, 'Now please marry us.'

'Are you not wed?' he asked, looking at the three sons.

'No,' she said simply, not wishing to disturb him with any report of their Indian marriage.

He asked them to kneel and opened his missal to the ceremony which binds Catholics, but when he saw the words and the three sons he realized how inadequate an ordinary ritual would be in this frontier of the human spirit. 'Heavenly Father,' he prayed, 'let us join on earth what You have already joined in heaven.' And he told them, 'You are married.'

The next months held many perplexities for the Steeds. They had supposed, when word of a Catholic Maryland was announced, that the colonies would experience the kind of wrenching terror that had swept England whenever a change in the national religion occurred, and Edmund at least looked forward with some relish to evening scores with certain hard-headed Protestants who had caused him trouble. But the sons of Lord Baltimore, who had inherited the palatinate when their father died prematurely, were not burners or executioners. After his initial swing through the new colony, Father Whitson returned to lay down the law. First he handed the Steeds a printed document:

> Catholics in the Palatinate are warned under the severest strictures from the Proprietor that they must not conduct Masses in public nor to the offense of any other religionists. No Catholic is to speak ill of anyone adhering to another religion nor to act in any way objectionable. There are to be no parades or public demonstrations, or gaudy churches or anything else that may offend. Priests are not to go about in ostentatious manner, nor are they to participate in the business of government. There is to be amity throughout the Palatinate and men of all religions are welcomed, so long as they confess to the Being of God, the Immortality of his Son, Jesus Christ, and the sanctity of the Holy Spirit.

'Those are the rules,' Father Whitson said, 'and they are to be obeyed, or the penalties will be severe.'

'Is the proprietor ashamed of being Catholic?' Ralph asked.

'He seeks a peaceable palatinate,' the priest said. 'And the conversion of Indians to the true faith.'

'We have no contact with our Choptanks,' Edmund said.

'Have many Catholics come to the other side of the bay?' Ralph asked.

'Scores. And each new ship brings others.'

'Then the judges and tax men and teachers will all be Catholic?'

'No. We shall not make the mistakes that New England has made. Maryland will not be a theocracy.'

Ralph did not know this new word, but he judged that it boded ill for his religion. 'What's the advantage?' he asked.

'Peace,' Father Whitson replied, and this was not an illusory goal, even though the lavish praise sometimes bestowed upon the palatinate for its tolerance was not always warranted. Maryland did honestly encourage peace with its Indians, and as a consequence suffered fewer wars than other colonies (but in a fit of desperation the government did arouse a crusade to annihilate the Nanticokes); and it surely proclaimed religious freedom in its noble Act of Religious Toleration (except that Jews and other heretics who denied the Trinity could be executed).

It took a long time for the Steeds to comprehend the philosophical structure of this new concept of colonization; they wanted a Catholic cross in the center of every settlement and a priest holding the gavel in all meetings, and it was difficult for them to believe that any system less root-and-branch than that could survive. The Catholics had won title to a new colony in America; let them enjoy it. But Father Whitson, keeping a stern eye on the Eastern Shore, decreed otherwise, and cathedrals were not built.

But on one point the Steeds and their priest agreed. Virginia was an enemy to be held at bay, and if gunfire was needed to accomplish this, they had the guns.

The trouble started this way. The royal grant establishing Virginia was one of the most generous and preposterous in history; it gave the tiny group of men climbing ashore at Jamestown domain over all lands between the Atlantic Ocean and the Pacific in an expanding wedge which encompassed almost everything north of Florida on the south—including half of Texas and all of California—and everything south of a line running from New York to a point far to the north of Alaska. In rough, Virginia was awarded nine tenths of what would later become the United States, plus a goodly share of Canada, and men like Captain John Smith intended that they keep what had been granted them. Certainly they would not permit a small island on the Eastern Shore to defect to Maryland, and the idea that a renegade like Edmund Steed, a Catholic to boot, should be conspiring to take Devon Island into the palatinate was repugnant.

The leaders at Jamestown sent an armed pinnace to capture Devon; a governor was aboard to assume political control, but he never landed. Edmund Steed, his wife Martha and their three sons lined the creek as the boat tried to make its way inland and killed two sailors. The *soi-disant* governor shouted that this was mutiny, whereupon young Ralph cried back, 'It's not. It's rebellion.' When one of the Steeds shot at the governor, the pinnace retreated.

War threatened, and reinforcements were dispatched from the western settlements of Maryland, but a sensible statesman in Virginia saw the folly of such action and met with good response when he proposed to the Maryland officials that the problems be adjudicated. Steed was sent for, and he crossed the bay expecting to be commended for his stubborn defense of the Palatinate, but was instead reprimanded. 'We wanted no killing,' Lord Baltimore's people said. 'We're sending a commission to Jamestown to solve this matter.'

'I'd be glad to go,' Steed said contritely.

'We certainly don't want you . . . or your kind. The proprietor in London has specifically enjoined us to send no one of Catholic faith lest it prove an irritation.'

'Damn!' Steed exploded. 'Is it a crime to be Catholic? Is it a crime to defend a Catholic colony?'

'Dear friend,' the man conducting the negotiations replied, 'it's never been a crime to be a Catholic . . .' and he proceeded with sanctimonious jabber about the new condition of things, and Steed thought: He cannot remember when it was a crime, but we Steeds can.

Even Father Whitson rebuked him for having opened fire upon the official vessel of the Virginia colony. 'Damn me!' Steed exploded. 'What would you have me do? Surrender my island to those pirates?'

'We would have got it back through negotiations,' the priest assured him.

'Never! You don't know those damned Virginians.' And from that moment the Steeds never referred to their neighbors down the bay without the descriptive and appropriate adjective *damned*. A man from Maryland had to watch his crab pots, or the damned Virginians would steal his catch; he had to guard his fishing grounds or they would be stripped; his oysters were under constant danger of theft; and every inch of soil was greedily sought after and plotted against by the Virginians. A Catholic like Steed, who presumed to match his bright tobacco with that of the York and the Rappahannock, had better be extra attentive, or the damned Virginians would steal him blind, and maybe burn his fields, or divert his ships.

If it was healthy to have an enemy, the Steeds had one.

In 1637, when Ralph was twenty-one, Father Whitson devised a way for him to start his studies in Rome. A trading ship had put into St. Mary's City and young Ralph was put aboard with a harsh memorandum from his father:

> On the voyage to Boston you must communicate your plans with no one from Virginia, or on some dark night they may toss you overboard, first because you're a Catholic, second because you defeated their attempt to steal our island. Now on the voyage from Boston to London you must remain silent, because the Puritans of that town would like nothing better than to feed you to the fish. They are your natural enemies. But it is on the voyage from London to Rome that you must be especially circumspect, because any descendant of Queen Elizabeth would find joy in destroying you.

When Father Whitson read this admonition, he told the young scholar, 'Utilize your time aboard ship in debate with others more learned than yourself, so that you may discover the temper of your mind.'

'Will they throw me overboard?'

'Would they dare?'

And so the first of the Steed boys was gone. In rapid succession the other two left, one for London to study law, one for Paris to make himself a doctor. It was significant in these early days of both Virginia and Maryland that children of the larger plantations often knew Europe better than they knew their own homelands; ships were constantly tying up at the family wharf and departing a few days later for London; obliging captains were glad to look after young scholars during the crossing and to introduce them to lawyers and doctors on the other side.

After some years abroad, the young people returned to the bays and rivers with boxes of books and memories of theaters and singing and ministerial exhortations. The three Steed boys would receive superior educations.

They were in Europe when a messenger posted across the bay in a shallop with news that changed much in Maryland: 'From London the proprietor has sent instructions that all free landowners of the palatinate are to assemble in St. Mary's City to approve such laws as Lord Baltimore has drafted.' Steed pointed out that with new indentured servants arriving from London he was not in a position to leave Devon, but the messenger informed him that the invitation was not an option: 'You will be there, Mr. Steed, on January 25 of the coming year.'

'For how many days?' Edmund asked with some apprehension, for without his sons at hand Martha might have difficulty running the plantation.

'For as many days as it takes to vote your approval,' the messenger said, and without attending to courtesies he was off to the other shore.

No member of the first four generations of Steeds in Maryland would ever travel anywhere except by boat: there were no roads. Two plantations might be a quarter of a mile apart by river but forty miles distant by land, assuming that the dense undergrowth could be penetrated. The early settlers were like fish; away from water they perished.

So Edmund Steed appointed two servants to polish up the handsome two-masted ketch he had recently purchased from a builder on the James, packed his best suit and ruff, and set out with razor and comb for the capital. It was a pleasant sail to St. Mary's City; down the Choptank, across the bay, down past the Patuxent, around Point Lookout and up the St. Mary's River to a well-protected anchorage where a score of wooden buildings had already appeared and where another score were building. It was going to be a beautiful little town on an equally beautiful little river, with only one drawback: it was perilously close to Virginia—just across the Potomac, to be exact—and could be assaulted at any time the Virginians chose to wipe it out. Under such circumstances it would not be the capital for long; the final center would develop far to the north, out of reach of Virginia militia.

Some distance inland from the river rose a palisaded fort, inside which stood the long rough buildings where one of the focal assemblies of colonial history would convene. Leonard Calvert, brother to the absentee proprietor—who had to remain in London fighting persistent enemies who kept trying to steal Maryland from the Catholics—was of the opinion that the great charter granted by King Charles meant what it said: 'The Proprietor will propose such laws as he sees fit, and an Assembly of freeholders will pass on their applicability.' Leonard, a sensible man who had often been rebuked by his lordly brother for being too lenient, proposed to lay before the citizens for their approval a draft of laws which the Calverts thought proper for the governance of their distant property.

The ordinary men who made up the assembly—factors and shipowners and farmers, but no priests—judged that even though the charter gave all prerogatives to the distant proprietor, they were in a better position to determine what was needed in Maryland. 'We will write the laws, and the proprietor will judge as to their efficacy.'

'It's to be the other way around,' Leonard Calvert pointed out. 'We propose and you dispose.'

'You have it backwards,' the stubborn assemblymen said, and a struggle with profound implications ensued. Lord Baltimore, in London, was one of the wisest and most conscientious of the colonial proprietors, and he saw danger in allowing a rabble to draft and execute laws; that was the responsibility of men with wealth and position. To the owner of a colony went the power to rule. Baltimore was never a despot, but neither was he a fool.

On the other hand, Edmund Steed, who by virtue of his early settlement at Devon was clearly the oldest Marylander in existence and one of the most devoted, saw that in a new world, new ways were essential. 'We must govern ourselves as far as occasion permits, and on the day we surrender our right to formulate laws for lands we know so well, we surrender our right to be free.'

'Do you oppose the Lord Proprietor?' he was asked.

'On all other points I submit to his superior judgment. He has erected this palatinate and made it a refuge. I bow before him, and before his brother, the lieutenant governor. But on the fundamental question of who should frame laws for a free palatinate, I bow to no one.'

'Not even the king?'

This was a fearsome question to put in that winter of 1638. For anyone to counter the will of the king, or even question it, was to run the risk of being charged with treason, and there were many in Virginia who waited to bring that charge against the Marylanders. But for a Catholic whose very life had been elevated by the acts of Good King Charles, to question would be ingratitude, the worst sin a gentleman could commit. Edmund Steed, aware of the difficult position in which he stood, replied, 'The king will quickly see that Marylanders are entitled to all the privileges of free men in England.'

'And if he doesn't?'

Steed would not be badgered into sponsoring treason. Ignoring the question, he began his patient work with the other delegates, reasoning with them night after night. Always he insisted that if they surrendered on this basic point, they would lose everything—'We are to be free men in a free society.' Others, watching his stubborn defense of their liberties, came to regard him as their leader.

Steed of Devon, they called him, and through the critical last five days of January he held his forces together, and into February and March and on into the hottest days of July. He was everywhere, pleading with his farmers and factors to stand fast: 'If we can last through August, we shall have won.'

The role of revolutionary leader was not one he had aspired to. Indeed, he was by nature pusillanimous. As a young man he had denied his Catholicism to avoid confrontation; in his early days at Jamestown he had participated in none of the cabals; he had fled to Devon to escape the embroilments of Jamestown; and he had shown little heroism in trying to hold on to Meg Shipton. His life had been quiet and withdrawn; he had not even allowed Simon Janney to discuss war with the Choptanks, yet here he was, Steed of Devon, stalwart defender of the Maryland conscience. From constant study of the classics he had become a classic man.

In London, Lord Baltimore refused to concede, and in the palatinate his brother Leonard was equally stubborn, so on a blistering hot day in August the test of strength occurred. In the rude building tormented by flies the speaker put the question: 'How many believe that the laws sent us by Lord Baltimore, and approved by his deputy, Leonard Calvert, our beloved lieutenant governor, must be approved by this assembly?' Calvert voted yes, and so did the secretary of the palatinate, who announced in a powerful voice, 'And I have in my hand the proxies of fourteen others.'

The speaker then asked for the votes of those who rejected Lord Baltimore's laws, preferring ones framed by themselves. 'How say you, Steed of Devon?'

Edmund rose, bowed respectfully to Lord Calvert, then looked at the men who had stood by him through the painful months. 'I say that our laws should be drafted here, by the people of Maryland.' Thirty-six others voted in favor of local rule. Maryland would be a self-governing colony.

There was no celebration that night; the victorious citizens did not feel that they had humbled a tyrant, for Lord Baltimore had never been one. They had merely established a principle, after nearly seven months of debate, and each man who went to his boat next day knew that he had done a good thing.

Edmund Steed, fifty-seven years old that hot summer, was tired when his men brought up his new ketch, and he fell back on pillows as the trip across the bay got under way. He had argued too long to find any triumph in his victory; he had seen too intimately the struggle that had taken place between two good principles. Each side had right and wrong, with his only slightly the stronger.

We have won freedom, he brooded, but if we abuse it, or vote for cheap personal advantage, it won't be worth having. We are familiar with the abuses of kings, but because what we now attempt is new, we can't foresee its abuses. They'll come.

He wished that his sons could be with him now, to discuss these great questions which had so exercised him during the fetid months in the capital. How good the clean air of the Choptank would be at the end of such labors. When the headlands guarding his island appeared and the ketch sailed between them, he felt as if he were entering the gates of a paradise few men would ever know: the broad river, the birds, the infinite life beneath the waves, the good fields and the worship of God.

As the ketch passed the western end of his island he noticed that recent storms had eaten away vast chunks of land; trees were falling into the bay at regular intervals and the fields on which tobacco should have been growing were collapsing in brown aggregations of mud.

'As soon as I reach home,' he muttered, 'I must attend to those banks.'

The commission was not executed, for as the ketch entered Devon Creek he experienced an overwhelming tiredness and fell back upon the cushions. One of the servants, noticing his collapse, hurried to him in time to hear a final injunction: 'Have them say Mass.'

Voyage Three: 1636

HOW LIKE AN ANIMAL HE LOOKS, THE JUDGE thought as he studied the prisoner in the dock. Not bold like a lion, nor graceful like a deer or a decent horse, but sly and mean and shifty. He's an animal, that's for certain, but what kind?

As the judge asked himself this question the prisoner's attention was directed not to the devastating evidence being marshaled against him, but on a fly which he had been trying to catch. Suddenly, with animal-like swiftness, he closed his hand and trapped it. Then he bent over to pull off the wings, one at a time. When the mutilated fly tried to escape, his tormentor reached out a thick, spatulate thumb, holding it over the fly for some moments, moving it about as the insect twisted. Then, grinning, he dropped his thumb heavily and crushed the fly. Only then did he look up at the judge.

'A ferret!' the judge whispered to himself. 'Damn me, he's a true ferret.' And in certain respects the judge was correct, for the prisoner had the pointed face of that crafty animal, the stunted ears, the long sharp nose. Pockmarked and with shifty eyes, he was repulsive, and the shock of uncombed blanched hair only added to his beastly appearance. When he grinned, his dark teeth looked pointed.

The judge adjusted his wig and scowled: A true animal, that one. Then he listened as the damaging record unfolded: three chickens stolen from the Widow Starling, lashes and two months in jail; silver-headed cane stolen from John Coolidge, Esquire, lashes and six months in jail; and now three loaves of bread stolen from baker Ford. His long experience on the London bench had taught him that persistent thieves rarely reformed and that the sooner they were permanently removed from society the better.

'It's a gallows offense, Timothy Turlock,' he growled, staring at the indifferent thief, 'and you shall be hanged.'

But before such a sentence was actually passed, the prisoner's mother, a short, wheezing woman of many troubles, arose and pleaded that her counselor, the Reverend Barstowe, be heard in extenuation. That angular clergyman rose and bowed deferentially; he had known young Turlock from birth and had an even lower opinion of him than the judge, but he did consider hanging too grave a punishment for mere theft, and he moved to the bench, where he whispered urgently to the judge.

'Well,' the judge finally announced to the waiting court. He sniffed three times, adjusted his snuff, and showed obvious self-satisfaction with the felicitous way in which he was expressing himself. 'You should be hanged, Timothy Turlock, but Reverend Barstowe has offered an ingenious proposal.'

He stared down at the prisoner, who gave no sign of being interested in any proposals, ingenious or not. He was twenty-eight, master of no trade, never employed steadily, a confirmed dependent on his hard-working mother, who had not taught him to stand straight or pay proper deference to his superiors, in addition to which he had pimples.

'Reverend Barstowe has a brother,' the judge said, 'captain of a ship plying to our colonies in Virginia.' Timothy stared at the ceiling; he had never heard of Virginia. 'And Captain Barstowe has out of the goodness of his heart volunteered to carry you to Virginia . . . for indenture to some planter there.' The prisoner showed no emotion.

'Turlock!' the judge thundered. 'Come to attention. Do you know what an indenture is?' He did not. He heard his mother on the bench behind him crying forlornly at the prospect of losing her son, so he assumed it must be some frightening punishment.

'It means,' the judge explained, 'that you will owe the gentleman in Virginia who buys your indenture seven years of just and fair labor.'

This sounded ominous to Turlock, and he could understand why his mother was weeping. 'After which,' the judge continued, 'you will be a free man.' He paused dramatically. 'A free man, Turlock, with all the rights and privileges accorded to free men.'

The word *free* galvanized the prisoner. He was not to spend more months in jail. He was not to be hanged. He was to be free, so that any punishment involved—the indenture the judge kept talking about—was irrelevant. 'Do you understand the terms?' He nodded vigorously. 'Seven years of honest labor.' He agreed heartily. 'And during those years, to learn a trade?' Oh yes. 'And instant death if you ever set foot in England again?' Indeed.

His mother, hearing the official words of her son's life banishment, broke into fresh tears, which irritated her son. He wanted this irritation to end, but there was more. Captain Barstowe was summoned, and he came forward like a mighty tyrant in some Asian country. He was accustomed to acquiring indentures in the London courts and was well acquainted with ways to make them yield a profit.

His calculating eye appraised young Turlock in an instant: Lazy, stupid, ill-bred, rebellious, a born troublemaker, probably eats like a pig. Well, seven years in the tobacco fields of Virginia will cure him. The captain estimated that he could sell this one for upwards of twenty pounds, for he was of workable age.

The judge addressed the captain. 'Do you promise this court to convey this prisoner to Virginia, at no cost to the crown?'

'Uh-huh.'

'Do you promise never to sue the crown for this prisoner's passage money?'

'Uh-huh.'

'And do you understand that you must recover your cost by sale of this prisoner's indenture to whatever gentleman in Virginia will have him?'

'Uh-huh.'

Normally at this point, in what had become a routine procedure in the English courts, the judge should have closed the hearing and ordered the papers of indenture drawn, but on this occasion the judge was perplexed, and he asked the sturdy captain, 'Do you really think you can find a buyer for this one?'

'In Virginia,' the captain said from long experience, 'they'll take anything.' So the indenture was drawn.

Captain Barstowe had been perceptive in his estimate of young Turlock, except that the young criminal proved even worse than expected. The ship had not been four days into the Atlantic before crew members came to Barstowe protesting that Turlock had stolen from them, and when his bag was searched, it was found to contain a staggering assortment of knives, caps and scrimshaw. There was only one solution: Timothy Turlock was lashed to the mast to receive ten stripes, but at the first blow he howled so piteously, and whimpered with such soul-searing anguish, that Captain Barstowe's judgment was addled. It was the custom in all English quarters for any man given the lash to bear at least the first six blows with gritted teeth, and some took a dozen in silence to prove their manhood; none on board could recall a grown man carrying on like Turlock, and after eight stripes accompanied by unbroken howling, Barstowe growled, 'Cut him down.'

Turlock whimpered all that day, but had a glorious revenge. Hiding in a corner of the galley, where he sought to steal a pair of sharp knives, he found himself next to a tureen of soup intended for the officers. Glancing quickly about to assure his safety, he ripped open his drawers, pissed in the soup, then took up a position near the mess, where he could watch with deep satisfaction as the captain dined.

When Barstowe's ship sailed into Jamestown in late 1636, he unloaded tableware and kegs of nails first, then paraded his seven indentures onto the wharf, offering them for sale at the various tobacco docks. Two women servants were gobbled up quickly, as were the two strongest-looking young men, but the captain found trouble disposing of his last three.

One man was suspiciously old, but was finally got rid of at a bargain price to a planter who required a clerk to keep track of his shipments to London. The second was so pitifully lame in his left leg that he would be of small service in the fields, but when he proved that he could write, a group bought his contract, intending to use him as schoolmaster to the children of three plantations.

That left vacant-faced Timothy Turlock, and on his sale depended the profit for this voyage. Captain Barstowe spoke well of his scrawny thief, emphasizing his youth, his amiability and the obvious fact that he was bright, of fine character and eager to learn. He found no takers. Canny plantation owners had learned to spot troublemakers in the flotsam sent out by the courts of London, and they would have none of this gallows bait. It looked as if Barstowe might have to give him away, but he had heard of a planter on a marshy estuary far west on the James who worked such miserable land that few ships ever called to offer him their servants. It was doubtful if he would long survive, but he did represent a last resort, and it was to his rickety wharf that Barstowe sailed.

'You're to be attentive,' he growled at Turlock, 'and mind your manners. This is your last chance.'

'Uh-huh,' Timothy grunted, staring with contempt at the wretched spot to which he was being taken. Not even in the worst of London had he seen a house so dilapidated, a setting so forbidding. To the door came a woman so scrawny that it seemed she must drop of mortal illness, but she looked strong and was keen-eyed. 'Ship's in!' she called to someone inside, and soon she was joined by a squat, heavyset, rough-mannered countryman who strode down to the wharf extending his blunt hand. 'Simon Janney's the name,' he said.

The bartering was painful. Janney, an extremely penurious man, set the tone by whining, 'I'd like an extra hand, but my wife's sick, my niggers eat me blind and the Indians . . .' He shook his head, then grudgingly admitted, 'I'll take him off your hands . . . if the price is low.'

'Now wait a minute, Janney. This man is prime.'

'If he was, you wouldn't be this far upriver.'

'He'll give you seven years' pure profit.'

'Seven years of trouble. But I must have someone.'

'You'll take him, then? Fifty?'

'Pounds? I haven't fifty pence.'

'What then?'

'That stack of tobacco leaves.'

The sale would have been concluded except that Mrs. Janney straggled down to the ship, studied the proposed hand and with a knowing trick pulled up his shirt to expose his back. There the lash marks stood, blue and purple. With a long finger she traced one and said, 'A bad one, this.'

As soon as the telltale marks were disclosed, Janney lowered the price he was offering, to which Barstowe objected vigorously, assuring the farmer that in Timothy Turlock he was getting a lad who could be depended upon to—His pitch was interrupted when Mrs. Janney exposed the last marks again, saying to Barstowe, 'Criminals like this shouldn't be sold at all,' but to her husband she whispered, 'Take him. He shows spirit.' She remembered her own crossing and the fact that she, too, had been last in her lot to find a taker.

So the sale was concluded: Timothy Turlock to the Janneys at a bargain price; half the stack of tobacco leaves to Captain Barstowe, who would peddle it in London for twice what the Janneys calculated.

The first job Turlock performed in the New World was binding those leaves which represented his purchase. His next was rebuilding the wharf, up to his knees in mud, after which he worked fourteen hours a day helping clear fields. Then he dredged a channel to drain a meadow, fenced the meadow and built a barn to house the cattle that grazed in the meadow.

By this time he was down to one hundred and nine pounds and looked exactly like a ferret, for the Janneys fed him no better than they ate themselves, and it became apparent to Turlock that this plantation held little promise. His term had six years, nine months to run, and he could visualize it as only an extended period of starvation and slavery. That was another irritation! Janney had acquired two slaves, but since he could profit from them only so long as they were healthy, they received better treatment than Turlock, who twice heard Janney tell his wife, 'Don't risk Toby on that. Send Turlock.'

And yet, he caught occasional insights that made him think Simon Janney had a certain affection for him. Once on a trip down the James they anchored off a great plantation with lawn running down to the river, and the master said, 'Tim, I've seen land on the Rappahannock twice as good as this. If we can get our present farm going, one day we'll own a better place than this.'

Turlock looked at his employer with a vacant grin, as if he could not visualize the dream that enthralled Janney, and this angered the countryman, who said in a burst of honesty and persuasion, 'Turlock, you could become a fine workman and some day own your own land.'

'You . . . feed . . . us . . . more,' Timothy said resentfully. The little thief lived almost at the subhuman level, and certainly at the subverbal. He never spoke in complete sentences and rarely used a word of more than one syllable. What he intended by this austere collection of four words was *If you feed us better food, I could work a great deal harder,* but to voice a subordinate clause beginning with *if* was quite beyond his capacity, and comparisons like *harder* and *better* were refinements of thought he could not master. He existed in a world of meaningful looks and mumbled monosyllables.

Janney, of course, had developed the ability to translate his grunts into workable if not sensible communication, and now said with a certain respect for Turlock's ability to work, 'Stay with us, Tim, after your term's over. We'll own the Rappahannock.'

Turlock did not even bother to grunt at this remote philosophical proposal, but at the end of that year Janney showed him something physical which excited his cupidity. For some weeks they had been collecting tobacco seed from various plantations, and now Janney announced that he and Turlock would take it across the bay to lands which, he said, 'we own over there.'

'Where?'

Janney could not be bothered to explain, but he assigned Timothy to the task of helping the slaves build a shallop for the plantation. It turned out to be a sorry affair, more holes than boards, but if Turlock bailed constantly, it did stay afloat. The first long trip was up the bay to Devon Island, where Janney had come to help burn off more acreage for tobacco, and what Turlock saw there was a revelation: a decent house, a wife who kept it neat and who educated her sons, a Papist chapel of their own, and other appurtenances which bespoke wealth. What disturbed Turlock, wide-eyed at the luxury, were hints he overheard indicating that his master, Janney, had almost as much wealth as Edmund Steed. Why . . . live . . . pig? he asked himself. Why . . . seven years . . . pig?

The idea gnawed at him, and when Steed said, 'Tomorrow we'll cross the channel and go to work,' he was resentful at having to quit this lovely spot. But when he entered the fields to the north, set down amidst beautiful rivers with unexpected vistas and grand variations, he gaped. Each field he moved to seemed more desirable than the preceding, with deep water at its edges, tall trees rimming its boundaries, and a multiplicity of wildlife. This monosyllabic criminal from the fens of London became the first white man to appreciate the glory of what lay hidden among the backwaters north of the Choptank: the dozen rivers, the score of creeks, the hundred hidden coves.

'God damn James River!' he cried as he viewed this paradise. 'My land.'

As the leaky shallop pursued its tedious way back home Turlock brooded upon the miserable situation in which he was trapped; the devastating impact of the Eastern Shore on his mind was not its beauty, which enthralled him, but the fact that it existed *now,* that a man of courage could enjoy it *now.* This realization would gnaw at him for a year, and back home he caused more and more trouble.

One August day in 1638, when Janney insisted that he work past sunset, he first grumbled, then refused. 'I can drag you into court,' Janney threatened, 'and make you work.' Then he assigned him a task too dangerous for his blacks, and Turlock revolted.

'Do you resist?' Janney asked.

'Uh-huh.'

'Get down there and chain that stump.'

'How?' Pimply-face snarled, and when Janney bent down to show him, Turlock grabbed a spade and bashed his master's skull. Then, satisfying himself that the fallen man was not dead, he kicked him twice on the point of the chin to keep him unconscious, then went whistling toward where the shallop was moored. On the way he stole a gun and all the tools he would need, tossed them into the boat, then ran to the house. After giving Mrs. Janney a lively kiss, he stole her scissors, her needles, two of her husband's shirts and three fishlines with hooks.

'Goodbye,' he mumbled, chucking her under the chin as he left for the river.

He calculated that even if Janney revived sooner than expected, he would not be able to make his way on foot to any plantation in time for the owners to accomplish much, and with the shallop gone, pursuit on the river itself would be impossible. For one solid day at least he had clear sailing.

What he did not take into account was the iron will of the Janneys; if they had survived Indian raids, they could survive servant rebellion. Mrs. Janney, when she saw the shallop disappear, ran about the plantation until she found her husband, lying prone in the mud, his face caked in blood. Screaming for Toby to come to her assistance, she dragged him home, bathed him, placed him in bed, and then set out on foot to the nearest plantation. She arrived at her neighbors well past dark, and informed them, 'Our servant tried to kill the master.'

From one plantation to the next, word spread that revolt had started. Like a fire burning wildly across dried evergreens, this dreaded message went; this was the consequence that all masters feared, the rebellion of either their servants or their slaves. When they caught Turlock they would kill him.

Timothy, assured that much must be happening at the plantation, kept his eyes to the rear, and when he saw various boats scurrying about guessed that an expedition was forming to apprehend him. Quickly he steered into one of the small estuaries that fed the James, unstepped the mast, and grinned contentedly as search parties swept by.

At dark he raised the mast and slipped silently downriver a dozen miles, then hid as dawn approached—and in this manner, reached the mouth of the James, where he put into operation a clever plan. Satisfying himself that the final plantation possessed a substantial sloop with a stout sail, he steered his shallop two miles back toward Jamestown, built a small raft, tied to it his hoard of tools, then crashed the stolen boat on a shoal, made his way through the shallow water and poled his raft downstream to the waiting sloop, which he appropriated. By dawn he was well into the Chesapeake.

His strategy worked. Searchers on the James spotted the wrecked craft and assumed that he had drowned. It was not till late afternoon that anyone missed the sloop, and by then he was well gone. All that was left to the frustrated plantation owners was to seek out a Jamestown justice, who signed a warrant for his apprehension, dead or alive. As he handed the document to Mrs. Janney he said, 'Bring him back and I'll hang him.'

Alone on the broad Chesapeake, his mast unstepped to prevent detection, Timothy Turlock paddled and pondered his situation. If he went back to England—hanging. If he went back to Jamestown—hanging. If he put into any Virginia river—chains and more hanging.

And then he saw, rising through the mists, the first faint outlines of the Eastern Shore, and he could visualize the cool rivers and peaceful coves he had known when burning fields for the Steeds, and this sanctuary became his target. It would be a new land, far from Virginia and mean-spirited masters. But could he survive alone? As he kept the sloop headed east he pondered this, and for the first time in his life tried to discipline into complete sentences the vagrant thoughts which hitherto had raced helter-skelter through his vacant mind.

Stop . . . Devon . . . see . . . Steeds? He judged not; Edmund Steed had looked like the kind of man who might be a magistrate, obligated to send him back. *Indians . . . here . . . like Indians . . . there?* He suspected the Choptanks might prove peaceful, else how could Steed live so easily? *What to eat?* On his earlier trip he had seen ducks and geese and the Steed servants had found oysters. *Where sleep?* Any kind of shack would equal what Janney provided, and from observing how Indians built their wigwams, he felt sure he could do as well. *Can . . . I . . . live?* This was the powerful question, and even though he summoned all his intellect to weigh the variables, he could reach no sensible answer. The effort pained him, quite exhausted his capacities, and he dropped these difficult thought processes. Instead he looked at the land ahead and grinned. *No chance . . . back there.* He was committed to the Eastern Shore.

To escape detection by any English ship putting into the Potomac, he unstepped his mast during daylight hours and lay in the bottom of the sloop, but once he reached the Eastern Shore, he moved northward at a steady clip, seeing numerous enticing bays. He became ravenously hungry, but his cunning warned him against landing here: too close to the James.

Later, when he felt that he was safely north, he beached his boat, hiding it among rushes, and foraged for what berries he could find. Using as bait the head of a fish he caught, he lured crabs; when toasted over a small fire they sustained him. At dusk he would come out of hiding and sail through the night, and in this cautious way approached the Choptank.

He did not venture directly into the channel south of the island, but lay to for several days, scouting the place. He saw smoke rise from the hidden house and movement of servants along the shore, and to his surprise the masts of two different boats, a bateau and a ketch. He supposed the latter must be an official craft come from Virginia to arrest him, so extra precautions were advisable.

He waited till one dark midnight when no lights showed on Devon, then slipped silently along the southern bank of the Choptank until he was well upriver. Then, in waning darkness, he darted across the river and hid along the northern shore, and as dawn approached he saw in the shadowy darkness something which gave him much assurance: a low marshland covering many acres, backed up by what was obviously fast land, for it was lined by towering trees standing dark against the sky. A night bird sang briefly and the broad river lay in unruffled stillness.

Home, the tired little thief thought, and carefully he edged his sloop along the rim of the marsh, not knowing how to penetrate it for the protection he needed. Then, at the eastern extremity, he located a commodious creek, not broad enough to invite inspection from searchers but wide enough to provide safe passage for someone wanting to hide. Lowering his mast to aid concealment, he paddled his boat softly into this passageway between the marsh on the south and solid ground on the north.

When he was far inland and secure from danger, he dropped anchor and stowed his paddle in the bow. He then fell asleep as the fading stars winked their careless approval. Toward noon he awoke with a curious sensation: he felt as if someone were staring at him. Rubbing his grimy eyes, he looked up, and there on the bank to which he had moored stood four Indian braves.

'Run . . . no . . . more,' he muttered. Rising on his knees, he grinned at the warriors and extended his open palms. 'See,' he said hopefully, 'no . . . gun.'

The Marsh

FOR TIMOTHY TURLOCK TO FLEE ALONE INTO THE Choptank marshes was an act of madness. In England he had not been a countryman, and in Virginia he had been so busy fighting the Janneys that he had not mastered the skills of rural life. Only one thing enabled him to survive: he had developed a passionate love of land and rivers, and intuitively sensed the steps he must take in order to live with them.

Accordingly, when the wandering braves found him at the edge of the marsh, he knew that he must throw himself into their hands, be as docile as possible and learn from them the tricks he would need. There was no Indian village of Patamoke on which he could rely; that site was a mournful echo populated by no one. The braves who had discovered Turlock had been on a casual hunting foray; for some days they remained with the runty Englishman, rather pleased that he was no larger than they.

From them he learned how to weave marsh grass into the walls of his hut and how to catch the few remaining crabs of autumn. Geese had not yet arrived from the north, so he could not trap them, but he did learn the rudiments of tracking deer.

They could not converse with him, of course, but his habit of talking in single words accompanied by grimaces and gestures prepared him admirably for speaking with Indians, who often did the same, so that by the close of the second day he had accumulated a vocabulary of a few words with which he would conduct most of his later intercourse with the Choptanks: *kawshek* for *oyster; tahquah* for *crab; attque* for *deer; nataque* for *beaver;* and the word which was going to prove most terrifying, *poopponu* for *winter.*

By the time the four braves had departed, they had provided him with an intensive course in survival which sufficed during the clement weather of September and October. Indeed, when the great geese did arrive, assuring him of food, he felt such confidence that he began preparing small fields for gardens, even though he had no seed or any comprehension of what to do if any fell into his hands.

But in late November, when the first really cold weather blew across the Choptank, he was appalled at its severity, and then began his dreadful testing, as cruel in its way as the starving time which had tested the first Virginians. He had no blankets, but there were pine boughs, and when these were properly interlaced he could creep under them and at least escape the gale. He also deduced that goose feathers, if they could be compressed into some kind of container, might provide warmth, and after many infuriating failures he discovered a way to make a small blanket from one of the shirts he had stolen from Janney. When tied ingeniously and stuffed with feathers, it was comforting. After a week he reasoned that he must throw out the big feathers with tough quills and use only the down; this conserved heat, so that on some nights he actually perspired.

Then came the snow. The Choptank was far enough north for the river to freeze once or twice each winter, and so situated that snow was frequent. He would fall asleep at dusk, his shirt-blanket about him, and during the night would become aware of an overwhelming silence: no sound of any kind, no birds, no boughs bending, no fall of any foot. And then he would hear that softest of all noises, the almost imperceptible touch of falling snow, striking pine needles and drifting slowly to earth, where it would cover his untilled gardens and smother his hut.

In the morning he would peer from his doorway and see only white, even the river's ice would be covered, and he would know that on this day he would be hungry and cold and bitterly alone.

The winter of 1638–1639 was unusually severe, and Turlock suffered through five snowfalls that depleted his pemmican and made it impossible for him to catch either fish or geese. When the sixth storm swept across the Choptank he was near dead, and when the river thawed he surrendered. He would sail down to Devon Island and give himself up to whatever charges the authorities in Virginia might want to bring against him.

Dolefully he stepped his mast, unfurled his stolen sail and left his sanctuary. Once in the Choptank with the island visible, he felt a sense of resignation; at least on Devon he would find food and warmth, and it might be months before the Steeds could deliver him to Jamestown. His spirits did not brighten, but did focus on the fact that during a postponement covering some months a clever fellow like himself might be able to think of something.

It was remarkable that Turlock had been hiding in the marshes for nearly half a year without those on Devon learning of his existence; after all, the two locations were only ten miles apart, but it must be remembered that the Indians had left Steed's employ, and the servants who had taken their places were not allowed to penetrate the back country. Therefore, when one of them noticed a strange boat putting into Devon Creek, considerable furor swept the settlement.

'Master Steed!' one cried as he ran toward the house. 'Boat! Boat!'

The master was absent in one of the fields, but from the trim door of the house a tall woman with a black shawl about her shoulders appeared, studied the snowy fields, then saw the boat. She was in her forties, with whitening hair and a skin still pallid. She moved as if the island belonged to her, as it did, and after satisfying herself that only one passenger occupied the boat, she sent messengers scurrying about the plantation.

As the sloop tied up to the wharf she saw an emaciated white man climb ashore. Walking unsteadily, he followed the footpath to the house, but had come only a short distance when he collapsed.

'Help him,' she told the servant at her side, and Turlock was dragged into the house, where Mrs. Steed could almost see the warmth penetrate his near-frozen bones.

'Who are you?' she asked when he had sipped some pork broth.

'Turlock.'

'Oh! You're the one who worked here with Simon Janney?'

'Same.'

Delicately she avoided disclosing that she also knew he was the one who had bashed Janney's head with a spade and stolen his boat.

'Janney . . . live?' Turlock asked.

'He did,' she said evenly, 'no thanks to you.'

'He . . . was . . . bad.'

She did not believe this. Both Janney and his wife had testified that neither had ever struck their fractious servant and that both had seen to it that he ate as well as they. Turlock had been presented to the court as an ingrate who—

'Master Steed is coming!' one of the men cried, and Turlock rose, expecting to meet Edmund Steed, with whom he had worked. Instead, a fine-looking young man of twenty-two entered, his cheeks red from frost, his hair tousled.

'This is my son Henry,' Mrs. Steed said. 'He interrupted his law studies in London when my husband died.'

Turlock knew he ought to say something about the death, but graciousness was not his specialty. 'Bad,' he grunted.

'You worked with my father when I was away?' young Steed asked.

'Uh-huh.'

There was an awkward pause, during which Turlock stared insolently at the glass window, the first he had seen in the New World. It ended when Mrs. Steed explained, 'We've discussed his attack on Janney.'

'A wonder you didn't kill him,' Steed said accusingly.

'No . . . good.'

'He was your legal master.'

'Liked . . . slaves . . . better.'

It was remarkable how quickly one became accustomed to Turlock's truncated conversation; when he provided brief verbal clues the educated mind leaped to fill the interstices, as if he were primal and restricted to the barest essential thoughts. The Steeds understood him readily.

Henry was about to lecture him when Mrs. Steed interceded; she said gently that what this repugnant little fellow needed was not moralizing but warm food, and she took him into the kitchen where pots were simmering and fed him. Then she led him to an empty bed, and he fell asleep under real covers.

When she returned to her remonstrating son she silenced him with an instruction she had received from her grandmother in High Wycombe: 'Look after the other man's belly and your own conscience.' She said, 'If a man comes to your door plainly starving, Henry, don't preach, feed him.'

'We've got to turn him over to the authorities.'

'Do we?'

The suggestion was so startling to young Henry, trained in law, that he began to expostulate, but his mother, thinking of the sleeping man, cautioned, 'Keep your voice down, son.'

And then she examined with him the ancient theory of sanctuary, whereby a man running from justice might run so adeptly that ultimately he entered into the place of refuge from which he could not be extracted. 'Men didn't devise that concept for nothing,' she said.

'There's no escape from justice,' Henry said.

'There is . . . if you reach sanctuary.'

This idea was repulsive and he began to argue forcefully, but his mother made two points: 'Henry, your father and I were often the objects of the law's persecution, but thank God, we found refuge.' And more telling, 'Just because you studied law, don't set yourself up as a little tyrant.'

Her son was prepared to accept this rebuke because of the extraordinary moral power his mother had demonstrated in the last months of her husband's life. While he was absent fighting for freedom in the Assembly, she had minded the plantation and kept the slaves productive. Her sons were unable to help, for they were in Europe and were still there when Edmund died.

Then she had faced real trouble: Simon Janney showed up with shadowy claims to all fields north of the island, said he could prove that he had worked them and had shipped their tobacco to Bristol under his name. She knew the history of the fields and knew his claim was fraudulent, but it required great and solitary effort for her to repel him. When the boys returned from Europe they were able to reoccupy the plantation only because their mother had been resolute.

'Simon Janney is a mean-hearted man,' she told her son.

'Do you think he whipped—What name did he give?'

'Turlock? I doubt it. Janney was never interested in revenge, only money.'

'Shall I surrender Turlock to Jamestown?'

'I think not,' she said, but in deference to her son's position as inheritor of the island she added, 'What do you think we should do?'

For five days Mrs. Steed and her son discussed the moral problems represented by Timothy Turlock's presence in their home, and that sly fellow knew what subject kept the pair engaged. Consequently, when the weather cleared and it looked as if spring would soon reach the river, he slipped away, after first ransacking Mrs. Steed's room to find some spools of thread which he needed. He also took her pins, some nails, a small hammer and a blanket, stowing them securely under the bench of his stolen sloop.

He was well down the creek before the servants noticed his departure, and the hue they raised surprised neither of the Steeds, 'Let him go,' Martha said. 'He carries with him his own punishment.'

'But he inflicts it on others,' her son said, 'never upon himself.'

Turlock spent that splendid autumn of 1639 in fortifying himself against whatever the winters of the future might bring. Using all the bits of cloth he could assemble, he made a facing for his stolen blanket; when the resulting pouch was carefully stuffed with goose down he would have a comforter as good as any in Maryland. He raised his bed, filling the space beneath with heavy goose feathers, and built a double wall inside the house, cramming empty spaces with more feathers. He added a new roof, thick with pine branches, and dug pits in which to store food, and drains to lead water and melting ice away from his hut. At the creek he built a wharf, following the pattern he had learned when doing this job for the Janneys, and even though he had no helper to drive the cedar pilings home, he so worried them and pounded them with a club that the points sank well into the mud.

But most of all this little man, barely a hundred pounds and sadly unfitted for outdoor life, mastered the forest, noting all things that occurred therein. He built trails and along them constructed traps of such ingenuity that he always had food; he cleared an area beneath the towering pines and moved his hut so that they might provide coolness in summer and protection against the snows of winter.

In these early days he saw the marsh merely as a surface thing, a mysterious hiding place in which water and land competed. Within it he found isolated islands firm enough to be tilled, and beside them swamps which would engulf the careless walker. At times he would perch on some hummock to watch the blue heron fishing, and he was delighted when the tall bird snatched a fish and sent it struggling down its gullet. He often saw foxes creeping through the grass, slyly watching for quail or rabbit, and at times large eagles would swoop down to grasp some prey he could not identify.

But the secret of the marsh, the aspect which captivated his imagination, was the fact that he could sail his sloop into it, unstep the mast and hide it so effectively that none could detect it from the river. Or he himself could dart along his camouflaged paths and lose himself just as effectively. Once when Indians came to barter he proved this. Running adroitly among the rushes, he called, 'Find me!' and they could not. When he emerged, grinning with his black teeth, they wanted to see how he had escaped, and when they saw, they marveled.

The Indians presented a problem. When he had learned more of their language, they warned him that they owned the marsh and the land he occupied and that if he wanted it he must buy it as Steed had done. When he objected, they took him far to the east where the werowance lived, and Matapank verified the Choptank claim. Turlock argued with them for some days and in the end had to concede that the land was theirs; to protect himself he said that he would buy it. Obtaining a well-tanned deerskin, he drew on it an outline of his property, showing the oblong marsh and the triangle of fast land, and he asked the leading Choptanks to make their marks; Matapank made his, and the little man with the cleft chin, and then the feeble white-haired giant and his daughter, Tciblento, the stately mother of two sons. When all had signed, Turlock made his mark.

But when the map was completed he realized that it represented no real authority, since it bore only unidentified marks and he had no way to indicate who had signed what. So it occurred to him that what he must do was carry the entire group of negotiators to Devon Island, where the Steeds could write the names and verify them. Matapank understood, and agreed to go; the man with the cleft chin was eager to go, white-haired and quick like a ferret; the giant would not leave his quarters, but Tciblento showed a surprising desire to visit Devon. So canoes were readied, but before they departed the white-haired old man halted proceedings to ask, 'And what does this stranger give us for signing his document?'

There was much discussion, during which the Indians proposed various items they needed. Turlock listened attentively, accepting some, rejecting others: 'I . . . get . . . that.' 'I . . . think . . . I . . . get . . . that.' And so on. At last an agreement was reached, and the convoy set forth.

It was a delightful trip down the river, with never a sign of human occupation on either bank, just the ospreys and the herons, with here and there a family of ducks that had lingered instead of flying north. When the canoes passed Turlock's marsh everyone commented approvingly, and finally Devon Island loomed ahead. Now Tciblento grew nervous, and when the canoes actually entered Devon Creek, she leaned forward to catch sight of the house and did not take her eyes from it while the canoes neared the wharf. Finally, servants saw the approaching procession and shouted to the master, and after a while young Henry Steed came down the pebbled path, and Tciblento fell back, said nothing, but kept her fingers to her mouth.

The signing was conducted on the table in the Steed kitchen, with Henry writing in the five names, adding a date, and asking his mother to testify to the accuracy and then his brother, after which he signed himself. In time the deerskin would be registered at St. Mary's City, but only after Turlock had cleverly altered the line showing the northern boundary, a trick which added another two hundred acres.

Then came the matter of payment. Leading the Indians apart from the Steeds, Turlock assured them that after the second full moon they could come to his marsh and he would deliver to them the specified number of axes, guns and other implements. Matapank and the little fellow with the cleft chin agreed, but Tciblento asked, 'Why not hand them to us now?' and he replied, 'Now . . . don't . . . have.'

So the Indians returned home empty-handed, but after the first full moon had waned Turlock went to work. At night he sailed his sloop to a cove on the far side of Devon, hid it among low-bending trees, and for three nights in a row crept inland to reconnoiter the Steed plantation. Then, in one busy night, he took axes from positions at which they would not be quickly missed; his guns he stole right from the quarters of those sleeping servants charged with hunting game; he filched three wheels, a hammer, a crowbar, two hoes, and when he had picked up several choice items for his own use, he crept back to his sloop and moved silently upriver to his marsh.

As he was about to unload his booty and carry it to his hut, it occurred to him that it might be more prudent to sequester it in the marsh. So with extreme care to leave no footprints, he picked and dodged his way into the heart of the swampiest section, where on a platform of sticks he cached his goods. Then he tiptoed out by a different course and sat innocently in his hut when an angry Henry Steed and three men came up the creek to search his place.

'Mr. Steed!' he pleaded, grinning at the plantation owner. 'What . . . I . . . do . . . stolen . . . axes? Have . . . my . . . own.' The servants verified the fact that Turlock's axes had never been Steed property, nor the guns nor the hoe.

'He's hidden mine somewhere,' Steed insisted, and his men searched the woods, but could find no sign of earth that had been disturbed. Steed directed them into the marsh, but when they tried to penetrate that wilderness they sank to their middles and he had to call them back.

'Think . . . Indians . . . took,' Turlock suggested, but the Choptanks lived too far away to be investigated, so Steed had to return to the island. As the ketch departed he warned Turlock, 'I know you're the thief. We'll catch you.'

He never did, but once Turlock had delivered his purchase goods to the Indians, he stayed clear of the plantation, having guessed that Steed would post sentries to apprehend him if he attempted new forays. The marsh and the fast land were legally his, four hundred acres of the former, nearly eight hundred of the latter, and he was determined that nothing, neither winter blizzards nor summer mosquitoes, would ever dispossess him.

When Turlock had occupied his marsh for well over a year he became aware that an occasional hunter or vagrant from the western shore had begun to camp at the abandoned Indian site of Patamoke and that a rude landing had been established inside the protective harbor. The Steeds at the mouth of the river did not seem to object; indeed, they profited from the accidental trade that came to their supply house on Devon, and no Choptanks were in the area to protest.

But the types of men who squatted on the ruins of the old village were so violent that trouble was inescapable; from their bloody experiences with Indians along the James they had learned to hate red men and were unable to distinguish the inoffensive Choptanks from the savages who had burned and slaughtered at Jamestown. Immediate war was declared against all Indians, and when a casual group of five Choptank braves wandered onto the ancient hunting grounds to the north of Patamoke, they were fired upon, and two were slain, including the husband of Tciblento.

A cry of anguish burst from the Choptank settlement when the three survivors stumbled back with reports of what had happened. Matapank, the werowance, was thrown into confusion by the tragedy; he realized that the unavoidable confrontation was at hand, but he had no concept of what he should do. Without a plan he assembled three counselors to accompany him on a visit to talk with the white men about the injustice they had done, but when this peace mission approached, the white gunners fired on them and Matapank was killed.

Now the burden that Pentaquod had sought to escape fell heavily upon him. The body of Tciblento's husband had not been recovered, so that funeral rites could not be conducted, and the beautiful woman was left without the consolation that might have come from a proper burial and the assurance of a secure life for her husband in the hereafter. She sat mourning with her sons, and nothing her old father could do assuaged her grief; her husband had been the first to fall in the warfare that she had known to be inevitable.

Pentaquod was further disoriented by the meaningless death of Matapank, to whom the mantle of leadership had been given almost a quarter of a century earlier; he had never been a strong werowance, but he had held the tribe together and should have attained old age as its respected leader. Now he was gone and the only force that could give these drifting little people the encouragement they required was Pentaquod, who was in his eighty-first year and eager for the grave. When the Choptanks came to him, begging his counsel, he not only retained his three turkey feathers, but in order to give his people courage he also agreed to wear, for the first time, the copper disk designating a werowance. Assisted always by Tciblento, he made the decisions required to give his adopted people courage.

In five canoes he and his wisest braves went down the Choptank to reconnoiter. They kept away from the camp, where the hunters were carrousing, and put into the marsh, where Turlock, a man they had learned to trust, kept himself aloof. Pentaquod, sitting in the fugitive's rude hut with Tciblento at his side, asked, 'Turlock, what do the white men want?'

'The river.'

'Why do they kill us?'

'You're Indians.'

'Must we quit this river and live as slaves under the Nanticokes?'

'They be killed too.'

'Must it be war? The war we have always sought to avoid?'

They talked for two days, with Tciblento acting as her father's memory, and then the whole entourage, including Turlock, proceeded downriver to Devon Island, where they consulted with the Steeds. Young Henry was of the opinion that the Choptank was permanently lost and that the Indians must move far to the east, to avoid trouble, but Turlock said that he had gone on two journeys in that direction, clean to the ocean, and had found white men gaining footholds there, too. At this doleful news Pentaquod asked what his little tribe could do, and Henry suggested that they move south and make common cause with the Nanticokes.

'And lose our freedom?' the old man asked.

'The Indians on the western shore have learned . . .' Henry began, but he did not finish, for what they learned was too painful to report: that wherever white settlers came, the Indian must abdicate.

At this gloomy point Mrs. Steed thought it desirable to introduce some less lugubrious topic, and she remembered how Tciblento had once been in love with Edmund Steed and had married instead one of the Choptank braves. 'How is your husband?' she asked brightly.

'The hunters killed him.'

'Oh, my God!' Mrs. Steed cried, as if Tciblento had volunteered proof of what the men had been discussing, and she felt such compassion for the Indian woman that she embraced her, resting for a moment on her shoulder.

'You shall stay with us through the winter,' she said softly.

'I must help my father.'

'He shall stay, too, in one of our houses.'

'These are the days when all are needed,' Pentaquod said, and when this was translated, Mrs. Steed reached up and kissed the old man. 'At least let your daughter stay,' she said, but Pentaquod took Tciblento by the hand and said querulously, 'There was a day long ago when I wanted her to leave, but now she is needed,' and silently the Indians went to their canoes as if preparing for a funeral journey.

In the three winter months of 1641 Timothy Turlock passed back and forth between Devon and the Choptank camp, bearing messages and trying to devise some kind of amicable arrangement whereby the Indians could survive in their small corner of forest, but the hunters were intractable; they intended driving out every Choptank and had already fired the opening salvos of warfare with the Nanticokes to the south.

In his discussions, Turlock met increasingly with Pentaquod, whose tear-dimmed eyes saw only the dissolution of his people. The old man was an infinitely greater philosopher than Turlock, who could barely grapple with an abstract idea, but they shared a love for the land that enabled them to communicate. Pentaquod tried to convince the ferret-faced little Englishman that it would prove as difficult for him to hold on to his land as it would be for the Choptanks to keep theirs.

'No hunters in my marsh,' Turlock boasted, using his hand to indicate the musket he would use to repel them.

'They aren't the enemy,' Pentaquod corrected.

'Who?'

'Steed.'

'No,' Turlock said firmly. 'Steed . . . peace.'

'Not warfare,' Pentaquod said. 'No guns. But he will always want more land. His barns will always be hungry. He will grab clear to the ocean, and you and I and all of us, even the hunters, will be consumed.'

During these fearful days Pentaquod brooded about the future of his tribe, but something immediate was happening which caused him deep personal concern. He had observed that Turlock lingered in the Choptank camp not so much to consult with him as to be near Tciblento, and one morning the appalling thought came to him: Great Spirit! He intends to marry her!

It was a pitiful mismatch: she was a head taller, beautiful where he was grotesque, poetic by nature whereas he could barely voice a complete thought, and forty-four while he was only thirty-two. What seemed strangest of all, the couple had practically no common vocabulary. How could they converse? How could there be any companionship?

And yet Pentaquod understood what impulses might be driving his daughter to this unlikely suitor. She stood at the parting of days, her husband slain, her tribe in disarray, her permanent home burned, the future a gray and dismal blank. It was not illogical for her to move with the strangers and make with them what life she could, but the necessity for such a decision was tragic.

Oh, Tciblento, he said to himself one morning, that you have missed a Susquehannock deserving of you, and the Steed that you should have married, and the worthy warriors that should have come . . . His shoulders trembled and tears filled his weakened eyes: How fearful that you should be driven to thinking of this pitiful man. Tciblento! You are the daughter of kings!

The wedding was a shocking affair, a travesty of ancient tradition: one morning the little Englishman mumbled, 'Time . . . go . . . marsh,' and this urge Pentaquod understood, for no man should remain long absent from his land. As the afternoon sun started dipping toward the west, Turlock merely left the wigwam and drifted casually toward his boat, indicating that Tciblento was free to accompany him, if she wished. Without saying farewell to her father, she silently fell in behind the little trapper and without ceremony of any kind entered the sloop. Her departure went unnoticed in the village; there was no celebration befitting the marriage of a princess, no beating of drums, no prayer by the shaman. This tribe was disorganized; the pressure from the Chesapeake was too pervasive.

Old Pentaquod, realizing that he would not see his daughter again, summoned her two sons, and holding them by the hand, even though they were grown now, walked to the shore and called after the departing sloop, 'Tciblento! What shall we do with your boys?'

But she was gone, gone from her tribe forever, and the boys would somehow be absorbed, and they would wander bewildered with the rest of the Choptanks, and in the end they would be hunted like deer and slain, and the needles of the pine would cover them.

Oh, Tciblento! The old man wept, and when the geese departed from the river his spirit followed.

A basic characteristic of the Eastern Shore was that significant events which happened elsewhere excited wild reverberations throughout the peninsula, but nothing which happened on the shore ever influenced history outside. This was demonstrated in January 1648 when a ship from Bristol put into Devon with a small group of indentured servants, a huge supply of trading goods for the Steed warehouse and a Catholic priest freshly ordained in Rome.

Ralph Steed, thirty-two, had done well in his studies and should have taken pride in being the first citizen of Maryland to achieve holy orders, but when he descended the gangplank it was obvious that he was disturbed. Grave of manner, his blond hair agitated by the wind, he kissed his mother soberly, greeted his two brothers, and said, 'Let us repair to the chapel.'

There he led a brief Mass attended by two sailors, after which he closed the doors and met solemnly with his family. 'Events of profound gravity are sweeping London,' he confided. 'King Charles is being hounded by Protestants, and a hideous person named Cromwell is threatening to capture the throne and have himself proclaimed king.'

'Are they going mad?' his mother asked.

'They are. And the consequences can be awful. Parliament is trying to revoke the Maryland charter. There's talk of sending the most dreadful commissioners here to wipe out Catholicism. We're in danger.'

He had only fragmentary information; aboard ship he had been treated with hostility by those who supported the Protestant Parliament in its fight with the king, and he had not been told some of the most disturbing news, but now the captain and the sailors were confiding everything to the Protestant stragglers who had come down from the camp to trade.

'Yes, sir,' the captain told them, 'there's fighting up and down England. A madman named Rupert is supporting the king, but General Cromwell is putting armies in the field to defend honest men. If Cromwell wins, the days of the Papist in Maryland will be numbered.'

Some of the sailors, rabid Parliament men, wanted to organize a kind of Protestant militia for the Choptank, to defend the new liberties being achieved in England, but their captain squelched this. 'The fight will be won in England,' he predicted, 'and that will determine what happens here.'

He was not correct in his prophecy. The planters of Virginia and Maryland were now and always would be staunchly royalist; they positively loved the king, any king, and the closer Parliament came to victory in England, the more fiercely did they defend Charles along the Chesapeake. To them the crown was a symbol of permanence, of the England they remembered, and Cromwell's insolence infuriated them—'How dare he move against the king!' And they circulated petitions attesting to their support.

But Father Steed, a solid scholar as well as a devout Catholic, perceived that a revolution of some magnitude was under way and knew that it must ultimately involve everyone in Maryland, not only the planters.

'We are king's people,' he told his family, 'and Catholics, and both attributes will place us under pressure. We must be prepared to defend ourselves.'

So Devon Island became a bastion guarding the Choptank. The three Steed brothers owned seventeen muskets but were hesitant to arm the servants, who were all Protestants, as were the hunters at the camp. All settlements in Virginia, of course, were vigorously anti-Catholic and could be expected to mount some kind of invasion. Indeed, the only hope of the Steeds was that stable citizens in Maryland-across-the-Bay would rally to the king's cause and maintain a rough stability until Englishmen in London subdued the Protestant threat and hanged Cromwell.

Ralph was the organizing genius. Staying in the background and allowing his younger brother Henry to assume visible control, he crossed the bay and quietly inspirited Catholics, assuring them that the present troubles were an aberration that must be resisted. He said further, 'We must not panic. It is inconceivable that Maryland, which allows religious liberty to all, should ever strike blows against the Catholics, who provided that liberty.'

But one night, as he was preaching thus, a Catholic housewife told him that renegades had broken into her home and burned her crucifix, and Ralph had shuddered with a premonition that the evils which he had been saying were inconceivable were already real. When he returned from his priestly duties he found that Henry had received news from England, and it was all bad.

'The Scots have sold King Charles to the Protestants for pittance. Prince Rupert has been driven from the land and is a pirate in the Azores. Commissioners of the vilest sort are being sent to subdue the colonies, and there has been rioting against Catholics.'

The Steed brothers might have acted imprudently except for the pacifying influence of their mother. Martha was fifty-four that year, white-haired, thin, but composed as always. She had survived many vicissitudes on this remote island and did not propose to surrender now to either panic or despair. Her Catholic family was destined to come under severe pressure; indeed, she had often wondered why this had not happened earlier, and she believed there was a non-hysterical way of combatting it. She told Ralph, 'Become invisible. You form too tempting a target.' She advised Henry to ease off on his trading lest he arouse the cupidity of the hunters at Patamoke. She also suggested that overtures be made to Turlock to see if he and Tciblento might move onto the island and man guns if violence occurred, and it was in pursuit of this proposal that Henry Steed, the fastidious manager of Devon, climbed into his bateau and had his servants sail him to the marsh.

What he found revolted him. At the head of the little creek which separated the marsh from fast land, there was a hut of the meanest sort, occupied by Turlock, his Indian woman and twin half-breeds that had been mysteriously born to them; Henry had supposed Tciblento to be far past childbearing age, but there the scrawny children were, playing on the earthen floor. Turlock, the master of this hovel, was in sad condition, emaciated, pimply-faced, ragged and with two teeth missing in front. To visualize him as a colleague was repugnant, but Henry had always respected his mother's counsel and began negotiations.

'Mother thinks it might be best if you moved onto Devon . . . with your wife . . . and children, of course.'

'How else?'

'We'd move out two of the servants. You could have a rather fine cabin.' He looked distastefully at the hovel.

'Trouble?' Turlock asked, chewing on a weed.

At first Henry was inclined to dissemble, but he suspected that Turlock might somehow have heard rumors from Jamestown, so he spoke openly. 'They've deposed the king.'

'What's . . . that . . . mean?'

'Got rid of him.'

'Good.'

'Real trouble may reach Maryland.'

'Uh-huh.'

'If you would help us, Turlock, we'd have the warrants for your arrest vacated.'

'Nobody . . . arrest . . . me.'

'One day they'll come for you. Trying to kill Janney. And they'll hang you.'

'Never . . . find . . . me.'

'Turlock, I'm offering you a sensible plan for restoring your citizenship. Come with me.'

The fugitive studied young Steed carefully, and instinctively drew the two boys beside him. 'Tcib, come here,' and he placed her behind him. 'Protestants fight Papist?'

'Yes.'

'I'm Protestant.'

'I know you are, Turlock. But you've seen Father Ralph, the good work he does.'

'Ralph is good.'

'So's my mother.'

'She was good.'

'She still is.'

'You're Catholic, Steed. I don't help you.'

Steed sat down on the only piece of furniture, a three-legged stool. He had not anticipated such a rebuff, but he needed this ugly fellow on his side and was prepared to humiliate himself by begging. 'Turlock, what happens in the next months will determine what happens on this river. Do you want to lose your land? Spend the rest of your life in jail? Or be hanged by the neck?'

'Protestants win, never touch me.'

'Dear friend,' Steed said hurriedly, 'you're exactly the kind of criminal these Puritans will hang! Believe me, Turlock, if you want to preserve your home here in the marshes, come with me and help my mother.'

Accidentally Henry had stumbled upon the two symbols that held meaning for the fugitive: his marshland and the kindness of Mrs. Steed. Grudgingly, and with the sorest doubts that he would be right in siding with a Catholic, he loaded the sloop he had stolen seven years earlier and took his family to Devon, where, as Henry had promised, they were housed in a well-built cabin. There he and the three Steed boys awaited the conflagration that was sweeping the western shore.

It reached the Choptank in a curious way. A twenty-six-year-old servant on the York River fell into an argument with his master, who lost his temper and whipped him severely. The man was so humiliated by this unwarranted punishment that he set fire to his master's house and fled; warrants had been issued for his arrest on the grounds that no matter what a master did to a servant, the latter must acquiesce, so, fearing that he might be hanged, the servant fled Virginia and found refuge at the camp on the Choptank.

There he inflamed four renegades with lurid reports of general revolution in Virginia, with Protestants burning Catholic homes, until one of the hunters cried, 'There's a whole Papist chapel on Devon Island, priest and all!' And canoes with five wild men set off down the river; the battle that Father Ralph had feared was ignited.

It was a grisly affair, and during the gunfire Timothy Turlock suspected that he was fighting on the wrong side. Still, his musket kept the marauders away from the Steed house, but since he had placed himself at the eastern windows, where the landing party would first assault, he was not able to protect the western end of the house, where the chapel stood. Father Ralph had taken his position at the altar, and when incendiarists approached with brands, he discharged his musket, accomplishing nothing.

Two stout hunters bashed in the doors and overwhelmed him. They certainly would have killed him, for they were infuriated by the sight of his priestly garb, except that Mrs. Steed screamed for help, and Turlock came rushing up, but not before the chapel had been set ablaze. As it burned, the invaders cheered and sought to cap their victory by destroying the Papist house as well, but resolute shooting by Turlock and his companions drove the rabble back, and at dawn, with the chapel smoking, the victors withdrew to their boats.

Father Ralph, bruised and shaken by the assault, gathered his family for prayers of deliverance, but Timothy Turlock and Tciblento did not attend. The fugitive had assembled his family and was now loading the two boys into his sloop; when Henry, stifling his pride, ran down to thank him for his help, he said merely, 'To hell with Catholics,' and returned to his marsh.

The effect of this battle on Father Ralph was crushing. The loss of the chapel in which he had prayed as a child was a heavy blow, but his mother reminded him that Lord Baltimore had counseled his Catholics against public displays of their religion lest they attract opposition, and she judged that the chapel had been ostentatious. What embittered him was the fact that Maryland, the colony in which Catholic proprietors had offered religious freedom to all, should be the scene of persecution of Catholics. But he was not sure of his position; at the height of the fracas in which his life had nearly been lost, he had heard his Protestant enemies shouting, 'This is for the thirty thousand you dirty Papists killed in Ulster.'

In Rome he had heard whispers that the Catholics of northern Ireland, sorely beset by Protestant tyranny, had revolted and slain many thousands of their oppressors. 'Is it to go on forever?' he asked his brothers. 'This fratricide?' For weeks he brooded about it, then decided that he must go to Jamestown to confront the terrorists who had sent this poison across the bay.

His brother Paul accompanied him to secure the quashing of the warrant against Timothy Turlock, and when they reached Jamestown they were told that each of their missions could be handled best by Councilman Matthew Maynard, so they marched to his home, where that portly gentleman caught his breath when they announced their names. He was further surprised to find that a Catholic priest in clerical garb had dared walk the streets of this town.

'Come in,' he said without enthusiasm. 'I think my wife would be interested in meeting you.' He said these words maliciously and dispatched a slave to summon Mrs. Maynard. Before either young man could state his mission, the counselor's wife appeared, a striking blonde in her late fifties wearing an impressive dress that must have come from London; it was not garish or blatantly expensive, but it was made of fine cloth and fitted well.

'I am sure you will be pleased to meet these young men,' the counselor said. 'This is Father Ralph Steed of Devon, and this his brother, Dr. Paul Steed.'

Mrs. Maynard betrayed no emotion other than the taking of a deep breath. Adjusting the heavy cloth of her dress, she addressed Ralph. 'I am most pleased to see you in Jamestown after all these years. I am Meg Shipton.'

It was Ralph who blushed. In fact, he trembled and would have sat had there been a chair at hand. He could say nothing, and Paul, who had never been allowed to hear of Meg, was left bewildered by his brother's extraordinary behavior. 'I am Paul Steed,' he said, half extending his hand to the mistress of the house. When she made no effort to take it, he added lamely, 'I've come to see your husband about a pardon for Timothy Turlock.'

'And who might he be?' she asked distantly.

'A very brave man who saved Ralph's life.'

'He saved your life?' She said the words almost sarcastically as she studied the priest. 'I am sure you feel indebted.' And with that, she swept out of the room.

'And now what can I do for you?' Maynard asked solicitously and with just the degree of unction necessary to make his question offensive.

'I ask that you vacate the charges against Timothy Turlock,' Paul said. 'He's reformed and lives a decent life.'

'What, might I ask, are the charges against him?'

'I'm not certain. Didn't Father say it was something to do with Simon Janney?' Paul looked at his brother, who was still in a state of shock.

'We have no Simon Janney,' Maynard said coldly.

'There were charges of some kind.'

'When?'

'When would it have been, Ralph?' Receiving no help from his brother, Paul stumbled on. 'Nine, ten years ago.'

'Time vacated them,' Maynard said austerely, and he dismissed Paul. 'Now what is it you seek, Father Steed, if that's the appropriate address?'

During the crossing from Devon, Ralph had composed an impassioned plea that Virginia stop sending agitators to the Choptank, a prayer that the freedom his family had always extended to others be extended to them, but the unnerving experience with Meg Shipton had disarmed him and he could find no words for her pompous and distasteful husband. 'I, too, speak for Turlock,' he mumbled.

'Noted,' Maynard said. After an embarrassing pause he said more unctuously than before, 'I had thought you might be wanting to issue a complaint about the burning of your chapel, but since that was a private affair, and on territory claimed by Maryland, however unjustly, I would find scant reason for listening.' He rose, indicating that the Steeds should leave, and without ever having presented their cases coherently, the young men were on the street.

Ralph was so confused by his meeting with the Maynards that he was useless to his brother. He moved in a daze, and when Paul proposed that they find something to eat, he could not respond intelligently; they returned to their ketch, where the servants were preparing chicken, and Paul ate while his brother stared at the river. Finally, after sending the men away, Paul asked harshly, 'Ralph, what's the matter?'

'That woman . . . Mrs. Maynard.'

'She treated you poorly, but what of that?'

'She's my mother.'

Now it was Paul's turn to fall silent. He gaped at his brother as if Ralph had profaned some precious icon, and found no words to express his astonishment. 'Yes,' the priest continued, 'Meg Shipton. I often wondered . . .'

Paul could not comprehend the vast human complication uncovered by this chance meeting, and when his brother tried to explain—the selling of wives, the abandonments, the lonely years on Devon, the escapes, the courage of their mother and the steadfastness of their father —he threw up his hands. It was monstrous, and the longer he thought about its complexities the angrier he became. As a doctor, he was familiar with specific situations and had learned to counteract them as best he could; behavior like Mrs. Maynard's was insufferable and he would not tolerate it.

Leaving Ralph still dazed in the ketch, he stormed back to the counselor's house and demanded to see husband and wife. 'I want a signed release for Timothy Turlock,' he shouted at Maynard. 'And I want you to talk with my brother like a decent Christian,' he told Mrs. Maynard.

'Young man—'

'And if you refuse, I shall inform everyone in Jamestown and all Virginia.'

The Maynards were uncertain as to what this ultimatum covered, the release or the visitation, and the counselor tried to utter some witticism, but Paul reached swiftly out and grabbed his wrist. 'You have one minute, sir, to send for my brother down there on the boat. One minute.'

Mr. Maynard now awoke to the fact that he had on his hands a dangerous type, and he dispatched a slave to fetch the priest. In the interval he wrote out a statement releasing Timothy Turlock from his indenture and excusing him for misconduct against his master. Then Ralph appeared, disheveled and looking like no priest.

'Mrs. Maynard,' Paul said, 'this is your son Ralph.'

'I am pleased to see you back from Rome,' she said icily.

It was a miserable scene, with no one prepared to make a sensible comment, and after several futile attempts to reconcile mother and son, Paul became enraged. 'God damn you both . . .'

'You could have your tongue branded for blasphemy,' Maynard warned.

'Damn you both!' he repeated, and the brothers left.

On the long, bewildering days of the sail back to Devon, Ralph sat slumped in the ketch, saying nothing, staring at the dark waters. After several useless attempts to console him, Paul left him alone, but on the night before reaching the island, when sleep was fitful, he thought he heard a click and rushed aft to find Ralph preparing to blow out his brains.

'Ralph,' he cried in terror, for what the young priest proposed was a fearful sin against humanity and the Holy Ghost: a suicide. Wresting the pistol from him, Paul slammed him backward, slapped his face and cursed him.

Ralph said nothing, seemed hardly to have known what happened, but the pistol was hidden from him. And when the ketch landed, and the brothers went ashore, they moved like old men with secrets too wretched to share. They could not tell their mother of the indecent scene with Meg Shipton, for that would pain her, nor could they share the incident with Henry, for he, too, had never been told of Ralph's parentage. All they could do was show the document freeing Turlock, and when Henry suggested that they deliver it to the marshes as proof of their willingness to help the fugitive, they could show no interest in either Turlock or his reprieve.

It was now that Father Steed entered upon the great years of his ministry to the Eastern Shore, traveling alone to the most dangerous parts of the peninsula, living fearlessly with Indians and renegades, performing marriages and christenings in the most unlikely spots, and at rare intervals consecrating some hidden room in a sprawling house to serve as chapel. There would never be many Catholics on the Eastern Shore, that was the religion of towns across the bay, but the ones who did brave the wilderness revered Father Steed as their conscience and their hope.

The lines in his face deepened. He grew careless of dress. And when it was proposed that because of his piety he move to St. Mary's City to serve the notable families there, he begged to be excused. 'I am at home in the back rivers,' he said—and it was along these rivers he traveled.

What was there about a marsh which gave it the power to enthrall a man? When Timothy Turlock received proof that he would not be hauled back to Jamestown for hanging and that his tenure of the marsh was secure, he experienced a resurgence of spirit that no one acquainted with his thieving ways would have credited.

'Tcib!' he shouted as the Steed ketch departed. 'We're safe.' Dancing a jig, he grabbed his sons, one under each arm, and ran down to where the marsh began. Pointing with his unshaven chin at the reeds and the twisted channels, he cried, 'Never lose it!'

In his appreciation of the marsh Turlock had advanced somewhat from the early days when he had seen it merely as a hiding place for animals as well as himself. Now he saw it as an empire, a reservoir of considerable richness populated by larger animals and tastier fish. He did not bother to differentiate the rushes and the various kinds of minute inedible crabs, nor did he have the knowledge to comprehend how the contrasting segments of life fitted together, each supporting the other; that complicated awareness would not come in his century. But what he could understand was that the marsh constituted a kind of outlaw state from which he could thumb his nose at the Steeds and any others who sought to enslave him in their ordered ways.

Once safe within its boundaries he was emperor. He had built himself a small rowboat, no more leakproof than the shallop he had helped build for Janney, and with his toes in the water that seeped through the cracks, he loved to creep down the hidden waterways that cut the marsh into principalities; as he progressed from one hummock to the next he watched the larger forms of life.

Deer were common, and he refrained from gunning them within the marsh, as if he recognized the right of animals to find sanctuary as well as he; his deer he shot inland among the trees. He grew familiar with muskrats, too, and watched where they built their conical lodges.

He was especially fond of the gaudy-colored turtle; it was not good for eating like the terrapin he caught whenever possible, and perhaps it was this uselessness that earned the slow-footed animal a particular place in his affection, for he often suspected that he, too, was good for nothing. He liked the songs of the frogs and laughed when his boys argued that the noises they uttered must be coming from some heavy bird.

'Frogs,' he told them, and not until he had trapped some and shown them how the moist creatures made their provocative sound would the boys believe. He felt a special identification with the osprey that swept in to filch fish the way he crept to steal; this was a fine bird, fiery and resolute, and sometimes when he saw it darting over the tips of the marsh grass he felt that he would like to be such a bird.

'Oh!' he cried to the boys. 'Watch him dive!' And he was gratified whenever the osprey flew off with a struggling fish.

The lesser life which kept the marsh viable he rarely saw, and its relation to the grasses he did not understand. Snails and jellyfish were none of his concern, but there was one creature that never failed to ignite his imagination: the great goose that came in October to fill the sky and command the streams. This was the symbol of the marsh's grandeur, the promise of its bounty.

As the days of summer shortened he would tell his boys, 'Some day now,' and each morning he would test the wind, and he could guess within two days of when the great birds would come sailing in, their raucous voices filling the air with protest as they argued where to land, and when they finally agreed upon his marsh he would run out as if to embrace them, for they shared this sanctuary with him, and like the deer, they were safe from his gun so long as they stayed here.

Once, caught up with emotion at the return of the birds, he flung his arms skyward as they wheeled in. 'Where were you?' he cried, but it was the boys who heard him, not the geese, and he was embarrassed that they should have seen him making such a fool of himself. He ducked into his leaky boat and rowed furiously into the remote waterways where cat-o'-nine-tails flourished, and there he found the new arrivals feeding and watched them through the chilly day.

In these years, and far into the future, the entire Chesapeake watershed contained only two established villages, and even these provided services more governmental than economic. Jamestown served as the capital of Virginia, St. Mary's City as the capital of Maryland, but as soon as more sensible locations were found—Williamsburg and Annapolis—the original villages practically vanished, proving that they had served no commercial function.

On the Eastern Shore the condition was even more pronounced, and there would be no town or village until the close of the century; even famous settlements like Oxford, Cambridge and Easton would not come till late, and this was understandable, for it was only at the ends of the innumerable peninsulas that pioneers settled. Since the farmers who occupied these headlands were largely self-sufficient, they felt no need for a trading center, nor could they have reached one by road if it had existed, for it was impossible to link the various peninsulas by trails, which would have had to traverse swamps, deep woods and broad creeks. Each family lived to itself.

But wherever men accumulate, towns begin mysteriously to form, and as early as 1650 the first tentative seeds of a community along the Choptank were being sown. Hunters and other drifters continued to prize the facilities they found at the ruins of the Indian village of Patamoke, where the splendid harbor provided access to the bay and protection from storms. Sometimes the site would be occupied four years in a row, then lie vacant for three. In some years only one casual hunter would stop by in early November, hunting geese, but it was known along the Eastern Shore as a place where anyone in extremity could probably find bread or a few ounces of gunpowder.

The Steeds watched carefully what happened at the old Indian site, for as good merchants they suspected that trade might one day develop there, and they intended to control it. Twice Henry Steed sailed into the harbor to ascertain whether the time was ripe for opening some kind of trading post, and it was clear to him that persons taking up residence on the peninsulas would find it easier to sail to some central point than to come all the way to Devon Island.

'For the present there aren't enough people to justify a post,' he told his brothers, 'but soon there will be.' What he did instead of opening a store proved his acuity: 'Paul, you must cross the bay and talk with the governor.' And when the talks were concluded, the Steeds had patents giving them title to the harbor and all the spacious lands surrounding it.

'Now,' Henry told the family, 'if anything does develop, we'll be in an excellent position.'

But no matter how extensive the Steed holdings became, Mrs. Steed could not rest easy. In 1638 she had repelled Simon Janney's claim against the northern fields, but she had not legally disposed of it, and now she warned her sons, 'Settle with Janney before he learns that we are prospering.' So once again Henry and Paul sailed the ketch to Jamestown, taking with them a remarkable cargo. Cash money was still murderously scarce, and none could recall when actual coins had circulated along the Choptank, for the good reason that Henry Steed had hidden every one that came his way. Secretly he had accumulated a hoard of Spanish and French pieces, plus a few shillings, and it was these he intended using as bait with Janney.

When they reached Jamestown they learned that the tough little countryman still occupied his mean farm upriver, so they steered their ketch to his wharf, but it was in such sad condition that they feared tying up to it. Anchoring in the stream, they rowed ashore and went to the hovel in which Janney, his toothless wife and their malnourished daughter lived. When Henry saw their condition he thought: The mention of hard coinage will speed this negotiation. But Janney proved an astute trader.

'I ought to know the fields, seein' they're mine.'

'I believe they're held in my father's name.'

'Use makes title.'

'There may be something to what you say.'

'Especially if I have it in writin'.'

'You do?' Henry asked cautiously.

'Letters,' Janney said, looking to his wife for confirmation.

'Letters prove nothing,' Henry said. 'You know I read law.'

'Then you'll know what a contract is,' Janney said.

For about an hour they parried in this manner, until Paul grew restless. 'I don't believe Mr. Janney has any proof,' he said peremptorily.

'But Henry believes. Don't you, Henry?'

'I would judge that you have some shadowy claim,' Henry conceded. 'Difficult to prove, but perhaps strong enough to cause us embarrassment in court.'

'Especially in a Virginia court.'

'I propose we discharge that claim. Now.'

'With what?' Janney asked.

'With money. With a substantial number of coins.'

He had stressed the fact of coins in order to impress Janney with the possibility of his getting hold of real money, but he was not prepared for Janney's next step. The canny farmer consulted visually with his wife and daughter; they nodded; he loosened a board in the floor and produced from beneath it a large clay pot, from which he poured onto the wooden table a hoard of European coinage more than twice as large as the one Henry Steed had accumulated. As he fingered the coins, lovingly and with pride, he said, 'We're planning to buy a place on the Rappahannock. Have been for some years. Now, if you're serious about clearing up your title, and you should be . . .' He allowed his coins to clink.

'How much do you want?' Henry asked coldly.

'The matter comes down to my signing your papers, don't it?'

'In part.'

'I'll sign and my wife will make her mark and my daughter Jennifer will sign. You'll be forever clear of us'—he hesitated, and no one breathed—'if you add substantially to our coins.'

Without hesitation Henry Steed took his purse by one bottom corner, turned it upside down and allowed all its contents to pour onto the table. 'I think that's substantial.'

'I think so too,' Janney said, and the quitclaim was signed.

On the trip home Paul said admiringly, 'That was daring,' and Henry said, 'Not if you knew I kept half our coins sewed along the waist of my trousers.' Then he became reflective. 'The important thing is that our patents are now without blemish, and, Paul, we must keep them that way. No mortgages, no loans, and above all, dear brother, no borrowing from Fithian. Promise me that you will never order from London one item you can't pay for. Marcus Fithian's the most honest man I know. I trust him with every leaf of our tobacco, and he gives me honest count, but for the love of God, never fall into his debt.'

He had met Fithian at the Inns of Court; the Englishman was one year older and many years wiser. The descendant of a family that had always specialized in financing trade, his ancestors had known the Fuggers and the Medici and had rarely been worsted by either. The young men had met in 1636, and for five months young Fithian had pumped Henry for knowledge of the colonies; he was pleased to hear that Henry had stopped in Boston on his way to London and had observed for himself the prosperity of that town, but Henry kept repeating, 'The true fortunes are to be made along the rivers of Virginia.' To test this thesis, Fithian had made a tedious journey in a tobacco ship to the York and the Potomac and had seen at once the chances for an industrial association that would profit both the remote planter in the colonies and the factor in London.

He was never avaricious, but four great plantations had already fallen into his hands because their undisciplined owners ordered more from London than they could pay for with the tobacco they shipped from Virginia. Fithian did nothing criminal, or even suspicious; he merely filled orders and kept meticulous balances, and when the former pushed the latter into debits, he foreclosed. He never tried to run a plantation himself; he knew he was unqualified for that exacting task: 'I wouldn't know the value of a single slave, nor a field of unripe weed.'

What he did, once he gained title, was send an underling to the colonies to seek out the best farmer available and sell him the land at great discount, trusting to keep that man's accounts for the next fifty years. It was in furtherance of this design that in 1651 he wrote to his friend Henry Steed:

> My cousin Lennox spent three weeks on your rivers and advises me that the farmer Simon Janney is hard-working, trustworthy and exceptionally well informed on tobacco. Do you concur? I have lately come into possession of a large plantation on the left bank of the Rappahannock which Lennox assures me is capable of cultivation, should it pass into the hands of the right owner. I have in mind to sell it to Janney at a price well below the market in hopes he can establish himself. Please instruct me by the captain of this ship. Can he pay a reasonable sum? Will he pay? Can he make land yield a profit?

To each of these questions Steed returned a strong affirmative, telling Paul as he did so, 'Where land is concerned, Simon Janney is almost as trustworthy as a Steed,' and he felt sure that the Rappahannock plantation was passing into excellent hands.

But repeatedly he returned to his basic thesis, which he preached to his mother and his brothers: 'Never borrow a farthing from London.' In all other respects they trusted their unseen partner: he sent them the desired cloth from Flanders, or crystal from Bohemia, or books from London. He arranged for their travel, kept their credits in the proper banks, and consistently knew more about their affairs than they. He was the absent partner at their feasts, the most trusted member of their acquaintances. They worked and ate on a river on the Eastern Shore, but spiritually they lived in London, thanks to the responsibility and integrity of Marcus Fithian.

There were other problems which could not be avoided. The Nanticoke Indians had behaved circumspectly when the first white men invaded their ancient territories, and had withdrawn, allowing the invaders a free hand in picking up the lesser sites along the southern rivers, and there had been no battles. But when additional invaders kept crossing the bay and pushing farther and farther up the rivers to appropriate really fine hunting lands, the pressure became unbearable.

Seven minor skirmishes marred relations in these years, and there would have been more if the Nanticokes had succeeded in persuading the Choptanks to join them. On various occasions emissaries were sent north proposing that the Choptanks fall upon Patamoke and eliminate it, but the peaceful little Choptanks refused—'We are not a warlike people. With our whites we are at peace.' And no arguments could goad them into attacking.

This earned the Choptanks no merit with the whites; an Indian was an Indian, and when a real battle erupted in Nanticoke territory, white settlers along the Choptank assumed that they must be the next targets; in anticipation they began firing at whatever Indians they spotted. In this they were encouraged by the harsh edict promulgated by the government:

> Notice to all citizens. The Nanticoke Indians have been declared the enemies of this Palatinate and as such are to be proceeded against by all persons in all ways.

As a result of this invitation to violence, a desultory warfare developed in which the whites repulsed any Indian who sought to establish contact with any settlement; the bewildered Choptanks would come downriver to ensure peace, and before they could land, guns would blaze at them, and they would retreat in confusion. On one such occasion the oldest son of Tciblento—a full-blooded Indian—was killed, and when runners went to Turlock's hut to inform her of this, she greeted them indifferently.

'Hatsawap was shot by white men.'

'What had he done?'

'Nothing. He came to talk peace.'

She did not react to this sad news, simply sat in her rags rocking back and forth on her haunches.

'Tciblento,' the runners said, 'you must talk with the white men. We are not at war with them.'

'But they are at war with us,' she said. They talked for a long time, recalling better days, and when Turlock came in from hunting in the marsh, dark and dirty, and wanted to know why the Choptanks were there, one of them said, 'Tciblento's son was killed by a white gunner.'

'They'll all be killed,' he said, and Tciblento nodded. She cooked a raccoon for them and they left.

The forest warfare did not diminish, for the Nanticokes did not propose to allow white men to dispossess them. They became skilled in ambushes and made life upriver difficult, so that in December 1652 the government issued the famous draconian orders which led to their elimination as a fighting force:

> The Nanticokes and their allies constitute a peril to this Colony and they must be disciplined. Declare war on them with every strength you have. Vanquish, destroy, plunder, kill or take prisoner. Do all these things to all or any of the said Indians you chance to meet. Put them to death or capture them alive at your pleasure. There must be no truce.

Now the hunters who clustered at Patamoke had their days of glory. They would hide behind trees that commanded well-known trails, and whenever an Indian appeared, man or woman, they would blaze away. The forests ran red with the blood of Indians, and fire consumed villages which had known no war.

The carnage was especially heavy among the confused Choptanks, who had given not a single cause for such bloodshed. In the entire history of the Choptank nation, no Indian had ever killed a white man or ever would, yet now they were hunted like squirrels. Tciblento's second Indian son, tall Ponasque, wise like his grandfather, and a companion climbed into their canoe and came downriver to plead for sanity, but as they passed the point east of Patamoke, three hunters spotted them. Taking careful aim at the young men, who could not take evasive action or protect themselves in any way, they began firing.

The first salvo fell short, and the leader of the hunters cried, 'Higher!' So they aimed higher, and now they shot over the canoe. 'Lower, just a bit!' And on the third fusillade pellets struck the Indian in the forward position and he fell sideways.

Two of the hunters cheered, but the leader warned, 'It's a trick! Hit him again!' So the hunters kept firing until Ponasque fell, too, and the canoe became so riddled that it sank with the dead bodies.

Now one of the lesser chieftains crept through the woods to plead with Turlock, and after he had informed Tciblento of her other son's death, and she had sat impassive as before, the Indian turned to Turlock and asked, 'What must we do?'

'Stay covered. I keep Tcib.'

'We'll starve.'

'Maybe . . . Tcib . . . too.'

'How long will this hunting last?'

'Year. Then . . . tired.'

'Turlock, let us go to the town and prove our peacefulness.'

'They . . . shoot you. Me, too.'

'You know their ways, Turlock. What can we do?'

'Nothing.'

And he was right. In those terrible years of elimination nothing that the Choptanks could have done would have convinced the white men that they were different. The pressure for land had begun, and this placed Indians athwart the ambitions and destinies of the newcomers, and no kind of truce could ever be engineered.

The little Indians moved through the forest in search of deer, but it was they who became the targets. Children would go out to play—no discipline could prevent them from doing so—and they became the goal in a deadly game. White hunters cheered as lustily when they gunned down a boy of seven as they did when they eliminated a woman of seventy, and always the perimeter was pushed back, back until the remnants huddled in their huts the way Tciblento huddled in hers.

In 1660, when Timothy Turlock was fifty-two, he received word which made the later years of his life more congenial than the earlier ones had been. Life in the marshes was never easy; true, there was always food, but if he needed even the smallest tool, he found it almost impossible to acquire the goods required for barter. Coins he never saw; over a period of nine years he never touched money except for the time he stole a pot containing a hidden shilling. So through the years he had stolen an amazing assortment of things. Whenever he approached a plantation his hawklike eyes roved as he identified items he might want to appropriate on some later visit, and a magistrate once said of him, 'If Tim Turlock were on his way to the gallows, his beady eyes would be locating things to steal on the way back.'

Miraculously, he kept his little family alive by subterfuges which required more work than if he had taken an honest job, and then his luck changed! The Indian wars, never of a magnitude equal to those on the western shore, were nevertheless nagging affairs, and hunters spent so much time shooting Indians that they overlooked the real menace that came creeping down from the north: wolves invaded the peninsula and a bounty was offered for their extermination.

> For every wolf killed the county commissioners will give rations of powder and pellet plus one hundred pounds of tobacco. Proof of killing shall be the right-front paw and the right jowl of the dead beast.

With an incentive like this, Turlock could swing all his powers into action, and he ranged the forests north and south, dealing destruction to the savage predators. He became so adept at tracking the large beasts, and so lethal in dealing with them, that admiring citizens who felt their cattle safer with him around said, 'Turlock succeeds where others don't because he lives like a wolf and thinks like one.'

What they were not aware of was that canny Timothy Turlock had convened a strategy session with his twin sons at which they had devised a naughty plan to subvert the new law to their advantage. 'Stooby fine in woods,' the admiring father had said in opening the meeting, and he was correct. Stooby, so-called because a hunter in Patamoke had said, 'That boy looks downright stupid,' had become at thirteen a master woodsman; he had inherited his father's natural cunning and his grandfather Pentaquod's inclination toward forest lore. He loved the deep quiet of this land, the way animals moved across it and the flight of birds as they searched for seeds. He was a much better hunter than his father and often detected the presence of wolves while Timothy was still fooling with his musket.

'Must be quiet,' Timothy would say like a miniature field marshal, but Stooby would merely point to where he had already located the wolf, and when they fired, it would be his gun that killed the predator.

'Stooby stay woods,' Turlock said. 'Charley watch town.'

The boys could not fathom his scheme, but when his beady eyes narrowed to slits and his grin disclosed the blackened teeth, they knew that good ideas were brewing. 'Charley, find where wolves bury.'

And then Charley understood! With a grin as malevolent as his father's he said, 'Night, I dig up paws . . . jowls.' And when he said this, the three Turlocks chortled, for they knew they had uncovered a gateway to endless riches: Tim and Stooby would kill wolves and deliver the emblems for bounty, and as soon as they were buried, Charley would come at midnight to dig them up, and they could be handed to the officials over and over . . . once the earth was blown away from their previous burials. The Turlocks were going to acquire a lot of tobacco.

On one trip north the hunting was poor; not even Stooby could locate wolves, and so the pair went farther afield than ever, a development that did not worry them, because they lived off the land and slept wherever dusk found them: a few pine branches, a fire in a hollow, and in the morning a dash of cold water in the face. But at one awakening Stooby warned his father, 'Beyond there, houses maybe.' He spoke in a curious amalgam of Choptank, gestures and short English words, but he never had difficulty in making himself intelligible; the hunters who had labeled him stupid had confused reticence with ignorance.

When they had progressed several miles without finding wolves, they did come upon a group of houses built by Swedes twenty years earlier, when that nation was endeavoring to secure a foothold in the New World. The Turlocks, naturally suspicious, scouted the settlement for some hours and satisfied themselves that ordinary men and women appeared to be following ordinary tasks, so toward noon they broke out of the forest, crossed land which had been lately plowed, and started shouting hellos.

Numerous people ran from the houses, and soon the Turlocks were surrounded by sturdy farmers and their wives talking a language Turlock had never heard before. Finally a lad was found who had sailed on an English ship, a blond boy about Stooby's age with a quick tongue, and he was most eager to talk.

'We're Dutch. From New Netherlands. And we've just knocked hell out of the Swedes.'

'What are Swedes?'

When this was interpreted the farmers chuckled, and one man pushed forward a strong-limbed young woman with the fairest blond hair Timothy had ever seen. 'She's a Swede,' the boy said, and bearded, filthy Turlock grinned at her.

They stayed at the Dutch settlement for six days, wearing the boy interpreter out with their questions, and for some reason which young Stooby could not analyze, his father consistently reported the condition of Patamoke to be better than it was and his place much superior to the hut in which they actually lived, but when the time came for departure, the boy discovered what the plot had been. In the woods, awaiting them on the path back to the Choptank, stood Birgitta, the Swedish girl, and by expressive signs she indicated that whereas life for a servant girl in the Swedish settlement had been hard, under the Dutch it had been hell. As the trio disappeared in the woods, she turned for one last look at her prison, made an indecent gesture and delivered what Stooby took to be a chain of Swedish curses.

They moved fast lest the Dutch try to recover their property, and for two days they exhausted themselves, so that when night came they simply collapsed, but on the third day they judged themselves to be free from capture, and they moved in stately fashion, with Stooby scouting for wolves and his father not caring much whether he found any or not. That night Timothy suggested that Stooby build his own sleeping quarters, then, carefully waiting until the boy had done so, he chose a spot far removed for the pine-boughed lean-to in which he and Birgitta would sleep.

The distance was not great enough; through the night Stooby heard strange sounds and riotous laughter, and jumbled words in Choptank and Swedish, and when day broke, the trio dawdled through the woods. For the second time in his life Tim Turlock had won the affections of a woman without actually wooing her and without knowing a dozen words of her language. He was able to do this because he existed on a primitive level in a primitive society where actions were more significant than words; his animal capabilities manifested themselves in a score of unspoken signals, and two women had been willing to gamble their lives on his ability to survive.

On the trip south he and the Swedish girl became robust companions; they had great fun together, day and night, and despite the difference in their ages, for she was not much older than his sons, it became apparent to Stooby that they intended staying together. He was not surprised, therefore, at what happened when they reached the marsh. His father went boldly to the hut, banged on the door, and shouted, 'Tcib, get out.'

The tall Indian woman, neat and disciplined even in rags, came bewildered to the door, saw the fair Swedish girl, and understood. It took her less than ten minutes to gather her pitiful belongings, and with no discernible recrimination she departed. She was no longer needed; she no longer had a home.

Charley elected to go with her, and when she started to walk through the woods he cried, 'No! That canoe is ours,' and he threatened to beat his father's brains out if any objection was made. Defiantly he paddled his mother down the creek to Patamoke, where she would shift from hunter to hunter.

Stooby never hesitated; he would stay with his father and hunt wolves, and on those increasingly frequent days when Turlock preferred to remain at home in dalliance with Birgitta, he hunted alone and did rather better than when his father impeded him. But now there was no Charley to dig up the emblems for resale, so Turlock himself had to go out at night and slink about the dumps, retrieving paws and jowls.

It is easy to reconstruct the history of Timothy Turlock during these years because his name appears with such troubled frequency in contemporary court records. The London judge's opinion that Turlock was a ferret, scurrying about just beyond the vision of man, was validated in these years. The marsh-dweller was now in his fifties, small, quick, sly, dirty of dress and habit, a frequenter of swamps, an invader of proper locations. That he should so often have been charged with stealing minor objects was not surprising, for Turlock was incapable of passing a usable object without appropriating it, but that he should also have won the affection of Tciblento and Birgitta was a mystery. One might have thought that this repulsive little man with the missing teeth would be last in any process of amatory selection; perhaps his sly insistence accounted for the mystery, or the fact that he openly lusted after women and allowed them to see it. In any event, he was a rebuke to proper Christians and a constant thorn in the side of the court.

He was, as the records prove, frequently fined and often whipped, but the latter punishment was a heavier trial to the community than to Turlock, for at the moment he was led from jail toward the post he began to utter such lamentations and shrieks of pain as to make a most unsavory spectacle, and since the judges knew that the whipping would have no effect on him, they were reluctant to sentence the community to such travail.

'We should have hanged him at the first session,' one of the commissioners said, following a miserable trial in which he stood accused of shooting a townsman who had tracked a deer into his marsh. But others felt that his existence was justified because he did kill an extraordinary number of wolves—'Like a carrion buzzard, he helps clear away the refuse of this town.'

So Turlock went his way, a curious little man who had already sired six bastards: two by Tciblento, one by Birgitta, and three by various indentured girls who had been publicly whipped for their transgressions. These six were the beginnings of that tremendous horde of Turlocks who would populate the Eastern Shore, each inheriting important characteristics from Timothy: they would love the land; they would want to live close to the water; they would develop companionship with birds and fish and animals; through the sixth generation none would be able to read or sign a name, and all would abhor such regularities as paying taxes and getting married.

And yet sometimes even that happened. Turlock had the brazen effrontery to go into Patamoke court and claim that he had purchased Birgitta's indenture from the Dutch, and when both she and Stooby confirmed this, the magistrates had to issue papers proving that he owned her services for seven years, but when she became pregnant they decreed that ownership did not include bedroom services. He was fined five hundred pounds of tobacco—which he obtained by selling one wolf's head five times—and Birgitta was publicly whipped.

She was not actually whipped; whimpering and sobbing, Turlock came into court volunteering to marry her if the lashes were forsworn, and reluctantly the judges allowed the wedding to take place. It was a strange affair: Charley and Stooby attended, as did their half sister Flora and the anomalous Tciblento, who sat through the ceremony looking at the floor.

She was living a strange life, sixty-eight years old, tall and dignified as ever, but obviously fallen upon evil days. No more the softly tanned deerskin dress or the edging of mink, no more the necklace of silvery white shells. She lived with strangers beyond the fringes of the harbor; her only consistent friend was Charley, a resentful, difficult boy who hated white men but strove to be like them. He was often in court.

One day when his mother was tending a shack for two hunters, he went into the forest for deer, and as he was returning, dressed in various rags such as dispossessed Choptanks wore, one of the very hunters with whom his mother lived shot at him, thinking him to be an Indian. The bullet went through his left shoulder but did not knock him down; stanching the blood with a dirty rag, he walked home, but fainted as he reached the shack. Tciblento tended him without tears. The hunter justified himself—'He looked like an Indian,' an excuse to which she made no response.

During these years she did not often see Stooby; he stayed with his father, probing the marshes and becoming the final authority on life along the water. He had already built himself one log canoe and was in the process of burning another; he spent more time on the river than on the shore, for although he had to live in the forest to shoot deer for food and wolves for profit, he lived on the water because he loved it. Sometimes he was absent for days, exploring the rivers running to the north, and if his father had been the first white man to appreciate the general wonder of this area, Stooby became the first, Indian or white, to know specific places, the marvelous points of land poking out like fingers into the gray water, the sleeping coves that hid behind them.

At twenty-three Stooby had committed himself to the river and the bay; they formed his empire, and on their broad bosoms he would always be at home. He lived by the tides, and the rising of the full moon, and the coming and going of water birds. He knew where oysters clung to sandy bars for protection and how crabs moved up and down the bay. In his mind he charted every spit, the convoluted entrance to every creek. He rigged his own sails and knew when to drop them in a storm, and he had such a sensitive feeling for boats that he could tell the instant one began to slip sideways or approach a hidden sandbar. He was a waterman, the first of his breed, a fish without gills, a marsh bird without pinfeathers.

An unusual man named James Lamb figured in many of Timothy Turlock's arrests. Forty-one years old when he appeared on the deck of a ship out of Bristol, he had crossed England on foot to escape detention in London and had reached the New World as a free man who had voluntarily fled a comfortable home because of an enlightenment which had altered his life. He had heard an itinerant preacher, one George Fox, a Quaker, explain the simple characteristics of a new faith, and he had been persuaded.

He was a gentle man, and his wife Prudence was even less pretentious than he. At the wharf in Jamestown they had purchased the indenture of a serving girl named Nancy, a child who had given them endless trouble through her propensity for allowing likable young men, and some neither likable nor young, to creep into her bed. The girl was haled into court, humiliated, whipped at the public post and warned by the commissioners that she might even be jailed, but she persisted in her lusty ways. A normal mistress would have disowned her, but Prudence Lamb could not. 'She is our charge,' she told her husband, and no matter what the ebullient child did, Mrs. Lamb protected her, paid her fines so that she could escape whippings, and assured her husband that Nancy would one day come to her senses, but when the young lady admitted Timothy Turlock into her bedroom for the second time, the Lambs judged that enough was enough.

'Thee cannot speak to him ever again,' Mrs. Lamb warned, and Nancy blubbered, 'There's no one else to talk with,' and the Lambs felt that it was their duty to find the girl some kind of companionship, and one day Mr. Lamb suggested Stooby Turlock as a proper companion, and Nancy whined, 'All he's interested in is turtles,' and as if she were a prophet, not six days later Stooby appeared at the Lamb home with a delicious diamondback terrapin, a gift, he said, because the Lambs had not taken his father to court for stealing a handcart.

Birgitta, bound to Turlock by servitude and marriage, looked on these irregular matters with the amused detachment of some ancient Norse goddess perplexed by the curious behavior of refractory earthlings. Her husband was repulsive and nothing would change him, but she could hope that one of these days he would be shot accidentally or hanged on purpose; then she would be free to make her own way in this burgeoning New World. She was certainly happier along the Choptank than she had ever been as a prisoner of the Dutch, and was developing a positive love for her lively daughter and her strange stepson Stooby. She understood the boy, and encouraged him in his pursuit of marsh and river. Sensing this, he invited her one day to accompany him on one of his explorations to the north, and without hesitation she grabbed Flora and climbed into the log canoe, spending three days in those exquisite streams which branched out from the right bank of the river.

'You have a paradise,' she told Stooby, and he nodded; he could not verbalize his feeling for these waters, but sometimes when he rounded a point and saw ahead of him an entire creek reaching far inland, his breath caught as if he were seeing a trusted friend after a long absence, and he loved his fair-haired stepmother for her understanding.

The people who understood the Turlocks best were the Steeds. Henry knew Timothy to be an incorrigible: thief, adulterer, liar, deceptor, vagrant and a dozen other characterizations, each repugnant to a proper household. He tolerated him because his mother, Martha Steed, insisted that he do so, but that did not prevent him from bringing charges against the offensive little cutpurse, and it sometimes seemed that Henry had to attend court monthly to testify. Consistently he won damages from the wastrel, and consistently Turlock paid in tobacco so rank, so filled with weeds that it had to be classified as trash. In no way could it be shipped to England for serious sale; to do so would be to destroy the good name of Steed.

Paul Steed, the doctor, saw a different aspect of the Turlocks, a functional one, as it were, for he was called upon to minister to babies sired by Timothy and to treat the various tragedies encountered by his wives and sons. One day he walked up the path from Devon wharf with heavy steps and head so bowed that his mother had to ask, 'Paul, what is it?'

'Tciblento's dying.'

'What of?'

'Some man thrashed her with a club.'

'Oh, my God!'

'But she was already dying . . . of us.'

'Paul, what do you mean?'

'She's the last of the real Choptanks, Mother. There was never any hope . . .'

Mrs. Steed proposed that Tciblento be brought to the island, where she could be properly cared for, but Paul said, 'No use. She can't live a week.'

'That week must at least be decent,' Mrs. Steed insisted, and she ordered the servants to prepare the ketch so that she herself could fetch the dying woman, but when she and Paul reached the hut they found Tciblento too weak to move. She had been, as Paul reported, in the process of dying when a drunken hunter for whom she was keeping house attacked her with an oaken club, breaking her jaw.

She lay on a paillasse of pine needles, gasping for breath, her face knocked awry but the grandeur of her dark eyes undimmed. When she saw Mrs. Steed, and recalled the handsome Englishman she had once loved and always, tears came into her eyes. She was too weak to turn her face away, but she was so ashamed that Mrs. Steed should see her secret, she closed her eyes and sobbed inwardly.

'Tciblento,' Mrs. Steed said, 'we're going to take you home with us.' The stricken woman summoned strength to shake her head no. She would stay here, in the low estate to which she had brought herself.

'Shall we send for Turlock?' Again the dying woman said no.

'Stooby? Wouldn't you like to see Stooby?' Tciblento nodded, so Charley was sent to fetch his brother, but the young waterman was absent on a probing of the coves, and Charley returned not with him but with Timothy.

Mrs. Steed would have preferred to bar the door to this reprobate, but Paul said, 'Oh, come in,' and Turlock came slouching to the low bed.

'Hello, Tcib,' he said. She looked up at him but could say nothing. Turning to the doctor, he asked, 'Will she . . .'

'No.'

'Well, Tcib, goodbye,' he said, and he was off.

She did not betray any sorrow in seeing him disappear for the last time. All things were disappearing, had been doing so for decades, and he was one of the least to be regretted.

There was a commotion now, for two officials were dragging into the hut the man who had clubbed her. He was an ugly fellow no better than Turlock, and when he stood before the dying woman he had so often abused he whimpered, 'Tell them I didn't do it, Tcibby,' and she looked at him and then at his arresters and told the latter that it had not been he. One of the men, knowing better, grabbed the cudgel and started belaboring him, inflicting real damage, but Paul interceded. 'Let him go,' he said, wresting away the club, and now the man whimpered for real cause and disappeared into the forest.

It was obvious that Tciblento could not survive the night, so Paul suggested that his mother sail back to the island in daylight, but she refused—'I cannot allow her to die alone.' And she stayed by the bed through the long afternoon, and when the sun set in the western bay she was still there, talking with the silent woman. 'There were good days on this river, Tciblento. I remember when you were married. You had Indian children, didn't you?' And the nothingness in Tciblento's eyes showed that she had died.

No muffled drums marked her passage. No handmaidens chanted of Pentaquod, who had saved their tribe, nor of the deeds of her sons, who had accomplished nothing. Her people were dispersed over wide areas, with no werowance to remind them of tribal ways. Many lay unburied in the strange places where they had fallen, and now she too, lay dead, in a hovel at the edge of a river her father had once ruled.

Voyage Four: 1661

FOR SOME TIME NOW THE COMMUNITY HAD BEEN suspicious of him. His master had confided to the governor that 'Edward Paxmore, whose indenture I purchased seven years ago, has taken to wandering about the colony without my permission, robbing me of labor justly mine.' As a result, spies watched his movements, reporting any unusual behavior to the committee of ministers, and the family from which he hoped to buy a piece of land for his carpentry shop when his indenture ended refused to sell.

Informers told the governor, 'He has traveled from Dover to Salisbury to Rowley to Ipswich and has been contentious in arguing with passers-by about the works of God.' Therefore, when Paxmore returned to Boston and reappeared at the house of his master, the sheriff was waiting to haul him off to court.

At the hearing, his master whined, 'Edward is a good carpenter who builds well. But in this final year with me he has taken to arguing about the works of God. He has cheated me of his labors, and I am sorely done.'

'What remedy?'

'Please, your honor, extend his indenture for another ten months. It's only fair.'

The governor, a thin, arduous man, was little concerned with financial restitution to masters; such cases were common and could be handled by ordinary judges. But this ominous phrase, 'arguing about the works of God,' disturbed him mightily, for it was clearly blasphemous and smacked of Quakerism. Within recent years the governor had ordered the hanging of three Quakers and had personally attended their executions. He had no intention of allowing this pernicious heresy to gain a foothold in Massachusetts, for it was an abomination.

The governor had a firm mind in all things, but he was perplexed by the man who stood before him, this tall, thin workman in homespun jacket too short at the wrists, in pants too skimpy at the ankles. He was awkward-looking, yet all had testified that he was an excellent carpenter. It was the Adam's apple and the eyes that troubled: the former jumped about like those in witches; the latter carried that intense fire which marked those who believe they have seen God. Such men were dangerous, yet this carpenter had such a gentle manner, was so deferential to the court and so respectful of his master that he could not be a common criminal. Deep matters were involved, and they must be gone into.

'Edward Paxmore, I fear you may have fallen into evil ways. I hand you back to the sheriff for presentation in court on Monday next for proper interrogation.' Having said this, he stared balefully at Paxmore and stalked from the room.

The trial should have been of little consequence, for Paxmore, thirty-two years old and with an excellent reputation for hard work, would normally have been rebuked for wandering and depriving his rightful master of his labor. The judge would add an additional six months to the indenture—never as many as the master claimed—and when these had been discharged, the carpenter would become a free man and a valued addition to the citizenry of Massachusetts.

But Paxmore's trial was to be different, for when the court convened on Monday morning Judge Goddard, a tall, heavy man who spoke in ponderous sentences, had the grim but satisfying task of putting final touches to the case of Thomas Kenworthy, confessed Quaker and recusant. On three earlier occasions Judge Goddard had ordered Kenworthy to be whipped and banished from Massachusetts, and thrice the Quaker had crept back into the colony.

Paxmore and his master were already seated in court when the sheriff brought Kenworthy in. The Quaker was a man of forty, thin, dark of face, with deep-set eyes and the manner of a fanatic who looked piercingly at people. His hands were bound and he seemed reluctant to step before the judge; the sheriff had to push him along, but when at last he was in place he stared defiantly at the judge and asked in a strong voice, 'Wherefore does thee judge me?'

And Goddard thundered, 'We have a law.'

'It is thy law and not God's.'

'Silence that man!'

'I will not be silenced, for God has ordered me to speak.'

'Stifle that blasphemy!' the judge roared, and the sheriff clapped his hand over the prisoner's mouth.

When silence once more prevailed in the small white room Judge Goddard resumed control of the case, placing his large hands on the table and looking with contempt at Kenworthy. 'Three times I have ordered you whipped, and three times you have continued your heresy. Do you learn nothing?'

'I have learned that God does not need governors or judges or ministers to speak to His people.'

'Sheriff, remove that man's shirt.'

The sheriff, a tall, lean man who betrayed a sense of satisfaction with his job, untied the prisoner's hands and ripped away the woolen shirt. Paxmore gasped. The man's back was a network of small round scars, but not like any he had seen before. These formed little cups across the man's back, and Paxmore would never forget the strange remark of the man at his elbow: 'You could hide a pea in each of them.'

Judge Goddard said, 'Are you aware, Thomas Kenworthy, of how your back looks?'

'I feel it each night before I go to sleep. It is the badge of my devotion to God.'

'Apparently you are of such a contumacious character that ordinary whippings have no effect on you. My order that you quit this colony has been ignored, three times. You have not only persisted in your Quaker heresy, but you have made so bold as to preach to others, infecting them, and there is no humility in you.'

'There is love of God in me,' Kenworthy said.

'Nor respect, neither,' the judge continued. 'In your three other trials you refused, did you not, to remove your hat in the presence of the governor and his court?'

'I did, and if I could have my hat now, I would wear it, for Jesus Christ so commanded.' His eyes fell on the hat Paxmore had worn into court, and in a sudden break-away from the sheriff he seized the hat and placed it defiantly on his head. The sheriff started to fight for possession of the hat, but Judge Goddard rebuked him, 'Let the criminal wear his hat, if it will help him hear my sentence,' then lowered his voice and said, more slowly, 'Thomas Kenworthy, it is my duty to pass sentence upon you.'

'God has already done so, and thy words are nothing.'

'You speak falsehood,' the judge thundered, allowing his voice to rise.

'I speak the instructions of God, and they are never false.'

'Do you then nominate yourself a minister, that you comprehend the teachings of God?'

'Each man is minister, yes, and each woman too.' Kenworthy turned to face the spectators, and because he stood nearest Edward Paxmore he pointed a long finger at him and said, 'This prisoner haled before the court is also a minister. He speaks directly to God, and God speaks to him.'

'Silence him again,' the judge shouted, and once more Kenworthy's hands were tied and his mouth covered.

Paxmore, trembling from the effect of having been twice involved in this trial, watched with fascination as the judge painstakingly arranged the papers on his table, obviously seeking to compose himself lest anger make him appear foolish. Taking a deep breath, he leaned forward to address the Quaker in measured phrases:

'The Colony of Massachusetts has been most lenient with you, Thomas Kenworthy. It has received your heresy and done its best to make you see the falsity of your ways. Three times it has allowed you to wander about our towns and villages, spewing your blasphemy. And you have shown no contrition. Therefore, the sentence of this court is that you shall be lashed to a great cannon and whipped thirty times, after which you shall be taken to the public square and hanged.'

The cruel sentence had no effect on Thomas Kenworthy, for he was already living in a kind of ecstasy in which whippings and gibbets were no longer of much concern, but it had a devastating effect on Edward Paxmore, who leaped to his feet and shouted at the judge, 'If you're going to hang him, why whip him first?'

The question was so explosive, and so obviously germane, that Judge Goddard imprudently allowed himself to be trapped into answering. 'To punish him,' he said spontaneously.

'Is not death punishment?' Paxmore cried.

'Not enough,' the judge responded. And then, realizing what he had done—that he had spoken like a fool—he bellowed, 'Lock that man up.' And he stormed from the small white room.

The sheriff took his two prisoners to the jail, a dank room below the level of the public streets, and there directed the blacksmith to apply one set of leg irons to the two men. When this difficult and untidy job was completed, and the two men were lashed together as one, the smith and the sheriff departed, leaving the condemned Quaker and the carpenter in semi-darkness.

Then began the dialogue of salvation. Thomas Kenworthy, one of the first Quaker preachers in America, a graduate of Oxford and a man versed in both Greek and Latin, interpreted the simple revolution in theology that had taken place in England less than twenty years before: 'George Fox is not a holy man, not a priest in any sense of that word, no different from thee and me.'

'Why do you use *thee?*'

'It was the way Jesus spoke to His friends.'

Kenworthy explained how Fox, this unpretentious Englishman, had come to see that many of the manifestations of religion were vain trappings and that the ritual was unnecessary: 'Thee does not require priests or blessings or ministers' sermons or benedictions or the laying on of hands. God speaks directly to the human heart, and the blessings of Jesus Christ are available to every man and woman.'

Paxmore noticed that Kenworthy never said *man* in the religious sense without adding *woman,* and the Quaker told him, 'When I was whipped in Virginia, one woman hung beside me at the tail of the cart, and she was braver than I could ever be. The cords hurt me, but they tore the woman apart, and she refused to whimper.'

'Does it hurt, the lashings?'

'In Virginia, I wept and cursed, but in Ipswich, God came to me and asked, "If my Son could bear His crucifixion, cannot thee endure a mere whipping?" '

Paxmore asked if he could touch the scars, and Kenworthy said no. 'It would make them too important. The dignity of my back lies in my heart, where I have forgiven the whipmen of Virginia and Massachusetts. They were like the Roman soldiers, doing their duty.'

He was describing to Paxmore the other tenets of the Quakers— equality of women, refusal to bear arms, tithing, no hymns or outward manifestations in worship, no priests, no ministers and, above all, the direct relationship of God and man—when the carpenter exclaimed, 'Thomas, I left Boston and wandered through the countryside because I was searching. Is this the revelation I was seeking?'

'It is no revelation, no mystery, and thee did not have to leave Boston to entertain it. It is the simple discovery that each man is his own pathway to God.'

Long after nightfall a jailer brought food to the prisoners, but neither could eat. Leg bound to leg, they wanted to talk about the spiritual revolution of which Quakerism was only a minor manifestation. 'There will be many others like me,' Kenworthy predicted. 'There will have to be, because God approaches people in different ways.'

'Is the governor right in his religion?'

'Of course he is. For him, what he says and what he believes in are altogether right.'

'Then why does he condemn— What was the word he used?'

'Quakers,' the Oxford man said. 'Our enemies accuse us of quaking in the presence of God, and we do.'

'Why does he condemn you to death?'

'Because he is afraid.'

'Is that why the judge ordered you to be whipped . . . and hanged?'

'It is. When he saw my scarred back in court, scars he put there, and realized how little effect they had had upon me— Edward, the last time in Roxbury, I did not even feel the cords . . .' In a sweep of spiritual insight he lost his line of thought, and his awareness of jail, and any sense of pressure from the leg irons. He tried to rise, then tried to kneel in prayer. Defeated in each effort, he sat on the bench and folded his hands over his heart, saying, 'If thee had not told me that thee had left Boston to go a-searching, I would not presume to tell thee what I am about to say, for I am putting a heavy burden on thee, Edward. But God has summoned thee.'

'I believe He has,' Paxmore said, and the two men talked through the night.

On Friday morning the blacksmith came in to cut the leg clamps, separating them, and while doing so, advised Kenworthy that he was to hang this day. From his leg the clamp was removed entirely, but on Paxmore's the iron cuff was allowed to remain and a seven-foot chain was attached to it. 'All prisoners must watch the hanging,' the smith explained, 'and with this chain the sheriff can hold you so that you don't run away.'

When the two prisoners were left alone in their cell Paxmore supposed that Kenworthy would want to pray, but the Oxford man was in such a state of exaltation that he did not need prayer to prepare him for the death that waited: 'We are children of God, and reunion with Him can never be painful. I go with additional peace in my heart because I know that thee has taken up the burden I leave behind.'

'Could we pray?' Paxmore asked.

'If you feel the need.'

'I have not the understanding you have—' He corrected himself, and for the first time used the Quaker expression: 'The understanding thee has.'

'Thee has, Edward. That is, the capacity for it. All men and women do. What is required is the unfolding of truth. And that will come.'

They knelt and Paxmore began a tortured prayer, but Kenworthy placed his hand on the carpenter's arm and said, 'The words are not necessary. God hears thee,' and the two men prayed in silence.

They were in this position when the jailers came. They were stocky men with powerful arms and seemed to enjoy their work, for they attacked it with a kind of easy joviality. 'Time's come,' the heavier of the two men announced, taking Kenworthy by the upper arm. The other grabbed Paxmore's chain and told him, 'The sheriff's handling you, special.' The two Quakers were separated for the last time, but not before Paxmore had a chance to cry, 'I will be on the scaffold with thee, Thomas,' to which Kenworthy replied, 'All Boston will be.'

Paxmore and three other prisoners—two men and a woman who had questioned some small detail of Puritanism—were led to the hanging ground, where a large crowd of watchers waited with varying kinds of delight. Some were fascinated by the gibbet from which a man would soon hang, others by the monstrous cannon to whose wheel the heretic would be lashed. Eight men of the town had already volunteered to pull the cannon and were busy attaching ropes to the carriage. But all experienced a heightened sense of existence, because their church was about to cleanse itself.

Paxmore, standing with the other prisoners who were constantly jeered at by the townspeople, looked in vain for Kenworthy; he was being held back until the colony officials put in their appearance, and now from the white church, where they had been praying, came the governor and Judge Goddard, dressed in black, followed by the town fathers, grim-lipped and ready.

'Bring forth the prisoner!' the governor shouted. It was clear that he intended to supervise personally the death of this obnoxious dissenter. When Kenworthy was produced, the governor went to him, thrust his face forward and demanded, 'Are you satisfied now that we have the power to silence you?'

'My voice will be stronger tomorrow than it ever was,' Kenworthy replied.

'To the cannon!' the governor cried, and the sheriff dropped the chain that held Paxmore and summoned three helpers, who came forward to grab the Oxford man and lash him, legs and arms far separated, to the iron wheel of the cannon, face inward.

'Jailer,' the governor commanded, 'thirty lashes, well laid on.'

The heavier of the two jailers stepped forward, and the town clerk handed him a length of wood to which had been fastened nine heavy cords of the kind used for guiding a light sail. Into each had been tied three stout knots, and as the jailer approached the cannon he snapped the whip expertly, close to the ear of the prostrate prisoner.

'That one don't count,' he said, and the crowd laughed.

'One!' the clerk intoned impassively, and the nine cords cut into the scarred back of the Quaker.

'Two!' the clerk counted, then 'Three!' and 'Four!'

'Make him cry out,' a woman in the crowd shouted, but Kenworthy uttered no sound.

'Seven' and 'Eight' passed with still no sound from the wheel, so the governor said, 'Pull the cannon forward,' and the men on the ropes strained until the wheel moved into a new position, exposing different parts of Kenworthy's body to the lash.

'Lay on, lay on!' the governor cried, and when the next strokes still failed to elicit any cry of pain from the prisoner, the governor stepped forward angrily and took the lash from the hands of the first jailer, handing it to the second. 'Lay on! Destroy that man!'

The second jailer, eager for an opportunity to display the kind of service he was ready to give his colony and his church, raised on his toes and brought the lashes down with savage force, causing Kenworthy's whole body to shudder. At the fifteenth stroke the body went limp, and as the enthusiastic jailer was about to apply the lash again, Edward Paxmore shouted, 'He's fainted. Stop! Stop!'

'Who cried out?' the governor demanded, and Judge Goddard, who had been watching Paxmore, replied, 'That one,' and the governor stopped to mark the culprit. 'We'll take care of him later,' he said. Then he cried, 'Men, move the cannon,' and the great wheel revolved.

By the twenty-fifth lash Thomas Kenworthy was nearly dead, but now the governor directed that the whip be turned over to a new aspirant eager to show how well he could strike, and pieces of flesh flicked off the bloody mass.

'Give it to him!' a woman called as the clerk finished his litany: 'Twenty-nine, thirty and done.'

'Water in his face,' the sheriff ordered, and after this was done, the limp body was cut down.

'To the gibbet,' the governor said, and he led the way to the hanging spot.

The water and the walk revived the prisoner, and after he was dragged aloft to the platform from which he would be dropped, he said in a voice which could be heard at some distance, 'Thee will be ashamed of this day's work.'

A minister who had watched the whipping ran to the scaffold and cried in fierce, condemnatory accents, 'Heretic, separatist! God has shown us the true religion and you traduce it. You have a right to die.'

'Hangman, to your task,' the governor said, and a black bag was placed over Kenworthy's head. As the radiant face disappeared, Paxmore whispered, 'Oh, God! He is not as old as I.'

The rope was lowered over the black mask, and the knot was located at the base of the neck. 'Let him die!' cried the woman who had shouted before, and the trap door was sprung.

On Monday, when Edward Paxmore, his left leg still in chains, stood before Judge Goddard, he did not present a pleasing sight. His wrists and ankles still protruded from tight homespun; his Adam's apple still bobbed like the cork on a fisherman's line; his eyes were still accusatory; but now his beard was scraggly, for he had not been allowed to shave, and he looked the perfect criminal. Without amenities the judge attacked. 'Well, Brother Paxmore, you had a chance to see what we do with heretics. Are you now willing to take an oath of allegiance to our religion and then leave Massachusetts forever?'

The proposal was so contradictory, so unlike the crystal-pure logic of Thomas Kenworthy—to swear allegiance to a religion and then to leave it—that Paxmore had to speak. 'Thy reasoning makes no sense,' he said.

'What's this *thy*. Are you already infected?'

'To the extent that thy mouthings seem confused and the work of the devil, not the words of God.'

The tall judge fell back in his chair. Not even Kenworthy had spoken to him in terms of such contempt, and for a moment he was discomposed. But his fury revived and he shouted at Paxmore, 'Are you, then, a Quaker?'

'I believe in a personal God, who speaks to me as he did to Thomas Kenworthy.'

'Thomas Kenworthy was lashed at the wheel and he is dead.'

'He lives in every heart that saw him die.'

'Hearts have no eyes. They cannot see.'

'And soon the people who watched Kenworthy die will grow sick of your beatings and hangings, and anathema will be on your name.'

'You know I can order you whipped?'

'And other judges like you ordered Jesus whipped.'

This was so blasphemous, an attack on both the colony and its church, that Goddard would hear no more. 'Drag him away, Sheriff,' and the burly sheriff took the judge at his word. Jerking mightily on the iron chain, he brought Paxmore to the floor, then dragged him feetfirst from the court. Before the hour was out Judge Goddard had penned this sentence:

> To the Constables of Dover, Roxbury, Rowley and Ipswich:
>
> You and every one of you are required in His Majesty's Name to receive into your custody Edward Paxmore, vagabond carpenter and suspected Quaker, and you are to convey him from town to town at the tail of a cart, and you and each of you are to whip him out of town with ten stripes well laid on, and this is to be done in accordance with the stated Law of Vagabond Quakers. And the constable of Ipswich is to see that Edward Paxmore is delivered over the border of Massachusetts and into the Colony of Rhode Island, where heretics abide. Dated, 17th March, 1661.

When the horrid terms of punishment were read to Paxmore in his cell, he fell to his knees and asked the spirit of Thomas Kenworthy to give him courage, but when the first lashes fell at Dover he found that he had no power of resistance, and when the twenty-seven knots cut into his flesh he cried aloud. At the tenth stroke he was a quivering idiot, and when the cold water, heavily salted, was thrown across his back he screamed and fainted.

He would never forget the terrible journey from Dover to Roxbury, struggling along at the tail of the cart. His body ached; flies nibbled at his wounds; his face became cloaked with dust; and during the entire passage villagers scorned him, and asked him if now he would repent and accept the true God.

When he reached Roxbury he was allowed three days' rest. The constable said, 'Just time enough for the scars to heal, so that I can whip them open again.' He thought of this statement a long time and wondered why people so attached to God should take such positive delight in crucifying a man who had precisely the same love for God, but with a different manner of expressing it. He even understood the punishment, for he had observed that all people allied to a church seek to protect it, but he would never understand the pleasure the Puritans took in the infliction of punishment.

The whipping at Roxbury was even more severe, for the constable studiously moved from side to side so as to cover his entire back with deep wounds. As the cart left town the driver called back, 'That was a good one, wasn't it. Our constable ties a double knot. You won't forget him soon.'

Paxmore, thinking himself close to death from the pain and the insects that gnawed upon him, reached Ipswich unable to move his legs; the cart dragged him into town. For five days he lay in a stupor, for the doctor gave it as his opinion that ten more lashes now would kill him, and when he recovered enough to understand what was happening, he heard from three different individuals that the whipping in this town was to be special, and everyone who spoke of it obviously relished the prospect.

Not only would Paxmore be whipped—and word had sped through the town that he might well die of his lashes—but a female Quaker had also been apprehended, and she was to be lashed too. Her name, Paxmore heard, was Ruth Brinton, and she had already been exiled from Virginia because of her brazen adherence to the Quaker heresy, and she had been whipped in Roxbury.

'Women we give only six lashes,' the jailer explained with a sense of real compassion. 'They can't stand much more, but they say this one is a vixen. She kept preaching while they beat her, and in Roxbury to silence her they had to beat her across the mouth.'

From Virginia! Could it be that this Quaker woman was the one of whom Kenworthy had spoken, a calm, determined, God-sent woman who exuded sanctity and gave men courage? He tried to interrogate the jailer, but the man only repeated that this one was a vixen, and that when she was whipped, the good people of Ipswich would see something.

This so agitated Paxmore that he demanded to see the local judge, and when that worthy man appeared in the cell, Paxmore said, 'To whip a woman is indecent and against the will of God.'

'We have a law,' the judge said.

'It cannot be the law of God.'

'Who are you to determine what God wills?'

'He speaks to me.'

The judge put his two hands before his face as if to ward off evil. 'It's a good thing, Paxmore, that you're leaving Massachusetts. We have no place for evil men like you.'

The carpenter, seeing that it would be no use to argue further with this righteous man, bowed his head and said, 'Allow me to take her lashes.'

'But the sentence has been written.'

'In the mercy of God, allow me to take her lashes.'

'That would accomplish nothing. After here she has six more in Duxbury.'

'Oh, dearest Father!'

'Are you appealing to God against God's law? We have a sentence on this woman, in writing.'

'Thee had better go,' Paxmore said, 'and hide thyself in a deep well, for God will surely seek thee out.'

These prophetic words disturbed the judge, and he said in a voice of reasoning, 'Paxmore, it would be fatal to give you six more lashes. The doctor told us you might not even survive the ten that are due you. Sleep in peace before tomorrow, and quit Massachusetts. You do not belong among the godly.'

When Edward Paxmore and Ruth Brinton were tethered to the same cart, they formed an incongruous pair—he tall and awkward, she small and delicately proportioned. But when the sheriff stripped them both to the waist, with watchers ogling in delight, their common heritage became obvious: each back was flayed and marked with indented scars. There was no man or woman.

Of course she drew the greater comment, for when the Puritans surged forward to see at close quarters a half-naked woman, with the great welts already marking her back, they shouted their satisfaction, and one cried, 'She won't forget Ipswich!'

Twice Paxmore tried to speak to the woman tied beside him, and twice the local judge ordered the constable to silence him, as if words passed between the two proscribed Quakers might contaminate the theocratic town. But on the third try he succeeded. 'Is thee the woman from Virginia that Thomas Kenworthy—' The constable struck Paxmore brutally across the mouth and shouted, 'Silence, infidel.' But the woman nodded, and through bloody lips Paxmore said, 'He was hanged,' and she replied, 'So shall we all be,' and the whippings began.

It was not customary for women to be lashed in Ipswich, so the crowd was large and appreciative. They watched approvingly as the nine cords cut into her back on the first three lashes, and then a whisper of suppressed excitement swept through the crowd as the fourth lash fell.

'She's bleeding in front!' a woman in the crowd shouted, and the spectators pressed forward to see for themselves where the tips of the lashes had laid open the breasts.

'Good blow, Robert,' a man called. 'Hit her again!'

'Oh,' the beaten woman moaned as the last two blows fell.

'Well struck, Robert. Now the man.'

Paxmore would not remember his punishment at Ipswich. The first blow pulled his face sideways, and all he could see was the Quaker woman beside him, a small, dark-haired woman limp and faint, with blood dripping from her breasts. That night they were parted, he to exile in Rhode Island, she to her final installment in Duxbury.

The subsequent history of Edward Paxmore in Massachusetts seems a grotesque nightmare. After his final whipping in Ipswich, the constable led him to the border of Massachusetts, and in the cold weeks of late March 1661, stole every piece of clothing he had and shoved him naked into Rhode Island. The citizens of the first village he came to were accustomed to receive such exiles from the theocracy to the north, and quickly dressed him in clothes too small. He was given a set of carpenter's tools and within four weeks was back in Massachusetts, a gangling carpenter preaching the Quaker doctrine and keeping himself in jeopardy.

Records show that he was arrested in Ipswich in 1662 and lashed through four towns before he was expelled once more into Rhode Island. The records do not show this, but again he arrived completely naked.

He returned to Massachusetts in 1663 and was again whipped through three towns and exiled, naked. In January 1664 he was back, his shoulders a mass of crisscrossing scars, his voice deepened and impassioned in the work of conversion. This time he was apprehended in Boston and taken before Judge Goddard, who was appalled at his appearance: he was emaciated from meals missed while fleeing; borrowed clothes many sizes too small hung curiously from shoulders which sagged as if borne down by unseen burdens; his eyes no longer flamed; and his deportment was much altered. He was not deferential to authority, he sought argument, and his colloquy with Judge Goddard, recorded both by officers of the colony and by crypto-Quakers eavesdropping at the court, was vigorous:

GODDARD: Why have you come back, when you have already received an even hundred lashes? Is your back so stout it can withstand everything?

PAXMORE: Why does thee persist in persecutions? Is thy heart so black it is impervious to a sense of guilt?

GODDARD: Why would guilt be upon me?

PAXMORE: Because thee acts in defiance of God's law and the king's.

GODDARD: Are you presuming to claim that the just law of the king is bad?

PAXMORE: I do so claim, but I am not required to, for the law itself states that it is bad.

GODDARD: Do you know that you speak treason? As well as heresy?

PAXMORE: If I speak against the king, I speak treason, this I confess, but the king himself will declare thy law void, because it is against his intentions and is bad.

GODDARD: Do you think that the King of England will alter a law because some fractious Quaker asks him to?

PAXMORE: No, because the reasoning of a just God asks him to, and he will obey.

GODDARD: You truly believe that the great law of Massachusetts will be changed to suit you.

PAXMORE: Not to suit me. To suit the everlasting laws of God.

GODDARD: You presume to interpret the wishes of God. What college in England did you attend? Did you study theology at Harvard? If so, what bishop ordained you to interpret God's law?

PAXMORE: I studied at night, in the cell of thy prison, and my teacher was Thomas Kenworthy, whom thee murdered.

(Everyone who attended this trial, Puritans and Quakers alike, remarked that when Edward Paxmore made this statement a pronounced change came over Judge Goddard. He dropped his sarcasm and lost his self-assurance. He also lowered his voice, leaned forward more, and engaged the prisoner in debate on a new level.)

GODDARD: You know that I do not want to order you whipped again.

PAXMORE: I am sure thee doesn't, good Judge, for the terror of Kenworthy's death rests on thy conscience.

GODDARD: Then why don't you remove your hat, as a sign of respect for this court?

PAXMORE: Jesus instructed us to remain covered.

GODDARD: If I send you in peace to Rhode Island, will you stay there?

PAXMORE: I must go where God sends me.

GODDARD: Thomas Paxmore, don't you realize that you're making it very difficult for the Massachusetts Colony to deal with you? Won't you leave us in peace?

PAXMORE: I bring peace.

GODDARD: A strange kind of peace. We have a good colony here, a good religion that suits us perfectly. All we ask is that you leave us alone, and all you do is preach treason and sedition and heresy.

PAXMORE: I come back to thy court, Judge Goddard, because I am instructed of the Lord.

GODDARD: What constructive message could you possibly bring?

PAXMORE: That thy sin of tenth March 1661 can be expiated. (At this strange statement the judge shuffled his papers.)

GODDARD: I did not sentence you on that date. Nor Thomas Kenworthy, neither.

PAXMORE: Thee sentenced the Quaker woman Ruth Brinton to be whipped through Boston and Ipswich and Duxbury. A woman . . . to be lashed naked. (There was a long pause.)

GODDARD: We must defend ourselves. Sedition and heresy eat at the roots of our society. Our colony and our church must defend themselves.

PAXMORE: The burden of that defense sits most heavily on thee, good Judge. I see in thy face the marks of sin. I shall pray for thee.

GODDARD: You leave me no escape, Edward Paxmore. I sentence you to be lashed to the wheel of the great cannon and to be whipped forty times, and then to be taken down and hanged.

PAXMORE: I forgive thee, good Judge. Thee bears a heavy burden.

The carpenter was dragged away to the cell in which his conversion had taken place, and he would have been hanged except that an unprecedented event took place. Late on the Wednesday night before the Friday hanging, Judge Goddard, tall and lonely, sought out the sheriff and directed that officer to open the cell door and then to lock it securely after the judge had entered to talk with the condemned man.

'Edward Paxmore,' the stern judge began, 'I cannot have your blood on my hands.'

'Good Judge, thee should have no blood on thy hands.'

'But suppose a citizen gives secrets to the French and by this act delivers the colony to the enemy?

'That would be treason.'

'Or if a tax collector murders a merchant to take his wife?'

'He has committed an offense against God's law.'

'Do you not confess that your treason is as great? A destruction of the church God has ordained for Massachusetts?'

'Does thee truly believe that God has personally ordained thy harsh and horrid church, so devoid of love?'

'I do. God is a stern taskmaster, as you have learned.'

'God is love, and if He does condemn the tax collector for murdering the merchant and hangs him, He does so in a forgiving mood, just as He forgave King David for a similar crime.'

'Paxmore, I cannot see you die. If I commit an illegal act, will you swear by the God you love not to reveal it?'

This offer presented Paxmore with a double difficulty: as a Quaker, he was forbidden to swear—that is, to use God's existence as security for what he, a mortal, was affirming; and as a Christian, he did not want to be the cause of another man's committing an unlawful act. But he felt deep sympathy for the travail Judge Goddard was undergoing, so he said quietly, 'I am forbidden to swear, good Judge, but I know thy torment, and I will affirm.'

'I accept.'

'I do so affirm.'

'And as to the illegality, the act is mine alone, Paxmore, and does not require your participation.'

'So be it.'

The judge summoned the jailer and caused the cell door to be unlocked. He then surprised that official by leading Paxmore from the cell and into a waiting carriage. Before the judge climbed aboard, he handed the jailer a handful of coins and swore him to secrecy. With that, the carriage headed for the harbor.

'You are to go to Maryland,' the judge said. 'There they are more tolerant.'

'Is not Maryland a part of Virginia? There they whip Quakers, too.'

'The two have broken apart,' the judge said, 'or so I am told.'

'There will be work in Maryland,' Paxmore said. But then he gripped the judge's hand. 'I am not fleeing death, for I am not afraid. Thee is sending me away.'

'I am,' the judge agreed, and after a pause he confided, 'The death of Thomas Kenworthy strangles me at night. Not the hanging, for he was a heretic and deserved hanging. But the whipping prior . . . the wheels of that great cannon . . .'

'Yet you sentenced me to that same cannon. Forty lashes . . . I would not have lived.'

'I did it because . . .' Goddard could find no logical explanation; perhaps he had done it to curry favor with the mob, more likely to justify the action he was about to take.

In the era when Massachusetts backed Parliament, and Maryland the king, it was not easy to travel from one to the other. Few ships sailed, for neither place produced goods required by the other and there were no roads, or carriages to ride upon them. On the other hand, it was easy to reach London, for it was the center of government, of manufacturers and learning; large ships, some surprisingly swift, crossed back and forth constantly and inexpensively, and many captains formed the habit of stopping en route at the fairest of the Caribbean Islands.

In 1664 Barbados was a lively metropolitan center, with ships from many nations in its harbor and fine stores along its waterfront. Books could be obtained and choice stuffs from France and Spain. Here legal papers could be cleared as easily as in London, and there were schools which the children of the American colonists could attend.

'I'm placing you aboard a ship to Barbados,' Judge Goddard said. 'From there you can easily get to Maryland.' The judge gave the captain money for passage, then handed Paxmore a purse, and while the carpenter tucked the money into his belt, the driver of the carriage rummaged in the boot of his vehicle to produce Paxmore's saws and adzes.

'It's better this way,' Goddard said. 'If you ever reappear in Massachusetts, I shall hang you before nightfall.'

'Why?'

'Because you are a threat to the tranquillity of our colony.'

'I would that I could rock it from its base.'

'I know. There will be others like you, but we shall prevail. Now go.'

Paxmore took his tools, bowed gravely to the judge who had saved his life, and climbed aboard the Barbados boat. At dawn the captain lifted anchor and the long, pleasant journey to the island paradise was under way.

In Barbados, Paxmore was kept in his cabin until inquiries had been made ashore, and after a while a bustling ship's chandler named Samuel Spence came aboard demanding in a stern voice, 'Where is this Edward Paxmore?' and when the carpenter was produced, Spence embraced him, crying, 'I am one of thy persuasion.'

'A Quaker? Is it possible?'

'In Barbados anything is possible,' and he led the bewildered carpenter down onto the quay and into a world Paxmore could not have imagined. There was a richness here that Boston had never known, and a freedom of spirit that was remarkable.

'Are not Quakers beaten here?' Paxmore asked.

Spence laughed and said, 'Who would bother? There's money to be made and work to be done, and each man prays as he will.'

'Thee meets in public?'

'Of a certainty.'

'Could we go to the meeting place?'

'On Sunday, yes. At least thirty will be there.'

'I mean now.'

'It would be to no purpose, Friend Edward. Is thee a good carpenter?'

'I do good work.'

'I can believe it. Thy tools are in excellent condition. We need a carpenter, and the wages are generous.'

'Wages?' In his entire life up to now, and he was thirty-five years old that year, he had never worked for wages, always as an indentured servant.

Spence moved him from ship to ship, mending spars, shaving away doors that had stuck and building cupboards in new spots. Within days Paxmore had three offers of permanent positions, and he had not yet seen the meeting house, but on Sunday, Spence took him to a shed attached to the home of a prosperous merchant, and there the Quakers of Barbados showed Paxmore for the first time what worship in the new style consisted of.

Four plain chairs were set against one wall, and on them sat three older men and a woman, all wearing hats. In the body of the shed benches were lined, with a rope down the middle indicating that men were to sit on one side, women on the other. The rest of the shed was severely plain, with no adornment of any kind, and as the meeting got under way the benches filled, and the Quakers kept their hands folded in their laps, looking straight ahead.

No one spoke. This was the holy time of which Thomas Kenworthy had told him, the time when the spirit of God descended and occupied both the meeting place and the hearts of those gathered therein.

Forty minutes passed, and in the solemn silence Edward Paxmore reflected on the curious destiny that had brought him here and would soon cause him to move on. His physical being cried out for him to stay here, in comfort and convenience, with an assured job and new friends who wanted him to stay, but the inner voice of which Kenworthy had spoken urged him to Maryland and the duties awaiting him there.

Eighty minutes passed, and still the Quakers sat in silence. Then one of the men on the facing chairs rose and said in a high voice, 'We have amongst us this day a friend from Massachusetts. How goes it there?'

For more than a minute Paxmore was unable to realize that he was being called upon to speak in a Quaker meeting, and he did not know what to do. He sat dumbly, whereupon the man with the high voice rose again and said, 'Friend Edward, thee would deprive us of needful knowledge. I pray thee, speak.'

So Paxmore rose and looked at the four silent figures on the facing chairs. He wanted to tell them what life in Massachusetts was like for a Quaker, to share with them the whippings, and the loneliness, and the exile of spirit. But in the churches of New England he had heard enough of ranting and of self-appointed men who had the answer for everything. He would never speak like that, nor raise his voice and shout God's thunder. He was done with ranting.

'In Massachusetts we do not meet like this,' he said quietly. 'There is a law, written down, which determines that Quakers are heretical and treasonous, and when caught they are tied to the tailgate of carts and dragged from village to village and whipped as they go.' He dropped his voice and added, 'Women and men alike, stripped naked to the waist and whipped.'

He stood silent, trying to control his emotions so that his voice would not rise, and no one in the shed made a sound. Finally he coughed ever so slightly and concluded, 'A meeting like this, in peace, sitting with Friends, is beyond the imagination of Quakers in Massachusetts, who sit in jail with their feet bound by chains. This is not only the First Day of the week. It is the First Day of my new life.'

No one else spoke, but when the meeting broke, the Quakers of Barbados clustered about Paxmore to ask if he had knowledge of this or that Quaker who had passed through the island on the way to Boston, and he was able to recite a doleful litany: 'He was hanged. She was tied to the great cannon and whipped. He is preaching in the fields near Ipswich, but I fear for him.'

And then an older man took him by the arm, and when they were apart, said, 'Thank thee, Friend Edward, for thy spiritual message, which heartened us. But did thee have to say, in public meeting, the word *naked?*' Paxmore said, 'I think it was necessary,' and the old Quaker said, 'Perhaps so, but to speak of a woman naked . . . even though it was not of her doing . . .' He was not at all sure.

On Monday, Paxmore became involved with a task that made little impression on him at the time but which would later exert an indelible influence on his life. An English ship put into Barbados carrying as passenger the captain of another vessel, and this man hurried to Spence's chandlery complaining that while approaching the neighboring island of St. Lucia he had been attacked by pirates. With ample muskets and fixed guns his crew had been able to hold off the pirates and even to inflict substantial damages.

'If no harm to thy ship, what's the problem?' Spence asked.

'During the fight, while the crew was occupied, our cargo of slaves revolted and ripped chains from the moorings.'

'They can be fixed.'

'But when we unloaded them they tore up the barracoon.'

'That's serious,' Spence said gravely. 'Can't have slaves rioting.' And he arranged for Paxmore and two other carpenters to return with the captain to St. Lucia to repair the ship and the barracoon.

It was a pleasant sail over the beautiful green-blue waters of the Caribbean, and Paxmore was in a happy frame of mind when the ship approached Marigot Bay, where the damaged vessel rested. He was not prepared for the beauty that awaited him: the entrance to the bay was scarcely visible from the open sea, but once attained, it spread before Paxmore's eyes a wonderland of green mountains, tropical valleys and blue water. It was one of the finest small harbors in the world, a place of enchantment, and here the wounded vessel waited.

It required only two days for the carpenters to repair the damage done by the pirates and the rioting slaves; then everyone moved ashore to mend the barracoon. This was a high-walled enclosure in which slaves from all ships putting into Marigot were deposited prior to reshipment to either Brazil or the English colonies of North America. Useless ones, or those who looked as if they might not survive passage to America, were jammed into whatever ship passed and sold in Haiti for six or eight months' service before they died.

The present cargo of slaves, having engineered a partially successful mutiny during the pirate attack, had gone on to rip away the top planking of the barracoon and showed promise of destroying the rest, if allowed. 'I don't want to shoot them,' the captain explained, 'but we can't let them break loose.'

'The whole should be reinforced,' Paxmore said, and the semi-pirates who operated Marigot agreed, so for three more days the carpenters worked, and during this time Paxmore had many opportunities to observe the extraordinary natural beauty of this place; its combination of steep hills and deep water entranced him, and he thought: Some day when Maryland is finished I would like to live here.

The barracoon, on the other hand, made little impression on him, and the slaves imprisoned within, none at all. In Boston he had had no chance to observe blacks. Occasional families had owned slaves, but in a city they were much like indentured servants and were treated in the same way. Now he saw several hundred crowded together and guarded by muskets, and his only thought was: They look sturdy, all of them.

To him black slaves were merely an extension of the indenture system of which he had been a part. In London, prior to sailing to the New World, he and his fellows had been sequestered in barracoons, and on landing in Boston he had been auctioned off. He had been a slave of sorts, and his slavery had been an avenue to a better life. The only difference between him eleven years ago and these blacks now was that their indenture was for life, and could be discharged by no passage of years, no amount of faithful servitude.

He could not comprehend the implications of this difference, because to him the idea of a perpetual indenture made common sense, for the black would enjoy a fixed position, a known security and a permanent master with whom he could establish a workable relationship. Paxmore could not, as he hammered the final boards of the barracoon into position, anchoring them with chains, perceive the dreadful moral problem that would arise if the permanent indenture of these blacks were extended to their children, and their children's children to all generations. That was slavery of a kind he could not envisage for himself.

But he felt no necessity to give the problem serious thought, and when the barracoon was mended he had three fine days to enjoy Marigot Bay before returning to Barbados, and he spent them well, imprinting on his mind the peculiarities of the tropics. But on the evening of the third day an English trading ship rushed into the bay with alarming news: 'Pirates are loose again. They raided Port Royal and were seen heading south.' So all slaves in the barracoon were hastily loaded into the trader and sails were raised for Maryland. It was on this ship that Paxmore embarked.

Once the slaves had been deposited in Jamestown, the ship proceeded to Devon with crates of furniture, and here he walked down the gangplank, wide-eyed, to inspect his new surroundings. He was met by a handsome gray-haired man nearing fifty, who extended his hand and a most cordial invitation: 'I'm Henry Steed, and if you're looking for work, I surely need a carpenter.'

'I was sent to the Quakers of the Choptank.'

'Hard people to work for. You'll do better here.'

'I am a Quaker.'

'In Maryland, no significance. I pay well, Mr. . . .'

'Paxmore.' He liked the concept of an employer's offering to hire a workman before asking his name. 'I would like to work for thee, but I am obligated to seek out the Quakers first.'

'And so you should, if promised.' And then, to Paxmore's surprise, Mr. Steed arranged for one of his own boats to forward Paxmore up the river to the spot where the Steeds had recently opened a large warehouse. 'It's called Patamoke Landing,' Steed explained. 'Few houses but much activity.'

'I am surprised thee would offer thy boat to a stranger,' Paxmore said.

'We are hungry for settlers. Quakers seem as good as any.'

When the bateau entered the harbor, Edward Paxmore saw a sight which put his wandering heart at rest: a secure haven from storms, a rude log hut serving as a tavern, two houses, a score of boats come in from neighboring headlands. Someone rang a bell, and people gathered from unexpected places.

'Are there any women among the newcomers?' two young men asked.

'Only a carpenter,' one of Steed's boatmen called back, and the young men departed.

'Mr. Carpenter! Mr. Carpenter!' an excited man shouted. 'My name's Pool.'

Bidding for Paxmore's services began before he landed, for others called out their names, advising him that he was needed, but he gave no sign of recognition, and when he finally stepped ashore, clutching his saw and axes, he said, 'I seek James Lamb.'

From a group of men standing beside the Steed warehouse, a man stepped forward and extended his hand. 'I am James Lamb and I welcome thee to Patamoke Landing.' He added that he had no need for a carpenter but that his fellow Quaker, Robert Pool, did.

A child, hearing this statement, called, 'Robert Pool, thee is wanted,' and a tall, serious man hurried up.

'I'm Pool, the man who hailed thee.'

For some intuitive reason Paxmore believed that he must keep close to James Lamb, and he told Pool, 'I have already spoken with Friend Lamb,' and Lamb understood the newcomer's hesitancy, for he told Pool, 'I shall be taking our friend to my house,' and then he asked, 'What is thy name?'

'Edward Paxmore.'

'The man from Boston?'

'Yes.'

'Oh . . .' Lamb said the word gravely, then quietly moved among the crowd, informing them that this was Paxmore of Boston, and a collection of Quakers formed a circle about the carpenter, asking questions that indicated both their familiarity with his history in Massachusetts and the deference in which they held him.

'How did thee hear of the whippings?' he asked simply.

'Two months ago a ship reached us from Boston,' Lamb said almost reverently, 'and it carried a Quaker woman who had suffered much in Massachusetts.'

'Ruth Brinton?' Paxmore asked.

'Yes,' Lamb said.

Paxmore surveyed the crowd more intently, then asked, 'Did she die?' And Lamb replied, 'No, she is at my house . . . sorely ill.'

The entire group of Quakers went immediately to the rough-wood house of James Lamb, and as they approached the low-slung door Lamb called, 'Prudence! Come here!'

From the doorway appeared a thin, handsome woman of forty, dressed in handwoven heavy cloth and a tight bonnet. She kept her hands folded over her waist and asked, 'What's thee want?' And then she appreciated how large the crowd was. 'What is it, James?'

'This is Edward Paxmore, from Boston.'

Prudence Lamb dropped her hands and stared at the carpenter. Tears came into her eyes, and she fell to her knees and bowed her head. 'Thee is a man of heroic resolve,' she said. 'Ruth Brinton has told us.'

And James Lamb helped his wife to her feet, and they went into the small house, and there lying on a bed was Ruth Brinton, small, frail and near death from her final course of beatings in Massachusetts. And when she saw the carpenter who had volunteered to take her lashes onto himself, she dissolved in tears, and from that moment her mending started.

The Cliff

ALL QUAKERS WHO LIVED NEAR THE LITTLE SET-
tlement at Patamoke were so pleased when Edward Paxmore married
Ruth Brinton, and so in debt to them spiritually for having fought the
battles of Quakerism in Virginia and Massachusetts, they banded together to give the couple a homesite. A small fund was collected and a
piece of land chosen near the harbor, but when the deed was about to
be transferred, James Lamb interrupted with the information that he
owned, beyond the marshes inhabited by the Turlocks, a headland he
had always intended occupying as one of the finest spots on the river, and
he would be pleased to yield this to the Paxmores.

The committee got into boats and sailed down the Choptank past the
marshes and to that cliff-protected headland which Pentaquod, eighty-
one years earlier, had chosen for his first home on the mainland. It was
still a stunning location, with incomparable vistas in three directions and
a warm sense of security among the tall pines and solid oaks. On this
headland one seemed part of a vast panorama of bays and rivers and
inlets and at the same time an intimate part of a small protected world.

'I do like this,' Paxmore said, but before he would make any commitment he deferred to his wife. 'What does thee think, Ruth?'

'Where will thy work be?' she asked, paying respect to the basic
Quaker tenet that in this world men and women must work. After
obedience to God, faithful performance of one's job is what counts.

'I would carpenter for the settlers, but we would have our permanent
home here—that is, if thee should want to live in a remote . . .'

'Oh, I should!' she cried with an enthusiasm she could not suppress.
She had seen too much of civil strife, and the prospect of living now on
a promontory which overlooked the world was irresistible. Here they

would build a home matched to the winds, on a plateau protected by cliffs. It was she who gave the place its name: 'Peace Cliff we shall call it.' And along the river it became a symbol of stability, the headland on which the Quakers lived.

They spent three days, with the assistance of friends, building an Indian wigwam at the far edge of the cliff, and as soon as they were alone Ruth Brinton began the rebuilding of her husband.

'Why does thee wear clothes which look too small?' and he replied, 'I like my wrists to be free so I can work with my hands.'

'But thee doesn't work with thy feet. Why wear such short trousers?' and he explained, 'A carpenter has to find his timber in many places and I want my ankles to be free.'

'Thee could still look a little neater,' she complained, but he kissed her and said, 'Thee's the neat one, little hummingbird,' and whenever he saw her, trim and delicate in her simple gray clothes, he felt a surge of love, and in time she surrendered; her husband was an ungainly carpenter who would never look neat, himself, but who had a positive passion for producing neat work.

In the autumn of 1664, in a burst of joyful energy, he demonstrated just how fine a carpenter he was: he built two edifices which would earn him a place in Maryland history, and a third object whose impact would vitalize the Eastern Shore. The first building was his own home; with the help of four Indians and two Quaker youths whose parents sent them to aid the newcomers, he cut and joined timber for a modest, two-room house. 'It would be pretentious and displeasing to God if we built larger,' he told Ruth Brinton, and she agreed. They used few nails and nothing imported from England, but built so carefully that their little Quaker house would survive for centuries. Secure on its headland and visible for miles along the river, it became the sturdiest of the Choptank homes.

The second building was more important, and since it was larger, it required the services not only of the four Indians and two youths but also of adult Quakers in the community. In Patamoke, James Lamb had acquired another piece of property which he was willing to cede to the Quakers generally if on it they would build a meeting house. This plain sect avoided the word *church* as smacking too much of architecture rather than purpose; Quakers built meeting houses, and the one Edward Paxmore designed for Patamoke, and built as a testimony of his appreciation for the haven they had provided him, was a masterpiece. In time it would become America's oldest surviving house of worship in continuous use, and each year of its existence it would be increasingly appreciated as a work of art.

It was set among trees, a marvelous start for any building. Once the land had been allocated, Paxmore spent three weeks analyzing it before he allowed his associates to chop down a single tree, and even then he adjusted his plans to the trees and not the other way around. He wanted a long lane leading to the door of the meeting house, and although it required some ingenuity to fit this lane among his trees, he finally succeeded, so that the entrance to the land became a kind of invitation to prayer.

Thus oriented, Paxmore felt at ease, and in an open space laid out a rectangular building with its central doorway in the middle of the long axis. It was a one-story building with a high roof and over the central doorway a rise in the roof, which produced a fine sense of symmetry. The windows were austerely placed so as to carry out the feeling of extended dignity, but it was the inside that captivated all who assembled here.

Directly opposite the door, and running for some distance left and right, rose a small platform reached by a flight of three spacious steps which ran the entire length. On this platform stood six of the simplest oaken chairs, each with curving arms; these were the chairs in which the elders of the meeting would sit, facing the worshippers. Those who occupied these chairs—on some Sundays only two, at other times six—would serve as the ministers and priests of this congregation. Unordained, and often self-nominated, they gave the meeting continuity and substance.

The body of the meeting house consisted of long rows of handsomely proportioned benches with a rigorous aisle down the middle: men sat to the right upon entering, women to the left, but there were many boys and girls in their late teens who mastered the trick of sitting partially sideways so that they could see and be seen across the aisle.

When finished, with all Quakers in the district having participated in the work, Patamoke Meeting, as the place was called, gave proof of what could be accomplished even in a wilderness if a simple workman who had mastered his tools was encouraged to follow his intuitive sense of proportion. He would not be able to construct a Gothic cathedral, which had come at the end of centuries of experimentation and accumulated wisdom in Europe, nor a great Catholic church like those now a-building in Italy, where the same kind of knowledge was available, but he would be quite competent to build a smallish house of worship which seemed to be a part of the forest and a logical outgrowth of the river, and such a building, if it were perfect in each detail and inwardly harmonized, would acquire its own cathedral-like beauty.

'It looks solid,' James Lamb said when it was finished, and on the first Sunday, which the Quakers called First Day, Paxmore occupied by general assent one of the six chairs. Next to him sat the oldest woman in the meeting, and then by quiet acclamation it was indicated that Ruth Brinton Paxmore, as she would be forever known, should sit on the facing bench, too, for she had given greater testimony than any other to the qualities of this new religion. It was these three who conducted the first worship in the plain new building, and for the entire hour and forty minutes no one spoke; all were content merely to savor this home in the wilderness.

The third bit of building that Paxmore engaged in during this hectic year set the pattern for the remainder of his life. It was experimental, beset with failures and wonderfully rewarding. Construction of the home and the meeting house had presented no problems; after all, in England he had progressed far in his trade and had mastered most of the tricks required for putting up a building that would not fall down, but he had never built a boat, and without a skilled ship's carpenter at hand to instruct him, there was little likelihood that he would stumble upon the many devices necessary in such intricate construction. But since he and Ruth intended to live the rest of their lives on the water, it behooved him to learn.

During that first autumn James Lamb had loaned him a small sloop, which he was free to use as long as he wished, but he knew that he was depriving Lamb of his property, and this galled. So as soon as the house was finished he told Ruth, 'I think I must build us a boat.'

'Does thee know how?'

'No. But I will learn.'

He sought as his teachers the Indians who had worked on the meeting house, and on various evenings he accompanied them as they searched his woods for the proper oak. He pointed out a splendid tree, and when they rejected it he wanted to know why. 'How would we get it to the river?' they asked in sign language, and he had to concede that there was no way so mighty a tree could be moved in one piece.

But along the northern boundary of his land, facing not the river but the small creek feeding into it, he did locate a satisfactory specimen which could be dropped in such a position that when burned and shaped, it could be rolled into the water, but the Indians cautioned him against this tree: 'Better choose pine.' And when he asked why, they said, 'Lighter wood. Easier to cut.' But he proceeded with the tree he had selected, explaining, 'I build with oak.'

What a universe of backbreaking work he took upon himself. On the third night Edward limped home and collapsed, keeping his hands over his mouth and blowing into them in an effort to reduce the callus-fevers that consumed them.

'What's wrong?' Ruth asked.

'Has thee ever tried to fell an oak?'

Ruth Brinton was an austere woman of fierce and burning rectitude; she walked with God and understood His plans for people. She had a dozen virtues, but the recognition of day-by-day humor was not one of them. 'Why would I want to fell an oak?' she demanded.

'I was only—'

'If I wanted an oak tree, I would go to those men whose job it is to fell them.'

'Ruth, I was merely—'

'But if the work is difficult and thee feels that I could help, I'd be glad to go with thee tomorrow—'

'Ruth! My hands are blistered. Has thee any bear fat?'

'Oh! Thee wants bear fat. Why didn't thee say so?'

When the tree finally fell, Paxmore understood better why the Indians had followed a system requiring several years to fell a tree: girdle it, burn it, allow the sap to stop running, burn it more, push it over. 'I haven't the time,' he explained to Ruth, but she had her mind fixed on more important matters.

'I've been thinking about the bear grease,' she said. 'I could fix thee a poultice which thee could carry, and during thy work thee could apply a little grease now and then.'

'The ax handle would slip.'

'Get one that doesn't,' she said, and some days later she handed him a carefully sewn bag containing a wad of cloth impregnated with bear grease.

By this time the Indians had removed the branches and were indicating how the ends of the massive trunk should be cut away to permit the molding of the front and rear ends of the canoe. This time Paxmore followed their advice and used fire instead of brute power, and when the twenty-two-foot segment rested beside the creek, he helped the Indians strip off the bark, disclosing a golden object so handsome that it already seemed half-canoe.

By flattening the side that remained on top, he achieved the rude outlines of what he sought, and then, while his Indians set fires to burn away the insides, he proceeded to that difficult task which he must master if he wished to become a boatbuilder: at each end of the log he began to hack away with an adze the unnecessary portions of wood. Working with extreme care, and never cutting away even a fragment until he was satisfied that its departure would enhance the curve of the canoe, he learned how the bow and stern of a boat should evolve naturally from the flow of the wood until each became suited to life in water. This technical skill he could master because he was a good house carpenter, but the intellectual trick the Indians showed him when the nearly finished canoe was rolled over, he could never have deduced himself, and it was this unexpected discovery which enabled him to become a master shipbuilder.

When the great hollowed-out log lay top down at the edge of the water, one of the Indians took a straight piece of timber and with an oyster shell drew a line down the length of the canoe two inches off dead center. Then, using the same implements, he drew a parallel line two inches to the other side of center, and when this was done he and his friends began to scrape away small fragments of oak along the outer edges of this four-inch center area, and after many hours of patient work, and the smoothing down of unwanted wood, they left a slightly raised backbone for the canoe, and Paxmore saw that this would always be the lifeline of the craft. It would give direction and stability; it would keep the canoe from drifting sideways when blown by wind; and it would serve as protection to the rest of the bottom when the canoe was hauled ashore.

In his personal life Edward Paxmore had discovered that a man lived best when he maintained some central belief upon which he could hang all action and to which he could refer all difficult moral problems; he was then vertebrate, with a backbone to sustain him, and he had observed that men and women who failed to develop this central belief wandered and made hideously wrong decisions because in time of crisis they had nothing to which they could refer instantaneously. He had found his backbone in obedience to God, in the simplest form possible and with the most direct access.

He now discovered that a boat also must have a backbone, a central structure of the greatest possible strength that ran the length of the craft without deviation and upon which all the rest depended. During the remainder of his life he would never construct a ship without a backbone of oak; upon this central and immutable fact he would build.

The canoe, with its two masts, was such a success that settlers along the river offered to buy it, but as he told Ruth, 'I haven't the strength to keep chopping down oak trees, nor the time to burn them out inch by inch.'

'Thee would if thee used the bear grease I gave thee,' she said.

What he could do, he saw, was encourage others to cut down oaks and pines and fashion planks from them, which he would then assemble into small boats. But no sooner had he jumped optimistically into this new field than he discovered that building a boat with planks was a task infinitely more difficult than hollowing a log; problems arose which were almost impossible for an ordinary housebuilder to solve. This was the enigma: lay out on a flat piece of ground a backbone of the length desired. To it attach ribs which form more or less the outline of the finished boat. So far so good. But now cut planks which can be attached to those ribs to form a watertight body which at the same time flows softly forward and back to form the bow and stern of the craft. It sounds easy; it is cruelly difficult to do. And when by chance and the blessing of a patient God you master the trick of cutting those planks, how do you secure them fore and aft to the bow and sternpost?

Many residents along the river complimented Paxmore on his canoe, but he realized that the merit was not his; the inherent nature of an oak tree had determined the general form the canoe would take. In building his first craft he couldn't have gone wrong, because the oak wouldn't let him. But in building a small boat, his planks of sawn timber would have no inherent form. He would need a clear concept of what he wished to accomplish, and he had none. So when his first rude boat was finished, no one stepped forward to bid on the monstrous thing; indeed, it barely stayed afloat, and when the sails were raised, it proved unmanageable. The only thing in its favor was the stalwart backbone; the subsidiary parts that determine quality were a mess.

He knew it. 'Look at that thing I call a boat,' he said to Ruth as it lay tied up to their wharf. 'A child could do better.'

'Dearest,' she said with that fearful simplicity which would enrage so many, 'when it comes to building a boat, thee is a child.'

So he determined to start over again as if he were indeed a child learning a totally new skill, and he studied his mistakes, seeing how he had asked wooden planks to perform jobs for which they were not fitted, but always he came back to the great fundamental: lay a solid backbone and see that everything relates properly to it.

He began with a much less pretentious craft, shorter and narrower in the beam, and spent all his time not on the flashy midsection, but on the bow and stern, agonizing over how he could bring all this planking to a finely shaped point, and when he finished he had a boat which didn't look especially attractive, for it had crudities innumerable, but which did sail. This time a man wanted to buy it.

'I'm going to build three more,' he told Ruth, 'and the last one I'm going to name the *Ruth Brinton.* That one will be very good.' And when the last caulking was hammered home he invited Ruth for a celebratory sail, but as they reached the center of the Choptank he said impulsively, 'We'll stop at Devon.' She protested, 'Not in this dress.' She made him return to Peace Cliff and wait till she had donned her best gray cloth and the little Quaker hat that accompanied it; but now when she sat beside her gangling husband he seemed so out of place that she said, 'Thee must dress also. It is the Steeds we're seeing,' and she would not allow him to untie the boat until he had changed.

They looked so proper as they sailed up Devon Creek, he tall and uncomfortable in the new suit she had woven, she prim and tidy with her hands folded, that servants alerted the Steeds, who brought their families to the wharf. 'What a fine boat!' Henry said, and he indicated that Paul should jump down to see if the fittings were as solid as they appeared. When Paul nodded, Henry said, 'Alice, why don't you take Mrs. Paxmore up to the house for tea. We're going for a sail.'

They went down the creek and out into the Choptank and finally the bay itself, with Paxmore tending sail and looking formal in his new suit and flat Quaker hat. When he brought the boat back, with Henry at the tiller, the Steeds were satisfied that this Quaker carpenter had mastered the art of building boats.

'I think we'd better have a drink,' Henry said as they climbed out of the *Ruth Brinton.*

'I don't drink,' Paxmore said.

'Not even tea?'

The carpenter laughed, and when they joined the ladies there was no talk of boats, because Mrs. Steed grabbed hold of Paxmore and told him excitedly, 'It's all arranged! You're to stay here for three days with this wonderful woman'—and she indicated Ruth—'and build me a special cupboard . . . here . . . for these.'

And she pointed to a nearby mantle on which stood, in orderly arrangement, a set of handsome pewter dishes, cups, knives and spoons. 'These are the *lares* and *penates* of the Steeds,' she said.

Paxmore's blank look indicated that he didn't know what she was talking about, but before she could explain, Ruth Brinton cut in with, 'Their household gods. It's a Roman phrase.'

Now Paxmore looked quizzically at his wife, as if the pagan gods to whom she had referred were blasphemous, but Ruth smiled primly and said, 'It's all right. Just means they're precious to the Steeds.'

He relaxed and asked Mrs. Steed, 'What kind of closet had thee in mind?'

'Here in the corner. Covered with this piece of glass we've just received from Holland.'

'That could be quite handsome,' he said as he studied the corner and the fine length of glass. 'Thee would want about six shelves?'

'We'll have to judge that as we proceed,' she said. Then, handing each of the Paxmores a piece of pewter, she confided, 'Grandmother Steed loved this. Once a year for as long as she lived she would serve a meal of deliverance. No glass or china, only the precious old pewter pieces. She did it to remind us of how they had lived in the difficult days.'

Paxmore, feeling the heavy ware, thought that a cupboard to conserve such pieces would be most sensible. 'I'll do it,' he told Mrs. Steed.

In the days that followed he and Ruth had their first opportunity to see a Catholic family at close quarters. Many aspects surprised the Quakers: the voluble prayers before meals instead of the solemn quiet of a Quaker family, the substitute for the Mass in which all members participated, the different Bible, and the perilous approach to paganism in their talk of saints and holy objects. They were particularly impressed by the tales of Father Ralph and his obvious sanctity.

'I think I would like Ralph,' Ruth said, and Paul replied, 'He never has much to do with women. He'd find you quite disturbing.'

'Why?' Ruth asked.

'Your outspokenness. Your willingness to participate in everything.'

'That's the Quaker way,' she said, and Paul replied, 'I know, and that's what Ralph would find disturbing. In his church women don't . . .' He found no way to finish his sentence, but Ruth, unwilling ever to let a challenge pass said, 'In ours they do.'

The Steed brothers found it easier to talk with Edward Paxmore, and one day while the women were admiring the distinguished manner in which the finished cabinet displayed the pewter, they took the carpenter aside and Henry, after coughing twice, said, 'Edward, I think you're ready to build us a ship.'

Paxmore never replied to any invitation in a hurry, and while the brothers waited he calculated how many hours it might take him to build a replica of the *Ruth Brinton.* 'I believe I could build thee a boat like the *Ruth Brinton*—'

'We don't mean a boat, we mean a ship.'

Paxmore was amazed at the proposal. 'You mean . . . a great ship . . . to cross the bay?'

'To cross the Atlantic,' Henry said, and once the words were out he became a persuasive visionary. 'Paxmore, if we owned a ship, we could send our tobacco directly to market and save enormous sums on rentals. We could return with goods for the stores at prices you wouldn't believe.'

'But I've never—'

'We've watched your progress in your last four sailing boats. You've come a far way, Paxmore.'

'That first was a bad job, wasn't it?'

'And we're convinced you're ready to build us a ship for London.'

'I've never built a ship,' Paxmore said quietly. 'I've never learned.'

'A man learns how by building it.'

What Paxmore said next proved that he was a true and cautious Quaker: 'Would thee risk thy own money in such a venture?'

'We would,' the brothers agreed.

Paxmore sat silent for a long time, then rose soberly and returned to the room where the ladies were. Walking directly to his wife, he took her by the hand and said, 'Ruth, we're going home . . . to build a great ship.'

Edward Paxmore was driven into an extended period of moral confusion through no act of his own; it was Samuel Spence's fault. That Barbados ship chandler never forgot that when his helper Paxmore sailed precipitately for Maryland because of looming pirate threats, he departed without having collected the wages due him, so in late 1666 Spence posted a letter, which, when it reached Peace Cliff, would cause the trouble.

In the meantime the lanky carpenter was adhering to the tradition of shipbuilders in early America. He did not establish an arbitrary yard and say, 'Here I will build my ship.' Instead he looked for a concentration of tall trees and there set up his works. The spot he selected was on the creek, close to where he had built his log canoe; it contained one of the most promising oaks he had ever seen, a giant in the sky, plus a substantial supply of pines. So one morning after praying for guidance and good health he started to fell the oak upon which his ship would depend.

With sweating toil he and his Indians swung their axes, and when at last the massive tree dropped close to the creek as planned, he stepped off the fifty-two feet he had decided upon for the backbone; but when he saw how vast a distance this was, he pressed his aching hands against his chest and thought: I can never build a ship of that size. But he was committed and knew that he would succeed only if he proceeded one careful step at a time. Accordingly, he began to chop away the branches, some as large as ordinary trees, and when the massive log lay exposed he studied it for two long days, trying to visualize the finished backbone that he would chop from it and the various ways in which the great body of the ship would relate to it.

With each crucial analysis he realized how ignorant he was, and on the morning of the third day, when he should have begun chipping away unwanted wood, he was paralyzed by self-depreciation. This task was too immense for a house carpenter. But as he sat upon the felled oak, he happened to see riding in the creek his original log canoe, and he asked the Indians to help him haul it ashore. Turning it upside down on the grass, he sat all morning studying the lines, and the subtle manner in which straight expanses of wood merged with round, and how various segments combined to form bow and sternposts, and from this most ancient of shapes, dating back ten thousand years or more, he began to appreciate what could be done and what must be done.

Halting all work except the felling of pine trees, he took a piece of pine and started to whittle a model of the large ship he wished to build, and on this task he spent the better part of two weeks, shaping here and retouching there until he had a miniature craft entirely pleasing to the eye.

But still he lacked confidence, so he had his Indians put the upturned canoe back into the water and in it he sailed to Devon to show the Steeds what he had in mind. As prudent men looking to the future, they had but one suggestion: 'If you make the ship broader at the midsection, it will be able to carry more goods.'

'The bulk would make it sail slower,' Paxmore pointed out.

'We have endless time,' Henry said, and Paxmore attached to the sides of his model thin strips of additional wood, which enabled him to carve a fatter form. When this was completed Henry Steed took a pen and lettered on the stern the name the ship would carry: *Martha Keene, Devon.*

'When the whole is done,' he told Paxmore, 'I'd like to have that model.'

'Thee shall,' the carpenter said, but on the sail back to his informal boatyard he had a beneficial insight: If I cut the model in half, lengthwise, I'll have not only a plan for the outside of the ship, but one for the inside, too. So when he reached the waiting oak he wedged the model into an informal vise and took down his saw, but when he started to make his cut he saw that to do it properly he must rip the backbone into halves, and this he was powerless to do.

Throwing down the saw, he thought, I could never split a backbone, and he pondered an escape, and gradually he uncovered a satisfactory compromise: I'll not touch the backbone. I'll saw alongside it, and this he did, producing not the true half-model required, but a workable approximation, and whenever he used this guide his fingers felt the unviolated backbone, and he was gratified.

Now he started his men hacking away at the oak, and as they worked he made a decision that would save hours of complex labor: The back of the ship will not be pointed. It will be flat.

He then moved to the other end, and here he faced problems of the most acute and perplexing nature: how to hook upon the fore end of the backbone the front end of the ship, which required a rising curve. While the Indians worked squaring away the long reach of the spine, he concentrated on this problem, and saw that if he could shape the forward end of the log into an upward curve, however slight, he would start with an advantage. So quickly he redirected the cutting so that the forward end would achieve the maximum upward sweep. He was not able to gain much, but when the backbone was finally finished, it did curve upward, and on this advantage he would erect the crucial forward thrust of his ship.

But with each success new problems evolved and now he must determine the precise manner in which the bow of his ship, the cutting edge which would breast the waves, would be put together. He had not the slightest instruction as to how this could be accomplished. He was a house carpenter, but like any prudent man he could sit down and apply what he knew about houses to ships, and the crucial fact he clung to was that an open rectangle could never be stable, because sufficient pressure at any one of the corners would collapse it, whereas a diagonal, if hammered securely into position, would permit enormous pressures to be exerted on the corners without collapse; the resulting triangles might break apart, or the wood might shatter, but they were stable.

Abstractly, the problem was simple: crisscross the interior of the ship with diagonals and no storm would ever be able to collapse its sides; of course, no cargo or passengers could be loaded either, because the interior would be consumed with diagonals.

So the problem really became this: how to achieve the rigidity of the diagonal without using ones which would prohibit the loading of cargo? Like most important difficulties, it was easily stated, laboriously solved.

He was at an impasse. How he wished that some great ship from London would sail into Devon so that he might inspect it. None came.

One page of a book from London would explain everything, but he had no such books. Bitterly he recalled his tedious days aboard the ships that had carried him from London to Boston to Barbados to Marigot Bay to Devon: I spent all that time on ships and saw nothing.

That was not entirely correct. He had seen a great deal about decking a ship and building bulwarks and finishing off the gunwales, but like an artist who rides a horse a hundred times, and never comprehends it until he tries to draw it, or like a novelist who has witnessed a human situation repeatedly but has not really understood it until forced to state in cold words what happened, he had lived in the heart of ships but had not seen them.

Ironically, during his confusion, the solution lay all about him . . . on the ground. As he paced at the forward end of his log, eyes fastened on the waiting curve, he happened to stumble, and when he looked down to see what had tripped him, he saw the massive roots of the oak sweeping sideways from the stump of the severed trunk. He stopped, studied the curious joint made by root and trunk, then knelt and began feverishly scraping away the earth, and when he finished he had laid bare one of the most powerful joints in nature, the flexed kneelike structure that is formed where a heavy root branches out from a main trunk, and as it lay exposed Paxmore realized that he had found the solution to his problem: instead of bracing his exposed bow with cumbersome diagonals, he would build into it this massive joint which contained its own bracing.

But when he turned to his Indians, about to ask them to help him dig out this knee, he found that they had gone; they were tired of building ships and would work no more. For him to continue without them would be impossible, so in profound anxiety he launched his log canoe by himself and sailed to Devon to ask the Steeds what he must do. When he reached there he found them occupied at the wharf, for a ship from Barbados had recently dropped anchor in Jamestown, and the Steed sloop had brought across the bay Samuel Spence's extraordinary letter and a cargo which Paxmore could not have anticipated:

> I have been haunted by the debt I owe thee in payment of the good work thee did for me, especially the rebuilding of that ship at Marigot Bay, and I have constantly wondered how to repay thee. Coins we have none, and our correspondents in London are in worse shape than we. They cannot hope to pay my bills, for the plague last year and the fire this have decimated them, and I had concluded that my debt to thee would have to stand undischarged, when a singular chain of circumstances put me in a position to aid thee.

> A gentleman of this island owed a debt to one of the London firms who owed me, and we agreed that he should simplify

things and pay me, but he had no money neither. He did, however, possess an interest in a slave ship due to arrive from Luanda, and when it put in to our port, he delivered to me a portion of his slaves.

I am making bold to send thee nine of these Negroes in discharge of my debt in hopes that thee will consider this fair exchange. Quakers who have passed through here advise us that thee has married Ruth Brinton, that stalwart spirit, and we send thee both our love.

The slaves had not yet been unloaded, and when Paxmore went to the sloop he found them huddled forward, and he wondered why, in the safety of harbor, they still clung together, but when he jumped down into the boat he saw that they had been chained to prevent disturbance during the passage across the bay. He stood for a moment scrutinizing these strangers: he saw their black forms, their promising muscles, the way in which the women held themselves proudly, even in chains.

'Cut them loose and I'll take them to Peace Cliff,' he called to Henry Steed, but Steed, who had often overheard Jamestown planters gossiping about their slaves, said cautiously, 'Safer to keep them bound till they're off the water,' and he directed his captain to sail the sloop to the cliff. There the blacks were marched onto the wharf, still in chains: six strong men, three women of childbearing age, all wearing iron collars. The Eastern Shore had received its first cargo of slaves, the lawful property of Quakers.

'All prime,' the captain said as he threw the chains back into the sloop.

'We can use them,' Paxmore said. The women he led to the house, where Ruth Brinton was on the floor, nailing together an extra table for her kitchen. She was astonished to see the blacks and asked, 'What are these?'

'They're ours.'

'In what way?'

'Samuel Spence, in Barbados, sent them in discharge of his debt to me.'

'And what are we to do with them?'

'They belong to us. They're our slaves.'

Ruth Brinton rose, wiped her hands, and studied the women. She could remember when she was that age, burdened with perplexities, and thought: How much greater theirs must be. To her husband she said, 'It would be quite improper for us to hold slaves. It would be against the will of God.'

And then began the great debate which would ultimately invade every legislature, every church and every home. Edward Paxmore cited three facts, the first two of which were economic and therefore of little persuasion where Ruth Brinton was concerned: 'Spence owed me the money and had the right to pay it in his way. Also, the slaves arrive just when we need them most. God must have sent them to help us finish the ship.'

His wife looked at him, aghast that he would offer such irrelevancies, but his third citation was moral, and not at all irrelevant: 'When I was an indentured servant in Massachusetts it was the custom for preachers to sermonize once each quarter on the duties of servant to master. How well I recall those thundering admonitions!' And he began to recite, as he remembered them, those compelling passages in which God specifically ordained and supported a system of slavery:

> 'Servants, obey in all things your masters, not with eye-service only but in fear of God.
>
> Servants, be obedient to them that are your masters with fear and trembling.
>
> Servants are to please their masters in all things, not answering again.
>
> Let all servants who are under the yoke count their masters as worthy of all honor.'

Ruth Brinton was appalled as she heard this recital; she could not believe that he was taking such teaching seriously. It was as if she were seeing for the first time the whole profile of her husband—and it was ugly.

'Edward,' she said with iron force in her soft words, 'does thee not realize that the whole teaching of Jesus is opposed to the slavery of one man to another?'

'I only know what the Bible says, and it says over and over that some men are to be slaves, and are bound to obey their masters.' Before his wife could interrupt he said, 'Now, the Bible also says that masters must be just, and that they must look after the welfare of the slave. The ministers in Boston used to emphasize that, too. In fairness to them I must say they always warned the masters to be gentle.' Then, in recollection of those distant sermons, he added, 'But I do recall that they warned us servants more sternly than they warned our masters.'

He would be a good master. He stopped all work on the ship so that stout cottages could be built for his slaves. He suggested to Ruth Brinton that she take the women into the house to do the heavy work, but she refused. She did, however, train one of them to look after her baby; the others grew vegetables and tended tobacco.

The men, tall and straight, proved excellent helpers at the ship, Abiram and Dibo showing such skill in ripping out planks that Paxmore established a sawyers' pit for them: huge pine logs were rolled into position atop a deep pit, in which Dibo stood day after day. Abiram, the stronger of the two, perched on the log, holding a long two-handled saw whose teeth he kept biting into a straight line along the pine. At the shout of an African word, Dibo in the pit would jump in the air, wrap himself about the saw's handle and exert all his weight in pulling downward. This descent of the saw made the cut; Dibo then pulled it loose, shouted another word, and Abiram would haul the heavy saw back into position. In this way, these two men hacked out the planks from which the ship would be constructed.

But when the time came to fit the timbers to the keel, and thus form the skeleton of the ship, Paxmore ran out of roots with which to brace his work. He searched the cliff area for oak roots formed into right angles, but found none; he did uncover a few of pine, but quickly learned that these lacked the requisite strength, and he was wandering far from his own lands when he came upon Stooby Turlock hunting wolves. He reported to his wife on this first meeting:

> 'He seemed a visitor from another world, a grown man of twenty-six with the ignorance of a four-year-old. However, when I indicated that I was searching for special tree roots, he understood at once and led me to at least nine oaks containing splendid specimens. He displayed such unusual knowledge of trees, that I invited him to work with me, but this word frightened him.'

When Paxmore required additional roots to frame out the ship, he looked for Stooby but did not find him. Learning that the young man lived in the marsh with his disreputable father, he sailed there one afternoon, failed to find the entrance, and was beating about the edges when a musket shot rattled past the canoe. Rising from the rushes like an apparition, Timothy Turlock shouted, 'Who that?'

'I'm looking for Stooby.'

Turlock spat in the water, then indicated where the entrance to his creek lay, and when Paxmore drew up to the rickety wharf the old man was waiting. 'Can I see Stooby?' the carpenter asked.

'Not here.'

'Why didn't you tell me—'

'You can wait.' He helped Paxmore from the canoe, then led him to a filthy shack in which a heavyset blonde was lounging. She made no effort to greet him, so he sat on a log which had been propped on tripod legs, and as he waited there he became aware that in one corner of the hut a young girl was standing.

'It's Nancy from James Lamb's!' he cried, rather pleased to find someone he knew. 'What's thee doing here?'

'She run away,' Turlock said. Paxmore could not know that this was the child with whom old Turlock had frequently been found in bed. He assumed that she had escaped for the usual reasons given by servants and slaves.

'James Lamb is a kind master,' he argued, and no one refuted him.

Stooby did not appear, and after a prolonged wait which grew more and more unpleasant, for the hut and its occupants were loathsome, Paxmore announced that he must get back to the cliff. 'Mr. Turlock, will thee please tell thy son I need more roots?'

'I may,' and the visit ended, but three days later Stooby came to the shipyard with word that he had located more than two dozen excellent specimens and that if Paxmore would assign three slaves to do the digging, he would deliver them to the site. It was in this offhanded way that Stooby began working for Paxmore, never on a regular basis, for he refused to be tied to any job; he simply responded whenever Paxmore needed special timbers or roots.

'He's really stupid,' Paxmore told his wife, 'and yet he isn't.' What he failed to discover was that whenever Stooby delivered wood, he studied with ratlike eyes every new step taken in building this ship. In the end, Stooby would know as much about building ships as Paxmore, and he would have taken one more giant stride toward becoming the complete waterman: he would know not only the waters but the ships that sailed them.

The most remarkable aspect of Edward Paxmore's shipbuilding was his collection of tools. Whatever he needed, he had to fashion for himself, and at the end of two years he owned an amazing collection of implements. He had, of course, his saws and adzes, those sovereign tools of the boatbuilder; Paul Steed, watching him carve a plank with delicate precision, told his brother, 'Paxmore could write his name with an adze.'

He made clamps for holding small items, gouges for tearing away unwanted wood, augurs for boring holes, and the most intricate saws. Since nails were precious beyond gold—all colonial construction depended upon what could be imported from England—he learned to carve small pieces of oak into nail-like forms; when they were hammered or screwed into position and water applied, they swelled and held disparate parts together almost as well as metal nails.

But always he lacked the essential tool without which the workman can never attain true mastery: he did not know the names of any of the parts he was building, and without the name he was artistically incomplete. It was not by accident that doctors and lawyers and butchers invented specific but secret names for the things they did; to possess the name was to know the secret. With correct names one entered into a new world of proficiency, became the member of an arcane brotherhood, a sharer of mysteries, and in the end a performer of merit. Without the names one remained a bumbler or, in the case of boatbuilding, a mere house carpenter.

Paxmore would always remember the July morning on which a two-masted Bristol tobacco trader put into Devon, and the joy with which he scrambled through all parts of the ship, asking the ship's carpenter what the various parts were. It was then that he began to unravel the mystery of names.

'*Trunnels* we calls 'em,' the man said of the tree nails Paxmore had been carving, and as trunnels they acquired added value, for this meant that they were part of an ancient heritage.

'It ain't *backbone*. It's *keel.* And the plank we attach on top for tying into is *keelson.*' But the word which pleased him most was the one the Englishman used for the bent roots upon which the stability of the ship depended. 'Them's *knees,* and you best cut 'em from hackmatack. Better'n oak.'

The measurements of a cut board were the *scantlings,* the squared-off rear was the *transom,* the piece of timber used to extend the bowsprit a *jib boom,* and the splice of timbers a *scarph.* But what astonished him was the fact that *floor* meant not an extended flat area, as in a house, but the small, rugged timber jammed up against the keel, on which the inner bottom of the ship was framed.

On this visit Paxmore picked up a hundred words, and with each, a new insight to his task, but none of his new knowledge disturbed him so much as what he discovered about the mast. For his ship he had trimmed a very tall pine tree into a perfect cylinder, and had erected it in an arbitrary manner at an arbitrary spot. Now he learned that he had done everything wrong.

'No! No!' the English carpenter admonished. 'Never a rounded base! Because if it's rounded at the bottom, how are you going to wedge it fast where it stands in its step upon the keelson? And if it's rounded where it passes through the deck, how can you caulk it to prevent leaks?'

He took Paxmore to the lowest section of his ship and showed him how the shipbuilders of the world stepped their masts. 'At the bottom, keep the tree a square. Then it can be set into this box, and knees can be thrown against it, and it can be wedged along straight lines, and no wind can move it.'

What a difference between a real mast and the one Paxmore had devised! The true one stood firm, wedged powerfully on all sides, four-square with the keel. His wobbled because its circular base provided no secure line for wedging.

'Now, at this height, as she approaches the hole through the deck, trim her to the octagonal,' and the Englishman showed what a handsome job the Bristol shipbuilders had done in modulating a square base into an octagonal riser; the eye could scarcely see where the shift had been made, and as the mast passed through the deck, a vital transit, it provided eight solid sides which could be wedged and waterproofed. Paxmore's was a leaky mess.

'It's only when we get up here,' the Bristol man said as they stood on deck, 'that you allow the octagon to become a circle,' and again the shift from one geometrical form to the other had been achieved with a lovely delicacy. 'You know why we want 'em round above deck?'

'No.'

'She don't fight the wind. And another thing, if your mast is truly seated and properly wedged, it'll stand of itself. The weight of the wind on the sail will push her down into the step and hold her there. Paxmore, don't let anyone guy your mast so tight it sings like a harp. The shrouds should be loose, always loose. They're not there to wrench the mast into position, only to give it help if a gale strikes.' And he led Paxmore to each of the shrouds protecting the mast and demonstrated how loose they were, bearing no pressure in times of calm but available in time of sudden stress.

And then he said something which quite staggered the novice. ''Course you placed your mast properly?'

'I centered it on the backbone . . . the keel . . . I mean the keelson.'

''Course. But I mean fore and aft.'

'I put it . . .' The vague look that came into Paxmore's eyes betrayed the fact that he knew nothing of sail capacity, or balance, or the moment of forces acting upon a ship under way, or the intricate problem of placing a mast so that winds upon the sail did not lift the bow or depress it or cause it to yaw.

'You know nothing of placing masts, do you?' the Bristol man asked.

'No.'

'Well, caulk her strong and pray she floats. Improvements come with experience.'

In December 1668 a pinnace crossed the bay, bringing to Devon Island a visitor who gladdened the hearts of everyone. He was Father Ralph Steed, fifty-two years old and gray from his labors throughout Maryland. He rested on the wharf to survey the impressive changes made at Devon since his prior visit: the substantial wharf, the broad paths leading to the constantly growing wooden house, the glassed-in windows, the second chimney bespeaking the added rooms, and above all, the sense of serene accomplishment. In his youth this had been a precarious foothold in the wilderness; now it was becoming the seat of country gentlefolk.

'I am especially pleased to see that you have got hold of some slaves,' he told his brothers. 'Properly utilized, they can be of great assistance to a plantation, and contact with their white masters does much to save their souls.'

It was a privilege to renew acquaintance with his brothers, and he was astounded by the fecundity of their wives: Henry had two sons and a daughter, Paul three boys and two girls, and this third generation already contained eleven grandchildren, not counting the many infants who had died. But the gem of the collection was a blond boy of seven, roguish and unfairly handsome, who took an immediate liking to his great-uncle and bowed with exaggerated politeness as he said, 'We are glad to see you in Devon again, Uncle Ralph.'

'That's Fitzhugh,' Henry said proudly, 'my grandson.'

'He'll be counselor-of-state, with his winning ways,' the priest said, holding the child by the hand as he told the brothers, 'It's remarkable and a thing pleasing to God that our family has always been able to find Catholic girls to marry.' But as he said this he winced and had to drop Fitzhugh's hand.

'Your hip?'

'Fell from a horse. It's nothing.' He made no complaints about his harsh life, but he did lodge one protest, and that most sternly. 'You haven't rebuilt the chapel!'

'It was too conspicuous,' Henry said, shrugging his shoulders in self-justification.

'I was conspicuous on every river,' Ralph chided, and no more was said about the chapel. But as soon as he reached the house with its handsome new porch he asked that the family be convened for the reading of a Mass, and when the brood was collected and he had greeted each new acquaintance, he offered a family celebration. Afterward he pointed to the corner cupboard containing the pewter and told his brothers, 'I like that. We had stern days and it's good to remember them.'

He was voracious in his desire for details regarding the operation of the plantation, and told Henry, 'It's a shame the Eastern Shore cannot grow sweet-scented leaf like Virginia. The Oronoco you grow over here always brings less in London.'

'It does well in France,' Henry said. 'They seem to like our heartier flavor.'

'I've brought with me some seeds of a tougher strain of sweet-scented. We should see if it will prosper in our soil.'

'It won't. We've tried all possible strains, and it's perverse. Sweet-scented, like beautiful ladies, grows only in Virginia. Oronoco, like real men, grows in Maryland.'

Father Steed also wanted to know how negotiations with Fithian were progressing, and Paul said, 'I visited him in London last year. He's older now and his sons are handling our affairs. Admirably, too.'

'He took possession of two plantations along the James last year,' the priest said. 'There was ugly talk, and I feared for our relations with him.'

'That's always been the story of the Virginia planters,' Paul said defensively. 'They earn a thousand pounds with their sweet-scented and order eleven hundred pounds' worth of goods. If they do this long enough, Fithian owns their land.'

'Are we in debt to him?'

'The other way around. We keep a cash balance in our favor.'

'How is that possible?'

'We've opened a warehouse at Patamoke Landing. People up and down the river come there to trade with us.' And he called for a bateau to take Ralph to the growing settlement. 'The long low building is ours,' he said as the boat entered the harbor. 'And that place by the wharf is a tavern. Only three houses so far, but I've deeded thirty acres to Lord Baltimore for the settling of a town, and he's promised to issue an ordinance appointing Oxford and Patamoke Landing ports of entry for ships in general trade.'

'Any industry?'

'None yet, but I've been contemplating giving that land over there to Edward Paxmore for a boatyard.'

'You've spoken of him several times,' the priest said. 'Who is he?'

'One of the best carpenters in England. Came to settle on our river. He's a Quaker.'

'He is?' the priest said. 'Oh, I should like to meet him. Wherever I go I hear of this new sect. Most contradictory reports. I'd like to meet one face-to-face.'

'That's easy. His boatyard is on the way home. He's building a ship for us, you know.'

'A real ship?'

'Wait till you see!' And on the way back the bateau diverted to the creek on whose banks Paxmore was completing his assignment.

'It's enormous!' the priest said as he looked up at the huge construction. 'How will you get it into the water?'

'From the stern we'll run ropes around pulleys attached to those oak trees,' Paxmore explained. 'Then we'll get all the men available, and while they pull in this direction, we'll knock out those timbers and the ship will edge forward in that direction . . . to the water.'

'And if it doesn't?'

'It must.'

Father Steed spent more than an hour inspecting the work, and he could not hide his wonder over the fact that his brothers were building a ship that could sail to London, but when he voiced this surprise, Henry quickly corrected him, 'It's not us. It's Paxmore.'

'I like that man,' Ralph said. 'Couldn't we meet with him?'

Henry took this question to the carpenter, who said, 'I couldn't leave now. I sleep here to be certain . . .'

'I meant, when the job permits,' Father Steed said quickly.

'Yes,' Paxmore said. 'I'm sure Ruth Brinton would want to talk with thee.'

'And who is she?' the priest asked.

'My wife.'

'Oh?' Ralph hesitated. 'It wouldn't really be necessary . . .'

'She talks much better than me.'

'I'm sure she does,' Ralph said, 'but I wanted to talk with you about Quakers.'

'It's about Quakers that she talks best,' Paxmore said, and it was arranged that when work permitted, he would sail with Ruth Brinton for a few days at Devon.

It was a visit which created a powerful impression on two families. The multiple Steeds had known Paxmore as a workman of high quality, while the Quakers had thought of the Steeds as business people on whom fortune had smiled; they were roused by Father Steed's stories of the repression experienced by his family, and when he spoke of the fire that had destroyed the chapel, Paxmore said impulsively, 'I could rebuild it. I've already built a Quaker meeting house.'

'What makes you a Quaker?' the priest asked.

Paxmore deferred to his wife, and the long dialogue was joined. It took place in the formal sitting room, with Father Steed, a wise, battle-worn, fat old man sprawled in an easy chair, representing the world's oldest Christian religion, and Ruth Brinton, a prim, bonneted woman in gray, perched on the forward edge of a straight-backed chair her husband had built, representing the newest. During parts of the conversation Henry Steed and Paxmore were present, but they did not interrupt, for they perceived that here were two theologians of high purpose comparing experiences after lifetimes spent in religious speculation.

QUAKER: You ask how I became what I am. When I was eighteen I heard George Fox preach, and he vouchsafed such an illumination that all distress vanished. His simplicity overcame me.

CATHOLIC: The world entertains many visionaries. Our church provides two or three a year, right down the centuries. And each has some one good idea, which prudent men should listen to. But rarely more than one. And that one can be fitted into the structure of the church. What was so special about George Fox?

QUAKER: His simplicity stripped away the unnecessary accretions of centuries.

CATHOLIC: Such as?

QUAKER: Thee asks. I would prefer not to embarrass thee, but thee did ask.

CATHOLIC: Because I feel a need to know. What unnecessaries?

QUAKER: Since God maintains direct accessibility with every human life and offers instant and uncomplicated guidance, the intervention of priests and ministers is unnecessary. The intercession of saints is not required. Musical chanting and pretentious prayers fulfill no need. God is not attracted by incense or ostentation or robes or colorful garments or hierarchies.

CATHOLIC: You pretty well abolish my church.

QUAKER: Oh, no! There are many in the world, perhaps a majority, who require forms and feel easier with rituals, and if this is the manner in which they approach God, then forms and rituals are essential, and thee would be delinquent if thee deprived them of that avenue to God.

CATHOLIC: But you feel there are others, perhaps a fortunate few, maybe the more intellectual.

QUAKER: There is no up nor down. In human beings there are differences which cause them to choose different paths.

CATHOLIC: But what is your path? Which parts of the Bible do you accept?

QUAKER: All of it. Every sacred word. And especially the teachings of Jesus Christ in the New Testament.

CATHOLIC: Do you then reject the old?

QUAKER: No, but we do not belabor it.

CATHOLIC: How specifically do you utilize it?

QUAKER: Thee touches a delicate point, Father Steed. There have been some among us and there are now . . . (Here Mrs. Paxmore hesitated, then spoke quickly with a certain confidentiality.) Indeed, my husband Edward is one of them who focus so strongly on the words of Jesus that they diminish the importance of the Old Testament—as if one could accept the New without comprehending the Old.

CATHOLIC: Would not this be serious error?

QUAKER: The same the Jews commit when they accept only the Old and ignore the New, as if one did not flow inevitably from the other.

CATHOLIC: And you?

QUAKER: Thy family asked Edward to build a shrine for thy pewter heritage, lest children born in ease forget. The Old Testament is a moral heritage upon which every word of the New is built. The New can never be understood except in reference to the Old.

CATHOLIC: Do you Quakers accept the divinity of Jesus?

QUAKER: Without question.

CATHOLIC: Do you acknowledge the Virgin Birth?

QUAKER: I have never heard it refuted.

CATHOLIC: But do you accept it . . . in your heart?

QUAKER: I do not ponder such miracles. There is too much work at hand, crying to be done.

CATHOLIC: You reject faith as the core of Christianity?

QUAKER: I base my life on James two-seventeen: 'Faith, if it hath not works, is dead, being alone.' I want faith, and I pray for its guidance, but the ultimate test for me is what the Christian does about it.

CATHOLIC: For example?

QUAKER: I can speak only for myself.

CATHOLIC: I'm interrogating a Quaker, not the Quaker abstraction.

QUAKER: I believe that jails as we have them now are a mortal sin against God. And I believe they must be changed for the better.

CATHOLIC: Is that single belief an adequate cause for initiating a new religion?

QUAKER: It is on such tendentious points that the soul of a revitalized religion rests.

CATHOLIC: And you would throw overboard the grand assembly of saints in order to reform a prison?

QUAKER: I would.

CATHOLIC: You would be making a poor bargain.

QUAKER: I would be directing my religion to the correction of a great evil, and God would approve.

CATHOLIC: What is this *thee* and *thou?*

QUAKER: It is the manner in which Jesus spoke.

CATHOLIC: And this hat on the head, even in church?

QUAKER: Jesus directed men not to uncover their heads in deference to any authority.

CATHOLIC: And this business of affirming in court rather than swearing?

QUAKER: Jesus directed us at many different places not to use God as reference for our actions. We attest on our integrity, and do not take refuge in His.

CATHOLIC: Is it true that your men will refuse to take arms in defense of our colony?

QUAKER: War is an abomination, and must be seen as such. This will be our greatest testimony. Does thee understand, Neighbor Steed, that for us it is not enough to believe that war is wrong—to have faith that it's wrong—we must also act.

CATHOLIC: Are there other areas in which you feel impelled to act?

QUAKER: There are. (It was obvious to the listeners that here Ruth Brinton wanted to cite a specific, but that some delicacy restrained her.)

CATHOLIC: What was it you wished to say?

QUAKER: Is thee inviting me to speak?

CATHOLIC: I am indeed.

QUAKER: I am convinced that one day all churches will see the immorality of slavery and will condemn it.

CATHOLIC: Slavery? Why, slavery's condoned in the Bible. Throughout the Bible. Old and New. Surely, Mrs. Paxmore, you don't reject biblical teaching?

QUAKER: I reject biblical interpretation which gives one man control over the life and destiny of another.

CATHOLIC: I'm really quite . . . You mean that all biblical teaching about the duties of the slave to his master . . .

QUAKER: It will be seen one day as terrible error which has been superseded.

CATHOLIC: Do you mean to say that my brothers are sinful because they hold slaves?

QUAKER: I do.

CATHOLIC: So you see, Henry and Paul, you're sinners. But, Mrs. Paxmore, doesn't your husband hold slaves?

QUAKER: He does.

CATHOLIC: And is he also a sinner?

QUAKER: He is. (At this point Edward Paxmore left the room, followed by the Steed brothers.)

CATHOLIC: Let me understand what you're saying, Mrs. Paxmore. You believe that on some day to come, the religious leaders of this world are going to convene and state that what the Bible has condoned since the days of Abraham, that what Jesus Himself approved of and against which He never spoke . . . You believe that our leaders are going to tell the world, 'It is all wrong?'

QUAKER: I expect to spend my life, Neighbor Steed, trying to convince my religion that slavery is wrong.

CATHOLIC: Aha! Then even your religion doesn't condemn it?

QUAKER: Not now.

CATHOLIC: And you would presume, one frail human being and a woman at that, to negate all the teaching of the churches and the Bible and human codes? How can you be so arrogant?

QUAKER: Because God speaks to me as directly as he does to your Pope. And if I see that slavery is a dreadful wrong, it may simply be that God has spoken to me first. I am the weak vessel He has chosen, and I can do no other than obey. (This topic was returned to numerous times during the three days, and many ramifications were introduced, but in the end Father Steed stood confirmed in his belief that God had ordained a society in which some were inescapably intended to be slaves, enhancing the general welfare, while Ruth Brinton remained equally convinced that slavery was inhuman and must one day be eradicated. At the conclusion of one intense exchange, Father Steed raised an interesting question.)

CATHOLIC: I know you said that you accept the New Testament, but do you accept all of it?

QUAKER: I do.

CATHOLIC: How about First Corinthians fourteen-thirty-five?

QUAKER: I don't know that verse.

CATHOLIC: 'It is a shame for women to speak in the church.'

QUAKER: We Quakers do not hold much with Saint Paul.

CATHOLIC: But was he not speaking for Jesus?

QUAKER: It is quite possible to love Jesus but to wonder about Paul.

CATHOLIC: If I understand what you said the other day, in your church women can serve as priests.

QUAKER: We have no priests.

CATHOLIC: I correct myself. Women like you serve as religious leaders?

QUAKER: We lead no one, but we do speak in meeting.

CATHOLIC: Is not that contrary to the teachings of Jesus?

QUAKER: To the teaching of Paul, and I reject Paul.

CATHOLIC: You think it proper for women to speak in church?

QUAKER: I do. And further, I think it most improper that thy great religion places women in such an inferior position.

CATHOLIC: Never! We revere Mary. We revere women as the foundation of the home.

QUAKER: But thee accords them no place in the church. Men priests speak to men, never women to women, or to men either. Does thee consider us incompetent?

CATHOLIC: No, but as I said before, all places in this world are ordained. Some are kings and they rule. Some are slaves and they serve. Some are women and they enjoy their special role, an honored one which does not include speaking in church.

QUAKER: Thy church could use Mary as a symbol of salvation, a repairing of the damage done to women.

CATHOLIC: Mrs. Paxmore, you seem prepared to give instructions to everyone. Slavery, women, prisons—what next?

QUAKER: As James said, faith without works is nothing. For the rest of my life I propose to work.

CATHOLIC: Do not underestimate the power of faith. Have you ever ministered to a dying man and seen the light come into his eyes when he hears from your lips that he is being embraced by the arms of his faith? Have you seen parents glow when they realize that their newborn is now baptized into their inalienable faith?

QUAKER: I believe in faith as a saving spirit, and the moments you speak of are sacred.

CATHOLIC: And don't take arrogant pride in your silence. There must be singing too. In every part of the Bible men and women go forth with drums and psalteries. And I think there must be ritual, the same Holy Mass said in the same language in all corners of the universe. It binds us together.

QUAKER: I have often thought that if I were not a Quaker . . . I thought this especially in Massachusetts where the religion was so dark and cruel. Once I looked up at the sheriff about to lash me and I could see no sign of God in that man's face. If I were not a Quaker, I think I would be a Catholic.

CATHOLIC: You reject Paul. But you accept Jesus?

QUAKER: I do. I do.

CATHOLIC: Then you must know that He ordained our church. He told Peter that he, Peter, was the progenitor, and that Peter's church would be the one and only church of Christ. What say you to that?

QUAKER: I say that forms change.

CATHOLIC: But never the one unchangeable truth, the one unchangeable church. (At this point Ruth Brinton shrugged her shoulders, a most impolitic response to what Father Steed had intended as a benediction, but when he saw her gesture he laughed.) My Massachusetts was Virginia. I was hounded out of Virginia.

QUAKER: I was shipped out . . . at the tail of a cart.

CATHOLIC: Could we pray? All of us? Bring in the children, too, and fetch Paxmore.

When the Paxmores returned to Peace Cliff, Ruth Brinton warned her husband, 'Edward, we must get rid of thy slaves.'

'They're on the edge of showing a profit.'

'Profit? Dear Edward, what profits a man if he gain the world and lose his own soul?'

'But the slaves are my property. The whole success of the boatyard depends—'

'Then quit the boatyard.'

'You mean, give up everything we've worked for? Ruth, these men are just beginning to master their trade. They'll prove invaluable.'

'Every day thee holds those people in slavery, thee endangers thy soul. Edward, get rid of them, now!'

'Others have begun buying slaves, seeing how well ours work. James Lamb—'

'We are not governed by what others do. We set our standards, and we are against slavery.'

'Thee may be, but I'm not. I worked for other men and found nothing wrong. Now other men work for me, and I feed them better than I was fed.'

Ruth Brinton became so angry that she shook her obstinate husband and cried, 'Doesn't thee see that this ownership is contaminating thy soul?'

'It's not contaminating Lamb's soul, nor Fry's, nor Hull's.'

She looked at her husband in disbelief and said no more, but that week she compiled a few notes to set her thoughts in order, and on First Day, at the Patamoke meeting house built by her husband, she delivered her historic address, the first anti-slavery message spoken in any church in America, but even these remembered words cannot convey the cold passion she used in uttering them:

'I see a day when the members of any Christian church will be ashamed to hold another man or woman in bondage. They will know without being told that so long as they keep one slave in their possession they are acting outside the will of God . . .

'I see a day when every member of this meeting will voluntarily award freedom to any slave within his or her possession. There will be no talk of selling them to gain a small profit, nor any talk of manumission after death. The freedom will be granted now, and totally, and without reservation, and on the day this is done every master will tell his wife, "On this day we did a good thing."

'I see a day when every black human being along this river is taught to read the Bible, and write his or her name, when families are held together and children are educated, and every man works for an honest wage. And this river will be a happier place when that day of freedom comes.

'God has sent us Quakers to Patamoke Meeting to give testimony on this fundamental point, and it may take years or decades or even centuries before we are competent to discharge our duties as leaders in this field, but the duty will always be here, silently, deeply, gnawing in our breasts, and the day will come when we shall ask in horror, "How could our ancestors have held other men in bondage?"

'I charge you now, "Go home from this place and set your slaves free." I command you in God's name, "Set them free and hire them for a wage." I call upon you, "Stop using black men and women to earn a profit. Start embracing them as brothers and sisters in God, endowed with every right you have . . ."

'We are a little gathering, a few people among many, but let us show the way to all.'

On Thursday following her homily Patamoke Meeting held its annual session for the governance of those Quakers who lived along the Choptank, and Ruth Brinton Paxmore's suggestion that slavery be condemned was put before the members in four proposals. Votes were never taken in Quaker assemblies; what was sought was the general 'sense of the meeting,' and discussion continued until this was uncovered and agreed upon. On this occasion consensus was quickly reached on Ruth Brinton's four concerns: 'That the Bible condemns slavery.' Not so, because too many passages in Holy Writ condone it. 'That no man or woman can be a good Quaker and hold slaves.' Not so, because too many fine Quaker families do just that. 'That those Quakers who do own slaves must set them free immediately.' Not so, because the Bible states specifically that men are entitled to ownership of their property. 'That Patamoke Meeting should speak out against slavery.' Not so, because it is not the business of any religion to reverse principles long established and accepted by good men and women everywhere.

When Ruth Brinton was thus rebuffed, her husband expected her to rage; she did not. As the other Quakers left the meeting house she nodded primly to each, and if occasion permitted, said a few gentle words. But when she reached home she assembled the black women who had been working for her and told them, 'From now on, thee works for wages. Each week I shall enter on this page the amount I owe thee, and on the day not far distant when all blacks are set free, I shall hand thee thy wages.' And that afternoon she began to teach them to read.

For some years England had been at war with Holland, a fact borne home to Marylanders when a Dutch fleet had sailed boldly into the Chesapeake, ravaging tobacco plantations and setting fire to shipping. When an attack was launched against Devon, Birgitta Turlock was certain that the Dutch had come to claim her as a runaway, but a group of colonial ships hastily assembled in Virginia, took after the Dutch, and they retreated.

To protect the valuable tobacco plantations from such depredation, London dispatched a forty-six-gun frigate to stand guard at the lower end of the Chesapeake, but the gallant Dutch, best seamen in the world at this time, sailed boldly back, captured the watch ship, and raided Devon once more.

These were troubled times, with strange alarms at sea, so there was little surprise one Sunday morning when a lone ship entered the Choptank, anchored in Patamoke harbor and set its entire crew on the wharf: a large-framed, grizzled Englishman, obviously the captain, and a young, alert Frenchman who could have been first mate. But there was surprise when they announced themselves as Quakers seeking the Patamoke meeting house, which they entered in time to hear Ruth Brinton deliver her arguments against slavery.

When prayer ended, they talked freely with the local Quakers. 'I joined thy faith in London when I heard George Fox preach. His logic would convert any man. My name is Griscom. This is my companion, Henri Bonfleur of Paris.'

The younger man said charmingly, 'There are many Quakers in France, thee knows,' pronouncing the first word as *zere* and the third as *men-ny*. He told Ruth Brinton that her message was inspired and must soon become general doctrine.

Then Griscom said, 'I'm looking for Paxmore, the shipbuilder,' and Ruth Brinton said, 'He's my husband,' and she summoned him. 'Our ship needs some repairs,' Griscom said, and Paxmore replied, 'We can't discuss that on First Day.' So on Monday he and the two visitors surveyed the repairs needed by the docked ship and decided that it would have to be sailed down the Choptank and up the creek to where the *Martha Keene* was about to be launched.

When they saw the stout ship that Paxmore was about to finish, they expressed their admiration: 'Better than most they build in London.' Without preliminaries they offered to buy it, but Paxmore dismissed such ideas, pointing out that it had always been intended for the Steeds. 'Ah yes!' Bonfleur said, 'we've heard of that great family.'

Griscom changed the subject by saying, 'If thee can rush our repairs, Paxmore, we're prepared to pay in coins.' Such an offer had never been made before, and the Quaker wondered if these strangers owned any coins, but Griscom settled that. From a pouch tied to his belt he produced an exciting jingle, then gave Paxmore a handful of Spanish dolares. 'Could we have the ship in two weeks?' he asked.

'That might be impossible. We have to launch this one first, and take it on runs . . . to see where it leaks.'

'Thy work won't leak,' Griscom replied with icy irritation. It was Bonfleur who suggested brightly that the delay might be profitable: it would allow them to explore the possibility of picking up cargo from an area of which they had heard so many fine reports.

'All our tobacco sails to Europe in ships already scheduled,' Paxmore pointed out. 'And in this one . . . when it's launched.'

The visiting Quakers ingratiated themselves with the local people, attending each First Day meeting and listening with careful attention if members spoke. They helped launch the new ship, suggesting useful tricks whereby the eighty-seven-ton craft could be eased into the water. During the first run out into the bay, they served as crew, working the sheets and watching with approval as the lateen mainsail took the wind. It was Griscom who suggested that a square mainsail might be better, and it was he who rigged it when the ship returned.

The new Quakers charmed everyone but Ruth Brinton, and this was curious, because it was on her that they spent their most obvious energies. They praised her talks in meeting and her cooking at Peace Cliff, but the more they tried to gain her approval, the more she resisted. 'No one seems to ask,' she whispered to her husband one night as the strangers slept on blankets in the kitchen, 'but where are their sailors? Surely they didn't sail that big ship of theirs alone.'

So next morning she asked Griscom, 'Where is thy crew?' and he explained, 'We knew repairs would take time. We hired the men out as husbandmen. At the York River.'

'Which plantation?' she asked, and without hesitation Griscom replied, 'Ashford.'

That night she whispered, 'Edward, they don't look like Quakers,' and her husband, chuckling, said, 'Are we so few that we must all look alike?' But at next meeting she kept her gaze on the strangers and reported, 'Edward, those men were not meditating.'

Her husband decided to ignore such speculation and directed all his attention to speeding up work on the strangers' ship, but the more he urged his slaves to hurry, the less inclined the new Quakers were to leave. They kept talking about the *Martha Keene,* which had departed on an exploratory voyage to Barbados under the command of Earl Steed, son of Henry and well versed in trade and ships.

On his return young Steed had much to discuss with Paxmore; as with even the most professional new ship, many minor things required correction, but because this was the first naval venture of a house carpenter, fundamental errors of some gravity had shown up, so it became imperative that Paxmore accompany Captain Steed on his next trial voyage, and rarely has a man taken a sadder sail.

The *Martha Keene* was sturdy; its keel was strong; and it was honestly built. But it could hardly be called a ship. From bowsprit to rudder nothing was right: the former had been incorrectly joined to withstand vertical pressures, the latter was improperly hung if maximum movement was desired. The tiller was not long enough; the boom was too loosely attached; the cleats were not properly positioned; and as anticipated, the mast leaked.

Paxmore took patient note of every complaint and added some of his own; when the list seemed complete he said quietly, 'Only sensible thing is to start over.'

'You mean . . . a new ship?'

'This one can never be mended.' He hesitated. 'It was built by a man who knew nothing.' Then he added firmly, 'But now I know.'

'No,' said Steed reflectively, 'this ship can be cured.'

'Never the mast.'

'Even that,' Steed assured him, and when they returned he worked as diligently as Paxmore to salvage his family's investment: a new jib boom was affixed to the bowsprit and joined properly; loose caulking was gouged out and hammered home correctly; additional knees were introduced; and all items on deck were so located as to provide easy access without hampering movement. Paxmore even proposed cutting a new pine from which a properly graded mast could be adzed, but this extravagance Steed would not permit: 'It will float.'

But when Paxmore saw his handiwork on the Choptank, he wanted to look away with shame, for it was a botch. Dumpy, heavy in the bow, slow to respond and with a creaking mast, it should not have been called a ship. A thing corrected was a thing weakened, and he wanted to rip it apart, board by board, and redo it properly. But even as it lay there, listing to port, he could see that within its misshapen body there lurked the concept of a true ship, and given another chance, he would bring that concept to reality. When the *Martha Keene* set forth on its next trial Henry Steed assured its builder, 'When it returns, make a few additional changes, and we'll take ownership,' but Paxmore gritted his teeth as he saw her lumber away from the wharf and muttered, 'I hope she sinks.'

If the colonies were impeded by lack of coinage, they were nearly destroyed by a lack of salt. Along the entire eastern coast there had been found no substantial salt deposits, and imports from the various mines of Europe were either prohibitive or unavailable. Every kitchen in Maryland suffered from this lack, and children could be seen dipping their hands into the bay in hopes of satisfying their hunger for this essential item. Men and women would sometimes dream of tasting a truly salted dish; their bodies suffered strange rashes; perspiration became acid and biting, much worse than the sting of mosquitoes.

Almost every infant industry at one time or another felt the need for salt, and because none was available, occupations that should have prospered never got started or withered. Henry Steed wrote to Fithians:

> We perish for lack of salt. Never has the bay produced a better catch of fish. Barrels of the best shad stand on our wharf. But because we have no salt, we cannot lay them aside for winter, and in February we shall go hungry when we could have dined like kings. Tears came into my eyes when I ordered my slaves to throw fish already caught back into the bay and to seek no more.

> When our fine new ship the *Martha Keene* crosses the Atlantic, could you find me a cargo of salt from the Polish mines? Regardless of cost? And will you please send documents explaining how best to evaporate salt from sea water?

When the instructions arrived, Henry Steed saw that here at last was an occupation ideally suited for the Turlocks. It required no great capital, little ingenuity and not much work. But when he went to the marsh, he uncovered a situation which he could not fully understand. Timothy Turlock, old and filthy and with no teeth at all, was in command of a hut as disordered as he. In one corner the blowzy Swedish girl Birgitta sat, apparently drunk. Her seven-year-old daughter Flora could have been a beautiful child had her hair been combed and her face visible; as it was, she seemed a sly little animal with all of her father's worst characteristics. It was the presence of a third female, James Lamb's servant girl Nancy, that disturbed Steed; she should have been at work, and here she was, a saucy little slattern idling her time with the Turlocks.

The only inhabitant who seemed even remotely responsible was Stooby; since Steed had last seen him the young man had suffered a savage case of smallpox and was deeply marked.

'I want you to start a salt bed,' Steed began.

'What?' The grunt came from Timothy and indicated his suspicion of anything a Steed might propose.

'A flat place into which you lead salt water. It's covered to keep out new rain, and after most of the water has evaporated, you boil the rest and we have salt.'

'Who wants salt?'

'Everybody.'

'I don't.'

'But can't you see? This would help us all, and you'd be able to sell it for whatever you need.'

'No needs.'

'But the others? Our fish industry. We have to have salt.'

'You make it.'

'No, Timothy. Our land is too high. Your land, here beside the marsh, it's just right.'

'You use our land.'

'No, we need someone to watch it constantly. Timothy, this would be so much easier than hunting wolves.'

'We like hunting.' He appealed to Stooby, who nodded.

'Stooby,' Steed pleaded. 'Can't you explain to your father that he's getting old. He can't go into the woods—'

'Better'n me,' Stooby said, sitting on his haunches as if that ended the conversation.

So Steed turned reluctantly to Nancy, asking her to convince the Turlocks that they should man the salt works, and she understood. In a semi-literate jargon she argued with them, explaining how easy the work would be and how rewarding the results. She made no headway with Timothy, but she did force Stooby to listen, and after a while he began to appreciate the possibilities.

'What?' he asked stolidly, implying by this single word his willingness to listen to the plan.

Steed, delighted that he had at last penetrated the indifference of this clan, took them all to the shore, where he sketched, in conformance to his instructions from London, a salt bed, in which water would be led from the Choptank onto a flat area for preliminary evaporation, then into successive beds for concentration, the last one being covered by a shed, beneath which the boiling would occur.

'Who pays?' Timothy wanted to know.

'I'll build the shed,' Steed said, so during the latter half of 1669 the Turlocks went into the salt business.

It was an aggravating affair. Water at the Turlock marsh contained only fourteen parts of salt per thousand, whereas at the mouth of the bay it contained twenty-nine, which meant that trying to make salt at the marsh was more than twice as difficult as it would have been in southern Virginia. The marsh also got more than its share of rain, so that constant additions of fresh water were diluting the process; and the raininess meant fewer hours of strong sunlight. And when in the last flat, under the shed, a pitiful amount of salt was finally made, it was not of a good coarse grain but was filled with sand.

'Hell with salt,' Turlock growled, and it was now that the trouble with Stooby began; it concerned Nancy.

When she fled from the Lambs she could, of course, have been apprehended by the court, and a magistrate wanted to do this, but Prudence Lamb said compassionately, 'It is better that she work out her own destiny.'

'With Timothy Turlock? She's been whipped twice for lying with him.'

'We have been able to do little for her,' Prudence said.

'But she owes you—what is it?—three years.'

'She owes us little.'

'You sign no warrant?'

'None. Perhaps God intended her for the marsh.'

But if Nancy had enjoyed some months of freedom in the cluttered hut, they had not been without conflict. Her original target had been Timothy; he was the only human being with whom she had ever felt much identification. When she was with him they laughed a lot, and once, when wolf hunting was good, he had even paid a fine to prevent her from being whipped.

But what she did not know was that Timothy already had a wife of sorts, the big Swedish girl whom he had indentured legally, and it was she who had title to the hut. Her child Flora was there, too, and things might have become difficult had Birgitta not been of ample heart. She saw no reason why Nancy should not move in, and if Turlock wanted to lie with her now and then, it was all right with Birgitta, for she had never intended staying permanently with this odious little man. She had been his mate for eight years but had always looked for a practical way of escaping; the presence of this gangling girl was of little consequence.

The trouble came from Stooby. He had always liked Birgitta; she had never treated him as an idiot and had sometimes tried to tell him of Sweden and the early days at the colony where they found her. He could not understand the nature of foreign countries but knew that the Dutch had been harsh masters and that Birgitta had fled them with enthusiasm. He was therefore irritated that his father should now be treating Birgitta unjustly, taking this new woman into the hut, and after watching the affair in silence for some time, his resentment rose until at last he confronted his father.

'You send her!'

'Nance?'

'Birgitta unhappy.'

'Who cares?'

'Unfair.'

'You shut!'

'Birgitta—'

'You shut!' The toothless old man grabbed for his musket and began clubbing Stooby with it, but the noise alarmed the women, who began shouting.

'Fool,' was all Timothy would say; his son said nothing, but that afternoon he disappeared.

He was walking disconsolately in the forest when Griscom and Bonfleur came upon him, and the Englishman cried with some excitement, 'It's the idiot!' And they took him to their ship, where they needed someone to clear away the mess created by Paxmore's black carpenters.

Stooby worked for the strangers during the time his father was trying fitfully to make salt, and the more he saw of the ship, the more suspicious he became of these men. From his long years in the woods he had learned to note and evaluate everything: the way moss grew, the color of toads, the inclination of pine trees, the roots of the larch. It was this skill that he now applied to the visiting ship, and at the end of a month he knew so much about the strangers that they would have been appalled. 'The idiot,' they called him, not realizing that in Stooby Turlock they had brought a natural genius into the heart of their project.

These were the small things he saw: flecks of dried blood where someone had been wounded; stains on the bulwark suggesting that large stores of powder had been kept there; nail holes where structures had once been attached; marks on the bottom deck where barrels had stood; shreds of rope where hammocks had been suspended, many of them; numerous repairs prior to the ones being made by Paxmore, indicating that the ship had suffered, at one time or another, much destruction; and the frequent utterance of one word he could not understand: Marigot.

But it was not the ship or the strangers that agitated him. It was his recollection of Nancy, and one afternoon when the strangers were not present he set forth in his canoe and returned to the marsh. Tying the canoe carefully to the rickety wharf, against the chance that he might have to escape in a hurry, he walked purposefully to the hut, kicked the door open and announced that he had come for Nancy.

She was seated in a corner, half dressed, playing a string game with Flora, and she looked up without concern. 'Hello, Stoob,' she said. He ignored her and walked to where his father lay on the floor, watching two bugs as they wrestled with a dead fly.

'Nancy is mine,' Stooby said.

'Go away.'

'You listen. Nancy is—'

Like a coiled snake, Timothy sprang from the floor, grabbed the musket with which he had once before repulsed his son and began smashing him about the head.

'No!' Stooby cried in a powerful, throaty bellow. 'No more!'

With violent blows he crashed his father back onto the floor, but Timothy had been in many fights, and using the musket to pull himself erect, he came at his son with every intention of killing him.

No more words were uttered, only suppressed grunts. The musket flashed out, catching Stooby in the jaw and drawing blood. Then the boy lunged at his father, caught him by the rag used as a shirt and drew him backward. As Timothy struggled to maintain his footing, his son brought his two hands up sharply, caught the gun and jammed it up against his father's chin, collapsing the old man's face.

But Timothy was not finished. Summoning his considerable strength, he swung the musket in a wild circle, hit nothing, bounced it off a broken wall and brought it to rest with a mighty bang against his own ankle. Suddenly he began to wail, as he had always done when being whipped, and his lamentations became torrential. Screaming and shouting, he lunged at his son, who calmly knocked away the musket and struck the old man on the chin with such force that he fell backward over a chair, banging his head on the floor and knocking himself unconscious.

Ignoring the inert body, Stooby went to the corner where Nancy sat and took her by the hand. 'You're mine,' he said, but as they were leaving the hut Birgitta said, 'No need to leave,' and with a sweep of her hand she indicated that they could have one of the curtained corners, and there they went while little Flora peeked to watch their love-making.

These long days when Edward Paxmore was finishing his corrections on the *Martha Keene* and repairing the mysterious vessel brought to his yards by Griscom and Bonfleur were difficult ones for his wife. Ruth Brinton, left alone at Peace Cliff, felt driven of God to do what almost no white person in the colonies had so far done: determine what kind of relationship ought to exist between the master and the slave. With all her suasion she had tried to get her husband to grant full freedom to the slaves he had inherited by accident, but he had kept insisting that they were his property, lawfully obtained, and that so long as he treated them humanely, as the Bible directed, he could not be at fault. Always he told his wife, 'I was a servant, I obeyed my master, and from him learned an infinite amount.'

'But thee was not a slave,' she argued. 'Thy term was definite.' He could not see where this made much difference because, as he pointed out, 'I would have been happy to prolong my indenture.'

'But always with the chance of terminating it, at thy request.'

'What difference?' he asked.

At Patamoke Meeting she encountered the same defeats. On four successive First Days she had ranted, and one member had warned Edward, 'Let not thy wife become a common scold.' She was infuriated, that was the only word, that the Quakers, who were so attentive to miscarriage of right, should be so obtuse on this great moral issue.

As for the other churches, what could one expect of them? They served the masters and preached whatever doctrine the plantations required. Even that noble soul Father Steed, who had done so much good in Maryland, was blind on this fatal topic. 'God appoints each man to his proper level,' he said piously, 'and like the slave, mine has been a lowly one, ministering to the wilderness. Mrs. Paxmore, I have gone months upon months without accomplishing one good thing. My life . . .' Often, for no apparent reason, he broke into tears, and she was not surprised when his younger brother came rushing to the cliff one day with the news that Ralph was near death.

'He says he would prefer more than anything else to talk with you.'

'I will come,' she said, thinking: If I were dying, he would surely come to me.

They had sailed to Devon, but when they reached the creek the wind was against them, so Paul ordered his slaves to row, and as they did, the great black muscles of their arms gleaming beneath the sweat, she could not see them straining; she could see only the three black women who worked for her and an anguish almost unbearable beset her, for she realized that she knew no more of her women than she did of these four strangers. Oh, she knew their names—Mary, Obdie, Sara—and roughly their ages; she was thirty-six and supposed that each of them was younger. Vaguely she knew that Mary was married to one of the men who worked for her husband, but she did not know which, and both Obdie and Sara had children, but under what arrangements she could not guess.

Dearest God, she thought as she sat in the bow of the sloop looking aft, we bring human beings to live amongst us and know nothing of them. Never once had she heard a Steed or any other owner say of his slaves, 'I told Amy and Obadiah to fetch it.' Always they said, 'I sent my slaves to fetch it,' as if they existed without names or personalities. Now, as Henry Steed hurried from the plantation house to help dock the boat, she looked not at him but into the faces of the four men who had rowed, and they were visages in a dream, without skeletal bones to lend reality, or blood to keep them warm, or any other substantial quality other than their age and their ability to work. These men are prime, she thought as she gazed into their faces, and that is all we care to know about them, but they are also human beings, and if we allow them to live among us without acknowledging that fact, we are breeding tragedy.

'Ralph is in sad condition,' Henry said, tears showing in his eyes. 'Be not too argumentative.'

'It is for argument that he summoned me,' she said. Primly, her neck clothed in gray, a Quaker bonnet on her head, her skirts lifted to escape the dust, she walked from the wharf to the house and up the stairs to the added room in which the priest lay. 'They tell me thee is poorly,' she said.

'I'm a small boat headed for the slip,' he said.

They talked for more than an hour, speaking of every contentious difference that lay between them, and at last she said, 'I am sorry, Father Ralph, that no Catholic prelate is available to talk with thee.'

He tried to blow his nose but was too weak. 'May I borrow your speech?' he asked, and when she nodded, he said, 'Thee is a priest.'

'I am a poor woman so tortured with sin that I fear I may not survive the night,' she said.

'Of what?'

'Of slavery. I am torn to shreds.'

'No need,' he whispered. 'No need. God saves the sparrow. He tends the slave.'

'I cannot leave it to God,' she said, her stern face dissolving in tears. 'Dear Priest, shrive my soul.'

'We've shared a river . . .' His voice trailed off. 'My brothers . . . call them . . .'

She hurried to summon the Steeds, and soon the small room was filled with brothers and wives and great-nieces. When he saw them—the off-spring of Edmund Steed, the faithful Catholic—he wanted to console them but could not form the words. Now Fitzhugh, ever more striking with his golden hair, moved to the bedside and grasped the old man's hand. 'Don't die,' he pleaded while his elders expressed their shock at his forwardness.

'Come back, Fitz!' Henry ordered, but the priest held the child's hand, and with this expression of love for his distinguished family, died.

For Ruth Brinton the next days were both a torment and a consolation. She turned to the cliff and began the task of discovering who these blacks were that shared the land with her. To her surprise she learned that Mary was thirty-nine, five years older than she had supposed. 'How does thee keep so young?'

'I work.'

'Is thy husband kind?'

'Best man God ever made.' Tears came into large black eyes.

'Does he love your baby?'

'He sing for her.'

Obdie had been taken from a village by a river, and her uncle had connived at her sale to Arab traders. 'He bad. He have seven wives.'

She had caused much trouble in the house and despised being told what to do. She said she was twenty-one, but there were serious discrepancies in her narrative: men in Barbados, men from Devon Island, a child born at Peace Cliff—it became quite complicated. Ruth Brinton tried to engage her in serious conversation, but Obdie suspected her of trying to establish some base from which new duties could be assigned, and she pretended not to understand. There wasn't much anyone could do with Obdie.

It was Sara who caused the confusion. She said she was about twenty-six and that so far she had had four children, two girls and two boys.

'Do you miss them?'

'Long time ago.'

'Do you believe in God?'

'Hmmmm.'

'Do you want to be free?'

Here Sara looked deeply into the eyes of her mistress and said nothing. A veil seemed to come across her pupils, as if she ran the risk of betrayal if her true thoughts were known. It was not an act of insolence, nor one of antagonism; it was just that subjects were being raised which could never be discussed honestly between white master and black slave, and it was dreadfully unfair of the white to raise them.

'Thee is the one who could learn, Sara.'

'Hmmmm.'

'Does thee want to read?'

'Yes.'

'Why?'

Again the veil fell across the eyes, and this time Ruth Brinton interpreted it as hatred. 'Oh, Sara, thee must not hate us for what we do.' There was no response.

Some days later Ruth Brinton went to the boatyard to see for herself what work their male slaves were doing. The visit irritated her husband, who was working on Griscom's ship, for he saw it as an interruption. He watched as his wife went to the sawyers' pit, and he observed with increased exasperation that she was staying there for the better part of an hour, just staring at the two men sawing planks from the heart of an oak log.

That night she said, 'Do Abiram and Dibo haul the saw every day?'

'It's what they're good at.'

'But the one down in the pit? Does he work there all summer?'

'Ruth! We sell the planks they cut—'

'Sell? Thee means we don't even need them for ourselves?'

'Where does our tobacco come from? We sell the planks.'

She said no more, for it was obvious that she was infuriating her husband. But on First Day she felt compelled of the Lord to speak in meeting. There was restlessness as she rose, and one woman went so far as to whisper, 'Would that she might hold her tongue.' But this Ruth could never do:

> 'I am lost in a dark alley of my own construction, and I simply cannot see the light. I am ashamed that my meeting has refused to assess the danger of the course we are on, and I think it most unchristian for us to dismiss as of no consequence the issues before us. I pray God for direction. I am a soul lost in sin and I pray for guidance.'

So many members of the meeting protested to Paxmore that when he and his wife reached Peace Cliff that evening he spoke to her with considerable harshness. 'Thee must stop dragging slavery into our prayers. The issue has been settled.'

'It has only just begun!'

'Ruth, the Bible has spoken. Our meeting has spoken. Thee heard what Father Steed said before he died. Does thee place thyself above all these?'

'I do.'

'Vain and arrogant woman.'

'No, Edward,' she said softly. 'I am beset with anxiety and I am trying to find the light.'

By common consent they halted conversation on this fruitless topic. These two, who had suffered so much for a common faith, loved each other with a slow, burning fire that would never be extinguished; their four self-reliant children were proof. Edward realized that he would never have loved Ruth so deeply if she had been less stubborn in her beliefs, less willing to endure punishment for them. And she could not forget that this quiet, ungainly carpenter had stubbornly returned to Massachusetts in face of promised death to testify to that same belief. As for his willingness to bear her stripes that day in Ipswich, she did not think of that now, for their love had moved to new levels.

At such moments of domestic conflict it was Edward's habit to quit debate and walk onto the porch, where he would stand for many minutes, contemplating the serenity of his river; it provided a calm greater than any he had known before; whenever he saw the marsh and the quiet trees he forgot his quarreling. On this night a dying moon rose in the east, throwing a silvery light over that placid stretch of water from the cliff to Devon, making it a peaceful lake of incredible beauty. 'This cliff was saved for Quakers,' he said. Then he returned to the kitchen to kiss his wife.

Ruth Brinton had discharged her irritation in a different way: she had hurried to her stove and begun cooking frantically, knocking pans and kettles awry, then chiding herself. Between peeling and baking she would think of what they had been arguing about, and she would smile, for she appreciated the fact that truth was revealed to human beings in different ways and at different times. She herself had been allowed, by God perhaps, to witness the future of whites and blacks on this river, and this clear vision impelled her to speak in meeting. If Edward did not see the dangers, if he remained confused over property rights and outmoded biblical quotations and the prosperity of his family at the expense of slave labor, she must be tolerant until such time as he, and other Quakers, saw what she saw.

She cooked a fine meal. They talked of the strangers' ship. He told her of how Stooby had quit working for the Englishman to live with Nancy and of how his twin brother Charley had come aboard. And they went to bed. But toward three in the morning, when herons begin to call, she was seized by a terrible shaking and sat upright in bed gasping for breath.

'Edward!' she cried in panic.

He wakened slowly and was appalled by what confronted him: his wife, her gown awry, trembling as if shaken by some storm. In a harsh voice she cried, 'I am strangled by sin.'

When many different people through many different generations experience common alarms, it is to be expected that in moments of extremity they will utter cries which are echoes of what has been said before. Ruth Brinton's confession of sin was phrased almost exactly in words used earlier by Edmund Steed at the conclusion of his unsuccessful attempt to deny his Catholicism: he strangled in sin and saved himself only by public disclosure and exile to Virginia. She cried, 'This day we must set our slaves free.'

'What is thee saying?'

'That before sunset we must divest ourselves of all slaves. It is the will of God.'

He tried to quieten her, intending to reason with her later, but she would not be consoled. 'We shall set our slaves free,' was all she would say.

Realizing that from this night there would be no retreat, he attempted several evasions. 'Let me draft a will which manumits them on my death.' No, such delay would be mere avoidance of the basic problem. 'Then let me hire them out to others—men of good deportment who will treat them well.' No, such hiring would not remove the blemish from us. 'Then let me sell them. I'll see Steed before noon. He needs help.' No, because that would be thrusting on others the sin resulting from one's own action.

But when he explained in the careful terms of husbandry that there was no conceivable way in which he could operate his business if he simply gave the slaves away, she stopped arguing and listened, and she saw that her imperative demands were placing on him a burden of moral and economic action for which he was simply unprepared. Tenderly she kissed him and said, 'Edward, I have forever known that thee will do right. By sunset this night there will be no slaves at Peace Cliff, nor ever again.'

'What I'll do—'

'Don't tell me. I can bear no more knowledge.' And she fell asleep.

Early next morning he set in motion his practical solution: he herded the slaves and their children onto a small boat and ferried them to Devon, where the Steeds said they would be delighted to purchase them. 'We daren't call it a purchase,' Paxmore warned, 'or Ruth Brinton would terminate the agreement.'

'There's other ways,' Steed said, and what he arranged was this: from London, Fithians would send Edward a crate of shipbuilding tools and Ruth Brinton a crate of theological works. 'And to make the sale more attractive, Edward, I'll cede you that good land east of Patamoke for a permanent boatyard.' Paul Steed promised to find such white servants and hired-out slaves as might be required in building the additional ships, and in this manner the Quaker Edward Paxmore divested himself of his slaves, turning a nice profit and acquiring a boatyard. On the morrow, when the *Martha Keene* was handed over to the Steeds, Paxmore would move his business to Patamoke.

There was an interruption, and surprisingly, it did not come from Ruth Brinton; she was satisfied that with the banishment of slaves from Peace Cliff she had accomplished as much as she could reasonably hope for in 1670. Later on, she assured herself, all people will awaken to the problem, and then perhaps even Edward will quit side-stepping moral issues.

The interruption involved violence. Men came running to the Steed warehouse, crying, 'Pirates have stolen the *Martha Keene!*' And others shouted, 'They've slain our sailors!'

When men from the warehouse ran to the shore they saw their ship, sails high, heading down the Choptank toward the bay, while on the wharf lay the bodies of three dead sailors.

In the next frenzied hours the people of Patamoke made a series of shocking discoveries. Jack Griscom and Henri Bonfleur had for some years been pirates; operating under various names, they had swept the Caribbean, chasing down Spanish vessels heading home from Panama, but accepting any accidental English traders who sailed into their path.

That much was learned from Stooby Turlock, who had watched and listened. When the citizens demanded angrily, 'Why didn't you warn us?'

he replied, 'Nobody asked.' The day was spent piecing together information about the pirates: they had no crew working ashore in Virginia; they had probably escaped into the Choptank at the end of some long and bloody chase; from the moment they saw the *Martha Keene* they had intended stealing her; and they were doubtless headed back to the Spanish Main for further depredations. Other shocks came as individuals catalogued their losses.

Edward Paxmore's ship had been stolen. On the eve of turning it over to the Steeds it had disappeared; two years of toil had come to naught.

Henry Steed came, distraught, to report that as the pirates were leaving the Choptank they stopped off at Devon and persuaded all slaves working on the island to join them in a break for freedom. 'When Abijah and Amos tried to persuade our slaves to stay with us, Griscom killed them both. All of yours fled, Paxmore.'

The wildest complaint came from Timothy Turlock, who rushed up the river in a canoe, shouting monosyllables that could scarcely be deciphered. Stooby did the translating and informed the listeners that the pirates had persuaded Charley to go aboard to help with the sails and had taken Birgitta as well.

'Did they kidnap her?' a woman asked.

'No!' Timothy blurted. 'She go!'

He wanted her back, and it was his noisy lamentation that goaded the others into action. Edward Paxmore said, 'We must get that ship.'

'How?' someone asked.

'Sail after her. Take her.'

'In what?'

'In their ship. It's smaller, but I fixed it well.'

Henry Steed was determined to recover his slaves, for they formed the backbone of his enterprise; indeed, they represented the profit of his plantation, and to lose them would be disastrous.

But the firm reasoning was done by young Earl Steed, intended captain of the ship that had been stolen: 'If we can put together a crew of sixteen, and assemble enough muskets, we can handle their ship better than they can manage ours, and we'll overtake them.'

'Where?'

This posed a problem. The pirates would have a day's head start, and the faster ship, but they would have only themselves, Charley Turlock and the Steed slaves to handle it. A resolute crew might overtake them. However, the pirates had a hundred possible destinations and the likelihood of locating them was not great.

Now Stooby spoke. Pockmarked, emaciated, poorly clad, he was an unlikely young man to battle pirates, but he had often been insulted by them and they had stolen a woman who had been kind to him. 'I listened. Often they said Marigot.'

'Marigot Bay!' Paxmore exclaimed.

'Where's that?' Earl Steed asked.

'Of course!' Paxmore said. 'That's where pirates raided the barracoons. It must have been Griscom and the Frenchman who bore down on us when I was there.'

He told them where Marigot was and outlined a plan whereby the Choptank men might slip in and retake the *Martha Keene*. Earl Steed, listening intently, judged that retaliation might succeed. 'Can we enlist sixteen?'

There was Steed himself, and Tim Turlock thirsting for revenge, and Edward Paxmore determined to recover his property. Henry Steed wanted to join them, but his son said, 'You're too old,' and Henry asked, 'But what about Timothy Turlock?' and young Steed said, 'That one has no age.'

Stooby insisted upon coming and produced three muskets for the arsenal. Twelve others volunteered, including a notable squirrel hunter with two muskets. Captain Steed told them, 'We must collect all available powder.'

'Why?' Paxmore asked.

'If we cannot recover your ship, I do not propose leaving it for them to gloat over.'

On the long sail to Marigot Bay, Captain Steed, twenty-nine years old, displayed a resolution which those who had known his father and his two uncles would never have suspected he had. He was not gentle like Father Ralph, nor fastidious like Uncle Paul, nor slightly pompous like his father; he was a new breed. To him, England was a respected family memory; he had been educated there, but it was not the *summum bonum*. For Earl Steed, destiny resided in Maryland, and if the mother country was too pusillanimous to protect her colonies from pirates, he would undertake the job.

Over his crew of fifteen he exercised the most rigorous control, impressing upon them the fact that the pirates had already killed five people in this one escape. He appointed Stooby cook, Paxmore the permanent lookout. He put Tim Turlock in charge of the kegs of powder and the muskets, while he himself managed the tiller and the set of the sails and charted the course to be followed.

The voyage had a strange impact on Paxmore, for now he had an opportunity to watch under sailing conditions how a well-built ship adjusted to the sea. The craft had originally been built in the Spanish Netherlands by Dutch carpenters who knew their jobs; it was now more than seventy years old, patched and repatched until the ancestral planks could scarcely be identified, but its lines had been so sweet, its joinery so right that it was still as sturdy as some rotund factor in his Amsterdam counting house.

When he was not on duty Paxmore studied the operation of the sails and confirmed the thesis of his Bristol instructor: the shrouds steadying the mast did not have to be pulled tight like the strings on a harp; they functioned best when slight strain or none was upon them. He also studied the action of the rudder and learned that it must not fight the sea but ride through it, giving direction, and at the conclusion of this inspection he marveled at how different a ship at sea was from one in a dock. All parts work together. You can hear them speaking.

Whenever he found a scrap of paper he sketched the manner in which a real ship was put together, and this information would become the foundation of his boatyard. He suspected that in the seventy years since this old wanderer was laid down, many improvements must have been devised in London or Boston, but these he would acquire later; what he had in this Dutch treasure was a bible of shipbuilding, and for an artist, which Paxmore was becoming, there could be no stronger foundation.

But now the island of St. Lucia loomed, and the time for study was past. It was Captain Steed's plan to lie leeward of the French island of Martinique to assure himself that no other piratical ships were moving in the Caribbean, and then to sail as swiftly and boldly as possible to Marigot, hoping to find the *Martha Keene* riding there, but when this plan was put into effect it yielded nothing, for Steed had sailed his craft too well: it had arrived two weeks before the pirates. The bay was empty.

He spent the time devising tactics that would give him an advantage when the pirates did arrive. He had to assume they would approach from the direction of Jamaica and Haiti, so he stationed his ship in a small bay which allowed it to be hidden while observing the entrance to Marigot. He then sent Stooby and Paxmore overland to scout the terrain at Marigot, and from the low mountains that rim that splendid harbor Paxmore looked down on the barracoon he had rebuilt, and the wattled homes where the pirates lived when ashore, and the desultory guards they mounted. He was pleased to see that the routine was careless, but it was Stooby who noticed the protected cove where small pursuit boats were tied. Without uttering a word, he indicated how someone must cut those boats adrift, and he spent a long time plotting paths to that spot.

When Paxmore returned with news that Marigot was sleeping peacefully in the sun and that the barracoons were empty, indicating that no trading ships were scheduled, Captain Steed said, 'All is in readiness for Griscom. He must come soon.' And on the morning at about the ninth hour, the *Martha Keene* hove into view, rolling easily on broad swells as it moved toward anchorage. Deftly it negotiated the entrance to Marigot, disappearing behind the headlands like a beautiful woman entering a night room. Stooby, watching from his mountain, waited until the pirates had rowed themselves ashore. He noted every man that went: Griscom loud and licentious, Bonfleur grabbing the waist of a woman not seen before, six white sailors, but no sign of Charley, nor of Birgitta, nor of any blacks. He carried this perplexing news to his captain.

It was Steed's firm decision that they must strike that night—'The pirates will be ashore, and if I know Griscom he'll be drunk.' He appealed to Stooby for guidance, and that cadaverous, pockmarked waterman said, 'Maybe Charley. Maybe two more.'

'Why won't the others come back?'

'Drunk.' Earl Steed, like the older men in his family, had considered Stooby Turlock an imbecile, and yet he was now prepared to rely on him, for the strange fellow had an animal cunning that produced startling results. Stooby looked at the world, digested what he saw, and reached conclusions. Now he told Steed of the cover where the pursuit boats lay —'I cut loose.'

Then Steed explained his tactics: 'At dusk we'll row this big ship down to Marigot. Stooby, you and Tom go overland to cut the boats adrift, then swim out and we'll pick you up in the rowboat. Squirrel Hunter, you're in charge of the rowboat. Paxmore and I will lead the boarding party. And when we get aboard, raise the anchor. Or cut the chain if necessary, and if this wind holds, we'll maneuver the *Martha Keene* out of the harbor, slap some sailors on her, and be off with both ships to Maryland.'

'And if there is a numerous guard aboard?' Paxmore asked.

'We cut their throats,' Steed said matter-of-factly, and when he saw Paxmore wince, he added, 'Remember, they've killed five of ours already. They'll kill all of us if we give them a chance.'

'And if they resist?' Paxmore asked.

'Stooby and I will fire on deck. Squirrel Shooter from the rowboat.'

'The shore will hear.'

'They'll find no boats. Stooby takes care of that.'

'And if the wind fails? And we can't move the ship?'

Captain Steed pointed to the barrel of powder resting in the rowboat. 'We burn her to the water's edge.'

'Agreed,' Paxmore said. Then, quietly, he said, 'I would not like to carry a knife or a musket.' When Steed assented, Paxmore said, 'But if we must burn the ship, let me light the fires.'

Steed nodded and said, 'Stooby, off to get those boats,' and the waterman was gone.

The others waited aboard ship till the agreed-upon hour, then launched the rowboat and held it close astern while Steed, Paxmore and Squirrel Hunter climbed down. Using small paddles instead of oars, they penetrated Marigot Bay, listened to the revelry ashore, and waited apprehensively until they saw, in the gloom, Stooby and his mate swimming toward them like a pair of beavers.

Steed was alarmed by what Stooby reported: 'Quiet, so we swim to ship. Almost empty.' One accidental glance by a watchman would have spotted the swimmers and ruined the expedition; what Steed did not consider was that no watchman would have spotted Stooby Turlock, who could slip through water without leaving wakes or splashes.

The five rowed silently to the offshore side of the *Martha Keene,* and when Paxmore held his hand out to prevent them from bumping, he could almost identify which plank he was touching and when it had been attached to the ribs. He patted the dark ship as if it were a pet.

It had been planned that at this point Captain Steed would take over, making crucial decisions as to whether a boarding should be attempted, but to his astonishment Stooby Turlock started talking in a loud voice, using a mixture of Choptank Indian and broken English that no one could have understood but his twin brother Charley, who ran to the side of the pirate ship, peered down into the darkness, and began calling back. The brothers spoke freely for half a minute, during which Paxmore was paralyzed with fright, after which Stooby cried almost loud enough to be heard onshore, 'Nobody here but Charley!' And he was up the side of the ship.

He was followed by Steed and Paxmore, and after a moment by the swimmer who had helped Stooby. Each was greeted by Charley's bear hugs and indecipherable gruntings, and after a delay the invaders attacked the problem of getting the ship under way and out of the harbor.

It proved impossible. The anchor could not be sprung loose. The sails were down and stowed. The invaders had not enough power to row the lumbering craft. And lights were beginning to show onshore.

'Ho, Charley!' came Griscom's deep voice. No response from the huddled raiders. 'Charley, you idiot! Who's there?'

Squirrel Hunter, who had been left guarding the rowboat on the offshore side, had pulled himself around the stern end of the *Martha Keene,* and now with the most careful and deliberate movements took aim at the pirate holding the lantern. With one shot he killed Griscom, and hell erupted. There were shouts and screams and running, and little Bonfleur had the good sense to stay hidden behind a tree, for when Squirrel Hunter grabbed his second musket, he picked off another pirate.

'We've got to burn the ship!' Steed cried, and Paxmore hauled up the keg of powder, but Stooby was already working with his brother, and deep in the bowels of the oaken ship—so strong, so ugly—they had spread powder from the pirate's store and without instruction had touched it off. A powerful flame surged out of the hatchways, with the twins appearing in its midst, slapping at their burning hair and chortling gleefully.

'Set fire!' Steed shouted to Paxmore, but there was no need. Stooby's blaze swept across the deck, reached Paxmore's keg and ignited an enormous fire.

'Out of the lights!' Steed shouted as gunfire started from the shore. Running to where he had left the rowboat, he started to climb down, but the boat was not there.

'Where in hell is the boat?' he bellowed.

'Here!' Stooby cried from the flaming darkness, and there it was, on the wrong side, in full target, with Squirrel Hunter and the two Turlocks gunning down pirates as if they were Choptank ducks.

'God damn it, bring that boat over here,' Steed roared, but Edward Paxmore warned him, 'No need to swear. This ship will sail no more.'

Captain Steed would never forget the return voyage from Marigot Bay. As he explained later to his father:

> 'The Turlocks stayed together like the witches in *Macbeth*, stirring an evil brew, and every six or seven minutes all three would roar with laughter and punch one another and roll about the deck and giggle with delight. And what, pray tell me, was the cause of their glee?

> 'Griscom and Bonfleur had proved to be monsters. They beat Charley and put burning tapers in his ears and made him dance while they drank, but every so often as we sailed Charley would remember how the squirrel hunter had shot Griscom dead and he would fall backward like Griscom and the three would roar with satisfaction.

> 'The pirates had stopped at Jamaica, where Griscom traded Birgitta to another pirate, and whenever Charley told of how in her farewell she approached the gangplank leading to the wharf at Port Royal and slapped Bonfleur in the face and pushed Griscom so that he fell backward, Timothy Turlock would bellow with delight, and slap his sons and roll on the deck, demanding that Charley repeat the story of her leaving.

> 'They stopped at Haiti, too, and when Charley reported what happened there, all the Turlocks chortled, because Griscom had talked our slaves into leaving with him by promising them freedom on his island . . . no work . . . good food . . . women . . . drink. Abijah and Amos knew that this was impossible, and they tried . . . Well, as you know, the pirates killed them. So at Haiti the slaves reached their paradise, and all were sold into that hell, and none will live a year. In this conclusion the Turlocks found great amusement.

> 'But it was to Charley that we owe our good fortune on this trip, because he had heard the pirates plotting to capture a salt ship out of Sal Tortuga, and I had not known that salt was mined there, so

we changed course and bought a shipload of the precious stuff, knowing that in Maryland it would be our fortune.'

Concerning Edward Paxmore's behavior, Steed could offer only sketchy reports: 'The first three days of our return trip he prayed for absolution, and when I asked why, he said, "I resorted to violence," and I reminded him, "But we took your ship from them," and he replied, "Yes, and I reveled when Griscom was shot, and for that I am ashamed." '

But after three days of moral confusion, Paxmore's countenance cleared and he began to put in order his marine drawings and fill the vacancies until he had as complete a manual of shipbuilding as could have been collected in America at that time. When this was done he fell into a positive euphoria, and one night, hungry for someone to talk with, he pestered Captain Steed on the quarterdeck: 'I know now that when a man finishes some important task, like writing a book, when the last word is written he wants to start over and do the job right.' Steed looked at the stars.

'When the *Martha Keene* caught fire and we watched the flames consume it, I was filled with satisfaction, even though it was my loss.'

'You'll cover all losses with our sale of salt.'

'It was my ship. I had toiled over it, dreamed upon it. My blood was in it, and when we launched it I had prayed it would float. But when it sank I was exultant, because I could start over and build a real ship.'

Captain Steed told his father, 'And there he stayed all night, striking his leg with his fist and muttering over and over, "A real ship, a real ship." When I went below for soup he was still there, moving his arms as if designing spars and curves.'

He was there when the captain returned to the deck, but he was not noticed, for a strange affair was taking place at the edge of the hold containing the salt. Timothy Turlock, recalling the hours of fruitless work he had spent trying to evaporate salt on the Choptank, was elated to think that on Sal Tortuga it could be mined like sand, and in the sheer joy of knowing that he would not have to work again, he was pissing into the hold.

'Get away from there!' Steed shouted. 'Charley, get that damned fool back from that salt.'

'Pop!' Charley grunted, adding words that were unintelligible. When his father refused to listen, Charley pushed him away. He stumbled, backed against the railing and fell overboard.

'Turn the ship!' Captain Steed shouted, but there was no way to do so. 'Get that boat in the water,' but it could not be lowered. Impassively, the ship moved on.

Steed ran to the railing and tried to throw the gasping old man a line, but it fell far short. The distance lengthened and the old man's arms grew feeble. When he realized that no turn could be made, no boat lowered, he began to laugh, and the last thing those on deck heard was his high, insane cackle as the wake pulled him under.

It was difficult for Ruth Brinton Paxmore to get the expedition into focus. When she sat with the Steeds before the pewter cupboard and listened to the celebrating, she simply could not understand how a voyage could be considered a success when it had ended in total failure, but Captain Steed was obviously pleased, her husband was euphoric, and even the Turlock boys seemed satisfied. It was mysterious.

'Thee still insists the expedition was a success?' she asked primly.

'We do,' Captain Steed said, gratified at the profit from his salt.

'But thee didn't get thy slaves back?'

'No, they were sold in Haiti.'

'And Turlock didn't get his wife back?'

'No, she was traded in Jamaica.'

'And Edward didn't get his ship back?'

'No, it was burned at Marigot.'

'And the Turlock boys didn't even get their father back?'

'No, he drowned in the Chesapeake.'

'And thee calls that success?'

She looked at the participants: Steed was placid and benign with his profits; the squirrel hunter basked in the glory of having killed Griscom and two others with only three shots; the twins were content with some mysterious inner gratification; and the eyes of her own husband were afire with victory. It passed belief, and she concluded that there was something in the world of men that enabled them to define *victory* in terms that no woman would ever understand. She thought she had better say no more.

But that night, when she was safely home at Peace Cliff with her husband, she was awakened by the terrible reality of the crime she had committed. In her righteousness she had driven Edward's slaves from the security and justice of her home; they had been passed along to Steed for money, and from Devon they had joyfully fled with the pirates, seeking freedom. In Haiti they had been sold back into the world's cruelest enslavement. There, in the most awful jungles of America, they would toil under the lash, and remember their childhoods in Africa, and their decent days with the Paxmores, and within a year they would be dead.

'Oh God, forgive us our sins!' she mumbled as the quivering began. She saw Mary straining in the Haitian fields, that good woman and her family perishing from exhaustion. 'You should be here with me,' she whimpered; even in slavery it would be better to work for people one could love, awaiting the day when wrongs were righted. 'Your death is charged against my soul,' she whispered.

Obdie would die in Haiti, and Abiram and Dibo, and Sara, too. 'Oh,

Sara!' she cried in the night. 'We need you.' Her death was lamentable, for she had learned to fight back. In her stubborn way she had conducted a secret life which no white would ever penetrate; she had been difficult and at times even ugly, but on this hideous night Ruth Brinton acknowledged that if she were a slave, she would behave like Sara. 'I would never stop fighting,' she said.

Her restlessness caused Edward to turn in his sleep, and desperately she wanted to talk with him, but she knew that on this night of reunion it would be unfair to throw her guilt on him, so she tiptoed away, wrapped herself in a coat and moved through the silent rooms in which black women had once talked with her. She went to where her own children lay, but when she looked down on them she could see only the black infants she had sent to their death: the children of Mary and Obdie. And she left the room of sleepers.

In the kitchen she opened her accounts book to the page on which she had entered the wages owing them; slowly the sums had grown against the day of freedom. The debts had not been paid and could never be.

In desolation of spirit she went onto the porch, seeking consolation from the river; but on this night the Choptank offered none. A considerable wind had begun to sweep in from the bay, agitating the river and throwing whitecaps. A dying moon hung in the east, casting gray light upon the marshes where geese huddled and on the tips of tall trees waiting to become ships. She looked west toward Devon, but it was hidden in the spray thrown by turbulent waves, and no birds flew.

'The Choptank knows,' she whispered. 'It feels the gathering terror.'

When the sun rose on the stormy scene, Edward found her shivering there, contemplating the spiritual disasters which the good people of this river would always bring down upon themselves.

Voyage Five: 1701

ON SEPTEMBER 14, 1701, ROSALIND JANNEY SET forth on one of the saddest journeys a woman can take. She was leaving her respected home, her family of distinguished ancestry, her two sisters with whom she had lived in harmony, and the dogs and horses that loved her. Such deprivation would have been adequate cause for lamentation, but in this instance she was also surrendering one of the loveliest plantations in Tidewater Virginia, with its own wharves and shipyard on the Rappahannock, and heading for some primitive wilderness in Maryland across the bay, and that was true misery.

But she was determined to make this sad journey in what her family would describe as good spirits. She had been born twenty-six years ago, an ugly child—'And that's a curse when it's a girl,' said her mammy—but in spite of her forbidding looks, her lively father had insisted upon naming her after one of Shakespeare's most beautiful and witty women. 'Fair Rosalind,' he called her, especially when guests were present, and all who heard this doting description had to be aware of its inappropriateness.

As a child, Rosalind burned inwardly at this teasing, for no matter what jokes her father made, no matter what passages he read from the play in which the real Rosalind appeared, she knew that her face was too large, and too red, and too filled with protruding teeth. When she reached the age of twelve and could read Shakespeare for herself in the heavy book Fithians had sent, she found the play ridiculous.

'Imagine,' she told her mother, 'wandering through a forest in boy's clothes, and talking for hours with a young man who'd fallen in love with you when he saw you as a girl, and he never suspects it's you.'

'You could dress in boy's clothes,' her mother said, 'and no one would notice.'

Smiling, she observed, 'But the real Rosalind was beautiful.'

'You'll be beautiful, too, when everything falls into place.'

Her younger sisters, who had grown into handsome young ladies, often repeated this promise: 'When you're older, Roz, everything will fall into place.'

This did not happen. She grew tall, but though she had no lack of appetite, her figure remained distressingly thin. She suffered the ignominy of watching suitors come in their shallops down the Rappahannock, but always for her sisters. When it became evident that the younger girls must make their matches now, while they were in full bloom, as it were, she graciously stepped aside, telling her parents, 'I think Missy should marry the Lee boy. He seems a proper match.' And she also urged the marriage of Letty to the Cowperthwaite lad.

Last year, at twenty-five, she had been aimless, a tall, awkward young woman, participant in no social life and left increasingly alone. She had turned to reading, and one afternoon when summer insects buzzed along the shores of the river, she took sardonic refuge in the play which had caused so much of her misfortune. 'What rubbish!' she sniffed as Orlando laid out the ludicrous plot. But then she came upon that scene in which Rosalind and her cousin discuss the fate of women, and it seemed as if Shakespeare had intended specifically for her every word these two intelligent creatures spoke:

CELIA: Let us sit and mock the good housewife Fortune from her wheel, that her gifts may henceforth be bestow'd equally.

ROSALIND: I would we could do so; for her benefits are mightily misplac'd; and the bountiful Blind Woman doth most mistake in her gifts to women.

CELIA: 'Tis true; for those that she makes fair, she scarce makes honest; and those she makes honest, she makes very ill-favourd'ly.

That's it! Rosalind Janney thought. Beautiful women are stupid, and the brilliant ones ugly. Well, I'm ugly and that entitles me to be brilliant. So I'll be damned brilliant.

From that moment her life changed. She saw no suitors, for she grew increasingly gaunt and mannish, but she did see how a plantation should be run. She mastered the art of raising sweet-scented tobacco, curing it in long, low sheds, packing it in hogsheads and loading it aboard the ocean-crossing ships that tied up at her father's wharves. She became adept in estimating whether the plantation tobacco would bring more at London or at Bristol, where ships from Virginia rarely put in. And to everyone's surprise, she became quite canny in the management of slaves, knowing when to buy or sell, and how best to utilize the hands assigned to various tasks. After a year of intense study she transformed herself into a proficient manager, never harsh or overweening but keenly aware of all that happened within her domain.

Her father, watching her single-minded concentration, understood the substitution she was making—the manager instead of the mistress—and it distressed him that a daughter of his should be forced into such an unproductive alley. He began to take special interest in her and to talk with her more than he had ever done with her sisters.

'Stop worrying, Fair Rosalind. It's my job to see you catch yourself a husband.'

'I've surrendered that longing.'

'Never! You're too precious a melon to lie wasting on the vine.'

She abhorred the image but said nothing that might displease her father; she did become embarrassed when she discovered that he had been discussing her with young men of the region, offering them a considerable portion of his holdings, including even a stretch of riverfront, if they would marry his eldest daughter. There were no takers, for even with six hundred acres plus a mooring on the Rappahannock, this ungainly girl was no catch, and she knew it.

She was therefore irritated when her father continued to press the subject. 'Fair Rosalind, you'll be married sooner than you ever dreamed.'

'What tricks are you dreaming of now?'

He did not reply. Instead he drew his forbidding daughter to him, pulling her into the shade of the spacious house he had built for his daughters and their mates. 'Sweet little Roz,' he whispered, half chidingly, 'did you think I'd allow the granddaughter of a Cavalier who rode with Prince Rupert . . .'

Rosalind's determination to live with reality meant that even her enthusiastic father's legends must be subjected to rational inspection. 'Our old goat never rode with Rupert, and in no possible way could he consider himself a Cavalier.'

'Your grandfather . . .'

'Was in charge of horses at an inn, and very daringly he gave Prince Rupert six of the best.'

'And on one of those six he rode off gloriously to fight with the prince at Marston Moor.'

'The dear bumbler never got close to Marston Moor, fortunately for us, because he was undoubtedly drunk . . . at least I never saw him sober.'

'If I say he was at Marston Moor, and if I say it often enough, he was.'

Like many families in Tidewater Virginia, the Janneys had decided that their glorious ancestor, Chilton Janney, had been a Cavalier dashing across England with Rupert in that unfortunate prince's futile attempt to defend King Charles I in his brawl with Cromwell's Roundheads.

Almost no member of Rupert's cavalry emigrated to Virginia after the decapitation of Charles, but many tidewater families, like the Janneys of the Rappahannock, claimed that they had done so. Their hearts were with Rupert even if their ancestors were not. They were entitled, by extension, to call themselves Cavaliers, for they firmly believed that if they had resided in England at that time, they would certainly have ridden with the prince, had he chanced their way. At any rate, they considered themselves Cavaliers and they behaved as such, and that's what mattered.

'I certainly don't intend to allow the granddaughter of a Cavalier to wither on the vine,' Thomas Janney said.

Rosalind, who had never been more deeply engaged in the business of living, thought: If anyone's withering on a vine, it's Letty. She reads nothing, is interested in nothing, and when she speaks it's sheer folly. Yet she's supposed to be luxuriating on the vine because she has a husband, and I'm withering because I don't. Aloud she said, 'For a woman of intelligence, this is an upside-down world.'

'What'd'ya mean?'

She had not intended to say what came out next, but she felt she must puncture her father's vanities. 'Why is it, Father, that when we discuss our family you always speak as if we began with Chilton Janney coming to the Rappahannock in the 1650s? Why don't you mention Simon Janney, who started us off on the James in 1610?'

It was traditional among the Janneys of the Rappahannock never to mention Simon, who had lived so miserably among the swamps of the James, and certainly not his wife Bess, a convicted fornicatress purchased from a ship captain. Secretly they were aware that aspects of Simon's history existed in court records—his acquisition of land, his purchase of slaves, his argument over the ownership of fields along the Choptank, and the manner in which he purchased from Fithians the great estate on the Rappahannock—but they preferred to think that these matters would remain hidden. However, against the possibility of discovery, they had manufactured for Toothless Bess an acceptable lineage: she was now 'Elizabeth Avery, daughter of a prosperous rural family in Hants.'

'We don't speak of those Janneys,' her father said stiffly, but it was known that when Simon and his scrawny wife assumed control of the present plantation, they brought with them their emaciated daughter Rebecca. She was there when Chilton Janney fled Cromwell's soldiers; he was her cousin, son of Simon's brother, who tended stables at an inn north of London, and he was a bright fellow, for he saw quickly that the prudent thing for him to do was marry this graceless girl with the three thousand acres.

He proved a first-rate husband, and after he began to feed his wife regularly, she rounded out into a respectable woman. They had four

children, among them Rosalind's expansive father, and now on plantations up and down the Rappahannock there were Janneys, offspring of
the Cavalier.

'Father,' she said as he left for the wharf, 'you're a rogue. Don't go
peddling me through the countryside.'

Her admonition was futile; a week later when a tobacco ship arrived
from London he announced to the entire family, 'Glorious day! We've
found a husband for Fair Rosalind!'

Cheers greeted this longed-for news and Rosalind's sisters left their
places to kiss her. 'Now our families can all live together,' Letty cried,
but her father dampened this enthusiasm by saying, 'Roz won't be living
here. She'll be across the bay . . . in Maryland.'

The Janneys gasped. Maryland! To exile the daughter of a Cavalier
family to Maryland was a sentence only slightly less formidable than
death, because Maryland was almost as deplorable as Massachusetts. In
fact, the news was so depressing that no one could think of a sensible
comment.

With studied care Thomas Janney spelled out the terms of the deal he
had arranged: 'He's a distinguished gentleman whose ancestors reached
the James River forty years before ours reached the Rappahannock,
which makes him gentry. He owns two thousand acres . . . an entire
island . . . plus another four thousand on a fine river . . . slaves, his own
harbor, acres of tobacco . . .' His voice trailed off in a way to suggest that
the bad news would follow.

'How old is he?' Missy asked.

'He's been married before.'

'Did he push his wife into the harbor?' Letty asked.

'She died in childbirth.'

'You haven't told us how old,' Letty pressed.

'He's got a splendid start in life . . . a substantial plantation . . . He's
forty.'

Another long silence, during which Janney could see his daughters
calculating how old the proposed bridegroom was in relation to their
father. 'He sounds ancient.'

'He is a husband,' Janney said, emphasizing the second word.

Now Rosalind spoke. 'Have you met him?'

'How would I meet him. He's over in Maryland.'

'How did you hear of him?'

'Fithians. I wrote to Fithians in London.'

'Oh, my God,' Rosalind exploded, 'now you're peddling me through
the streets of London!'

'Watch your blasphemy! It don't become a lady.'

'I'm no lady. I'm a woman outraged because her father has been
hawking her like a shipload of tobacco.'

'We've been trying to find you a husband,' Janney said stiffly, and when he appealed to other members of the family, the young people nodded; they, too, had been making offers up and down the tidewater.

'How much did you authorize Fithians to pay . . . if someone would take me?' Rosalind asked icily.

'Fithians assures me that your future husband requires no dowry!'

Rosalind arranged her knife and fork in a precise pattern, then asked, 'One thing's important. Is he of good repute?'

'He is. Fithians have done business with his family much longer than ours. They reminded me . . .' His voice trailed to a whisper. 'His family had dealings with . . . Old Simon.'

'Shouldn't you tell me his name? If I'm to be married to him.'

'There is one thing more, Roz. He's Papist.' And before any of the family could protest, he added, 'But he's promised that you won't have to convert.'

'Generous,' Rosalind said bleakly, and then her father passed along a letter forwarded by Fithians in which the bridegroom had put his promise in writing:

> I, Fitzhugh Steed, do hereby promise that my wife Rosalind will never be pressed to convert to Catholicism. My pledge and bond,
>
> Fitzhugh Steed

'He's a Steed!' Missy cried joyously, and each of the young people recalled friends who had connections with this distinguished family. Almost every Catholic home along the great rivers of Virginia had sent children to marry the Steeds, and Letty cried, 'Oh, you lucky girl!' But Rosalind looked straight ahead, for she had not intended marrying a man of forty.

So on a September day in 1701 Rosalind Janney left her lovely home and walked soberly down to the family wharf, holding fast to the hands of her weeping sisters. At the final stretch of lawn she looked with apprehension toward the pinnace which had been packed the day before with those personal things she was carrying to her new home, but in its place stood a lovely snow, its three masts yellow, its trim red, its body brown and its water line a shimmering blue. On its stern, lettered in gold, stood the name *Fair Rosalind*. It was a magnificent gift, large enough to sail to London; she would descend upon her new home in grandeur.

Her sisters kissed her farewell; her brothers-in-law did too, with a sense of relief. Her father clasped her and said, 'Always remember, you're a Janney of Virginia. Your grandfather rode with Prince Rupert. Be proud. Be a good wife. And teach your children that they come of good blood. They're Cavaliers.'

She watched her kind family standing on the wharf until they became distant figures in a twilight fairy tale. When they vanished she studied each house, each tree along this river she loved so much, and then the river vanished, and finally Virginia itself, lost in mists, and she began to weep.

Now they were on the bay, that grand, forbidding body of water, and she sensed that her life was being wrenched in half: the sweetness of the past was irrecoverable, the humiliation of the present inescapable. To leave Virginia for the wilds of Maryland! The gentility of the Rappahannock for God knows what savage river! And the sweet English chapel for the Romish Mass! Dear God, in neither Virginia nor England can a Papist hold office, and here I am marrying one! Was ever a young woman forced into a worse marriage?

To her unlistening slaves she cried, 'It's awful for a woman to be put up for sale.' It was this last word which turned her attention to them: How would these sailing the snow find passage back to Virginia? And she asked the white captain, 'How will the sailors get home?'

'They belong to the ship,' the captain said, and it was only then that Rosalind realized that her father had given her not only this handsome new ship, but also the twelve slaves needed to man it. She had expected to take her three sewing women. But the men as well! This was the dowry of a princess.

Next morning, like a good manager, she concentrated on the sailing of her snow; if this was to be her ship, she needed to know its secrets, and that was not easy, for this was a most unusual craft. It had a standard foremast, square-rigged of course, and a mainmast also square, and with such sails she was familiar. But immediately behind the mainmast, and almost touching it at points, rose a curious third mast from which hung fore-and-aft sails, and as soon as she understood the benefits arising from this unique combination, she knew that few ships afloat could outmaneuver hers.

She was in good spirits when her snow pulled into the lee of Devon Island, breasted the eastern headland and turned west to find the creek. As it progressed slowly inland she had a chance to inspect her new home: a giant oak, a lawn as fair as any in Virginia, a rambling wooden house that bespoke decades of exciting living, and on the wharf a handsome man of forty, fair-haired, relaxed in manner, and from the way he carried himself, probably vain and self-indulgent. Beside him stood a petite young girl, and it was she who first offered greetings. Curtsying prettily, she extended her hand and said, 'I'm Evelyn, your new daughter.' The man smiled and reached out to help. 'Hullo,' he said. 'I'm Hugh Steed.'

Rosalind, looking at the handsome pair, knew how plain she must appear to them; she felt that they were part of the conspiracy, the beautiful people allied against the ugly, but she would be perpetually grateful that if they were disappointed, they had the breeding not to show it. She tried to smile. 'I'm Rosalind Janney.'

But when she stepped onto the wharf and stood beside these resplendent people, she experienced the full shame of being an unprepossessing bride. She felt faint and wondered if she could carry this thing through, this marriage arranged by Fithians across the ocean, but then she gritted her teeth, allowed Fitzhugh Steed to kiss her, and thought sardonically: Courage, lass. You're the granddaughter of a Cavalier who rode with Rupert at Marston Moor.

Rosalind's Revenge

WHEN ROSALIND JANNEY WALKED FROM THE wharf on Devon Island toward the plantation house and saw its random form, with afterthought additions sprawling across the rise, she had the strange feeling that she had been ferried up the bay to bring order into this household, and that without her it would not be achieved. The Steed house needed pulling together, and so did its inhabitants. Gathering her skirt in her left hand, she marched to the task.

Fitzhugh, punctilious in his attentions and gracious in trying to make his proposed wife feel as if she were indeed mistress of the island, led her onto the wooden porch, paused so that she could look back upon the creek and its activity, and said grandly, 'It's all to be yours. It cries out for your attention.'

At this show of generosity she wanted to grasp his hand, but the presence of slaves lugging bundles restrained her. Instead she smiled, showing the firm white teeth that always looked so big. 'Governing a plantation is a monstrous job. You seem to have done well without me.'

He chuckled and told his daughter, 'Show your new mother to her quarters,' and he was gone, his lace-touched coat bobbing in the sunlight.

Evelyn Steed was even more gracious than her father. She was a pert little princess, bubbling with self-assurance and positively eager to help this newcomer establish herself properly. Taking Rosalind by the hand, she led her through dark hallways to a spacious bedroom overlooking the creek, and then, when it might have been time for her to drop Rosalind's hand, she caught the other one and squeezed it tightly. 'We've needed you so much,' she cried impulsively. 'We're all so glad you've come.'

'You're a surprise,' Rosalind said with catching breath, touched by the girl's sincerity. 'I wasn't aware your father had so lovely a daughter.'

'And Mark? Did they hide him from you, too?'

'Who's Mark? Your brother?'

'Older than me and at St. Omer's.'

'Where's that?'

'In France. All Catholic boys study at St. Omer's. If their fathers have ships. Or access to them.'

'I like the way you use the word *access,* Evelyn. You sound as if you'd had good schooling.'

'Father loves to use big words. Says a gentleman should speak precisely.' With this, she pirouetted about the room, then stopped suddenly and once again grasped Rosalind's hands. 'It's been most awfully lonesome here—with Mother gone, Mark in France . . .'

'Your mother . . .'

'Died. Seems years ago.' Again she pirouetted lightly. 'And Father's been fully as lonely as I.' She came to rest directly opposite Rosalind and asked, 'How old are you?'

'Not old enough to be your mother, not too old to be your sister.'

'I like riddles! Let me guess.' She circled Rosalind, surveying her from all sides. 'You're twenty-seven.'

'One year too much.'

'That's a jolly age. But isn't it rather late to be married?' Without waiting for an answer, she asked, 'Were you married before?' And again without waiting: 'You see, Father's already eager to marry me off, and he's been writing to the Claxtons across the bay. Do you know them? In Annapolis?'

'How can I answer if you ask so swiftly?' And Rosalind pulled the excitable girl onto the bed beside her, and there they sat with their feet dangling, grappling with importunate questions.

'My marriage has come late, Evelyn, because I was ill-favored. My younger sisters were as pretty as you, and they married near your age. I've not been married before. And how would I possibly know any Claxtons in Annapolis when I'm from Virginia, which is a long way distant.' But then she became aware that she was speaking crisply and even with a certain irritation, so she softened her voice and asked, 'Is he a pleasing young man?'

'Never saw him. Never saw any Claxton. It's all being done with letters.'

'As in my case,' Rosalind said.

'You, too?' The girl's curls flashed in the air as she swung about to look at Rosalind and laugh. 'So you're a letter bride!'

'By way of London.'

'What do you mean?'

'Your father inquired of Fithians if they had a bride and they wrote—'

'You're Fithians too?' Evelyn cried gleefully, and she danced about the room, making mock introductions: 'Miss Fithian, meet Miss Fithian!' But her laughter died abruptly as she said softly, 'Maybe it's permissible to be a letter bride when you're twenty-six. At my age I'd like at least to see him.'

'So you shall!' Rosalind said impulsively, remembering her own reactions to a similar situation.

'Don't give in,' the girl pleaded. 'Please don't give in.'

'Now just a moment, Evelyn. We're not forming a team against your father.'

'He's a darling . . .' She hesitated. 'What am I to call you? Mother? Or what?'

'You're to call me Rosalind. I'm Rosalind Janney, soon to be Steed.'

The new snow was dispatched to Annapolis to fetch a priest, and on the fourth day of Rosalind's stay at Devon she was tended by Evelyn, who helped dress her for the wedding. 'I confess I'm most nervous, Evelyn. I've no concept of what a Catholic ceremony is.'

'Me neither,' the girl said. She was unusually flushed, more excited really than her mother-to-be, and it was not long before Rosalind learned why.

'Father Darnley's from Annapolis. I'm sure he'll be able to tell me about Regis.'

'Who?'

'Regis Claxton. The boy I'm to marry some day.'

'Do ask,' Rosalind said, 'and if you feel any embarrassment, I will.'

'No fear! I want to talk with him.'

So Rosalind was dressed by Evelyn and her own three black maids, and although her size prevented them from making her the traditional delicate bride, the laces they attached to her and the flowers they placed in her arms did create a sense of festivity, and she did not feel apologetic when she left her bedroom and walked to where Fitzhugh and the priest waited.

The ceremony surprised her; it was almost indistinguishable from her sisters' in the Church of England, and Father Darnley, a big, relaxed man, did everything reasonable to make her feel at ease. When the prayers ended she asked to speak with him and Fitzhugh alone. 'Our children shall be reared as Catholics. And I will want to attend Mass with my husband, but I think it best that I do not convert.'

'There'll be no pressure from me,' Steed assured her.

'Nor from me,' Father Darnley echoed. He had lived in Maryland too long to retain the missionary zeal of his youth and in recent years had seen too much of the fatal struggle between Catholic and Protestant to believe that the old days of Catholic domination would ever return.

'Do you realize,' he asked, as he folded his ceremonial garments, 'that when our capital was moved from St. Mary's City to Annapolis, guards were posted at the central square forbidding any Catholic to walk on the street facing the new buildings . . . lest we profane them?'

'Can that be true?' Steed asked.

'It's still true,' Darnley affirmed, whereupon both he and Steed broke into laughter.

'My footfall endangers the state!' Steed shook his head, then warned his new wife, 'You see the infamous circle you're joining.'

'My sisters kissed me goodbye as if I were quitting the known world.'

'In a sense you were,' the priest said. 'But you'll find solace living here in Maryland—with the Steeds and their promise of greatness, and the Catholics and their promise of immortality.' He hesitated just long enough to convey the impression that what he had said was jest. 'I'm famished. We must all eat . . . and I wouldn't be offended if we also drank.'

Rosalind arranged it so that Father Darnley sat next to Evelyn, and during the festivities, managed by eleven blacks, she kept an eye on her new daughter and saw with satisfaction that a lively conversation was under way. Toward the end of the banquet she moved to the other side of the priest and asked, 'What have you been able to tell her of the Claxtons?'

'A splendid Catholic family, well regarded in Annapolis.'

'And Regis?'

'A fine Catholic.' He said this with falling inflection, as if that were all he could say of the young man or all he wished to say.

'But not an exciting prospect for a husband?' Rosalind asked bluntly.

'Exciting? No. Trustworthy? Yes.'

'I see,' Rosalind said, and from the manner in which Darnley turned from her to attack his persimmon pudding she knew that he would confide no more. In his human alphabet young Claxton rated zed.

Now the day ended. Slaves carted away the remnants of the feast and fires were lit in the black quarter, where women, coming in from the fields, were offered pieces of the wedding cake. On Devon Creek the first wild geese of autumn convened noisily and the first really cold breeze swept in from the bay. The priest sat alone in the inglenook, and in her bedroom Evelyn let down her hair and contemplated the unhappy news she had heard that day regarding her intended husband.

In the bridal bedroom Fitzhugh Steed, forty years old, experienced a kind of relief. From the moment his first wife had died, a supremely silly child unequal to the task of living on an island and rearing two children, he had known that he must remarry: the plantation had grown too large and too diverse to be easily handled, and if he wanted it to prosper, he must pay full attention to it rather than to the distracting problems of a household.

Many families in both Maryland and Virginia had wanted to align themselves with the Steeds of Devon, and various marriages had been proposed, but he wanted no more fatuous brides; one was enough for a lifetime. He required someone exactly like Rosalind: older, of good family, and safely past the age of romantic folly. He needed someone to oversee Evelyn's getting married and Mark's introduction to the management of the plantation. As for himself, he had worked out various arrangements, which were proving satisfactory, and sought no additional entanglements from a new wife, but he also recognized that if he did remarry, he would have to honor certain implied obligations, especially those relating to the bed, and he proposed doing so, even though he felt more propelled by duty than by passion.

Therefore, while Rosalind undressed behind a screen he quickly slipped out of his marriage suit and jumped into bed, where he awaited her. When she carried her candle to the nightstand, her dark hair flowing over her shoulders, she looked almost presentable, and from his pillow he cried, 'Roz! You're downright beautiful!' And he reached out his hand. She would never forget that gesture; she often wondered what force of character had been required for him to make it, but she was grateful that he had done so.

'I want to be a good wife,' she said as she blew out the flickering light.

'You're going to be the best,' he assured her, pulling her into the bed.

On the wintry afternoon of New Year's Day, March 25, 1702, Rosalind informed her apathetic husband that she was pregnant, and in the following September she gave birth to a son, Samuel. Often, in later years, she would wonder what miracle had allowed her to have children by her strange and diffident husband; actually, she would have three, two boys and a girl, and each pregnancy would seem an accident, the result of a performance which had no meaning and certainly no spiritual significance. She once summarized her position: If Fitzhugh owned a valuable cow, he would feel responsible for getting her bred to a good bull. He feels the same about me. But then she frowned: 'I'm worthy of better than this'—and she vowed that she would always manifest that worthiness.

After the birth of her first child, Rosalind annoyed her husband by insisting that she be allowed to inspect all the Steed holdings. At first Fitzhugh supposed that this meant the barns and fields on Devon Island, and he was annoyed when she told him one morning, 'Today I should like to see the warehouse at the landing.' When she surveyed the settlement now known in official documents as Ye Greate Towne of Patamoke she was impressed, for although it was little more than a village, it had a bustling quality. The tavern at the waterfront was commodious; the Steed warehouse was imposing; the Paxmore Boatyard quite filled the eastern end; and a bright new courthouse complete with whipping post, stocks, pillory and ducking stool was being built. The town contained only one street running parallel to the harbor, and it was broken by a large square left open but surrounded by posts set in earth.

'That's our slave mart,' Fitzhugh said proudly. 'We do an honest business there.' But Rosalind thought: Compared with the way we managed our plantation on the Rappahannock, you do no business at all. But that will change.

Her energies were directed to Devon Island, and the more she saw of the slipshod way in which the various Steeds discharged their responsibilities, the more astonished she became that it survived. There was little orderliness and less logic; the six thousand acres were planted helter-skelter, and the eighteen white servants and thirty-five slaves were assigned arbitrarily to tasks which might or might not prove productive. The two ocean ships rarely left either Devon or Bristol with full cargoes, and no one assumed responsibility for their thrifty utilization. It was rule by hazard, and the fact that Devon continued to exist was due more to its magnitude than to its husbandry.

Rosalind proposed to change this. She started first with the house itself, a rambling affair which had grown to unmanageable dimensions. Summoning the Paxmore brothers from their boatyard in Patamoke, she asked their advice as to what might reasonably be done to bring coherence to the place, and she kept close to them as they studied the situation. They warned her that they were reluctant to take on new assignments, for the building of large ships and small boats occupied their whole attention. The older brother, who did all the talking, said, 'But we're indebted to the Steeds for our business and we feel obligated. Let's see what can be done.'

They were not excited by the possibilities; too many of the accidental excrescences would have to be torn down, but at one point she heard the older brother say, 'It's a shame there isn't a strong central structure. Then we could telescope.' She asked what this meant, and he said, 'Come with us to the cliff, and we'll explain.'

So for the first time she sailed across the river to Peace Cliff and walked up the oyster-shell path to the unpretentious, restful house that stood on the headland, and as soon as she saw it she understood what the brothers meant when they said *telescope*. The humble house built by Edward Paxmore in 1664 was still sturdy, but after his death the growing families of his four children merited additional space, so a larger block of four rooms had been added, with a higher roof line. And when the boatyard prospered, a real house had been added, with an even higher roof line.

The result was a house tall and solid to the left as one approached it, joined by a lesser middle section, which was joined by a noticeably smaller third. The three buildings resembled a collapsible telescope. 'A giant could shove them all together,' Rosalind said approvingly as she studied the design. 'It's neat, efficient, pleasing to the eye, and perfect for this cliff.'

She was even more impressed by the simple manner in which the three parts functioned, and when she finished examining the last tidy room she asked, 'Could you do the same for me?'

'No,' Paxmore replied. 'Thee can build this way only if the first house is solid and uncluttered.'

'Is ours quite hopeless?'

'Not at all! Thee has a superb location . . .'

'I know the location's good. What about the house?'

'It can never enjoy this simple line,' he said. 'But it can acquire its own charm.'

'How?'

'Tear down the ugly parts.'

It was as simple as that. To achieve a fine house it was essential that the ugly parts not be amended, but torn down completely. This Rosalind was willing to do, but always as she worked with the slaves as they ripped away excrescences, she kept in mind that solemn purity of the Quaker house, and when the time came to start rebuilding she asked the Paxmore brothers if she might return to the cliff to refresh her memory of what she was after.

It was on this second visit that she met Ruth Brinton Paxmore, now a woman of sixty-nine. 'This is our mother,' the younger Paxmore son said, and from the first moment Rosalind liked this prim old lady dressed in the austere gray of the Quakers.

They had talked for less than ten minutes when Ruth Brinton interrupted the pleasantries. 'Has thee any plans at Devon for the manumission of thy slaves?'

'The what?'

'When does thee plan to give thy slaves freedom?'

The question was so startling, covering as it did a subject which had never been discussed in Rosalind's hearing, that she was unable to respond, but her confusion was alleviated by the older son, who explained, in obvious embarrassment, 'Mother's always asking people about slavery. Thee mustn't mind.'

'But thee must mind,' the old woman retorted. 'This is a question we must all face.' She spoke with such sincerity, with such obvious fire of conscience, that Rosalind said abruptly to the brothers, 'Go about your business. Your mother and I wish to talk.'

They spoke for two hours, discussing first the trivialities of the kitchen and next the profundities of the church. 'I had the blessed fortune of knowing thy husband's great-uncle, Father Ralph. We often talked of Catholicism and he almost persuaded me that if I were not a Quaker, I ought to be a Catholic. I think thee would be wise to rear thy children as Catholics. It's the Steed tradition. My children have married Quakers, fortunately, but I'd not be distraught if it had been otherwise.'

'How many children did you have?' Rosalind corrected herself: 'Do you have?'

'Two boys, who run the boatyard. A daughter, and then very late in life another daughter. Their husbands work in the yard, too.'

'How fortunate!'

In these two hours Rosalind learned more about the Steeds than she ever had in conversation with her own husband: the rare quality of Father Ralph; the fastidiousness of Henry, who had built the family fortunes; and the curious behavior of his son, Captain Earl, who had fought pirates, and established the shipping contacts, and lived as much in England as in Maryland. 'He loved the sea and should not have been required to supervise a plantation. It began its downhill course under Captain Earl.'

'He must have died young.'

'As a plantation manager he died young. Almost at the start. But as a sea captain he must have reached fifty.'

'Then what happened?'

'The scourge of our seas. Pirates. Two of them crept into this river.'

'Yes. Evelyn told me of them. She said they were Quakers.'

The old lady laughed, and Rosalind was surprised at the vigor of her responses. 'Quakers, indeed! They were fraudulent in all things and stole from everyone. Captain Earl pursued them and killed the Englishman Griscom. The Frenchman Bonfleur escaped and went on to be the intolerable fiend he still is. Year after year he sought revenge, and then one day he caught thy father's ship off Barbados . . . What I mean, Captain Earl was thy husband's father. He captured it, the ship, that is, killed three of the passengers and sent three back to inform Maryland that Earl Steed had been tortured for two days, then thrown to the sharks.'

'My God!' Rosalind sought for a handkerchief, which she held to her mouth. 'My husband never told me . . .'

'Thee would be well advised, Rosalind, not to use the name of the Lord in vain. This is not Virginia, and thee could find thyself in trouble.'

'Was there no reprisal?'

'Four vessels built by my sons have been taken by pirates. They ravage at will.'

'You speak as if they should be punished . . . even hanged. I thought that Quakers . . .'

'We seek peace. But we also protect ourselves against mad dogs. I've always felt that when thy father killed that monster Griscom, he could well have slain Bonfleur too.'

'Isn't this a remarkable confession, Mrs. Paxmore?'

'It's extremely difficult, Rosalind, to reconcile belief with human passion.' She hesitated, frowned, and fell silent.

'What example were you about to give?'

'Is thee competent to hear?'

'I am.'

'I'm sixty-nine . . .'

'And that excuses your frankness?'

'I think so.'

'Then tell me the unpleasantness.'

'It's not unpleasant, Rosalind. It's the kind of problem by which God tests us.'

'For example.'

'I think thee must assume responsibility for thy husband's other children.'

Without altering the even tone of her voice, Rosalind asked, 'Where are they now?'

'In the marsh,' Ruth Brinton replied. 'In the swamps of human despair.'

'What marsh?'

'The Turlock marsh—the one around the bend of the Choptank.'

And she proceeded to instruct Rosalind in a subject which had never been alluded to at Devon. 'A prisoner named Turlock escaped to the marsh many years ago, before Edward and I reached here.'

'What did he do there?'

'He bred. With any woman he could lay hands on he bred an assembly of infamous children—halfwits, criminals, devious young people . . . and some worthy of salvation.'

'Why should I become involved with these children?'

'Because . . .' She hesitated, then said quickly on a new tack, 'Old Turlock found a Swedish woman somewhere, and she had a slattern daughter named Flora, and Flora had a slattern named Nelly, and it's this Nelly . . .'

'Where did my husband meet her?' Rosalind asked quietly.

'In the marsh.' The old woman spoke with no condemnation. 'He's not to blame, Rosalind. As thee undoubtedly knows, his wife was a poor thing, able to perform only one job, the production of two handsome children. Evelyn's fine, as thee knows, but Mark is a champion. So their father drifted to the marsh, and that's where his three children are.'

'Was this long ago?'

'It's now. One's a mere babe.'

For some inexplicable reason, Ruth Brinton was able to divulge a fact like this without appearing to be scandal-mongering; perhaps it was because she offered witness with such unfaltering integrity. At any rate, she informed Rosalind of the prolonged liaison and of the children that had resulted. It was these children and not the behavior of the parents which concerned the old moralist.

'Nelly Turlock's not qualified to rear them. With her they'll become marsh deer.'

'What's she like?'

'Beautiful, of course.'

'Did she ever live at Devon?'

'Heavens, no! Fitzhugh would no more think of allowing her on the place . . . It's as if she were one of his slaves. He might lie with her, but he certainly would never . . .'

'You've given me much to think of,' Rosalind said.

'Thee will live a long time on this river,' the old woman said, 'and encounter many obligations. Thy husband. His children. Thy own. Life consists of sending everything forward. Everything.'

'I came to see your house,' Rosalind said as she bade the old Quaker goodbye, 'but what I saw was my own.'

On the sail back to Devon she tried to evaluate what she had learned, seeking to formulate some kind of rational response: Evelyn Steed was an admirable child worthy of deepest love, and Mark, whom she still had not met, promised to be her equal; Fitzhugh was revealing himself to be exactly as represented, a self-indulgent, moderately capable man content to simulate the management of either a plantation or a marriage; her own child gave promise of being intelligent, and on him, plus the others that might follow, she would have to rely. She could see nothing to be gained by confronting Fitzhugh with her knowledge of his conduct, nor was she distraught by this uncovering of his behavior. On plantations in Virginia owners often became embroiled with pretty, nubile slaves, and prudent wives had learned that ignoring the problem was the sanest way to handle it, and the most efficacious; the infatuation rarely lasted long enough to become publicly embarrassing, and if children did result, they could either be masked in the general plantation population or quietly sold off farther south.

She would survive Nelly Turlock, except for one ugly word used by Mrs. Paxmore. Rosalind had asked whether Fitzhugh's relationship with the Turlock girl had occurred long ago, and Ruth Brinton had replied, 'It's now.' She thought: If it's continuing, with me in the house as his wife . . . And she began to construct an edifice of moral outrage, augmented by her sudden recollection that Mrs. Paxmore had said that one of the marsh children was a mere baby: It must have been conceived while I was living with him! Her fury started to mount, but soon she burst into robust laughter. Damn my stupidity! I argue myself into believing it's nothing more serious than bedding down with a slave . . . what happened in the past was no responsibility of mine. But because it's happening in the present, I'm outraged. I shall ignore it equally.

And it was with these thoughts that she began her long retreat from Fitzhugh Steed. If he preferred to frolic in the marsh rather than live seriously at the plantation, and if he needed the transient beauty of this wild creature rather than the stately assurance of an educated wife, so much the worse for him. She began building those sturdy defenses with which women protect themselves from the debacles of the bedroom. Henceforth her focus would be on gardens.

The launching of her famous garden was delayed, for as she began to stake out its paths she chanced to look up, and there stood her daughter Evelyn, now seventeen and blooming like the lovely flowers of autumn. 'How awful!' Rosalind cried impulsively, rising to embrace her daughter. 'I'm worrying about a garden and ignoring the most precious blossom of them all.' She kissed Evelyn, and at table that night told Fitzhugh, 'Tomorrow we start to find a husband for this girl.' And he replied, 'No worry. I've sent across the bay to fetch the Claxton boy.'

But when the Steed slaves reached Annapolis with the invitation, the young man told them, 'I'd not like to cross the Chesapeake till the weather settles,' and they returned without the Claxtons.

When this heroic response was repeated at table, Evelyn blushed; she had sailed the Choptank in all weathers. Rosalind said angrily, 'Good heavens! If I were a young man about to meet my love for the first time . . .' She paused to calculate what she might do, then added slowly, 'I do believe I'd head into the heart of a hurricane.'

'I think you would,' Fitzhugh agreed. 'But Regis will arrive in good time, and our chick will be married.' Two weeks later, when the bay was calm, a boat arrived from Annapolis bringing not Claxton but Father Darnley, who informed the Steeds that 'young Regis and his mother will be crossing any day now.'

'A sorry situation,' Rosalind grumbled. 'The priest appearing before the prospective bridegroom.' But Fitzhugh reminded her, 'The Claxtons are an important family and must be treated with respect.'

'Why in damnation does a boy have to be brought to his wedding by his mother?' No one responded, for Evelyn was mortified and Fitzhugh was irritated by his wife's outspokenness, and Father Darnley, who served the Claxtons as their priest, deemed it prudent to convey nothing of his thoughts on the matter.

'Very good soup,' he said, and when Rosalind tried to catch his eye, hoping to enroll him in her cause, he stared at his plate. But when the meal ended he could not escape, for as he headed for his evening prayers in the inglenook, she grasped him by the hand and muttered, 'Father, this wedding must not take place.' Still he said nothing.

So when the bay was calm, like a pond protected by woods, the Claxtons came over, but their meeting with the Steeds was not congenial. Mrs. Claxton, from an upstart family with ample lands, led her chinless son Regis up the path from the Devon wharf and shoved him in position to be greeted by his intended bride. He simpered in embarrassment and mistook Rosalind, his future mother-in-law, for Evelyn; the vast discrepancies in their beauty seemed not to register, and when his mother corrected him he simpered again.

Could such a one come seriously to court my daughter? Rosalind thought, and she began the maneuvers which were intended to send this ungracious pair home empty-handed. 'Do come in,' she said expansively. 'This is my husband, Fitzhugh, and I'm sure you know from Fithians' letters that this must be Evelyn.' She lavished praise upon the Claxtons, assuring them that their fame had circulated throughout the Eastern Shore. 'You're known as one of the really great families of Maryland, and we're honored that you've come to visit us. Father Darnley told us of your piety, too.'

Evelyn, of course, saw that her mother was teasing the Claxtons into fatuous reactions, and they complied. 'We're really not one of the principal families. The Dashiells own a much larger plantation.'

Rosalind paid special attention to the young man, showering him with ironic flattery, against which he could not defend himself. At one point she said, 'Father Darnley told us you're an outstanding huntsman,' and he replied, 'One day I shot three rabbits,' and she said, 'Remarkable!'

That first afternoon had been painful enough, but as the visit progressed, things deteriorated. Mrs. Claxton showed herself to be a ninny, and her son seemed determined to prove that he had inherited her salient qualities. Even Evelyn, once so hopeful that Regis might be the one to lead her to a new life across the bay, surrendered such dreams and confided to her mother, 'He is really impossible.'

But during supper on the evening before the wedding was to take place, Fitzhugh coughed impressively and said, 'Mrs. Claxton, I think you and your son should prepare to drink a toast.'

'To what?' the giddy visitor asked.

'To tomorrow. When Father Darnley marries Regis and Evelyn.'

This blunt announcement, which the Steed women had not been invited to discuss, caused a flurry, and Regis had the good grace to get up and move to Evelyn's side, where he took her hand and kissed her awkwardly.

Rosalind noticed that when this happened, the girl flinched, so that night in Evelyn's room she said harshly, 'You cannot allow this wrongful thing to proceed.'

'I am powerless to stop it.'

Rosalind shook her. 'You are never entitled to use that excuse. Any human being with strong character can oppose wrong.'

'I'm seventeen!' Evelyn wailed. 'And Father worked hard to arrange this marriage.'

Rosalind broke into ridiculing laughter. 'Dearest child, age is nothing. Your father's vanity is nothing. All that matters is that you build the best life possible. That you become the best human being possible. With Regis Claxton you'll have no possibilities. The wastage will be appalling.'

'But I might never marry. Here there are no Catholics.'

'There were no Catholics for your father, either, and he took me. Believe me, Evelyn, you're a special girl. You have a particular beauty. Men will seek you out, and there's no law which says they have to be Catholics.'

'He was the only one Fithians could find.'

'Fithians! God damn Fithians.'

The force with which Rosalind uttered these words startled the girl, and she turned to ask her mother directly, 'Has it been so bad?'

'Not as you think,' Rosalind replied. 'Your father's been most kind, Evelyn, as you've had opportunity to witness. But the system! This writing of letters of application to Fithians in London! This stupid arranging of lives according to external patterns . . .' Rosalind began to stalk about the room, a towering figure of rebellion.

'Is it Nelly Turlock?' Evelyn asked.

Rosalind stopped abruptly and stood at some distance from the bed, her arms akimbo. She had never spoken of Nelly to her daughter, for she had not been sure that the girl knew of her father's misbehavior, but now the subject had been broached. 'Who bothers a moment about Nelly Turlock? Your father's found a certain comfort in the marshes, and I'm unconcerned.' She paused. 'Have you seen the children?'

'They're adorable. The loveliest white hair. I suppose you've heard what they're saying about Nelly?'

'I've heard all the dismal stories, Evelyn, and they impress me little. When you marry there'll be the big house where you live with your husband, and there'll be the little house where he lives with one of the slaves or one of the Turlocks and the two need never meet.'

'I doubt that Regis would take one of the slaves.'

'That's what's wrong with him,' Rosalind said. 'In fact, everything's wrong with him, and I plead with you not to marry him.'

'He's my best chance,' the girl cried in true anguish, stuffing her face into her pillow.

Now Rosalind took the sobbing Evelyn into her arms. 'We're talking of a human life. Yours. You'll live many more years, and they must account for something. You must be a woman of character.'

It was clear that these words meant nothing to the bewildered girl, so Rosalind shook her, making her attend. 'Two images flood my mind, and

I want them to flood yours, too. The first concerns my sisters, Missy and Letty. They were lovely girls, much like you, and they had untold possibilities, but they scurried into meaningless marriages, with meaningless young men, and now they lead meaningless lives. I could weep with pity when I think of them. The other image involves a woman you know, Mrs. Paxmore.'

'The old woman who rants about slavery?'

'No. The old woman who has never feared to testify concerning life. As a consequence, she has a beautiful home, fine children and better grandchildren. And most important of all, a beautiful soul. Be like her, don't be like my sisters.'

At last Rosalind had said something that Evelyn could comprehend. 'Are you trying to become like Mrs. Paxmore?' she asked.

Rosalind considered this. Never before had she expressed her intentions openly, for she had known no one with whom she could talk sensibly, but now she recognized the relevance of Evelyn's question. 'Yes,' she said slowly, 'I suppose I do want to be like her.' Then her voice became harsh. 'And tomorrow you can judge whether I have succeeded.'

When Evelyn tried to probe the meaning of this threat, Rosalind bent down and kissed her. 'You are infinitely precious to me, and I cannot stand idle and watch you waste your talents on a dunderhead. Indeed, I cannot.'

At breakfast next morning she warned her husband that this foolish marriage must not go forward, but he ignored her protests on the grounds that to halt things now would be embarrassing. She tried to point out that a moment's trivial embarrassment was less significant than a lifetime of wastage, but he had already summoned the priest and the servants. The Claxtons came down late, hoping to make a grand entrance, but when Rosalind saw them she could not stifle her laughter. 'Fitzhugh,' she whispered, 'you can't go ahead with this.'

'Everyone's here,' he said brightly, stepping forward to greet Mrs. Claxton.

But when he led the two young people into position before Father Darnley, Rosalind cried in a loud voice, 'Stop this farce!'

'What . . .' Mrs. Claxton made a strangling sound and looked as if she might faint.

'Get them out of here!' Rosalind ordered. 'Out, I said! All of you, out!'

The slaves responded first, retreating through an open door. The white indentures followed, shoved along by Rosalind, who then faced the bewildered Claxtons. With her arms bent at the elbow, as if her fists were eager to strike, she said quietly, 'The farce is ended. Take yourselves home across the bay.' And she did not let up until her visitors were on the porch with their bags beside them.

'This is infamous!' Mrs. Claxton protested as Fitzhugh attempted to console her, but Rosalind would permit no conciliation.

'You are to go home,' she said sternly. 'This has been a dreadful mistake, and I have behaved poorly. But you must leave.' And she stood in the doorway as if guarding it lest they try to return to the house. Tall and resolute, she glowered at them like some clear-seeing goddess, and after a while they crept to their sloop, whose bow headed toward Annapolis.

Fitzhugh was outraged by his wife's behavior and might have tried to chastise her, except that Father Darnley was watching, doing his best to appear dissociated from this scandal; but as the priest went to the sloop, which would take him, too, back to Annapolis, Rosalind involved him in her strategy. 'Sweet Father, you know what happened. Now find us a bridegroom for this girl.' He affected not to hear, so she placed herself before him and said, 'Tell the young men that I shall settle upon her a great share of my own dowry. But for the love of God, do something to save this soul.'

When the sloops were gone and the Steeds were left to absorb the reverberating shocks Rosalind had generated, Fitzhugh started to fulminate, believing that to be his duty as man-of-the-house, but his attempts were so ludicrous that Rosalind ignored him. Clasping his daughter— really her daughter—she whispered, 'On this day we did a good thing. Fifty years from now, gentle flower, you'll look back and laugh, and bless me, for I have saved your life.'

In February 1703, when annual storms swept the Chesapeake, a small boat put into Devon Creek bearing a solitary traveler, a young man, his hair tousled by wind and rain. Finding no one at the wharf, he pulled his homespun jacket about his damp shoulders and started toward the house.

Belatedly an indentured servant spotted him and started shouting, 'Stranger coming to our landing!' And down the servant came to warn the young man that this was Steed property.

'I know,' the young fellow said, plowing straight ahead. 'Father Darnley sent me.'

From the doorway Rosalind Steed heard these words and rushed out into the rain to greet the stranger. 'We are so glad to meet you,' she said in great excitement, clutching the young man's arm and leading him to the porch. She watched admiringly as he stamped his feet and swung his arms to brush away the rain.

'Name's Thomas Yates, James River. Father Darnley told me you have a—'

Rosalind interrupted, for she saw no need to mask her delight. 'Eve-

lyn!' she cried triumphantly. 'A young man's come to see you . . . through
the storm.'

Now she was free to tend her garden. Her daughter was married. Her
son was doing well at the college in France. And her husband had
resumed his routine of some days on Devon, some in the marsh. Even
the warehouse in Patamoke was flourishing.

She made it clear to the workmen that she did not wish a formal
garden in the English style, like the ones she had known along the
Rappahannock. She respected geometrical patterns and understood why
they were favored by ladies whose fingers never touched soil; through a
change of seasons and alternating blooms such gardens could be attractive, but she loved to work the soil, and to see large results, and this
produced her basic strategy: My principal flowers will be trees. Because
when you plant trees, you're entitled to believe you'll live forever.

So first she studied what trees were already in place, and fortunately,
scattered in the space between the wharf and the house stood maples and
elms of magnitude, and these she trimmed and cultivated to serve as
cornerstones of her planting. Her pride was a white oak of majestic
proportion: thirty feet at the base, nearly eighty feet tall and more than
one hundred and forty feet in the spread of its mighty branches. It
provided enough shade to protect an entire lawn; it had already been
sovereign when Captain John Smith named the island, and to it the other
trees related.

The lawn contained no red maples, so her opening operation in the fall
of 1703 was to transplant three such trees, two of which promptly died.
'You can't move trees of that size and expect them to live,' her husband
warned her, but she moved three more, just as large, and these lived. In
spring they were harbingers, in autumn the glory of the landing, visible
from all parts of the creek as one approached by boat.

Upon this solid foundation she composed the rest of her stupendous
garden: dogwood for spring, mountain laurel for summer and huge
plantings of pyracantha for autumn, at which time the dogwoods would
reappear with clusters of red berries.

'No tulips, no hollyhocks,' she said. 'And for heaven's sake, no box.
I want nothing that has to be coddled.' She avoided also the peony, the
tall magnolia, the phlox and hawthorn. But she was not averse to decora-
tion, for when her large plantings were in position she said, 'Now for the
jewels,' and in two dozen practical places she planted holly trees—two
male, twenty-two female—expecting bright berries of the latter to provide glow at sunset. And when the hollies were started—some to grow
forty feet tall—she added her final touch, the extravagant gesture which
would make this stretch of lawn her timeless portrait: in seven open areas

where the sun could strike she planted clumps of daylilies, knowing that when they proliferated the areas would be laden with tawny-colored flowers of great vitality and brilliance. July at Devon Island would be unforgettable; the daylilies would see to that.

In 1704 and 1705 her gigantic gardens were sprawling disappointments, for the transplanted maples were husbanding their strength and the daylilies had not begun to multiply—fifty would eventually result from one original—while the rudely transplanted dogwood seemed half dead. Small gardens with small flowers can be transformed in a matter of months; gardens focusing on trees require years. But by 1706 all parts seemed to merge: the oak dominated, its indented leaves bright in the sun, and the maples lent color. But it was the procession of the seasons that gratified: the shimmering white dogwoods of spring; the undisciplined daylilies of early summer; and in the autumn the exuberance of the pyracantha, that noblest of shrubs; and the turning colors of trees set against the permanent green of the enduring pines.

Her garden was a triumph, as durable and generous as she, but sometimes she felt that it displayed its greatest glory in midwinter, when bitter winds swept in from the northwest and snow covered all, with only the pines showing color: now the dogwood slept, and the hidden roots of the daylilies, and the visible buds of the laurel. Even the oak was barren, but then as she walked among the bare limbs she would catch sight of the hollies, those fine and stubborn trees to which the birds of winter came, seeking red berries, and her heart would leap and she would cry: 'When the last berries are gone, spring begins and all this starts again.' And she would run in the snow and visualize the beautiful gardens of summer, with the laurel as pale and lovely as any iris.

The garden of her personal life was not flourishing. Her husband now offered no excuses for his frequent absences, and she had to suppose that he was spending them at the marsh. She had never seen Nelly, but chance comments from infrequent visitors kept reminding her that the girl was beautiful and lively—'She boasts an excellent figure, and why she isn't married is a mystery.' The best explanation came from an acidulous woman whose husband managed the Steed offices in Patamoke: 'She's a Turlock, and they rarely wed.'

Rosalind had made cautious inquiries as to Nelly's children and learned that they were rollicking rascals, with their grandmother's Swedish blond hair and blue eyes—'Which is a wonder, seeing that they're mostly Turlock.'

'What do you mean?' Rosalind asked.

The conveyor of this information was a woman who envied the Steeds and now pondered how best to wound the mistress of the island. Biting her lower lip in study, she started to speak, then hesitated, then babbled on, 'You know, of course, that Flora Turlock, that's Nelly's mother . . . Have you ever seen her, Rosalind?'

Mrs. Steed shook her head, and the woman said, 'Of course not, how would you? *You* don't go to the marsh.'

Rosalind smiled, offered more tea and asked, 'What were you trying to say?'

'It's rather ugly, but it's true. Nelly's mother was Flora. Her father was Charley.'

'Charley who?'

'Charley Turlock—Flora's brother.' The woman held her teacup to her lips, then added, 'Her brother. She had a baby by her brother.'

Without considering what she was saying, Rosalind replied, 'I read somewhere that the Pharaohs of Egypt married their sisters.'

'Are you defending such behavior?'

'Not at all. I'm merely saying . . .' She left the sentence unfinished, for it occurred to her that no words would satisfy this woman, and that whatever was said would circulate viciously throughout the community.

'You know, of course,' the woman continued, 'that Flora was publicly whipped for her sin?'

'There seems to be a great deal of women being whipped in Patamoke.'

'But . . .'

'And I wonder if it does any good.'

'Mrs. Steed . . .'

'And that damnable ducking stool. They reserve it for women, too, and I suppose that if I weren't the wife of Fitzhugh, I'd be lashed to it and ducked in the Choptank.'

This was heresy, and the visitor assessed it as such; by the shocked look on her face she betrayed her plan to report widely what Mrs. Steed had said, but Rosalind was not finished. 'I really don't care whether you repeat what I just said or not. The whipping of women and the ducking stool are the hideous acts of frightened men, and I am sick of them.'

Four days later Fitzhugh returned from Patamoke, distraught. 'In town the talk concerned your challenge to the authorities.'

'You mean what I said in defense of Flora Turlock?' She paused, then added, 'Nelly's mother. Your Nelly's mother.'

This name had never before been spoken in Fitzhugh's presence, and he was incensed at what he considered his wife's lack of good breeding. 'Wives don't speak of such things. You be careful what you say about whippings . . . and the ducking stool.'

'Are you threatening me, Fitzhugh? You must know that's idle.'

'I'm reminding you that the magistrates can sentence you, if they wish.'

'They'll not wish,' she said brightly. 'They'd be loath to humiliate you.'

'And what do you mean by that?'

'That so long as you live I can say what I wish.' Staring at him as if he were a stranger, she added, 'You're no longer my husband, Fitzhugh, but you are my protector. And under your protection I shall do as I please, and it pleases me to warn you that the punishments you men mete out to women are barbarous and must be stopped.'

'When you speak like that, Rosalind, you are very unwomanly. For you deal with things that should not concern a lady.'

Fitzhugh was wrong in thinking that because his wife was ungainly she was unfeminine. No lady on the Choptank awaited the arrival of the next fashion doll more eagerly than she, for whenever she learned that a ship was scheduled to arrive from London, she contrived to be first aboard to catch the precious prize.

Since it would have been impractical for the London fashion houses to publish books showing their creations, and since the newspapers and magazines which reached the colonies were deficient in illustrations, it had become the custom for merchants to construct articulated dolls, fourteen inches high, and dress them in exact replicas of the latest mode. Sandaled and bewigged, these enchanting little figures were boxed and shipped abroad, so that women in the remotest backwaters could know the proper length of hem.

In May 1706 the snow *Fair Rosalind* made a scurried trip from London and put into Devon with one of the most tantalizing dolls ever to have crossed the Atlantic. It showed a trim little lady wearing a pale-blue coif adorned with six tiny rows of lace and a dress that caught the breath because of its innovation. Over a gold-brocaded stomacher hung a noble sacque made of heavy bombazine. Rosalind had seen sacques before and liked their normal flowing lines, but this was different, because just below the hips it flared outward at least eighteen inches on each side.

'How do they do it?' she asked her fascinated sewing slaves as they fingered the cloth, trying to detect how they must cut it to duplicate the model. Deftly they lifted the layers, and what they uncovered evoked gasps of admiration, for the heavy fabric rested upon four hoops made of delicate, bent wood.

'How wonderful!' one of the slaves cried, dropping the skirt, raising it, dropping it again.

'We can make!' another said enthusiastically, following one of the seams with her finger.

But Rosalind had developed a sure sense of what to wear and what to avoid, and she disappointed the slaves by saying, 'Not for me. Those hoops would make me look even bigger.' The women sighed as she cut the hoops away with her little scissors, but they had to agree that when the heavy sacque was allowed to fall free, it looked better for a tall woman.

'That's to be it,' she said, and before the doll had been in America two hours, its lines were being reproduced not in heavy bombazine but in soft dimity, and when the new dress was finished, and the lace cap made, and the slippers covered in red, she presided at her table with added assurance, for she knew she was dressed as well as the most fashionable women of London.

Thoughts of England reminded her of Mark, and she became impatient for his return. She knew him only as the initiator of letters from Europe, but his manner of writing was so distinct, and his wit so apparent, that he was becoming a real person whom she knew she would like:

> I am informed through my skill at reading letters upside down as they rest on other people's desks that Fithians have arranged for Tom Yates to assume control of eleven thousand acres on the James. They've warned him that he may be overstretching himself, and I wonder too, but at the foot of their copy of the letter the senior Fithian wrote: 'This young lad seems a good sort. I think we shall be safe in extending him credit.' What gave me assurance was that in their last order, Tom and Evelyn asked for three crates of books.

She was therefore delighted when, in January 1707, Mark tested his luck once more by slipping a letter home with the captain of the swift-darting snow *Fair Rosalind.* When accepting the letter the captain warned, 'It'll take God's luck for us to sneak our way past the devils.' But he had escaped the pirates, and when his gaily painted snow tied up at Patamoke, there was much admiration for his daring, and Fitzhugh showed Mark's letter through the town and said, 'The boy's coming home on the October convoy.' And townspeople replied, 'Pray God the ships get through.'

It seems incredible, but in these years the Chesapeake shivered under a state of siege; more than a hundred pirate ships—English from Jamaica, French from Martinique—clustered at Cape Henry, waiting to pounce on any merchant ship from Virginia or Maryland foolhardy enough to risk running the blockade. And if the frightened merchantmen remained huddled at their wharves, the pirates ventured arrogantly into the bay, ravaging any plantations on exposed headlands. Many an English family on the James River, or the York or Rappahannock, experienced the terror of seeing French pirates sail boldly to their wharf, storm ashore and plunder the plantation. Silverware, tobacco and slaves were taken, and sometimes the home was burned. Farmers were slain and valuable ships were stolen from their moorings.

It was an age of terror—when a pirate might sail a ship with forty guns and a crew of two hundred, and nothing on the Chesapeake could withstand their assault. Nor was the British navy of much help; it was engaged in that wild and futile War of the Spanish Succession; its ships were needed to support the Duke of Marlborough as he fought in Flanders against the French, and none were available to confront the pirates of the Caribbean. Any English ship leaving either London or Annapolis ran the risk of almost certain capture, and if resistance was offered, it was likely that all passengers would be either shot or hanged.

The distraught colonists, whose existence depended upon commerce with London, devised a strategy that was furiously expensive but also effective: English ships would cross the Atlantic only in giant convoys, one leaving London in October, another departing the Chesapeake in May. During the remainder of the year no ship would venture forth, except swift blockade runners like the *Fair Rosalind.* These took enormous risks, trusting upon their speed to outrun the waiting pirates; if they succeeded, their profits were exorbitant.

Mark Steed left England in the October convoy. His ship, a two-masted brig built years ago by the Paxmore brothers, was owned by his family, but he sought no special privilege; he was an ordinary passenger making a dangerous transit. As his ship sailed down the Thames he became aware that seven others seemed to be moving in concert, and their presence lent assurance; but as they left the Thames and entered the Channel he realized that the convoy was not to be a mere eight ships. Some fifty waited in the roads, and all turned gracefully to the south, dotting the Channel with their sails.

'Magnificent,' Mark said to a gentleman returning to Annapolis.

'We've still to pass the coast of France,' the gentleman warned, and as the convoy stood off the cliffs of Dover, with the menacing shores of France quite visible, young Steed was gratified to see two English warships move up to give protection. 'With them on our flank,' the gentleman said, 'the French will never dare.'

The impressive convoy now turned westward for the run down the Channel, but winds failed and the sixty ships idled on the glassy sea, almost touching one another as they drifted. Sailors were assigned to guard the rails, so that if two ships appeared near collision, they could push them apart with little apparent energy. Night fell, and slim lights showed from distant portholes.

'Ahoy!' the watchmen cried whenever some ship moved too close, and if the cry was repeated, sailors ran to the railing to push the invader away, and all seemed like an assembly of toys set adrift in a basin by children.

But when the wind rose, and the convoy could move on toward Plymouth at the end of the Channel, Mark gasped at what awaited. There, in the roads where the Spanish Armada had been defeated by Drake and Hawkins, stood no less than a hundred and sixty ships, their sails aloft, their captains waiting for the signal.

'I never knew there were so many ships!' Mark cried to his fellow passengers. And then, to cap his astonishment, a squadron of nine warships left Plymouth and moved into position at strategic points about the vast convoy.

A gun fired, its echoes muffled by the thousand sails. A blue pennant ran up the commodore's halyard, and each of the warships responded with a gun salute. 'Look smart!' the captain of Steed's brig shouted, and his vessel, along with the more than two hundred and twenty others, turned with the wind and set out for the New World.

It was an unforgettable passage, an assembly of riches, a convocation of daring spirits. At no time could Mark look from the railing of the brig and see less than fifty sails scattered upon the horizon, and at night he could see the same number of lights, except when fog settled over the Atlantic. Then, in the gloom, the commodore's ship would fire its gun at intervals, and the heavy air, bearing down upon the waves, would deaden the sound. Sometimes it seemed as if the gun had exploded only a field away, and then Steed would clasp his hands about his chest in the cold November air and experience a sense of well-being that he had never known before.

'We've passed the French coast,' he muttered to himself, but now came the greater risk.

It was customary for the annual convoy to sail not directly to the Chesapeake, for that route was impossibly stormy, but to head for the calmer waters of Barbados, where regrouping was possible, and from there to proceed north past the pirate strongholds and on to the Chesapeake. The disadvantage of this route was that its final stages traversed waters infested by pirates. However, with the warships constantly circling the huge fleet, it was sometimes possible to make the transit while losing only a few ships.

'But the strictest discipline must be observed,' said the young ensign dispatched from the commodore's brigantine. 'If there is any straggler, he will be lost.' At Barbados he issued printed instructions and said that signals would be changed for this part of the voyage: 'Two guns and red pennant mean that the faster ships must luff and wallow in the wind until the slower catch up. If any ship, and yours looks to be a fast one, passes the commodore's, it will be sunk. Understood?'

The captain nodded, so the young man continued, 'We enter dangerous waters. Keep a constant lookout. We know that Carpaux is on the prowl and so is Jean Vidal. What's worse, we have information that Bonfleur now has three swift ships under his command. Look smart.'

Carpaux had often invaded the Chesapeake, and Vidal was fierce, a young firebrand out of Martinique known to burn ships and cast away passengers, but it was Bonfleur who had become the constant terror. He was an old man now, sixty-four, and the survivor of numberless attempts to catch him. He was the scourge of the Caribbean, the burner of Panama, the destroyer of Belize. He had fought for so long and so viciously that no English tactic could surprise him, and for the past forty years he had preyed upon the Chesapeake, invading the rivers and setting the plantations aflame.

He had often sailed in concert with Stede Bonnet and L'Ollonais, smaller in stature than either, more brutal than both. Once he had gone into Cartagena alone, with only thirty-seven men, and had captured the entire city, divesting it of a fortune and slaying more than a hundred. In 1705 he and the two other ships that often sailed with him cut out eleven merchantmen from the October convoy, burning them all and killing scores.

The French offered him sanctuary at Martinique, because they hoped he might inflict great damage on the English, but just as often he captured French ships and put them to the sword, or Spanish, or Dutch. He was without morals, or pity, or remorse, a vicious old man who had seen a score of pirates hanged by the various authorities; his war against all civilized nations was endless. In the late days of December 1708 he commanded ninety-one guns and seven hundred men, and he had boasted that he would 'cut the English convoy to ribbons.'

The commodore had other plans. He intended shepherding his huge collection of sail past Point Comfort and into the relative safety of the Chesapeake, and to accomplish this he must tighten his formation so that his warships could act in concert if an attack came. Accordingly, he flashed his signals, but when the two hundred and twenty ships moved closer, minor collisions, and some not so minor, became inevitable. The winds would change and ships would have to tack, and as they did so they would climb slowly upon the backs of smaller ships, and spars would shatter and sails would be lost.

Then the commodore would signal: 'Faster ships luff!' and those like the one Mark Steed rode would turn with the wind, and hoist a staysail and ride sideways to the waves, rolling like pith balls in a shallow saucer, hour upon hour, and all except the most practiced hands would become sick from the pitching motion, but the convoy held.

Off the northern coast of Haiti, where the wind was brisk, the pirates decided to attack: Carpaux down from the Carolinas, with Vidal and Bonfleur out from refitting in Martinique, descended upon the stragglers, eleven pirate ships with two thousand fighting men and more than two hundred cannon. And they might have succeeded had not the commodore anticipated their bold action. Swinging his own ship about to confront the pirates, he signaled all warships to follow and invited any merchantmen with heavy guns to move on his flank. Steed's ship was one of the latter, and it sped at the two pirate vessels commanded by Carpaux.

It was a short, violent engagement. The huge pirate guns ripped into many of the lumbering merchantmen, but destroyed none. The commodore's flotilla ran directly at the pirates, scattering them and sinking one of the craft attached to Jean Vidal. The big merchant ships with heavy armament fired resolutely at the swifter pirates and in time drove most of them off, but Henri Bonfleur, victor in many such battles, knew that no convoy was safe if it could be scattered, and with great heroism directed his three ships to cut directly into the heart of the vast collection.

He sailed through it like an avenging spirit, spitting fire and threatening the very existence of this massive assembly. But when he came to the brig in which Steed rode, he found that captain not turning to flee but bearing directly down upon him. It was obvious that the two must crash, but Steed's captain refused to waver. On and on his bowsprit came.

'Prepare to crash!' the mate shouted, and Steed braced himself as the forward part of his ship raked the pirate, knocking men down and tearing away much of the rigging.

'Prepare to repulse boardings!' the mate cried, and Steed grabbed a pin, brandishing it as if it had a chance to repel a pirate's pistol. Some of Bonfleur's men did try to board, hideous creatures with beards and knives, but the English sailors repelled them as the two vessels ground and scraped their way free.

At this moment young Mark Steed caught full sight of the pirate captain: a smallish man with a beard flecked in gray, a heavy sweater about his neck, two pistols dangling useless at his knees, words screaming from his ugly lips. He was so repulsive that Steed felt driven by some avenging force to hurl his belaying pin, but his aim was bad and it clattered harmlessly to the deck. As the two vessels ripped apart, leaving the pirate ship sorely damaged, Bonfleur glared momentarily at his opponent, then ignored him in the business of saving his ship.

This proved impossible, for two of the commodore's vessels bore down on the wounded pirate ship and began peppering it with such heavy gunfire that it was plainly doomed. But not Bonfleur. One of his subaltern ships, aware of the master's peril, swung boldly in a circle that brought it along the lee side of Bonfleur's sinking vessel, and as it swept past, pirates reached out and grabbed Bonfleur, pulling him to safety.

'Convoy reform,' signaled the commodore, and as night fell, it reassembled, deck close to deck, while warships prowled the edges.

The pirates had been driven off. The merchantmen turned north, and before the new year they sailed into the Chesapeake. As the vast congregation moved up the bay, cohorts dropped off for the James, and the York, and the Rappahannock, and the Potomac, and wherever they touched shore people came from many miles to receive that year's mail from England and a joyous sight of friends they had not seen for six or seven years. Guns were fired, and far up the rivers planters told their friends, 'The convoy's here!'

On the third day of passage up the bay, Steed's ship left the dwindling assembly and turned toward the Choptank. Slaves on watch at the western end of the island lit fires. Other slaves, observing them, set their stacks of wood ablaze, and before long someone at the plantation was firing a cannon, so that people in the big house could run to the north shore and watch their ship as it came home, safe from perils, safe from pirates.

Triumphantly the brig breasted the eastern approaches and entered the creek, where ropes were thrown ashore so that slaves could haul the vessel homeward, and from the deck Mark Steed, twenty-seven and skilled in religion from France and law from England, looked out to greet his new mother.

She saw him then as she would always remember him: a young man, young in appearance, young in bravery and cleanliness of spirit. 'Here comes the salvation of the Steeds,' she murmured as he approached.

He was that. Where his father was indolent, he was concentrated, and where his uncles had confused concepts for running a plantation, he adhered to a few basic principles. When he tried to explain them to the older Steeds he quickly realized that they had no comprehension of what he was trying to do; the one who understood was Rosalind.

'In all things we must be self-sufficient,' he told her, and she knew he was right. 'Never again must we buy just slaves . . . men and women who can do nothing special. I want every indentured servant and slave on this plantation to be an expert, and if we can't train them, we'll sell them off and buy others already trained.'

The Steeds now had twenty-seven white workers and sixty-eight blacks, whom they divided among three work camps: one for the gardeners and the men who worked the ships; one at the west end of Devon for the tobacco fields; and one on the mainland growing nothing but tobacco. There was a fourth gang consisting of four blacks who could be assigned anywhere; they worked perpetually at burning down trees so that new land might be brought into cultivation after the greedy tobacco plants had consumed the richness of existing fields.

These were the specialists that Mark and Rosalind developed: weavers to make the huge amounts of cloth needed each year by the Steeds and the other slaves; lacemakers for the finer cloth; tailors; tanners, shoemakers; barbers; cabinetmakers; sailors; caulkers; timber men to bring huge trees to the pits; sawyers; carpenters; foundry men; ropemakers; fishermen; coopers; and most important of all, skilled handymen who could be relied on to fix almost anything. After all, the Steeds were running what amounted to a small town, and it was Mark's responsibility to see that it functioned.

He was surprised when his new mother insisted upon one other specialization: 'I should like to have two slaves skilled in making bricks.'

'Whatever for?'

'I shall be needing bricks.' So Mark, laughing at his indulgence, sent across the bay to St. Mary's City, where building had stopped with the loss of the capital, and bought two slaves well versed in brickmaking. It was a good investment, for these two found clay deposits with enough trees nearby to furnish charcoal, and before long a steady supply of light-red brick was forthcoming.

Mark wondered what his mother intended doing with them; some she used to build a moss-grown terrace adjacent to the house, and others were laid in pleasant walks among the flourishing trees. But such diversions utilized only a small portion of the product; the rest was carefully stored until the pile became impressive.

'Shall we put the men to other work?' Mark asked.

'Never.'

'But what shall you do with the bricks . . . thousands of them?'

'They shall be very useful, Mark.' And the piles grew.

No aspect of the Steed operations failed to interest her. When she discovered that her family's ships were often laid up because worms had eaten out the bottoms, she consulted with the Paxmores, who told her, 'Against the shipworm we can do nothing. It flourishes in these waters and eats wood the way thee eats hominy.'

'Can't we paint something on the wood to protect it?'

'Tar and pitch help,' they said, and forthwith she put teams of mainland slaves at work cutting pine trees and rendering pitch and turpentine to treat the bottoms. This was effective, but only so long as the tar held the pitch close to the treated wood; a very heavy application might last four months.

'Is there some way we can hide the wood?' she asked the Steed captains, and they said that copper sheathing helped but that it was prohibitively expensive. She imported large sheets on the next October convoy, and when they were hammered onto the bottom of the largest ship, the hungry worms were rebuffed. But as her captains had warned, this was too expensive for the colonies. Lead sheathing might work, but there was no lead.

Grim-lipped, as if the shipworms had declared war on her personally, she started afresh to study them. Teredos they were called, two-inch whitish creatures with shell-like noses that could bore through oak. When she crept beneath a hauled ship to inspect their work, she saw that they had perforated planks, boring in all directions until the wood was pocketed and ready to fall apart. No wood was safe from their attack, only copper or lead could stop them.

But then two accidental bits of information came her way. One of her captains said, 'They're always worse in July and August. That's why it's a clever trick to send the eastbound convoy out of these waters in May. The worm can't get at them during the summer.' Equally helpful was the comment by the older Paxmore: 'We don't suffer from the worm as much as others, because our boatyard is upstream, in fresher water.'

From these clues she devised the strategy that saved the Steed ships: 'Mark, come June, I want our captains to move their ships far up the Choptank. They're to stop there during July and August—and you watch, we'll not have a worm.'

The captains grumbled at such preposterous instructions from a woman, but they complied, and to their amazement they learned that Rosalind was right: in fresh water new teredos did not breed, and old ones already attached to the bottoms died and fell away. By this clever shift in anchoring, the Steeds saved many pounds formerly spent on refitting, and their ships sailed faster because the wood was clean.

Mark tended all financial matters, spending much time at the family warehouse in Patamoke casting up accounts. He was there when Nelly Turlock appeared one morning to select numerous swatches of cloth; she thrust the door open with a flourish of her right arm and strode to the middle of the room as if she were part owner. She was a striking woman, the same age as Mark but much more worldly, for when she realized that this new young man was the son of her protector she made a special effort to attract his favorable attention and refused to be waited upon by servants.

'I need three yards of fearnought for Charlie's hunting pants,' she said with a gentle smile, as if laughing inwardly at some joke she understood but Mark did not. As he rolled out the rough double-thick woolen which could withstand thorns, he tried to watch her undetected, but she caught his eye and smiled again.

'And some of this Irish frize.' She dropped her voice and added by way of explanation, 'That's for my winter coat. The kersey is for me too.' While he measured off these fabrics she rummaged among his goods and came up with a heavy bolt of Osnaburg, good for making stout skirts against the cold weather.

'How many lengths do I need?' she asked sweetly, holding one end against her shoulder.

'Take ample,' Mark advised, but the slave who customarily attended the cloth interrupted, 'She take half again. For shoulders.' And Mark said, 'I think he's right,' and he smiled at her as he cut the goods.

She ordered much more, but when he had summed the numbers, she made no offer to pay. 'Put it in the book of Mr. Steed,' she said, and with an arrogant reach of her left forefinger she riffled through the pages to identify the one on which the accounts of Fitzhugh Steed were kept. When Mark entered the latest purchases he saw that the total debt was considerable, and it occurred to him—judging solely by what she had bought this day—that she was feeding and clothing the entire Turlock establishment.

He did not feel competent to discuss this matter with his father, but he did go to Rosalind—'It's nothing better than stealing, what that woman's doing.' And this opened the problem of Fitzhugh's deportment.

Rosalind said, 'Mark, it's quite simple, really, and I make no protest. Not even about the thefts.'

'But he's behaving like such an ass.' When Rosalind objected to this harsh evaluation, Mark continued, 'I can understand his philandering while Mother was alive. Things were really rather dreadful. And after her death, there need be no restraint. But now he has a wife—a perfectly fine wife . . .' He shook his head in disgust and walked toward the window.

'Mark, listen. He fell into bad habits bit by bit. And bit by bit it's corroded him. I suppose you know he and Nelly have three children.'

'Children! My God!' This intelligence so disturbed him that he paced the room, then stopped before his mother to say bitterly, 'They're my brothers and sisters . . . in a manner of speaking.' This image amused him and he broke into nervous laughter. 'This is really quite silly, isn't it?'

'Yes. It's what any woman must live through . . . as best she can. That is, when she's not pretty—I mean, when she's ugly.'

'Mother!' The cry was an honest protest, and the confusion on Mark's face proved this. His new mother was only six years older than himself, and this spare differential caused perplexity, but she was many years wiser, and her judgments often disclosed a profundity which surprised him. The simple fact was that he liked her. She possessed all the attributes he had wanted to find in his father, and none of the debilitating weaknesses which made the elder Steed such a pathetic figure.

'Every year you'll become more beautiful,' he said. 'And Father won't be here to see.'

'He'll outlive both of us,' she predicted.

'I didn't mean that.'

When Mark sailed back to Patamoke to enlarge the warehouse, he hoped that Nelly Turlock would not sashay in, demanding dividends for her family. But she continued to appear, insolent, provocative and infuriatingly self-assured. She seemed to have a nose capable of seeking out any item imported from London and an appetite so voracious that a good portion of every new shipment seemed destined for her. One afternoon Mark calculated that Nelly Turlock consumed slightly more than twice as much Steed income as Rosalind, but when he presented these figures to his mother, she pointed out, 'There are more Turlocks in the marsh than Steeds on the island.'

This was not exactly true. Henry and Paul, sons of the original Edmund who had settled at Jamestown in 1607, had produced eight children between them—Mark's grandfather, Captain Earl Steed, was one of them—and these children had not been tardy in begetting offspring of their own, so that Devon Island housed many Steeds in the plantation hall and an equal number in smaller satellite cottages. In fact, the island was becoming so cluttered that Rosalind decided something must be done. Her husband humphed and garrumphed in his normal fatuous manner and said, 'Any Steed can live on this island as long as he wants to,' but Rosalind paid little attention. Instead she appealed to Mark, and her reasons for wanting to depopulate the burdened island were so cogent that he gave enthusiastic support.

So this second wife, this outsider from Virginia, assembled the clan in the room with the pewter dishes and spread out her plan: 'The big house will remain here . . .' (Some of the Steeds would later recall that when she said this she hesitated, as if uncertain about the continuity of the house.) 'And the young people of the next generation who will be managing the estates can remain here. By that I mean Mark . . . and his wife, when he takes one. We'll keep the Heron Cottage for members of the family, and Holly Hall, but the other cottages we'll convert to slave quarters.'

This produced noisy comment, but she was obdurate. 'Those little houses must go. They're hovels.' When family protest subsided she said, 'Mark and I have been exploring our lands. On the north bank of the Choptank are many excellent sites. Each family should choose the one it prefers. Six hundred acres of cleared land will accompany every house you build.'

Now the argument became vigorous, with a dozen Steeds rejecting the plan, but Rosalind plowed on. 'I've found one location superior to all others, and it seems to me that two or even three families could move there with gratification. Indeed, it seems finer than the island. With proper husbandry it could become a paradise.'

The undercurrents of protest quieted. The Steeds were not happy with Rosalind's dominance in matters so vital to the family, but they knew that she was no fool, and if she was stating that one of the mainland sites was more appealing than the island, they would listen. 'Sail to the western end of Turlock's marsh and enter Dividing Creek. Go beyond the cove and on the western bank you'll find a deep entrance to a splendid creek. Proceed up it for half a mile and you'll come to a fork. It's the land between the arms of that fork I'm recommending. They tell me an Indian chieftain used to live there, and it's named in the deed our family bought from Janney as the Refuge.' With these words she launched a treasure hunt, for numerous Steeds sent their sloops up Dividing Creek to evaluate the majestic triangle once occupied by Pentaquod of the Choptanks.

It was incredible how this choice fragment of land, denuded of every primeval tree by the clearing fires of 1631, had revitalized itself. For eight years the fields had produced moderately good Oronoco, but tobacco depleted minerals so swiftly that in the end the Steeds found it more profitable to abandon the peninsula and burn trees in other locations so that new fields still rich in nutrients could be developed.

On the abandoned fields birds had dropped seeds unharmed by passage through their bowels, and these had become cedars that grew like weeds. In time a few oak and hickory seeds took root, and with every autumn wind some loblolly blew in. Then holly berries arrived, brought by birds, and by the end of fifty years the land was once more as magnificent as in those far-off days when Pentaquod first identified it as his home; the giant oaks four hundred years old were gone, of course, and the monstrous old loblollies, but only an eye long accustomed to forests would have marked their absence, for the land was recovered: fire and overcultivation and the deprivation of minerals and leaching and every kind of abuse had failed to destroy this splendid soil. All that was required to renew it was the quiet passage of seventy years, during which it had lain dormant, restructuring itself.

How beautiful it was when the young people of this fifth generation of American Steeds came to rediscover it: deer abounded and beaver; geese and ducks vied for a place to rest; the last bears and wolves in the area made it their home; and in the small marshes at the heads of the embracing streams a thousand different kinds of life proliferated. Once again it was a paradise with vistas of enchantment, and as each night ended, with the sun struggling to break loose in the east, blue herons would fly back to their ancient home, probing the muddy bottoms of the creeks and crying in the darkness when they found succulence.

On the occasions when Fitzhugh stayed at Devon, life on the island could be most pleasant. He was a congenial man who loved his children and who savored the routines of plantation living; he was excited whenever a new shipment of slaves arrived from Haiti or when one of the family ships set forth with its hogsheads of Oronoco for London. He was especially delighted when, on those happy days which occurred once or twice a year, some incoming ship brought letters from Europe; then he would arrange them carefully on the big table in the kitchen, and without opening them, try to guess who had written and with what information.

He was courteous with his wife and insisted that all others who came into contact with her be the same. In a kind of banter he called her 'Mistress Roz' and seemed pleased with her management of the plantation. At least, he never interfered or tried to countermand her orders, but his acquiescence was tinged with condescension, as if her duties were some unimportant game in which he had no interest.

Since they no longer slept together, his attitude toward her was that of an indulgent uncle, and this she had to accept if she wanted to enjoy any kind of life at all on Devon. So she did accept, without complaint, realizing that he treated her thus because he knew himself to be incompetent. She made the hard decisions because all his life he had inclined toward the easy ones, and in doing so, had dissipated whatever character he might have had.

Rosalind, for her part, treated her husband with deference and catered to his vanities. He was the master; the children were to respect him; and when the yearly issues of the *Tatler* arrived, he of course got to read them first. Invariably she addressed him by his full name, Fitzhugh, and saw to it that the children spoke of him as Father. She paid exaggerated attention to his opinions and often seconded them enthusiastically in front of the children, while intending to ignore them as soon as he was gone.

Fitzhugh had never experienced any kind of love for his wife; to him she was a big, awkward woman with a voice two levels too strong, and he would have been astounded to discover that she possessed all the emotions of a pretty young thing of seventeen. She, in the first months of their marriage, had truly loved this flashy, careless fellow and had been ecstatic in her first pregnancy, and even when she had fully discovered his incapacities, she still had tried to retain her love for him; but now she reacted to him pretty much as she might to a big and lively puppy: he was fun to have around the house but hardly of any consequence.

On those disappointing terms the Steeds existed. But their lives were not tragic. Indeed, an uninformed spectator might have judged the Steed household to be one of constant merriment, for Rosalind saw to it that spirits were kept high. In this she was abetted by her husband, for he delighted in playing games with his children and teasing them into one preposterous situation or another. With little help from his first wife, he had reared two fine offspring in Mark and Evelyn, and now he was doing the same with the three children of his later years. He taught them word games, and the locations of strange countries and the characters of mythology, and he never gave them anything or shared ideas with them before making them engage in his game of Many Questions.

'I have brought something special from the store. Many questions.'

'Is it made of paper?'

'No.'

'Can I chew it?'

'You'd be sick if you did.'

Sometimes he would fend them off for half an hour, always sharpening their wits, then catching them in his arms when they solved his riddles.

He also ensured that the big house contained ample supplies of food, assigning two slaves to the job of hunting game. In the course of a week the Steeds might eat venison, lamb, muskrat, duck, turkey and occasionally pork. But the dish he relished above all others was shad, backed with onions and savory. When it was served, the children protested at the bones, but he muzzled them with the assurance that 'shad makes the brain grow, because if you're not smart enough to miss the bones, you're not smart enough to eat it.'

He, not Rosalind, tended to supervise the kitchen, and he taught the three slaves who worked there his preferences in baking breads and making calf's-foot jelly. He was especially attentive to the ways in which they served the two permanent staples, oysters and crab, and allowed to his visitors that nowhere in Maryland could one find better crab cakes than at Devon.

For him no banquet deserved the name unless in addition to the six meats and seven vegetables and eight desserts, it contained either platefuls of oysters or dishes of crisp crab cakes; and usually, when the table was completely set, he would lean back and in his hearty way tell any guests, 'When Mistress Roz came across the bay to marry me, her family in Virginia accompanied her to the boat, weeping. "You're going to Maryland! You'll starve!" And here she is, starving.'

Fitzhugh also took charge of the wine cellar, and saw to it that it contained bottles of Burgundy, a cask of port and a tun of Madeira, and when neighboring plantations ran short of either of the last two, he generously supplied them until the next ships arrived with replenishments. He supervised his slaves in the making of cider, which his family consumed in copious amounts, but he alone prepared the three drinks for which Devon became noted. Syllabub was served at most meals: 'One part milk, one part cream; one part ale, flavored with lemon and lime, topped with cinnamon bark.' Possets were drunk before retiring, for they were conducive to sleep and good digestion, but persicot was reserved for festive occasions. Kept in cruets, a golden amber in color, it was served after the dessert to leave a pleasant tingling in the mouth. Of it Fitzhugh said, 'For six weeks I warn the slaves to set aside every peach and apricot pit, and cherry, too, and when I have enough I cut each one in four parts, and steep them in French brandy with cloves and cinnamon. After three months I add some sugar water, and the longer this stands, the better it becomes.'

Rosalind tended the more mundane matters, particularly the medical care of all who pertained to the plantation; on some mornings the little house behind the mansion became an infirmary, with three Steeds, four other white planters and a dozen slaves in line for her ministrations. From long experience with plantation life, she had assembled those remedies best calculated to cure the ills that accompanied the cultivation of tobacco on remote fields: ipecac to induce vomiting, laxative salts for opposite effect, oil of juniper for the chest, spirits of saffron to control spasms, and glyster for burns.

Her sovereign specific was hot linseed oil, applied liberally and covered with cloths; this subdued congestions. She also used tartar emetic with great frequency to cure what she called distress, and in a small bottle which she alone controlled, she kept laudanum to use when amputations or tooth extractions were necessary.

For the Steed plantations, unlike some across the bay, were centers of work. Any of the Steed boys approaching manhood had learned how to tend fields, and make casks, and cure Oronoco, and figure profits. At some point or other, most had worked in the family warehouse at Pata-moke, and many had sailed as ordinary seamen to Bristol. The scorn in which many English gentlemen held trade was no part of the Steed tradition; their family had prospered not primarily from tobacco but from the myriad activities associated with it, and in some years when Oronoco sold for little in either Bristol or London, the Steeds continued to make a satisfactory income from their barrels, their beaver pelts, their ships and, above all, their warehouse. It was difficult for anyone to live along the Choptank without paying tribute in some form or other to the Steeds.

It was a good life, but sometimes when Rosalind looked at her florid husband playing with the children, she could not escape thinking: If only he had the capacity to know that an ugly woman can also be a loving human being! At such times she would harbor deep resentment that God had not made her beautiful, but when her hurt was deepest she would swear grimly: I'll not surrender. I'll not sink to his level. Ugly or not, I'll be the best person I can.

Among the visitors to the Patamoke warehouse was a petite, solemn Quaker girl of eighteen. Dressed in prim gray, with a bonnet whose strings fell untied about her shoulders, she had that clarity of skin which makes any woman beautiful; in her case her small features were so harmoniously balanced and pleasing that whenever she entered the store Mark Steed, if he happened to be there that day, would remark upon the difference between her and the rambunctious Turlock woman. He also compared her with his mother, and from something his mother had read him from Shakespeare, thought: Since she's pretty, she's probably stupid.

To test this he tried on several occasions to engage her in conversation, but failed. She had come to the store for specific items required by the shipbuilders and was not to be diverted. In the bright fabrics from Paris she could express no interest, and neither she nor any of the other Paxmores needed the lace of Bruges or the copperware of Ghent. She seemed almost retarded, a gray shadow appearing mysteriously at the town wharf in a shallop sailed by her brother, saying nothing, never smiling, never responding to gallantries.

Once at home he remarked upon her strange behavior, and Rosalind asked bluntly, 'When are you getting married, Mark?' and he replied, 'When I left London, I had a kind of arrangement with Louise Fithian.'

'London? I'd have thought you'd want a local wife.'

'Louise is a dear, really she is.' And he expounded on her qualities with an enthusiasm which pleased his mother.

'Have you a silhouette?'

He did. It had been cut by a Frenchman skilled in using small scissors, and showed a standard profile, a standard pouting beauty. 'She seems quite attractive,' Rosalind said with no enthusiasm. Then, returning the silhouette, she mused, 'I wonder if it's a good idea to import a wife from London. I do wonder.'

'The sainted Edmund imported Martha by mail. Never saw her before she stepped on his wharf.'

'She was a fugitive. Driven from home. By her religion.'

'That's another problem. There are no Catholic girls on the Choptank.'

'The Fithian girl can't be Catholic.'

'No. But I know her.'

'You also know the Paxmore girl.'

'The little gray one?'

'Not so gray, Mark.'

And she insisted that he accompany her to Peace Cliff, and when he had tied their sloop at the Paxmore wharf and climbed the low hill to the telescope house, she led him not to young Amanda, who watched with keen interest, but to old Ruth Brinton, who was raging.

'How terrible!' she stormed. 'In the square facing the courthouse.'

'What happened?' Rosalind asked.

'To sell human beings under official sanction.'

'Mrs. Paxmore,' Rosalind interrupted. 'It's always been done and it's done humanely. Now stop ranting.'

'But yesterday they sold a mother north, a father south, and a nine-year-old daughter upriver.'

'We do not do that on the island,' Rosalind said quietly.

'We all do it, my dear friend, if one does.'

'No!' Rosalind protested. 'Each family lives by its own standards, and no Steed has ever abused a slave. We need them and we love them.'

'But if a human family can be dragged onto a dock at the very door of the house of justice . . .' The old woman began to tremble, whereupon Amanda moved to quieten her. Speaking defensively she said, 'On this point Grandmother is never satisfied.'

'Nor ever will be,' the old woman snapped.

'The meeting has rebuked her many times,' Amanda said. 'But on she goes. A voice in the wilderness.' She said this with such simplicity that she resembled some Hebrew maiden in the Old Testament.

'I wanted you to meet my son Mark,' Rosalind said.

'I've heard he's a fine lad,' Ruth Brinton said.

'Where would you have heard that?'

'Amanda told me. She sees him when she goes to fetch nails.'

Rosalind noticed that the little Quaker girl did not blush, she looked straight ahead without apologies; but Mark blushed profusely, and Rosalind thought: He should. It's a very human reaction and it differentiates him from his father.

On the sail back to Devon, Rosalind said nothing, but once she had her son alone in the house she said firmly, 'I wanted you to see a real woman,' and she told him briefly of Ruth Brinton's travail in Massachusetts and of the exemplary life she had lived in Patamoke, serving as the conscience of both the Quaker and the general community.

'You don't fool me, talking about old Mrs. Paxmore. You wanted me to see Amanda . . . in her home.'

'I did indeed. I wanted you to see what a home of integrity could be.'

'I'd be afraid of touching a Quaker. That Amanda could be a fierce woman in a household. Did you see how she took command when you were badgering the old woman?'

'I wasn't badgering her. It's just that on slavery—'

'You were badgering her. And you're doing the same to me.' He decided to have no more to do with the Paxmore girl, and now when she entered the warehouse he found excuses to avoid her. She was a prim, difficult and, in some undefinable way, repelling young woman, and he was afraid of her.

His problem of finding a wife was handled in an unusual way. On the October convoy Fithians sent Rosalind a disturbing letter:

> This may be highly improper, for you are no longer involved in Virginia affairs, but we deem it prudent to warn you in severest confidence that the financial safety of the Janney plantation on the Rappahannock is in jeopardy. The yield of their fields has diminished and the quality of their sweet-scented has fallen. In each convoy they send us poorer tobacco and larger orders for more expensive goods. Stating it frankly, they are on the verge of bankruptcy, and no one in Virginia seems to be aware.

> We have watched with admiration the manner in which you and Mark have cultivated your Maryland plantation, making it one of the best. Your diversification of interests has accounted for much of your success, and we notice that you rarely order anything which does not contribute to the further success of your operations. Could you and Mark not go down the bay and initiate the same program for your sisters and their husbands? Twice in the past we have had

to repossess what is now the Janney plantation and we do not wish to do so again in the near future. Louise Fithian sends her regards to Mark and wishes him well in this venture.

So the slaves were ordered to ready the *Fair Rosalind,* and on it Rosalind and Mark made the long sail to the Rappahannock. The degree of business deterioration they found, and the inability of the Janney sons-in-law to rectify it, were not the memorable aspects of this trip; Rosalind's remorseless disparagement of her younger sisters was.

Missy and Letty were now in their early thirties, each the mother of children and each as vacuous as a woman could be. They affected ignorance of all plantation matters, and when Rosalind spoke harshly of the looming catastrophe, the best they could do was whimper. They never appeared in their kitchens, leaving such matters to their slaves; knew nothing of family expenditures, and considered the Janney ships as mere conveyors of merchandise from London to their drawing rooms. What had to leave the plantation for London did not concern them.

The appalling part, to both Rosalind and Mark, was that they were rearing their attractive daughters for the same kind of life: rise at ten; eat heavily at noon; do a little sewing, but never on any garment of practical use; sleep through the afternoon; visit; chatter; change clothes; overeat at night; drink a little sherry while the men drank port; and never, never enter a shed in which tobacco was being cured.

It was Mark who detected the awful penalty exacted by this system. 'The wastage of the wives can't be prevented. It's the destruction of the men that's so painful. If your sisters tell me one more time, "Rosalind can manage such affairs, she was the clever one," I'm going to strike someone. Either one of them could have been as clever as you, Rosalind. They could have been, I know it, and they've wasted their lives, and their husbands' lives and now the plantation.'

'You're not entirely correct,' Rosalind said. 'For a woman to become as fine . . . No, I mean that for a woman to achieve her capabilities, she must have an example. She cannot discover truth by herself.'

'What example had you?'

'William Shakespeare.'

'What does that mean?'

'It means that I was an ugly child—had no young men pursuing me —and in God's grimness I could do nothing but read. I read all of that heavy book you see on the table near the window, and I warrant it hasn't been opened since I left.'

'I couldn't understand Shakespeare,' Mark said honestly.

'Nor could I . . . the first two times. Character consists of what you do on the third and fourth tries.'

'I want to get out of here, Rosalind. There's nothing we can do for these doomed people.'

'Now we face the third and fourth try,' his mother said, and they spent two agonizing months trying to reorient the Janney plantation. Mark worked with the sons-in-law, both older than himself, showing them how they must supervise their distant fields and balance their funds: 'Order from Fithians only those things that will enable you to create new wealth on the land you already have. Either you produce more wealth here or you perish.'

Rosalind was much harsher. Without betraying Fithians' confidences, she forced her sisters and their husbands to construct a four-year accounting and showed them the awful downward drift of their fortunes: 'No more clothes from Europe, only the raw cloth. You can learn to sew. No more expensive trips. Your children can learn in Virginia what they require. Three slaves in the house. All the others at productive work.'

'What work?' Letty simpered.

'Damn it! God damn this foolishness! You ask what work? And your accounts show that you buy shoes, you buy barrels, you buy jackets, you buy furniture that Fithians import from Flanders. Stop it! Stop all this idiotic buying and make the things yourselves.'

'I can't make furniture,' Letty said.

'Then teach your slaves to do it.'

'How?'

'There are books. If you'd been importing books . . .'

'That's for you to say. You were always the clever one.'

In disgust Rosalind turned her back on her lovely sisters; they were beyond salvation. But their husbands still had a chance—'If you work diligently for five years, you may salvage this place. If you don't, it will go bankrupt, and on one of the convoys Fithians will send you not great packages of lace and silk but a manager to supervise the sale to someone better qualified.'

Tears filled her eyes as she left her childhood home, that lovely, quiet place where the lawns stretched forever, but this sentimental farewell did not dampen her fury, and when the Steed sloop was well down the Rappahannock she sat with Mark and talked boldly. 'When this boat reaches Devon, I shall get off at the headland and walk the rest of the way.'

'Why?'

'Because it's going to carry you to Peace Cliff. And it's there you will disembark. And you will walk up that hill and ask Richard Paxmore for the hand of his daughter Amanda.'

'But . . .'

'Mark, you've seen the alternative. If strong men like you don't marry the finest women available, what will happen to humanity?'

'She's not Catholic.'

'I have no comment. I simply have no comment because that's not a relevant statement.'

'But Quakers . . .' He paused. 'Look at the old woman. She's all fire.'

'I'm all fire. When I'm seventy the people of the Choptank will hate me. Because I will never stop being as strong as I can. I will not tolerate surrender, and I will not stand by and watch the best of the Steeds, their one great hope, make foolish errors. Louise Fithian just died. Now get yourself a real wife.'

Amanda was not surprised when Mark Steed came to her door proposing marriage, and later when Rosalind arrived to arrange details, the prim little girl confided, 'I realized these things take time.' In her strong-willed way she announced one decision which took her family by surprise: 'Mark's Catholic, so we'll be married by a priest.' And it was the Paxmores' sloop, not the Steeds', which sailed to Annapolis to fetch Father Darnley.

In these momentous affairs Fitzhugh Steed took no part. Regarding the troubles at the Janney plantation he said, 'They're your family, Roz. Straighten 'em out.' And when his son announced that he was marrying the Paxmore girl, he said, 'One woman's about as good as another. I never suffered from marryin' a Protestant.'

He had grown careless in speech, affecting the dialect used by local watermen. Days would pass without his being seen at Devon, and Rosalind became accustomed to watching him climb into a bateau alone and head down the creek toward the marsh. He never spoke of the Turlock girl, and surprisingly, Rosalind had not yet seen her. With Mark spending increased time with his new wife, there was little opportunity for him to tend the growing warehouse in Patamoke, and thus Rosalind's source of information on her husband's mistress evaporated.

It was a strange world she occupied: wife to a man she scarcely knew and whose bed she no longer shared, organizer of a vast plantation belonging to others. Now, with her stepchildren launched into lives of their own, her entire emotional life concentrated on her three children. Samuel, aged eight, showed signs of becoming another Mark; he was intelligent, quick to respond and lively, but he already had his father's inclination toward irresponsible gallantry, so that Rosalind often wondered if he would ever establish a solid base to his life.

Pierre, almost two years younger, named for a friend her husband had relied upon while at St. Omer's, was quieter, a stalwart little fellow with reddish hair. He seemed to love animals and the quiet places in the wooded garden his mother had created, and he had a passion for speaking French with his father. Rosalind never felt that she knew Pierre, for he had a stubborn character and withheld confidences, but what she saw of him she liked. 'He'd make a good Quaker,' she said of him once when he had obstinately refused to obey.

Rachel was fun, a laughing little girl of five who gave every indication of becoming a giddy woman, like her aunts at the Janney plantation. She flirted with her father, on the rare occasions she saw him, and was fiendishly skilled in manipulating her older brothers. She seemed much above average in intelligence and delighted in using words more complicated than she could understand. 'Pierre is apprehensive,' she once said, intending to say that he was being difficult. Whenever Rosalind caught the child playacting or abusing her privileges, she thought: When she grows up she'll acquire common sense. Rosalind put great store in common sense and prayed that all her children would achieve it.

The affection she displayed for them sometimes surprised those who visited Devon, for it was common belief that intelligence forestalled love; this reasoning prompted many in Patamoke to justify Fitzhugh's dalliance with the Turlock girl—'He must have a very cold bedroom at home, with that one.' Yet here were three delightful children belying that assumption, for they were the offspring of Rosalind's passion, not his.

She was, indeed, the best mother that either the Janneys or the Steeds had so far produced, a loving, careful, understanding woman who had a clear vision of what her children might become. She taught them their numbers and insisted that they read at a level constantly higher than apparent capacity. She badgered her husband about finding a tutor for the family, pointing out that if a satisfactory one were imported from England, all the Steed children on the mainland could move to the island and learn their Latin, but Fitzhugh growled, 'You worked like hell to get 'em off the island, now you propose bringin' the kids back.' And he refused to find a tutor.

She felt uncertain of her capacity to teach her sons beyond the rudiments, and as she was casting about for alternatives, she heard of the Jesuit mission recently established at Bohemia, an isolated manor at the northern fringe of the Eastern Shore. It had been located in this unlikely position so as to avoid attention from crusading Protestants who had a penchant for burning Catholic buildings and abusing Jesuits whom they suspected of trying to lead Maryland back into Catholicism. She knew she should look into the situation at Bohemia, but put off doing anything about it.

And then one cold December morning in 1710 she wakened to find the island covered with snow. She was at her window looking out upon the heavy fall as it accented the bright berries of the holly and set in bold relief the stark branches of the oak, when she saw her three children, well bundled by their slaves, explode from the front door and run helter-skelter through the drifts. She was amused at first, and watched with interest as they disappeared toward the wharf, only to come charging back. Rachel protested tearfully that her brothers had struck her with snowballs; but when they stopped to comfort her, she ground her mittens into their faces, smearing them with snow she had kept hidden behind her back.

And in that childish play, with the red sun of late December shining on their faces, they warned Rosalind that the time had come when she must move them away from Devon and out into the mainstream of mathematics and Shakespeare and the Catholic philosophers. The boys were only eight and seven, but already the years were wasting.

As soon as the snow stopped falling, she ordered the slaves to prepare the sloop, and on the first bright day when the winds abated she packed her sons into warm clothing and placed them aboard. It was indicative of her determination that she did not bother to consult Fitzhugh on this drastic decision, but even if she had wanted to she could not have done so, for he was in the marshes.

They sailed north past the latitude of Annapolis, and then past the mouth of the beautiful Chester River, and on to the Elk, which led them to the Bohemia River, up which they sailed as far as possible before reverting to oars. The persons they asked regarding the Jesuit settlement viewed them with alarm and would reveal nothing, but at last the sloop tied up at a wharf beyond which it could not proceed, and here a woman grudgingly conceded, 'The Papists is yonder,' and she indicated a pitifully small footpath leading into the forest.

Two slaves walked ahead, brushing the snow from the low-hanging branches, and two others followed, carrying the small possessions of the boys. In the middle strode Rosalind, her skirts tied above her knees with cords, her hands clutching Samuel and Pierre. In this manner the Steeds approached the Jesuits.

One priest was in attendance, and he was supervising a holding of more than eight hundred acres, a few in tillage, most in unexplored woodland. The mission church was small and wooden; the rectory in which the priest and his helpers lived was little more than a windblown shack.

'We have no school here,' the priest apologized.

'I did not expect one,' Rosalind said.

'What can we do with your sons?'

'You can teach them to work . . . to read Latin . . . to become fine young men.'

She was so persuasive, and she offered so heartily to pay the Jesuits for their trouble, that the priest could not arbitrarily refuse her. He invited her party of seven to stay with him that night; the slaves could sleep in corners of the mission, the Steeds on the floor before the hearth. As the short day ended, and the fire threw shadows on the glazed-paper windows, they talked of Maryland and the Steeds: 'I've heard of your family. Didn't your husband attend seminary in France?'

'He's not the seminary kind,' she said gently, pulling her long limbs tightly to her to conserve warmth. 'But he did study in France, and so did my son Mark . . . at St. Omer's.'

The priest looked askance at this; her age belied a son old enough to have graduated from St. Omer's. 'My stepson,' she explained. 'He married a Quaker girl. And I'm not Catholic, either.'

'But you would bring your sons here . . . ?'

'Father. I do not want my sons to be barbarians. It's as simple as that.'

'I suppose it is,' the priest replied, and he began reciting the reasons why it would be both impractical and impossible for them to remain at the mission: no place for them, inadequate food, no schoolbooks, no teachers, no stability in the wilderness. He went on and on, and when he was finished, Rosalind said, 'Good, I'll leave them with you and be gone in the morning.'

It was merciful that she forced the Jesuits to keep her sons, because on the return trip, when her sloop was about to enter the Choptank, the slave who was steering suddenly screamed, 'Pirate ships!' And dead ahead, bearing down on them at a distance of about two miles, came two Caribbean ships lined with portholes bearing guns and decks crowded with marauders. They had chosen the winter to invade the bay, gambling that no English warships would be on station, and now, with their monstrous advantage in guns, they were free to ravage as they willed.

Rosalind, hastening to the bow of her sloop, made a rapid calculation born of years upon the bay: 'The wind favors us. We can scuttle into the river ahead of them.' And without further hesitation she directed the captain to trim sails and bring the swift-moving sloop onto a breathtaking course that would speed her into the Choptank.

As they approached the island they screamed and flashed signals, hoping to warn the Steed hands of the impending danger, but they were not seen or heard. So they sped up the river, looking constantly behind and seeing at last, with sickening fear, the two pirate ships nosing their way into the channel. The four slaves, who had learned that pirates relished capturing blacks as easily transferrable property for sale in Haiti, were more apprehensive than Rosalind, and when the mainland cut off the wind, they rowed vigorously, hoping to maintain their distance from the looming ships.

To forestall the sloop, the lead pirate ship fired a salvo, the heavy iron balls splashing into the waves not far from where Rosalind stood directing the flight. The reverberations echoed through the wintry air, and now those on the island were made aware of the danger pressing down upon them.

For several minutes, while the great ships came closer, nothing happened. And then Rosalind saw with relief that someone onshore was launching a longboat, manned by ten slaves, and when it sped toward the sloop, Rosalind saw that Mark Steed was in the bow, shouting directions to the rowers. In less than ten minutes, Rosalind calculated, the fresh rowers would be aboard the sloop and escape would be possible.

But now the pirates fired a single round, coming perilously close to Mark's longboat, throwing water over him, obscuring him for a moment, and Rosalind screamed, 'No!' But when the splash died, she saw that Mark was still in command, and she fell on one of the benches as if it had been her life that had been saved.

The reinforcements enabled the sloop to maintain distance from the pirates and reach an improvised landing short of the creek. There Rosalind and Mark scrambled ashore, with Mark shouting, 'Leave the boats! Save yourselves!' And he waited till all fourteen slaves had vanished in the woods. He was standing there as the pirates sailed ominously by, taking their time to effect a comfortable landing, for they knew they could not be opposed.

Rosalind and Mark hurried by forest paths to the cleared tobacco fields and across to the plantation house, shouting commands to all they met: 'Pirates! Come to the big house!'

When they reached that vulnerable fortress Rosalind quietly asked for her daughter, and when Rachel was produced, golden-haired and sleepy from her nap, Rosalind embraced her and said, 'You must be brave now,' and she asked where Fitzhugh was, and the child said, 'He hasn't been here since you went away.'

She told Mark to fetch Amanda, and when the little Quaker wife waddled forward, heavy with child, Rosalind said, 'You must hide in the far root cellar. Pirates do dreadful things to young women, even in your condition.'

She then asked if any other Steeds were on the island, and was gratified to find that none were; they would escape this day's travail and be ready to rebuild. 'If pirates come,' she said grimly, 'they also go. Our task is to keep them from destroying everything.'

Now the hulking ships were in the creek, arrogantly threading their way into waters that would have proved forbiddingly dangerous if English warships had been in pursuit. The island had no defenses, and when the lead ship drew close to the wharf it loosed a volley which tore through the upper rooms of the wooden house, shattering everything.

'Oh God!' Rosalind cried from her position on the porch. 'This is going to be worse . . .'

Now the first pirates were storming ashore, lean men with beards and flashing swords. Ten came and then forty and then a hundred, scattering through the trees, tearing all things apart. The slaves they did not harm, herding them in great batches toward the ships, but the slave houses they set afire.

Then they came toward the big house, eighty or ninety of them, hungry for spoils, dedicated to destruction. They approached viciously, hoping that someone would try to oppose them, for they had the wild courage of those who know that the enemy is unarmed. One caught a brand from a flaming slave hut and ran toward the house.

'No!' Rosalind screamed. She did not mean that the pirate should not enflame the house; she meant that Mark should not try to oppose him. But he moved to intercept the incendiarist, brandishing a pistol, and when the pirate kept coming, with the torch before his grizzled head, Mark took aim, fired and killed him.

Frenzy erupted. Other pirates, seeing their comrade fall with blood spurting from his forehead, became avenging monsters. Four leaped upon Mark, stabbing and shooting long after he was dead. Another, rushing like a maniac toward the house, swung his rifle in a great arc, catching little Rachel above the ear and demolishing her skull. This one then turned on Rosalind, striking her many times with the butt of his gun and knocking her senseless.

When she awoke she was propped against a tree; slaves had imperiled their own lives by dragging her to safety. As her eyes focused she saw the Steed plantation in flames: the big house, the slave quarters, the little houses in which the lesser Steeds had been invited to live; even the wharf. And on the porch of the gutted building from which all items of value had been stolen, she could see the shattered body of her daughter committed to the flames.

Only when the ravishment was complete did the captain of the pirates come ashore. Rosalind watched with cold hatred as he strode arrogantly among the trees she had planted. She would never forget him, a small, wizened old man walking with mincing steps and smirking at the destruction his men had wreaked. He came to where she lay and ordered his men to haul her upright. Then, walking about her as if he were in a slave mart, he said, 'I'm Henri Bonfleur. I've met your family before.' Viciously he struck her across the face, then said quietly to his men, 'Turn her loose. She's too ugly to bother with.' He placed his right foot in her stomach and pushed her backward. As she lay on the withered grass he looked down at her and said, 'Don't send ships this time to Marigot.' He was about to pass on to inspect the booty, but instead he turned and kicked her again and again. 'Your men killed Griscom. Now see the fire!' Contorted with hatred, he passed on, and when an underling asked, 'Shall we kill her?' he snarled, 'No, let her live to enjoy this day.'

Bitterly Rosalind watched as the pirate ships triumphantly withdrew. Then slowly, painfully she pulled herself up and walked with faltering steps to where the few remaining slaves were hidden. She directed them in digging two graves in the family cemetery beyond the oak, and there she buried the children on which her hopes had rested: Mark, who was not of her body but who was of her mind and her character, and little Rachel, whose naughty spirit might have enabled her to become an inheritor. As the earth fell upon their uncoffined bodies, she almost strangled with grief, and in that fearful moment swore that she would be revenged: 'Pirates, run where you will, we'll find you!' All her actions became subservient to this consuming hatred: pirates must be driven from the sea and hanged. It was intolerable that they should be able to invade private homes with impunity, and if the government in London could not protect this bay, she would.

She summoned the two ships owned by the Steeds and had them refitted with banks of concealed cannon. She increased the number of sailors per ship and had them trained in repelling boarders. Guns and cutlasses were ordered by the barrelful and in the late summer of 1711 her stratagems bore fruit. One of the ships was accosted by a swift-moving pirate brigantine whose fore-and-aft sails allowed her to maneuver in light winds. What the pirate did not know was that the Steed captain sought to be overtaken, for when the brigantine was close at hand he revealed the bank of heavy guns whose fire tore away the superstructure of the pirate ship.

The pirates were not seriously dismayed by this, for their basic tactic was to grapple merchant ships, board them, and subdue the crew in hand-to-hand combat; but this time it was the merchant sailors who did the boarding, and with their cutlasses and pistols, killed many of the pirates. Nineteen they chained belowdecks, hauling them and their ship back to Devon.

'You must turn them over to the authorities,' Steed warned, but Rosalind said, 'On this island you're the authority.' He asked her what she meant by this, and she snapped, 'You're a justice. Pass sentence.' When he refused, she directed that the pirates be removed to Patamoke, where she demanded that the courts sentence these murderers to death, and when this was done she watched the building of the gallows at the wharf, and she was waiting there when the pirates were led forth.

To each of the nineteen she said, as he passed by, 'If you see Bonfleur in hell, report what happened.'

These hangings created a scandal. On the one hand, they were illegal, for pirates were the responsibility of the province and all agreed that Mrs. Steed should have forwarded them to Annapolis. But on the other hand, pirates had ravaged the Steed plantation and had slain two of Mrs. Steed's children, not to mention abducting more than twenty of her slaves, and her revenge was obviously pleasing to the general populace. Furthermore, it showed what a determined woman could do. She became a heroine, but when broadsides were published detailing the victory of her ship and the hanging of her pirates, she was not satisfied. She ordered thousands of these sheets for distribution in all Caribbean ports. She wanted Bonfleur and Carpaux and Vidal to know specifically who it was that had hanged their fellows. She challenged them with the knowledge that she would not rest until they, too, were hanged.

Her stern example goaded the authorities into assembling a small fleet of privateers commissioned to destroy, once and for all, the pirate nests throughout the Caribbean, and when volunteers were called for, she offered the Steed vessels. She told her captains, 'No more casual tobacco trips to London. We'll fight in the Caribbean till the last devil is hanged.'

Her husband protested, 'What will happen to our crops?'

'They'll rot,' she said curtly. 'They certainly won't be ferried to London in our ships.' And when he complained of this wastage, she said contemptuously, 'If you had any manliness, Fitzhugh, you'd be serving on one of the ships.'

'Me?'

'Yes! Have you no sense of justice? Do you allow a fiend to burn your home and kill two of your children and make no counter? Do you want me to captain one of the ships? By God, I'll sail that sea till I catch him by the neck.'

'Catch who?'

'The pirate. Any pirate. The great inhuman pirate that terrifies us, and comes up our bay to burn and slaughter.'

'You must learn—'

'I've already learned. I've learned what a weak, sick thing you are. I've stomached your behavior in the marsh. I've forgiven you for not being here when the place was burned. And I can even understand why you did not particularly grieve when your children were slain. But sheer cowardice I cannot tolerate.'

'But, Rosalind—'

'Do you get aboard that ship? Or do I?'

She was two inches taller than her husband, a few pounds lighter, but the difference in character was immeasurable. She saw the world as a unit, all parts interrelating, and for a boy of promise not to know Latin was exactly as grave an omission as for a father not to be concerned about the totality of his family. She had never made much of courage or the customary manifestations of manliness, no more than she had thought much of the so-called womanly virtues; there was no great advantage, she thought, in being able to coquette or bake a crumpet, but there was an immortal advantage in being a decent woman or a proper man.

I don't want revenge to even things out, she told herself after her husband had reluctantly departed, but I do want it to tidy up the world. Piracy cannot be tolerated.

Hoping that the new American measures might bring the intolerable situation on the Chesapeake under control, she turned her attention to Devon. She did not want ostentatious gravestones for Mark and Rachel, but she did want reminders of the imperishable love she had felt for these two excellent children; she would never see better and their loss would never be far from her thoughts. Their graves lay beside the oak, and sometimes she would go there and reflect upon her insufferable loss, but her tears were few, for she was not one to weep easily. On occasion she would think of the fine black women who had worked in her kitchen and done her sewing, and she would ponder their fate: raped and ravaged by the pirates and sold in Haiti. Then the cruelty of the world would overwhelm her, and she would drop her head and think of nothing, and after a long while she would sigh and return to her tasks.

Principally she must rebuild the house, and whenever she placed a pencil on paper she felt the loss of Mark. How she wished that he were there to help; he would know the measurements and the cost of brass. She sometimes speculated on why she had such an affection for this lad; he was not her son nor of her blood; perhaps it was because he represented all men, all husbands, all generals and captains, and the world would be far better if more were like him.

With no children of her own at hand, she lavished her attention on Amanda Paxmore Steed, as she was invariably referred to in the community, and as the time approached for her delivery, Rosalind speeded the rebuilding of her house so that a special room for children might be available. In fact, she became so oppressive in her attentions that the Quaker girl said one day, 'Rosalind, I'm going back to Peace Cliff.'

'But you're a Steed.'

'No. I'm a human being. And thee is stifling me.'

'What a preposterous—'

'Rosalind, I'm doing this so that I can have a fine, normal son. And after he's safely born and truly started, we'll come back. Of course we'll come back.'

The firm set of her jaw warned Rosalind that she had better concur, and quickly, or she would lose a grandson. 'An excellent idea,' she said. 'You'll be out of the way while the builders are busy.'

She did not employ an architect. And she was further hampered by the loss of the trained slaves stolen by the pirates, but through judicious purchases in Virginia she did acquire some fine masons, bricklayers and carpenters, and these she gave instructions as to how her house was to be built: 'It's to occupy the same site as before, but it's never to be cluttered.'

She drew plans for every façade, every room, and when the ground was cleared and the sawn timbers were drying in the sun, she announced her basic decision: 'We'll build of brick.'

'We don't have enough for a whole house.'

'We'll fire them.' And she doubled the brick crew, and the staff cutting trees for the charcoal, and in time she collected a substantial pile of reddish bricks to augment those she had been saving during the preceding decade.

But when the foundations were in and the first two courses of bricks laid, she did not like the result: 'There's something wrong. They don't look the way they should.' Deep in her mind she had a memory, from somewhere along the Rappahannock, of what a brick wall should be, and hers fell short.

Was it the color? Or the thickness of the oyster-shell mortar? Or the depth of the indentations between the courses? She could not tell, so she sailed to Patamoke and inquired of everyone she met, and finally a newcomer from Holland said he felt sure he knew what the matter was, and he sailed back to Devon and inspected the wall: 'It's simple. You're not even using the English bond.'

'What?'

He showed her how the bricks in her courses had been laid always with the long face outward, which resulted in monotony and lack of sturdiness: 'You must follow either the English bond or the Flemish.' And he demonstrated how, in the former, one course was composed only of bricks laid lengthwise, while the course above and below used bricks with only their ends showing. This alternation was most pleasing, and Rosalind said, 'That's what we want. Simple, we'll tear out that second course and relay it end out.'

'But the Flemish bond is even better,' the Dutchman said, and he showed her a simple yet charming way of alternating in every row a long brick with an end one, so that the wall became not only extra sturdy but also pleasing to the eye.

'I like that!' she cried, but before she could give her slaves instructions, the Dutchman said, 'What's best is when you use light-colored local bricks for the long stretchers and blackish Holland-type bricks for the short headers.'

Two days were wasted while he searched the Choptank for some of the darker bricks, but when he located a few they produced a pattern so pleasing that Rosalind agreed she must have such a house. It took her more than two years to assemble the dark bricks she needed, but when enough had been collected she was prepared to go ahead with her house.

Construction was interrupted by an event which set cannon reverberating around the bay. The flotilla of privateers assembled by Virginia and Maryland planters had up to now accomplished little; there had been desultory forays against the pirates but no engagements of significance. Invasions of the Chesapeake had been halted, but on the high seas the pirates still burned and murdered with impunity. And then, in November of 1713, five American vessels converged on four pirate ships lurking near Martinique, and after a running fight, drove them into Marigot Bay. There a furious hand-to-hand fight ensued, with all the pirate ships being destroyed. Ninety buccaneers were hauled in chains to Williamsburg, and when they were sorted out for hanging on the docks of London, it was found that one old man masquerading as a deck hand was actually Henri Bonfleur, now sixty-nine, toothless and steeped in cruelty.

It was Fitzhugh Steed who brought the exciting news to Devon. He was accompanied by a lieutenant who bore testimony to his courage in the fighting, and when this pair walked slowly up from the wharf to the improvised wooden shack in which Rosalind lived alone, they were taken aback by the ardor with which she greeted them. Embracing her husband joyously, she cried, 'Is Bonfleur really in chains?'

'We saw him selected for London,' Fitzhugh replied, sinking into a chair.

Clenching her hands and striding about the room, oblivious of the presence of the lieutenant, she muttered, 'God has delivered him to us.' Then she came to her husband and said, 'We must leave for Williamsburg at once.'

'Why?'

'To get Bonfleur.'

'For what?'

'To hang him.' Before her husband could protest, she added, 'He's to be hanged from a gibbet I will erect on those ashes,' and she pointed toward the vanished porch where Mark and Rachel had been slain.

'That's past now,' Fitzhugh said from his chair.

'It's just beginning!' she stormed as she moved about the room. 'We'll catch them all, and hang them all.'

She could not be dissuaded from her determination to see Bonfleur executed at the scene of his infamy, but Fitzhugh refused to accompany her to Virginia. 'You're mad. Where's your womanly self-respect?' She replied that she was acting as an outraged mother, 'The mother of your children, by the way.'

At Williamsburg the English authorities in charge of the warfare against piracy were aghast at her proposal that Bonfleur be surrendered to her, but after they had watched her in court, stern as hammered iron, they had to concede that it had been her determination alone which had driven this cruel pirate from the seas. And when they listened to her recite the devastation he had visited upon Devon, they knew it would be appropriate if he were hanged there—'But not on the island itself, for that would be interpreted as private vengeance. Publicly at Patamoke, with drums beating.'

'Thank you,' she said quietly, with no sign of triumph. But as she stalked from the courtroom like an avenging Greek goddess, one of the judges whispered, 'That one carries a heart of brass. Thank God she's not stalking me.'

In the days when Bonfleur was being processed for his trip up the bay, she had free time, and it occurred to her that Williamsburg stood not far from the James River, where Tom and Evelyn Yates had their plantation, so on the spur of the moment—in the way she did most things—

she sailed to the Yates home to see her daughter Evelyn. And when she saw how this family had attained order and prosperity and three fine children, she was overcome with emotion and tears appeared upon her cheeks as they sat in the wintry sunshine.

'What is it, Mother?' Evelyn cried, fearing that the journey to Virginia and the excitement of the trial had impaired Rosalind's health.

'This is what life should be,' her mother replied. 'A woman and her children. Not the pursuit of pirates.'

Evelyn broke into relieved laughter. 'You fraud! Always you will be pursuing some enemy. Remember that day you drove the Claxtons away?' She kissed her mother and added, 'Said you were saving my life. Well, you did.'

Rosalind recalled that day and sighed. 'I was so ugly in my hardness. But so right.' With a broad sweep of her arm she indicated the Yates children and the growing prosperity of the land: 'This paradise of action compared to Regis Claxton and his puny fears.' She wiped her eyes and said, 'But I was also right when I declared war upon Bonfleur. And now I must go home and hang him.'

She insisted that the wizened pirate be brought up the bay chained in the hold of her snow, but when that trim little craft came into the channel north of Devon she directed the Englishmen to produce him on deck so that he could review the scenes of his earlier triumphs. 'There you landed, Bonfleur, and those jagged walls are the ones you burned. That tall oak marks the grave of my children. And ahead is Patamoke, which you also ravaged, years ago, and this marsh we're passing is where you stole the Swedish girl. Can you even remember her?'

Bonfleur, holding his chains, glared at his tormentor. 'I remember that winter's night when my men wanted to kill you and I stopped them. Sad mistake.' She sent him below, and when he was brought forth at Patamoke she stood by the gibbet in December cold, never averting her gaze from his cruel face. When he was truly hanged, his lashed feet dangling in the night, she said, 'Now we go after the others.'

When she sailed back to Devon she found that Fitzhugh had left. He had taken all his clothes and guns to the marsh, from which he refused to return. It created a scandal, and had it not been for his exalted former position, he would probably have been publicly whipped. Father Darnley was brought over from Annapolis to reason with him, but when the priest sat in the little marsh hut, Steed told him, 'I'll never go back. This one'—and he indicated Nelly Turlock—'doesn't read books or pepper me with questions.'

When Father Darnley returned to Devon he told Rosalind, 'We can still hope he'll change his mind and resume his responsibilities.'

'Not him,' she said firmly. 'He's a sad weak man lacking in character. Quite unable to accept responsibilities.'

'He fought the pirates.'

'Only because I goaded him.'

'Have you, perhaps, goaded him too much?'

'No, it's like two people on a dark road with only one lantern. One forges ahead and does the work. The other refuses to keep up.'

'But if he can't keep up? If he needs our help?'

'He doesn't care to keep up. He never cared for his home, nor his wife, nor his ships, nor anything.' She realized the harshness of her assessment and added, 'I am not abandoning him, Father. Long ago he abandoned himself. He's even abandoned the church. I am now the Catholic. He's . . .' She waved her long hands expressively, signifying emptiness.

A few weeks later Father Darnley was ferried back; Fitzhugh had died. He had been hunting with his marsh children when he stopped abruptly, wiped perspiration from his eyes, and told his oldest boy, 'I think the time has come to lie down.' The Turlocks were prepared to bury him in the woods, but Rosalind recovered the body for interment beyond the oak. At graveside she did her best to present the image of a grieving widow, but her thoughts were harsh: You'd be entering the good years of your life, if you'd allowed me to be a partner. And as Father Darnley spoke well of the dead profligate, sanctimoniously citing a fictitious record at St. Omer's and his reputed bravery in fighting pirates, Rosalind became preoccupied with the jagged outline of her new house: From here you can't determine whether it's being built or being torn down. It's caught in a moment of time, indecipherable. But I can tell you, the family's being built. The boys at Bohemia will see to that.

With two of her children, Mark and Rachel, dead and with the other three absent from Devon—Evelyn down the bay, Sam and Pierre still with the Jesuits at Bohemia—Rosalind's restless energy and her need to give love had to find new channels, and one April day in 1714 as she was leaving the warehouse in Patamoke she was led by accident to that spot across from the courthouse and the slave auction where the whipping post stood close to the stocks. There, to the delight of threescore witnesses, a girl of eighteen was being lashed with strokes from the cat-o'-nine-tails. Her back was already bloodied when Rosalind reached the scene, and at the eighth stroke she had fainted, but the crowd urged the jailer to proceed in the manner the judges had decreed: 'Well laid on.'

'What did she do?' Rosalind asked, looking compassionately at the bleeding figure, nude to the waist, as it hung limp from the crossbars.

'Tom Broadnax's serving girl.'

'But what did she do?' Rosalind recognized the name of a leading citizen, but this did not help in determining his servant's crime.

'Had a bastard child of her body.'

'What?' At thirty-nine Rosalind had become impatient with indirection. She demanded to know what crime this girl had committed that would justify such savage punishment.

'It's what they say in court. *Bastard child of her body.*' And it was this arcane terminology that set her investigating.

She went to the courthouse, where records of proceedings and punishments, neatly written by the clerk, were kept in a large folio, but when she asked to see the book she was told that was impossible. Drawing herself up to her considerable height, she thundered at the small man tending the book, 'Nothing's impossible. I demand to see that book.' And she wrested it from him, taking it to the window so she could inspect its heavily ruled pages.

What she saw regarding the case of Betsy, Thomas Broadnax's serving girl, disgusted her: 'It's a novel. A French novel in four chapters.' She was correct, for the relevant entries read:

26 March 1714. Today being the first day after the New Year, Thomas Broadnax did complain to the court that his indentured girl Betsy has become increasingly obstinate and loath to obey, and he beseeches the court to warn her that she must give faithful service throughout the New Year.

28 March 1714. Thomas Broadnax did present to the court testimony against his indentured servant girl Betsy that without being married she was about to bear a bastard child of her body.

29 March 1714. Thomas Broadnax did appear in the court with testimony that his serving girl Betsy has borne a bastard child of her body. The court sentenced said Betsy to be whipped with eighteen lashes, well laid on, same to be applied when she was recovered from her delivery.

3 April 1714. Thomas Broadnax did appear in court with information that the child borne of his indentured servant girl Betsy is a girl. The court assigns said bastard child to the care of Thomas Broadnax, to work for him till the age of twenty-one, he to supply her with food, lodging and dress.

It was a series of decisions which could have been matched in any Eastern Shore courthouse during these years, and Rosalind appreciated this; the customs may have been barbaric but they were generally approved. What made this case abhorrent was that following each of the four entries came the signatures of the justices, led by the name of the presiding judge: Thomas Broadnax. He had been displeased with his serving girl; he had brought charges against her in his own court; he had sentenced her to a public whipping; and he had assigned to himself the infant's unpaid services for twenty-one years.

'What horrible questions flood the mind!' Rosalind muttered as she returned the record to the apprehensive clerk, and for days she could not dispel either the image of Betsy hanging to the crossbar or her imaginings as to how she had got there. Having no other pressing concerns, she stayed in Patamoke, trying to find Betsy and talk with her, but that unfortunate girl was locked up in the Broadnax home, trying vainly to wash the salt from her wounds. So Rosalind sought out the judge and found him in his fields, a burly man dressed in black and dignity: 'She was a faithless girl and merited her punishment.'

'But she still works for you?'

'Her indenture has three years to run.'

'Are you not afraid that she will poison you? For the terrible things you've done to her?'

'Poison? Mind your tongue, Mistress Steed.'

'Yes,' she said boldly, 'if you had treated me that way, I would seek revenge.'

'Yes, you're a great one for revenge. Do you know what they call that pompous house you're building? Rosalind's Revenge. You were irritated that your husband . . .' His voice trailed off, allowing the insinuation to cut.

'Broadnax, you're a fool. What's worse, you're a sanctimonious fool.' It was these words which brought Rosalind Steed into the Patamoke court, and as in the case of Betsy, her accuser, adverse witness and dispenser of justice was Judge Thomas Broadnax:

> 17 April 1714. Thomas Broadnax did testify to the court that Rosalind Steed did, in the affairs of the indentured serving girl Betsy, who had to be whipped for her foul misbehavior, call said T.B. a fool and averred she might poison him. Said R.S. to pay a fine of three hundred pounds of tobo to said Broadnax.

The sentence was signed by Thomas Broadnax, Chief Judge.

Rosalind took the certificate for her tobacco personally to the judge's home, and when the door was opened for its delivery, Betsy stood there to receive it. The girl had been made aware of Mrs. Steed's intercession on her behalf, and now burst into tears, which Rosalind halted brusquely. 'Let me see your back,' she said.

'Oh, he would kill me if he came in.'

'Nonsense! He's at the courthouse.'

'His wife is worse.'

'Does she starve you?'

'She does. And whips me, too.'

'But you did have the baby?'

'I did. Precious little else to do in this house.'

'The father?'

Betsy looked away. She would not speak, nor would she uncover her back, but with an unexpected move, Rosalind caught her and pulled up her blouse. There the horrid marks remained, deep and livid. For some moments Rosalind stared at them, and against her will tears came into her eyes. She was ashamed of herself, and mumbled some excuse as she dropped the blouse.

'Who's there?' came a harsh voice from a nearby room, and quickly Betsy straightened her clothes and replied, 'Delivery of the tobacco paper.'

'What are you saying?' came the stern voice, and soon Mrs. Broadnax, an unforgiving woman of fifty, stormed into the hallway about to abuse her servant when she saw Mrs. Steed. 'I'm surprised you'd come here, poisoner and all.'

'I've brought the fine, as your husband directed.'

'Leave it and go. We're not impressed with your kind.' And four days later Rosalind discovered how vengeful the Broadnaxes could be, for she was back home at Devon when a shallop sailed up to the wharf bearing a solitary man whom she had not previously met but of whom she had heard occasionally.

He was thin and straight from much living in the woods. He walked with quiet grace, as if he commanded the trees through which he moved. His face was deeply pocked and his hair was white, revealing the seventy-three years which his bearing belied. He spoke with difficulty, as if words —any words—were alien to him, and occasionally he introduced Indian phrases which Rosalind had not heard before.

'Stooby,' he said, assuming that she would know him to be a Turlock.

'Turlock?'

'Mmmm.' To any of her questions, he replied in a grunt, indicating affirmation or denial, and after a few minutes with him it was easy to determine which.

'I am very pleased to see you, Stooby. My son Mark told me many good things—'

He brushed aside her graciousness, for his message was imperative: 'They whipping Nelly.'

'Who's Nelly?' she asked impulsively, then pressed her right hand over her mouth to correct her stupidity.

'Steed's girl. Broadnax whipping her.'

'What for?'

'Three children. Your three children.'

And slowly the horror of the visit became clear: Judge Broadnax, infuriated by the insolent manner in which Rosalind Steed had responded to her penalty, and enraged by his wife's account of how the tobacco fine had been delivered, had decided to strike back. He had come into court and personally charged Nelly Turlock with 'having borne three bastards of her body,' and had sentenced her to ten lashes, well laid on.

'When does it take place?'

'Three days.' And then Stooby said something which revealed that even he could see the insane vengeance in this act: 'Many years nothing. Your man dies—whipping.'

'Yes. Broadnax would never have dared while my husband was alive. Nor Mark, either. They'd have shot him.' Then, for a reason she could not have explained, she asked, 'Was Charley . . .' She did not know how to phrase her question. 'Were Charley Turlock and Flora Turlock Nellie's parents?'

'Mmmm,' Stooby said. 'Little house. We all live . . .'

'Did you think it wrong, Stooby?'

'Little house . . .' He said this with such finality that it was apparent he did not wish to explore further the strange behavior of his brother: the hut in the marsh had been small, and in it strange pairings had occurred. But then his reserve broke and he clutched Rosalind's hand. 'Whipping, you stop.'

'I shall if God gives me strength.' And all that day, after Stooby had gone, she devised stratagems to halt this miscarriage of justice, but she was powerless and knew it. Then, while there was still only an hour and a half of daylight, she thought of a way to shame the town into stopping this senseless beating of women.

Calling her six strongest slaves, she ordered them to prepare her fastest sloop, and when her head sailor protested, 'It'll be dark,' she overrode him. 'We're only going to the cliff,' she said, and off they set with a fair wind pushing them at six knots.

Waiting impatiently for the journey to end, and counting the fading light as if it were coins falling into a jar, she wondered if she had ever seen this river more benevolent: spring touched the trees along the shore, and the breeze threw tips of waves, white in the sunset. In the distance a fishing boat made for Patamoke, and as the day died the last geese of the year settled in coves to rest before their long flight north. She thought: How peaceful this river, and how wrong some of the things we do on its banks.

Her calculation as to time proved correct, for she reached Peace Cliff well before dark and was able to direct the slaves to find quarters at the logging camp farther up the creek. She climbed up to the gray-brown telescope house, where, as she had hoped, Ruth Brinton Paxmore sat in the gloaming, watching the river she loved so much—'I saw thee coming and made little wagers as to when thee would arrive.'

'I come on most serious business.' And she outlined the deplorable thing that was to happen two days hence at Patamoke.

'Thomas Broadnax thinks he is Nebuchadnezzar,' Ruth Brinton said.

'But it's so hideously wrong, Mrs. Paxmore. Year after year these men assemble and dole out whippings to women who could not have babies without their connivance. But never are the men punished. Good God, my husband stalked this river with impunity, and never a hand was laid on him, but the minute he dies these awful justices grab for the woman and sentence her to be whipped. Why? Why?'

'Thee has come to the right person to ask,' the frail old woman said, rocking back and forth in the gray light that seemed a part of her gray costume.

'What do you mean?'

'I was whipped out of Virginia. I was whipped through Massachusetts at the tail of a cart.'

'You—Ruth Brinton? You?'

The old lady rose, went to the window, where glimmers of light still rested, and opened her blouse, disclosing the welts that neither time nor the dimming of memory would heal.

'Oh, dear God!' Rosalind whispered. She stood transfixed, the awfulness of such whippings somehow intensified by this evidence on the body of a very old woman. She then saw with excruciating clarity that men ordered only young women to be stripped, as if the sexuality of the act were impossible if the victims were older—like their mothers or grandmothers. The punishment was therefore not merely a whipping; it was an act of lust, a purging of heated thoughts.

And in that revelation she discovered how it could be halted. Her proposal was daring and fraught with much danger, but that it would be effective she had no doubt: 'Ruth Brinton, on Thursday when they whip Nelly, you and I will stand forth and bare our backs too, and insist that they whip us, as well, for we share in her guilt.' This was so strange a statement that she added, 'On behalf of the town we share.'

'I'm eighty-one.'

'It is testimony that is needed.' By some happy chance Rosalind had hit upon the one word that had the power to activate the fighter in the old woman: *testimony.* A human being, to live a meaningful life, was required to bear testimony; in prayer, in the husbandry of the home, in the conduct of public life, a man or woman must at critical moments testify publicly as to fundamental beliefs. Ruth Brinton had always done so, which was why she was regarded throughout the Eastern Shore as a Quaker saint, difficult at times, stubborn always, but a testament to man's striving for a saner life.

'I'll help,' she said. That night the two women shared the same bedroom, and before they fell asleep Ruth Brinton confided, 'I shall do this,

Rosalind, because it was thee who saved Amanda's life when the pirates came. Thee offered thine to save her, and there is no greater love.'

They spent the next morning, Wednesday, in prayer, and at noon, with the most serene equanimity, they went down to the Paxmore wharf and climbed into Rosalind's sloop. Ruth Brinton's sons were at work in the boatyard in Patamoke, so there was no one to prevent the old lady from leaving, and it was with a kind of spiritual exaltation that they sailed out into the Choptank, past the Turlock marshes and into the town harbor. As they tied up they chanced to see Judge Broadnax, stout and severe, but he refused to acknowledge them; on four different occasions he had been forced to fine the Paxmore brothers for refusing military service, which caused him to have an even lower opinion of Quakers than of Steeds.

They slept that night at the Patamoke home of the Steed who was running the warehouse, and on Thursday morning they had prominent places at the whipping post, mingling with those excited citizens who had come to see the Turlock woman finally punished. The sheriff promenaded as if he were the hero of the occasion, snapping his nine-tails and looking toward the door of the jail from which the criminal would be hauled.

At ten o'clock the door opened and Nelly Turlock appeared in a brown shift which could easily be stripped away. Faint with terror, she was led slowly to the whipping post, and as she passed, some in the crowd cheered and some muttered curses; as long as Fitzhugh Steed had protected her she had been insolent, but now revenge had come.

Rosalind had not seen her before this moment; she seemed quite beautiful, but slatternly, and so dazed she did not seem to recognize who was taunting her in the crowd, nor who was suffering with her.

Now came the time to bind her to the stake, and when this was done the sheriff reached up and pulled away her shift, leaving her naked to the waist, but before he could apply the first of his ten lashes an extraordinary thing happened. Mrs. Steed left the crowd, walked boldly to the whipping post and pulled down her blouse, standing half naked beside the sentenced girl. And while gasps of outrage were still echoing, old Ruth Brinton Paxmore stepped beside her, repeating the performance. When her withered back was disclosed, cries of disgust issued from the crowd.

'Take them away!'

'Profanation!'

The display of the three half-naked women had precisely the effect that Rosalind intended. One was young and wanton and deserved whipping, but the other two were different: Rosalind was a lady, she was tall, her breasts were large and not seductive; and as for Ruth Brinton, she was a great-grandmother, horribly out of place in such a scene. The time when men would have enjoyed seeing her whipped was long past: her breasts had withered; she was disgusting, a travesty.

'Take them away!' a woman shouted. 'Obscene!'

Then Rosalind spoke, not covering her breasts with her hands but standing clear: 'I am as guilty as she. You must whip me, too.'

And old Ruth Brinton added, 'This whipping of women must stop.'

But now Judge Broadnax appeared, quivering with rage because of an interruption he had not sanctioned. 'What happens here?'

'Two others demand to be whipped.'

'Then whip them!' But he had delivered his verdict before seeing who the voluntary victims were, and when he saw Rosalind and Ruth Brinton standing beside the post, naked to the waist, he was shocked. 'Cover them and take them away!' he thundered, and when this was done he ordered that the lashes begin, but with every fall of the cat, Rosalind and Ruth Brinton screamed in anguish, as if the knotted cords had fallen on their backs, and their cries echoed, and after that morning there was no more whipping of women in Patamoke.

The incident had one unexpected consequence. Stooby Turlock sailed back to Devon to talk with Mrs. Steed, but this time he came attended by others; as he walked up the gravel path to the half-finished house he brought with him three blond children between the ages of seventeen and ten. They were clean, and obviously under severe instructions to behave themselves, and when Rosalind appeared, Stooby said, 'I bring his children.'

Gravely Rosalind shook hands with each of the stiff, suspicious young people, then inquired, 'You say . . .'

'Fitz's.'

She asked their names, then suggested that they walk in the yard, and when they were gone she asked, 'Why did you bring them here?'

'Nelly gone. Never come back.'

'She ran away?'

'Mmmm.'

Rosalind coughed and groped for her handkerchief. Little wonder that a woman who had been so humiliated should want to quit the river. 'I would have stayed and fought them,' she told Stooby when she had wiped her nose. 'I would have strangled Broadnax in his own—'

Stooby put his hands over his ears. 'Don't say. Next they whip you.'

'You don't have to listen, Stooby, but Thomas Broadnax walks in danger. Now, what about these children?'

'No mother. No father. They stay here.'

And with this simple declaration, Stooby Turlock posed a moral problem for Rosalind Steed: what to do with the bastard children of her dead husband? The whole testimony of her life dictated that she assume responsibility for these three, and the vanishing of her own children was an added persuasion. But she also had a sense of harsh reality and knew that these children had been born in the marsh, of the marsh. Their father was a weak man, lacking in character, and their mother was worse. In these children there was not good blood. They promised small likelihood of achievement; intuitively she sensed that with them she could accomplish nothing.

She had come to believe that the human stock populating this world was wondrously uneven. When she goaded her son into marrying Amanda Paxmore, there was not even a remote chance that the little Quaker girl would turn out badly; she came from solid stock, with the personal fire of old Ruth Brinton in her veins and the irreducible integrity of Edward Paxmore. She trusted that her sons at Bohemia would grow into stalwart men upon whom Devon could depend. But the children of her silly sisters across the bay—what timid and fragile things they would be!

The three Turlocks now wandering in the yard came from damaged sources, and she was convinced that no matter how much love and force she applied to them, she and they would end in heartbreak. They belonged to the marsh, and to move them elsewhere would be cruelty.

'Take them back, Stooby,' she said.

'I seventy-three,' he said. 'Soon I die. The children?'

'They'll find a way.'

'Please, Mrs. Steed. Your children, not mine.'

'No,' she said firmly. She would not try to share the reasoning behind her decision, nor would she retreat from it, but when Stooby pointed out that he had not the wherewithal to rear the children, she promised, 'I'll pay for everything.' And when she saw him leading the children back to the sloop, his shoulders sagging and his white hair shining in the sun, she was satisfied that whereas he must be disappointed now, he would in the long run see that she was right.

She kept her word. She followed what was happening in the marsh and saw to it that Stooby had the funds needed to raise the abandoned children, but when she heard that he had given them the name Steed, she sent word that this was not wise, and thereafter they were lost among the Turlocks.

Stooby did not die soon, as he had feared. Because of his sturdy life in the woods, and his lean competence in caring for himself, he lived on and on, giving Nelly's children the love they needed and an introduction to swamp life. By the time the boys had left their teens, they were accomplished watermen, and because they had acquired Stooby's intense interest in birds and river things, they became the principal suppliers of soft crabs and oysters, roasting ducks and turtles for soup.

Rosalind, watching their sensible progress, thought: I was so correct in not taking them from their natural home. That day they were like waves which had ventured far inland, making a mark they could never again achieve. Now they've receded to their tidal level, and there they prosper.

Her own sons prospered too. In December of 1718 they returned from Bohemia polished young scholars, for the Jesuits had taught them Latin, Greek, Italian and French, and they were as familiar with Thucydides and Cicero as they were with the Douai Version of the Bible. They knew little of hunting geese or trapping beaver, but they understood the niceties of St. Thomas Aquinas and were, as the letter from the Jesuits said, 'ready for the rigors of St. Omer's.'

Rosalind agreed that they must continue their studies in France— 'Where in today's world could a young man find better instruction?' But the thought of sending them across the Atlantic on the May convoy struck terror in her heart, for these were the years when the most hideous pirate of all ravaged the Chesapeake. After the mass hangings of 1713 there had been a diminution of piracy, but in 1716 a dark meteor had blazed across the Caribbean, Edward Teach, a man of horrible cruelties known as Blackbeard. In Jamaica he had roared, 'Warn that Bitch of Devon we'll be along to revenge the good men she hanged.'

Twice he had ventured into the bay but had kept to the Virginia shore, wreaking enormous devastation, and at each burned plantation he told some victim, 'Tell the Bitch of Devon we haven't forgotten her.'

Rosalind's response had been instantaneous. She had offered the English navy her five ships, and the financial returns from three convoys had been sacrificed while her captains prowled the Caribbean, searching for Blackbeard. That canny criminal, trained as a British privateer in the War of the Spanish Succession, eluded them, and then in late 1718 word reached Virginia that he had holed up in a North Carolina inlet. Volunteers were called for, and Rosalind sent her ships, but no word had filtered back to the bay.

'You can't sail to France,' she told her sons, 'as long as Blackbeard roams. He's sworn to kill you, and me as well, and we must wait.'

In the interim she held the boys close to her. They were the descendants of men who had resisted pirates, and if she had asked them to sail against Blackbeard, they would have done so, but she was satisfied to keep them at Devon. Samuel was almost seventeen, still outgoing and occasionally fractious; Pierre evaluated problems more sagaciously and remained more cautious in his responses, but she was pleased to see that each respected the other and consciously made concessions in order to sustain the bond. They formed a strong pair, and Rosalind thought: They'll be able to run Devon once they get back from France.

While everyone waited for news from Carolina, she instructed her sons regarding the plantation: 'Don't ever make our garden pretty. And when you marry, promise me you'll never allow your wives to plant these lovely paths with box. It smells and is the mark of those who have never really loved gardens. They make a game of box, mazes with it, and waste their gardeners' time keeping it trimmed.'

Pierre asked what plants she did respect, and without hesitation she replied, 'Pyracantha. It's gangling and sturdy and most handsomely colored.' Sam said, 'You're describing yourself,' and she confessed to the similarity.

They were together when the geese prepared for their long flight north, and although she was moved by their departure, the boys were not, and this frightened her. 'You must live close to nature. Books and priests are not life. The coming and going of the crabs down there in the river . . . that's life.'

She led them to all parts of the plantation, pointing out the characteristics of the soil, the life history of the various plants she was endeavoring to grow, and always she managed to pass the marsh which stood at the head of the creek, reaching messily inland with its incredible burden of complicated life. She was there one day when herons came, their long awkward legs projected in front as they landed on the shallow water. 'Those are the birds I love . . . so patient . . . so permanent.' Her sons began to see their patrimony through her eyes, and to appreciate the heavy responsibility they must assume on their return from St. Omer's.

'And while you're looking at the plants and birds,' she told them, 'keep an eye free for the girls. Which ones would fit in with an island? Which would be solid companions? And good mothers like Amanda? Try them all but pick the winner.'

And then, when it seemed that the May convoy would not dare to sail, the *Fair Rosalind* rushed north from Carolina with news that caused citizens to drop to their knees in the middle of the road and give thanks: 'Blackbeard is dead!' Rosalind Steed's ships, supported by others from the colonial navy, had pocketed the pirate in a cove where Lieutenant Robert Maynard had engaged him in hand-to-hand combat and slain him with a cutlass. The pirate's severed head, which had uttered so many threats against the Bitch of Devon, took its last ride stuck to the end of a Steed bowsprit.

When the news reached Patamoke, guns were fired and Rosalind ordered all members of the Steed family to attend the public prayers held on the wharf, and there she stood, solemnly holding the hands of her sons, as the minister cried in exultation, 'The long siege has ended! Tonight we sleep in peace! No town on the Chesapeake has done more to vanquish pirates than ours, and standing amongst us is a woman who never faltered in that fight.'

On the peaceful sail back to Devon, Rosalind told her sons, 'If you ever engage in a notable enterprise, and you will, see it to the finish.' Sam asked, 'Is that why the Refuge Steeds call you Rosalind Revenge?' But before she could respond, Pierre said, 'I shall think of you as Rosalind Steadfast,' and she replied, 'That I like better,' and she thought: I do not want my sons to think of me as always fighting against men—their father, Bonfleur, Blackbeard, Judge Broadnax. I could have been friends or partners with any of them. If they had let me. If they had been decent human beings.

In May, when the great convoy finally assembled—two hundred and thirty ships this year—she had no hesitation in placing her sons aboard, for she was satisfied that when their studies were completed they would return to assume their responsibilities as the new Steeds of Devon.

With her sons gone, she was totally alone. There was the house to complete, but that scarcely engaged all her energies. What she needed was life, the growing of children as well as the prospering of trees, so in humbleness of spirit she asked her slaves to ready the small shallop, and when a calm day arrived she got into it by herself and sailed across to Peace Cliff, where she walked unannounced up the low hill to the telescope house. There she sought Amanda and made peace—'I need you at Devon. And I think Beth needs the island.'

Her granddaughter was a lively child of eight, with amber braids peeking out from beneath her Quaker bonnet. When she curtsied and shook hands, Rosalind thought: This one's bound to be a notable woman. She's just the age to profit from the relaxation of a Catholic home after all this Quaker severity. But Amanda was thinking: Rosalind's the most honest and courageous woman I know, but she is dominating. We'd not be on Devon a week before she'd want us both to become Catholics.

So she said no. 'I respect thy intentions, but I sense that things will be much safer if Beth stays here. This is her destined life, and Devon could only be a distraction.' She would permit no extended discussion, and in the end Rosalind had to go back down the hill, get into her shallop and sail home alone.

As she crossed the Choptank, with the gentlest of winds pushing her along, she reflected on the irony of recent events: Stooby wanted to give me Fitzhugh's three children, but I refused them on the proper grounds that they could never fit into Devon patterns, and I was right. Now I seek my husband's granddaughter, and Amanda refuses on grounds which I suspect are equally right, that she wouldn't fit into the Devon pattern. Well, I have my sons, and they're the best of the lot . . . bred true . . . offspring of Cavaliers.

It was possible that her preoccupation with children sprang not from love, for which she had always possessed an enormous capacity, but from a necessity to feel herself involved in the ongoing processes of life, and it was a happy accident that just as her family existence became most empty, an event occurred which propelled her into the heart of Choptank affairs.

At the home of Judge Thomas Broadnax, husband and wife combined to terrorize the little bastard girl consigned to their permanent care. They had given her the name of Penelope, shortened to Penny, and had made of her the most abused and menial kind of serf. They provided barely enough clothes to keep her warm and only such food as she required to stay alive. Together they believed that their harshness was ordained by God as punishment for the child's having been born out of wedlock, and that when they chastised her, they were doing His work.

For any infraction of the intricate laws they laid down, she was beaten. If she dared to protest, she was chained to the wall of a dark closet, and beaten afresh when released. Her arms bore permanent scars, and if any older person made an unexpected move toward her, she cringed. Judge Broadnax always explained to her, in heavy legal terms, why it was proper for him to beat her until the blood flowed and why it grieved him to do so, but it was Mrs. Broadnax who terrified her. The judge's wife could be a demon, striking and scratching and screaming until the child trembled whenever she had to approach her with a heavy tray of food, which Mrs. Broadnax gorged while the hungry child stood attentive at her elbow.

One day, when the persecutions became unbearable, the little girl ran away from the Broadnax home, fleeing aimlessly to any refuge that might preserve her from the judge's fury. By accident she stumbled into the Paxmores' boatyard, but when the older brother saw her, and realized that she had run away from the Broadnax home, he became quite frightened, for the harboring of a runaway indentured servant was a principal crime, and he would have none of it. Brusquely he shoved the child away, knowing that if he kept her, he would be subjected to the judge's wrath.

Bewildered, the little girl wandered down the road until she came to the Steed warehouse, and there Rosalind happened to be inspecting some fearnought in which to clothe her slaves, and when she saw the battered child, and the scars along her arms, she impulsively caught her up and kissed her and told her, 'You've nothing to fear. Cardo, give this child something to eat.'

It was only when Penny was stuffing herself on cheese that Rosalind discovered who she was. 'Judge Broadnax! He beat you like this?' She had barely established the facts of his brutality when Mrs. Broadnax stormed into the warehouse, demanding to know whether her runaway servant answering to the name of Penny had been seen . . .

'There you are, ungrateful child!'

But as she reached to recover the little criminal Mrs. Steed interposed: 'You'll not touch this child.'

'She belongs to me. She's a disobedient hussy.'

'Do not touch her.'

Mrs. Broadnax, not catching the ominous quiet in Rosalind's voice, imprudently came at Penny, intending to twist and pinch her arm as she led her away. Instead she was confronted by the powerful form of Rosalind Steed, who with one substantial shove sent her sprawling backward among the barrels, over which she stumbled, landing flat on the floor.

'Don't touch her,' Rosalind repeated in a voice of terrible power, 'for if you try again, I shall kill you.'

It was a fearful statement, heard by several, and these witnesses could also testify that after having said this, Mrs. Steed gathered the child into her arms and carried her to the town wharf, where they went aboard the Steed sloop, despite the fact that Mrs. Broadnax warned her in a loud voice which she must have heard, 'If you harbor that child, you'll rot in jail.'

The warrants were sworn, and the constable's boat sailed out to Devon with them. Satisfying himself that the child Penny was indeed on the island, he mournfully came back—'It's shameful to arrest a woman like Mrs. Steed. But she's done wrong and I suppose she must pay.'

The trial was a sensation, long remembered in Maryland records. Judge Thomas Broadnax presided, seeing nothing wrong in acting as adjudicator in a controversy involving his wife, and he was properly grave in manner. He allowed the prosecutor to develop the contentious history of this difficult Steed woman—her outbursts against authority, her specific threat to kill the judge's wife, and especially her disgraceful behavior in disrobing at the public whipping of the Turlock woman, a known whore. As each new bit of evidence unfolded, with the various Steeds in the audience crimson with embarrassment, the judge became more pontifical and serenely compassionate: 'Do you mean to say that a gentlewoman like Mrs. Steed uttered such profanity?' He shook his head in sad disbelief.

But he was miscalculating his adversary. During the first day Rosalind sat silent as the hurtful evidence piled against her. She realized that she was being tried not for kidnapping an indentured servant but for an accumulation of petty offenses against the male community: that she was a Protestant who more or less adhered to the Catholic faith; that she had defended the Turlock woman; that she had sometimes driven hard bargains in the purchase of land; that she had sent her sons to Bohemia and then to St. Omer's; and most of all, that she had been an outspoken woman when she should have been silent. Curiously, not less than six witnesses testified to the fact that she was building an outrageous house; that seemed a real sin.

At the close of that first day it was apparent that Judge Broadnax would be justified in sentencing her to jail or at least to the ducking stool, but when the second day began, the climate changed. With remorseless force Rosalind produced witnesses willing at last to testify against their infamous judge: he had beaten the child senseless during a dinner; he had forced her to work shoeless in the snow; he had provided one dress, and one only, which she had to wash on Saturday nights and wear still damp to church on Sunday. On and on the cruel testimony came, as if the community wanted to purge itself of secret connivance. On several occasions Judge Broadnax tried to halt the testimony, but his companion justices, tired of domination and seeing a chance to rid themselves of his obstinacy, overruled him.

One of the most telling witnesses was Amanda Paxmore Steed, who took the stand to describe in quiet detail the condition of the little girl when Mrs. Steed invited her to Devon to see for herself. Amanda, a small woman in demure gray, created such a powerful impression, and was so relentless in her description of the bruises and the scars, that women in the audience began to cry.

Judge Broadnax interrupted to point out that the Bible instructed masters to chastise their servants if they misbehaved, and he might have carried the day, for Maryland society in 1720 allowed little sympathy for runaway servants; by custom they were thrashed and returned to their masters with the duration of their indenture lengthened. Any who connived in their delinquency were sent to jail. 'We are here to preserve the sanctity of contracts,' Judge Broadnax reminded the jury. 'What would your farms and businesses be worth if the servants you honestly acquired were allowed to roam free? Tell me that, if you please.'

At this critical moment, when the trial hung in the balance, as if justice were truly blind, Rosalind introduced three witnesses it had taken her much trouble to find. They had known Broadnax's servant girl Betsy, mother of the bastard Penny, and on five separate occasions she had confided to them certain facts about Penny.

'Judge Broadnax,' Rosalind asked quietly, but with a menace and contempt she took no pains to hide, 'do you really want these women to testify?'

'You bring liars into the court,' Broadnax thundered. 'It's to no purpose, but if they want to make fools of themselves . . . and of you, Mrs. Steed . . .' He shrugged his shoulders, and the first woman, a servant of no repute, took the stand.

'Betsy told me that it was the judge who came into her bed.'

The next woman, of no better reputation, testified, 'Betsy told me the judge had his way with her.'

And the next woman said the same, and then Penny herself was put on the stand, to say in a weak, small voice, 'Before my mother died she told me the judge was my father.'

When Rosalind's turn came she admitted all charges against her: in anger she had said that the judge ought to be poisoned, and in greater anger she had struck Mrs. Broadnax and threatened to kill her—'But I did so because there was evil amongst us.'

'How did you know that?' one of the subsidiary justices asked.

'I knew when I read the record. And you should have known when you allowed the record to be written.'

'What record?'

'Of this court.' And she recited, as best she could, the hideous record of a judge who had testified against his own servant's pregnancy, had caused her to be whipped, had taken her child into a lifetime of servitude and had then abused that child most cruelly. 'In beating the child, Judge Broadnax was punishing himself for his own sin. In abusing this little girl, Mrs. Broadnax sought revenge against her husband. There is ugliness here and guilt, but not mine.' The decision of the justices can be read in Patamoke records to this day:

> 11 November 1720. In that Rosalind Steed of Devon has been found guilty of making violent threats against Thomas Broadnax of this town and his wife Julia, and because of her constant harranguing, she is sentenced to three submersions on the ducking stool.
>
> Thomas Broadnax, Presiding
> Alloway Dickinson, Justice Quorum
> Samuel Lever, Justice

The Choptank was cold that day. A wind blew in from the west, throwing small whitecaps and warning boats to stay ashore. The air was somewhat warmer at the inner harbor, where the long-beamed ducking stool was located, but the water was icy. A huge crowd gathered at the shore to watch the Steed woman receive her punishment, but there was no elation among the watchers. There was general agreement that the justices had acted properly: Penny had run away and had to be returned as an admonition to other servants; Mrs. Steed had harbored her and that was clearly a crime; and she had been an abusive woman, throwing her tongue into places it wasn't needed. But her crime had been trivial in comparison with Judge Broadnax's, and he was not only unpunished but he had the little girl back to abuse as he wished for the next twelve years. There was something badly askew in Patamoke, and the citizens knew it.

So Rosalind marched to the ducking stool in silence, chin high, still opposing Broadnax in all things. She remained arrogant as they strapped her into the chair, and refused to close her eyes at the final moment. Instead she took a deep breath and stared at Thomas Broadnax with a hatred that almost inflamed the November air. And then the chair ducked toward the dark water.

What happened next became the subject of endless repetition and delighted discussion. It was the custom when ducking a difficult woman who had irritated the men of town to hold her under water until her lungs nearly collapsed; it was a terrible punishment, accented by strangling and mocking voices. But on this day, by previous arrangement among the townspeople, the stool went in and out of the water so swiftly, and the act was repeated with such dispatch that, as one woman said approvingly, 'She scarce got wet.'

When the men swung the stool inboard and unleashed their victim, the crowd cheered, and women ran forward to embrace her, and Judge Broadnax thundered, 'That wasn't a ducking! The order of the court said clearly—'

But the people had left him. They were with Rosalind, congratulating her and kissing her, while he stood by the harbor—alone.

It was the custom on the Eastern Shore to give the homes of leading citizens names, and some were of such wry charm that they would persist as long as the land endured: a contentious man finds peace at last in a remote farmhouse and christens it the Ending of Controversie; a parcel of land is conveyed under debatable circumstances and the home built on it is named Crooked Intention; not far from Devon Island a man builds his dream home and names it the Cross of Gold, but he does so in French, Croix d'Or, and before long it becomes Crosiadore; and along the Choptank three contiguous farms summarize the colonial experience: Bell's Folly, Bell's Persistence, Bell's Triumph.

It was understandable, therefore, that the name given in derision to the brick mansion on Devon Island should become permanent: *Rosalind's Revenge*. At night, in taverns, some would argue that it stemmed from the builder's remorseless pursuit of the French pirate Bonfleur. Others remembered that the words were first uttered when Fitzhugh Steed quit the island to live openly with the Turlock girl. But most believed, or wanted to believe, that it represented Mrs. Steed's triumph over the cruel judge, Thomas Broadnax: 'He had the power to order her ducked, but she went in and out like a mallard and lived to see him flee the town in disgrace. We started to laugh at him and his bitch wife, and this they could not endure. Rosalind had her revenge.'

It was a strange house, totally wrong and out of balance. The Flemish bond, instead of producing a beautiful façade, looked heavy and lacking in grace. But perhaps the fault lay in the basic design, for which Rosalind was to blame. Various observers, including the Paxmore brothers, had pointed out that what she was building was nothing better than an unadorned cube: 'Each of the four sides is a square of identical size. This is monotonous and adds no beauty.' One of the brothers reminded her of the traditional Choptank wisdom: 'At first, a wee bit house for you and the wife. When babies start coming, a little larger. And when money comes, you add a real house. That way, each part lends beauty to the rest.'

She had ignored the criticisms and for nine years had obstinately pursued her plan of erecting a perfect cube on the foundations of the original Steed home. But when observers saw the mistake she was making with the two chimneys, they had to protest. One of her ship captains, who had seen the fine homes of England, pointed out, 'To give balance, the chimneys must stand at the two ends of the house, not side-by-side along the rear.' He took paper and drew a sketch of what he had in mind, and it was superior to what she was doing. 'At least,' he pleaded, 'if you won't put the chimneys in their proper place, put some windows in the side walls. Create a pleasing balance.'

She ignored his recommendations, and in 1721, ten years after she started, she had her cube completed. Only one aspect was satisfactory: the front façade did have a classical balance, with a central doorway of austere cleanliness, flanked on each side by a pair of well-proportioned windows. On the second floor appeared five windows, smaller than those below but centered exactly, the middle one positioned over the doorway. Somehow these ten nicely related openings, framed in white against the Flemish bond, gave the cube stability and quiet elegance—without them the house would have been a total disaster; with them it was merely a failure.

Ruth Brinton Paxmore gave her last testimony one cold First Day in November 1721. She was eighty-eight years old, but able to walk unaided from the town wharf to the meeting house and with firm step to ascend to the waiting chair on the facing bench. She wore gray as usual, and a small bonnet with the strings loose over her shoulders, a custom she had borrowed from her granddaughter Amanda.

Her appearance evoked mixed emotions among the Quakers of Patamoke: she was the leading voice on the Eastern Shore, a woman of demonstrated sanctity, but she was also a bore. In spite of admonitions and incessant defeats, she persisted in dragging slavery into almost every private conversation or public statement. The Patamoke Meeting had repeatedly rejected her suggestion that the ownership of slaves disqualify a Quaker from membership in the society. The Yearly Meeting of the Eastern Shore had done the same, as had the larger general meetings in Annapolis and Philadelphia. The Quakers were eager to point out that a slaveholder must treat his slaves well, as the Bible directed, and they developed a further doctrine which irritated many non-Quakers: the just ownership of slaves must see to their Christian salvation and to their education. But for the radical reforms Ruth Brinton wanted to initiate, there was no support, and she was deemed a nuisance. 'She's our hair shirt,' many said, and when she rose to speak, they squirmed:

> 'The facts are few and stubborn. Slavery in all its manifestations must be eradicated. It is not profitable to the farmer nor fair to the slave. Every aspect of society is impeded by its existence, and if we on the Eastern Shore persist in this extravagance while other sections rely upon free labor, we must slide backward.
>
> 'For a long lifetime I have listened attentively to arguments thrown against me and I find substance in none. The Quaker program must be simple and straightforward. While the African is still a slave, educate him. As soon as possible, manumit him. If that is impractical, at thy death set him free in thy will. And within a decade state so that all can hear, "No man or woman who owns slaves can be a Quaker." '

Primly, as if indifferent to the reception of her revealed message, she resumed her seat, and two days later died.

Her death had unanticipated consequences for Rosalind. Four days after the burial in the little graveyard behind the meeting house, Amanda arrived at Devon bringing Beth with her. The bright little girl was now ten and ready for solid instruction in the books which had made Rosalind so firm of character. 'We want to live with thee,' Amanda said in the reserved and precise manner of her grandmother, 'and Beth and I both deem it timely to employ a tutor.'

'We'll buy one,' Rosalind said abruptly, and she took Amanda and the child to Annapolis, where numerous young men more or less qualified as teachers were offering their indentures for sale. 'We'll buy the best,' Rosalind said, 'and he can set up a school for all the Steeds,' and this she did. The young man was a gem, a graduate of Cambridge in England and a practicing Catholic. Philip Knollys was the kind of brash young fellow who knew nothing in depth but everything at a level which enabled him to expostulate with bounding confidence. He was only slightly brighter than Beth, but he did know how to keep boys and girls free of riot, and as soon as he established his noisy, effective school for the seventeen Steed children, Rosalind told her cousins from the Refuge, 'Here's a young man we must keep.'

These were happy years for Rosalind. She positively cherished Amanda as one of the most sensible young women she had ever known, and with her took an almost malicious pleasure in being a renegade Protestant who loved the complexity of Catholicism. Beth, of course, was enchanted by Knollys and under his tutelage was inclining toward Catholicism; when her uncles returned from St. Omer's they found her well advanced in Catholic doctrine.

'It's a shame girls can't be educated,' Pierre complained to his mother. 'Our little Beth is quicker of mind that we were.'

Little Beth had her own plans for further education; as soon as she reached seventeen she informed her mother and grandmother that she intended marrying the tutor. He was summoned, and stood facing Rosalind and Amanda with charming arrogance; he was all of twenty-nine and with one year to run on his indenture, and Rosalind asked, 'Is it proper for a man still a servant to seek the hand of a young woman he is obligated to teach?'

Before he could respond, Beth interrupted, 'Thee is asking three separate questions. How can he possibly answer in one swoop?'

'What three questions?'

Like a little lawyer, her chin jutting toward the bench, she replied, 'First, is it proper? Anything in good conscience is proper. Second, does he have a moral obligation to me as his student? He has, and he has discharged it. Third, does his being a servant disqualify him? It does. But that can be quickly remedied.'

'How?' Rosalind asked contentiously.

'Terminate his indenture. Now.'

Amanda agreed, and when that was done the little girl rushed to Knollys' arms and embarrassed him with kisses.

The wedding was held under the oak, with Father Darnley, an old man now, officiating in half-drunken jollity. Amanda was shocked, for Quaker weddings were solemn, but since Father Darnley had married her many years ago, she was willing to grant him indulgence.

Now Rosalind had time to proceed with the building of her home, and when a new tutor was purchased to take over the Steed school, Mr. Knollys was free to help. He had a considerable knowledge of geometry and carpentering and gladly assumed control of the slaves assembled for the final effort. As the months passed, and Rosalind revealed her intentions, Knollys caught her infectious enthusiasm and assured everyone in Patamoke, 'It's to be the finest home on the Eastern Shore.'

Those who had laughed at her stumpy original cube with its misplaced chimneys and unsatisfactory end walls could see at last what she had always intended. Using it as the solid center of her construction, she built at some distance east and west two slightly smaller cubes, each containing two rooms downstairs, two up, but with much lower roof lines than the main building. When they were finished they looked as peculiar as the central cube: squat, heavy buildings without any pleasing adornment except the rigorous arrangement of their front façades, where four windows somewhat smaller than those in the main house gave balance.

When asked what the two strange appendages were, Rosalind replied,

'Rooms for the children we're all going to have.' And the children did come, so that the new tutor was kept busy instructing a seemingly endless supply of Steeds, while Rosalind continued medicating them. To her emergency supplies she had added ginseng drops, most effective in treating the flux, and Venice treacle for childhood coughs. A woman in Patamoke had introduced her to burnt hartshorn, a bitter substance which produced good results when used to combat congestions, and it was now possible to get steady supplies of turmeric from London, and this was certain to cure weaknesses of blood. But the medicine which made life among the mosquitoes bearable was the new one called simply 'the bark.' It was that, the bark of some magic tree, extremely bitter, which attacked all fevers and ate them up.

'A child can be prostrated with fever, shaking as if a dog worried him, and five applications of the bark puts him on his feet again,' Rosalind told the Steeds at the Refuge, and when they followed her advice, they found that their summers were twice as comfortable as they had been previously. The bark was a miracle, and on Devon Island only Mrs. Steed was allowed to dispense it, which she always did with a promise: 'Enjoy its bitterness. It's going to fight on your behalf.'

And then, in 1729, she disclosed the final plan for her home. Using a huge pile of bricks assembled over the past two years, and goading Knollys' slaves to extra efforts, she made various bold moves. At the original cube she tore out large segments of the two end walls, and at each of the flanking buildings she did the same. It looked as if she were determined to wreck the very buildings she had worked so long to construct, but when all was prepared, she put the slaves to the exciting task of erecting two low, compact passageways, each with three windows, which bound everything together. These new additions were not large enough to be considered houses, but they were built with such solidity that they were obviously parts of the whole. When challenged as to what they were, Rosalind said, 'On sunny days I shall sit in these warm, comfortable rooms and sew.' These were the lovely connectives that bound the cubes together into one magnificent home.

When the rubble was cleared, and the lawns raked, and low shrubs put in place to hide the scars of building, Rosalind's Revenge stood revealed, and no part of the beautifully balanced five-part structure was more ideally suited to its purpose than the original cube which had evoked such cynical merriment. Now it was clear why she had placed her chimneys at the rear: the passageways could not have been added if the chimneys had been at the end walls. And it was also manifest why the end walls had been left so bleak: she had always intended that they be pierced for the passageways.

How stately the great house was, with five separate roof lines, with twenty-four matched windows in a façade that moved forward in the center, slightly back at each end, and well back at the passages. Especially satisfying was the manner in which the house fitted the trees, which she had planted well before the building was begun, so that when a visitor arrived at the wharf and looked northward, he saw a stretch of lawn not too spacious, a collection of trees not too numerous, a house not too ornate, so that he was tempted to exclaim, 'How well-proportioned it all is.'

What the visitor could not see was that in a corner of the main room Rosalind had caused a cupboard to be built, and here she preserved the pewter dishes rescued when the pirates burned the preceding house. A few of the pieces had been somewhat melted by the flames, but all were serviceable, and each March, as the old year ended, she liked to assemble all Steeds for a banquet of gratitude that the year had passed without disaster. Then she would allow the children to eat off the pewter plates, and feel the dense hand of history, and she would tell them, 'You can never foresee how a house or a human being is going to turn out till the work is completed.'

And when the Refuge Steeds had departed in their boats, she gathered her own family to instruct the children in their heritage and told them of how Edmund Steed had come to America with a courageous Catholic heart to build this plantation, and of how his wife Martha Keene had fled England to share the wilderness with him, and then she told them of King Charles, whose head had been chopped off, and this part the children loved for its gruesomeness as she described the falling of the ax. Then, with just the right mixture of high adventure and travesty, she told them who Prince Rupert was, and of how he had galloped back and forth across England to save his king, and then she asked, 'And who do you suppose rode with him?'

'Chilton Janney!' the children cried.

'Yes, your great-great-grandfather. He was a Cavalier and he rode with Rupert at Martson Moor.'

And then one of the children would say, 'But you always said he was dead drunk.'

'I never saw him sober,' Rosalind would confess.

'And he wasn't a real Cavalier,' another child would say, and she would reply, 'In his heart he was.'

At various places in this chronicle certain phrases have been used relative to the Choptank which might lead one to think it a peaceful stream: 'She got into her shallop and sailed to Peace Cliff' or 'They sailed idly down the river past the marsh.' And for twenty-nine days out of thirty these descriptions were apt and these actions possible. The Choptank was a splendid body of water; indeed, that spacious area between Devon Island on the west and Patamoke to the east was practically a lake, and on pleasant days an experienced sailor like Rosalind Steed could traverse it with impunity.

It was on such a day in October 1732 that she left Rosalind's Revenge, walked down to the wharf and asked the slaves to prepare her shallop —'I'm sailing to Patamoke.' One of the older slaves said, 'Better tomorrow. Clouds over the bay.' She rejected this advice—'We always have clouds somewhere.'

As she sailed down the placid creek she came upon a cove black with geese, home from the north, and she thought how beautiful they were, but then a solitary heron came to the edge of a small marsh to fish for crabs, and she thought: I always wanted to be a stately goose but was destined to be an awkward heron. Well, the goose comes back now and then with a show of glory, but the heron stays forever.

The river was incredibly beautiful as she entered it for the easy run to Patamoke; the banks were lined with oak and maple turning myriad shades of red, and above them, on the cliff, stood the gray loveliness of the Paxmores' telescope house, so different from the manor she had built, so perfect in its Quaker dignity, and she thought: A remote corner like this, and within a few miles, we have two of the most handsome houses in America. Her eyes lingered on the gray house and she could visualize old Ruth Brinton moving about the plain kitchen, and tough-minded little Amanda learning her lessons of integrity.

But as she passed the cliff and headed for the marsh the sky darkened and from the bay came winds of force. And then, within the space of minutes, a storm of tremendous fury engulfed her little world. Rain came down in slanting sheets; the wind roared to forty miles an hour, then fifty; whitecaps as huge as those thrown up by the ocean ripped across the river; and her shallop was tossed and tortured.

Within the first half-minute she had the sail down and the shallop running with the wind: I'll let it push me ashore . . . anywhere. I'll get drenched walking to land, but no matter. She was following standard procedure for the Choptank; since the entire Eastern Shore was alluvial, a sailor never had to fear putting his craft upon the rocks, for there were none. When trouble threatened, the waterman allowed his boat to move toward shore till it scraped bottom, then he got out and walked through the waves to safety.

But on this October day the waves would not permit this escape; they tossed the shallop until Rosalind had to relinquish the rudder and cling to the sheerstrake to avoid being washed overboard, and when in this position she saw a succession of really monstrous waves coming at her, she realized what peril she was in.

We'll see it through, she said to herself, bracing for the shock of the first wave, and by strength alone she clung to the violently pitching boat.

When the last of the big waves roared by she gasped: That was a near thing, very near. And she began to take deep breaths, watching in dismay as her mast crumpled, dragging the boom into the water. There was still a good chance that she could ground the boat and struggle ashore, so she returned to the rudder stick, endeavoring to restore the shallop to a reasonable course, and she might have succeeded had not a mighty gust swept in from the bay, throwing the entire river in confusion. Waves moving in one direction were tormented by new ones raised by the howling wind; the shallop rose on one heading, twisted in midair, turned and tumbled violently.

Rosalind was thrown clear, but she still fought to reach shore, which she had every chance of attaining, except for the broken mast which struck her from the rear, tangling her feet in its swirling lines, dragging her down and down.

Turlock children, surveying their marsh after the storm, spotted the wrecked shallop and yelled to their elders, 'Boat ashore!' And when all the family ran into the marsh prepared to steal any movable parts, they found Mrs. Steed half buried in the sand, her hands engaged in the shrouds she had been fighting when she died.

Voyage Six: 1773

ONE OF THE MOST IMPORTANT JOURNEYS EVER undertaken along the Chesapeake was also one of the shortest. It covered less than twelve miles, but when its ugly mission was completed, a revolution had been launched.

The Lords Proprietor of Maryland had always enjoyed the right of advowson, a feudal privilege which they sometimes discharged in ways that could not be fathomed. All citizens of the colony conceded that the lords had the right to appoint their own clergyman to any Church of England vacancy which occurred, but no one could comprehend how even an absentee owner who lived in London without ever having seen Maryland could have appointed to the rural church at Wrentham a man so totally devoid of religious conviction as Jonathan Wilcok.

This monster arrived at the rich living located a few miles north of the headwaters of Dividing Creek one November day in 1770, two hundred and eighty pounds of blackmail, simony and self-indulgence. The blackmail accounted for his having obtained this enviable sinecure: he had caught young Lord Baltimore in a situation which was not only compromising but also downright perilous unless secrecy were maintained, and when he pointed this out to the profligate he also suggested, 'If you were to give me the living at Wrentham north of the Choptank, I'd be no threat to your safety.'

The simony consisted of his selling at maximum profit to himself all services of the church. He would not marry, christen or bury without substantial fees, which had to be paid in choice tobacco, and he also abused his position by driving the hardest possible bargains in acquiring real estate for his private use. There was no transaction so venal that he would not resort to it, if only it showed promise of gain.

But it was his self-indulgence which put him in bad odor with his parishioners. Possessed of an appointment from which no force on earth could remove him—neither the Bishop of London who despised him, nor Lord Baltimore, who feared him, and certainly not his flock, who had no rights at all except to pay his handsome salary and keep silent—he was free to behave as he wished. This included getting mildly drunk seven nights a week, siring two bastard children, maintaining a foul-mouthed wife and a mistress, and propelling his vast and sweaty bulk into any problem whose resolution might yield him an advantage.

It was loathsome that the Church of England should suffer from the misbehavior of Jonathan Wilcok, but traditions of the time absolved him, and if the scandals he generated did damage the church, they did not obliterate the splendid work done by other devoted clergymen whose appointments had been similarly made. The Rector of Wrentham and his brethren represented the Established Church of Maryland; their existence was approved by king and Parliament and their conduct was beyond reproof. On balance, they performed acceptably, in the proportion of seven worthy ministers to three rectors of Wrentham.

At dawn on a cold day in January 1773 this clergyman, now well over three hundred pounds in weight, rose early, bundled himself in swaths of homespun, over which he slipped a clerical garb with stiff collar and white tie, studied himself admiringly, and said to his adoring wife, 'Today we bring some order into this community.' Then he informed his four slaves that he would be sailing to Patamoke for the court session due to convene at noon. 'Imperative I be there. The future of the Choptank is at stake.'

So the slaves readied two horses and brought out the rude palanquin which hung suspended between them. Then they informed the rector, "All's ready, Master,' and he waddled to where his contraption waited.

It would have been quite impossible for him to walk on his own from the church to the head of Dividing Creek, a distance of three miles, but he was able to negotiate the few steps to the palanquin. However, when he got there he was incapable of climbing in, for the thing swayed and refused to stay steady. So one of the slaves stood between the two horses, quieting them and the palanquin; two took the rector by his arms and moved him backward while the fourth remained in front, pushing on his huge belly.

'Now!' the men cried, and with remarkable skill they engineered their master into his conveyance. Grunting and sweating even on this cold morning, the rector cried, 'Forward!' and one of the slaves walked ahead, leading the two horses, while two others pushed from behind; the fourth man was supposed to jump into any emergency to ensure that the fat man did not fall out.

In this manner the pilgrimage reached the stream where the episcopal barge waited, and there new complexities arose, for the mammoth clergyman now had to be eased out of his palanquin, walked across a slippery wharf and let down into the boat. Finally this was accomplished, to the accompaniment of directions shouted by everyone, and as soon as the rector landed safely in the barge he made himself at ease, lay back on seven pillows and roared, 'On to Patamoke.'

When he arrived at that thriving commercial center, children and idlers passed the word, 'Here comes the Rector of Wrentham!' and all ran to the wharf to enjoy once more the extraordinary manner in which he would be brought ashore. It required the services of six men: from the barge the four slaves pushed and grunted while on the shore two others threw down a rope, which was passed around the fat man's back and under his armpits, each of the men retaining one end. Then, as the men on shore counted, 'One, two, three!' everyone exerted maximum force and grandly the rector rose from the barge as if on wings and slid ashore.

Again, as soon as his feet found security on the wharf, he became composed and grandiose, the traditional figure of a benevolent clergyman. Throwing his coat about him, he nodded graciously to the townspeople and walked with ponderous dignity toward the courthouse, his porcine face wreathed in condescending smiles. As he entered that low stone building he noted with pleasure that all was in readiness: the bench was occupied by justices well disposed to his cause; the three culprits were waiting to receive their just punishments.

The defendants were an unlikely trio, with nothing but their common guilt to form a bond between them. Even in dress they were distinct. Simon Steed, aged forty-three, was a tall, austere, thin-shouldered man who treated the court, the spectators and his fellow criminals with equal disdain. His clothes followed the French style, a taste he had developed at St. Omer's. His wig was powdered; his stock was starched; his shirt had fourteen buttons and was touched with lace; his blue velvet coat came almost to his knees; and his pants ended just below, marked by small silvery buckles. At his wrists a fringe of gray lace protruded, lending an air of elegance when he moved his arms. He was a gentleman, the wealthiest man in the community, and to see him standing in the dock like a common criminal was exciting to the townspeople, but from the deference they paid him it was obvious that their sympathies lay with him and not with his accuser.

Beside him stood a man just turned forty, distinguished by the fact that he wore a broad-brimmed flattish hat which he refused to remove even when nudged by the court attendant. This was Levin Paxmore, one of the principal supports of Patamoke Meeting and head of the Paxmore Boatyard, whose workmen were putting in doubled hours during these years of stress. He was a somber man, dressed in a long gray coat marked by nine frogs, with no lace at the wrists and no silver buckles on the shoes, but he, too, displayed a kind of elegance, for the cloth of his coat and pantaloons was of the best. He was obviously offended at being summoned to court and refused to acknowledge the gestures of good will thrown his way.

The third man had often stood before this bar. Thin, quick of movement, rascally of eye, he captained a miserable old sloop that traded the Chesapeake. He came from the marsh and was dressed accordingly: improvised shoes made of animal hide; no stockings; baggy pants held about the waist by a tattered rope; heavy woolen shirt but no coat; no hat; and a dark beard. He was Teach Turlock, and even his name was an offense to this community, for a rapscallion father had named him after the pirate Blackbeard, 'a man who knew what he was up to.' Forty-one years ago, when the prisoner had been named, Blackbeard was still a fearsome memory, for he had ravaged the oceans, and two gentlemen had gone into court to force old Turlock to give his son a proper name, and the court had so ordered: on the record his name showed as Jeremiah Turlock, but universally he was known as Teach, which even his enemies had to admit was proper, for he displayed most of the enduring qualities of that pirate.

The social and moral principles of the three defendants were as varied as their clothing. Simon Steed was an avowed supporter of the king; he had little patience with those agitators in Massachusetts and Virginia who were uttering treason, and he hoped devoutly that ill-intentioned men in both America and England might soon be brought to their senses. Levin Paxmore held aloof from political discussion; he felt that God ordained governments and that men had no right even to comment, let alone protest. It was Teach Turlock who represented the new spirit abroad in the colonies; he was a potential revolutionist, not from principle but from an ugly desire to get even with those stationed above him. When men talked in whispers about rebellion, he fingered his gun.

Only the intrusion of some alien force as powerful as the Rector of Wrentham could have enlisted these three unlikely companions in a common cause, and now that gigantic, puffing servant of the church wheezed his way to the front of the court, gingerly lowered himself into a broad chair and signaled to the justices that the trial should begin.

The tax collector testified first. 'Time out of mind, all good citizens of this district have delivered to me before the last day of December thirty pounds of choice tobacco to be handed over to the Rector of Wrentham as his salary for maintaining the Established Church in our district.'

'Has this always been the law of this colony?' the presiding judge asked.

'Your father's day and mine. Your honors handed me the tobacco, as honest Christians should.'

And the three judges nodded self-righteously.

'Has anyone failed to pay?' the presiding judge asked.

'These three.'

'You're the tax collector. Why didn't you take action?'

The tax collector blushed uneasily, looked down at his feet, then said in a high, whining voice, 'The other rector told me, "Leave them alone, damned Papists and Quakers. God will punish them." But our new rector'—and here he looked approvingly at the fat man—'he intends to straighten things out.'

'How?' the judge asked.

'Each of these three must pay ten years of tithes. Our rector insists upon it as his due.'

'And you asked these men for their tobacco?'

'I did.'

'And did Simon Steed refuse to deliver his three hundred pounds?'

'He did. Said he was Catholic and refused to pay.'

'Did Levin Paxmore fail to deliver?'

'He did. Said he was Quaker.'

'And did Teach Turlock also refuse?'

'He did.'

'And did you ask each of these men on three separate occasions, as required by law, to pay their assessments?'

'I did.'

'And did each refuse three times?'

'They did.'

The constable testified that as soon as the tax collector notified him of the delinquencies he personally did his best to collect the three hundred pounds, but had been rebuffed. 'Mr. Steed, if it please the court, was grandly indifferent . . . refused to notice me . . . told one of his men, "Get that fellow off my property." Friend Paxmore, the one with the hat on his head, behaved quite different. I've had to arrest him before for not serving with the militia, and when he saw me coming he asked in a low voice, "What does thee want this time?" and when I told him "Three hundred pounds for the chapel," he said, "Thee knows I can't pay that." '

'And what did you say?'

'I said, "Thee knows it's off to jaily-baily." '

The audience laughed, and even Paxmore allowed a faint smile to relax his lips.

'Did Turlock offer to pay?' the judge asked.

'He offered to shoot me.' This, too, occasioned laughter, but the constable added, 'He had no gun and I judged it was only a manner of speaking.'

'But he did offer to shoot you?'

'In words, yes.'

Now came the time for the rector to testify. Ponderously he struggled out of his chair, adjusted the white stock beneath his pendulous throat and said in precise, educated manner, 'Time out of mind it has been the revered custom in this colony for every man, woman and child above the age of sixteen to help pay the rector's salary. This provides funds for the poor, maintains the church buildings for worship, and gives proof that all citizens pertain to the church and volunteer to protect it. If even one person refuses to pay, the entire structure of our Christian faith is put in jeopardy, and this the courts have always recognized. These three men have persistently denied the right of the church to collect its just fee, and I demand that they be fined ten times thirty pounds and sentenced to jail for their contumely.'

'You've heard the charges,' the judge said. 'Turlock, have you aught to say?'

The waterman shrugged.

'Friend Paxmore, can you offer any justification?'

The tall Quaker shook his head.

The judge then asked Steed, but before the planter could respond, the rector objected. 'Your honor, it would be wise, I think, not to allow this man to speak in open court. He was educated in France, where he imbibed the pernicious and debilitating doctrines of atheism. He has imported the books of Voltaire and Montesquieu and has loaned them to any who could read French. He has even gone so far as to find a copy of *Candide* done into English, and this, too, he has disseminated. Whatever he chooses to say will be seditious and irrelevant.'

But the justices agreed that Steed be allowed to speak, and in the quiet, forceful manner he had developed for dealing with all problems, he proceeded to interrogate the rector. 'Do you hold that even Catholics and Quakers must pay the yearly tithe?'

'I do.'

'Even when tobacco is so hard to come by?' Before the rector could respond, Steed asked, 'Where would Teach Turlock get tobacco?'

'Others do.'

'You haven't answered my question. Where?'

'I am not concerned with the household problems of Teach Turlock.' And by the distasteful look he threw at the waterman he indicated that he had never been interested in Teach's moral problems, either.

'In a time when tobacco can scarcely be found, all other branches of government have agreed to accept their assessments in flax . . . or corn . . . You alone insist on tobacco. Why?'

'Because the Lords Baltimore entered into a solemn covenant with God to give Him thirty pounds of choice tobacco per head per year.'

Steed walked to where a farmer and his wife sat. Standing beside them, he asked the rector, 'Did you accept from this man part of his farm in payment of his assessment?'

'He offered it.'

'How many acres?'

'Sixty-seven.'

'Do you now own, in your name, not the church's, a total of three hundred and seventy acres of the best Choptank farmland?'

'The rector of any parish has the right to live in a comfortable house and farm his land.'

'Three hundred and seventy acres' worth?'

'It's land that has come to me honorably.'

'Did you propose last year that I cede you fifty-three acres west of Dividing Creek?'

'You owed it to me.'

'And how large will your holdings be at the end of this year?'

The rector appealed to the court, and the justices agreed that this was inflammatory, whereupon Steed started a new tack. 'What charities have you paid for in the last twelve months?'

'If anyone had come to me—'

'Didn't Peter Willis come to you?'

'He was notorious. To have given him aid—'

'Whom did you aid?' Steed's fastidious use of the word *whom* irritated the clergyman, who railed, 'Whom? Whom? And whom are you to question me in this way?'

Very quietly Steed said, 'I merely wanted to know what charities.'

The fat clergyman appealed again to the court, and again they sustained him. 'Mr. Steed, the Rector of Wrentham is not on trial. You are.'

'I apologize,' Steed said humbly. 'But I must ask one more question, which is perhaps even more intrusive than the preceding.'

'Watch your deportment,' the presiding judge warned.

'Rector Wilcok, these are difficult years. Strange voices are being raised in the land—'

'He speaks sedition!' the rector warned.

'The time may soon be at hand when England will need every champion—'

'He speaks French sedition!'

'Do you not think it might be prudent if, in such difficult times, when you already own so much property—'

'Sedition! Sedition! I will not listen to such questioning.'

The justices agreed. 'Mr. Steed, you have far exceeded the proprieties. You have raised questions of the most pernicious tendency and have sought to bring into the quiet precincts of this court the passions which excite the multitudes outside. You must sit down.'

'Those passions, sir—'

'Constable, sit him down.'

That officer was not required; Steed bowed to the justices, bowed to the rector, and with a grace that could only be called exquisite, wheeled and bowed to the farm couple whose lands had been stolen from them. Then he returned to his chair with the other prisoners, where Levin Paxmore clasped his hand.

'The prisoners will rise,' the presiding judge intoned, and when they were before him he said gravely, 'Especially in these troublous times is it necessary that the traditions on which our colony is based be observed with extra diligence. Time out of mind good men have paid part of their increase to the church which protects and guides them. Now more than ever we need that protection and guidance, and for anyone, Catholic or Quaker, to deny that obligation is a shocking breach of citizenship. Simon Steed and Levin Paxmore, you are each ordered to deliver to the church at Wrentham three hundred pounds of tobacco well and truly casked.'

The dissidents nodded.

'And as for you, Teach Turlock . . .' At this portentous opening, the disheveled waterman turned to the spectators and grinned, as if to say, 'It's me they're talking of.' The judge continued, 'You have no tobacco, nor any means of acquiring any. You have no personal goods worth the taking, but you do have a deficit of three hundred pounds, so this court orders that you cede to the Rector of Wrentham eighty acres of the fast land you hold north of the marsh.'

The grin vanished. The scrawny waterman looked in dismay at the bank of justices, appealing silently this terrible verdict: they were wresting from him land which he cherished, which his ancestors had acquired from Indians and protected with their lives against wolves and mosquitoes and tax collectors and Steeds who had wanted to plant it in tobacco. A strangled cry rose from his throat. Throwing himself toward the bench, he cried, 'No!' The constable pulled him away, but in doing so, thrust him in the direction of the rector, who was at the moment hauling his ponderous bulk out of his chair.

Without considering the wrongful thing he was doing, Turlock leaped at the fat man and started beating him about the face. The court became an uproar, and after the constable and two farmers had quieted the fiery waterman, the presiding judge said balefully, 'In jail, six weeks.' And the waterman was dragged away.

When the court was cleared of spectators, the justices accompanied the rector to the wharf, where with the aid of six men he was loaded back onto his barge. The presiding judge walked along the shore, throwing obsequious farewells to the clergyman, but his two companions stood soberly on the quay and one said, 'Next year, believe me, I will no longer enforce the claims of that pious wretch.'

'It's the law.'

'Then the law must be changed.'

'Such thoughts are dangerous, Edward,' and the second judge looked to see if anyone had heard the treason.

'These are dangerous times. I'm an Englishman, born, bred and consecrated, but recently I've begun to fear that London . . .'

'Be reasonable. Teach Turlock deserved jail . . . for a score of reasons.'

'But not to have his land taken.'

'What does he care for land?'

'Did you see him when Arthur delivered the sentence? And Steed and Paxmore? They're good men.'

'They're dissidents. The time is coming when all must pull together.'

The judge who spoke first looked toward the main street of Patamoke, then indicated that his companion must look, too. What they saw was Simon Steed and Levin Paxmore walking arm and arm, deep in conversation. 'Do you realize,' the first judge asked, 'that here this day we've performed a miracle?'

'A strange word, *miracle.*'

'Yes, we justices have made it inevitable that three men as unrelated as Steed, Paxmore and Turlock will unite on common ground. I warn you, we'll see the day when those three and others like them will strip the fat Rector of Wrentham of all his lands, and after that they'll—'

'Edward! I pray, don't finish that sentence.' The second judge put his hands over his ears to blot out his associate's final judgment.

'Ideas will be set in motion which all the justices in this county will be powerless to halt.'

Three Patriots

THE TWO JUSTICES WERE WRONG IF THEY AS-
sumed that Steed and Paxmore were talking treason. They were discussing commerce, and when they reached the boatyard Paxmore invited his
co-defendant into the plain wood-walled office from which he conducted
his business.

'What makes thee think that vessels will be at a premium?' Paxmore
asked as they sat on chairs he had carved from oak.

'The hatred I saw in Turlock's eyes . . . when the justices took his land.'

'The Turlocks are always savage.'

'But this was different. This was a declaration of war, and frankly,
Levin, I'm afraid.'

'Of what? Turlock's powerless . . .'

'Of the spirit. There's an ugly spirit abroad, Levin, and sooner or later
it will engulf us all.'

'And that's why thee wants vessels? Against days of riot?'

'Exactly. I think the day will come when people like you and me who
want to maintain ties with England will be pushed to the wall by the
canaille.'

'Thee has the advantage of me. I didn't study in France.'

'The mad dogs . . . the Turlocks. Soon they'll be shouting that the
colonies should break away from England. England will resist, as she
should. And I'm afraid there might even be war.' He hesitated, looked
nervously at the floor and whispered, 'If war does come, we shall need
ships.'

Paxmore, seeking to ignore the awful freight of those words, took
refuge in nautical pedantry. 'Friend Steed, thee uses terms carelessly. A
ship is a very large vessel with three masts or more. Nations own ships.
Businessmen own *brigs* and *sloops.*'

Steed, also eager to avoid talk of war, asked, 'Which should I build?'

'Neither. Thee wants a *schooner*. Able to move about with speed.' And each man sucked in his breath, for each knew that a commission had been offered and accepted, and this was no trivial matter, for if Steed was prepared to pay for a schooner, he must allocate to it a substantial portion of his wealth, and if Paxmore undertook to build it, he must put aside the lesser projects on which his normal income depended.

So the two men sat silent, contemplating the obligations they were about to assume, and finally Steed spoke. Moving briskly to the desk, he jabbed it with his forefinger. 'Speed, Levin. Above all else, we must have speed.'

Now it was Paxmore's turn to act decisively, and for him this was an intense process. Without rising, he began to twitch his body, turning his shoulders and edging his elbows back and forth in a performance that might have seemed grotesque to someone unfamiliar with what he was doing. Years before, Steed had told men at the store, 'When Levin Paxmore thinks of a schooner, he becomes that schooner.' And now the canny builder wrestled with those problems which had agitated the most ancient shipwrights. Finally, at the end of his contortions, he said, 'Thee can have speed, but thee can't have speed and maximum cargo. I can pull the lines out this way'—and he indicated the length of the intended vessel —'but that means I must squeeze her in here, just where you'd want to stow the hogsheads.'

'Forget the hogsheads. This schooner will be hauling compressed cargo of treble value.'

'We should keep the freeboard low, but the masts must be extra tall. We'll need a spread of canvas.'

'I'll want a very stout superstructure.'

'That'll decrease speed.'

'But I must have it. For the cannon.'

At this word Paxmore placed both hands on his desk. 'I can't agree to put cannon aboard one of my vessels, Simon.'

'I wouldn't ask you to. But you build stoutly, so that when you're through I can place the cannon.'

'I could not agree—'

'You leave the spaces—four of them.'

'But that would make it top-heavy,' Paxmore warned, and as soon as he spoke these words he realized that Steed had tricked him into connivance on a military matter, and he drew back. 'I am not building some great ship of war,' he warned, and quickly Steed assented, 'Never! Ours is to be a small schooner of peace.'

For two days the men planned the vessel that was to become the hallmark of the Paxmore yards: sleek, swift, maximum canvas, minimum beam, sharply formed bottom, lively tiller, fantastically protruding bowsprit. It was to be a schooner defined by a businessman, executed by a poet, and at every critical point each man made his decisions in reference to a view of the future that he had constructed after the most careful analysis of what he saw happening in the colonies.

Simon Steed saw that hotheads like Teach Turlock were going to nudge the colonies closer and closer to a confrontation with the mother country and that agitations of vast dimension were going to disrupt trade and the normal use of oceans. This probability influenced him in two ways. He knew that in time of turmoil adventurous traders prospered, for they were willing to buy and sell when others were immobilized by anxiety. And he was also spurred to daring ventures by remembrance of his grandmother's stubborn fight against pirates; like her, he believed that the seas must be kept free. He was therefore willing to take risks and was prepared to pay not only for the vessel he and Paxmore were planning, but for three others in swift succession, for he saw that with a fleet of four he could trade in these troubled times with sharp advantage. But that he would do so under the British flag, now and forever, he had not the slightest doubt.

Levin Paxmore, in his forty years at Patamoke, had built many ocean-going vessels, but they had been stodgy affairs: snows with ridiculous paired masts, and brigs with stumpy ones. He had always known that better craft lay waiting to be built among the oaks and pines of his forests, and sometimes when he had seen a large British ship putting into the harbor outside his boatyard, her lines trim and her three masts justly proportioned, he had felt pangs of artistic regret: I could build better than that, if anyone would buy. Now he had his customer, a man with insights at least as profound as his own, and he was eager to start. He would do so as a Quaker pacifist who abhorred war, and it never occurred to him that cooperating with Steed would lead him step by step to compromise those convictions.

So these two men of good intention launched their project believing that they could pursue it without surrendering past allegiances. Dimensions of their schooner had not been agreed upon, but at the close of that second day they proposed that on the morrow they would lay out the specific measurements; however, shortly after dawn two slaves sailed to the ramp at the boatyard with the exciting news that a trading vessel had put into Devon from London, bringing Guy Fithian and his wife on an inspection tour.

'Were they made welcome?'

'Master Isham's wife, she said come in.'

Simon Steed had never married and at forty-three had no interest in doing so; he ran the family business, read speculative books sent over from Paris, and allowed his younger brother Isham and his wife to supervise the social life of the Steed empire. If Isham had extended the courtesies, there was no need to quit the exciting business of laying out a great schooner, so Simon told his slaves, 'Sail back and assure Fithian I'll be there by nightfall.'

'No, Master. He say come now.' And one of the slaves handed Steed a brief note from his brother advising him that grave news had arrived from London. His presence was mandatory.

So Steed told Paxmore, 'We have two hours to do the work of two days. What size shall our new craft be?'

The two men, in shirt sleeves even though the January day was brisk, began to step off the proposed dimensions. 'I'll want her longer than before,' Paxmore said. 'I've been thinking that we must go to eighty-four feet and some inches.' And he drove two pegs to indicate that considerable distance.

'Longer, rather than shorter,' Steed said, and he moved the pegs slightly.

'Narrow in the beam, something under twenty-one feet,' and again Paxmore drove his pegs.

'I like that,' Steed said. 'Gives just enough room to swivel the cannon.'

The Quaker ignored talk of ordnance, but standing in the middle of the design, he said, 'I think we must go to a depth of eight or nine feet in the hold. Of course, Steed, you won't be able to navigate in the shallow waters of the bay.'

'We keep to the channel . . . to the ocean. Make her bottom as sharp as you need.'

'I calculate she'll come in at a hundred and sixty tons.'

For the remaining two hours the men reviewed all aspects of their decision, and when they were satisfied that they had reached a sensible compromise on many conflicting demands, Paxmore called one of his nephews and said, 'Martin, that large oak we've been saving. Start it into a keel,' and before Steed left the boatyard the reassuring sounds of an adze were echoing.

On the brisk and pleasant sail back to Devon he tried to guess what kind of information might have caused his brother to send that imperative note: Since it came from Fithians, it must have originated in London. And since there's no longer war with France, it must concern the colonies. Something about politics. Then he frowned. Could it possibly be business? Surely, Parliament can't have passed legislation damaging to our trade.

He was convinced that London would not be so foolish, and his reasoning was original: The one staff the king must lean upon is the support of men like Paxmore and me. Only we can hold the rabble in restraint. And at this thought he flinched, for the sloop was passing Turlock's marsh, and he visualized that hot-eyed radical wasting in jail, planning vengeance, and this encouraged him to summarize ideas which had been brewing for some months: Society must be a compromise between new, untested men like Turlock, who want to destroy old patterns, and old, tried men like Paxmore and me, who tend to cling too long to the patterns we're trying to protect.

He speculated on this for some minutes, and true to habit, whenever he dealt with large concepts such as *society, mankind* and *change* he began to think in French, and this was the fatal canker in his character: by every external sign he was fitted to be an English gentleman, except that he had learned to read French books, and these had corrupted him.

He was enormously captivated by Montesquieu and had spent one summer evaluating the Frenchman's challenging theory that the governance of man is best served by dividing authority into three insulated compartments: executive, legislative, judicial. It had never occurred to him that those were the functions of government, but under Montesquieu's exquisite tutelage he saw that this was the case.

But as soon as he reached this conclusion, he drew back from its logical consequences: The best way to attain this balance is by following the English system. A just king, a stalwart Parliament, a wise group of judges. It was contradictory: in all his practical applications he was an Englishman; in all his basic attitudes toward goodness of life he was a Frenchman. And now he turned practical: It would be a tragic day if our colonies ever felt tempted to break away from England, and when his boat touched the Steed wharf he bounded up the path, hungry to discover what kind of crisis had brought Guy Fithian across the Atlantic.

People inside Rosalind's Revenge heard him coming and hurried to the door to meet him, and there for the first time he saw Jane Fithian, many years younger than himself, gay and blond and lovely on the arm of her capable husband. She was so compelling in a light-blue dress of India cloth with its bodice of delicately applied lace, that she seemed to float toward him, extending her hand and saying in a soft voice, 'Hullo, I'm Jane Fithian.'

'Welcome to Devon, Mrs. Fithian.'

'Oh, no!' She laughed merrily. 'I'm his sister, not his wife.'

At these words he blushed so deeply that everyone watching, even the slaves, knew that he was excited by this elfin English girl, and as soon as he found himself alone with Guy he asked, 'Why did you bring her?' and Fithian replied with no embarrassment, 'Because it's high time you were married, Simon.' The words, and the intention behind them, were so bold that Steed blushed again and was about to protest when Fithian said, 'What really brings me is disaster . . . twofold.' And he proceeded to spell out the worsening situations which had made an ocean crossing imperative.

'The fall in tobacco prices means that many of the great plantations with which we've done business . . . well, they're bankrupt.

And if we continue to extend them credit, we'll be bankrupt too.'

'We're solid,' Steed said defensively.

'Would to God all the American plantations were in your condition. You and Isham know how to work, how to keep things in balance.' He shook his head gravely. 'Simon, would you have any interest in taking over Janney's—that big plantation on the Rappahannock?'

Without a moment's reflection Simon said, 'No.'

'Isn't it somehow related to your family?'

'Vaguely. But of no interest to us. Is that why you came?'

'Janney's is only one of a score. Do you realize that factors like us own most of Virginia? I represent a consortium. Six London factors, and we're being asked to absorb American debts amounting to millions. You call these places Maryland and Virginia. They're really Fithians and Goodenoughs.' In great agitation he moved about the room, shaking his head and saying, 'We own the damned plantations, and we don't want to. Simon, at least come with me to see what can be done about Janney's. You owe me that.'

Again Steed protested that for an Eastern Shore man to fiddle with a plantation in Virginia was insanity, but Fithian stopped him short. 'Like it or not, Simon, we're all caught up in insanity.' And the gravity with which this trusted old friend uttered these words forced Steed to listen.

'You feel safe because you run your plantation and stores prudently. Well, government in London seems determined to drive you out of business. Yes, you as well as the lazy Janneys.'

'What now?'

'Tea. They're going to cut your throat with tea. And if that succeeds, then step by step everything else.'

'Why tea?'

'Because the East India Company—'

'I know. I know. One of the poorest-run companies in the world. But it has that government monopoly.'

'And it's going to exercise it. The trick is this. If you American traders want to buy tea in London, you'll pay a heavy tax. The India Company won't. You'll not be able to compete. The company will land its tea on your docks and undersell you.'

When the intricacies and injustices of this device became clear, Steed slumped in his chair, pressed his hands to his forehead and said, 'It looks to me as if Parliament is determined to crush the very people in the colonies upon whom England must depend.' And with obvious frustration he reviewed the succession of acts already discriminating against the merchants of Maryland: the restrictions in trade, the unjustified taxes, the advantages awarded London monopolists at the expense of colonial businessmen, the preposterous shipping laws, the arrogance of the tax collectors.

'Have you set forth to destroy your friends?' he exploded.

'I think we have,' Fithian said, and with this he lowered his voice, and the conversation left mercantile affairs in which he and Steed were threatened with heavy losses, and entered upon those questions which touch the soul. 'What England should do right now, Simon—before summer—is say to the colonies with smiling good will, "Go your way, children. Grow strong and later on share your munificence with us." '

Steed said nothing. The idea was so radical, so contrary to his own conclusions, that he could barely digest it. So Fithian continued, 'If we do that, we shall bind you to us forever. You'll bank in London, and buy your goods there, and send your sons to Oxford. Believe me, a union like that could be a powerful force in this world.'

'Do many think like you?' Steed asked.

'You would be sick to hear the idiots. They can't visualize any future different from the past. I argue the future of Atlantic trade and they hear nothing. This fellow Burke argues the legal position and they don't hear him either.'

'Is no concession possible?'

'They'd all be possible if men were sensible. We'll make the trivial ones. But the substantial ones that could remake the world? Impossible.'

'So we planters will be driven back and back?'

'Yes. Because you're visible.'

'It would be fearfully wrong if Parliament continued to abuse us merchants. We're your link to sanity. We're loyal to a man. We love England, but we'll not be endlessly abused.'

And so the discussion continued, the Englishman advocating separation, the colonial renewing his allegiance. It ended when Fithian said abruptly, 'Enough of this. You must come with me to Janney's.'

'I've warned you. I won't touch it.'

'But for your own sake, you must see the problem. Besides, I want to show Jane the Virginia shore.'

'Is she going?'

'Of course. I want her to know you. I want her to marry you.'

'You shock me.'

'She's my baby sister. A precious, wonderful child. And we've been affiliated with the colonies for so many generations, I thought it time we made the bonds closer.'

'I'm Catholic.'

'We have an ample supply of Protestants in the other branches of the family.' He tapped Steed on the chest. 'All of us need new blood, new ideas. And you need a wife.' Steed started to protest, but Fithian stopped him. 'I sit in London and read letters from all over the world, and after a few years I build an image of the writers. And the image I have of you, Simon, is of a stolid, honest, unexciting calculator who is sometimes deeply moved by contemporary happenings, but dry of heart. Don't miss life because you contemplated it only from a distance.'

The sail to the Rappahannock was a peaceful winter idyll: geese flew overhead in vast congregations and the sky was a lambent gray; occasionally some ship bound for Baltimore would appear through the soft haze, its nine sails barely filled, and after a while it would pass on. The weather was brisk, and each morning Jane Fithian's cheeks were a bright English red, and she would apologize, 'I'm sure I must look a perfect milkmaid.'

She was a witty girl, well able to participate in the learned discussions her brother conducted. 'I think the king should send two armies to the colonies, one to march from New York north and the other from New York south. Then we'll see what headstrong rebels are capable of.' She said such things to tease Simon, who was twenty-one years her senior, but she did not succeed.

'Your armies, my dear Miss Fithian, would never reach either Boston or Philadelphia. We're not children, you know.'

'You're barbarians, that's what you are, and if we stopped our ships for even six months you'd perish . . . for lack of food . . . and ideas.'

'And if we stopped our ships for six months, Fithians would crumple . . . for lack of money.'

'We'd be sillies, each of us, to act so stupidly,' she admitted, 'and I'm sure we won't.'

But when they reached the Janney plantation and she saw its sad condition, she was deeply agitated. 'They seem such fools, all of them. Oh, Guy, if only we could stay here a year or two to straighten them out!' Her brother pointed out that the fault lay not only with the unfortunate Janneys but with the policy-makers in London. 'I'm to blame, too, for extending them credit.'

Only Simon remained untouched by the swift fall in the Janney fortunes. 'They've always been inept, and now fate in the form of ten-percent interest has overtaken them.'

It was his opinion that Fithians should foreclose, take control of the vast lands, and sell them cheaply to some better managers.

'We can't do that,' the Englishman protested. 'Because if we forced Janney's into bankruptcy, we'd have to follow with at least nineteen others. What would be the result? Panic in Virginia. And Fithians with more plantations than it could supervise.'

'What shall you do?' Steed asked.

Guy Fithian, spiritual and legal representative of many English businessmen, lowered his head, rubbed his chin and said, 'Pray. That's what we'll do, pray.'

'For what?'

'Well, my first prayer has been that I could find someone like you to manage Janney's. And the nineteen others. To tide us over the period before the war starts.' At the mention of war, Simon winced. 'And next I'd pray that after the war the free colonies will honor their debts.'

'Don't speak as if war were inevitable,' Steed said.

'It is,' Fithian said quietly.

And after they had inspected a batch of plantations tottering on abysses which the owners barely comprehended, Jane asked her brother, 'Can't we do something?'

'As I said before, we can pray.'

'So the war I spoke of in jest is to be a reality?'

'I think so,' her brother said.

The visits to the grand plantations were like a dream: slowly the sloop would climb the rivers; slaves would be waiting at the wharves to catch the lines; ahead would stretch the impeccable lawn; off to one side would stand the slave quarters; and in the midst of all would rise the mortgaged mansion, sometimes with columns gleaming in the wintry sun. The reception was invariably generous, with fine drinks and small talk of London, but in the eyes of the owners there would be a quiet terror in the presence of this factor who owned the place.

Guy Fithian was not a destroyer; he was there to see if some reign of reason could be installed to save both the ostensible owners and himself, but there was never a rational plan. 'The slaves have to be fed, Mr. Fithian. Tobacco is sure to recover. We don't know how to raise corn or wheat. There's been some talk of growing apples, but only for cider. And each month our debts seem to grow heavier.'

Yet it was these good people, so sorely abused by London, who most enthusiastically supported England and the king. 'There will never be rebellion here. In Richmond and Williamsburg there has been talk. Jefferson isn't reliable and Patrick Henry is a born troublemaker of no substance whatever. No, sir, Virginia stands fast with the king.'

'That's more than I would do,' Fithian told Steed as they prepared for the sail back to Devon. Steed did not respond, and Fithian, in an abrupt change of subject, asked, 'And what of Jane?'

'In these uncertain times . . .'

'That's when you must get your personal affairs in order. Do you intend marrying her?'

'Good heavens!'

'Simon, for the past six weeks we've been visiting people unable to make decisions. Don't become like them in your old age.'

The mention of age was unfortunate; it gave Simon an excuse. 'After all, I'm forty-three and she's only twenty-two. I'm old enough—'

'A splendid excuse,' Guy snapped. 'And I can think of a dozen others. And none apply.'

'Why not?' Simon asked almost petulantly; he did not like being ridiculed.

'Because we live in an age of tension. Everything's uncertain, and at such times wise men attend to basics . . . like marriage.'

Steed said, 'I'll think about it on the sail home.' And when the island loomed far to the east, hiding in river mists, Guy called him to the rear of the sloop and asked, 'What's the decision?' and Steed said hesitantly, 'I might as well,' and Guy shouted, 'Jane, come here!' and when she joined them, red-cheeked and lively, her brother said, 'Simon wants to marry you,' and she kissed Steed and poked him in the ribs and said, 'You didn't have to propose. I was going to do it when we reached the island.'

Steed was relieved that a major decision had been reached so painlessly; the more he had seen of Jane in the Virginia mansions the more he had grown to love her. She was a crisp, enticing young woman, with a strong mind and a lively interest in the Fithian enterprises. He was sure that she could have married a younger man—several in Virginia had seemed eager to propose—and was flattered that she had chosen him. 'You could have brought order into any of those plantations,' he told her as they walked up the path from the wharf. 'I want you to manage this one.' But in obedience to some deep sense of propriety she said, 'I didn't come to manage. I came to love.'

But beyond such practical considerations, which were English in nature, Steed also felt drawn to Jane sexually, and was neither reluctant nor embarrassed to express this longing, a fact he attributed to his French inheritance. Jane became increasingly desirable when they went to bed in the large square room once occupied in bitter loneliness by Rosalind Janney Steed, and one night when low flames spiraled in the bedroom fireplace she said, 'You thought your life had ended, didn't you, Simon? But it was just preparing to begin,' and she laughed.

While Simon Steed had been absent in Virginia, conducting his reticent courtship, Teach Turlock fumed in jail, and to every prisoner who shared his cell he spoke veiled treason—'Maybe we got to drive the fat rector out of Maryland. This land stealing.' He suggested that judges were thieves, too, and whenever any Englishman was mentioned, even the king, he spoke harshly.

Some of his fellow prisoners, aware of the way his thoughts were tending, tried to mollify him by arguing against his excesses, but he rejected their counsel. 'The time is comin' . . .' he said, and told those close to him that when he got out of jail, Englishmen had better watch out.

The jailer got a taste of his hardening attitude when papers were delivered for Turlock to sign; they transferred title to eighty acres to the Rector of Wrentham, but when Teach understood this he refused to make his mark—'No rector takes my land.'

'But the court says you must sign,' the jailer said patiently as the clerk nodded.

'To hell with the court.'

The two officials gasped, for such language was not used in Patamoke. The law in such cases was precise: for speaking disrespectfully of any court, imprisonment; for a second offense, branding the tongue with a flaming iron; for a third offense, hanging.

'Say nothing of his blasphemy to the justices,' the jailer pleaded when he and the clerk were alone. 'He's a crazy man who loves his land.'

But of course the justices had to be told that Turlock had refused to sign, and they became angry. Two appeared in prison to warn him of the jeopardy in which he was placing himself, but he sat grim-lipped and dirty, his hands tucked beneath his bottom lest he be tempted to take the quill. 'We can prolong your sentence. Or take your sloop,' they warned.

But he was obdurate, and neither cajolery nor threats induced him to accept the pen, so the justices retired, and shortly thereafter he was informed that his sentence had been doubled; he must remain in jail till April.

He began to laugh at the justices, at the rector and at himself. He realized that things had gone sadly wrong and there wasn't much he could do about it. At this point he could have been saved from rebellion; a single conciliatory gesture would have mollified him. Instead his wife visited the jail with news that the surveyors had marked off the eighty acres—'Not swampy land toward the creek. Best land. With the big trees.'

Surprisingly, he did not rage or become abusive. After his wife left he merely sat on his stool, benumbed, churning inwardly, so that one of the prisoners said, 'When they take a piece of his land they take a piece of his guts.' When two justices appeared, accompanied by the constable, bearing documents for him to sign, he allowed them to pinion him, and hold his right arm, and force his fingers to draw the sprawling X's which took away his land. But later, when the justices reviewed all that had happened, they remembered that during the enforced signing Turlock had studied with animal fierceness the two documents—'He couldn't read but he was memorizing how the papers looked.'

On April 6, 1773, he was released and on April 7 the rectory at Wrentham was ransacked. At first the fat clergyman could not ascertain what had been stolen, for his candlesticks and silverware seemed to be intact, and it was several days before he realized that his title to the eighty acres at the marsh was missing; when he was satisfied that this was the case, he summoned his slaves and directed them to get him to Patamoke as expeditiously as possible. Huffing and puffing, he informed the justices that Turlock's title had been stolen, and when the justices said, 'We'll have the clerk draw you a copy,' they found that theirs was gone too.

'It was Turlock!' the clerk remembered. 'He was here the day after he was released from jail. Asked to see the deed he had signed.'

'You know he couldn't read.'

'I forgot. I was called away . . .' His voice trailed off as he tried to recall that day, and then he understood the trick that had been played on him. 'It was Mrs. Turlock! She came to the other door. Asked if her husband was here.'

'And you didn't ascertain whether the deed was returned to the files?'

'Who steals deeds?'

Obviously Turlock did, so the justices ordered duplicates to be drawn, but when the constable went to the marshes to inform Teach that the court had fined him twenty additional acres for burglary, and that these must be added to the rector's holding, he flew into a rage so violent that any prospect of getting him to mark the transfer was futile. 'I was lucky to escape with my life,' the constable reported, so the justices took it upon themselves to sign the deed, and Turlock was cheated of another portion of his land.

In fury he retreated to his sloop, black and near the end of her days: her back was hogged; her sails were torn; her bottom was riddled with worm; but Turlock had learned to sail her with surprising skill and had even taken her to Barbados for contraband rum and to Sal Tortuga for salt.

The sloop merited a crew of ten, but often she sailed with only two, for Turlock could stay awake for days on end, or mostly awake, keeping his old wreck afloat. On his present trip he carried a crew of eighteen, for he had in mind much more than a smuggling trip to Barbados. At night he slipped out of the marsh, down past Devon and into the broad reaches of the Chesapeake, where he proposed to stay for some time.

A vessel of quite different character was following the same plan. Lieutenant Copperdam, of His Majesty's Royal Navy, had for some months been dominating the Massachusetts coast and had apprehended various American craft attempting to evade customs. It was his habit to board the vessel, confiscate its contraband, and send the sailors off to London in chains. This high-handed behavior had so infuriated the citizens of Massachusetts that Copperdam had decided to test his fortune in the Chesapeake.

The first colonial vessel he spied was a broken-down, hog-backed sloop limping along with every sign of running contraband. At first Copperdam considered letting her pass, for in that condition it could not be carrying much, but since there was nothing else on the horizon, he moved in for an easy capture.

However, as he closed in on the derelict, its sides opened suddenly and six cannon flashed out. Fire was withheld, and Copperdam saw to his astonishment that the enemy intended boarding and fighting hand-to-hand. Too late he tried to pull away, but in doing so, ran aground, whereupon the shallow-drafted sloop came close and put its men aboard.

And then a miracle happened! Instead of capturing the English vessel and arresting its crew, the invaders merely ransacked it for anything of value and sailed boisterously out into the Atlantic. Lieutenant Copperdam, in reporting his humiliating experience to the English authorities in New York, said, 'It was like wrestling a porcupine barehanded. They said she carried a crew of only eighteen. Seemed more like eight hundred.' When they asked about her captain, he said, 'Bearded, barefooted, filthy, and never said a word.'

And as he was reporting, another English ship came into New York with a similar tale. 'A black sloop which seemed about to sink hailed us, emptied our hold and sailed away.'

'Was the captain barefooted, heavy beard?'

'The same.'

When this description circulated about the Chesapeake, knowing sailors realized that Teach Turlock had declared private war against the English, and they speculated on how soon that war would become general. Plantation owners, appalled at the possibility of an open breach with England, growled, 'What's the damn fool done? Issue his own letters of marque and reprisal? He ought to be hanged.' But one dark night the black sloop came creeping into the Choptank, and before dawn the local watermen had taken off her booty, stepped her masts and hidden her within the marsh. Turlock was their champion.

As the year 1773 drew to a close, Levin Paxmore worked fourteen and fifteen hours a day. The transom of the building vessel had already been carved and painted— *Whisper*— and the keelson had been fastened to the keel. The two huge masts had been shaped—square to octagon to circle —and the steps into which they would ultimately be fitted had been carpentered. But the planking was far behind schedule. The reason was an old one: cutting pine boards to the right thickness, shaping them to the intricate flow of the schooner's silhouette, and matching a larboard plank to one already cut for the starboard were both time-consuming and difficult. There was a limit to what sawyers could do in a day, and a ship of this size expended timber at a rate of something like six times that of the smaller boats Paxmore had been accustomed to build.

And yet, every new scrap of information which filtered in to Patamoke confirmed Steed's original conviction that the job must be finished quickly. As Paxmore told his wife, 'The omens are frightening. Yesterday an English warship came all the way to Patamoke. Pestering me to learn if it was one of ours that had assaulted Lieutenant Copperdam! Wanting to know why I was building the *Whisper*. Taking notes on everything.'

'What does thee think will happen?' Ellen asked.

'My mind is blank. I work from day to day.' He paused, then added, 'The only thing I'm sure of is that when I finish this one, another will be needed.' Again he hesitated. 'What I've done is, send my men into the forest. They've cut three more keels and six more masts, and now I'm looking beyond those to the others that must follow.'

'Does thee see war?'

Paxmore looked about the kitchen to assure himself that none of the children were listening, then said, 'I see confusion.'

'Then why are so many vessels needed?'

'I don't know. But in times of confusion . . .'

'Levin, it's often in such times that the good work of the Lord is done.'

'No!' he cried, leaving his chair and walking about the room, waving his hands as if to prevent her from saying what he knew she was determined to say. 'I cannot wrestle with thy concerns this night.'

'Levin, the time is at hand. God projects us into difficult times so that we may bear His testimony.'

She spoke with such sweet persistence, and with such logic, that he surrendered. Falling into a chair beside her, he asked, 'What now?'

'Last year in Patamoke Meeting the motion failed by only thirteen voices. At the Baltimore Yearly Meeting it failed by less than a hundred. It's an obligation that God puts upon us to see this thing finished.'

'I won't propose it.'

'Levin, I've proposed it three times. People expect me to. But if thee rises this time, it will be fresh . . . a new voice . . . thy support alone will convince half the opponents.'

'Ellen, I'm too tired. I work all day at the yard, all night at my plans. Arguing with thee puts a knot in my stomach.'

'But, Levin, the time has come. A great drum beats out the schedule and we must move forward . . .'

'Thee sounds quite militaristic.'

She ignored this, and said, 'When Ruth Brinton demanded that Edward Paxmore manumit his slaves, he protested that doing so would ruin his business. It had the opposite effect. When Thomas Slavin set his free, his neighbors predicted he would go bankrupt. Now he owns twice the land.'

'I cannot prescribe for others.'

'That's what testimony is,' Ellen said with profound conviction. 'I do not testify in order to shame my neighbors. I testify because God will allow me to do no other. It is wrong for Quakers to own slaves. It is wrong to keep Negroes in ignorance. It is wrong to separate families. It is wrong to buy and sell human beings. And if thee refuses to lead this movement, then thee condones wrong.'

'I will not do thy work in meeting,' he said, and when Ellen continued pestering him he stomped from the house and sought refuge at the boatyard, where he could grapple with problems that had a specific solution. He remained there for several hours, inspecting with approval the massive schooner that was taking final shape, and as he saw her looming from the shadows, he projected her into the water, two masts erect, and it occurred to him that if speed was the principal requirement, it could be assured by quitting the rigorous custom of rigging every schooner with large triangular fore-and-aft sails and substituting a much more subtle design: Gaff-rig the fore-and-afts so that the top of each mast becomes available for a pair of square-rigged sails, and add another jib forward. With such a mix . . . With a dowel he sketched on the floor such a rigging, and it looked fine, but when he imagined himself in the bowels of a schooner so rigged, he began to sense limitations.

So he adjusted his ghostly sails, shifting them to unseen spars: I want this schooner to be able to maneuver in whatever wind, and for that there's nothing beats the square sail. They can halt a ship in midflight. Or even back it up. But I also want to sail close to the wind, and for that we must have bigger fore-and-afts. On and on he went, investigating in the abstract the properties of sail, but the more rationally he thought, the tighter became the knot in his stomach, until at last he shivered in the night, so oppressive were the problems besetting him.

Suddenly he cried aloud, 'I will not testify in meeting,' but even as he uttered these evasive words he had to acknowledge that Ellen's harassment about slavery was not the cause of his moral confusion. That sprang, curiously enough, from his speculations about rigging, and it was a perplexity that could plague only a Quaker: Speed and maneuverability! No man would require both if he were merely importing goods from London. He'd have that double need only if he intended using his vessel in war. What I'm building is a ship of war.

Overcome by this realization, he fell on his knees, clasped his hands and began to pray: I'm not building ships of war. I'm not building platforms for cannon. Almighty God, I'm a poor man trying to live with my neighbors in accordance with Thy law. Exert Thy full power to keep us at peace. He prayed for a long time, asking guidance as to what he must do with this schooner, and the three others coming in its train. He would not build for war, and yet every improvement he had made on the *Whisper* made her more war-worthy.

He was on his knees when the door to the big shed opened, admitting a man who seemed to be carrying an armful of tools. Had he been headed the other way, Paxmore would have suspected him of stealing them, but obviously he was bringing them back—and this was perplexing. Maintaining silence, Paxmore watched as the man drew closer, and saw to his surprise that it was Gideon Hull, one of his best workmen and a Quaker to be trusted; he was indeed carrying a heavy armload of shipbuilding tools.

'What's thee doing, Gideon?' he asked in a quiet voice.

The workman dropped the tools, whipped around in dismay and saw Paxmore kneeling in the shadows. Neither man spoke, so Paxmore began picking up the tools. 'What were they for, Gideon?'

'I was bringing them back.'

'I would have loaned them, if thee had asked.'

'Not for my need, Levin.'

'Whose then?'

Hull stood mute. He knew that if he said one word, the whole story would unravel, and this he did not want, for it involved others. But Levin Paxmore, like his wife, was persistent, and after many questions, Hull was worn down. 'It's Teach Turlock. He's back in the marsh with a cannonball through his side. We slipped out to help him mend it.'

'We?'

'Leeds and Mott.'

Paxmore was shocked. Three of his best men involved in aid to an outlaw! Realizing the legal dangers involved in such criminal behavior, he was about to berate Hull when it occurred to him that he was at least as guilty and perhaps more so: In this yard we're building ships for war. Our acts are treasonous, and helping a pirate mend his sloop is the least of our wrongdoings.

Now Hull was bragging. 'Everyone knows it was Turlock who did in Copperdam. He's already sold two cargoes of captured goods in Baltimore.'

'How did he get a cannonball through his strakes?'

Hull refused to divulge additional details, and Paxmore judged it best not to press the point. 'Did thee patch him?'

'He's headed for the Chesapeake right now,' Hull said with grim satisfaction. 'I'll stow these.' And without further comment he replaced the valuable tools, bowed to Paxmore and left the shed.

Paxmore remained till dawn, deeply agitated by Hull's action, and then he saw the three great oak trees waiting to be hewn into keels, and he recalled the dictum of his forebears: A Paxmore ship keeps an unsullied keel. The vessels he had built had all contained such keels, heavy and true and unpenetrated, and this had accounted for the fact that they had not become hog-backed or old before their years.

But the keel of his personal life was far from steady; his ship was generating a high degree of sway. On the slavery issue, he knew that his wife was right and that the time had come for Quakers to announce forthrightly that the ownership of slaves disqualified a man or woman from membership in the society, but he also knew that one man could do only so much, and his job was building schooners against the impending crisis. But in doing this he tacitly approved the warfare which he saw as both deplorable and inescapable. Patriots tended to be irresponsible people like Teach Turlock; they sought to inflame the populace to acts that would be regretted. Honest men like Steed and Levin Paxmore avoided such excesses, and he prayed they always would.

But on this night he had discovered how easily one could be tricked into aiding rebellion, and he was confused. He ended his long vigil with one more prayer: Almighty God, keep these colonies on an even keel.

The precarious balance was shattered during the balmy spring of 1774. Guy Fithian, with the best intentions and a desire for commercial gain, sent his brother-in-law Simon this enthusiastic letter:

> Light at last in the darkness! As I told you when we visited Virginia, I have been distressed by the action of Parliament in granting a tea monopoly to the East India Company. Things were managed poorly by the Company and to the disadvantage of honest traders like ourselves. I am glad to report that I have found a way to circumvent the Company's monopoly, so that you will now be able to sell tea in your part of Maryland with a tax much lower than before and with considerable profit to both you and me. I have therefore taken the liberty of loading your old snow *Fair Rosalind* with three thousand, two hundred pounds of the choicest leaf. Since your snow is not a fast ship, it will doubtless arrive after these letters, but I am sure you will have no trouble in disposing of her cargo at these attractive prices.

Steed did not anticipate any trouble in the sale of his unordered cargo: Fithians would send leaves of first-rate quality; it was eagerly wanted by his customers; and as London pointed out, under the new system it actually cost less than tea imported from Holland or France. But in the interval before its arrival he began to encounter difficulties at home.

Jane Steed was proving to be even more delightful a wife than he had anticipated; she was a fascinating companion, a delightful hostess. Whatever dress fell into her hands she improved, and her three slaves seemed to enjoy sewing her old clothes into new patterns, or tricking them out with bits of lace and satin. She was also innovative in kitchen affairs, dressing duck and venison in rich new ways, and finding delicious uses for hominy. She made good gravies and used nuts and fruits to advantage. Devon had never known better meals than the ones she supervised, and when visitors from Europe spent a month or so at Rosalind's Revenge they always complimented the Steeds on the excellence of their table. 'Simon's the one to thank,' Jane said modestly. 'He lived in France, you know, and learned the secrets of good cooking.' This was an amusing deception; Simon shared the honest American attitude toward food— 'Have plenty and cook it till it's black.'

In the early days of their acquaintance Jane had sometimes ridiculed her future husband's colonial pretentions at learning; after she had lived with him for a while she found that he actually did read five languages: English, French, German, Latin and Greek. His library did include the best available books in each of those languages, and all had been studied. His knowledge was extraordinary and she was pleased to see that it had not made him a radical; in all judgments he was conservative, and when she spoke forcefully in defense of England, he supported her.

But Jane had become increasingly distressed by one fact which had not impressed itself upon her during the brief days of their courtship: Simon was in trade. He had stores in Patamoke, Edentown, Oxford and St. Michaels. He and his brothers had actually worked in these stores, serving the general public, and nephews of the family now served in them, mastering the skills which had kept the family prosperous for more than a century and a half.

Not only did the Steeds have stores, but they also offered for general sale the handiwork of their slaves. The Steed Negroes made barrels, as blacks did on all plantations, but when they had made enough for the family's use, they went on making them, and young Steed managers went about the Chesapeake peddling them. They sold lumber, too, and extra cloth woven by the Devon slaves. What was even more demeaning, on two different occasions Simon had loaded one of his ships to the gunwales, sailed her to Martinique and sold her 'cargo-and-bottom' to an enterprising Frenchman who in one swoop gained possession of some hogsheads of tobacco, some naval stores much needed in the islands, and a sound Paxmore-built ship. On the first of these unusual deals Steed had gained a thousand pounds, paid in Spanish coins, and on the second, a thousand five.

Jane found such dealings distasteful. Gentlemen did not engage in trade; they left the running of shops and the haggling over prices of individual items to folk of lesser category. In fact, a true gentleman rarely carried money on his person and never discussed it with others. The actual handling of money—the passing of coins from one person to another—was contaminating, and she found it abhorrent that her husband was engaged in this dirty business.

'Fithians does nothing else,' Simon protested one day.

'Ah, but we do it in general, never the specific.'

'I don't see the difference,' Steed said.

'You would if you'd been educated in England. Trade is repulsive. Gentlemen restrict themselves to the management of great businesses.'

On this point she was obdurate, and Steed discovered that to the English gentry the retail sale of a single item was gauche, while the wholesale movement of a thousand such items was acceptable. 'It comes down to one simple question,' his wife said. 'Do you meanly bow and scrape to everyone who has a shilling, or do you handle your business affairs like a gentleman . . . with yearly accounting in a dignified manner?'

'Is that what your brother does?' Simon asked.

'Of course. I doubt if he's ever handled money in his life. There are books and yearly accountings and it's all settled by clerks who write letters.'

Steed laughed. 'When we were in Virginia, didn't you see that those fine people were in danger of losing their plantations because they knew nothing of business? And that we Steeds have saved ours because we did? We know how to run stores, and work slaves to a profit. Every one of my nephews knows how to make a barrel, as I did at their age.'

'Don't you feel'—she groped for a word—'dirty? Doesn't this store-keeping make you feel degraded?'

'Not when it keeps us solvent. And able to buy the books we want.'

If, as Jane charged, she was 'besmirched by the dirty fingers of trade,' she had to admit that the trade was not parochial. To be sure, the family fortunes rested upon the Eastern Shore emporiums and collateral manufacturing operations, but the levels of profit were determined by exports to Europe: tobacco, naval stores and timber to England; fish, flour and meat to other countries. It was not unusual for a merchant ship to arrive in the Chesapeake with commercial documents from as many as fifty different European cities inquiring about shipments of Steed materials. In Great Britain the letters might have come from towns like Oxford, Cambridge, Edinburgh; in Spain, from cities such as Barcelona, Cadiz, Seville; in Portugal, from Lisbon or the salt town St. Ubes; in Belgium, from Ghent, Ostend, Ypres; in Holland, from Amsterdam, Utrecht, Haarlem; and in France, because of Simon's study there, from any of thirty-four cities like Bergerac, Dunkirk, Metz, Besançon and, especially, Nantes. To work on Devon Island in 1774 was to be in contact with the most sophisticated centers of Europe.

But in the spring of that year one commercial event superseded all others: the arrival at the mouth of the Chesapeake of the creaking, waterlogged old snow *Fair Rosalind,* laden with packets of tea which had evaded the normal tax in London. All that was required to make this transaction legal was the payment of a small token tax designated by Parliament to act as proof that the colonies were still subservient to it. In Boston in the preceding autumn there had been minor trouble over this petty tax, and one consignment of tea had actually been thrown into the harbor, but those tempers had subsided and Marylanders loyal to the king trusted that there would be no trouble in their colony.

In fact, the responsible planters to whom Steed spoke welcomed the arrival of this cheap tea. The justices expressed strong pro-British sentiments and told him, 'High time the mother country exerted her authority. You did a good job, Steed, bringing in this tea.'

The Paxmores were disturbed. They loved their tea, and since they drank nothing stronger, had felt deprived when denied it. But like Quakers in general, they brooded about potential consequences of even the most transparent act, and this tax on tea was far more complicated than that. 'I want the tea,' Levin Paxmore said, 'but to be forced to pay a tax about which I was not consulted goes against the grain of my republican principles.' He concluded that he should pay the tax, drink the tea and tremble over what might happen next. 'I know what Steed will do. I know what we will do. But who can predict what the Turlocks might do?'

Who, indeed? Since that fateful day in 1765 when Parliament arbitrarily imposed a Stamp Act requiring a trivial fee on commercial and legal paper, newspapers and almanacs, Teach Turlock and Marylanders like him had sensed intuitively that Britain was trying to place its collar upon the colonists, and he resisted like an untamed dog. He had never used one of the items taxed—how could he, being illiterate?—but he had known danger when it appeared—'It ain't right.' He had continued to resist each subsequent act of Parliament which infringed his freedom, for he saw with primitive logic that if London succeeded with the tea, it would transfer its strategy to other areas until all rights were strangled.

Teach could not have expressed even one of his conclusions in a reasoned sentence, but his crafty, analytic mind recognized tyranny in whatever subtle form it took. 'The rector, the king alike. He steals my land. He steals my taxes. Together they steal my freedom.'

He represented the thinking of most colonists, and now when he sailed his black schooner boldly into the Choptank they applauded, for he was their spiritual champion even though his lack of education prevented him from being their spokesman. He trailed the *Fair Rosalind* right to her berth at Patamoke; he did not enter the inner harbor, but anchored in the Choptank, where he could watch the celebration on shore as the tea-ship docked, delivered its papers to the authorities, and welcomed aboard the English tax collector, who inspected the tea, calculated its value and submitted a bill to Simon Steed as the consignee. Only when the tax was paid, and the submission to England legalized, did Turlock row ashore.

His arrival caused a commotion, for his daring behavior at sea had elevated him to the rank of hero, but he did not look the part. He was forty-two years old, extremely thin, bearded, barefooted, dressed in two rough garments which fitted him poorly, and quite dirty from months at sea. He wore no belt, but the rope that held up his trousers also held two pistols, and when he slouched along, these moved awkwardly, banging against his raw hipbones. He wore no hat, but since he was taller than most men, his shaggy head was prominent, bespeaking a rough kind of leadership.

'Where's Steed?' he asked as soon as he reached the customs office.

'He went to his store.'

Moving with the easy rhythms of a man who had slipped through marshes and along forest trails, he walked toward the Steed emporium with three of his sailors trailing behind, but when he reached the store he told his men to wait as he went inside. Steed was not visible. 'Where is he?' Turlock asked, and the young Steed nephew who was managing the place indicated a room in the rear.

'Hullo, Simon.'

'Turlock! Aren't you brave, coming into port?'

'The tea.'

'What about it?'

'You paid the tax?'

'As required.'

'Don't sell it.'

'But it's paid for. People want it.'

'Simon, don't sell it.'

They talked in this manner for some time: a plea from Turlock not to sell, a reply from Steed that it was a normal business transaction. They got nowhere, so Turlock shrugged his shoulders and left, but when Steed employees sought to unload the tea and take it to the family warehouse, Turlock's sailors prevented them. There was a scuffle, nothing much, and the young Steed manager ran to the wharf, calling upon *Fair Rosalind*'s crew to drive off the troublemakers, but when the crew moved forward to help unload the tea, the gaunt figure of Teach Turlock interposed.

'Don't touch,' he said quietly. He made no move toward his guns. He merely stood barefooted at the wharf-end of the gangplank and advised the Steed sailors to drop their bundles of tea and withdraw. They did.

All that day Turlock stood guard, and at dusk a rowboat from the black sloop came ashore with nine more of his sailors, who positioned themselves about the gangplank.

The next two days saw increased tension. The justices came to the wharf and warned Turlock that he must not interfere with the unloading of a cargo properly paid for and properly taxed, but the resolute captain merely said, 'No tea.' There were no army units stationed in Patamoke, and the constable's single deputy could in no way oppose the will of these brigands, but if the general public could be mobilized, the freebooters could be disciplined and the tea could be landed.

So the justices appealed to the people of Patamoke—and a strange thing happened. The people listened respectfully, weighed what the learned men had to say—and concluded that they were wrong and Turlock was right. One man reminded the crowd, 'They took his land and he takes their tea.'

'We're not talking about land,' the justices complained. 'We're talking about tea.'

Now Turlock spoke. 'No tea. No tax. Soon we lose everything.' The parliamentary complexities were beyond the understanding of common people, but they grasped the danger in this insidious tax, and the attempts of the justices to enlist them in opposition to Turlock failed.

He did not gloat at their defeat. Instead he walked quietly to the Steed store and there initiated a discussion which was to determine the subsequent behavior of all who lived along the Choptank. Neither Steed nor Turlock allowed the argument to become heated, and such threats as were made were couched in the subdued terms used by two long-time adversaries striving to reach a sensible solution to their impasse.

'The tea will be landed,' Steed warned. 'Soldiers will be sent from Annapolis.'

'They'll find no tea.'

'Why not?'

'We talk today. We talk tomorrow. Tomorrow night we burn your snow.'

'That's destruction!'

'It's old. Seventy years. All patches.'

'You'd burn the *Rosalind?*'

'Simon, it's war. In Barbados, men from Massachusetts told me.'

'England will crush us. Teach, if you burn my snow, England will drive you from the seas.'

For the first time in their discussions Turlock smiled, a grimy, hairy, self-confident smile. Four times now he had gone up against the English in naval actions, and while it was true that on three of those occasions they had forced him to run, he was confident that when a hundred privateers like himself were at sea, there would be no chance of eliminating them all. He did not try to rebut Steed's arguments; he smiled.

And in that quiet arrogance he conveyed a message to the merchant that no words could have achieved. Steed said, 'You think war is inevitable?' 'Mmmm.' 'You think we can win?' 'Mmmm.' 'You think the seas can be kept open?' 'Mmmm.' 'You think Boston is going to stand firm?' 'Mmmm.'

Again and again these two men, who had operated together only as co-defendants in the tithe case, reviewed the situation, and after two hours had passed, Steed said, 'I'd like to bring Paxmore in,' and Turlock nodded. So the Quaker was sent for, and he appeared, gray and cautious.

'Turlock thinks there's bound to be war,' Steed said.

Anxiety showed in Paxmore's face, and he said, 'Oh, I hope not.'

'You afraid?' Turlock growled.

'Yes, because England will destroy us.'

'But what if we don't have actual war?' Steed asked. 'Just irritations. Can we keep the sea lanes open?'

Now Paxmore was obligated to speak as a proud shipbuilder. 'The *Whisper* will not be taken. Her speed will astonish.'

'When will she be ready?'

'Three weeks.'

'And you'll start on the others?'

'I already have.' And with this admission Paxmore knew that he had committed himself to war. He wiped his forehead.

The three men sat in the small office, and no one spoke. Flies buzzed and Turlock followed their flight from window to door to ceiling, waiting for the frightened leaders to make sensible comment. Finally Steed asked, 'Paxmore, if war does come, can we win?'

'No.'

'But you seem resigned to have it come?'

'England'll win, but she'll learn that she must treat us better.'

'Exactly how I feel,' Steed cried. 'We'll have war. Turlock will see to that. But there's no chance we can win. We might gain some minor concessions.'

'We'll win,' Turlock said with great force.

'How?' the other two asked.

'By holding on. Tomorrow night we start. We burn the *Rosalind.*'

'You what?' Paxmore cried.

Turlock rose to his full height and looked serenely at his two frightened neighbors. 'When we stood in court we knew this would happen. Build your schooners, Levin. Simon, you arm them. This is war. Tomorrow night it reaches Patamoke.' He turned and left.

Paxmore, shaken by the possibility that the snow might be intentionally burned, asked, 'Did he mean it?'

'He did. It's a symbolic act, and I shall make no move to stop it.' He allowed time for this to register, then said, 'And neither shall you, Levin. We sail to Peace Cliff . . . now . . . to look for spars.' And to protect himself, he announced to various persons in the store that he and Paxmore were headed for the woods in back of Peace Cliff, to look for tall trees. They were on the porch of the telescope house, watching night shadows fall across the river, when the sky behind them brightened, with flickers of reddish light darting upward from the eastern horizon. Paxmore bowed his head in silent prayer, but Steed watched the flickering shoots until they died.

'We've started something of magnitude,' he said, but Paxmore, terrified at the consequences, remained silent.

It was characteristic of the Steeds of Devon that once they settled upon a course, they maintained it until a conclusion was reached, and in the agitated weeks following the burning of the tea, Simon hardened his thinking about the threat of war. 'I shall always remain loyal to the king,' he told his wife.

'I should hope so,' she said, as if there were no alternative.

'But if Parliament persists in transgressing our natural rights . . .'

'What natural rights do colonials have?'

'You sound like the member of Parliament who said, "In London the thinking head, in America the working hands and feet." '

'Of course! The purpose of a colony is to provide wealth to the homeland, and I think it shameful the way you allowed a filthy pirate to burn your tea.' She had no words strong enough to condemn his supine surrender.

'The people refused the tea.'

'They'd have taken it if you'd shown any fight.' She railed at the pusillanimity of the authorities and said that three English soldiers in uniform could have stopped the whole affair. 'What's more,' she added, 'I think that Turlock told you about the burning in advance. So that you and that sickly Paxmore could scuttle out.'

Ignoring this clever deduction, he said, 'My real irritation stems from the fact that the colonies are not being used properly. The only possible justification for England's owning a colony in a new land is to experiment here with methods that can't be introduced in the home country.'

'You do talk the greatest nonsense, Simon.'

'I want to keep Maryland a part of England, but only if we retain the right to our unique development.'

'Maryland develops as England develops, and that's that. Your job is to serve the king.'

An opportunity to serve arose in the summer of 1774, when a committee of eleven leading citizens of Patamoke and surrounding territories convened to discuss events occurring at scattered points throughout the colonies. Two of the members had some time earlier volunteered to serve as local reporters to the Maryland Committee of Correspondence, whose job it was to maintain contact with committees of like intention in other regions. Inflammatory documents from Boston had been forwarded to South Carolina, and the correspondents in that state reported how they, too, had resisted the importation of tea.

In July the Patamoke committee sent a deputation to Devon to discuss the possibility of Steed's chairing a meeting that would review the situation in the colonies and draft a statement of local intention. Two boats sailed into the creek, and when the somber men came up the brick-lined path to the big house, Jane Steed was stiffly courteous. In times past she had entertained these men on happier occasions and knew them by name, but now she could guess at their purpose and it repelled her. 'Come in, gentlemen,' she said with obvious reserve. 'Place your hats on the table. My husband will join you shortly.'

The men were pleased at another chance to see the leading mansion of their district and commented idly on the fine decorations. Jane stayed with them briefly, then excused herself, for she wanted no part in this seditious gathering, but when her husband appeared, he got right to the heart of the matter. 'I'm sure you haven't come so far on trivial affairs.'

'We have not,' the leader said, and he asked the two correspondents to outline the present condition of the colonies.

'In Massachusetts, endless problems with the governor. In South Carolina, near-rebellion. In New York, confusion. And in Virginia . . .' Here one of the writers paused, dropped his pompous style and said, 'Gentlemen, we can thank God for Virginia. That colony has notable patriots.'

'What are they doing?'

'Writing. Arguing. Defending all of us with their cogency.'

'Who?'

'Jefferson . . .'

'I have little regard for him,' Steed said.

'Madison, Wythe.'

'Has Byrd spoken?'

'He has not. He seems afraid.'

'That bodes ill. The Byrds are the best of the lot.'

'And the most timorous.'

'So what do you propose for the Eastern Shore?'

'For the entire shore, nothing. For Patamoke, everything.'

And these quiet, conservative businessmen, most of them self-taught, expressed their fears and hopes. Events were deteriorating. As in New York, all was confusion. The colonies were like a rudderless ship wallowing in the troughs, and it was incumbent upon men of good will to state their positions. This the men of Patamoke were prepared to do.

'We shall convene a meeting in the courthouse, Thursday instant,' one of the merchants said. 'We think you should preside, Simon, and that we should state our determinations.'

'This is a grave matter,' Steed said. 'If we sign and publish a document that . . .'

'We run risks,' the spokesman said.

'But,' one of the correspondents interrupted, 'by Thursday night we could have our resolutions flying to all the colonies. Men in New Hampshire would know where we stand, and in Georgia, too.'

Steed thought: He wants to dispatch letters because his job is to dispatch letters. Aloud he said, 'We will be placing our necks on the chopping block, you know that.'

The chairman caught the significance of Steed's use of *we* and *our*. 'Then you will be with us?'

'I will.'

'Thank God. We did not want to move without you.'

But when the eleven patriots had gone, fortified perhaps by Steed's acceptance but frightened for sure by his mention of the chopping block, Jane demanded to know what had taken place, and when Simon told her, she was furious. 'What are you doing, you pitiful little tradesmen? Are you challenging the king?'

'I hadn't thought of it that way,' Steed said quietly.

'You'd better! A gang of foolish, untraveled boors and clods from Patamoke are going to tell the King of England what to do? Is that what you propose?'

'I hadn't expressed it that way.'

'How do you express treason?'

Simon pondered this question for some moments, then said, 'I'd rather imagined that a group of men on the scene wanted to advise Parliament of certain facts which might otherwise be overlooked.'

'What presumption!' Jane cried. 'You! You are going to advise Parliament!'

'If I lived in England, I would be in Parliament. There is no one in Parliament, Jane, who even approaches my knowledge of Maryland.'

'That's sheer vanity, Simon.'

'Let me express it another way. Every one of those eleven men who met here knows more about what to do in Maryland than any member of Parliament.'

'John Digges! He collects muskrat skins!'

'And he knows muskrats, and how to tan them, and sell them, and what's good for others like himself.'

'Simon, if you presume to meet with those men and send insulting resolutions to the king, I would expect soldiers to come here and arrest you and maybe hang you.'

'I run the risk of just that,' Steed said, but no amount of railing altered his decision.

On Thursday morning he asked two slaves to sail him to Patamoke, where he landed at noon. After reporting at the store to satisfy himself that no tea was on the shelves, he repaired to the boatyard, where Paxmore had the *Whisper* almost ready to launch; it was a handsome vessel, and the thin lines of caulking along the bottom formed beautiful patterns. But when Steed asked if Paxmore proposed to join the meeting at the courthouse, the latter said firmly, 'No. Thee is heading for waters in which I cannot follow.'

'I'd like to have your signature,' Steed said.

'My wife wanted me to attend, too, but I'm not one for signing petitions. I don't know where all this is going to lead.'

'You heard Turlock. It leads to war. And war leads to nothing. But we're on a course that cannot be altered.'

Paxmore repeated that he would not participate in the meeting, but he surprised Steed by showing him three keels chopped out of oak and a pile of spars waiting along the edge of the shed. On the day the *Whisper* was launched, a new schooner would be started.

Fourteen men convened. Steed did not speak; he sat severely alone on the dais, and when the clerk started to take down what the various speakers said, he shook his head firmly and the writing stopped; he explained that he wanted no permanent record of who made which proposals, lest at some future date it be used nefariously.

The assembly was as ridiculous as Jane had predicted: a group of partially educated farmers and petty tradesmen presuming to advise a king, but they wrestled with explosive ideas, and the simple truths they elucidated would form one of America's significant summaries of grievances. When the speeches ended, Steed rose and reminded the committee, 'We are here to asseverate our allegiance to the king, and to seek his understanding cooperation. I will not sign unless we include an affirmation of loyalty.' All agreed, and when this was provided, the document was read:

'Alarmed at the present situation in America, and distressed by the incessant encroachments upon our liberties, we are determined not only to complain but likewise to exert our utmost endeavours to prevent the enforcement of such encroachments as deprive us of our cherished birthright as Englishmen. Motivated by the warmest zeal and loyalty to our Most Gracious Sovereign, we are determined calmly and steadily to act in concert with our fellow subjects in the colonies to pursue every legal and constitutional measure to prevent the loss or impairment of our liberties; and to promote an ever closer union and harmony with the mother country, on which the preservation of both must finally depend.'

Thirteen men walked forward, one by one, to sign, and then the pen was handed to the chairman, who signed boldly in the place reserved for him, Steed of Devon, and before the sun had set, the two energetic correspondents were on the way to Annapolis with the document which they labeled *The Patamoke Determination.*

In the early months of 1775 Teach Turlock's private war against England came to an abrupt halt. He lost his sloop.

He was drifting lazily back from Barbados with a legal cargo of sugar, salt and slaves when he was hailed by an English customs frigate whose captain wished to conduct a routine search. Since Turlock carried no contraband, he should have submitted, but he was so antagonistic to authority that he resisted. When the English captain ran out his guns, Turlock fled.

In a decent vessel the waterman would have escaped, for he was much the better sailor, but his old, hog-backed sloop was in sad shape and was quickly overtaken, but with dusk approaching, there was still a likelihood that Turlock would escape, so the frigate began firing, and one heavy ball struck Turlock's mainmast, shattering much of it and leaving the topsails flapping in the wind.

This enabled the English captain to close, but instead of finding a chastened merchantman waiting to be boarded, he found a little battleship preparing for hand-to-hand combat. 'Put down those guns!' the English captain called as the ships were about to touch, but before he could repeat the cry, shots were being exchanged and a full-scale naval engagement was under way.

The English won. Three of Turlock's sailors were killed, and when the rest had been herded aboard the frigate, the old black pirate sloop was set ablaze and Turlock, in captivity, had to watch it sink into the Atlantic, while his crew was chained for transport to London.

'Piracy, mutiny, firing on His Majesty's ship,' intoned the captain. 'You'll be hanged, every one.'

But as the frigate entered the North Atlantic it was overtaken by a speedy privateer out of Boston, and now a second battle ensued, with the English losing. The American prisoners were unchained, and after the English vessel had been stripped, it was turned over to Turlock and his gang, who now had a fine London frigate in place of their hog-backed sloop, and with it they captured an English trader making for Plymouth.

But when they sailed victoriously into the Chesapeake they were met by a Virginia patrol boat; it led them to Jamestown, where their prize was confiscated by the government. They were shipped back to Patamoke, where Turlock announced, 'Fought two battles. Lost two ships. Wound up flat on my ass.'

For several weeks he tried to find a vessel, but although he was a hero to the mob, he was a pirate to the gentry, and it was they who were the owners. So he retired to the marsh, and was hunting squirrels one day when he happened to look across the waving grass and saw, returning from a surreptitious voyage to Jamaica, the finest schooner he had ever seen, Mr. Steed's *Whisper,* long and slim and heavy with sail. It sped by the marsh, seeming to float above the waters, and as it disappeared toward Patamoke, Turlock said, 'That's my next command.'

His campaign started that day. When Simon Steed came down to the wharf to inspect his schooner, there was Teach Turlock, bowing properly and saying, 'Fine schooner, sir. If you let me take her out . . . profits . . . profits.'

The idea was so preposterous that Steed ignored it, but when the *Whisper* was empty, there was Turlock suggesting, 'They'd never catch me in this.'

Steed did not propose to risk his heavy investment on a barefoot rogue, but one day when he visited his Patamoke store Turlock presented him with a substantial reason: 'Soon we have war—real war—and do you think he can captain the *Whisper?*' And with his thumb he pointed toward Captain Allworthy.

The question had perplexed Steed. Allworthy was a substantial man and a good sailor, but he was hardly right to command an important vessel if war threatened. He would not be valiant in running blockades, and so the first seed was sown.

It germinated some days later when the *Whisper* began loading spars to be sold in France, for as Steed watched on the wharf, Turlock sidled up to him and said quietly, 'Let me sail to France. Learn the waters. Then give Captain Allworthy the new one Paxmore's building.'

The idea was so sensible that Steed hesitated for a moment and looked into Turlock's eyes. What he saw was a dedication so powerful that on the spur of the moment he capitulated. 'All right. Get aboard as second mate. See what you can learn.'

When the *Whisper* sailed down the Choptank toward the bay, Teach Turlock was aboard, bearded and barefooted, feeling her sway, sensing her power and her problems. As they passed Devon Island he saluted and muttered, 'Simon Steed, you're goin' to be proud of what this schooner does,' and at night he would lie in his hammock, tracing her lines from memory, recalling how each rope passed through the blocks and where it was secured. And he could feel each of her movements and how she took the various waves.

Most interesting was his relationship to Captain Allworthy, of whom he had spoken so poorly. He paid the man great respect, following him when possible and listening to all he had to say, for he realized that this man knew the sea. For generations, dating far back before the first words of the Bible were composed, certain men like Allworthy had attained through study and experience a sense of what a wooden ship could do. This knowledge, transmitted from one generation to the next—Phoenician to Greek to Gaul to Anglo-Saxon to the herring fisherman off Newfoundland—constituted the lore of the sea, and when its customs were observed, the ships came through; when they were not, the ships landed on rocks. And no captain in that unbroken succession could have explained what exactly he knew. On this voyage, Teach Turlock joined the procession.

When the *Whisper* came home to Patamoke, he stood by the wheel, his heart racing with excitement, for he saw that Paxmore had launched the next schooner; its masts were already in place. He said nothing, but watched like a marsh eagle as Captain Allworthy went down the plank to report to Mr. Steed, and he held his breath as the owner came aboard.

'Well, Mr. Turlock, are you ready?'

'I am.'

'The *Whisper*'s yours.'

'You'll hear good reports of her,' Turlock said.

But later, when he sailed a small boat out to Devon Island to discuss strategies, he ran into trouble, for Jane Fithian was disgusted that her family was placing a major schooner in the care of such a man. 'Look at him! Can't read or write! Barely speaks two words together. He's the worst sort of American.'

When Simon tried to explain why Turlock was precisely the kind of man needed in these uncertain times, she said indignantly, 'Can you imagine him arriving in London and meeting with the captain of a proper English ship? Laughable.'

'In the years ahead, Jane, my captains won't be going to London.'

'Are you speaking more treason?'

'I'm facing facts. Teach Turlock is the man we need.'

'Then may God have mercy upon us.'

'And on England.'

He said this with such depth of feeling that even she could see that he had reached a great fork in some imaginary road he had been traveling, and for a moment she wanted to share his experience; instead she said, 'To throw Turlock into the Atlantic with an armed schooner is like throwing a lighted bomb into the bedclothes of King George.'

And the more he reflected on this remark, the more apt it seemed. But even he was not prepared for some of the things his unpredictable captain was capable of, because when the time came for sailing, Steed went aboard for a last-minute inspection, and what he saw pleased him. The sailors were content to work for a local hero like Turlock, and under his direction they had trimmed the *Whisper* excellently. The hogsheads were lashed with extra care, and all was shipshape, but as Steed was about to depart, satisfied that at least the traditional amenities were in order, he spied in a corner of the captain's room a red-headed boy who could have been no more than seven.

'Who's that?'

'Matt.'

'Who's he?'

'My son.'

'He's not sailing with you?'

'Got to learn sometime,' and he told the boy, 'Take Mr. Steed to the gangplank,' and the little fellow moved down the passageways with an expertness that showed he had already memorized his portion of the *Whisper.*

The fact that Jane Steed argued with her husband about colonial behavior toward England did not mean that their married life was either tense or unpleasant. She loved her pompous husband and considered his attempts at being an English gentleman amusing. He was generous and kind-hearted, and he indulged her in the petty expenditures which gave her so much pleasure. From the first she had wanted a slave who could sew in the French manner, so he had bought her one in Annapolis. When she heard that an actual theater had been erected in that city, she wanted to cross the bay to see for herself, and he took her. And when she protested if anyone called her an American or a Marylander, insisting that she was English, he agreed: 'Jane's from London. A Fithian, our factors.' And whenever he said this, she seemed to glow and feel better, for she always thought of herself as an English gentlewoman.

For his part, he loved her more than he had when they first traveled together in Virginia. Her smile was so genuine, and it irradiated her face so totally that it kept him enchanted. She was kind, and laughing; any room she entered was illuminated, and it pleased him to see the way men inadvertently followed her with their admiring eyes. Under her care, Rosalind's Revenge became the outstanding house on the Eastern Shore insofar as generous hospitality was concerned, and when she became visibly pregnant both she and Simon moved with stately pride, and his love for her increased.

'When I think of the years we might have been married,' he said ruefully one day, and she answered, 'There was no possibility that we could have been wed a day earlier. I wasn't ready.'

When he asked her how it was that a girl so charming had been free to come to America, 'I mean, why weren't you married already?' she said, 'From the time I was a little girl Guy told me that my fate was to come to America and marry you. He used to bring your letters home and let me read them . . . tobacco and pig iron . . . I became an expert on the Maryland plantation.' She smoothed the apron over her protruding stomach and said, 'He also told me you were rich and kind.' She reached up and drew her thumbnail down his chin. 'And he said that in France you had acquired perfect manners. He made you sound irresistible. So I waited.'

'You saved my life,' he said simply, and she accepted this, for she could see the change that had come over him since her arrival. She knew that prior to her visit his life had been trapped in an iron routine: each day he had risen, read in the classics, written his letters to Europe, breakfasted, and gone about the business of managing a great plantation. He had assumed that this was his permanent destiny and that if he conserved the wealth of the plantation, it would pass into the hands of his nephews, who would live much as he was living.

Jane's arrival had revolutionized that staid routine. She had driven him to new occupations, such as boating for pleasure and having neighboring plantation couples in for six or seven days. Also, the orders being carried to London by the Steed captains were much different now, and when the fine furniture arrived the interior of Rosalind's Revenge became as elegant as the exterior.

'You launched a revolution,' he told her affectionately one morning in February, but instead of acknowledging his compliment as she usually did, she startled him by saying abruptly, 'Don't use that word around me. These damned colonies want nothing but revolution.'

Eager to assure her, he said that whereas Maryland might kick up its heels, it would never break away from the king. 'We might have arguments,' he said quietly. 'And maybe even an exchange of fire. But we'll always honor our loyalty to the king.' She rejected this, claiming that everything the colonials were doing implied disloyalty to the king, but he reminded her that in *The Patamoke Determination* it was he who had insisted on the sentences reaffirming loyalty.

'Words!' she said, and the force with which she spoke made him realize that she had for some time been brooding about the actions of the colonies. Some days later Simon was handed an unsealed letter for transmission to London. It was addressed to Guy Fithian, and since it was a family custom for both Jane and Simon to add postscripts to each other's letters to Guy, he casually unfolded the paper and was shocked by its contents:

> Life here becomes almost unbearable. The average Marylander is a peasant with no appreciation of manners and no desire to acquire any. Conversation is so boring I could scream. No politics, no fashion, no gossip, no comment on the life of a city. I crossed the bay to see what they call their theater. Sheridan, and not one person on stage could act and the violins were out of tune.

> I haven't had a decent piece of beef in two years, and if anyone gives me oysters again, I shall throw them in his face. Horrible food. But I could bear this if the citizens were civil, but all the whispers are of war against England and of ships clashing at sea. Simon, good man that he is, assures me that this pitiful country of his will always remain loyal to our beloved King; but why the King should want it is beyond me. I say cut it loose and be damned.

> Guy, tell me why it is that we English were able to subdue the Scottish rebels in '15 and '45 and the French in '63, and now permit these ridiculous colonials with no fleet, no army, no cities and no leadership to give us trouble? Why doesn't the King send a troop as he did with Scotland and knock these silly people about the ears? I warn you, if these rebellious fools, and you should see the idiot Simon has put in command on one of his ships, if they take steps against the King I shall jump on the first English ship that touches here and come home till the idiots are disciplined. I am having a baby soon and will bring it, too.

Soberly, his jaw quivering, he carried the letter to his desk, lit a taper, melted the wax and sealed it, without adding the customary postscript. He placed it with the substantial pile of correspondence intended for Europe, leaving it on top so that Jane could satisfy herself that it had been posted. He said nothing to her about its contents, but he did become trebly attendant, listening to her complaints about their neighbors and responding to each of her small demands.

When word reached the Chesapeake of how conditions in Massachusetts had deteriorated after Lexington, with rebels continuing to fire upon the king's men, Jane fell into a despondency from which Simon could not lure her. She began ranting openly against the drabness of Maryland life: 'No breeding, no sense of station. And those damnable month-long visits by plantation boors. And what I simply cannot abide a day longer, the monotony of the greasy cooking.'

Steed deemed it wise not to remind her that only a month previous she had been praising Maryland cooking. Instead he did his best to placate her, but nothing offset the fact that insolent colonials had fired upon the king's troops. Her impressions were intensified when Captain Turlock sailed into Patamoke with triumphant news about the *Whisper*. In a moment of thoughtlessness Simon invited him to Devon, where his crude manners and peasant gloating infuriated Jane. Turlock said, 'This schooner can do anything! Fore-and-aft sails, close to wind. Big ones upstairs, before the wind like a hawk.' Enthusiastically he reported on a close brush with an English frigate and on how the *Whisper* had shown her heels.

'Did you fire on the king's ship?' Jane asked.

'Didn't need to.' Turlock recalled the encounter and grinned, his broken teeth showing through his beard. 'Matt stood aft, laughing at the Englishmen as we pulled away.'

'Who's Matt?' Jane asked.

'My son.'

'How old is he?'

'Soon to be eight.'

Jane gave a little shudder and left the room.

'I think you'd better get back to the *Whisper*,' Steed said, and in some confusion the lanky captain left. He had expected dinner, but at the wharf he assured Simon, 'I'm ready to sail any time,' and they stood beside the vessel and talked over plans.

'Always the same problems,' Steed said, one foot on the gunwale. 'No salt. No money.'

'In Jamaica they say the Portuguese port St. Ubes has plenty of salt.'

'Our ships have never sailed there. Too close to England.'

'I'd like to try St. Ubes. Big cargo, big profit.'

'You willing to risk it?'

'With *Whisper*, yes.' So it was agreed that Turlock would try a risky passage to a new port whose salt mines were reputed to be the best after the ones in Poland and Austria.

When Steed said that his perpetual problem was money, he did not mean that the Devon plantations were in financial straits; they were building two more Atlantic schooners and the manufactures were doing well. The problem was: the rich men of the English government refused to coin sufficient currency to enable the colonies to function. For a century tobacco had been utilized as coinage, but with the dreadful slumps in recent years, it no longer served as currency; instead business was conducted with the aid of an incredible mélange of paper documents and European coins. Letters of credit from one merchant to another were circulated like pound notes, and none were more highly sought than those of John Hancock, Robert Morris and Simon Steed. But these were scarcely adequate to meet the needs of a burgeoning commerce, so every colonist had to contrive one trick or another to get his hands on real money.

'Were you able to acquire any coins?' Steed asked.

'That's what I really came for,' Turlock said, and he took Steed to a bench beside the creek, and there, when they were alone, he confided, 'We took a merchantman. Spanish. Look.' And carefully he unwrapped a large cloth packet which had been secreted in his coat. Loosening the ends, he spread a hoard of gold coins in the sunlight.

'You have big-joes!' Steed said excitedly, for it had been some time since he had seen these splendid gold coins of Portugal; they had been minted in 1723 during the reign of King João and bore his bewigged portrait and name in Latin, Ioannes, from which the American name derived. A whole coin, heavy and worth about thirty dollars, was called popularly a big-joe; when sawed in half, which was usually the case, it was a half-joe.

'And these,' Turlock said proudly, sifting the pile to show the Spanish doubloons, the English sovereigns and the mass of livres tournois, the smaller French coin which circulated the world as a standard.

'It was a worthy trip,' Steed said, and as he retied the packet, returning it to his captain for deposit at headquarters in Patamoke, he reflected on how strange it was that the capture of a merchant ship should be celebrated on Devon: What our family used to condemn as piracy we now praise as patriotism.

The long voyage that Captain Turlock started in late 1775 was notable for a chaotic chain of events: the vast profits earned on Portuguese salt, the running fight with the English frigate *Chancery,* the two months in a Lisbon jail for lack of proper papers, the capture of a rich merchantman heading home from Peru, the start of Matt's education.

His teacher was the second mate, a Choptank man named Mr. Semmes who had been taught to read by the fat Rector of Wrentham. When Captain Turlock learned that his mate had studied with the rector, there was salty discussion of that churchman's habits and Mr. Semmes said, 'He taught me to read, hoping to acquire thereby a servant for nothing. When I said I was going to sea, he sought to have me arrested as a deserting bondsman.'

'Did you punch him in the nose?'

'No.'

'Pity.'

Mr. Semmes had a fine sense of the sea, and one day as young Matt was lugging him his breakfast he caught the boy's arm and asked, 'Do you intend being a captain?' and Matt said, 'I do,' and Mr. Semmes said, 'Then you must learn to read and write,' and the boy said, 'Cap'm doesn't read or write,' and Captain Turlock knocked the lad down and growled as he got up, 'I'd be a better captain if I did.'

So the lessons began. On a flat board Mr. Semmes drew the alphabet and the numbers, and for three days Matt memorized them. Within a brief time he was writing not only his own name but also those of the crew; he would lie on a hatch cover and write down the name of every sailor who passed, and before long he knew the spelling of each.

But what fascinated him was the ship's log, for he realized that it recorded facts much more important than names. 'The life of the ship is written here,' Mr. Semmes said as he made his entries, and Matt tried to be present whenever the observations were recorded: 'Course East-north-east. Day calm. All canvas.' And to understand better what the words meant, he mastered the compass and could box it as well as any sailor, rattling off the hundred and twenty-eight points as if playing a game. 'Listen, Mr. Semmes, I'm going to do the Second Quarter.' And he would stand at attention and recite in a monotone, 'East, East one-quarter south, East one-half south, East three-quarters south, East by south. And now the hard one! East-south-east three-quarters east.' And as he completed each quarter, Mr. Semmes would applaud.

The day came when Captain Turlock shot the noonday sun, then walked to where the ship's log was kept, and instead of barking his data to Mr. Semmes he gave them to Matt and watched with glowing eye as his red-headed son wrote in large childish letters: 'Latitude 39° 10′ North. Longitude 29° 15′ West approx.' Teach entered his positions in this form because with the aid of a good sextant captured from a Spanish merchantman he could be sure of his latitude, but lacking a reliable clock, he had to guess his longitude.

But when he saw the entry completed, as well as Mr. Semmes could have done, he had to turn away lest he betray his emotion, for Matt was the first in his lineage going back five thousand years who could write, and his arrival at learning seemed much like the arrival of the colonies at nationhood: prospects unlimited lay ahead.

In the spring of 1776 it became apparent that the contentious lawyers of Massachusetts and the philosophical patriots of Virginia were determined to take the thirteen colonies out of the British Empire, and nothing that the more prudent loyalists of Pennsylvania and Maryland might caution was listened to. Echoes of meetings occurring in Philadelphia, in which men as stable as the Marylander Charles Carroll were actually discussing revolution, filtered down to the Eastern Shore, but they were not credited, for most of the citizens in towns like Patamoke or on plantations like Devon wanted to remain attached to England. They saw every reason for doing so; they calculated each advantage.

Levin Paxmore was typical. As a Quaker he had lived to see his religion accepted without serious restraint; true, he had to pay a fine for not drilling with the militia, and he still had to contribute thirty pounds of tobacco each year to the Church of England, but he viewed these only as irritating impositions. He was free to pray as he wished, to marry whom he liked, to speak his mind in meeting, and to rear his children in his faith, and these were freedoms to be cherished. His business also prospered under English rule; for the past nineteen years he had risen every morning with more work to do than he could complete, and while he often had to wait for payment because no money circulated, he was never defrauded. Right now, things were better than they had been in many years; he had finished two schooners for Simon Steed, and had two more under way, with additional inquiries from officials in Philadelphia. For some time he had known that gunfire with the English was inescapable, but he still trusted that it would be brief and without damaging consequences. But now he began hearing rumors of actual separation, and some of his more apprehensive neighbors were talking about returning to the homeland, England, if the troubles worsened. When two Quakers from the meeting approached him with a sensible plan for repatriation, he assembled his family in that spare room at Peace Cliff in which Ruth Brinton Paxmore had laid down the principles by which her brood would live. 'I believe we should stay with the land,' he said. 'Our task is to bring God's commonwealth into being here.'

'Even if Maryland separates from England?' Ellen asked.

'There will be no separation,' he said firmly. 'I expect trouble, perhaps serious trouble, but we will always be English.' And by holding up his left hand, as if to silence further comment, he forestalled his wife's question as to why, if they were to be English, he was building ships intended for use against the English.

For Simon Steed such decisions were more difficult. His whole being was tied to Europe; his business interests focused in England, for which he felt the warmest ties. In London, Fithians held his wealth; in Berk-shire, his forefathers had defended the faith; and while his own education had been in France, it was to England that he looked for fundamental leadership. Up and down the Atlantic coast thousands of men like him were casting up their spiritual accounts and deciding to remain loyal to the king. In Simon's case the impetus to do so was greater, because he was married to an English girl who desperately wanted to go home.

Steed was distressed that she retained her animosity toward the colo-nies; she now abhorred the Eastern Shore and what she termed its provincialism. Her husband's repeated assertion that from here she could keep in touch with the entire world did not satisfy her. The Americans she saw were boors, and were threatening to become traitors as well. The horrible Captain Turlock who brought his big-joes to their counting-house never confessed what English ships he had robbed to get them, and to think of those miserable idiots that she had seen in Virginia presuming to govern a new nation was absurd, the height of folly.

The birth of her daughter had not been easy, and the infant was proving difficult. Jane was convinced that it was Choptank water that irritated the baby, and she grew to loathe the ugly name of that river which surrounded her on all sides. 'Thames, Avon, Derwent, those are real rivers. Who ever heard of a river whose water was always salt?'

'At Edentown it's fresh,' her husband pleaded.

'And who ever heard of mosquitoes on the Thames?' she fumed. 'Simon, I warn you, if those fools in Philadelphia utter one word against the king, I'm going home.'

In July the shocking word reached her that men in Philadelphia, including Charles Carroll and Samuel Chase of Maryland, had not only declared their independence of England but had also dared to put in writing the insulting list of charges against the king. 'The impudence!' she stormed. 'Those pretentious upstarts!' When her rage subsided she said coldly, 'You watch, Simon. We'll punish you the same way we did the Scots.' And from the moment news of the Declaration reached her, she directed all her energy to preparations for flight. She refused to remain in this rebellious colony and relished the prospect of English warships coming up the Chesapeake to discipline it.

Teach Turlock did not hear of the formal Declaration until late Au-gust, but this did not signify, for he had been conducting his private war for more than a year now. In January he had been so bold as to venture into the Thames on the gamble that the *Whisper* had not yet been identified as a privateer, and he had been right, but trade with the colonies was so depressed that he was unable to pick up any profitable shipments and had left England with empty holds. When he reached St. Ubes he found that merchant ships had loaded all available salt, and it became apparent that the profits for this voyage would be limited to what he might steal from French or Spanish merchantmen.

He met none, so the *Whisper* drifted back and forth across the Caribbean, but when it put into Martinique on the chance of picking up even the most trivial cargo, French captains advised him that the thirteen colonies had become the United States of America and were engaged in open warfare against the mother country.

'United!' Turlock snorted, remembering Maryland's constant feuding with Virginia. 'We'll never be united.' Then his chin firmed, making his beard bristle, and he told the French with joy, 'Now it's real war!' And he stormed back to his schooner.

North of Barbados he captured and sank a small English trader, setting her crew adrift in lifeboats. He then cruised northeast to intercept any English ships bound for Martinique or Guadaloupe, and here he caught another small English trader, again setting her crew adrift in sight of land.

His third capture occurred almost in the shadow of Caracas; it was a Spanish ship well laden, and after it was robbed, it was set loose. And his fourth interception was a substantial English merchantman heading out of Panama for Jamaica. That night young Matt Turlock wrote in the log the words that glorified the privateer: 'For each gun, one ship.' The *Whisper* carried four cannon, and with them it had captured four prizes. No privateer could do better.

In triumph Turlock sailed home to the Chesapeake, and his feats were trumpeted from shore to shore. He had a small casket of big-joes and livres tournois, but when he spread them on the desk at the countinghouse, his employer came with perplexing news: 'Captain, the Council of Safety at Annapolis has requisitioned the *Whisper*. You're to carry the families back to England.'

'Which families?'

As Steed tried to explain, his voice choked and he turned away to compose himself, but when he turned back to talk with his captain, his face flushed and he hurried from the countinghouse.

'What's happened?' Turlock asked the man who came to count the coins.

'Families loyal to the king are being taken back to England.'

'Steed going?'

'No, but his wife is . . . and the baby.'

Turlock could not fathom this. In his world a man told a wife what to do, and she did it unless she wanted a beating from the broad side of a shovel. For a wife to leave her husband for another country and to take a child along was unprecedented. 'Not right,' he muttered as the coins were removed.

But it happened. The *Whisper* sailed to Baltimore, where two families came aboard; one woman knelt down and kissed the deck, crying, 'It's a blessing to be on an English ship,' but then she saw Captain Turlock and asked tearfully, 'Is he taking us to England?'

At Annapolis nine families joined, and from the tidewater plantations another six; at Patamoke two groups were taken on, with slaves carrying vast amounts of luggage. As the trim schooner moved down the Choptank, a barge moved out from Devon Island containing Jane Fithian Steed, her infant daughter and her husband. A rope ladder was lowered from the *Whisper,* but before Mrs. Steed could climb up, her husband caught her by the arm and said, 'I'll join you in England. For the present I must tend the plantation.' But she said sternly, 'You'll never come to England, and I'll never see Maryland again.'

'But what . . .' Before he could frame his question she was clambering aboard the rescue ship, and when she reached the deck her husband lifted their baby in the air and passed it along to sailors leaning down to take it. Slaves tossed up the luggage and the *Whisper* moved on, leaving the barge drifting in midstream.

But the passenger list was not complete. As the *Whisper* headed for the bay, a speedy sloop appeared from the direction of Patamoke, firing a small gun to attract attention, and when it drew alongside, passengers saw that the fat Rector of Wrentham was appealing to be taken aboard —'I want no more of these foul colonies. I'm an Englishman.' And ropes were lowered so that twelve men could haul him up, after which some nineteen boxes and parcels followed.

Only when he was securely on board, with no possibility of retreat, did he discover that the owner of the schooner in which he was fleeing was Simon Steed and her captain Teach Turlock, whom he had defrauded. He hastened below, and was seen no more on deck.

On the voyage to London young Matt was given the job of caring for the Steed baby, and he quit bringing food and tea to the mess and carried milk and crackers to the child, for whom he acted as nurse and watchman. There were women who could have performed these tasks, but some were stricken with seasickness and others were busy caring for Mrs. Steed, who collapsed in the captain's cabin as soon as the *Whisper* cleared the Chesapeake, and none could have cared for the baby better than Matt.

He fed her, carried her about the deck and kept her amused with little games. She was less than a year old, and when she wanted to crawl toward the bulkheads, he watched her carefully. While she slept in her basket he felt free to pursue his studies with Mr. Semmes, but he had pretty well exhausted what the mate knew, and he now found a gentleman from Annapolis who was returning to a Sussex home he had left fifty years earlier, and this man delighted in teaching him advanced figuring and verb forms.

On most days, however, Matt and the baby stayed in the bow, riding it up and down as the long swells of the summer Atlantic slid past. These were days he would treasure, when whole new fields of knowledge were opening up, when he had some appreciation of the mournful tragedy which had overtaken these good families, and when he tended the Steed baby, who rarely cried and seemed to enjoy being with him.

But what Matt would remember most was something that occurred not on deck but below. One morning as he was watching over Penny Steed he noticed that his father was nowhere to be seen, and after a while Mr. Semmes came forward to ask in a low voice, 'Will Master Turlock accompany me?' and Matt went belowdecks, where he heard gurgling sounds.

They came from the cabin occupied by the Rector of Wrentham, and when he went inside he found the fat clergyman in a furious sweat, with his father standing over him. A paper prepared by Mr. Semmes lay on a table before the unhappy man, and Captain Turlock was saying, 'Sign it or I'll throw you to the sharks.'

'I won't give up my rightful land,' the fat cleric whimpered.

A sharp blow to the back of his head provoked new groans, and the rector cried, 'You're killing me!' and Turlock said, 'The only escape is to sign.' With his left hand he thrust the quill at Wilcok and growled, 'Sign it, or feed the sharks.'

'I'll sign!' And with the quill he fixed his signature to this paper:

> Aboard the *Whisper*
> 10 August 1776
>
> Of my own free will and without constraint from anyone, I do hereby confess that I obtained from Captain Teach Turlock of Patamoke 100 acres of his best land through fraud, deceit, malversation and theft, and that I return to the said captain the entirety.
>
> Jonathan Wilcok
> Rector of Wrentham

Witness: John Semmes
         Matthew Turlock

When the company left the cabin and climbed the ladder to the deck, Captain Turlock took his son to the wheel and showed him a box in which the ship's papers were kept. 'This one we guard with our life,' he told his son.

For Levin Paxmore the years 1776–1777 were a disaster. Under goading from Simon Steed he finished four copies of the *Whisper*, but learned with dismay that three of them had been quickly captured by the English and converted into British men-of-war to prey upon the colonists' shipping. The fourth, the schooner *Good Hope,* was sent into the Atlantic with an untrained crew of Choptank farmers and was promptly sunk, causing sharp-tongued Ellen Paxmore to tell her husband, 'I warned thee not to build ships of war. Thee has sent forth a covey, and all have been lost.'

'Not Turlock's,' he said, at which she reminded him caustically, 'But that was not built as a ship of war.'

She pestered him to cease his support of this futile fighting; on all sides the British were victorious, and she interpreted the quick loss of the Paxmore schooners as proof that God looked unfavorably on the rebellion. She predicted that it would soon collapse.

But her husband worked on. 'It's my job,' he said as he laid down the keel for his sixth schooner, already named by Isham Steed the *Victory.*

'Does thee foresee victory?' Paxmore asked as the transom was carved.

'Not in battle. But I think we shall prove our points to the king and enjoy many more freedoms when this is ended.'

In these early years of the rebellion Simon Steed faced tantalizing decisions. In order to pay for the war, both the government of Maryland and the Continental Congress issued paper money; patriots were exhorted to turn in their metal coinage and accept these promissory notes, and many did. Crusty men with only a few shillings in hard currency would troop to the customs house and trade their good money for bad and were applauded for their patriotism.

'Shall we surrender our metal?' Isham asked one afternoon when pressures to do so had been exerted by justices and Annapolis officials.

'Not yet,' Simon said stubbornly, resisting all arguments. As he told Isham, 'This paper money's worth nothing. We'll hold on to our coins and watch the paper collapse.'

And he was right. Within months the paper was depreciated, first $1.50 in paper to $1 in coins, then $2.50 and soon $10 paper to $1 real. When this level was reached, and patriotic pressures continued, Isham asked, 'Couldn't we buy some now?' but Simon merely glared at him, then predicted, 'We'll see the paper sell at thirty to one,' and before the year was out it stood at forty.

'Now?' Isham asked, but again Simon shook his head, but one day he did come into the office showing excitement. 'The paper has fallen, eighty to one. Now's the time to buy.'

'But won't it collapse altogether?' Isham asked. 'Five hundred to one?'

'No,' Simon explained. 'Maryland's a proud state. We'll redeem our paper. Buy as much as you can get.' And at eighty to one the Steeds began to turn in their solid currency, and Simon was correct. Maryland was proud, and she did redeem her paper at forty to one, which meant that Simon had doubled the family fortune. That he had done so at the expense of sentimental patriots did not concern him, for, as he said, 'the management of money is a skill and must be practiced as such.'

For Captain Turlock the early years of the revolution were a kaleidoscope: a tropical dawn off Panama waiting for an English merchantman; a quick run to New York with provisions; long, easy trips to St. Ubes for salt; a foray into the English Channel in pursuit of an English sloop, a visit to Nantes for the hardware and cordage sorely needed at Baltimore.

The *Whisper* became known as 'the schooner with the red-headed boy,' for several captains reported that when the American freebooters stormed aboard they were accompanied by a young lad who kept goading them. 'He wears a woolen cap pulled over his ears and speaks in a voice unusually deep for a child his age. At first I thought him to be a dwarf, but when he marched up to me and said, "Captain, you are taken," I found him to be a child. Remarkable.'

Captain Turlock had only a vague understanding of how the war was progressing; he knew that General Washington was pinned down somewhere in the north and that the Americans seemed to lose more battles than they won, but when a captured English sailor said defiantly, 'When this war's done, traitors like you and Ben Franklin will be hanged,' he asked, 'What ship does Captain Franklin sail?'

To the surprise of his crew, the war taught him caution. Not for him the gallant foray into enemy ports, or the futile contest against superior strength. The *Whisper* had speed and maneuverability, and these could be used best in hit-and-run tactics; he was not afraid to run and was perfecting at sea the same strategy that American generals were adopting on land: the sudden thrust, the quick retreat, the waiting, the cautious move.

For in any planning he had to bear in mind that whereas the *Whisper* could depend upon her speed to escape from the average English ship, three duplicates with identical capacity had been captured by the enemy and now flew English colors. His constant fear was that some day in the Caribbean the three other Paxmore schooners would converge and hunt him down. That explained his caution and why he sometimes returned to the Chesapeake empty, and sometimes even with expensive damages that had to be corrected.

And then early in 1777, when prospects were most bleak, Mr. Steed had an opportunity to observe at firsthand the skill of his barefoot captain.

A Lieutenant Cadwallader had come south from New York with an urgent message from General Washington, whose prospects for holding out against the English were fading: 'The general feels certain we can't survive another year unless France joins us. And with substantial assistance, mind you. Steed, you must go to France.'

'I thought Franklin was there.'

'He is. Doing excellent work in Paris. But the business leaders—the solid men in ports like Nantes—they're convinced we've no chance of winning.'

'I'd not be effective,' Steed said, thinking of his own uncertainty about the war.

'But you could talk to them. You must go.'

'I'll try.' And after Cadwallader had moved on to the southern ports, Steed thought: How ironic. The English Protestants of Philadelphia and New York always sneered at us Catholic boys who went to school at St. Omer's—'Why not attend a true college like Oxford?' But now it's the Frenchman who becomes essential. He had no stomach for this mission and no hope that it would succeed. He believed the colonies to be doomed and wondered only what kind of peace England would grant. But he had a high sense of duty, and since he had been handed this ticklish job, he would do his best.

It was easy for Cadwallader to say, 'Go to France,' but it was not easy for Captain Turlock to get there, for when the *Whisper* reached the exit to the Chesapeake she found waiting a cluster of English guard boats, each with two heavy guns—'Seven of 'em,' young Matt called from his position forward.

'I see 'em,' his father replied.

'What do we do?' Steed asked.

'We wait.'

'For what?'

'The precious moment,' Turlock said, and they waited.

For five tedious days the *Whisper* sailed slowly back and forth inside the protection of the headlands, while the British vessels held to the open sea. On two occasions American privateers arrived from the east, spotted the British guard boats and retreated to try other ports along the coast, but the *Whisper* could not employ that stratagem. She was trapped in the Chesapeake, and until her captain devised some trick for escape, she had to stay trapped.

During this grating delay Simon Steed conducted himself like the patient negotiator General Washington had assumed him to be. He was forty-seven years old, stiff, erect, proper, deeply wounded by the flight of his wife and desolate over the absence of his daughter. He never complained. At the start of the voyage he had told his captain that speed was essential, and he assumed that Turlock appreciated this. It was now the waterman's responsibility to break through the blockade, and no one aboard the *Whisper* knew better than he how to accomplish this.

'What we're waitin' for, Mr. Steed, is a stout wind from the west, risin' at two in the mornin'.'

'What will that prove?'

'You'll see.'

And on the seventh day, at dusk, Captain Turlock met with Mr. Semmes as the sun sank over Virginia, and they studied the clouds, and Turlock said, 'Tonight, I think.' They went to the owner and said, 'Maybe tonight. It'll be risky.'

'Cannon fire?'

'Much,' Turlock said, and as darkness fell he alerted his gunners, who moved extra balls into place and additional bags of powder. At midnight Steed could see no alteration in the wind, but at one o'clock, with a waning moon showing in the east, he felt a slight agitation moving across the calm waters of the bay, and then a scattered gustiness, followed by dead calm. He supposed that the long-awaited night wind had died down, but Captain Turlock, long familiar with the Chesapeake, moved among his men to say, 'Before dawn. We'll be in the middle of them.'

What he was counting on was that if the wind rose sharply, as he was certain it must, it would strike the Chesapeake thirty or forty minutes before it reached the Atlantic; indeed, in the darkness the British would not even know it was on its way unless they were more weather-wise than he, and without visible indications, that would be unlikely. In that half-hour of superior wind, he proposed to have his schooner at top speed, bearing directly down on the middle of the blockade. If he collided with some enemy vessel, the fight would occur there, with always a possibility of escape. What he hoped was that the *Whisper* could snake her way through the congregated ships and kick her heels in the broad Atlantic.

At quarter to two the wind rose substantially and Turlock told his men, 'At four it'll be near gale. We go.'

All practical sail was raised, that is, the three jibs forward, the two fore-and-afts and the two lower square sails. The two peak squares would be held in reserve until the last minute, when top speed would be needed; raising them in the strong wind that seemed about to break would prove dangerous, and Turlock did not want to run that risk until the moment of flight. Then he would risk everything.

At half past three he stood just west of the entrance to the bay, hiding as it were among the low Virginia hills, but now he swung the *Whisper* directly east, and as she picked up speed in the pale, moonlit darkness he cried, 'Mr. Semmes, all sail!' and young Matt hauled on the lines as the square topsails rose majestically into canvas-snapping position.

'Man the guns!' Turlock cried, and with his ship as ready as it would ever be, he sped eastward toward the open ocean.

It was four-twenty that morning before the British blockaders became aware that a major schooner was bearing down upon them. Bugles blew and orders were shouted, but with their mainsails down, the watching boats could not respond quickly, and there was confusion. On came the American vessel, nine sails aloft in the heavy wind, her deck awash, her bow cutting the choppy waves.

'Fire!' the English captains bellowed, and cannon roared—to no effect.

'Hold fire!' Turlock cried. His job was not to sink or damage blockade boats, all he wanted was to avoid them; and this he did with matchless skill until that moment when the captain of the seventh English boat, seeing in the pale light that this daring fool was about to escape, ordered his helmsman to put about and throw his ship directly into the path of the escaping schooner.

'Cap'm!' Matthew screamed.

There was nothing Captain Turlock could do but forge ahead, hoping that his superior weight and expanse of filled sail would inflict greater damage than he received. 'Stand to crash!' he shouted, and Simon Steed, owner of this fine ship, winced.

But at the last moment, when the bowsprit of the *Whisper* was practically jabbing at the larboard flank of the English vessel, Turlock spun the wheel as violently as he could to starboard, an action which in the open sea would surely have capsized the schooner, considering the huge spread of sail she was carrying in this wind. But now, as he had calculated, his swift schooner crashed sideways into the smaller English vessel, larboard to larboard, and there was a crunching of timber as the blockader held the *Whisper* erect. The impact was so sudden, and of such brief duration, that the *Whisper* seemed to bounce away, largely undamaged.

Now Captain Turlock spun the wheel again, this time to larboard, and as his ship scraped clear of the sorely wounded enemy, with the wind almost abeam and strong enough to throw the *Whisper* down, the bow turned majestically; the pressure on the sails abated, the ship righted itself, and Turlock told Mr. Semmes to fetch his son. When Matt appeared, flushed with victory, his father said, 'At the start of the fight I thought, "My son's a damned fool." '

'Why?'

'Standin' in the bow like a stupid figurehead. But when it came time to hoist the sails, there you were, workin' the ropes.' Matt smiled. 'And when the cannonballs came crashin' through, you didn't hide.' Captain Turlock reached down and rumpled his son's red hair. 'You're goin' to be a sailor.'

Toward the end of the voyage Steed suffered one bad day. He was casually inspecting a chart showing the entrance to the Loire River, on which Nantes stood, when it occurred to him that at that moment he was only a short sail south of England, and he began to see the pleasant images that name evoked: his English wife, his daughter, the honest men at Fithians, the serenity. He thought how startled Captain Turlock would be if he said, 'Let's sail north two days and we'll be in England.' And he thought: When the war's over I may move to England. Jane would be happy there, and Isham could run the plantation.

And as soon as he formulated these thoughts it became clear that he was visualizing not the total victory that Lieutenant Cadwallader had spoken of, the kind that General Washington apparently wanted, but a kind of negotiated truce, from which the relationships that existed before the war could be reestablished: That's what I want. The colonies and England back together, but on a better footing. And then he acknowledged why he wanted it: Because we can't defeat England. We're destined to live with her. And I wish this damned war would end. He looked north and muttered, 'England, England!'

In the meantime he was obligated to wheedle from France as much help as possible, so that the colonists could win some battles and appear at the bargaining table in good posture. I'll do my job, he promised himself, unaware that even at this critical moment he still called his new nation *the colonies*. He was destined to be a poor ambassador.

He was standing there, aloof and overwhelmed with loneliness, when young Matt Turlock left his lookout position and came to talk with him. 'We'll soon be sighting France,' the boy said. Steed ignored the comment, so Matt asked directly, 'Didn't you live in France?'

'I did.'

The red-headed boy was not abashed by this cool reception. 'Up there's England,' he said. The lonely figure made no response, so Matt continued, 'They'd like to know where we are. They'd like to capture this ship.' Again no response, so the boy babbled on, 'I sailed to England once, Mr. Steed.' Silence—except for the cry of a seagull. 'Remember, I took Mrs. Steed and Penny to London.'

At the mention of his daughter's name, Steed lost his indifference. 'Did she sail well?' he asked.

'She stayed in a basket forward. I guarded her.'

'You did? No one told me that.'

'Yes, Mrs. Steed kept to her cabin, sickly I think. But Penny and I stayed forward day after day. She loved the sea.'

'And you cared for her!' Steed shook his head, then fumbled in his pocket, producing at last a bright half-joe. 'I should like to give you this for your trouble,' he said, handing Matt the coin. The boy offered no mock protestation; he knew the value of a Portuguese joe and pocketed it with a big 'Thank you, Mr. Steed.'

'Where did she stay?' Steed asked.

'The basket stood here. I brought it out every morning.'

And for the rest of that day Simon Steed remained in the fore part of the ship, looking first to the north toward England, then to the deck where the basket had rested.

They entered the Loire at St. Nazaire, where a rude fort pretended to guard the integrity of the river, but it was doubtful if the guns so proudly visible could deliver much weight. A French pilot came aboard to help them negotiate the beautiful river, but he added to Steed's pessimism by reporting, 'We give the colonies little chance. It's ships that will prevail, and England has them.'

When they reached the wharf at Nantes they found that French merchants were vigorously excited about the caviar he was bringing but contemptuous of his principal mission. 'We see no hope for the Americans. Actually, Steed, we think you'd be better off remaining with England.'

'Then why do you fight to protect your independence? War after war, and always against England.'

'We're a nation. With an army. With ships. Your destiny is colonial.'

Wherever he went in Nantes it was the same. Every French merchant hoped that something evil would befall the English, and if the colonies chanced to be the agency for the disaster, fine. Steed heard many expressions of brotherhood and good will, followed by hard-headed calculations that England must win the war. When he dined with the Montaudoins, dictators of the Loire economy, their nephew, who had known Steed as a student, had copious praise for the southern colonies: 'Gracious land, splendid people. We're so happy to have you with us, Simon.'

'Will you report your enthusiasm to Paris?' Steed asked bluntly.

'Socially, of course. Politically? I'm afraid, dear fellow, you haven't a chance.'

Dutifully he went to each of the firms with which he had done business —the Baillys, the Brisard du Marthres, the Pucet Fils—and from each he heard the same story: 'The colonies cannot win. Accept the best peace available and get on with it.'

He took the long overland journey to Lorient, a port in which the more adventurous firms maintained headquarters, but they, too, were doubtful: 'We French are practical. If there was any chance you could maintain your independence of the English, we'd back you ten thousand percent. There is no chance.'

The firm of Berard, with which Steed had conducted much business, organized a formal dinner honoring Steed, not as a political negotiator but as a valued customer, and when the important gentlemen of the area were assembled, a Monsieur Coutelux summarized their attitudes:

'We have followed with extreme attention events in the colonies and have noted with approbation your determination, starting in 1774, to free yourselves of commercial domination by London. Your resistance to the various taxes, your insistence that you be free to ship tobacco direct to France instead of through Bristol, your strong inclination toward a French style of self-government—all this encourages us. You are on the right track, Steed. But when you challenge English military might, especially her naval superiority, you are being downright foolish, and you must not expect us to support you in your folly.

'Understand, Steed, we're as opposed to England as ever. We merely wait the proper moment to give her the *coup de grâce*. It may come in Spain, or Italy, or some unknown place like India, but somewhere, somehow we're destined to rule Europe and she's destined to a minor role. But the timely spot cannot be the colonies. You haven't the manpower, the army, the manufacturing or the navy. Your best chance, and I tell you this from the bottom of my heart, is to go home, make peace with London, and await the day when France gives England the mortal thrust. Then, and only then, will you be free.'

Disheartened, Steed returned to Nantes, went aboard the *Whisper* and consulted with his crew. 'I must stay in France until help is assured. But you're free to roam. Captain Turlock, are you willing to risk another run through the blockade?'

'Always.'

'Your luck may run out.'

'I've tricks I ain't used yet.'

So it was arranged, on credit, that Captain Turlock should load the *Whisper* with cloth, brass fittings, salt, ships' compasses and all the compact manufactured goods for which the starved colonies yearned, hurry home and return to pick up Steed. So on a bright day Turlock sailed down the Loire and out into the Atlantic.

When he was gone, Steed began his serious work. Patiently he returned to each merchant, explaining in colloquial French why the colonies deserved help in their resistance to England. 'I know we've been fighting them since 1775, with no results. But we're still in the field, and we're getting stronger. Believe me, dear friend, we're getting stronger.' When they laughed, he asked, 'Then why did you entrust your cargo with my captain? Because you know he'll penetrate the blockade. In seven months he'll be back for another shipment. You know that.'

He returned to Lorient, went down the coast to La Rochelle, and the more he talked the less he accomplished. He was, perhaps, too French to argue well the cause of the colonies; he could not convey the thundering actuality of the Blue Ridge farmer or a Massachusetts weaver. And then, when his fortunes were at their lowest, he was rescued by a fellow American who spoke the vernacular.

Benjamin Franklin, chief advocate in France for the colonies, came down to Nantes to meet with the leaders of that city and Lorient and La Rochelle. The Montaudoins placed at his disposal a small château, in which he held court, and there Steed met him.

He was well past seventy, bald, paunchy, squint-eyed, and as lively as a chestnut on a griddle. He affected a costume that was aggressively American, including a coonskin hat and a gnarled cherry-wood cane. He spoke abominable French with a vigor that made his pronouncements sound fresh and challenging. At the big dinners he gave he rejected sentimentality and never spoke of America's valiant struggle; he appealed always to the fundamental interests of France, and the more mundane he made them the better.

'We're doing your dirty work, and all we seek is tangible support. We seek the privilege of trading freely with your port cities, with profits for you. We want to establish in the New World a counterbalance to the Old, and this will be of advantage primarily to you.'

He was an amazing man. He had brought down from Paris a mysterious woman introduced merely as Madame de Segonzac; her identity and her relationship to Franklin were not explained, but Franklin paid her deference and relied on her to persuade his guests. He also delighted in walking through the streets of Nantes and visiting those shopkeepers who had imported for the occasion the remarkable mementos then flooding Paris: teacups with Franklin's portrait set in porcelain; snuffboxes decorated with enameled coonskin caps; silken pillows with embroidered portraits; and broadsides containing his bespectacled countenance and quotations from *Poor Richard*. It was these homely, pragmatic aphorisms which endeared this uncouth American to the French; in his barbarous way he spoke their language. But nothing he accomplished in Nantes surpassed his performance one afternoon when he was strolling along a crowded street near the wharf. There an enterprising merchant from Corsica had imported three of the large china chamber pots containing on their sides portraits of Franklin, and on their insides glazed representations of the coonskin cap. Hundreds had been sold throughout France, but these were the first in Nantes, and when Franklin saw them he stopped, spoke to the Corsican, and watched approvingly as one of the pots was placed in the middle of the street. Then, as sailors guffawed, he showed them what he would look like sitting on his own crockery. There was much cheering, and within two days the story had reached most of the western ports.

In his large meetings he never seemed serious, but he always was. He conveyed only one message: The United States shall prevail. And before he had been on the seacoast a week he began convincing those sturdy merchants that it was in their interest to back the fledgling country, not because the United States was relying upon philosophical principles derived from France, and not because there was an inherent brotherhood between the two countries, but because by doing so, the French could gig the English and at the same time earn a batch of livres tournois.

For two months Franklin and Steed worked together, and after Turlock had brought the *Whisper* back to Nantes and the time came for parting, the older man said, 'Simon, your help has been invaluable.'

Steed, aware that he had supported Franklin only half-heartedly, since he did not believe in an ultimate American victory, mumbled, 'I accomplished nothing. It was you they wanted to hear.'

'I was the clown, attracting their attention. It was imperative that you be there to represent the other side of our effort.' He laughed, then chucked Steed under the chin as if he were a boy. 'You were the respectable element, and believe me, Steed, the French businessman hungers for respectability. They never deal with banks that are on the verge.'

Then he became serious. With a firm hand he pulled Steed around until they were facing. 'When we started our work you didn't believe we could win. I could see it. Do you believe now?'

'I'm confused. It seems to me we should stay with England.'

Franklin did not protest. 'Let's go to your schooner,' he suggested, and when they sat in Captain Turlock's cabin he said forcefully, 'Simon, we're destined to win. I know our armies are in retreat everywhere and we've no navy. But the great sweep of human desire fights on our side, and we cannot be defeated.' He pointed out the cabin door and said, 'Look at him. The new American.' And there stood Captain Turlock, barefooted, grimy from working on his ship, clothed in near rags, but ready to storm his way into Bristol port if asked. 'Why did you choose him for your captain?' Franklin asked.

'Because he knows . . . he knows what a ship can do.'

'General Washington chose you to come here because you know. You know what a plantation can do. Now open your eyes, son, and see what a collection of men like you and Captain Turlock can accomplish.' He rose in a state of euphoria and orated as if he were trying to persuade the merchants of Nantes: 'We can remake the world. Simon, we're going to win.' And from that moment in Nantes harbor, Simon Steed never doubted; he cast aside his cautious love for England, his romantic longing for the old securities, and leaped into the full tide of the revolution.

As a result of what he and Franklin achieved in the next week, the solid business community of the French coast awakened to the probability that the United States might indeed win their war of attrition and become a major commercial center. Opposition to French involvement in what had hitherto been regarded as merely another idealistic uprising diminished, and the way was paved for the vigorous participation of that remarkable trio of French military geniuses who would join Lafayette in helping the United States maintain its independence: Rochambeau, Bougainville and, above all, De Grasse.

When the time came for Steed to sail back to Devon, Franklin confided, 'I've written to the Congress suggesting that you be named agent for the southern states.'

'For what?'

'For the acquisition of supplies.'

'I don't understand.'

'Ships. Men like Captain Turlock. Scatter them over the face of the ocean. Bring in muskets and powder and chain and cloth for uniforms. Steed, an army survives on things . . . like chickens and brass cannon. Get those things.'

Simon Steed was the kind of man to whom such a specific suggestion was a command, and on the spur of the moment he asked Franklin, 'What should I take back now?' and he was astonished at the reply: 'Nothing. Leave Nantes with empty holds.'

'Such a waste . . .'

'Speed to St. Eustatius.'

'That tiny island?'

'Tiny but powerful. It's owned by the Dutch, and we've been assembling there a body of munitions you'd not believe.'

'What do we use for money?'

'Credit. Your credit.'

'Seems very risky.'

'We're engaged in a risk so grave it terrifies me. Your risk comes at St. Eustatius.'

So they parted, each man engaged in a gamble of staggering dimension: to fail meant ruin and death at the hangman's trap; to win meant the establishment of a nation founded on new principles whose possibilities were only dimly understood. In the hostile port of Nantes, where no man believed America could survive, Simon Steed had convinced himself of those new principles, and to them he was willing to dedicate his fortune and his life.

'We'll sail tonight,' he told Captain Turlock.

'Empty?'

'Yes. To St. Eustatius.'

'Never been there,' Turlock said, but he was ready to go.

That any mariner could find St. Eustatius was a miracle, but a greater miracle awaited him when he did find it. For it was one of the smallest islands on earth, a volcanic, rocky pinpoint lost in a cluster of islands north of Guadeloupe. Captain Turlock, seeking it through a bank of clouds, had almost decided it did not exist, when his son cried, 'Cap'm, land to starboard,' and there, emerging from the sea like a mysterious sentinel, rose the jagged shores of St. Eustatius.

As the *Whisper* maneuvered to enter the minute harbor Simon Steed was overwhelmed by what he saw: a shoreline crowded with great warehouses; so much cordage and cotton that bales were left standing uncovered; no police, no soldiers, no naval guns protecting the place; and in the cramped waters between the headlands not less than sixty vessels. He found out that five or six heavily laden ships put into port daily bringing goods from Europe and Africa, while an equal number left carrying those goods to the embattled American colonies. As one British admiral, furious at the insolence of the place, complained, 'It's the richest small island that ever was on earth.'

It existed in a fairy-tale atmosphere; it was owned by the Dutch, who were at war with nobody, but the goods coming to it were dispatched by merchants of all nations: Russia, Sweden, Portugal and, especially, France and England. This last was particularly aggravating to the British: English chandlers who refused to supply English warships in Plymouth surreptitiously consigned their best goods to St. Eustatius, where they were sold to American vessels fighting England. Also, many a stout merchantman sailing from London with papers for Italy or Greece changed course dramatically south of the Channel and hied off to St. Eustatius, where profits were trebled.

Captain Turlock could not tie up to any dock; thirty vessels were ahead of him. But from his anchorage he rowed ashore to purchase the materials of war needed along the Chesapeake: the strongest English cordage, double-thick French brassware, muskets from Austria and salt from Poland. He bought wisely, from a score of different merchants speaking many different languages, and when the bills were totaled he had Mr. Steed issue letters of credit. With the *Whisper* loaded as heavily as its timbers would allow, he hoisted anchor and set out for America, having no idea of how he would penetrate the English blockade or what port he would put in to if he succeeded.

It was a bright, sunny run before the wind, but it ended abruptly, for a major English squadron patrolled the Chesapeake and not even a canny dissembler like Turlock could slip through. He sailed north toward Boston, but was intercepted by an American frigate, a pitiful affair with untrained crew and few guns, whose captain cried on speaking-trumpet, 'Turn back! You can't get into Boston.' So the *Whisper* and its priceless cargo drifted south, hoping to land somewhere in the Carolinas, but they, too, were rimmed by English warships, and at a meeting of desperation Turlock told his owner, 'Mr. Steed, the best we can do is beach her somewhere in the Delaware Counties. Carry the goods overland.' Mr. Semmes agreed that no other strategy was practical, so Steed had to approve. 'But you'll lose twenty percent in pilferage,' he said. To which Turlock answered, 'You'll add forty percent to the price.'

So the *Whisper* moved cautiously north, well out to sea where the

Chesapeake squadron would not detect her, and when the latitude of Lewes on the Delaware coast was reached, she turned abruptly west and sped toward shore. There, at the mouth of a small stream, she dropped anchor, boats were lowered and unloading began. Before the first cargo was got ashore men from the Delaware Counties appeared and parties were organized to portage these crucial military supplies across the peninsula to the eastern shores of the Chesapeake, from which they would be ferried to Baltimore.

'You will be paid,' Steed promised the Delaware men.

'Pay or no, we'll get to Baltimore.' They were men who had been fighting the English for three long years; victory seemed farther away than ever but surrender was a word they did not use.

When the schooner was emptied, Steed told his captain, 'Go back to St. Eustatius. Make as many voyages as possible.' And thus the golden ferry between the Dutch entrepôt and the colonies began. In the years that followed, whenever a cargo slipped through the English blockade, Simon Steed took control. He recorded each item, awarded it the highest value possible, turned it over to the fledgling government, and allocated to himself a handler's fee of thirty percent above the inflated cost of the goods. If the war dragged on, and if Captain Turlock continued his daring escapades, the Steeds would be millionaires, and not in dollars, in pounds sterling.

But in late 1777 events took a bad turn; daring English sea captains converted the Chesapeake into an English lake. They sailed boldly to the head of the bay, landed an enormous army there and marched on Philadelphia, hoping to cut the colonies in half, knock out those in the north, then the remainder in the south.

Word reached the Choptank that a massive battle had been fought along the banks of a stream called Brandywine, and that Philadelphia had fallen, and that General Washington had escaped annihilation only by retreating to the environs of an iron mill called Valley Forge. That he could recover sufficiently to oppose the English was doubtful; the collapse of the revolution was at hand.

A squadron of English ships sailed boldly into the Choptank, anchored off Patamoke and bombarded the town. When no opposition appeared, landing parties came ashore and a lieutenant trim in gold and blue announced, 'We have come to burn that infamous nest of sedition, the Paxmore Boatyard,' and with flaming torches his men set fire to the wooden sheds and retired.

There was on the ways at this time the nearly completed *Victory;* her spars were not yet in place and there was some minor caulking to be done, but she was almost a schooner and was desperately needed. So when the flames were hottest, and it seemed that this precious vessel must go to ashes, Levin Paxmore, his dark hair outlined by the fire, rushed into his doomed boatyard and began chopping away the struts that held the *Victory* on the ways, trusting that once it was set free, it would slide down the railway and launch itself into the harbor, where any flames attacking it could be quenched.

When it became apparent what Paxmore intended, men of the town gathered to cheer him on, unmindful of the final salvos fired by the retreating English ships, but none volunteered actually to move in among the flames to help chop away the struts, for the heat was too fierce.

Ellen Paxmore, infuriated by the bombardment and alerted by the fires brightening her sky, had come to the boatyard and had quickly understood what her husband was attempting. She, too, was appalled at the thought of this fine schooner's being burned, and when no one else would help Levin, she grabbed an ax and disappeared into the flames, but she had chosen a spot which no one could have conquered; the fire was raging and she had to withdraw.

A slave named Pompey—a name awarded in ridicule by some plantation scholar trained in the classics—watched Mrs. Paxmore's valiant attempt, and now quenched with his bare hands the sparks that threatened her gray dress. After he had done this he grabbed her ax and dashed into the flames, where he chopped away two of the struts.

'It's moving!' the crowd roared, and slowly the *Victory* crept down the ways, gathered speed and splashed into the harbor.

Now men were more than willing to leap into small boats and crowd the prematurely launched vessel, splashing water upon the flickering flames and securing the hull to shore. Levin Paxmore, assured that his new schooner was safe, even though his boatyard was in ashes, walked painfully home, expecting to have his burns immediately cared for. Instead he was confronted by the most profound discussion of his life, for his wife awaited him, her own burns unattended:

ELLEN: Did thee notice, Levin? The only man brave enough to help was the slave Pompey?

LEVIN: I didn't see.

ELLEN: Thee never sees. Pompey sprang into the fire. Pompey helped me fight the flames eating at my dress. Pompey chopped away the struts. Does this mean nothing?

LEVIN: It means we saved the *Victory*.

ELLEN: It means he is a man, a good man. Can thee not see the terrible wrong in holding such a man to slavery?

LEVIN: My hands ache.

ELLEN: My heart aches. Levin, I cannot abide another day in this condition. These colonies are fighting for freedom. Men like Simon Steed perform miracles in the name of freedom, but they ignore the gravest problem of all. Right on their home doorsteps.

LEVIN: Pompey's a good slave. When he's rented to me I treat him justly.

ELLEN: By what right has thee been ordained to treat justly or unjustly? Is thee a God because thee is white?

LEVIN: What does thee want me to do?

ELLEN (lowering her voice and taking her husband by his burned hands): Come First Day, I want thee to rise and propose that henceforth no Quaker who owns a slave can remain a member of our meeting.

LEVIN: Thee has tried that gambit a dozen times.

ELLEN: But thee has not, and thy word will carry substantial weight.

LEVIN: I am busy building schooners. Steed has said, extravagantly I suppose, that they are helping to ensure freedom.

ELLEN: A greater war than that on the Chesapeake is being fought.

LEVIN: What does that mean?

ELLEN: Surely these colonies will have their freedom, one way or another. England or a confederation, what does it signify, really? But the freedom of men . . .

LEVIN: That, too, will follow . . . in due course.

ELLEN: It will not! (Here her voice rose again.) More than a hundred years ago in this town Ruth Brinton Paxmore begged the Quakers to set their slaves free. Nothing happened. Fifty years ago thy grandmother made the same plea, with the same results. Fifty years from now my granddaughter will throw the same words into the wilderness unless we take—

LEVIN: Slavery will die out of its own weight, thee knows that.

ELLEN: I know it will persist forever unless good people fight it. Levin, on First Day thee must testify.

LEVIN: I cannot inject myself into an argument which does not concern—

ELLEN: Levin! This day a black man saved me, leaped among the flames like a salamander. Would thee leave him there in the fire?

LEVIN: I cannot follow when thee engages in hyperbole.

ELLEN: And I can no longer rest in this house so long as even one member abides slavery. Levin, I must make my bed elsewhere.

LEVIN (dropping his head onto the bare table): I have lost my yard, my tools. And my hands are burning with fire. I need help, Ellen.

ELLEN: And thee will lose thy immortal soul if thee turns thy back on Pompey. He, too, needs help.

LEVIN (leaping to his feet): What does thee demand?

ELLEN: Thy testimony . . . in public . . . come First Day. (Silence, then in a gentle voice.) Levin, thee has been preparing for this day. I've seen thee watching the black people of this town. The time has come. I think the fire served as a signal . . . to the future.

LEVIN: Can thee put some bear grease on my hands? They burn. Terribly they burn.

ELLEN (applying the grease): This means that thee will speak?

LEVIN: I have not wanted to. In these affairs God moves slowly. But

Pompey is a decent man. Thee says it was he who chopped away the restraining poles?

ELLEN: He did. But he does not warrant thy support because of his acts. He warrants it because of his existence.

LEVIN: I suppose it's time. I'll testify for thee.

ELLEN: Not for me and not for Pompey because he helped. For the great future of this nation—the future that Ruth Brinton saw.

So on a First Day in late 1777 Patamoke Meeting was startled to find itself in the midst of a debate that would tear the church apart. The members had come to the ancient meeting house expecting that words of consolation might be offered to Levin Paxmore over the loss of his boatyard or prayers celebrating the town's deliverance from the English. Instead, after nine brief minutes of silence, Levin Paxmore rose, his hands bandaged, his hair singed:

> 'The Bible says that sometimes we see through a glass darkly. For me it required a great fire which destroyed my handiwork, but in those flames there moved a figure comparable to Shadrach, Meshach and Abednego. It was the slave Pompey, owned by a member of this meeting who hires him out to others. I did not see what Pompey accomplished, but I am told he was most valiant and it was to him that the merit goes for saving the schooner.

> 'In the days since the fire I have been asking myself how it could be that a slave with nothing to gain and all to lose should throw himself into my fire, to save my schooner? And the only answer that makes any reason is that Pompey is a man exactly like me. He breathes like me, and eats, and works, and sleeps when he is tired. How do I know? Because I saw him by the wharf yesterday, and his hands were bandaged like mine. The fire burns him as it burns me. [Here he held his bandaged hands aloft, and many began to feel uneasy.]

> 'Therefore, today I reverse everything I have previously argued in this meeting. Slaves must be set free. In the name of God and Jesus Christ they must be set free, and no man dare call himself a Quaker and a slaveholder, too.'

The meeting broke up in consternation. Levin Paxmore was its most prosperous member, and also one of its sagest. Those opposed to change had always counted on him to support them: 'Let us move slowly. Let us study this for the next Yearly Meeting.' And now he had broken the covenant and called bluntly for immediate manumission on pain of expulsion.

At the Quarterly Meeting in December 1777 the Quakers of the Choptank became the first important religious group in the south to outlaw slavery among its members. In spite of Levin Paxmore's unflinching leadership, the issue was bitterly fought and it required two days for the clerk to ascertain the sense of the membership; even then seven obdurate men stormed from the hall vowing to surrender Quakerism rather than their slaves.

It had required more than a hundred years for this most liberal of the southern Christian sects to decide that human slavery was inconsistent with Christian principles; the more conservative sects would require an additional century.

When the decision was announced, Levin Paxmore touched his scarred hands and told his wife, 'The burning has stopped,' and she knew why.

For those Americans who lived within the benediction of the Chesapeake, the culminating crisis of the revolution occurred in 1781. Indeed, the future of America and perhaps of the world then stood in peril, for it seemed that the attempt at self-rule must be crushed, and with it the hopes of millions in Europe for a better pattern of life.

In that year the English army, consolidated at last under a succession of daring generals, began to chew the south apart. Victory upon victory crushed General Washington's lieutenants in Georgia and South Carolina, and it became clear that a few colonial farmers, no matter how brave, were no match for hundreds of well-trained English regulars supported by large guns.

And when General Cornwallis began ravaging Virginia, and Admiral Rodney assembled a fleet of battleships in the Caribbean, ready to invade the Chesapeake, it seemed obvious that the rebellion was doomed. New York lay in English hands; Philadelphia was neutralized; Boston and Newport were powerless to send support, and no major port along the Atlantic was open to American vessels, even if any had succeeded in penetrating the blockade.

Men had begun to talk openly of defeat and started calculating among themselves what kind of terms they might be able to wheedle from the victorious English. Even General Washington had faltered in his dogged optimism, sending Steed of Devon a letter which summarized the times:

> Where pray God is the French fleet that you and Franklin assured me would spring to our defense? Without their aid and without it soon, I fear we are doomed. My men mutiny. More deserters leave camp than recruits arrive. They have no food, no guns, no uniforms to sustain their dignity, and above all, no pay. Only the iron will of our junior officers holds this army together, and there is little hope

that they can sustain this miracle throughout the balance of this year.

Friend Steed, we must have immediate help from France. Have you any practical way of rushing this message to Paris? If so, depart at once and tell them the whole fortune of the war hangs in the balance, which must dip against us if our impoverishment continues. We need arms and food and cloth and money and particularly a French navy to offset the strangulation that threatens. I implore you, Steed, do something.

There was nothing he could do. He could send no imploring letters to Nantes, for no mail could penetrate the blockade. He could not try to slip across to France himself, for Captain Turlock was absent in the Caribbean. And he could not even board his family sloop and sail to Virginia to help fight Cornwallis, because English patrol boats dominated the bay. Powerless, he had to stay on Devon, watching the disaster; he was not even aware of the greater disaster that had overtaken his two schooners at St. Eustatius.

Captain Turlock, in the *Whisper,* had been highly pleased with Simon Steed's nephew, Norman, as skipper of the new *Victory.* He was venturesome yet obedient to signals, daring yet prudent in protecting his ship. 'He'll make a fine captain,' Turlock told his son as they watched the young man.

Together they had made three runs to St. Eustatius, transporting enormous cargoes, which Simon Steed sold at profit to the hungry armies of General Washington. They were now beginning a fourth sally, and if they could somehow smuggle the two schooners into Boston or Savannah, they stood to make a fortune. So as they drifted easily southward through the Virgin Islands, keeping watch for any English prowlers, Captain Turlock invited his colleague aboard the *Whisper* for a final consultation. 'The trick this time, get in and out as fast as possible.'

'Always before we've taken time.'

'Something warns me things are different,' Turlock said.

'How?' the younger man asked.

'England is getting ready for the kill. Too much movement.'

'I saw nothing coming down.'

'Me neither,' Turlock grunted. 'But things are changed. In fast. Out fast.'

Norman Steed could not comprehend how a man could see nothing and be told nothing and yet sense that somehow the world had changed. He paid his respects to Captain Turlock and rowed back to the *Victory,* but when the two schooners passed St. Maarten, that strange island half French, half Dutch, he saw that Captain Turlock had launched a boat, which came scudding across with an imperative: 'At St. Eustatius the *Whisper* is to enter first. Keep a close watch.'

But when they approached the golden isle nothing had changed. There were the forested masts, the bustling porters, the reassuring Dutch flag drooping heavily in the still air. Indeed, there was so little breeze that when Captain Steed's *Victory* reached the entrance in good condition for an easy turn to starboard, the vessel made that turn, which put her into the harbor some distance ahead of the *Whisper*. But as the sleek new schooner moved to anchor, for there was still no room at any of the wharves, a shattering gunfire broke out, the mast of the *Victory* was carried away, and her young captain lay dead with two musket balls through his chest.

It was Captain Turlock's intention to storm into the harbor and revenge this craven act, but no sooner had he broken out his four guns than Mr. Semmes cried, 'Captain! Those ships are all English!'

And that was true. Admiral Rodney, commander of the Caribbean squadron, had at last grown choleric over the insolence of the Dutch in maintaining this treasonous entrepôt, and with a squadron large enough to blow the island out of the sea, had captured it. Then, craftily, he kept the Dutch flag flying, luring freebooters like young Norman Steed into the range of his guns. St. Eustatius was no longer golden; it was lead and iron.

In a rage, Teach Turlock turned the *Whisper* away, leaving young Steed dead, the *Victory* lost and her Choptank crew headed for the Old Mill prison at Plymouth. Numbed with fury at having been so tricked, he stormed through the Caribbean, tackling any English vessel he came upon. On one glorious cruise, years before, he had taken one prize for each of his four guns, the best a freebooter could hope for. Now he took two for each gun, and the booty in the bowels of his schooner became enormous . . . and a tantalizing misery.

For he could land it nowhere. The principal reason why he had been free to rampage through the myriad islands was that England had moved her major battleships northwestward to encase the colonies in a rim of iron. The strangulation that General Washington had feared was under way, and there was no device by which Teach Turlock could land his captured booty.

And then, one day in late August as he languished off the Carolinas, hoping to find some refuge, he overtook a small fishing boat containing American watermen, and they gave him tremendous news: 'The French have come!'

They told of General Lafayette, that conceited but brave man, who had marched into Virginia, restoring order and maneuvering so brilliantly that he had General Cornwallis cooped on the York Peninsula. They spoke of a powerful effort, through all the colonies, to reinforce

Lafayette and bring the war to a conclusion. And then they reported the most electrifying news of all: 'They say a French fleet has arrived to clear the Chesapeake!'

'That means we can get home!' Turlock cried, and within five minutes he was clearing his decks for a swift dash north.

How beautiful the *Whisper* was as she sped toward Cape Hatteras, wind to larboard, her bow cutting into the waves, her decks aslant, and young Matt forward peering for sight of Cape Henry. Gulls followed, wheeling and dipping, and sun glistened on the lines. It was good to be heading home in time of trouble, to stand with one's own kind against the enemy.

Off Hatteras they intercepted another boat, and its occupants confirmed the incredible: 'French ships guarding the bay! You'll have easy entrance!'

Now that the shoals of Hatteras were safely passed, Captain Turlock piled on more sail, so that the *Whisper* leaped through the waters, making the speed that Levin Paxmore had predicted, but as the rich voyage neared completion Turlock knew that it was not one of triumph, for he had lost his sister ship, and he damned the English, hoping that the French would smash them.

Then came the cry—forward—from young Matt: 'Cap'm! Battleships! All English!'

And there, moving majestically toward the entrance to the Chesapeake came four great ships of the line: *Royal Oak,* 74 guns; *London,* 90 guns; *Invincible,* 74 guns; *Intrepid,* 64 guns. With grand indifferent motion they rolled in the swells, indomitable, relentless. They saw the *Whisper* but ignored her; they knew they could not catch her in the open sea. Their job was to crush the French intruder; that done, annoying craft like the *Whisper* could be easily handled. She would be driven from the seas.

But now Matt cried again: 'Cap'm! More!' And seven more gigantic ships loomed from the horizon, the most powerful ships of the English navy.

'Cap'm! More coming!' And eight more towering vessels, terrifying to the sailors on the small *Whisper,* hove into sight: *Monarch, Centaur, Montagu, Ajax.* They came like platforms of death, monstrous engines of war rolling in the sea like whales impervious to the small fish surrounding them. When the line had passed, Captain Turlock asked Mr. Semmes to make an entry in the log:

4 September 1781. At dusk well east of Cape Henry we were passed by nineteen great ships of the English line, heading for the Chesapeake. May God in His mercy strengthen the French, for tomorrow we live or die with their ships.

The French could not have been in a weaker position to engage the English squadron. Some days earlier Admiral de Grasse had arrived at the mouth of the Chesapeake with a squadron of twenty-four ships, but imprudently he had anchored his flotilla inside the headlands; worse, he had given liberty to almost half his crew, who were now foraging the shores of the bay for food and water. Still worse, since none of his ships were copper-sheathed like the English, they were perishing from the worms. And worst of all, his position allowed him no room in which to maneuver. He was trapped, and when scouting boats rushed in with news that Admiral Rodney was bearing down with the entire Caribbean squadron, he realized his peril.

If De Grasse had been a prudent man, he might have surrendered then and there, for the enemy had every advantage except one: the British ships were sleek-bottomed and free of worm; their crews were complete and battle-hardened; they had the advantage of the wind and ocean space in which to maneuver; and they had guns of shattering power manned by the best seamen in the world. The only disadvantage the English suffered was that Admiral Rodney, a tested leader in battle, was not aboard the ships; his place had been taken by an indecisive gentleman of little battle experience named Gatch.

The accident which caused this substitution was one of those misadventures which occur from time to time, as if to prove that human history can never be an exact science: the English government had sent to the Caribbean their best admiral, Rodney, and a plethora of their best ships. Victory over De Grasse was ensured. But when Rodney captured St. Eustatius he became so bedazzled by the riches there and so mortally tempted by a chance to steal some four million pounds for himself, that he dallied among the warehouses and wasted time among the overflowing shops, and in the end even requisitioned a small squadron of the best battleships to convoy him back to London in style. His absence, and especially the absence of the diverted ships, gave the trapped French squadron one slim chance of escape.

Captain Turlock, of course, did not know of Rodney's absence, and when dawn broke on the morning of September fifth he shuddered. Watching from a safe distance to the east, 'like a gnat watching eagles,' he said, he saw the great ships of the English line form like an arrow and move toward the mouth of the bay, where the trapped French ships could be destroyed one at a time. 'It's to be a massacre,' he told Mr. Semmes, and to his son he said, 'When you become a captain, never let yourself be caught at the mouth of a bay.' Then, remembering his disaster at St. Eustatius, he added, 'Nor at the mouth of a harbor, either.'

'Look, Cap'm!' Matt cried, and in the distance, barely visible, came the first of the French warships.

'My God!' Mr. Semmes cried. 'They're going to run it!'

There they came, a line of vessels with almost no chance of escaping, with no room for subtle maneuvering or the arts of war, just forging blindly ahead, out of their trap and trusting for a chance to reach the open sea: *Languedoc,* 80 guns; *Saint Esprit,* 80 guns; *Marseillais,* 74 guns.

'Look!' Matt shouted, and there came the most powerful ship afloat, the gigantic *Ville de Paris,* 110 guns.

'They're going to make it!' Mr. Semmes cried, slapping Captain Turlock on the back, but the captain said nothing. For more than an hour he just stood there, staring at this incredible scene of twenty-four disadvantaged French warships turning the tide of battle by an act of supreme courage. When the last of the line stood free, away from the confines of the bay and ready to form a battle line, he turned to Mr. Semmes and said, 'We saw it. No one will believe us, but we saw it.' Like a deer breaking loose from dogs, De Grasse had leaped his barriers and gained space.

Belatedly the English admiral responded. His prey had sprung the coop, but there were tested maneuvers for countering the move. 'Wear all ships!' he signaled, and the men aboard the *Whisper* gazed in grudging admiration at the manner in which the heavy English battleships responded. At one moment they were headed directly into the mouth of the Chesapeake, a minute later they were jibing, and four minutes after that they had turned inside their own wake to head in precisely the opposite direction, taking a course which must produce a collision with the French ships, unless the latter bore away.

By this maneuver the English regained their advantage. They had the wind off their larboard quarter; their heavy guns bore down upon the French; they retained the choice of movement. 'Watch!' Captain Turlock whispered to his son. 'You'll never see this again.'

Majestically, ponderously the two lines of ships drew together; at top speed they moved at less than three miles an hour, but their weight was so formidable that Matt could almost hear the crunching of spars.

Each line was about five miles long. At the rear they were four miles apart, which meant that these ships would not close fast enough to participate in the battle. But the lead ships moved ever closer . . . four hundred yards apart . . . two hundred . . . a hundred . . . and finally close enough for pistol shots.

'When are they going to fire?' Matt asked.

'Soon enough,' his father said, and of a sudden a massive burst of flame exploded from the English ships, and cannonballs ricocheted with fearful effect across the French decks. The battle for the future of America had begun.

Matt would never forget the impact of that first English salvo. Wooden cannonballs had been used in hopes they would throw jagged splinters through the bodies of French sailors, and that is what happened. Before the smoke had cleared, the decks of the French ships were red, and young sailors sped about with buckets of sand to help the gunners maintain their footing, but before the latter could prepare their guns, a second volley of wooden balls exploded, adding to the devastation.

'Why don't they fire back?' Matt cried in frustration.

'They fight different,' his father explained. 'Watch the English spars.' And when Matt did, he saw that whereas the French gunners accomplished little in disrupting the decks of their enemy, they were beginning to knock down his masts and sails.

'Who's winning?' Matt cried.

'No one knows,' his father replied, and for two agonizing hours under a dying summer sun the guns roared, and the implacable ships moved ever closer; even pistols reverberated. The lead ships of the English line created unimaginable devastation on the French decks, already undermanned, and for a while it seemed that the French must crumble. But toward dark the terrible efficiency of their gunfire began to take its toll. Down came the soaring English masts, down fluttered the gallant sails. One English ship after another began to limp, and then to falter, and finally to fall away.

It was a curious fact that in this culminating struggle of the revolution, this engagement foreseen by Washington as the one which would determine everything, not a single American participated. Gunners from Marseille and Bordeaux took part and young officers from Kent and Sussex, but no Americans. There were no sailors from Nantucket, nor sharpshooters from New Hampshire, nor sloops nor frigates from Boston. The fate of America was being determined by Frenchmen engaged in mortal collision with Englishmen.

When the day ended, neither fleet had won. No colors were struck. No ship was sunk. Of course, the English admirals decided to burn the *Terrible,* sorely damaged, but later this was held to be a craven act. Captain Turlock, who was close enough to see the *Terrible* while she lay wallowing, gave it as his opinion that 'six watermen from the Choptank could have sailed that ship to the Channel and captured four prizes on the way.' But she was burned.

This engagement was one of the decisive battles of history, for when it terminated, with the French line of battle still impregnable, the English had to withdraw, leaving the Chesapeake open to the French fleet. Rochambeau was now able to bring thousands of French soldiers south for the final thrust against Cornwallis; the iron blockade of the Atlantic ports was broken.

It became a battle without a name, a triumph without a celebration. It accomplished nothing but the freedom of America, the establishment of a new system of government against which all others would eventually compare themselves, and a revision of the theory of empire. The only American in a position to perceive these consequences as they happened was a barefooted waterman from the Choptank who watched on the morning of September 6, 1781, as the great ships of the English line turned slowly north in retreat.

'Now we can go home,' he told Mr. Semmes. 'They won't be back.'

Among the French soldiers unloaded by Admiral de Grasse's fleet was a young colonel bearing the illustrious name of Vauban, a collateral descendant of that Marshal Vauban who in 1705 had laid down the rules for siege warfare. Young Vauban had come to America to embellish his reputation, and was overjoyed to discover that General Cornwallis had retreated into a fortified position from which he could be expelled only by a protracted siege. Throwing himself upon General Washington, he proclaimed, 'Mon General, I shall show you how to subdue this English-man!' And before permission was granted, this energetic young man had put together a makeshift team whose bible would be *Rule of Siege,* a handbook compiled by himself on the principles of the great Vauban and printed in Paris. As soon as he saw where Cornwallis had holed up, he knew what had to be done.

'General Washington, it's all really very simple. A classic siege.'

On his own recognizance he crossed the Chesapeake to enlist the aid of Simon Steed. 'I need an interpreter so that I can talk with the men, and you speak French. I need a hundred more workmen who can also fire rifles, and I have been told that your Choptank men are the best.'

As to the former request, Steed pointed out that he was fifty-one years old and scarcely the man for hand-to-hand combat, to which young Vauban said airily, 'My great-great-grandfather conducted major sieges when he was seventy. All you have to do is talk and find me a hundred men.'

For enlistment of the sharpshooters, Steed sought the help of Captain Turlock, who said, 'Hell, we got a hundred Turlocks who love to fight.' Actually, when he loaded the *Whisper* with men and ammunition, there were eleven Turlocks aboard, a collection of scoundrels so mangy that Colonel Vauban said, 'You're bringing me rats.' When Steed translated this, Turlock said, 'Muskrats. Wait'll you see them dig.'

From all parts of the Eastern Shore similar contingents set out for Yorktown, and when Vauban assembled them he said in flowery exuber-ance, 'Men, we're about to show America what a siege is.'

He wore a white-and-gold uniform which he studiously protected from smears, so that the ragged and often shoeless watermen scorned him, but when they had finished digging the trenches he devised, they found to their surprise that approaches to the English fortifications had been so cleverly planned, they could move with impunity, for the English marksmen could never get a good shot at them.

It became apparent to Simon Steed that General Cornwallis was doomed; the French soldiers, who dominated the action, had only to march in and take the place, and in staff meetings with General Washington he said so. This infuriated Colonel Vauban. 'Gentlemen! We must conduct the siege properly,' and out came the handbook explaining how a gentleman behaved in the final stages of a siege. 'We must show force,' he said, 'and then we must breach the wall.'

'We don't have to breach the wall,' one of Washington's aides protested. 'We can starve them out.'

'Starve!' Vaugan exploded. 'Gentlemen, this is a siege!' And he proceeded to position his watermen outside the walls of the English fort and lead them in a manual of arms which he had devised. The men were bearded, filthy, ragged and insolent, but they went through the motions on the grounds that 'this one knows something.' When English marksmen on the parapets began firing at the ragtag colonials, Vauban ignored them haughtily and continued his drill. At the conclusion he said, 'Now they know our strength. They're cringing.'

He told the committee of generals that according to the rules, they must now expect certain developments: 'General Cornwallis is obligated to try a sortie. Tonight.'

'That would be suicidal!' a rough-shirted American general protested.

'But he must!' Vauban said. And leafing through his manual, he found the passage regulating the deportment of the commander being besieged:

> 'The honor of arms requires that the officer besieged make at least one honest effort to break through the lines of the besieging enemy and to inflict as much damage on the siege installations as practical. To avoid such sorties is to surrender any claim to honor.'

'But we'll shoot his ass off,' the American said.

'That's no concern of his!' Vauban said, aghast. 'It's a matter of honor.'

'Honor hell, he's whipped.'

Such a statement was outside the pale, and Vauban ignored it. 'The second obligation is ours. We must attempt to breach the fortifications. I shall start in the morning.'

'We don't need any breach,' the Americans argued, and they were right. With the Chesapeake under the control of Admiral de Grasse's ships, Cornwallis was doomed. Within a week he must surrender, and breaching the fortifications was a senseless exercise, but again Vauban produced his *Rule of Siege:*

'For the attacking general to refrain from breaching the fortifications, or at least attempting to do so, is to disclose a deficiency in honor. To win the siege with any show of dignity, he must assault the walls.'

That night, as Vauban had predicted, General Cornwallis mounted a sortie. His men marched straight into American fire, and they kept coming until they reached a battery of cannon, which they spiked. They then marched back inside their walls, and the siege continued. By noon the next day the cannon were back in operation, and only eleven Englishmen and four colonials were dead.

To Vauban's disgust, the breaching of the fortifications was not necessary. He had his men primed for it, all eleven Turlocks ready with charges of powder, and the clever trenches dug, but before the men could swing into operation, General Cornwallis surrendered. Now came Vauban's finest hour.

The question arose as to how the English should turn over their fort and their guns to the victors, and fiery debate ensued, at the center of which stood Colonel Vauban, aided by his interpreter, Simon Steed. General Cornwallis demanded full military honors, including the traditional right of marching his men, flags unfurled and muskets ashoulder, out through the fortifications while the English band played some American tune to show respect for the valor of those who had forced surrender.

'No! No!' Vauban protested, and with Steed supporting him in a mélange of French and English, he whipped out his book and turned to one of the profound passages:

'At the end of the siege, if it be successful, the defeated general is entitled to march his men through the walls, their flags proudly unfurled, their arms in position, and it is traditional for the band of the defeated side to play, as the men march, some military tune treasured by the victors, as testimony to the valor of the assault.'

The English at the meeting jumped on this as justification for just what General Cornwallis was demanding, but now Vauban asked Steed to read the rest of that passage:

'But this tradition is honored only if the defeated army can march through the walls using a breach which they forced the attacking army to make. If the surrender takes place while the walls remain unbreached, this can only mean that the defenders showed a lack of determination in defending their position, and they surrender all claim to honors. They march unarmed, with flags furled. Their band is not allowed to play a tune of the victors, for they have proved themselves deficient in military honor.'

After hearing these harsh words, one of the English generals leaped forward and struck the book from Steed's hands. 'There was no deficiency of honor, sir.'

But Colonel Vauban interceded. Going to the Englishman, he said, 'I tried my best to breach the walls for you. But they wouldn't help.' He indicated the Americans. 'And your Cornwallis was too quick with the white flag. One more day and I would have made the breach.' He kissed the general and retired, his eyes filled with tears, but he would not allow the English to come through the undemolished gates with military honors. Their guns were stacked, their flags were furled, and their band had to play one of their own tunes, *The World Turned Upside Down*.

But the English generals had their revenge. That night they refused to dine, as the honors of war demanded, with the American victors. 'The Americans didn't defeat us. The French did.' They dined with Rochambeau and his staff, but as they drank wine afterward Colonel Vauban said, 'The barefoot men I brought across the bay are a sad lot. Filled with lice, and not one of them could read. But they had their own kind of virtue. I doubt that free America will be a pleasant place. But it will develop its own virtue.'

Victory should have brought Simon Steed honors and rewards. It didn't.

In Nantes he had served the colonies well, and in smuggling needed supplies he had been most ingenious, sacrificing four of his ships in doing so. Also, he had brought more than a hundred men to the final siege, where he had served with General Washington, and when offices were being handed out at the end of the war he felt entitled to one in which he could at least recoup the costs of his four schooners. He got nothing.

There were too many rumors that he had profited outrageously from the war; his speculation in the various paper issues was known and in some quarters grudgingly admired, for consistently he had guessed right, doubling his investments whenever he did so. But his dealing in soldiers' scrip was another matter, for here he was making profit on the heroism of others.

Actually, the charge was unfair, as the case of Wilmer Turlock proved. He had fought through the first five years of the war, always complaining but always present. He had also volunteered for the final siege at Yorktown and for his services had received a printed promise from the Continental Congress that at some future date he would receive $480. The trouble began when he told his Uncle Teach, 'I need the money now.'

'They ain't payin' it now.'

'How'm I goin' to get it?'

'There's men buyin' the notes on speculation,' the captain said.

'Who?'

'Sam Deats, upriver.'

Turlock had gone to Deats, a miserable man, who snarled, 'I'm payin' one for eight.'

'What's that mean?'

'For your four-eighty I give you sixty.'

'That's robbery!'

'I didn't ask you to come here. I'm takin' the risk, not you.'

'But Congress will pay.'

'Then wait for Congress and don't bother me.' And when Wilmer went to other speculators, he found them offering one for ten.

It was then that his uncle suggested, 'Go to Devon. Simon Steed's a difficult man but he's honest,' and the young soldier sailed down to the island, where Mr. Steed drew up a paper on which Wilmer made his mark:

> On January 19, 1785, I approached Simon Steed, begging him to accept my Warrant of Pay. Mr. Steed advised me three times to hold on to it, assuring me that Congress would pay, but when I said I had to have my money now, he warned me that he could pay me only one in six. I told him others were paying only one in eight or one in ten, so he took my Warrant for $480 and handed me $80, which I willingly accepted.

Steed had a pile of such receipts and they proved that he had invariably advised the young soldiers to hold on to their scrip, and then paid better than the going price. But in the end one fact stood out: because he had hard money when the soldiers had none, he had been able to buy their scrip for one sixth its value. And when Congress redeemed the scrip at par, as he always predicted it would, he earned six hundred-percent interest for what amounted to a loan of fourteen months.

But even this tight-fisted action would not have been disqualifying; throughout Maryland and the other new states many financiers had profited in this manner, but Simon's case was tainted by his larger dealings with the government itself. In 1777 in the city of Nantes, Benjamin Franklin had proposed that Simon serve as purchasing agent for the fledgling government, and commissions had been issued appointing him to this post.

All agreed that Steed had performed ably, smuggling in necessary supplies in his various ships. Indeed, his *Whisper* had become legendary for her feats in slipping into and out of St. Eustatius; her contribution was heroic, and without the sinews of battle she delivered to

Baltimore and Boston, the course of the war might have been altered.

But now it was being divulged that whenever one of Steed's schooners put in at St. Eustatius, this kind of transaction took place: Two bales of prime cordage from the Low Countries, purchased at £ Sterling 50. Same sold at Baltimore for £ Sterling 120. Commission to Simon Steed for procuring and handling same, 33 1/3% or £ Sterling 40. Thus, on one shipment of cordage costing 50, Steed made a final profit of 110. True, he took risks with the *Whisper* and he did have to pay the captain and crew, but even with those deductions, his profit had been stupendous.

When calculations were completed, Congress found that this unassuming Eastern Shore gentleman had milked the government of more than four hundred thousand pounds sterling, and his name became anathema: 'Richer than Simon Steed.' 'Patriotism for sale at six cents on the dollar.' Any hope that he might have had for preferment in the new government vanished.

He retired to Devon, living alone in the great house, spending his afternoons wandering aimlessly in the spacious wooded garden designed by his Grandmother Rosalind. The oak grew nobler with each passing decade and in autumn the pyracantha flamed. The hollies were substantial trees now, the females laden with red berries, the males stern and aloof like their master. And in the early summer when the burnt gold of daylilies flooded the banks, Simon believed that no spot in Maryland could be more handsome.

At such times, when nature was so benevolent, he thought of his missing wife and daughter; his loneliness did not make him bitter, for he understood why Jane Fithian had found rural America so distasteful, but he did sometimes indulge himself in wry amusement: She scorned us. Used to ask how louts like Washington and Jefferson could presume to negotiate with a king. We negotiated.

He missed Penny. Each year during the long war—nine of them, from 1775 through '83—he had managed somehow to deliver into England letters of credit upon which his wife and daughter could draw, and all that he received in return had been one silhouette showing a child of five wearing pigtails. He had sent it to Annapolis to be encased in gold, and now it hung on a chain near his bed.

Often since the end of war he had contemplated quitting Maryland altogether and going to England to live with his family, or perhaps taking them to France, but after consulting by mail with Guy Fithian he rejected that plan, because the factor wrote:

> I can serve you best by frankness. My sister is not entirely herself, despite the fact that we have given her the best care that England can provide. She slips into such furious tirades against the traitors in America that seeing you again would be disastrous. Penny thrives

and gives no evidence of following her mother into partial but heartbreaking insanity. She loves you for the money you send each year.

When he reflected on this painful situation he sometimes thought that he had been taxed too heavily for his patriotism: he had lost his wife, his daughter, his nephew, his fleet and his honor.

How lonely he became, holding more than two hundred thousand pounds sterling and only God knew how many livres tournois and Spanish doubloons and Portuguese big-joes. Two or three times a year he would entertain at Rosalind's Revenge, and then boats from all over the Chesapeake would congregate in Devon Creek, and slaves would carry portmanteaus to the big rooms and the two wings would be filled, and forty would sit down to dinner in that splendid dining hall erected by Rosalind Janney Steed, and Simon would preside, listening to the small talk but not engaging in it.

Early on the morning of Wednesday, April 15, 1789, a gentleman in uniform named Major Lee hurried down to the dock at Mount Vernon in Virginia, where two rowers were waiting to ferry him across the Potomac River.

As soon as they deposited him on the Maryland shore he ran to where two other men in military uniform were waiting with fresh horses. Major Lee vaulted into his saddle and set off in a gallop for Annapolis. At every inn or crossroads church where people might be gathered, he called out the exciting news, 'General Washington's to be our President.' Invariably, cheers rose from the listeners, and as he dashed on, Lee could see the Marylanders scattering to inform their neighbors of the good news, indeed, the only news that would have made any sense on that historic day. Who but Washington had the measure of acceptance and skill required to launch the new Constitution?

At the state house in Annapolis, Major Lee discovered, to his pique, that news of the election had already been disseminated, but he was pleased to observe the cheering crowds who came out to greet him as a messenger who had actually seen Washington at Mount Vernon.

'He'll stop by here tomorrow on his way to the capital,' Lee assured his listeners. 'He begins his reign as soon as he takes the oath in New York.'

But Major Lee had not ridden from Mount Vernon in order to converse with the politicians of Annapolis. After congratulating them on the way in which their representatives had helped select the new President, he spurred his horse to the dock, where a pinnace manned by four sailors waited. Jumping in, he directed the men, 'Down to Devon Island. Quick.'

The sailors raised small sails on the two short masts, then sprang a jib forward, but the wind was chancy and even after they had cleared the mole guarding the harbor they made only fitful progress, and nightfall found them drifting aimlessly on the broad expanse of the Chesapeake. Stars appeared occasionally, dim and distant above the flapping canvas, but no wind rose to help them make the crossing.

At four in the morning Major Lee asked the captain of the pinnace, 'Shall we row?' and the captain studied the situation, looking into the darkness in all directions.

Before committing his men to the ugly chore, he asked, 'Will we be sailing north immediately?'

'We spend only a few hours at Devon. Then north.'

'Then I won't ask the men to row out of the calm. The wind will rise.'

'But when?' Lee asked in the darkness.

'It will rise,' the officer assured him.

So Lee fretted through the long night, and at five-thirty, when light was beginning to show in the east, he fell asleep. When he woke, the day was about him and a brisk wind pushed in from the northwest. The captain of the pinnace did not say, 'I told you so.' He was satisfied that his men had escaped the job of rowing that heavy boat out of the doldrums.

It was eight in the morning when the pinnace sighted Devon, and as soon as it entered the creek slaves hailed its arrival, shouting, 'Master! Master!' but imparting no specific news. When the pinnace worked its way up to the Steed wharf some thirty persons waited to greet the major, who ignored them, pushed his way through, and ran up to Simon Steed, embracing him. 'General Washington sends his regards. He's to be our new President!'

A cheer rose from whites and blacks at this reassuring news, and Steed nodded gravely, as if the cheers had been intended for him. To the crowd he said, 'How could we have chosen any other?' and they all cheered again.

Major Lee brought heady news: 'The general is crossing from Annapolis to Chestertown and hopes to converse with you there before he proceeds to New York and his new duties.'

As these words were said, Steed felt a glow of renewed confidence; doubtless the new President had decided upon some position of significance for his Eastern Shore deputy. And as the crowd milled about Major Lee, seeking added information, Steed withdrew, as if in a trance, speculating on what his responsibility might be: I've worked with ships all my life and could handle the navy. Or I'd be adequate in some post dealing with commerce or the nation's money.

His reverie was broken when Lee tugged on his arm. 'The general wants Paxmore and Turlock, too.'

This diluted sharply the intimacy of the meeting, and Steed asked in some dismay, 'Shall we be going in your boat?' and Lee further dampened the excitement by saying, 'No, I'm to pick up some others on the way,' and Steed thought to himself: It's not to be a meeting. It's a convention.

'I'll ready my sloop at once,' he told Lee, who reminded him, 'Be sure to fetch Paxmore and Turlock.'

Simon broke out a small boat and sailed directly to Peace Cliff, where he informed Paxmore of the meeting, and together they sailed to the marshes. At first they had difficulty finding the entrance to the myriad streams that segmented the marsh, but Paxmore remembered certain landmarks that led to Turlock Creek, which they penetrated cautiously, as if trying to avoid an ambuscade. Through the years men along the Eastern Shore had learned to approach this place with care.

'Halloo!' one of Steed's sailors called. There was no response.

'Call again,' Steed ordered, but the slave was reluctant to do anything that might anger those hiding in the marsh. 'Give the call!' Steed commanded.

'Halloo!' the slave trumpeted, and the echo had barely died when a shot rang out. The men in the boat could hear the pellets rip through the dried grass.

'Stop where you are!' a ghostly voice warned.

'Captain Turlock!' Steed called back. 'It's me. Steed.'

A second shot ripped through the grass and this angered Steed. 'Damn it, man! President Washington wants to meet you. In Chestertown.'

From the marsh a disembodied voice called, 'Cap'm Turlock, he ain't here.'

'Where is he?' Steed called into the emptiness.

'On the porch.' And from the grass appeared a lanky youth of nineteen, carrying a musket, a marsh dog at his heel. He wore few clothes, no shoes, no hat. He was a surly waterman, but when he saw Steed his begrimed face broke into a broad smile and he said, 'I knowed you at Yorktown.'

'Did you fight there?'

'Didn't fight. Wore my ass off diggin' trenches.'

'Where's Teach?' Steed asked, and the young man led the way through devious trails to the cabin.

There, barefooted, dressed in patched homespun, scratching his beard, sat the man who had terrorized the Caribbean. 'Mr. Steed, it's good to see you!'

'President Washington wants us to visit with him in Chestertown.'

'When?'

'Tonight.'

'We better get movin',' and the grizzled captain left the porch, spent a few minutes inside the cabin, and reappeared in a passable costume:

baggy homespun trousers, heavy shirt woven from flax and cotton, shoes made from muskrat skins and a coonskin hat.

He showed the Steed slaves a shortcut through the marsh, and within an hour the three men were aboard the sloop, heading northwest for Knapps Narrows, where Steed announced the news to the people of Bay Hundred. Once in the Chesapeake, they sped north for the difficult passage at Kent Narrows, proposing to reach Chestertown at about the same time that Washington would be landing for his overnight stop.

But bad luck overtook them in the lee of Kent Island; the brisk wind was masked by trees, and a whole afternoon was idled away, with Steed growing more and more impatient. 'Can't you move this boat?'

'The men could try rowing.'

'Then get them to rowing.' But this accomplished little, and the day ended with the Choptank men wasting their time at the mouth of the Chester River, while the new President celebrated with friends in Chestertown.

At dawn the next morning Steed was beside himself with frustration. 'Can we get horses?' he asked his captain.

'No horses, no roads.'

'Well, damn this wind.'

It was ten in the morning before the trio reached Chestertown, and as Steed had feared, Washington had left at dawn for Warwick, the next stopping place on the way to New York. Steed asked the innkeeper if three horses could be found, and the man replied, 'Washington's men took 'em all.'

'Find some!' Steed commanded.

'Who's to pay?'

'I'll pay.'

'And who are you?'

'Simon Steed of Devon.'

The innkeeper nodded and said, 'In that case the farmers may have something.'

'Get them here.'

So the innkeeper sent two of his helpers to round up some horses, but the owners came with them, demanding payment in full for the unlikely beasts. They were not for hire. 'I'll buy them,' Steed said, but Levin Paxmore would not allow this. 'Thee is charging outrageous prices,' he remonstrated as the two farmers stared at him. 'Mr. Steed requires these horses to overtake General Washington . . . for a most important meeting.'

One of the farmers pointed at Teach Turlock and grinned. 'He's goin' to see Washington?'

'He is,' Paxmore said quietly. 'He was a notable fighter in the late war.'

'What's 'is name?'

'Teach Turlock.'

The farmers gaped, then began shouting to bystanders, 'Hey, this is Teach Turlock!' And they grabbed the captain's hand, shouting excitedly, 'You damned near burned up this bay with the *Whisper*. Captain Turlock, you were a mighty man.'

And one of the farmers said, 'If you want to rent horses, Turlock, you can sure rent 'em from us,' and the three Choptank men set off in pursuit of their President. At Georgetown they crossed the Sassafras River, galloped north to Cecilton, then followed a mean and dusty road into Warwick, where crowds of farming people clustered at the crossroads.

'Where's the general?' Steed asked.

'He's stopping at the Heath place.'

'I saw him ride in,' a woman said reverently, and children shouted, 'He's sleepin' in that house.'

In the road, his arms crossed, stood Major Lee, protecting the farmhouse in which his general slept. When Steed rode up, the major indicated that he must dismount and leave his horse behind. 'We missed you,' he said.

'Damned wind.'

'Yes, it started to die just as we cleared the Narrows.'

'Slept standing up, cursing the wind,' Steed explained.

'The general will be pleased you came. He asked for you repeatedly.' At this gratifying news Steed beamed, but what Lee said next deflated him. 'The general yearns for a good card game, and when he rises he'll be eager to play. Catch some sleep on the bench, Steed. He may want to play all night.'

This kind of visit was not what Simon had envisaged. Indeed, through the long windless night he had rehearsed the topics he wished to discuss with the new President, and cardplaying was not one of them. But he was determined to accomplish two goals on this trip: to present himself in the best possible light, and to nail down some assurances as to how the Eastern Shore was to be governed.

Accordingly, he did not accept the bench offered by the major; instead he carried his canvas bag out to the wash house, where he soaped down, combed, touched himself with perfume and donned fresh clothes. When he was finished he presented the fine figure of a fifty-nine-year-old patriot eager to serve in whatever capacity the new President might determine.

Washington did not arise till about six-thirty in the evening, at which time Major Lee informed him that the Choptank men had arrived. Without attending to his dress, Washington hurried from his sleeping quarters, saw Steed standing at attention and acknowledged him briefly, then spotted Levin Paxmore, the shipbuilder, and hurried to him. Grasping his fire-scarred hands, Washington said, 'What sturdy ships you build.'

'Four of them ended fighting for the English.'

'Ah, but the *Whisper* that fought for us helped determine the battle. Keep your hat, Friend Paxmore. You've earned the privilege.'

He then spotted Captain Turlock and stood before him admiringly, hands on hips, unable to speak. Finally he grasped the waterman by the shoulders, pressed them vigorously and said, 'I confess a special fondness for brave men,' and he began to recite some of the adventures Turlock had experienced. 'They almost trapped you at St. Eustatius, didn't they?'

'They did get my sister ship. That was a sore defeat.'

'We've all had them,' Washington said. 'You should be an admiral, sir.'

'I can't read or write,' Turlock replied.

Washington laughed and asked, 'What do you plan to do now?'

'A little fishin',' Turlock said, and Washington guffawed.

'Major Lee!' he called in a resounding voice. 'Take note of this man, and note him well. The only one in America who doesn't seek an appointment.' He laughed again, then bowed deeply, adding, 'You were most helpful, Captain.'

Then he returned to Colonel Steed, saying heartily, 'Damned glad you overtook us, Steed. I am most hungry for some cards.' And he led the way to a small room which Major Lee had arranged for this night. It contained a table, six chairs, two lamps on high stands and three spittoons. Two planters from the Warwick area had been waiting since five and were eager for the game to start. A Colonel Witherspoon who was riding with Washington took a chair, but when the general and Steed sat down, there remained one empty space.

'I do like six to a game,' Washington said. 'Friend Paxmore, would you take a hand?'

'I would not,' the Quaker said.

'How about Major Lee?' Steed asked.

'I will not allow him to lose any further,' Washington said.

Colonel Witherspoon pointed at Captain Turlock. 'Do you play?'

'Some.'

'Sit down,' and Turlock took the sixth chair. When the first hand was dealt he looked at his cards and muttered, 'Jesus Christ!' Washington stopped arranging his cards and stared at the swamp man, and Colonel Witherspoon said reprovingly, 'We don't use oaths, Captain Turlock.'

'You would if you saw these cards,' Turlock replied, and Washington smiled.

After the third hand the general said graciously, 'Steed, I am gratified to an extent I cannot express that you have seen fit to visit with us. One of my first tasks in New York will be to ask the Congress to recompense you for your lost ships.'

'I would be grateful,' Steed said, and then he waited, knowing that this was the moment in which the new President ought to say something about an assignment in the forthcoming government, but nothing was said, and Turlock ruptured the spell by grunting, 'Your deal, General.'

As midnight approached, Major Lee led Levin Paxmore out of the house and onto the roadway, where they talked for some hours, while the locals sat along the road, watching the house where their beloved hero was meeting in high consultation with the leaders of the region. 'Gad, how I'd love to be in that game,' Lee confessed.

'Thee likes cards so much?'

'I'm a fanatic, but I seem always to lose, and the general's forbidden me to play.' They walked along the dark road for some minutes, then Lee said, 'Of course, he always loses too. But he says the difference is he can afford it.'

'Does he play so much?'

'Before the war, almost every night. He kept an account book of each night's play, and it shows that he lost heavily. During the war I never saw him play but once. During the cold days at Valley Forge. And of course he lost. He'll lose tonight, you can be sure of that, and I'll enter it in the book. *Chestertown, lost three pounds, sixteen shillings, nine pence.*'

'This is Warwick.'

'They all seem the same. We approach the towns. The people storm out. They drown him with adulation. This land has never seen a hero like Washington, nor will again.'

'Is he so fine?' Paxmore asked.

'You saw him. Six feet four. He towers above ordinary men.'

'I mean morally.'

'He puzzles me,' Lee confessed. 'He places his whole destiny in the hands of God, serves Him with devotion. But like a soldier, not a puling clergyman.' In the darkness Major Lee permitted silence to indicate his confusion.

'Will he make a good President?'

'The finest. No man could prove his equal. He stands alone, a monument to integrity.' Another pause and then, 'But there are contradictions. You know, of course, that he gained enormous approval by his refusal to accept any salary as general of the colonial armies. That's right, never accepted a shilling of pay. Said over and over that a patriot should serve his country in time of danger and pay no heed to the cost.'

'That was admirable,' Paxmore said, but he did not point out that in the dark days of the war he had built three ships for the Continental navy, in addition to those for Steed, and that since the revolutionaries had had no funds, he had borne most of the cost himself. Also, his boatyard had been burned and his best workmen conscripted into the army.

Even had he enjoyed cards, he would not have dared to play this night, for the war had left him largely impoverished; but to learn that General Washington had also served without pay was heartening. But then Major Lee added, 'What Washington did was refuse a salary but demand an expense account. I helped him make it out, and he listed everything—his son's expenses, wine for the mess, a carriage for himself and four more carriages for his friends, rations, guns, braid for his jackets, axes for the woods. Thinking back on those accounts, they were extraordinary.'

'I could make out such an account for my shipyard,' Paxmore said, 'and would do so, if asked.'

'Yes,' Lee conceded. 'Each item submitted was an honest figure. But whether some of them should have been submitted remains dubious. All I know is that when there was talk of Washington's becoming President, he again volunteered to serve without pay—just expenses. And the committee told him with some firmness, "Oh no, sir! This time you must accept a salary!" They told me later, "No new nation could survive another of his damned expense accounts." '

They now turned and walked back down the road past the house where the players were intent on their cards. They could see General Washington studying with some disgust a hand which Captain Turlock had just dealt, and Paxmore asked, 'Is he capable of governing? I mean, soldiers are sometimes both obstinate and deficient in knowledge.'

'He's not read much,' Lee confided. 'I rarely see him with a book. He's certainly no Adams or Jefferson, but maybe they read too much.'

Up and down the silent road they walked, touching upon all aspects of the new position that Washington was moving into: the military appointments, the finances, the judgeships, the building up of a merchant navy, the admission of new states carved out of the western lands, the entire gamut of government—while the general continued playing cards.

'I never knew my father,' Lee confided toward two in the morning. 'So perhaps my good opinion of the general is weighted in his favor. But I've served with him since I was a boy in 1774, and no finer man ever walked on the soil of this continent. He may not prove to be a capable President, but he'll be a just one. And he'll provide a symbol, stronger and brighter every year.'

He reflected on this, and after they had passed the cardplayers again he said, 'At the meetings related to the revolution we had many fine orators, and I heard most of them. I never heard a finer intellect than that stubby little lawyer from Philadelphia, James Wilson. Ben Franklin could make a point, too, and John Adams could be devastating. But the best speech I ever heard was given by George Washington, who never said much.

'It was in 1774, I think, when the British were bombarding Boston and we in the south didn't know how to respond. That day the oratory contained much fire and more confusion, but when everything seemed to be lost in chaos, Washington—I think he was only a colonel then . . .' He hesitated. 'Virginia militia, it must have been.

'Anyway, when it seemed that we must allow Boston to fight alone, this man stood up and spoke one sentence. Just one sentence, and when he sat down the whole history of the colonies was changed.'

'What did he say?'

' "Gentlemen, I will raise one thousand men, outfit and pay them at my own expense, and march myself at their head for the relief of Boston." '

Paxmore said, 'I think I need sleep. I shall be going inside.'

Major Lee said, 'I'll keep guard out here.'

When Paxmore entered the gaming room it was half after three and Teach Turlock had only a few shillings on the table. 'If you president as well as you play cards,' he said admiringly to Washington, 'this country will be all right.'

Turlock lost that hand and decided to quit the game. 'Come on, Friend Paxmore,' he said, 'we'll catch some sleep.' And he lay down on the floor outside the door while the Quaker made his way to a back room where a dozen men were stretched out.

Now came the part that General Washington enjoyed most. It was four in the morning, deadly quiet in all parts of the night except in this room where the candles flickered. The game was down to just four players, one of the local landowners having dropped out, and each surviving player knew the established peculiarities of the others. Simon Steed played an absolutely straightforward game, no bluff. Colonel Witherspoon played for every advantage, studied each card, each adversary with minute attention and won more than his share of hands. The planter was a good player, willing to take extraordinary risks if he detected even a slight edge in his favor. And General Washington was proving himself to be what he always had been: a cautious, stubborn defender of his shillings, a niggardly man when it came to betting, a daring man when he saw a chance to win a big pot, but so transparent in his positions that he was destined always to lose if the game continued long enough.

'Your majesty,' Steed said at five in the morning, 'I think I have the better of you.'

'I do not take kindly to that appellation,' Washington replied, holding his losing cards close to his sweaty shirt.

'Sire, this country yearns for royal trappings,' Steed insisted.

'I prefer mister.'

'The people will not permit it. Believe me, Sire, we Americans may have thrown out one set of royalty, but we are most hungry to adopt another . . . a better, that is. And you're that better.'

Washington tapped his chin with his cards. 'Others have said what you say, Steed, and there's much common sense in what you advise. It may well be that in the end we shall have to have a royalty. But in this game you must not address a man as Sire when you intend to cut his throat. What cards are you hiding against me, Steed of Devon?'

The game broke up at a quarter to six. Major Lee, hearing the commotion, came to the door of the room to announce, 'The horses are ready, sir.'

'We'd better be on our way to Wilmington,' Washington replied. 'Shall we take thirty minutes to wash up, Witherspoon?'

'Did you lose again?' Lee asked impishly.

'You can mark me down in the book,' Washington replied, 'as having lost two pounds, twelve and three.'

'Warwick has proved costly,' Lee said.

'It was worth it to meet once more my comrade in arms at Yorktown,' Washington said, throwing his long right arm about Steed's shoulder, and with that, he retired to the washhouse. There would be no confidential talk of government position, but Washington was not an unfeeling man and when he returned from his toilet and saw the bleak look on Steed's face, he went to him, took him by the hand and said bluntly, 'My dear friend, I would give an arm to have you at my side.' He paused. 'But the scandals. Impossible. Impossible.' And he marched to the horses.

But before he reached them he was stopped by Teach Turlock, who produced from a filthy bag a paper which he had cherished since 1776; it was the Rector of Wrentham's cession of Turlock's hundred acres. 'Please, General Washington, restore my land.'

The President studied the paper, asked Turlock and Steed a few questions, then called for Major Lee to bring him a quill. Sitting on a bench at the door to the farmhouse he added this endorsement to the precious document:

To my old comrade in arms, Governor John Eager Howard

Rarely have I seen a document so shot through with fraud and force and forgery as this, but rarely have I heard supporting evidence from reliable witnesses as solid as that which bulwarks this claim. I pray you, lend good ear to the supplication of the Patriot, Teach Turlock, that his lands be restored.

Geo. Washington

In the roadway a throng of hundreds waited to applaud their hero, and in his red-and-blue riding coat he made a handsome figure, bowing gravely right and left. Major Lee provided a small stool to help him mount, and when he sat astride his large chestnut, he looked more noble than ever.

'Great wishes, Sire,' Steed called, tears beginning to form.

'We shall face difficult tasks, all of us,' Washington said as he rode off, attended by cheers that would not cease till he reached New York.

The three Choptank men, without having consulted one another, mounted their horses and followed for some miles as if drawn by a powerful magnet. When the time came to turn back, Major Lee rode up to bid them farewell. To Steed he said, 'The general asked me to say that you will have access to him as long as you both shall live. He prizes you as one of the true servants of this nation.'

But to Levin Paxmore he whispered, as their horses moved in the early sunlight, 'I spoke perhaps too freely under the stars. You'll keep what I said confidential?'

'I shall honor thy request,' Paxmore said, whereupon Lee pressed into the Quaker's hand a personal communication from Washington. Paxmore waited to open it until he had returned to his desk at the boatyard. Then carefully he unfolded the paper, spread it smoothly, and read:

Friend Paxmore

You must submit at your earliest convenience a true accounting of the costs you incurred in building ships for our cause, less whatever funds were advanced you by the Congress. And I shall do my best to see that you are paid in full, because all free men stand in your debt.

Geo. Washington

That day Levin Paxmore compiled an honest account of every shilling he had spent on the revolution, including the replacement of his sheds and a wage for his wife, and when President Washington signed the authorizing bill, Paxmore was paid in full, and it was this military money that formed the foundation of the Paxmore fortune.

Voyage Seven: 1811

WINTER ALONG THE EASTERN SHORE WAS USU-
ally clement. An occasional freezing of some salt-free river, or a desultory fall of snow which soon melted, indicated that winter was at hand,
but because of the modifying effects of both the Atlantic and the Chesapeake, temperatures never dropped very low.

But in January 1811 there came a sudden snowfall of some inches, and
farmers along the shore stayed indoors until it passed. Thomas Applegarth, twenty-seven years old, unmarried, tenant on a farm near Patamoke owned by the Steeds, used these days of enforced idleness to study
a book lent him by Elizabeth Paxmore, for whom he sometimes did odd
jobs. It was a geography of the eastern states, and what impressed him
was the manner in which the mountains of Pennsylvania drifted in a
marked direction from northeast to southwest. Even the dullest mind
would have deduced, from this new map, that some extraordinary force
had determined the lay of these mountains, but what that might have
been, Applegarth had not enough training to detect.

Yet as he studied the map he vaguely recalled something he had read
recently about events that had occurred long ago in Europe, but what
precisely they were he could not remember. And then, toward dusk, as
it came time for him to tend the cattle, he put down his book, went out
and walked along a frozen path to the barn, and as he did so he came
upon a small accumulation of ice under a tree, and suddenly the whole
mystery of the Pennsylvania mountains and the formation of the Chesapeake became clear to him, as if someone had struck a monstrous match
in a darkened valley: Ice! That's what it was that scarred the mountains
of Europe. And that's what dug out our valleys in America!

He could not grasp what an ice age was, nor the vastness of the sheet that had at one time lain over Pennsylvania, but he saw clearly one fact: that the ice sheet must have contained within it an enormous quantity of water, and when the ice finally melted, that water must have formed a gigantic river, parent to the present Susquehanna. And that river, nothing else, had reamed out the Chesapeake Bay and deposited the silt which had become, in time, the Eastern Shore.

His concept was so grand, and its parts fell together so neatly, that as he milked the cows in the shadows thrown by his lantern he existed in a kind of glory. 'That's how it must have happened,' he whispered to himself. 'The world up north was imprisoned under a mantle of ice, and when it melted, it scarred the mountains and filled the valleys with tremendous rivers.'

The idea so preoccupied him that on the first clear day he drove down to Peace Cliff to return Mrs. Paxmore's book and ask her whether she believed it was possible for America to have experienced an age of ice.

'A what?' she asked.

'I read that northern Europe—well, this was long ago—it had ice on it.'

'I suppose Russia has ice every year,' she said.

'No, this book said that the entire land had ice hundreds of feet thick . . . all over it.'

'Nothing could have lived,' she protested.

'That's exactly it,' Applegarth said. 'The ice had to be very thick to gouge out the valleys.'

'To what?'

'Have you ever looked at the mountains of Pennsylvania?' he asked.

'I've never been to Pennsylvania.'

'I mean a map.'

'I've never seen a map of Pennsylvania.'

'There's one here in your book.'

'There is?' It irritated the Quaker woman to think that there could be either maps or ideas with which she was not familiar, and she took the book from Applegarth rather rudely and thumbed through it. 'Why, so there is,' she said, and she studied the map with care.

'See how the mountains all run in the same direction?' the farmer said.

'What's that signify?'

'They were gouged out by a heavy layer of ice moving southwest.'

The idea was so novel that Mrs. Paxmore had nothing in her past reflection by which to judge it, but she was one of those Quaker women to whom all knowledge was important, so she stood firmly on her left foot, with her right cocked at an angle, and considered the remarkable thesis that her odd-job man was proposing, and the more she pondered his words, the more inherently reasonable they became. 'It could have happened that way,' she said.

'And if it did,' Applegarth continued, 'then the whole valley of the Susquehanna, as we know it today . . . Well, it must have been a stupendous river. A hundred times bigger than we see it.'

With a solid finger he outlined on the map the principal features of his theory, coming at last to the Chesapeake itself. 'Our bay must have been the mouth of that immense river. What do you think of that?'

In the weeks that followed, and during the long winter nights, Thomas Applegarth and Elizabeth Paxmore studied whatever they could find about ice ages and mountains; they found little. Speculation about the formation of earth features had only just begun in the United States; the fascinating revelations which were being evolved in Europe could not have been known in Patamoke, but one day Mrs. Paxmore did turn up an interesting piece of information.

A professor of moral philosophy at Yale University had been dabbling in scientific matters. And he came up with the interesting concept that a river like the Hudson in New York could best be understood as 'a drowned river valley.' The phrase captivated Mrs. Paxmore and she discussed it with her husband.

'Isn't that a splendid imagination? A river valley which has been drowned, inundated by the sea!'

'Sounds to me like a sad misuse of words,' her husband said. 'A pig can drown. Or a little boy who falls out of his canoe. Because they stop breathing and are drowned. But how could a river drown? Tell me that.'

'It doesn't drown,' she replied. 'It is drowned.'

George Paxmore leaned back to consider this foray into logic. Then, with a brusque wave of his hand, he dismissed the Yale professor, the Hudson River and the Chesapeake. 'No educated man would condone such grammar.'

But when Mrs. Paxmore brought her new theory to her odd-job man, he visualized its application immediately. 'It's what happened!' he said excitedly. 'In the later years, when the ice had mostly melted, the river would begin to lose its force, and the ocean would creep in, and the river mouth would be drowned under the weight of salt water.' It was a concept so intellectually beautiful, and so respondent to observable facts, that it seemed the clincher to previous speculations. He now saw the Susquehanna system in grand design, the remnant of a river which had once drained a major portion of an ice-laden continent, a majestic river which in the end had seen itself overcome by the ever-encroaching sea. He resolved to look into this matter further, when spring came.

Mrs. Paxmore, whose geography book had launched these speculations, pursued her own investigations, looking into all the books she could find and talking rather obsessively to those members of the community better informed than she. She was surprised one evening when her husband pushed back from the table and said, 'Thee may have been right, Elizabeth. I've been studying our bay . . . Well, I've been endeavoring to reconcile what I see with that interesting thesis thee propounded some weeks back. And the more I contemplate, the more I have to conclude that thee has hit upon something.'

He outlined the steps of this thinking: that if the ancient river had indeed been drowned, the resulting bay would be determined partly by the river and partly by the ocean, rather than entirely by the latter. This would mean that there ought to be an orderly progression from entirely fresh water at the mouth of the Susquehanna, where it debouched into the bay, to entirely salt water at the spot where the bay debouched into the sea. 'And that's what I find,' he concluded. 'Most interesting.'

'Thomas Applegarth has been talking about making an expedition to the headwaters of the Susquehanna,' she said. 'I think we ought to help him.'

'We could give him time off. Find some other handyman.'

'I mean with money.'

George Paxmore formed his hands into a little cathedral and contemplated them for some time. Money wasn't wasted on the Eastern Shore, least of all by a Quaker. His wife was making a serious proposal, but it was sensible. Knowledge must always be pursued. 'I think we could let him have twenty-five dollars,' he said.

'Does thee want to tell him?'

'I think thee should. It's been thee who has encouraged him.'

Elizabeth decided that they should both inform their handyman that their family would like to support his scientific investigations to the extent of twenty-five dollars. He was unprepared for this bonanza and for some moments could not respond. Then he said, 'I have fifteen of my own, and I can save at least twenty more by the end of February. I'd like to see the upper river before the snow has melted.'

So on the first of March, 1811, Thomas Applegarth, a farmer of Patamoke on the Eastern Shore, took off in a small sloop and headed for the present mouth of the Susquehanna River. The winds were not propitious, and he required three days to reach Havre de Grace. There he deposited his boat with the owner of a shipyard, and with sixty-three dollars in his pocket, started his exploration of the river.

For fifty cents he employed a man with a canoe to take him as far north as the turbulent rapids at Conowingo. At this point he allowed the canoeist to return home, while he struck out on foot along the left bank of the river, that is, the one to the east. Frequently he was forced to leave the river, for the going was too rough, and on some nights he slept quite a few miles inland from the banks.

But whenever he was able to walk alongside the river itself, or plunge into its icy waters for a cleansing bath, he felt himself to be in some mysterious way purified and closer to the secrets of the past. At the infrequent ferries he would ask to help the rowers, spending whole days moving from shore to shore, so that by the time he reached the first important ferry at Columbia he was a practiced riverman.

But it was not until he had hiked past Harrisburg and got into the mountainous section of Pennsylvania that he began to see the evidences he sought. It was clear to him that in times past this mighty river had been ten or fifteen times as wide as it now was; proof existed in the flat, smooth benchlands stretching east and west from its banks. Surely they had once been the bed of that mighty, long-vanished stream which had carried away the waters of the melting ice. Each day was a revelation, a proof.

When he reached Sunbury, 215 miles from Patamoke, he faced a difficult decision, for north of that settlement were two Susquehanna Rivers. One would take him west to Williamsport, the other east to Wilkes-Barre, and no one whom he consulted could tell him definitely which was the senior river. To his amazement, no settler in Sunbury had explored to the headwaters of either.

'Which throws the bigger body of water?' he asked.

'Come a flood, either does right smart,' the most knowledgeable man replied.

'If you were going to the headwaters, which branch would you take?'

'I ain't goin'.'

'But which would you guess?'

'It don't concern me.'

He located a woman who said, 'In times of freshet, the east branch seems to bring down the biggest trees—liken as if it had come the longest distance.'

'Or it came through the most wooded land.'

'I was takin' that into my calculations,' she said.

Since this was the only substantial evidence he had uncovered, he said, 'That sounds sensible. I'll go east.'

So on the last day of March, Applegarth started the long, difficult journey to Wilkes-Barre, and from there, north to the Indian settlement at Tunkhannock. The going was extremely rough; no boats were able to move upstream, and for long distances there was no road beside the river. For three days he struggled through uncut forests, determined to stay with the river, but in the end he had to abandon this resolve and move onto established roads, regardless of how far adrift they led him.

He felt as if he were exploring virgin land, and sometimes when he had been distant from the river for several days, he would come upon it rushing southward, and he would cry aloud with joy at having discovered an old friend: 'There you are! Beautiful river, holder of secrets!'

He would take off his coat and shoes and step into the waters, and sometimes they would feel so enticing that he would plunge in, forgetful of his clothes, then march along the riverbank until his pants and shirt dried on him. Occasionally he would ride with some farmer going to market; more often he walked alone, for days on end, always probing farther toward the source of his river.

On the long and winding stretch from Tunkhannock to Towanda, a distance of nearly forty miles as he wandered, he met no one, at times splashing his way right up the margins of the river in lieu of roads. He ate sparingly, an end of bread and some cheese, and lost seven pounds doing so. It was in this time of loneliness that he conceived his plan for putting on paper his reflections about the Susquehanna and its relation to the body of water he loved so strongly, the Chesapeake. He would spend whole days formulating a single passage, trying to make it sound important, like the reading he had done that winter. He sensed that there was a proper way to report an expedition: he must never claim too much; he must present his conclusions tentatively, so that others who came later could refute him if the facts they discovered were better than his. He was especially aware that he was dealing with conjecture, and he sensed that responsible men identify conjecture and differentiate it from fact.

Kicking at the river, and splashing its cool water over himself even to his hair, he cried to the forest, 'I am searching for the soul of this river,' and he covered the last miles in Pennsylvania as if enveloped in a kind of glory, the splendor a man sometimes experiences when he is engaged in seeking for a source.

He was some miles into New York before he met anyone who could give him advice, and this man had no idea as to where the little stream known as the Susquehanna might begin. 'Somebody who hunts deer might know,' a farmer told him, and the man's wife suggested Old Grizzer. Applegarth found him on a shabby farm, a man in his late sixties with no teeth and no hair on his head but a massive lot over his face.

'By God, sonny! I've always wanted to know where that danged stream began myself. For two dollars I'll take you as far as I know, and for two more dollars we'll go plumb to the beginning, even if'n it's up in Canady.'

So they set out on a twenty-eight-mile journey, an old man who knew the terrain and a young man who knew the river. They went along cornfields which had not yet been plowed for spring planting and through woods which only the deer and crazy coots like Old Grizzer had penetrated. And always the Susquehanna was tantalizingly ahead of them, growing narrower until it was no more than a creek, but persisting in a fiendish determination to survive.

'By God, sonny, this is a damn stubborn trickle,' the old man said. And on the fourth day he said, 'Sonny, I made a bad bargain. This damned river has no beginnin' and I'm tuckered out.' But when it dawned on him that he must hand back the two dollars he had collected as guide, he found new resolve. 'I'll go a little farther. There's simply got to be a spring up here somewheres.'

So they continued for another day, until they found what might in an emergency have been considered a spring. 'Would you call that the source?' the old man asked.

'I might,' Applegarth said, 'except for that stream leading into it.'

'Goddamn,' the old man said. 'I was hopin' you wouldn't see it.'

'I'd like to follow it a little farther,' Applegarth said.

'You do that, sonny. As for me, I'm announcin' here and now that this is where the Susquehanny begins. Right here.'

'You wait. We'll go back together.'

So the old man made himself comfortable beside the bogus source while young Applegarth strode north, following the trickle of water. He slept that night under an oak tree, and before noon on the next day, May 4, 1811, he came to the ultimate source of the river. It was a kind of meadow in which nothing happened: no cattle, no mysteriously gushing water, merely the slow accumulation of moisture from many unseen and unimportant sources, the gathering of dew, so to speak, the beginning, the unspectacular congregation of nothingness, the origin of purpose.

Bright sunlight fell on the meadow, and where the moisture stood, sharp rays were reflected back until the whole area seemed golden, and hallowed, as if here life itself were beginning. Thomas Applegarth, looking at this moist and pregnant land, thought: This is how everything begins—the mountains, the oceans, life itself. A slow accumulation—the gathering together of meaning.

There is no need to remember the name Thomas Applegarth. Neither he nor any of his descendants figure in this story again. He was merely one of a thousand Americans of his time who were trying to fathom the significance of things: the explorers, the machinists, the agriculturists, the boatbuilders, the men and women who were starting universities, the newspaper editors, the ministers. They had one thing in common: somewhere, somehow, they had learned to read, and the demands of frontier life had encouraged them to think. From this yeasty combination would spring all the developments that would make America great, all the inventions and the radical new ways of doing things and the germinal ideas which would remake the world.

(Of course, this encouragement of creativity never applied to blacks. They were seldom allowed to read, or pursue mathematics, or discharge their inventive skills. The social loss incurred by our nation because of this arbitrary deprivation would be incalculable.)

In 1976, when a congregation of Bicentennial scholars sought to assess the contribution of that little band of unknown philosophers like Thomas Applegarth, they wrote:

A minor classic is that book which occasions little notice when published, and no stir among the buying public. It appears in one small edition, or maybe two if members of the author's family buy a few extra copies, and it dies a quick and natural death. But as the decades pass we find that everyone in the world who ought to have read this book has done so. It enjoys a subterranean life, as it were, kept alive by scholars and affectionate laymen of all nations. They whisper to one another, 'You ought to read this little book by So-and-so. It's a gem.' And after a hundred years we find that more people have read this little book by So-and-so than have read the popular success which was such a sensation in its day. What is more important, the people who do read the little book will be those who do the work of the world: who educate the young, or make national decisions, or endeavor to reach generalizations of their own.

A perfect example of the minor classic is Thomas Applegarth's *To the Ice Age,* published in an edition of three hundred copies at Patamoke in 1813. Applegarth had no formal education, so far as we can ascertain. He was taught to read by Elizabeth Paxmore, a Quaker lady living near Patamoke. It was she who awakened his interest in scientific matters.

At the age of twenty-seven this Maryland farmer set out with some sixty dollars to explore the Susquehanna River, with a view to proving to his own satisfaction whether northern Pennsylvania could at one time have existed under a sheet of ice. His general observations were extraordinary for his age. He seems to have anticipated theories far in advance of his time and to have foreseen quite accurately what later exploration would prove. His specific conclusions, of course, have long since been superseded, a development which he predicted in a remarkable passage on the nature of discovery:

The speculative mind of man moves forward in great revolutions, like a point on the rim of a turning wheel, and if now the point is forward, it cannot remain so for long because the wheel, and the cart which it carries, must move ahead, and as they do so the point on the rim moves backward. This oscillating movement whose temporary position we can rarely discern, is what we call the process of civilization.

What Applegarth did do which has never been superseded was to view the Susquehanna riverine system, past and present, as an ecological whole. In this day this word had not been invented, but he invented the concept, and no team of contemporary engineers and environmentalists has ever had a clearer picture of the Susquehanna and its interrelationships. He has been an inspiration to generations of American scientists, and no one who has followed his sixty-dollar exploration to that final day when he stood at the veritable headwaters of the Susquehanna can forget his description of that moment:

I stood in that meadow with the sun reflecting back from the isolated drops of water and realized that for a river like the Susquehanna there could be no beginning. It was simply there, the indefinable river, now broad, now narrow, in this age turbulent, in that asleep, becoming a formidable stream and then a spacious bay and then the ocean itself, an unbroken chain with all parts so interrelated that it will exist forever, even during the next age of ice.

The Duel

IN THE WAR OF 1812 AMERICAN FORCES WON EX-
hilarating victories on the open ocean, in Canada, on Lake Erie and at
New Orleans, but on the Chesapeake Bay they were nearly annihilated.
A group of brave and cunning British sea captains roamed the bay,
making it an English lake populated at times by as many as a thousand
ships, small and great, eager to 'discipline the Americans and teach
Jonathan his manners.'

Among the more impetuous leaders of the British effort in 1813 was a
young man of twenty-eight, totally contemptuous of the former colonials
and determined to avenge their victory over his father at the Battle of
the Chesapeake in 1781. He was Sir Trevor Gatch, son, grandson and
great-grandson of admirals.

His promotions had been meteoric, as might be expected of a young
man with such a heritage. At the age of eleven he had gone to sea in his
father's flagship. At fifteen he was a full-fledged lieutenant in command
of a patrol boat, and at nineteen was awarded the rank of captain, an
august one in the British navy. He was a slight man, not much over five
feet three and considerably under nine stone. He had watery blond hair,
somewhat feminine features and a high-pitched voice, but despite his
trivial appearance, he had acquired by virtue of a ramrod posture and
love of command a formidable military presence. He had a passion for
discipline and his inclination to flog was notorious, but men were proud
to serve with him because he was known to be a lucky captain whose bag
of tricks rescued ships that would otherwise have been lost. His men said
of him, 'I'd sail to hell with Clever Trevor,' and his promotion to admiral
was assured.

His fiery temperament could best be explained by family tradition. The

Gatches had come originally from Cornwall, 'the peninsula that wishes it were the sea,' and generations had sailed from Plymouth, attracting the favorable attention of kings. In the late 1500s Queen Elizabeth had wanted to establish in northern Ireland a congregation of families loyal to her Protestant cause, and first among her choice were the contentious Gatches. Secure in an Irish castle, honored by King James I with a baronetcy which would subsequently produce two lords, the Gatches had continued at sea, fighting in support of Marlborough off Flanders, at the capture of Jamaica and against Admiral de Grasse at the Battle of the Chesapeake.

In 1805 it had been expected that Sir Trevor would serve beside Nelson at Trafalgar, and he did, a twenty-year-old captain in charge of a ship-of-the-line with seventy-two guns. When his foremast and spars were shot away, he responded by grappling his ship to a wounded French battleship and pounding it to pieces from a range of inches. Now he was in the Chesapeake, thirsting for the sight of any American vessel, determined to be an admiral and a lord.

In late August 1813 he was anchored near what had once been Jamestown, Virginia, when a spy slipped across the bay with intelligence which caused him to leap in the air with excitement: 'The *Whisper* was badly damaged in its last running battle and is now at the Paxmore Boatyard in Patamoke, seeking repairs.'

'The *Whisper!*' Gatch cried when he gained control of his enthusiasm. 'We'll find her and destroy her.'

Urging his rowers, he sped in his longboat to the admiral's flagship and there sought permission to raid the Choptank, destroy the *Whisper* and hang her captain. The British command, having kept watch on this swift schooner for two generations, gave enthusiastic consent, and the admiral, fresh from having burned plantations throughout the tidewater, added his benediction: 'God speed you, Gatch, and have the band play when he dances on air.'

So Captain Gatch in the *Dartmoor,* eight guns, accompanied by seven small craft, set out to chastise the Americans and sink the *Whisper.*

The spy who had informed the British of the *Whisper*'s plight left tracks as he set out to cross the bay, and a clever waterman from the Wicomico River south of Patamoke deduced what he was about, and this second man came north to alert the Americans along the Choptank: 'The British fleet is being informed that the *Whisper* is in the boatyard.'

This worrisome information was of vital importance to two quite different men. Captain Matthew Turlock, owner of the *Whisper,* was a red-headed, red-bearded waterman of grizzled appearance and conduct. Forty-five years old, he had been fighting at sea since the age of seven, and with the passage of those years had developed a conviction that the principal responsibility of a sea captain was to save his ship; cargo, profit, schedules, even the lives of his men were subsidiary to the great command: 'Save your ship.' And he had done so under difficult circumstances and in varied weather. He had seen many ships lost, but never one under his command. Now, trapped on shore for overhauling, the *Whisper* was in peril, and he intended saving her.

The other American troubled by the news was George Paxmore, the young Quaker now in charge of his family's boatyard, for he realized that if the British sailed into the Choptank and found the *Whisper* on blocks in his shed, they would burn both it and the yard; as a boy he had often heard the story of how in 1781, two years before his birth, a British raiding party had come into the river and set aflame the Paxmore yards, and he did not wish a repetition.

So as soon as the loyal spy delivered his news, these two men sprang into action. 'First, we must get her off the ways,' Paxmore said. He was a spare young man, serious of purpose and extremely energetic. With a huge mallet he crept among the timbers, knocking away the lesser supports, then climbed into the sides of the slipway, directing the removal of the principal props.

Captain Turlock, meanwhile, had assembled his crew and had them ready to improvise a jury rig which would get the *Whisper* moving through the water, even though her masts and spars were not yet in position. When the men were instructed, he joined Paxmore in knocking her free and watched with satisfaction as she slid into the harbor. As soon as she struck water, he directed twenty-eight of his men in two longboats to start rowing, and slowly they edged the beautiful hull out into the Choptank, where low, slapdash masts were erected, enabling the heavy schooner to move toward the marshes.

Now came the stratagem on which the success of this venture would depend. While the *Whisper* slowly made her way downstream, George Paxmore led twoscore men into the woods, where their axes bit into the stout trunks of the loblollies. Satisfied that they would fell enough green trees, Paxmore hurried back to the boatyard, where he conscripted another two dozen men to haul sawed timbers to a rude warehouse standing some two hundred yards upriver from the main building. As soon as the lumber arrived, and ladders were provided, Paxmore jumped into a small sloop and sailed out into the river.

Up and down he went, following with careful eye the work of the two crews. Late in the afternoon the first group of men began arriving at the yard with their felled loblollies, and these they nailed against the face of the main shed, masking it and forming in its place a mock forest: It doesn't look real to me. We're going to need twice as many trees.

He then sailed closer to the warehouse, whose front was being made to look like a boat shed: That timber will fool nobody. Much too fresh.

So he sailed back into the harbor and all that night supervised the chopping down of additional trees, the smearing of watery paint upon the new boatyard, and when at dawn he went back onto the Choptank he was satisfied that he had done as good a job as possible: It may fool them. It may not. There's nothing more I can do.

But then he thought of something positively vital: Back to shore! Quick! Quick! And when the sloop reached the wharf he leaped ashore and ran to the real boatyard, shouting to the tree cutters, 'Go back and fetch any dried branches.' To the carpenters he cried, 'Help me with the turpentine,' and they were sweating like pigs in the hot August sun when sentinels cried, 'They're coming up the river.'

The British bombardment of Patamoke on August 24, 1813, was a savage affair. Captain Gatch had intended landing just below the town and investing it on foot, so that he could lay waste the infamous place at leisure, but a squadron of watermen who had been hunting rabbits all their lives—including some thirty Turlocks from the marshes—set up such a resolute fire that Sir Trevor had to confess, 'Damn me, they fight like Napoleon's best.' And to his dismay he had to stand well out in the river and bombard the place with long guns, because the riflemen on shore were beginning to pick off his sailors.

'Set fire to the whole town!' he shouted in his high voice, and flaming shot was directed at the principal buildings. This set no spectacular fires, so he directed his men to turn all their efforts to the boatyard, where he thought the *Whisper* lay, and when red-hot cannonballs were thrown into that sprawling structure, a fire of great intensity erupted and the British sailors cheered, and Captain Gatch cried, 'Damn me, we've got 'em this time.' It was his opinion that the incendiaries had struck the turpentine and oil supplies being used to repair the *Whisper.*

As the tumbling flames rose and twisted in the air, destroying the shed and all within, Sir Trevor stood very erect and smiled grimly. To his aide he said, 'My father was humiliated at the Battle of the Chesapeake. And a generation of our lads have tried to pin down the *Whisper,* but now, by gad, she's done for.' And at noon he ordered his flotilla to sail back down the Choptank, keeping well off the points, where the local militia was still troublesome.

'Shall we fire some farewell shots at the town?' the aide asked.

'That we shall!' Sir Trevor replied, and nineteen heavy shots were lobbed into the town, creating havoc while the British sailors cheered their victory.

But as they withdrew, the spy who had brought them here, knowing the tricky manners of Choptank people and especially the Turlocks, kept his eye fixed on the marsh, and while Captain Gatch was sharing a bottle of rum with his gunners, this man cried, 'Captain, there's the *Whisper!*' and Gatch choked.

It was the *Whisper,* hidden among the marsh grasses where no Englishman would have spied her. But now, at two in the afternoon, Sir Trevor stood face to face with the ghost of the schooner he had sunk a few hours earlier.

'Man all guns!' he commanded, and the entire flotilla drew up in a line close to the marsh, for there was now no headland from which the militia could operate, and slowly the heavy cannon were wheeled into position.

The first salvo struck home, and planks were ripped from the decking. The next hit the port side of the anchored schooner in the area known as 'between sea and sky,' and the damage was tremendous.

On the fifth salvo an outlook shouted, 'She's taking water. Heavy list to port.'

And then, as the smaller English guns began to tear apart the stricken *Whisper,* the lookout cried, 'There's a man aboard. Red hair, red beard.' And the gunfire centered on this big, dodging figure, and finally a cannonball struck him in the left arm, pinning it against a bulkhead, and the outlook could see blood spurting, and he cried, 'He's hit, sir. He's down.' And when Captain Gatch took the glass, he saw the schooner listing to port, the shattered wood, the smear of blood, and on the deck a severed hand.

'He's dead,' he announced to the crew, and forthwith he directed boats to be lowered and men to row ashore and burn the *Whisper,* that it should never torment the seas again. And the fires were set, and the shattered mast and the severed hand were consumed, and vengeance was had for all the sins this sleek schooner had committed.

Next morning, as the victorious British squadron navigated the channel north of Devon Island, the spy said, 'That's where the Steeds live. They owned the *Whisper,*' and Captain Gatch cried, 'It's a far distance, but another prize to any man who hits it.' So the guns were fired and great cannonballs were lofted toward the house, but only two reached it. At the end of an arching flight, they lodged in the bricks at the top of the second story, near the roof, where they remained imbedded, having accomplished nothing.

The British bombardment of Patamoke affected three local citizens in contrasting ways. Paul Steed, grandson of Isham and great-nephew of Simon, now headed the vast plantation system, assisted by various older cousins of the Refuge Steeds, and at twenty-two he was young enough to have enjoyed the cannonading of Rosalind's Revenge. Indeed, during the barrage he had danced gleefully as the balls passed overhead, missing their target, and when two did finally hit, doing no real damage, he shouted in triumph, 'They're powerless! Look at them scuttle away.' And he had grabbed a musket and run to the northern shore, firing ineffectively at the flotilla. The pellets from his gun fell a good mile short of the English vessels, but later he would boast to the community, 'We repelled them.'

Paul was the first male Steed who had failed to obtain at least part of his schooling in Europe, usually at the great Catholic seat St. Omer's, but he had been educated more or less effectively at the new college at Princeton in New Jersey, where large numbers of southern gentlemen were now being trained. The strong Presbyterian bias of the college had had a deleterious effect upon the pure strain of Catholicism which the Steeds had hitherto cultivated, and young Paul's character had suffered thereby. He was not sure what he believed in; he lacked conviction on the simple basics and his vacillations expressed themselves in his reluctance to marry or assume real responsibility for the management of the plantation.

In fact, the Steeds of Devon were in danger of becoming just another tidewater family in grand decline, and Paul showed no capacity to reverse this doleful trend. The problem was an intellectual one; Paul and his generation were the first to miss the easy transport back and forth to Europe; family ships no longer left family wharves for regular and relatively quick passages to England and France; children could no longer simply run down to the waterside for a visit to London, and this lack of civilizing impact was damaging the fiber of the young. It was not that Europe offered a superior culture, or an education more subtle than what a bright lad could acquire at Yale or William and Mary; what Europe provided was the challenge of different ideas expressed in different languages by men reared in different traditions, and Paul Steed was a prime example of the damage done when these broad new ideas were no longer a part of a young man's education. From now on, the great families of the Chesapeake would become parochial.

But the young master had spirit. When the British were safely out of sight he brought ladders and inspected the two cannonballs lodged in the northern wall of his home, and when he saw that they were well wedged in among the bricks, he summoned slaves to plaster in the broken spaces so that the balls might be permanently housed where they had struck, and it became a ritual whenever guests stopped by the Revenge for Paul to take them upstairs to his bedroom and there show them the half-projecting missiles of the British raid.

'That devil Gatch was trying to kill me in bed,' he would say laughingly, 'but Clever Trevor miscalculated and fired too high. Three feet lower and the cannonballs would have come crashing through that window and killed me as I slept.' He never revealed that the had made this room his only after the attack.

George Paxmore was elated that the British had spent their gunfire on his deceptive warehouse, which burned with little loss, and none on his camouflaged boatyard, which survived untouched. In fact, he was so gratified that he paid each man who had cut trees or timbered the warehouse a bonus of one week's pay. 'Thee performed a miracle,' he told them. 'Without thy fine effort, Paxmore's would have been finished.'

But he also suffered a psychological defeat, because the *Dartmoor,* which had done this damage to Patamoke and burned the *Whisper,* was a Paxmore product. His grandfather, Levin Paxmore, the famous designer, had built it back in the 1770s, and on it had lavished his most attentive care; it was the last of the well-regarded *Whisper* class that had performed so ably.

It had been christened the *Victory* and had stumbled into a trap laid by Admiral Rodney at St. Eustatius. Captain Norman Steed had been killed by musket fire and the *Victory* had been captured. Rechristened the *Dartmoor* and fitted with six powerful guns, it had enjoyed years of distinction as a member of the British fleet and had helped defeat the French at Trafalgar.

For some years now it had been Captain Gatch's preferred vessel, for in it he could move with startling speed, rushing at larger ships and subduing them before they had a chance to maneuver their powerful guns to repel him. The *Dartmoor* was by no means deficient in gunfire; recently Captain Gatch had mounted two additional heavy guns forward, making eight in all, and he had spent weeks training his gunners how best to use their weapons.

So during the hours the flotilla had stood off Patamoke, pumping in devastation, Paxmore was confused: he was embittered to see Captain Gatch trying to burn down his boatyard, but at the same time he appreciated the opportunity to study the *Dartmoor* professionally, and he had to concede that many of the alterations Gatch had introduced had strengthened the ship: He's raised the timbered sides to give his gunners added protection. And moved his cannon to lend added weight forward. That keeps his bow down. Provides the gunners a more stable platform. But then his practiced eye spotted the danger: I do believe he's made her ride too low in the bow. He must watch. Finally he made a curious concession: In battle she must be formidable. Hesitation. But of course she wasn't built for battle.

He had argued himself into the corner that bedevils everyone charged with planning a ship or making a decision: each improvement carries with it the seed of its own self-destruction; a vital balance has been altered and the consequences cannot be foreseen. Yet change is essential, inescapable; the burden of the thinking man is to calculate the probable good against the possible bad and to decide whether the change will be worth the risk. Captain Gatch had gambled that weight forward would provide him with better gunnery, and the accuracy of his recent fire confirmed that decision.

At the height of the blaze and the screaming, George Paxmore concluded: I have in mind a vessel that will treble the *Whisper*'s advantages but increase her risks only slightly. And he began to pray audibly that Captain Gatch's outlooks would miss the camouflaged boatyard, for he was eager to start construction, and when the flotilla withdrew he was not ashamed to fall on his knees and give thanks for his deliverance.

Then rumors began to flood Patamoke: 'The *Whisper* was detected.' 'The spy ferreted her out as she hid among rushes.' 'Gunfire at shore range destroyed her.' 'In the end she was put to the torch.'

When Paxmore heard this he became so agitated that his wife asked, 'George, what's the matter? We've saved the yard,' and he replied, 'They sank the *Whisper*.'

'No!' she cried, running out to survey the river as if it might contain contrary evidence, but it was gray and unconcerned.

Then workmen came to confirm the report. 'Captain Turlock's killed and burned with his ship.' And there was lamenting, for all men who have worked a ship and known her qualities come to love her, and her untimely death is deplored. They began to recount her exploits, and Elizabeth Paxmore served the first of that year's cider, and George Paxmore blew his nose and bit his lip and said, 'Matthew Turlock was the best waterman this river ever produced,' and they began to reminisce about him.

But Matthew Turlock did not die in the burning of his ship. When his left hand was blown away, he was sickened by the pain and the sight of his own blood and came close to fainting. Perhaps this was his salvation, for as he lay on the deck, trying to stanch the flow, he became invisible to the British sharpshooters.

When he saw that the *Whisper* could not be saved, he crawled to the landward side and dropped off into the marsh, still trying to wrap his shirttail about his wound, and when the shore party came to burn the vessel, he was hiding in the grasses. Later he staggered to fast ground, where two Turlock boys watching the fire discovered him. Others were summoned to drag him to safety, but he would not leave the shore, remaining there as his splendid schooner burned to the waterline.

The *Whisper*! Proudest vessel in America's resistance to the king, the wandering command of his father, his own home from the age of seven, the scourge of corsair, the insolent taunter of English admirals, the swift, sleek progenitor. How pitiful to see her dying in the shallows of a marsh, gunned down without the power to respond. Salt tears wetted his beard and he fell unconscious, which allowed his kinsmen to carry him to safety.

Rachel Turlock, seventy-seven years old and leader of the clan, took one look at the bleeding stump and said, 'Hot shovel.' No doctor was close enough for summoning, and the wound was bleeding too profusely to be stanched by ordinary means. 'Hot shovel,' Rachel repeated, and a fire was spurred and a spade laid on till the iron was red-hot. Then five Turlock men held Matthew pinned to the earthen floor of the hut while Rachel supervised one of her grandsons as he took the spade from the embers, spit on it to test its incandescence, then applied it with great and pressing force against the jagged stump. Matthew, feeling the pain course through his body, fainted again, and when he revived saw that his stump had been smeared with bear grease and swathed in dirty cloths.

And as he felt the dull pain surging through his arm, a Turlock from Patamoke ran in with the harshest news of all: 'When they fired the last salvo they hit your home.'

'Was Merry hurt?'

'Killed.'

And in the fury of knowing that his wife, too, was lost, as well as his ship and his left hand, Matt Turlock swore to get revenge, and the duel began.

When the stump had hardened, Matt kept it wrapped in canvas, knocking it against tables and chairs now and then to toughen it, and after a while the scar became like bone and he judged that the time had come.

He went to the box in which he kept his treasure: the deed to his land, the quitclaim signed by the Rector of Wrentham and President Washington, the bag of European coins, all silver. It was this silver that he took to a craftsman in Patamoke with the instruction 'Melt 'em down,' and when enough silver quivered in the pot he explained the device he wanted.

'Make me a heavy cup—it's got to be heavy—to fit over this stump. Leave two holes for rawhide thongs . . . tied at my elbow.' When the cup was cast, he found it to be exactly what he wanted, but he had further requirements: 'On each of the compass points a star, on the flat side an eagle.' So with heavy hammers the workman fashioned four stars on the cuff, then added a handsome eagle on the flat side covering the end of the stump. When the rawhide thongs were attached at the holes, and tied above the elbow, he found himself equipped with a heavy weighted metal cup which could be lethal in a fight.

'Silverfist,' the sailors of Patamoke called him, but they did nothing to challenge him to use his heavy left arm. Matthew was forty-five when he lost his ship, a tall, rugged, red-bearded waterman with deep-set eyes hidden by shaggy red eyebrows. He had sailed the Chesapeake since birth; indeed, he had gone alone upon it at the age of four, and he intended to continue. What he needed now was a ship.

When he stopped at the office of George Paxmore he found the Quaker builder eager to replace the *Whisper*. Indeed, the young man was so distressed by the burning of his family's masterpiece that he seemed willing to proceed without a specific commission. But not quite. After he brought his enthusiasm under control he asked, 'Has thee money to pay for the it?' And he was relieved when Turlock said, 'Enough.'

Paxmore did not want to hear any specifications from the captain; his only desire was to build a ship which would excel, but as he grudgingly divulged his plans he did occasionally stop to ask, 'Does thee understand what I'm after?'

Surprisingly, Turlock was content to let him have his way, for he had learned from his father that the *Whisper*'s applauded merit lay one fourth in what Turlock did with her, and three fourths in what Levin Paxmore had built into her. 'All I want,' he told young Paxmore, 'is the best your family ever built.'

'That's what thee'll get, but the cost will not be slight,' and he produced a paper on which he had figured to the last trunnel. 'It totals $2,863.47.'

'What dimensions?' Turlock asked.

'Eighty-two feet nine inches length, twenty-three feet six inches breadth. Draws ten-six in the bow, fourteen-eight in the stern.'

'Good. I do not want it bow-heavy.'

'Nor I,' said Paxmore. Then he waited for a confirmation, but instead of speaking, Matt Turlock drew from his waist a canvas bag laden with silver coins and began to count, pushing them into piles with his silver-tipped left hand. When the sum amounted to a thousand dollars American, he said, 'Build it. I have the balance.' And he disappeared.

In early 1814, when it was finished, Paxmore said, 'This one will sail in any breeze, but with a quartering wind she'll clip along,' from which his men called her their clipper, and it was this name that Paxmore painted on her transom. But when Turlock saw it he said firmly, 'I name my own ship,' and it was repainted the *Ariel:* 'The spirit of the sea. This one lives close to the heart of oceans.'

He recruited a knowing crew of thirty-four and told them one cold January day, 'We'll try her on the Choptank,' but when he had her moving, he nosed her into the Chesapeake, then edged her down the eastern margin of the bay far from the dozing British ships of war, and when she reached Cape Henry he startled the men by sailing into the broad Atlantic, shouting, 'Look at how she takes the waves!'

It was three months before he returned to the bay, bringing with him a crew hardened for war. He brought no booty; the *Ariel* had captured two small English merchantmen but had got little from them, just enough to feed the crew. At Patamoke he asked Paxmore to make a few alterations, picked up a commission from Paul Steed, and set forth again on his quest.

He was moving briskly down the bay when the lookout called, 'Two British craft three points off starboard,' and when Matt took the glass his breath caught in his throat, for he saw that the lead ship was the *Dartmoor,* flagship of his mortal enemy, Captain Gatch. 'He has eight guns to our two,' he cried to his men. 'And maybe two or three more on the little ship trailing aft. But we can do it.'

Allowing his sailors no time to calculate what this enormous advantage might mean to Gatch, Matt gave one swift glance at his chart and satisfied himself that the battle could be confined to that broad stretch of bay between the York River on the west and Cape Charles on the east, and he was pleased that he would not have to worry about British support ships rushing in from the James River, for its mouth lay well to the south. Fate had given him room, a brisk wind off the western shore and a trusted crew. He asked no more.

Crisply he told his men, 'We'll cut that one out and sink her,' and he indicated the trailing sloop with the four guns. Having given this brief command, he swung the *Ariel* onto a starboard tack that would carry him between the two British vessels, and well aft of the more dangerous one in the lead. He calculated that he would dispose of the sloop before Captain Gatch in the *Dartmoor* could swing about and bring his guns to bear.

Now the *Ariel* leaped through the water, her low decks awash, her tall masts straining under the weight of sail, and so expertly did the clipper move that Turlock succeeded in the first part of his plan: his two guns punished the lesser vessel and stopped her in the water, whereupon he swung about and bore down upon her. Nine Choptank men swarmed aboard, scuffled, killed when necessary and set the ship ablaze.

There was no way to recover them without stopping dead in the water and allowing the *Dartmoor* to fire at will, so Turlock waved to his men and watched approvingly as they launched rowboats. They were out of the fight.

When Captain Gatch swung the *Dartmoor* about, intending to run down the impudent American ship, he saw with amazement that it was captained by a man he thought he had killed long since—'Good God! It's Turlock!' Spotting immediately that Turlock had only two guns while the *Dartmoor* carried eight, he shouted, 'That's the new thing they call the clipper. We sink her now!'

Every advantage lay with Gatch. By swinging north he had acquired the weather gauge; he had eight well-trained gunners and an eager crew who believed in his invincibility. What was more important, at the bombardment of Patamoke he had outsmarted Turlock and felt confident he could do so again. He could not lose and told his men so.

Before Turlock could untangle himself from his engagement with the first British vessel Captain Gatch bore down on him from the north, sails tightly controlled and the four port guns exactly trained. The pass was a masterpiece of seamanship, and Gatch's gunners, secure on their steady platform, devastated the *Ariel*'s decks; they did not, however, damage either mast, so that Turlock had an opportunity to head eastward and prepare himself for the next assault. With some dismay he noted that neither of his gunners had even fired at the British ship during the first sally. He did not propose to have this happen again; he would choose the time and condition of the next contact.

Accordingly, he danced about in the eastern portion of the bay, keeping careful eye on the *Dartmoor* but also watching with satisfaction as the British sloop burned to the waterline: You've lost half your command, Gatch. Now the other half.

As he waited for an opportunity that would permit him to keep the *Dartmoor* to port, he ordered his gunners to swing their swivels to that side and warned, 'This time we must hurt them.' To his sailors he said, 'We'll give them full musket fire.'

Obedient to his plan, the *Ariel* moved with great speed on a starboard tack, almost throwing itself across the path of Gatch's schooner, and as it passed, it delivered a withering fire from all kinds of weapons. One cannonball glanced off the foremast, causing some of the forward canvas to lose wind; muskets ripped across the deck. It had been a notable exchange and no American sailors had been lost.

At this point it would have been prudent for Turlock to retire; he had hurt his enemy, and there was no reasonable hope that in a prolonged battle his lightly armed clipper could continue to rake the heavier *Dartmoor*. But Turlock was not thinking prudently; he was so bent upon revenge that safe escape was no part of his plan. 'Shall we finish them off?' he cried to his men, and they shouted their assent. So he altered course, moved down along the west coast of the bay and proposed to come at the *Dartmoor* on a rushing port tack, with a quartering wind.

But Gatch discerned the plan and conceded that for the moment, with his foremast scarred, he had the slower vessel, so he prepared to pass starboard-to-starboard and to rake the insolent American foe with a hail of fire not to be forgotten. Turlock's men quickly understood the tactic and realized that all depended upon their successful passage of this fiery deluge. They wheeled their two guns into maximum position and lined the starboard bulwark with muskets of every description. This would be a test of wills.

It was a test of captains, too. Gatch had the advantage of fire superiority; Turlock had the wind, the speed, the taste of partial victory. And each had the support of his crew, the English knowing that Clever Trevor was a lucky leader, the Americans relying as they had always done on the courage of Silverfist.

How beautiful the two Paxmore schooners were as they maneuvered through the Chesapeake, the old *Dartmoor* as fine as the bay had produced, the new *Ariel* a sprite foretelling a future when clippers of this design would command the seas from China to Murmansk. They sped across the bay like those bugs of summer which dance upon the water, their miraculous feet never breaking the surface. Their masts were raked, their lines severely clean; they leaped forward as if eager for a test of strength, and during one fearful moment Gatch thought: My God? Does he intend to ram? He judged the American capable of any folly.

But at the last moment Matt Turlock veered to bring his starboard across the path of the *Dartmoor,* and the firing began. The American gunners were good, and they were resolute, killing two English sailors; but the heavy guns of the Dartmoor were terrifying, and they ripped the *Ariel.*

Wood shattered. Men were thrown helter-skelter. The clipper seemed to shiver, and a yard came crashing down. This time the English fire had been irresistible, and the fragile *Ariel* was doomed.

That is, she would have been doomed if Turlock had been stupid enough to wait for a third test of arms. He was not. A quick survey satisfied him that she had been sorely damaged and that on any further runs her advantages of speed and maneuverability would be lost. Without hesitation he fled.

'Now we have her!' Gatch shouted as his men cheered. And he prepared to chase the wounded *Ariel* to her hiding place in the Choptank and destroy her as he had done her predecessor.

But it was not Captain Turlock's intention to hide anywhere. Without reflecting on where or how he would refit, he limped toward the entrance to the bay, trusting as his father would have done forty years earlier that somewhere in that great ocean the *Ariel* would find refuge. Wounded, her spars in disarray, her decks cluttered with debris, the ship crept out into the open ocean, where not even a swift *Dartmoor* could catch her and where she could heal herself.

'She'll sink out there,' Sir Trevor prophesied as he watched her go, but he did not believe his own prediction; he suspected that somehow Matt Turlock would mend that sleek clipper and that somewhere on the oceans of the world the two vessels would meet again. Nevertheless, when he reported the battle to the Admiralty he claimed a victory. 'True, we lost one small sloop of no consequence, but the *Ariel* we punished, and this is important, for the Americans had begun to place great store in their new clipper. We drove her from the seas.' He now had two victories over Captain Turlock and no defeats, and when his men rejoined Admiral Cockburn's fleet for the attack on Washington, they boasted, 'Clever Trevor knows how to handle Americans. He smashes 'em.'

Of all the places in the Atlantic to which Matt Turlock might have gone to mend his ship, he chose the least likely. He sailed to St. Eustatius, that insignificant Dutch island in the north Caribbean. No longer was it an entrepôt of swarming wealth; one of the peace treaties that periodically swept Europe had returned the island to the Dutch and it was once more what it had been down the centuries: a sleepy, unimportant little harbor with two or three shops that did a pitiful business. Of course, along the shore there still stood those immense warehouses which for a few exciting years in the 1770s had housed the wealth of the world, but now they were empty and mice gnawed their timbers.

The few artisans on hand were glad to find work and in a desultory way repaired the *Ariel,* so that by the end of three weeks she was as stout as ever, but what to do with her became a problem. She could not sail back to the Chesapeake, for in mid-1814 that body of water became so infested with British battleships that no American craft could move, and that condition would prevail for more than a year. Other logical ports were blockaded, so the tedious business began of drifting back and forth across the ocean, hoping for profitable trade.

Captain Turlock made one successful run from the French island of Martinique to the Spanish port of Veracruz in Mexico, and there he loaded timber intended for Halifax, but a British gunboat had identified him as American and driven him from shore. He disposed of the untrimmed logs far across the sea in Portugal, but was able to find no cargo there destined for any port that he could enter. With a swift clipper and a crew of thirty-four to feed, he was being driven from the seas.

So one day as he was drifting aimlessly across the Atlantic he recalled his final trip in the *Whisper:* he had deposited a cargo of meat at Havana and was about to quit the port when a ship chandler rowed out to advise him that three slaves were waiting to be smuggled to Virginia, and that a substantial freight charge would be paid if he delivered them. He did so, and the money had added substantially to his profit, so now he began casually inquiring about the slave trade, and learned the basic principles: 'Fill your ship with any kind of trading goods, run to Africa, pick the slaves out of the barracoons, ferry them to Brazil, take rum and sugar to any commercial port—and repeat the process.'

Blockaded by the British from honest trading, he was tempted by the easy money to be made in Africa but was restrained from sailing there by his awareness of the law. Since 1792 American ship captains had been forbidden to import slaves into the new nation and were indicted for piracy if they tried. In 1808 all importation, regardless of what nation owned the vessel, was outlawed, and Maryland, with her own surplus of slaves, even forbade their purchase from neighboring states like Virginia.

And yet the trade continued. Daring captains could snatch enormous profits by sneaking to Africa, unloading their cargoes in Cuba or Brazil, or even smuggling prime hands to secret landing spots in the swamps of Georgia. It was this nefarious trade that Matt Turlock decided to enter.

'Not permanently,' he assured his mate, Mr. Goodbarn, as they headed for Africa. 'Just a trip now and then till peace returns.' And when they reached the Portuguese harbor of Luanda in Angola he explained to the local factors, 'I'm not a slaver. Just this one trip to Brazil,' and a Senhor Gonçalves said, 'Good! I have two hundred and sixteen awaiting passage.'

But when Gonçalves inspected the bare structure of the *Ariel*'s holds, he laughed. 'If you propose to carry slaves, you've got to have proper pens.' He hired a team of Portuguese carpenters familiar with this procedure, and they swarmed into the bowels of the ship, installing massive barricades, and one afternoon, as the sound of hammers reverberated through the ship, Turlock had a premonition: They're nailing down my destiny. He realized that once his ship was fitted for the slave trade, the impetus to continue would become irresistible: You don't refurbish your entire hold for one trip. But regardless of the money involved, he swore: Once this war ends, out come those partitions. We go back to honest cargo.

When the job was done, Senhor Gonçalves invited him below to approve what the carpenters had achieved, and he was shaken by the gloomy massiveness of the bulwarks, the cramped space allotted to the slaves. Where the foremast came through the deck to seat itself in the keelson, a stout wall had been built. Where the mainmast came through, a vertical grating had been erected, and a short distance aft of that, another wall terminated the holding area. But what astonished Turlock was that between the bottom of the hold and the deck, a whole new floor had been laid, and the heights of the ceilings were unbelievable—'In the lower hold it's got to be less than four feet.' ('Just under,' Gonçalves said.) And here in the upper it can't be more than four-eight.' ('Four-ten,' Gonçalves said proudly, showing Matt that a man could more or less stand erect if he kept his belly bent.)

'What you have,' he continued, 'is four compartments. Two above, two below. Room for four hundred sixty slaves in all. You throw the most powerful ones, the troublemakers, down there. The others you keep up here.'

Turlock felt strangled, as if he had constructed a jail for himself; he was aghast at what these carpenters had done to his ship. He wanted to quit the slave trade right there, but Senhor Gonçalves said reassuringly, 'Captain, they had to make two layers so you could load more slaves. That's where the profit is. And they had to make them solid. You must remember that for a hundred and fifteen days strong black men will stand cursing behind those bars, trying every trick to break them down and mutiny your ship. In this trade we've learned one thing. If they do break loose—and sooner or later they'll break even these bars—the only thing to do is shoot them . . . fast.'

When the slaves were herded onto his ship, and thrown below into the four compartments, Turlock suffered additional revulsion, thinking that no proud waterman from the Choptank would accept such indignity; within the first minutes there would be riot. But these aren't watermen, he rationalized, and when the hatches were battened down and the holds sealed except for small openings into which food and water would be delivered, he raised anchor and set sail for the Brazilian port of Belém, some distance east of the Amazon. When he landed there in January 1815 the Portuguese plantation owners were delighted to get the slaves and assured him that his profits would be prodigious, but as often happened in such cases, payment was delayed, and he was forced to lay over.

The more he saw of this steaming tropical town and its relationship to the Amazon, the more he liked it. He began to frequent a tavern called Infierno—its door was guarded by two devils carved in ebony, and they seemed to wink at him when he entered, as if they were a foretaste of what slavers could expect in afterlife—and there he heard fantastic stories about the Amazon: 'Thirty percent of all the water that enters the oceans of the world comes from here. Sixty miles out at sea the water is still fresh. Throw down your buckets and drink. No man has ever gone to the end of the river. It has birds and animals that would stupefy you.'

He was listening to such a monologue when an English sailor made an unbelievable statement: 'Our men marched to Washington, burned the city and captured the whole American government. The United States is no more.' When Turlock shouted his disbelief, the sailor said, 'Ships like yours will be driven from the sea. They're hanging captains like you . . . right now.'

Even after he had collected his money, Turlock sat day after day in the Infierno, seeking information. He could not believe that a nation so promising could have collapsed, but before he departed on his third voyage to Africa a French officer arrived at Belém with confirming news: 'You Americans must learn never to challenge England without our help. Now you've lost everything.'

For the first time in his life Turlock was bewildered. He needed the easy money provided by the slave trade, but he also needed information about home. He felt that if America had succumbed to the British he ought to be on hand to aid the new system, whatever it was to be. He knew that the wounded country would need practiced men and sturdy ships to develop its commercial interests.

So in spite of attractive commissions from Brazilian slave dealers, he sailed not to Africa but to the Chesapeake. He arrived there in April 1815, to find no English warships on patrol, no impediment at the capes. Gingerly he sailed into the bay, hailing the first ship he saw. He and the other captain spoke each other.

'Defeated? Hell, no! We drove the redcoats back to London.'

'I was told that Washington was burned.'

'It was, and not a thing was lost. We'll build it better than before.'

'England is not ruling us?'

'Nor ever will.'

The ships passed. Turlock stood by the railing, the speaking-trumpet in his right hand, his silver fist hammering rhythmically at the wood.

When he reached Patamoke he found that he was regarded as a hero, the man who had kept the American flag aloft. He did not tell his neighbors of his second defeat by Captain Gatch nor of his ignominy as a slaver. He was so relieved that America was still free that he accepted the plaudits.

In triumph he became a moody man, as effective at forty-seven as he would ever be. But he had no wife, no home, really, no job; and he could never erase from his mind those drifting months on the Atlantic when he had not even a port he could claim his own. He thought: I'll stop at Patamoke for a while—give the *Ariel* a good mending. Then something'll turn up.

In the meantime there was considerable excitement on Devon Island, and he found himself sailing down there more and more.

As soon as the war ended, Penelope Steed Grimes had informed her London circle that she was taking her pretty daughter Susan to Maryland, in the Americas, to be married. For some years she had been in communication with her distant family, the Steeds of Devon, and had known of her father's death. Simon Steed had been well regarded by Fithians, her London family, for he had been generous in supporting her. When she married Captain Grimes, Simon had sent five thousand pounds, a tremendous sum which had helped her husband buy a colonelcy in a good regiment. He had died fighting Napoleon, but by then Simon was dead, too.

Her correspondent at Devon had been Isham Steed, her grandfather's brother, a delightful old man who had visited London in 1794 to attend Penelope's wedding to Captain Grimes; he had enchanted the community as a witty, well-educated gentleman who could laugh at American pretensions. He liked Penelope and through the years had kept her informed about the Steed half of her heritage.

He had written, proposing that young Susan come to America and marry his grandson Paul. At first the idea had seemed preposterous to Penelope. 'They're cousins, in a manner of speaking. And Paul's gone to some silly school in America where he's learned nothing, I'm sure.' She rambled on, as she often did, but in the end began to take seriously her great-uncle's suggestion.

Fithians assured her that the Steeds were one of the soundest families in America, and that if rumor could be trusted, Simon had doubled his fortune in the rebellion. The family was stable, as witness Uncle Isham, and now that peace had settled over the area, life in Maryland could be quite acceptable. A portrait painter had shipped to London a likeness of young Paul, and when everything was added up, a Steed-Grimes marriage seemed practical, despite the consanguinity.

So in the summer of 1816 Penelope Grimes, lively widow of forty-one, took passage on one of the Steed ships accompanied by her daughter Susan, aged twenty, and after a crossing as placid as the good relations now existing between England and America, the ship dropped anchor at Devon. Susan, standing at the rail, saw with delight that Rosalind's Revenge was as handsome a plantation home as she had been promised. 'It's protected by a hundred trees! It's a splendid place!' Her musical voice carried over the water, and as she came toward him, Paul was even more charmed by her dainty style, the beauty of her features.

Days of exploration and enchantment followed, with Penelope as pleased as her daughter by the unexpected suavity of Devon. 'Really, it could be transplanted right into rural England and no one could detect the difference. Susan, we've come to a little paradise.'

Both women were fascinated by the idea of literally owning servants who could be told what to do without fear of their departing in a huff. But even so, when old Isham and young Paul appeared one day leading a shy black girl of thirteen, neither of the English visitors was quite prepared when faced with the actuality of slavery.

Shoving the little girl forward, barefoot and dressed only in a slip, Paul said, with obvious pride, 'She's yours, Susan. Name's Eden.'

'Eden what?'

'Just Eden. Slaves don't have names,' and Isham added, 'She sews beautifully. And she's young enough to train in the ways you desire.' Eden, her smooth and beautifully composed features betraying no sign of understanding, stood silent as the Grimes women inspected her.

'She's a gem!' Penny said, but her daughter was confused as to what one did with a slave. 'How do I . . .'

'You own her. She sleeps outside your door,' Paul explained. 'She does whatever you wish. Because she belongs to you.' Turning to the black girl, he said abruptly, 'Back to the kitchen,' and the girl vanished.

'Paul!' Susan said when the girl was gone. 'What a sweet gift! And the glorious parties you've been having.'

'There's to be more,' he assured her, and that night Susan met for the first time some of the Steed captains. Among them was Matthew Turlock, not at present working for the Steeds but a figure of some importance in the community.

'This is our local hero,' Paul said with a faint touch of amusement. 'He fought the British.'

'I'm sure he fought well,' Penelope said as she took his right hand. 'I'm told some of your seamen were quite heroic.'

'Yes,' Susan burbled. 'My cousin's married to Sir Trevor Gatch and he told us . . .'

At the mention of Gatch's name Captain Turlock stiffened. 'He was a formidable enemy,' he said. 'He's the one who fired the cannon at this house.'

'This house?' Penelope said in disbelief. 'Did the war reach here?'

'It did,' Turlock said.

'You must see what your friend Sir Trevor did to us,' Paul cried, his voice rising rather higher than he had intended, and with a lamp he led the way upstairs to his room, where the two cannonballs were lodged in the wall near his bed. 'Had Captain Gatch lowered his sights three feet, I'd have been killed.'

'Oh, look at those dreadful things,' Susan cried. 'Coming right into the room. Could I see them?'

She looked about for a chair to stand on, but then turned abruptly to Captain Turlock and said, 'Lift me up. I must see them,' and before anyone could protest, she had placed herself in front of the bearded waterman and drawn his arms about her. With a heave he projected her toward the ceiling, holding her aloft without difficulty, and as she traced the outline of the iron balls she cried, 'Oh, Paul! You could indeed have been killed.'

When Captain Turlock put her down he turned to Mrs. Grimes and apologized. 'I would not have presumed . . .'

'It's nothing,' Penelope said. 'Susan does as she wishes, and no harm.'

'We're mightily pleased that she's to live among us,' he said gallantly, and he was so polite, so rough and authentic, that Mrs. Grimes began to take an interest in him; all during that first dinner she talked principally to him, learning of his years at sea and of the adventures to which Paul had alluded. On their third dinner together she asked some really personal questions, but she was hardly prepared for the astonishing fact he revealed: 'I've never forgotten you, Mrs. Grimes. When you left Devon for your exile in London . . .'

'I hardly call it an exile, Captain.'

'You quit your home. That's exile.'

'I found a new home. That's good sense. But when did you and I ever meet?'

'When you left for London, you sailed on my father's ship. And I sailed too. And it was my job to care for you.' He paused, recalling those exciting days when he and America were fledglings and everything was new. 'I kept you in a basket, forward, and fed you and took you to the women when you cried.' He said this so simply, and with such remembered affection, that Mrs. Grimes was moved. 'We called you Penny then. I was eight.'

'And so much would happen to us both,' she said impulsively. 'How did you lose your hand?'

'Captain Gatch shot it off. The day he laid those eggs in the wall upstairs.'

She laughed at his expression, then asked, 'So you've been fighting the English all your life?'

'Not viciously,' he said. 'It was long drawn out . . . year after year we . . .'

'But you hate Captain Gatch viciously, don't you?'

'I do. That war never ends.'

He took her about the bay, pointing out the plantations on Dividing Creek owned by the other branches of the Steed family, and then sailed her to Patamoke, where he showed her his clipper, the *Ariel*, on blocks at the Paxmore Boatyard. 'Look at those clean lines. They move through the sea the way a heron moves through air.'

'And what's a heron?'

He started to explain when George Paxmore, tall and grave of mien, his flat hat perched on his head, came from the boatyard with a problem that obviously was serious. 'I must talk with thee, Matthew.'

'When I've finished showing Mrs. Grimes the river,' Turlock said. 'Her daughter's to be the new mistress at Devon.'

'Fortunate girl,' Paxmore said, not removing his hat or extending his hand. 'You'll come back?'

'I will.'

'What's a heron?' Penelope asked again when the solemn Quaker had left.

'Have you never seen a marsh?'

'No, but I've been told you live in one. I should very much like to see it.'

So on the sail back to Devon he detoured at Turlock's Creek and led the sloop into those narrow and exciting waters where the sparta grass grew eight feet high, creating a world of mystery, and as they sailed silently in this wonderland a heron flew past, legs dangling far behind the tail feathers, and Matthew said, 'There he goes, the great fisherman. Our Indians called him Fishing-long-legs.'

'Did you have Indians . . . in the old days?'

'We have Indians now . . . in the new days.'

'What do you mean?'

'I'm part Indian. Three times members of my family—far back, of course.'

'You're part Indian!' She was fascinated by this exotic information and intended advising her daughter of it as soon as she got back to Devon, but before this could happen, there was a detour.

'I used to live up there,' Matthew said, indicating the log cabin which Turlocks had occupied for two centuries.

'I'd love to see it. Can we walk?'

'If you don't prize your shoes.'

'I don't!' And she was out of the sloop before he was, running up the path to the rambling house in the woods.

A Turlock woman of indeterminable character appeared as the voices drew close to her cabin, and two children kept behind her skirts. 'Oh, it's you, Matt,' she said. 'What brings you here?'

'This is Mrs. Grimes. Her daughter is marrying Paul Steed.'

'Lucky girl.'

'Mrs. Grimes, this is one of my cousins, name of Bertha.'

Penelope tried to say something gracious, but the impact of the cabin and its occupants was too powerful. This was America, the America cartooned by British wits, and it repelled her. 'I think we'd better go back.'

'You wanna see inside?' Bertha asked, kicking open the door.

'No, thank you. They're expecting us.' And she retreated.

This incident should have prepared Turlock for what happened. At Mrs. Grimes' insistence he had stayed at Devon three days, during which he had an opportunity to watch both Penelope and her daughter more carefully. Young Susan was still an unformed child; with a good husband she might become a strong woman; with an essentially weak man like Paul Steed she would probably relax and become quite ordinary. But at twenty she was beautiful and alert. He wished her well.

Penelope was a mature woman endowed with that easy charm which comes from living on four thousand pounds a year. Her hair was neat; her teeth were good; her skin was not ravaged; and she was semi-educated. Above all, she was responsive, eager for new adventures in this new world. If some of it, like the Turlock cabin, repelled her, she could still see the merit of life along the Choptank and understand the forces that had framed the various Steed captains. None was more impressive than Matthew Turlock, and by various actions she let him know she thought so.

Therefore, at the conclusion of the third day the captain went to his room, washed carefully, inspected his nails and presented himself to Mrs. Grimes. He spoke simply. 'I've been thinking that you might consider remaining in America . . . might even have thought of . . . Well, the *Ariel* does belong to me . . . I've been careful with my money . . .'

Mrs. Grimes broke into a nervous but not disrespectful laugh. 'Is this a proposal, Captain Turlock?'

'It is.'

As a lady of breeding she tried to restrain her nervous laugh, but it broke through as an insulting giggle. 'Me? Live in Maryland? For the rest of my life?' She controlled herself, then placed her hand on his arm, saying, almost in a whisper, 'I'm a Londoner, Captain.' Then she added something which under more relaxed circumstances she never would have said: 'Can you picture me in a cabin? With Bertha?'

'I do not live in a cabin now,' he said gravely, keeping his silver fist behind him, lest that, too, offend.

'Dear Captain Turlock,' she began, but then the nervous giggle returned. She felt ashamed, tried twice to compose herself, then rose and kissed him on the cheek. 'It's quite impossible . . . Indians . . . in London . . .' With a flutter of her hand she indicated that he should go, and with a deep bow he did.

As soon as he left she informed the Steeds that she would be sailing for London immediately. 'I've behaved poorly, and I'm ashamed of myself.'

'Did that Turlock embarrass you?' Paul Steed asked menacingly, as if he might conceivably run after the captain and thrash him.

'No. He paid me the honor of proposing.'

'Proposing?' When the household was informed of this gaucherie the laughter was general, except for Susan, who said, 'I'd love to have him for my daddy. That great silver fist hammering on the table, laying down the law.'

'He's a waterman,' Paul said, and the packing began, but before Mrs. Grimes could sail, old Isham Steed died, and after his funeral, when his papers were inspected lest promissory notes of value be overlooked, Paul came upon a copy of his letter to President Jefferson, and when this was circulated within the family, Mrs. Grimes gained a better picture of the Indians her daughter's new family had known in previous centuries:

> Devon Island, Mlnd.
> 13 July 1803

Dear Mr. President,

Immediately upon receipt of your request that I send you a report on the Choptank tribe I assembled an impromptu commission consisting of the best informed citizens of this area to inquire into the matters you raised. None of us is an expert, and none speaks the Indian language, but we and our forebears have lived with this tribe for generations, so although our information is not scientifically precise, it is the best available. With that apologia I proceed.

At this date we know of only one Choptank Indian surviving on this planet. She is Mrs. Molly Muskrat, aged 85 or thereabouts, infirm of body but tantalizingly clear of mind. She lives on 16 acres of moderately good land on the left bank of the Choptank River across from our capital city of Patamoke. She is, so far as we can ascertain, a full-blooded Choptank, the daughter of a well known workman in these parts and the descendant of chiefly families. She has most of her teeth, a remarkably full head of hair, and a lively interest in things. She was delighted to talk with us, for she is aware that she is the last of her people. Her age is of course uncertain, but events which she saw personally occurred about 80 years ago, so we are not hesitant to give her age as about 85.

Legend puts the apex of Choptank society in the first decade of the 17th Century, when the tribe numbered some 260 souls, 140 living in a village on the site of the present-day Patamoke, and 120 farther upriver close to where Denton now stands. They were inferior in number, power and importance to the southerly Nanticokes, and sharply so to the tribes on the western shore of the bay.

A persistent tradition among the Choptanks claimed that the great man in their history was one Pentaquod, a mythical figure supposed to have reached them from the north. Mrs. Muskrat believes him to have been a Susquehannock, but this seems unlikely, for Captain Smith encountered a real werowance named Pintakood, and doubt-less she has the two names confused.

They were a peaceful tribe and never warred against the whites. Indeed, the highlight of their tribal history came in 1698 when the Maryland government accused them of having killed a white farmer in an argument over a cow. Although it was later proved without question that the affray had involved Nanticokes, not Choptanks, a tribal council was held and the werowance of that day told his people, 'It is obligatory that someone offer himself as the perpetrator of this crime and allow himself to be hanged, so that the rest of us can have peace.' Two young men stepped forward, got in their canoes, paddled down river and surrendered themselves voluntarily to be hanged.

They adjusted poorly to civilization. Originally possessing some of the finest land in Maryland, they were constantly pushed back until our ancestors had to confine them in pitiful enclaves, where they lingered. A man named Turlock, whose voluminous family had infusions of Choptank blood at three different periods in history, summarizes the local understanding of what white men did to this tribe: 'We married some, we shot some, the rest we starved.'

Inch by inch they lost their lands, for they never comprehended what leases or mortgages or sales implied, and when they were located near their river, an ugly situation developed. White men told them to fence their fields the way decent farmers always did, but when the Indians complied, other farmers would knock down the fences so their cattle could graze, and then sometimes the infuriated Indians would shoot the invading cow, and endless difficulties would ensue. There was no possibility that white men and Indians could live side by side.

They were not killed off in war, for there was never a Choptank war. They simply lost their desire to live. Their families grew smaller. Men married later and later, for they had no hunting grounds. And in the end only a few old women survived. They seemed to adjust better than the men. And now there is only Mrs. Muskrat.

Reflecting on the vicissitudes that have overtaken her people, she told us, 'No matter how poor the land you gave us, there was always someone who wanted it.' She showed us seven different offers to buy her 16 acres, but said, 'I won't sell. I shall die on the banks of my river.'

In our appendix we give a list of all the Choptank words that Mrs. Muskrat could recall, plus some that have entered into our English language. She told us that the word *Choptank* meant *where the water flows back strongly,* but she could explain nothing, and I would point out that while there is a tide at Patamoke, it is not a considerable one. We have no other guess as to the etymology.

And now without being familiar or presuming upon our friendship, I must confess, Tom, that all of us who studied law with you under George Wythe while at William and Mary are proud of your accomplishments, and if fate decrees you serve a second term as our President, an eventuality which seems probable, we are certain that you will discharge your duties then as capably as you do now.

> Your debating partner,
> Isham Steed

Postscriptum. I purchased from Amsterdam the telescope you recommended and have had hours of enjoyment exploring the heavens, as you predicted I would.

If Matt Turlock was disgruntled when he sailed away from Penelope Grimes, her nervous laughter rankling in his memory, he was enraged when he left George Paxmore. He had sailed directly to the boatyard to inspect repairs to the *Ariel,* but found the clipper back in the water without having been touched.

'What's wrong?' he asked gruffly.

'Everything,' Paxmore said, and when he showed no signs of further explanation, Matt grabbed him harshly and asked, 'Where's the carpenters?'

'They're not working. They won't be working.'

'And why not?'

'Because they went below, Matt. We all went below.'

'And what happened below?'

Paxmore called one of his workmen, a Quaker mechanic of noted skill and piety. 'Tell Captain Turlock what thee saw, Lippincott.'

'I saw the cramped hold of a slave ship,' Lippincott said. He stared defiantly at the red-headed captain and walked away.

'Matthew, thee's become a slaver.' Before Turlock could respond, Paxmore said with deep resentment, 'Thee took the finest clipper I ever built . . .'

'And what are we going to do about it?' Turlock asked as if issuing a challenge.

'I have this proposal, Matthew. If thee will allow my men to board thy clipper and tear out those slave quarters, we'll do the work for nothing and then make the other repairs. If thee refuses to quit the slave trade, we'll never touch our vessel again, even if she were sinking of the worm.'

Twice rejected in as many days was too much for Turlock. Shoving Paxmore aside, he growled, 'I'll have her mended by carpenters of courage—who know what the world is and how damned difficult it is to find a cargo and an open port.'

But Paxmore would not be so easily repulsed. Returning to where Turlock stood glowering at the *Ariel,* he said quietly, 'Matthew, I would to pray with thee. And so would Elizabeth. Come to our home.'

'I need no prayers. I need a carpenter.'

'We all need prayers.'

'Get away from here, Paxmore. You make me sick.'

'Then I shall do the praying.'

'Don't bother to pray for me. I need it no more.'

'I shall not pray for thee. I shall pray for myself. I shall ask for forgiveness for having built the clipper. You have defiled . . . it's no longer a vessel of mine.' Gravely he looked at the beautiful clipper, the epitome of his family's tradition, and with an awkward movement of his left hand, erased it from the harbor. It was contaminated and would never again enter the Paxmore yards.

With a slave ship that ran the risk of daily capture, Matt Turlock furtively sailed the Atlantic, trying to devise a way of slipping into St. Eustatius for a much-needed overhaul. When he finally reached there he had to supervise the work, and did much of it himself, but when he and the Dutch carpenters were through, the *Ariel* was in maximum condition, with a third gun carriage on deck and strengthened bulwarks below, each with riveted iron rings for the secure fastening of chains.

When the job was completed he told the Dutch chandler, 'With this we'll make a hundred trips to Africa.'

'Lucky if you finish one. The British battleships have begun their patrol.'

'Idiots! They'll never halt the trade. Not while Brazil and America are hungry for slaves.'

'They've made four, five captures already. A Captain Gatch brought one—'

'Who?'

'Captain Gatch . . . *Dartmoor* . . . eight guns.'

'He came here?'

'He captured a Spanish slaver, brought her here to mend the damage his guns had done. Too deep. We could do nothing.' He said *ve coot do nossing,* and Turlock smiled. 'So Gatch sailed her out there and burned her.'

'He's in these waters?'

'He is. And he'll hang you even if your hold is empty . . . if you're a slaver, that is.'

'Will he be coming back to St. Eustatius?'

'They cover the entire ocean.'

When Turlock sailed, he lingered in the vicinity, praying that Sir Trevor would return with some capture, but he did not. So Matt ran to Luanda, ducked in close to shore and swiftly loaded two hundred slaves to be smuggled into Georgia, and on his next trip, more than three hundred for Havana.

It was in this port that he met Spratley, a small, gap-toothed, foul-smelling, foul-talking British sailor from the dregs of London. He had jumped ship in Haiti and with extraordinary conniving had made his way to Cuba. Matt was standing in a waterfront tavern when he sidled up, tugged at the sleeve covering the silver fist and whispered, 'You're Captain Turlock, yes?'

'I am,' Matt said, looking down at the unsavory stranger.

'I'd like to sail with you.'

'I need no one.'

'You need me.'

Matt drew back, studied the unlikely applicant and laughed. 'You'd ruin any ship you touched.'

The sailor returned the laugh, then mumbled, 'That's what Captain Gatch said.'

'Sir Trevor Gatch?'

'Clever Trevor. You seek him. I seek him.'

'How do you know I seek him?'

'Everyone knows.'

'And you?'

'I want to kill him. I want to hold his head under a bucket of slime and watch his eyes as he gags for breath.'

'Because he whipped you,' Turlock said, making no effort to hide his contempt. 'What's your name?'

'Spratley.'

'Well, Spratley'—and he grabbed the man by his shirt, dragging him close—'I'd whip you too, for a no-good. Now get away.'

But Spratley had seen how Captain Turlock reacted at the name of his enemy, and he was certain that he had found his next employer. 'I know what you don't know, Captain.'

'What?'

'I know where Captain Gatch is.'

'You do?'

'Captain, I'm dyin' for a drink.' And as they sat in the cantina, Spratley told of his experiences with Gatch. 'He looks trim and proper ashore, or in battle. All erect and that. But on the long reaches he's a demon. Want to see my back?'

'I told you I'd have flogged you,' Turlock repeated. He had learned from long experience never to credit tales of brutality at sea; the narrators were invariably scoundrels who had deserved punishment, afloat or ashore. But when Spratley told of how Captain Gatch had led the shore party that had impressed him on the streets of London, and of how Gatch had refused to pay his men on the principle of 'Keep the pay and keep the man,' and of the ranting tirades Sir Trevor was accustomed to deliver, Turlock's appetite was whetted, and against his own best judgment he signed the sniveler.

He held him in contempt, yet repeatedly on the return voyage from Cuba to Luanda he sought him out, eager to hear any rumors concerning the man he had sworn to defeat, and as Spratley talked—'If we grapple, let me board first. I want to sink my knife into that one'—Turlock saw that this little wharf rat was as deeply committed as he.

Actually, the little Englishman proved to be a good sailor; he understood his duties and performed them well. He was a gunner, too, and pleaded with Turlock to let him man the third gun—'I want to shoot his eyes out.'

'You said you wanted to lead the boarding party.'

'I want to kill him,' Spratley said, and he was so convincing that Turlock broke his rule, and began to sympathize with him, and asked to see the scarred back the little fellow had been so eager to show, and when the crisscrossed welts were visible, Turlock almost retched.

'What happened?' he asked.

'Ten strokes one day. Twenty another. Then a hundred.'

'No man could survive a hundred.'

'That's what the mate said, but Clever Trevor shouted, "I'll cure him or I'll kill him." '

'Cure you of what?'

A strange look came into Spratley's eyes and he said, in what seemed to be honest bewilderment, 'I don't know. He was in one of his moods.' He thought about this, then added, 'At nineteen strokes the mate stopped it.'

Turlock nodded. 'No man could . . .'

'He's at the Bight of Benin.'

'Why didn't you tell me sooner?'

'Sooner, you wouldn't have believed me.'

'How long will he be there?'

'That's his station. A year at the Bight. Then back to England.'

'Does he roam?'

'Greatly. I escaped in Haiti. For seven weeks we chased an American ship.' Then he added a fragment which clinched his veracity. 'You know he despises Americans. Ungrateful rebels, he calls you.'

'Did he ever mention me?'

Spratley laughed. 'Said he'd beaten you twice and would do so twice again, if he didn't kill you first.' The little fellow laughed again. 'That's when I started watching for you. They told me of your silver fist—that you don't kill easy.'

But as the *Ariel* approached the coast of Africa, Captain Turlock had a most disturbing nightmare. He wasn't really asleep, just dozing in his hammock, when a nebulous thought swept across his mind: Spratley had been deposited in Havana by Clever Trevor, and everything which happened subsequently had been an intended hoax. He was being tricked into entering the Bight of Benin, where Gatch would have a flotilla waiting, a hundred guns to three.

So without reflection he rushed forward to where Spratley was sleeping, knocked him from his hammock and began hammering him with his silver fist. When the bewildered seaman tore free he cried, 'Captain! Captain!' and Turlock came to his senses.

But this did not help Spratley, for Turlock grasped the back of his neck and began hammering his face against the bulkhead until Mr. Goodbarn ran down to see what was happening. 'Leave us alone,' Turlock shouted, and in the darkness of the fo'c'sle he accused the Englishman, 'Gatch put you ashore, didn't he? He rehearsed you in all you've said, didn't he?' He laid Spratley's duplicity before him, but the man was bewildered, unable to grasp the accusation.

Nevertheless, Turlock had to believe that the nightmare had come as a warning, and he refused to sail north to Benin; he anchored boldly at Luanda, defying any British patrol boats that might be on station to suppress the slave traffic. And just as boldly he went ashore, dickering with the Portuguese for the slaves they had collected from the interior. And when he had accumulated some five hundred at a good price, he personally supervised their loading and raised anchor for a speedy run to Havana. He knew he should have thrown Spratley onto the beach, but he kept him, and the more he listened to the tales of Gatch's insanity, the more satisfied he became that Spratley was no more nor less than what he had said from the beginning: a London alley rat impressed into the naval service and abused there till the moment of desertion. That he thirsted for revenge on his cruel captain, there could be no doubt.

So from Havana, Turlock sailed not for Luanda but for Benin, and since Belém lay on the direct route, he stopped there to take on an additional supply of powder and ball, for with the third gun he now carried, the usual supply might soon be depleted in battle. Spratley was enthusiastic about the idea of more ammunition and told the men how he proposed to use it: 'One! Down go Sir Trevor's sails. Two! Down goes Sir Trevor's mast. Three! Down goes Sir Trevor.'

To obtain ammunition, Turlock had to anchor some distance from the harbor, away from normal traffic, and one steaming afternoon when he was satisfied that his men could handle the loading, he rowed ashore to renew acquaintance with the Infierno, whose ebony devils winked at him as if he were their brother. He winked back, and then, according to his custom, studied the sky before going inside—'Storm could be rising. We'll stay here some days until it passes.' And he was sitting relaxed with a mug of spiced beer when a mild commotion occurred at the door; he heard loud voices and a scuffle and looked up to see that Captain Sir Trevor Gatch had entered, accompanied by five of his officers. For a brief moment he considered flight, before the Englishman could see him, but as soon as he contemplated this action he rejected it. Seating himself firmly in his chair, he placed his silver fist on the table where it could not be missed.

The officers swaggered in, looked insolently about but did not identify him as Matt Turlock, but as they seated themselves one young man did ascertain that the lone drinker was probably an American, and told his mates in a loud voice, 'Wherever one goes, Americans.'

Captain Gatch had his back turned and could not see Turlock, but when they were served he asked superciliously, 'Did you say, Compton, that we share this place with Americans?'

'I did, sir.'

'Unfortunate.' Turlock ignored the remark, but soon Gatch returned to the subject. 'One would have thought that Americans would stay clear of the seas, after the drubbing we gave them.' Still no response, so he added, 'Especially since we captured two American slavers last week and sent them home for hanging.'

The officers laughed and this encouraged their captain, who said, in a voice so loud and squeaky-high that no one could ignore it, 'Slavers and grubby merchants, that's what they are.'

'Who are?' Matt asked quietly.

Gatch tightened, his military composure manifesting itself in his straightened shoulders. More quietly now he said, 'The Americans are. They're good for absolutely nothing but—'

He did not finish his sentence, because Turlock interrupted sharply, 'You, sir, are a damned fool.'

Gatch leaped up, whirled about, and found himself facing Captain Turlock. He showed no surprise, nor did he retreat. He looked at the red beard, then down at the silver fist. He realized that his group overpowered Turlock, six to one, and that some kind of magnanimity was called for, but he also hated this man and could not control himself. 'I take it, Captain Turlock, you're out to seek a third thrashing.'

With a great swing of his left arm, Turlock brought his weighted stump about, catching Sir Trevor a blow on the shoulder which glanced upward, striking the top of his head and knocking him down. Four of the officers leaped at Turlock and might have killed him, except that Captain Gatch, from his fallen position, restrained them. 'Let him go, the boor. We don't want him. We want his filthy slaving clipper.'

The young officers dropped their hold on Turlock, allowing him to return to his table for his cap. When he had paid his bill he backed slowly toward the door as Captain Gatch announced to the bar's patrons, 'Tonight we drive one more slaver from the Atlantic.' Then Turlock slammed the door and dashed toward the wharf, leaping into his rowboat and pulling furiously. Against the darkening sky he could see the six Englishmen running toward the *Dartmoor,* hidden around a bend in the opposite direction.

His arms wearied, but as he pulled the boat through the water he began shouting, *'Ariel!* Up sails! Up anchor! We go!'

'We can't go!' a voice called back. 'Steve Turlock's ashore with a party of three.'

Rowing faster than he had ever done before, Matt bellowed, 'We sail without them!' And as soon as the rowboat banged against the side of the *Ariel* he supervised the attaching of lines, and sailors hauled the boat aboard, with him in it. Leaping onto the deck, he shouted, 'Get her under way! Out to sea!'

Mr. Goodbarn, a cautious man, ran up to ask, 'What's happening, sir?'

'Gatch! The *Dartmoor*'s hiding upstream.'

Mr. Goodbarn choked, then pointed out, 'Sir, we aren't forced to leave port. The Brazilian government won't allow Gatch to attack us so long as we stay inside.'

'I want him outside,' Turlock said as the ship began to move.

'Halloo, *Ariel!*' came voices from the shore, and Turlock bellowed back, 'Swim!' and Steve Turlock leaped into the bay, followed by his companions.

'Our papers haven't been cleared,' Mr. Goodbarn warned.

'To hell with papers.' And gradually the *Ariel* caught the late-afternoon breeze and began moving more swiftly, and a Brazilian guard boat sailed out to protest the departure, but its attention was distracted by the fact that the English ship of war was also leaving without proper clearance.

The *Ariel* had a slight start, which it improved when the shore was left behind, but the *Dartmoor,* hoping to increase speed as the winds strengthened, did not propose to allow her enemy clear sailing. In the fading daylight a salvo of well-aimed shots tried to knock down the *Ariel's* rigging, but fell short. Before the gunners could reload for a second try, the *Ariel* had moved out of range and during the long night she stayed ahead.

At dawn the two vessels retained their relative positions, because no matter how swiftly the *Ariel* sailed, the rising wind enabled the *Dartmoor* to keep pace, and a worried Mr. Goodbarn told his captain, 'Sir, they're keeping up.'

'That's what I intend.'

'But in this heavy wind they may overtake us.'

'I want them to,' Turlock said, and Mr. Goodbarn, whose neck would also be stretched if the *Ariel* was captured, looked back at the menacing *Dartmoor* and shivered.

'Break out the topsails, Mr. Goodbarn,' Turlock said.

'Sir, the wind is rising.'

'That's what we want,' and Turlock watched approvingly as the two square sails climbed to the tops of their masts. 'Now we'll see if he's a sailor.'

It was a dark overcast day, with a heavy breeze from the shore, and for nine hours the two ships pounded eastward, decks awash and the wind beginning to howl. At dusk they remained separated, and through the long night Captain Turlock kept all sails aloft, even though the *Ariel* was listing perilously to starboard. Twice Mr. Goodbarn asked if he wanted to lower the topsails and twice he asked, 'Has Sir Trevor lowered his?'

In the darkness the *Ariel* began to shudder from the impact of tall canvas and rough seas, and some of the sailors expressed apprehension: 'He's drivin' us to the bottom of the sea.'

'He knows what he's doin',' one of the Choptank men replied, but as he spoke the schooner took a sickening drop to starboard, twisted in the trough between the waves and roared upward with a sudden wrench to port. 'Jesus!' the Choptank man said.

The only sailor who actually relished the chase was Spratley, who remained at his gun as if action were imminent, staring back in the darkness to catch sight of the *Dartmoor.* When dawn broke under scudding clouds, and the sun appeared for a brief moment, throwing the pursuers into golden relief, he shouted, 'We still have 'em!' as if he were a fisherman teasing an important catch closer to the rowboat so that a net could be dropped. When Captain Turlock passed, inspecting the deck, Spratley winked at him and said, 'This day we'll take him,' and Matt nodded.

All that day the chase continued, and whenever it looked as if the *Ariel* might spring clear, through the excellent management of its sails, Turlock dropped off the wind a point or two, enabling the *Dartmoor* to catch up. One of the sailors complained, 'Damn it, we should be half a day ahead of them,' but Spratley corrected him, 'We don't want to be ahead. We're sucking that bastard into the jaws of hell.' And he stayed by his gun.

During the third night Captain Turlock had to catch some sleep, so he turned the *Ariel* over to Mr. Goodbarn, telling him, 'I think you know what to do,' and the mate nodded. At dawn the *Dartmoor* had moved closer, and when Turlock saw this he was pleased. All that day he sailed through the growing storm in such a way as to keep the British schooner in a position from which she might want to use her guns, but since he did not lower his sails, Captain Gatch could not lower his, either.

At noon Captain Turlock studied the *Dartmoor* through his glass and asked Mr. Goodbarn, 'Has she moved her cannon forward?'

'Two of them. The rest are fixed.'

'But they are forward?'

'They are, sir.'

'Good. Does she seem a mite heavy in the bow?'

'She always has been, since the British captured her.'

'You can see it, too?'

'She's heavy, sir.'

'I thought so. Gatch is a fool.' And he ordered Spratley's movable gun to be shifted far aft. Then he swung his clipper slightly so that it made maximum speed.

A ship, like a human being, moves best when it is slightly athwart the wind, when it has to keep its sails tight and attend its course. Ships, like men, do poorly when the wind is directly behind, pushing them sloppily on their way so that no care is required in steering or in the management of sails; the wind seems favorable, for it blows in the direction one is heading, but actually it is destructive because it induces a relaxation in tension and skill. What is needed is a wind slightly opposed to the ship, for then tension can be maintained, and juices can flow and ideas can germinate, for ships, like men, respond to challenge.

At three that afternoon Captain Turlock, ignoring the signs of fierce wind about to sweep the South Atlantic, had his maximum sails aloft, his course laid so that the wind came at them from two points forward of the starboard quarter. He maintained a port tack, for like every other ship that sailed, the *Ariel* performed slightly better on one tack than the other, and her greatest speed came on the port. From his long acquaintance with the *Whisper,* he suspected that the *Dartmoor* sailed best on her port tack, too. So the two ships were now in a posture of maximum performance.

The duel began. No gun was fired, because Captain Turlock kept tantalizingly just out of range, but from the manner in which he sailed, it must have seemed on the *Dartmoor* that he was about to fall behind, so that the eight heavy guns could riddle him. At any rate, the *Dartmoor* maintained pursuit, and as Captain Turlock watched her plow into the growing waves, bow down, he told Mr. Goodbarn, 'Before sundown.'

At four the wind started to blow in gusts so strong that the mate said, with some urgency, 'We've got to lower the topsails.'

'They stay,' Turlock said.

'You're placing our ship in great danger, sir.'

'And his,' Turlock said.

At five the sky began to darken and by five-thirty it was as foul a day as the *Ariel* had seen. Spratley, convinced that the two ships must close before dark, had ordered his helper to bring six more cannonballs on deck, and the two other gunners had done the same, but when Turlock saw this he was aghast. 'All extra cannonballs to the bottom of the hold! And everything else of weight!' For the next fifteen minutes the crew stowed everything movable belowdeck, with Captain Turlock yelling into the hold, 'Place it all aft! Everything aft!' And as the men did this, he told Mr. Goodbarn, 'We'll stay stern-heavy. Let him have the bow.'

It wasn't enough. Turlock, testing the deck with his feet, sensed that his ship was in peril, so he shouted, 'Spratley's gun! Overboard!'

'Oh, sir?' the little Englishman protested, but Mr. Goodbarn and his men edged the heavy gun to the rail and pushed it over. As it sank unused, Spratley groaned.

Just before darkness set in with that incredible speed it shows in the tropics—daylight one moment, night the next—the sun broke out beneath the cloud cover and illuminated the *Dartmoor* as if she were a golden ship painted upon a porcelain plate used by a queen, her spars, her sails, her decks aglistening. Only for a moment did the light prevail; then, as it began to fade and great winds roared across the ocean, the lovely schooner began to bury her heavy nose in a towering wave, digging deeper and deeper, until she had buried herself completely.

Not a cap floated on the dark Atlantic. The sun vanished. The gold was gone.

From the *Ariel* rose a spontaneous shout, then individual cries of victory, and Spratley danced about the remaining cannon, crying to the captain, 'Down he goes!' But Turlock, agitated beyond control, swept his left arm in a violent circle, knocking the gunner to the deck. 'You weren't fit to tie his shoe.'

Spratley was not to be denied his victory. Leaping to his feet and ignoring the captain, he set a match to one of the guns, and a cannonball shot out across the turbulent waves, skipped once and sank to join the *Dartmoor* in the vast, dark caverns of the sea.

'You may drop the canvas, Mr. Goodbarn,' Turlock said. 'This night we'll ride a gale.'

Voyage Eight: 1822

IN THE REMOTE WASTES OF NORTHERN CANADA,
where man was rarely seen except when lost and about to perish, a family
of great geese, in the late summer of 1822, made their home on a forlorn
stretch of Arctic moorland. Mother, father, six fledglings: because of a
freak of nature they had come to a moment of terrifying danger.

The two adult birds, splendid heavy creatures weighing close to fourteen pounds and with wings normally capable of carrying them five
thousand miles in flight, could not get off the ground. At a time when
they had to feed and protect their offspring, they were powerless to fly.
This was no accident, nor the result of any unfortunate experience with
wolves; like all their breed they lost their heavy wing feathers every
summer and remained earthbound for about six weeks, during which
they could only hide from their enemies and walk ineffectively over the
moorland, waiting for their feathers to return. It was for this reason that
they had laid their eggs in such a remote spot, for during their moulting
period they were almost defenseless.

Onk-or, the father in this family, strutted about the bushes seeking
seeds, while his mate stayed near the nest to tend the fledglings, whose
appetites were insatiable. Occasionally when Onk-or brought food to the
younglings, his mate would run long distances as if pleased to escape the
drudgery of her brood, but on this day when she reached the top of a
grassy mound she ran faster, flapped the wings she had not used for six
weeks and flew back toward her nest, uttering loud cries as she did so.

Onk-or looked up, saw the flight and sensed that within a day or two
he would be soaring too; always her feathers grew back faster than his.
As she flew past he spoke to her.

Maintaining a medium altitude, she headed north to where an arm of the sea intruded, and there she landed on water, splashing it ahead of her when her feet slammed down to act as brakes. Other geese landed to eat the seeds floating on the waves, and after weeks of loneliness she enjoyed their companionship, but before long she rose on the water, flapped her long wings slowly, gathered speed amidst great splashing, then soared into the air, heading back to her nest. From long habit, she landed short of where her fledglings lay, moved about unconcernedly to deceive any foxes that might be watching, then collected bits of food, which she carried to her children. As soon as she appeared, Onk-or walked away, still unable to fly, to gather more food.

He and his mate were handsome birds, large and sleek. Both they and their children had long necks feathered in jet-black, with a broad snowy white bib under the chin and reaching to the ears. When their wings were folded, as they were most of the time, the heavy body was compact and beautifully proportioned, and they walked with dignity, not waddling from side to side like ducks. Their heads were finely proportioned, with bills pointed but not grotesquely long, and the lines of their bodies, where feathers of differing shades of gray joined, were pleasing. Indeed, their subdued coloring was so appropriate to the Arctic moorland that an observer, had there been one, could have come close to their nest without noticing them.

On this day there was an observer, an Arctic fox who had not eaten for some time and was beginning to feel the urge of hunger. When from a distance he spotted the rough nest on the ground, with the six fledglings tumbling about and obviously not prepared to fly, he took no precipitate action, for he had learned respect for the sharp beaks and powerful wings of full-grown geese like Onk-or.

Instead he retreated and ran in large circles far from the nest, until he roused another fox to make the hunt with him. Together they returned quietly across the tundra, moving from the security of one tussock to the next, scouting the terrain ahead and developing the strategy they would use to pick off these young geese.

During the brightest part of the day they lay in wait, for long ago they had learned that it was easier to attack at night, when they would be less conspicuous against the Arctic grass. Of course, during the nesting season of the geese there was no real night; the sun stayed in the heavens permanently, scudding low in the north but never disappearing. Instead of blackness, which would last interminably during the winter, there came only a diffused grayness in the middle hours, a ghostly penumbra, with geese, young and old, half asleep. That was the time to attack.

So as the sun drifted lower in the west, on a long, sliding trajectory that would never dip below the horizon, and as the bright glare of summer faded to an exquisite gray matching the feathers of the geese, the two foxes moved slowly toward the nest where the six fledglings hid beneath the capacious wings of their mother. Onk-or, the foxes noted, lay some distance away with his head under his left wing.

It was the plan of the foxes that the strongest of the pair would attack Onk-or from such a direction that the big male goose would be lured even farther from the nest, and as the fight progressed, the other fox would dart in, engage the female briefly, and while she was awkwardly trying to defend herself, grab one of the young geese and speed away. In the confusion the first fox might very well be able to grab a second fledgling for himself. If not, they would share the one they did get.

When the foxes had attained a strategic position, the first made a lunge at Onk-or, attacking from the side on which he had tucked his head, on the logical supposition that if the great goose were not instantly alert, the fox might be lucky and grab him by the throat, ending that part of the fight then and there. But as soon as the fox accelerated his pace, knocking aside grasses, Onk-or was awake and aware of what was happening. He did not try evasive action or do anything unusual to protect his neck; instead he pivoted on his left leg, swung his moulted wing in a small circle and with its bony edge knocked his adversary flat.

Onk-or knew that the fox would try to lure him away from the nest, so instead of following up on his first blow, he retreated toward the low pile of sticks and grass that constituted his nest, making sharp clicking sounds to alert his family. His mate, aware that the family was being attacked, drew the fledglings under her wings and studied the ominous grayness.

She did not have long to wait. As the first fox lunged at Onk-or again, the second swept in to attack the nest itself. She had only one flashing moment to ascertain from which direction the attack was coming, but she judged accurately, rose, spread her wings and pivoted to meet the fox. As he leaped at her, she struck him across the face with her powerful beak, stunning him momentarily.

He soon recovered to make a second attack. This time she was prepared, and a harsh swipe of her wing edge sent him sprawling, but this terrified her, for instinct warned her that he may cunningly have seemed to fall so as to distract her. If she struck at him now, he would slyly dart behind her and grab one of the fledglings. So as the fox fell, she wheeled on her right foot, placing herself and her extended wings between him and the nest. As for the rear, she had to depend upon Onk-or to protect that from the other fox.

This he was doing. In the half-light he fought the clever fox, fending him off with vicious stabs of his beak, knocking him down with his powerful wing thrusts and filling the Arctic air with short cries of rage and challenge. The fox, who had never been confident that he could subdue a grown male goose, began to lose any hope that he could even hold his own against this infuriated bird. Furthermore, he saw that his partner had accomplished nothing at the nest and was, indeed, absorbing an equal thrashing.

Hoping in vain that the two geese would make some fatal mistake, the two foxes battled on for a while, recognized the futility of their attack and withdrew, making short, chattering noises to one another as they did.

When daylight came the two parent geese knew how necessary it was that their six children proceed with the business of flying. So on this day Onk-or did not leave the nest to forage for his family; he stayed by the odd collection of twigs and grasses and nudged his children out onto the moorland, watching them as they clumsily tried their wings.

They were an ungainly lot, stumbling and falling and vainly beating their long wings, but gradually attaining the mastery which would enable them to fly south to the waters of Maryland. Two of the young birds actually hoisted themselves into the air, staying aloft for short distances, then landing with maximum awkwardness and joy.

A third, watching the success of her siblings, flapped her wings clumsily, ran across the rocky ground and with great effort got herself into the air, but as soon as she did so, Onk-or felt a rush of terror, for he saw something she did not.

Too late! The gosling, unable to maintain flight, fluttered heavily to the ground, landing precisely where the two foxes had been waiting for such a misadventure. But as they started for the fallen bird, Onk-or, with supreme effort, flapped his wings not yet ready for flight, rose in the air and endeavored to smash down at the foxes. His wings were not equal to the task, and he, too, fell, but before the dust was gone from his eyes he was on his feet, charging at the two foxes. Insolently, the first fox grabbed the gosling, killing it with one savage snap of the jaws, and sped away. The second fox ran in circles, tantalizing Onk-or, then disappeared to join his partner in their feast.

What did this family of seven think as they reassembled? Onk-or and his mate were unusual in the animal kingdom in that they mated for life. They were as tightly married as any human couple in Patamoke; each cared desperately what happened to the other, and Onk-or would unhesitatingly sacrifice his life to protect that of his mate. Four times they had flown together down from the Arctic to the Eastern Shore, and four times back. Together they had located safe resting spots up and down eastern Canada and in all the seaboard states of America. Aloft, they communicated instinctively, each knowing what the other intended, and on the ground, either when nesting in the Arctic or feeding along the Choptank, each always felt responsible for the safety of the other.

In this habit of permanent marriage they were like few other birds, certainly not like the lesser ducks who mated at will, staying close to each other only so long as their ducklings needed protection. It was a curiosity

peculiar to the great geese. Beavers also married for life—perhaps because they had to live together during their winters in lodges frozen over
—but few other animals. Onk-or was married to his mate, eternally.

His first response, therefore, as the foxes disappeared with one of his
daughters, was an intuitive checking to assure himself that his mate was
safe. Satisfied on this crucial point, his attention shifted to his five remaining children. They must learn to fly—now—and not stumble into
traps set by enemies.

His mate, who had remained on the ground during the loss of the
fledgling, had not been able to ascertain what was happening with the
foxes, for the incident had occurred behind a cluster of tussocks, and for
one dreadful moment she had feared that it might be he the foxes had
taken. She was relieved when she saw him stumbling back, for he was
half her life, the gallant, fearless bird on whom she must depend.

But she also possessed a most powerful urge to protect her offspring;
she would surrender her own life to achieve this, and now the first of
them had been stolen. She did not grieve, as she would have done had
Onk-or been killed, but she did feel a dreadful sense of loss, and like her
mate, determined that the other five must quickly learn to fly. In the days
to come she would be a ruthless teacher.

As for the goslings, each knew that a fox had stolen the missing child.
Each knew that tragedy, from which their parents tried to protect them,
had struck, and the nascent urges which had caused them to attempt
flight were intensified. They had never made the long pilgrimage to the
feeding grounds of Maryland, but intuitively they knew that such
grounds must be somewhere and they should ready themselves for the
incredible migration. They were determined to master their wings; they
were determined to protect themselves from foxes.

Of course, these birds were too young to have selected partners, nor
had they associated with other geese. But even at this early stage they
were aware of the difference between the sexes, so that the three young
males were looking for something quite different from what the two
remaining females were awaiting, and as other families of geese flew
overhead, each fledgling could differentiate the children in that tentative
flock. They knew. At seven weeks it was incredible what these young
geese knew, and if by some ill chance both their parents should be killed,
leaving them orphaned in the Arctic, they would know how to fly to
Maryland and find the Choptank cove that had been designated as their
home. All they needed for maturity was the strengthening of their wings
and the selection of a mate from the other fledglings born that year. They
were a doughty breed, one of the great birds of the world, and they
behaved so.

In mid-September, as in each year of their lives, Onk-or and his mate
felt irresistible urgings. They watched the sky and were particularly

responsive to the shortening of the day. They noticed with satisfaction that their five children were large and powerful birds, with notable wing spans and sustaining accumulations of fat; they were ready for any flight. They also noticed the browning of the grasses and the ripening of certain seeds, signs unmistakable that departure was imminent.

At all the nests in the Arctic this restlessness developed and birds bickered with one another. Males would suddenly rise in the sky and fly long distances for no apparent reason, returning later to land in clouds of dust. No meetings were held; there was no visible assembling of families. But one day, for mysterious reasons which could not be explained, huge flocks of birds rose into the sky, milled about and then formed into companies heading south.

This southward migration was one of the marvels of nature: hundreds, thousands, millions of these huge geese forming into perfect V-shaped squadrons flying at different altitudes and at different times of day, but all heading out of Canada down one of the four principal flyways leading to varied corners of America. Some flew at 29,000 feet above the ground, others as low as 3,000, but all sought escape from the freezing moorlands of the Arctic, heading for clement feeding grounds like those in Maryland. For long spells they would fly in silence, but most often they maintained noisy communication, arguing, protesting, exulting; at night especially they uttered cries which echoed forever in the memories of men who heard them drifting down through the frosty air of autumn: *'Onk-or, onk-or!'*

The wedge in which Onk-or and his family started south this year consisted of eighty-nine birds, but it did not stay together permanently as a cohesive unit. Sometimes other groups would meld with it, until the flying formation contained several hundred birds; at other times segments would break away to fly with some other unit. But in general the wedge held together.

The geese flew at a speed of about forty-five miles an hour, which meant that if they stayed aloft for an entire day, they could cover a thousand miles. But they required rest, and through the centuries during which they had followed the same route south and north they had learned of various ponds and lakes and riverbanks which afforded them secure places to rest and forage. There were lakes in upper Quebec and small streams leading into the St. Lawrence. In Maine there were hundreds of options and suitable spots in western Massachusetts and throughout New York, and the older geese like Onk-or knew them all.

On some days, near noon when the autumn sun was high, the geese would descend abruptly and alight on a lake which their ancestors had been utilizing for a thousand years. The trees along the shore would have changed, and new generations of fish would occupy the waters, but the seeds would be the same kind, and the succulent grasses. Here the birds would rest for six or seven hours, and then as dusk approached, the leaders would utter signals and the flock would scud across the surface of the lake, wheel into the air and fly aloft. There they would form themselves automatically into a long V, with some old, sage bird like Onk-or in the lead, and through the night they would fly south.

Maine, New Hampshire, Massachusetts, Connecticut, New York, Pennsylvania! The states would lie sleeping below, only a few dim lamps betraying their existence, and overhead the geese would go, crying in the night, *'Onk-or, onk-or,'* and occasionally, at the edge of some village or on some farm a door would open and light would flood the area for a while, and parents would hold their children and peer into the dark sky, listening to the immortal passing of the geese. And once in a great while, on such a night, when the moon was full, the children would actually see the flying wedge pass between them and the moon, and hear the geese as they flew, and this matter they would speak of for the rest of their lives.

No goose, not even a powerful one like Onk-or, could fly at the head of the wedge for long periods. The buffeting of the wind as the point of the V broke a path through the air turbulence was too punishing. The best a practiced bird could do was about forty minutes, during which time he absorbed a considerable thrashing. After his allotted time in the lead position, the exhausted goose would drop to the back of one of the arms of the wedge, where the weaker birds had been assembled, and there, with the air well broken ahead of him, he would coast along in the wake of the others, recovering his strength until it came his time again to assume the lead. Male and female alike accepted this responsibility, and when the day's flight ended, they were content to rest. On especially favorable lakes with copious feed they might stay for a week.

During the first days of October the geese were usually somewhere in New York or Pennsylvania, and happy to be there. The sun was warm and the lakes congenial, but as the northwest winds began to blow, bringing frost at night, the older birds grew restive. They did not relish a sudden freeze, which would present problems, and they vaguely knew that the waning of the sun required them to be farther south in some region of security.

But they waited until the day came when the air was firmly frosted, and then they rose to form their final V. No matter where the lake had been upon which they were resting, the geese in the eastern flyway vectored in to the Susquehanna River, and when they saw its broad and twisting silhouette, they felt safe. This was their immemorial guide, and they followed it with assurance, breaking at last onto the Chesapeake, the most considerable body of water they would see during their migration. It shimmered in the autumn sun and spoke of home. Its thousand estuaries and coves promised them food and refuge for the long winter, and they joyed to see it.

As soon as the Chesapeake was reached, congregations of geese began to break off, satisfied that they had arrived at their appointed locations. Four thousand would land at Havre de Grace, twenty thousand at the Sassafras. The Chester River would lure more than a hundred thousand and the Miles the same. Enormous concentrations would elect Tred Avon, but the most conspicuous aggregation would wait for the Choptank, more than a quarter of a million birds, and they would fill every field and estuary.

For more than five thousand years Onk-or's lineal antecedents had favored a marsh on the north bank of the Choptank. It was spacious, well-grassed with many plants producing seeds, and multiple channels providing safe hiding places. It was convenient both to fields, so that the geese could forage for seeds, and to the river, so that they could land and take off easily. It was an ideal wintering home in every respect but one: it was owned by the Turlocks, the most inveterate hunters of Maryland, each member of the family born with an insatiable appetite for goose.

'I can eat it roasted, or chopped with onions and peppers, or sliced thin with mushrooms,' Lafe Turlock was telling the men at the store. 'You can keep the other months of the year, just give me November with a fat goose comin' onto the stove three times a week.'

Lafe had acquired from his father and his father before him the secrets of hunting geese. 'Canniest birds in the world. They have a sixth sense, a seventh and an eighth. I've seen one smart old gander haunts my place lead his flock right into my blind, spot my gun, stop dead in the air, turn his whole congregation around on a sixpence, without me gettin' a shot.' He kicked the stove and volunteered his summary of the situation: 'A roast goose tastes so good because it's so danged hard to shoot.'

'Why's that?' a younger hunter asked.

Lafe turned to look at the questioner, studied him contemptuously as an interloper, then explained, 'I'll tell you what, sonny, I know your farm down the river. Fine farm for huntin' geese. Maybe a hundred thousand fly past in the course of a week, maybe two hundred thousand. But that ain't doin' you no good, because unless you can tease just one of those geese to drop down within gunshot of where you stand, you ain't never gonna kill a goose. They fly over there'—he flailed his long arms—'or over here, or down there, a hundred thousand geese in sight . . .' He startled the young man by leaping from his chair and banging his fist against the wall. 'But never one goddamned goose where you want him. It's frustratin'.'

He sat down, cleared his throat and spoke like a lawyer presenting a difficult case. 'So what you got to do, sonny, is pick yourself a likely spot where they might land, and build yourself a blind—'

'I done that.'

Lafe ignored the interruption. 'And hide it in branches that look live, and all round it put wooden decoys whittled into at least eight different positions to look real, and then learn to yell goose cries that would fool the smartest goose ever lived. And if you don't do all these things, sonny, you ain't never gonna taste goose, because they gonna fly past you, night and day.'

The attractive thing about Lafe was his unquenchable enthusiasm. Each October, like now, he was convinced that this year he would outsmart the geese, and he was not afraid to make his predictions public at the store. 'This year, gentlemen, you all eat goose. I'm gonna shoot so many, your fingers'll grow warts pluckin' 'em.'

'That's what you said last year,' an uncharitable waterman grunted.

'But this year I got me a plan.' And with a finger dipped in molasses he started to outline his strategy. 'You know my blind out in the river.'

'I stood there often enough, gettin' nothin',' one of the men said.

'And you know this blind at that pond in the western end of the marsh.'

'I waited there for days and all I got was a wet ass,' the same man said.

'And that's what you'll get in that blind this year, too. Because I'm settin' them two up just like always, decoys and all. I want that smart old leader to see them and lead his ladies away.'

'To where?' the skeptic asked.

Lafe grinned and a deep satisfaction wreathed his face. 'Now for my plan. Over here, at the edge of this cornfield where everythin' looks so innicent, I plant me a third blind with the best decoys me or my pappy ever carved.' And with a dripping finger he allowed the molasses to form his new blind.

'I don't think it'll work,' the cynic said.

'I'm gonna get me so many geese . . .'

'Like last year. How many you get last year, speak honest.'

'I got me nine geese . . .' In six months he had shot nine geese, but this year, with his new tactics, he was sure to get scores.

So when Onk-or brought his wedge of eighty-nine back to the Choptank marshes, dangerous innovations awaited. Of course, on his first pass over Turlock land he spotted the traditional blind in the river and the ill-concealed one at the pond; generations of his family had been avoiding those inept seductions. He also saw the same old decoys piled on the bank, the boats waiting to take the hunters into the river and the dogs waiting near the boats. It was familiar and it was home.

Giving a signal, he dropped in a tight, crisp circle, keeping his left wing almost stationary, then landed with a fine splashing on an opening in the center of the marsh. He showed his five children how to dispose themselves, then pushed his way through the marsh grass to see for himself what feed there might be in the fields. His mate came along, and within a few minutes they had satisfied themselves that this was going to be a good winter. On their way back to the marsh they studied the cabin. No changes there; same wash behind the kitchen.

As the geese settled in to enjoy the marshes, the young birds heard for the first time the reverberation of gunfire, and Onk-or had to spend much time alerting them to the special dangers that accompanied these rich feeding grounds. He and the other ganders taught the newcomers how to spot the flash of metal, or hear the cracking of a twig under a gunner's boot. And no group must ever feed without posting at least three sentinels, whose job it was to keep their necks erect so that their ears and eyes could scout all approaches.

Eternal vigilance was the key to survival, and no birds ever became more skilled in protecting themselves. Smaller birds, like doves, which presented difficult targets for a hunter, could often trust to luck that an undetected human would miss when he fired at them, but the great goose presented such an attractive target either head-on or broadside that a gunner had the advantage, if he were allowed to creep within range. The trick for the geese was to move out of range whenever men approached, and Onk-or drilled his flock assiduously in this tactic, for any goose who frequented the Turlock marshes was threatened by some of the most determined hunters on the Eastern Shore.

By mid-December it was clear that the geese had outsmarted Lafe Turlock once again; none had landed at the blind in the river and only a few stragglers had landed at the pond. By the end of the first week Onk-or had spotted the cornfield trick, and Lafe had been able to shoot only three geese.

'Them damn honkers must of got eyeglasses in Canada,' he told the men at the store.

'You was gonna feed us all this winter,' one of the men reminded him.

'I will, too. What I got to do is make a few changes in my plan.'

He assembled his five sons, plus four other crack shots, and told them, 'We are gonna get ourselves so many geese, you'll have grease on your faces all winter. We do it this way.'

An hour before dawn he rowed his youngest son out to the river blind, before which they strung a dozen decoys haphazardly. He told his boy, 'I want for the geese to see you. Make 'em move on.'

Another son he placed at the pond, with the same careless arrangement and the same instructions. 'Of course, son, if you get a good shot at a goose, take it. But we ain't relyin' on you.'

At the cornfield he posted yet a third son, expecting him to be seen. The six other men he took on a long walk through loblolly, ending at a cove where he said the canny geese would have to land. 'The trick is to think like a goose. They'll leave the cornfield, fly in a half-circle, see the decoys beyond the pine trees and come down here.'

When they came down, they were going to land in the middle of a fusillade from the four fastest guns, followed immediately by a second round from the three slower guns, during which time the first four would load again to pick off the cripples, by which time the slow guns could reload to do any cleaning up.

'This is guaranteed to get honkers,' Lafe promised, 'if'n that damned big bird don't catch on.'

The geese were slow this morning in going to their feeding stations. There was fractiousness among the younger birds, but the elders did not protest, for mating time was approaching and there were many second-year geese who had not yet selected their partners, so that confusion was inescapable. But toward six-thirty Onk-or and another old gander began making the moves that would get the flock started. Restlessness ceased and eighty-odd birds began moving into positions from which they could take to the air.

Onk-or led the flight, and within moments the flock had formed into two loose Vs which wheeled and dipped in unison. They headed for the river south of the marsh, and Onk-or saw that some hunter was still trying vainly to lure geese into the old blind located there. The big birds landed well upstream, fed for a while on grasses, then took off for better forage. They flew to the pond, where there was futile gunfire, and then toward the cornfield, where Onk-or quickly spotted the lone gunner stationed there. He swung away from the corn, flew left, and saw some geese feeding in a stream lined by pine trees. Since the geese already down proved that the area was safe, he would land his flock there.

The geese came in low, wings extended, feet ready for braking, but just as Onk-or prepared to land, he detected movement among the pine trees lining the shore, and with a brilliant twist to the north he swung out of range, uttering loud cries of warning as he did so. He escaped, and those immediately behind made their turns, too, but many of the trailing geese did not react in time; they flew directly into the waiting guns and furious blasts of fire knocked them down.

Seven geese were killed, including two of Onk-or's children. It was a disaster, and he had been responsible. It must not happen again.

At the store Lafe basked in his victory. 'To catch a honker you got to think like a honker,' he told his listeners, but his glory was short-lived, because for the rest of the season he got no geese from his own marshes, and only two when he led an expedition farther upstream.

'I never seen honkers so cagey,' he snarled. 'I'm goin' to hire me them trolls from Amos Todkill.' So in January 1823 he sailed up to Patamoke to dicker with Todkill, who specialized in combing the marshes for wounded young geese, which he domesticated, using them as living lures to bring wild geese directly into the muzzles of waiting guns.

Todkill said he'd allow Turlock to rent fifteen of his tame geese, three days for a dollar and a half. 'Pretty steep,' Lafe complained.

'But you know they're foolproof. "Never-fails," we call 'em.'

Todkill tied their legs, tossed them into his boat and sailed back to the marsh. 'I want me fifteen or sixteen reliable guns,' he announced at the store. 'I laid out real money for them damned trolls, and I expect some honkers in return.'

He enlisted a veritable battery, whose members he stationed at strategic spots so that the crossfire from the muzzle-loaders would be impenetrable. He then spread four dozen of his most lifelike wooden decoys, after which he released Todkill's fifteen live ones. 'As pretty a sight as a honker ever seen, and as deadly,' he said approvingly when all was in position.

Then he and the sixteen other hunters waited. Nothing happened. Occasional geese from the marshes flew past, ignoring the trolls, who cackled to lure them down. Once or twice substantial flocks, headed by the old gander, came tantalizingly close, then veered away as if in obedience to a signal, and the three days passed without one good shot at a honker.

Onk-or from the first had spotted the bizarre assembly of wooden decoys and live trolls, and it was not long before he discerned the guns hiding among the rushes. He not only kept his own geese from the lethal area; he also alerted others, so that Lafe and his artillery could not possibly get themselves the geese he had promised.

At the store one of the hunters said, 'Them trolls fooled me, and they fooled Lafe, but they sure as hell didn't fool that old gander.'

'What they did,' Lafe said, 'was waste my dollar-fifty. It was only through the help of prayer that I kept from stranglin' them birds before I gave 'em back to Todkill.'

The men laughed. The idea of Lafe Turlock's hurting a goose, except to shoot it, was preposterous. He loved the big birds, fed them cracked corn when snow covered the ground, rescued cripples the end of the season and turned them over to Todkill. Once, after a big revival meeting, he said, 'The life of man is divided into two seasons: "Geese is here. Geese ain't here." ' So when the men joshed him over his costly failure, they were surprised that he did not fight back.

He remained silent for a good reason: he was ready to shift into phase three of his grand design. Assembling his sons in early March, he told them, 'Turlocks eat geese because we're smarter'n geese. And a danged sight smarter'n them dummies at the store, because I know somethin' that would rile 'em, if'n they had brains to understand.'

His sons waited. He looked out the door at the March sky and confided, 'I been trampin' through the woods, and I think I found me the spot where they does their courtin'.' He was referring to those few geese who had either been wounded by ineffective gunfire or seduced by the clemency of the Choptank; they would not be flying north with the others, but would remain behind, raising their Maryland-born families in marshes to the south. And when they mated, they would be vulnerable, for as Lafe explained to his sons, 'Geese is just like men. When their minds get fixed on ass, caution goes out the window, and come next week we're gonna knock down enough careless geese to feed us through July.'

It was in the deepest nature of a Turlock to be sanguine where hunting and fishing were concerned: the oysters were down there but they could be tonged; the crabs might be hiding but they could be caught. 'How we gonna do it, Pop?'

'Strategy,' Lafe said.

Onk-or, too, was thinking strategy. He must get his flock through the frenzy of this season without loss, and to accomplish this he must keep them away from the mating grounds, for he had learned that when young geese gawked at their contemporaries in the mating dance, they grew inattentive, and their elders were no better, for they, too, stood about cackling and enjoying the proceedings, unmindful of lurking guns.

So for both Lafe and Onk-or the last days of winter became critical, for the man had to find the mating ground, and the goose had to keep his family away from it. Nine days went by without a loss to the Turlock guns.

'No fear,' Lafe assured his boys. 'Honkers has got to mate, and when they do, we come into our own.'

He had anticipated, almost better than the young geese, where those who did not fly north would conduct their courtships, and there, along a grassy field deep in the woods, he placed himself and his sons, each with three muskets. The young geese, responding to their own inner urgings, were drawn to this spot, and there they began their dances.

Two males would focus upon one female, who would stand aside, shyly preening herself, as if she held a mirror. She would keep her eyes on the ground, pretending to ignore events which would determine how she would live for the remainder of her life.

The males meanwhile grew more and more active, snapping at each other and hissing, advancing and retreating and putting on a great show of fury. Finally one would actually attack the other, flailing with wings extended six or seven feet, and crashing heavy blows upon the head and shoulders of the other. Now the fight became real, with each heavy bird attempting to grab the other's head in its powerful beak.

According to some intricate scoring system, it would become apparent to both contestants, to the rest of the flock and especially to the waiting female that one of the fighting birds had triumphed. The other would retreat, and then would come the most moving part of the dance.

The victorious male would approach the waiting female with mincing steps, swaying from side to side, and as he drew near he would extend his neck to the fullest and gently wave it back and forth, close to the chosen one, and she would extend hers, and they would intertwine, rarely touching, and they would stand thus, weaving and twisting their necks in one of the most delicate and graceful manifestations in nature.

As the dance approached its climax, the young geese of Onk-or's group started instinctively toward the mating ground, and although Onk-or and his mate moved frantically to intercept them, they bumbled their way into the open area.

'Now!' Turlock signaled, and the guns blazed. Before the startled geese could take to the air, the six Turlocks dropped their guns, grabbed others and blazed away, dropped them and reached for their back-ups. Geese fell in startling numbers, and by the time Onk-or could get his flock into the air, enough lay dead to stock the icehouse.

When they reassembled in the marsh Onk-or discovered that one of his sons was dead, and he was about to lament when he found to his terror that his wife was missing, too. He had seen geese falter and fall into the grass offshore, and he knew intuitively that the men would now be combing that margin to find the cripples.

Without hesitation he left his flock and sped back to the mating ground. His arrival disconcerted the men who, as he had expected, were searching for wounded birds. Flying directly over their heads, he landed in the area at which he had seen the geese falling, and there he found his mate, sorely crippled in the left wing. It was impossible for her to fly, and within minutes the dogs and men would find her.

Urging her with heavy pushes of his bill, he shoved her through ill-defined waterways, heading her always toward the safety of the deeper marshes. When she faltered, he pecked at her feathers, never allowing her to stop.

They had progressed about two hundred yards when a mongrel yellow dog with an especially good nose came upon their scent and realized that he had a cripple somewhere in the bushes ahead. Silently he made his way ever closer to the wounded goose, until, with a final leap, he was upon her.

What he did not anticipate was that she was accompanied by a full-grown gander determined to protect her. Suddenly, from the water near the cripple, Onk-or rose up, whipped his heavy beak about and slashed at the dog. The startled animal withdrew in shock, then perceived the situation and lunged at the gander.

A deadly, splashing fight ensued, with the dog having every advantage. But Onk-or marshaled all his powers; he was fighting not only to protect himself but also to save his crippled mate, and deep in the tangled marsh he attacked the dog with a confusing flash of wing and thrust of beak. The dog retreated.

'There's a cripple in there!' Turlock shouted to his sons. 'Tiger's got hisse'f a cripple.'

But the dog appeared with nothing except a bleeding cut on the head. 'Hey! Tiger's been hit by a honker. Get in there and find that cripple.'

Three boys and their dogs splashed into the marsh, but by this time Onk-or had guided his damaged mate to safety. They hid among the rushes as the men splashed noisily, while the mongrels, not eager to encounter whatever had struck Tiger, made little attempt to find them.

A week later, when the crippled wing had mended, Onk-or herded his geese together and they started their mandatory flight to the Arctic: Pennsylvania, Connecticut, Maine, and then the frozen moorlands of Canada. One night as they flew over a small town in central New York they made a great honking, and citizens came out to follow their mysterious passage. Among them was a boy of eight. He stared at the shadowy forms and listened to their distant conversation. As a consequence of this one experience he would become attached to birds, would study all things about them, and in his adult life would paint them and write about them and take the first steps in providing sanctuaries for them, and all because on one moonlit night he heard the geese pass overhead.

Widow's Walk

ROSALIND'S REVENGE DID NOT HAVE A TRUE widow's walk. That agreeable architectural device had flourished mainly in New England, where the family of a sailing man was accustomed to erect on the roof of its home a square, fenced platform from which the wife could look down the bay to spot the arrival of her husband's vessel, coming home after years of whaling in the South Pacific. The name *widow's walk* derived from romantic tales of those loyal women who continued to keep watch for a ship that had long since gone to the bottom of some coral sea.

But the big plantation house of the Steeds did have an improvised widow's walk. In 1791, when Isham Steed followed the advice of his college mate Tom Jefferson and bought himself an Amsterdam telescope, he wanted to erect it in a place from which he could follow the stars, so he cut a hole through the roof and built there a platform, fencing it with low pickets and making it a pleasant spot from which to view not only the heavens but also the sailing ships moving up and down the bay.

During one unseasonably warm day at the end of March in 1823 Susan Grimes Steed went up to this fenced area and fell languidly into the wicker chair she kept there. For nearly a quarter of an hour she stared at the bay, hoping to spot some tall ship coming home to Baltimore, but her attention was distracted when she heard a rustling in the air above her. Looking up, she saw that great numbers of geese were assembling in elongated Vs; from all the coves and corners of the Choptank they rose in preparation for their long flight to Canada.

Knowing that this time the geese were truly leaving and would not be seen again till the cool days of autumn, she rose from her chair and pressed her hands against the picket fence. 'Oh God! That I were flying with you!' She lifted her right hand and waved the distant birds on their way, watching them until they became invisible at the horizon.

She sank back onto her chair and gazed blankly at the bay. No boats were discernible; no ships came in from Spain; only the vast expanse of water, unruffled clear to the western shore, stretched before her, and the ennui which had possessed her for some months increased.

But then, at the southern extremity of the water visible from the roof, she saw what might be a ship—at least, it was a moving speck, and she kept her small telescope focused on it for a long half-hour.

It could be a fishing boat, she mused, eager to find any mental exercise to occupy her mind. No, it's a ship. It's a ship with three masts. And at the word *masts,* the obsessive sexual fantasies returned.

She interpreted the ship as a man coming up the bay to lie with her, to wrestle with her furiously, to tear her clothes away and chase her through the woods of Devon. As the images continued, her lips became dry, and when the homecoming ship stood opposite the island, its sails set for Baltimore, she rose from the chair and stood by the fence, her eyes fixed on the tall masts, her body aching with desire.

I wish I were on that ship, she lamented, and as it drew away, its masts gray against the sun, she imagined herself in the captain's cabin, and he naked and hungry for her.

This is sickness! she thought, shaking her head violently. She drew her tossed curls across her eyes, as if to shut out the dreaded visions, but they still persisted, and she leaned heavily against the fence, allowing its points to jab her hands.

She remained in this position until the ship vanished, taking with it her phallic imagery. Only then did she climb down the ladder and walk slowly to her bedroom, where she lay on the silken coverlet, staring at the two cannonballs imbedded in the wall: If only they had come lower to strike him in his bed . . .

But she was horrified at the thought that she could wish her husband dead, and she threw her arms across her face and cried aloud, 'What a wretched woman I have become.'

'Did you call, ma'am?' Eden asked from the door.

'No. Go away.' The black girl disappeared, and she was left with her fantasies.

They stemmed from her savage disappointment in her husband. She now saw Paul Steed as a dilettante, a waster of himself and of everything with which he came into contact; always he stood in demeaning contrast to her, for she had inherited her Grandfather Simon's highly organized directness of purpose. When she first appeared at Devon she may have seemed a giddy girl, but she had never intended remaining that way. She suspected that this alteration had surprised and in a sense disappointed her husband, for shortly after their marriage he had told her, 'When we first met at the wharf you were a beautiful, innocent child. Let's not allow the years to change us.' But she had changed, and he had not.

And yet, she had to confess that in the early days of their marriage he had been almost exciting. He obviously loved her and had her pregnant almost immediately. Initially they had enjoyed their large bed, but quickly it had become a site for routine performances on his part, if not hers. Two other pregnancies had followed—how, she sometimes wondered—and by the end of the fifth year, the marriage was routine, and flat, and terribly dull.

She had become aware of his moral weakness when he began spoiling the children through lack of force, and weakening the family's business through lack of attention. She had tried to be a good mother, disciplining the children when he would not, but this led them to look exclusively to her for guidance: Paul should be talking with them. Damn it, we have three of the finest children in Maryland and he ignores them. There was a son six, a daughter four and a rambunctious son of two, and each seemed bright beyond expectations; already she had taught Mark, the oldest, to read and cipher, and the girl was aping him with surprising ease.

'We ought to be a happy family,' she muttered one day. 'The ingredients are in place.' But Paul engaged so small a portion of her interests and capacities that she felt unused, as if she were a reservoir of great potential but with no outlets. He was a silly man, and she often wondered what the professors at Princeton could have taught him, if they had bothered with him at all. His ideas were fragmentary; his goals wandering; his beliefs evanescent. He commanded little respect among the Steeds and had little chance of keeping the plantation system under control.

She was nearing thirty, at what should have been the threshold of her mature life, and the prospect of living it with a man who wasted his talents terrified her. It was not that she found herself ill-at-ease away from London, as her mother had done. She liked Maryland, and on the eve of her departure from England, all members of her family had warned her that she must not follow in the footsteps of the unfortunate Jane Fithian Steed. Old Carstairs Fithian told her, 'Your grandmother was my sister, and both Guy and I tried to prepare her for the colonies. Warned her that she must make the concessions, not her husband. She must not expect London and she must not expect her hard-working husband to be a Paris dandy. Your grandmother was a headstrong girl, fought America at every turn, and in the end surrendered control of her mind. If you marry young Steed, you must make adjustments to his standards.'

None needed to be made, at least in the fields which had caused Grandmother Jane to destroy herself; Susan loved the freedom of Maryland, the varied types of people she met along the Choptank, the new kinds of food, the fun of visiting Annapolis. Especially she liked the bay and the wild life that abounded along its edges; Devon Island still contained more than a score of deer, and when geese occupied the river they enchanted her: A group of old gossips chattering in the sunlight.

Her malaise was not based on selfishness, or petty indulgence. She was a good hostess, and when plantation neighbors came to stay for a week or two, she made them feel they were conferring an honor on her by their presence; she saw to it that their children were entertained, and that the slaves took them for donkey rides to the end of the island or on boating trips out into the bay. Under her management there was much happiness at Rosalind's Revenge; she was an excellent chatelaine and had she been fifty-five or sixty, there would have been no problem. Unfortunately, she was twenty-nine.

In February that year she had slipped into a destructive habit. While lying in bed one night, fretful over her husband's inattention, she happened to stick her left foot out from under the covers, as if she meant to leave the bed, and the sense of freedom generated by this simple act amazed her: If I wanted to, I could put out my other foot and forsake this place.

So she adopted the habit of sleeping with one foot free. One morning Eden came upon her dozing thus and reprimanded her, 'Ma'am, you catch cold,' but she offered no explanation, and Eden noticed that she continued to keep one foot uncovered.

The cannonballs presented a problem, too. From various bits picked up from the slaves, it was obvious that Paul had not been sleeping in this room at the time of the early-morning bombardment, and that when he ran to the shore, brandishing his musket, Captain Gatch's flotilla had long since gone. Yet there the two balls remained in the wall, cemented in place for the neighbors to admire, a celebration of his heroism.

She remembered the first time she had inspected them. 'Is there a chair I might stand on?' she had asked, but before anyone could answer, she had turned, and Captain Turlock had lifted her, and she had felt the silver fist pressing against her leg—

I've got to stop this! But her mind was unable to comply.

With the geese gone, the days lengthened and the bay warmed. Now she went to the roof almost daily, relaxing in the wicker chair like a sea captain, using her telescope to follow the ships moving north and south, and trying vainly to detect what was happening on the western shore. She could see the outline of trees and on clear days could even identify specific buildings, but the people occupying them remained invisible, two or three degrees too small to be distinguished.

'Come forth, damn you!' she sometimes cried, as if the farmers were maliciously hiding from her. Then she would lean back and stare at the sky—birdless, cloudless, infinitely remote—and she would think: I'm as invisible to them up there as the people across the bay are to me.

But whenever she began feeling overwhelmed by self-pity she would rush down from the roof and start to work in her garden, that vast semi-wild space with the trees and the flowering shrubs, After the first summer in 1816, when the amber daylilies had exploded all over the lawn, she had patiently worked to confine them to limited areas, digging out the wanderers and rimming the desirable clusters with pebbled borders.

This was hard work and would normally have been turned over to slaves, but she loved flowers, especially the robust daylilies, and on some days she worked till dusk, weeding and digging and replacing pebbles. She did not try to prettify the place. Old Rosalind Janney Steed had left written instructions for all the women who might follow her as mistress of this garden:

> I pray you, no roses, no mazes, no formal footpaths, no marble statues from Italy, and, for the love of God, no box.

But trees died, and unless their departure was anticipated and others planted to take their place when they were gone, a forested garden would, over the course of two or three generations, fall apart. Susan was determined that when she left hers, it would be good for another fifty years.

She was there, one day, working on the borders, when she noticed a large cavity in one of the cedars that lined the outer limits of the garden, and when she dug her little rake into it, she saw that it was doomed. So she walked into the woods north of the house, looking for small trees which she might use to replace the dying one, and she had gone some distance toward the north shore of the island when she saw in the channel something that both delighted and distressed her: it was the clipper *Ariel,* coming home at last. She was delighted that she would be able to talk with Captain Turlock again; she was distressed that she had not been on the roof to celebrate its arrival in the bay, for it was this ship that she had been awaiting since the breaking up of the ice.

She did not wave at the clipper, nor did she step out from among the pines; she merely stood in the shadows and watched every aspect of the returning ship, trying to imagine what seas it had sailed, with what cargo, and into what distant ports where English was unknown.

She remained there for more than an hour, moving ever closer to the shore so that she could see around the trees and follow the progress of the stately clipper—past Peace Cliff, past the Turlock marshes where the geese had stayed, and on toward Patamoke. One thing she had seen gave her comfort: the *Ariel* was dirt-smeared and would have to remain in port some weeks for cleaning.

Captain Turlock had sailed back to Devon for two reasons: he wanted to know whether Paul Steed had accumulated any tobacco for shipment to France, where the Steed ships did not usually go; and he wanted to renew his acquaintance with Mrs. Steed. On his last visit, eight months ago, he had been flattered by her attention. It had been more than casual, of that he was convinced; and often during the long reaches across the Atlantic, or when lying to off Africa, a haunting couplet drummed through his head, forcing him to recall the provocative manner in which she had looked at him, as if inviting him to approach her:

> Many a glance too has been sent
> From out the eye, love's firmament . . .

He was tormented by the images aroused by those glances, and usually closed off his reverie by castigating himself: You're fifty-five years old. She's a child. But the thought persisted that she represented his last hope for a woman who could gratify this special hunger. He was most eager to see her again.

So when his sloop tied up at the wharf, he leaped ashore with more than customary spirit, and although he hurried to the office from which Paul managed the plantation, his attention was focused mainly on the garden in hopes that Susan might be working there. She was not visible, and this disturbed him, for she must have known that he was coming.

And then, just as he was about to enter Paul's office, he chanced to look upward, and there on the roof, behind the picket fence, Susan, in a gray-blue dress and a shawl about her hair, her hands fixed upon the low fence, was staring down at him. She gave no sign of recognition, simply stood there, leaning over and watching him. He, too, made no sign, for he could not tell who else might be looking, but before he entered the office he did scratch at his nose reflectively, using his silver fist.

Paul had no consignments for Paris. 'Wheat sells there no better than in England, but I'll tell you what I could use, Captain Turlock. Twenty casks of salt.'

'I'll bring it on the next voyage.'

'When will that be?'

'We'll leave next week.'

'You leaving so soon?'

'Patch up the *Ariel* and off we go.'

'I hope we'll see something of you before you sail.'

'That would be most pleasant.'

'And you'll break bread with us today, of course?'

'I should like to.'

Paul finished some papers, then led the way to the front porch, where Tiberius, an elderly slave dressed in livery, opened the doors for the two men. 'Is Mrs. Steed in?' Paul asked, and the servant replied, 'She's on the roof.'

'Damn the roof. Send Eden to fetch her,' and shortly thereafter Susan came down the stairs, her shawl gone, her eyes ablaze.

'Here's Captain Turlock back home again,' Paul said, and she said, looking at Turlock, 'I trust you had a good voyage.'

They dined not in the big room but in one of the connecting ways built by Rosalind Steed more than a century past. It served the exact purpose she had planned; the sun came in upon a small table to which three chairs adjusted nicely, and those occupying the chairs could look out and see the garden trees so close they seemed to be at hand.

'I do love eating here,' Susan said as four slaves brought the food, and then she said no more, for the men began to talk, and Captain Turlock told of his new adventures, and after he had spoken of a dozen places, none of which she would ever see, she did ask one question. 'Didn't you say when we first met, years ago, that you were engaged in a kind of duel with Captain Gatch, who was married to one of my cousins? You never did tell me what happened?'

Turlock coughed slightly, adjusted himself in his chair and said, 'We fought each other for years. And in the end nobody won.'

'But I heard he had died . . . at sea.'

'He died gallantly, Mrs. Steed. Trying to do what could not be done.'

'How do you mean?'

'He tried to make his schooner sail faster than she could.'

'What an odd way to die. Did you hear that, Paul?'

'His schooner sank,' Paul snapped. 'That's the way I heard it years ago.' He reflected on this for a moment, then added, 'Took his whole crew down with him.'

'Was that part of the duel?' Susan asked.

Turlock coughed uneasily. 'It was his character, ma'am. He had to do what he did.'

A slave came to advise Mr. Paul that he was needed at the office, so he excused himself, but Susan and the captain remained in the sunlit passageway, and she spoke with great caution, for she did not want to betray the depth of her concern, but at the same time she wanted him to know that the concern was there. She said, 'A man from Patamoke who sailed on the *Ariel* told me that you had engaged Captain Gatch in a running battle, somewhere here, and that he had defeated you in much blood.'

'He did.'

'But in the end . . .'

'I survived.'

'And he didn't. Was it because you were more clever than he . . . braver?'

'It was a duel, ma'am.'

'I wish I had been on that ship.'

'We don't allow women, ma'am.'

'I mean his. When he was chasing you. And you lured him on.'

'What are you saying?'

Susan laughed nervously. 'Captain Turlock, I do know all about the opening battle. He outgunned you, and you ran away.'

Turlock broke into a broad grin. 'That I did.'

'But you waited for him in Brazil . . .' She was not sure what she wanted to say next, but then a flood of words came upon her. 'When you told us those inconsequential things about the Amazon—the birds, the bigness, you were really trying to impress me . . . not about the Amazon, about the battle.'

'Why would I do that?' he asked evenly.

'Because you know that I . . .' She looked at him steadily, but then a movement on the lawn distracted her, and she said lightly, 'Look! Paul has to go to the other shore.' And they sat side by side, looking across the garden as Paul went down to the wharf. After the sloop moved off, a slave ran to the house and spoke with old Tiberius, who came to inform his mistress: 'Master, he got to go to the wharf distant.'

'The table can be cleared,' she said quietly, and when the room was silent she thought for a long time as to what she must say next. 'Do you remember how we first met?'

'On the porch, wasn't it? With your mother.'

'I mean, when we became aware of each other.'

'I have no clear recollection . . .'

'You do. I know you do. You remember it as vividly as I do . . .' She hesitated, and it was he who answered, 'It was the cannonballs. You wanted to see them, and I lifted you . . . and from that moment you have never left my arms.'

'I should like to see them again,' she said softly, and taking him by the hand, she led him from the passageway and into the empty hall and up the stairs to her bedroom, and there she drew his arms about her and raised on tiptoe and said, 'You'll have to lift me.'

His arms closed, and as he raised her in the air she pressed against him ever more tightly, then threw her arms about his rumpled head and whispered, 'Don't let me go, Matt,' and when he lowered her, they fell, intertwined, toward the bed.

It was unfortunate that the slave girl Eden could not have remained ignorant of what had happened in the room, but late in the afternoon, at her accustomed time for turning down the beds, she blundered in to find them naked. With no embarrassment she nodded gravely to her mistress, turned and left.

In the weeks that followed, when Captain Matt came to Devon on amusingly improbable excuses, or Mrs. Steed sailed to Patamoke ostensibly to shop and stay overnight with friends, Eden realized how ardent their affair had become. And she supposed that Mr. Steed must know what his wife was doing.

All during the month of June, Paul feigned ignorance, conducting his life in his usual fashion, but when Captain Turlock insolently dispatched the *Ariel* to Africa under the command of First Mate Goodbarn—so that he might remain free to dally on shore—Paul could no longer keep up the pretense. He became moody and was remiss in meeting his business obligations; those slaves who had to approach him for instructions, he dismissed snappishly. He refused to confront either Susan or the captain directly; he allowed his bitterness to fester, and this made him increasingly difficult.

He manifested this in a way no one could have predicted, he least of all. The Steeds had always been known throughout the Eastern Shore for the benevolent manner in which they treated their slaves; indeed, this had long been a family doctrine: 'Devon slaves eat well and wear warm clothing.' They were not often punished and never whipped. This tradition was honored even by the remote Steeds at the Refuge, for if anyone there abused his slaves, he was summoned to Rosalind's Revenge and warned, 'Steeds don't do that, and if you persist, you'll have to leave the Choptank.'

But now Paul Steed, the master of Devon and exponent of the family, took to striking Eden for fancied misbehavior. His fury against her was heightened every time Susan was not at home; he would demand an explanation from Eden, and when she merely hung her head, sulking and silent, he would lose control of himself, and would beat her about the head until her violent sobbing brought him to his senses. But one morning, when Susan was again absent from his bed, he summoned Eden, and when she persisted in her silence, he became so enraged that he produced for the first time a heavy strap, with which he lashed her furiously.

'Master, I don't know what she do!'

'You do, you hussy!' And he continued to beat her, begging for the truth yet fearing to hear it.

From that day he played the game of wanting to know where his wife was and what she was doing, and he kept beating and questioning Eden, always terrified that she would tell him. Eden was twenty years old, as delicate of feature and clear of skin as when Grandfather Isham had presented her to Susan as a family gift. She had not yet borne children, a suspicious fact, but she had mastered the intricacies of plantation life better than any of the other slaves. She could sew handsomely and tend a room and look after the children when their nursing slave was busy. She had made herself a valuable adjunct to the big house, like a piece of comfortable furniture, and for Paul Steed to whip her was a humiliation.

But there was nothing she could do. She was Steed property, for life, and if he was displeased with her, society allowed him to thrash her until she collapsed in a heap.

Her plight was intensified by the fact that she knew what her mistress was doing, and approved. When Paul struck her, she could take inner consolation from the fact that his wife was cuckolding him, and that the other slaves knew it. When he fell into a fury and lashed her with extra harshness, she could grit her teeth and think: He knows why he does this. And she abetted her mistress in the connivances, and came to look upon Captain Matt as a hero for bringing excitement and love into Rosalind's Revenge.

Ultimately Susan had to find out what was happening to her maid; one day she saw Eden wincing as she lifted a portmanteau filled with clothes for a week-long stay in Patamoke, and she asked, 'What is it, Eden?' and when the girl said nothing, Susan lowered her smock and saw the welts. 'My God! What's happened?' And the disgraceful story unfolded. Then she became bitterly angry at her husband and upbraided him instantly: 'Whatever got into you, to strike my girl?'

He offered no sensible reply, but said something about her insolence, and neither of them elected to state the actual cause, although each knew clearly what it was.

But Susan was a woman of spirit; she took Eden to Patamoke and sold her to a planter who would treat her decently, but as soon as Paul heard of this he caught up with them, shouting at the new owner that he had no right to buy his slave, that she belonged to Devon, and he demanded her back. When the man stuttered, 'But I paid four hundred . . .' Paul slapped the money into his hand—and Eden became his property.

On the sail back to Devon he kept telling Eden that he had never meant to harm her, that he actually liked her and considered her one of his best servants. He promised not to pester her again about Mrs. Steed's whereabouts, and he made other resolves, all tending to prove that he would henceforth be a considerate master. But she had been at Devon only a few days before he came raging into the big room upstairs, again demanding to know where Susan was, and when Eden remained silent, he began whipping her with a strap, and she would not cry out, until the strap fell from his hand and he whimpered, 'Eden, I do not mean to hurt you. But where is my wife?' And when she looked at him, without sneering, without contempt, only with sadness, he tried to make amends, but she winced as blood trickled down the middle of her back, and he saw this and took her in his arms and whispered, 'I didn't mean to hurt you. I didn't mean . . .' And he fell with her onto the bed, and tore away her clothes and wiped her bruised back and consoled her and stayed with her there, day after day.

Now it was summer. Cardinals flashed among the trees and blue herons tiptoed sedately where the geese had once congregated so noisily. Slaves trapped soft-shell crabs with gratifying frequency, and insects droned in the afternoon sun. Mosquitoes became a major problem, but Paul had devised a canvas sack into which men and women alike could thrust their feet, shoes on, and then draw it tight about the waist. With this protection, only the hands and face needed personal attention, and two slaves were stationed in rooms where people met, waving fans to keep the fierce insects away.

Susan enjoyed the fanciful stories about mosquitoes. Mr. Landis from the Miles River told of overhearing two that had carried off one of his calves and were about to eat it. The first said, 'Let's drag it down to the Choptank and eat it on the beach,' but the second said, 'No! Down there the big ones would take it away from us.'

In July the weather became brutally hot. Whole days would elapse without a breeze and ships would sit becalmed in the bay, their captains cursing for a zephyr. When the ships did move, they left wakes that remained visible for miles as waves moved out from the bow. Over the river settled a shimmering haze, and few birds were willing to brave the intense heat that reflected from it. Sometimes, just before sunset, osprey could be seen patrolling the glassy river, searching for fish.

The loblollies stood motionless, hours passing without a needle dipping, and human life appeared to be in suspension too. Tiberius, keeping watch at the door, dozed in his chair, not wishing to speculate on where his mistress might be this time; he liked Susan and had known the generous manner in which she treated the slaves. He had watched her being kind to Eden and attentive to the black children when they fell ill. As for Eden herself, he had always considered her a choice human being, better fitted than most of the slaves to protect herself, and if she had chosen her present course to escape the beatings that were being inflicted upon her, he was not going to protest. Sometimes, when she stayed for protracted periods in the big bedroom with the master, he wished that she had remained in the fields, living a more normal life of husband and children, but in no way could he blame her.

'Girl got only so many chances,' he told her once when he carried food to the big room and found her alone. 'Best she take 'em.' When their paths crossed, as they did more infrequently now, he treated her with respect.

Matt and Susan spent the long summer in a dream world of content.

They were most often in his small house in Patamoke, and on her first night there Susan asked, 'Captain Gatch really did bombard this house, didn't he? Is it true that one of the cannonballs killed your wife?'

'Who told you that?'

'Eden.'

'Five struck. You can still see where they ripped away the wall.'

'You didn't feel it necessary to keep them plastered in place? To demonstrate how brave you were?'

'Forget him, Susan.'

During the hottest days of August they reveled in a passion which seemed inexhaustible; after their wild wrestling matches, and their sleep, Susan would pester him by drawing one thumbnail across his forehead, onto his nose and down upon his upper lip. 'Waken up, Matthew. Day's awasting.'

One afternoon he looked at her in drowsy disbelief. 'Did your mother ever tell you . . . This sounds ridiculous, but I proposed marriage to her.'

Susan squealed with delight and belabored his chest with her fists. 'You horrible old man! You went to bed with my mother?'

'God, no! You can't imagine how proper we were.'

'Did she ever come here? Like this?'

'You're a naughty girl. I wanted to marry your mother. She was quite handsome, you know.' He began to chuckle. 'Did anyone tell you that I tended her when she was a baby?' Then the wonder of having Penny Steed's daughter in bed with him became overwhelming, and he had no more to say.

Susan guessed what thoughts were going through his mind. 'You were saved for me. My mother did the scouting, like an Indian. Dear God, I wish we were both just beginning—with a whole life ahead of us.'

If they were unrestrained in their love-making, they endeavored to preserve at least a show of decency in the community. They behaved circumspectly, never flaunted their affair in public, and gave the townspeople an opportunity to ignore it if they wished. Indeed, Susan looked more like a devout housewife than a mistress, and after five or six days of self-indulgence in the Patamoke house, she would discreetly slip back to Devon, where she resumed her role of dutiful mother.

Paul's public spectacle when buying Eden back was the only incident so far which had created anything close to a public scandal, and it had been quickly superseded by Matt's dignified deportment. It was a curious affair, and for the present it remained within manageable limits. As one knowing Patamoke housewife predicted, 'Summer will end, and the *Ariel* will return, and Captain Matt will sail, and that'll be the end of it.'

The burden of the two misalliances fell most heavily on Paul. Never a man of outstanding character, he now revealed himself as exceedingly weak. There were rumors that he was conducting an extended affair with his wife's black maid, and people were mildly amused. But the business health of the plantation began to decline, and what small attention he paid to Devon consisted of storming into the office, ranting at the help and making silly decisions. The young Steeds from the Refuge who were doing most of the work had begun whispering among themselves as to the possibility that he might have to be replaced. 'He's not only tearing his plantation apart. He's beginning to affect ours, too.'

His most difficult problem, of course, was with Eden. In bed she could be wildly exciting; out of bed she was an aggravating enigma, and he often felt that as she moved about the room, tidying up the wardrobe in which Susan's dresses were kept, she was laughing at him. Once when Susan had been absent for five days, an immense gloom settled over him, and he began to shout at Eden, 'My wife belongs here—not you,' and he raised his hand to strike her. But this time she insolently grasped his wrist and said, 'No more, Master,' and she stared him down, and slowly his arm dropped to his side. In other ways, too, she asserted herself, demanding prerogatives, but in her physical relations with him she was impeccable. 'You want to stay longer, honey? All right, we stay, and pretty soon you sleep again.'

When he wakened she would be sitting on the edge of the bed, her hands folded in her lap. He noticed that never did she presume to wear any of Susan's clothes, even though he invited her to do so. 'That dress comes from Paris. Try it on, Eden.'

'No, that's Missy's.'

'It would fit you, almost.'

'Go back to sleep.' He spent much of this hot spell sleeping, but occasionally he would engage in a burst of reading: John Locke and Alexander Pope and David Hume. Then he would talk of great plans for a new theory of plantation management, but soon he would be asleep again. He admired Pope and tried reading passages to Eden, choosing those isolated lines which compressed so much of English commonplace morality:

> 'For fools rush in where angels fear to tread . . .'
> 'Hope springs eternal in the human breast . . .'
> 'A little learning is a dangerous thing . . .'
> 'The proper study of mankind is man . . .'

Eden would listen attentively, but whether she caught any of the poet's intended meaning Paul could not say; she was a good audience, and if Tiberius came to the door with a pitcher of lemonade, she cautioned him to leave it quickly, without interrupting.

But one afternoon in August, when the heat was almost unbearable,

Paul was reading aloud from Pope when he came upon a quatrain which he started boldly, stumbled over, and finished in confusion:

> 'Vice is a monster of so frightful mien,
> As to be hated needs but to be seen;
> Yet seen too oft, familiar with her face,
> We first endure, then pity, then embrace.'

He dropped the book, looked at Eden as if he were seeing her for the first time, and suffered a visible revulsion. 'Get out of here! Damn you, leave this room!' And he grabbed the strap, intending to belabor her about the back and face, but again she resisted. Slowly, showing fierce contempt, she retreated toward the door, opened it quietly and withdrew into the hall, while all the slaves working in the house could hear the master's cries of rage: 'Don't you ever come back here, you whore!' He pursued her down the hall, lashing at her with the strap in such a way as to be sure to miss. When she reached the main stairs used by the white folk she descended slowly, and Tiberius cried loud enough for the master to hear, 'Don't you come down them stairs, Sassy.' And he pretended to slap her, pushing her into the back part of the house.

That night she was back in the big room, smiling at the cannonballs as her master wept and begged forgiveness.

As happened so often in Patamoke, it was the Quakers who brought a touch of common sense to the ridiculous goings-on along the river. One morning, at the close of summer, George Paxmore knocked on the door of Captain Turlock's home and said, 'Matthew, my wife and I want to talk with thee.'

'Talk ahead,' Turlock snapped, holding the door so that his visitor could not peer inside.

'At our house. Elizabeth's waiting.'

'I don't believe I care to speak with Elizabeth. She talks and never listens.'

'As a friend, I beseech thee to come with me,' and he took Turlock by the arm and led him away.

The walk to the Paxmore house near the boatyard was an awkward one. Neither man wished to say anything substantial where full attention could not be paid, so Paxmore contented himself with observing that the ships heading for Baltimore seemed far more numerous than previously, and he gave it as his opinion that this new port had driven Annapolis out of business. 'And Patamoke, too. We won't see ships like yours coming here much in the future.'

'As long as I sail her you will.'

When they passed the *Ariel,* home from Africa, Paxmore asked, 'Why did thee allow Mr. Goodbarn . . .' But this was coming too close to the agenda and he did not finish his sentence.

When they reached Paxmore's town house, a small white affair near the harbor, George deferred to the older man; after all, Captain Turlock was fifteen years his senior. 'Please enter. We're happy to have you as our guest.'

Elizabeth Paxmore, all in gray, still had the fair complexion of her youth, unsullied by powders or rouges; she was an attractive woman of thirty-nine, and Turlock found himself thinking: Damn, if I wasn't mixed up with the other one, she'd be most acceptable. He bowed and took the chair she offered, noticing that their home was austere yet relaxing, with just enough chairs carved by the master, just enough decorations embroidered by the mistress.

GEORGE: We want to beg thee once more, Matthew, to quit thy abominable trade.

MATT: What trade?

GEORGE: Slavery. Thy ship trades nothing else.

MATT: I've just been plaguing Paul Steed to give me a shipment of wheat.

GEORGE: We know how thee trades a little wheat for a great many slaves. We know of thy stops in Africa and Brazil.

MATT: What business—

ELIZABETH: We're neighbors, Matthew. What thee does affects us, too.

MATT: It shouldn't.

ELIZABETH: It's inescapable. Thee is my brother. Thee sails my ship. Thee brings thy slaves into my shadow.

MATT: I'd say you were sticking your nose into my affairs.

ELIZABETH: I am indeed. If thee won't care for thy immortal soul, I must.

MATT: And I suppose God directs you to do this?

ELIZABETH: He does, Matthew. He directs thee, too, but thee doesn't listen.

MATT: How can you be so goddamned certain—

GEORGE: If thee has a poor argument, Matthew, thee doesn't strengthen it with profanity.

MATT: Excuse me, ma'am.

ELIZABETH: Would thee like some tea?

MATT: That I would.

GEORGE: Slavery is a terrible wrong. It does hideous things to people, maladjusts them. (At this, Matt Turlock looked down at his hands, thinking of what Susan had told him about her husband's strange behavior.)

ELIZABETH: We cannot speak with thee logically, Matthew, unless thee acknowledges that slavery is this great evil. Thee sees that, doesn't thee?'

MATT: I see that fields need people to work them, and the best hands ever invented for that task are the niggers of Africa. God would not have allowed—

ELIZABETH: He works mysteriously. I sometimes think He has allowed this present generation to exist so as to prepare us.

GEORGE: Thy trade is corrupting thee, Matthew. Thee isn't the man for whom I built the *Ariel.* Time has corroded—

MATT: It corrodes all of us. You as well as Mrs. Paxmore.

GEORGE: We have striven to adhere to the principles of humanity.

MATT: As you define them. Tell me this, do you really believe that you will live to see the day when slavery is outlawed in Maryland?

GEORGE: It's been outlawed on the high seas. Sooner or later the British patrol will capture thee, and hang thee.

MATT: They'll never. And you'll never see the end of slavery.

ELIZABETH (adjusting in her chair to signal that she was changing the subject): When George says that thy profession corrodes, he refers to thy regrettable behavior with the Steeds.

MATT: That has no relationship—

ELIZABETH: It does. A human life is all of a part. What thee does in Africa determines what thee will do in Patamoke.

MATT: I think you're being damned fools.

GEORGE: We see a human soul destroying itself. Our anguish is no less than thine.

MATT: I feel no anguish, not in Africa nor in Patamoke.

GEORGE: Thee does, Matthew, because I feel the agitation, and I am thy brother. Elizabeth and I love thee. We love thy strength and willingness. We ask thee as friends and associates to quit this evil. Be done with it all. Get back to the sea. Burn the *Ariel* for its contamination. I'll build thee a new ship, a better. Matthew . . .

ELIZABETH: Will thee pray with us?

MATT: Pray when I'm gone.

ELIZABETH: When will thee be gone?

MATT: In about one minute.

ELIZABETH: I mean from Patamoke.

MATT: That's my affair.

ELIZABETH: It's not at all. Can't thee see what thee's doing to the Steeds?

MATT: I did not ask—

ELIZABETH: But thee can't consciously goad two human beings into destroying themselves. Matthew, we're talking about two immortal souls.

MATT: You take care of your soul, Mrs. Paxmore. I'll take care of mine.

ELIZABETH: I shall pray that God sends thee light. I shall pray.

MATT: You know what I think, Mrs. Paxmore? I think you're a goddamned busybody. You pray for yourself, and let me alone.

He stomped from the trim house, disgusted with its occupants, but on his way to his home, where Susan waited, he reflected on his family's long acquaintance with the Paxmores, and on the stories he had heard about the Quakers, and it occurred to him that Quaker men were cursed with some of the sharpest-tongued busybodies God ever put on earth. From rumors about town, he understood that they even got up in church and spoke their minds, but as far as he was concerned, these women represented only austerity, preaching and sanctimoniousness. But it was strange—generation after generation these quiet women with their demure bearing and fearless intelligence seemed to make the lasting wives. Their husbands appeared to love them as much at seventy as they had at seventeen: I wonder if there's something to the way they're brought up? Always speaking their minds and taking part in things? Compared to the Steed women, or the Turlocks, these Quaker wives seemed to function at full capacity till God struck them dead.

Any incipient compassion Turlock may have held for the Quakers vanished that afternoon when a deplorable scene took place at the harbor. While he was away from town visiting the widow of a Turlock who had died at sea, George Paxmore chanced to meet Mrs. Steed coming from a shop, and the evangelical mood possessed him so strongly that he accosted her. 'Susan, would thee do me the honor of a brief visit?'

'I do not care to go to your house,' she said sharply, 'in view of what you've said about Captain Turlock.'

'I did not invite thee to my house. To my clipper.'

This so surprised her that she half assented, but when she reached the harbor and from the rowboat saw that he was headed for the *Ariel*, she refused to get in. 'That's not yours. It's Captain Turlock's.'

'I built it,' Paxmore said, and he took her arm and persuaded her to join him. On the short trip to the *Ariel* he said nothing, but when the sailor on duty asked his mission, he said, 'To inspect my clipper,' and he handed Susan up the ladder.

He allowed her only a brief moment on deck, during which she admired the neatness of the vessel; then he led her to the hatch and asked for a ladder. When the sailor brought it, he adjusted it so that Susan could climb down, and when she stood on the 'tween deck he joined her.

It took her some moments to adjust to the darkness; then, as her eyes began to pierce the gloom, she heard Paxmore say, 'In this compartment forward of the mast, where you can't even stand up, one hundred and sixty slaves.'

'No!' Vaguely she had known that Matt was a slaver, just as she knew vaguely that during the Revolution he had seen great battles, but one fact was as nebulous as the other. To her he was merely Matt Turlock who sailed the oceans; slavery at sea was no more a reality than slavery at Devon Island. She could not have told Paxmore, at this moment, how the Steed slaves lived; they existed and formed no part of her consciousness.

'And aft of the mainmast, eighty more.'

'My God!'

'Yes, only by calling on the mercy of God can we comprehend what this ship means.' And he forced her to lie on her stomach and peer down into the lower hold. 'Forward, a hundred and twenty men. Aft, another hundred.' She started to rise, but he held her down. 'Look at the headroom in which a woman with child must try to stand.'

She was about to respond when she heard a roaring voice from aloft: 'What in hell are you doing down there?'

Calmly George Paxmore replied, 'I am showing your lady how you earn your livelihood.'

With a towering oath Matt Turlock leaped into the hold, grabbed Paxmore by the neck and rushed him toward the ladder. 'Out! You preachifying rogue!' And after he had shoved the unresisting Quaker onto the deck he sped up after him and pushed him toward the gangway. 'Off this ship forever.'

'It's mine too, Matthew.'

This was said with such self-righteousness that Turlock quite lost his head and launched a violent kick at the departing boatbuilder. He missed, and Paxmore said, 'God condemns thee and thy slave ship.' And he rowed ashore.

Two sailors helped Susan climb out of the hold, and Turlock expected her to be shaken by what she had seen, but instead she was obviously flushed with erotic excitement.

'I've always wanted to visit the *Ariel,'* she said. 'It's a powerful experience.' And she allowed him to lead her to his cabin, and she could not feast enough on the charts, the carved ivory, the gimbaled bed. This was the essence of Matt Turlock.

'Paxmore did me a favor, showing me belowdecks.' She sat on his bed and studied him as if for the first time.

'He said this morning I was destroying you.'

'No! You're creating me. Matt, it was seven years ago that you lifted me up to see the cannonballs. Every day since then I could feel the pressure of your arms because you held me longer then necessary. You held me because you wanted me . . . and I've always wanted you.'

On that first afternoon in the big bed at Rosalind's Revenge he had

asked her, 'Shall I untie the thongs and take off the fist?' and she had
protested, 'No! I want to feel it across my body . . . everywhere.' Since
then, whenever they began to make love she kissed the silver eagle as a
kind of salute; it became the symbol of their passion.

Now she kissed it again and whispered, 'Poor Paxmore, he must have
thought that showing me the slave quarters would kill my love for you.
I love you even more for your dangerous life. Now I know why you
require a silver fist.'

Later, when they were resting in the gimbaled bed, there came a loud
clattering on deck, and before she could slip into her clothes the door
to Matt's cabin burst open, revealing her husband, finally enraged to the
point of madness. He had an ax and was screaming threats of murder.

There was a wild scramble, and shouting that could be heard onshore.
She would never be able to sort out precisely what happened; she did
remember Matt's throwing himself across the bed and knocking away
the weapon Paul carried. In the end, Matt, with only a towel about him,
grabbed Paul and tossed him into the harbor, and most of the townspeople were on the wharf by the time he swam ashore. A woman who had
watched the scene from a rowboat summarized it: 'Both of 'em was
naked.' The scandal was now public property.

When the young Steeds working in the Devon office heard of this disgraceful exhibition—even slaves were joking about it—they knew that
they must act. Instructing one of the blacks to inform Paul of their
departure, they marched soberly down to the wharf, climbed aboard a
sloop and set out for the Refuge. As they sailed past Peace Cliff they
rehearsed what they must say, and by the time they reached the marsh
and entered Dividing Creek they were prepared.

Gravely they stopped at each of the Refuge plantations, advising one
senior or another that he must come immediately to Herbert Steed's big
house, and there they unfolded the shameful story.

'Before I tell you what happened yesterday in Patamoke, I suppose
you know that Paul's flown apart . . . as if struck by a bomb.'

'I don't know,' Herbert Steed replied somewhat stuffily. He was a
rotund, pompous man who sniffed before each sentence.

'He's taken to beating Eden, that's his wife's maid, with a heavy strap.'

'Striking a slave!'

'And after he beats her, he lies with her.'

'You haven't told the women?' Herbert gasped.

'Everyone knows. You must be aware that Aunt Susan is practically
living with Captain Turlock.'

This rumor had reached the Refuge, and Herbert Steed already knew
what he thought about that: 'Swamp trash.'

'Yesterday things reached a climax. After practically condoning the affair for these months, Paul storms into Patamoke, tries to murder Turlock, and ends being thrown into the harbor.'

To everyone's surprise, Herbert broke into laughter. 'Paul Steed thinking he could commit a murder. He couldn't swat a fly. I'm surprised the maid—what's her name?—allows him to beat her.'

'She doesn't any longer. One of the slaves told me she grabbed his wrist and said, "No more," and he was afraid to continue.'

Now the young men resumed the serious discussion. 'The scandal we could absorb. But Paul's destroying the Devon plantations. And before long his pathetic decisions will begin to affect yours, too.'

'How do you mean?' Herbert asked sharply; where money was involved, he was involved.

'Take the stores. No one's really supervising them. Clerks wander in at nine o'clock. Last month I visited all four—fly-ridden, filthy, didn't look like Steed property at all.'

The other nephew broke in: 'Are you aware that the field-clearing gang hasn't burned an acre this year? No one's hammering at them.'

'Enough!' Herbert said. And he underwent a remarkable transformation: his shoulders squared; his eyes focused sharply; and his mouth set grimly. He was fifty-three years old and for some time had believed that he had retired from daily responsibilities, but the possibility that the Steed plantations might collapse galvanized him. Briskly he rose from his chair and announced, 'I'm taking charge of the Devon plantations—now.'

He had allowed no discussion from his cousins. Packing a few things in a canvas bag, he went to the sloop and was about to depart with his nephews when a prudent thought occurred: 'Timothy, run back and fetch us three good guns.' And when these arrived they set sail for Devon.

Late that afternoon Paul Steed rose from his bed, left Eden and drifted aimlessly down to the office, where to his surprise he found the man they called Uncle Herbert, a pompous, seemingly futile type, installed in his chair. 'What're you doing here?' he asked with trembling authority.

'I've come to run things,' Herbert said.

'What things?'

'Paul, go back to your whore. And don't you ever again allow Captain Turlock to set foot on Devon Island.'

'Are you commanding me?'

'Paul, get out of here. You are no longer in charge.' Instinctively the two younger Steeds moved to positions behind their uncle, and the trio presented such a formidable wall of opposition that Paul could summon no strength to combat it.

'You'll not succeed . . .' he began to bluster, but Herbert Steed left his desk, walked quietly to the former master and escorted him to the door. 'Go back to the girl, Paul. That's to be your life from here on.'

Ejected from his office, he stumbled toward the Revenge, passing through a garden of remarkable beauty without seeing it. He entertained the vain hope that when he met Eden she would somehow inspire him to oppose this capture of his prerogatives, but when Tiberius opened the outer door, uttering his usual gracious words, 'Do come in, Master Paul,' he kicked it shut and stomped away.

He walked not to the wharf, where he was no longer welcome, but westward toward those wheat fields which had always been the most productive; generations ago the Steeds had learned that to produce tobacco, a field required years of rest now and then, or the alteration of crops rich in nitrogen, and these fields had been kept vital. As he wandered through them he felt pride that he had kept them still viable: Maybe the best fields in Maryland.

But when he reached the western end of the island he was astonished to discover that the fields seemed much shorter than they had been when he was a boy, but this was so improbable that he wondered if he were remembering properly. Shouting for the overseer, he was able to rouse no one, so he went to the edge of the land, kicking at the soil and inspecting the line where the waters of the bay touched the island, and as he was doing this he saw one of the slaves fishing. The man supposed the master had come to spy on him and started running, lest he be punished, but Paul cried, 'Stop, Stop!' and when the man ignored his shouts, Paul set out after him, but the slave was speedy in retreat, and Paul could not catch him.

So he resumed his solitary wandering and came upon that stand of pine in which he and his cousins had camped as children, listening to the thunder of the bay as the stars appeared: My God! So many trees have gone! And below him, in the waters of the Chesapeake, lay rotting pines.

Again he shouted for the overseer, and this time an older slave appeared. 'Yassah, what you need, Mastah?'

'This shore? Is it falling away?'

'Yassah, every year, more 'n more.'

'Those trees. There used to be a little forest, didn't there?'

'Yassah. I was boy, trees out to there.' And he indicated a spot so far distant in the bay that Paul gasped.

'Don't you do anything about it?'

'Nosah, nothin' you can do.'

Paul dismissed the slave and continued his walk, witnessing always the encroachment of the bay, and it seemed that in his brief lifetime a valuable portion of the island had disappeared: I must do something about it. I must talk to the people who look after these fields.

When he returned to headquarters he found considerable excitement. Captain Turlock had sailed a small boat down the Choptank, bringing

Mrs. Steed to her home, but Herbert Steed had forestalled him at the landing, refusing him permission to come ashore. There had been a scuffle; the two younger Steeds had supported their uncle; and Turlock had struck one of them with his silver fist, throwing him into the creek before marching solemnly up the path to the big house, arriving there just as Paul returned from his western explorations.

'Good afternoon, Paul,' Turlock said.

The confused events of these past days were too much for Steed—his demotion, the falling away of the land, and now this arrogance—and he lashed out stupidly. 'Damn you, I'll thrash you . . .'

'You'll what?' Turlock asked.

Steed made another lunge at him, then flailed his arms helplessly. The captain pushed him away twice, and when this did not halt the ridiculous attack, swung his left arm almost gently and with his silver fist pushed, rather than knocked, Paul to his knees. He was about to help the fallen man rise when he heard an ominous command from behind: 'Stand where you are, Turlock.'

Still offering Paul help, he turned his head to see Herbert Steed standing on the gravel path, flanked by two nephews, one dripping, and all with guns. 'What in hell?'

'Off the property,' Herbert Steed said quietly.

'Put those guns down,' Turlock snapped, turning his attention from Paul and allowing him to fall backward. 'What do you think you're doing?'

'I know what I'm doing, Turlock. I'm counting to five, and if you're still on that porch, I'm going to blow your guts out. Boys, get ready to fire.'

And he began to count: 'One, two, three—'

'Steed!' Turlock bellowed. 'You're acting like a—'

Very calmly Herbert interrupted his count. 'Do you think any jury would convict us? After that?' And with a look of sickening disgust he pointed with his gun at Susan. 'Four. Aim at his guts, boys.'

Before Herbert could utter the command to fire, Captain Turlock backed off the porch, looked contemptuously at the fallen husband and started slowly down the graveled path. He had gone only a few steps when Susan uttered a cry and started after him, but the three Refuge Steeds interposed with their guns. 'You stay!' Herbert commanded. 'The circus is over.'

And he barred the way. When Turlock reached his sloop he got in and slowly moved it toward the creek, but three days later he was back, bringing with him the casks of salt Paul Steed had ordered. Herbert appeared at the wharf with the purchase money, but Turlock ignored him, allowing Mr. Goodbarn to handle that negotiation. 'I'm going to the big house,' Turlock said.

'No, you're not,' Herbert Steed replied quietly.

'I guess I am,' Turlock said, and three of his sailors produced muskets to neutralize the men in the headquarters building. While they stood guard, Matt Turlock walked gravely up the path, noting the last daylilies as they withered on their brown-green stalks. At the door he knocked politely and informed Tiberius that he had come to pay his respects to Mrs. Steed.

Up to this moment Susan had been unaware of his arrival, but as his voice echoed through the hallway, she rushed from her upstairs room and ran down the flight of stairs, throwing herself into his arms. Her husband followed.

After embracing Susan, Turlock half pushed her away. 'I'm sailing for Africa. It'll be years before I return.'

'Oh no!' she cried, clinging to him again.

'I must. We've hit the end of the road here, all of us.'

'Matt, no!' She grasped his arms, begging him not to go, but he was resolute. To Paul he said, 'I'm sorry. I hope that in the future things will be better for all of us.'

Paul made no response, but Susan refused to accept this as the end of summer, the end of all she had so desperately dreamed of. 'You can't go, Matt,' she pleaded. Then an alluring idea came to her. 'I'll go with you. Eden! Pack the bags!' And she broke away from the two men and dashed upstairs, calling for her maid.

'I must stop her,' Matt said, and he bounded up the stairs after her, overtaking her in the bedroom as she began to pull down boxes and bring out her dresses. Eden, standing in a corner, watched the hullabaloo, slim and silent and unsmiling.

'Susan!' Matt said harshly. 'It's over. There's no way you can board my ship.'

'But I . . .'

'Unthinkable.' He brought her away from her frantic packing and held her by the shoulders. Ignoring Eden, he said tenderly, 'Susan, you've been the most precious thing in my life.'

'I must stay with you,' she whispered. 'There's nothing in life, Matt. Nothing. These last three days . . .' She shivered.

'We begin over again, all of us.'

'There can be no more beginning.'

'You could help Paul regain control of the—'

'Him?' The withering scorn bespoke more than the end of summer, but Matt was obdurate. He started for the door, but she uttered such a pitiful cry that he had to stop. Then she threw herself at him, whimpering, 'Matt, lift me up as you did that first day.' Clutching his hand, she dragged him toward the bed and waited for him to put his arms about her as he had done so long ago.

Slowly he lifted her until her shoulders were on a level with the imbedded cannonballs. 'Hold me long, as you did then,' she pleaded, but he began to lower her. Frantically she clutched at him, failed to stop him, and found herself slipping down. Her feet were again on the floor; her life was over.

She made no protest as he left, but did listen as he said to Eden, 'Look after her. She's worth loving.'

With heavy step he stalked down the stairs, bowed to Paul Steed, and returned to his sloop. 'Back to the *Ariel*,' he told Mr. Goodbarn. 'We sail in the morning.' The sailors dropped their guns as Matt saluted the three Steeds watching from the office doorway.

The *Ariel* left Patamoke the next day at dawn, heading for London-Luanda-Belém. She had assembled commissions which would keep her at sea for four years, and as she sailed slowly down the river Captain Turlock looked for what he suspected might be the last time at the familiar sights, the beacons that had guided his life. Abeam lay the Paxmore yards where his clipper had been devised; how grieved he was that his association with these honest Quaker builders had been ruptured; no one tended to the welfare of ships as they did.

There was the family swamp; Cousin Lafe would be tracking deer through the tall grasses; herons would be fishing in the shallows. And on the rise stood Peace Cliff, that noble, quiet haven so different from the gaudy show of Devon. He remembered when George Paxmore's mother had invited him to that telescope house and given him a book to take on his journeys during the war. 'Thee doesn't have to attend school to learn. A ship can be a school, too. But if thee doesn't learn, thee dies young.'

He had decided not to look back at Rosalind's Revenge, lest it haunt his dreams, but when Devon Island lay to port his eyes were lured to that stately house, and he saw what he feared he might see. On the widow's walk, her blue dress standing out in the breeze, stood Susan, her face not discernible from this distance but her handsome figure unmistakable. For as long as the *Ariel* remained in contact with the island, Captain Turlock stared at that solitary figure. He would never know another like her; she had been the capstone of his desire, a woman of exceptional passion and love. Inadvertently he looked away for a moment in the direction of his cabin: God, how I wish she was waiting in there.

Shaking his head at the impossibility, he looked once more toward Devon—and she had disappeared! Disappointed, he shrugged his shoulders. I shouldn't have thought she'd go down before we passed from sight.

She hadn't. Learning that the *Ariel* would leave Patamoke at dawn, she had slept fitfully, her left foot free of the light coverlet, always prepared to flee that horrid bed. At dawn she had risen and called for Eden to bring her the blue dress that Captain Turlock had commended at their first serious meeting. Eden, passing easily from maid to mistress to maid, sought out the fragile dress and helped Susan into it, then combed her hair and wove blue ribbons in, knowing that Mrs. Steed was preparing for a farewell rite.

Susan could eat no breakfast, and when the day was bright she went up to the roof, and sat there in the hot September sun looking eastward up the Choptank toward Patamoke. Lashed to the wicker chair, lest it blow away, was her small telescope in its waterproofed bag. Removing the glass, she studied the river; no bigger than a dot on a piece of paper was the *Ariel* when she first identified it. Then it expanded, with real sails and visible bulwarks. Now she could lay the telescope aside and watch the beautiful clipper, five sails aloft, as it breasted the island. She could not with her naked eye particularize among the moving figures, but with her telescope she saw Captain Turlock, the sun glistening now and then from his left hand. What a compelling man he was, that shock of red hair, the beard, the massive fist; he had told her during her last impassioned stay at his house in Patamoke that he was beginning to feel an older man: 'When I was young I could have romped with you four days running, with no interruption for food.'

As he moved down the straits she remembered every word of encouragement he had ever spoken to her: 'You're like an inexhaustible spring at the edge of a desert.'

And there he went. The *Ariel* was leaving the strait now and entering the bay, but still some moving forms remained visible. 'Oh God! Don't take him away!' she cried aloud.

'He is away!' a voice said behind her, and she turned to face her husband.

With a wild brush of his hand, Paul Steed swept the telescope out of her grasp and watched as it tumbled noisily down the sloping roof, clattering at last to the ground.

'You whore!' he said. 'Crying your heart out for such a man.' He pointed toward the departing slaver and said scornfully, 'A great hero! A man who peddles human flesh.'

Humiliated by his sneering and outraged by the destruction of her telescope, she whipped about and lunged at him with no clear understanding of what she hoped to accomplish; she wanted vaguely to hurt him, to erase that sneering. Paul saw her make this motion, and whereas he had been afraid to confront either Matt Turlock or Uncle Herbert, he was willing to fight Susan. With a harsh blow of his two hands clasped, he knocked her toward the fence, where she toppled for a moment, lost her balance and started falling from the roof.

Fortunately, her right foot caught in the pickets, and this saved her. But when Paul saw her dangling there, her foot wedged, her head down toward the edge, he lost what little sense he had and yanked the foot loose. Holding it, he cried, 'Go to Captain Turlock!' and with a thrust he shoved her down the sloping roof, watching as she disappeared over the edge. Her screams began as she disappeared from sight and ended in a piercing shriek as she struck the ground.

Paul, not fully aware of the hideous thing he had done, listened to her fall and then, with an impetuous cry, leaped after her. He did not clear the fence. His toe caught; he stumbled, slammed down hard on the slates of the sloping roof, tumbled for some feet, then pitched over the edge and down to the ground.

It is not easy to kill a human being. A would-be murderer stabs his target six times and fails to strike a vital organ. A crazed woman, run amok, shoots a man three times at point-blank range and punctures him in different places but with little damage. The two Steeds, tumbling from their widow's walk, had caught momentarily on rainspouts edging the roof, and then fallen heavily into flower beds.

Herbert Steed, hearing the commotion shortly after reporting for work, ran out from his office and called to his nephews, 'What are those damned fools doing now?'

Then Tiberius came running from the porch, shouting, 'Sir, sir, they done suicide.'

This brought all the slaves running, and by the time Uncle Herbert and his nephews reached the scene, Eden was cradling Mrs. Steed in her arms and saying softly, 'You not goin' to die. You not meant to die yet.'

When the situation was unraveled, and it became obvious that neither Paul nor Susan was fatally injured, the problem arose as to what should be done with them. Herbert Steed summed it up when he said, 'That damned fool never did anything right. Now he leaves it to us to see they walk again.' And he supervised carrying them up to the big bedroom, where a slave woman cared for them till a doctor could be fetched. When he arrived, by sloop from Patamoke, he found that she had set the bones and washed the cuts with warm soapy water.

'Not much more I can do,' he said, but he did inform Uncle Herbert that he need not worry about Paul. 'His hip'll mend. Leg'll be a bit short, but no harm. The one to watch is Mrs. Steed. Seems to have a badly twisted spine.'

His prognoses were correct. Paul did heal, but with a short left leg and a permanent crick in the neck that caused him to look at life sideways. Susan, however, was left an invalid; critical bones in her back were permanently affected, and although she could manage a few steps about her room, she was quite incapable of sustained movement.

Uncle Herbert, to the surprise of his family, had developed a willingness to make large decisions on everything. 'That pair can't possibly bring up their children. I'm sending the two oldest to that school Mrs. Paxmore runs at Peace Cliff.' When Susan protested, he said sternly, 'Quakers are a sorry lot, but they know how to teach. Your Mark seems to have a brain, and she'll cultivate it, God help the lad.'

Susan was not demanding, but she did require constant attention, and Eden provided it; indeed, she cared for Paul too, and as the pair grew more crotchety, she grew more understanding. She still had no husband, no children; she adopted the crippled Steeds as her family and treated both with equal compassion. Paul could become quite ugly, making preposterous demands, but she ignored him for the weak, sad thing she knew him to be, and when he pestered her, she lightly dismissed him and went about her chores.

Her affection centered on Susan, whom she dressed with care and tended with the forgiving love a mother bestows upon a sickly child. It was she who insisted that Susan return to the roof. 'If'n it pleasures you, the way it used to, you oughta go. We can carry you.'

'I don't want my wife on that roof . . . ever again,' Paul blustered, but Eden told him, 'Hush.' She summoned two slaves to carry the crippled woman to the widow's walk, and there she rested during three seasons of the year, and even in winter when soft days came she sat in the wicker chair, using a new telescope Uncle Herbert had bought her, watching the tall ships as they passed up and down the bay.

And on certain days, when strength returned, she would draw herself upright, and grasp the pickets, and follow the ships intently. Then the phallic symbolism of the masts would possess her, as it had long ago, and she would scour the southern portion of the bay and cry, 'Bring him back!'

She was in this mood one October day in 1825, her eyes fixed on the south, when she heard a distant rustling over her shoulder, and without changing the direction of her sight she whispered, 'They're returning. The geese are here again.' And she stood there, looking to the empty south, as the first flock flew overhead, their noisy cackling announcing with joy the fact that they were home.

Voyage Nine: 1832

BY THE END OF THE THIRD DECADE OF THE NINE-
teenth century the black nations bordering the Gulf of Guinea in western
Africa were a highly sophisticated group. The Ibo, Benin, Yoruba and
Fanti had come to understand the tragedy of slavery and were able to
take imaginative measures to protect their people from it. The old days
when ruthless gangs could swoop down upon an unsuspecting village to
carry off its best young men and women were largely gone.

But since the trade remained highly profitable, there continued to be
daring slave-collectors willing to run the risk of capture by British patrols assigned to stamp them out, and these predators were now forced
to trap their blacks in remote villages far south of the Congo, where
native leaders were often ignorant and susceptible to subornation. Here
companies of cruel businessmen prowled the jungles, forcing their way
far upstream to the headwaters of little-known rivers to track their
prey.

One knowing trader, Abu Hassan by name, followed a complicated
route to catch his slaves. He entered the Congo River where it debouched
into the Atlantic, far south of the Gulf of Guinea. Ignoring the bordering
lands, for they were held by the Kongo peoples, as sophisticated as the
Ibo or Yoruba to the north, he traveled three hundred and sixty miles
up the Congo to where an enormous river came in from the south, the
Kasai, but he took no slaves here, either, for these lands were held by
the clever Kuba. However, after paddling three hundred and fifty miles
up the Kasai, he came upon a gigantic river called the Sankuru, but even
here he did not try to capture slaves, for this river was guarded by the
Luba nation. But after traveling five hundred miles up the Sankuru, he
found his target, the Xanga River, enormous in breadth and length, but

so remote that no captain of a slaving ship had ever heard of it. Along the upper reaches of the Xanga many small villages clustered, their people unaware of slave markets.

It was to these villages that Abu Hassan came in the spring of 1832. He was a tall, sad man, wearied by forty-seven years of difficult and dangerous African trading. He dressed in Arab robes, covered by a glowing white burnoose, and he was always the gentleman, cleansing his hands after any unpleasantness. He spoke many languages—Arabic, French, English and, especially, Portuguese and the various Congo dialects—and was able to conclude business deals with either a Xanga chieftain or a Boston slaver. He had been born on the opposite side of Africa, in an Arab settlement north of Mozambique, and had worked at first in transporting slaves down to the Indian Ocean for shipment to Arabia, where the demand was constant, but when the catching of blacks became increasingly difficult he had been drawn deeper and deeper into the heart of the continent, until the day he discovered that it would be simpler and more profitable to march his slaves west to the Portuguese seaport of Luanda, where ships intended for Cuba, Brazil and the United States clustered.

In 1832, as he slowly made his way up the rivers in canoes containing an amalgam of cheap trading goods, he did not know that he was heading into confrontation with a gifted young Xanga named Cudjo, who lived in a village close to where that river flowed into the larger Sankuru. Cudjo was in trouble.

For some time his own people had been suspicious of him. Spies had watched his movements, reporting anything unusual to the village headman, and in the tribal councils his advice had been ignored. Even more alarming, the family of the girl Luta, whom he had chosen to be his wife, suddenly refused him permission to buy her.

He was being driven to the conclusion that he might have to quit this tribe which had done everything but proscribe him publicly, for he had often watched what happened to men declared outcasts and was determined to escape the penalties they had suffered.

Despite his perilous position, he had no desire to leave this lovely river along whose banks his ancestors had been so happy. Vaguely he knew that the Xanga ran into larger rivers and they into still larger; to live in his village was to see the quiet traffic of a continent and to be in touch with a multitude of tribes north and south.

And in addition to the river, there were the associations in the village. His forefathers as far back as memory recorded had been primal figures, strong in war and voluble in peace. They had governed their portion of the river, dispensing justice to their people and assuring adequate food supplies. In the normal course of affairs he would take their place and become the dispenser of government.

The trouble which had mysteriously arisen to threaten him started not with opposition in his own village but from quite another quarter. In the old days Arab traders had come up the Xanga in leisurely fashion, stopping perhaps for a score of days to exchange goods and gossip, but recently a new type of trader had appeared, the man named Abu Hassan, for example. He arrived with canoes, talked secretly with the headman, traded in a jiffy and was gone. He also introduced unfamiliar goods: rifles and beverages and cloth of a different make. He was arrogant and gave commands, and those porters who enlisted to help him get his goods to market did not return to their villages.

Cudjo had taken a quick dislike to Abu Hassan; the older traders had accepted whatever the villagers offered for barter, but this new breed stated in strident terms what they required, and the black people felt obligated to provide it. Cudjo tried to persuade his people that they must oppose such domination, but he was only twenty-four years old and the sager heads would not listen. He sometimes wondered why they were so insistent upon defending Hassan when his total effect was so negative, and he persisted in his opposition.

Indeed, he made himself something of a nuisance, a troublemaker who would not long be tolerated, and some months ago, when Abu Hassan came up the Sankuru with his canoes, Cudjo had been prepared to oppose him when the trading commenced, but to his surprise the Arab did not stop. He continued right up toward the headwaters of the Xanga, pausing only long enough to confer quietly with the three headmen and give them presents.

'He will trade with us on the way back,' the village leaders explained, and the convoy passed on.

'We should not trade with him,' Cudjo protested, and the elders looked at each other knowingly.

It was now that he became aware of plots against him. The tribal leaders began to meet surreptitiously, refusing to admit him to their discussions, and he was particularly disturbed when Akko, a young man no older than himself, was accorded preference.

This Akko was a shifty manipulator, more given to clever tricks than to hard work, and Cudjo knew that the tribe would find itself in difficulty if it followed advice from this man. But Akko was adroit in managing things to his advantage, and it became clear throughout the village that the elders had determined to elevate him into a position of leadership that should more properly have gone to Cudjo.

Now, when word came that Abu Hassan was coming down the Xanga with his men, Cudjo saw that the decision had been made: Akko was put in charge of assembling the village's goods for trading, a position of trust, while Cudjo was isolated from any important task. He had to sit in bitter idleness as Akko collected the ivory, the feathers, the partially cured leather and the powdered horn of the rhinoceros, so valuable in trade to the east: it enabled old men to marry young girls.

In his idleness Cudjo decided upon a curious stratagem. He would on his own recognizance journey up to the headwaters of the Xanga to ascertain what trade goods Abu was demanding this time, and he would then come back and alert his tribesmen as to what items were of particular value, so that they might have on hand substantial supplies of these preferred goods when the Arabs arrived. This would prove his willingness to serve, even though Akko had been promoted over him.

He was a powerful young man, able to paddle his river craft up the Xanga or run for long spells after he had beached his boat and started overland. He had strong legs, a very thick neck and shoulders more solid than most. If the contest between him and Akko had come down to fighting or wrestling, he would have won easily.

So he found no difficulty in ascending the river, and on the sixth day hid his canoe and walked through the deep forest, peering through leafy protection to observe what was happening in the village where the Arabs traded. There stood the huts, the piles of ivory, and the striped tents from which the traders conducted their business and in which they slept at night.

The first thing he noticed was the unusually large number of Arabs accompanying the expedition. In the old days, when some wandering tradesman reached the village, he brought at most one assistant, relying upon black porters to carry out the elephant tusks. Even Abu Hassan, on his two earlier trips, had brought only two white helpers; this time he had nine. Cudjo peered around to see what enormous mound of trade goods justified such a company, but he could detect nothing.

The second inexplicable thing was a substantial fire that was burning near one of the tents, in front of which sat two white men, their faces smeared as if they were playing at being black. Of this strange behavior he could make nothing.

Because of his uncertainty over what was happening, he slept that night in the woods, and when he wakened before dawn he saw to his surprise that the fire had been allowed to die down. As he watched, the Arabs came out of the striped tents to start the fire again. This was indeed mystifying; in his village fires were tended at night to keep animals away, and allowed to die at daybreak.

When the sun rose, two events took place in rapid order, and the peaceful world he had known was shattered. From the south, where there were only the poorest villages with little to trade, came a doleful line of twenty-two black marchers, each bound to the other by chains and bands of iron about the neck. They moved in silence, guarded by three new Arabs bearing long guns and whips.

When this file approached the village, a signal was sounded, and the black headmen, assisted by their cronies, blocked off escape routes and designated various strong young men and women to be pinioned. While Cudjo watched in horror, the black leaders turned these young people over to the Arabs, who drove them to the tent where the fire had been burning. There two Arabs, assisted by black helpers, fastened iron collars about the necks of the captives and linked them together by chains, which were then hammered shut.

One young black, apparently as strong as Cudjo, perceived that when the elders nominated him it meant trouble, so he broke loose and would have run to the forest, except that Abu Hassan himself raised his gun, aimed it with great precision and shot the man dead. A young woman began to scream, and as long as that was all she did the Arabs ignored her, but when she tried to run to the body of her dead companion, Abu Hassan swung the butt of his rifle in a fierce circle and knocked her unconscious. An iron collar and chain were fastened to her as she lay in the dust.

Nineteen of the finest young people of the village were so collected and chained. The black headman also offered to sell six others, but they were not strong and the Arabs rejected them. One of these, a woman with child, tried to stay with her enchained husband, and when she became difficult, Abu Hassan shot her.

The chain binding the nineteenth prisoner was now welded to the dragging chain of the twenty-two brought north from the impoverished villages, and a procession containing forty-one future slaves started its long march west to Luanda, the Portuguese port on the Atlantic Ocean where cargoes of slaves would be collected in the barracoons until enough had been gathered to fill a ship headed for Cuba.

Cudjo, watching as the Arabs in charge of the enchained slaves lashed their charges to get them started right, trembled with rage. The best young people of the river were being taken, and they had been designated for this fate by their own leaders, who were now rewarded for their duplicity with a trivial collection of beads and cloth and iron axes. Abu Hassan had brought his nine assistants not to trade but to forge iron collars and to drive long lines of slaves into the barracoons. When the procession was gone, Abu Hassan and his helpers loaded their canoes and prepared to descend upon Cudjo's village.

To forestall them, he departed swiftly and sped through the jungle on foot, hoping to reach his sequestered boat before the Arabs progressed to that point, for if they got started down the river first, he would not be able to pass them and alert his village. Therefore he ran until his lungs were on fire.

He reached the river in good time, broke loose his hidden boat and started paddling furiously. Never before had he been so aware of the Xanga, its bending trees and darting birds. It was a river to cherish, and all who lived along it were now in peril.

Without rest he kept his powerful shoulders working until at last he rounded the bend which protected his village. Some children saw him approaching, paddling as if fiends were at his back, and they shouted that Cudjo was returning. This produced an unexpected result: the old men of the council hurried to the shore, suspicious of what message he might be bringing. And when his boat neared the landing, it was they who moved in to surround him.

'Abu Hassan!' he cried, but before he could speak further he caught a glimpse of some man, Akko it must have been, sneaking up behind him. As he turned to meet this adversary, the man brought a heavy club down upon his head and he lost consciousness.

When he awakened he found himself gagged and bound by a heavy iron collar from which a chain led to a tree. He was guarded by an Arab with a gun, and there was no way he could communicate with his villagers; if he tried to scream, the gag muffled his voice; if he tried to escape the Arab, the iron collar choked him. But he must in some way arouse the young men and women to the peril about to engulf them.

Before he could devise any tactic, he had to watch in horror as the village leaders assembled the people, while the Arabs, including even the one who had been guarding him, took up positions with their guns ready. He tried to shout a warning, but he could make no noise. He turned his attention to the chain where it was twined about the tree, but even he could not break it loose.

Helpless, he saw the village elders begin to nominate the young people they were willing to sell: this stout lad, that promising girl, the young man who had stolen the cow, anyone the village wished to get rid of. Then he gasped. The old men designated Luta, the girl he had tried to purchase for his wife. She screamed, but Abu Hassan clubbed her into silence.

At this point Cudjo managed to work the gag out of his mouth, and with great brassy voice, shouted, 'Resist them! Don't accept the chains!'

Abu Hassan, hearing the dangerous alarm, directed one of his men to silence the black, but when the Arab approached, Cudjo summoned extra-human powers and shattered his chain at the tree. Swinging the loose end about his head, he rushed at the man and felled him. He then raged toward the doomed prisoners, trying to rouse them to revolt, but before he could take more than a few steps, Abu Hassan raised his gun to shoot him. This proved unnecessary, because Akko, for the second time, clubbed Cudjo and he fell to his knees, and quickly his dangling chain was welded to that of a man he had known since childhood. Together they would make the long march to the sea.

Twenty-three men and women comprised the convoy, but the smiths had prepared twenty-seven collars, and to march with a partial complement, utilizing guards, would be a waste. So when the column was formed and about to start west, Abu Hassan brushed aside the village elders whom he had paid for their help, and pointed to three likely young men and one healthy-looking woman.

'Add them to the chain,' he ordered, and the guards grabbed the four and pinioned them until iron collars could be clapped about their necks. The first to be trussed was Akko.

'Not him!' one of the faithless chiefs called. 'He's my son!'

'Take him,' Hassan ordered, and the welding was completed. But when the old man saw his son in chains, destined for a land no one could comprehend except that it was far away, he began to wail, and grab Hassan, and make a nuisance of himself.

Hassan shoved him away, but now the parents of the other three unexpected captives began to mount a confused demonstration, and there was such noise that Hassan lost his temper and made an extraordinary decision.

'Take them all to Luanda.'

'The entire village?' one of the blacksmiths asked.

'Everybody!'

'It's six hundred miles. They can't possibly live.'

'Some will.'

So the entire village was whipped into line behind the chained young people. One hundred and nineteen infants and elders started an impossible trek through the Congo jungles toward a goal most of them would never reach. Up front, two armed Arab guards. Beside the chained prisoners, two others with guns ready. Then the mass of villagers guarded by Abu Hassan himself, with two guards straggling at the rear, ready to gun down anyone attempting to flee. The two remaining Arabs had gone down the Xanga toward the Congo with canoe loads of ivory and rhinoceros horn.

It was a preposterous march, a petulant act of vengeance not uncommon in these waning days of the slave trade. In 1832 every step in the vile business was cynical, ruthless and illegal. Black leaders sold their followers for baubles; Arabs chanting the Koran organized the marches; Christians intent on saving souls managed the barracoons; renegade captains transported the slaves in proscribed ships; and in Cuba pariah dealers risked buying them on the chance that they could be smuggled into the southern states, where importation of new slaves was forbidden.

Of course, the kidnapping of blacks out of Africa had long been outlawed, by the United States in 1792, by Great Britain in 1807, by France in 1815, but such restriction merely made the rewards for contraband extra tempting; plantation owners in the Caribbean, Brazil and the southern states continued to offer extravagant bids for prime hands, and recreant captains could always be found willing to run the blockade.

It was on his segment of the massive gamble that Abu Hassan was now engaged. He had set out from the Xanga with twenty-seven prime blacks in chains and one hundred and nineteen as an undifferentiated mass. He hoped to get at least twenty-two of the chained slaves to Luanda and not less than thirty of the others. If he could do that, he could show a fine profit, what with the earlier shipments he had dispatched from villages farther south. In fact, if he ran into no unusual difficulties, he stood a chance to fill an entire ship with his slaves alone, in which case he could dicker with the captain for a maximum price.

He was not concerned, therefore, when the older villagers began to die off. As a matter of expediency, he was even willing to abandon those who must soon die, so as the line of marchers forded one river after another, it became smaller and tighter. It was a good march, one of his best, for he had not yet lost a single black in chains, and they were the ones on which his basic profit would depend.

For the blacks so chained, the march was a hideous experience. For more than forty days in heat and rain each man would march and sleep and evacuate his bowels attached to two others; for a young woman chained between two men the journey was almost unbearable, but on the procession went.

Cudjo, chained somewhere near the middle, bore the long trek better than most, but it became apparent to the guards that in spite of his chains he endeavored constantly to maneuver himself so that he could kill Akko, the unfortunate who had twice betrayed him. Akko appealed to the guards for protection. They would have preferred shooting Cudjo, but he was too valuable a property, so they contented themselves with lashing him, or beating him in the face with their gun butts whenever he made a move toward his enemy.

Forestalled in that direction, he was equally powerless to aid Luta, who was chained to Akko, for any move in her direction was interpreted by both Akko and the guards as an attack on him. Once one of the Arabs smashed a gun into Cudjo's instep, and it seemed for a while that Abu Hassan might have to shoot him because he fell so lame that he could not keep up. But he summoned new reserves and dragged his painful foot along.

His mother and father died almost together on the thirtieth day. Abu Hassan, looking at the wasted bodies, was not unhappy to see them fall. Fifty-one had died off, leaving only the strongest, and it seemed likely that he would be reaching Luanda with far more than the mere thirty extras he had calculated.

But on the fortieth day heavy rains struck, and fevers from the swamps caused severe loss of life. Two of the women in chains died and twelve of the others, so that Hassan's potential profits were slashed. This enraged him, and when the chains on the two dead women had to be removed, he abused the blacksmith so severely that the poor man simply ripped the collars off, lacerating the corpses horribly. The file moved on.

On June 10, the fifty-ninth day, Abu Hassan led his company into the outskirts of Luanda, the thriving Portuguese city perched on the edge of the Atlantic Ocean. Leaving his charges in an improvised encampment near the city, he went alone into Luanda to arrange for the orderly sale of his blacks. He discovered to his irritation that no slavers were in harbor at the moment, because two British warships were patrolling the seas to keep away any captains who might be thinking of a quick and profitable dash to the slave ports of the Caribbean. His only alternative would be to throw his slaves into one of the barracoons run by the Jesuits near the shore, so he tried to discover which of the huge pens contained his earlier shipments from Xanga, and at last found them.

'Good passage for us,' his guards reported. Since they had started from the villages farthest south, where rivers feeding into the Congo system were shallower, they had not suffered heavy losses; also, they were herding only younger blacks in prime condition, so that their survival rate ought to have been superior.

'Less than ten percent loss,' they said, congratulating themselves.

'Come out and pick up the new arrivals,' Hassan directed, so the guards accompanied him to the temporary encampment, where with long-practiced eyes they evaluated the huddled blacks.

'The twenty-five in chains look good,' they told Hassan. 'These forty-one others? Not worth much.'

'They'll help fill the ship,' Hassan said defensively.

'They won't last long in Cuba,' the slavers said professionally. 'Not many of them will be smuggled into America.'

'They'll help fill the ship,' Hassan repeated.

'Shall we strike off the chains?' one of the guards asked.

'No. It could be many weeks before a ship puts in,' Hassan warned. 'The damned British.'

He was right in his guess that the British would keep his slaves penned up, but he would have been outraged had he known why. There was in the complement of priests running the barracoons a young Portuguese of peasant stock; he was called Father João and he suffered from an incurable affliction: he took Jesus seriously. What he witnessed of the slave trade sickened him, and at great risk he had devised a system of signals to alert the British cruisers whenever the barracoons were filled, or whenever some especially daring slave ship was about to make a sortie into shore for a quick load of slaves.

On the evening of the day when the first chain of Xanga slaves arrived, Father João had placed in the branches of a tree a white cloth, whereupon a lookout on the cruiser *Bristol* reported to his commander, 'Sir, slaves have reached the barracoons.' No international commission had designated the *Bristol* to be the watchdog of the seas; an inflamed public opinion had demanded that the trade be halted, and this the captain was prepared to do.

For two weeks his heavily armed ship patrolled the coastline of Portuguese Angola, enforcing respect from the captains of several fast ships which lurked beyond the horizon. If the *Bristol* challenged them to stand by for inspection, they did so, knowing that if their holds did not actually contain slaves, the watchman could do nothing. The slave ship might contain rings for fastening chains, and a 'tween deck for stowing blacks, from which even an idiot could deduce its business, but if it contained no actual slaves in bondage, it committed no offense, and while the English officers might look with scorn at the Americans operating the ship, they were powerless to do more.

The blockade continued, with the British grim-lipped, the Americans cursing, the Arab businessmen desperate over the costs of feeding their slaves, and the blacks in the barracoons trying in vain to protect themselves. Since those great pens had no roofs, when rain came, as it often did from clouds scudding in from the Atlantic, they could only huddle together and wait for it to stop. When it did, the sun beat down with tropical ferocity, and now Abu Hassan began to fret, for not only did some of the older villagers begin to die, but his prime stock in chains began to fall sick.

On no one did the degradation of the barracoon fall more heavily than on Luta. For more than thirteen weeks she had been chained between two young men only slightly older than herself; all her bodily functions were available for their inspection and theirs to hers. Beatings she did not have to fear; occasionally the Arab guards could bear no longer the tedium and the complaining, and they would go temporarily beserk, striking out at anyone, but intelligent slaves learned how to draw back from such short-lived assaults.

But against the terrible indignity of being close-chained in a waiting pen, Luta had no defense. She might have died from sheer surrender of spirit had not Cudjo watched her from his distance, lending her encouragement and strength. Sometimes he would shout across the chains to her, words of fire and assurance, until one of the guards poked him with a musket, warning him to be silent. Then, during the long rains, he would simply watch her, and gradually she let him know that she was now determined to survive this awful experience, and he shouted for all to hear that he loved her.

Six weeks had now elapsed since the various chains of slaves from the Xanga had been thrown into the barracoons, and Abu Hassan was beginning to suffer from the cost of maintaining his property. He was faced with a difficult dilemma: feed them less and save coins, or continue to feed them so that they would look better at the auction in Cuba. He rejected each alternative, retreating to a stratagem he had used once before: he sold the entire contents of his barracoon to the Jesuit fathers who owned it. 'Let them take the risks,' he told his assistants.

So the Arabs quit themselves of the Xanga slaves, pocketed a fair profit, and went to the bazaars to collect trade goods for the subornation of other tribes south of the Congo. Abu Hassan knew of nineteen other rivers feeding into the Sankuru, each with a cluster of pitiful small tribes whose elderly leaders might be tricked into selling their best young people into the slave trade.

'We'll be back,' he assured the Jesuits. He could foresee the lucrative trade continuing indefinitely into the future; the British might try to interrupt it, for reasons he could not fathom, but there would always be daring ship captains willing to take the risks attendant upon enormous profits. 'I just wish one of them had hurried up,' he said ruefully as he led his team out of Luanda. 'We'd be leaving with bags of gold.'

The Jesuits to whom he had sold his consignment did not wish to be in the slave trade; it was just that they owned the barracoons and had found that quite often it was to everyone's advantage for them to step in as middlemen, pay the Arab slavers a reasonable fee, and themselves assume the risk of feeding the blacks and eventually delivering them to some ship captain for a small but comfortable profit.

It was not this profit that the Jesuits sought; while they had the savages in their charge they Christianized them, and this was commendable because it meant that any blacks who might die on the long passage to Cuba would do so in the arms of Christ. Their souls would be saved.

So now the beatings stopped and kindly young clerics raised on farms in Portugal visited the barracoons daily, explaining in mangled African phrases how Jesus watched over everyone, even those in chains, and how in a later and better life the slaves would meet Him personally and see for themselves His radiant generosity. Cudjo braced himself against the earnest young Portuguese, but Luta started talking with Father João, and the honest compassion that glowed in his eyes made his words consoling; when she pieced together all that Father João promised, it made sense, for she had always believed that there must be some god who ordained the movement of the stars and of people and even of the animals in the forest. And that this god or collection of gods should have sent a special son as intermediary was not difficult to accept. That this son should have been born of a virgin posed no insurmountable problem for her; in recent weeks, chained to her two companions, she had often wished that she could be incorporeal.

So intently did she listen to the young priest that Father João reported enthusiastically to his superiors, 'We are making many converts in the barracoon. The girl who calls herself Luta is ready to embrace the true religion.'

So in the late afternoon of a day which had seen both storms and blazing heat, two older Jesuits appeared in the barracoon, stepping gingerly among the lazing bodies until they reached the spot where Luta stood in chains. Moving her two companions aside as far as their chains would permit, the priests addressed her and asked if she was prepared to accept Christ as her preceptor. When she nodded, they expressed true joy of spirit and told her that Jesus would now take her into His personal charge, and that she would know life everlasting. Her trials on earth she would be able to bear because of the paradise that would follow hereafter; in her new home she would find God's love and attention.

They then blessed her and asked her to kneel, which she did with difficulty, since her chain-companions had to kneel with her. This in turn caused the slaves attached to those two to kneel, until at last all the surviving blacks of this chain were on their knees while the girl Luta was taken into the church. Cudjo, who had to get down with the rest, would have objected if the recipient of this grace had been anyone but Luta; he felt that if she needed this assurance, he would do nothing to distress her.

'You are now a child of God, the beloved of Jesus,' the older priest intoned, and after he left, the twenty-five slaves got up off their knees and the two men chained to Luta looked at her with special interest to see if the blessings of the priests had in any way affected her. They could detect only the quiet resignation she had always manifested.

A curious change now came over the blacks in the barracoon: they had grown so satiated with the mindless routine of storm and sun, they began hoping that the thing the priests called a ship might come to Luanda. No one in the pens could imagine what new terrors this ship might bring, but they sought it. Cudjo was actually hungry for change.

At dawn on the second day of August a ship of much different character arrived off Luanda. It was low and sleek. Its sails were rigged in the hermaphrodite manner—four very large jibs attached to the long bowsprit, four square sails at the foremast, two fore-and-aft at the main— which meant that it could exact the maximum advantage from any wind. The main thing, however, was the impression it created of meaning business; the slave dealers on shore told each other, 'Now something will happen.'

By eight o'clock that morning a small boat let down from the ship, darted into a cove and deposited on shore an older man, stooped of shoulder and slow of gait, but his arrival reassured the slavers. 'This one means to buy,' they said as he walked purposefully along the shore.

'Hello,' he said as he came to the square, 'I'm Goodbarn, from the *Ariel*, Captain Turlock.'

'We recognized you,' the chief agent said.

The visitor fell into a rattan chair and asked for a drink. He seemed tired and much aged since they last saw him, so they were not surprised when he said, 'This is our last trip. We're going to load maximum and strike for a big profit.'

'The barracoons are filled.'

'We want no old, no sick.'

'For you, Mr. Goodbarn, we have hundreds of strong young niggers.'

'We're going to load four hundred and sixty belowdecks. And we'll risk fifty-seven topside. Those must be in chains so we can bolt them down.'

'Large shipment,' the agent said.

'We intend to retire rich.'

'How old is Silverfist?'

'Well past sixty, but you'd never know it.'

'When do you propose loading?'

'Today.'

'That would be impossible.'

'You said they were waiting.'

'Yes, but we couldn't get the red chair set up in time.'

'To hell with the red chair,' Goodbarn said. He was tired and even more eager than his captain to be done with this last gamble.

'Without the red chair, there will be no departure of slaves from this port, I can tell you that.'

'When can we do it?'

'Tomorrow, but what plans have you for slipping into shore?'

Goodbarn took a long drink of warm beer, held it in his mouth and looked out toward the bay. 'We came here in 1814 to refit the *Ariel* for slaving . . . for that one trip. Eighteen years later we're still slaving, telling ourselves this is the last trip.' He looked about cautiously and indicated that he wished to speak alone with the agent. 'You asked what our plans are? Captain Turlock reasons that some spy on shore is flashing signals to the British patrol. Don't laugh. Nothing else explains the promptness of their reaction whenever we attempt a landing.'

'Quite impossible,' the agent said. 'The Portuguese officials—'

'So what we're going to do is pay a Spanish captain to make a false run some miles up the coast. The *Bristol* will follow and we'll sweep in.'

'The English commander's too clever for that trap.'

'It won't be a trap. Because today you will march three hundred slaves north to where the Spaniard might land. And if the *Bristol* refuses to follow, the Spaniard loads his slaves, sells them in Havana and splits with us. However, my good friend, we'll make this so real that the *Bristol* will have to sail north.'

'Who pays for marching the slaves . . . in case the *Bristol* trails them?'

'I do. We have a great risk in this voyage, a great chance of profit. Captain Turlock is always ready to pay money to make money.' And he poured onto the table a small pile of silver coins.

When the dealer hefted them, counted them and considered the complicated offer being made he nodded, then called to the others, 'We can move the red chair out tomorrow. The *Ariel* will load five hundred and seventeen at nine o'clock.'

At noon three hundred other slaves started marching north to serve as decoy; at one Father João spotted them and flashed a signal to the British; at two the *Bristol* sailed north.

In the barracoons the slaves from which the *Ariel* would select her cargo were carefully readied for shipment. Each received a bucketful of fetid water in the face, another in the middle of the back. Additional buckets were left standing in the center for those who wished to cleanse themselves further; Cudjo and Luta did so. While they were washing, priests brought in extra tubs of food, something that had never happened before, and Cudjo whispered, 'They want us to look clean and healthy. Tomorrow we'll be sold.' That night the slaves went to sleep knowing that in the morning something of significance must happen.

At dawn they were marched out of the barracoons and down to the wharf, where Cudjo saw for the first time a burly red-bearded old man with a silver knob for his left hand; and the imperial way the man stood, shoulders stooped but eyes flashing, indicated that he was master. When Cudjo observed the manner in which other whites deferred to him, he whispered to the slaves on his chain, 'Watch out for that one.'

Now the old man moved with precision down the long files of unshackled blacks, accepting some, rejecting others: 'Yes, yes, yes, not that one.' From the assured manner in which he made his decisions, Cudjo guessed that he had often engaged in this process.

When he had approved some four hundred blacks, he turned briskly to those in chains, but before he started down the line he called to another elderly man in a black suit—'Goodbarn,' Cudjo heard him say —and together they inspected the sturdy slaves. They accepted most, but when the big man came to the slave next to Cudjo, a big fellow who had been ailing since he reached the barracoon, he saw at once that this one was not a good risk, and he indicated that he must be removed from the chain, but Goodbarn, if that was his name, explained why this could not be done, and the big man shrugged his shoulders.

He now came to Cudjo, and for some inexplicable reason grabbed him by the chin, stared into his dark eyes and said something to his associate. He obviously did not like what he saw in Cudjo's face, and again asked if both Cudjo and the ailing slave could be cut loose, but Goodbarn said no. With his hand still at Cudjo's chin he growled some warning and thrust the slave back.

When he finished checking the chained slaves, he ordered Mr. Goodbarn to assemble all he had approved; he marched with them, nodding his head and saying short words to Goodbarn. Then he withdrew a short distance, surveyed the mob and nodded. The purchase was agreed upon.

Now the spiritual part of the long voyage from the Xanga villages began. The five hundred and seventeen chosen slaves were herded into a small area, where they stood with their backs to the sea facing a handsome red chair which had been placed on bales of merchandise, forming a kind of rude open-air cathedral. To it came a procession of priests making way for a tall and somber man dressed in red. When he had been assisted onto the platform containing the chair, he raised his hands and the crowd fell silent.

'You are about to start a journey to an unknown land,' he said in Portuguese. 'But wherever your fate takes you, God will be watching over you, for you are His children. He will guide and comfort you.' He continued for some minutes, while Mr. Goodbarn fumed, always looking at the ocean. The bishop was of the opinion that the blacks were actually lucky to be making this journey, for they would be moving into areas where God prevailed, and there they would learn of His boundless charity.

But now came the significant part of the exercise, the symbolic moment which justified the establishment of the barracoon and its more or less humane management. The bishop extended his arms to their widest and cried, 'In the name of Jesus Christ, I baptize you into the Holy Christian Church. If perchance you should die on the journey you are about to undertake, you will be received into heaven and sit upon the right hand of God.'

When he had finished making the sign of the cross, seven priests hurried through the massed slaves, anointing them with holy water and assuring them of life eternal. When this was completed, the bishop gave the entire assemblage his blessing, wished the ship's crew a safe passage, and climbed down off the bales of cotton. As soon as he was gone, Mr. Goodbarn shouted, 'Now get these black bastards on board. Quick!'

The slaves were turned about, to face the ocean, and for the first time they saw the ship that would carry them to the blessings of which the bishop had spoken, but they were permitted to inspect it for only a moment, because members of the ship's crew began thumping them in the back and shouting, 'Move on! Move on!'

They ran a gauntlet of sailors and slavers, all urging them toward the ship, up whose gangplank they were rushed. On deck stood Captain Turlock, his red beard flecked with gray, his silver fist shining in the hot sun. With sure eye he studied the slaves to check whether sickly substitutes had been inserted, and with a heavy swipe of his metaled hand he moved the unchained slaves toward the hold.

There Mr. Goodbarn supervised their allocation to one of the four compartments, taking pains to ensure that powerful men and possible troublemakers were sent to the lowest hold. Belowdecks a Mr. Jenkins supervised the welding of such chains as had come below, and when these men were finished with their tasks, four hundred and sixty slaves were stowed in quarters that might have accommodated sixty men in reasonable decency. The grating at the mainmast was bolted shut. The passageway between the two levels was locked. The white men climbed out on a ladder, which they drew up behind them. And the hatch leading to the deck was bolted from the outside. In gloom, and seasickness, and filth the blacks would sail.

Meanwhile, on deck, Captain Turlock was trying to do something he had never done before: find space for fifty-seven men and women, most of them in chains. These he bolted to the bulwarks, port and starboard. The others he ordered to huddle forward, with a guard instructed to shoot them if they gave trouble.

'It's our last trip,' he told Goodbarn. 'See it goes well.'

It started poorly. Father João's false signal had sent the *Bristol* on a wild chase to the north, but as soon as the priest realized he had been tricked and that the *Ariel* had slipped into shore, he boldly unfurled a large sheet, which alerted the *Bristol* to the invasion. Now it came rushing south, determined to intercept the slaver before it could get out to sea.

'*Bristol* coming!' Captain Turlock's lookout cried.

'All hands!' Turlock shouted, and no other orders were necessary, for each American sailor knew that he must get this clipper out of Luanda or risk years in a London jail.

With astonishing speed the crew had the *Ariel* ready, and while Portuguese wharfmen, eager to keep slavers coming to their port, threw off the lines, Mr. Goodbarn supervised trimming 'the slaver's delight,' as the hermaphrodite rigging was called. 'If'n a morfidite can't get you goin' in light airs, nothin' can.'

The *Bristol,* already under way, would enjoy an advantage, especially with her formidable guns, but the *Ariel* did not propose to allow her within range, and in the early stages of the contest nullified the *Bristol*'s running start by catching an offshore breeze which carried her well out to sea. Father João, watching the two ships, prayed the breeze would drop so that the slaver might be taken. But his prayer was not answered. The breeze maintained and Captain Turlock cleared the harbor.

'Raise the topsails,' he told Mr. Goodbarn, and when they were aloft, the ship leaped forward, but it had to keep to a course which brought it close to the *Bristol,* which had swung its guns into position.

Among the slaves bolted to the deck topside were Cudjo and Luta, and the former, always alert to what happened about him, deduced that the disciplined behavior of the American crew meant that they faced some kind of danger, so he pulled himself erect, as far as his chain would allow, and peered over the gunwale. 'Oh!' he gasped, for there, not far away, he saw a much larger ship, its sails rounded with wind.

Till this day he had never seen a ship, so he could not understand its characteristics, but he knew intuitively that this other vessel was the cause of the apprehension he saw in the faces of his captors. For only a brief moment was he able to study the relative position of the two ships, for Captain Turlock bellowed, 'Mr. Jenkins, get that big one down!' And Jenkins clubbed Cudjo with a belaying pin. But after he fell to the deck Cudjo was able to shout to the other blacks, 'That one is trying to capture this one!'

Slaves in both gangs scrambled to their feet to see what Cudjo meant, and this concerted movement of the blacks terrified the white sailors, for they had been taught from their first day aboard the *Ariel:* 'The thing to fear is not storms or British cruisers, but a rebellion. Stamp it out before it gets started.'

'Mr. Jenkins,' Mr. Goodbarn shouted, 'knock those slaves down!'

With belaying pins the sailors swept along the gunwales, knocking the slaves away, then belaboring them as they lay on the deck. The white men had no reluctance to break heads, for they knew that a certain number of deaths could be expected, and they might have killed Cudjo except that Captain Turlock shouted, 'Mr. Jenkins! Back to the lines.'

The savage beating silenced the blacks, but Cudjo continued to watch the British ship as the *Ariel* rolled in the open sea, disclosing a brief glimpse now and then, and he was delighted to see the other ship moving closer. But now puzzling things began to happen. A series of clever maneuvers by the man with the silver fist began to move his ship away from the pursuer. A gun, much bigger than any ever used by Abu Hassan, was fired and a bullet of immense size, judging from the sound it made, whistled through the ropes overhead.

One of the slaves chained directly to Luta looked over the gunwale and saw what was happening. 'They're firing a big gun at us!' he shouted.

'Get him down!' the captain shouted.

Deprived of their lookout, the cowering blacks could no longer follow the action, and their desire to know became so great that Cudjo defiantly stood erect—in time to see the British ship give up the chase. It fired two cannon at the fleeing *Ariel,* but the shots fell harmlessly into the ocean, and the American sailors broke into a cheer.

Cudjo knew that the chase was over. He knew that this red-bearded man had unusual powers. Above all, he knew that any chance for escape was lost.

Once the *Ariel* cleared Africa and the lurking menace of the British cruisers, the daily routine was established. Each dawn some sailor threw several buckets of salt water over the chained blacks. About an hour later buckets of swill were placed where the slaves could feed themselves. Toward noon the covers leading to the fetid hatches were removed and a work party consisting of unchained slaves from the forward contingent was sent below to collect the bodies of any who had died during the preceding twenty-four hours. These were thrown into a rope basket, which was hauled aloft and emptied over the side of the ship; on several occasions young men and women chained aft would spot the corpses of their parents.

At dusk the swill buckets were again brought out, but the constant motion of the ship was so sickening to the slaves that most of them, including Cudjo, became violently ill at each sight of food. They vomited and excreted and then lay in the filth until the morning bucket of water sluiced at least some of it away. Cudjo, growing constantly thinner, wondered what the conditions below must be. He found only two clues: at noon, when the hatch covers were removed, the heated stench was so awful that the white sailors kept wet rags about their noses, and once when the slaves forward went down to drag out the corpses, they passed Cudjo and he asked, 'What's it like?' and an old man said, 'Let them kill you up here.'

Sick as he was, Cudjo followed with intense interest everything that happened on deck. He began to appreciate Captain Turlock's capacities, and how he varied the set of his sails. He understood the duties of the helmsman and even learned the English words used to direct his actions: 'Steady on' when the ship's wake showed indecision, or 'Hard starboard' when the great boom was to be swung to the other side in order to catch the breeze more efficiently. He was able to determine the relative importance of the sailors, and who it was that took command when the captain slept. He learned the bells and spent many fruitless hours trying to determine what was in the black box before the tiller that the captain and the helmsman studied so attentively. It did not yet occur to him that this had to do with direction, for he always knew where north was except when fog settled upon the ocean, but he did notice that the white men consulted this box much more frequently at those times when he himself was disoriented, and from this observation he reached one conclusion: the black box had something to do with preventing the ship from becoming lost. Abu Hassan had once brought to the Xanga villages a trading product that had stupefied and delighted them: a magnet with a collection of iron filings. Only once had Cudjo been allowed to work the magnet before the filings were lost, but its mystery had stayed with him. He now concluded that in the secret box there must be a magnet which pulled the ship in the right direction.

But as he became familiar with the operation of the ship, he also became obsessed with what must be happening belowdecks, and once when the covers were removed so that six corpses could be hauled out, he strained at his chains, hoping to catch at least a glimpse of the horror he knew existed, but he could see nothing. However, his act did not go undetected, for Captain Turlock saw what he was doing and ordered Mr. Jenkins to strike him down.

As he lay unconscious on the deck, Turlock stood above him and said to the trembling slaves, 'You want to see what's going on below. Damn me, you'll see, right now.'

He ordered the forward hatch opened and had his men throw all the unchained blacks below. If their friends caught them, fine. If they broke their backs, to hell with them. He then commanded his carpenter to unbolt the chains holding the two groups aft, and when this was done he ordered his men to throw those blacks below; the two men chained to Cudjo were responsible for dragging him along.

He awoke in the bowels of the ship. Darkness and horror reigned, and when a storm arose, the shapeless mass of arms and legs and torsos rolled back and forth. The free-moving older slaves from the forward part of the deck found what space they could in the area, which was so cramped that standing erect was impossible; they had to lie flat day after day.

The chained slaves faced a more difficult problem. Since they had to move as a unit, all they could do was crouch miserably in corners vacated by the numerous dead, but during the first night below, Cudjo was able to move close to Luta, and for the only time since their capture they had a chance to talk.

'I wanted to come down here,' he told her.

'Why?'

'Because I know how to sail this ship.'

'What good?'

'Because we shall take this ship away from them and sail home.'

'How?' She pointed to the stifling hold filled with emaciated shadows.

'We will take this ship!' he repeated stubbornly, and during the long, sick night he moved among the others in this upper hold, whispering to them. One told him a remarkable thing: 'In the hold below, which is worse, a man from another village, he calls himself Rutak, has been saying the same thing.' The informant led him to a gap in the planking; Cudjo lay prone, his chains forcing the men nearest him to lie down with him, and he whispered, 'Is Rutak there?' and after a while a heavy voice replied, 'I am Rutak.'

They talked for nearly half an hour, and in the upper hold at least six slaves could hear what Cudjo was saying, while in the lower the same number could overhear Rutak, so that before the night was over, all the blacks were aware that Cudjo and Rutak intended something.

Among those in Cudjo's chain gang who could not help but hear what was being said was Akko, the young man whose trickery had been responsible for Cudjo's capture. As the son of a village leader, he had always known preferment, so that the experiences as a chained slave on the march from the Congo, and the indignity of the barracoon, and now the horror of this ship had a deeper effect on him than on most of the others. He was shattered; his deepest sensitivities were profaned and he was prepared to avenge them.

Shifting his chains, and dragging his two arm-companions with him, he approached Cudjo and said in the dark, 'I will help you take the ship.'

This offer, so unexpected, presented a difficult dilemma. Two months ago Cudjo had wanted to kill this man; now the arrival of worse agonies had obliterated from Cudjo's mind any thought of mere revenge for personal wrong. But could he trust a man who had betrayed him? In the darkness he could not see Akko or estimate his sincerity, but he did know from his own case that the events of slavery were so compelling as to force a change in any man or woman. He jerked his chains and took Akko by the hands. 'We will need you,' he said.

At noon on the next day, when the hatches were opened, the bright sunlight illuminated the upper hold in which Cudjo and his companions huddled. The space was four feet ten inches high, with no ventilation. One corner was set aside as a latrine, but the urine filtered through onto the heads of the blacks below. Any who died within a twenty-four-hour period were piled in another corner. When the hatch to the lower hold was opened, Cudjo saw that it was sheer hell. He shuddered. Every detail was worse.

And then Captain Turlock, who was always watching, chanced to look into the hold and saw to his horror that the chained slaves thrown down yesterday had not been bolted fast. 'They've been free to roam the whole damned ship!' he screamed, and the carpenter was summoned.

'Fetch the smith and go down there and bolt those niggers down!' he cried, and even when these two specialists, protected by four ordinary sailors with belaying pins, were at their tasks, he continued to rant: 'You let those niggers who have seen everything up here congregate freely down there—who knows what might happen?'

He looked down to see how the work was progressing and saw staring up at him the big warning face of Cudjo, his mortal enemy. 'No!' he cried. 'Don't put him in the upper hold with the others who were on deck. Put him and his gang below, and stretch them out tight.'

So Cudjo, Luta and Akko were thrown even lower into the innards of the ship they had determined to capture, and the blacksmith attached the loose ends of their chain to rings that were the maximum distance apart. Now this batch of slaves would not be able to scratch away lice, or rub their eyes, or feed themselves, or tend to their bodies in any way. The rings of the chain were hammered shut. The cover to the lower hatch was closed. The cover to the upper hatch was restored to place, and a solemn darkness prevailed.

In this darkness Cudjo, Akko and Rutak conspired. The latter was a powerful man who had already devised a way whereby he might be able to break his chains loose from the bulkhead, and when, with the help of all the free-moving men in the hold, he did so, he showed Cudjo and Akko how to break theirs, too. It then became necessary for the three men to detach themselves from the others, but to break the chain itself proved impossible. They therefore decided that in their escape attempt they would transform their impediment into an advantage. They would utilize the two chains as a weapon, and they trained their two groups, always stooping, never able to stand, in intricate maneuvers which would be supported by the free-moving slaves.

When their plan was perfected, Cudjo and Rutak huddled for hours with their lips close to the ceiling boards, instructing the men and women above them.

On the day they had designated for their noontime attempt, a heavy storm arose and sickness belowdecks became epidemic; even Cudjo and Rutak were retching. They were able to vomit nothing because they had eaten so little, and they decided to surrender any thought of going ahead with their plan.

It was Akko, the thin, wiry little man who resented confinement profoundly, who persisted. 'The whites will be as sick as we are,' he argued. 'They'll be inattentive. This day was delivered to us by the gods.' He reasoned so persuasively that Cudjo and the others slowly saw that a storm was the best possible time for their attempt. Accordingly, Cudjo and his men edged open the hatch leading from their hold, whereupon his chain gang and Rutak's climbed silently into the upper hold. There four sturdy men had organized their part of the operation.

As they waited in the pitching darkness they formed a strange army: four hundred and seventy-nine unarmed blacks, the strongest impeded by chains, proposing to overwhelm four canny officers and thirty-two sailors armed with guns, knives and belaying pins. The slaves knew that many of them would have to die if this ship was to be taken, but they were certain that many of their captors would die, too.

Removal of the dead was delayed on this day because of the storm, and it was not till well past two that Captain Turlock ordered his men to open the hatches. Since there were now no slaves on deck to serve as corpse collectors, it had become the custom for two sailors to descend in the rope basket that would later be used to haul out the dead. Once below, the sailors were also expected to check the security of the slaves, going into each of the holds. Because of the stench, this duty was not appreciated.

On this stormy day two grumbling sailors descended in the basket, inspected the upper hold and found that the two chain gangs had escaped from below. They were unable to report this alarming knowledge because as they started to open their mouths, huge hands engulfed their faces and they were strangled.

With remarkable self-discipline, Rutak and his men climbed silently into the basket, marked the time it had always taken to collect the corpses, then signaled in the accustomed manner for the men on deck to winch the basket out. At the precise moment that Rutak's team cleared the hold, but before anyone on deck could sound an alarm, Cudjo and his gang grabbed the bottom ropes of the basket and swung themselves on deck. In less than ten seconds the two groups of chain-bound blacks surged over the deck.

Victory would be impossible unless they used their chains effectively, and this they did. Sweeping in curved arcs toward the sailors, they entwined them, decapitating some, wounding others and allowing them to fall to the deck, where they were strangled by the unchained blacks.

Most skillful of the leaders was Akko, who had an innate sense of what the chains could accomplish; he and Luta killed three sailors. It was also Akko who first saw Captain Turlock rushing onto the stormy deck, pistol in hand. He saw Silverfist coolly survey the scene to decide where he was needed most; huge Rutak was running berserk, but Turlock apparently judged that others could handle him. Then he spotted Cudjo, the man he had feared from the start, and he knew that he must kill this one or lose his ship.

'Cudjo!' Akko shouted as the captain pointed his pistol, and when Cudjo did not hear, he and Luta swarmed over the redhead from behind.

Entangling him in their chains, they tried to strangle him, but failed. He fell heavily to the deck, shouting, 'Mr. Goodbarn! Help!' But the mate had already been slain.

So Akko, Luta and Turlock rolled on the deck, and with his flailing pistol and silver fist he held them off. Struggling to regain his footing, he lurched to one knee, pointed his pistol straight into the chest of Akko and discharged it. Then, with his silver knob, he began to beat Luta in the face, gradually crushing it to a hideous pulp.

Shoving their bodies aside, he started down the deck to rally his men, and he might have succeeded had not Cudjo turned to see the death of Luta. With a great cry he dragged his chain-mates with him, and they leaped upon Turlock, bearing him down. Cudjo jammed his knees into the captain's chest, applying pressure until he heard bones crack.

This should have killed him, but with a tremendous burst of energy he kicked Cudjo away, regained his feet and started swinging his left arm in lethal arcs, but as he started down the deck to rally his men, a sudden gush of blood burst from his mouth. Pressing the back of his right hand against it, he saw that it could not be stanched. 'Mr. Goodbarn,' he called with weakened voice, 'don't let them take the ship!'

But now Cudjo came at him again, assisted by his mates, and Turlock waited till he was close in. Then he lashed out at him with his silver fist, clubbing him over the head with his pistol, but Cudjo bore in, screaming a victory cry. Enmeshing him in the chains, he knocked him down and strangled him.

He was beating Turlock's bloody head against the decking when Rutak bellowed, 'Cudjo! Mind the ship!'

It had been agreed from the first hour of the conspiracy that Cudjo would capture the helm, but the death of Luta and his revenge upon Turlock had diverted him. As he shook his head, endeavoring to orient himself, the helmsman discharged his musket almost in the face of a slave attached to Cudjo's chain, but that black man, with an extraordinary intensity of purpose, continued his forward motion and swept the helmsman into his chained arms, bearing him to the deck and dying on his chest. The helmsman tried to break loose, but three unchained women fell upon him and tore his throat.

The sight of this violence cleared Cudjo's brain and he leaped, as well as his chains would permit, to take command of the helm.

Now all the blacks were out of the hold, and they simply overmassed the sailors. The carpenter, who had nailed them to the bulkheads, had his head torn off; the blacksmith, who had cut away the chains of those who died so that they could be pitched overboard, was now wrapped in chains of his own, weighted with whatever iron could be found, and tossed screaming into the sea.

It was Rutak who stopped the killing, and ordered, 'Throw all the white men into the hold. Half on the bottom, half on top.' He then directed that the dead sailors be tossed into the stormy sea, and this was done, except that when four blacks grabbed Captain Turlock by hands and feet, Cudjo halted them. 'He was brave,' he said, and he looked into the glaring eyes of the dead man and placed his two hands under his back. Gently the tired old body was dropped into the Atlantic, an ocean it had fought for so many years. The silver fist, so valuable it could have ransomed many of the slaves, went useless to the depths.

Now came the sadness of bidding farewell to the forty-eight slaves who had given their lives for freedom. Each survivor had known at least one of the dead as a friend, but none experienced the confusion and anguish that Cudjo did when Akko and Luta were cut loose from the chains in which they had lived side by side for one hundred and sixty-four days. The dead man had been the cause of grief, the wise plotter, the heroic warrior at the climax. The dead woman . . . she would forever be the echo of that peaceful village along the Xanga. He looked away as their bodies were consigned to rest in an ocean they had never known.

He left the burial scene and returned to the helm, determined to get this ship somehow to safety. In the dark hold he had assured the slaves that if they captured the ship, he would know how to sail it.

He knew. As the storm worsened he ordered even the reefed sails to be taken down, and when his black crew could not immediately comprehend his orders, he left the tiller and showed them. The steering of the ship he turned over to the man from the upper deck who had led him, on that first fateful night, to Rutak in the deck below.

When the ship steadied, and when Rutak and his enterprising assistants had explored all quarters, experimenting with the compact and varied foods found below, Cudjo turned his attention to the mysterious box which he knew he must master if this adventure was to succeed. He could make nothing of it. Around the black face within the protecting arc appeared figures in white, but they were a mystery. A long needle rested in the middle of the mysterious thing, and it moved.

Cudjo concluded that there must be some relationship between the motion within this black box and the wind, or perhaps the sails, or the sway of the ship, and it was not until the next night, when the storm had cleared and the stars came out in unaccustomed brilliance, that he was able to solve the riddle. He allowed Rutak to steer for some unknown destination, one sail set, while he attended to the black box, and late on this starry night, when every hypothesis had proved faulty, for the movement coincided with no phenomenon that he could detect, he happened to look up at the stars with which he had been so familiar in the jungle, and when he located that faithful star by which men traveled at night, he suddenly realized that it controlled the dancing needle, so that no matter where the needle seemed to point, it maintained a constant direction.

What to do with this knowledge he could not decide, because he had no concept of the world or where on this great ocean he wished to go.

Rutak and the other freed men and women now came to him to discuss this very question: Where are we to go? He was powerless to answer them, and their combined speculations provided no answer.

They knew that Arabs were their mortal enemies, lurking and tricking to drive them into slavery. They knew that persons who spoke what was Portuguese were also their enemies, eager to sell them into slave ships. The priests confused them; some had helped and even stayed in the barracoon when they took sick, but others had been responsible for their going aboard the ship; the chief in red who had hurled so many final words at them and then dashed them with water, they could not fathom at all. The one thing they were certain of was what Cudjo reported: there was on this ocean at least one ship which had intended to befriend them. Their job was to find that ship.

So they kept to the arbitrary course which Cudjo had set that first starry night; they would sail north, always north, and as the weeks passed they became efficient in raising sails and reefing them. They deciphered what an anchor was and how to use it, and they dragged up from the holds three sailors to instruct them in ropes. These sailors, each a veteran of five or six slave crossings, were surprised at the order the blacks were able to maintain; they had been taught that slaves were animals.

But the sailors would not help the blacks navigate their prize. They deduced that since the weather was growing colder they must be heading north, but since they never saw the stars they could not guess how far. They also judged that only those crewmen jailed belowdecks survived, which meant that the mutineers had killed at least nineteen Americans. They went below, determined to recapture the ship and hang every damned nigger, but Rutak, having masterminded a piracy of his own, did not intend to encourage another. Accordingly, he ordered forty blacks, men and women alike, to bunk belowdecks to monitor the holds, and these suspicious watchmen, having escaped from the horror which the whites had maintained in those cramped quarters, were determined that there be no repetition.

It was late in October 1832 that the Baltimore clipper *Ariel,* well out from the coast of Morocco, was hailed by the French corvette *Bordeaux.* The captain of the ship being overtaken did not, of course, know what it meant to be hailed by a warship and was at a loss as to how he must respond. He judged the best thing to do was to keep plowing ahead and avoid a collision.

In the end the corvette did four things in rapid succession: it fired a shot across the bow of the *Ariel;* it fired another shot; it then closed and shouted instruction in both French and English; and finally it launched two rowboats containing twenty sailors heavily armed, and when they boarded the strange ship they shouted back in French, 'It's manned by blacks! They speak no civilized language!'

When officers came aboard, it took them only a few minutes to realize that they were on a ship which had suffered mutiny; belowdecks they uncovered the seventeen prisoners, and a tale of horror began to unfold.

'We were sailing peacefully westward.'

'Where to?'

'Cuba.'

'A hold full of slaves?'

'Well, yes.'

'Acquired where?'

'Arab slavers had marched them into Luanda.'

'I think you sent shore parties into Africa to capture them.'

'Oh no, sir! On my honor. The Portuguese sold them to us. You know, the bishop on the red chair who blesses them before we take them aboard.'

'How many?'

'Five hundred and seventeen.'

'Good God! We find only four hundred and thirty-one.'

'You know niggers. They do die fearfully.' The spokesman saw that when this was interpreted, it created an unfavorable impression, so he quickly added, 'And don't forget, many were killed in the mutiny.'

Yes, a major ship had been taken on the high seas, and all its officers slain. This was a matter of the gravest import; its ramifications could be evaluated only by a court of law. So the captain of the *Bordeaux* placed a cadre of men aboard the *Ariel* to trail along until both ships could reach a French port, but only two days' progress had been made when the British cruiser *Bristol* hove into sight, identified the *Ariel* as a slave ship the British had been trying for many years to arrest, and demanded of the French that she be turned over to them.

An international incident threatened, but the two captains who had faced each other in distant wars realized that this was an impasse which must be handled by compromise, and a sensible one was worked out over port and pudding in the *Bristol:* the French had captured the ship and it was clearly their prize, and if the court dealing with mutiny awarded it to them, the sleek clipper would become part of the French war fleet. The mutinous slaves, who had murdered not less than nineteen American seamen, including four officers, would be turned over to the British, who had a traditional interest in suppressing the slave trade and who could be trusted to handle this complicated case intelligently. The seventeen American survivors would, of course, be set free by the French, but they would be retained by the English as witnesses in the trial of the rebellious slaves, and later as defendants themselves against the charge of slaving.

The *Ariel* did enter the French navy, where her high degree of speed and austerity of design captivated all who served in her. The infamous 'tween-deck was removed, and the main deck was raised slightly to accommodate eight carronades. She sailed the Atlantic for years, often on station to interdict the slave trade, and in due course made a return journey to the very town in which she had been built.

The slaves were returned to their chains and transported by the *Bristol* to Plymouth, where on June 13, 1833, an extraordinary court delivered an extraordinary verdict:

> It is established that the clipper *Ariel* of American registry had been engaging in the slave trade for many years, at considerable profit to her owners and crew. Otherwise, in this incident the ship was well handled and in the best traditions of the sea. No evidence was presented to us proving either undue cruelty or sustained severity. The crew, from Captain Matthew Turlock down to the messboy, was responsible.

On or about August 1, 1832, the *Ariel* arrived off Luanda, Portuguese Africa, for the obvious purpose of collecting a shipment of slaves from the barracoons in that city. These slaves, an incredible five hundred and seventeen in number, had been collected among the villages strung along the Xanga River, one of the minor tributaries of the Sankuru, itself a tributary of the Congo. They were the property of the Arab slaver Abu Hassan, whose activities have been reported earlier in the British courts.

The *Ariel* loaded its forbidden cargo despite efforts by His Majesty's cruiser *Bristol* to prevent such slaving, and then made its escape under the *Bristol*'s guns and in full knowledge of its illegal behavior. On September 22 the slaves imprisoned in the hold mutinied and took the ship. More than a month later, on October 24, it was captured by the French corvette *Bordeaux*, a remarkable fact being that its sails were properly set and it was being handled in shipshape manner. This court declares said clipper *Ariel* forfeit and congratulates the *Bordeaux* for having taken possession.

Now as to the individuals involved. We find the seventeen surviving American sailors guilty-by-participation in the crime of slaving. Had the voyage proved successful, they admit they stood to share the money gained by the sale of their slaves in Cuba. Each and severally are sentenced to two years in jail.

The slaves present a more difficult problem. There will be many in this nation and elsewhere who will feel that their attempt to escape from bondage was commendable, but the solemn fact is that in doing so they engaged in an act of mutiny on the high seas, they stole a ship which had been duly registered, and they murdered four officers and fifteen men. Can the seafaring nations of the world condone behavior which strikes at the very heart of naval tradition? This court thinks not.

Because of his leading role in the mutiny, the slave known as Rutak shall be hanged. The slave known as Coboto shall be hanged. The slave known as Betana shall be hanged . . . [and so on, through a list of nineteen slaves.]

The slave known as Cudjo, who appears to have played a major role in the mutiny, also played a major role in saving the ship. He and all others shall be transported to Havana, and delivered to their rightful owners.

This harsh decision raised, as might have been expected, an outcry in both England and France, but the objections came from only a limited number of critics. In the former country the year 1832 was one of vigorous political reform, always opposed by the grand Duke of Wellington, and also one in which the anti-slavery movement gained the momentum which would within the year prohibit the ownership of slaves throughout the British Empire. The citizenry was so preoccupied with doing good for blacks in general that it had no energy left to protect the rights of specific blacks.

In France, the nation was bending every effort to digest the peculiar behavior of their new king, Louis Philippe; nominated by the radicals because he was a revolutionary, he quickly became the darling of the conservatives because he had always been at heart a reactionary. Alternately confused and elated, the citizens of France could not care what happened to a gang of slaves, especially since their aborted action enabled France to gain a fine warship.

On June 15, 1833, Cudjo and four hundred and eleven other blacks were marched out of Plymouth jail and loaded onto a British ship bound for Cuba, where in a large shed at dockside they were put up for sale.

Word had circulated, of course, that these were the mutineers who had murdered the crew of the *Ariel,* so an ugly fascination attended their sale, and more buyers than usual pressed in upon the auctioneer, but they had come to gawk, not bid. Plantation owners were loath to bring onto their land slaves known to cause trouble, and speculators feared that none could be smuggled into America, where an uprising of slaves led by the preacher Nat Turner had ended in the slaughter of fifty-five Virginians. American slaveholders were terrified.

At the sale, Brazilian traders bought the lot except for six of the strongest young men. After the most careful inspection, these were picked off by a thin American who wore a white linen suit buttoned almost to the chin. He sucked constantly upon a silver toothpick and spoke softly in the manner of a gentleman: 'Name's T.T. Arbigost, Savannah, Georgia, and I pay cash.' When the auctioneer asked, after the sale, why he had purchased the six men who promised to be most difficult, Arbigost said, 'I have ways of training them. What I figure is, I can smuggle them into Georgia, then slip them into the market, one at a time . . . different parts of the country . . . nobody need ever know they were mutineers.' He paid over his money, marched his six slaves, including Cudjo, to his sloop, dragged them belowdecks and ordered his carpenter to secure them. This man was a powerful fellow from the interior of Georgia who hoped one day to run his own plantation and had specific theories about handling blacks. With the aid of four stout sailors he spread-eagled Cudjo on the lowest deck of the ship, where the headroom was only eighteen inches. He ordered his men to strap down each ankle, extending the legs as far as possible. He did the same with Cudjo's wrists. Then, about his neck he fastened a heavy iron collar from which led two small chains. These he bolted to the deck. And when the powerful slave was thus secured, the carpenter began to kick him, cursing the while and daring him to try mutiny aboard this ship. And he continued doing this until Cudjo fainted. With a farewell series of kicks, the carpenter growled to the remaining five, whom he pinioned in similar fashion, 'Now let's see you mutiny.'

It was in this posture that Cudjo, twenty-five years old, slipped into America.

The Slave–Breaker

MOST NATIONS HAVE AT ONE TIME OR OTHER BOTH condoned and practiced slavery. Greece and Rome founded their societies on it. India and Japan handled this state of affairs by creating untouchable classes which continue to this day. Arabia clung to formal slavery longer than most, while black countries like Ethiopia and Burundi were notorious. In the New World each colonial power devised a system precisely suited to its peculiar needs and in conformance with its national customs.

The most practical was that in Brazil. Since Portuguese women were discouraged by their Catholic faith from emigrating to a savage new country, Portuguese men found their wives in the slave population, and a curious, strong and viable society developed. Slaves were slaves and were treated as such until they produced beautiful daughters; then suddenly they became the parents of the bride. At fourteen the master's son was given his own slave, the prettiest black woman of eighteen on the plantation, and it became her pleasurable task to introduce the lad into an essential meaning of slavery.

The most reasonable system was the English. Since many of the best young men had to find their destiny in a life overseas, it became traditional for many of the best young women to follow them; although marriage with slaves was unthinkable, reasonably decent treatment was obligatory, and it was not surprising that England became the first great power to outlaw slavery at home and discipline it abroad.

The French were perhaps the best administrators of their slave system; it was a cross between the total assimilation of Brazil and the rigid exclusionism of England, and resulted in a kind of amiable non-rigid society in Guadaloupe and Martinique, where a family of some distinction might have a cousin married to a former slave. In fact, there were persistent rumors that Joséphine de Beauharnais, the exquisite Martinique girl who married Napoleon to become empress of France, had slave blood in her distant background. The lot of the French slave was by no means pleasant, and there were insurrections in these islands too, but they were handled with compromise and concession.

The most stolid, unrelieved system was that of the Dutch. They treated their slaves no worse than others, but they did so with such relentless pressure and lack of grace that slave rebellions in their colonies became frequent. To be a slave on a Dutch island was to live without hope; day after relentless day the sugar mills revolved, grinding the blacks into sullen submission until they could bear no more. Then the fiery insurrection, the savage reprisals, and the continued grinding of the mill.

The Spanish were an anomaly. In Mexico and Peru their primary slaves were Indians, whom they baptized and annihilated. Blacks fared comparatively well in some of the Spanish possessions, where they often served as teachers, minor administrators and family friends. In the Spanish islands their life in the sugar fields was horrible and brief. Many who had known servitude in islands like Cuba thanked their forgotten gods when fate moved them to the United States.

By all standards, and in the opinion of all, the one island which represented human slavery at its absolute nadir was Haiti. Here, under a remote French administration, accountable to no one, a band of cruel exploiters accepted those fractious slaves whom no one else could handle, worked them sixteen hours a day like animals, fed them little, beat them constantly, and buried them after four or five years. For a slave to be assigned to Haiti was a sentence of lingering death.

American slavery covered such a vast area that no generalizations could be easily made. In the northern tobacco states with temperate climates, like Virginia, it duplicated the best aspects of the English pattern; in the more remote lower states, like Mississippi and Louisiana with their steaming sugar and indigo fields, the worst features of the Dutch and Haitian systems flourished. And the cotton states, like Georgia and Alabama, offered some of the best, some of the worst.

Maryland was in a category by itself. Indeed, it encompassed two categories: the western shore, whose plantations were much modified by anti-slavery pressures from Pennsylvania; and the Eastern Shore, which remained insulated from outside pressures and resembled a fiefdom of the Carolinas. In 1833 the apex of Eastern Shore slavery occurred on the vast Steed holdings.

There were four major plantations: the great one on Devon Island, with its satellite operations north of the Choptank, and the three fine establishments at the Refuge, with their outlying fields reaching to the Miles River. Together they covered a vast extent of land, well over thirty thousand acres, which were worked by six hundred and ninety-three slaves. And these slaves, who soon would total more than eight hundred, were kept under control by eighteen white men.

No one could ever see all the Steed slaves. Some worked in fields so remote they rarely encountered a white overseer. Others tended the various stores. The fortunate ones, insofar as food and clothing were concerned, worked in the four mansions. Others specialized in trades requiring the most sophisticated skills; they stayed in hidden shops all their lives. But most worked the plantation crops: wheat, corn, vegetables, a little tobacco. They hoed and weeded and harvested, and they did this till they died.

They lived, for the most part, in collections of rude, dirt-floored wooden cabins whose boards did not fit and through which the winds of winter swept. They were allowed some wood to burn, but not much. They were given some food to eat, but never much. They were medicined when they fell ill, but only by the overseer or his wife. And they were given clothes, one reasonably good outfit for special occasions, one fitting of work clothes for all other days of the year. They had no church, no hospital and, above all, no school.

The first slaves had reached Devon Island in 1670; it was now one hundred and sixty-three years later and almost nothing had changed. If those first blacks could come back and walk up from the wharf some Tuesday night, by Wednesday morning they would find themselves fitting easily into the system. Actually, no slaves direct from Africa had reached Devon in more than eighty years; new arrivals had been born in America, often on plantations noted for their success in breeding blacks.

At Devon their lives were governed by overseers; on remote plantations a Steed slave might spend three years clearing new fields and breaking them in without ever having actually seen a member of the Steed family. Overseers were usually German or Scot; they had a pragmatic approach to life, and the Lutheran religion of the former and the Calvinism of the latter prepared them to believe that sinners should be punished. Thus they were always ready to chastise the tardy slave and keep the field hands working; also, they tended to be honest.

On the island itself in the year 1833 the overseer was a Mr. Beasley, a Scotsman with an impeccable reputation for strictness and fairness. He knew each of his slaves by name and tried to assign them tasks for which they were preeminently suited. In his early days on a Virginia plantation he had often whipped slaves, because the master there demanded it; but after he fell under the influence of the Steeds, he never struck a slave again. He did, however, demand instant compliance, and if a slave

proved refractory, Mr. Beasley recommended sale to some other plantation. He also liked to see his slaves attending the prayer meetings he
conducted—'The word of God is soothing to a troubled spirit.'

Some of the distant plantations had known overseers of quite a different stripe; some were true horrors, lashing and beating and knocking
down; but when verified reports of their savage behavior reached Mr.
Beasley, he dismissed them on the spot, so that the Steeds were justified
in boasting, as they did repeatedly, 'Our slaves are the best treated in
Maryland. They're not beaten and they're not abused.'

The pitiful fact about slavery as it existed on the Steed plantation was
its banality. On white and black alike the heavy encumbrances of custom
pulled everyone down to a mournful level in which the most extraordinary situations were accepted as inevitable. An unbroken chain of black
men and women was purchased for the plantation or bred there, and they
existed through the centuries without family names, or recorded histories, or education, or variation, or hope. The male field hands formed an
interminable succession of Toms, Jims, Joes; at the big house classical
names were preferred, for these gave a kind of distinction to social life:
Pompey, Caesar, Hannibal, Napoleon, Brutus. Women in remote fields
often bore names that were rarely spoken by their white overseers: Pansy,
Petty, Prissy, Pammy, Puss. Generation after generation they were
judged to be alike: treated alike . . . dressed alike . . . ignored alike
. . . and buried alike.

The whites who supervised this system also became alike in their ways.
Most wives were kind and condescending, but also careful to ensure that
a new crop of seamstresses was growing up in the slave quarters. The
plantation owners were aloof but considerate; they would be shamed if
anyone circulated reports that they were treating their slaves poorly: 'We
endeavor to be good masters, and we discharge any overseer who touches
a slave.' The fact that at Devon the master himself had gone mad for a
spell and had actually whipped his slave girl Eden was referred to only
obliquely: 'We ran into a small problem but corrected it.' The real burden
under which the white masters lived was psychological: they came to
believe that they were inherently superior and that they were ordained
to hold in their hands the destinies of those less fortunate.

The white Steed overseers occupied a curious position, half slave, half
free. In a hundred years no overseer had ever eaten a meal at a Steed
table, nor had any ever sat in the presence of a Steed without having been
invited. It would have been unthinkable for Mr. Beasley to break either
of these customs.

Along the Choptank there were five levels of social life, and the members of each understood their place. First came the Steeds and similar
planters; infinitely below them came the slaves. In town there were the
merchants and artisans such as the Paxmores, referred to by the slave-

holders as 'those poor unfortunates.' In the country lived the solid farmers on whom the society depended; and everywhere there appeared the unspeakable white trash, like the Turlocks, often referred to as 'Oh, them.'

One aspect of slavery baffled explanation: along the Choptank only one family in eight owned slaves, yet all believed that their existence depended upon the continuance of slavery. It was as if the Steeds had used witchcraft to persuade the slaveless farmers to defend a system which benefited not them but the rich, and when George Paxmore tried to argue that the economic life of the river would be enhanced if black men were set free to work for wages, he was considered an irresponsible fool, not only by the Steeds, who owned slaves, but especially by the Turlocks, who owned none and whose relatively low position was caused primarily by the region's insistence upon slave labor.

'All I need to know about niggers,' Lafe said when the mutiny aboard the *Ariel* became known in Patamoke, 'is that they murdered my cousin Matt. One of 'em looks at me with a crooked eye, he dies.'

The Steed system of slavery was a gentle one, and it bore satisfying fruit. It was seen at its best at Christmastime; then, by long tradition, the slaves received one week of holiday, and Mr. Beasley saw to it that in each of the communities hogs were barbecued over a pit fire, with dozens of chickens roasting on the side. At the big house candies and pies were made. Hundreds of loaves of bread were baked, and the Steed women took care that every slave got his new set of work clothes; boys who had reached eighteen during the year were given their first suit of good clothes and girls of that age were given two dresses.

Mr. Beasley, strict teetotaler though he was, allowed bottles and even kegs of whiskey to be brought onto the grounds, and festivities were endless: cockfights, races, wrestling matches, sewing bees, baking competitions and all sorts of games for children. Each plantation had at least one man who could fiddle, and sometimes he played for nine hours at a stretch. Often the white folk from the big houses would come to watch the dancing; chairs would be brought out and the owners would sit approvingly as their slaves enjoyed themselves.

No work was done during this festive period, only the inescapable routines like milking cows and gathering eggs and carrying out the chamberpots from the big house. It was a joyous time, and fifty years later blacks in some far part of the nation would remember plantation life: 'If'n no Christmas, I think I'da died.'

The Steeds enjoyed the holiday almost more than their slaves; it enhanced the illusion that they were good masters. The gaiety in the dark faces proved that life in the shanties could be tolerable, and the obvious delight when the new clothes and the extra food were distributed proved that on these plantations at least, the slaves loved their masters.

There was only one ominous cloud: Elizabeth Paxmore, the Quaker lady, had been caught teaching black children how to read and write. She did not, of course, admit them to the informal school she conducted for plantation whites at Peace Cliff, but she did welcome them to the shed in back of the telescope house, even though this flouted local custom. What was worse, she had allowed two older blacks to slip into her classes and was teaching them how to read the Bible, and each of these students belonged to the Steeds.

When word of this criminal behavior reached Uncle Herbert, who now supervised the entire Steed operation, he was aghast. He asked his nephews if he was correct in assuming that slaves had never been taught to read the Bible, and they assured him he was. He then summoned Mr. Beasley, who stood with hat in hand to receive his instructions: 'You've got to go and reason with that difficult woman. We can't afford a scandal . . . God knows we've sent our own children to her. But we do want a stop to this pernicious business.'

So Mr. Beasley got into his sloop and sailed over to Peace Cliff. Bowing politely, he said, 'Mrs. Paxmore, I come on unpleasant business.'

'Thee always does,' she said crisply, but with a touch of dry humor. She was now forty-nine years old, trim and erect as an elm tree, and almost as pretty. Her features had attained a lovely calm, as if conforming to the gray dresses she wore, and her manner had softened. She was disarming, a woman of middle age who had the alertness of a girl. Smiling warmly, she invited Mr. Beasley in, sat him down and faced him in a straight-backed chair. 'Now tell me thy problem.'

'Ma'am, it's about those two slaves you're teachin' to read the Bible.'

'Is it wrong to teach another human being to read the Bible?'

'Mrs. Paxmore, you don't seem to understand that since the trouble with Nat Turner over in Virginia . . . Things aren't the same, and this meddling with slaves has got to stop.'

Elizabeth Paxmore folded her hands in her lap and said firmly, 'It will not stop.'

Mr. Beasley ignored this challenge and pleaded, 'You've also got to quit teaching our nigger children.'

Mrs. Paxmore started to respond, but the overseer said hurriedly, as if he had memorized his arguments, 'All the states agree that slaves must not read the Bible. They center on certain verses and it disturbs them. The proper thing is for a white minister to explain the Bible . . . or the master of the plantation.'

'Don't they center on certain verses?'

'But they give a balanced view. That God ordered the world. That some were intended to be slaves.'

'And that the slave must obey the master?'

'Of course. The Bible says that specifically.'

Mrs. Paxmore looked at the overseer compassionately and asked,

'Does thee think that I will stop disseminating the word of God?'

'You'd better. The word of God must be taught only by those capable of explaining its true meaning.'

They had reached an impasse. Mr. Beasley had nothing more to say. Politely he excused himself, placed his hat on his head and walked down to his sloop. At first Mrs. Paxmore felt that she had bested him, but in the end he triumphed, for she never saw any of her students again, men or boys. She waited for them to appear in the shed behind the house, but they never came. One day in Patamoke she stopped a Steed slave to ask where her students were, and the woman was too frightened to reply, there on the street where she could be seen by the Steed personnel at the store, but with a movement of her eyes she indicated that she would meet Mrs. Paxmore later, behind a wall.

'They was sold south.'

This phrase represented the ultimate terror among slaves—the sugar plantations of Louisiana, the cotton fields of Mississippi—and Mrs. Paxmore, suddenly weak, leaned against the wall, her hands over her eyes. The two young men so hopeful, the children just beginning to learn their letters . . .

'They was all sold south.'

It was into this society that Cudjo came in mid-December 1833, and his arrival created a sensation, for he was the first native from Africa that anyone then living at Devon had ever seen.

He reached the Choptank illegally. After Mr. Beasley expelled the two Bible-learners, he hurried them to Baltimore, along with four children separated from their parents, intending to sell the lot south. But as he approached the auction hall he was intercepted by a slave dealer from Savannah who introduced himself as 'T.T. Arbigost, with a most interesting proposition.' Mr. Beasley did not like such men or their connivings, but Arbigost whispered, 'Why pay the auctioneer an unnecessary commision?'

'What did you have in mind?'

'Sell your slaves to me, privately.'

'You won't offer as much.' Mr. Beasley had good reason to be suspicious of Georgia traders, and Mr. Arbigost, with his white linen suit and silver toothpick dangling from the corner of his mouth, seemed especially suspicious. But he offered an attractive barter: 'Now, I know that the niggers you want to dispose of are troublemakers. I can see that. But I'll take them off your hands in a way that you'll come out ahead. For the two men, I'll give you one of the finest prime niggers you ever saw, docile, good at machines. And for the four children, I'll give you my two women.'

'That hardly seems—'

'Plus four hundred dollars.'

It was a trade, and after Mr. Arbigost shifted his silver toothpick, he confided, 'Tell you the truth, Mr. Beasley, I'd put the two wenches at work in the fields. Proved themselves a little sassy in the big house.'

'You have the same kind of trouble with your buck?'

'No, sir!' He moved close to the overseer and dropped his voice to a whisper. 'I personally smuggled him in. Right off a ship from Africa.'

Mr. Beasley had never worked a slave direct from Africa, and asked, 'Is that an advantage?'

'Yes, yes!' Mr. Arbigost cried enthusiastically. 'Means he hasn't learned the ways that get niggers into trouble.'

Enticed by the prospect of dealing with a new kind of slave, Mr. Beasley inspected the man being offered. Looked to be about twenty-five, sturdy, good teeth, huge biceps. His face had that placid gaze of complete resignation which overseers preferred. 'Shall I chain him to the boat?'

'Chain him, Mr. Beasley? Do you expect a fine boy like that to mutiny? Look, he's as gentle as a lamb.' Mr. Arbigost poked Cudjo in the ribs, and he was gentle.

The three slaves were led to the wharf, and the long, easy sail to Devon began. Cudjo would remember every detail: the bigness of Baltimore harbor, the multitude of ships resting there, the spaciousness of the bay, the beauty of the Eastern Shore as it rose gently on the horizon, the calm of Devon Island. He also studied the four half-naked slaves operating the boat, and thought: I sailed a ship larger than this. But he noticed that the men seemed at ease, and their backs were not striped like his.

Upon delivery at Devon he was assigned to one of the outlying plantations from which the two men who had been caught learning to read had come, and there, far from the clement eye of the Steeds, he was placed under the supervision of a Mr. Starch, fiercest of the overseers. All incoming slaves served their apprenticeships with Starch, who had a knack for breaking them into the Steed system. When he first saw Cudjo and his impressive physique, he assumed that here was a man who might prove difficult, but during his weeks in Georgia the big Xanga had mastered the strategy for being a slave.

He obeyed. Grasping situations more quickly than most, he studied to determine what pleased an irascible overseer, and he provided it. He did so for a powerful reason: he was determined to learn. His thirty-three days in command of the *Ariel* had taught him a lifetime of lessons; that he could operate a complex machine, that he could handle people, that he must learn to read, that he must learn to figure, that his life would be meaningless unless he learned somehow to be free. Most of all, he had acquired that inner confidence which can make a man infinitely more powerful than the accidents of birth would normally permit. No amount of temporary abuse was going to divert him from his twin goals of learning and attaining freedom.

Slavery he did not understand, except the fundamental truth that blacks were slaves and whites were not and that whatever the latter said was correct. Even during his brief stay at Savannah he had watched with amazement as white men gave blacks the most faulty and ineffective instruction for doing a job; even the stupidest black could see that it wouldn't work, but even the wisest black could not correct the white master. 'Yassah! Yassah!' was the first English word Cudjo had learned, and he used it constantly without feeling any sense of debasement. If 'Yassah' was the password to existence, so be it.

Whites and blacks alike were fascinated by this stranger from Africa, the former hoping to find proof that blacks were born savage and rescued only by slavery, the latter trying to discover something about their origins. He disappointed both groups, for he was not savage, nor was he interested in Africa; his problem was America. During his apprentice-ship in Georgia he had picked up enough English to communicate, and as soon as he was settled in as one of Mr. Starch's field hands he began asking questions: 'Who d'big boss?' 'Where he live?' 'Anybody here can read?'

When this last question was asked, the other slaves showed fear. They explained that Cudjo's predecessors had been caught reading and had been sold south. With a hundred stories they impressed on him that the worst thing in the world that could happen to a slave was to be sold south, and after he had listened to a plethora of such tales he said, 'I been south.' And he indicated that there were many things worse.

Whenever he saw a scrap of writing he studied it, hungrily, trying to decipher its mystery. His first solid instruction came when barrels were packed with goods for London. Then a slave from the cooperage appeared with an iron stencil and a pile of wood shavings. Lighting a small fire, this man threw on heavy timbers until he had a fine blaze, into which he thrust the iron stencil. When it was red-hot, he pressed it against the head of the barrel, allowing it to sizzle until the notation was deeply burned: DEVON PLNT FITHIANS LONDON 280 LB.

He memorized the rubric, unable to decode even one fact it repre-sented. Nevertheless, he could reproduce it, letter for letter, which he did in the sand when no one was looking. Then, from something Mr. Starch said, he deduced that this barrel was intended for London, and he felt a strange sensation of triumph, for he had been in London. That much he knew.

He also heard the overseer from another plantation say, 'I wonder, Starch, if that far barrel contains a full two-eighty pounds,' and Mr. Starch had gone to it, tapped on the figures and said, 'When we brand it two-eighty, we mean two-eighty.' Cudjo looked quickly away, but as soon as the men left, he hurried to the cask, studied the marks that Mr. Starch had struck, and learned that 280 was said two-eighty. In the next few days he wrote these symbols in the dust many times and pronounced them. They were the opening wedge.

When the next barrel was filled, and the lid was about to be hammered down, he stood by the barrel and asked, so that Mr. Starch could hear, 'This one got two-eighty?'

Without thinking, the overseer responded, 'It better.' Then he stopped, looked at Cudjo and shook his head. But he remembered him.

The sense of power that came with knowing that this barrel was headed for London and that it contained two-eighty was so exciting that Cudjo looked for other writing to decipher; there was none. So he began to inquire as to how the two banished slaves had learned, and slowly he discovered that a white woman named Mrs. Paxmore had taught them. Quickly he dropped all questioning, lest some clever slave deduce his plans, but in an entirely different part of the field he asked in subtle ways who this Mrs. Paxmore was, and he was told.

One day in early December 1834 he slipped away from work, ran down to the bank of Dividing Creek, swam across and ran along the eastern edge of the creek until he came to Peace Cliff. Without hesitation he ran up the hill, reached the back door, banged on it and waited.

A woman appeared, middle-aged, thin, dressed severely in gray. The thing he would always remember was that she was neither surprised nor frightened, as if accustomed to the arrival of disobedient slaves. 'Yes?'

'I learn read?'

'Of course.'

Carefully closing her kitchen door, she led him to the shed in which she had given earlier instruction and placed him on a chair. 'Which plantation do you come from?' This was too difficult, so she asked, 'Who d'big boss?'

'Mastah Starch.'

She leaned back, made a little temple of her fingers and said quietly, 'Does thee know the words *sold south?*'

'I been south.'

She bowed her head, and when she raised it Cudjo could see tears in her eyes. 'Thee still wants to learn?'

He nodded, and without further comment she took down a hornbook —a shingle into which the alphabet had been burned—but before she could say anything, he wrote with his finger the words branded on the tobacco casks. She could not follow him; fetching a pencil and paper, she said, 'Write.'

For the first time in his life Cudjo put words on paper: DEVON PLNT FITHIANS LONDON 280 LB. She smiled. She could guess with what effort this illiterate slave had memorized those letters, and she was about to explain them when he stopped her and pointed to 280. 'Two-eighty,' he said, and she congratulated him.

She then went to each group of letters, and he exulted when he discovered which of the symbols signified London. He repeated the name several times, looked at her and laughed. 'I been London.' She thought this unlikely and assumed that he was confusing the name with some locality in the south. Carefully she explained what London was and where, and he cried, 'I been London,' and with a few words and gestures he convinced her that he had indeed been in this great city which she had never seen, but when she asked how he had got there, some inner caution warned him that no one must ever know, and he feigned an inability to comprehend her question.

She shrugged her shoulders and proceeded with the lesson, pointing to the five Ns, and demonstrating that this symbol had the same sound in each of the four words in which it appeared. Cudjo repeated the instruction, and on the second repetition a light actually broke across his face, irradiating the room. That was the secret! All these symbols carried their own sound, and reading was nothing but the decipherment of those sounds.

All that afternoon he and Mrs. Paxmore went over the letters of the rubric from the barrels until he had mastered each. Intuitively she knew that it was more important to do this than to start with the alphabet, for Cudjo himself had brought her this problem; it stemmed from his life, so its solution would have treble meaning.

When day ended she returned to the hornbook and made the sounds of the letters, and he already knew letters like the D in Devon and F in Fithians, but when she got to L he was confused. In LONDON it had been pronounced the way she said it now, but in LB it had the sound of P. He repeated the sound: 'Pound. Pound.'

She stopped, looked at the rubric and realized that there was no simple way in which she could explain what an arbitrary abbreviation was. 'You see . . .' She retreated to the word PLNT and explained that this was merely a short way of writing *plantation,* and this he understood readily. But then there was the problem of LB meaning *pound.*

'Learn the letters,' she said, thrusting the hornbook at him, and before he left she asked him to read the alphabet, and he got twenty-one of the letters right. He was, she told her husband that night, one of the brightest human beings she had ever tried to teach.

Now it was Christmas, and the slaves had their week of holiday. While others gorged on roast pig and drank their whiskey, Cudjo stole away to Peace Cliff, spending hours on the lessons Mrs. Paxmore set. He met Mr. Paxmore and their handsome young son Bartley, and was invited to have Christmas dinner at their table. It was a sober affair, with silences he could not understand, but there was a spiritual warmth and the food was plentiful. Bartley was especially attentive, a boy of fifteen eager to know about the world.

'Thee was in the south?'

'I been.'

'What was it like?'

'Work, no food, Mastah whip.'

'Is it better here?'

'Yes.'

'Will thee get married some day?'

This was beyond Cudjo's understanding, and he looked down at his plate, the first he had ever seen. 'Get him some more turkey,' Mrs. Paxmore said, and as soon as the meal was over, Cudjo wanted to go back to the learning shed.

'Bartley will take thee,' she said, and the boy proved as capable a teacher as his mother. His pleasure was to have Cudjo recite the alphabet as fast as possible; they had races, and it became apparent that Cudjo had mastered every letter, every sound, but when they reached the numerals he was confused.

Bartley was good at arithmetic and had often helped his father calculate tonnages at the boatyard, so he was able to explain it, and if Cudjo had been noteworthy in his ability to learn letters, at figures he excelled. In three intensive days, during which he saw little of Mrs. Paxmore, he mastered the principles of simple figuring.

'He's quite remarkable,' Bartley told his parents as the black man hurried back to the plantation at the end of the holidays.

It was remarkable, too, that Cudjo could continue learning when he had so few materials to work with; he knew every grain that marked the hornbook. He could write in his sleep the message burned onto the back: 'Pack my box with five dozen liquor jugs.' Mrs. Paxmore had informed him that this sentence was unusual in that it contained every letter of the alphabet; he recited it to himself at all hours, seeing the twenty-six letters pop up in order.

But he required something more substantial, and in March of 1835 Mrs. Paxmore said, at one of their infrequent meetings, for Mr. Starch had become suspicious of his new hand and was keeping closer watch, 'Thee can return the alphabet now. Thee's ready for a book.' And she handed him a small, poorly printed volume called *The Industrious Boy's Vade Mecum.*

Cudjo held the book in his two hands, stared down at it, read the title almost accurately, then raised it to his face and pressed it tightly against his cheek. 'I gonna know every word.' And he pointed to *Industrious* and Mrs. Paxmore explained that he was industrious in that he studied and learned so well. He then pointed to *Vade Mecum* and she started to explain that this was Latin, but she realized from teaching children that this was supererogatory; all he needed to know was the meaning. 'It means *go with me*. It's your helper.' But when he opened the book it fell to a page containing mathematical problems, many of which Bartley had already taught him, and he began to rattle off the answers at a speed that Mrs. Paxmore could not have matched.

'A miracle has happened in that shed,' she told her husband that night. Then she smiled at her son and said, 'Thee is a better teacher than I,' and she burst into tears. 'Imagine, preaching to people that Negroes can't learn.' She sat quite still for some time, then started tapping the table nervously with one finger. 'I shall never understand,' she said.

It was the book that became Cudjo's undoing. It was so small that he could hide it in his trousers, not in the pocket, since his pants had none, but along the flat of his left rump, held there by a string passed between the middle pages. He was able to share his secret with no one, for he knew that if it were discovered that he could read, he would be sold south, so he looked at the book only when he could find a few minutes alone.

The book had been written for boys nine and ten years old and told of selected heroes upon whom the boys should pattern themselves: Robert Bruce and the spider; Roland and the last battle; George Washington at Valley Forge. The level of difficulty was exactly right for Cudjo, but his quick mind soon absorbed the moral messages and he yearned to talk with someone about Robert Bruce, and why he was fighting. There was no one. So he memorized the selections, finding great pleasure in the simple poems which adorned the text:

> Brave Robert sat within his cell
> And watched the spider spinning well,
> Until he heard the battle call.
> He won the day, so must we all.

But one November morning when the barrels were being rolled down to the plantation wharf, Mr. Starch heard Cudjo reading off the consignment brand: 'Devon Plantation. For Fithians in London. Two hundred eighty pounds.' He leaped from his horse and grabbed Cudjo. 'Where did you learn to read?'

'I no read, Mastah.'

'You just read that marking.'

'I heard you speak it, Mastah.'

'You're a liar. You stand here.' And he rode among the slaves, asking questions, then came back roaring, 'You've been seein' Mrs. Paxmore.'

'No, Mastah.'

'You damned liar!' And he leaned over in his saddle and began whipping Cudjo across the shoulders. Cudjo naturally drew back, placing himself out of reach, and this enraged the overseer. Leaping from his horse, he lunged at the slave, ordering him to take off his shirt to receive the lashes he deserved. Cudjo delayed, so Mr. Starch ripped away the shirt, and in doing so, disclosed the end of string protruding from the top of the pants.

'What's that?' he bellowed, and with a powerful yank on the trousers, he tore them down and the hidden book fell to the ground.

'Damn you!' he thundered, and he whipped Cudjo till his arm tired. Throwing the slave into the plantation sloop, he sailed to Devon Island to report the infraction to Mr. Beasley, but Uncle Herbert intercepted him at the wharf. 'What brings you here?' he asked.

'Caught this slave readin'. He's been to Paxmore's.'

'Oh dear!' Steed sighed. 'We really must do something about those damned Quakers.'

'Where's Beasley?' Starch asked.

'Retired. And if you handle yourself well, you can take his place.' Uncle Herbert paused portentously, then added, 'And perhaps mine, too, in due course.'

Starch, inspired by this intimation, said brusquely, 'First thing we do is whip this one into shape.'

'Sell him south. I want no nigger on my place that can read.'

'I'd say yes,' Mr. Starch said hesitantly. 'But . . .'

'But what?'

'He's awful good at fixin' machines. Has a true talent.'

'What do you propose?

'He's worth savin', Mr. Steed. He really is.' Mr. Starch coughed, then said, 'What I say is, rent him out to Cline for a year.'

Uncle Herbert made a temple of his fingers and bit the steeple. To send a slave to Herman Cline was a fearful decision, to be made only in the worst cases. 'We Steeds try to keep clear of men like Cline.'

'But he cures niggers.'

'You think he can cure this one?' Before Mr. Starch could respond, Herbert added, 'I despise niggers who can read.'

'Cline will put an end to that, believe me.' So Starch sailed south to fetch him.

Cline lived on the Little Choptank River, south of Devon. There he and his wife occupied a stretch of low, wet land, half field, half swamp. On the scantiest of savings he had managed to buy at bargain prices four slaves whom no one else could handle, and by terrifying them with whip and fist, had converted them into acceptable workmen. They had drained some of the swamps, creating a fairly productive farm, and his success with these renegades conferred on him a title which meant money: Cline the Slave-Breaker. Planters in the region came to believe that for $150 Herman Cline could break the spirit of even the most difficult slave and transform him into a docile servant.

He appeared one morning at the wharf, forty-seven years old, not overly tall or powerful. As he slouched up the path to the office, in his battered hat, ragged shoes, torn pants and loose homespun shirt, he carried a large wad of tobacco in his left cheek and a carved club in his right hand. It was unusual in that it terminated in a six-foot rawhide whip, tipped at the end. He held the club loosely, so that the rawhide draped twice in graceful loops; when he spoke he pointed the club at the listener, making the lash sway in the air. He was unshaved, unwashed and underfed, but his eyes moved with such quickness, taking in all aspects of a situation, that he created an impression of extraordinary energy and limitless will power.

'I'm here,' he said.

Uncle Herbert found him so distasteful that he made no attempt to welcome him, but this did not disturb the slave-breaker. He had business to do and wished to finish it. 'Same terms as before. I get to work your boy one year. You pay me fifty dollars when I bring him back. Five months later, if'n he's cured, you owe me the other hundred.' Steed nodded, and Cline shifted his plug of tobacco, looking for somewhere to spit. Steed indicated the door, and when this was attended to, Cline added, tapping his left hand with the head of the club, 'And if'n he ain't broken when I hand him back, you keep the hundred.'

Uncle Herbert wished to be no part of this ugly transaction, so Mr. Starch said, 'Agreed, Cline. But this time you've got a tough one on your hands.'

'Them's the kind I like.' He grinned in anticipation of the challenge, then added, 'You agree like before. If I have to kill him to cure him, no fault of mine.'

'That risk we take,' Starch said, and when Cudjo was dragged forth, Cline took one look at him and realized that this was going to be a difficult year. He said nothing; simply marched the big Xanga to the wharf, indicated that he was to get into the sloop, and got in after him. But before casting loose, he suddenly swung his club and began belaboring Cudjo over the head, knocking him down with the first blow and continuing to thrash him as he lay in the boat, striking particularly at his face.

Mr. Steed and Mr. Starch, on the wharf, were startled by the violence of the attack, but the latter said, 'That's the way he always begins.'

'It's rather horrible,' Herbert Steed said, but his overseer nudged him. 'Look behind. It's good for our niggers to be reminded of what can happen.'

And there on the grass behind the wharf stood seven or eight slaves from the big house, watching everything but saying nothing. Mr. Starch, spotting the girl Eden, went to her and grabbed her by the arm. 'Don't you be so sassy to Mr. Paul, or you gonna spend a year with Mr. Cline.'

She did not try to escape his grasp, nor did she respond in any way to his threat. She merely looked at the retreating boat as it headed south for the Little Choptank.

Herman Cline was a good farmer. Taking nine hundred acres of lowland that no one else wanted, he had patiently cut off the trees from one high spot after another, constructing by this method a series of scattered fields. By careful husbandry and incessant toil he had coaxed these fields into producing substantial crops, and if he could accomplish as much in the next twenty years as he had in the past twenty, he would one day have a farm capable of yielding real income.

His help consisted of his wife, his two horselike daughters, the four slaves he had purchased and five other slaves who had been sent to him for discipline. These nine blacks lived in a small shedlike building with no window, no wooden floor, no furniture of any kind except a row of nails on which to hang their clothes. There was no fireplace, no utensils for cooking; their food was delivered in a bucket, from which they ate with their hands.

On the Cline farm there was no Sunday. Half an hour before dawn on three hundred and sixty-five days a year, including Christmas, Mrs. Cline beat a length of iron, warning the slaves to be ready for work in thirty minutes. They toiled till sunset, with ten minutes' rest at noon, and after dark each was responsible for certain additional tasks, such as chopping wood or cleaning the pigpens. The four slaves Mr. Cline owned were expected to work like this for the remainder of their lives.

The five other slaves were treated with additional harshness. Every morning of the year Mr. Cline recited some arbitrary excuse for thrashing at least one of them: 'The pigs wasn't cleaned properly.' On the third morning it was Cudjo's turn: 'I caught you lookin' at my daughter. When she passes, you look at the ground.' With his rawhide lash he beat Cudjo twenty times, then asked, 'What you gonna do when my daughter passes?'

'Look down,' Cudjo said.

'You say *Mastah* when you speak to me,' and he lashed him ten more times.

For food the slaves got a bucket of cornmeal mush, day after day after day. Every third day each got a strip of cured pork, which he hung on the nail assigned to him, gnawing from it at a rate to preserve something till the next strip appeared.

The morning beatings were only the beginning. All day long Mr. Cline prowled his fields, descending upon his workmen at odd moments, or at odd bends in the road, leaping at them for their sloth and thrashing them till they bled. They must work every minute, and care for every item on the farm as carefully as if it were their own. Mr. Cline had one custom often seen among slaveholders: he would take a long rest in the afternoon, then an hour before quitting time he would appear lively and fresh. Scratching himself, he would leap into the middle of whatever job was under way, and would work like a demon for twenty minutes, till the sweat poured down his face. Then he would stop and say, 'That's the way a real man works, damn you.' And he would select some slave who had lagged and would lash him ten or twelve times, shouting at him, 'I've shown you how to work, now, damn you, do it.'

Christmas showed the Cline system at its worst. The nine slaves would know that elsewhere along the Choptank other slaves were enjoying a week of festivity, but his worked every day. On Christmas Day, half an hour before dawn, as usual, the iron gong would ring, the slaves would emerge from their earthen-floored cabin, and they would be led to some particularly odious task. At high noon Mrs. Cline would ring the gong again, and her husband would come to the slaves and say, 'Well, you've done no work at all, but today's Christmas.' When they reached their miserable shed they would find a bucketful of mush and on a greasy piece of paper one roasted chicken.

When Cudjo saw this on Christmas afternoon he had to control himself from bursting into bitter laughter. 'At Devon plantations we has whole hogs and piles o' chicken!' He was so outraged that he refused to fight for a fragment of this treat. He ate his mush and watched the other eight slaves tearing at the small bird.

Mr. Cline did not hand out new clothing at Christmas, either. Each of his nine slaves had one costume, and that was all. He wore it every day, until it hung from his frame in tatters. Then Mr. Cline would scream, 'You smell like an ox. Why don't you care for your things!' and he would thrash the offender with the cowhide, and grudgingly throw the new clothes at him.

The seasons along the Little Choptank were horrendous. In summer the mosquitoes were so numerous that hundreds would settle between elbow and wrist, all biting at the same time. In winter a fierce wind blew in from the bay and swept down on the unprotected shed in which the nine slaves huddled. It came through cracks in the walls like a string of needles, punishing the skin. When the temperature was two degrees below zero the slaves slept on the floor, each with a single thin blanket. They worked barefoot in the fields; the soles of their feet had cracks a quarter of an inch wide and the same deep.

Why did nine powerful black men allow Herman Cline, who weighed less than any one of them, to mistreat them so brutally? The question can be answered only within a larger context. From Africa about eleven million slaves were exported, and more than half found cruel masters; the reasons for their submission are complex and terrifying. Primarily, they could be kept under control because they never functioned as a unit of eleven million human beings; they were parceled out, a few at a time, a hundred here, threescore there. And after they had been hidden away, all agencies of society conspired to keep them in bondage.

The white men of Patamoke stood ready and even eager to thrash any black who opposed a master. The laws of Maryland approved such discipline, and the sheriffs helped enforce it. Each minister in slave territory intoned the ancient lessons from the Bible: ' "And that servant which knew his master's will and did not do it shall be beaten with many stripes." Those are the words of Jesus Himself.' White men lounging at the stores, women chatting at their sewing circles, children studying at school, and especially judges protecting the law, all supported the system and united to warn slaves that they must obey.

Such reasoning still fails to explain why the specific nine black men in the frozen hut tolerated Cline's brutality. His four personal slaves had served under other masters only slightly less cruel, and they felt certain that if they were shifted to any similar farm, they would be treated much the same. So they endured. The five plantation slaves hired out for discipline were mortally shaken by Cline's savagery, but they knew their sentences were finite; if they could survive this terrible year, they could hope for a better life in the future. So they, too, endured. But the basic reason why Cline could walk alone among his powerful blacks was that except for Cudjo, all had been indoctrinated since birth with one fundamental fact: if they gave him trouble, he had the right to kill them.

There were laws denying this, of course. They were proudly displayed in all slave states, and Maryland's code was one of the most humane: no slave could be abused; he had to receive proper food, clothing and shelter; none could be mutilated; and if a slave was killed, the perpetrator was held responsible. On the large public plantations the slave codes were generally respected, but since everyone acknowledged that Mr. Cline's farm was a kind of correctional institution, the code did not apply there.

Proof of this came one April morning in 1836, when Cudjo's term with the slave-breaker was nearly half completed. A difficult black man from a plantation on the Miles River, who had been sent south for disciplining, was so badgered by Mrs. Cline, who had ordered him to sweep the yard where the chickens ran, that he finally had to say, 'But, Missy, I done clean it.'

'Don't you sass me!' she screamed, and grabbing a heavy stick, she began thrashing him, and the noise was so great that Mr. Cline came running up, and his wife cried, 'He threatened me!' And her husband bellowed, 'I'll learn you to strike a white woman.' He ran indoors for his leather whip, and he rained such a series of blows on the slave that the man, desperate, leaped into the water of the Little Choptank, whereupon

Mr. Cline roared, 'Tryin' to escape, eh?' And he fetched his musket, took aim and blew the man's head apart.

There had to be an inquest. A judge and a sheriff from Patamoke studied the facts, heard from Mrs. Cline herself that the slave had threatened her, and quickly reached a verdict which the clerk did not even bother to record: 'Mr. Cline did only what had to be done.'

In the following days he vented his wrath especially on Cudjo, for he sensed that whereas he had terrorized the big Xanga, he had not really broken him; the Steeds had many plantations, and if he did a good job on Cudjo, he could expect repeat business. So he watched Cudjo constantly, thrashing him without reason, depriving him of his share of food and assigning him the most onerous tasks. One June night toward eleven, when Cudjo had been working since five that morning with only ten minutes' rest at noon, Mr. Cline caught him nodding at the special task of washing down the farm boat, and he leaped upon him with the cowhide, thrashing him for his indolence. Cudjo finally fell to his knees, unable to bear any more, and as he lay in the mud by the wharf, Mr. Cline said, 'Now maybe you'll tend to what I say.' And Cudjo was left to crawl back to the shed, sleep on the bare earth and be ready for work in the early dawn.

What was the effect of eleven months of such treatment? Each morning Cudjo rose with the determination that he would compose in his mind before noon a dozen sentences, using as many difficult letters as possible. And this he did: 'The lamb see the fox and jump quick to the stove.'

In the afternoon he reviewed the histories of Robert Bruce, Roland and George Washington, inventing incidents which happened to them while they were slaves: 'Roland say to Mastah, "Horse run down there."'

And after grabbing from the swill bucket such mush as he could, and gnawing on his end of bacon—which no other slave ever touched, not because they feared punishment but because this was a decency all had agreed upon—he did sums in his head, adding lengthy columns.

And one September night, as he lay on the cold earth, he imagined that it was shifting under him and that he was again on the rolling ship. He recalled those splendid days with Rutak when they were meeting and solving so many strange problems, and the old sense of competency returned and he consoled himself with the idea that he was an able man, and he said aloud, 'This gonna end. I gonna be free once more.'

He had barely uttered these words when an intractable slave new to the Cline farm told him in the darkness, 'Place to run, ever you get a chance, Pennsylvania.'

He had heard this name before. Among all slaves in the south this was the sacred word, for if you got to Pennsylvania, which lay to the north, there was hope. Cudjo told the newcomer of Mrs. Paxmore, and the man assured him, 'In Pennsylvania many peoples like her.'

'How you know?'

'I been there.'

'How come you here now?'

'White men capture me. Sell me back.'

To this awful news Cudjo had nothing to say. To be free and then to be betrayed must be the worst experience of all, but he began to whisper to himself, as thousands of slaves did in the night, 'Pennsylvania.' He tried writing it in the dust, when no one was looking, and he got most of the letters right. Freedom lay to the north. You reached Pennsylvania by escaping north.

Whenever he said the word he had difficulty getting to sleep, no matter how exhausted he might be, for he kept thinking of those days when he was captain of a ship; then, too, escape lay to the north, and sometimes he would rise from his earthen pallet and look at the north star and feel it luring him on.

In November 1836 Mr. Cline loaded Cudjo in his boat and sailed north to Devon, where he marched him, obviously subdued, up to the office. 'Mr. Steed, I bring you a corrected nigger.'

'Did he prove difficult?'

'One of the worst. Surly.'

'But you broke him?'

'I did.' He stood uneasily in the presence of gentry and waited for Mr. Steed to broach the subject of money, but Uncle Herbert took perverse pleasure in discomfiting this white trash. He pretended to go back to his papers, then looked up as if surprised to see Cline still standing there.

'What was it you wanted?'

'The money. Mr. Starch said . . .'

'Oh, of course! But Mr. Starch isn't here at the moment.'

Cline saw this as an attempt to evade a just obligation, rather than the teasing it was, and his face darkened, his hands tightening as they did when he faced a difficult slave, but before he could engage in any stupid act, Mr. Steed called, 'Mr. Starch!' and while he waited for the head overseer to report, he smiled condescendingly at Cline.

When Starch arrived, Steed asked, 'What arrangements did we make for paying Cline?'

'Fifty now. A hundred later if the nigger's broken.'

The slave-breaker sighed and relaxed his fists. Contemptuously Mr. Steed counted out fifty dollars and with a ruler shoved the money at Cline, who gathered it up, nodded and started back to his boat.

'Horrible type,' Uncle Herbert said as he disappeared.

'But necessary,' Mr. Starch said. Then, remembering that he had not asked Cline one important question, he ran to the door and called, 'Cline, in your opinion, what's the nigger good for?' and the man called back, 'Fixin' things.'

A year before, Mr. Starch had discovered Cudjo's mechanical ability and was now pleased to have Cline confirm that judgment. 'We can use him on the far plantation,' he told Uncle Herbert. 'We need mechanics there.' But this plan was frustrated by an intrusion that neither man could have anticipated.

Paul Steed, increasingly aware of his uncle's advancing years and waning energy and realizing that he must himself soon resume management of the vast holdings, had begun to take interest in various decisions. So when Eden said that morning, 'I hear they brought that man Cudjo back. They say he good at fixin' things,' he limped down to the office and asked, 'Have we a slave here called Cudjo?'

Uncle Henry, surprised at Paul's appearance, said yes, there was such a man, adding, 'But Starch is taking him across the river.'

'No,' Paul said crisply. 'I shall need him at the forge.' And when the slave was removed from Starch's sloop, Paul led him to a small dark building well to the west of the mansion where a very old slave called Hannibal operated a smithy, sharpening scythes, mending wheels and shoeing horses. In one corner stood a forge, square and solid and close to the earth; it was activated by a great bellows made from two cowhides and fed from a pile of charcoal stacked in another corner. It was a tight, unified place, blazingly hot in summer, protected in winter, and Cudjo quickly mastered the intricacies of working iron. One day as he hammered on the iron rim for a wheel he looked up to see in the doorway to the smithy a handsome woman, older than himself, smiling.

'My name Eden,' she said. When he made no response, she said, 'You can read. Mrs. Paxmore tell me.' And from her skirt she produced a book, which she offered him.

It terrified him. A book no different from this had sentenced him to a year in hell; he had barely escaped with his life. But she held it out, a gift from her and Mrs. Paxmore, and with trembling hands he took it, and after a long moment he brought it to his cheek and held it there, and hot tears ran across its binding.

'What book is it?' she asked.

He spelled out the letters: *Lessons from Plutarch.* With great pain he handed it back. 'No,' he said.

'Cudjo, you can have it. Mastah say all right.'

'Mastah Herbert?'

'No, Mastah Paul.' And she said, 'He want to see you—now,' and she led him to the big house, which he had never before been allowed to approach, and at the entrance Tiberius, an old man now but still impressive in his blue-and-gold uniform, told him, 'Son, yo' keeps yo' hands at yo' sides, and yo' doan' bump into nothin'.' He brought Cudjo through the door and into the stately grandeur of the hall. 'This way,' he said, leading the two slaves into the gracious western corridor built generations earlier by Rosalind Janney Steed.

At the entrance to a beautifully proportioned room, with sunlight streaming in through lace curtains, the old doorman announced, 'Mastah Paul, Missy Susan! I has the hona' to present yo' two slaves, Eden and Cudjo.' Bowing grandly, he retired.

In the room sat two thin, proper-looking people. On the table at the master's elbow lay a stack of books; the table at which Miss Susan rested in her ponderous chair held a tea service. 'Mastah Paul,' Eden said, 'this here Cudjo. He be the one can read.' Her forebears had lived on Devon Island for more than one hundred and fifty years and in that time had evolved the charming speech patterns used by slaves and poor-white farmers, with its truncations, its special words, its simplified verb forms and musical cadences. It was an imaginative speech, and Cudjo had acquired the rudiments.

'Come in, Cudjo.' The frail man held his head to one side; with a pale hand he indicated where Cudjo should stand. 'I'm your master, Cudjo. From now on you're to do as I say.'

'Yes, Mastah.'

'Is it true what Eden tells me? You can read?'

It was a moment of anguish. Before, when a white man discovered that he could read, he had been sent to Mr. Cline for a year. If he confessed now, he might be sent back, with little chance that he could survive, for Cline would have lost his fee. He stood dumb.

The small man in the chair took the book from Eden and pressed it upon his slave. 'Read the title,' he said, pointing to the letters.

To be able to read was a gift almost as precious as freedom itself, and desperately Cudjo wanted to exhibit his knowledge, but he was so terrified of Mr. Cline that he could not move his lips.

'It be all right,' Eden said, and proudly Cudjo read *'Lessons from Plutarch.'* He pronounced the last syllable to rhyme with *starch,* and Paul corrected him.

Susan asked from her chair, 'Do you know who Plutarch was?' and only then did Cudjo see that she was crippled, for she moved in her chair with difficulty and seemed unable to use her legs.

'No, ma'am.'

'Are you a good workman?' And before he could reply, she added, 'I mean with tools . . . machinery?'

'Yes, ma'am.'

'I want you to build me a chair . . .' And she explained her long-cherished dream: a chair which she could propel about the room with her own hands and which would assist her in standing whenever she felt strong enough, and she had barely finished her instructions when Cudjo fell on his knees, peered under the chair and began making suggestions as to how her desires could be fulfilled.

'My God, Paul,' she said with enthusiasm, 'he's the first to understand what I've been trying to say.' Then she laughed and said teasingly, as if she loved her husband, 'No, Paul. Don't posture. You didn't understand, either.'

Paul blushed, then said to Eden, 'You told me the truth. This man is skilled.' And to Cudjo he said, 'You may have the book. My wife will give you others if you can build her chair.'

But on the way back to the forge books were forgotten. Eden, speaking rapidly and with tremendous force, said in low, guarded words, 'Cudjo, I know 'bout you.'

He became afraid, supposing that somehow she had learned of his part in the mutiny. No. She was speaking of how he had managed to survive Cline. 'Slaves sends the word. You very pigheaded.'

He said nothing. Then, to his surprise, he felt her taking his hand and pressing it to hers. 'Cudjo, you, me, we's gonna run away.'

He looked straight ahead, for these were hanging words when spoken by the wrong person. She had seemed so familiar with the big house that she could well be a spy, the kind that betrayed those blacks who sought escape. But she kept talking in that low, imperative voice. 'You look hard on everythin' in the big house. Learn everythin'. You, me, we gonna run to Pennsylvania.'

The word exploded through the afternoon shadows. Pennsylvania! How many times had he whispered that magic name!

Now she said hurriedly, 'We neva' rest, Cudjo. We got to be free. I has money saved . . . pistol . . . knife. Never I come back here.' She spoke with a fury that he had never before heard from a woman; she was like great Rutak in the mutiny, a force of irresistible moral power. She was prepared to kill—herself or others. She was a wild animal in her determination to be no longer caged.

'I been waitin' for you, Cudjo. I see Cline 'most kill you in the boat. I watch and tell myself, "If'n he come back alive, he be the one." ' She fell silent, and began to tremble with the fire of her long-suppressed resolution to be free. Then she clasped his hand tighter and whispered, 'I needs one body to help me . . . to look . . . to tell me when.' She hesitated. 'You is the one, Cudjo.'

Now he was able to speak. 'I knows Cline's farm. Look my back. I afraid.' He was not fearful of flight or of punishment if he failed; what he did fear was admitting into his confidence any other human being. He could trust no one, for he could hear deep within his memory that slave talking in the night at Cline's farm: 'White men capture me. Sell me back.' There was only one power in the world that he could trust, and that was himself.

So he rejected Eden's proposal, turned her away coldly. With fury she threw the Plutarch to the ground and ridiculed him as he scrambled to recover it. 'What for you learn to read? What good it do you, you ain't a free man?'

The first meeting ended dismally, but next evening, as Cudjo washed up after his work at the forge, Eden came again to the door and said boldly, 'Hannibal, you ever go fishin' yonda?'

'Sometimes.'

'Go fishin',' and when the old man was gone she came to Cudjo and pulled him down to the straw on which he slept and began kissing him and fumbling with his clothes, and when for the first time in his tortured life he experienced the mystery of what a woman could be, she pulled his hands across her naked back so that he could feel her scars, and quietly she asked, 'You think on'y you's been whipped?' As his hands lingered there, she resumed her litany: 'We gonna go north. Mastah Paul try to stop us, Mastah Starch try, we gonna kill 'em.'

So the plans were laid, and when Hannibal straggled back from the creek with no fish, he looked down upon the lovers and said, 'That's nice. Miss Eden, ever'one been axin' when you gonna ketch yo'se'f a man. I mighty pleased this night. I mighty pleased.'

Paul and Susan Steed were also pleased when their pretty slave began frequenting the forge in which the new hand, Cudjo, slept. They had often speculated as to why this fine woman had never married; at thirty-four she was even prettier than she had been as a young girl. Her reserved, stately bearing excited admiration whenever she appeared at a dinner party to attend Miss Susan.

Everyone remarked on how gentle she was with her crippled mistress, and how she volunteered to do whatever would make Susan's life easier, and they were amused at how Eden handled Paul Steed. With the passage of years he had lost his querulousness and now accepted the consequences of his extraordinary behavior on the roof. His left leg was shorter than his right, but with the aid of a built-up shoe he walked with only a slight limp, and although his neck did incline sharply toward the right, as if to give his body a compensating balance, it did not prevent him from doing what he loved most: reading the shelves of great books he had acquired at Princeton. Thucydides, Plato, Montesquieu, Rousseau, Locke, Adam Smith, Plutarch—he had become as familiar with their thoughts as if they had lived down the Choptank a few miles and met with him on sunny afternoons.

He had a poor opinion of divines as writers and held the typical collection of sermons to be trash; he enjoyed a good sermon, but since there was no functioning Catholic church close to Devon, he could not indulge that preference very often. The Steed family did, of course, do as it had done through the centuries: invite clergymen to stay at the island and instruct the family in the teachings of Catholicism—and one summer Paul quite astounded the more conservative Steeds by prevailing upon an itinerant Methodist rabble-rouser to spend five days at Devon, preaching to the slaves by day and debating with the Steeds at night. It was an instructive experience, and when the man, a gaunt fellow from Virginia, departed he took with him one hundred dollars contributed by Paul.

The crippled Steed had become, in short, a southern gentleman of the best type: he did no work; he read incessantly; he spent much time contemplating the problems of the South; and he was increasingly infuriated by the basic unfairness of the North-South relationship: 'The criminals at the North make us sell our wheat and cotton to Europe at cheap prices, but will not permit us to buy our manufactures cheaply from England. No, they pass a high tariff, keep out cheap European products and force us to buy from Massachusetts and New York at extremely high prices. Northerners are strangling us, and if they continue, they will place the Union in jeopardy.'

Susan had become a lovely English cameo, a quiet little lady perched in her chair, bestowing on all a calm sweetness. She paid much attention to her dress, wanting always to look her prettiest, and in this she was abetted by Eden, who said, 'Git yo'se'f six new dresses from Bal'more.' And if Susan would not order them, Eden did.

It was this freedom of action that got the slave girl into trouble. One morning when she came back to the big house after having spent the night with Cudjo, Susan reprimanded her, slyly, 'Make him marry you, Eden. Girls always regret it if they allow the men to take advantage.' And she felt so warmly toward her slave that she said, 'Eden, take those two dresses we got from London. Let out the seams and wear them yourself.'

'You mean it, ma'am?'

'Yes, I do. You've been so kind, and maybe when Cudjo sees you in a new dress it'll open his eyes.'

So Eden took the expensive dresses, lowered the hems and fitted them to her own handsome figure. Unfortunately, when she first wore the ecru, whose exquisite pale-brown color complemented her own, the first person she met was Mr. Starch, who was beginning to feel his power as future manager of the Steed plantations.

None of the Devon Island slaves liked him; they considered him better suited to handling one of the remote plantations where his ugly manners would remain hidden, and they also feared the changes he might initiate. He was aware of this disaffection and was determined to stamp it out in these final days of his apprenticeship, so now when sassy Eden came down the graveled walk in her new finery he supposed that she had somehow stolen it from her mistress. 'She's an insolent one,' he muttered as she walked past. He stopped his own work to watch her sashaying over to the forge, and her self-confidence so infuriated him that he took an oath: First thing I do is get rid of that one.

On the first of April 1837 Herman Cline returned to collect his final hundred dollars for breaking Cudjo, and when he entered the office, Uncle Herbert kept him standing, whip under arm, then looked up and asked, 'Yes?'

'I've come for my hundred.' Uncle Herbert said nothing, so Cline asked anxiously, 'You found him proper broke, I trust?'

'Yes, yes.'

'Then I can have my money?'

'Of course you can,' and Steed counted out the money and once again shoved it forward with a ruler, as if offering it in person might make him partner to Cline in the dirty business. The slave-breaker counted the money, which irritated Steed, then stood uneasily at the desk, showing no intention of departing.

'What is it?' Steed asked, obviously irritated.

Cline shifted his weight awkwardly, then said slowly, 'I got me a peculiar problem.'

Uncle Herbert's attitude changed dramatically. Leaning forward almost with eagerness, he said, 'Perhaps I can help.' It was the type of response Steeds had been making since their plantations began; from Edmund on down they had invariably been concerned about problems along the Choptank, and as Uncle Herbert grew older, his interest in these timeless difficulties increased. He supposed that Cline wanted advice as to how best to develop a farm which was mostly marshland, and he had many ideas on the subject. 'I'd like to hear your problem, Cline.'

'Well . . . it's thisaway. I got me four bucks, difficult niggers nobody else could handle. Bought 'em cheap and whipped 'em into slaves of real value.'

'Everyone knows you can do that. What's the problem?'

'Well . . . it just occurred to me and the missus the other day that we're wastin' half the value of them niggers.'

Herbert Steed thought he saw what was coming next, and he decided to cut that approach quickly. 'No, we wouldn't want to rent them, Cline. They work for you, but I doubt if they'd work for us.'

'Wait a minute, sir. Wait a minute. That wasn't my idea at all. What I was wonderin', you got any young nigger women you want to sell? Ones givin' you trouble. I need me some breeders.'

'What was that?' a voice asked from behind the slave-breaker.

'Oh, Mr. Starch! I come for my money.'

'You earned it. Cudjo's quite tractable these days, thanks to you.'

'He stayed to inquire,' Uncle Herbert said, 'if we had any young females we might sell him . . . as breeders.'

'I was wonderin' when you'd come to that,' Starch said. 'Otherwise you're wastin' your bucks.'

'Jist what the missus and me figured. You got any troublemakers you wanta shed?'

'No . . .' Mr. Starch hesitated. Then the picture of sassy Eden in her stolen dress flashed across his eyes and he said slowly, 'But you might come back the first of June. Maybe we could do business then.'

When Cline departed, Uncle Herbert asked, 'What'd you have in mind?' and Starch said that on the far plantation at Broad Creek he had a hussy that was giving trouble, and that here on Devon he had been thinking for some time that this girl Eden ought to be cleared out.

Herbert Steed snapped his fingers. 'My own conclusion. That nigger is getting more and more uppity.' He drummed on his desk, then asked, 'What brought her to your attention?'

'As I was comin' along the walk I see her sashayin' past in a dress I know she stole from Miss Susan.'

'Send for her.'

Slaves were dispatched to fetch Eden, and they found her at the forge, interfering with the work of Hannibal and Cudjo. 'Where'd you get that dress?' Herbert asked severely as she entered the office.

'Miss Susan, she give it to me.'

'She never!' Starch broke in. 'You stole it.'

Ignoring Starch completely, and looking squarely at Uncle Herbert, Eden said with great firmness, 'I not steal nothin'. You knows that.'

Pulling her around to face him, Starch bellowed, 'Don't you ever speak in that tone. Now get out of here, and get out of that dress.'

When she was gone, Uncle Herbert said, 'You're right, that sassy item goes down the bay to Cline's. He'll cure her.'

But Eden did not go to her quarters and take off the dress. Instead she appealed to Miss Susan, and soon a slave came knocking at the office door with an imperative message: 'Miss Susan, she wants to see you gen'lmen.' And when they reached the mansion this frail lady told them sharply, 'I gave the dresses to Eden, and she's to keep them.'

So on the way back to the office, Starch said glumly, 'She'll never let us sell Eden to Cline,' but Uncle Herbert said softly, 'She doesn't own Eden any longer. She sold her to get her away from Paul, and he bought her back. She's Paul's slave, not Susan's.' At this news, Starch chuckled. And it was agreed that they would rush Eden to Cline's before Paul could intervene.

Cudjo, unaware of what had happened, was directing his full attention to Miss Susan's chair. He made the wheels so large that they would pass over bumps easily, then rimmed them in oak. The axle he hammered out of his best iron, finishing the ends in fine squares on which the wheels would fit. He caned the back of the chair and double-caned the bottom, but his ingenuity showed itself in the way he devised a lever which, when pushed forward, would tilt the chair so that Miss Susan could get out of it in a standing position. It was quite inventive, and as it neared completion, numerous visitors were brought to the forge to inspect it.

Herbert Steed said, 'It was worth paying Cline his hundred and fifty to save this nigger. He's earned it back with this one chair.' Later Mr. Starch told his employer, 'Only thing I don't like about Cudjo, he's messin' around with Eden. We better move her out even faster.'

'Cline's due back about the first of June.'

But Starch, eager to shed this possible troublemaker before he assumed control of the plantation, quietly dispatched a sloop to the Little Choptank, advising the slave-breaker that if he were to appear about, say, the first week in May, he could pick himself up a couple, three good breeders, cheap.

By the middle of April the magic chair was finished, and on the fifteenth it was presented to Miss Susan in the sunny room in the west wing. Cudjo wheeled it in proudly, its many coats of varnish shimmering in the sun. Gently he lifted the crippled mistress, placing her on the carefully prepared seat. 'It be mighty strong, but 'most sof' as a kitt'n.'

She adjusted her weight and felt how comfortable everything was. 'Fo' movin' the chair, this wheel,' and he showed her how to guide it up and down the pleasant passageway connecting the west wing to the center section. She had longed for such a chair and moved it with agility, her face beaming. 'You be pretty good, Miss Susan. But now de bes' part.'

He pushed the chair to the window, from which the garden was visible, and explained the mystery: 'Grab hol' on this handle, push down, and the chair lif' you to yo' feet.' As the chair moved upward, bringing her to a standing position, a look of astonishment came over her face, but she said nothing, merely took Cudjo's hands to indicate that he must repeat his instructions, and again she stood.

'Now let me try,' she whispered, and he returned her to the table at which she had sat immobile during the fourteen years of her infirmity. Gingerly she turned the big wheels, advancing herself to the window. Braking the chair, she leaned down on the lever and felt the chair ease her forward. Reaching for the sill, she stood erect, then stepped the short distance to the window, from which she looked out at the garden in which she had worked so assiduously. No one spoke. Tears came to her eyes, and finally she turned to her husband. 'I should have had this chair a dozen years ago.' And she thanked Cudjo and told Eden, 'Tell Mammy in the kitchen to serve something special at the forge tonight,' and there was dancing when the two roast chickens arrived.

But in the morning a slave who had been absent for some days crept to the forge with frightening information. 'I been sail down Cline's farm, Little Choptank.' Instinctively, Cudjo shuddered at mention of that hell. The man continued, 'Eden, they done sold you to Mr. Cline.'

'What?' Cudjo cried.

'Yas'm. Cline, he tell me to say thet he comin' one week to fetch her.'

As soon as the informant was gone, Cudjo told Eden what he had never shared before. He described the harsh reality of the Cline farm: the mean shed in which she would sleep; the horrible Cline women, each one worse than the other; the leather strap; the gruesome food; the years with no rest even at Christmas. 'A man cain't hardly live one year that way. You gonna kill yorese'f before you take it.' His lips closed, for he dared not speak as he visualized the alternative: she would be goaded to some terrible act for which she would be hanged at some mournful crossroads.

'Eden,' he said quietly, 'you cain't go.' And the plotting began.

Applying finishing touches to the chair became a valid excuse for Cudjo to appear at the big house, and during one trip, while Paul and Susan went upstairs to nap in the bedroom with the two cannonballs, Eden led Cudjo not to the sunroom where he usually worked, but to the little-used east wing where, in a small curtained room, she had long ago found an empty cupboard in which to secrete her cache against the day of her escape; it contained a pistol, a saber, knives, a rope, and a surprisingly large collection of coins in a small canvas bag.

Cudjo was terrified. 'Eden, Mr. Cline if'n he fin' a slave wid jes' the blade of a knife, he beat him fo' three days till he cain't walk or lif' his arm. You be killed fo' sure fo' this.'

'If'n a body try to stop me, I gonna kill 'em. Mastah Paul come at me, he gonna be dead.'

'Eden, doan' say that. Mastah Paul, he be good to us.'

'He good now. But how long?' And she slipped his hand under her blouse so that he could feel the familiar welts across her back. 'Who you think done that?'

Incredulously, Cudjo asked, 'Mastah Paul?'

'Long time ago.'

'Eden, ever'body know niggers at Devon doan' git whipped.'

'I got whipped,' she said simply, and she convinced him that if anyone, even Miss Susan, tried to hold her in bondage any longer, that person was going to be slain.

'But Miss Susan yore frien'. She give you the dress you wearin'.'

'Nobody my frien'. You talk like this, even you ain't my frien'.'

The plan they devised was to wait for the good weather in May, when it would be warm enough to sleep in the fields. They would keep to the eastern side of the bay, for they had heard that it was easier to slip past Wilmington than Baltimore, and with luck they could be in Pennsylvania within two weeks. Once there, they had no doubt that they could earn a good living, for Eden knew how to tend a home and Cudjo could work at almost anything.

They calculated that Mr. Cline would come to fetch Eden on the first of May, since plantation business was often conducted on such days, so during the final week of April they set a firm date for their flight. 'Five days we go,' Eden said, and from this decision there would be no turning back.

On the morning of the fourth day, as Cudjo distractedly worked at the forge, old Hannibal moved close and whispered, 'I spec' you headin' no'th first night you is able.' Cudjo kept hammering at a shoe, and the old man said, 'I spec' you takin' Miss Eden wid you.' Again no comment, so the old man started to withdraw, but stopped and said, 'You got my prayers, son. You doin' right.'

One cruel aspect of the flight was that neither Eden nor Cudjo could ask a single human being exactly where Pennsylvania was, or what to expect if they got there. Every slave could narrate a dozen pitiful stories of attempts betrayed by supposed friends: 'Field hands git together, gonna speak up to the overseer, hopin' to make things mo' better, but a house girl warn the mastah they plottin'. He sell 'em all.' Or the case of Ol' Jesse: 'He cain't stand no mo', he headin' no'th. Got all things fixed, but this young buck he mad at Jesse, he tell the overseer, and Jesse, he dead from the beatin'.'

Those seeking freedom were exposed—by accident, by hateful revenge, by their own incompetence. To move from southern Maryland to the border of Pennsylvania was an act requiring supreme courage and maximum strength; to escape all the way from Alabama or Louisiana called for a determination which could hardly be described. Furthermore, for a male and female to make the attempt together demanded not only courage but also an incredible amount of luck.

Eden was five years older than Cudjo, and major decisions were left to her, but she was impressed by Cudjo's innate power; she did not yet know that he had taken over a full-rigged ship and sailed it successfully for more than a month, but from various hints she had picked up, she judged that in his previous life he had been a man of great courage. To him fell the job of ensuring that the minor details were cared for: the file, the bag for food, the two walking staves.

By sunset on April 28 every precaution had been taken, and the two slaves ate supper together at the forge. Old Hannibal ate with them, and toward the end of the simple meal tears came into his eyes, and Cudjo forced him to go out and look for more charcoal lest Eden guess that he had penetrated their secret. He came back with an armful of coal, his emotions under control.

And then, with no introduction whatever, Hannibal blurted out,

'Pennsylvania be ten days no'th.' No one spoke. Poking at the fire, he added, 'I hea' say, "Doan' go tuh Wilmington." Headin' west, they be alota' Quakers.'

Again there was silence, and after a long while Eden leaned over, kissed Cudjo goodnight and walked slowly to the big house, knowing that by this time tomorrow night they would have stolen a skiff, piloted themselves far up the Tred Avon River and found a hiding spot near Easton. As she turned to look at the garden and the peaceful scene at the wharf, she swore to herself: Nothin' gonna stop us. Not dogs, not death. When she sauntered into the house she saw that Miss Susan was already upstairs and that Mr. Paul was reading, as usual, in his study.

When he heard her come in he looked up from his books and asked, 'That you, Eden?' Then he turned his crooked neck and glanced at her in a strange way; it was as if this night were fourteen years ago and he was preparing once more to thrash her with the strap. But it wasn't exactly that kind of look, either. It frightened her, and she ran up to her room thankful that after tomorrow she would never again see this twisted little man.

On the final morning Cudjo and Eden went about their affairs with a special innocence. They forced themselves to speak naturally, but their voices were so low that on several occasions Miss Susan had to tell Eden to speak up. The noon meal passed without incident, and so did the afternoon naps, but toward five Cudjo ran to the big house, quaking. 'What you want, Cudjo?' Tiberius asked, protecting his door.

'Got to see Eden.'

'She wid Miss Susan ove' in th' east wing tryin' yo' chair.'

This was the worst possible news, for that was where the escape material was hidden. Not knowing what he might have to do, he hurried into the east corridor, and as he entered the room saw Miss Susan steering right for the cupboard containing the gun and the knives. 'Miss Susan!' he blurted out. 'I got tuh talk wid Eden.'

'Come right ahead,' she said, almost with gaiety, and showed him how competent she was becoming by wheeling about and leaving the room. As soon as she was gone, Cudjo whispered in an ashen voice, 'Mr. Cline, he come afo' time tuh git you.' They looked out one of the small windows and saw a sloop at the wharf and the slave-breaker walking up to consult with Uncle Herbert and Mr. Starch.

Eden did not falter, nor did she utter a cry. She merely grasped Cudjo by the arm and whispered, 'They nevah gonna take me.'

'Let me think,' Cudjo said. 'You hush. I got tuh think.' She could almost see the host of ideas running through his mind, and for the first time realized that he had other capacities beyond his ability to master machines. 'Ain't nobody gonna touch that pistol, 'cause maybe they search us. Ain't nobody gonna run away, 'cause we has got to follow a plan.' His right fist trembled as he banged out the alternatives. Then, as he stared at the menacing sloop, he thought he saw a solution. 'Eden, sun gonna go down pretty soon. Cline, he not gonna sail back tonight. He be sleepin' here wid Starch. You an' me we jes' settle down. Darkness comes, we wait one hour. Then we steals the boat and gits goin'.'

Ignoring his counsel against any suspicious act, Eden went to the cupboard and took one of the knives. 'We try your plan, Cudjo. But if'n it doan' work, ain't nobody gonna take me.'

Breathing deeply to control his apprehension, Cudjo kissed her and went back to the forge. He was right. Mr. Cline had completed the purchase of Eden and the two fractious girls, but since it was growing dark, he was invited to spend the night with Mr. Starch; the fugitives had their reprieve. But just before sunset Mr. Cline told Uncle Herbert, 'I'd like to satisfy myself that this here Eden is still of breeding age. I don't want to take home somethin' that's too old to be of service.' So Uncle Herbert dispatched two slaves to the big house with orders to fetch Eden.

But when the messengers reached the mansion they were halted by Tiberius. 'Yo' stan' back. Mastah Paul just send a man to fetch Cudjo, an' I ain't movin' from here till he git back.'

When Cudjo learned that he must go to the big house, he started to tremble, not that he feared for himself, but he could almost see the sanguinary events that might soon take place. That he would support Eden to the hanging tree, he had not the slightest doubt. Secreting a sharpened file in his pant leg, he walked quietly to the mansion.

There old Tiberius was grumbling to the slaves who had been sent to fetch Eden. 'What take you so long, Cudjo? You in trouble! You git in here!' And he led the way to the sunroom. Pushing open the door, he shoved Cudjo inside.

There sat Mr. Paul and Miss Susan, and near them was Eden, and when Cudjo stole a glance at her, she gently touched her bodice, indicating that her knife was ready. He allowed the fingers of his right hand to rest on the sharpened file; she nodded, waiting for the signal.

None came. Clearing his voice, Paul Steed said softly, 'My wife and I are so glad to see you.' With a gesture of his right hand he added, 'You may sit down.' Cudjo hesitated; he had rarely sat on a chair, and never on one covered in brocade. Paul laughed and said, 'Sit down. It won't bite.' So the two slaves sat on silk.

'My wife and I have been thinking about you,' Paul said quietly. 'We've never known anyone kinder than Eden.' He nodded toward her. 'And last week Miss Susan proposed . . .'

'What I proposed . . .' she started to say, then abrupty turned and wheeled herself about the room, braked the chair and ejected herself into an upright position before Cudjo. From this standing position she said, 'We propose, Cudjo, to manumit Eden. And you we shall allow to buy your freedom.'

Freedom. The word sounded like thunder in his ears, yet it had been said so gently by the very people they were prepared to kill. In deep confusion Cudjo looked at Eden, but she sat with her hands folded in her lap, her eyes cast down.

'It'll work this way,' Paul said in his slow, scholarly manner. 'We manumit Eden with this paper, which we shall both sign tonight. She is freed, in grateful appreciation of the extraordinary services she has provided my wife.'

'I free?' Eden asked quietly.

'You are free.' He coughed, for what he had to say next was both painful and embarrassing. 'We both owe you a great deal, Eden. In a dark period of our lives—'

'What Mr. Steed is trying to say,' his wife broke in, 'is that we want to repay you for your loving kindness.' Before Eden could speak, she added, 'Of course, I very much want you to stay on and help me. I still need you, even with Cudjo's new chair.'

Paul had control of himself again, and said, matter-of-factly, 'We'll pay you a small salary, which we'll hold for you. And when it reaches three hundred dollars, you can buy Cudjo's freedom.'

'I already got twenty dollars,' Eden said.

'You have twenty dollars?' Paul gasped.

'Yes. Since I born I save every penny.' She made a gesture with her hands, as if catching something. ' "Here, Eden, for holding the horse." '

'My advice would be, hold on to those dollars. You'll need them when Cudjo sets up for himself.'

'What you mean?' Eden asked.

'When he's free you'll go to Patamoke, likely, and he'll work in the boatyard, likely. Or maybe as his own carpenter.'

'When I be free?' Eden asked in a firm, unexcited voice.

'You are free now,' Paul said. 'Cudjo will be free shortly . . . when you've earned his price.'

And having said this, he produced a document of manumission which he and his wife had agreed upon, but before they could sign it, there came a loud fracas at the door, and Uncle Herbert accompanied by Mr. Starch entered the house and demanded of Tiberius where the girl Eden was. Voices were raised, and soon Herbert came bursting into the sunroom, with Mr. Starch close behind. 'There you are!' Herbert cried with some petulance. 'Why didn't you respond when the slaves came?'

Paul and Susan were dismayed at this intrusion, and the former said, 'Really, Uncle Herbert, my wife and I were having—'

'We're not interested in you or your wife,' Herbert said insolently. 'What we want is that girl.'

'For what purpose?' Paul asked, twisting his head with difficulty to look at him.

'Mr. Cline wants to inspect her. To see if he thinks she can breed.'

'What?' Susan asked from her chair.

'She's been sold to Cline. Leaves in the morning.'

'You dare not sell my slave.'

'Mrs. Steed, this girl isn't your property any longer. Hasn't been for years. She's owned by Mr. Steed, and I've decided to sell her.'

Before Susan could protest this astonishing information, Paul said quietly, 'There was no consultation with me.'

'Of course not,' Uncle Herbert said condescendingly. 'Mr. Starch and I never bother you with details. We run the place and do what we think's best.'

Paul stood up, and suddenly his shoulders squared and his voice firmed. Looking his uncle directly in the eye, he said, 'Uncle Herbert, you and Mr. Starch no longer run the plantation. Your responsibility ends as of this night.'

'But, Paul, I've been showing Mr. Starch how to handle things when I—'

'When you what?'

'When I retire. I'm sixty-seven, you know.'

'And you have just retired.' Moving briskly, he went up to his uncle and grasped both his hands. 'You were of great help, Uncle Herbert, in the days of my confusion. Devon would have collapsed without you. But now the confusion is ended, and so is your tenure. You must leave the island tomorrow.'

'But Mr. Starch requires—'

'He requires nothing. Do you think I'd place Devon in hands like his? Mr. Starch, you have left my employment. I'm sure Mr. Herbert will find a place for you on one of the Refuge plantations.'

'But, Mr. Paul—' Starch began in a whining voice.

'I've no need of you, Mr. Starch, nor of anyone like you.'

'Who's to run the plantation . . . and the stores?' Uncle Herbert asked, a fat, pompous old man undergoing an intense deflation.

'Me,' Paul said. 'With my wife's help.'

'Your wife?' As if drawn by magnets, Herbert and Starch looked at the fragile figure in the chair, but as they did, she set the brake, activated the lever, and to their astonishment rose to an upright position and without assistance walked to them.

'Yes,' she said, 'we've ignored this magnificent plantation for too long.'

Uncle Herbert started to comment, but his words gagged in his throat. Finally his eye fell on Eden. 'Well, the sale of that one's been concluded. Mr. Starch, keep her under guard tonight.'

But when the overseer moved toward the slave girl, Paul cried, 'Stand back, damn you. Starch, I said you'd left my employ.'

'What're you going to do about the girl?' Uncle Herbert asked.

'We're about to manumit her,' Paul said, and with slow, patient force Susan walked to the desk.

'But we've already sold her! Paul, this girl is a troublemaker.'

'I know she is not,' Paul said quietly

And then Herbert lost his control. 'Better than anyone you know her —and you should damned well be ashamed of yourself.'

'I am,' Paul said. 'I have been for fourteen years.' Susan took his hand and said, 'And now we shall sign the paper. Uncle Herbert, since you were technically in charge of Devon when this document was drawn up three days ago, I should think it wise to have you witness it.'

And she asked Eden to wheel the chair closer, and she sat down, obviously fatigued, took the pen and signed away their property rights in the slave girl. Paul dipped the quill in the ink and signed. Then he motioned to Uncle Herbert, who huffed and hawed until Paul said quite sharply, 'We want your signature, Herbert. Your last official act on Devon.' And when the gray-faced man reluctantly signed, Paul said, 'You look very tired. I should have relieved you of this tedious burden three years ago.'

Mr. Starch, who was outraged by everything that had happened, could be silent no longer. 'To behave like this in front of two slaves ... By God, sir, it's indecent.' And he stomped from the room.

'He's right,' Herbert said, looking with disgust at Eden and Cudjo. Then, turning his back on them, he stood facing Paul and Susan. 'I did my best to save your plantation.'

'You were needed,' Paul said. 'But now Devon requires a new kind of leadership.'

'And you think you're prepared to provide it?'

'I do. With Susan's help.'

Scornfully, Herbert turned to her. 'He certainly gave you good leadership, didn't he? Headfirst down the roof.'

'The years pass,' Susan said quietly. 'Passion is spent and wisdom prevails. We're going to make Devon even a greater plantation.'

'Not with him at the head,' Herbert snapped, and with disgust at the weaknesses of his family, he stomped from the room.

After he slammed the door, there was an awkward silence. Paul knew that he should never have spoken thus to a white man in the presence of slaves, but it had been done, and Eden, understanding his thoughts, began tidying the room, as if this had been an ordinary day. 'Cudjo, neaten them books.' And as the two slaves moved about, Paul said, 'Tomorrow our work begins.'

And Eden said, 'Tomorrow could we be takin' my paper an' carryin' it to the courthouse? An' it be wrote in the book?'

'Oh yes!' Mrs. Steed cried. 'I'll sail with you.' When her husband looked up in surprise, she said, 'I feel so much better, Paul. And I want to see these people married. I insist that Eden start her new life correctly.'

Paul nodded, and when Eden glanced at him she saw that in his eyes there was that same enigmatic look she had seen the night previous, when he had so frightened her. And she realized that it could never be deciphered: he had beat her, and loved her, and set her free.

She would not thank him for his generosity. Arranging the final pillow, she stalked from the room, but Cudjo went to each of his benefactors, bowing his great torso and saying, 'We thanks you.'

They slept at the forge that night, bewildered, torn apart by a confusion of emotions they barely understood. Toward dawn Cudjo asked, 'Afore we sails to Patamoke, mebbe I goes to cubboard. Git shed o' the pistol an' knives.'

But Eden had a different vision: 'Never. Some day we gonna need 'em.'

Voyage Ten: 1837

IT WAS A TRIP THAT BARTLEY PAXMORE WOULD
remember for the rest of his life. By 1837 roads of a rough, inadequate
nature linked together the small towns scattered across the Eastern
Shore; it was now possible, though hardly comfortable, to drive a wagon
from Patamoke to the county seat at Easton.

But those isolated homes that stood at the remote ends of peninsulas
were still accessible mainly by boat. Of course, rude trails led up the
middle of each peninsula, but it was difficult for a horse to negotiate
them. From the Paxmore house at Peace Cliff to Patamoke was an easy
seven-mile sail; using tortuous land trails, the distance was a rugged
thirteen miles.

So when young Paxmore, eighteen years old and self-reliant, decided
to leave Peace Cliff to visit a settlement at the headwaters of the Miles
River, he naturally elected to go by the small sloop-rigged boat his family
owned. He told no one of his plans or his departure. He simply went
down to the dock at dawn one Thursday morning and set forth.

It was not until dinner—that is, the midday meal—that he was missed.
Younger children were sent running to the dock, and they returned with
the expected news. '*Emerald*'s gone!' they shouted, and when the meal
resumed they asked many questions as to where Bartley might have
taken it. His gray-haired parents stared straight ahead, refusing comment, but toward the end of dinner George Paxmore could contain
himself no longer. Slapping his big right hand on the table so that the
dishes jumped, he cried, 'I will be danged!' and hurriedly left the table
lest he explode with laughter.

Elizabeth Paxmore tried to quieten the children, who burst forth with
a dozen questions. Amy, the youngest girl, was of the opinion that he

had gone to Oxford to buy hogs, at which suggestion her mother smiled. But she would not tell the children where, in her opinion, their brother had gone.

He was, at that moment, breasting Blackwalnut Point at the southern tip of Tilghman Island, setting his jib and mainsail for the long run to the north. He lolled in the rear of the boat, tiller tucked under his left arm, the lines to the sails lashed close to his right hand. The wind was coming so briskly off the port quarter that he was able to keep the *Emerald* well on course. And there he sat through the long afternoon.

From Peace Cliff to the head of Miles River was a distance of forty-seven miles, and he would not be able to cover this before nightfall, because the course, like all on the Eastern Shore, required many different headings, and for a considerable distance he would sail due south in order to make north. What might happen to his wind in that stretch, no one could predict, but it would certainly be a combination of reach-and-beat for the last twenty miles.

He was not concerned about the necessity of spending the night in his boat. He would merely move inshore, tie the bow to some projecting tree and catch what sleep he could. He was not hungry now, nor would he be at sunset, for his mind was so agitated that to think of food would have been repugnant.

He had seen Rachel Starbuck only once, at the Yearly Meeting of Quakers held in the revered old meeting house called Third Haven in Easton. The Paxmore clan had not tried to reach the meeting by cart; they had piled into the sloop, left the Choptank at Oxford and made their way up the glorious Third Haven Creek and into Papermill Pond, where they tied up to the dock belonging to Mordecai Swain. They walked to the meeting house and as they entered, Bartley groaned. The perplexed Quakers were still debating the problems of slavery, for the outlying meetings were well behind Patamoke in grappling with them, and families like the Paxmores had to be patient while the others caught up. But Bartley was astonished to hear Swain arguing from the front bench that Quakers must do nothing to alienate the great plantation owners who still held slaves in bondage:

> 'In the long run, dear friends, and it is the long run we must bear in mind, we shall never succeed in abolishing slavery unless we have the open-hearted cooperation of those good Christians who now own slaves. We have convinced ourselves. Now we must convince them, and we shall not do so by proclaiming the destruction of their property rights.'

In uttering the phrase *property rights* Swain had unthinkingly adopted the vocabulary of those who defended slavery—'This slave is my lawful property and you cannot deprive me of his labor'—and the meeting rebuked him. Three different speakers chided him for falling into error, after which he rose again, speaking in a soft, conciliatory voice:

> 'It is precisely because slavery is protected by law as an inviolate property right that we face difficult problems when dealing with it. All sensible men, North and South, agree that it is immoral. But it is also legal, and it is this legal justification which ensures its persistence. To combat it, we must use only legal means. And that requires convincing slaveholders that society in general has changed, that what is legal should now become illegal. It is a matter, I insist, of persuasion.'

Before Swain could retake his seat a man Bartley had never seen before leaped to his feet with un-Quaker force and launched into a vigorous plea that the meeting commit itself to a course exactly opposite to what Mordecai had proposed. He proposed that Quakers urge slaves to run away from their masters and then assist them in fleeing to freedom in Pennsylvania. Bartley could feel a stir of excitement sweep Third Haven as the man spoke, and he whispered to his father, 'Who is he?'

'Very strong-minded man from Miles River. Name of Starbuck.'

And then, as Bartley looked more closely at the impassioned speaker, he saw, sitting in the row opposite, in the women's section, a young girl of exceeding beauty. She had wide, dark eyes and light-brown hair, and was wearing a gray dress with a white collar and a blue-and-yellow bonnet. She and her mother were gazing so steadily and with such pride at the speaker that Bartley guessed they were his family; he could not take his eyes away from the Starbuck girl.

She was younger than he, he supposed, but her face showed unusual maturity and great firmness of character. As she listened to her father speak she leaned forward as if to urge him on, but Bartley saw that her mother, almost as pretty as she, placed a restraining hand on her elbow, pulling her back into a more ladylike posture.

He heard no more of the debate. No matter, he thought. It would continue in dull repetition for the next twenty years. He could see only the Starbuck girl, and if he listened intently he fancied that he could hear her breathing. She was the most compelling human being he had ever seen, and he was dizzy from watching her.

At the noon break he surprised himself by walking boldly up to her and asking, 'Is thee Speaker Starbuck's girl?'

'I am.'

'I'm Bartley Paxmore. From Patamoke Meeting.'

'I know,' she said, and the fact that this incandescent girl had taken the trouble to find out who he was quite immobilized him. He stood there in the sunlight, on the meeting-house steps, and could think of nothing to say.

'Would thee like to take lunch with us?' she asked, and when he fumbled for some kind of answer which would indicate that he had no packed lunch of his own, she said quietly, 'We always bring more than enough,' so he joined them.

It was a feast. The Starbucks had five children, two of them married, and after introductions had been made Bartley had to say, in acute embarrassment, 'No one told me thy name.'

'Rachel,' she said.

It was of Rachel he now thought on his long run to the north. From that day three months ago she had filled his mind; indeed, he could think of nothing else but her superb figure in the gray dress, moving among the trees at Third Haven, her pretty face tucked in under the blue-and-yellow bonnet. Memory of her captivated him, and he could see her in the waves as they sped by his boat; he could feel the pull of her smile in the lines leading to the sails. He had never before heard a name so totally appropriate, so euphonious as Rachel Starbuck.

He spent that summer's night moored to a fallen tree on the shore opposite St. Michaels, and since he could not sleep, he watched the vagrant lights of the little fishing village, the comings and goings of men with lanterns, and he thought: Soon I shall have a home of my own, and I shall go to the barn at night to fetch the eggs for Rachel. And the image was so felicitous that he broke into song:

'She's the bonniest lass in the field.
I'm the ruggedest man in the fight.
To me those lips their kisses will yield.
The robins sing, "She is thine tonight." '

He chuckled: Father would berate me if he heard me singing such military words. And then the moving lights across the broad river began to vanish, and all were asleep except him, and his heart beat like a hundred hammers, because ere this new day ended he would be docking his boat at the home of Rachel Starbuck.

He reached the farm at eleven in the morning, and the two younger Starbucks spotted him as soon as he pulled his boat toward shore. 'It's Paxmore!' they shouted, and their cries brought their sister to the door, and when she saw who had come, she knew at once what his mission was. Without pressing down her apron, or in any way prettifying herself, she walked down the path to meet him, holding out her hand to bid him welcome.

He was faint with emotion and could scarcely voice his words. 'Is thy father home?' he asked abruptly.

'He is,' she said.

Without saying another word, Bartley Paxmore strode to the farm-house, entered and sought out Micah Starbuck. In the Quaker tradition, he addressed the older man by his first name. 'Micah, I have come to ask for thy daughter.'

The abolitionist put his fingers together and drew his mouth in as if to whistle. 'Well,' he said to Paxmore's surprise, 'she's got to go some-time. What does thee say, Chick?'

Rachel reached out and took Bartley's hand. 'I think I'm ready.'

'We'll give notice to the meeting on Sunday,' Starbuck said, and it was as simple as that. When Prudence Starbuck came down from work she had been doing upstairs, she was informed of her daughter's engagement. 'We've heard thee's a fine young man, Bartley,' she said.

'Thank thee, Prudence,' he replied. Things that he had dreamed of with such ardor were happening so fast, he became quite dizzy and did not know what to do next.

'And now thee may kiss her,' Micah said, and Bartley trembled and leaned forward awkwardly and kissed Rachel on the cheek.

'Thee'll do better later on.' Micah laughed, and Bartley felt his knees begin to buckle and he asked, 'May I sit down?'

No matter what happened in the ensuing years, Bartley Paxmore would remember that at the age of eighteen he had been so in love with Rachel Starbuck that when he touched her with his lips he almost fainted. He had come forty-seven miles unannounced to claim her, drawn as if by a score of magnets, and the fire of that day would never burn down to gray ash.

Next day the Starbucks arranged to have the announcement of the engagement read at two successive meetings, with the marriage to take place as soon thereafter as possible. This meant that Bartley had best stay at the farm during these eleven or twelve days, and what happened accidentally on the sixth day changed his life.

The family was at supper, some hours before dusk, when Micah heard an unusual commotion near the hen coops, and when he sent his youngest son to investigate, the boy returned and stood stiffly in the doorway, his feet planted together, his hands at his side as if reporting significant news to a king or a general.

'Another black man. Hiding in the rushes.'

No one spoke, but all rose quietly to watch as Micah left the room. After a brief absence he returned and said simply, 'Thee knows what to do.'

Supper was forgotten as each member of the family moved quietly and purposefully into action. Prudence, the mother, swept all the food on the plates into a bowl, which she handed to Rachel. 'He'll be starved,' she said, and Rachel left. Mrs. Starbuck and her other daughter moved about the room, arranging things to create an impression of casualness; from past experience they knew that on this night their home would be harshly inspected. When she was satisfied that things were right, she stood before Bartley and said almost sternly, 'It now depends on thee.'

'What am I to do?'

'Control thyself. Thee may have to endure strange insults, Bartley. Is thee strong?'

'I'll try.'

'Trying isn't good enough,' and she instructed Rachel, 'Watch over him.'

After some time Micah returned to the house. 'He's been beaten horribly.' When his wife asked if she should poultice him, he said, 'No, he can live with what he has. We're taking him to the other woods.'

What this meant Bartley did not know, but what happened next astonished him. Starbuck took his youngest son, a boy of ten, and said, 'Thee will stay with him, Comly. And at dawn thee'll lead him by the back roads to Pidcock's farm on Wye Island.'

'Yes, sir,' the boy said, and went upstairs, returning with a sweater, which he tucked under his arm, for it was not yet cold.

'Thee,' Starbuck cried peremptorily to his intended son-in-law, 'grab a spade and bury those disgraceful rags. Spread cow manure over the spot to hide the scent.'

In this accidental manner Bartley Paxmore found himself involved for the first time in abetting the flight of a runaway slave. At Peace Cliff his family had been philosophically committed to exterminating slavery in general; the Starbucks were willing to risk their lives to aid an individual black man. Actually, he caught only the briefest glimpse of the slave who caused this commitment. Starbuck had ripped away the man's rags and was about to hand him a pair of sturdy pants and a woolen shirt, but now the slave stood naked in the twilight, a powerful man not much over twenty, his sides and back cut with lashes. They looked at each other for only a moment, face-to-face in shadows, and then Starbuck told his ten-year old, 'Guide him to the far woods.' And the child said, 'I'll take him up the middle of the stream, to throw the scent in case they bring dogs.' And the slave was gone.

Now the Starbucks gathered in the kitchen to wait. They sat in prim silence, and Bartley thought: This is another Quaker meeting. But soon they heard the sheriff shouting and footsteps running toward the house. The slave-trackers kicked open the door and began crying, 'Where's the nigger?'

Three snarling dogs entered on a leash, and Bartley was distressed to see that they were in charge of a Patamoke man who would know him, old Lafe Turlock from the swamps, gap-toothed, lean and hungry for the reward he would get if he caught the runaway. He hunted slaves because he hated them, ever since one had slain his cousin Matt during the mutiny of the *Ariel,* and he boasted, 'I got me the best nigger-huntin' dogs on the Eastern Shore. Give my dogs a shoe or a shirt, and they'll track a runaway to Canada.' Instinctively Bartley moved behind Rachel to prevent Lafe from spotting him.

The sheriff said, 'We know goddamned well, Starbuck, that you help niggers run to Pennsylvania. But this time we aim to get our man back. He belongs to this fine gentleman here. Paid four hundred dollars for that buck, and he's entitled to recover.'

The owner stepped forward, a wiry man in worn and ragged clothes, carrying in his left hand a bull whip, the rawhide folded twice and dangling easily at his knee. His teeth were black from chewing tobacco and his slouch hat drooped low about his eyes. 'I'm Herman Cline, Little Choptank, and you, goddamn you, yo're hidin' my nigger.'

'Describe him,' the sheriff said.

Looking directly at Starbuck, Cline said, 'Answers to the name of Joe. Big man with scars on his back.'

'There would be scars,' Prudence said quietly.

The three men turned toward Mrs. Starbuck, their eyes flashing the hatred they felt for such an intruder, and Herman Cline asked, 'Where you got him hidden?'

'I've seen no slave,' Prudence said.

'You swear to that?' the sheriff asked.

'I will.'

The sheriff laughed. ''Course you will. Because they kept the nigger out with the chickens.'

'Let's get goin',' Lafe said, pulling his dogs into position. So in the fading light the slave-trackers inspected the chicken yard and the barn and the fields, looking assiduously for telltale signs. At one point the dogs passed directly over the spot where the clothes lay deeply buried, but they detected nothing.

Suddenly the sheriff whipped about, caught Bartley by the arm and shouted, 'Who in the hell are you? Some northern agitator?'

Micah started to explain, 'He's come to marry my daughter—' but Lafe Turlock broke in, 'I know that one. He's a Paxmore. Very bad lot.'

'Another goddamned Quaker!' the sheriff growled, shaking Bartley as if he were a recalcitrant child. 'Where is he?'

'Who?' Bartley asked, trying to break free.

'Don't you wrastle with me!' the sheriff bellowed. 'I'm the law!' and he struck Bartley across the face.

This was too much. Bartley formed a fist and would have smashed it in the sheriff's face, but Micah had foreseen this possibility and caught the young man's arm to restrain him. 'Lucky for you, son,' the sheriff said menacingly. 'You touch me just once, I gun you down. Now where you got that nigger?'

'Mr. Starbuck,' Cline said in his whining voice, 'we're reasonable men.

We know my nigger is on your property. I seen him swim across the Little Choptank, and Lafe here seen him row across the Big Choptank in a stolen boat.'

'That's right,' Lafe said. 'My dogs picked up his scent and led us right to your doorstep, Mr. Starbuck. You got that nigger, and we know it.'

'That runaway belongs to Mr. Cline,' the sheriff said. 'And I have me a court order directin' you or any other loyal citizen to help me recover Mr. Cline's property. If you choose to disobey the laws of this land—'

'What is thee doing?' Micah shouted. And Bartley turned to see that Lafe Turlock was about to throw a lighted brand into the barn.

'You hand over that nigger,' he threatened, 'or up goes the barn.'

The sight of flame, and the possibility that a barn of good timbers might be burned, outraged young Paxmore. With a leap he broke away from the sheriff and threw himself upon Turlock, carrying him to the ground, where he pinned his arms, knocking away the brand. This so angered the sheriff that he jerked at his belt to free his gun, but Micah prevented this drastic action.

'There is no slave on this property,' he said calmly.

'Like your old woman, you'd swear to anything,' the sheriff said, almost pleased, in a way, that Micah had stopped him from using the gun; he did not want to kill young white men.

'I think he's in the woods over there,' Lafe said, dusting himself off and recovering his dogs.

'Why don't your goddamned dogs find him?' Cline cried in a burst of petulance.

'Because they prob'ly led the nigger up the stream. To kill the scent.'

'Then get your damned dogs in the stream to find it again when he climbs out,' Cline groused. Turlock ignored the stupid suggestion; never had he worked on a slave chase with a more unpleasant man. Normally a hunt was more like a festival, with drinks and eats and each man urging the others on, and all encouraging the dogs. But Cline—he was a mean one.

It was now dark, and the slave-trackers were frustrated. 'Let's go back to Patamoke,' one of the men suggested, but the sheriff would not quit. 'Ever'one into the kitchen,' he ordered, and when the Starbucks were seated, he said, 'Goddamnit, we know that nigger is here somewheres. I personally seen him run onto your property, Starbuck, like he knowed that if he could reach here, he was safe. By the time it took us to reach here, you hid him. And by God we're gonna find him.'

And they proceded to ransack the place, turning out every chest. Once the sheriff grabbed the smallest Starbuck girl, screaming at her, 'You took food out to him, didn't you?'

'No,' she said. 'He wasn't ever here.'

In the end the men had to admit defeat, but the sheriff warned Micah, 'I'm gonna keep an eye on you. Because I know you help niggers escape north. And that's against the law—the law of Maryland, the law of the United States and the law of common decency.'

Herman Cline looked at Mr. Starbuck with pleading eyes, and when he realized that this would accomplish nothing, he turned on Lafe and sneered, 'You and your damned dogs.' He had paid Turlock ten dollars —without recovering his slave.

As the trio departed, the sheriff took Paxmore by the arm. 'Son, you was near killed this night. You're marryin' into a bad lot. One of these days I'll be throwin' you in jail.'

The marriage took place on Monday afternoon following the second Sunday. Quakers from many farms assembled at Third Haven, women to the left, men to the right. There were two rows of facing benches; on the upper sat two elderly men and two women of about the same age. They were not related. The men wore their hats. On the lower row sat Bartley Paxmore, bachelor of Peace Cliff, age eighteen, with his hat on, and Rachel Starbuck, spinster of Miles River, age sixteen, wearing a blue-and-yellow bonnet.

For the first twenty minutes of the ceremony no one spoke. Some flies trapped in the meeting house, buzzed lazily but gave no offense. Outside, the birds of summer chattered, but at such a distance that they could hardly be heard, and they, too, gave no offense. Men and women looked straight ahead, recalling other marriages in which they had participated, but no one moved.

Finally Bartley Paxmore rose and intoned those fateful words which send a tingle up the spine of any Quaker: 'In the presence of God and these our friends assembled, I, Bartley Paxmore, take thee, Rachel Starbuck, to be my wife . . .' There was more, arranged as each particular meeting determined. On this day Paxmore said, 'For better or worse, for richer or poorer, in sickness and in health, until death do us part.' Trembling, he sat down.

After a long pause Rachel rose and said clearly, 'In the presence of God and these our friends assembled, I, Rachel, take thee, Bartley . . .' Her promises were somewhat different, and when they were made she sat down.

After a protracted silence the young couple rose and Paxmore placed a gold ring on her finger and kissed her. Then they sat, and again there was silence.

Twenty minutes passed, and then one of the old women on the facing bench rose and said in firm voice:

'Marriage is a holy sacrament ordained by God and precious in His sight. But it is also the union of two lively young bodies, and if we forget that, we lose the mission of God. Rachel and Bartley, find joy in each other. Have children. Have laughter in thy home. Love each other increasingly, for when the ardor of youth is gone, the remembrance of great love will continue and make all the years of thy life glorious. In this meeting house today are many old couples whose lives have been made bearable and fruitful because of the passion they have known each for the other, and it will be so with thee when thee looks back fifty years from this day.'

She sat down, and no one gave any sign of either approval or disapproval of her remarkable words. They were her summary of what a marriage consisted of, and she had felt led by God to share them with this beginning couple. After silence had maintained for some minutes a very old man, much older than the woman who had spoken, rose and said in a high clear voice:

'Prudent men in all nations and all religions have found it improper for a married couple to spend more than twenty percentum of their family income on rent. Never take out a mortgage for any cause except the purchase of a farm, and never pay more than five percentum for the mortgage. And never, never sign the note of a friend. For sixty years I have watched men sign for their friends and always it ends in disaster. The note is lost, the friend is lost, the money is lost, and only grief remains. Rachel, never let thy husband sign a note for a friend. If the other party needs the money and merits it, give it to him. But don't sign his note.'

When the old man sat down a neighbor whispered to him, and after a moment's reflection the old fellow rose again to add this postscript: 'It would also be permissible to take out a mortgage to buy a town property but only if it were essential to a business, and never for more than five percentum.' When silence was restored, the meeting sat immobile until a younger woman with a wavering voice rose to say, 'When thee has children, for that is the purpose of a marriage, be certain that they are taught to know Jesus. It is a fearful thing to rear children who know not the Christian faith.' That was her complete speech, and there would be no more.

Finally the two old men on the topmost bench rose and shook hands. Then all the Quakers shook hands with their neighbors, and each moved forward to sign the marriage document, which would be deposited in the place of record in Easton. When the signing ended, Bartley Paxmore had been duly married to Rachel Starbuck.

The Railroad

BY THE MIDDLE YEARS OF THE 1840s CITIZENS LIV-
ing along the Choptank had separated into two well-defined groups
epitomized by the two leading families of the region. Paul and Susan
Steed had become the acknowledged champions of those wealthy plantation owners who were convinced that Maryland must follow the guidance of the Carolinas and Georgia, even if this meant dissolving the
Union, while George and Elizabeth Paxmore were spokesmen for that
great body of middle-class farmers and businessmen who felt that the
Union was something unique and precious which must be preserved. In
financial and intellectual power the Steed faction predominated; in stubborn moral force the Paxmore group would prove important.

Most of the time the Steed-Paxmore paths diverged, the former attending to their plantations, the latter to the building of ships; but at unpredictable times their interests converged, and then there was trouble.

In these years Devon became one of the best-regarded plantations in
America. Three reasons accounted for this. First, Paul Steed gave it
statesmanlike management, seeking out the best overseers in Maryland
and Virginia and paying them well. He himself now owned nearly nine
hundred slaves and used them to maximum advantage. There were no
beatings, no savagery; after he discovered how Mr. Cline operated his
correctional farm on the Little Choptank, no more Devon slaves went
there. His wise decisions helped his plantation to prosper; he alternated
crops, kept his ships busy and extended the number and range of his
stores. His years of quiet study had enabled him to become an expert,
and he was often seen limping about the remotest corners of his mainland
plantations, pushing his twisted neck into all sorts of problems, which
he took delight in solving.

Second, on a trip across the bay in 1842 he chanced to see the operation of the Baltimore and Ohio Railroad, and was so enchanted by the prospect of linking the nation together by rails that for no reason at all other than scientific curiosity he rode the train to Harpers Ferry and back. That experience convinced him that the only hope for the peninsula of which the Eastern Shore was a part lay in binding its three segments together by means of an extensive rail system.

From the earliest days of the nation anyone with an intelligence equal to that of sparrows had realized that the peninsula ought logically to be united as one state, but historical accident had decreed that one portion be assigned to Maryland, whose citizens despised the Eastern Shore and considered it a backwater; one portion to the so-called State of Delaware, which never could find any reasonable justification for its existence; and the final portion to Virginia, which allowed its extreme southern fragment of the Eastern Shore to become the most pitiful orphan in America.

All who lived in this tripartite travesty kept hoping that in the forthcoming year the three sections would be united to form a viable state with its own interests, history, traditions and prospects. Year after year it failed to happen. Paul campaigned in Congress for the sensible realignment and everyone he approached agreed that the change should be made, but nothing was done, for, as Senator Clay told him one afternoon, 'My dear Steed, the most permanent thing in this world is a temporary arrangement.'

But now, with the possibility of a rail system running the length of the peninsula and connecting with the North at Philadelphia and the South via Norfolk, the Eastern Shore had a bright future, and the organizer and marshal of that future would be Paul Steed. It was in pursuit of this grand design that he and Susan began to invite the leaders of the nation to visit with them at Devon. The Steed sloop would cross the bay, sail down to the mouth of the Potomac, then up to Washington, where it would wait to carry famous senators and congressmen to Rosalind's Revenge for a week or ten days' entertainment. While the visitors philosophized, Paul would bring in leaders from the Choptank to talk persuasively with them.

The locals cited every reason that a logical man could devise as to why the three fragmented parts should be united, and they accomplished nothing except the pleasure of meeting great men and listening to them talk. How often in those pregnant years did the senators speak for two minutes on the problem of uniting the Eastern Shore, and then orate for five hours on the insoluble problems of slavery!

Third, it was in this field of burgeoning interest in slavery that Steed did most to bring favorable attention to Devon. He began innocently: a long, analytic letter to Fithians in London explaining that whereas it might be appropriate for England to abolish slavery, it would be suicide for the American South to do so. Noel Fithian replied with a scholarly analysis of certain weaknesses in his friend's reasoning, and Paul sent back a rebuttal.

Later he corresponded with gentlemen in Massachusetts, Ohio, Louisiana and, especially, South Carolina. His letters were so beautifully composed and so instinct with logic and high argument that they circulated among friends of the recipients, and chance readers from different parts of the country wrote Paul suggesting that he compile his letters and offer them as the statement of a southern realist, but it was not until Senator Calhoun of South Carolina wrote, that Steed became actively interested. With his customary perspicacity, the great defender of states' rights and slavery told Paul:

> I have rarely come upon a group of letters which so succinctly states the moral position of the South. You are cogent and unswerving in your defense of our position, and it would be salutary if you could collect the other letters I hear you have written and present them in compact form so that those at the North who wish to understand our reasoning can find it handsomely expressed.

In 1847 Paul issued his collection of twenty letters, *Reflections of a Maryland Planter,* which evoked such enthusiastic praise in the South and such rebuttal at the North that many readers wanted to know how a parochial planter like Steed, stuck away in one of the most remote corners of the nation, could have mastered so much learning. The explanation was simple.

In the dark years of his soul's retreat, when all along the Choptank he was ridiculed for his relations with the slave girl Eden and his reluctance to intervene in his wife's scandalous behavior, he found consolation in the work of three authors who had molded his education. Jean Jacques Rousseau reminded him anew of the honorable condition in which men might live if they attended to the basic lessons of the soil. From Rousseau he derived his passionate love of human freedom and his determination to protect it in both the South and the North. Plato reminded him of those noble propositions upon which any orderly society must be founded. But he learned most from the novels of Sir Walter Scott.

Like many southern gentlemen, he found in Scott's works a defense of those principles upon which the nobility of southern life was based: the brave laird of good intention, the chaste woman who inspires him and whom he protects, the loyal serf whose willing work enables the laird to monitor the land, and the allegiance of all to the ideals of an unselfish chivalry. On one memorable afternoon in 1841, as he sat in the lace-curtained room reading *The Heart of Midlothian,* he rose to his feet and took an oath: Here on this island I can be a new Guy Mannering, a local Quentin Durward.

From that solemn moment he dedicated himself to achieving Plato's good society, Rousseau's freedom and Walter Scott's chivalry. It was inevitable that his letters should epitomize these beliefs, and in his first epistle to Noel Fithian, when he addressed himself to the most difficult topics that were troubling the nation, he was not afraid to spell out his personal convictions:

> . . . The Negro is genetically inferior, requires a master, has many fine qualities when properly guided, and cannot exist outside of some slave system.

> . . . Contrary to what certain mal-intentioned people are saying, slavery is an economic asset, for it enables landowners to keep in cultivation acreage which could not otherwise be utilized. No white man could possibly work outdoors in areas like the Carolinas, Alabama and Louisiana.

> . . . It is entirely possible for a system of slavery in the South to coexist with a system of free labor at the north, providing always that the north does not continue to insist upon low prices for our southern raw materials and high prices for its manufactured goods.

> . . . It is also possible for slavery to exist side-by-side with a system of gradual manumission of slaves, for this has been tried with great success. The logical goal would be to train Negroes in the trades so that they could work anywhere in America. It will probably require about two hundred years for them to achieve the necessary level of education.

> . . . It is essential to the orderly working of the system that those Negroes who run away from their lawful masters be returned to them, regardless of where in the United States they flee. The right of property is sacred and must be honored by federal as well as local law.

> . . . There has been talk of secession from the Union, but this will occur only if those at the north persist in enforcing high tariffs, in encouraging abolition, and in giving refuge to runaway slaves. If these antagonisms can be halted, the two sections can co-exist profitably and enjoy a limitless future.

In his twenty letters, Paul invariably referred to the South, capitalized, and its unhappy persecution by those 'at the north,' not capitalized, as if the former were a spiritual entity and the latter a chance combination of miscellaneous agencies. But he never ridiculed the northern position and in Letter VIII actually stated it rather better than some of its own apologists. The letter which gained widest circulation, however, was

XIII, in which he dealt head-on with the charge of southern cruelty to the slave. This was reprinted a thousand times in southern newspapers, and served as the focus for a thousand rebuttals in northern ones. A particular paragraph became famous:

> There has been brutality, but never on the plantations of my family or my friends. There has been inattention to the requirements of food and clothing and protection from the elements, but not on any plantation I know. And there has been unconscionable whipping of refractory slaves, but the planter guilty of such offense is scorned by his equals, avoided by his associates, and haunted by his own conscience. His lot is ostracism among his own kind and scorn from the general public. The only way he can redeem himself is to give long and continued evidence that he has quit his evil behavior, for if he were to continue after having been rebuked, he would be outlawed by the body of gentlemen.

In a later section of the same letter he did admit that unspeakable types such as Mr. Cline existed, and that on their farms ugly incidents had sometimes taken place, but he dismissed their brutality with a phrase that gave scant consolation to the Negroes who suffered under their lash: 'They dare not associate with gentlemen.' He implied that this was punishment enough; but he also added that every southern state had strict slave codes, 'which all but the most depraved observe,' and he cited Maryland's to prove that under its benevolent protection a slave might have to work hard, but he was well fed, warmly clothed, comfortably housed and defended against abuse.

By accident, the other letter which achieved considerable notice outside the book was XIX, which he had composed in a fit of some irritation. The slave Frederick Douglass, who had been born on a plantation just off the Choptank, and who had served at various sites adjacent to the Steed holdings, had escaped north and been adopted by the more unsavory elements of the abolition movement. In 1845 he published a scurrilous book purporting to give a true account of slavery in the Choptank district, and through it he had achieved a certain notoriety as a speaker in northern churches. The South was both vexed and damaged by this book, for Douglass wrote compellingly; it was believed in Patamoke that some white man must have written the book for him. So in a letter to a friend in Ohio, Paul Steed demolished the pretentions of this rabble-rouser. He savaged him on four counts, which he outlined at the beginning of his letter:

> *First,* you must not believe that his writing proves that blacks can achieve a high level of mental ability, for he is mostly white, as he

himself confesses: 'My father was a white man. The opinion was that my master was my father.' Obviously any intellectual powers he may demonstrate derive from his white parentage.

Second, he is an imposter, for he has always sailed under assumed names, first calling himself Bailey, then Stanley, then Johnson and next Douglass. What name can we expect him to steal next? 'The real Mr. Johnson had been reading *The Lady of the Lake* and suggested that my name be Douglass. From that time until now I have been called Frederick Douglass.'

Third, he is an atheist, so that no evidence he offers of mistreatment need be accepted. Who has ever uttered more horrible profanation than this: 'The religion of the South is a mere covering for the most horrid crimes, a justifier of the most appalling brutality, a sanctifier of the most hateful frauds, and a dark shelter under which the darkest, foulest, grossest and most infernal deeds of slaveholders find the strongest protection.' Is this not the Anti-Christ speaking?

Fourth, he is a self-confessed forger: 'The week before our intended start to freedom I wrote several protections for each of us.' What he means is that he forged five passes to deceive the authorities and signed them with the honorable name of William Hambleton of St. Michaels, misspelling the name in his ignorance.

The lasting value of Steed's letters lay in his discussions of management and economics. These occurred in no specific letter but infused them all; he displayed himself to be the best type of plantation owner—informed and desirous of operating his large holdings at a profit to everyone. In a dozen unplanned ways he disclosed his determination to provide his slaves with decent living arrangements and a carefully regulated share of the good things that resulted from his management. Each slave received more clothes than on other plantations, more food. He was especially attentive to the sanctity of family life and abolished the old custom, adhered to by Uncle Herbert, of selling a refractory husband south without regard for the wife and children kept behind. He explained his reasoning:

A healthy slave represents both a substantial investment and a good opportunity to turn a profit, but the investment is destroyed and the profit lost if the slave is in any way incapacitated by ill treatment, and by this I mean not only physical abuse but also the mental wounding that can occur through separation of families or inattention to the slave children. If the dictates of humanity do not protect the slave, the principles of prudent husbandry should.

The letter that was most difficult for northern analysts to digest was XX, for in it Steed explained to Noel Fithian his theory that freedom in the United States depended upon the continuance of slavery. He cited some fifteen cogent arguments, drawing upon the experience of Greece, Rome and early America. He was convinced that free men could flourish only if supported by a slave class and argued that it was not the freedom of the white gentleman that he was defending, but the welfare of the slave. Never did he waiver in this conviction; never did he admit the slightest concession which might disprove his thesis. One of his citations gained wide circulation:

> The freedom enjoyed by citizens of the United States, to the envy of the known world, was engineered primarily by gentlemen of the South who owned slaves. Of the men who wrote the Declaration of Independence, those who made the greatest contribution were slave-owners. Of those who framed our Constitution the majority of true intellects came from the South. Of the twelve Presidents who have guided our nation to its present level of enviable success, nine have been slaveholders and their leadership has been the sanest and the most appreciated by the nation at large.

He argued that it was only the gentleman, set free from mundane matters by the hard work of his slaves, who could properly assess the movements of society and separate good from bad. He said it was the wives of those concerned gentlemen who inclined society toward the higher values:

> It has been the women of the South who have kept aflame the beacons of our nation: charity, gallantry, compassion, grace, and all the other amenities. They could do this because they were set free —by the existence of family slaves—to attend to matters of greater moment than washing and cleaning. It is not the women at the north who have established norms for our national behavior, for they have been preoccupied with petty matters. It is our gracious ladies of the South who have set the patterns.

And again he returned to his basic theme that it was the existence of slavery that enabled black men and women to be free:

> So what we find is that the black woman of the South is more free to pursue her true interests of motherhood and family care than the so-called free woman at the north who works in some mill under conditions that prevent her from enjoying life. True freedom is found in a disciplined society in which each participant has a place and knows what that place is.

He saw himself as the 1847 inheritor of Pericles of Athens, and Marcus Aurelius of Rome, and George Washington of Virginia, and he endeavored to hold himself to the austere standards set by those men. 'Their freedom to move in the world,' he often said, 'was based upon the existence of slaves who performed the lower categories of work.' But he was not insensitive to the nagging question of the abolitionists: 'Must the slave live his entire life without hope?' He addressed himself to this matter toward the end of Letter XX:

> You will remember, Noel, the fine slave girl Eden who attended you when last you visited us. She was in all ways a superior person, and the loving care she lavished on Susan after our accident was the principal reason my wife survived. We set Eden free, and paid her a salary which she could accumulate for the purchase of her husband, that fine Xanga mechanic you commented upon at the forge. They now reside in our village of Patamoke, where the husband has built a good business as carpenter and general fixer. Eden, it may interest you to know, voluntarily offered to continue her work at Devon and nurse Miss Susan, who under her care can now walk with a proficiency you would not believe. I venture to suggest that both Eden and her husband are happier here in Maryland than they could possibly have been in Africa.

In fact, Paul Steed convinced himself that he protected the freedom of all men, especially the freedom of the slaves under his control. 'I serve as their master for their own good,' he reasoned, and he was so forceful in propagating this theory that everyone along the Choptank came to believe that 'our slaves are happier under our benevolent care than they would be if they were set free.' Everyone believed this, that is, except the slaves themselves and workingmen like George Paxmore.

Paul Steed had long been aware that he must one day have trouble with the Paxmores over the question of slavery, and in late 1847 he was visited by Thomas Cater, the postmaster at Patamoke. Mr. Cater sailed down to Devon, wearing his dark suit and a darker frown, to place before Mr. Steed evidence that the Quakers at Peace Cliff were receiving seditious mail. 'I wouldn't have believed it, sir, had I not seen it with my own eyes,' and he threw on the desk a heavy envelope that had been sent from the North with a copy of the *New York Tribune,* a provocative journal dedicated to stirring up trouble.

'There it is,' Mr. Cater said gingerly.

Steed would not touch it, for Maryland law explicitly forbade the circulation of any material 'calculated to stir discontent among our colored,' and men had been sent to jail for ten years for the offense. At first the law had applied only to inflammatory rags like *The Liberator,* but now it covered even reasonable papers that questioned in any way the morality and economics of slavery.

'What shall I do with it?' Mr. Cater asked.

'The law says you're to burn it.'

'Each time it arrives?'

'You have no obligation to encourage black uprisings.'

Mr. Cater, not wanting to take the offending journal back to Pata-moke, asked Mr. Steed if he could have a match, and when this was provided he went onto the lawn, knelt down and set the newspaper afire. When only black ashes remained he returned to the house. 'I'll take note of everything they receive and keep you informed.'

Steed's concern over Paxmore's possible treason was put aside when word reached Devon that Senator Clay had at last found a date on which he could cross the bay to discuss the proposed railroad. Extraordinary preparations were made for his comfort, for he was an old man now and travel would be difficult; he was not really a senator any longer, but he retained the title and had such power that if he approved an Eastern Shore railroad, his former colleagues in the Senate would probably support it. So the big guest bedroom in the west wing was readied with flowers; slaves were drilled in how to attend the famous Kentuckian; invitations were dispatched to important citizens in the area; and Susan Steed wheeled her chair into distant parts of the mansion, attending to those small details which accounted for the social distinction of the Steeds.

It was midafternoon when the sloop arrived with the senator, and when he stepped ashore, a tall, thin, distinguished man of seventy-one, with handsome flowing hair and wide, expressive mouth, he brought a dignity which bespoke his years of service to the nation. Characteristically, he paused at the wharf, surveyed the plantation, making a quick assessment of its management, and started up the graveled path, his step firm and even eager.

'You keep a fine establishment,' he said approvingly to Paul, who had to hurry on his shortened leg to keep up. 'I miss my farm in Kentucky —the animals especially. I like good husbandry. It marks a good mind.'

When he approached the mansion, old Tiberius stepped forth in his blue uniform and white gloves, bowing from the waist. 'Yo' is welcome to Rosalind's Revenge,'

'What revenge did she take?' Clay asked, stopping on the porch to study the plantation from this perspective.

'Several,' Paul explained. 'She hanged the pirate Henri Bonfleur.'

'I've heard of him,' Clay said, admiring the manner in which the garden led down to the creek.

'And it was her ship that captured Blackbeard. Cut his head off, you know. She was a terror.'

'And did she build this beautiful house?'

'She did.'

'Used the Flemish bond, I see.' Nothing escaped this great man's eye. When he saw Susan Steed approaching him in her wheelchair he became all grace, and hurried forward to assist her as she projected herself upward. 'How excellent of you to invite me to your shore,' he said, not grandly but with the intense warmth of a Kentucky farmer who liked to see well-stocked plantations.

'We've invited some of our leaders to meet with you,' Steed said. 'Their boats will be arriving.'

'That pleases me.'

'Would you like to repair the damages of the trip?' Steed asked.

'No. I travel well. But I would like to hear your statement of the matters which bring me here,' and he made his way instinctively to the sunroom, where the late-afternoon light filtered through the lace curtains, making the room warm and hospitable. There, in a comfortable chair, he drank two whiskeys, then asked, 'And what of this railroad?'

Steed had prepared a map showing the Eastern Shore, and whenever he looked at it his anger rose. 'Sir, it should be obvious to anyone that this peninsula ought to be one governmental unit.'

'I tried in vain,' Clay said, chuckling at the obstinacy he had met when sponsoring a bill to bring the three parts of the peninsula into one state. 'But have you ever tried to tell one sovereign state anything? Let alone three.' He shook his head, then studied the map. 'What have you in mind?'

'Simply this.' And with bold strokes Paul outlined what he thought should happen: 'Let the federal government authorize one solid railroad line from Wilmington due south to the tip of Cape Charles. That will unite the whole peninsula to Norfolk across the bay. Then let individual towns build spurs into that major line. And up here, a ferry that will run to Baltimore.'

'Steed, you make enormous good sense, as always. But you overlook one salient fact. The metropolis of this region is destined to be Baltimore, and since wheat has supplanted tobacco as your major crop, Baltimore's whole preoccupation will be with the West, not the South. When we complete a great railroad to Chicago, the westward pull will be irresistible. Look to Baltimore, not Norfolk.' He was eager to expand on this, but guests began arriving, solid businessmen from various parts of the Choptank, and Clay greeted each with courtly deference, listening carefully as Steed explained who they were.

After a substantial dinner, with three kinds of wine, Mrs. Steed wheeled her chair away from the table and said, 'Ladies, I think we should leave the gentlemen to their cigars,' and off she led them.

'Mr. Steed's been telling me about his hopes—your hopes, that is—for a railroad,' Clay said with an inflection which implied that he supported the idea.

'Yes!' various voices cried, and when the map was fetched, each man explained what he and his group were willing to contribute to the grand design.

'Surely, there would be no way for the rails to cross the Choptank,' Clay said.

'Quite right, sir,' a merchant from Dorchester County agreed. 'What we plan is to bring this spur to Patamoke, and end it there. Terminal. On our south bank we build due east and hook on to the main line.'

'Of course, Senator Clay,' a Patamoke man interrupted, 'there'd be a ferry across the Choptank. Is now, for that matter,' and he indicated where the little ferry ran.

'It seems a splendid concept,' Clay said.

'You'll help us?'

'I shall indeed.'

This commitment delighted the Eastern Shore men, because the word of Henry Clay was like bars of gold in a safe built on rock. He was a politician who got things done, the expediter, the slaveholder who understood the North, the one man who saw the nation as a whole.

But the Choptank men wanted to be sure that Clay would be in a position to deliver on his promise. 'Is it true that the Kentucky legislature will send you back to the Senate?'

The bluntness of this question, touching as it did on the delicate matter of his uncertain future, must have embarrassed Clay, but he did not show it. Turning to his questioner, he said softly, 'From the time I first served in the Kentucky legislature, sir, I have always been at the call of my country. And even though I am now an old man, if Kentucky wishes to summon me to duty, I shall respond.' And then he added, 'If I am returned to the Senate, I shall support your railroad. But I want not only your relatively short spurs. I want a whole network of rails, binding this nation together. I want an end to North and South, West and East. Most particularly, I want an end to our bitter rivalry over slavery.'

Railroads were not mentioned again. 'You good men of Maryland stand at the border between the rivalries. Some like Steed are southern planters. I imagine that most of you have no slaves.' He asked for a show of hands, and two thirds of the men indicated that they held none.

'So you men at the margin, tell me what we must do to bind this nation together.' He leaned forward, an old man, really a very old man, for he was worn out with fighting, and pointed to each man in turn, seeking advice.

The responses were varied; some men wanted slaveowners to be given the right to carry their slaves into all the new territories opening in the West; some wanted the tariffs imposed by New England congressmen to be lowered; two men suggested that a timetable be set at the end of which all slaves should be set free, say a hundred years from now. And all agreed that the differences currently existing between North and South be dampened.

Now Clay began close questioning. 'Let us suppose that a slave runs away from this plantation.'

'It does happen,' Paul conceded, leaning forward to catch Clay's handling of this ticklish problem.

'Let us suppose further that Mr. Steed's slave gets as far as Boston.'

'Some go to Canada,' one slaveowner said quickly.

'Should Mr. Steed be encouraged—nay, should he be legally permitted —to go to Boston and recover his slave?'

It was unanimously agreed that he had that right; even the two men who thought that at some distant date all slaves should be set free agreed that under current law Steed had the right to recover his property. 'But now,' Clay said, 'we come to the sandy part. When Mr. Steed arrives in Boston, is he allowed to enlist the help of the United States marshals stationed there? Or the local police? Or the services of any chance bystander?'

To each of these questions, unanimous affirmatives were given, but before the senator could respond, one of the more liberal men added a word of caution: 'I'd like to reconsider my answer on that last question. About enlisting the aid of bystanders. Wouldn't that be provocative? I mean, the acts would be visible . . . in public?'

Clay leaned back as the men hammered out their reactions to this hypothetical case, and he was impressed that in the end all agreed that the return of a man's lawful property was obligatory. Three times Clay proposed illustrative cases with slight variations and three times the men of Choptank affirmed their early decision: a man's property was inviolate, and if it ran away, the entire force of society should be mustered for its return.

Now the doors to the dining room swung open and old Tiberius appeared. 'Gen'lmen, de ladies is comin' back.' And he stood aside as Susan wheeled herself into the room, a wrenlike little woman with unextinguishable charm. Within a few minutes she established the fact that she knew as much about this problem of sectionalism as any of the men, except the senator, but custom had dictated that she retire from the serious part of the conversation.

The company slept that night in the mansion, and at breakfast Senator Clay resumed his interrogation of the gentlemen. All morning he talked with them, and at the noonday meal, and all afternoon. An hour before dusk he said that he would like to inspect the plantation, and he walked about two miles, checking everything. At one point he told Steed, who limped along beside him, 'One of the best things I've done in my life was import good cattle from England. Nothing strengthens a nation more than a solid agriculture.' He approved of Steed's management and surprised him by saying, 'I've studied your *Reflections,* Steed, and am pleased to see that you practice what you preach.'

That night Clay was ready for another three-hour session, but the railroad was mentioned only once. 'Tell me, gentlemen, when we do build this road, will it drag your sympathies south toward Norfolk or north toward Philadelphia or west toward Baltimore and Chicago?'

'We'll always be southerners, sir,' Steed said.

Clay started to respond, but Tiberius was throwing open the doors and in came the ladies. On this night Susan said, 'You know, Senator, that I'm an Englishwoman.'

Clay rose and bowed. 'Your country sends us brave generals and beautiful women.'

'And I sometimes think that this rivalry between South and North is folly.'

'I think so too, ma'am, like the difference between Ireland and England.'

'Ah, but they're two different countries.'

'And we must strive to see that South and North do not become two different nations.'

'That we must!' one of the businessmen cried.

Clay reached for the silver bell resting at Paul Steed's elbow and rang it. When Tiberius appeared, he asked, 'Good Tiberius, could you bring glasses for the ladies?' When this was done, and the wine had been passed, Clay proposed a toast. 'I have rarely talked with more sensible citizens than those gathered here tonight.' He hesitated. 'Are you a citizen, Mrs. Steed?'

'For many years,' she said.

'Ladies and gentlemen, to the Union!'

They drank in silence, all in the room looking over the rims of their glasses at this extraordinary man who had made himself a symbol of all those forces which were striving to hold the nation together: Clay the Compromiser, Clay the man who came to listen.

In the morning, as he walked slowly down to the wharf, he told Steed, 'Getting your railroad will not be easy. Our first priority is to finish the rails to Chicago.'

'Then?'

'I can look only one year ahead, Steed. I'm always terrified by the next twelve months.'

The Paxmores, of course, were never invited to social affairs at Rosalind's Revenge, and this was understandable, for their attitude toward slavery was so at variance with that of the planters, neither side would have felt comfortable. The slaveowners, being gentlemen, would hesitate to irritate the Quakers by reciting the problems encountered in trying to manage slaves economically, whereas the Quakers, not being gentlemen, would have no reluctance in heckling the slave people about the moral inconsistencies in the system.

'It's almost as if they reject the established law of the land,' Paul complained, and Susan replied, 'They feed their prejudices on that foul literature sent down from Boston and New York. They simply refuse to accept the testimony of their own eyes.'

'Such as what?'

'Such as the way nine hundred slaves live with us in harmony.'

She had identified the tragic difference that separated the two families: the Steeds pointed to their well-run plantation and believed that it compensated for horror camps like Herman Cline's, while the Paxmores pointed to one horror camp on the Little Choptank and judged it to counterbalance the hundreds of well-run plantations. There was not much meeting of minds.

The difficulty Paul Steed had foreseen arose after the Paxmores had purchased a subscription to *The Liberator* and demanded that Mr. Cater deliver it to them, something he was forbidden to do. Therefore, whenever the steamboat from Baltimore arrived with editions of either the *New York Tribune* or *The Liberator*, he had burned them—'No sedition in Patamoke.'

When George Paxmore satisfied himself that United States mail was being destroyed, he protested, but Cater warned him, 'Friend Paxmore, you don't seem to realize I'm acting in your defense. Suppose I hand you the papers? And advise the sheriff? Off you go to jail.'

The Paxmores lodged a protest in Annapolis, and were advised: 'Postmaster Cater is obeying the law.' They wrote to the Postmaster General in Washington, who tossed their complaint to an underling, who answered: 'Those at the North can insist that we carry their mail to the South, and this we do, but it is understandable if southern postmasters burn it in conformance to local law.'

This reply so outraged the Paxmores that they sought final arbitrament from that unflagging champion of New England rectitude, John Quincy Adams, once President of the Union, now its principal defender in Congress. He had been looking for just such a case to exploit, and dispatched an investigator, a gentleman from Illinois, to verify the Paxmores' charges. The marshal, an anti-slavery man, returned to Washington with proof that the postmaster had been burning United States mail.

A scandal might have resulted, because Adams, a cantankerous, mutton-chopped old warrior of eighty-one, was determined to fight such impropriety. This was not necessary. A compromise was arranged whereby Postmaster Cater was removed from his job at Patamoke and offered a much better one by the patriots of South Carolina, where he continued to burn any mail he considered seditious.

His departure had a strange aftermath. When Cudjo gained his freedom, he moved into Patamoke and started a business of his own. He was a carpenter, a mechanic, a boatbuilder, a fixer, a gardener, an extra hand on boats tonging oysters. He was offered a permanent job at Paxmore's boatyard, but he had such an insatiable desire for freedom that he wanted to be his own boss, even though that meant occasional periods of slack employment.

Since Eden continued to work at Rosalind's Revenge, so as to be close to crippled Susan, a curious household developed. For about two weeks of every month Eden lived with Cudjo in the shack in Patamoke, helping to raise their two sons; then she would board one of the Steed boats and go back to Devon for a couple of weeks, and it was during one of these trips that Paul Steed told her, 'Eden, now that you and Cudjo are free, you've got to take a last name.' This was a reasonable suggestion in that the possession of such a name was one of the marks of a freed black, but neither Eden nor Cudjo had ever had a name.

'I got no idea,' Eden said.

At the moment she spoke Paul happened to be looking at a letter and was irritated to think that the Paxmores had been able to embarrass a postmaster who had been doing such a good job. Then the idea came to him: 'Eden, Mr. Cater was moved south. His name is needed no more.'

So Cudjo and Eden became the Caters, and whenever the Steeds mentioned the name, it reminded them of their antagonism to the Paxmores.

Paul Steed tried three times to lure Daniel Webster to Devon, and to do so was important, for in the fight for the railroad, support from the great New Englander was essential. He was the most powerful man in the Senate and commanded the most faithful following among the leaders of industry.

He was too busy with governmental matters to make the long journey from Washington, even though it was understood that Steed would send the plantation boat to fetch him. And then one day, unannounced, a Mr. Walgrave from New Hampshire appeared at the island with exciting news: 'If you could see your way clear to invite to the meeting these gentlemen . . .' And he handed Paul a list of names representing the most prosperous businessmen of the Eastern Shore, Delaware and Baltimore.

'I would be proud to invite such men,' Steed said. 'But would they come?' And Mr. Walgrave, a small fussy man who spoke in whispers, said, 'I think they might be interested in talking directly with the senator. I think you'll find them receptive.'

'If you feel so certain,' Paul said in some perplexity, 'why doesn't Senator Webster himself . . .'

'Oh no!' Walgrave whispered. 'That would be highly improper. But if the invitation came from you . . .'

'I'll certainly try,' Paul said. 'This railroad . . .'

'Oh!' the New Hampshire man said, 'you'll find the senator most interested in railroads. Yes, indeed.'

So the invitations went out, and almost every man who received one replied that he would indeed like a chance to visit with the great senator. Arrangements were made to sleep the visitors in all parts of the mansion, in the office and even in two overseers' cottages freshened up for the occasion. Guests began arriving two days before the scheduled conference, and maps were placed at convenient places for study of the intended routes. There was much talk about a spur that would tie into a ferry to Baltimore, the men from that city insisting that trade be siphoned there rather than north to Philadelphia, and concessions were quickly agreed upon.

On the day prior to the meeting, Mr. Walgrave appeared, all blandness and confidential whispers. He assured each man that Daniel Webster was crossing the bay to see him personally, because the senator had such high regard for that man's business judgment, and he spent the evening germinating enthusiasm for the arrival of the great man.

At breakfast he outlined, in his soft voice, what the procedure of the day must be, and at ten, when the boat came up the creek, he was at the wharf leading the cheering party. 'Hip, hip, hooray!' he cried, encouraging the slaves waiting to catch the ropes to join in.

When the steamboat tied up, Mr. Walgrave was first aboard, and after deckhands had moved ashore with the luggage, he cried—whispering no longer—'Here comes Senator Webster!' And from the cabin stepped a burly man with a huge, balding head, piercing eyes and dark cavities below his cheekbones. His mouth turned down in a perpetual sneer, and like an emperor he strode to the gangway, descended to the wharf and moved forward briskly to shake hands with his host.

'My good friend Steed,' he cried to a man he had never before met, 'how fine of you to meet our little boat.' He shook hands solemnly, passed along to each of the welcoming committee, stood for a moment enraptured by the prospect, and said in a deep rumbling voice that seemed to echo among the trees, 'Gentlemen, I am eager to talk railroads.'

In the session before lunch he was overpowering, not because of his voice, which he kept low, and not because of his massive form, which he moved little, but solely because he was a man of compelling intellect. A planter from across the Choptank would start almost humbly to explain the advantages of having a railroad . . .

'Mr. Stallworthy, you need not hesitate with me. I have no constituent in Massachusetts whose business does not profit because of the railroad. I believe that every American industry . . .' His syllables rolled out magnificently, carrying with them a sense of conviction which heartened his listeners.

And he mastered data. If someone spoke of Baltimore's vested interest in the Eastern Shore, Daniel Webster had the figures supporting this claim, and he became a more clever advocate than the Baltimorean. He was a businessman himself, ingrained in the processes of buying and selling. But in the session after the noonday meal he displayed the other aspect of his policy: 'It is essential, I believe, that we construct every possible railroad line running north and south, for these are the sinews that will bind our nation together.'

When he began to expatiate upon the problems of the Union, he spoke like a god, and Steed reflected on the fact that he was so persuasive in his personal commitments, whereas Henry Clay had been so aloof and intellectual. 'We need them both,' he muttered to himself as Webster forged ahead, brushing aside difficulties which Steed knew could not be so easily disposed of.

But he was at his greatest during the evening meal. Sitting at Susan's right, he discoursed on his vision of a more powerful Union, stretching to all parts of the continent, provisioned by the southern states, supplied with manufactures by the northern, and provided with raw materials by the western. In the midst of his flowery oration he dropped his napkin, placed his two hands on the table and said in a resonant voice, 'Gentlemen of the South, I am here to learn from you what it is you desire from that Union.'

Old Tiberius appeared to lead the ladies to their coffee, but Webster interrupted, 'I believe the ladies should stay,' and he personally superintended the placement of Susan's chair.

The discussion was far-ranging. He had not come, like Henry Clay, to listen, but rather to catch fleeting images of problems, which he would grasp, rephrase and make a permanent part of his arsenal. No slaveowner proposed any action but that Daniel Webster understood his dilemmas, sympathized with them and gave assurance that he would do his best to alleviate them. When the probing question that Henry Clay had raised —What is to be done about the fugitive slave?—was brought up by Steed, Webster brushed it aside in four forceful words: 'Return him, of course.' How, and under what circumstances and with what effect upon federal law-enforcing agencies did not concern him.

He retired early, quitting the room like a spent tornado, his massive head bowed as if overcome by the burdens of office. At the door he turned, smiled at Susan and looked every man in the eye. 'Gentlemen, and beautiful ladies, tonight your railroad is much closer to Patamoke than it has ever been.'

When he was gone, leaving a conspicuous void, the party started to break up, but Mr. Walgrave signaled imperiously to Paul that Tiberius ought to lead the wives to their coffee. When the doors to the dining room were closed and cigars were lit, Mr. Walgrave from the head of the table said in his whispery voice, 'Gentlemen, now we get down to business.'

'What do you have in mind?' a merchant from Patamoke asked.

'Senator Webster, gentlemen. That's what I have in mind.' And he proceeded to make a speech which astounded everyone in the room except one of the men from Baltimore. Steed observed that this gentleman kept puffing on his cigar and looking disdainfully at the ceiling, and Paul got the impression that he had heard it all before:

> 'Gentlemen, let's not mince words. You know and I know that Daniel Webster is the one man in the United States Senate who represents our interests. Now, don't tell me that he's a high-tariff man and therefore can't represent the interests of you southerners. He alone has kept the tariff within reasonable limits. But more important, he has supported every good piece of business legislation that has come before Congress in the thirty-eight years he has been serving you.'

One guest pointed out that he had served Massachusetts, not Maryland, that indeed he had been an enemy of the principal laws that might have helped planters. Of such a claim Mr. Walgrave was contemptuous:

> 'Unworthy, sir, unworthy. Senator Webster may have had to vote, as a good New Englander, against one or another of your bills, but has he not consistently voted for the business interest? Are you each not better off because he has been your watchdog in the Senate, striking down those bills which served only to excite the rabble at the expense of the businessman?'

He went around the room, one man at a time, and proved that Webster had done his duty, for he queried each man on particular mercantile bills which Webster had sponsored to aid that man's business. Each had to confess that Daniel Webster had been the guardian of plantation owners as well as factory owners. Then he came to the point:

> 'So I am here tonight, gentlemen, to enlist your support for this man who has supported you so staunchly. I am about to collect pledges from you to enable Daniel Webster to pay off a few of his personal debts, so that he can continue in the Senate as your champion. I want each of you to ask yourself, "What has this great man's effort in the Senate been worth to me?" and I want you to contribute accordingly.'

One of the planters from north of Patamoke asked, 'How much did you have in mind?' and without hesitating a second, Mr. Walgrave whispered, 'Five hundred thousand dollars.' This evoked gasps, so he added quickly, 'Gentlemen, as you know, Senator Webster lives expensively. He has farms, relatives. He entertains much in Boston and New York. And when you come to Washington, you'll wine and dine with him. His expenses are large because his heart is large.'

Temporarily the meeting broke up into small groups, in which discussion was vigorous, and Mr. Walgrave made no attempt to interrupt this necessary process of opinion-formation, as he termed it; he had conducted numerous such meetings in all parts of the nation and had found that he never got really big pledges unless the local businessmen were given ample time for arguing among themselves. And it was big contributions he wanted.

'Are you asking us for the whole half million?' a planter asked.

'Heavens no!' Walgrave said. 'Understanding supporters from all over the nation are making their contributions.'

'Isn't such a collection forbidden by the Constitution?' a lawyer from Patamoke asked.

'It certainly is!' Mr. Walgrave agreed instantly. He had learned that this was the way to handle this difficult question, which always arose during these fund-gathering sessions.

'Then why are you asking us . . .'

'My dear friend, if you contribute—well, let us say, two thousand dollars tonight and expect Senator Webster to vote yea or nay on some bill that interests you, that would be bribery, subornation of the Senate, and it would certainly be punishable at law. But Senator Webster does not, nor has he ever, engaged in bribery, or the sale of his vote. All I promise you tonight is that if you see fit to support this great man, and keep him in office . . .'

'He has nobody running against him.'

'Thank God for that. No, he's not up for reelection, and if he were, no one in Massachusetts could defeat him.'

'Then why does he need . . .'

'Sir, he serves us all as Senator. He represents the entire nation. His living expenses . . .'

'They must be pretty high, to need half a million.'

'They are,' Mr. Walgrave snapped, and then he dropped back to his whispery voice. 'They are because he must work extra hard to protect men of property. Gentlemen, you support Daniel Webster or you throw your fortunes to the wolves.'

Now was the moment to whip these potential contributors into an orderly session. Speeding about the table, he placed before each man a carefully printed slip of paper on which to write the amount of money he was willing to contribute, and Webster had been so impressive, so comprehending of their problems, that each man but one signed a pledge. Paul Steed gave three thousand dollars.

'You haven't signed,' Mr. Walgrave said to the man who had been staring at the ceiling.

'No,' the man responded. 'I gave three years ago, in Pittsburgh . . . remember?'

'No, I do not remember,' Mr. Walgrave said with a certain asperity.

'That night you were collecting from the iron and steel men . . . four hundred thousand that time.'

Mr. Walgrave took note of the man. Under no circumstances would he ever be invited to another social evening with Daniel Webster.

For Eden Cater the 1840s were a time of perplexity. She was a freed woman with a good husband, two fine sons and a compassionate mistress who needed her. Miss Susan, with the aid of various devices built for her by Cudjo Cater, moved rather well about the mansion, and as she grew older, she grew more kind and understanding: 'I'm English, you know. Our ladies are supposed to acquire a certain grace.' She spoke often of the Fithian women in London, and of the quaint ways in which they had supervised her childhood: 'We had nannies, you know, and they always spoke French to us and slipped us novels to read. "So zat you will know how to make love . . . when ze time comes." '

She always added, as Eden listened to her monologues, 'But then, of course, I'm half American, too. And American women who live on islands are supposed to acquire a certain courage.' On some days she even went out into the garden, where she would sit in her wheelchair and watch as the slaves edged the walks. She was a gentle mistress, and the slaves treated her indulgently: 'Yes, ma'am. Yeeeessss, ma'am.' But they kept the garden pretty much as they wanted it, with the looming pyracantha reaching out for any passer-by and the tawny daylilies in place behind the iron rims in which their beds were now enclosed to prevent wandering.

Paul and Susan had added numerous hollies to the pattern, and these ingratiating trees, red in autumn, green in winter, gave the lawn a new touch. Indeed, Paul had perfected a holly which threw enormous clusters of bright red berries and was selling rooted plants to his neighbors under the name of Susan Fithian. Places all up and down the Choptank were burgeoning with Susan Fithians—'A hearty tree. They'll stand any adversity.'

Eden was not really needed at the mansion; two younger slaves had been trained to tend Miss Susan, but whenever she left for Patamoke to spend time with her family, she was missed. 'She's so understanding,' Miss Susan told the other girls. 'Sometimes behaves as if this were her house, not mine.' Upon reflecting on this phenomenon, she added,

'That's understandable. She was born on this island. Started living in the mansion the same year I did.'

Eden was drawn to Patamoke not only because of her family, but also because she sensed that movements were afoot which must soon engulf her and Cudjo. She loved to sit on the bench before their cabin in the evening and exchange ideas with him, for she developed her understandings at the mansion, he at the boatyard.

Their conversation followed strange patterns, for she had learned gentleman's English at Rosalind's Revenge, while he had picked his up from the fields and Cline's shed, intermixed with readings from Plutarch. Their pronunciation varied, too, with Eden speaking a soft, drawling tongue, while Cudjo's was crisper and more barbarous. Each pronounced the repetitive short words—the, these, they, them, that, then, there— with the hard *d* sound, and they used other interesting variations and contractions, but the important fact was they conversed on a high level of interest and taught their sons to do the same.

Suppose that Cudjo wanted to say *Why don't they just wait? He has the time.* It was likely to come out *Howc'm dey doan' jes' bide? He hab de time.* It might be truncated, but it was neither illiterate nor humorous.

On one trip home, Eden told her husband, 'When them great senators an' whatnots comes to Revenge they talks about railroads for ten minutes an' slavery for ten hours. Cudjo, they hopelessly confused.'

'What you think?'

'All the good white men, like Mr. Steed an' this Clay an' Webster, they wants to do the right thing. You can hear that in they voices. But they doan' know nothin', Cudjo. Fact is, I think they knows less than you an' me.'

'The others?'

'Most of the big owners—along the Choptank—they plain stupid. They think nothin' ever gonna change.' She repeated her ideas to her sons, then returned to Cudjo. 'At the bottom of the heap you got Lafe Turlock an' Herman Cline. Slave-trackers. Cudjo, you best watch out for 'em. They gonna try kill us . . . some day.'

'Why us? We ain't done nothin'.'

'Because we're free. They hates all black folk, but us free ones they hates the most.'

Cudjo asked how she assessed the Paxmores, and she said, 'They tryin', Cudjo, but they all mixed up.'

'They sure help me.'

'But they think they can change things by bein' nice. Miss Elizabeth, Mr. George, they doan' want to harm nobody. Turlock and Cline, they want to harm ever'body.'

'But Mr. Bartley an' Miss Rachel, they somethin'. You remember that night the slave come to our door?'

How well she remembered! It had been a watershed night for the

Caters. This slave had swum across the Choptank, an amazing feat, and had come dripping to their door. Cudjo, aware that he might be sold back into slavery if caught helping a runaway, wanted to turn him away, but Eden laid down the law. 'I often think what happen, we have to run away that night Miss Susan sign my paper. I can see the dogs . . . us in the swamp . . . no friends.' She had pulled the slave into their cabin and said, 'Cudjo, ain't never no slave come to this door an' failin' to find help.'

'This here Bartley,' Cudjo resumed, 'maybe he doan' want to fight, but he ain't afeert of nothin'. Me an' the slave is runnin' north. Lafe Turlock an' his dogs on our trail. Lafe, he shoot at me. Bartley, he step out from behind a tree. They wrassle. Lafe sic his dogs on Bartley. Rachel, she come out an' bust the dogs with her oar. Ever'body arrested but me an' the slave. We gits to Pennsylvania. Bartley, he gits two weeks in jail.'

'Yes,' Eden said reflectively, 'on the little things they strong. But come the big ones, they gonna be like all the rest.'

'Never old Mrs. Paxmore. She teach me to read. Ever'body warn her, "You teach nigger to read, you in trouble." But she teach me.'

Eden refused to comment on this special woman, the quiet one who had dared so much. But as for the other whites, they were stumbling in darkness toward a conflict that Eden saw as inevitable—"Cause when I listens at the mansion, Cudjo, all I hear is that even the senators, they doan' know what comin' down the road.' But Eden knew.

The final weeks of 1849 were a shambles. The Senate, led by Daniel Webster and Henry Clay, recently returned to it by the legislature of Kentucky, was preparing a vast compromise acceptable to South, North and West which would abolish sectional rivalries, the threat of secession and the possibility of war. Rarely had two great leaders toiled toward a more desirable end.

But the House of Representatives was in disarray. Through fifty-eight agonizing ballots extending over weeks it had been unable to elect a Speaker, its members snarling each at the other like alley dogs. And no solution was in sight. The cause, of course, was slavery, as it would be through the next decade. The House, being less philosophical than the Senate, simply could not reconcile its sectional differences, and the futile debate droned on.

During this impasse one of the greatest intellects our Senate was to produce sent word to Paul Steed that since he had long wanted to meet the writer of the *Reflections,* he was prepared to cross the bay, even though his health was not the best, and on a sunny day in late December the Baltimore steamer drew up at the wharf and discharged one of the majestic figures of American history.

There was certainly nothing majestic about his appearance. He came from his cabin slowly, leaning on the arms of two sailors. He wore a long black cloak with an extra shepherd's flap about the shoulders; the fact that he wore no hat allowed his huge mane of white hair to stand out in many directions, but it was his sunken face and burning eyes that created the most lasting impression, for they formed a kind of death mask.

'My God!' Paul muttered as he came down the gangplank. 'He's dying!'

This was John C. Calhoun, United States Senator from South Carolina, incandescent defender of the South. He was five years younger than Henry Clay but looked ninety-five years older. Yet as soon as he was satisfied that his feet were on firm ground, he moved forward eagerly to grasp Paul's hand.

'My dear Steed,' he said in low, guarded tones, as if he knew he must husband what little strength he had, 'I am pleased to meet a man I have admired so much.' As they walked to the mansion, followed by the plantation owners who had come to honor this champion of their cause, he paused from time to time, catching his breath, and in these intervals he allowed the slaveowners to congratulate him on his various stands in the Senate. Steed was touched to observe the love in which they held him.

It was nearly noontime when the assembly reached the mansion, but Calhoun wanted to start right in with meetings, so the men gathered in the main room while the women refreshed themselves. The men were barely seated when Calhoun startled Paul by saying abruptly:

'Steed, I want you to drop this nonsense about railroads. They're a northern invention calculated to woo the South away from her ancient virtues. You run a railroad down this peninsula, you turn good southern soil into northern shanties. The future of the South lies with agriculture and a stabilized slave economy.'

He said not another word about railroads, and before Steed could challenge this dismissal, the gaunt old man surveyed the assembled planters as if checking for loyalty. Then, satisfied that he spoke with friends, he stated his philosophy:

'We of the South face a grave crisis in the forthcoming session of Congress. Clay and Webster are plotting, I feel sure, to bring forth some monstrous omnibus bill which will give the North everything and the South nothing. We shall be stripped of our God-given rights. We shall be excluded from the territories. Texas will be cut in half solely because it's a slave state. There's talk of forbidding the sale of slaves in Washington. Demeaning to the nation's capital, they claim. On all fronts we're in retreat.'

When the slaveowners asked what they must do, he looked at each man with his flashing, deep-set eyes, then asked whether they were determined to protect their rights. In unison they replied, 'We are,' and he spread forth his program of defense:

> 'We must insist upon the right of taking our slaves with us into all the territories. We must keep Texas of maximum size. We must not surrender on Washington, for it is our capital, too. And above all, we must demand of Congress that it pass a fugitive slave law with teeth. If one of your slaves, or mine, runs away to the North, the full power of the federal government must be brought to bear upon that slave, and he must be returned to his rightful owner.'

Admiring discussion of this strategy ensued, with one planter after another lauding Calhoun for his clear vision, but he brushed aside the encomiums, shifted in his chair, and proceeded to the main body of his thought:

> 'I take my stand not as a southerner but as a man concerned with the destiny of my country. We're different from other nations. We're a minority, and the day will come when the other nations of the world will combine against us, simply because we are a minority dedicated to freedom while they rely on cruel oppression of their peoples. In those days a great philosophical debate will develop as to how the rights of a minority can be preserved against the overwhelming pressures of a majority. The United States will stand alone, gentlemen, and it will then confront the problem that we confront today. How can a righteous minority protect itself against the thoughtless tyranny of the majority?'

He spent a glowing half-hour developing this theme, that what the South faced in 1849, the entire nation would face in 1949. He was dazzling in the brilliance of his arguments, his marshaling of classical antecedents. He was the fiery protector of liberty, the man who saw the future almost as a revelation. Then he spread his trembling hands on the arms of his chair and said, 'There, gentlemen, is the problem on which we are engaged.'

Old Tiberius appeared at the door with news that dinner was spread, and the men trooped in to try the terrapin, the oysters and the venison. It was a relaxed, gracious meal in which politics arose only when one of the wives told the senator of the unfortunate affair with Postmaster Cater. 'All he was doing was protecting us from the filth spewed out from New York and Boston.'

'Did the good man find a job elsewhere?' Calhoun asked.

'Yes, in South Carolina.'

'We have always been the last refuge of free men,' Calhoun said.

The talks continued through the afternoon and all the next day. Calhoun let his listeners know that he felt the United States to be at a point of peril; there was a real possibility that the South might have to sever the Union because the North refused to respect its rights. And as he talked every man who listened realized that here was a senator who was wrestling in the closing days of his life with the most profound problems; he was a man who lived in a world different from theirs, in which facts impinged on concepts and concepts on the structure of national life. He lived at a degree of intensity that none of them could equal, and one planter from Dorchester County said, as he guided his sloop back across the Choptank, 'He's like a volcano that's been shooting fire so long, it's split its sides.'

When the guests were gone, Paul supposed that the tired old man would want to spend a couple of days in rest, but that was not Calhoun's style. 'Steed, you brought me only southerners, men and women already converted to our side. I'd like to meet some of your northern apologists. I need to know what they're thinking.'

'You mean now?'

'I mean this afternoon. When I return to Washington, if the House can ever organize, I enter a great debate on the future of this nation. I'd like to know what the ones on the other side are saying.'

'The only . . .' A daring idea flashed into Paul's mind. 'Senator, we have a family of Quakers just across . . .'

'Fetch them. I've never talked with Quakers.'

So a boat was dispatched to Peace Cliff, and at two that afternoon it returned with four Paxmores: George the boatbuilder; Elizabeth the quiet spokeswoman; young Bartley, afire with ideas; and Rachel, daughter of the avowed abolitionist Starbuck. They seemed very prim as they marched up the gravel path to the house they had not visited in many years, the women in gray and bonneted, the men in black with flat hats perched above their austere faces, but all four walked with an eagerness that pleased Calhoun. 'They look like early Christians in Rome, marching to the lions.' He laughed, then added, 'Well, today I'm their lion.'

In his thank-you letter to Steed, Calhoun would write: 'I have rarely met a woman who impressed me so favorably as your Elizabeth Paxmore. At first she seemed prudish and severe, but when I listened to her gentle explanations, so forcefully yet intelligently expressed, I found myself wishing that she were on our side. You said you rarely see this family. If you see Elizabeth, give her my regards.'

The session was memorable in that it occupied itself with only the most vibrant differences between the sections, as if all participants agreed that the afternoon was too precious to waste in trivialities:

CALHOUN: I think we can start best by agreeing that the Negro is an inferior human being, destined to serve the white man in a secondary capacity.

ELIZABETH: That I refuse to concede. I teach Negroes. Yes, against the law. But I do teach them, and I assure thee, Senator, they learn as rapidly as thy son.

CALHOUN: It grieves me to think that you put yourself outside the law, Mrs. Paxmore, as if you knew better than Congress.

RACHEL: On this we do know best.

CALHOUN: So young, so self-assured?

RACHEL: Tormented, Mr. Calhoun. I seem to know nothing these days except the inevitability of conflict.

CALHOUN: How old are you, ma'am?

RACHEL: Twenty-eight.

CALHOUN: You should be tending your babies. Now if, as I insist, the Negro is inferior, then the best process ever devised for handling him is slavery. It provides his freedom.

BARTLEY: How can a sane man think that?

CALHOUN: Because the finest minds since the beginning of time have thought it. Jesus Christ, Plato, George Washington. Slavery was devised by ancient wisdom and has never been improved upon.

BARTLEY: Is thee satisfied with the way it operates in South Carolina?

CALHOUN: It's the salvation of South Carolina, the basis of all our progress.

ELIZABETH: Does thee teach thy slaves to read the Bible?

CALHOUN: The slave requires no learning. The Bible must be interpreted for him. Is that not right, Steed?

ELIZABETH: Before Paul answers, I think I should warn thee that I know how he interprets the Bible when he reads to his slaves. 'Slaves, obey thy masters.'

CALHOUN: That's what the Bible says.

RACHEL: But it says so much more.

CALHOUN: And the unbridled teaching of that *more* will only unsettle the slaves, confuse them. We have learned, over the past two centuries, how best to handle Negroes. They're children, delightful children when they're not misled by some half-educated preacher like Nat Turner.

ELIZABETH: They are men and women, just as capable of comprehending the Bible as thee or I.

CALHOUN: There you are in error. I can look forward to the day, one hundred years from now, say 1949, when some kind of freedom may have been won by the Negro, but I assure you, Mrs. Paxmore, that on that day toward which you look, the Negro will not be free in his own mind. He will live not off the charity of the plantation but off the charity of the government. He will never be able to govern himself, or save money, or regulate his life. He will huddle in your cities and receive his charity, and be the slave he has always been.

ELIZABETH: Senator, he will be attending Harvard and Princeton, with thy grandchildren, and there will be scarce, if any, distinction between them.

CALHOUN: No black man will ever master enough knowledge to enter Yale, which I attended.

RACHEL: What about Frederick Douglass. Has thee read his book?

CALHOUN: Steed here has settled Douglass. Proved his book was written by white men.

RACHEL: Sir, does thee always ignore evidence that goes against thy prejudices?

CALHOUN (speaking to George): Do Quaker husbands . . . I've never met Quakers, before, you know. Do you always allow your women to carry the debate?

GEORGE: It's very difficult to halt them, sir. Especially when they're right.

CALHOUN: Do you agree with these women?

GEORGE: Totally.

CALHOUN: Then I fear we're in for dangerous times. Over the last two days I spoke with the plantation owners of this region. They agree with me heartily. Don't you see the conflict you're sponsoring? I was taught that Quakers love peace.

ELIZABETH: We do, and are constantly drawn away from it. By slavery.

CALHOUN: You know, of course, that in some states you could go to jail for teaching Negroes. Steed, you must be aware of that. (Before any of the Paxmores could respond, he abruptly changed the subject.) Have any of you read Mr. Steed's fine book on this subject?

RACHEL: We all have. Out of respect for a distinguished neighbor.

CALHOUN: And how did his impressive logic affect you?

RACHEL: As the mutterings of a good-hearted, totally confused gentleman, who will not know what happened when the hurricane strikes.

CALHOUN: Are you four abolitionists?

RACHEL: I am. The others—

CALHOUN: Please, young lady! Let them speak for themselves.

ELIZABETH: We do not categorize ourselves.

CALHOUN: But it was you who received through the mails the seditious literature.

ELIZABETH: Senator, freedom is not sedition.

CALHOUN: It is when it deprives Steed of his rightful property.

ELIZABETH: Paul Steed cannot own human beings.

CALHOUN: The law says he can. Congress says he can.

RACHEL: Then the law must be blown aside, the way winds of autumn blow the leaves away. Once they were green, and once they served a useful purpose, but now it's winter and they've fallen.

CALHOUN: Instruct me. If Congress passes a law with strong teeth, requiring citizens in all parts of the nation—I mean Boston and Philadelphia and Chicago . . . These citizens must by law return all runaway slaves to their rightful owners.

RACHEL: My God!

CALHOUN: You're not averse to taking the name of the Lord in vain.

RACHEL: Is thee contemplating such a law?

CALHOUN: It will be registered before this time next year. And what will you Paxmores do about it? I need to know.

GEORGE: We will resist it with every fiber in our bodies. I say that as a resident of Patamoke. Thee can imagine what it will be like in cities like Boston. The entire—

CALHOUN: Even if it's the law of the land?

GEORGE: If thee passes such a law, Senator, it dies of its own weight that afternoon.

CALHOUN: It will carry jail sentences for those who interfere.

GEORGE: Build very large jails, Senator.

CALHOUN: I understand this might shock certain . . . well, Quakers like yourselves. But with the passage of time?

GEORGE: Every day will intensify the resistance. I assure thee, Senator, thee cannot enforce such a law.

CALHOUN: Then you foresee what I see? The possibility of war between the sections?

RACHEL: We do.

CALHOUN: But I thought that Quakers . . .

ELIZABETH: Like thee, Senator. We live in confusion. We know of thy intense patriotism in 1812. And of thy strong Union sympathies in the years that followed. Thee was a different man, then.

CALHOUN: The intransigence of the North forced me to alter.

ELIZABETH: It must have been at terrible philosophical expense. (Calhoun shrugged his shoulders.)

GEORGE: It's been the same with us. Our family has invariably preached peace. But we had to go to war against the pirates. We had to build ships to fight the English in 1777. Our ships went back to war in 1814. And now we face an ever more terrifying possibility. It's not easy to be a Quaker, and I suppose it isn't easy to be a senator.

CALHOUN: You'll make no concessions?

RACHEL: None.

CALHOUN: You, young man. You haven't said much.

BARTLEY: I'm looking ahead. There isn't much I'd want to say. (He indicated that under these circumstances, with Paul Steed listening, he had better remain silent.)

CALHOUN: By this you want me to understand that you've already begun clandestine operations—the spiriting away of slaves belonging to other people.

BARTLEY: If a runaway comes to my door, I shall always assist him.

CALHOUN (to Elizabeth): Surely, if you follow the principles you've stated, you would not encourage runaways . . . or aid them?

ELIZABETH: My religion would not allow me to steal another man's property. But I would educate the slave so that he can gain his own freedom.

CALHOUN: I'm glad to hear someone who defends property.

RACHEL: Does thee really believe, Senator, that thee can perpetually hold millions of Negroes in chattel bondage?

CALHOUN: It's the law of nature, ma'am, and the law of this Union.

RACHEL: Then war is inescapable.

CALHOUN: Do you, the youngest person here, take it upon yourself to declare war?

RACHEL: No, sir. Thee did that.

CALHOUN: What do you mean?

RACHEL: When thee said that slavery was immutable.

CALHOUN: It is, my dear young lady. It's the law of God, the law of any reasonable man. The Negro must be kept, he must be guided, he must have his food and clothing provided by someone.

ELIZABETH: I can name one Negro right now who would be worthy of sitting with thee in the United States Senate.

CALHOUN: No such Negro exists or ever will. Tell me, Mr. Paxmore, how do you see the next decade developing?

GEORGE: I heard at my boatyard in Patamoke that when Daniel Webster was here . . .

CALHOUN: Did he visit you, Steed?

GEORGE: He's supposed to have said, in answer to a direct question, that he would support a fugitive slave law with real teeth. He said that. Daniel Webster.

CALHOUN: For once he showed good sense.

GEORGE: When I heard this I concluded that there would be such a law, and that it would result in warfare between the sections.

CALHOUN: Do you think the southern states will secede?

GEORGE: Everything thee has said today leads to secession.

CALHOUN: What could the South do, Mr. Paxmore, to alleviate the pressures that seem to be driving all of us in that direction?

RACHEL (whose intrusion irritated the Senator): Offer a plan for the assured liberation of all slaves. Not immediately, perhaps, but certain.

CALHOUN: I take it you read *The Liberator*.

RACHEL: When the postmaster allows me to have a copy.

CALHOUN: Which is not often, I pray. So you want us to surrender our property? Throw away the fruit of our labors? Steed here has nine hundred slaves, which he has paid for in the sweat of his brow. All of them to go?

RACHEL: There can be no lasting peace until they do.

CALHOUN: And go to what? To freedom as you and I know it? Never. If they ever do go, which God forbid, it will be to a new definition of slavery—deprivation, ignorance, charity in some new form. (Here he paused. Then he addressed Elizabeth.) If you know so much about the wrestlings of the Quaker conscience with the problem of war, then you must also know how assiduous a minority must always be in defending its rights. By and large, the people of this nation have not liked Quakers. Their pacifism in 1812 when we were striving to protect this Union irritated me considerably. But you have persisted because you knew that a prudent minority must defend itself against the tyranny of a majority. Isn't that right?

GEORGE: We have endeavored to exist without irritating others. That may have been our strength.

CALHOUN: Precisely. The South is a minority striving to defend its rights. Because we have controlled the Senate, we've been able to do so. And I can see a time coming when the United States will be a minority among nations, and on that day it will use every device that the South uses now to protect its rights to existence. I fight for the future, Mr. Paxmore. I have a vision which—

RACHEL: Does it include perpetual slavery for the black man?

CALHOUN: The Negro will always be in slavery. I prefer the southern version to that which those at the North will impose.

They ate an early evening meal, listened to the bitter winds blowing in from the Chesapeake, and went to bed. In the morning everyone assembled at the wharf as John Calhoun departed for the Senate, and the great battles which loomed there, and his impending death. As the dark coat and the bushy head disappeared into the cabin, Rachel Starbuck Paxmore said, 'One of the finest this nation has produced, and wrong in everything.'

No authoritative copy of the odious legislation reached Patamoke until the first week in October 1850, but when it arrived by packet from Baltimore for posting at the courthouse, everyone could see what Daniel Webster had done. George Paxmore, at the boatyard, refused comment until he had a chance to discuss the new law with his wife. At noon he left his desk in charge of his workmen, most of whom favored the bill, and sailed home to Peace Cliff, where he assembled his family in the kitchen.

'They've passed something even worse than we had imagined,' he reported, taking out the notebook on which he had scribbled the main features of the bill.

'Is it law?' Rachel asked.

'The law of the nation. Any slaveholder can go anywhere in the United States and recover whatever black man or woman he claims to be a runaway.'

'Even to cities like Boston?'

'Everywhere. States, territories, District of Columbia. Or land not yet a territory. All he has to do is state that the Negro is his, and his claim is established. The black man cannot testify on his own behalf. He cannot summon other witnesses.'

'What can he do?'

'He can listen attentively as the judge delivers the sentence returning him to slavery. Even manumitted men and women can be dragged back. Every United States marshal is charged with enforcing the law. And a new horror has been introduced. Every citizen must, on pain of going to jail, assist the marshal in capturing the runaway, or arresting the freedman, if the marshal orders him.'

'Such a law is unthinkable,' Elizabeth said, shaking her head in disbelief as she sat by the stove, hands folded.

'It's obviously not unthinkable,' her husband said with unusual anger. 'They've passed it. But we can make it unworkable.'

'George! We must not be hasty,' Elizabeth said. 'We must pray for counsel.'

'What did thee have in mind?' Bartley asked his father.

'We shall oppose it,' Rachel interrupted. 'With every power we command, we shall oppose it.'

'That we shall,' George said, his white hair quivering as his body tensed.

'I think we should pray,' Elizabeth said, and for some minutes they sat in silence, after which she said, 'I must exact a promise from each of thee. There will be no violence. We cannot solve this problem with violence.'

'But if a slave runs to our door, surely thee will help him escape?' Rachel asked.

'I will not deprive another man of his lawful property.'

'But will thee step aside while Bartley and I . . .'

To this, Elizabeth agreed, and their home became a haven for the oppressed. Even in the Deep South word was passed: 'You get Choptank, high white bank, Paxmores.' If the slave could reach here, Bartley and Rachel would somehow spirit him to the Starbucks, where young Comly would lead him north to Pennsylvania.

The attitudes of the five Quakers involved in this escape route varied. Elizabeth, the tireless woman who had been fighting slavery for half a century, believed that moral suasion was sufficient; she would teach slaves at considerable risk to herself; she would feed them at her expense; she would clothe them with shirts she had sewn; and she would medicine them and bind their wounds. But she would not encourage them to quit their masters, for that was deprivation of a legal right. She remained what she had always been: the quiet, traditional Quakeress, the teacher, friend and comforter, but no more.

George Paxmore would always contribute money; he would hide fugitives; and on occasion he would himself guide them to the Starbucks'. But he abhorred violence and would not even stay overnight with the robust Starbucks, who did not.

Bartley Paxmore, at thirty-one, was the new-style Quaker, engaged actively in fighting slavery and willing to take great risks with either his own life or that of fugitives. He was excessively daring and had pieced together an escape route right up the peninsula through the heart of the Refuge plantations. He had already made seven trips to the Starbucks' and supposed that he would be making more, but like his father, he eschewed violence and would not go armed.

His wife Rachel was quite different. Like all the Starbucks, she saw slavery as the ultimate abomination and would make no concessions. If a slaveowner were to overtake her while she was leading slaves north, she would kill him; consequently, Bartley never allowed her to slip into dangerous situations. She was the goader, the encourager, the unfailing enemy of the slave-catcher, and it was often her unalloyed courage which gave escapees heart to try the last ten miles to the border.

Comly Starbuck not only refused to reject violence, he expected it, and was always prepared to fight his way clear if slave-catchers moved in. He was a sturdy young man, larger and stronger than Bartley, and dedicated to quite different ends: 'When the South secedes, as it will, there must be a vast uprising of the slaves. Then we will tie this evil into knots.' He expected one day to enlist in a northern army.

The principal opponents of the liberationists fell into three groups. There were the big plantation owners whose wealth was tied up in Negroes and who could always be counted upon to finance a chase. They were not brutal men, but they were deeply perplexed as to why a gang of northern agitators should be so bent upon depriving them of their lawful property. They wanted peace with the North, wanted trade to continue and multiply. The more prudent saw that as the United States stretched westward, the non-slave states must one day outnumber the slave by a large margin, and when that time came they wanted their inherited rights to be respected. On every subject except slavery they were reasonable men; like Paul Steed, their spokesman, they believed that for all men to be free, black men had to accept slavery.

At the bottom of the pro-slavery men were the professional trackers like Lafe Turlock with his dogs and Herman Cline with his rawhide.

They hated blacks. There were not many like these two, but every town on the Eastern Shore provided its quota. One of the easiest recreations to organize along the salty rivers was a nigger chase.

In between stood the majority, a group difficult to decipher. They were white; they owned little land or other forms of wealth; few had slaves, and then only one or two. But they had been convinced by southern philosophers that their welfare depended upon the perpetuation of slavery, and they took it unkindly when folks at the North spoke ill of their peculiar institution. They were motivated not by a fear of slaves but by their dislike of freed blacks, whom they saw as shiftless, undisciplined and profligate. One farmer spoke for all when he said, 'With a slave who knows his place I got no quarrel, but I cannot abide a freed nigger who can read. He means trouble.'

This middle group was shocked when people actually living in the South, like the Paxmores, spoke against slavery and rejoiced when blacks escaped. These people did not hire themselves out as slave-catchers, but if a chase developed, they joined, and when the slave was treed and the dogs were barking, they derived as much enjoyment as when a raccoon was trapped. But if anyone suggested that the Eastern Shore might have to quit the Union in defense of slavery, these men and women grew reflective and said, 'We stand with Daniel Webster. The Union must be preserved.'

In the 1850s, following the passage of the Fugitive Slave Act under the sponsorship of Senators Clay and Webster—Calhoun felt it was not stringent enough—a subtle, undeclared war erupted between the slave-owners and the enemies of the peculiar institution. It was fought incessantly; a slave would run away from some plantation in South Dorchester, make his way to the Choptank, know from secret instructions where the Paxmores lived, and at dead of night cross the broad river, go ashore at the foot of the white cliffs showing gray in the moonlight, and climb to the kitchen door.

In later years white men and women would often ask incredulously: Why did the blacks accept slavery? In the decade from 1851 to the end of 1860, some two thousand made their way up the Eastern Shore, fighting against incalculable odds, trying to beat their way to freedom. An old woman in her seventies would say some morning. 'I gonna die free.' And off she would go. Children would be told in awesome tones, 'You make one sound, we all gonna be killed.' They died in swamps; they drowned in rivers; they were hanged from trees; they were burned at stakes. But on they came, and some stopped briefly at the Paxmores'.

For the second time in history a Turlock was learning to read. Young Jake, eleven years old, was getting up each morning, washing his face at the bench behind the cabin at the edge of town, and trooping off to school. The existence of this academy, and especially the presence of its remarkable teacher, was one of those accidents which alter the face of history—not big history, like wars and elections, but the little history of a town like Patamoke or a river like the Choptank.

Paul Steed had become more and more a man of powerful character, and despite the infuriating indifference of the federal government, he persisted in believing that a railroad could be built down the spine of the peninsula, but he wondered how, when the work began, the construction companies would find enough skilled labor to build the tracks. Slaves with mules could do the grading, but it would require a lot more than slaves to do the actual building.

His problem was solved when the Baltimore newspapers began running stories about the famine in Ireland and of the forced exodus from that starving land. One night in his study he told Susan, 'Damn! We could sail to Ireland and pick up a thousand men!' He became so excited by the prospect that he could not sleep. After they retired, she heard him roaming up and down all night, talking to himself.

In the morning he boarded one of his ships loading wheat, ordered the captain to be ready to sail at noon, regardless of cargo, and by nightfall was at the mouth of the Chesapeake, having left behind orders that huts be erected in Patamoke to receive the immigrants he would import.

When he landed at Cork he saw a sight which would haunt him for the rest of his days: lines of families near death from starvation waiting hopelessly for food, or transportation to anywhere. 'They'd sail to the ports of hell,' the English dockmaster told Steed.

'I could find places for three hundred men.'

'Must take families.'

'I didn't want women and children.'

'Nobody does, but if you leave them behind, they die.'

So Paul stood at the foot of the gangplank and watched as seventy-seven families came past him, glassy-eyed and with an appalling number of emaciated children. He tried to choose families with grown sons, but the dockmaster did not allow much selection, and in the end Steed had a conglomerate mix of some men who might possibly build a railroad and many dependents who might possibly survive on what their fathers were able to earn.

'Home fast!' Steed told his captain, and when the ship had weighed anchor he started his duties as head feeder of the starving. He worked in the kitchens twelve and fifteen hours a day, helping to prepare food and devising ways of doling it out in proper portions so that no one gorged himself to death. His limp and his twisted neck became the Irishmen's symbol of salvation, and when Sunday came, he organized prayer services for the three hundred and seven Catholics he was importing to his homeland.

There was no priest aboard, and Steed was reluctant to lead devotions, but he did find a glib-tongued spindle of a man named Michael Caveny to whom praying was as natural as cursing:

'Almighty God, who sent His plague to Egypt and His famine among the Hebrews, so that the earth trembled with punishment, we know that Thou didst also send the years of plenty so that Thy people flourished. By Thy grace are we embarked upon this holy vessel which will carry us to paradise undreamed of where food is plentiful and where our children can romp in green pastures without fear of want.'

On and on he prayed, a mellifluous outpouring of imagery and biblical fragments, so filled with hope that Steed could hear sobs from every part of the crowded deck. At the peroration, in which God and babies and lambs and feasts of thanksgiving intermingled, Paul found himself wiping his eyes, and that day released double portions of food.

Michael Caveny—his name had originally been Cavanaugh, but centuries of abbreviation had shortened it to its present musical form—was an uncommon man. At thirty-nine, with three children, he had known the torment of hunger but never despair. He had done things to feed his children which in later years he would erase from memory, not wishing to saddle his family with such images, and he had forced them to survive in conditions which had exterminated scores of his neighbors.

He was a lyrical man to whom the slightest manifestation of nature became justification for protracted prose poems: 'Look at the fish flying through the air! God sends them aloft with a song, and the Devil pulls them back into his hot frying pan.' The more Steed saw of this man the more he liked him, and by the time the ship reached Patamoke, Michael Caveny had been designated foreman of the railroad crew.

This proved an empty honor, for there was no railroad. The nation was too preoccupied with building really important lines to the West to allocate any funds for an inconsequential line down the Delmarva Peninsula, as it had been aptly named from the first syllables of the three states which shared it. The railroad did not reach Chicago until 1853, and it had to probe south, too, for despite the apprehension of Senator Calhoun that it might bring northern heresy with it, merchants of the South insisted that they, too, have iron tracks on which to move their goods. So once again the Eastern Shore was ignored. But this was not all loss, for in the resulting isolation, it was able to confirm and deepen its unique patterns of life.

The decision not to build left Paul Steed with his horde of unemployed Irish Catholics crowded into a block of hovels along the northern edge of town. They had no priest, no occupation, no savings, and only such clothing as the plantation owners in the area could provide, but within weeks it was astonishing how many of them found jobs. Eleven left town to become overseers; they became famous for two characteristics: they kept an eye out for the prettiest slave girls, and periodically they went on titanic drunks, but they were basically good men, and when they were fired from one plantation they quickly found jobs on another—'McFee swears he'll stay sober this time, and I think we ought to give him a chance.'

Paul Steed, of course, offered Michael Caveny a good job at Devon, but to his surprise, the doughty little Irishman refused. 'I have a feeling, Mr. Steed, that St. Matthew himself would be honored to work for you, but my place is in town, with my people. We've to build a church and find ourselves a priest, and I've the little ones to think about.'

'You've already done wonders with them.'

'Ah, truer words were never spoken, Mr. Steed, but now I'm pondering their education. Patamoke school needs a teacher and I'm of a mind to apply.' Steed warned him that local Methodists might be reluctant to hire a Catholic, but Caveny said sweetly, 'True as the word of God, but I'm sure you'll be giving me a fine recommendation.' And that was how young Jake Turlock awoke one morning with orders to report to Teacher Caveny.

'If'n them Papist kids kin learn to read,' his Grandfather Lafe said, 'so kin you.'

The instruction which Jake would remember longest came not in reading but in geography. Mr. Caveny had acquired fifteen copies of a splendid little book called *A Modern Geography,* published in New York City in 1835. It had been compiled by a Professor Olney, M.A., and it summarized the latest information on the world, with engaging woodcuts illustrating how a tiger eats a man in India or malamutes haul sledges in Siberia.

The most valuable contribution appeared on the last page of each section, in a paragraph captioned *Character,* for here, in a few solid words, Professor Olney told the students what they might expect of the inhabitants of each country. Professor Olney, himself of British extraction, reminded the students of what their ancestors had been like:

English: Intelligent, brave, industrious and enterprising.

Scots: Temperate, industrious, hardy and enterprising. Distinguished for their general education and morality.

Welsh: Passionate, honest, brave and hospitable.

Jake recognized that these favorable terms described the people he knew in Patamoke, and when he recited the descriptions to his grandfather,

Lafe growled, 'That professor knows what he's talkin' about.' However, when Olney had to deal with non-British peoples, especially those with Catholic backgrounds, he was more severe:

Irish: Quick of apprehension, active, brave and hospitable. But passionate, ignorant, vain and superstitious.

Spanish: Temperate, grave, polite and faithful to their word. But ignorant, proud, superstitious and revengeful.

Italians: Affable and polite. Excel in music, painting and sculpture. But effeminate, superstitious, slavish and revengeful.

Jake saw nothing in these descriptions to complain of. Certainly, the Irish living on the north edge of town were passionate, ignorant and hospitable, but Mr. Caveny took a different view. 'I want each boy to take his pen and line out the words after *Irish,* because the writer knew very little of his subject. Write in "Witty, devout, generous to a fault, quick of mind, faithful to the death. But violent-tempered, especially when mistreated by the English." ' For the Italians and the Spaniards, no corrections were needed. But it was when Olney reached the lesser breeds that he really unloosed his venom:

Arabs: Ignorant, savage and barbarous. Those on the coast are *pirates;* those in the interior are *robbers.*

Persians: Polite, gay, polished and hospitable. But indolent, vain, avaricious and treacherous.

Hindoos: Indolent, spiritless and superstitious. Mild and servile to superiors, haughty and cruel to inferiors.

Siberians: Ignorant, filthy and barbarous.

Mr. Caveny required his students to memorize these perceptive summaries, and in each examination he would pose some question like this: 'Compare an Englishman with a Siberian.' And Jake would respond, 'Englishmen are brave, intelligent, industrious and generous, but Siberians are ignorant, filthy and barbarous.' He had never seen a Siberian, of course, but he felt certain that he would recognize one if he ever got to Siberia. They rode in sledges pulled by dogs.

In his book Professor Olney did not characterize Negroes who lived in America, but of those who remained in Africa he said succinctly, 'An ignorant, filthy and stupid people.' Mr. Caveny said, 'While that description is certainly true of Africa, it would be desirable for us to construct our own description of the Negroes here in Patamoke,' and on his blackboard he wrote down those words which the boys contributed as describing the blacks they knew; henceforth in any examination when Caveny asked his students, 'What is the character of the Negro?' Jake and the others were expected to frame their answers from this description:

Negroes: Lazy, superstitious, revengeful, stupid, irresponsible. Apt to run away, but they love to sing.

For as long as Mr. Caveny's pupils lived they would think of the British Turlocks as brave, honest, hospitable, industrious, temperate, hardy and enterprising, and the black Caters as beyond redemption, except for their ability to sing.

The town of Patamoke had now assumed its final shape. Everything centered on the harbor, which provided not only a good anchorage for ships but also a focus for all life within the town, now composed of 1,836 citizens. Businesses lined the north rim of the harbor. On the street behind this thoroughfare stood three impressive governmental buildings —the courthouse, the jail and, in between, the new slave market, a spacious area covered with a roof but not walled in along the sides.

Along the eastern edge of the harbor stood the rambling buildings of the Paxmore Boatyard, and to the west, as so often happened in American towns, gathered the better residential homes; the combination of a grand view of the river and the clean breezes from the south made this area desirable, and here the white owners of the town lived. In between were the small houses of the artisans, the mariners, the retired farmers and the boardinghouse keepers.

These major dispositions had been agreed upon more than a century ago; what made Patamoke of 1855 different was that two new vital elements had been added. To the north, beyond the business district, the Irish families clustered, and they had had either the gall or the gumption to build for themselves a rather large Catholic church, in which services were conducted by a flamboyant priest from Dublin. As several towns-men observed, 'In the old days Catholics were gentlemen who dined with candlelight on Devon Island. Now they're real people, and very noisy.' The Steeds viewed this new development not with outright distaste, but with a large degree of bewilderment. None of the family was easy with the brash young priest, for he preached a Catholicism quite strange to those whose forebears hobnobbed with the Lords Baltimore.

The other innovation stood on a marshy point east of the boatyard, where a collection of cabins and shanties had grown up. It was called Frog's Neck and was occupied principally by freed blacks, with a few lean-tos for the slaves who were hired out by the day to businesses in Patamoke. Sometimes a man or woman would work away from the home plantation for two or three years at a time, never seeing a salary, which was paid directly to the owner. However, if an enlightened owner like Paul Steed rented out one of the Devon slaves, he saw to it that the slave received part of his wage, and several had earned enough in this way to purchase their freedom. There was formal contact between the black area and the boatyard, some with the business section, quite a lot with the residential area in which many of the slaves worked, but absolutely none with the Irish district.

There was, of course, a final area, but it was not delineated. Its inhabitants lived where they could, some with the Irish, some in shacks within the business district and some with the blacks. These were the poor white trash. There were forty-one Turlocks scattered about Patamoke and no one could unscramble the relationships that existed among them.

It was a good town, and during those very years when extreme passions excited the rest of the nation it flourished in peace. A pragmatic harmony infused the place, accountable in major part to the exemplary behavior of its two principal citizens. Paul Steed ran a good plantation at Devon and a better store in Patamoke; he gave employment to many of the Irish and good prices to all. He was firm in his support of slavery as a principle and of the Whig Party as the salvation of the country, but most of all he was a force for balance. When in town over the weekends he attended Mass, sitting alone in the second row of benches, an austere, proper little man with his head cocked to one side as if he were weighing what the priest said.

The other leader, George Paxmore, was an old man now, straight and white-haired at seventy-two. He no longer worked at the boatyard on a daily basis, but he did come in from Peace Cliff now and then to satisfy himself that the building of ships was progressing in an orderly manner. At the yard he tended to employ blacks rather than Irishmen, but he had helped the latter substantially in building their church and he subscribed generously to any collections they made for their many charities. He deplored their drinking, envied their lightness of heart. It was he who arranged for Michael Caveny to become town constable, and never regretted this act, for Caveny proved himself to be a rough-and-ready character who preferred to talk a man into proper behavior rather than use a gun—'Sure, a man like you who beats his wife should grow a larger beard, Mr. Simpson, for how dare he look at his face in a mirror?'

The settled relationships of this little town were shattered one hot afternoon when T.T. Arbigost, in his white linen suit and silver toothpick, drifted into the harbor aboard a dirty steamer from Baltimore, unloading seventeen slaves, whom he stowed in the pens at the market.

This done, he brushed himself off, looked contemptuously at the miserable ship he had left, and dispatched information to Devon Island that he had acquired a fine lot of primes from the plantations of southern Maryland.

Since the Steed plantations could always use more hands, Paul sailed to Patamoke prepared to buy the lot, but when he inspected them they appeared to be in such excellent condition that he could not fathom why Arbigost had brought them here rather than to the more profitable markets in Louisiana.

'Well, yes,' the unctuous dealer agreed, rocking back and forth in his chair at the market. 'That's the penetrating kind of question I'd ask if I came upon fine specimens like this.' With his riding crop he pointed casually at the blacks standing in the pens.

'No doubt they've proved intractable,' Steed suggested.

'There you're wrong!' Arbigost said with an ingratiating smile. 'Would I risk a trip across the bay in that . . .' With his toothpick he indicated the ship.

'What's your secret?'

'Money, Mr. Steed. Plain, ordinary money.'

'You'd get more in Louisiana.'

'And lose it on the cost of the trip. Mr. Steed, wherever I went in Baltimore they told me, "Steed of Devon, he needs slaves." You're well known, sir.'

Paul wanted to make the purchase, but when he inspected the men he could not accept the testimony standing before him. 'These are intractable men that you've smuggled in from Georgia.'

'Mr. Steed!' the wily dealer protested, and cleverly he evaded the matter of provenance, concentrating on the question of tractability, and it was what he finally said in pursuit of this strategy that inflamed Patamoke. 'Have I ever in my life sold you a recalcitrant nigger?' He paused dramatically to allow Steed time to acknowledge his exemplary behavior, then revealed an additional bit of evidence in his favor. 'Remember when I sold your Mr. Beasley that fine Xanga who answered to the name of Cudjo and was so good at machinery? Mr. Beasley had identical doubts about the Xanga, but I assured him then, as I assure you now, that Cudjo was broken . . . that he would prove to be a good slave.' He smiled, poked Paul on the wrist with his toothpick, and added, 'What I didn't tell Mr. Beasley then, because there was no need for him to know, was that it was this very Cudjo who led that famous mutiny aboard the *Ariel.* Remember?'

'The *Ariel?*'

Mr. Arbigost nodded. 'Bloody affair. Entire ship taken.'

Steed sat heavily upon the block from which the slaves would be auctioned if he did not buy them at private treaty. 'That ship was built

here. The dead captain was from this town.' It was incredible! Cudjo
Cater had led that mutiny, and Paul Steed had set him free.

'But didn't he turn out to be an excellent slave?' Mr. Arbigost whee-
dled. 'And I promise you, Steed, these men will prove the same, because
on my farm we have ways of training slaves.'

Paul wanted to run away from this insidious man in his prim, high-
buttoned suit, but he needed slaves, and now Mr. Arbigost shifted his
silver toothpick to the corner of his mouth and made a striking offer: 'We
could haggle over individual men—up this, down that—but as gentlemen that would be unsavory. For a flat twenty-one hundred dollars each
they're yours.'

After the slaves had been marked for shipment to the far plantations,
Steed warned Arbigost that it would be prudent if nothing was said about
Cudjo and the *Ariel.*

'I've already told the men handling the slaves.'

'Then we're in for trouble,' Steed said, and he decided not to return
to Devon but to sleep in Patamoke. He was at the house adjoining the
store when Lafe Turlock, accompanied by his five sons, grown men now,
stormed up to the door, demanding to see him.

Lafe was an old man, bent of shoulder and slack of jaw, but he had
the marsh fire. 'Steed, they tell me it was yore nigger Cudjo that took
the *Ariel.*'

'So Mr. Arbigost reports.'

'We're gonna hang him. He killed my cousin Matt.'

'Why are you telling me?'

'Because we want you to come along. Hold back the constable.'

'I think Mr. Caveny will do his duty.'

'We think so, too, and we don't want no trouble.'

'Aren't you threatening to cause a good deal of trouble?'

'All we're gonna do is hang a nigger. We ain't gonna rile up the
community.'

'I should think that would rile the community considerably.'

'Not when we tell 'em what he done.'

Paul retreated into his house and asked the Turlocks to join him.
Going into the kitchen, he whispered to his serving girl to run and tell
Mr. Paxmore and Cudjo Cater what was afoot. Then he returned to talk
with the Turlocks. He accomplished nothing. Lafe insisted that he would
personally tie the rope about Cudjo's neck, and the boys urged him on.

So the meeting broke up, with Steed refusing to join the lynching
party. When he last saw the gang of six they were fanning out across the
community to assemble their mob.

Paul thought for some minutes as to what he must do, and in the end
decided to seek Mr. Caveny. The constable had been alerted to the
Turlock uprising and instantly recognized that here was the first test of

his power in this town. To him the *Ariel* was merely another ship, the mutiny a trivial incident far less significant than the starvation he had seen in Ireland. He calculated that most of the citizens of Patamoke would feel the same way and that he would be allowed a relatively free hand in dealing with this rambunctious family.

But when Mr. Steed arrived, obviously frightened, the planter's anxiety infected the constable. Then Mr. Paxmore walked in, tall and quiet. 'We want no riots,' he said. 'Mr. Caveny, is thee prepared to defuse this mob?'

'It's only six,' Caveny said.

'There will be more,' Paxmore said. 'We'd better go out to Frog's Neck.'

So the three men walked slowly and without visible agitation through the streets from the jail to the marshy point, and there they found that all the blacks had fled except Eden and Cudjo Cater.

'We stayin',' Eden said as the three white men approached.

'Thee must show no weapons,' Mr. Paxmore warned.

'We stayin',' the black woman said, and it appeared from her manner that she was well armed. Cudjo said nothing, just stood by the door of his cabin.

'Were you aboard the *Ariel?'* Steed asked.

'I be.'

'Oh, my God!' Steed shook his head. This was going to be a bad night.

Then the Turlocks appeared, and it seemed as if half the town sided with this wild family. But as they came nearer, Paul saw something which enraged him even more. Marching in front, side by side with Lafe Turlock, was Mr. Arbigost, who obviously felt that the disciplining of blacks anywhere, anytime, was his concern.

'Arbigost!' Steed shouted. 'What in hell . . .'

'We want that nigger,' Lafe roared, but Mr. Steed ignored him. 'Arbigost! What are you doing with these men?'

And now the heat of the evening was diverted from Turlock to the stranger in the white suit, and a brief, impassioned dialogue took place, during which tempers had a chance to subside.

'Gentlemen!' Mr. Caveny said when the first exchange ended. 'Sure, it would be a shame to spoil a summer's evenin' like this. I'm proposin' we all go back to town and have free drinks on Mr. Steed.'

'I want that nigger.'

'Lafe,' Mr. Steed said. 'That was a long time ago. Cudjo has proved himself—'

'I'm gonna hang that nigger, what he done to my cousin Matt.'

It was the utterance of this great name that terminated the riot, for when it was spoken, all turned to stare at Paul Steed, and many in the crowd recalled his shame. Captain Matt, that big, brawling redhead who had once tossed Steed into the harbor.

Steed, well able to guess what the would-be rioters were thinking, took Lafe by the arm, turned him around and said quietly, 'Why don't we all go to the store for a drink?'

When the mob receded, Eden went back into the cabin, took the knife from her bosom, the revolver from her dress, and with no display of emotion, placed them on the table. When Cudjo saw them he was terrified by what might have happened, and he sought to sweep them away, but Eden covered them with her arms.

It was in March 1857, when it seemed to everyone in America that the compromise worked out by Henry Clay and Daniel Webster before they died was going to save the nation—everyone, that is, except the bull-headed abolitionists, who would accept nothing less than the shattering of the Union—that Chief Justice Roger Brooke Taney, a Maryland man, read a decision in the Supreme Court which destroyed the shaky edifice behind which the conciliators had been working. In simple, incontrovertible terms the learned Chief Justice, one of the strongest men ever to serve on the court, spelled out the future.

The case, like all those which make significant law, was muddled. This slave Scott, had been born in a slave state, carried into a free one, then carried into a territory where slavery was prohibited, back into a state where it was permitted, and finally into Massachusetts, where slaves were automatically free. What was his status? The court could logically have decided almost anything.

Chief Justice Taney and his associates found an easy, if evasive, escape; they announced that since Dred Scott was black, he was not a citizen of the United States and had no right to defend himself in a federal court. His status reverted to what it had been three decades earlier. He was born a slave and must remain so through life.

If Taney had let the matter drop there, he would merely have deprived one Negro of his freedom, but the old fire-eater had been at the heart of political strife all his eighty years, and it was against his character to hide. He decided to grapple with the most explosive issue of his age. He would settle once and for all this pernicious problem of slavery. Backed by Justices who themselves owned slaves, as his family always had, the old man threw into his basic decision a group of obiter dicta which startled the nation: no arm of government anywhere within the United States could deprive an owner of his lawful property; the Missouri Compromise was void; Congress could not prevent slavery in the territories; and individual states were powerless to set black men free.

When the decision reached the Choptank the plantation owners were delighted; all that they had ever wanted from the federal government they now had, and it seemed to men like Paul Steed that divisive argument must cease. At the Steed stores throughout the region he posted copies of the decision and told his overseers, 'Now we can fight the runaway problem with a real weapon. Explain to your slaves that even if they do happen to escape for a few days, they must eventually be returned. The problem is settled for all time and we can go forward with our work.'

The middle group of citizens was pleased with the decision; it would end strife. The Irish were unconcerned. And freed Negroes, such as Eden and Cudjo Cater, realized that they must walk very carefully indeed, for at any moment someone might claim them as slaves, produce spurious documents in court and whisk them away to some cotton plantation. Eden checked her manumission papers, but she checked her guns and knives more carefully.

It was the Paxmores who were shattered by this extraordinary decision, and when they received a copy they came upon that amazing passage in which Chief Justice Taney wrote:

> Slaves have for more than a century been regarded as beings of an inferior order, so far inferior that they had no rights which the white man was bound to respect.

When George Paxmore heard these awful words, he bowed his white head and could think of no way to contradict them. Twice he started to speak, but it was useless. If the highest court in the nation judged that a black man possessed no rights which a white man had to respect, there was no hope for this country. It must subside into barbarism.

Rachel Starbuck Paxmore led the fight against the Dred Scott Decision. Wherever she went she preached against its inhumanity. She rose in meeting and harangued those Quakers who had assumed that with the earlier compromise, some kind of peace had been attained. She argued with customers in Steed's store. She wrote letters. She quoted Taney's pernicious words as proof that the Union must soon be dissolved—'We cannot abide such theories. Men and women of good conscience must rise up and shatter them.'

And the sad aspect of her crusade was that Chief Justice Taney never said those words. He merely quoted them as opinions of a former generation, but when this correction was pointed out to Rachel, she snorted: 'He may not have said them, but he wrote his decision in consonance with them.'

In October of that year she found her chance to rebut the Dred Scott Decision. She was seated at home, on Peace Cliff, with her husband and the older Paxmores. They had been reading together some writings of Horace Greeley, from New York, and George Paxmore was finding cause for hope in his reports. 'Greeley thinks there's a subsidence of passion.' And Elizabeth said quietly, 'I should certainly hope so.'

Rachel was about to turn down the lamps and lead the group to bed when a knock came at the door. Without speaking, she returned the lamp she was carrying to its table, carefully turned up the wick, then told the others, 'We have work to do.'

When she boldly opened the door, she found such work as the Paxmores had never faced before. There stood nine huge black men, looming in the darkness. 'We is from Cline's,' the spokesman said, and when Elizabeth saw his lacerated and bleeding back she gave a weak cry and fainted.

'I di'n mean to scare her,' the wounded black started to say, but Rachel took him by the arm and motioned him into the house. With her elbow she indicated that George should tend his prostrate wife; then she led the other eight massive slaves into the kitchen. They filled the room and looked with dismay at the fallen woman; she was old and frail, but when she was revived she steadied herself at the table and with a weak hand turned the first black around so that she could inspect his scarred back.

'Dear God,' she whispered. 'We must get these men to freedom.' All her life she had been opposed to abetting runaways; her religious principles told her that slavery could be eradicated by slow persuasion. She had been willing to teach and encourage and help; now, at her first sight of a truly beaten slave, she moved to new understandings.

'We not stand no more,' the lead-slave said.

'Thee didn't kill him?' George asked cautiously.

'No matter,' Elizabeth said sharply, and with that, she began moving about the kitchen, preparing food. As the slaves gorged themselves, she hurried upstairs to gather together the clothes Rachel had been collecting for such an emergency.

'We goin' north,' one of the slaves said.

'Of course you are,' Rachel said, 'but how?' Nine big men! How could they slip past the guards who prowled the highways?

It was Bartley who came up with the plan, and he did so with such quiet authority that he convinced everyone it would work. 'Clearly, we can't sneak so many past the watchers. And we can't risk holding them here and slipping them through one at a time. So what we'll do is this. Rachel, get thy brother Comly and hurry to Philadelphia to arrange for our arrival. George, slip into town and have Parrish print up an announcement for an auction. Patamoke slave market. Describe these nine men and Eden Cater.'

'Why Eden?' his father asked.

'Because I'm going to drive these men north as my property. Openly. Purchased at public auction, as the bill of sale will say. I'm taking them to my plantation on the Sassafras, and if a woman is moving with us, it will look more natural.'

'Thee will have to leave tonight,' Rachel warned. 'Cline will be after thee.'

'Mr. Cline, he think we cross de bay,' the lead-slave said. 'Cline follow our tracks, he in Virginia.'

This false lead gave Bartley's stratagem a frail chance. Before dawn Rachel was on her way to the Starbucks' and George was sailing to Patamoke to get the printing done. Bartley said that he would bed the slaves down in the woods behind the house, but his mother would not allow him to remove the wounded man before she had poulticed his bleeding back. The big man lay on the floor and she knelt to cleanse the wounds, a white-haired old lady of seventy-three morally outraged by the fundamental savagery of a system she had thought she understood.

In Patamoke her husband found the Quaker printer John Parrish and confided the family's plan. Working feverishly, Parrish set type for a public auction presumed to have been held in this town four days ago. He used a woodcut of a male slave resting on a hoe. The seller was T.T. Arbigost of Georgia, and among the slaves was an older female answering to the name of Bessie, and she was described in some detail.

While this handbill was being printed, and a bill of sale filled out, George moved quietly to the Cater cabin, knocked politely and waited for Cudjo to open the door a crack. 'Cline's slaves have run away.'

Cudjo said nothing, but the powerful muscles in his neck tightened. He listened as Paxmore explained his son's proposal, then said enthusiastically, 'Eden come home tonight, we both go.'

'No. Bartley fears that would be too conspicuous. Someone would notice thy absence. Thee must be here when Cline comes through, two or three days from now.'

Again Cudjo said nothing, but Paxmore could see his hands clenching. 'Dear friend, thee must not touch Mr. Cline. Our task is to get his slaves to Pennsylvania.'

'You want Eden come to Peace Cliff?'

'Immediately.'

'She be there. Them slaves, they reach Pennsylvania.'

So the expedition was readied. Rachel was on her way to Philadelphia. Elizabeth turned over the money she had been saving for garden seeds, and Bartley stayed with the slaves, coaching them as to how they must repeat 'Yassah' to anyone who questioned them. Then Eden arrived.

She had sailed her own skiff down the river, dressed like the maid in the broadside. She was tense, and eager to be on the way; when she looked into the faces of the escapees she assured them, 'We gonna reach Pennsylvania,' but her manner was so aggressive that Bartley would not accept her as a member of his group until Elizabeth had searched her, taking away the pistol from her dress and the knife strapped to her leg.

'There must be no violence,' Bartley warned the slaves. 'We shall be protected by the grace of God.' But Elizabeth, standing at the door to the kitchen as the slaves filed past, told each one, 'Don't let them capture thee.'

The chain of slaves, bound together by a lust for freedom, marched silently to the river, where Bartley had anchored a large ketch, and in this they sailed quietly up the Choptank, keeping to shore farthest from Patamoke. When they were well upstream he beached the ketch and told the men, 'Now starts the dangerous part.'

It was a perilous journey, one white man, nine black, and one slave woman. They walked single file, hoping to avoid towns and inquiries. Toward noon on the first day, when they were safely past Easton, they were stopped by a farmer who asked where they were headed, and Bartley replied, 'Sassafras,' and the farmer said, 'I hope you got some niggers there you can trust,' and Bartley said, 'Tom and Nero's real good hands.'

They slept in fields, but as the peninsula narrowed they could not avoid towns, so after the most minute coaching, Bartley led his file right down the middle of a community, turning now and then to inspect his blacks as if he owned them.

'Where you headin'?' a law officer asked.

Since they were now north of the Sassafras, Bartley answered, 'Head of Elk. Got a lot of plowin' to do.'

The officer studied the slaves and asked, 'You got papers for these niggers?'

'Sure have,' and while the blacks stood at rigid attention, trying not to show their fear, Bartley produced the documents John Parrish had forged.

'Good-lookin' wench,' the officer said.

'She can cook, too,' Bartley said.

'We see a lot of runaways up here. Keep your eyes peeled with this lot.' Gratuitously he gave the last slave in line a vicious whack with his club, and for a moment Bartley feared the whole deception might fall apart, but the slave grabbed a lock of hair at his forehead, bowed several times and mumbled, 'Yassah. Yassah.'

Now came the nerve-racking part. They were north of Head of Elk, not far from the Pennsylvania border, but it was precisely here that mercenary slave-trackers patrolled the roads, expecting to catch fugitives grown careless in that last burst for freedom, and as Bartley had anticipated, some of the men wanted to break away, each making the final attempt on his own.

He argued against this, warning the slaves that if they dispersed, they would lose the advantage of all he had done. To his surprise, his most ardent supporter was Eden, who told the men, 'Doan' be stupid. You is five miles from freedom. Keep brave.'

But one slave named Pandy refused to share the corporate risk. He predicted that so large a group would be spotted. He would make the last push by himself, and off he went.

Bartley was uncertain what he would do if challenged in these last few miles, and he was therefore dismayed when he saw coming at him on horses three men who were obviously slave-trackers. 'What you doin' with all them slaves?' the leader demanded.

'Takin' them to my place at Risin' Sun.'

'Why you this far east?'

'Bought 'em in Patamoke. Much cheaper than Baltimore.'

'That's right,' one of the men said.

'You got any papers provin' they're yourn?'

'All in order,' Bartley said. He was trembling, for he knew that these eight slaves did not intend being taken prisoner, and he feared Eden's violent action if any attempt were made. He scuffed dirt with his toe as the men read the sale documents, feigning indifference. *God, would this moment never pass?*

'They don't look like Georgia niggers to me. They look like ordinary Maryland field hands.'

'They been broken,' Bartley said, and he raised the shirt of the slave who had been most recently beaten. The slave-trackers, seeing the welts, realized that here was a difficult nigger. The leader, with a powerful kick of his boot, knocked the slave into the dust, while the other two riders showed signs of wanting to snatch the whole file. If the fallen slave had made the slightest response to the kick, there would have been a general battle, with lives lost, but the fallen man groveled there, and the riders passed on.

When they were gone, Bartley cried, 'As fast as possible. North to the line.' And they had made much progress when to the rear they heard the clatter of hoofs; the trackers were bearing down upon them.

'We knowed you was escapin'!' they shouted as they reached the last slave in line.

Now it was Eden who took command. With a wild leap she threw herself upon the lead rider, knocking him to the ground. He fell in an awkward position, which allowed her to grab a stone and drop it on his head. When she looked up, she saw that the Cline slaves had pulled the other two riders off their horses, too, and before Bartley could intervene, the three men were trussed.

'Take their horses,' Eden said, but Bartley warned the slaves most passionately that if they moved the horses into Pennsylvania, they would be hanged.

'Stealing horses is a terrible crime,' he said, and Eden began to laugh, but Bartley continued, 'They will never let you go. Men will track you to France to punish a horse thief.'

'Take 'em in the woods,' Eden told the slaves, and the three trackers were hauled away. Eden would not allow Bartley to follow, and he waited in agony until the men reappeared. He would not, however, allow the horses to be taken.

'Turn them loose,' he insisted, and when this was done, everyone started running toward the border, but they were stopped by a harrowing sight. Toward them came two slave-trackers lashing a black man with a rope around his neck and his hands tied behind his back. It was Pandy, whom Mr. Cline had been abusing for seven years. He had been within a mile of freedom when he stumbled into just the kind of trap Bartley and Eden had foreseen.

Now he passed his mates, his eyes down. He had betrayed himself, but he would not betray them. 'What you got there?' Bartley asked casually.

'Goddamn runaway. Means fifty bucks apiece for us.'

'He looks a mean one.'

'Where you headin'?'

'Risin' Sun.'

'Not too far, but watch them niggers. They do like to run.'

'I got me two guards,' Bartley said.

'Guards!' The men laughed. 'You cain't trust no nigger.'

They passed on, back to the farm of Herman Cline.

For the last mile none of the slaves spoke, and Bartley saw that most had tears in their eyes, but when they were well into Pennsylvania one of the men began to sing:

> 'Sweet Jesus, guard him.
> Sweet Jesus, save our brother.
> Sweet Jesus, let us die in sleep.
> Sweet Jesus, take us home.'

In Philadelphia the abolitionists who spent their time and money rescuing slaves were agog. The telegraph from authorities in Wilmington had brought news of a criminal escape: a white man and a black woman had led eight male slaves to freedom by overpowering three slave-catchers near the Pennsylvania border and tying them upside down from a large oak tree, where they were not found until their horses returned to the stable, alerting search parties. Everyone in the North was awaiting disclosure of who the escapees were.

Bartley had foreseen just such a commotion, and as soon as he set the eight men on the path to Kennett Square, where Quakers would be waiting to absorb them into the established system, he and Eden crept west to the little village of Nottingham. There they threw themselves upon the trustworthiness of a Quaker family named Hicks, whom they had to take into their confidence—'It would be fatal if thee noised abroad how we forged the documents. Mrs. Cater and I need new clothes, new documents and enough money to get us both home through Baltimore.' Papers were forged and tickets purchased for a gentleman returning to

Richmond with his wife's maid. And the two conspirators went south.

Now Rachel and her brother took over. They were a resolute pair, and when the slaves arrived in Philadelphia they quickly dispersed them to various hiding places so that no one could deduce that these were the men who had so humiliated the trackers. Rachel, always anticipating trouble, floated one story that the eight slaves had reached Lancaster and another that they were already in New York, where she had arranged for abolitionists to hold a supposed party at which the eight were to be exhibited.

But she had underestimated the enemy, for as she walked down Market Street after having made arrangements to ship three of the men to Boston, she saw to her horror that Lafe Turlock and Herman Cline were coming toward her, with two policemen in tow. Turning quickly, she pressed herself against a shop window and watched as they passed from sight. That night she read in the paper their advertisement:

RUNAWAY

Eight Prime Slaves Four Marked with Scars Back and Face
One hundred dollars reward for every one returned to
Herman Cline of Little Choptank, Maryland, who can be
reached at Mrs. Demson's Boarding House on Arch Street.

Under the law, every citizen of Pennsylvania was obligated to assist Herman Cline in recovering his slaves. Some informant had alerted him to the fact that despite the false leads spread by Rachel, the fugitives had reached Philadelphia and were in hiding there. Federal marshals were already searching rooming houses, and a pro-slavery group of southerners residing in the city had augmented the reward being offered by Cline. It could only be a matter of days before the runaways were apprehended, and men were already speaking of the fact that they must first be returned to northern Maryland for punishment due them for having strung up the trackers.

But the abolitionists were not powerless, especially with Rachel Paxmore goading them on. What they did was to find a Quaker printer not only willing but positively eager to help them. He printed large handbills, four hundred of them, proclaiming the arrival in Philadelphia of the notorious slavers, Lafe Turlock—with a graphic description—and Herman Cline, one of the cruelest masters in the state of Maryland. The poster showed woodblock caricatures of the odious pair and ended with this admonition:

Every citizen is warned to be on watch for these monsters, these body-snatchers. Wherever they go on the street, shout warnings of their passage. Wherever they stop to eat, advise everyone within hearing of their identity. Mark where they sleep and let us know. And if they even approach a black citizen, shout and call for help, because these men will snatch freed Negroes if they cannot find their former slaves.

These handbills were distributed to every inn, every dining place, tacked onto poles and pasted on storefronts. Every leader of the abolitionist movement received four copies, which were to be displayed in prominent places.

Rachel and her brother Comly later told their mother what had happened in the ensuing days. 'We knew where they slept, at Mrs. Demson's, so when they appeared on the street, we had packs of young people standing there, who surrounded them, shouting, "Slavers! Slavers!" Wherever they stopped to eat, we stood near their table and stared at them. If they wanted an ale, they could have one only if every person at the inn knew who they were, and many men would spit on the floor and refuse to drink while they were in the place. We made them anathema.'

Lafe Turlock and Herman Cline! They withstood the torments for three days, then quit the city. They thought at first of trying to find their slaves in New York, but one of the abolitionists shouted at them while they were dining, 'Don't think you can escape us! We've warned the committees in Lancaster and New York.'

So in the end they had to take passage back to Baltimore. As their boat pulled away from the city, Cline looked at the skyline and almost wept. 'Just think, Lafe! I work my heart out in those swamps. I get a decent start in life. And then my property runs away. Nine prime slaves. More than twenty thousand dollars. My goddamn niggers are hidin' in that city, somewheres.'

Lafe said, 'It was them signs. They riled the people against us.'

'A man's whole savings wiped out. Damn, it seems unfair.'

But the reward for the eight slaves still stood, and Rachel was aware that numerous adventurers lusted for this money. 'What can we do?' she asked members of the Philadelphia rescue committee.

'There is only one sure thing,' a wise old Quaker gentleman assured her. 'Thee must get them to Canada.'

'But I thought Boston . . .'

'They are not safe even there. A black man can find safety nowhere in this country. He must go to Canada.'

So Rachel Paxmore and her brother arranged to spirit the eight slaves out of the country. It took time and money and courage. An improvised path had evolved without conscious direction: 'There's a doctor in Doylestown, and then you go to Scranton, and beyond New York the safe spot is the home of Frederick Douglass in Rochester.'

Rachel stayed with the men all the way to the Canadian border, and only when they were safely across did she permit the tension which had gripped her for three weeks to show itself. She sat on a fallen tree and wept, her shoulders quivering with the anguish that assailed her. 'Sister,' said Comly as he sat on the log beside her, 'it's ended. They're safe.'

But she said, 'How despicable. That men in the United States who seek freedom must flee to Canada to find it.'

The flight of nine slaves from Herman Cline's farm on the Little Choptank so angered the other owners in the region that they convened at Devon Island to consider what steps they might take to prevent similar losses of their capital.

'Cline lost twenty thousand dollars in one night,' a planter from St. Michaels said. 'A repetition could wipe us little fellows out.'

'Has any serious thought been given to driving the Paxmores from this territory?' asked a burly man who had been forced to chase two of his slaves all the way to the Pennsylvania border before retrieving them. 'Things have been a lot better along the Miles River since David Baker . . .' He left it there, not wanting openly to suggest that the Paxmores be gunned down.

'What we might do,' one of the the Refuge Steeds suggested, 'is use religion. Remind the slaves of their moral obligations to us.'

This proposal met with general approbation, and many of the planters turned to Paul Steed. One asked, 'Paul, couldn't you give a series of sermons? I'd sure love to have you come to my place and talk to my hands.'

Others seconded this suggestion, but Steed demurred. 'I don't speak well in public. The audience stares at my crooked neck and doesn't listen to what I say.'

'Some truth to that,' the man from St. Michaels agreed. 'But the idea of church services is still good.'

And then someone remembered a tall, thin, fire-eating Methodist-Protestant minister from across the bay; he'd had outstanding success with revivals and delivered what was regarded as 'the best nigger sermon in the business.'

'Are you thinking of Reverend Buford?' Paul asked, and when the planters said that was the man, Paul said, 'I know him. He stayed with us here at Devon.'

'He's not Catholic,' a planter said.

'I wanted to argue religion with him. He's powerful.'

It was agreed that two Choptank men would cross the bay to enlist the aid of Reverend Buford, and when they saw him at the little town of Hopewell on the James River they were reassured that he was the man they wanted. Tall, funereal, with a mop of black hair and a stupendous Adam's apple that punctuated his simplest remarks, making them seem more vivid than they were, he was, as they had remembered, a fiery man. 'What we want,' they told him, 'is your best nigger sermon.'

He was reluctant to leave Virginia, where he found much work to do, but when he heard that the invitation came from Paul Steed, he said with some eagerness, 'I'll come. Most intelligent Catholic I ever met.'

'Well, he needs you, and so do we all!'

'Nigger trouble?'

'Nine of Herman Cline's prime hands run off. Eight was traced to Philadelphia.'

'They were recovered?'

'Nope. Abolitionists up there run him and Lafe Turlock out of town. Slaves vanished into thin air. Lost twenty thousand dollars in one night.'

'I've heard of Cline,' Buford said. 'Some of our people send their slaves to him, and I have no intention of crossing the bay to aid a monster. Probably deserved to lose his slaves, all of them.'

'Reverend, it isn't Cline we're worried about. It's us. Decent men like Paul Steed are in danger of losing their entire investments. We need help. Pacification.'

'We all need it,' Buford said with surprising anxiety. 'Who can tell where the passions of this day are going to lead? I pray every night for guidance.'

'And we pray for your guidance,' one of the planters said. 'Come over with us and help quieten things.'

'If you thought it would do any good, I'd be willing to give my *Theft of Self* sermon.'

'That's the very one we want. I heard you give that at Somers Cove three years ago. Very powerful.'

Reverend Buford started delivering *Theft of Self* at the smaller plantations east of Patamoke, intending to build expectations as he moved always closer to the main centers of population. The format was invariable. In the late afternoon, when the day's work was pretty well concluded, all slaves were assembled in some tree-lined open space. Buford insisted that every white person on the plantation be in attendance, seated in the shade and dressed in their Sunday clothes. He started his preaching from a rostrum, but as his enthusiasm grew, he moved about quite freely, using wild gestures and imploring tones.

His message was simple and effective. He did not dodge the issue that had brought him to the Eastern Shore:

> 'I know and you know that the other week nine slaves ran away from their master, trying to find what they called freedom in the cities of the North. I suppose there could even be some of you

standing before me now who have had such thoughts. I confess that even I might have them, were I one of you. But what does God say about such behavior?'

With tremendous force he lined out the teaching of the Bible on slavery. God ordained it; Jesus approved of it; St. Paul said it was one of the gateways to heaven. He was especially strong when he reached the matter of punishment, for some slaves were beginning to ask why it was, if God was all-merciful, that He encouraged beatings? Like all preachers who gave nigger sermons, he lingered over Proverbs 29:19, which stated specifically that a slave 'will not be corrected by words, for though he understand he will not answer.'

And he developed the further thesis that when a master struck a slave, he was doing the work of God Himself: 'God directs the master to punish you with stripes when you do not obey.' He also spent much time on that curious passage at First Peter 2:18, beloved of southern preachers. This little book was one of the most trivial in the Bible, yet chance passages from it condemned a race.

> 'What does the Bible tell you? That you must obey your masters, and not only your good masters, but especially your bad ones, because when you submit to their punishment, you build up gold in heaven. And the Bible says, furthermore, that if you are punished unjustly when you have done no wrong, and I know this sometimes happens, causing great animosities, you must submit with a glad heart, because God sees and makes allowances for you in heaven. That is the law of the Bible.'

All their lives the slaves had heard about Proverbs and Peter, and now even though Reverend Buford glossed them with his special rhetoric, they grew restless. Some stared at the violent movement of his Adam's apple and whispered, 'He gonna choke hisse'f!' and others began to fidget. Buford knew how to handle this; he had two additional arrows in his quiver, and when he shot these at the slaves, they listened, for the first contained a definite threat:

> 'You look at Mr. Sanford sitting there and you think, "He has it easy!" But you don't know that Mr. Sanford has obligations at the bank, and he must gather up the money, a dollar at a time, working hard to do so, and pay that money to the banker, or he will lose this plantation. The banker will come down here and take it away and sell every one of you to Louisiana or Mississippi.'

He recited other heavy obligations of the white folk sitting in the shade; this one had examinations to pass at Princeton, that one had to care for the sick, and he, Reverend Buford, was obligated to the fine people who ran his church. The world was crammed with duties, and some of the lightest were those borne by slaves.

It was his second arrow that gave Buford his peculiar force in pacifying slaves, and it was from this that his famous sermon took its name:

'At dinner today Mr. Sanford told me that he had never had a finer bunch of slaves than you. "They work hard," he told me. "They mind the crops. They wouldn't steal a single one of my chickens." Yes, that's what Mr. Sanford told me. He said that you were the most honest slaves in Maryland, but then he added something which shocked me. He said that some of you had been thinking of running away. And what is running away, really? Tell me, what is it? It is theft of self. Yes, you steal yourself and take it away from the rightful owner, and God considers that a sin. In fact, it's a worse sin than stealing a chicken or a cow or a boat, because the value of what you have stolen is so much greater. Mr. Sanford owns you. You belong to him. You are his property, and if you run away, you are stealing yourself from him. And this is a terrible sin. If you commit this sin, you will roast in hell.'

At this point Reverend Buford liked to spend about fifteen minutes describing hell. It was filled primarily with black folk who had sinned against their masters; there was an occasional white man who had murdered his wife, but never anyone like Herman Cline, who had murdered two of his slaves. It was a horrendous place, much worse than any slave camp, and it could be avoided by one simple tactic: obedience. Then the preacher came to his peroration, and it became evident why he insisted upon the attendance of the white masters:

'Look at your master sitting there, this kind man surrounded by his good family. He spent long years working and saving and in the end he had enough money to buy you. So that you could live here along this beautiful river rather than in a swamp. Look at his beautiful wife, who comes out at night to your cabins to bring you medicine. And those fine children that you helped to bring up, so that you would have good masters in the years to come. These are the good people who own you. Now, do you want to injure them by stealing yourself, and hiding yourself up North where they cannot find you? Do you want to deprive Mr. Sanford of property he bought and paid for? Do you want to go against the word of God, the commands of Jesus Christ, and make those fine people lose their plantation?'

He preferred at this point for the owners to start weeping, for then some of the older slaves would weep, too, and this gave him an opportunity for a ringing conclusion, with the white folk in tears, the slaves shouting, 'Amen! Amen!' and all ending in a rededication to duty.

It was a fine thing to hear Reverend Buford speak; he delivered his *Theft of Self* sermon at eight major plantations, ending at Devon Island, where Paul Steed entertained him in the big house prior to his performance.

'You've matured since we last met,' Steed said.

'You've become quite a manager,' Buford responded. 'Last time it was all books. This time all work.'

'What do you hear in Virginia?' Steed asked.

Buford was no fool. He circulated in the best circles and kept his ears open. 'We find ourselves resisting agitators from both ends.'

'What do you mean?'

'The abolitionists pressure us from the North to free our slaves, and the secessionists from South Carolina pressure us to leave the Union.'

'What will you do?'

'Virginia? We'll make up our own minds.'

'To do what?'

For the first time during his foray to the Eastern Shore, Reverend Buford was at a loss for words. He leaned back in his chair, looked out at the lovely gardens, and after a long hesitation, replied, 'If men like you and me can keep things calmed down just a little longer, we'll stabilize this agitation. We'll strike a balance between North and South. Then we can proceed in an orderly—'

'Slavery?' Steed broke in.

'In a hundred years it will fall of its own weight.'

'Have you read Hinton Helper?'

'Yes, and I've read your retort.'

'Which do you prefer?'

Again the gaunt reverend fell silent, finally mustering courage to say, 'Helper. We'll all be better off when slavery ends.'

'I have close to a million dollars tied up in my slaves.'

'*Tied up* is the right phrase.'

'Then why do you continue to give your sermons?'

'Because we must all fight for time, Mr. Steed. We must keep things on an even balance, and believe me, having several million former slaves running free across the countryside will not maintain that balance.'

'Answer me directly. Are the Quakers right? Should I free my slaves now.'

'Absolutely not.'

'When?'

'In about forty years. Your son Mark seems a steady young man. He'll want to free them, of that I'm sure.'

'And my million dollars?'

'Have you ever really had it? I preach often at Janney's big plantation on the Rappahannock—'

'Some of my forebears were Janneys.'

'I think I heard that. Well, they're supposed to have a million dollars, too. And they have difficulty finding a few coins to pay me. They're rich, but they're poor. And history has a way, from time to time, of shaking the apple tree, and the weak fruit falls off and the owner sees that he never had very many apples to begin with. Not really.'

'Here you shall be paid,' Steed said, producing a handfull of bills. 'I find talking with you most refreshing. I can't understand how you can preach the way you do.'

'I'm an old man in an old tradition.'

'You're barely sixty!'

'I go back to a different century. And I dread the one that's coming.'

His sermon on Devon Island was by far the best of his tour, but it differed from the others because Paul and Susan Steed consented to sit in the shade only if he promised not to refer to them in any way. He therefore had to renounce his heroics and attend to his logic, and he made a stirring case for slavery as an orderly method of fulfilling God's intentions. At Steed's request he also stressed the duties of the master to the servant, quoting biblical verses he usually overlooked, but his peroration had the same fire as before, and when he ended, his listeners were in tears and some were shouting, and as he left the podium many blacks clustered around to tell him that he certainly knew how to preach. But as he moved toward the wharf, where a boat waited to deliver him to Virginia, he was accosted by two white people whom he had not noticed during his sermon. Somehow they had slipped into the edges of the crowd.

'I'm Bartley Paxmore,' the man said, extending his hand. 'This is my wife Rachel.'

'I've heard of you two,' Buford said guardedly.

'How could thee distort the word of God so callously?' Bartley asked.

'Good friends,' Buford said without losing his temper, 'we all need time, you as well as I. Are you prepared to bring down the holocaust?'

'I would be ashamed to delay it on thy terms,' Rachel said.

'Then it will not be delayed,' Buford said. 'You'll see to that.' And he was so eager to escape the tangled passions of the Eastern Shore that he actually ran to his boat and jumped in.

When Elizabeth Paxmore, in her sickbed, heard Bartley's report of Reverend Buford's *Theft of Self,* she asked for her Bible and spent a long time leafing through it, sidetracked constantly by coming upon some passage she had memorized in her youth.

At last she cried, loud enough for everyone in the room to hear, 'I've found it!' And when her family gathered, even the grandchildren, who would remember this event well into the next century, she asked, 'Why do they persist in censoring the one verse in the Bible that seems most relevant?' And she read from Deuteronomy 23:15:

> 'Thou shalt not deliver unto his master the servant which is escaped from his master unto thee: . . . thou shalt not oppress him.'

She said that she wished her family to continue abetting the runaways, even if it took them away from Peace Cliff during what all knew was her last illness. 'I will be able to fend,' she assured them.

In 1859 two contradictory events provoked Paul Steed into sitting down and evaluating the economic base on which the Devon plantations rested. The first was the excitement aroused throughout America by the forceful book of a North Carolinian, Hinton Helper, who had the temerity to title it *The Impending Crisis,* as if slavery were in desperate trouble. In this uncompromising work Helper, a southerner with sound credentials, argued that the South must always suffer in competition with the North if it persisted in using slave rather than free labor. He marshaled statistics tending to prove that plantation owners would gain if they freed all their slaves, then hired the men back.

In Maryland the book caused a mighty stir, for these were the years men were choosing sides, and northern propagandists cited Helper to prove their claim that border states would be wise to stay with the Union. Legislation was passed making it a crime to circulate either Helper or *Uncle Tom's Cabin,* and when the freed black who lived next to Cudjo Cater was caught reading a copy of the latter, he was sentenced to ten years in jail.

Many southerners wrote to Steed, reminding him that since his *Letters* had made him a champion of the slaveowners, he was obligated to rebut Helper; the petitioners argued: 'We know that Helper has used erroneous facts to bolster his fallacious conclusions, and it's your job to set the record straight.'

He would have preferred to avoid the fight, but a second event intervened, and this forced him to do precisely what his correspondents wanted: undertake to weigh dispassionately the pros and cons of the slave system. What happened was: Southern agriculture had suffered badly in the prolonged depression of the 1840s, and many plantations had neared collapse; it was this period that provided Helper with his statistics, and they certainly did prove that slavery was a burden; but starting in 1851 a veritable boom had developed, and in years like 1854 and 1856, southern producers of tobacco, cotton, sugar, rice and indigo reaped fortunes.

Now the value of slaves increased; when Paul found it advisable to rent a few from neighbors, he discovered to his amazement that he must pay up to one dollar a day for their services, and provide food, clothing and medical supplies as well. During harvest the price jumped to a dollar-fifty, and he began to wonder whether returns from his crop warranted such outgo:

So I retired to my study and with all available figures before me tried soberly to calculate what the experience of the Steed plantations had been in bad years as well as good. I owned, at the beginning of 1857, a total of 914 slaves, distributed by age, sex and worth as follows:

THE STEED SLAVES

Classification	Male Number	Male Value Each	Female Number	Female Value Each	Total Value
Infants, 0–5	44	0	47	0	0
Children, 6–13	135	300	138	250	75,000
Prime, 14–52	215	2,000	161	1,800	719,800
Older, 53–66	72	1,200	65	300	105,900
Ancients, 67–	16	0	21	0	0
	482		432		900,700

Any slaveowner will quickly see that my figures are conservative, and I have kept them so on purpose. In this analysis I wish to offer the lowest possible value for my slaves and highest possible maintenance costs, for if under such circumstances they still produce a profit for the plantations, then slavery will have been demonstrated to be economically feasible. Therefore I should like to append a few notes to the above table:

Infants. Obviously they are of considerable value, and to quote them as zero is ridiculous, but infants die, they become crippled, they prove themselves useless in other ways, so it is prudent to carry them on the plantation books at no proven value.

Children. Healthy children are bringing much higher prices these past few years than shown, especially those in the later ages. Were I so inclined, I could sell the Steed children south at prices considerably in advance of these, but at Steed's we do not sell off our children.

Prime. Figures at Patamoke sales have been consistently higher than these, as proved by the rental prices in the past few years. If an owner in Alabama can rent out a prime hand for up to $400 a year, and if the slave has forty good years, his actual value could be astronomical.

Older. These figures may be high. I could not sell our older slaves south for such prices, because they would not last long in the rice and sugar fields, but for what one might call domesticated service in a city like Baltimore, they could fetch even higher prices than I show.

Ancients. Every slaveowner will remember older Negroes who served handsomely into their eighties. Our plantation has a door-man who answers to the name of Tiberius who is one of the adorn-ments of the island. Departing guests invariably praise him for his courtly style, and when visitors return to their homes their letters usually include some reference to Tiberius. If slaves have been well treated in their prime, they provide years of appreciated service in their seventies, but on the auction block they would bring nothing, so I list them at that.

Artisans. I do not include in my analysis any classification for the highly skilled mechanics who can contribute so much to the success-ful operation of a plantation. At Steeds we have perhaps two dozen men who would bring more than $3,500 each if offered for sale, and three or four who would fetch twice that. The plantation manager is slothful if he does not ensure the constant development of such hands within his slave force, for to purchase them on the open market is expensive when not impossible.

So the value of the Steed slaves is over nine hundred thousand dollars, using the most conservative figures, and something like one and a quarter million with top evaluations. But what does this figure really mean? Could I go out tomorrow and realize nine hundred thousand dollars from the sale of my slaves? Certainly not. To place so many on the auction block at Patamoke would destroy all values; what I really have in my slaves is not a million dollars, but the opportunity to earn from their labor a return of about thirteen percent per year.

Warfare uses a concept of value which covers this situation, *the fleet in being.* Such a fleet is not actually at sea, and it is not fully armed or manned, and no one knows its exact condition, but in all his planning the enemy must take it into account, because the ships do exist and they might at any time coalesce into a real fleet. As they stand scattered and wounded they are not a fleet, but they are a fleet in being. My 914 slaves are wealth in being, and it often occurs to me that they own me rather than that I own them, for as I have shown, I cannot sell them. Indeed, it is possible that the Steed family will never realize the nine hundred thousand dollars existing in these slaves; all we can do is work them well and earn a good yearly profit from that work. Thirteen percent of nine hundred thousand dollars is a yearly income of $117,000. Now I confess that rarely do we accomplish that goal, but we do well.

He then went on to cite his expenses—about $122 a year per slave, for he fed and clothed better than average—the loss through accidents and many other factors. In the end he proved that by the most careful husbandry, which included giving his slaves at least as much attention as he gave his hogs, it was possible to utilize them more profitably than hired labor. He refuted each of Hinton Helper's main arguments, and added a clincher:

I would concede to Mr. Helper that if a plantation owner were going to be lazy, or indifferent, or cruel to his slaves, or inattentive to every small and irritating item of management, he might do better hiring his help rather than owning it. But the true southern gentleman accepts not only the possibility of making a just profit but also the obligation to create on his plantation a harmonious style of life, in which each man and woman has duties to perform and rewards to enjoy. He likes to have his slaves living near him, to observe their families growing and to share in their recreations. He takes pride in the fact that they take pride in whom they work for; often he hears his slaves boast to Negroes from other plantations, 'This is the best place to work.' I direct my plantation to seek that approval, and I produce a good profit for everyone while doing so.

Without reservation, I would throw open the Steed plantations for comparison with the labor-mills at the north. My slaves live freely in the open air, eat good food, are warm in winter, and are cared for by my doctors. In every respect their lot is superior to that of the so-called free labor at the north, which rises before daylight, works in horrible conditions, and goes home after sunset to a foul bed. When unprejudiced men compare the two systems, they must conclude that ours is better.

By May of 1860 the United States was in such confusion that European nations began to speculate on when a war would start and which side they ought to back. Both London and Paris received ominous reports from their envoys, the French ambassador having written:

> The presidential election this autumn cannot escape chaos. There may be as many as five contending parties, for the Democrats are in pitiful disarray and will not be able to agree on any one man. Expect them to present two candidates, one North, one South and to lose the election thereby. The Whigs have become the Constitutional Unionists and have no possibility of winning. But the Republicans are also split and may also have to offer two candidates, so that 1860 may well go down in history as the year in which nobody won.

Because of a constellation of contradictory reasons, most European nations sided with the South and actively hoped it would win. England perceived the northern states as being the real inheritors of the original colonies, and any animosities held over from 1776 and 1812 were vented on them. Also, British industrialists relied heavily on southern cotton, and goaded their government into openly supporting these states. Austria backed the South because it was viewed as being the home of gentlemen and fine horses. And France was strongly pro-southern because this region was civilized, whereas the North was not. Russia and Germany vaguely wanted to teach the upstart nation a lesson.

When Europe decided that war was inevitable, it became necessary to form some estimate of the South's chances of winning, and in late May the French government dispatched one of its lesser naval vessels on a casual tour of seven southern ports, chosen rather skillfully to reveal a wide scattering of opinion. Remembering the amiable relations France had once enjoyed with the Steed family, whose sons had attended St. Omer's, officers directed the little ship to end its voyage at the port of Patamoke, where the local gentry were to be entertained and queried.

The ship was the *Ariel,* captured from the slaving fleet in 1832 and refashioned into a corvette of eight guns. She was an old ship now, but her timbers were so solid and her keel so unblemished that ambitious men liked to serve aboard her, and her captains, usually younger men, often found quick promotion. Her present commander, Captain de Villiers, did not know the Chesapeake, but his great-uncle had served under De Grasse; the name kept recurring in family records.

His arrival at Patamoke was not announced. Paul Steed was pushing his wife's chair on a promenade through the north garden when the *Ariel* passed up Devon channel, and although both the Steeds had once been involved with this ship, they did not recognize her as she passed. The French Ministry of Marine had raised her bulwarks to accommodate the guns and had replaced the old hermaphrodite rigging with full brig dress.

But when the vessel approached Peace Cliff, old George Paxmore, who had built her, studied her with his glass, as he did all ships of size coming upriver, and cried to his son, 'Bartley, I do believe it's the *Ariel.* Look what they've done to her!' Bartley joined his father on the porch as the elegant ship sailed past; he had not been born when she was launched in 1814, but family conversation had acquainted him with her history, and he could now appreciate the compact design and the flow of wood and sail which had made the ship memorable.

It was not until the *Ariel* had berthed that she created her real impact, for her name proclaimed her saga, and citizens from all parts of town streamed down to see this legendary vessel. A score of Turlocks came; their family had once owned the *Ariel.* And young men whose fathers had worked upon her came down to study her lines. As they watched, a very old man, crotchety and pushing people aside, moved to the edge of the wharf.

It was Lafe Turlock, seventy-seven years old and long retired from chasing runaways. He had sold his dogs and given his tracking boots to his grandson, but when he saw the *Ariel* his eyes beamed. 'She was my cousin's ship. Finest sea captain this river ever produced. Killed by niggers I won't name.'

Through the long afternoon and into the evening the townspeople gaped at the beautiful little ship, recalling her escapades. They watched admiringly as young Captain de Villiers came ashore to pay his respects and dispatch a boat to convey his greetings to the Steeds. He sought the Paxmores, too, but the young men who ran the boatyard warned him, 'Steeds and Paxmores do not meet at social affairs,' and since this was precisely the kind of subtlety that Captain de Villiers wanted to investigate, he said graciously, 'Oh, I intended inviting your distinguished uncle to the ship, not to Devon.'

'He would be delighted to come,' the young man said.

'And you. And your wives.'

So it was agreed. On the first evening the ship's officers would be taken to Devon for a gala party with the leading planters. On the second evening the Paxmores and their friends would be entertained aboard the ship that old George had built. And on the final evening the Steeds and a few choice friends of similar persuasion would attend a farewell party aboard ship. By that time Captain de Villiers would have a sense of loyalties along the Choptank.

During each afternoon the ship was opened to the general public, and a host of Turlocks trooped over the deck that their cousin Matt had once ruled. They relived his exploits and listened, jaws agape, as Lafe pointed out where the gallant redhead had fallen—'The niggers was so dumb they didn't even cut off his silver fist.'

There was one family that did not board the ship. Cudjo Cater and his children stayed onshore, for as Eden explained, 'They sure ain't gonna want to see us on that ship.' Cudjo took his sons to a point along the shore from which they could see the spars, and as they stood there he told them of his adventures.

'You was tied down?' they asked.

'Chained an' bolted,' Cudjo said.

'You mean the roof only this high?'

'Lower. Put your hand lower.'

'Nobody cain't live that low.'

'We did,' Cudjo said.

'An' then you come up stairs.'

'On deck. Rutak, he lead the way. Don't never forget his name. Bravest man I ever knowed. You here on earth because of Rutak.'

The boys saw the people of Patamoke streaming aboard, and said wistfully, 'Wish we could go.'

'No way you go aboard that ship,' Cudjo said, and he took the boys to Eden. 'I want them in the house,' he said. 'Ever'body just keep quiet ain't nothin' gonna happen.'

The gala at Devon was one that the families would talk about for years. The French officers were resplendent in their gold uniforms and glistening swords; Paul and Susan were fastidious as hosts, conversing with the visitors in French, then translating for their Choptank guests. Susan was so exhilarated that she dispensed entirely with her wheelchair, walking proudly to her place at the head of the table, assisted only by her husband's arm. Old Tiberius, past eighty now, officiated with an elegance that few French major-domos could have equaled, and extravagant toasts were proposed to the grandeur of France.

'Maryland is of the South?' Captain de Villiers inquired.

'All who matter.'

'And if—well, if trouble comes?'

'Every man in this room . . . Ask my son Mark. He runs the plantations now.'

Mark Steed was forty-three, as handsome in his subdued way as the attractive captain was in his. 'We'd follow the lead of South Carolina, all of us.'

When the others nodded, De Villiers pointed out, 'Yes, but you're men of substance. What of the general populace?'

Paul Steed, with his traditional capacity to ignore the middle majority —those stubborn Methodists who had warned that they would abide with the Union—promised the captain, 'In all Patamoke, ninety-five percent would rush to fight with the South—for freedom.'

The talk was good, and one course followed another, passed on silver trays by slaves wearing white gloves. At one point Captain de Villiers asked, 'If I were obligated to advise my uncle in the Ministry, how could I explain the superior strength of the South?'

'The gallantry of its men,' Paul Steed replied. 'You are dining with gentlemen, Captain, and these men abide by their word. If they go to war against the North, it will be to the death.'

The captain raised his glass for the final toast: 'To the gentlemen of the South!'

His dinner with the Paxmores was less congenial. Once old George had explained how the ship had been built, and had taken the officers into the hold to show them the devices he had used to avoid cutting into the keel, there were no light topics to discuss. Captain de Villiers had the distinct impression that Quakers, whom he had never encountered before, paid little attention to light topics. Indeed, the evening dragged, until he cleared his throat and asked, 'If things deteriorate . . . I mean, if war comes—'

Rachel Starbuck Paxmore, now a prim and lovely woman in her forties, interrupted, 'We would support the North, unflinchingly.'

'But the generality?'

'I believe that more than half would join us. The good Methodists love our Union.'

'At Devon, I was told otherwise.'

'At Devon, dreams prevail. Do not be misled by dreams.'

'But the business leaders, even those without slaves, they agreed.'

'That's why a war would be so terrible. Dreams fighting against reality.'

'If war should break out, could the North force the South to remain in the Union?'

'We pray it will not come to that,' Bartley said.

'And so do we all,' De Villiers responded. He was relieved when the evening ended, but as the determined Paxmores walked to the gangway, and he saw the trimness with which they carried their austere bodies, he felt that he might have had good conversation with these people if he had chanced to strike the proper notes: But with men who don't drink and women who don't flirt, what can one do?

At the railing he asked, 'You'll be back tomorrow?' and Rachel replied, 'No, but it was gracious of thee to ask.'

The third night posed a difficult problem for the Steeds. It was one thing for them to invite the French officers to Devon for festivities; it was quite another to sail into Patamoke and publicly board the vessel which had once been so intricately intertwined with their lives. Susan's notorious love affair had culminated there; from the decks of the *Ariel,* Paul had been tossed into the harbor with most of the populace of Patamoke looking on.

With the delicacy that had governed their lives since the accident on the widow's walk, Paul refrained from raising the question as to whether it would be proper to attend the final dinner, but Susan felt no such restraint. 'Paul, I'd love to see that ship again.'

'Would it be proper?'

'Paul!' Placing her hand gently on his arm, she laughed. 'We've been highly proper these last thirty-seven years and I doubt if there's a person in Patamoke . . . No,' she said defiantly, 'I don't give a damn if everyone in Patamoke remembers us and the *Ariel!* I want to see that ship.'

So toward noon of the last day they packed their finest clothes in valises and boarded the Steed sloop, and yard by yard as the little boat moved down the creek and into the river, Paul could see his wife's animation increasing. She was like a schoolgirl slipping away to her first assignation. 'Paul! I'm sure it's right for us to be going. It was a ship that meant much to us, and I'm an old woman now and I desire to tie down the past.'

She was a finely tuned person, Paul thought, resilient, lively, a cherished companion. Their passage up the river was an epithalamium, a restatement of the abiding love that had marked the later years of their lives, and when the *Ariel* became visible, each was able to view what had happened on it as an incident, important but by no means overwhelming.

The state dinner did not begin well. The wind died and mosquitoes attacked ferociously, but Captain de Villiers had come prepared. As soon as the planter guests were aboard, he ordered the crew to hoist anchor and move the *Ariel* out into the middle of the river, where the number of insects dropped sharply. Then he announced, 'Good news, ladies. Our French chemists have perfected a miracle. They call it *essence de citronelle.* You will love the smell of its oranges and lemons, but the mosquitoes won't.' And he directed his staff to spray the area where the guests would sit, and the evening became a gallant affair, the last of its kind these planters would know for many years. The ladies were beautiful, and behaved as if their slaves would be tending them forever; the men spoke well of their adversaries at the North and told De Villiers, 'We must all pray that common sense prevails.' And the moon shone on the Choptank in full-rimmed splendor.

But the man who gained most from this last evening was not seen by either the guests or the crew. He was standing onshore, in the darkness provided by a tree, watching the ship he had known so well. When he had first marched to it in chains, the gangplank had been on that side. He had spent his learning days chained to the bulwark on this side. His first pen belowdecks must have been back there. The second, where he plotted with Rutak, had been below that.

There was the hold from which he had stormed with Luta . . . When he thought of her, always in chains until her dead body was cut loose, he could think no more. Only his eyes continued the memory. Over that railing he had thrown her into the sea. He had to sit down. His head sank so low he could no longer see the ship.

After a long time he looked aft, to the tiller he had mastered and the compass whose secrets he had unraveled. How tremendous those days had been, sailing north. He rose to his feet in great excitement and imagined the sails being raised at his command: Rutak! The ropes! And up the topmost sails had gone, and he had sailed that ship.

Transfixed by the beauty of his vessel, he stayed in the shadows, tending it until the anchor was raised. He watched as it made its way back to the wharf, and he named each guest who departed down the gangway. Then the night fell silent, except for the half-hours when the bells sounded. How well he knew them! In the darkest hours, chained to the bottom of the ship, he had followed the bells; their stately rhythm had governed his life.

Midnight struck, and two and four, and the ship lay sleeping at the wharf. He watched as the summer sun began to rise, back up the Choptank, throwing its rays deeper and deeper into the river. Voices drifted softly across the water, and soon townspeople began to gather along the shore to watch their ship depart.

Lafe Turlock came to remind his myriad grandchildren that once this ship had belonged to them, and the anchor was raised for the last time, and Captain de Villiers appeared on deck, and slowly the beautiful corvette entered the river and sailed away. But the man who had once really owned this ship, by right of capture, remained in the shadows, watching till the tips of the masts vanished from sight.

Captain de Villiers left Patamoke with the opinions of everyone who would be involved in the forthcoming struggle—except the slaves and the freed blacks. It had never occurred to him that he might have sought their judgment, too.

When the dinner guests disembarked, two remained behind. Captain de Villiers insisted that Paul and Susan Steed spend the night in his cabin. 'I will deposit you on Devon Island, then head for France.' So these two went once more to that cabin which had been the scene of their scandal.

'It seems so long ago,' Susan said as the door closed. 'But our lives have not been wasted.'

Paul could think of no appropriate response, but he was so restless that he did not yet wish to retire. 'I was so proud when you said you wouldn't need the chair tonight.'

'I would not want to come aboard this ship . . .' Her voice trailed off.

'I thought the conversation on these two nights . . . No wonder my ancestors preferred France.'

'You're just anti-British, Paul. Always have been.'

'There's something in the way a Frenchman wears a uniform . . .'

Susan sank down upon the bed she had once known so well and stared at the cabin door. 'The terror this ship has known.' She reflected on this, then said, 'It just occurred to me, Paul. I didn't see Cudjo or Eden on the wharf.'

'Probably didn't even know it was in the harbor.'

'Do you suppose he really did capture it? And kill . . .'

'Somebody did.'

'Would a gang of uneducated black slaves be able . . .'

'They sailed it, didn't they?'

'I suppose you were aware that Captain de Villiers was probing us?'

'His government wants to know. A hundred years ago France made all the difference on the Chesapeake. It may do so again.' He thought about this for some moments, then added, 'I think we planters got our points across.'

'He spoke as if war were inevitable.'

'I think it can be avoided. If only we could muzzle agitators like the Paxmores.'

'I wonder what they told him? You know, he saw them separately, last night.'

'From something he dropped, I judge they bored him to death. They don't drink, you know.'

Susan could not sleep, and in the darkest part of the night she walked by herself to the door, opened it slightly and looked out toward the spot where one of the men said that Captain Matt had been overpowered. She wanted very much to go out and touch the planking, but she was dressed only in her shift and deemed it best not to startle the night watch.

'What you doing, Sue?'

'Paul, as soon as they drop us at Devon tomorrow I want your help on one thing. Have Eden and the boys take me up to the roof. I want to see this ship go down the bay.'

'That's reasonable,' Paul said, and Susan came back to bed and they fell asleep.

In the morning they sent a boy to fetch Eden; she could ride back to the island with them. She boarded the ship with pride, surveying everything so that she could later report to her husband, and when the French captain bade farewell to the Steeds at Devon, she marked his behavior. He noticed this and gallantly helped her onto the wharf, but in an instant she was gone. Her mistress had given firm orders during the passage: 'As soon as we touch land I want you to instruct the boys to carry me to the roof.'

She was there when the *Ariel* passed down the channel and into the bay. It was not the ship of old; she could not decipher what changes had been made in the sails, but it was still a vessel that ventured upon the great oceans, and its slow passage down the bay excited her as nothing had done in years.

'What grace,' she said. But as it disappeared behind a distant headland a powerful new ship came north on its way to Baltimore, and she was transfixed by its majesty. It was one of the four-masted clippers used in the China trade. It had been built in New Bedford, and carried twice as much sail as any ship ever built on the Choptank.

'Look at it!' she gasped as it moved resolutely up the bay, and when Eden wanted her to leave the roof, she insisted upon staying. 'Look at this tremendous ship, Eden!' They stood side by side for nearly an hour, and as they watched, the breeze fell, whereupon the sailors hoisted what Choptank people knew as 'the light airs,' those ballooning stunsails attached to the ends of the spars; when they were added to the full complement already aloft, they gave the ship an appearance of being decorated with lace, floating in an indiscernible wind.

'It's so lovely,' Susan said. 'And so very big.'

'They builds 'em up North,' Eden said.

The four-master disappeared too, and Susan said, 'You may call the boys now,' and when, exhausted, she was tucked into the big bed, Eden feared that she might never rise from it again, and tears welled in her eyes.

'What is it, Eden?' the frail old lady asked. When no answer came, she said, 'To see a ship like that . . . Two ships like that . . . It's enough for a lifetime.'

When South Carolina proved its willingness to fight the North by bombarding the federal positions at Fort Sumter in Charleston Harbor, a thrill swept the plantations of the Eastern Shore and responsible men assumed that Maryland would quickly join the rebellion in defense of freedom. As Paul Steed told the other planters, 'The governor's from a town not far from Little Choptank. His heart's in the right place.' So Patamoke waited for the declaration of war.

It did not come. The slave-owning counties realized that their destiny lay with the South, but the greater bulk of Maryland lay close to Pennsylvania and had been corrupted by northern sentiment. Then, too, since the capital at Washington was completely surrounded by Virginia and Maryland, it was imperative to the northern cause that Maryland at least remain in the Union; incredible pressures were exerted, especially by the new President, Lincoln, and it looked as if the state would be torn apart.

This did not happen. Through vacillations, which Paul Steed watched with dismay, Maryland inclined first this way, then that, and in the end wound up on the northern side.

That is, the official posture was with the North, and a regiment from the Eastern Shore even fought in blue, 'to their everlasting disgrace,' Steed said, but honest plantation owners and their supporters sided with the South, as did the marsh folk. For emotionally, Maryland was a southern state, always had been; its traditions, sympathies and economic interests lay south.

Therefore, when northern regiments were formed, partisans of the South retaliated by surreptitiously shipping volunteers into Virginia, where they proudly enlisted in the southern armies, and it was on a mission of this sort that Colonel Rupert Janney started out from the Rappahannock to consult with his distant cousin, Paul Steed, up the bay.

He sailed furtively, on his own vessel of one hundred and ten tons, because federal gunboats had already begun to patrol the Chesapeake, and it was assumed that many of the major battles in the forthcoming war would be fought there. With his map cocked on his knee, he directed his captain how to find the Choptank and negotiate the channel into Devon Creek. As soon as the gangplank was down, he leaped ashore in full uniform, crying, 'Where's Steed?'

Colonel Janney was a handsome man, some forty-five years old, slim, clean-shaven, gracious of manner. 'I'm really in the cavalry, Paul. Like my forebears before me. I was named, you know, after Prince Rupert, your ancestor and mine. He never wavered and I'm sure you won't, either.'

Janney was an intense man, inspirited by the looming battles. 'I'm serving with a man named Jeb Stuart, the Prince Rupert of our day. He knows horses, Paul. And tactics. We shall cut the Yankees to ribbons and be off before they know we were there.'

It was difficult to keep Colonel Janney pinned down to one topic; he had read Steed's book of letters and his important pamphlet on the economics of slave ownership. 'I've been proud to call you cousin. You see things so clearly. Imagine a renegade like Helper arguing that slaves are a financial detriment, when you and I know that our plantations . . . Is it true that you own nearly a thousand slaves? Incredible.' He paced the large dining room, then asked abruptly, 'What'll you do now . . . this big house and all . . . Susan gone?'

'My son Mark . . .'

'He's the one I came to see.'

'You want to take Mark with you?' Paul asked the question without betraying the emotion it caused.

'He's the type we seek. If gentlemen don't lead, the rabble won't follow.'

'I'm sure Mark will want to aid the cause of freedom.'

'Exactly. Paul, what you said in your book . . . That was a damned good book, Paul. Summed things up rather neatly, I thought. You and I are fighting for human freedom. It's all in the balance—the good life, the decent management . . . When can I see Mark?'

'He'll be in the office.'

'He wasn't when I landed.'

'Probably checking the slave row.'

'You've got to watch 'em.' He strode about the room, then came to rest with his second important question: 'How many effectives you think I can take back with me?'

'You mean from this region?'

'Exactly. I hear you have some great riflemen over here. I want 'em all.' He spoke with such enthusiasm and had such energy that Paul wondered how he could have allowed his plantation to remain in a state of disrepair.

'I should judge that most of the watermen would want to join you. They're excellent with guns and they love battles.'

'Will you help me enlist them?'

'Anything for the cause.'

'Good. Jeb Stuart's goin' to need horses.'

'He'll have a hundred from me. Send me the papers.'

'Paul, I knew as I came up the bay . . . When can we enlist the men?'

'Today.'

'Damn it, Paul, if you were younger and . . .' He looked at his cousin's twisted neck. 'What happened?'

'Fell off a roof.'

'Jesus Christ! You mendin' your own roof? What you got slaves for?' He looked at the neck and the shortened leg. 'Wonder you weren't killed.'

'My leg caught on the spout.'

'We'll put that down as a miracle.' When Mark returned to the office, Janney bombarded him with reasons why he should join the southern cavalry, but Mark cut him short: 'I've already joined the infantry.'

'What?' his father asked.

'Yes, I've written to Beauregard in Richmond. I'm to be a major, and I'd like to cross the bay with you, sir.'

'First we've to enlist the troops.' So the three gentlemen sailed to Patamoke, where Colonel Janney harangued a rousing assembly at the wharf: 'Men, the freedom of this nation depends on you. The decency we have known is being challenged by forces of repression. I invite you to join me in our crusade to protect the rights of honest men.'

Sixty-seven men, a fourth of them Turlocks, volunteered, and as they were making their marks on the enlistment rolls, Janney saw Bartley Paxmore and two Starbuck boys looking on. 'They're fine young men,' he said to Paul. 'Why aren't they joining us?'

'They're Quakers,' Steed explained.

'Hmmm!' Janney snorted. 'Won't fight for us and afraid to fight against us. A sad lot.'

When the enlistees were marched aboard, and all was prepared for the dangerous run to Richmond, Colonel Janney faced the captain of the ship, saluted and cried, 'Move down the river. We hazard the crossing in darkness.' He then went to the railing, a handsome man in pearl-gray uniform with a bright red sash about his waist, and saluted Paul, who saluted back. He then strode to the bow of the ship, where he stood erect, the wind in his black hair, memorizing each maneuver against the day when he might, for some unforeseen reason, have to take a Confederate ship down a river. He almost glowed in the afternoon sun, an efficient, daring officer eager to get back on his horse and ride north.

Like every man aboard that ship, he was convinced that he was engaged upon a sacred mission to defend human liberty. Of the sixty-eight men who left the Choptank, counting Mark Steed, only two owned slaves, but all were persuaded that only by enforcing slavery permanently could the freedom of the nation be preserved.

From the wharf Paul cried to his son, 'Take care, Mark. We'll need you when this is over.'

On September 22, 1862, President Lincoln publicly proclaimed a course of action he had decided upon earlier: all slaves within the states at war against the Union were to be free on January 1, 1863. 'Thank God!' Paul Steed cried when he heard this doleful news. 'At least the idiot had sense enough not to touch ours.' He was right. Lincoln, who had a personal aversion to blacks and feared they could never be absorbed into a white society, wanted to see them settled somewhere out of the country. He had prudently refrained from liberating those living in important border states like Kentucky and Maryland, whose governments sided with the North; only slaves in states like Alabama and Louisiana were freed. In his relief, Paul wrote to his son, then campaigning along the Mississippi:

> By his intemperate action he runs the risk of alienating the European powers, and throwing them into the war on our side, for they will see emancipation as an excitation to servile rebellion. Will Austria want black freedom in America to ignite fires of resistance in her vast holdings? I assure you, Mark, that Lincoln has made a fearful mistake, but thank God he did not touch the Devon slaves. He had too much sense for that.

The proclamation, which had no force and did not free one slave, did have the power to depress slave prices in border states. Plantation owners along the Choptank asked themselves, 'If he has the power to free slaves in the Carolinas, why not in Maryland?' And within one month the value of a prime slave dropped from a high of $2,300 to a low of $900. By the end of December it was $600. In this brief space the Steeds lost seventy percent of their negotiable wealth.

In June the blow fell which the Maryland planters had feared. A scruffy Union vessel put into Patamoke, and a major from Connecticut, wearing a dirty blue uniform, began enlisting slaves into the northern army. He made a show of seeking permission from the owners and handing them certificates guaranteeing a later reimbursement of $300 per slave, but few believed such promises would be honored.

The invitation to flee servitude and fight against the South was irresistible. Nearly two hundred Steed slaves asked Paul's permission to enlist, and he was powerless to refuse. But only the strongest were accepted, and when these were marched aboard ship, even those who had been rejected cheered, as if this expeditionary force were destined to win freedom for all blacks.

Paul Steed, watching in dismay as his slaves sailed away, found some solace by comparing this dirty ship, this scruffy major and these black recruits with the Confederate enlistment program conducted earlier at this wharf: That major's a disgrace. Colonel Janney wouldn't allow him near his horse. And as for the Negroes who wanted to be soldiers—one Turlock could gun down the lot.

Cudjo Cater, hearing the commotion, left his cabin, and with Eden and his two sons trailing behind, reported to the recruiting officer, 'I can work a ship.'

'Grandpop, you're too old,' the northerner said.

'I can work machines.'

'Grandpop, take a look at the kind of boys we want,' and when Cudjo continued pestering him, he pointed to rejectees half the old man's age. 'Now go back to your master.'

'I'm free.'

This meant nothing to the recruiter, but then he spied Cudjo's two sons. 'Now there's the type we want. You want to fight for freedom?' he asked the boys.

Eden pushed them forward. 'They good fighters,' she said.

So the two Cater boys were taken, but when the day ended, there was Cudjo, still trying to enlist. This amused the recruiter, who whistled for the major. 'This man says he's got to come with us.'

The Connecticut man came to the recruiting area, inspected Cudjo's teeth and snapped, 'Hell, this man must be over fifty.'

'I can work machines.'

'We don't need mechanics, old fellow. We need men who can march. Now go back to your master.'

As the ship sailed, Cudjo looked at the willing young men lining the railings and wondered how many of them would be able to march six hundred miles with chains about their necks . . . and still have strength to capture their ship.

With the strongest male slaves gone and only the rejected and the women left to work his vast plantations, Paul made an effort to keep alive the spirit of Devon. Each night he allowed old Tiberius, now approaching ninety, to lead him into the dining room in which he had so often entertained. Alone at the head of the table, he would sit erect as two elderly servants in white gloves brought him his meal. Invariably he would look at the chair in which John C. Calhoun had once sat; it stood apart, protected by a betasseled cord of gold.

How sardonic it was, Paul thought, that the three greatest men he had known—Clay, Webster, Calhoun—had each sought the presidency, and been rebuffed: Always we elected men of lesser quality. Dolefully he counted off the grim procession of incompetents who had occupied the White House during these years of crisis: Van Buren, with no character; General Harrison, with no ability; John Tyler, God forbid; Polk, who allowed everything to slip away; General Taylor, lacking any capacity for leadership; the unspeakable Millard Fillmore; Franklin Pierce, who was laughable; James Buchanan, who could have averted this war; and now Abraham Lincoln, traitor to all the principles he once professed.

He recalled fondly the moral greatness of Clay, the grandeur of Daniel Webster, the intellectual superiority of Calhoun, and shook his head: Why must we always reject the best?

And then, when his spirits were at their lowest, the southern armies launched a chain of victories, culminating at Chancellorsville, down the bay, and his hopes revived. General Lee, through sheer brilliance, was defeating superior northern armies, and Mark Steed wrote from one battlefield:

> It confirmed our belief that any company of fifty southern men can outfight any Yankee contingent three times that large, and it gave us vital encouragement to invade the north and put an end to this war. Then we shall know our old freedoms, and you and I shall rebuild the plantations.

In late June of that year excitement on the Choptank grew, for word filtered back that southern armies were involved in a stupendous march north in an effort to create a pincers which would curl back to engulf Philadelphia, Baltimore and Washington itself. The end of the war seemed at hand.

Now Paul climbed to the widow's walk where his wife had once kept vigil, and fixed his gaze northward, across the bay, toward those unseen battlefields just beyond the horizon, where, as he told his planter friends, 'Our destiny is being hammered out.' It was tantalizing; events of supreme significance were under way, but he could hear only echoes, as if the Eastern Shore were not allowed a vital role.

In the first days of July a hush fell over the bay. Mosquitoes swarmed and slave women fished for crabs. Rumors crept in that a mighty battle was engaged at Gettysburg, a few miles north of the Maryland border.

And then the blows fell: 'Pickett led his men where no men could go, and they almost made it . . .' 'Lee almost made it, but he's in retreat . . .' 'Lee says we can hang on, but any chance of invading the North is lost . . .' 'In the Shenandoah they are burning . . .' 'Major Mark Steed died a hero's death . . .'

Paul continued to frequent the widow's walk. He would stand at the railing and survey his domain, thousands of acres beyond the range of vision. But most of the slaves were gone; Susan was gone; Mark would not be back; the railroad was still unbuilt.

During the first cold days of November 1864 Lafe Turlock sat in his cabin near the marsh and heard the geese conversing. 'I'm gonna get me so many of them geese,' he promised his great-grandsons, 'that you gonna have grease all over yore face.'

He was eighty-one years old and as thin as the upper trunk of a loblolly. His old passions were gone: he had no dogs; he no longer went out at night to watch fires as they consumed houses; he fished little and had nothing to do with tonging oysters. But when the geese came back each autumn, his juices flowed, and he oiled his guns.

With most of the good hunters absent on Virginia battlefields, the goose population had risen from the normal eight hundred thousand to nearly a million, but it was still as difficult as ever to lure a particular flight over the spot where you were hiding. He told the boys who clustered about him in goose season, 'The old ones tell the young, and you ain't gonna ketch yorese'f a goose lessen yo're smarter'n I think you are.'

What he would have enjoyed would be to go out with his sons, but most of them had died off, or his grandsons, but they were dying in Virginia. 'How many you calculate we lost?' he asked the men at the store. 'I count nineteen Turlocks dead. Christ A'mighty, the geese is runnin' wild.'

He was not certain he could rely on the young boys; they could barely heft their guns. Still, they could fill spots in the blinds and maybe luck something. He had them out before dawn; in goose season school was unimportant. And when the geese looked as if they might be coming in, he disciplined them sternly: 'You cain't hit no goose at a hundred yards. You got to lure him down.' With ancient skill he blew upon his whistle, and the geese were tempted. They came in low, and when they were in dead-sure range he shouted at the boys, 'Now!'

It was a bad year, but the Turlocks would eat.

Voyage Eleven: 1886

THE WORST STORMS TO HIT THE CHESAPEAKE ARE the hurricanes which generate in the southeast, over the Atlantic Ocean. There they twist and turn, building power and lifting from the waves enormous quantities of water that they carry north in turbulent clouds.

They first hit Cape Charles, at the southern end of the Eastern Shore, then explode ferociously over the waters of the bay, driving crabbers and oystermen to shore. Their winds, often reaching a fierce ninety miles an hour, whip the shallow waters of the Chesapeake into waves so violent that any small boat runs a good risk of being capsized.

In late August of 1886 such a hurricane collected its force just south of Norfolk, but instead of devastating the bay, it leapfrogged far to the north, depositing in the Susquehanna Valley an incredible fall of rain. In less than a day, nineteen inches fell on certain parts of Pennsylvania, and all things were flooded, even into New York State. Harrisburg felt the lash as its waterfront homes were submerged; Sunbury was inundated; poor Wilkes-Barre watched the dark waters engulf its jetties; and even Towanda, far to the north, was swamped by raging floods from streams that a day earlier had been mere trickles.

From a thousand such rivulets the great flood accumulated, and as it crested on its way south to the Chesapeake, it buried small towns and endangered large cities. On it came, a devastating onslaught of angry water, twisting and probing into every depression. Past Harrisburg it swept, and Columbia, and over small villages near the border of Pennsylvania. Finally, in northern Maryland, it exploded with destructive fury into the body of the Chesapeake, raising the headwaters of that considerable bay four and five feet.

For three days the storm continued, producing strange and arbitrary results. Norfolk was by-passed completely: merely a heavy rain. Crisfield had no problems: a slow rain of no significance. Devon Island and Patamoke were barely touched: their biggest problem was that they had no sun during three days. But the great bay itself was nearly destroyed: it came close to being drowned by the floods cascading down from the north. It lay strangling in its own water.

To understand what was happening, one must visualize the bay as carefully structured in three distinct dimensions. From north to south the waters of the bay were meticulously graduated according to their salt content, and any alteration of this salinity was fraught with peril. At Havre de Grace, where the Susquehanna debouched into the bay, there should have been in autumn three parts of salt per thousand; there was none. On the oyster beds near Devon Island there ought to have been fifteen parts per thousand to keep the shellfish healthy; there were two. And at the crabbing beds farther south the crustaceans were accustomed to nineteen parts; they had to contend with less than six. All living things in the bay were imperiled, for the great flood had altered the bases of their existence. The protection provided by salt water was being denied them, and if relief did not come quickly, millions upon millions of bay creatures were going to die.

Prompt restoration of the traditional north-south relationship was essential, but the bay was also divided into a bottom and a top. The lowest area contained deep, cold, very salt water, often deficient in oxygen, moving in from the Atlantic Ocean, bringing many life-sustaining components. Deep down, it tended to move in a northerly direction, and its presence was essential for the health of the bay. On top rested the less salt, less heavy, warmer water replenished by the sun and containing a good oxygen content. It tended to move in a southward direction, sliding along on the top of the cold water. It carried with it many of the lesser forms of marine life on which the crabs and fish lived, and it deposited the nutrients which the oysters lower down required.

But these two vast layers of water should not be considered unrelated, like sheets of mutually exclusive steel moving in opposite directions, each independent of the other. Convection currents, generated by the sun, could at any given point draw the cold layer up and force the warm layer down. A strong surface wind might encourage such an interchange; the passing churning propeller of a large ship could augment the normal pressures that from below and above were constantly working on the two layers, causing them to mix.

But in general the water down deep was colder and saltier and slower; the water near the surface was warmer and less salty and more filled with oxygen. There was another difference: the water on the surface moved freely, even capriciously, over the entire surface of the bay; but the deep water held close to the invisible channel cut some hundred thousand years ago by the prehistoric Susquehanna as it drained away the waters of the first ice age. At the bottom of the Chesapeake, running its entire length and reaching well out into the Atlantic, this primeval riverbed existed, sixty feet deeper than the shallow waters surrounding it, but as clearly defined as when first reamed out by tumbling boulders.

Any sharp dislocation of the upper and lower levels of the bay would have disastrous consequences, for over the millennia marine life had learned to accommodate to the conditions as they existed, and there were many creatures living in the upper layer of warm, light water who could not survive if the cold, heavy water of the bottom suddenly engulfed them.

There was a final division, this one between the western half of the bay and the eastern. The former was fed by five substantial rivers—Patuxent, Potomac, Rappahannock, York, James—some of which drained large inland areas reaching westward to the Blue Ridge Mountains. The huge flow of fresh water contributed by these rivers made the western half of the bay much less saline than the eastern, more silty, more filled with accidental non-marine vegetation, and in general more active.

The so-called rivers of the Eastern Shore did not deserve that name. They were not rivers in the customary sense: they drained no large upland areas; they had no great length; they had no fall; they did not collect fresh water from large drainage areas; they were tidal for most of their reach; and they were notably salty for much of their distance and brackish the rest. They were really tidal inlets—*estuaries* was the proper name—probing arms of the bay, which curled inland, creating flats and marshes.

Since they deposited only a fraction of the water produced by the western rivers, the eastern half of the bay had to be saltier, more torpid, more given to marshes, and much more productive of those small salt-water plants that sustained marine life. Also, another natural phenomenon contributed to the saltiness of the eastern half; the whirling motion of the earth applied a constant force that pushed the heavier water to the east, so that if a scientist drew isohalines—lines connecting all points west to east that had identical percentages of salt water—they would tilt conspicuously from southwest up to northeast. This meant that a line drawn due west from Devon Island, with its fifteen parts of salt per thousand, would find water much less salty in the middle of the bay and notably less so on the western shore. In fact, to find water on the western shore with a salinity equal to Devon's, one would have to drop twenty-five miles south.

Watermen skilled in reading the variations of the Chesapeake kept in mind that there were really three distinct segments: the moderately deep riverine western part; the very deep central channel followed by the steamers, which represented the course of the prehistoric and now drowned Susquehanna; and the exciting estuaries of the eastern portion, where plankton and menhaden and crabs and oysters abounded.

An Episcopal clergyman in Patamoke with time on his hands and a fine Princeton education behind him, carried this analysis to its logical conclusion:

> We have three dimensions. North-south, west-east, top-bottom. If we divide each of these into ten gradations, o through 9, we can construct a numbering system which will locate precisely where we are in this diverse body of water. The northernmost, westernmost, shallowest point at that spot would be o–o–o. The southernmost, easternmost, deepest point at that spot would be 9–9–9. Thus we really have one thousand distinct Chesapeakes. Devon Island, which is a focus for us, would be less than halfway down the bay from north to south and would be classified as 4. It stands not quite at the extreme eastern edge, so gets an 8. The bar where the oysters grow is at the bottom, which gives a 9. Therefore, the position in which we are interested is 4–8–9.

What happened in 1886 at Chesapeake Bay Number 4–8–9? The magnitude of this storm broke all existing records not by trivial percentages but by huge multipliers. For example, the greatest previous discharge of fresh water at the mouth of the Susquehanna had been something like 400,000 cubic feet per second, and that represented a devastating flood. Now the disgorgement was more than three times as great, an unheard of 1,210,000. This produced a volume of non-salt water so prodigious that it shifted the isohalines seventy-two miles southward, which meant that the waters about Devon Island had become practically salt-free.

When the storm broke, there existed on a small subterranean shelf at the western edge of Devon Island—point 4–8–9 by the clergyman's calculation—a congregation of oysters which had fastened themselves securely to the solid bottom. Here some of the largest and tastiest oysters of the bay had produced their generations, while the minute spat drifted back and forth with the slow currents until they fastened to the bottom to develop the shells in which they would grow during the years of their existence.

Along this shelf, well known to watermen from Patamoke but kept by them as a secret, oysters had thrived during all the generations watermen had tonged the bay; no matter how many bushels of large oysters were lifted from this location, others replaced them. This was the shelf that could be depended upon.

In its original stages the flood from the Susquehanna did not affect these oysters. True, the salinity of all the water dropped, but at the depth at which they lived the loss did not, in these first days, imperil them. But there was another aspect of the flood which did. The Susquehanna, as it swept down from New York, picked up an astonishing burden of fine silt; for example, a house along the riverbank in Harrisburg might be inundated for only seven hours, but when the owners returned they would find in their second-floor bedrooms six inches of silt. How could it possibly have got there? Well, each cubic centimeter of seeping brown water carried its burden of almost invisible dust lifted from the farms of New York and Pennsylvania, and it was this dust, suspended in water, that was left behind.

The silt that fell in the bedroom of a butcher in Harrisburg could, when it dried, be swept away, but the silt which fell on a bed of oysters could not.

Down it came, silently, insidiously and very slowly. In four days more silt fell than in the previous sixty years. The entire Choptank as far east as Patamoke was chocolate-colored from the turbulent mud, but as soon as the waters began to calm themselves, their burden of silt was released and it fell persistently and inescapably onto the oysters.

At first it was no more than a film such as the propellers of the evening ferry might have deposited on any night. Such an amount caused no problem and might even bring with it plankton to feed the oysters. But this thin film was followed by a perceptible thickness, and then by more, until the oysters became agitated within their heavy shells. The spat, of course, were long since strangled. A whole oncoming generation of oysters had been suffocated.

Still the fine silt drifted down, an interminable rain of desolation. The bottom of the Choptank was covered with the gray-brown deposit; whole grains were so minute that the resulting mud seemed more like cement, except that it did not harden; it merely smothered everything on which it fell, pressing down with fingers so delicate, its weight could not be felt until the moment it had occupied every space with a subtle force more terrible than a tower of stone.

The oysters could have withstood a similar intrusion of sand; then the particles would have been so coarse that water could continue to circulate and plankton be obtained. Submersion of even a month was tolerable, for in time the sand would wash away, leaving the shellfish no worse for their experience. But the flood-swept silt was another matter, and on the tenth day after the flood, when the brown waters bore their heaviest burden of mud, even the mature oysters on the Devon shelf began to die. No lively water was reaching them, no plankton. They were entombed in a dreadful cascade of silt and they could not propel themselves either to a new location or to a new level. Secured to their shelf, they had to rely on passing tides that would wash the silt away. But none came.

On the twelfth day the waters of the Chesapeake reached their maximum muddiness; silt from midland Pennsylvania was coming down now, in a final burst of destruction, and when it reached the relatively calm waters of the Choptank, it broke loose from its carrying waters and filtered slowly down to the bed of the river. This was the final blow. The oysters were already submerged under two inches of silt; now three more piled on, and one by one the infinitely rich beds of Devon Island were covered by an impenetrable mud. The oysters perished in their shells.

In time, say a year and a half, the currents of the Choptank would eat away the mud and once more reveal the shelf upon which untold generations of new oysters would flourish. The shells of the dead oysters would be there, gnarled and craggy and inviting to the young spat that would be looking for a ledge to grab hold of. The spat would find a home; the nourishing plankton would drift by; the oyster beds of Devon Island would exist once more, but for the meantime they were obliterated in the silt of the great storm.

Another resident of the Chesapeake was also intensely affected by the hurricane of 1886, but he was better able to cope with the disaster, for he could move, and by taking precautions, adjust to altered circumstances. He was Jimmy, the time-honored Chesapeake name for the male blue crab, that delicious crustacean upon which so much of the wealth of the bay depended.

While the storm still lay off Norfolk, gathering speed and water, Jimmy, resting in the grassy waters at the edge of Turlock Marsh, perceived that a radical change in the atmosphere was about to occur. And it would probably arrive at the worst possible moment for him. How could he know these two facts? He was exceedingly sensitive to changes in atmospheric pressure or to any other factors which affected the waters of the bay. If a storm of unusual force was developing, he would be made aware by the sharp drop in barometric pressure and would prepare to take those protective measures which had rescued him in the past. Also, he knew intuitively when he must climb painfully out of his old shell, which was made of inert matter that could not grow in size as he grew. He had to discard it and prepare himself for the construction of a new shell better fitted to his increased body size. The time for such a moult was at hand.

When the storm broke, and no great body of water fell on the Choptank, Jimmy felt no signals that a crisis was at hand, so he prepared to shed his old shell, an intricate process which might consume as long as four hours of painful wrestling and contortion. But before the moult could begin, he became aware of a frightening change in the bay. The water level was rising. The salinity was diminishing. And when these two phenomena continued, and indeed accelerated, he became uncomfortable.

During any moult, which might take place three or four times a year as he increased in size, he preferred some secure place like the Turlock

Marsh, but if it was going to be flooded with fresh water, it could prove a deathtrap rather than a refuge, so he began swimming strongly out toward the deep center of the bay.

A mature crab like Jimmy could swim at a speed of nearly a mile an hour, so he felt safe, but as he cleared Devon Island and was hit by the rush of saltless water, he felt driven to swim with frenetic energy to protect himself. He would not drop dead in the first flush of fresh water, and he could adjust to surprising variations in salinity for brief periods; but to exist in the way for which his body had been constructed, he needed water with a proper salt content.

But moving into the deeper water meant that he would lose the protection of the marsh for his critical moulting. He would have to go through this complex maneuvering out in the bay, where he would be largely defenseless. But he had no other option.

The silt posed no insurmountable problem. It obscured his vision, to be sure, but it did not settle on him or pin him to the bottom, as it did the oysters. He could flip his many legs and swim clear, so that he was not yet in danger at this stage of the flood, but he did sense that he had to swim down toward the ocean to find the salinity necessary to his survival.

These matters assumed little importance in view of the crucial one at hand. Swimming easily to the bottom of the bay, he found a sandy area, a place he would never have considered for a moult in normal times, and there began his gyrations. First he had to break the seal along the edge of his present shell, and he did this by contracting and expanding his body, forcing water through his system and building up a considerable hydraulic pressure that slowly forced the shell apart, not conspicuously, but far enough for the difficult part of the moult to proceed.

Now he began the slow and almost agonizing business of withdrawing his boneless legs from their protective coverings and manipulating them so that they protruded from the slight opening. With wrenching movements he dislodged the main portion of his body, thrusting it toward the opening, which now widened under pressure from the legs. He had no skeleton, of course, so that he could contort and compress his body into whatever shape was most effective, but he did continue to generate hydraulic pressures through various parts of his body so that the shell was forced apart.

Three hours and twenty minutes after he started this bizarre procedure, he swam free of the old shell and was now adrift in the deep waters of the bay, totally without protection. He had no bony structure in any part of his body, no covering thicker than the sheerest tissue paper, no capacity for self-defense except a much-slowed ability to swim. Any fish that chanced to come his way could gobble him at a gulp; if he had been in shallower water, any bird could have taken him. In these fateful hours all he could do was hide.

And yet, even at his most defenseless moment his new armor was beginning to form. Eighty minutes after the moult he would have a paper-thin covering. After three hours he would have the beginning of a solid shell. And in five hours he would be a hard-shelled crab once more, and would remain that way until his next moult.

But as he waited deep in the bay for his new life, the results of the storm continued to make themselves felt, and now the water was so lacking in salt that he felt he must move south. He swam forcefully and with undiverted purpose, keeping to the eastern edge of the bay where the nutritive grasses produced the best plankton, and after a day he sensed the balance of the water to be more nearly normal.

He was not given time to luxuriate in this new-found security of proper water and a solid shell, for urgings of a primordial character were assaulting him, and he forgot his own preoccupations in order to swim among the grasses, looking for sooks which had been by-passed in the earlier mating periods. These overlooked females, on their way south to spend the winter near the entrance of the bay, where fertile sooks traditionally prepared to lay their eggs, sent out frantic signals to whatever males might be in the vicinity, for this was the final period in which they could be fertilized.

Jimmy, probing the marshes, detected such signals and swam with extraordinary energy into the weeds, from which a grateful sook came rushing at him. As soon as she saw that she had succeeded in attracting a male, she became tenderly passive and allowed him to turn her about with his claws and mount her from behind, forming with his many legs a kind of basket in which he would cradle her for the next three days.

This was her time to moult, and Jimmy gave her a protection he had not enjoyed. Covering her completely, he could fend off any fishes that might attack or beat away any birds. Turtles, too, could be avoided and otters that loved to feed on shell-less crabs. For three days he would defend her, holding her gently as she went through her own difficult gyrations of moulting.

When she succeeded in escaping from her old shell, she allowed Jimmy to cast it aside with his feet. She was now completely defenseless, a creature without a skeleton or any bony structure, and at this moment it became possible for the two crabs, he with a shell and she without, to engage in sex, an act which required six or seven hours.

When it was completed he continued to cradle her gently for two days, until her new shell was formed. Only when he felt it secure beneath him did he release her, and then the two crabs separated, she to swim to the lower end of the bay to develop her fertilized eggs, he to the northerly areas to spend the winter in the deeps.

But in 1886 it was not to be as simple as that, for when the Susquehanna broke its banks, flooding the land on either side of the river for a distance of miles, a vicious problem developed: the flood waters upset privies, flushed out septic pools and cleaned out manure dumps, throwing into the swiftly moving waters of the river an incredible accumulation of sewage. In each town that the river inundated on its rampage south, it reamed out the sewage ponds until at the end, when it emptied into the Chesapeake, it was nothing but one mighty cloaca carrying with it enough poisons to contaminate the entire bay.

The effect was worsened by the fact that in the big cities the river picked up huge quantities of industrial waste, especially the newly developed oils, which spread the poisons over the entire surface of the bay. Rarely had the Chesapeake been called upon to absorb such a concentration of lethal agents. It failed.

From the mouth of the river to the mouth of the bay the entire body of water became infected with a dozen new poisons. Those fortunate oysters which managed to escape the silt did not escape the fatal germs, and that October all who ate the few oysters that were caught ran the risk of death, and many died. The bluefish were contaminated and typhoid spread where they were eaten. The crabs were sorely hit, their delicate flesh acting as veritable blotting paper to absorb the germs. In New York and Baltimore families that ate them died.

The fishing industry in the Chesapeake was prostrated, and two years would pass before fresh waters from the Susquehanna and the Rappahannock and the James would flush out the bay and make it once more habitable for oysters and crabs.

Jimmy, seeking refuge at the bottom of the bay, and his impregnated mate, heading south to breed her young, had conducted their mating in an eddy of water heavily infected by the sewage of this vast cesspool, and they, too, died.

The Watermen

THE GOLDEN AGE OF THE EASTERN SHORE CAME
in that four-decade span from 1880 to 1920 when the rest of the nation
allowed the marshy counties to sleep undisturbed. True, in these years
the world experienced panics and wars, and revolutions and contested
elections, but these had almost no impact on the somnolent estuaries and
secluded coves. Roads now connected the important towns situated at
the heads of rivers, but they were narrow and dusty, and it took wagons
days to cover what a speedy boat could negotiate in an hour. When roads
paved with white oyster shells did arrive, at the end of this happy age,
they were usually one car-width only and formed not a reasonable means
of transportation but a lively invitation to suicide.

There was, of course, excitement, but it rarely arrived from the outside
world. A black male servant was accused of assaulting a white woman,
and a lynching party composed mainly of Turlocks and Cavenys broke
down the jail to string the accused from an oak tree, but Judge Hathaway
Steed proposed to have no such blot on his jurisdiction; armed only with
a family pistol, he confronted the mob and ordered it to disperse. The
terrified black man was then transported to a neighboring county, where
he was properly hanged.

The Eastern Shore baseball league, composed of six natural rivals,
including Easton, Crisfield, Chestertown and Patamoke, flourished and
became notorious for having produced Home Run Baker, who would hit
in one year the unheard-of total of twelve round-trippers. A luxurious
ferryboat left Baltimore every Saturday and Sunday at seven-thirty in the
morning to transport day-trippers to a slip at Claiborne, where the
throngs would leave the ship and crowd into the cars of the Baltimore,
Chesapeake and Atlantic Railroad for a two-hour race across the penin-

sula to Ocean City on the Atlantic. At four forty-five in the afternoon the railroad cars would refill, the train would chug its way back to Claiborne, passengers would reboard the ferry and arrive back at Baltimore at ten-thirty at night—all for one dollar and fifty cents.

One of the adventures which caused most excitement came in 1887 when a ship commanded by Captain Thomas Lightfoot, a troublemaker if there ever was one, docked at Patamoke with its cargo of ice sawed from the fresh-water ponds of Labrador. When the sawdust had been washed away, and the blue-green cakes were stored in icehouses along the riverfront, Captain Lightfoot produced an object which was to cause as much long-lasting trouble as the golden apple that Paris was required to award to the most beautiful goddess.

'I've somethin' extra for you,' Lightfoot announced as he directed one of his black stevedores to fetch the item from below. 'Before it appears I wish to inform you that it is for sale, ten dollars cash.'

A moment later the stevedore appeared on deck leading by a leash one of the most handsome dogs ever seen in Maryland. He was jet-black, sturdy in his front quarters, sleek and powerful in his hind, with a face so intelligent that it seemed he might speak at any moment. His movements were quick, his dark eyes following every development nearby, yet his disposition appeared so equable that he seemed always about to smile.

'He's called a Labrador,' Lightfoot said. 'Finest huntin' dog ever developed.'

'He's what?' Jake Turlock snapped.

'Best huntin' dog known.'

'Can't touch a Chesapeake retriever,' Turlock said, referring to the husky red dog bred especially for bay purposes.

'This dog,' said Lightfoot, 'will take your Chesapeake and teach him his ABC's.'

'That dog ain't worth a damn,' Turlock said. 'Too stocky up front.'

But there was something about this new animal that captivated Tim Caveny, whose red Chesapeake had just died without ever fulfilling the promise he had shown as a pup—'Fine in the water and persistent in trackin' downed birds, but not too bright. Downright stupid, if you ask me.' This new black dog displayed a visible intelligence which gave every sign of further development, and Caveny announced, 'I'd like to see him.'

Captain Lightfoot, suspecting that in Caveny he had found his pigeon, turned the Labrador loose, and with an almost psychic understanding that his future lay with this Irishman, the dog ran to Caveny, leaned against his leg and nuzzled his hand.

It was an omen. Tim's heart was lost, and he said, 'I'll take him.'

'Mr. Caveny, you just bought the best Labrador ever bred.' With grandiloquent gestures he turned the animal over to his new owner, and the dog, sensing that he had found a permanent master, stayed close to

Tim, and licked his hand and rubbed against him and looked up with dark eyes overflowing with affection.

Tim paid the ten dollars, then reached down and patted his new hunting companion. 'Come on, Lucifer,' he said.

'That's a hell of a name for a dog,' Turlock growled.

'He's black, ain't he?'

'If he's black, call him Nigger.'

'He's Old Testament black,' Tim said. And to Captain Lightfoot's surprise, he recited, ' "How art thou fallen from heaven, O Lucifer, son of the morning!" ' Turning his back on the others he stooped over the dog, roughed his head and said in a low voice, 'You'll be up in the morning, Lucifer, early, early.'

Lightfoot then startled the crowd by producing three other dogs of this new breed, one male and two females, and these, too, he sold to the hunters of Patamoke, assuring each purchaser, 'They can smell ducks, and they've never been known to lose a cripple.'

'To me they look like horse manure,' Jake Turlock said.

'They what?' Caveny demanded.

'I said,' Turlock repeated, 'that your black dog looks like a horse turd.'

Slowly Tim handed the leash he had been holding to a bystander. Then, with a mighty swipe, he knocked Turlock to the wet and salty boards of the wharf. The waterman stumbled in trying to regain his feet, and while he was off balance Caveny saw a chance to deliver an uppercut which almost knocked him into the water. Never one to allow a fallen foe an even chance, Caveny leaped across the planking and kicked the waterman in his left armpit, lifting him well into the air, but this was a mistake, because when Turlock landed, his hand fell upon some lumber stacked for loading onto Captain Lightfoot's ship, and after he had quickly tested three or four clubs he found one to his liking, and with it delivered such a blow to the Irishman's head that the new owner of the Labrador staggered back, tried to control his disorganized feet, and fell into the Choptank.

In this way the feud between Tim Caveny, owner of a black Labrador, and Jake Turlock, owner of a red Chesapeake, began.

The first test of the two dogs came in the autumn of 1888 at the dove shoot on the farm of old Lyman Steed, who had spent his long life running one of the Refuge plantations and had now retired to a stretch of land near Patamoke.

Nineteen first-class hunters of the area convened at regular intervals during the dove season to shoot this most interesting of the small game birds: gentlemen like Lyman Steed, middle-class shopkeepers and rough watermen like Jake Turlock and Tim Caveny. For a dove shoot was one of the most republican forms of sport so far devised. Here a man's worth was determined by two criteria: the way he fired his gun and how he managed his dog.

Each hunter was allowed to bring one dog to the shoot, and the animal had to be well trained, because the birds came charging in at low altitude, swerved and dodged in unbelievable confusion and, on the lucky occasions when they were hit, fell maliciously in unpredictable spots. If there was a swamp nearby, as on the Steed farm, the doves would fall there. If there were brambles, the dying doves seemed to seek them out, and the only practical way for the hunter to retrieve his dove, if he hit one, was to have a dog trained to leap forward when he saw a dove fall from the sky and find it no matter where it dropped. The dog must also lift the fallen bird gently in its teeth, carry it without bruising it against thorns, and drop it at the feet of his master. A dove hunt was more a test of dog than of master.

Jake Turlock had a well-trained beast, a large, surly red-haired Chesapeake, specially bred to work the icy waters of the bay in fall and winter. These dogs were unusual in that they grew a double matting of hair and produced an extra supply of oil to lubricate it. They could swim all day, loved to dive into the water for a fallen goose and were particularly skilled in breaking their way through ice. Like most of this breed, Jake's Chesapeake had a vile temper and would allow himself to be worked only by his master. Every other gunner in the field was his enemy and their dogs were beneath his contempt, but he was kept obedient by Jake's stern cry: 'Hey-You, heel!'

His name was Hey-You. Jake had started calling him that when he first arrived at the Turlock shack, a fractious, bounding pup giving no evidence that he could ever be trained. In fact, Jake had thought so little of him that he delayed giving him a proper name. 'Hey-You! Get the dove!' The pup would look quizzical, wait, consider whether he wanted to obey or not, then leap off when Jake kicked him.

So during his useless youth he was plain 'Hey-You, into the water for the goose!' But at the age of three, after many kicks and buffetings, he suddenly developed into a marvelous hunting dog, a raider like his master, a rough-and-tumble, uncivilized beast who seemed made for the Chesapeake. 'Hey-You! Go way down and fetch the dove.' So when this red-haired dog swaggered onto the dove field this October day, he was recognized as one of the best ever trained in the Patamoke area.

Lucifer, Tim Caveny's Labrador, was an unknown quantity, for he had never before participated in a dove shoot; furthermore, he had been trained in a manner quite different from Hey-You. 'My children were raised with love,' the Irishman said, 'and my dog is trained the same way.' From the moment Lucifer came down off Captain Lightfoot's ice ship, he had known nothing but love.

His glossy coat was kept nourished by a daily supply of fat from the Caveny table, and his nails were trimmed. In return he gave the Caveny family his complete affection. 'I believe that dog would lay down his life for me,' Mrs. Caveny told her neighbors, for when she fed him he always looked up at her with his great black eyes and rubbed against her hand. A peddler came to the door one day, unexpectedly and in a frightening manner; Lucifer's hackles rose, and he leaned forward tensely, waiting for a sign. Startled at seeing the man, Mrs. Caveny emitted a short gasp, whereupon Lucifer shot like a thunderbolt for the man's throat.

'Down, Lucifer!' she cried, and he stopped almost in midair.

But whether he could discipline himself to retrieve doves was another matter. Jake Turlock predicted widely, 'The stupid Irishman has spoiled his dog, if'n he was any good to begin with.' Other hunters who had trained their beasts more in the Turlock tradition agreed, adding, 'He ain't gonna get much out of that what-you-call-it—Labrador.'

But Caveny persisted, talking to Lucifer in sweet Irish phrases, trying to convince the dumb animal that great success awaited him on the dove field. 'Luke, you and me will get more doves than this town ever seen. Luke, when I say, "Fetch the dove!" you're to go direct to the spot you think it fell. Then run out in wide and wider circles.' Whether the dog would do this was uncertain, but Tim had tried with all his guile to get the animal in a frame of mind conducive to success. Now, as he led him to Lyman Steed's farm, he prayed that his lessons had been in the right direction, but when he turned the last corner and saw the other eighteen men with their Chesapeakes awaiting him, eager to see what he had accomplished with this strange animal, his heart fluttered and he felt dizzy.

Pulling gently on the rope attached to the dog's collar, he brought him back, kneeled beside him and whispered in his lilting brogue, 'Lucifer, you and me is on trial. They're all watchin' us.' He stroked the dog's glistening neck and said, 'At my heel constantly, little fellow. You don't move till I fire. And when I do, Luke, for the love of a merciful God, find that dove. Soft mouth, Luke, soft mouth and drop him at my toes, like you did with the rag dolls.'

As if he knew what his master was saying, Luke turned and looked at Tim impatiently, as if to say, 'I know my job. I'm a Labrador.'

The field contained about twenty acres and had recently been harvested, so that it provided a large, flat, completely open area, but it was surrounded by a marsh on one side, a large blackberry bramble on another, and a grove of loblollies covering a thicket of underbrush on a third. The doves would sweep in over the loblollies, drop low, hear gunfire and veer back toward the brambles. Placement of gunners was an art reserved for Judge Hathaway Steed, who hunted in an expensive Harris tweed imported from London.

The judge had been a hunter all his life, raised Chesapeakes and sold them to his friends. He had acquired a much better intuition concerning doves than he had of the law, and he now proposed to place his eighteen subordinates strategically, about sixty yards apart and in a pattern which pretty well covered the perimeter of the field. Toward the end of his assignments he came to Tim Caveny. 'You there, with the what-you-call-it dog.'

'Labrador,' Caveny said, tipping his hat respectfully, as his father had done in the old country when the laird spoke.

'Since we can't be sure a dog like that can hunt . . .'

'He can hunt.'

The judge ignored this. 'Take that corner,' he said, and Tim wanted to complain that doves rarely came to that corner, but since he was on trial he kept his mouth shut, but he was most unhappy when he saw Jake Turlock receive one of the best positions.

Then everyone stopped talking, for down the road edging the field came a carriage driven by a black man. On the seat beside him sat a very old gentleman with a shotgun across his knees. This was Lyman Steed, owner of the field. He was eighty-seven years old and so frail that a stranger would have wondered how he could lift a gun, let alone shoot it. Behind him, eyes and ears alert, rode a large red Chesapeake.

The carriage came to a halt close to where Hathaway Steed was allocating the spots, and the black driver descended, unfolded a canvas chair and lifted the old man down into it. 'Where do we sit today?' Steed asked in a high, quavering voice.

'Take him over by the big tree,' Hathaway said, and the black man carried the chair and its contents to the spot indicated. There he scraped the ground with his foot, making a level platform, and on it he placed the owner of the farm and one of the best shots in this meet. 'We's ready,' the black man cried, and the judge gave his last instructions: 'If you see a dove that the men near you don't, call "Mark!" Keep your dogs under control. And if the dove flies low, absolutely no shooting in the direction of the man left or right.'

The men took their positions. It was half after one in the afternoon. The sun was high and warm; insects droned. The dogs were restless, but each stayed close to his master, and the men wondered whether there would be any doves, because on some days they failed to show.

But not today. From the woods came six doves, flying low in their wonderfully staggered pattern, now in this direction, now swooping in that. Jake Turlock, taken by surprise, fired and hit nothing. 'Mark!' he shouted at the top of his voice. Tim Caveny fired and hit nothing. 'Mark!' he bellowed. In swift, darting patterns the doves dived and swirled and twisted, and three other hunters fired at them, to no avail, but as the birds tried to leave the field old Lyman Steed had his gun waiting. With a splendid shot he hit his target, and his big Chesapeake leaped out before the bird hit the ground and retrieved it before the dove could even flutter. Bearing it proudly in his mouth, but not touching its flesh with his teeth, he trotted back, head high, to his master and laid the bird at the old man's feet.

'That's how it's done,' Tim Caveny whispered to his Labrador.

There was a long wait and the hunters began to wonder if they would see any more doves, but Hathaway Steed, walking the rounds to police the action, assured each man as he passed, 'We're going to see flocks.'

He was right. At about two-thirty they started coming in. 'Mark!' one hunter shouted as they passed him before he could fire. Jake Turlock was waiting and knocked one down, whereupon Hey-You leaped out into the open field, pounced on the fallen bird and brought it proudly back. Jake looked at Tim, but the Irishman kept his eyes on the sky. He did whisper to Lucifer, 'Any dog can retrieve in an open field. Wait till one falls in the brambles.'

On the next flight Tim got no chance to shoot, but Turlock did, and this time he hit a bird that had come over the field, heard the shooting and doubled back. This dove fell into brambles. 'Fetch the dove!' Jake told his Chesapeake, but the bushes were too thick. That bird was lost.

But now another dove flew into Tim's range, and when he fired, this one also fell into brambles. 'Fetch the dove!' Tim said calmly, his heart aching for a good retrieve.

Lucifer plunged directly for the fallen bird but could not penetrate the thick and thorny briars. Unlike Turlock's Chesapeake, he did not quit, for he heard his master calling softly, 'Circle, Luke! Circle!' And he ran in wide circles until he found a back path to the brambles. But again he was stopped, and again his master cried, 'Circle, Luke!' And this time he found an entrance which allowed him to roam freely, but with so much ranging he had lost an accurate guide to the fallen bird. Still he heard his master's voice imploring, 'Circle, Luke!' and he knew that this meant he still had a chance.

So in the depth of the bramble patch, but below the reach of the thorns, he ran and scrambled and clawed and finally came upon Caveny's bird. He gave a quiet *yup,* and when Tim heard this his heart expanded. Lucifer had passed his first big test, but on the way out of the patch the dog smelled another fallen bird, Turlock's, and he brought this one too.

When he laid the two doves at Tim's feet, the Irishman wanted to kneel and kiss his rough black head, but he knew that all the hunters in his area were watching, so in a manly way he patted the dog, then prepared for his moment of triumph.

It was a custom in dove shooting that if a hunter downed a bird which his dog could not retrieve and another man's dog did fetch it, the second hunter was obligated to deliver the dove to the man who had downed it. It was a nice tradition, for it allowed the second man to make a show of carrying the dove to its rightful owner while all the other hunters observed his act of sportsmanship. Implied in the gesture was the challenge: 'My dog can retrieve and yours can't.'

Proudly Tim Caveny walked the hundred-odd yards to where Jake Turlock was standing. Lucifer started to follow, but Tim cried sharply, 'Stay!' and the dog obeyed. The other hunters took note of this, then watched as Tim gravely delivered the bird, but at this moment another hunter shouted, 'Mark!' and a whole covey flew over.

Automatically Jake and Tim fired, and two birds fell. Jake's Hey-You was on the spot, of course, and proudly ran out to recover the dove his master had knocked down, but Lucifer was far distant from where his master had shot, yet he was so obedient to the earlier command, 'Stay,' that he did not move. But when Tim yelled, 'Fetch the dove,' he leaped off his spot, rushed directly to the fallen bird, and carried it not to where Tim was standing, but back to his assigned location.

The hunter next to Tim on the down side of the field called, 'You got yourself a dog, Tim.'

When Caveny returned to his location and saw the dove neatly laid beside his pouch, he desperately wanted to smother the dark beast with his affection; instead he said merely, 'Good dog, Luke.'

'Mark!' came the call and up went the guns.

The day was a triumph. Luke hunted in marshland as well as he had in brambles. He proved he had a soft mouth. He circled well in woods, and on the open field he was superb. And with it all he displayed the bland, sweet disposition of the Labradors and the Cavenys.

It was the tradition on these dove shoots for one member at the end of the day to provide refreshments. At quarter to five, religiously, the hunting ceased. The dogs were put back on leashes, and if the owners had come by wagon, were stowed in back while their masters ate cold duck and drank Baltimore beer. Turlock and Caveny, having come on foot, tied their dogs to trees, and as they did so the former muttered, 'Doves ain't nothin', Caveny. It's what a dog does in ice that counts.'

'Lucifer will handle ice,' Tim said confidently.

'On the bay proper, my Chesapeake is gonna eat 'im up. Out there they got waves.'

'Your Labrador looks like a breed to be proud of,' old Lyman Steed said as the black servant carried him into position to share the duck.

'Possibilities,' Judge Hathaway Steed said. 'But we won't know till we see him after geese.'

Each man complimented Tim on what he had accomplished with this strange dog, but each also predicted, 'Probably won't be much on the bay. Hair's not thick enough.'

Tim did not argue, but when he got Lucifer home he hugged him and gave him chicken livers, and whispered, 'Lucifer, geese is just doves, grown bigger. You'll love the water, cold or not.' During the whole dove season, during which this fine black dog excelled, Tim repeated his assurances: 'You're gonna do the same with geese.'

The test came in November. As the four men and their dogs holed up in a blind at the Turlock marshes, Jake reminded them, 'Geese ain't so plentiful now. Can't afford any mistakes, man or dog.' He was right. Once the Choptank and its sister rivers had been home for a million geese; now the population had diminished to less than four hundred thousand, and bagging them became more difficult. Jake, a master of the goose call, tried from dawn till ten in the morning to lure the big birds down, but failed. The hunters had a meager lunch, and toward dusk, when it seemed that the day was a failure, nine geese wheeled in, lowered the pitch of their wings, spread their feet and came right at the blind. Guns blazed, and before the smoke had cleared, Jake's Chesapeake had leaped out of the blind and with powerful swimming motions had retrieved the goose that his master had appeared to kill. Lucifer went into the water, too, but many seconds after Hey-You, and he was both splashy and noisy in making his retrieve of Tim's goose.

'Sure doesn't like cold water,' Jake said contemptuously.

'Neither did yours, when he started,' Tim said.

'A Chesapeake is born lovin' water, colder the better.'

It became obvious to the hunters, after eight mornings in the blind, that while Tim Caveny's new dog was exceptional with doves on warm days, he left much to be desired as a real hunter in the only form of the sport that mattered—goose on water. He displayed a discernible reluctance to plunge into cold waves, and they began to wonder whether he would go into ice at all.

Talk at the store centered on his deficiencies: 'This here Labrador is too soft. Can't hold a candle to a Chesapeake for hard work when it matters. You ask me, I think Caveny bought hisse'f a loser.' Some hunters told him this to his face.

Tim listened and said nothing. In his lifetime he had had four major dogs, all of them Chesapeakes, and he understood the breed almost as well as Jake Turlock did, but he had never owned a dog with the charm of Lucifer, the warmth, the love, and that meant something—'I come home, the room's bigger when that dog's in it.'

'Point is,' the men argued, 'a huntin' dog oughtn't to be in a room in the first place. His job is outside.'

'You don't know Lucifer. Besides, he's sired the best lot of pups in the region. This breed is bound to catch on.'

The Patamoke hunters were a suspicious clan. The most important thing in their lives, more important than wife or church or political party, was the totality of the hunting season: 'You got to have the right gun, the right mates, the right spot, the right eye for the target and, above all, the right dog. And frankly, I doubt the Labrador.' The pups did not sell.

Tim had faith. He talked with Lucifer constantly, encouraging him to leap more quickly into the cold water. He showed what ice was like, and how the dog must break it with his forepaws to make a path for himself to the downed goose. Using every training trick the Choptank had ever heard of, he tried to bring this handsome dog along step by step.

He failed. In January, when real ice formed along the edges of the river, the men went hunting along the banks of the bay itself, and when Jake Turlock knocked down a beautiful goose, it fell on ice about two hundred yards from the blind—'Hey-You, get the bird!'

And the big Chesapeake showed what a marvelous breed he was by leaping into the free water, swimming swiftly to the edge of the ice, then breaking a way for himself right to the goose. Clutching the big bird proudly in his jaws, he plunged back into the icy water, pushed aside the frozen chunks and returned to the blind, entering it with a mighty, water-spraying leap.

'That's what I call a dog,' Jake said proudly, and the men agreed.

Lucifer did not perform so well. He retrieved his goose all right, but hesitantly and almost with protest. He didn't want to leap into the water in the first place; he was not adept at breaking ice; and when he returned to the blind, he ran along the ice for as long as possible before going back into the freezing water.

'He did get the goose,' Jake admitted condescendingly, and for the rest of that long day on the Chesapeake the two dogs performed in this way, with Hey-You doing as well as a water dog could and Lucifer just getting by.

Tim never spoke a harsh word. Lucifer was his dog, a splendid, loving, responsive animal, and if he didn't like cold water, that was a matter between him and his master. And toward dusk the dog found an opportunity to repay Tim's confidence. Jake had shot a big goose, which had fallen into a brambled sort of marsh from which Hey-You could not extract it. The dog tried, swam most valiantly in various directions, but achieved nothing.

In the meantime Lucifer remained in the blind, trembling with eagerness, and Tim realized that his Labrador knew where that goose was. After Hey-You had returned with nothing, Tim said softly, 'Luke, there's a bird out there. Show them how to get it.'

Like a flash the black dog leaped into the water, splashed his way through the semi-ice into the rushy area—and found nothing. 'Luke!'

Tim bellowed. 'Circle. Circle!' So the dog ran and splashed and swam in noisy circles and still found nothing, but he would not quit, for his master kept pleading, 'Luke, circle!'

And then he found the goose, grabbed it in his gentle mouth and swam proudly back to the blind. As he was about to place the goose at Tim's feet, the Irishman said quietly, 'No!' And the dog was so attentive to his master that he froze, wanting to know what he had done wrong.

'Over there,' Tim said, and Luke took the goose to Jake, placing it at his feet.

The feud between the two watermen continued. The men at the store fired it with unkind comments about Lucifer's deficiencies, but once or twice Caveny caught a hint that their animosity was weakening, for at some unexpected moment a man would see in Tim's dog a quality which made him catch his breath. Outwardly every hunter would growl, 'I want my dog to be rough and able to stand the weather and ready to leap at anyone attackin' me,' but inwardly he would also want the dog to love him. And the way in which Lucifer stayed close to Tim, anxious to detect every nuance in the Irishman's mood, tantalized the men at the store. All they would grant openly was, 'Maybe Tim's got somethin' in that black dog.' But Jake Turlock would not admit even that. 'What he's got is a good lap dog, and that's about it. As for me, I'm interested solely in huntin'.'

Aside from this disagreement over dogs, and a fistfight now and then, the two watermen maintained a warm friendship. They hunted together, fished together and worked the oyster beds in season. But it was the big gun that cemented their partnership, giving it substance and allowing it to blossom.

In these decades when the Eastern Shore flourished, the city of Baltimore also flourished. Some discriminating critics considered it the best city in America, combining the new wealth of the North with the old gentility of the South. The city offered additional rewards: a host of German settlers who gave it intellectual distinction; numerous Italians who gave it warmth. But for most observers, its true excellence derived from the manner in which its hotels and restaurants maintained a tradition of savory cooking: southern dishes, northern meats, Italian spices and German beer.

In 1888 the noblest hotel of them all had opened, the Rennert, eight stories high, with an additional three stories to provide a dome at one end, a lofty belvedere at the other. It was a grand hostelry which boasted, 'Our cooks are Negro. Our waiters wear white gloves.' From the day of its opening, it became noted for the luxuriance of its cuisine: 'Eighteen kinds of game. Fourteen ways to serve oysters. And the best wild duck in America.' To dine at the Rennert was to share the finest the Chesapeake could provide.

Jake Turlock and Tim Caveny had never seen the new hotel, but it was to play a major role in their lives. Its black chefs demanded the freshest oysters, and these were delivered daily during the season by Choptank watermen who packed their catch in burlap bags, speeding them across the bay by special boat. When the boat was loaded with oysters, its principal cargo, the captain could usually find space on deck for a few last-minute barrels crammed with ducks: mallards, redheads, canvasbacks and, the juciest of all, the black. It was in the providing of these ducks for the Rennert that Jake and Tim began to acquire a little extra money, which they saved for the larger project they had in mind.

One night at the store, after arguing about the comparative merits of their dogs, Jake said, 'I know me a man's got a long gun he might want to dispose of.'

Caveny was excited. 'If you can get the gun, I can get me a couple of skiffs.'

Turlock replied, 'Suppose we get the gun and the skiffs, I know me a captain who'll ferry our ducks to the Rennert. Top dollar.'

Caveny completed the self-mesmerization by adding, 'We put aside enough money, we can get Paxmore to build us our own boat. Then we're in business.'

So the feuding pair sailed upriver to the landing of a farm owned by an old man named Greef Twombly, and there they propositioned him: 'You ain't gonna have much more use for your long gun, Greef. We aim to buy it.'

'What you gonna use for money?' the toothless old fellow asked.

'We're gonna give you ten dollars cash, which Tim Caveny has in his pocket right now, and another forty when we start collectin' ducks.'

'Barrel of that gun was made from special forged iron. My grandfather bought it from London, sixty-two years ago.'

'It's been used.'

'More valuable now than when he got it home.'

'We'll give you sixty.'

'Sixty-five and I'll think about it.'

'Sixty-five it is, and we get possession now.'

Twombly rocked back and forth, considering aspects of the deal, then led them to one of the proudest guns ever to sweep the ice at midnight. It was a monstrous affair, eleven feet six inches long, about a hundred and ten pounds in weight, with a massive stock that could not possibly fit into a man's shoulder, which was good, because if anyone tried to hold this cannon when it fired, the recoil would tear his arm away.

'You ever fire one of these?' the old man asked.

'No, but I've heard,' Turlock said.

'Hearin' ain't enough, son. You charge it with three quarters of a pound of black powder in here, no less, or she won't carry. Then you pour in a pound and a half of Number Six shot, plus one fistful. You tamp her down with greasy wadding, like this, and you're ready. Trigger's kept real tight so you can't explode the charge by accident, because if you did, it would rip the side off'n a house.'

The two watermen admired the huge barrel, the sturdy fittings and the massive oak stock; as they inspected their purchase the old man said, 'You know how to fit her into a skiff?'

'I've seen,' Turlock said.

But Twombly wanted to be sure these new men understood the full complexity of this powerful gun, so he asked them to carry it to the landing, where he had a fourteen-foot skiff with extremely pointed bow and almost no deadrise, chocks occupying what normally would have been the main seat and a curious burlap contraption built into the stern area.

Deftly the old hunter let himself down into the skiff, kneeling in the stern. He then produced a double-ended paddle like the ones Eskimos used, and also two extremely short-handled single paddles. Adjusting his weight and testing the double paddle, he told Jake, 'You can hand her down.'

When the two watermen struggled with the preposterous weight of the gun, the old man said, 'It ain't for boys.' He accepted the gun into the skiff, dropped its barrel between the chocks, flipped a wooden lock, which secured it, then fitted the heavy butt into a socket made of burlap bagging filled with pine needles.

'What you do,' Twombly said, 'is use your big paddle to ease you into position, but when you come close to the ducks you stow it and take out your two hand paddles, like this.' And with the two paddles that looked like whisk brooms, he silently moved the skiff about.

'When you get her into position, you lie on your belly, keep the hand paddles close by and sight along the barrel of the gun. You don't point the gun; you point the skiff. And when you get seventy, eighty ducks in range, you put a lot of pressure on this trigger and—'

The gun exploded with a power that seemed to tear a hole in the sky. The kickback came close to ripping out the stern of the skiff, but the pine needles absorbed it, while a veritable cloud of black smoke curled upward.

'First time I ever shot that gun in daylight,' the old man said. 'It's a killer.'

'You'll sell?'

'You're Lafe Turlock's grandson, ain't you?'

'I am.'

'I had a high regard for Lafe. He could track niggers with the best. Gun's yourn.'

'You'll get your fifty-five,' Jake promised.

'I better,' the old man said ominously.

Caveny produced the two skiffs he had promised, and their mode of operation became standardized: as dusk approached, Jake would inspect his skiff to be sure he had enough pine needles in the burlap to absorb the recoil; he also cleaned the huge gun, prepared his powder, checked his supply of shot; Tim in the meantime was preparing his own skiff and feeding the two dogs.

Hey-You ate like a pig, gulping down whatever Caveny produced, but Lucifer was more finicky; there were certain things, like chicken guts, he would not eat. But the two animals had learned to exist together, each with his own bowl, growling with menace if the other approached. They had never engaged in a real fight; Hey-You would probably have killed Lucifer had one been joined, but they did nip at each other and a kind of respectful discipline was maintained.

Whenever they saw Jake oiling the gun, they became tense, would not sleep and spied on every action of their masters. As soon as it became clear that there was to be duck hunting, they bounded with joy and kept close to the skiff in which Caveny would take them onto the water.

Duck hunting with a big gun was an exacting science best performed in the coldest part of winter with no moon, for then the watermen enjoyed various advantages: they could cover the major part of their journey by sliding their skiffs across the ice; when they reached areas of open water they would find the ducks clustered in great rafts; and the lack of moonlight enabled them to move close without being seen. The tactic required utmost silence; even the crunch of a shoe on frost would spook the ducks. The dogs especially had to remain silent, perched in Caveny's skiff, peering into the night.

When the two skiffs reached open water, about one o'clock in the morning with the temperature at twelve degrees, Tim kept a close watch on the necks of his two dogs; almost always the first indication he had that ducks were in the vicinity came when the hackles rose on Hey-You. He was so attuned to the bay that one night Tim conceded graciously, 'Jake, your dog can see ducks at a hundred yards in pitch-black,' and Turlock replied, 'That's why he's a huntin' dog, not a lap dog . . . like some I know.'

When the ducks were located, vast collections huddling in the cold, Turlock took command. Easing his skiff into the icy water, he adjusted his double-ended paddle, stayed on his knees to keep the center of gravity low, and edged toward the restive fowl. Sometimes it took him an hour to cover a quarter of a mile; he kept the barrel of his gun smeared with lamp black to prevent its reflecting such light as there might be, and in cold darkness he inched forward.

Now he discarded his two-handed paddle and lay flat on his belly, his cheek alongside the stock of the great gun, his hands working the short paddles. It was a time of tension, for the slightest swerve or noise would alert the ducks and they would be off.

Slowly, slowly he began to point the nose of the skiff at the heart of the congregation, and when he had satisfied himself that the muzzle of the gun was pointed in the right direction, he brought his short paddles in and took a series of deep breaths. Then, with his cheek close to the stock but not touching it, and his right hand at the trigger, he extended his forefinger, grasped the heavy trigger—and waited. Slowly the skiff would drift and steady, and when everything was in line, he pulled the trigger.

He was never prepared for the magnitude of the explosion that ripped through the night. It was monstrous, like the fire of a cannon, but in the brief flash it produced he could always see ducks being blown out of the water as if a hundred expert gunners had fired at them.

Now Caveny became the focus. Paddling furiously, he sped his skiff through the dark water, his two dogs quivering with desire to leap into the waves to retrieve the ducks. But he wanted to bring them much closer to where the birds lay, and to do so he enforced a stern discipline. 'No! No!'—that was all he said, but the two dogs obeyed, standing on their hind feet, their forepaws resting on the deadrise like twin figureheads, one red, one black.

'Fetch!' he shouted, and the dogs leaped into the water and began their task of hauling the ducks to the two skiffs, Hey-You always going to Turlock's and Lucifer to Caveny's.

Since Tim's job was to man his shotgun and knock down cripples, he was often too busy to bother with his dog, so the Labrador had perfected a tactic whereby he paddled extra hard with his hind legs, reared out of the water and tossed his ducks into the skiff.

In this way the two watermen, with one explosion of their big gun, sometimes got themselves as many as sixty canvasbacks, ten or twelve blacks and a score of others. On rare occasions they would be able to fire twice in one night, and then their profit was amazing.

As soon as the two skiffs reached Patamoke, the watermen packed their catch in ventilated barrels, which they lined up on the wharf. There they purchased from other night gunners enough additional ducks to make full barrels, which they handed over to the captain of the boat running oysters to the Rennert, and at the end of each month they received from the hotel a check for their services.

Night after night Jake and Tim lurked at the edge of the ice, waiting for the ducks to raft up so that the gun could be fired, and as the barrels filled with canvasbacks and mallards, so their pockets filled with dollars, and they began to think seriously about acquiring a real boat in which they could branch out.

'There's a man on Deal Island, got hisse'f a new kind of boat,' Turlock said one morning as they were packing their ducks.

'What's special?'

'Claims it's the best type ever built for the Chesapeake. Made especially for drudgin'.'

Time out of mind, watermen of the Chesapeake had used two words with unique pronunciation. There was no such thing as an oyster, never had been. It was an arster, and to call it anything else was profanation. And a man did not dredge for arsters, he drudged them. Jake and Tim proposed to become arster drudgers, and the boat they had in mind was ideal for their purpose.

It put in to Patamoke one day, and Turlock ran to the Paxmore Boatyard and asked Gerrit Paxmore to join him in inspecting it. 'This is quite remarkable,' the Quaker said. And he began to analyze what the Deal Island men had done.

'Very shallow draft, so it can go anywhere on the flats. Single mast far forward, but look how it's raked! Gives them a triangular sail. More room on deck. Also allows the tip of the mast to hang over the hold, so that they can drop a line and haul cargo out. Enormous boom to give them drudging power. Very low freeboard, so they won't have to hoist the arsters too far, and it looks like it could sleep six.'

But then his practiced eye saw something he definitely did not like. 'She has no protruding keel, which accounts for her shallow draft, but she does have a retractable centerboard. I don't like that, not at all.'

'She has to have,' Turlock said. 'To counterbalance the sail.'

'I know, but to insert a centerboard, you've got to penetrate the keel.'

'What's the fault in that?'

'At Paxmore's we never touch the keel.' He looked at an old boat tied to the wharf, its backbone hogged. 'Our boats don't do that.'

He would not discuss the new craft any further, but returned to his yard; Turlock, however, asked the captain if he could serve on the next oystering, and the Deal Island man said, 'Come aboard,' so Jake dredged for six days, and when he came ashore he told Caveny, 'That's the finest boat's ever been built. It helps you work.'

So they went back to Paxmore, and Tim listened as his partner extolled the new craft. 'Mr. Paxmore, that boat helps you drudge. You can feel that huge boom bendin' to the job.'

But Paxmore was adamant. 'I would never feel comfortable, building a boat whose keel had been half-severed.'

'Suppose you don't feel comfortable? How about us? We're buyin' the boat.'

'I build by my own principles,' Paxmore said. 'If someone else can use my boat when she's built, good. If not, I'm ready to wait till the proper buyer comes along.'

Jake stepped back, looked at the self-satisfied Quaker and said, 'You'll go out of business in six months.'

'We're in our third century,' Paxmore said, and he would not discuss boatbuilding any further.

As a matter of fact, the question almost became academic one wintry February night when the two watermen had crept out to a spacious lagoon in the ice; there must have been three thousand ducks rafted there beneath a frozen late-rising moon. Caveny became aware of how cold it was when Lucifer left his spot on the gunwale and huddled in the bottom of the skiff. Hey-You turned twice to look at his cowardly companion, then moved to the middle of the bow as if obliged to do the work of two.

Jake, seeing this tremendous target before him—more ducks in one spot than they had ever found before—decided that he would use not a pound and a half of shot but almost twice that much. 'I'll rip a tunnel through the universe of ducks.' But to propel such a heavy load he required an extra-heavy charge, so into the monstrous gun he poured more than a pound of black powder. He also rammed home a double wadding. 'This is gonna be a shot to remember. Rennert's will owe us enough money to pay for our boat.'

Cautiously he moved his lethal skiff into position, waited, took a deep breath and pulled the trigger.

'Whoooom!' The gun produced a flash that could have been seen for miles and a bang that reverberated across the bay. The tremendous load of shot slaughtered more than a hundred and ten ducks and seven geese. It also burst out the back of Jake's skiff, knocked him unconscious and threw him a good twenty yards aft into the dark and icy waters.

The next minutes were a nightmare. Caveny, having seen his partner fly through the air during the brief flash of the explosion, started immediately to paddle in the direction of where the body might fall, but the two dogs, trained during their entire lives to retrieve fallen birds, found themselves involved with the greatest fall of ducks they had ever encountered, and they refused to bother with a missing man.

'Goddamnit!' Caveny yelled. 'Leave them ducks alone and find Jake.'

But the dogs knew better. Back and forth they swam on their joyous mission, gathering ducks at a rate they had never imagined in their twitching dreams.

'Jake! Where in hell are you?'

In the icy darkness he could find no way of locating the drowning man; all he knew was the general direction of Jake's flight, and now, in some desperation, he began sweeping the area—with almost no chance of finding his mate.

But then Lucifer swam noisily to the skiff, almost reprimanding Tim for having moved it away from the fallen ducks, and after he had thrown two ducks into the skiff, he swam casually a few yards, grabbed the unconscious and sinking Turlock by an arm, hauled him to the skiff, and returned quickly to the remaining ducks.

When Tim finally succeeded in dragging Jake aboard, he could think of nothing better to do than to slap the unconscious man's face with his icy glove, and after a few minutes Jake revived. Bleary-eyed, he tried to determine where he was, and when at last he perceived that he was in Caveny's skiff and not his own, he bellowed, 'What have you done with the gun?'

'I been savin' you!' Tim yelled back, distraught by this whole affair and by the mangled ducks that kept piling into his skiff.

'To hell with me. Save the gun!'

So now the two watermen began paddling furiously and with no plan, trying to locate the other skiff, and after much fruitless effort Jake had the brains to shout, 'Hey-You! Where are you?'

And from a direction they could not have anticipated, a dog barked, and when they paddled there they found a sorely damaged skiff almost sinking from the weight of its big gun and the many ducks Hey-You had fetched.

On the doleful yet triumphant return to Patamoke, Tim Caveny could not help pointing out that it had been his Labrador who had saved Turlock's life, but Jake growled through the ice festooning his chin, 'Granted, but it was Hey-You that saved the gun, and that's what's important.'

The partners now had enough money for a serious down payment on an oyster dredger, but before they made a contract with any boatbuilder, Jake wanted Tim to sail aboard one of the Deal Island innovations, so they shipped with a mean-spirited gentleman from that island, and Tim came home convinced that no boat but one of that type would satisfy him.

But he had also learned that the best boats on the bay were those built by Paxmore's, always had been, and he was not willing to settle for second-best. He therefore launched a campaign to convince his partner that they must do business with the Quaker, no matter what his idiosyncrasies. 'Let him build the boat however he wants. He'll do it right.'

Jake was obdurate. 'The three boats I seen are just what we want. I won't have no details sacrificed to any square-headed Quaker thinks he can improve the breed.'

For a week the two watermen could not even agree to take their big gun out for ducks, and no barrels were shipped to the Rennert. Then Tim counted their savings, concluded that it was safe to go ahead, and reluctantly agreed that since Paxmore refused to make what they wanted, they must give their commission to some other builder. Tim was not happy with this decision but was prepared to go ahead with it. And then one morning, as they argued as to which of the alternative builders they would employ, a boy came with news that Mr. Paxmore wanted to see them.

It was a strange but very Choptank trio that convened. Gerrit Paxmore was the youngest of the three—stiff, wearing black shoes, heavy black trousers and waistcoat. He suffered from a forbidding countenance that rarely broke into a smile, and he spoke precisely, as if recording every word against some possible future challenge, at which time he would be prepared not only to explain it but to fulfill it. Patrons soon discovered that to do business with Paxmore was not easy, but it was reassuring.

Jake Turlock had his family's leanness, height and sour visage. He wore run-over shoes, baggy trousers, torn shirt and smashed hat, items which he rarely changed. He could read and write, having been well taught by the first Caveny from Ireland, but he posed as an illiterate. He hated Negroes and Catholics but found himself consistently thrown in with them, and much to his surprise, liked the individuals with whom he worked. He was, for example, convinced that Tim Caveny, as a Papist, was an insidious type, but he had never discovered any other man with whom it was so comforting to work. Tim had forced him to save money; had saved his life when the big gun blew out the back of the skiff; and up to now had proved reliable in emergencies. But Jake felt certain that when a real crunch came, Caveny would be found wanting.

Tim was much like his father, old Michael, the schoolteacher of indomitable optimism. He was inclined to be pudgy, lazy and preposterous. He loved his church and his family; but he loved even more the concept of sticking everlastingly to the job at hand. He was, in his own way, as much a puritan as Gerrit Paxmore, which was why these two men understood each other. Tim was invariably willing to bet his money that *his* nigger would outfight the other, that *his* dog would retrieve more doves, that *his* boat would outsail any other on the bay. He existed in a world of perpetual challenge, in which he constantly faced men who were bigger than he or had more money. But since he was Irish, a reliable margin of good luck hung over him like an aura. He strove for the best, and the best sometimes happened.

It was he who opened the conversation that morning. 'Mr. Paxmore, we've decided—'

'We've decided nothin',' Turlock interrupted.

'Perhaps I can assist thee,' Paxmore said gently. 'I've consulted with my men, and we want to try our hands at one of these new boats. What does thee call them?'

'Skipjack,' Turlock said.

'After the fish that skips over the water,' Tim interposed. 'And it does, Mr. Paxmore. This boat skims.'

'So we've decided, here at Paxmore's . . .' He coughed, placed his hands on the desk as if confessing all, and said, 'We'll build thy boat.'

'Centerboard in position?' Turlock asked.

'Of course.'

'How much?' Caveny asked.

'We think we can do it . . .' With almost a visible shudder he looked at the two supplicants, who could not possibly have the money required, then said in a whisper, 'We could do it for twelve hundred dollars.'

As soon as the words were uttered, Tim Caveny slapped down a bundle of bills. 'We can pay five hundred and forty dollars on deposit.'

This was more than twice what Paxmore had expected, and with an astonishment he could not control he asked, 'Where did thee acquire so much?' and Caveny said, like a fellow industrialist, 'We've been savin' it.'

Jake Turlock hated to surrender cash. 'Would it be cheaper, Mr. Paxmore, if me and Tim was to provide you with your timber?'

'It would indeed!'

'How much cheaper?'

'Thee would include keel, mast, boom?'

'You give us the length. We have the trees.'

Paxmore studied a paper which betrayed the fact that he wanted to build this boat no matter what the profit: he had a complete sketch of an improved skipjack, waiting to be transformed into a sleek bay craft. 'Mast, at least sixty-five feet tall, two feet in diameter at the thirty-foot mark, to allow for trimming.'

'I have my eye on just the tree,' Jake said.

'Boom fifty-three feet.'

'That's awful long for a boom. Longer than the boat itself.'

'That's the design. Bowsprit a good twenty-two feet.'

'She's gonna be very top-heavy, with those dimensions,' Turlock said.

'She'll be ballasted,' Paxmore assured him, but he had not yet said how much reduction he would allow if Turlock cut the timber from the woods behind his marsh.

'The savin's?' Jake asked.

'Thee will save three hundred and fifty dollars.'

'Tim,' the waterman said, 'get us some axes.'

The work the two men did in the ensuing weeks was awesome, for not only did they chop down oaks and loblollies during the day; they also took their long gun out each night, because only by constantly supplying the Rennert with barrels of ducks could they discharge the remaining debt on the skipjack. In addition to all this, Tim Caveny, in any spare moments, was constructing something that was about to shock the bay.

He worked in secret with his oldest boy, hammering at pipes, spending hours at a forge in town. The only indication Jake caught that his partner was up to something came one dawn when he helped lift mallards and canvasbacks from Tim's skiff. 'What you doin' with them extra struts?'

'I got me an idea,' the Irishman said, but he confided nothing.

And then one night as the watermen went down to their skiffs, Caveny revealed his masterpiece. From the front of his boat protruded not one but seven guns, each with a barrel two inches in diameter. They fanned out like the tail of a turkey gobbler, coming together where the triggers would normally be. There were no triggers. 'That's my invention. What we do is load the seven guns—powder, pellets and tampin', all in order.'

'How you gonna fire 'em? Jake asked.

'Ah ha! See this little iron trough?'

Jake had seen it, and had wondered what purpose it served; he could not have anticipated the insane proposal that Tim now made.

'The trough fits in here, just below the powder entrances to the seven guns. We fill it with powder all the way acrost. At this end, we light it. Whoosh! It fires each of the seven guns in order, and we kill so many ducks we're gonna need two extra skiffs.'

'It'll backfire and scorch you to death,' Jake predicted.

'It ain't yet.'

'You mean you fired this battery?'

'Three times. And tonight we fire it at the biggest mess o' ducks we can find.'

They paddled down the center of the Choptank, seeking a strong field of ice across which they could push their arsenal. North of Devon Island, where the rivers penetrating inland clustered, they found some, pulled their skiffs onto it and started the long, patient movement inland. Hey-You and Lucifer, each in his own skiff, made no noise, and when the hunters reached open water, everyone remained quiet for about half an hour, adjusting eyes to the darkness and allowing whatever birds lurked ahead to quieten.

Hey-You's hackles rose, and Tim whispered, 'It's a congregation!'

'We'll move together,' Jake proposed.

'But I'm to shoot first,' Tim said.

'Damned right. I'll be there to catch you when it blows you apart.'

The plan was for Tim to ignite his powder trough and, at the explosion of the first gun, for Jake to fire his monster. They calculated that Tim's seven guns backed up by Jake's would fire so nearly simultaneously that a curtain of lead would be thrown across the bay; few fowl would escape.

Each man eased himself into his skiff, instructed his dog where to sit, and started to work the small hand paddles. One could barely see the other, but an occasional hand signal indicated the preferred course, and slowly they approached the resting ducks. There were so many that Tim could not even estimate their number; all he knew was that they presented a worthy target.

As the time for lighting his powder train approached he muttered a brief prayer: 'Dearest God who protects watermen, don't let nothin' spook 'em.'

The ducks slept. The two skiffs moved silently into position. The dogs sat with every muscle tensed. And the men lay prone, their faces close to their guns. There was no moon, no snow.

Gently, but with his hands trembling, Tim Caveny spread the calculated amount of powder along his iron trough, checked it to be sure it nestled properly under the orifices of his seven guns, then lit the right-hand end. With a powerful flash, the powder leaped from gun to gun, and as the first one exploded, Jake Turlock fired his monster.

From the point of view of massacring ducks, the timing had been exquisite, for the powder had ignited three of Tim's guns before Jake could fire his. This meant that at the first flash, hundreds of ducks had risen into the air, only to be knocked down by Jake's great gun, then punished by the last four guns in Tim's arsenal.

Never before had there been such carnage on the Chesapeake. In fact, the two dogs brought so many ducks to the skiffs that they showed signs of sinking; the watermen ferried dead birds to the ice shelf, stashed them and returned to fetch others. The dogs were exhausted.

Next morning, when the count was made, the partners had sixty-nine canvasbacks, thirty-two mallards, thirty blacks, twenty-nine teal and thirteen geese that they could ship to Baltimore. In addition, they had twenty-two pintails which they would sell for a few pennies each to the Negroes living in Frog's Neck, and a score of mergansers, which no one would eat because they fed on fish. Tim's imaginative arsenal, so dangerous to use, so lethal when used, had proved its merit, so the two watermen continued to fell trees by day and fire their cannon at night. Whatever money they obtained from Baltimore, they turned over to Paxmore.

As winter ended and the ducks flew north, Gerrit Paxmore finished building his first skipjack, and when it was launched he told the two watermen, 'This boat will sail better than any in the bay.' Turlock and Caveny were prepared to believe this, but they were taken aback when the Quaker added, 'I've kept thy money in our office. I'm prepared to hand it back, because thee doesn't have to take this boat . . . if thee doesn't wish.'

'Why wouldn't we?' Turlock asked angrily.

'Because,' Paxmore said quietly, 'I've done something with the centerboard.'

The three men went aboard and climbed down into the hold where they could inspect the bottom of the boat, and there Turlock and Caveny saw the damnedest thing their eyes had ever met. Instead of placing the centerboard in the middle of the keel—cutting a slim hole fourteen feet long right through the heart of the oak, then building around it what boatmen called the trunk to keep out the water—Paxmore had left the keel untouched, as the tradition of his family required, but had cut a hole parallel to it, thus offsetting the centerboard some eight inches to starboard.

'You goddamned fool!' Turlock shouted. 'This boat's off center. It'll never . . .'

'Friend,' Paxmore said gently, 'thee has no need to swear. Thy deposit is waiting.'

'But goddamnit, I asked you plain and simple about the centerboard. And you told me in your own words . . . Didn't he, Tim?'

'He sure as hell did. Why, this damned thing—it's a cripple.'

'Please, gentlemen. Speak less roughly. Thy money—'

'To hell with our money! We want our boat.'

'Thee is not obligated . . .'

It was dark in the bowels of the skipjack and the three men seemed like angry ghosts. The centerboard was sadly awry; indeed, to call it a center anything was ridiculous. The whole balance of the boat was destroyed, and Caveny could visualize it sailing crabwise down the bay. Tears came into his eyes, and he showed Paxmore his hands, blistered for months. 'We chopped every goddamned timber in this boat. And what do we get?'

'A ——— washtub,' Turlock said, using the foulest word he could conjure.

It was this ultimate obscenity that awakened Paxmore to the fact that he was in real trouble. He had assumed that by merely offering the men their money, he would be relieved of difficulties with his unusual craft; certainly he could peddle it to someone else, perhaps at a minor loss, and with the funds thus received, pay the two watermen for their work in felling trees.

'No!' Turlock said grimly. 'We want our boat and we want it now. You take that goddamned centerboard out of there and you put it in here, where it belongs.'

'That I will not do,' Paxmore said, and as he spoke his right hand fell protectively upon the unblemished keel, and only then did Tim Caveny realize that this unpleasant Quaker loved the new craft as much as he and Jake did.

'What we might do,' Tim suggested, 'is take her for a trial.' Turlock did not want to do this, lest he like the results, but Paxmore encouraged the idea. However, Tim had an additional idea: 'Suppose we do accept it, damaged though it is? How much reduction in cost?'

'Not one penny,' Paxmore said. 'This is the finest boat on the bay, and if truth were told, thee should pay me an extra two hundred.'

'You are a son-of-a-bitch,' Turlock growled, and as he climbed out of the hold he said, 'I want to be let off this boat. I want nothin' to do with a goddamned washtub.'

'Let's give it a trial,' Tim pleaded, and he began to haul the mainsail, and every pulley, every rope worked so perfectly that he said, 'They're right. A sail like this does raise easier.'

They raised the jib, too, and then they swung the gigantic boom, two feet longer than the boat that supported it, and they could feel the power of the canvas overhead. There was a good breeze, and Caveny and Paxmore moved the skipjack into the middle of the Choptank—Turlock wouldn't touch sail or wheel—and she began to lay over to starboard, and the water broke white, and seagulls followed the new craft, and after a long while Turlock muscled his way aft and shoved Caveny away from the wheel.

Paxmore sat on the hatch covering, saying nothing. He could feel his boat responding to the waves and could visualize just how she accommodated to the wind. When Turlock called from the wheel, 'I think she needs more ballast forward,' Paxmore said, 'I think so, too.'

They christened her the *Jessie T,* after Jake's mother, and before she took her first trip oystering, the conventions governing skipjacks were installed: 'No color of blue ever to board this boat. No red brick ever to be used as ballast. No walnuts to be eaten. No hatch cover ever to be placed on deck upside down.' And because of the extremely low railing and the massiveness of the boom, larger by far than that on any other type of vessel sailing the Chesapeake: 'Above all, when you work on deck, mind the boom!'

The *Jessie T* was worked by a crew of six: Captain Jake Turlock, in command of the craft and responsible for her safety; First Mate Tim Caveny, who took care of the money; three Turlocks, who manned the dredges in which the oysters were caught; and the most important member, the cook. From the day the boat was planned to the moment when the three Turlocks were hired, there had been only one candidate for cook: a remarkable black man renowned along the Choptank.

He was Big Jimbo, an unusually tall Negro, son of the slaves Cudjo and Eden Cater. From his father he had learned to read and from his mother to carry himself with fierce pride. He was a gentle man, given to humor, and because of his rare ability with a ship's stove he knew that he was as good as the captain and better than the crew.

He resolved one possible difficulty the instant he came aboard. On a skipjack the three crewmen slept forward in cramped quarters. The captain, cook and mate—in that order—divided the three good bunks aft among themselves, and it had become traditional for the captain to choose the extra-long bunk to the starboard, the cook to take the next best one to port, with the mate getting the somewhat less convenient bunk across the back of the cabin; but on the *Jessie T* things worked out a little differently: one of the Turlocks who should have slept forward was a close cousin of Jake's and he announced that he would sleep aft, because he was sure the nigger wouldn't mind berthing in the smaller quarters.

So when Big Jimbo came aboard he found his bunk taken. Without even a second's hesitation, he politely lifted the gear out, placed it on deck and said, 'Cain't no man cook if'n he sleeps forward.'

He had made a mistake, and a serious one. The gear he had thrown out of the aft cabin was not the intruder's, but Tim Caveny's, the co-owner of the skipjack. When the Turlock lad had decided to move aft, Tim had seen a chance to promote himself into a better bunk, so he had preempted the cook's and had diverted Jake's cousin into the shorter aft bunk. When Tim saw his gear being thrown on deck, he started to raise hell, but Big Jimbo said softly, 'Mister Tim, if'n that's yours, I do apologize,' and he was more than polite in returning it to the cabin, where he placed it not in the bunk that Tim had chosen, but in the aft one.

'I sort of thought I'd sleep here,' the Irishman said tentatively, pointing to the cook's longer bunk.

'Cook sleeps here,' Big Jimbo said, and he used his words so sweetly that even the displaced owner was charmed. And then, before any ill feeling could develop, Jimbo assembled the crew on deck and said, 'I brung me some milk and some cream, so we gonna have the world's best arster stew. You want she-stew or he-stew?'

'You cain't tell a she arster from a he,' one of the Turlocks said.

'I ain't talkin' about the arsters. I'se talkin' about the eaters.' He smiled benignly at the watermen and asked, 'What's it to be, she or he?'

'What's the difference,' one of the men asked.

'That ain't for you to ask.'

'We'll take he.'

'Best choice you ever made,' Jimbo said, and he disappeared down the hatch leading to his wood stove.

A she-stew was the traditional one served throughout the Chesapeake: eight oysters per man, boiled ever so slightly in their own liquor, then in milk and thickened with flour, flavored with a bit of celery, salt and pepper. It was a great opening course but somewhat feeble for working-men.

A he-stew was something quite different, and Big Jimbo mumbled to himself as he prepared his version, 'First we takes a mess of bacon and fries it crisp.' As he did this he smelled the aroma and satisfied himself that Steed's had sold him the best. As it sizzled he chopped eight large onions and two hefty stalks of celery, holding them back till the bacon was done. Deftly he whisked the bacon out and put it aside, tossing the vegetables into the hot oil to sauté. Soon he withdrew them, too, placing them with the bacon. Then he tossed the forty-eight oysters into the pan, browning them just a little to implant a flavor, then quickly he poured in the liquor from the oysters and allowed them to cook until their gills wrinkled.

Other ship's cooks followed the recipe this far, but now Big Jimbo did the two things that made his he-stew unforgettable. From a precious package purchased from the McCormick Spice Company on the dock in Baltimore he produced first a canister of tapioca powder. 'Best thing ever invented for cooks' in his opinion. Taking a surprisingly small pinch of the whitish powder, he tossed it into the milk, which was about to simmer, and in a few minutes the moisture and the heat had expanded the finely ground tapioca powder into a very large translucent, gelatinous mass. When he was satisfied with the progress he poured the oysters into the milk, tossed in the vegetables, then crumbled the bacon between his fingers, throwing it on top.

The sturdy dish was almost ready, but not quite. From the McCormick package he brought out a packet of saffron, which he dusted over the stew, giving it a golden richness, augmented by the half-pound of butter he threw in at the last moment. This melted as he brought the concoction to the table, so that when the men dug in, they found before them one of the richest, tastiest stews a marine cook had ever devised.

'Do we eat this good every day?' Caveny asked, and Big Jimbo replied, 'You brings me the materials, I brings you the dishes.'

Dredging oysters was hard work, as events during the winter of 1892 proved. The season was divided into two halves, October to Christmas, when the oysters were plentiful, and January to the end of March, when they were more difficult to find. Since the *Jessie T* had an all-Patamoke crew, it returned to that port each Saturday night, bringing huge catches of oysters for sale to the local packing plants, and because those who sailed the skipjack were devoutly religious—even the profane Turlocks —they did not sneak out of port late on Sunday afternoon, as some did, but waited till Monday morning, an act of devotion for which they expected God to lead them to the better beds.

Captain Jake had enjoyed Christmas and was sleeping soundly this first Monday after the New Year, but at three o'clock in the morning his daughter Nancy shook him by the shoulder and whispered, 'Daddy! Time to sail.' He muttered a protest, then sat bolt upright. 'What time?' he asked, and she replied, clutching her nightgown about her throat, 'Three.'

He leaped from bed, climbed into five layers of protective clothing, then went into the next room, where he kissed his two other children as they slept. His wife was already in the kitchen brewing a pot of coffee and pouring out a quart of milk for him to take to the boat. She also had some strips of bacon and a handful of onions to be delivered to Big Jimbo for that day's stew.

Through the dark streets of Patamoke, Captain Jake headed for the wharf, and as he approached the swaying masts of the oyster fleet, he saw converging on the waterfront a score of men dressed like himself, each bringing some item of special food. They moved like shadows in the frosty air, grunting hellos as they met, and when Jake reached the *Jessie T* he was pleased to see that Big Jimbo was already aboard, with a fire well started.

'Brung you some milk,' he said, half throwing his parcel onto the swaying table. The cook grunted some acknowledgment, then reached for a bucket of choice oysters that had been set aside for this occasion. Placing a well-worn glove on his left hand, he began shucking the oysters, tossing the meat into one pan while pouring as much of the liquor as possible into another. 'Things look good,' Captain Jake said as he deposited his gear and went on deck.

Mate Caveny was prompt, and while he and the captain cleared the deck, the three Turlock crewmen came aboard, stowing their gear forward in the mean quarters. 'Cast off!' Jake called, and when his lines were clear and his two sails aloft, his skipjack began its slow, steady movement out to the center of the river, then westward toward the bay. Three hours later the sun would begin to rise, but for the present they would be in darkness.

It was very cold on deck. A brisk wind swept in from the bay, coming as usual out of the northwest, bitter cold from Canada. Captain Jake stayed at the wheel, standing before it and moving it with his left hand behind his back. The Turlocks patrolled the deck, while Caveny stayed below helping the cook.

Past Peace Cliff they went and into the channel north of Devon Island. Blackwalnut Point appeared in the dim light, while ahead lay the great bay, its waters ruffled by the heavy wind. It was cold, dark and wet as the tips of waves broke off to become whipping spray that cut the face.

But now Big Jimbo rang his bell, and all but the youngest Turlock moved below; he watched the wheel, standing in front of it, as the captain had done.

In the cramped cabin below, Big Jimbo had prepared one of his best he-stews, and when crackers were broken over the bottom of their bowls and the rich mixture poured in, the men's faces glowed. But as in most skipjacks, no one moved a spoon until the cook had taken his place at the small table and reached out his large black hands to grasp those of Captain Turlock and Mate Caveny, whose free hands sought those of the two crewmen. The circle thus having been completed, the five watermen bowed their heads while Captain Turlock uttered the Protestant grace:

> 'God is great. God is good.
> And we thank Him for our food.
> By His hand we all are fed.
> Thank Thee, Lord, for daily bread.'

When he finished, all the men said 'Amen,' but they did not relax their hands, for it was now Tim Caveny's responsibility to intone the Catholic grace:

> 'Bless us; O Lord, for these Thy gifts which we are about to receive from Thy bounty, through Christ our Lord, Amen.'

Again the men said 'Amen,' but still they kept their hands together, for in addition to the two formal graces, it was the custom aboard the *Jessie T* for Caveny to add a personal prayer, and in his rich Irish accent he now asked God for special attention:

> 'We have observed Thy day with prayers and have sought Thy blessing upon our families. Now we ask that Thee guide this boat to where the arsters sleep awaiting our coming. Lord, make the harvest a rich one. St. Peter, guardian of fishermen, protect us. St. Patrick, who crossed the sea, watch over this boat. St. Andrew, who fished the Sea of Galilee, guide us to our catch.'

'Amen,' the watermen whispered, and spoons dipped into the golden-flecked stew.

They needed prayers, for their work was both hard and dangerous. When Captain Jake felt that the *Jessie T* was properly positioned over the invisible beds, he ordered Caveny and the three Turlocks to drop the two dredges, one port, one starboard, and when these iron-pronged collectors had bounced over the bottom long enough, he tested the wires holding them, calculating whether the load was adequate, and when he was satisfied, he ordered the dredges hauled aboard.

Now the muscle-work began. Port and starboard stood two winches, powered by hand, and around the drum of each, the wire leading to its dredge was wound. Then the men, two to a winch, began turning the heavy iron handles, and as the drums revolved, the lines holding the submerged dredges were hauled aboard. Danger came when the iron prongs of the dredge caught in rock, reversing the handle and knocking out men's teeth or breaking their arms. Few watermen ever worked the oyster bars without suffering some damage from reversing handles; one of the younger Turlocks carried a broad scar across his forehead—'I like to died from bleedin'. Lessen I had a head like rock, I be dead.'

When the dredges finally climbed aboard, dripping with mud and weed, their cargo was dumped on deck, except when the load was simply too dirty to work; then the men engaged in a maneuver that almost jerked their arms from their sockets. Alternately lowering the dredge into the sea a few feet, and yanking it back, they sloshed the great net up and down until the mud washed free. Only then were they allowed to bring it aboard with its load of oysters and shells.

Quickly the dredges were emptied onto the deck, then thrown back for another catch. As soon as they were back in the water, the watermen knelt on the deck to begin the sorting, and with deft hands well scarred by the sharp edges of oysters, they picked through the mass of dead shell and weed, isolating the living oysters which represented their catch. Their fingers seemed to dance through the debris, knowing instinctively whenever they touched a good oyster; with curious skill they retrieved each one, tossing it backward toward the unseen piles that mounted as the day's dredging progressed.

It was a custom aboard the skipjacks for each of the four men sorting the catch to throw his oysters into the corner of the boat behind him; this distributed the weight of the catch evenly across the deck of the boat, fore and aft, port and starboard. When the long day ended—dawn till dusk, six days a week—the *Jessie T* was usually piled high with oysters, yet riding evenly in the water because of the planned way they had been stowed.

Toward the end of each day Captain Jake, who did none of the sorting, began to look for a boat flying a bushel basket high from its mast. This was the buy-boat, and there was usually one in the vicinity. When it came alongside, the men aboard the *Jessie T* had to work double-fast. Into the iron measuring bucket dropped onto their deck by a boom from the buy-boat they shoveled their catch, and each time the iron bucket rose in the air and returned to the buy-boat, depositing the oysters into its hold, Tim Caveny at the railing would cry 'Tally one!' then 'Tally two! —and so on until the fifth bucket, when he would shout 'Mark one!' Then he would begin again with 'Tally one!'

At dusk he would report to his crew, 'Twenty-two and three.' This meant twenty-two marks plus three tallies, or one hundred and thirteen bushels. And each man would then calculate what that day's work had brought.

The *Jessie T* worked on shares. The skipjack itself received one third, divided evenly between the two owners, Jake and Tim, but they had to pay for the food, the cordage, the dredges. The captain received a third, which again he had to split with Caveny, who could just as easily have served as leader. And the four crewmen split the remaining third among them, except that Big Jimbo was recognized as such a superior cook that he received a little extra from everyone.

His position was anomalous. The four Turlocks hated Negroes and never hesitated in voicing their disgust. 'Goddamned spades killed my cousin Captain Matt—one of them gets out of line with me, he's dead.' They often made this threat in the presence of Big Jimbo, indicating they knew damned well he was descended from the murderer; but the cook himself was prized as a friend, as a most willing helper on deck and as the best galley-man in the fleet. 'When you sail *Jessie T,* man, you eat. Our nigger can outcook your nigger ever' time.'

The extraordinary contribution of Big Jimbo was demonstrated one gray February morning when the men were at breakfast, with the youngest Turlock at the wheel. The skipjack was heeling to starboard, so that the dishes on the crowded table were sliding, and Captain Jake called up through the cabin door, 'All okay up there?'

'All's fine!' the man at the wheel shouted back, but soon thereafter he cried in some alarm, 'Cap'm! Very dark clouds!' And then immediately, 'I need help!'

Captain Jake started for the ladder, but Ned Turlock, one of the three crewmen, beat him to it. With a hearty bound, the young man leaped up the four steps and made the deck just in time to be struck in the face by the flying boom, which had been swept across the deck by a change in the storm's direction. Ned was knocked into the turbulent water and was soon far aft of the skipjack without a lifebelt, but Captain Jake, taking command of the wheel, swung the boat about while everyone worked the sails in an effort to bring it under control.

As soon as the skipjack steadied and was on a course that might bring her near the thrashing waterman, who was struggling to stay alive, Big Jimbo tied a rope about his waist, then asked Tim Caveny to fashion a kind of harness, with smaller ropes lashing him about the shoulders and holding him to the main rope. When this was tested, the big cook checked to be sure that the loose end of the rope was secured to a mooring cleat, and then, without hesitation, plunged into the deep, icy waters. His arms thrashed wildly as he tried to stabilize himself, and one of the Turlocks cried, 'Hell, he cain't swim neither,' and Captain Jake growled, 'Niggers cain't never swim. Watch him with the hook.'

Big Jimbo, kicking his feet and flailing his arms, moved closer to the drowning man, but the force of the waves and the irresistible movement of the skipjack prevented him from making the rescue, and it seemed that Ned Turlock must drown. But on deck Captain Jake was willing to take great risks, so in the midst of the furious squall, he brought his boat around, almost capsizing it, and headed on a tack that would intercept his cousin in the water.

With a giant embrace, Big Jimbo caught the exhausted man, clutched him to his bosom and pressed water from his lungs as the men aboard the *Jessie T* pulled on the rope to drag the two men aboard. At supper that night, after the oysters had been sold and the profits calculated, the six watermen joined hands as Caveny poured out their thanks:

'Almighty God, Thou didst send the storm much like the one that swamped the fishermen on Galilee, and in Thy wisdom Thou didst sweep our sailor Ned from us. But just as Thou didst rescue Jonah after forty days and forty nights in the belly of the whale, so didst Thou urge our nigger Big Jimbo to dive into the rolling waters to save Ned. St. Patrick, patron saint of fishermen, we thank thee for thy intervention. Greater love hath no man.'

When the prayer ended, everyone had objections: 'The forty days and forty nights were Noah and the ark, not Jonah.'

'They were both a long time,' Caveny said. 'I thought Ned was gone.'

'Last week you said St. Peter was our patron saint.'

'A fisherman needs all the help he can get,' Caveny said.

'You should of finished the last bit.' And Captain Jake misquoted, ' "Greater love hath no man than this, that he lay down his life for his brother." '

'I didn't forget. I just thought Ned might take it unkindly, bein' told he was brother to a nigger.'

With the near-drowning of Ned Turlock, the suspicion that the *Jessie T* might be a bad-luck boat gained so much credence that Captain Jake found it difficult to enroll a crew. One cynic at the store reminded the men, 'Like I told you, that skipjack was doomed from the start. Its centerboard is out of whack. Side-assed, you might say.'

And one of the Turlock boys who sailed in it confided, 'Thing you really got to watch is Captain Jake. In the fall, when arsters is plentiful, he pays his crew a salary. Come winter, when they ain't so many arsters, he smiles at you like an angel and says, "Boys, better we work on shares this time." I ain't sailin' with him no more.'

When an Eastern Shore skipjack found itself unable to enroll a crew, it was traditional for the captain to make the big decision, which Captain Jake now did: 'Caveny, we sail to Baltimore.'

With only Ned and Big Jimbo to help, they headed across the bay, past Lazaretto Light, past Fort McHenry, where the star-spangled banner had flown that troubled night, and into one of the finest small anchorages in the world, Baltimore's inner harbor. Its merit was threefold: it lay right in the heart of the city; it was surrounded by hotels and stores and warehouses immediately at hand; and it was so protected by their tall buildings that no storm could imperil a ship docked there. Also, it was a joy for any ship's cook to enter this harbor, because on the waterfront stood the huge McCormick Spice Company, its odors permeating the area, its shelves crammed with condiments the cooks sought.

As the *Jessie T* approached her wharf in the corner formed by Light Street, where the white steamers docked, and Pratt Street, where the skipjacks tied up and the saloons clustered, Captain Jake warned his companions to be especially alert. 'We may have to pull out of here in a hurry,' he said. 'Jimbo, you guard the boat while Tim and me goes ashore to tend to our business.'

'Cap'm,' the big cook said, 'I watch the boat, but first I got to get me some spices,' and as soon as the *Jessie T* made fast, Big Jimbo was off to McCormick's, returning with a small, precious package which he stowed below.

Now Turlock and Caveny started toward the row of saloons, and as they swaggered ashore, Jimbo called out, 'Good luck, Cap'm. I be waitin'.'

There was one saloon, the Drunken Penguin, at which captains needing crew often had success, so it was natural that the two watermen should head there. 'What a fine sign!' Caveny exclaimed as he saw for the first time the besotted penguin leering at him. Turlock, ignoring the art criticism, banged into the swinging doors with his shoulder, and smashed his way into the darkened bar, standing for a moment to survey the familiar scene. When he moved to a table at the rear, two young men who recognized him as an Eastern Shore skipper quietly rose and slipped out a side door.

He and Caveny had a beer, then a plate of food from the free lunch. 'Many people droppin' by?' Jake asked the bartender.

'Nope,' the barman said, wiping a glass much longer than required. 'They's mostly at the other places.'

'They'll be comin' in,' Jake said as he attacked his food. 'Tim, fetch me another pickled egg.'

There was no action that first afternoon, and Caveny suggested they explore some other bars, but Jake refused. 'In other years I've found what I wanted here. We'll find it this time, too.'

Toward dusk laborers from sites nearby dropped in for their evening beer, and Caveny said, 'Reminds me of those great opening lines of Grey's *Energy:*

'Homeward at the close of day
The weary workmen come.
Tired with their honest toil
And all lit up with rum.'

Midnight approached and nothing happened. 'I told you they was at the other bars,' the barman said.

'I heard you,' Jake grunted, and that night he and Tim slept sitting at their table. Dawn broke, and along Light Street came carriages with passengers for the early steamers, and soon Pratt Street was alive with draymen. The heavy business of Baltimore was under way.

At about nine o'clock in the morning the two watermen were wide awake, and Tim suggested, 'I ain't never seen Hotel Rennert. Let's see where our arsters goes.' So the two watermen walked a dozen blocks in the clean, brisk air, crossed a park and stood on the Belgian blocks that surfaced all the streets near the great hostelry. 'Magnificence brought down from heaven to earth,' Caveny said. When Turlock made no reply, the Irishman pointed to the towering façade and the beribboned doorman. 'It's an honor to provide arsters to such an establishment.' Again there was no response, so Tim plucked at his captain's sleeve. 'Jake, I think St. Peter, patron of us sailors, would look upon it kindly if we had a beer at the Rennert, seein' as how we help keep it in business.'

'St. Peter might look kindly, but that flunky wouldn't,' Jake said, pointing to his rough clothes and Tim's unshaven face.

'There's always welcome to an honest workman,' Caveny replied, and he strode up to the doorman and said, 'My good man, Captain Turlock and I provide the arsters used in your establishment. Would you extend the courtesy of allowin' us to enjoy a beer?' Before the surprised functionary could respond, Caveny said grandly, 'At our expense, of course.'

'Are you indeed oystermen?' the doorman asked.

'That we are,' Caveny replied, 'best of the bay. Which is why Rennert buys from us.'

'Gentlemen, the oyster bar is through that door. I feel sure you will be welcomed.'

Gingerly Jake Turlock entered the mahogany-lined room. There was the glistening bar of which he had heard, the black man shucking in the corner, the chalked board proclaiming the many varieties of oysters available, and three men in business suits having an early snack. It was a handsome room, ideal for the purpose to which it was dedicated.

'My good man,' Caveny said to the barman in charge, 'my mate and I catch the arsters you sell here.'

'Is that true?' the bartender said.

'As true as I stand before you like the honest fisherman I am.'

'And would you be wantin' to sample the oysters you've caught?'

'God forbid that we should come all the way to Baltimore to eat arsters. What we want is a cold beer.'

'And that you shall have,' the barman said. 'Compliments of the Rennert.'

'We can pay,' Caveny said.

'I'm sure you can, but we rarely see our oystermen, and this beer is on the house.'

Caveny sipped his beer as if he were a gentleman, making various observations on the quality of the hotel. As he placed his glass on the bar, depositing it gently with ten fingers embracing it, he asked, 'Would you be offended, sir, if we tipped rather more handsomely than is the custom?'

'From sailors like yourselves . . .'

'Watermen,' Caveny corrected, and onto the bar he tossed a sum of coins which would have covered not only the two beers but also a generous tip. 'This is a grand hotel,' he told Turlock as they returned to the street, but Jake merely said, 'Back to the Drunken Penguin. You never know when they'll straggle in.'

The first prospect arrived at two that afternoon, an Englishman about twenty-four years old, seedy, bleary-eyed, underfed. He had just enough money to purchase a beer, which entitled him to gorge on the free lunch.

Turlock, watching his ravenous appetite, nodded to Caveny, who moved to the bar. 'From the fair city of Dublin, I'm sure.'

'London,' the Englishman said.

'None finer in the world, I always say. Would you be offended if I suggested another beer?'

The young man was not disposed to argue about such an invitation, but when the drink was paid for, and the glass stood empty on the bar, he discovered the heavy cost of this courtesy, for suddenly he was grabbed from behind by the strong arms of a man he could not see, and his generous friend Timothy Caveny was bashing him in the face. He fainted, and when he revived, found himself bound hand and foot in the cabin of a strange boat, with a very large black man standing guard and threatening to knife him if he made one move.

Jake and Tim returned to the Drunken Penguin, resumed their seats at the back table and waited. After dark a young man came into the bar, loudly announced he was from Boston, waiting for his ship to arrive from New Orleans; he lounged awhile, had a desultory beer and picked at the spiced beets, licking his fingers as he finished. He was a sturdy young fellow, and Caveny doubted that he could be easily subdued, so as the Bostonian looked aimlessly about the bar, Tim approached the bartender to make a whispered offer. It was accepted, and when Tim took his place at the young man's elbow to propose a drink in honor of the great port of Boston, where Tim had served in many different ships, the glass was ready.

The Bostonian took one sip, looked at the bubbles, then placed the glass on the bar. 'Drink up!' Tim said brightly, gulping down a large portion of his own drink.

'I'd like a pickled beet,' the young sailor said.

'Best food in the world with beer,' Caveny said as he passed the glass bowl along.

The sailor ate two beets, took three gulps of his beer and fell flat on the floor. 'Grab his feet!' Captain Turlock ordered, and watchers at the bar, who had seen this operation before, stepped reverently back as Jake and Tim lugged their second hand to the *Jessie T.*

When a crew had been conscripted in this way, a captain was afraid to put into port over weekends lest his men desert. He stayed out on the Chesapeake during the whole fall season, loading oysters onto the buy-boats, picking up fresh food from them when necessary and watching his shanghaied men every minute to prevent their escape.

'Don't feel sorry for yourselves,' Captain Turlock told the two men. 'You get paid just like everyone else. By Christmas you'll be rich.'

The impressed seamen had to work like slaves. They threw the dredges into the water; they pulled them up; they sloshed them when there was mud; they stayed on their knees hours and days at a time picking through the haul; and when the buy-boat came, it was they who shoveled the oysters into the metal buckets.

Oystermen had a hundred clever tricks for hoodwinking shanghaied helpers: 'Well, you see, the earnin's I've been quotin' ain't clear profit. You've got to pay for the clothes we provide, the gloves, and so forth.' They also had to pay for their food. Also deducted were fees for mending the dredges, the cost of new ropes.

Captain Turlock favored a simpler method: 'You men are gettin' richer by the day.'

'When can we go ashore?' the Englishman asked.

'You mean, when can you leave our boat?'

'In a manner of speaking, yes.'

'At Christmas,' Turlock promised, and Caveny added, 'On that holy day all men yearn to be with their families.'

During the third week of December, when ice formed on fingers, the two impressed seamen came to the aft cabin and demanded to speak with Turlock. 'We want your promise that we'll be off this boat by Christmas.'

'You have my solemn promise,' Turlock said. And then, to make the deal binding, he added, 'Mr. Caveny will swear to that, won't you, Tim?'

'As sure as the moon rises over Lake Killarney,' Caveny assured him, 'you'll be off this boat by Christmas.'

Two days before that holiday, when the last buy-boat had loaded itself with oysters, Captain Turlock convened his crew in the galley and said brightly, 'Jimbo, if one of the lads could fetch you some milk at Deal Island, could you make us a mess of he-stew?'

'I likes to,' the big cook said, and Turlock studied the two shanghaied crewmen. 'You go,' he said to the Bostonian. Then, as if changing his mind for some deep philosophical reason, he said to the smaller man,

'Better you take the pail. I want to talk wages with this one.' So the Englishman grabbed the pail and went on deck.

Caveny, Jimbo and Ned Turlock followed him up to maneuver the *Jessie T* into the dock at Deal Island, so that the Englishman could step ashore to find his milk. While this was under way, Captain Turlock engaged the Boston man in serious conversation. 'Where will you be headin'' with the pay we're givin'' you?'

'Home. I've a family waiting.'

'They'll be proud of the money you're bringin'' 'em.' The young man smiled bitterly, and Turlock said reassuringly, 'You mustn't feel angry. This is the way of the sea. You've learned about arsters and you've saved some money.'

Such moralizing was repugnant, in view of Turlock's harsh commands on this cruise, and the Bostonian rose in some anger to go above, but the captain detained him by holding on to his arm. 'Sit down, young fellow. We've taken a lot of arsters this trip and you'll be takin'' a lot of money to Boston.' He added other sanctimonious truisms, at the end of which the young man said, 'Captain Turlock, you're a fraud. You're an evil man, and you know it.' In disgust he moved toward the ladder, but this time Turlock interposed himself physically, saying, 'I cannot allow you to depart in bitterness . . . before we've discussed your wages.' And the talk continued.

On deck the others understood why their captain was keeping the Bostonian below, for when the Englishman started ashore with his pail, Caveny yelled, 'The house at the far end,' and as the young man started off toward the little fishing village, the Irishman gave a signal, and Ned Turlock at the wheel swung the skipjack away from the dock and back into the bay.

'Hey!' the young man shouted as he saw his boat, and his wages, pull away. 'Wait for me!'

There was no waiting. Relentlessly the oyster boat left the island and the young man standing with his empty pail. He was beached, 'paid off with sand,' as the watermen said of this common practice, and if he was lucky, he could straggle back to Baltimore at the end of two or three weeks, without recourse or any chance of ever recovering his wages for long months of work. Tim Caveny, watching him standing by the shore, said to his two companions, 'I told him he'd be ashore by Christmas.'

When the *Jessie T* was well out from the dock, so that the abandoned man could no longer be seen, Captain Turlock bellowed from below, 'Mr. Caveny, come down here and pay this man!'

When Caveny appeared in the galley, Turlock said forthrightly, 'This man has honest grievances, which he's expressed openly. Calculate every penny we owe him and pay him in full. I want him to remember us with kindness.' And he went on deck, where he took the wheel.

With all the Irish charm at his command, Caveny reached for his account books, spread them on the table and assured the Bostonian, 'You've worked hard and you've earned every penny,' but as he was about to start handing over the cash, there was a wild clatter on deck. Noises that could be not be deciphered shattered the air and from them came Captain Turlock's agonized cry: 'On deck. All hands.'

The young sailor from Boston leaped automatically up the companionway, not noticing that the paymaster remained stolidly at the table. Bursting through the cabin door and leaping forward to help in whatever emergency had struck, he arrived on deck just in time to see the massive boom sweeping down on him at a speed that was incredible. With a great cry he thrust his hands before his face, failed to break the blow and screamed as the thundering boom pitched him wildly into the muddy waves.

Now the four Patamoke men lined the railing of their skipjack and shouted instructions: 'You can make it to shore. Just walk. Put your feet down and walk.'

They were distressed when he flopped and flailed, too terrified by his sudden immersion to control himself. 'Just walk ashore!' Captain Turlock bellowed. 'It's not deep!'

At last the young fellow understood what the men on the disappearing boat were trying to say. Stumbling and cursing, he gained his footing, found the water no deeper than his armpits and started the long, cold march to Deal Island.

'It's a Christmas he'll never forget,' Tim Caveny said as the sailor struggled to safety. There were now only four to share this season's riches, and when they gathered for their evening meal, two days before Christmas, they joined hands and listened attentively as Tim Caveny prayed:

> 'Merciful and all-seein' God who protects those who go upon the waves, we are poor fishermen who do the best we can. We go forth in our little boat so that others can eat. We toil in blizzards so that others can bide at home. We thank Thee that Thou hast brought us safely through this long and dangerous cruise, and we ask Thy continued blessing on our wives and children.'

Oyster dredging had ended for 1892; this night the buy-boats would rest in Baltimore. Tenderly the *Jessie T* came about, steadied her sails and headed home. The watermen would always remember that Christmas as one of the best in their lives, for the weather was crisp, with a bright sun during the day and a helpful mistiness in the moonless nights. They had a lot of hunting to catch up with, because guarding their shanghaied crew had prevented them from enjoying their guns during the prime months of November and December; they went out every night.

It was during the sail back home one morning that Tim Caveny cleverly put his finger on the considerable danger they might run if Captain Jake proceeded with his plan for restaffing the *Jessie T*, now that the Englishman and the Bostonian had departed. Turlock had mentioned the problem to Big Jimbo, who said, 'You ain't got no trouble, Cap'm. I knows two men likes to drudge.' But when the cook returned with the would-be crew, Tim saw that each was very big and very black.

Without bothering to take his partner aside, he asked, 'Jake, you think it smart to hire 'em both?'

'They look strong.'

'But it would make three white, three black. And you know how niggers like to plot against white folk.'

Jake studied the three black men, and although their faces were placid, he could easily visualize them launching a mutiny. Turning to Big Jimbo, he asked abruptly, 'Weren't it your daddy that murdered my grandfather's brother?'

'Maybe it was your grandfather stole my daddy as a slave,' the cook replied evenly.

'Tim's right,' Turlock snapped. 'We'll take one. Catch us another white man in Baltimore.'

So on the first day of dredging, the *Jessie T* was not on station. She was delivering a load of ducks to the Hotel Rennert in Baltimore, and after this was accomplished, Turlock and Caveny returned to the Drunken Penguin to inspect what the waterfront had to offer. They had not long to wait, for into the bar came a giant German wearing one of those gray sweaters with a double-folded neck and pants so thick they looked as though they could withstand a hurricane. He was obviously hungry, for he wolfed down three pickled eggs before the bartender could pour his beer, and while he was gulping a sandwich, Captain Turlock struck him on the head with a bottle. When he collapsed in the sawdust, Caveny ran into the street and whistled for Big Jimbo to come drag him out.

He was still unconscious when the *Jessie T* sailed, but when the skipjack cleared the Lazaretto, Jake summoned the Turlock boy from his position forward and said, 'Take the wheel. This one may be trouble when he wakens.'

With Tim's help he spread the unconscious German on the deck, then grabbed a belaying pin and advised Caveny to do the same. When they had secure positions from which they could defend themselves, Turlock called for the black sailor to throw a bucket of water over the German's face, but just as the young fellow was about to do so, Jake prudently called for Big Jimbo. 'Better stand here with us. This one could be mean.' So the cook joined the circle, and the water was thrown.

The fallen sailor shook his head and gradually awoke to the fact that he was aboard a moving ship. When he sat up, wiping the salty water from his face, he stared at the circle of faces, two white, two black. Assuming that Turlock was the captain of this craft, he asked in heavy accents, 'Where'm I going?'

'Arsterin', ' Jake replied.

The German was obviously disposed to fight, but he saw the belaying pins and reconsidered. 'How long?' he asked.

'Three months. And when we pay you off, we bring you back to Baltimore.'

The German remained sitting, and after he had pressed the water out of his sweater he said, 'Otto Pflaum, Hamburg.'

'Glad to have you, Otto. Coffee's on.'

He was a splendid addition to the crew, a man of powerful energy and surprising dexterity in sorting what the dredges hauled up from the bottom. Knowing nothing of the bay's traditions, he did not think it unusual when the *Jessie T* remained on station, week after week; he enjoyed it when the buy-boats visited to pick up the catch, for this meant that for the next few days the food would be superior, and he had a ravenous appetite.

'You let him, he stay at table twenty-four hours each day,' Big Jimbo said admiringly.

'Only decent thing on this boat, the cook,' Pflaum said.

In the winter of 1893 the crew of the *Jessie T* came to appreciate how lucky they were to have found big Otto Pflaum, for once more they were confronted by their ancient enemy: boatmen from Virginia creeping in to encroach on Maryland waters, even though a compact between the two states clearly reserved those oyster beds for Eastern Shore watermen.

The Virginia men had three advantages: since their state was larger, they were more numerous; their boats were much bigger than the skip-jacks; and for a curious reason no one could justify, they were allowed to use fueled engines while Marylanders were restricted to sail. Their swift, piratical craft could strip an oyster bank in an afternoon.

Naturally, the Choptank men tried to hold the invaders away, but the Virginians were able sailors and knew how to muscle the smaller skip-jacks aside. They also carried rifles, and since they were not afraid to use them, gunfire was common; two Patamoke men had already been killed.

At first there had been no retaliation from the skipjacks, but the past year, after several blatant attacks, some of the Choptank boats had gone armed, and sporadic firing had broken out. In spite of the fact that Patamoke boats sailed under a constant threat of open warfare, Captain Turlock had been reluctant to arm the *Jessie T.*

'Our job is drudgin' arsters, not fightin' Virginians,' he told the men at the store.

'What you gonna do, they come at you with guns?'

'Stay clear.'

One of the captains said, 'Strange to hear you say that, Jake. Wasn't your kinfolk them as fought ever'body on the bay?'

'Yes, and we're mighty proud of what they done, pirates and British and all.'

'Then why don't you arm yourse'f?'

'Because a skipjack ain't no man-o'-war.'

So the *Jessie T* remained unarmed, and Jake's strategy worked, for he moved onto the beds early each Monday, and after prayers hauled his dredges back on deck with huge catches. When the Virginia boats began to encroach, and he satisfied himself that they were armed, he withdrew, content to work the smaller beds inside the Choptank. But his retreat merely emboldened the invaders, and before long they were brazenly aprowl at the mouth of that river.

The Virginians were led by a daring boat whose arrogance was infuriating. It was a large bateau named the *Sinbad,* distinguishable for two features. For its figurehead it carried a large carved roc, the legendary bird with great talons; and the entire boat was painted blue, a color forbidden to skipjacks. The *Sinbad* was formidable.

This winter she challenged the *Jessie T,* almost running her down on a sweep across the beds. 'Stand clear, idiot!' the Virginia captain bellowed as he bore down.

'Run into him!' Ned Turlock shouted to his uncle, but the *Sinbad* was much too heavy for such tactics, and prudently the *Jessie T* retreated.

This encouraged the other Virginia dredgers; with impunity they paraded over the Maryland beds, scraping them clean with their powered boats. It was a sad experience for the Choptank men, made worse by the fact that Virginia buy-boats moved in arrogantly to collect the stolen oysters for sale in Norfolk.

Something had to be done. One evening four Patamoke skipjacks assembled at one of the beds to discuss strategies that might restrain the Virginians, and one captain who had a safe crew, in that none had been shanghaied, said that since he was going ashore, he would telegraph the governor of Maryland, requesting armed force to repulse the Virginian invaders. But when Pflaum heard the conversation he demanded loudly, 'They go ashore. Why we have to stay out?' and one of the captains, aware of Pflaum's status, quickly explained, 'Because your boat gets the biggest oysters.' Later the *Jessie T* crewmen laughed at the big German as he stood alone in the bow, trying to unravel this curious explanation.

The telegram achieved nothing, so the skipjacks that had put into Patamoke for the weekend acquired rifles, which they were prepared to use, and for two days Captain Jake was content to allow the other Patamoke skipjacks to patrol the Choptank while he sailed unarmed, but when the Virginians detected this strategy, they came right at the *Jessie T* and muscled her off the good beds.

Otto Pflaum had had enough. Storming into the cabin at dusk, he shouted, 'You, damned Turlock. You don't go into Patamoke, you afraid I jump ship. You don't buy us rifles, you afraid of *Sinbad*. By God, I no sitting duck, let them others fire at me, bang-bang. I want a gun!'

He got one. Next afternoon when the *Jessie T* tied up to a Baltimore buy-boat, Captain Jake asked if it had any extra guns for sale, and five were procured, so that on the following morning when the blue-hulled *Sinbad* bore down with her engine at top speed, it found Otto Pflaum standing forward and shooting at them with a repeating rifle.

'He hit them!' Ned Turlock shouted as the surprised Virginians scattered about the deck.

For the next few days oystering was pleasant, and as they sailed back and forth across the beds, Captain Jake had time to reflect on the excellent job the Paxmores had done with the *Jessie T: She* has her centerboard off to one side, but she sails better'n any boat on the bay. He remembered telling Caveny, 'No man in his right mind would build a boat with the mainmast so far forward, but it works. And do you know why? Because it's raked so far aft.' It was a curious mast: it not only rose from the innards of the boat at a severe angle, so that it appeared almost to be leaning backward, but its top bent forward, producing an arc which seemed certain to break it. The mast thus fought against itself, leaning backward but curving forward, and it was this tension that made it so powerful; from it hung one of the largest sails ever used on a small boat, and because of the mast's design, the sail rode up and down with ease. It's a beautiful boat, Jake thought. Damned shame it can't just mind its business and drudge arsters.

But under the leadership of the enraged *Sinbad,* the Virginians had mounted a concerted effort to drive the Marylanders away from their own beds, and any skipjack that volunteered to challenge them received rough treatment. Gunfire became commonplace, and Captain Jake was always inclined to retreat, to protect his boat, but Otto Pflaum and young Ned Turlock would not allow the *Jessie T* to be taken off station.

It became a target for the *Sinbad.* 'Move back, you bastards!' the captain of that vessel would bellow as he brought his engine to full speed.

'Don't alter course!' Pflaum would shout back, and the *Jessie T* held fast as Pflaum and Ned Turlock stayed in the bow, blazing away at the invader.

Nothing was accomplished, but one night as the crew assembled for prayers, Ned Turlock said, 'Uncle Jake, when you got yourself this German, you got somethin' good.'

The camaraderie of the cabin was a strange affair, as Ned pointed out one night, 'Never thought I'd serve with two niggers, and both of 'em real good at arsterin'.' He was seated between the cook and the black sailor, eating from a common pot. 'Where'd you learn to sail?' he asked the younger man.

'Big Jimbo, he teached me.'

'He ain't got no boat.'

'He brung me to the *Jessie T.* When you was duck huntin'.'

'You ain't never been on water, prior?'

'Nope.'

'Danged, you learn fast. You watch, Jake, these goddamned niggers gonna take over the world.'

'You sailed, prior?' Caveny asked the German.

'Many ships,' Pflaum replied.

'You jump ship in Baltimore?'

'Want to see America.'

'This is the best part,' Ned broke in.

'And you're earnin' good money doin' it,' Captain Turlock said. All the men engaged in this conversation would later remember that whenever Jake stressed wages, Otto Pflaum listened intently, keeping his hands clasped over his belly, saying nothing.

'He was special attentive,' Ned Turlock would report at the store.

He was attentive, too, when the *Sinbad* swept back into action, for when the Virginia guns blazed, and a bullet struck Ned, knocking him perilously close to the railing, Pflaum stuck out a massive paw, dragging him to safety. Then, using his own gun and Ned's, he launched a fusillade at the Virginia boat.

'I think he got one of them!' Caveny cried, for in the heat of battle Otto performed heroically.

It therefore posed a grave moral problem when the time approached to throw him overboard. In whispered consultations Caveny said, 'We got to remember he saved Ned's life, more or less.'

'That's got nothin' to do with it,' Captain Turlock growled. 'Cruise is endin'. We got to get rid of him.'

Caveny brought Ned into the discussion, expecting him to vote for keeping Pflaum aboard and paying him honestly, but the young man was a true Turlock, and said, 'Overboard. We need his share.'

So it was agreed that during the first week in April, as the cruise ended, Ned would take the wheel, Caveny would keep the German in the cabin talking wages while Captain Turlock and Big Jimbo waited on deck with belaying pins in case anything went wrong when the boom swept Otto overboard.

It was a gray day, with the wind blowing, as it did so often, from the northwest. The bay threw muddy spray, and the dredges were stowed port and starboard, having crawled across the bottom for three unbroken months. Everyone was tired and even the buy-boats had retreated to their summer anchorages. The long voyage was over and the oystermen were heading home to divide their spoils.

Tim Caveny was in the cabin, his books spread on the table, explaining to Pflaum how the money would be divided. 'We had a good season, thanks much to you, Otto. We handle the money like this. One third to the boat, which is only proper. One third to the captain. One third to you, and young Turlock and the two niggers, with ever'body throwin' in somethin' extra for the cook.'

'That's fair. Best cook I ever sailed with.'

'I'm now going to pay you in full—'

'All hands!' Captain Turlock shouted as a tremendous clatter echoed on deck.

Later Caveny confessed, 'It could of been my fault. You see, I knew the call was comin', so I didn't react. In a flash Otto saw I had no intention of goin' on deck, even though there was supposed to be an emergency. So he give me a look I'll never forget, hitched up his pants, pushed his right hand into his belt and went slowly up the ladder. You know what happened when he reached the deck.'

What happened was that Otto knew the boom would swing in upon him; he was ready when it came, grabbed it with his left arm, swung far out over the bay as it swept past, and with his right hand produced a pistol, which he aimed at Captain Turlock's head.

'One of the most devious tricks I ever saw,' Turlock said later, for as the boom rode out to starboard, Otto Pflaum slowly made his way forward along it till he reached the mast. With great caution he lowered himself onto the deck, walking slowly aft toward the cabin. He kept his pistol aimed at Captain Turlock's head, and when he drew even with Jake he said, 'I stay in cabin. Alone. You take this boat to harbor. Quick.'

With calculated steps, feeling his way as he went, he backed to the cabin door, opened it, shouted down the hatchway, 'Caveny, you got two seconds to get out or I kill you!' He waited for the terrified Irishman to scramble onto the deck, then descended slowly into the cabin, locking it behind him.

For a day and a half the five men on deck went without food or water. They sailed the *Jessie T* as rapidly as possible back to Patamoke, angry and cursing at the duplicity of this German who had pirated their boat, and when they docked at the wharf, and Caveny had been allowed back into the cabin to pay Pflaum his wages, the big German crawled up the ladder, pistol in hand, and made his way slowly to the side of the skipjack. Without a farewell of any kind, he gingerly stepped backward off the boat, still pointing his gun at Turlock's head, and made his way to a waterside bar.

'How I catch a ship to Baltimore?' he asked the girl waiting tables.

'*Queen of Sheba,*' the girl explained. 'When she comes down from Denton.'

She was exceptionally pretty, a girl of nineteen who prided herself on her appearance. 'What's your name?' Pflaum asked, flushed with his share of the oystering wages.

'Nancy Turlock. My father owns that skipjack.'

'He's a fine man,' Pflaum said. And for two days he remained at the bar, waiting for the *Queen of Sheba,* telling extraordinary yarns to Captain Turlock's daughter.

On the final afternoon as Otto Pflaum purchased his ticket to Baltimore, with Nancy Turlock at his side in the yellow cape he had bought her, he noticed a commotion on the roadway leading to the wharf, and went with Nancy to see what was happening.

It was an amazing sight. A teamster, his cart loaded with casks, stood in the middle of the road near the heads of his two horses, while an elderly woman dressed all in gray and wearing a peculiar style of cap berated him so vigorously that Pflaum thought she might actually strike him with her furled umbrella. It was bizarre. The drayman cowered before her onslaught, even though he weighed twice what she did. The horses whinnied at the excitement. Children gathered in clusters to enjoy the scene. And the frail old lady moved about with a vigor that would have been surprising in a young man.

'What is this?' Pflaum asked, bewildered by the confusion.

'Just Rachel,' the Turlock girl said.

'Rachel who?'

'Rachel Paxmore. She taught me to read. In the old days she made speeches about freeing slaves. We think she's nutty, but no one tries to stop her.'

Slaves having been freed, she had taken to reprimanding teamsters caught abusing their animals.

Whatever slight reputation the *Jessie T* might have earned by her good oystering was destroyed when Otto Pflaum loud-mouthed it in the Patamoke bars that Captain Turlock had tried to drown him and that he, Pflaum, had been forced to capture the skipjack and hold it against five opponents for more than a day.

'Jake botched it,' the other watermen said, and again none would sail with him.

Normally, Turlock and Caveny would have gone to Baltimore to shanghai a crew, but they were afraid that Pflaum might be lurking there, so they swallowed their pride and permitted Big Jimbo to sign up another of his blacks. Thus the *Jessie T* became the first Patamoke boat to have three whites and three blacks; it was a cohesive crew, for Big Jimbo disciplined his recruits, warning them, 'You do right, they gonna be lots of black watermen. You mess around, no niggers never gonna see inside of a skipjack.'

But any pleasure Captain Jake might have found in his crew was dissipated when he brought the *Jessie T* into port one Saturday in late

December to learn that his daughter Nancy had run away to Baltimore. 'I grew suspicious,' Mrs. Turlock said, 'when she started ironing her clothes. Then I noticed that whenever the *Queen of Sheba* came to the wharf she asked a lot of questions. So I kept a close watch on her, but last Tuesday she fooled me by ridin' up to Trappe and takin' the packet there. She's gone, Jake, and do you know who with?'

'Lew?' Jake asked. Turlock girls had a habit of running off with Turlock men.

'Would to God it was. It's that Otto Pflaum.'

'God A'mighty!' Jake cried, and he was all for sailing immediately to Baltimore to recover his girl, and Tim Caveny encouraged him, but they were prevented from leaving by shocking news that reached them. Two skipjack captains had sailed into Patamoke with the superstructures of their boats chopped up. 'We was drudgin' proper in our waters off'n Oxford when the Virginians swept in. *Sinbad* leadin'. They like to shot us clean outa the water.'

'You mean, they came into our river?'

'That's where they came.'

'Anybody hit?'

'Two of my crew in hospital.'

'What are we gonna do?' the embittered skippers asked.

'Do? We're gonna drive them right out of the Choptank.'

On Monday morning the *Jessie T* sailed out of Patamoke with a grim crew. All six men were armed, and Big Jimbo assured Captain Jake that his two black sailors were first-class squirrel hunters. If there was to be battle, the skipjack was ready.

But it was hardly prepared for what the Virginians did. Four of their power-driven boats lay off the point of Tilghman Island, and as the *Jessie T* moved down the Choptank, these adversaries, led by the *Sinbad,* moved in upon her, judging that if they could knock Jake Turlock out of the river, they would have little trouble with the rest of the fleet.

It was a most uneven fight. Captain Jake stayed at the wheel, while his five crewmen, including Big Jimbo, stationed themselves along the rail. The Patamoke men fought well, and some of their fire pestered the Virginians, but the invading boats were too swift, their gunfire too concentrated.

On one pass, bullets ripped into the stern of the *Jessie T,* and Captain Turlock would have been killed had he not dropped ignominiously to the deck. Infuriated, he bellowed for Ned to take the wheel, while he crouched behind one of the dredges to fire at the *Sinbad.*

At this moment one of the Virginia boats swept in from the port side and rained a blizzard of bullets at the skipjack. Jake, kneeling behind the dredge, saw one of Big Jimbo's men spin in the air, lose his rifle overboard and fall in a pool of blood.

'Christ A'mighty!' Jake cried, forgetting his own safety and rushing forward, but as he did so, sailors from the blue *Sinbad* fired at the wheel, thinking to gun down the captain. Instead they hit Ned Turlock, who stumbled to one knee, clutched at the wheel, sent the skipjack turning in a circle, and died.

It was a terrible defeat, and there was nothing Captain Jake could do to retaliate. He had to watch impotently as the Virginia Squadron raced on, seeking other skipjacks that might want to contest its presence. None did.

As the *Jessie T* started her mournful retreat to Patamoke, the four survivors gathered in the cabin for prayers, and Caveny thumbed through his Bible for that passage taught him by an old sailor with whom he had first served on the Chesapeake:

> ' "The fishers also shall mourn, and all they that cast angle into the brooks shall lament, and they that spread nets upon the waters shall languish."
>
> 'Almighty God, what have we done to deserve Thy wrath? What can we do to regain Thy love? Blessed St. Andrew, patron of fishermen, accept into thy care the souls of Ned and Nathan, good watermen of this river. Blessed St. Patrick, dry the tears of their women, and protect us.'

The *Jessie T* would have to find a new crew, and gloom was deep upon the Choptank as its watermen studied what they must do to repel the invasion from Virginia.

Jake Turlock was gray with rage. He showed the fury that had sustained his forebears in their dogged fights against pirates and British warships, for not only had he been forced to witness the murder of his two crewmen, but he had also seen the insolent Virginians invade his own river. He took a violent oath to be revenged, and with his whole being engrossed in trying to come up with a plan, he forgot his dog, paid no attention to the geese inhabiting his marsh and even allowed his long gun to go unattended.

But it was crafty little Tim Caveny who devised the tactic whereby they could punish the *Sinbad,* and it was so bizarre and daring that when Jake heard it, his jaw dropped. 'You think we could handle it?'

'Positive,' Tim said, his eyes dancing with joy as he visualized the surprise he had fashioned for the Virginians. 'But since they operate with four powerboats, we better find five or six Choptank crews willing to work with us.'

When Turlock approached the other skipjack men, he found them hungering for a final showdown. 'And that's what it's gonna be,' Jake assured them. 'They can have their engines. What me and Tim's got cooked up is better'n engines.'

But as New Year's Day approached, with the start of the winter dredging, Turlock had to face up to the fact that the *Jessie T* suffered from one deficiency. 'Tim, we got to have up front a man with no nerves.'

The two watermen fell silent as each reviewed the strategy, and finally Jake said hesitantly, 'What we really need—'

'Don't tell me,' Caveny broke in. 'Otto Pflaum.'

'The same. And damnit, I'm gonna swallow my pride and go fetch him.'

They crossed to Baltimore, going straight to the Drunken Penguin, where they elbowed their way in. Big Jimbo, of course, could not accompany them inside, but he did wait in the shadows nearby, in case things got out of hand. They were seated innocently at their customary rear table, drinking beer like two ordinary Eastern Shore watermen, when Otto Pflaum appeared. He still wore his extra-thick pants, his heavy sweater with the double roll at the neck, and he looked formidable. As soon as he saw the Choptank men he assumed that they had come to take his girl away, so he did the prudent thing. Without taking his eyes off his enemies, he grabbed a bottle, smashed the end on a table, kept it pointed outward from his right hand, and advanced. Then, with his left hand, he broke the end off another bottle. Thus armed, he approached, whereupon Caveny asked in a voice of gentle Irish reasoning, 'Otto, dear friend, don't you trust us?'

The big German said nothing. He moved closer, placing himself in a position from which he could jab a jagged bottle into each face. Then he stopped, keeping the bottles close to the eyes of the men who had tried to kill him.

'Otto, sit down and talk with us,' Caveny pleaded.

'You want to hire me again?'

'Yes!' the Irishman said eagerly.

'Same wages as before? A swingin' boom?'

'Otto, you misunderstood . . .' Caveny was eager to explain that a failure in communication had been responsible, but the German pointed the broken bottle at him and growled, 'Shut up.'

'We need your help,' Turlock said.

'Doin' what?'

'Sit down. Put the bottles away.' Jake spoke with such authority that the big sailor obeyed. 'How's Nancy?' Turlock asked.

'She's pregnant.'

'You married yet?'

'Maybe later.'

'Otto, we need your help. You got to sail with us again.'

'Plenty sailors, why me?'

'The Virginians. They're drivin' us from the bay.'

Turlock had said the only words that could have excited this giant. Pflaum had seen the arrogant *Sinbad* and had fought against her, so he relished the prospect of renewed combat.

'This time, no boom?'

'There was none last time,' Caveny said gravely. 'A sudden wind.'

'This time, pay before I leave Baltimore.'

'Wait a minute!' Caveny exploded. To make such a demand was tantamount to an accusation against the integrity of the *Jessie T,* but Pflaum was adamant: 'We give the money to Nancy. But she gets it before we sail.'

This was agreed, and on the last day of the old year the *Jessie T* returned to Patamoke for the unusual fitting out that Jake and Tim had contrived.

When Otto Pflaum saw the magnitude of the big gun that Jake proposed for the bow he was staggered. 'That's a cannon!' Jake said nothing, merely pointed to the small cannonballs intended for the gun, and before Pflaum could comment, he showed him three more long guns, several kegs of black powder and larger kegs of lead pellets.

'What you tryin' to do, destroy the *Sinbad?*'

'Exactly,' Jake said grimly. He then invited Tim Caveny to show Otto the real surprise, for onto the skipjack the Irishman had lugged three of his deadly spray guns, each with a battery of seven barrels and a capacity of many pounds of shot. Otto was captivated by the ingenious manner in which Caveny intended igniting his guns, and cried, 'You must let me fire one,' and Caveny said, 'Our plan is for you to fire two.' But Jake interposed, 'No, we'd better save Otto for the two big guns forward.'

'Do I aim at the cabin?'

'At the waterline. I'm gonna sink her.'

So Jake spent the first two days of January training his accomplices; practice rounds were fired far up Broad Creek so no one could spy, and when he was satisfied that his men could handle their arsenal, he headed for the Choptank.

The guns were kept under tarpaulin, so that the *Jessie T* looked like merely one more Maryland skipjack trying to earn an honest living. The plan was for two relatively unarmed boats from Patamoke to move in the van in a casual approach to the oyster beds that were in contention, and to allow the *Sinbad* to drive them away. Then, when the Virginia vessel came at the *Jessie T* to complete the sweep, it would be Jake's responsibility to bring his boat as close as possible to the enemy, keeping the blue *Sinbad* to port, for the guns were concentrated on that side.

This would be a risky maneuver, because the *Sinbad* sailors had proved they would not hesitate to gun down the opposition, but Captain Turlock had anticipated the most dangerous moment: 'You men at the guns stay low. It'll be hard to hit you. I'll stay at the wheel and take my chances.' He had improved the risk by building about the wheel an armored semicircle behind which he could crouch; his head would not be protected, but as he said, 'If they're good enough to hit me in the head from their shiftin' boat, they deserve to win.' It was a confident crew of eight—four white, four black—that entered the bay and headed south.

Two days passed without incident, except that the *Jessie T* caught so many oysters it was an embarrassment. 'We cain't side up to a buy-boat, or they'd see the guns and the extry two men. On the other hand, if we pile them arsters right, they'll form us a fort.' So the deck was rearranged to permit the gunners to hide behind their catch.

On the third day the ominous blue *Sinbad* entered the Choptank, prowled the edges of the Patamoke fleet, then made a direct run at the two lures set up by Captain Turlock. As expected, the Virginia boat drove the smaller skipjacks off, then came directly at the *Jessie T.* 'Thank God!' Turlock called to his men. 'We pass her to port.'

The hidden gunners kept low. Jake hunkered down behind his iron battlement, and the two boats closed.

The first fire came from the *Sinbad.* When its crew saw that the *Jessie T* was not going to back off, their captain cried, 'Give them another whiff.' Shots ricocheted about the deck, ending in piles of oysters. The fusillade accomplished nothing except to anger the Choptank men and make them more eager to discharge their battery.

'Not yet!' Jake called, and his men stood firm while the *Sinbad* grew careless and moved much closer than she should have. 'Wait! Wait!' Jake called again, kneeling behind his armor plating as bullets whined by him.

As he hid, he caught the eye of Otto Pflaum, finger on the great gun once owned by the master-hunter Greef Twombly. He saw with satisfaction that Pflaum was not only ready with this gun, but prepared to leap to its lethal brother propped against the bulwark.

'Now!' Jake shouted, and from the entire port side of the skipjack a blaze of powder exploded, sending a devastating rain of lead across the deck of the *Sinbad* and punishing her at the water line. Those Virginians who were not knocked down were so confounded that they could not regroup before Tim Caveny fired at them with another of his seven-gun monsters, while Otto Pflaum leaped to a second long gun and aimed it right at the gaping hole opened by his first.

The *Sinbad,* mortally wounded, started to roll on its port side and its crew began leaping into the water and shouting for help.

'Let 'em all drowned,' Turlock snapped, and with grand indifference the *Jessie T,* her centerboard side-assed, as her detractors charged, withdrew from the battle.

It was a triumphal return such as few naval centers have witnessed, for the victorious vessel came to the dock laden with oysters, and as Tim Caveny called out details of the battle, Otto Pflaum counted the iron buckets as buyers on dock hauled them ashore: 'Tally three! Tally four! Mark one!'

At the close he informed his fellow crewmen, 'Damn near record. Thirty-nine and three!' But the *Jessie T* had earned more that day than one hundred and ninety-eight bushels of oysters. It had won the right to say that the riches of the Choptank would be harvested in a responsible manner.

The victory of the Choptank men led to a series of events that no one could have imagined.

The fact that Captain Turlock was now able to berth each weekend at Patamoke allowed him and Caveny to go duck hunting, with such good results that the two watermen accumulated surplus income in the Steed bank.

Since Jake Turlock had grown sick and tired of hearing the men at the store downgrade his boat—he loathed especially their contemptuous description 'the side-assed skipjack'—he decided to get rid of her and buy the partnership a real boat with its centerboard where it ought to be. When he approached Gerrit Paxmore with this proposal he found the Quaker willing to listen. 'I've been pondering this matter, Jacob, and have concluded that I've been obstinate in refusing to build in the new manner. There is a difference between an ocean-going schooner, whose keel must be kept inviolate, and a skipjack destined for bay use only, where the strain is not so great. I'd like a chance to build thee one to thy design.'

When the contract between Paxmore and the Turlock-Caveny partnership was drawn—'a first-class skipjack with centerboard trunk through the keel, $2,815'—Gerrit Paxmore asked the owners of the *Jessie T* what they intended doing with their present skipjack, and Turlock said, 'I suppose we'll find a buyer somewheres, even if she is side-assed,' and Paxmore replied, 'I think I can take it off thy hands,' and Caveny asked, 'You got a buyer?' and Paxmore said, 'I think so,' but he would not divulge who it was.

So the new skipjack was built, superior in every way to the *Jessie T,* and when it had been launched and given a couple of trial runs out into the bay, Jake and Tim concluded that they had bought themselves a masterpiece, and the former said with some relief, 'Now we can hire a white crew. You, me, three Turlocks and Big Jimbo in the galley.'

'Them niggers wasn't so bad,' Caveny recalled.

'Yes, but a white crew's better. Less likelihood of mutiny.'

'The niggers fought well.'

'Yes, but a white crew's better.' Jake paused, then added, ' 'Course, I'd not want to sail without Jimbo. Best cook this bay ever produced.'

But when he went to Frog's Neck to advise Jimbo that the new skipjack would be sailing on Monday, he found to his dismay that the big cook would not be assuming his old place.

'Why not?' Jake thundered.

'Because . . .' The tall black was too embarrassed to explain, and Turlock heckled him, charging cowardice because of the gunfight, a lack of loyalty to his crew mates, and ingratitude. Big Jimbo listened impassively, then said in a soft voice, 'Cap'm Jake, I'm takin' out my own skipjack.'

'You're what?'

'Mr. Paxmore done sold me the *Jessie T.*'

The information staggered the waterman, and he stepped back, shaking his head as if to discharge evil invaders. 'You buyin' my boat?'

'Yes, sir. From the day I could walk my daddy tol' me, "Git yourse'f a boat." He had his own ship . . . for a while . . . as you know.'

'What ship did Cudjo ever have?' Turlock asked in disgust, and Big Jimbo thought it best not to pursue the topic. What he did say was this: 'He tol' me, time and again, "When a man got his own boat, he free. His onliest prison the horizon." '

'Hell, Jimbo, you don't know enough to captain a skipjack.'

'I been watchin', Cap'm Jake. I been watchin' you, and you one o' the best.'

'You goddamn nigger!' Jake exploded, but the words denoted wonder rather than contempt. He burst into laughter, slapped his flank and said, 'All the time you was on deck, doin' extry work to help the men, you was watchin' ever'thing I was doin'. Damn, I knowed you niggers was always plottin'.' In the old camaraderie of the cabin, where these two men had worked together, and eaten and slept, Jake Turlock punched his cook in the back and wished him well.

'But you got to change her name,' Jake said.

Big Jimbo had anticipated him. When he and Captain Jake went to the Paxmore Boatyard to inspect the refitted *Jessie T* they found the old name painted out, and in its place a crisp new board with the simple letters *Eden.*

'Where you get that name?' Jake asked, admiring the condition of his old boat. 'That's a Bible name, ain't it?'

'My mother's name,' Jimbo said.

'That's nice,' Jake said. 'I named her after my mother. Now you niggers name her after yours. That's real nice.'

'She give me the money to buy it.'

'I thought she was dead.'

'Long ago. But she always collectin' money . . . fifty years. First she gonna buy her freedom, and the Steeds give it to her. Then she gonna buy Cudjo's freedom, and he earned it hisse'f. Then she gonna buy her brother's freedom, and Emancipation come along. So she give me the money and say, "Jimbo, some day you buy yourse'f a boat and be truly free." '

In October 1895 the skipjack *Eden* out of Patamoke made its first sortie on the oyster beds. It was known throughout the fleet as 'the side-assed skipjack with the nigger crew,' but it was in no way impeded, for Captain Jimbo had to be recognized as a first-class waterman. There was, of course, much banter when the other captains gathered at the store: '*Eden* like to went broke last summer. Cap'm Jimbo tooken her up the Choptank to fetch a load o' watermelons to the market in Baltimore, but when he got there the crew had et ever' goddamned melon.'

There was no laughter, however, when the black crew began to unload huge quantities of oysters into the buy-boats. And the bay might have been outraged in the fall of 1897, but not really surprised, when Randy Turlock, a distant nephew of Captain Jake's, showed up as a member of the *Eden*'s crew, which now consisted of five blacks and one white.

'Why would a decent, God-fearin' white man consent to serve with a nigger?' the men at the store raged at the young waterman.

'Because he knows how to find arsters,' young Turlock said, and in the 1899 season Big Jimbo's crew was four blacks and two whites, and thus it remained as the new century dawned.

Onshore, relations between whites and blacks did not duplicate what prevailed in the skipjacks. When oyster dredging, a waterman was judged solely on his performance; if he said he was a cook, it was presumed that he could cook; and a deck hand was expected to muscle the dredges. A man won his place by exhibiting skills, and his color did not signify.

But when he stepped ashore the black oysterman could not join the circle at the store, nor send his children to the white man's school, nor pray in a white church. For seven months he had eaten shoulder to shoulder with his white crew mates, but onshore it would have been unthinkable for him to dine with his betters. He had to be circumspect in what he said, how he walked the pavements and even how he looked at white people, lest they take offense and start rumors.

The permanent relationship between the two races was underlined at the start of the century when a gang of venal Democratic politicians in Annapolis proposed an amendment to the Maryland constitution, revoking the right of blacks to vote. This was done for the most corrupt of reasons—perpetuation of thieving officeholders—but behind the most honorable and persuasive façade. The gang did not offer the amendment under its own besmirched name; it employed the services of the dean of the law school at the university, a handsome man with a mellifluous three-barreled name, John Prentiss Pope, and he devised a simple formula for perpetually denying the ballot: 'Any Maryland resident is entitled to vote if he or his ancestors were eligible to do so on January 1, 1869, or if he can read and interpret a passage of the Maryland constitution.' It was especially effective in that it avoided the necessity of stating openly that it was anti-Negro.

'What we intend doin',' the Democrats explained when they visited Patamoke, 'is end this silly business of niggers traipsin' to the polls like decent people. You know and I know they ain't never been a nigger qualified to vote, nor ever will be.'

The campaign became virulent. Newspapers, churches, schools and congregations at country crossroads united in an inflamed crusade to restore Maryland to its pristine honor: 'We gonna end this farce of niggers pretendin' they got the brains to comprehend politics. End nigger votin' and reinstate honest government.'

Not many blacks voted, actually, and some who did accepted money, but the basic argument against them was they supported the Republican party because Abraham Lincoln had belonged to it, and he had freed the slaves. Endlessly the Democrats had tried to lure black voters into their party, but had failed; now the blacks would vote no more. The unfolding campaign indicated that the amendment would carry, for Democratic orators stormed the countryside, proclaiming, 'If a respected professor like John Prentiss Pope says niggers shouldn't vote, you know what your duty is on Election Day.'

The Steeds favored the amendment because they remembered John C. Calhoun, spiritual leader of their family; he had claimed that the governing of free men should be restricted to those with education, moral principle and ownership of wealth. 'I am not against the black man,' Judge Steed said at one public meeting held in the Patamoke Methodist Church, 'but I do not want him casting his ballot on issues which concern only white men.'

The Turlocks were savagely supportive of the proposed restrictions and campaigned up and down the river for its passage: 'Niggers killed our cousin Matt. They're slaves at heart and better be kept that way.' Even the family members who had shipped with Big Jimbo aboard the *Jessie T* or served under him on the *Eden* were vehement in their pronouncement that no black had the intelligence to vote; their experiences to the contrary aboard a skipjack were ignored, and the men ranted, 'They're animals. They got no rights.' Only Jake Turlock suffered confusion on this matter; he knew that Big Jimbo was the most capable man ever to serve on the *Jessie T,* more reliable even than Tim Caveny, but whenever he was tempted to concede this, he recalled the description of blacks that he had memorized so well in school, and he could see the words inflamed in his copybook:

Niggers: Lazy, superstitious, revengeful, stupid and irresponsible. Love to sing.

No black who had ever served with him had been lazy, but in his mind all blacks were. No blacks had been as superstitious as a skipjack captain who would allow no blue, no bricks, no women, no walnuts, no hold cover wrong side up. No blacks had been so vengeful as the German Otto Pflaum, and as for stupidity and irresponsibility, these words could never remotely be applied to Big Jimbo or the black watermen he enlisted, yet Jake believed that all blacks were flawed by those weaknesses, because in his childhood he had been so taught. One night after a hectic meeting at which he had spoken in defense of the amendment, he said to Caveny, 'Come to think of it, Tim, I never heard a nigger sing aboard our skipjack, but it's well known they love to sing.' 'They're a bad lot,' Caveny replied. 'Cain't never tell what they're up to.'

The Cavenys, now a growing clan along the river, had always been disturbed by the presence of blacks in their community. 'We didn't have no niggers in Ireland. Wouldn't tolerate 'em if they tried to move in. They ain't Catholic. They don't really believe in God. Ain't no reason in the world why they should vote like ordinary men.' The entire Caveny brood intended to vote for the amendment and could imagine no reason for doing otherwise.

The other residents along the Choptank were almost universally opposed to black franchise, and this illustrated a singular change that was modifying Eastern Shore history: during the Civil War well over half the Choptank men who had served did so in the Union army, but now when their descendants looked back upon that war they claimed that well over ninety-five percent had fought with the Confederacy. The reasons behind this self-deception were simple: 'No man could have pride in havin' fought for the North, side by side with niggers. My pappy was strictly South.' Patamoke families were proud if an ancestor had marched with Lee or ridden with Jeb Stuart, ashamed if he had served with Grant, and it became common for families to lie about past affiliations.

Because of this selective memory, the Eastern Shore converted itself into one of the staunchest southern areas, and people were apt to say, 'Our ancestors had slaves and fought to keep 'em. Emancipation was the worst evil ever to hit this land.' It was these belated southerners, egged on by plantation families whose ancestors had honestly sided with the South, who now united to keep blacks from their schools and churches;

they joined in mobs to discipline them when they became fractious; and gleefully they combined to adopt this amendment which would rescind the right to vote. Indeed, it seemed as if this might be the first step in a return to the good, rational days of the past, when blacks knew their place and when life on the Eastern Shore was placid and orderly—'We end this votin' nonsense for niggers, we can restore some peace and quiet in this community.'

The only people who opposed the new law were the Paxmores and a few dissidents like them, and even these would have been muted by the unanimity of the community had it not been for a formidable school-teacher. Miss Emily Paxmore was one of those tall, gangly women of indefinite age who seemed destined from birth to be spinsters; she might have taught music, or served as clerk in some uncle's store, or concentrated her efforts on whatever church she attended, but in her case she found a place in the schoolroom, where she taught with a persistence that amazed both the parents and their children.

She was a large woman who favored severe clothes, a hairdo drawn taut, and a frown which repelled parents on first acquaintance, then softened as she spoke about the educability of their children. When she first heard of the proposed legislation, she supposed that the reporter was teasing her because of her known sympathy with blacks, and she made a frivolous response: 'To even consider such a law would be like turning the calendar back two hundred years.'

This unfortunate remark became a rallying cry for the advocates of the amendment, who declared, 'That's exactly what we want. The way things were two hundred years ago, before the niggers fouled them up.'

When Miss Paxmore realized that the sponsors of the bill were serious, she directed her formidable energy to resisting them. She rose in meeting to enlist the support of her fellow Quakers, but found a surprising number sympathetic to the bill, supporting the theory that Negroes were not capable of understanding issues.

She convened public meetings, but made the serious mistake of inviting northern ministers and politicians to address them, for this tactic lost more votes than it gained—'We don't need northerners comin' down here to instruct us on how to vote.'

She moved about the town, relentlessly buttonholing anyone who would listen, but she accomplished nothing. In despair she traveled across the bay to Baltimore for consultation with opponents of the bill, and there found only gloom. 'The situation is this, Miss Emily. All the Eastern Shore favors the legislation. All the southern counties, loyal to the Confederacy, will vote for it. The far western areas, where a sense of freedom has always maintained, will support the Negro's right to vote, and so will much of Baltimore. But if you add our votes and theirs, they've got to win.'

Maryland became a test case for black rights; orators from many southern states came north to excite voters against the dangers of black franchise, and sabers rattled as ancient battles were recalled. Each week it became increasingly apparent that the amendment was going to be adopted and that in Maryland, at least, blacks would revert to the conditions they had occupied during their centuries of slavery.

Emily Paxmore returned to Patamoke a defeated woman, and men at the store chuckled as she picked her grim way back to her home near the school. And then, four weeks before the plebiscite was to take place, she had an idea, and without conferring with anyone, she boarded the *Queen of Sheba* and sped to Baltimore. Breathlessly she told the men and women running the campaign against the amendment, 'It's quite simple. We can defeat this fraud by a tactic that will prove irresistible.'

'What could possibly turn the tide?'

'This. From today on we never mention the word Negro. Instead we hammer at the fact that this amendment will deprive Germans, Italians, Jews and even Irishmen of their right to vote. We'll make them fight our battle for us.'

'But the amendment doesn't say that,' a gentleman versed in law objected.

Miss Paxmore tensed. 'Few Germans or Italians or Russian Jews were eligible to vote on January 1, 1869. Think of that!'

'But we all know that the law is not to be applied against them.'

'I don't know it,' she said primly. 'And I'm going to shout from every housetop that this is a plot to disfranchise immigrants.'

'Wouldn't that be dishonest?'

Miss Paxmore folded her hands, considered the accusation, and replied, 'If I am telling a lie, the other side will be able to refute it . . . six weeks after the election.'

She was on the street twenty hours a day, a tall, furious woman dressed in gray, asking her impudent question in the German district and the Italian: 'Does thee think it proper for good people who pay their taxes to be denied the vote?' She wrote advertisements that appeared in the papers, challenged legislators of German and Italian extraction to open their eyes to the danger threatening their families, and spent her evenings in Baltimore's Third Ward, haranguing Russian Jews: 'They are plotting to rob thee of thy rights. Thee must fight this law.'

Advocates of the amendment were appalled by the fire-storm this gangling schoolteacher was igniting, and they dispatched John Prentiss Pope to assure all immigrants that his amendment would be applied judiciously. Party hacks circulated through the wards, whispering that 'our amendment won't never be used against your people. It's meant only for *them.*' And they would wink.

But Emily Paxmore had an answer for that. 'They come like the snake in paradise and whisper, "We promise we won't use the new law against thee." But I can assure thee that they have plans right now to disfranchise every Jew, every German and every Italian. Once this amendment passes, thy vote is lost forever.'

This accusation was almost criminal; obviously no such plans existed, nor had they even been suggested when the measure was first proposed. 'Oh, we might want to use it some day against those damned Jews in the Third Ward. Cut them down to size. But never against the Germans.' Supporters became frantic when Miss Paxmore circulated charges that the proposed new law would be applied immediately to eliminate the Irish vote.

'This damned woman is destroyin' us with her lies!' one Democratic leader thundered, and he assembled a group of six to confront her in the small hotel from which she worked. When she met them in the lounge, six pillars of ward politics, she found them geared for battle. 'If you repeat those lies against us, we'll take you to court. Throw you in jail.'

'What lies?' she asked simply, her hands folded in her lap.

'That the Germans will be disfranchised.'

'Won't they be? The law is most explicit as thee has written it.'

'But it's not intended for Germans.'

'Who is it intended for?'

'Them.'

'Is thee afraid to speak their name? Does thee mean the Jews?'

'Now damnit, Miss Paxmore, there's not a word in our amendment that works against the Jews.'

'My dear friends, every word could be applied to Jews who immigrated here from Poland, or the Baltic, or Rumania.'

'But we're not going to use it against them. We promise you . . .'

Coldly she recited the terms of the proposed law; it could easily be applied to Jews and Catholics without good education and especially to Hungarians and Lithuanians and most particularly to Poles and Italians. Concluding her citation, she said, 'It's a cruel law, gentlemen, and thee should be ashamed of thyselves.'

They were not ashamed. 'Miss Paxmore, you know damned well how this amendment will be used. If a nigger tries to vote, we give him the constitution, and I'm the judge and I say, "You didn't pass." If a German reads it, I say, "You pass." '

'For such duplicity thee should be doubly ashamed. How can the black man ever—'

'Goddamnit!' a burly political leader exploded. 'We're gonna throw you in jail for libel and perjury and defamation of character.'

Emily Paxmore was not intimidated. Looking at each of the men, she asked, 'What character?'

Another leader waved his copy of the amendment and said almost plaintively, 'It's unfair, Miss Paxmore, for you to lie about our intentions. You know in your heart we would never use this bill against good people . . . only niggers.'

Emily Paxmore grabbed the paper from his hand and placed it over her bosom. 'This amendment, if it passes, will one day be applied against persons like me. But I see from thy expressions that it's going to be defeated, and for that I thank God, because it's a criminal effort.'

She was right. When the ballots were counted, Choptank voters had supported the amendment overwhelmingly, as had the rest of the Eastern Shore. Those southern areas on the mainland where slaves had been common also voted to deprive the blacks of their rights, but in the remainder of the state the plebiscite was determined on the principle that Miss Paxmore had enunciated: 'Do you want to disfranchise immigrants?' Blacks were never mentioned, and from the western counties where Germans had settled came a heavy vote against the amendment; in polyglot Baltimore it was overwhelmed. The proposal lost. Blacks could continue to vote.

When Emily Paxmore came home, she never spoke of her frenetic campaign. She returned to her teaching, producing young scholars whose lives would stabilize the Eastern Shore, but one afternoon when her brother Gerrit visited her, she responded openly to his interrogations. 'I did lie, Gerrit, and I'm sorely troubled by it. They had no plan to disfranchise Germans or Jews. And I did make the accusation too late for them to combat it.'

'Why did thee do it?'

'Because each soul on this earth faces one Armageddon. When all the forces are arranged pro and con. Now comes the one great battle, and if thee runs away or fails to fight with vigor, they life is forever diminished.'

'Thee sounds mighty military, for a Quaker.'

'Armageddon is even more compelling when it's a battle of the spirit. This law was wrong, Gerrit, and I stumbled upon the only way to destroy it. I'm ashamed of the tactics I used, but if the same situation were to occur again . . .' Her voice drifted away. She took out her handkerchief and pressed it to her nose. Blinking her eyes several times, she said brightly, 'But it won't occur again. Armageddon comes once, and we'd better not back off.'

In August 1906, when the two watermen were in their grizzled sixties, Caveny came running to the store with exciting news: 'Jake, I think we got us a contract to haul watermelons from Greef Twombly's place to Baltimore.' This was important, for oystermen spent their summer months scrounging for commissions that would keep their skipjacks busy; the shallow-drafted boats carried too little freeboard to qualify them for entering the ocean, or they might have run lumber from the West Indies, as many schooners did. Also, the boom was so extended that in a good gale, when the starboard was underwater, the tip of the boom tended to cut into the waves, too, and that was disastrous.

So the watermen prayed for a cargo of farm produce to Baltimore and a load of fertilizer back, or coal to Norfolk, or pig iron from the blast furnaces north of Baltimore. Best of all was a load of watermelons from far up some river, for then, with a crew of three—Turlock, Caveny and a black cook—the skipjack could earn real money, passing back and forth across the oyster beds it had worked during the winter.

At the start of this unexpected bonanza Jake was in such a good mood that as the lines were about to be loosened, he impetuously called for his dog to come aboard, and when the Chesapeake leaped across the open water to scramble aboard, Caveny asked, 'What goes?' and Jake said, 'I got a hankerin' to take my dog along.' Before the sentence was finished, Caveny had leaped ashore and was bellowing, 'Nero! Come here!' And his voice was so penetrating that almost at once his Labrador dashed up, prepared for whatever adventure was afoot.

It was a pleasant cruise. The skipjack sailed slowly up to the far end of the Choptank to Old Man Twombly's farm, where they found Greef and the watermelons waiting. His first cry from the rickety wharf concerned the gun: 'How's the big one doin'?' And before he threw a line, Jake yelled back, 'We're gettin' about seventy-seven ducks a go,' and Greef replied with some contempt, 'You ain't usin' enough shot.'

While the loading took place, the skipjack's black cook caught himself a mess of crabs from the stern and fried up some crisp crab cakes. Greef brought down some cold beer and sat on deck with the watermen and their dogs, remembering old storms. Greef made the men a proposition: 'Five years ago I planted me a line of peach trees, just to see. They're producin' major-like, and I want to risk a hundred baskets stowed on deck. You sell 'em, you keep half the cash.' But when the peaches were aboard and the skipjack was ready for sailing, the old man took Jake aside and whispered, 'With that gun, you load her right, you tamp her right, you ought to catch ninety ducks on the average.'

The passage across the bay was aromatic with the smell of peaches, and when the cargo reached the Long Dock, the A-rabs were waiting with their pushcarts, pleased to receive fresh melons but positively delighted with the unexpected peaches.

With their windfall profits, the two watermen trekked to the Rennert for a duck dinner, then visited Otto Pflaum and his wife, loaded up with fertilizer and sailed for home. As they quit the harbor they chanced to find themselves at the center of a triangle formed by three luxurious bay steamers, now lighted with electricity, and they admired the scintillating elegance of these fine vessels as they set out to penetrate the rivers which fed the bay.

'Look at 'em go!' Jake cried as the vessels went their individual ways, their orchestras sending soft music over the water.

'Classic ships,' Caveny said, and for most of an hour the Choptank men regarded the ships almost enviously.

The oystermen could not have imagined that these large ships would one day disappear entirely from this bay, as the Paxmore schooners had vanished and the Paxmore clippers. The classic ship that night was not the gaudy steamer but the quiet little skipjack, the boat conceived on the Chesapeake, tailored to its demands and adapted in every part to its conditions. It would endure after everything on the bay that night had gone to rust, for it was generic, born of the salt flats and heavy dredging, while the brightly lighted steamers were commercial innovations useful for the moment but bearing little relation to the timeless bay.

'They disappear mighty fast,' Caveny said as the lights merged with the waves.

Now the watermen were alone on the bay, and before long the low profile of the Eastern Shore began to rise in the moonlight, a unique configuration of marshland and wandering estuaries. 'We really have the land of pleasant livin',' Turlock mused as his skipjack drifted in the night airs, but when they approached Devon Island he fixed his gaze at the western end of the island, where a multitude of trees lay wallowing in the tide.

'I never noticed that before,' he said. 'That island's gonna wash clean away, one of these storms.'

The watermen inspected the erosion, and Caveny said, 'I read in a book that all our land on the Eastern Shore is alluvial . . .'

'What's that?' Turlock asked suspiciously.

'Land thrown here by the Susquehanna, when it was fifty times as big. You know what I think, Jake? I think long after we're dead there ain't gonna be no Eastern Shore. The land we know will wash into the ocean.'

'How soon?' Jake asked.

'Ten thousand years.'

Neither man spoke. They were sailing over oyster beds for which they had fought, beds whose icy catch had numbed their hands and cut their fingers, bringing blood to their frozen mittens. Beyond that spit, barely visible in the night, the *Laura Turner* had capsized, six men lost. Over there the *Wilmer Dodge* had foundered, six men gone. Around the next headland, where ducks rafted in winter, the *Jessie T* had driven off the invaders from Virginia.

Softly the skipjack entered the Choptank. Jake's Chesapeake still patrolled the bow, ready to repel invaders, but Caveny's Labrador lay prone on the deck, his head close to Tim's ankle, his dark eyes staring up at the Irishman with boundless love.

Voyage Twelve: 1938

A BASIC TENET OF QUAKERISM WAS THAT IF A MAN or woman tended the divine fire that burned within each human breast, one could establish direct relationship to God without the intercession of priest or rabbi. Songs and shouted prayers were not necessary to attract God's attention, for He dwelt within and could be summoned by a whisper.

Nevertheless it became a custom in all meetings for certain devout souls to be recognized as possessing special devotion, and they became known as ministers. In the traditional sense of this word they had no right to it, for they did not attend seminary, nor were the hands of some bishop placed upon them, bestowing a divine gift, the legitimacy of which extended back to Jesus Christ. In all other religions, the priest thus legally ordained could expect to be supported economically by his parishioners, and to do their spiritual work for them.

In the Quaker faith the minister had no legitimacy other than his or her own behavior, and no fixed income other than what he or she could earn by hard work. A Quaker acted like a minister, then became one.

During the Great Depression of the 1930s the Quakers of Maryland, Delaware and Pennsylvania discovered that they had in their midst another in that majestic line of Quaker preachers. Woolman Paxmore, then in his fifties, was a tall, gaunt, prophetic man with an unusually large Adam's apple that jutted forward as if he had two noses. He had spent his life as a farmer, but his commitment to God was so overpowering that even while young he began traveling to various towns, and wherever he appeared at First Day worship the congregation let him know that they would be disappointed if he did not speak.

He had been aptly named after one of the first Quaker ministers born in America. John Woolman had been an inspired man, a humble New Jersey tailor who from the age of seven had known himself to be called by God. Each year his simple rustic life gave further evidence of his exceptional faith: he ministered to the poor, elevated the status of blacks in his part of New Jersey, traveled up the Susquehanna to check on the government's treatment of Indians, and went on his own meager funds to England to study conditions there, always evidencing a simple belief in the goodness of God.

His namesake, Woolman Paxmore, led much the same kind of life. He, too, ministered to the poor, finding homes for no less than thirty orphaned children. He had gone to states like Oklahoma and Montana to see what could be done to help the Indians. And in his fifty-sixth year his thoughts turned to Berlin, the capital of Nazi Germany.

He was working in the field one day, harvesting corn on the north bank of the Choptank, when a powerful, straightforward thought occurred to him: Jesus Christ was a Jew, a real Jewish rabbi with a long nose, and no living man ever accomplished more on this earth. For Adolf Hitler to persecute the spiritual descendants of Jesus is wrong. It is all wrong.

That week he began preaching this simple message: to discriminate in any way against the Jew is to deny the heritage of Jesus Christ. He took his message to the rural meetings of Pennsylvania and down into New Jersey, where John Woolman had preached, and to all the meetings in Delaware. He drove a small Chevrolet, and on Saturday afternoons Quakers in out-of-the way places would see him coming, a tall, ungainly man, hunched over the wheel of his car, peering sideways as he moved slowly into town, looking for some address which he remembered imperfectly.

He would stop the Chevrolet anywhere, leave the motor running and walk about the streets, importuning strangers, 'Could thee perhaps tell me where Louis Cadwallader lives? There's no such person in this town? Could it be Thomas Biddle?'

When he found the person he sought he was greeted with warmth, and other Quakers in the neighborhood were summoned to an informal supper. Some of his finest preaching was accomplished in these quiet Saturday nights when Quakers met over a cold ham dinner to hear the reflections of their distinguished minister. Such gatherings often ended with slabs of apple pie and glasses of milk, and the rural folk would listen intently as Paxmore brought his discussion to an end: 'I believe that if three or four of us went to Herr Hitler and pointed out to him the grievousness of his behavior, he would understand. I think God would show us a way to rescue those tortured people, and bring them out of Germany as He once brought their ancestors out of Egypt.'

'Does thee think Herr Hitler would listen?'

'He has not succeeded in gaining control of Germany by being a stupid man. And wise men listen. He will listen to us if we approach with simple testimony.'

He became obsessed with the idea of going to Germany and talking directly with Hitler, and as he moved about the eastern states he convinced two other Quakers of the practicality of his plan: a merchant in Pittsburgh said he was prepared to go, and a renowned schoolmaster from a small town in North Carolina said he had an inner conviction that Hitler would listen. So in October 1938 these three elderly Quakers assembled in Philadelphia and discussed plans for their visit to Berlin.

Woolman Paxmore, as the acknowledged preacher, laid the spiritual groundwork: 'We shall tell him in plain words, but without rancor, that what he is doing is wrong, that it can in no way aid Germany, and that it must be an affront to the Christians of the world.'

It was the Pittsburgh merchant who assumed responsibility for the logistics of the trip: 'Well-minded Friends in Philadelphia have contributed generously. We'll go to New York this Friday and sail on the *Queen Mary* to Southampton. British Friends will meet us there and we'll spend three days in London. We proceed to Harwich and cross the Channel. In Berlin a group of German Friends will house us, and we have already applied for a meeting with Herr Hitler.'

And so they set out, three tall Quakers with no credentials other than their simple faith. The third day of their ocean trip was a Sunday, and the schoolteacher proposed that they hold a Quaker meeting in one of the cabins, but Woolman Paxmore protested, 'It seems ostentatious for us . . .'

'How ostentatious, if we meet in private?'

'Because there is a formal meeting in the salon,' Paxmore replied, 'and we should support it.'

The three Old Testament figures, dressed in black, added grace and color to the services conducted by an Episcopalian minister from Boston, but were surprised when at the end of prayers the clergyman said, 'We are honored this morning by having within our congregation one of the distinguished religious leaders of America, Woolman Paxmore, the Quaker preacher from Maryland, and I for one would consider it an honor if he and his two companions would hold a Quaker service for us this afternoon.'

This proposal met with enthusiastic support. At the Sunday meal many of the first-class passengers came down to the tourist class in which the three Quakers were traveling to urge that Paxmore conduct the services. 'We've never attended a Quaker meeting,' the passengers said. 'It would be a rare privilege.'

So in the late afternoon a group of some sixty people assembled in the salon which had been used for the morning services. Three chairs had been arranged at the front of the room, and it had been supposed that

Woolman Paxmore would occupy the middle chair, as a place of honor, but it was his custom always to award that chair to whatever man or woman had assumed the responsibility for the housekeeping details of the meeting, and now he insisted that the Pittsburgh merchant take it, for he had provided funds for the trip.

For ten minutes the three men sat silent. After twenty minutes there was still no sound, and visitors who had never participated in a Quaker meeting grew uneasy. They did not shift or shuffle, but it was plain that they expected something to happen. There was no singing, no collection, no prayer, no sermon. Thirty minutes elapsed, and forty. Then the Episcopalian clergyman rose and said briefly, 'Brother Paxmore, we do hope you will feel called upon to speak with us. We have heard that your messages are inspiring.'

This was very un-Quakerish and it caught Paxmore by surprise; he had been overawed by the responsibility he had assumed, that of serving as the conscience of Christianity, and had felt that it would be intemperate of him to speak at such a hallowed moment. The journey was engaged; the obligation had been assumed; there could be no turning back; words were no longer needed.

But he was a true Quaker, a man of total simplicity, and whereas he had felt it improper to speak, it was not intemperate of the Boston clergyman to point out that the assembled group had hoped to hear what a Quaker preacher might be like. His personal inclination was not to speak, but if others demanded that he do so, he would.

Nodding gravely to the clergyman, he rose, but the ship was moving through vast and easy swells and was unsteady, so he grabbed at the chair and stood behind it. Tall, black-suited, gray of head, angular of face and bony-handed, he stood in the swaying salon and said, 'Women and men must meet the challenge of whatever specific time they have been chosen to fill, and the inescapable challenge of our time is the treatment Herr Hitler is according the Jews of Germany.' He predicted that if Hitler were allowed to mistreat the German Jews, he would soon extend such acts to the Jews of Austria, Poland and France. 'And then he will turn his attention to other non-conformists, like the Seventh Day Adventists and the Quakers. And pretty soon the malignancy will encompass thee, and thee, and thee.' With these words he pointed his massive right hand at specific members of the congregation, and three passengers with German backgrounds, who felt that Hitler had done much to restore the dignity of Germany, rose in anger and left the salon.

Woolman Paxmore did not even notice. He was in the process of developing an idea which he knew to be just and inspired by God, so he continued, 'But if men of good will were to go to Hitler and remind him of the fact that Jews and Jesus are descendants from a common stock, this infernal slippage into barbarism might be halted.'

He then proceeded to expound the concept that had become a fixation with him: 'Thee must acknowledge that Jesus Christ was Himself a Jew. Living in Palestine under the hot sun, he was probably darker than many American Negroes. And his features could not have been the sweetly simple ones of our religious calendars. He was a Jew, and he doubtless looked much as thy tailor or doctor or professor looks today. If Jews have large noses, he had one. If they are swarthy, he was swarthy. If they talk with their hands, he did so too. During much of his life Jesus Christ was a Jewish rabbi, and if we forget this, we forget the nature of Christianity.'

At this two more passengers departed. Ignoring them, Paxmore concluded, 'We believe that if these simple truths can be pointed out to Herr Hitler, he will have to concede them.' He did not spell out what good might thus be accomplished, but his logic had been so forceful that when, at the close of the hour, the meeting ended, various listeners crowded about him to ask what proposals he intended making, if he did meet Hitler.

'Very simple,' he explained. 'We shall beseech him to turn the Jews loose, let them emigrate.'

'To where?' a businessman asked.

'Where?' Paxmore asked in astonishment. 'Any country would be glad to receive them.'

'Do you think that?' the businessman pressed.

'Of course. Wouldn't thee welcome the arrival of such a group? Educated men and women? Children with fine schooling? There's no limit to what they might accomplish in America. And I'm certain that France and England will feel the same.'

Out of politeness the businessman did not comment, but he did look at his wife and shake his head. 'These religious nuts,' he whispered to her as they left the salon. 'We have them with us always.'

'But it was interesting,' his wife replied.

'Fascinating,' he agreed. 'I like their idea of talking directly with God. I've always thought you didn't need all the priests.' He paused for a moment, then said, 'I suppose that if you do talk directly with God, you could get hung up on the Jewish thing. Jesus may have started as a rabbi, but he was smart enough to quit.'

Another passenger stopped to talk with Paxmore. This man was a Jew, a merchant from Baltimore, and he asked, 'Let's suppose for the moment that you can get to Hitler, and let's suppose he listens, and then let's suppose that he is willing to make some gesture. What are you prepared to offer him?'

'We'll take all the Jews he doesn't want and settle them in some other country,' he repeated patiently.

'Do you really believe the other countries will accept them?'

'It would be inhuman to do otherwise.'

To this the man from Baltimore made no comment. Instead he changed the subject dramatically. 'Have you given any thought, Reverend Paxmore . . .'

'I'm not a reverend,' Paxmore corrected.

'In my book you are. Have you given any thought to the possibility that Hitler might offer to release the Jews—some of the Jews, that is—providing the outside world puts up a certain sum of money?'

'That would be blackmail!'

'Precisely. And you must be prepared to meet it.'

Woolman Paxmore fell silent. It was difficult for him to believe that the leader of any state would resort to blackmail, and after some contemplation of this evil possibility he summoned his two colleagues. 'This gentleman has raised a most disconcerting point. Will thee explain it to my friends?'

As the other passengers left the salon the three Quakers sat down with the Jew from Baltimore, and he explained in cruel, harsh terms the blackmail he expected Hitler to propose.

'Thee speaks of him as a monster,' Paxmore objected.

'He is. Reverend Paxmore, I think it a certainty that if you good men do not rescue the Jews of Germany, they will all be executed . . . hanged . . . shot.'

'That's infamous!' Paxmore protested. He rose in great agitation. 'Thee speaks as if we were dealing with a madman.'

'You are,' the man from Baltimore said. 'And what are you prepared to offer him?'

The thought was alien to anything that Paxmore had contemplated. Offer him? They were coming to offer him the truth, a glimpse of God's eternal message of justice and salvation.

'Dear friends,' the Jew said at the conclusion of their abortive discussion, 'he will ask you for money.'

'Where would we get money?' the schoolteacher asked.

'I could sell Peace Cliff,' Paxmore said simply, with no doubt in his mind that saving human lives was more important than holding on to his ancestral home beside the Choptank.

'Dear friends,' the Jew said, 'Hitler will want far more money than you could ever raise. But if he does demand it, remember that I and my acquaintances stand ready to collect whatever ransom he demands.' He shook hands with the three Quakers, giving each a business card.

When the missioners reached Berlin they were greeted with contempt by German officials and with amused condescension at the American embassy. 'You've come to persuade Herr Hitler to treat the Jews more kindly?' one young secretary from Virginia asked.

'We have,' Paxmore replied. 'I trust thee will do everything possible to speed our mission?'

'Look, our ambassador can't even get in to see him. Small chance for you.'

'We'll wait,' Paxmore said.

They stayed in Berlin, trying to make contact with the few Quakers who lived in that city, but the German Friends were not eager to expose themselves as associates of the three strange men from America. One family, however, had English roots—a daughter had married a Quaker from London—and they discounted possible danger. They came to the hotel where the Americans were staying and met openly with them.

'We are the Klippsteins,' the father said stiffly.

'The name sounds Jewish,' Paxmore said.

'Way back.'

'Are you at a disadvantage?'

Herr Klippstein considered this question a moment, then relaxed his stiffness and broke into a smile. 'We are condemned three ways,' he said, indicating to his family that they should sit. 'We were Jewish. We are Quaker. And we have always been liberals.'

'Condemned is a harsh word,' Paxmore objected.

Now Klippstein's levity vanished. 'Within two years we will all be dead . . . if you do not help us.'

'Dead! That's impossible. We're dealing with human beings.'

'You mean *they're* human beings? Or *we're* human beings?'

'Herr Paxmore,' Frau Klippstein interrupted. 'This is no ordinary problem.' She spoke English haltingly; her sentence came out, 'Ziss iss not ord-i-nar-y prrroblim.' She said that each day the restrictions grew harsher.

'That's what we've come to talk with Herr Hitler about,' Paxmore explained. 'To convince him that he must release the Jews . . .'

Herr Klippstein laughed. 'No possibility,' he said.

'But the foreign ambassadors? Don't they take action?'

'Most of them approve of Hitler. They believe he is good for Germany. Because most of them despise Jews . . . and Quakers . . . and liberals of any sort.'

'Certainly not the American ambassador.'

'I don't know him. I do know some of his staff. They would help no one who was not rich and well educated and socially important. They're as bad as the English.'

'The English embassy won't help?'

'Herr Paxmore!' Klippstein went on to advise the Americans to go back home. No one in authority would see them, of that he was convinced.

But in the middle of the fourth week a uniformed messenger appeared at the hotel to inform them that at two o'clock that afternoon Hermann Göring would see them. This news did not surprise Woolman Paxmore, who had always believed that he and his two associates would ultimately see Hitler and convince him that he must release the Jews. 'We'll see Göring today and he'll probably arrange for us to see Hitler tomorrow,' Paxmore told his companions.

A Rolls-Royce called for them at half past one, and they were driven through magnificent streets to a palace where hordes of uniformed personnel protected the dignity of the Third Reich. Paxmore was impressed. 'Aren't they handsome-looking young men?' he said to the schoolmaster from North Carolina.

The three Quakers were ushered into an enormous room decorated with colorful maps that were works of art rather than accurate depictions. They showed the consolidation of the German empire, with heavy Gothic lettering that made them doubly impressive. At the far end of the room—twice the length of the biggest room any of them had ever seen before—stood a white desk covered with small golden ornaments. The schoolteacher whispered, as they approached it, 'Looks very unfunctional.'

The three were brought to a position some ten feet short of the desk and told to wait. Paxmore noticed that they were standing on a white carpet, and reflected on how difficult it must be to keep such a thing clean.

After a fifteen-minute wait, during which the three tall men talked quietly among themselves, while six uniformed guards looked at the ceiling, a door opened and an enormous man dressed in white and gold strode into the room, followed by a most beautiful blond woman in a riding habit.

An interpreter leaped to position between the two and said, 'This is General Göring and Madame Göring.' Then the general began to speak, in deep, reassuring syllables. 'The general says that he has always known of the Quakers. They have in Germany a splendid reputation for fairness and honesty. He knows of the good work your people have done throughout the world, without ever taking sides or embarrassing local governments. He welcomes you with open arms to Germany.'

Woolman Paxmore thought it obligatory to acknowledge these generous words, but Göring stormed ahead. 'General Göring says that he brought his wife along because as a Swedish lady, which she is, she, too, has heard of the Quakers and wanted to see some.'

'You have Quakers in Germany,' Paxmore said. The interpreter thought it wisest not to repeat this, and Göring continued, 'So because of your fine reputation, the Third Reich will always be most eager to cooperate with you in any practical way.'

'We have several suggestions—' Paxmore began.

'Gentlemen,' Göring interrupted in English, 'let's be seated.' He led them to a corner of the great room to a table where tea had been arranged. The interpreter said, 'The general knows you are not English, but perhaps . . . some tea . . .'

'Please do!' Frau Göring said in English.

'I doubt if there are many Quakers in Sweden,' Paxmore said.

'I've not met them, if they're there,' Frau Göring said in perfect English. She was a charming woman and offered each of the Quakers tea and small sandwiches.

'We don't come as Quakers,' Paxmore said.

'But that's what you are?' The interpreter's voice rose. 'That's why the general consented to see you.'

'Of course we're Quakers,' Paxmore conceded, indicating the other two men. 'But we come as Christians, General Göring, to beg you to allow the Jews to leave Germany.'

The huge man chortled, then spoke rapidly in German, which the interpreter summarized sporadically. The upshot was the Jews of Germany were completely free to depart at any time, to take with them all their possessions, to settle in any nation that would accept them. 'But no nation wants them,' Göring concluded.

Woolman Paxmore coughed. Taking a sip of tea, he controlled himself, then said quietly, 'Our evidence is that almost no Jews are allowed to leave Germany, and only then if they pay considerable amounts of money to do so.'

Göring did not flinch. He said, 'Of course we expect to be indemnified for the free education we've given them. Truly, Herr Paxmore, you wouldn't expect us to let these able and brilliant Jews depart without some kind of compensation? To take their skills, which we gave them in our free schools, to serve our enemies?'

'You have no enemies,' Paxmore said.

At this, Göring exploded. Reaching out, he slapped Paxmore resoundingly on the knee and said, 'You peace-loving Quakers! You see nothing. We're surrounded by enemies, ravenous enemies . . .'

The interpreter could not handle the word *ravenous* and fumbled with it until Frau Göring interrupted. 'Ravenous enemies, Herr Paxmore. And they are ravenous.'

'They could be converted into friends,' Paxmore said quietly. 'And the way to achieve this is to make a gesture toward the Jews.'

'We intend to make gestures toward the Jews,' Göring said, laughing at his joke.

'And if it is reasonable for your government to demand . . .' He stopped. The only word he could think of was *ransom,* ransom money for the Jews, but he knew he ought not to use that word.

'Ransom money,' the North Carolina schoolmaster blurted out.

The interpreter fumbled with the word, trying to soften it, but Frau Göring broke in again. 'It's not a ransom, Herr Paxmore. It's rather a repayment for the free education they've received.'

'That was the expression I was searching for,' Paxmore said honestly. 'And if it is such payment that is preventing the emigration of your Jews, I can promise you that the required funds will be forthcoming.'

General Göring asked that this information be interpreted again, and after he had satisfied himself that he understood what the Quakers were proposing, he asked Paxmore bluntly, 'You are prepared to put up the money?'

'Yes.'

'How much?'

This stumped Paxmore, who had never discussed such matters seriously with anyone. 'A million dollars,' he said, amazed at himself for having mouthed such a figure.

'A million!' Göring repeated. 'A million . . . hummmmm.'

The meeting broke up. 'You are to stay close to your hotel,' the interpreter said. The man was a Prussian, educated in military schools, and everything he said carried an ominous reverberation.

Two days later a pair of black military cars drove to a rear entrance to the hotel and the three visitors were told to pack small overnight bags. 'I will inspect them,' the same interpreter said, and he went to their room as they packed, watching carefully as each item was placed in its bag. He then led them quickly down a back stairs and into the cars. They were driven to an airfield where a small plane with only four passenger seats waited. The interpreter came along, saying nothing until they were well airborne; then he said crisply, 'You are going to meet der Führer . . . at Berchtesgaden . . . and when you are brought into his presence you are to stand at attention, your hands at your sides, and say nothing. Do you understand, nothing.'

Woolman Paxmore wanted to respond to such a ridiculous instruction, but the merchant from Pittsburgh nudged him, so he said nothing. But when the interpreter wasn't looking, he shrugged his shoulders so that the schoolmaster could see. That man raised his eyebrows and smiled.

They landed at an airfield near a lake and were ushered immediately into a Rolls-Royce, which started a steep climb up a road of exquisite beauty. 'We are going to the Eagle's Aerie,' the interpreter said with the proper amount of awe, and after a long ascent through forested trails the car broke through to a view of staggering grandeur.

'My goodness!' Paxmore said. 'Anyone would like to live up here.' The mountains, the vast expanse of forest, the limitless plains of Germany below, how different they were from the small, flat fields of the Eastern Shore! 'This doesn't look much like the Choptank,' he said to no one.

'This way,' the interpreter said, leading them into a salon even bigger than Göring's. They had not yet adjusted to it when they were surprised by General Göring himself, who entered from a far door wearing a Bavarian knee-length hunting costume and heavily ribbed lederhosen.

Taking huge strides, he came to greet the three Quakers, saying in English, 'Gentlemen! So soon we meet again!' He actually embraced Paxmore, slapping him vigorously on the back. In German he said, 'Der Führer was captivated by your idea, gentlemen. He wants your specific comments.'

And before the Quakers could respond to this, Herr Hitler appeared, a smallish man with very black hair, wearing a simple brown uniform lacking in either medals or pretension. When the two German leaders stood side by side, they seemed like typical huntsmen, their intelligent faces beaming with excitement.

And now Hitler spoke, in a rather high, thin voice, and the interpreter took over. 'Is what General Göring tells me still true? You can collect one million dollars to pay for the Jews' education?'

'Yes,' Paxmore said firmly. At that moment he had not the slightest idea as to where he could collect a million dollars, but his life had been spent in making commitments which were to be discharged later, and in doing so, had found that for a worthy cause God somehow found ways to fulfill the most demanding pledge. 'We will get the money.'

'Then I think we can let you have your Jews,' Hitler said. 'We've calculated the cost of their education. In your dollars . . . What was it, Hermann?'

'Five thousand dollars a Jew,' Göring said.

Paxmore was not good at arithmetic and he stumbled for an answer as to how many Jews one million dollars would rescue. 'Two hundred,' said the schoolmaster.

'Outrageous!' Paxmore protested. 'Herr Hitler—'

'Silence!' the interpreter shouted.

Paxmore ignored him and moved close to the dictator. 'It ought to be fifty thousand, at least. Compassion would dictate at least that many.'

The interpreter refused to translate this audacious demand, but Hitler saw the effect his proposal had made on the Quakers; indeed, in naming it he had suspected that it would be unacceptable. Now he calmed the interpreter and instructed him to ask, 'What number did you have in mind?'

'Fifty thousand,' Paxmore said firmly.

'I doubt if we have that many who would want to leave,' Hitler said.

'Thee would gain great credit, Herr Hitler,' Paxmore said in his voice of quiet reasoning, 'if thee made a gesture of such dimension.'

And the fact that this unkempt, gangling man would use persuasion and an appeal to self-esteem impressed the dictator. On the spur of the moment he snapped, 'Forty thousand,' and with that, he marched from the room.

'You've struck a great bargain.' Göring beamed. 'As you have seen for yourself, Der Führer is a man of deep compassion. Tell the world this.

Report it to the world.' With a salute, which seemed totally out of place, he waddled off after his leader.

In this way Woolman Paxmore and his two tall friends bought the lives of forty thousand Jews. They gathered the million dollars from diverse sources, solely on the strength of their reputations and the assurance that they would do what they said they would do.

And for the rest of his life Paxmore would meet men and women with heavy accents who would seek him out to tell him, 'You saved my life. My group was the last to escape from Germany. The rest are all dead, in the ovens.' And they would try to kiss his hands, but he would pull away.

The affair of the German Jews gave Woolman Paxmore no sense whatever of accomplishment, and he better than anyone else knew that in this affair his hands were not for kissing, for when he and his two friends had collected the money and arranged for the rescue of the forty thousand, he could find no country that would admit them, and he spent nearly half a year traveling from capital to capital begging the various governments to accept these people saved from extinction. In the end he failed, both with his own government and all others, so that of the forty thousand who were entitled to escape, having been paid for, only twenty-five thousand did reach safety, because the others were acceptable nowhere.

Ordeal by Fire

IN 1938 A STRIKING BOOK WAS PUBLISHED IN PATAmoke. Its merit did not lie in its literary style, which stressed cuteness and a blizzard of exclamation points. Nor was it memorable for any philosophical revelations, because it consisted of unrelated little episodes chosen at random and arranged without regard to chronology.

It was called *A True History of Patamoke* and had been composed, or perhaps assembled, by Judge Hathaway Steed's older son Lawton. Since the development of the town was seen through the romantic experiences of the tobacco-raising families, there was much material on haunted rooms, beautiful young wives and Cavaliers. To read the book gave the impression that one could understand the history of the Choptank only if one visited seventeenth-century plantations.

What made the book outstanding was an amazing accomplishment: it recorded three hundred years of history without once mentioning the blacks who had shared that history and played a major role in it. There were whole chapters about pretty Steed women, and the reforms essayed by dissident Paxmores; there were even condescending paragraphs about the Turlocks, especially those of a piratical turn, but about the slaves who enabled the system to function, there was absolutely nothing.

To take only one example. The Caters had made themselves a powerful force in Patamoke history: Cudjo's rise exemplified an era; Eden had led fourteen escape missions into Pennsylvania; Captain Jimbo sailed his skipjack through two generations of watermen, becoming known as the premier skipper in the fleet—but the family was not even mentioned. It would not be correct, however, to claim that the name Cater was ignored in the history; on page 118 appeared this paragraph:

In 1847 the postmaster Thomas Cater found himself in trouble with local fanatics who sought to import through federal mails copies of seditious literature, which he lawfully sequestered!! The agitators protested so vehemently and continuously that in 1849 this good man was forced out of his position, but Patamoke residents of a more sober mind were gratified to learn that he had received a much better position in South Carolina, where he joined the Confederate forces, rising to the rank of major!!!

Ignoring the Caters might have been justified on the ground that no one black family dominated, but Steed also ignored the black Methodist ministers who had served this community so constructively, often stabilizing it through turbulent decades when they were lucky to receive one hundred dollars a year in salary. He overlooked, too, the small businessmen, the workers who staffed the oyster canneries, the blacks who served as foremen in the tomato plants, and the men who loaned money, serving as crisis banks to keep the community functioning.

Of the black schools that tried to educate the children of former slaves, there was not a word, nor any record of the baseball teams that could usually defeat the white. There was no account of the late-summer rallies, when the nights were filled with music, nor of the powerful black evangelists who could make hellfire sizzle at the edge of the pine grove.

In obedience to the national custom, the black experience was erased, not because it was unimportant, but because in the mind of a man like Lawton Steed it had never existed, and visitors from other parts of the nation who read this book pleasantly after their crab-cake dinners at Patamoke House could be excused if they left with the impression that the Choptank had been explored, settled and developed by far-seeing white men who did all the work, after which a gang of blacks mysteriously appeared out of nowhere, with no history, no traditions, no significance and no rights. In 1938, when the *True History* was published, Patamoke contained 6,842 citizens, of whom 1,984 were black. Twenty-nine percent of the population, in the thinking of civic leaders, did not exist.

The *Patamoke Bugle* reflected this tradition; months would pass without a single mention of the black community, and if notice was taken, it was invariably an amusing account of some disaster at the African Methodist Episcopal Church or a hilarious report of a gambling riot. It was forbidden ever to use the honorifics Mr., Mrs. or Miss when referring to a black, and except for reporting court cases, their social life was ignored.

The blacks lived behind the boatyard east of town, severely restricted to that area in which occasional freed slaves had taken residence since 1700. In the intervening years Frog's Neck had altered little: houses were still small, often without windows; some were painted when employers gave leftover pails of paint to men and women who had served faithfully; and there was a truncated baseball diamond on which black players perfected their skills. But it was a world apart, with its own church, school and customs. It had no doctor, no dentist, but it did have a black policeman who exhibited incredible tact in maintaining a semblance of order.

If the *True History* contained nothing about blacks, its attitude toward them was intimated in two paragraphs, which gained favorable comment from the locals:

> So for several happy decades beginning around 1790 the Eastern Shore enjoyed a stable society marked by graciousness, stability, patriotism and order!! It was possible to maintain these noble traditions of England because everyone possessed honest and untainted English blood. Our great plantations set the style for the lesser orders to follow. Each man knew his proper place and the obligations that went with it.

> This lovely ideal was shattered by two disastrous events! The Emancipation Proclamation and the influx of peasants from Ireland and Jews from the less desirable countries of Europe!! Like locusts they destroyed a graciousness of life they could not comprehend, introducing abominations like labor agitation, income taxes, women's suffrage, Communism, Bolshevism and the New Deal!!!

In 1938 Patamoke was a closed little world, with its own customs, shibboleths and strengths, but in it blacks could achieve a life that was marginally satisfactory if they devised strategies of survival. To do so was difficult, for they were required to suppress ordinary human emotions in order to escape notice in a white environment. On no one did the problems of survival fall with heavier force than on Jeb Cater, a thin, medium-sized man of forty-two who occupied a two-room shack in the Neck.

This year Jeb had special problems. Not only was his employment more precarious than usual, but his wife was pregnant, so that the money she would normally have earned was missing. During the final months of the year Jeb worked fourteen and eighteen hours a day at any available jobs, and even then could scarcely keep his family of four alive—'What we gonna do, our son arrives, on'y God knows.'

He already had two daughters, Helen, aged nine and almost old enough to work steadily, and Luta Mae, aged seven, who was so troublesome that it seemed she might never hold a steady job, and it was his conceit, nurtured during the long hours of his toil, that his next child must be a son. His wife Julia chided him on this: 'You takes what you gets an' you likes it.'

Julia had grown up in Frog's Neck and had known Jeb all her life; they were the same age and had started courting at fifteen. She had been a large girl, with a strong mind, and once she settled on Jeb as her probable mate, she did everything to prevent his escape. He had wanted to try his luck at some job in Baltimore, but she had prevailed upon him to stay at home. During the last days of World War I he had talked of running away to the army, but she had stopped this abruptly by threatening to elope with his older brother.

She ran her only real risk when this brother left town, found a job somewhere and returned with good money, inviting Jeb to join him. 'Your brother ain't gonna amount to nothin', money or no money,' she had argued, trying to hold her man, and when Jeb reminded her that only a year ago she had threatened to marry the brother she was now condemning, she sniffed, 'Me marry that no-good. Jeb, you fool easy.'

This was a good description of her husband: he fooled easy. He believed that tomorrow would be better, that he would find a permanent job with a decent wage, that the girls would study in school, and that his next child would be a boy. He also believed in the ultimate goodness of the United States and had been ready to fight the Kaiser to defend it. He had inherited from his predecessor Cudjo Cater that solid will power that enables men and nations to survive, and from Eden Cater the personal courage to keep trying. He was, in many respects, the finest black man in Patamoke, but in spite of this, he could never find steady work.

In winter months he labored aboard a white man's skipjack dredging oysters. In the summer he ran a trotline, trying to catch crabs. He was a master of neither profession and earned little, but it was in the two in-between seasons that his family felt the pinch of real poverty. In spring he helped the skipjack captain haul timber to Baltimore, and in autumn he lugged his tools into the surrounding woods to split firewood. For a cord of pine he earned twenty-five cents, for a cord of oak, fifty.

Regardless of what he did, he came home exhausted, for he worked hours that no white man would have tolerated, and always at the most demanding tasks. If the skipjack loaded timber, it was Jeb who carried it aboard at the river ports and unloaded it in Baltimore. His hands were calloused, his back slightly bent, but on and on he worked, a machine that was employed at slight cost and would be discarded at the first sign of slowing down.

Despite his unstinting labor, he would still have been unable to support his family had not Julia worked as hard as he. She never complained, for she was gratified at having captured Jeb, and this was understandable, because not only did the black community respect him as a leader, but he was also the best husband in Frog's Neck. At home he had a placid disposition, and in public a willingness to share his meager funds with any family facing trouble, and Reverend Douglass said of him, 'I preach charity according to the Bible, but it's Jeb who demonstrates what the word means.' He was a good father, too, spending much time with his daughters, and if young Luta Mae was proving fractious, it was not because her parents ignored her; they loved her deeply and did their best to quieten her rages when she felt herself abused by white folks.

'Luta Mae,' her father told her repeatedly, 'you ain't got to fight the white folks. You got to side-step 'em.' It was Jeb's belief that if a black person minded his ways, he would run into very little trouble with whites.

'Turlocks hate us colored,' he warned his daughters, 'so the smart thing, stay shed of 'em. Cavenys too. Just you stay clear, like me, an' you find no trouble.'

Repeatedly he assured his family that the bad old days when Turlocks and Cavenys could rage through the countryside were gone: 'Ain't been a lynchin' along the Choptank in twenty years, and they ain't gonna be if'n you side-step 'em.' The Turlocks and Cavenys recognized Jeb's qualities by observing many times, 'He's a good nigger. Knows his place.'

Jeb realized that the heaviest burden in the family fell on Julia. She held three jobs. In winter she shucked oysters at the Steed sheds, working the midnight shift so that gallon cans of fresh seafood could be shipped out at dawn. In summer she was invaluable at the crab-picking company, and in autumn she worked double shifts at the Steed tomato cannery, peeling by hand the extra-fancy size for cold-packs.

In addition to this, she did sewing for several white families and stood as one of the great pillars of the African Methodist Episcopal Church. She was Reverend Douglass' principal support and also one of the lead sopranos in his choir. She was positively convinced that God took a personal interest in her church and her family, and although she was well aware from stories handed down from the time of Cudjo and Eden that Christianity had often been used as a prison for blacks, she also knew that God had not only arranged for Emancipation by sending Abraham Lincoln to earth, but had also given blacks their A.M.E. Church as proof of His concern.

From Monday morning at midnight till Saturday afternoon at six Julia Cater worked as few people in the world were required to work, but as Sunday approached, and the wooden church waited for her to decorate it with whatever flowers the season provided, she knew that God Himself waited to participate in her thanksgiving that another week had passed without major disasters.

Lesser disasters were with her constantly: 'Ain't no more crabs comin' in, Jeb. Nex' week the las'.'

'Maybe Mrs. Goldsborough, she want some sewin' done.'

'Tomato peelin' start late this year. Meanwhiles we got to eat.'

From anxiety to anxiety the Cater family moved from year to year, but in late 1938, with Julia unable to work at the cannery until her child was born, and with Jeb earning almost nothing on the skipjack, a major crisis developed, and at last, desperate, the husband and wife decided to seek advice from Reverend Douglass.

'We ain't got a penny, and no food in the house,' Julia told the minister. Jeb sat, silent, looking down at his work-worn hands.

Reverend Douglass leaned back in his chair, saddened as always by the story heard so often in Frog's Neck. But this time he felt overcome by it, for these were the Caters, who had labored so faithfully to keep their family together, who despite their pitiful, hard-earned income had always contributed to his salary, had even whitewashed their shack to preserve an appearance of decency and dignity.

He could see them now, entering his church, Jeb a few steps in front in a clean suit, then Julia, prepared to sing her praises to God, and the two girls, pretty and spruced up for the Sabbath. They were the backbone of his congregation—and now they were starving.

Reverend Douglass mulled over the possible ways he could help the Caters. He knew that in the Steed stores or at the Paxmore Boatyard there were no jobs for additional blacks; each establishment had its quota who swept and lugged and cleaned and muscled things about, but those jobs were treasured from one generation to the next, even though the pay was minimal. Sometimes in cases of extreme indigence the black community coalesced like corpuscles about the wound and somehow the patient was saved. But in these harsh days the families had scarcely enough for their own, and the reverend knew it would be useless to ask for help from them. The only thing left was the traditional Patamoke recourse: the Caters could go to either the Steeds or the Paxmores and plead for help.

But when he suggested it to the Caters, Julia said, 'We's proud,' and then, unable to bear the thought of begging, she went on, 'Maybe they get me some sewing, and Jeb could fix barns. Or the girls could help at the cannery.' And still Jeb said nothing.

Finally Reverend Douglass said, 'I'll go to the Steeds and ask for help.'

'Better the Paxmores,' Julia said, and it required rigid self-discipline to prevent tears.

Reverend Douglass left the Neck and drove out to Peace Cliff to talk with Woolman Paxmore, just home from Berlin, where he had helped save twenty-five thousand Jews, and the kindly Quaker said, 'John, I simply have no money left.'

'Mr. Paxmore, this worthy family is in deep trouble.'

'John, I'm powerless.'

'But the woman's about to have another baby. We can't let her go hungry.' Reverend Douglass, realizing that no white family could comprehend the perpetual crisis in which blacks lived, cried with heartbreaking force, 'These good people are starving!'

Woolman Paxmore pressed his hands against his eyes, and because he was a minister, snatches of biblical phrases tumbled through his head. He thought of Jesus aiding the poor and admonishing his followers to care for the downtrodden, and it grieved him that whereas he had been able to help the Jews in Berlin, he could not do the same for the blacks here in Patamoke. Painfully he dropped his hands and looked at Reverend Douglass, whom he accepted as a messenger from God. 'Obviously, we must do something,' he said quietly. 'But what?'

And then he remembered a canning jar in which his wife stored small coins against some day of great need, and he left the room to find that jar, but as he rummaged about, his wife heard him and asked, 'What is it, Woolman?' and he said, 'The Caters. Those good, dear people.' And she said nothing as he took her coins.

The meeting at which the two ministers rescued the Caters occurred on Friday. Next day the *Patamoke Bugle* carried the latest in its series of hilarious make-believe anecdotes from the black community:

> Reverend Rastus Smiley of the Riptank A.M.E. Church appeared in the law offices of Judge Buford seeking aid. 'Jedge, I'se got to have yore help. I'se been accused unjustly, and if'n you doan' pertecks me, I'se gine ter jail.'
>
> 'What are you accused of, Rastus?'
>
> 'White folks claims I done stole two hogs, three turkeys, and four chickens.'
>
> 'And you're willing to swear you're innocent?'
>
> 'On de Bible, Jedge Buford.'
>
> 'I always feel obliged to defend a gentleman of the cloth, but Rastus, you never have any money. What are you prepared to give me for my services?'
>
> 'One hog, one turkey and two chickens.'

Amos Turlock was in a bitter mood. Rocking back and forth in his shack north of the marsh, he brooded upon the sad condition into which his life had fallen. He was only twenty-nine, a tall, lanky waterman who shaved only on Sundays; one of his incisors had recently broken and other front teeth threatened to follow. Sucking on the empty space, he gazed dispassionately at his weatherbeaten wife as she plodded about the kitchen, preparing his greasy breakfast. 'I jes' cain't believe it,' he said more to himself than to her. 'Goddamnit, he's my own brother-in-law and he hadn't oughta behave thisaway.'

'Ain't he more your cousin?' his wife snarled. 'Din' his pappy marry your aunt?'

'Point I'm tryin' to make, if a body would listen, Hugo Pflaum ain't got no right atall.'

He rocked on, contemplating the inequities of life, and he had many to protest. For one brief spell at the turn of the century his branch of the Turlocks had been smiled upon—'We had the brick house in town. Gran'daddy Jake had his own skipjack.'

'Yesterday you claimed Sam Turlock was your gran'daddy.'

'He was, goddamnit, on my mother's side . . .' He stopped in disgust. It was impossible to conduct a serious conversation with this woman, one of the Turlocks from upriver, but after a dull silence he resumed his litany. 'Yep, we had our own skipjack, and you know what, Cass, I think that son-of-a-bitch Caveny stoled it from us. Yes, sir, you ask me, he flashed some papers in court, but I think he forged 'em, and the judge let it slip by.'

He rocked in silence, shaking his head over paradises lost: the brick house had been sheriffed out at a forced sale; the skipjack was now operated by Cavenys alone; his children could barely read; and were it not for the marsh and the game it provided, the family would barely be able to exist, even with public charity. And now the final indignity! His own cousin, Hugo Pflaum, had announced in the *Patamoke Bugle* that he intended to confiscate every long gun on the Choptank, and at the store had specifically boasted, 'If I don't do nothin' else, I'm gonna get my hands on The Twombly.'

'Goddamnit!' Amos cried, rising from his chair. 'We been warned. Cass, get the children in here. I want to talk with ever'body, serious.'

Whenever he stood up and spoke in that tone, she knew he meant it, so she stopped frying the eggs and shouted from the door, 'Kipper, Betsy, Ben, fetch Nellie and come in here.' Four separate protests greeted this cry, and she yelled, 'I meant what I said. Your pop wants to talk to you.'

Four bedraggled children came in from the muddy yard, and if old Captain Jake could have seen them—he the master of his own skipjack and dominant waterman of the Choptank—he would have been appalled at how swiftly his family had descended, and he would have been perplexed as to the reasons. For one thing, he had married his full cousin, so that each inherent weakness in the Turlock strain had been magnified. And he had scoffed when Miss Paxmore warned him that his children were not learning to read. Furthermore, while Tim Caveny had hoarded every penny, like the penurious Papist he was, Jake had squandered his on family ventures of no merit. He had not lived to watch the sad transfer of the skipjack to sly Timothy, but in his last days he had often suspected that this might happen.

Why did a family rise and fall and sometimes rise again? Luck played an enormous part. For example, if Jake Turlock had lived as long as Tim

Caveny, he might have held his sprawling family together, and saved both the brick house and the boat, but he had drowned one bitter night when a super blast from the long gun caused him to lose his balance and capsize his skiff.

But a family rises or falls primarily because of the way it marshals its genetic inheritance and puts it to constructive use. No family along the Choptank had a more vigorous life force than the Turlocks; they were not handsome like the Steeds, nor clever like the Cavenys, nor powerfully built like the two generations of Pflaums, nor intellectually solid like the Paxmores, but they possessed a wonderful capacity for survival. They were lean, spare, simple and clean of mind, with strong eyes and teeth, had they cared for them. And all members of the family possessed an animal cunning that protected them. With their genetic gifts they should have owned the river, and Turlocks like Captain Matt of the slave trade and Captain Jake of the oyster dredging had done so.

Amos could have owned it, too, for he had inherited every innate capacity his forebears had possessed, but fatal inbreeding had encouraged family weaknesses to multiply, while its virtues receded. He had wanted to repurchase the house in town when the price was reasonable, but he never got around to it, and now they wanted eleven hundred dollars. He had intended to buy back his family's share in the skipjack, and he could have done so, for Caveny offered it, but now a skipjack was selling for six thousand and there was no possibility of repurchase. He had also talked of sending his children seriously to school, but at their first protests had allowed them to swarm in the marsh.

Now they stood before him, four marsh rats as disorganized and hopeless as he. 'Serious business, and I want you to listen. None of you, and this includes you too, Cass, is ever to mention The Twombly. You don't know nothin' about it. You don't know where I keep it. You don't even know whether I still have it or not. And goddamnit, you are never to let anyone know that I use it.' He stared balefully at each of his children, then at his wife. 'Because if you blab, even once, Hugo Pflaum is gonna come here and take The Twombly away, and that means you and me ain't gonna eat no more duck.'

In 1918 the government of Maryland had outlawed possession of long guns, for it could be proved that these lethal weapons were slaughtering ducks at a rate which prevented replacement. A census had been conducted, and the location of every gun specified; they were known by name—Cheseldine, Reverdy, Old Blaster, Morgan—usually referring to the family which first owned them, for no matter how many hands a gun passed through, it was always referred respectfully back to its original owner.

The 1918 census had shown seventeen long guns on the Choptank, and diligent pressures from Maryland's game wardens, primarily Hugo

Pflaum, had reduced the number to four. The Herman Cline, once owned by the slave-breaker on the Little Choptank, had been confiscated, and the Bell, a beauty from Denton. The Cripton family had gone to great lengths to protect their monstrous gun, Cripton, even threatening to murder Pflaum if he persisted in his attempts to impound it, but in the end he had tracked it down to a corncrib.

Amos Turlock ominously remembered the photograph which the *Bugle* had displayed of the capture. There was Hugo Pflaum, a stubby man with broad shoulders and no neck, holding in his right hand Cripton, twelve feet tall, with its barrel reflecting sunlight. His left hand grasped Abel Cripton, hat pulled down over his face to avoid the shame of having lost a gun which had been in his family for over a hundred years.

Turlock had cut the picture from the paper and tacked it to the kitchen wall, where it still hung in tatters; when he was drunk he liked to spit at it, for Hugo Pflaum, with his bull neck, was his enemy, and The Twombly was in peril so long as he operated.

The Twombly, oldest and best of the Choptank arsenal, had taken its name, of course, from old Greef Twombly upriver, whose ancestors had imported it from England in 1827. Its barrel was still as clean as when it left its London foundry; its oak stock had been replaced four times but was still as thick as a man's thigh. Hugo Pflaum, studying his census of the guns he was supposed to capture, said of The Twombly, 'It's been used on this river for a hundred and eleven years. I figure it's been fired on an average of three times a week, twenty-five weeks a year. That's over eight thousand shots. Now, if they kill even fifty ducks with each shot, and that's low, why, it means that this gun has removed about four hundred thousand ducks from circulation, and it's got to stop.'

Hugo's estimates were conservative; when a voracious old man like Greef Twombly owned a gun as good as this one, he didn't restrict its use to three nights a week, and when it passed into the hands of a confirmed waterman like Jake Turlock, he didn't average a mere fifty birds a shot. A more accurate count would be that this famous old gun had slaughtered nearly two million ducks and geese, and this helped explain why the bird population had declined so severely in recent decades.

'Hell,' Amos complained at the store, 'last year me and Abel Cripton, we sat in our goose blind at the marsh for two straight weeks—and how many geese you suppose flew over? Not twenty.'

He was right. Where the Choptank region had once entertained more than a million geese each year, now fewer than twenty thousand appeared, and these kept to the marshes south of the river. The depopulation was incredible, and many gentlemen who had paid substantial sums for their English and Austrian shotguns rarely found an excuse to use them for anything but doves. The geese were gone; the ducks were going, and it was Hugo Pflaum's job to see that reasonable hunting procedures encouraged their return.

This was the meaning of Amos Turlock's lecture to his family: 'I don't give a damn for them fancy foreigners who come in here to steal our ducks with their expensive guns. They miss, they ain't gonna starve. But if we don't get our ducks regular, you and me, we ain't gonna eat.'

The oldest boy, Ben, knew where the gun was hidden, but even before Warden Pflaum began to apply pressure, he had deduced, with shrewd Turlock wisdom, that the day must come when someone would try to take The Twombly away, and he had never spoken of it to anyone. What was more remarkable, he had begun marking Pflaum's movements. He and the other children knew the warden as Uncle Hugo and often stopped by his farm, where Mrs. Pflaum, their Aunt Becky, could be counted upon to provide them with German cookies. They enjoyed listening to Hugo tell tales of Germany, where his father had lived in the country before running away to sea.

'In Germany,' Uncle Hugo explained, 'they keep the forests as clean as the park before the courthouse. My father said a custodian would be shot if his woods looked like the ones around here. A park, that's what a German woods is. And when you grow up you should make the woods in back of your place a park.'

Ben said, 'We like it the way it is. So do the deer.'

'You must tell your father he can't shoot those deer any more.'

Ben said nothing, but intuitively he knew that this husky, amiable man with no neck was his family's enemy, and he watched how and where he went.

One night in October 1938 Ben whispered to his father, 'Hugo's up to Denton, lookin' for the gun that's supposed to be there.'

'Good,' Amos said, and when night fell he and Ben hurried along a footpath that led into the heart of the marsh, then ducked off to one side, doubled back, moved along a path that was barely discernible and came finally upon a wooden structure not two feet high and absolutely invisible from any distance. It rested on poles, to keep salt water away, and had a lid, which Amos lifted quietly. Inside, in a nest of greased burlap, lay The Twombly, its barrel wiped clean, its heavy stock solid and new. Almost reverently Amos hefted it, carried it in his arms and headed for the waiting skiffs, but as he climbed easily into his, placing the gun in position, he heard a noise, grew tense, then laughed.

'Come on, Rusty,' he said, and his red Chesapeake leaped into the boy's skiff and they were off.

On January 1, 1939, Julia Cater gave birth to a boy, who was taken to the A.M.E. Church in Frog's Neck and christened Hiram, a biblical name meaning 'most noble,' and on the way home from church Jeb Cater was stopped by the captain of a successful skipjack. 'Jeb, we goin' out and we stayin' out. You want to cook?'

It had happened just as he predicted: 'Things is gonna be tough for the rest of this year, Julia, but come 1939 they gonna fall in place.'

He was not happy about leaving home for a protracted absence right after the birth of his son, and his apprehensions were doubled when Julia took a job shucking oysters—'Don't you think you oughta stay with the boy?' His wife ridiculed this—'We got a chance to earn some money, we takin' it.' She would work the midnight shift, hurry home and supervise the girls as they dressed for school, then tend the baby and have him ready for Helen to watch over while she slept.

The girls, of course, attended the black school held in a crumbling building at the far end of the Neck. It contained twenty-two desks for forty-seven students, so the teacher had to exercise some ingenuity in keeping her pupils juggled between sitting and standing classroom periods. She taught seven grades, and when a black child left her care that child usually had all the education it would get. There was one broken blackboard, but months would pass with no chalk. There was no ink, but ingenious boys collected berries from which a pale stain was extracted. Pencils were precious and some students would spend whole weeks without one, but what most irritated little Luta Mae was the fact that she was now in Grade Three without ever having had a book. The school had books, outmoded editions handed down from white schools in the neighborhood, but they were so few that only certain students could obtain one, and so far the luck of the draw had worked against her.

'Harry he gets one and Norma Ellen she gets one,' she complained to her mother, 'but I never gets one.'

'Maybe next year, in Grade Four, you'll be lucky,' Julia said. She refused to believe that the teacher was discriminating against her daughter, and when Luta Mae said harsh things, Julia reprimanded her, 'You wait till your daddy gets home in March . . .'

At the end of the oyster season Jeb Cater came home, tired from his hard work but well nourished because he had been the cook. His broad face beamed with pleasure as he gave Julia his wages, but any thought of disciplining Luta Mae vanished when he saw his son. 'That boy growin' like a weed! He gonna be the best.'

For hours at a time he played with Hiram, not throwing him in the air as some fathers did, for the boy was too precious for such rough treatment, but talking to him as if he understood. 'Hiram, you gonna go to school. You gonna learn to go out into the world. Come time you gonna enlist in the army. Who knows, you might be a general in France.'

There were no aspirations too lofty for this child, and Jeb's heart expanded with hope when he saw how well formed the child's body was, how bright his eyes, but after his exultation he found that a son altered his life in disturbing ways.

During the years when he had only daughters he could ignore the handicaps under which all blacks existed, but with a son he was constantly reminded of the discriminations, for whereas he had been required from birth to adjust to them and had grown inured to injustice, it galled him to realize that his son was doomed to an endless repetition of such unfairness. These were the specifics he began to list, not commenting upon them even to his wife, but marking them in his mind:

. . . It was customary, in Patamoke, for a black to step aside on the town pavements when a superior white person passed, even going into the gutter if necessary.

. . . It was traditional for a workman like Jeb to touch his cap when a white man approached and to lift it completely off the head for a white woman. The white thus deferred to could pass on without acknowledging in any way the black man's courtesy.

. . . There were no black doctors in the region, no dentists. A black could get minimum medical care from white doctors, especially in the case of communicable diseases which might spread to the white community, but the system was a bad one, lacking confidence on both sides.

. . . Few blacks ever assembled in a building that was painted. The church, the school, the corner store, the homes were gray and rotting.

. . . Streets on which whites lived were paved; those for blacks were dusty and rutted.

. . . All things pertaining to blacks were diminished. The school had only seven grades instead of twelve. The school year consisted of only one hundred and ten days instead of one hundred and sixty-six. Five blocks of black homes had one streetlight instead of ten. And the playground for children in the Neck was a small back lot instead of a ten-acre field with a full-scale baseball diamond.

. . . Almost every really desirable aspect of Patamoke life was proscribed to blacks. They were not welcomed in the library, nor in the big stone churches, nor in the motion-picture theater (except in a high and dirty balcony), nor in the courthouse, nor in the new school, nor in the recreation areas, nor in the public meetings, nor in the better law offices. If they were seen at night walking along the better streets, they were questioned, and at the ball park they had to sit in the unshaded bleachers, in a section severely roped off.

. . . What infuriated the two Cater girls was that when they had saved their pennies and marched proudly to the Gold and Blue Ice Cream Parlor, the man behind the counter took their money, treated them courteously and gave them at least as generous a scoop as he gave white children. But once the cone was in their hands, they had to leave the parlor, walking past the lovely iron tables where white children sat, and if they so much as nibbled at the dripping ice cream while they were inside the store, the owner would chide them gently, 'No, no. You mustn't eat the cone in here. Only outside.' So the girls would carry their cones grimly to the door, quit the premises and eat on the street. Luta Mae, eight years old, resented this expulsion. It wasn't the fact that she had to eat outside that embittered her—'It's them tables, Mom. All white and lacy-like with the clean glass tops and the kids sittin' there.' For some years her dream of paradise was a cloudy space filled with endless iron tables, all painted white, at which angels sat in easy relaxation, not eating ice cream necessarily, 'Just sittin' there at the clean tables.'

. . . Jeb's major irritation was one he could explain to no one, but it was so real it gnawed at him when other far more important deprivations went unchallenged. Each summer a crescendo of excitement was orchestrated by a smallish white man who arrived in town from Baltimore, Mr. Evans. He went first to the *Bugle,* whereupon florid stories began to appear on the front page: 'Show Boat to Offer Six Sure Hits.' Then he employed two black boys to help him poster the town: 'Show Boat. Two Weeks. Solid Hits.' Finally he made a deal with Steed's whereby he could plaster one side of their store with really large full-color announcements of the stars and the plays they would be presenting: *Stella Dallas, Romeo and Juliet, Up in Mabel's Room, Red Stockings* and *Uncle Tom's Cabin.* Seats were scaled from a dollar down to fifteen cents for children at matinées.

Excitement rose in the week prior to the arrival of the boat, for then the *Bugle* told of the fabulous successes the various actors had enjoyed in Europe and New York, and at Steed's a desk was set up inside the door where seats for specific performances could be reserved. It was then that the blacks in Frog's Neck began to lay their plans; they could not reserve seats, of course, for they were restricted to a hot and narrow balcony, but they could express their preferences: 'Gentlemen from Baltimore say us colored gonna like this here *Skidding.* Very funny little boy, make you laugh.'

The two favorites among the residents of the Neck were *Stella Dallas* and *Old Time Minstrels,* and each year Jeb Cater bought tickets for the latter. 'I likes that there play about the girl, she break a man's heart, but I prefers the minstrels.' He did not try to explain why he liked the night of minstrelsy, but it had nothing to do with the fact that blacks were portrayed, nor that the humor was broad and easily understood. What pleased him was that the white manager, realizing that his all-white cast lacked certain proficiencies, always hired Will Nesbitt, a local black, to play the bones and do the shuffle.

The bones were four time-hardened cow-ribs, about seven inches long, one pair for the right hand, another for the left. When properly wedged between the thumb and fingers they could be rattled like castanets, and a good performer could beat out amazing rhythms with this musical instrument. Will Nesbitt could beat a real tattoo, and it was this bold and basic rhythm that established the quality of a good minstrel show.

So on two nights during the show-boat stay, the blacks of Patamoke could watch their own man perform. Nesbitt had no lines to speak, no role in the broad comedy, but he was part of the show, and when he was invited to step forward and do the coon shuffle, ridiculing the feckless behavior of black workmen, it was a moment of joy. Black athletes could not perform with whites, nor black singers in a white choir, nor black spellers against children their age from white schools, but on the show boat Will Nesbitt could do the shuffle, and that was something.

Why, then, was Jeb Cater infuriated by the show boat? Because it contained only a few seats for blacks, and those far from the stage and smelly. They could not be reserved; to be assured of one meant that some member of the family must stand in line for hours, and even then, white men from the big houses were free to barge in ahead to purchase seats for their black help.

If there was one function throughout the year to which the blacks of Patamoke should have been invited on equal terms, it was the show boat, especially to its nights of *Old Time Minstrels,* but it was precisely these that were handled most callously. Even so, in the summer of 1939, Jeb Cater was prepared once again to go through the misery of trying to land two tickets for the minstrelsy.

Early Monday morning of the third week in July whistles started blowing on the Choptank, and a puffing little tug appeared in the channel, hauling behind it a monstrous old barge on which a theater had been erected. The whole appearance of the two boats evoked nostalgia and romance: the little tug straining against the cables; the captain tooting his whistle; the lovely dip of the line as it fell beneath the water; the blunt nose of the scow; the small, vigorous band on deck, hammering out strong tunes; the waving of the cast as they recognized old friends; and the bright colors of the theater itself, red and gold in the sunrise.

With what care the tug brought its heavy burden into the harbor, stopping its forward motion lest it crash into the wharf, then nudging it cautiously into position. Lines fore and aft! Lines binding it to the posts! Lines bringing it close so that gangways could be lowered! And then the gangplanks, one amidships for white patrons, another aft for blacks.

The management, on its nineteenth visit to Patamoke, was clever enough not to offer the minstrelsy during the first days. These were reserved for the new comedy *Skidding,* the old favorite *Stella Dallas* and the risqué farce *Up in Mabel's Room.*

On the first night of *Old Time Minstrels* Jeb got in line too late to find a seat, but on the second he sent Luta Mae to stand for him while he went crabbing, and it was his intention to hurry home, sell his catch, wait for Julia to finish work at the cannery and then take her to the show, but she surprised him by announcing firmly, 'Don't want to see no more pretendin'. You wants to go, you takes Helen.' To his surprise, she also refused—'Too many peoples.'

So at dusk he went to the wharf and found Luta Mae fairly close to the ticket window, not the big one where the real seats were being sold, but the little one in the rear for blacks. Standing beside her, he moved along with his black neighbors, put forty cents on the lip of the window and got his two tickets, twenty-five cents for himself, fifteen cents for Luta Mae. Gingerly they climbed the steep stairs, entered the little balcony, said hello to their friends, then awaited the lowering of the lights.

It was magical! Worth all the waiting and the conniving and the humiliation. 'Ain't this somethin', Luta Mae?'

'Look at them uniforms!'

The band consisted of four members who played a staggering variety of instruments and played them well. When they reached the finale to the *William Tell Overture* they were so versatile they sounded like a company of forty, and then the curtains parted, and there was the familiar half-moon of black-faced performers, with a most handsome white gentleman in the center asking his unctuous questions:

'Mr. Bones, do I understand that you took after your good friend, Rastus Johnson, with a razor?'

'Dat's a fact, Mr. Interlocutor.'

'And what, if I may be so bold as to ask, was the reason?'

'He done sneak into mah house and steal mah wife's nightgown.'

'Come now, Mr. Bones, you don't chase a man with a razor merely because he stole your wife's nightgown.'

'Yeah, but she was in it.'

A minstrel show consisted of two halves: the first featured the circle, with the interlocutor exchanging jokes with his two end men, Mr. Bones and Mr. Sambo. It was in this part that various actors did their specialties, and shortly before intermission the time came for Will Nesbitt to appear. 'Now you watch this, Luta Mae. This the good part.'

Nesbitt was a tall, thin black man with practically no hips, and when he came jigging on stage, rattling out a rhythm with his bones, the black gallery roared. Luta Mae was entranced by the clicking and the lovely intricacy of his steps as Nesbitt performed in near-darkness, with a beam of light chasing him about the stage. 'It's wonderful!' she cried, clasping her father's arm.

'He the real thing,' Jeb whispered.

But when the second half started—a playlet with the cast in white face —Luta Mae could not make the adjustment. 'Where all the colored, Daddy?'

'Them was the colored,' Jeb explained.

'Why they white?'

'They're actors,' Jeb whispered, but before he could give a better answer the highlight of the show approached. It consisted of a lone white dancer, very capable, who came on stage in white tails and top hat to sing *Me and My Shadow,* and as he danced, Will Nesbitt, all in black, appeared behind him, imitating every step like a real shadow, and for some minutes the two artists dueled in the shimmering light to the words and music of one of America's most effective songs, with the white dancer executing difficult steps and the black equaling them.

Now stagehands moved a short flight of stairs into position, and as he danced nimbly up them, the white man sang that effective passage about his loneliness as he climbed the stairs at midnight, to find only an empty room.

Up after him came his black shadow, and on the relatively small top stair the two men engaged in a competition, until at the end Will Nesbitt let go in a furious improvisation, which the white man watched in admiration, finally wiping his brow and asking the audience, 'Ain't he somethin'?' The balcony exploded with cheers, in which the white audience joined, for Will Nesbitt with his flying feet was something to see.

The concluding number was a resumption of the circle, with some of the actors in black face, some in white, and Will Nesbitt the only real black, off to one end rattling his bones and doing a reprise of his shuffle.

'Are the men in the circle real colored?' Luta Mae asked.

'No.'

'But the man who beat the other man in the dance, he is?'

'He sure is.'

The girl pondered this, then asked, 'If the real colored is the best, why they use make-believe for the others?'

Jeb had no explanation.

On the Eastern Shore, aviation played an emotional role, not an economic one. When Charles Lindbergh soloed across the Atlantic back in May 1927, the area had gone wild with enthusiasm, for it seemed as if the Chesapeake had leapfrogged from the age of the sailboat into the age of air, leaving the railroad and the automobile to other parts of the

United States. Roads were still bad, someone having invented a one-lane disaster paved with oyster shells that crumbled under the weight of a car. But the airplane!

Jefferson Steed revised his Great-Grandfather Paul's enthusiastic belief that the Eastern Shore would be saved by the railroad. 'I can foresee,' Jefferson sonorously proclaimed at the Fourth of July celebration, 'the day when our peninsula is united by swift-flying airplanes that link us to all parts of this great nation.' He lost a bundle sponsoring a commuter airline that failed five weeks after it started.

The air age would have its greatest impact on two persons: Isaac Paxmore, the boatbuilder, and John Turlock from the cabin in back of the marshes.

In 1938 Paxmore, watching a barnstorming plane fly up the bay, said to his sons and nephews, 'If we've built boats all these years, we can certainly build a flying boat.' He was sixty years old when he uttered these words, but the principle of flight so enchanted him that he began forthwith to draw the plans for an airplane made of highly finished light wood, powered by the best engine he could buy from experts in the field and pulled through the air by a laminated propeller which he would personally construct.

His cautious sons considered him irrational, but his nephew Pusey, son of the preacher Woolman Paxmore and a well-disciplined young man who had excelled at Harvard Law, saw possibilities in the flying boat and encouraged his uncle. 'I think we ought to try. There's bound to be a big market in the Navy for airplanes that can land on water, and I had a classmate at Harvard whose father makes airplane engines. Place called Scanderville.'

'Where's that?'

'Pennsylvania.'

'Is that where the prison is?'

'The same. His factory's a branch of Lycoming, and they build a good engine.'

So in 1939 young Pusey Paxmore donned his best blue suit and reported to the factory in Scanderville, where he purchased two Lycomings, which he brought home by truck. A handsome seaplane waited to receive them, its pontoons ruggedly attached, its surfaces sanded to a glossy finish by workmen long accustomed to building fine boats.

'This is the start of a whole new adventure,' Isaac said. 'This broad river was made for seaplanes.'

When the time came to test-fly the contraption, and the tanks had been filled with gasoline, an aviator from Washington crossed the bay in his own powerboat, studied the seaplane and pronounced it at least as good as any being made elsewhere. 'It seems to have the proper lines. Now we'll see.'

He asked if Isaac wanted to accompany him, but the old Quaker said, 'Pusey wishes to go. He supervised buying the engines.'

'He got good ones. Hop in.'

So Pusey Paxmore, a conservative Quaker dressed in a three-button suit, jumped into the second seat and held his breath as his uncle's invention gathered speed on the Choptank, threw a monstrous wake, then raised onto the step, rode on it for a few moments, finally breaking free of the water and sailing into the air.

The lasting impact of this flight did not, however, concern either Isaac Paxmore or his nephew Pusey. The trial run was without incident, the test pilot pronouncing the craft airworthy; he predicted great things for the Paxmore seaplane and expected to see it adopted by both the commercial and military fleet. Neither of these prognostications came to pass because the Paxmores lacked both the funds and the determination to proceed in aviation; their prototype remained a dazzling toy, much enjoyed along the river until its engines rusted away during World War II.

But on his third trial run, the pilot from Washington invited any local who might want to try aviation to accompany him, and to everyone's surprise Amos Turlock's younger brother, John, stepped forward. He was then an aimless young man of twenty-seven who had tried his hand at various employments and failed in all. He liked hunting and oystering and that was about it.

But he was adventurous and he wanted to see what flying was like, so when volunteers were called for he stepped vigorously forward and was selected. Fastening the belt so that he would not fall out, he grinned somewhat stupidly at the hangers-on who chided him, waved to a girl he had been courting, and kept his head cocked so as not to miss anything.

The next half-hour was a religious experience, so profound that it altered his life—'With me everythin' dates from 1939. Before, nothin' happened except the time I trapped a skunk. After, my eyes were opened.'

What happened was that he saw for the first time the Eastern Shore of Maryland; indeed, he may have been the first human being ever to have seen it properly. 'What I mean, I was up there in the sky, lookin' down on land I thought I knew, but it was all so different I couldn't believe my eyes. I just gawked and gawked, and then I had this clear vision, like I was in a dream, and I shouted out loud for all the heavens to hear, "Jesus Christ! We got a paradise and we don't know it." '

What he saw below him was that enchanting mixture of broad estuaries, nestling coves and long fingerlike peninsulas providing a shoreline hundreds of miles in length, a magical blend of land and water equaled nowhere else in the United States. 'Lissen, you know-it-alls,' he told the men at the store, 'you could drive these roads a lifetime and never know

what the real Eastern Shore is like. You could sail it till the canvas rots
without appreciatin' what you have. Only when you're up there in the
sky, like I was, can you see how the parts lock together.' Once when he
spoke thus, he leaped from his bench, threw his hat in the air and cried,
'Me and the wild geese! We're the only ones that know.'

But John Turlock had more than mere enthusiasm; he had seen not
only the beauty of the shore, but also its possibilities, and one evening
after he had extolled its splendor to the skeptics at the store, he sat in
the cabin with his brother Amos and began scribbling on a piece of paper.
After a while he shoved his work across the table. 'How you like that,
Amos?'

J. Ruthven Turlock
Your Real Estate Counselor
Patamoke, Maryland
Paradise for Sale

'Your name ain't Ruthven,' Amos growled.
'Sounds better. People will notice.'
'What people?'
'Rich people.'
'What'll you do with rich people, John?'
'Name's Ruthven. What I got in mind is those rivers I saw from the
air. Peachblossom, Tred Avon, Miles, Wye. Amos, there's enough empty
land borderin' those rivers to keep a real estate man with imagination
busy for the rest of his life.'
'It's there, but who's gonna buy it?'
'Millionaires. They're gonna grow tired of cities. They'll want places
like those for their kids and their yachts.'
'Insane,' Amos said.
'Tomorrow morning you and me are goin' in town, and I'm gonna rent
me an office. Stay with me and in ten years we'll both be millionaires.'
'You're crazy! Rich people with yachts buyin' this marshy land?'
Amos Turlock was too canny to be lured into a sure money-loser like
that.

The abortive adventure into aviation had produced a secondary impact
on another young man from the Choptank, for when the trial flights
ended, the pilot had told Isaac Paxmore, 'You got yourself a great plane.
Thing to do, sell it to the Navy.'
'How do we do that?' the cautious Quaker asked.
'Send one of your boys to the Navy Department in Washington. Lobby
the admirals.'
'I don't think my sons . . .'

'That kid in the blue suit. He was real smart about seaplanes.'

'My brother's son.' A happy idea broke. 'He's a lawyer. Solid young man. We could send him.'

It was in this way that Pusey Paxmore, Harvard Law 1938, reached Washington. His father's excellent reputation for work done in Germany, and his own wide acquaintance among the young lawyers then flooding the administrative agencies, assured his success, and very quickly he discovered that whereas he could not sell his uncle's seaplane, he could sell himself.

The first person to suspect that Hiram Cater was suffering from mastoiditis was the woman who served as midwife for Frog's Neck. Full-fledged doctors, of course, were not really available to the blacks, primarily because the doctors were white and did not relish having blacks traipsing into their offices where white patients might see them, but also because the fees charged were so high.

'This here boy got infection of the ear,' the midwife said during the second day of the child's howling.

'Cain't see no pus,' Julia said when she returned from her work bobbing crabs.

'It don't show like a ordinary boil. Down deep.'

'What do we do?' Julia asked, moving her big body wearily about the kitchen after the long day at the crab cannery.

"Mostly they uses hot oil,' the midwife said, and the two women prepared an unction, but they could not judge a proper temperature, and when they poured it into Hiram's ear, the baby screamed.

Jeb was attempting to sleep after his own long day at the crab lines, and the crying brought him angrily into the kitchen. 'What you doin' to that boy?'

'We fixin' his ear,' his wife explained.

'Sound like you're tearin' it off,' Jeb said, taking the boy into his arms.

Either the hot oil was working, bringing pain before relief, or it had missed the deep infection altogether, but whatever the situation, Hiram's screaming increased. Jeb, unable to bear it, and racked by his own pain at his son's suffering, carried the boy out into the yard and held him gently against him as he walked up and down, but when the howling went on, unabated, he shouted, 'I'm takin' this boy to the hospital.'

Through the dusty paths of the Neck he carried his crying baby, and onto the paved streets of the white section. Three times blacks stopped him to ask what he was doing, and to each he said, 'My boy's dyin' of pain. Goin' to the hospital.'

Patamoke Hospital was a rambling two-story red-brick affair which had grown by increments through the decades to serve a fairly large surrounding community. It was staffed by dedicated local doctors and nurses with a southern concern for the welfare of their neighbors, and although the medical system was not well prepared to care for blacks, when one was sick enough to require hospitalization, the system grudgingly moved into operation even if the patient was too poor to pay. The problem was: how did the black patient get into the hospital?

Jeb Cater, for example, carried his child through the imposing white columns of what was obviously the entrance, but there he was stopped by a nurse who said, 'In back. In back.'

She did not explain where in back the colored entrance was, and the building was composed of so many ells and alleys that Jeb could not easily find it. A black drayman hauling away soiled linen directed him, but when he reached the small door where the garbage was collected, he found it locked. The drayman left his truck to help Jeb attract attention, and after a while the door was opened. As soon as he gained entrance, good and reassuring things began to happen.

'This child has an ear infection,' a white nurse said, holding Hiram as carefully as if he were her own son. 'What treatment have you been giving?'

Jeb did not understand the question and hesitated; the nurse categorized him as another ignorant nigger and asked gently, 'Have you given him any medicine?'

'They puts in hot oil.'

She looked at the ear and said, 'Probably didn't do any damage. The doctor's got to look at this.'

'I wants the bes' doctor,' Jeb said, and a few questions satisfied the nurse that whereas this black father could pay something, he could certainly not pay a proper bill, so she made the necessary notes on the entrance card. Then she used the telephone to summon a young doctor, who used a tightly wrapped cotton swab to test the baby's ear.

'Mastoiditis,' he said.

'Is that bad?' Jeb asked.

'Could be. If we don't tend it.' And with care and understanding, the young doctor explained that Hiram was suffering from an inflammation and possibly an abscess of the inner ear. There were ways to reduce the infection short of surgery, provided it had not penetrated bone, but if it had, an operation might be necessary. His words were so simple and comforting that Jeb was filled with emotion and sought to thank him, but this the young man would not allow—'We're here to cure your boy. We'll do everything possible.' He said nothing about fees or modes of payment; he simply took the child in his arms and left the room.

It was what happened next that made this day inerasable. When the doctor left the reception room for blacks he did not, of course, walk up the stairs to the second floor, where the expensive rooms were, or even to the ground floor, where white charity cases were handled. Instead he walked down a flight of stairs to the boiler room, and beyond it to a small, cramped section whose ceiling was crisscrossed with pipes and whose illumination came from one unshielded light bulb dangling from a wire. The place had no windows.

It was here that Hiram was placed in a crib. When the doctor left, assuring Jeb that nurses would be there soon to care for the child, the father sat by the crib and looked at the accommodations, and as he did so he became aware that along the wall small cots held blacks requiring serious medical attention, and the meanness of the room, the confined anger it contained possessed him, and the longer he waited, the deeper his anger became.

It was forty minutes before the nurse appeared, and each of those minutes impressed on him anew the wrongness of this place. He did not want a sunny room high in a tower for his son; he knew he lacked the money to pay for such accommodation; but he did want decency: All my life I work for whatever wages white man give me. He decide my pay. If'n I ain't got money to pay for a good room, that his decision. This cellar ain't right.

The furnace providing hot water to the hospital came on and a low rumble filled the room, and then a flood of unnecessary heat, which clung to the cots, since no ventilation carried it away. After a while a black nurse appeared—she wasn't really a nurse, of course, because black girls were not allowed to enroll in local training courses—and she lifted Hiram gently, advising Jeb, 'You stay here, you likes. We be back with good news real soon.'

So he remained in the ward, talking with the bedridden, and each sick man or woman was so grateful at being in the hospital that none complained. And after a long time the nurse returned with Hiram, informing Jeb, 'We's gonna keep him four, five days. He gonna be all right.'

Jeb wanted to thank someone, press someone's hand in gratitude, but there was no one; he wandered aimlessly up the stairs, looked about the reception room and went home.

Four of the doctors who administered Patamoke Hospital were outraged by such treatment of black patients; they had been educated in America's best medical facilities—Jefferson in Philadelphia, Massachusetts General—and they knew that what they were doing was barbarous, but they were impotent. When it was proposed that blacks be moved into the general wards, the whites of Patamoke raised such a fury that the orderly operation of the hospital was jeopardized.

'Any sensible man knows,' Amos Turlock raged at the store, 'that nigger blood is contaminated. Infected with cholera and suchlike.'

The young doctor who had treated Hiram Cater with such affectionate attention once tried to explain that blood was blood, but Amos was too smart to be taken in by such spuriousness. 'You put nigger blood with white, it coagulates.'

The young doctor asked how it was that throughout the history of the Eastern Shore white blood and white genes had infused successfully with black, as the most cursory glance at the variations in color within the black community at the Neck would prove—

'Don't come at me with arguments like that!' Turlock bellowed. 'What happens is, the white blood is destroyed. Cholera and all that.'

Amos Turlock was deathly afraid of cholera, and he and others like him did not propose having it introduced into Patamoke Hospital. 'They handle it just right like it is. No need to change. Keep the niggers in the cellar. And sterilize everything three times before it comes back upstairs.'

It was December, but Hugo Pflaum was sweating with excitement. Deep in the basement of Patamoke Courthouse he fidgeted in his swivel chair and looked with pride and chagrin at the row of fifteen photographs hanging in black frames against his wall. 'There they are,' he muttered nervously, 'fifteen guns they said could never be captured, and Father and I brought 'em all in.'

They formed a gallery of which any game warden could be proud, fifteen long guns that had terrorized the Choptank: 'Cheseldine, we found it hiding beneath a pigsty back in 1922. Reverdy, my father ran up and wrestled its owner in 1924.' At the next photograph Hugo paused with real affection, for it showed the first gun he had captured by himself. 'Took it along the Little Choptank. Herman Cline, once owned by the famous slave-breaker.'

But then his face darkened, for he had come to the two empty spaces reserved for Gun Sixteen and Gun Seventeen, and he could hear the acid voices of the men at the store chiding him, and not in jest: 'Hugo, you're mighty enterprisin' when it comes to confiscatin' other people's guns, but the men have begun to notice that you don't touch the guns operated by your own fambly.' 'Yes, Hugo, how come your brother-in-law Caveny, he's allowed to keep his gun? And Brother-in-law Turlock feels free to fire The Twombly when he wants.'

Amos Turlock's gun was always referred to in this way, as if the honorific *The* proclaimed its noble heritage, oldest long gun in Maryland. Hugo realized that his reputation for integrity depended upon his bringing in that gun, and he complained to his wife, 'My own relatives are making me look like an ass, Becky, and it's got to stop. You march over to your brother Amos and your sister Nora and warn them that I got to lift their guns.'

He had spoken with such wounded dignity that she had gone to Amos, who had dismissed her with a snarl. 'He comes at me, Beck, he's gonna be delivered at your doorstep on a slab, feet first, and that ain't idle chatter.' So she had warned Hugo, 'Stay clear of Amos, he's mean.'

She had better luck in arguing with her sister Nora Caveny. 'You got to help us capture the big gun, Nora. The old days are gone, and it would be a dreadful thing if your boy Patrick was arrested.' The warning had been effective, and now Hugo waited in his office for the information which had been secretly promised; within the week he would have the Caveny in his possession!

Here came his informant, Nora Caveny, his sister-in-law and mother of that fine lad who was studying at St. Joseph's College in Philadelphia. She was trembling. 'I slipped into the courthouse as if I was payin' me taxes,' she said, out of breath. 'I would be mortified if anyone saw me.'

'You're doin' the right thing, Nora. Not only is the gun confiscated by law, but you've seen yourself how it near blinded your husband and how one like it killed old Jake.'

'It's a monstrous weapon, Hugo, and has no place in the hands of a young man intended for the priesthood.'

'How's he doin'?'

'Honors, and after Christmas vacation he enters St. Charles Borromeo.'

'In Rome?'

'Not likely. Philadelphia. But if he does well there, he might make it to Rome.'

'You must be proud.'

'All mothers should have such sons.' She lowered her voice. 'And I intend protectin' mine.'

'Where does he have the gun?'

'I'm not allowed to know. Before my husband went to jail he took Patrick aside and showed him where the precious thing was hidden. You'd think it was gold. Some of the Turlock men upriver know where it is and I think they use it at times. But no women are told.'

'You think Patrick's planning to use it tonight?'

'I'm sure of it, Hugo. I heard him talkin' with Jimmy Turlock, and you know him. All he thinks about is trappin' muskrats and huntin' ducks.'

'Where will they be goin'?'

'That I don't know. There's no ice, and Jimmy owns no marshland.'

'Wish I had a better clue than that.'

'The only other thing I know . . .' She hesitated, wondering if what she was about to say carried any significance. 'I heard him tell Jimmy to leave his Chesapeake behind. They wouldn't be in heavy water.'

'That's important,' Hugo said. 'Means they're not headin' for the bay. That cuts my responsibilities in half.'

'One thing,' Nora said as she studied the rogues' gallery. 'You promised there'd be no photograph in the paper.'

'I did, Nora.'

'Him intendin' for the priesthood, it wouldn't be proper.'

'There'll be a photograph, of course. Has to be, to show the others they can't use that kind no more. But I'll take it with just me and the gun. It'll hang over there.' When it was properly in place, there would be only one vacancy, reserved for The Twombly, and as Hugo prepared to slip home for a long nap prior to his night's work, he felt gratified that a photograph of the Caveny would soon be in place, but he feared that the seventeenth spot might remain vacant for a long time.

The waning of the Depression brought Julia Cater a perplexing dilemma: because she was recognized as a reliable housekeeper, white families invited her to work for them, and had she done so, she might have earned somewhat more than she did in the various canneries. The Steeds could have used her in their town house and the Paxmores who managed the boatyard asked her several times to work at their home. Even the Cavenys who had the line of trucks wanted her, but always she refused.

Two good reasons kept her at her burdensome tasks: she found solid joy in working with other black women and singing with them through the long, hot hours at the steam tables; and she was the best hand along the Choptank at bobbing crabs.

Watermen like her husband brought their crabbing boats to the wharf by noon, and when the live animals were hauled ashore in baskets, Julia's manager would be on hand to buy several barrels of the biggest crabs for the special process he had invented. It was always with a sense of pride that he delivered the big crabs to Julia's table—'We got some beauties again!' And he would have his men throw the live and kicking animals into the vats of boiling water.

When Julia lifted them out with her net they were a beautiful red, and it was on these fine specimens that she went to work. Deftly she pulled away the bony carapace, the swimmers and the apron. After scooping out the entrails, she placed the crab with its delicate meat in a kettle of boiling crabapple vinegar, and after the crabs were well infused with this tangy flavor, she took from a carefully guarded closet a small folded packet of spices, which she had concocted from powders bought by the manager at McCormick's in Baltimore. Only Julia knew the proportions for this mixture; other houses tried to capture the lucrative business of bobbing crabs, but theirs never matched the ones Julia made.

After the mysterious packet was emptied into the boiling vinegar, the crabs remained in the brew only a short time, so that a fresh, tantalizing flavor would be imparted rather than a drenching superabundance. Then the crabs were lifted out and set on racks to drain, after which Julia took each one individually, inspected it, adding lumpy claws to replace any that may have been lost in fighting and wrapping the whole in parchment.

The end product was a bobbed crab, much sought after in Baltimore and New York saloons. The customer paid seventy-five cents for this tidbit, which he could eat either cold as it came from its parchment or grilled with a little butter and pepper. Either way, the spicy, delicious meat was one of the finest delicacies of the Eastern Shore, and Julia Cater, better than any other worker in the canneries, knew how to make it.

She was a culinary expert, one of the best in America, and for her efforts was paid eighty cents a day for a ten-hour day.

With this money, plus the funds her husband added, she kept her family together. The girls were growing older now, and thank God they were responsible. Helen, approaching eleven, was already talking about finding her own job in a cannery, and nine-year-old Luta Mae, although rather forward in protesting injustices, nevertheless, was willing to run errands for white folks and pocket the pennies they offered. What reassured Julia was the girls' sense of duty; their father was usually absent on some skipjack and their mother was gone the greater part of each day, so that if the sisters had any tendency toward delinquency, they would have had easy opportunity to go wrong. Instead, they minded the home, tended their brother, progressed in school and sang in church.

The singing was important. 'If'n a colored girl cain't sing,' Julia often said, 'she dries up her soul.'

At the crab cannery, and while working on tomatoes, Julia sang. In the kitchen with her daughters she sang. And in church on Sundays and Wednesdays she poured out the love she felt for God and His miraculous world. Her voice was strong, like her body, and often when she sang she allowed her head to fall backward, as if she desired her song to go straight upward. Closing her eyes, she would clench her hands before her and sing her praises.

Had her wages been doubled at the Steeds', she would not have wanted to work in silence, one lone black woman moving through hushed rooms. The way to clean a room was to move at it slowly with your two daughters, each with a cloth, each with her own contribution to the singing. The only decent way to bob a crab was in the presence of a score of women, their voices rising in song, their bodies swaying to the music, breathing with it, passing the long hours of toil to its rhythms and reassurances.

And it was not all work music, by any means. Sometimes toward the end of a season, when Julia realized that her man would be coming home one of these days and that Hiram with the scar at his ear all mended would run forth to greet his father, Julia would burst into song whether there was anyone to join her or not.

In the spring of 1940 the Steeds belatedly came to grips with the problem of their vanishing island. Jefferson Steed, the congressman who now occupied Rosalind's Revenge, awakened to the fact that not only were the western fields in critical danger, but the mansion itself ran some risk of being undermined and toppled. Frantic steps were taken to shore up the western banks, where erosion was rampant, but no sooner had bulkheads been installed at great cost than diverted currents began eating away at the northern shoreline, and the southern, too.

The spectacular storms that occasionally swept the Chesapeake usually generated in the Atlantic, south of the bay, and when they roared inland they deposited a lot of water; there was always some flooding but never any real damage to the shoreline. It was the less conspicuous storms that did the damage, the persistent ones that came without fanfare from the northwest, blowing for days and even weeks at a time, creating substantial waves to nibble away at the northwestern tips of the islands and peninsulas.

The Eastern Shore consisted of a vast, flat alluvial deposit sent down by glaciers as they melted at the ends of the various ice ages. The highest point in the Patamoke area was Peace Cliff, and within a radius of twenty miles from the town a searcher would find not a single rock, and barely a pebble. Everything was sandy clay. Of course, into it had been mixed vegetable matter, oyster shells and fine gravel brought down by the Susquehanna, but in effect, Devon Island, as representative of the whole, was cruelly vulnerable to the pounding waves.

They did their damage not by breaking upon the face of the shore, thundering it to shreds; they broke some distance out, then rolled in at surface level, gradually undercutting the bank at water line. At times the cut would extend two or even three feet under what appeared to be a solid extension of land with tall trees upon it, but it was doomed, for its base had been hollowed out.

Then, when some storm of unusual force swept in, the huge block of sandy soil, plus its burden of trees and grassy banks, would shudder, tremble for a moment, and slowly collapse into the bay. At Devon Island this remorseless erosion had been continuing in its silent, steady way since long before the day Captain John Smith first mapped the place in 1608. Much of the island had already disappeared, and heroic steps were required if the remainder was to be saved.

'What we'll do,' Jefferson Steed said, 'is throw bulkheading of a sturdier type about the entire northwest sector.' His foreman pointed out that this would be exceedingly costly, but Steed said, 'We've been selling off the mainland plantations at a good profit, and anyway, if we don't pin the shoreline down, we're going to lose the mansion.'

So an engineer was called in, and he spent more than a hundred thousand dollars to protect the island; but his wooden wall had scarcely been completed when a stubborn four-day nor'wester hammered at it. 'Thank God, it's standing,' Steed said as he and the engineer surveyed their work, and he was correct; the pilings had been so deeply driven and so clevery tied together with planking that the new bulkheads resisted the storm.

'But look over here,' the engineer said with dismay.

And what Jefferson Steed saw took all the assurance out of him. For the storm, powerless to knock down the bulkheading, had simply cut around behind it, forming a deep channel between the wooden wall and the island, and the current thus created was so swift that it eroded the sandy soil almost as effectively as the waves had done, but from a different direction. At many places it was impossible to step from the remaining soil onto the bulkhead, so wide had the channel become.

'What in hell can we do?' Steed asked.

'We could try to enclose the entire island in one unbroken wall,' the engineer replied.

'At what cost?'

After some silent calculation the man said, 'Two million dollars.'

'Good God!' And for the first time Steed faced the possibility that his family might actually lose this island. 'The whole damned thing could go . . . the Revenge . . . everything.'

Numbly he walked to the northern shore and pointed to a new type of erosion beginning there. 'Looks as if new currents were butting at us, all the time.'

'They are,' the engineer said.

This fatalistic remark angered Steed, and he demanded, 'Well, what are you going to do about it?'

'Nothing,' the engineer said.

'You mean . . . all we did last year was fruitless? This year, too?'

'Seems so. But I assure you, Mr. Steed, it could not have been anticipated.'

'That's what we hire engineers for. Damn it, we've wasted a fortune. What's going to happen?'

Carefully the engineer studied the northern bank, shaking his head dolefully when he realized the awful rate at which it was slipping back into the bay. With Steed he got into a small powerboat to circumnavigate the island, and it was apparent that even the small wake thrown by this boat imperiled the shoreline, for its waves cut at the vital line where the impacted sand met water.

'You can imagine the damage done by the wake of a big vessel,' he told

Steed. Each foot of shoreline was under attack; each year the island would grow smaller as its borrowed sand slipped back into the bay.

'What's it all mean?' Steed asked.

'It means that Devon was doomed from the day it was created. The entire Eastern Shore was, if we accept the evidence.'

They were now at the southeastern corner of the island, the spot from which the roof line of Rosalind's Revenge was most compelling; just enough of the house itself was visible to give the structure substance, but the feature that caught the eye was the widow's walk, that rectangular superstructure with the low balustrade. That this should go down with the crumbling island was unacceptable, and Steed shook his head.

Twice he tried to speak, but his throat filled and words fell back. Afraid that tears might come to his eyes, he reached for his handkerchief and mumbled, 'Excuse me, please,' and the engineer had the decency to look away.

The separation of races which had always marked the Eastern Shore continued unabated into the 1940s and long thereafter, and the loss to the community of what might have been accomplished by joint effort was staggering. Choirs would have been sweeter, taxes could have been kept lower if black incomes had been allowed to rise, baseball teams would have been more capable if black players had been accepted, and in almost every enterprise the results could have been more productive if black energies had been enlisted.

But tradition demanded that the two communities exist side by side in a kind of armed truce, with all the arms in possession of the whites. Enforcers of the policy fell into two groups: at the apex of society the Steeds and their fellow planters—'We took the name *planter* in the good old days when our slaves raised tobacco, now we grow mainly tomatoes, but we hold on to the name'—believed that blacks were suited only for labor and that society prospered when they were held to it; at the base of the pyramid the Turlocks and Cavenys defined and enforced the working rules.

'Niggers is meant for Frog's Neck,' Amos Turlock said many times. 'Let 'em come out in the mornin' to work in the canneries, but let 'em by God get back home, come nightfall.'

The Turlocks were not altogether idiotic in their enforcement. 'Best thing this town ever did was hire that nigger cop. One of the finest men in this town. He sees to it that when the niggers cut somebody up, it's their own kind.' They also felt that the blacks should have a school. 'Not a real school. Ain't no black in this world fit for college, but they got a right to an education. Six, seven grades. They got to learn how to read.'

So the races lived in their separate vacuums except for those rare and hallowed nights when someone organized a rally. This event usually occurred in summer. Hand-lettered signs would appear in the window at Steed's, and on posts along the waterfront:

MONSTER RALLY
A. M. E. CHURCH GROUNDS
SATURDAY NIGHT

In the black community no signs were necessary, for everyone knew that upon the success of this rally depended the amount of good work their church could do in the coming season. It was to the white community that the signs were addressed, especially the Turlocks and Cavenys, for if they paid their admissions in sizable numbers, the affair was bound to be a success; the Steeds and Paxmores would contribute whether they came or not, but it was more fun if the Neck was filled with Turlocks, for as Jeb Cater said, 'They knows how to enjoy theirselves.'

On Saturday, July 20, 1940, the big rally of the summer was to be held; on Thursday and Friday all families related to the A.M.E. Church attended their customary tasks. Jeb Cater was responsible for roping off a substantial portion of the Neck, which could be entered only upon payment of an admission. The Will Nesbitt Band practiced unaccustomed numbers because a rumor had circulated that Father Caveny, fresh from his ordination, might attend. Other men gathered chairs, swept the grounds and strung lights.

The women of the black community, after long hours in the canneries, were busy cutting chickens for frying, and chopping okra to be boiled with tomatoes and onions, and baking the goodies which white children liked so much. To Julia Cater's small home black watermen brought baskets of crabs and celery and onions and bags of flour, for by tradition she was in charge of making the reigning treat of any rally—the crab cakes.

Congressman Steed said of her cookery, 'I've attended rallies and political meetings up and down the Eastern Shore, and I calculate I've eaten at least two hundred crab cakes a year for forty years. That's eight thousand cakes, and year by year I've graded 'em on a scale of ten. Most public restaurants are serving trash that rates no higher than two-point-zero. A shred of crab meat, a loaf of bread, deep-fried in rancid fat and doused with catsup. What a travesty! Now, my Aunt Betsy made a crab cake that rated eight-point-seven. Gobs of lump, all back fin, delicately sautéed. Never had enough.

'But for real Eastern Shore crab cake, you've got to go to Julia Cater over in Frog's Neck. You see a poster announcin' a rally where she's doin' the crab cakes, you owe it to yourself to go, just for her masterpieces. Score? Nine-point-seven, highest ever awarded.' When someone asked why, if Julia's cakes were so fine, he rated then only nine-seven, he explained, 'The perfect crab cake would have just a touch of onion. Julia refuses.'

Once a newspaper in Baltimore had carried a front-page picture of Congressman Steed bending over a stove while Julia Cater demonstrated how to make her specialty. 'What she does,' the story said, 'is use the finest crab meat, just a smidgin of chopped celery, well-beaten eggs to hold the meat together and bread crumbs dried in the sun to give the cake substance. A touch of pepper, a touch of salt and something from a brown paper bag which she refuses to identify, and *voilà!* Crab cakes Eastern Shore, and this reporter never had better.'

On Thursday and Friday the three Cater women worked till their fingers were numb, picking crabs. Other women volunteered to help, but Julia felt that this was her opportunity to serve the Lord with what she did best, and all through the night she and her daughters deftly picked at the crabs and sang. 'Crab meat so good,' Helen explained, 'crab, he don't want to give it up.' The work was both tedious and difficult, a constant picking for the elusive lumps of meat that distinguished the best cakes. 'I seen crab cakes,' Julia said, 'they was a disgrace. All dark meat in tiny shreds, I wouldn't put 'em in a pan, let alone eat 'em.'

By Saturday morning the Cater women had buckets of pale-white crab meat sitting under cheesecloth cover in the cool of the house. During the heat of the day they slept, and at five in the afternoon they began their labors, and as the golden-brown cakes began to come from the fire, round like small tomatoes and lumpy where the good crab meat showed beneath the breading, they were pleased.

At dusk two black men took their positions at the improvised gateway leading to the rally grounds, and as people came down the road from town, these men collected forty cents from grownups, twenty cents from children, and from time to time when some white man who had favored the rallies through the years made an appearance, the older of the two collectors would take him aside, toward a clump of bushes, and there would present him with a bottle of whiskey and invite him to take a swig.

'We appreciate your comin',' the douanier would whisper, and often he would drink with the white man, sharing the same bottle.

One man who never missed a rally was Amos Turlock—'Best damned cookin' in the county, and them niggers know how to sing.' For his modest admission, Amos was offered a gluttonous supply of food: fried chicken, cantaloupe, tomato-and-onion salad, numerous pies, tables of sandwiches and, of course, the crab cakes.

Visitors gorged themselves from five till sunset, then Will Nesbitt and his nine-piece band played loud and bouncy music. During this part of the rally Nesbitt's men stuck to music they had been playing at such affairs for a decade, waiting until Father Caveny appeared for their special numbers.

At intervals the choir sang, led by Reverend Douglass, who had a good voice. These men and women offered mainly religious music, running through a ritual of hymns often unfamiliar to the white guests, but sooner or later strong voices like Julia Cater's would slip into the popular spirituals, and sometimes the whole crowd would join in the singing, and at such moments of fusion any thought of white or black would vanish.

It was about nine o'clock when word sped through the crowd that Father Caveny was coming, and he knew what was expected of him, for he brought with him a small black box, which perplexed the whites in the audience but delighted the blacks. He passed easily through the crowd, a fair-haired young man of twenty-six, dressed in clerical garb, the local lad who had done well in college and even better in the seminary. Patamoke was proud of young Patrick Caveny, but it was also bewildered by his unpredictable behavior.

Nodding to the Steeds and his other white parishioners as if he were on a promenade in his church, he circulated for a while among the blacks, then allowed himself to be edged toward the bandstand. People started to applaud, and Will Nesbitt came down to invite him to join the band. This brought cheers, and after smiling easily to the crowd, and asking for one more bite of crab cake, he unlocked the black box.

Inside lay an unassembled clarinet in four pieces, and slowly, with Irish dramatics, he took them out and carefully fitted them together: bell, body, mouthpiece, reed. After testing the assembly, he asked one of Nesbitt's men to sound a note, which he sought to match. Satisfied with the condition of his instrument, he nodded to Nesbitt, and the band picked out the seven lovely notes of a song the blacks loved, 'Bye, Bye, Blackbird,' and when they sounded, the audience cheered.

Father Caveny did not play during the first part of this admirable song, but when the music reached what was called the bridge, or, as some termed it, the break, the band stopped and on his clarinet he played the lonesome wail of a black man trapped in the north and yearning to return home.

Then the band joined in, and ten minutes later the rally at the A.M.E. became a riot.

The Steeds and other proper Catholics were embarrassed by the gyrations of their priest, and the congressman's aunt said, 'If you ask me, he's getting much too close to the niggers in all respects,' and one of her generation said, 'Shameful, for a man of the cloth to be playing a clarinet the way he did in high school.'

But when the rally was over, and Reverend Douglass had counted the dimes and quarters on which his church must exist for the coming season, and when the pots were cleared and the ropes taken down, it was Jeb Cater who summed up the evening: 'Quakers like Woolman Paxmore, the finest man in town, they loves black people in big doses—like all the blacks in Alabama or Georgia—but Father Caveny, he loves us one by one . . . just as we are . . . here in Frog's Neck.'

On February 22, 1941, Amos Turlock's photograph appeared on the front page of the *Patamoke Bugle,* but not in the form that Hugo Pflaum had planned. He wanted grizzly Amos standing on one side, The Twombly in the middle, and himself on the other side, the clever game warden who had confiscated the last and most famous of the long guns.

No, it was quite a different kind of portrait. Unshaven Amos stood with an ordinary shotgun in one hand and a dead goose in another; the caption read:

Local Hunter Bags Goose
in Family Marsh

The story went on to tell of how Amos had prowled the marshes for five months, hoping to get one good shot at his elusive target, and several hunters were quoted in praise of his determination:

> 'If any Patamoke man was destined to get a goose this year,' said Francis X. Caveny, himself a gunner of note, 'it would have to be Amos Turlock, for he knows more about the habits of this bird than any other local resident.'

There was additional material recalling the years when quite a few geese used to visit the Choptank, and Amos was congratulated editorially for reminding Patamokeans of those good old days:

> To Amos Turlock and to men like him, we say Bravo! And even though we might be fatuous, we would like to voice the hope that one day the multitudes of geese that once inhabited our region will return. Certainly we applaud the efforts of good sportsmen like Amos Turlock who strive so diligently to help us keep the ducks we still have. Hang your goose high, Amos, and eat it in good health!

No black in Patamoke could exist through a period as short as six days without being reminded of the distorted society in which he lived. This was brought home to the Caters on the afternoon of the day when they heard the exciting news that Amos Turlock had actually shot a goose.

What happened on this particular afternoon was that Julia was fortunate enough to get an appointment with the traveling black dentist who had come down from Baltimore. For some time she had been having serious trouble with her teeth, and since dental care was totally beyond the reach of local black families—white dentists would not treat them and there were no black practitioners—she had watched her teeth deteriorate when she knew that with proper attention they might be saved.

'Bad case here,' the overscheduled visitor said. 'Only thing I can see, have them all out.'

'But, Doctor—'

'They could have been saved. Maybe they still could be if I could see you once a week for six months. Impossible. Better have them all out.'

'But—'

'Lady, we have no time to argue. I can pull them for you, take an impression, and mail you a set of real fine teeth from Baltimore. Forty dollars and you have no more trouble.'

'But—'

'Lady, make up your mind. I don't get back this way again this year.'

'Could I come back?'

'Look, if you don't have the forty dollars now, I'll take a deposit and trust you for the rest. Reverend Douglass told me—'

'It's not money!' she interrupted sternly, and then all the fight went out of her. The years of trying to hold her family together, of trying not to get too fat the way some black women did, the anxiety over her teeth and the recent behavior of Luta Mae and the education of her son. It was too much, too much. The remorseless, never-ending struggle was too much.

Resigned, she lay back in the chair, but when the first whiffs of gas reached her nostrils she instinctively fought against them. 'I ain't gonna faint!'

'Now, now,' the dentist said, softly stroking her hand.

Really, it was much less painful than she had anticipated, and the dentist laughed when he helped her from the chair. 'If the teeth don't fit, I'll tell you what. I'll wear them myself.'

But when she reached the street, and felt the vast emptiness in her mouth, she could not hold back the tears. 'Dear Jesus, I won't never be able to sing no more.'

If anyone had sought to compose an honest history of Patamoke, he or she would probably have felt obliged to include a passage on the spiritual experience of the region, and a curious problem would have presented itself, because it would have been difficult to identify any of the presumed leaders as the man or woman who had done most to inspirit the area.

For example, a traditionalist might want to nominate William Penn, the stately Quaker from Philadelphia; he came to Patamoke in the late 1600s, bowing pompously to the locals and offering evidence of his spirituality, but it would be difficult to enshrine him, for to the average Marylander, Penn was a conniving, thieving, lying rascal who had done his darnedest to steal the northern part of the colony into Pennsylvania, and succeeded. Paul Steed, in writing of that period, said:

> The worst enemy Maryland ever had was William Penn, that sanctimonious Quaker and self-styled religious pontificater. Had my forebears not been on their guard, Penn would have stolen the fairest portion of our colony, all the way down to Devon Island. He came to Patamoke once, ostensibly to pray with his local religionists but obviously to spy out what parts to steal next. A more devious man never appeared on the Choptank.

Animosity toward Penn's memory was kept alive by two unfortunate incidents: in 1765, when Charles Mason and Jeremiah Dixon surveyed the line allocating land between Maryland and Pennsylvania, they started from a point not far from the Choptank, and it was soon rumored that Pennsylvanians had suborned them to draw a line favorable to Penn's people; and in 1931, when a professor at Penn State College wrote a book explaining that the Chesapeake Bay should never have been so named since it was merely the extended mouth of the Susquehanna River, the *Patamoke Bugle* thundered: 'First they steal our land and now they want to steal our bay. We say, "To hell with Pennsylvania and its thieving ways." '

A more acceptable case could be made for Francis Asbury, that inspired English clergyman of limited education but unlimited devotion to the precepts of John Wesley who came to Maryland in the 1770s. A man of indefatigable will, he traveled each year more than five thousand miles, laboring to establish in the nation about to be born the new religion of Methodism. His harsh style was particularly effective on the Eastern Shore, which he traipsed from end to end, shouting hellfire and providing the simple citizens with a brand of religion much more appealing than the stately proprieties of Episcopalianism, a rich man's faith, or Catholicism, which had become severely formalized. Asbury stopped at Patamoke three times, creating a frenzy among the watermen with his revelations of heaven and hell, and it was principally because of his enthusiasm that the Choptank became in effect a Methodist river. Of one visit he wrote in his diary:

> I arrived at Patamoke, a fair town on a fair river, on fire to save the souls of these rude men who fished the bay as the followers of Jesus fished the Galilee, but the first man I fell in with was one Turlock,

who annoyed the patrons of our tavern by his noisy eating, his loud drinking, his smoking and his riotous behavior. He appeared as forgetful of eternity as if he had been at the most secure distance from its brink. The reprobate had the effrontery to tell me in a loud voice that his father had lived to be 109 and had never used spectacles.

Having been greeted by a man so steeped in sin, I was eager to get about the business of saving this place, but I found that Satan had arrived before me, diverting the good people of Patamoke with a play, which they attended noisily and with apparent delight. I was sore distressed.

George Fox, the founder of Quakerism, visited Patamoke in 1672, but he made no lasting impression, and the saintly Father Ralph Steed had endeavored to establish Catholicism in the most remote corners of the region at about the same time, but his influence had been felt more on the western shore. Ruth Brinton Paxmore, in that same period, had been a powerful force for good, but her personality was so abrasive that she could not be considered symbolic of the region. Woolman Paxmore, as we have seen, was a more gentle type, but he exercised his influence principally in other parts of the eastern seaboard and was not thought much of at home.

No, the man who gave the Eastern Shore its most profound spiritual lift was Jefferson Steed, and what he did was stop planting tomatoes.

In the late 1940s he perceived that those portions of the vast Steed land holdings which had for the past half century been devoted to tomato growing were shortly going to show a loss. The huge tomato canneries scattered along the banks of Eastern Shore rivers were outmoded; much better factories were being installed in New Jersey and the West. Also, the ground had been worn out by constant assaults from the tomato plants, notoriously hungry for minerals, and poor soil meant weak plants susceptible to infestations of insects. Even more important, with labor rushing away from farms and to war plants and new projects like the proposed Bay Bridge, it was no longer economical to raise tomatoes, so on a day fateful in the history of the Eastern Shore, Jefferson Steed told his foremen, 'No more tomatoes.' When they protested that the great iron-roofed canneries, looming out of the marshes along the estuaries, could be put to no alternate use, he replied, 'Let 'em rust to hell. They've served their day.' And a way of life vanished.

'What will we grow?' the foremen wanted to know.

'Corn,' Steed said.

The men, all practiced farmers, could not believe what they were hearing. They had always grown modest amounts of corn for their dairy herds, but if they added acreage that had formerly grown tomatoes, new markets would have to be found. 'Where will we sell the stuff?' Steed replied, 'Eastern Shore people love horses. And what's left over, that's my headache.'

So at considerable risk of financial disaster, Congressman Steed planted his tomato fields with a hybrid corn developed by agronomists at the University of Maryland, and it grew well. But the remarkable yields he achieved came not from this good seed but from the daring decision he made when planting: 'From the time the first Englishmen raised corn in Maryland we've planted it three feet apart in rows widely separated. Always thought it had to be that way. But if you ask me, it was only so that horses could move between the rows to cultivate. With these new chemicals we don't have to plant that way.' And boldly he had seeded his corn so tightly that even a man had difficulty passing between the stalks.

It worked. And in the fall when black field hands swept down the compacted rows, piling the ears in stacks three times as large as predicted, Steed knew he had a good thing.

'Now all I have to do is find a market,' he told his manager, and by questioning fellow congressmen he uncovered patrons eager to buy his surplus at the low prices he was able to offer, and soon other farmers along the Eastern Shore were converting from tomatoes to corn; in the late summer the far fields were burdened with stalks eight and ten feet high, laden with heavy ears. Steed's gamble was one of the shrewdest ever made in Maryland agriculture, and farmers who might have lost their land had they stayed with tomatoes became moderately rich on corn.

But a lucky stroke in rural economics would not qualify a man for sanctification; what Steed did next, in the late 1950s, was to pension off his field hands and purchase a squadron of gigantic automatic corn harvesters, which saved him a great deal of money and allowed him to harvest his fields speedily on Monday and his neighbors' on Tuesday. The harvester meant that large-scale agriculture was now possible, for gang-plows prepared the fields in spring, huge multiple disks worked it in late April, harrows with enormous teeth kept the land clean, and metal dinosaurs crawled over the fields in autumn, harvesting the corn.

Where did the spiritual significance in such an operation lie? The black field hands had harvested corn slowly but with almost perfect efficiency; the mechanical pickers swept rudely down the rows, leaving in their trail about three percent of the corn missed. It fell as broken ears, or grains knocked off, or stalks left at the end of rows too tightly packed against the hedges for the machine to reach, or one or two rows left standing down the middle, not worth the driver's turning his huge machine around for.

Steed and his managers were not slothful; they realized they were losing corn, but when they calculated what they would have to spend to garner the stray bits, they found that it was cheaper to leave it. 'Let's admit that the loss in harvesting by machine is three percent. But even when you add to that the depreciation and the gasoline, the machine harvester is a bargain. So we'll forget the fallen grains.'

It was one of the happiest decisions a Steed ever made regarding his land, for when the bright yellow grains lay on the ground in autumn, reflecting back the paling rays of the sun, geese flying overhead began to see them. At first a few stopped on their way to customary wintering grounds in North Carolina, and a thrill shot up and down the spine of the Eastern Shore—'Geese comin' back! Henry seen at least forty at the far end of his field.'

Housewives going to market would suddenly stop to stare at something their grandmothers had spoken of but which they had never seen. 'I was turnin' the corner off Glebe Road, and there in the field stood—well, it must of been a hundred fat geese feedin' on the Childress farm.'

One autumn at least forty thousand geese came to fields along the Choptank, and legends of the time when nearly a million came were revived, and fifty Turlocks began to grease their guns.

By 1960 two hundred thousand geese were spending their winters along the endless streams feeding into the Choptank, and in the years ahead the population would reach the levels Captain John Smith had observed in 1608. Rafts would form east of Patamoke, ten thousand geese drowsing on the water, and something would alert those at the edge, and they would rise, and all would follow, and then the scouts would satisfy themselves that the danger was not real, and they would settle once again upon the river, and all the rest would follow; it was like a magic carpet somewhere east of Baghdad, rising and drifting and falling back.

At the store, huntsmen summed up the consequences: 'Elmer's carvin' decoys again. They's five Turlocks advertisin' their services as guides. That black man at the garage is offerin' to pick feathers off'n a goose for twenty-five cents, and Martin Caveny rented his waterfront to a dude from Pittsburgh for nine hundred dollars.'

But always when the hunters explored this fascinating subject of how the return had vitalized the Eastern Shore—'Ever' damned motel room rented for the season'—the moment would come when they would fall silent from the wonder of it all, then some old man would shake his head and say, 'Beats all, the geese came back.' And again no one spoke, for the old man had summarized the best thing that had happened to the Shore in a hundred years.

When Hiram Cater was seven years old his serious education began, not in spelling or arithmetic but in the brutal tactics of survival in a white world. His mother, who could remember lynchings along the Choptank when black men who may or may not have been guilty of something were summarily hanged, was his principal instructor: 'Your job to stay alive. Keep away from notice. Doan' do nothin' to attract attention. If a Turlock or a Caveny come your way, you step aside. Doan' never challenge a white man.'

At the slightest indication that young Hiram was developing a temper, she warned him, 'All right you hit Oscar. He black. But doan' never hit a white child, because his papa gonna make big trouble.'

And she was especially careful to admonish her son about speaking to white girls: 'They doan' exist. They ain't there. You doan' go to school with them, you doan' go to church with them, and in town you keeps strictly away.' As she watched her son, she was gratified that the two halves of Patamoke were separated; with luck, he need never come into contact with a white girl.

Her doctrine was: 'It doan' exist.' Anything that irritated or denigrated was to be cast out of mind, and no insolence from whites was sufficient cause to retreat from this basic strategy. If Hiram had no books in school, forget it. If when he did get his hands on a book, it was in tatters from long use in white schools, ignore it. If the school had no glass in its windows, keep your mouth shut, because nothing can be done about that. The most automatic human responses were to be muzzled, kept down in one's stomach. The one response to humiliation was a grin, a step aside, a descent into the gutter so that the white woman could pass, a repression.

'That's how it gonna be all your life,' Julia Cater told her son, and she was preaching old black wisdom, for through the generations that was how black women enabled their sons to survive so that they could grow into black men.

Hiram's natural protests, uttered from the day this indoctrination began, received scant support from his father. 'You do like your mama say, you stay alive.' On the skipjacks, Jeb had mastered the trick of getting along with white crewmen. 'I does the job better, and when trouble starts I keeps my eyes down.' As a consequence, he was known favorably as a good nigger, and after a while he found little resentment in playing this role. 'Man got to stay alive. Man got to have a job. You listen to your mama, Hiram, you gonna be a smart man some day, maybe have your own skipjack.'

The effect on Hiram of this constant repression of natural instincts was minimal, for he found within the black community adequate outlets for his boisterous spirits. If he wanted to fight, Oscar was at hand, slightly larger, slightly better with his fists. If he wanted to play rough games, many boys his size frequented the school grounds and at times their contests became almost violent. By no means did his mother's preaching make him into a subdued child, nor one afraid of social conflict. Instead this walling him off from the white community forced him to become an even stronger personality within the black.

Like his father, he had a rugged medium build. His skin was darker than that of many with whom he played, bespeaking an unmixed ancestry reaching back to Africa, but of that continent and Cudjo Cater's adventures there, he knew nothing. He was a child of the Choptank, without heritage, or language, or knowledge of social custom, and it was likely that this condition would maintain for the rest of his life, as it had for his father.

One preachment of his mother exerted a profound influence: 'You brush your teeth, you ain't gonna lose 'em the way I done los' mine.' Cleaning his teeth twice a day became a solemn ritual which he observed through choice and not because his mother forced him. As a result, he noticed that his teeth were whiter than those of his playmates and much brighter than those of white children, who were allowed unlimited quantities of candy.

He was allowed almost nothing. His sister Luta Mae saved their pennies and on festive days would lead him to the Blue and Gold Ice Cream Parlor, where they would agonize over which of nine flavors to choose for their cones; he thought of these days as the best in his life and felt none of his sister's resentment that when the cones were bought they could not be eaten at the lacy iron tables. He wanted to be out on the street, where the cool touch of the cream on his lips contrasted with the hot breeze from the river.

When Luta Mae was twelve, a big bright girl with energies and imaginings far surpassing those of her older sister, she told Hiram extraordinary stories—of how she flew one day with Charles Lindbergh all through the sky, and of how she had once owned a Chevrolet and driven it over the oyster-shell roads, and of how she had met this older boy Charley and of their going through the countryside and doing everything they damned well pleased. One's mind was dusted out when one talked long with Luta Mae, for her enthusiasms flourished and carried her to perimeters far beyond the Choptank.

When she was thirteen she confided to Hiram that she would refuse to end her education when the black school terminated at the end of the seventh grade. 'I am going to Salisbury. I am going to the black high school and get all A's. And then I am going to college.' She had fallen under the spell of a Miss Canby, who taught in the Patamoke black school, and from her had learned to speak white man's English, with no contractions or gutter slang. She affected ladylike pronunciations, too: *skoo-well* for *school* and *Feb-ru-ar-y,* with all letters vocalized in a manner few college professors could equal. She was reading Langston Hughes and the life of Frederick Douglass, who had grown up nearby.

And always she seemed to be dragging Hiram along behind her, as if it was his education that mattered; but when their mother heard of this, she became agitated.

'Doan' you listen to Luta Mae,' Julia warned. 'She got special problems.'

And then, suddenly, the Eastern Shore was gripped by an excitement that preempted even Julia's cautionary preachments. World War II had come and gone, scarcely touching the Shore; no munitions plants sprouted, nor any big military installations. Life hardly changed in spite of the convolutions at Berlin and Hiroshima; the only excitement came when a U-boat crept close to the Virginia Capes and sank some freighters. It was believed that the real mission of the submarine was the bombardment of Patamoke and the destruction of the Paxmore Boatyard, and when cynics said, 'Not likely they'd bother,' older men reminded them, 'That's what they said before the British bombed us in the War of 1812.'

The war had passed without invasion of the Choptank, and things were back in their somnolent grooves when the Maryland legislature, composed principally of men from the western shore, passed a bill authorizing the construction of a mighty bridge right across Chesapeake Bay. Imaginations were inflamed by the possibilities: 'Is it feasible for man to construct a bridge five miles long across a major arm of the Atlantic Ocean? It is and we shall do it.'

The announced justification of the bridge was that it would provide an alternate route between Washington and New York, but the real purpose was to enable Monday-to-Friday bureaucrats in Washington and Baltimore to get more speedily to their summer resorts along the Atlantic Ocean, and this meant that the sleepy fields of the Eastern Shore, so long protected from outside influences, would be converted into snarling highways for pleasure seekers. Where gracious living had prevailed, gas stations and quick-food counters would clutter the landscape.

Almost unanimously the Eastern Shore opposed this bridge, and heated meetings were held at which local patriots explained that the bridge would really be paid for by watermen who did not want it and by farmers whose ancient holdings would be contaminated by it. Screamed the *Bugle:*

> This is confiscation of the most brutal sort. Against our permission and with our own funds, our way of life is being despoiled. Where we once had a few-score automobiles on our lovely back roads, we will now have thousands. Our most precious corners will be invaded by any boob from Baltimore who has a second-hand car. Noise, contamination, rowdyism and the influx of strangers who do not

comprehend our values will be the consequence. No greater disaster than this damnable bridge has ever faced our land of peaceful living, and we oppose it with all our energy.

The timeless proposal that the Eastern Shore detach itself from Maryland to form a new state was revived, and agitated meetings were held in Delaware and Virginia to speed the plan, but as always, it came to naught; Maryland did not want the Eastern Shore, did not understand it or care to pay for its upkeep, but it was determined that it not become part of any other state. So a bridge was authorized that nobody on the Eastern Shore desired in order to destroy a way of life that everyone wished to preserve; and rich northerners who had bought estates along the rivers bewailed its arrival the way rich southerners had once lamented the departure of slavery.

One group of people along the eastern rivers was delighted with the prospect of a bridge, but they kept their counsel and waited. They were the blacks who saw in the building of the bridge a chance for employment that had otherwise eluded them—'Now we gonna get jobs. They gonna need a lot of men to build that bridge.' Will Nesbitt quietly told his band members that night clubs would be needed to entertain the workmen, and he proposed playing in them. Reverend Douglass looked into the possibility of finding jobs for most of his unemployed parishioners and came back from engineering headquarters in Baltimore excited about the prospects.

'Jeb,' he told Cater, 'I'll give you a recommendation as one of the best workmen in this area. You're older and more responsible, and I'm sure you'll land a good job.'

So Jeb surrendered his position on the skipjack, informed his family that from now on he was a bridge builder, and rode with Will Nesbitt to the construction center at the eastern end of the bridge. While the band leader negotiated for a possible location in which to play, he reported to the hiring office, where lines of men waited for employment, and he saw with growing reassurance that many were being hired. The chalked sign said that drivers, dozers, office help and field bosses were needed, plus other specialties which he could not decipher, like sand-hogs.

A lot of jobs were being distributed, but not to blacks. When he reached the office a brisk young man asked, 'You work on a bridge before?' When he said no, the young man said, 'Sorry, nothing.'

At that moment of his rejection, two buses drew up, one from Boston, one from New York, and Jeb saw that the construction company was importing white men from distant cities rather than employing blacks who lived near the site. And the men had come not just for specialized jobs he could not perform; he lingered and heard them given the precise kind of work that he could have done: drivers, shovel men, watchmen, tool cleaners.

Will Nesbitt had no better luck. Roadhouses were being opened, but they were importing white talent, and when the two black men drove back home they carried a bitterness which was hard to mask. Nesbitt said, 'I seen them buses bringin' in the white men. Seems like from birth they just doan' want us. They doan' let us go to school, then they tells us, "You ain't been to school." '

Jeb restrained his anger, as he had disciplined himself to do, but the more Will talked of the discriminations they faced in all acts of life, the sadder he became, because he saw this perpetual unfairness saddled onto his son and then onto his son's son, through the generations. He did not, however, report the incident of the buses to his family, but Will Nesbitt spoke of it throughout the Neck, and on Thursday night Luta Mae came storming home, slamming herself about as she did when suffering outrage.

'I was informed,' she said with schoolmarm prissiness, 'that no blacks were being employed at the bridge.'

Jeb said nothing, but Luta Mae persisted. 'Was I informed correctly?'

'Well . . .'

'Goddamnit!' the girl cried.

'Luta Mae! Doan' you ever blaspheme in this house.' It was Julia speaking.

'Mother,' Luta Mae cried, whipping about and pushing Julia back, 'you keep your Bible-mouthing to yourself. We're talking about vileness.' And Julia watched, amazed, as her daughter argued with her father like some embittered man.

'Tell me the truth, Father. Did they send buses to bring in ordinary workmen?'

'Yes, yes. That's what they done.'

'And those white men took jobs that you could have filled?'

'That's what they done.'

'Goddamnit!' the girl cried with a savagery her parents had never seen before. 'That bridge should be burned to the ground.'

'It ain't built yet,' her father protested, but she brushed him aside and was seen no more that night, nor on Friday or Saturday. On Monday the papers carried a story that the hiring offices at the eastern end of the bridge had been consumed by fire. Officials believed that it must have been started by a cigarette thrown carelessly into a wastebasket.

When Jeb and Julia heard of the fire, and saw Luta Mae returning home with smugness etched beneath her dark eyes, they could guess what had happened but were afraid to voice their fears, for what their daughter had done led to prison. But Will Nesbitt stopped by the shack and said knowingly, 'Damned hiring office burned. A good thing.'

He waited for Jeb to respond, but Jeb was too smart to say anything.

When the bandleader left, Jeb fell onto his knees, bent his head and began to pray, and before he had started his supplication Julia was beside him, praying that their family might safely negotiate the threatening years.

The return of geese to the Eastern Shore brought two men into confrontation. Amos Turlock believed that the huge birds had come back to him personally, and since his ancestors had hunted geese on the Choptank for more than three hundred years, he proposed to continue. Furthermore, he intended using the long gun which had blazed across these waters since 1827, and when the geese began to invade his marsh, as they had in his grandfather's day, he figured it was time to check on The Twombly, hidden like the infant Moses in rushes.

Hugo Pflaum, the game warden responsible for the Choptank, began receiving indications that his brother-in-law Amos might be on the prowl. One resident reported having heard a tremendous blast at midnight 'like the echo of Confederate cannon at Chancellorsville,' and another had seen mysterious lights toward two in the morning, moving slowly up and down the river. Backwoods families began having goose with greater regularity than their legal huntsmen could have provided, and there were telltale traces of fresh corn on fields which geese had picked clean two months before. Worst of all, whenever Amos appeared at the store, he was smiling.

The law prohibiting his behavior was explicit, and he was breaking it in seven respects: he was using a long gun absolutely outlawed since 1918; he was using a night light which blinded the geese, something no decent gunner had done in the past hundred years; he was shooting at night, strictly forbidden; he was baiting his marsh and the field back of his cabin with great quantities of ripened corn; he was hunting out of season; he had no license; and he was selling dead geese commercially. But he committed all these crimes with such innocent deception that Pflaum could never catch him.

'The average crook,' Hugo reported to his superiors in Annapolis, 'lurks furtively, leaves a blazing trail that anyone could follow, and makes a score of mistakes. I've captured all the great guns but Turlock's. I've arrested twenty-three farmers baiting their fields, and I doubt if there are three night-lights operating in the entire area. But this damned Amos Turlock, he does everything, every night, and I cannot catch him.'

'The stories coming out of Patamoke, Hugo, are damaging your reputation,' the regional manager said. 'You want extra men?'

'That I could use.'

So two extra wardens were dispatched to Patamoke, dressed flashily like ordinary dudes out of Philadelphia, and they approached Amos with an interesting proposition that he act as their guide for some goose hunting.

'It's out of season!' he snapped.

'We know that. But in Chestertown they assured us—'

'In Chestertown they don't know a goose from a duck.' He dismissed them, then ran to the store to warn his cronies. 'Two new wardens in town.'

'How'd you know?'

'They walked like wardens.'

So he laid low, and after two weeks the strangers returned to Baltimore, assuring the head office that they had thrown the fear of God into Amos Turlock. That night with one mighty blow The Twombly slew sixty-nine geese, and Turlocks eight miles upriver feasted.

The explosion of the gun was clearly heard in several homes facing Devon Island. 'Sounded like maybe an airplane busting apart in the sky. We ran out, but it was all dark. Then we saw this light in Broad Creek and my husband got his field glasses, but by then the light had vanished.'

When Hugo returned to his office in the basement of the courthouse he studied his maps and concluded that Amos had shifted his operations away from his own creek and out into the spacious reaches of the major rivers. 'Well,' he muttered to himself, 'that means he's got to travel some distance with his cannon. That gives me a chance.'

Early one morning he slipped downriver in his powerboat to inspect the setting in which he would lay his traps, but on the return trip he spotted something which disturbed him almost as much as the reemergence of The Twombly. On the sloping field leading down from the Turlock cabin hundreds upon hundreds of wild geese were feeding, their fat bodies moving in the wintry sun, their long black necks extending now and then to watch for any trespassers. They had apparently been there a long time and gave every indication that they intended remaining; Amos had certainly baited this field with shelled corn.

Cautiously Hugo beached his boat, climbed ashore and moved toward the field. As he did, the goose sentinels spotted him, satisfied themselves that he had no gun, and quietly herded the flock to another part of the field. They maintained a distance of about forty yards; if the warden stopped, they stopped. If he moved, they gave him space, and this allowed him to inspect the field.

Not a grain of corn was visible; the geese were eating grass. If the field had been baited, it had been done with such exquisite timing that by two hours after sunrise every grain was gone.

But just as he was about to leave in disgust, Hugo decided to move to where the geese now clustered, eating furiously, and as before, when he made a motion toward that area, the stately geese retreated just far enough to keep out of range. Again he found no corn, but he did find something almost as interesting: on a bramble in the middle of the area in which the geese had been feeding most avidly he spied two heavy threads used in weaving canvas.

'Damn!' he growled, his thick neck jammed down into his collar as he stared at the signals: At midnight he rolls a hunk of canvas out here, covers it with corn, attracts a thousand geese, then rolls it up before dawn and leaves no sign. Except these. Carefully he lifted the strands of cloth from the bramble and decided that each night for the next week he would inspect these fields for corn spread out on canvas, which left no telltale marks.

'Hey!' a harsh voice called as he placed the evidence in his wallet.

It was Amos Turlock, with two of his sons. 'What you doin' on my land?'

'Inspecting the clever way you bait your geese.'

'No baitin' here.'

'The canvas, Amos. That's an old trick and it'll put you in jail.'

'What jury . . .' He allowed the sentence to hang, and Pflaum backed off. What jury, indeed, would indict a Choptank Turlock on the evidence of two strands of canvas webbing? In fact, what jury of men from the store would indict him if he marched along the wharf with The Twombly and sixty dead geese? Half the jury would expect to get one of the geese when they delivered their verdict: 'Innocent.'

Hugo realized that since Turlock had been alerted, it would make no sense to try to catch him at the baiting game, but if the wily old fellow could be tricked into using his gun, then Pflaum could confiscate it on sight without the necessity of a jury trial. So he allowed Amos to think that his focus was on canvas baiting; indeed, he came out two nights in a row to let the Turlocks know he was watching their fields, but what he was really watching was the cabin for some sign of where the family kept their long gun. He detected not a single clue.

On St. Patrick's Day, after drinking several beers with young Martin Caveny, and nodding to Hugo Pflaum as he prepared to drive his eighteen-year-old Ford back to the cabin, Amos Turlock took a long nap, from about seven in the evening till midnight. He then rose, looked for his son Ben and his Chesapeake Rusty and led them into the marsh. The dog had long since learned to make no sound as they approached the area where the gun was hidden, but when he saw it safely loaded into the skiff that Amos used, he leaped joyously for the sturdier skiff in which Ben would ride to pick up the dead geese. He was so intent on helping his masters on another hunt that he failed to notice the faint scent of a stranger, a man in a rowboat lurking off the end of the marsh.

The three craft moved silently out into the Choptank, drifted westward for some time, the two skiffs oblivious of the trailing boat, which kept at a safe distance. At about three in the morning, when the crescent moon had set, the skiffs rounded a point not far from Peace Cliff, where the Quaker boatbuilders lived, and there on the bosom of the river waited a raft of some thousand geese chatting quietly in the night. The skiffs separated, the one with the dog lagging behind to wait for the explosion.

The major skiff, the one with the gun, eased its way toward the raft, making more noise than old Jake Turlock would ever have made. Now the justification for this carelessness became evident: Amos Turlock flicked a switch and a huge headlight set in a triangular, mirrored box flashed on, illuminating the masses of geese and freezing them into position. The light came at them so suddenly and with such reflected force that they were powerless to move. Aiming the skiff right at the heart of the motionless geese, Amos took a deep breath, kept his body away from the recoil of his monstrous weapon and pulled the trigger.

Only when the two skiffs were loaded with the seventy-seven geese and Rusty was back aboard, did Hugo Pflaum reveal himself. He had them now. At night. Long gun. Light. Seventy-seven birds. Out of season. He could put these two in jail for life, but when he moved in to make the arrest he found his cousin Amos Turlock pointing a large shotgun right at his chest.

'Hugo, you ain't seen nothin'. You wasn't out here tonight.'

With considerable courage Pflaum pointed his flashlight at the gun he was so determined to capture. There it was, resting insolently in its chock, its heavy butt jammed into the burlap bag of pine needles, the ancient slayer of waterfowl, the perpetrator of outrage. But protecting it was his brother-in-law Amos with a shotgun and a snarling Chesapeake.

'Hugo, be a bright fellow and head home. Me and Ben won't humiliate you. We won't say a word at the store.'

Pflaum took a deep breath and rested on his oars, keeping his flashlight focused on The Twombly. He was almost close enough to touch it. Damnation, he did want to drag that gun into custody, to be photographed with it, to terminate its scandalous life on this river. But he heard Amos Turlock's soft, persuasive voice: 'Make believe you never seen it, Hugo. Go on home.'

With a regret that would burn for the rest of his life, the game warden dimmed his flashlight, cranked his outboard and started the noisy trip back to Patamoke.

The quality of any human life is determined by the differential experiences which impinge upon it. For example, J. Ruthven Turlock's entire history past the age of twenty-seven had been altered by the accident of that seaplane ride; without it he might never have appreciated the grandeur of his native land and gone wandering after something better; with it he found a key to life.

The same seaplane exerted a contrasting influence upon Pusey Paxmore. Without his subsequent involvement as a lobbyist in Washington he would probably have been satisfied with a moderate success in providing legal services to the Steeds and those wealthy newcomers lured into the area by J. Ruthven; with it he became a fixture in the nation's capital, valued for his Harvard excellence, respected for his Quaker character.

In 1958, when Hiram Cater reached the age of nineteen, Will Nesbitt, leader of the band and always rich in propositions that might help his friends, brought an interesting one to the senior Caters: 'Sign at the post office claims a Marine Corps recruiter gonna be visitin' Salisbury armory Wednesday and Thursday.'

'What that mean to us?' Jeb asked.

'It mean your son Hiram ought to haul hisse'f to the armory and enlist.'

'What chance he got?' Jeb asked in some bitterness. His son had graduated from high school in Salisbury and for two years had been bouncing from one pitiful job to another. 'On'y steady job a colored boy can get, mowin' lawns, May till September.'

'My friend,' the musician said expansively, 'I was told for sure, they gonna take a handful of coloreds. Sposin' they can find some well qualified.'

'Ain't none better qualified than Hiram,' Julia said, and she was right. Her son was quiet, well behaved, quick to learn and trustworthy. She often told her neighbors, 'If'n that boy be lucky enough to be born white, ain't no job in town he couldn't get. And maybe a scholarship to college as well.' But when she pondered what the black college south of Salisbury had done to Luta Mae, she doubted the value of an education. 'We send her there a fine, respectable girl. She come out a radical, livin' somewheres up in New York, rantin' about burnin' down the world.'

Jeb ignored his wife's lamentation and asked Nesbitt, 'You feel sure Hiram can make it?' He wanted neither his son nor his family to undergo unnecessary mortification, and if what he feared was true—that the invitation to blacks was merely a display of tolerance to be ignored if any promising young Negroes actually applied—he felt that his son should avoid such humiliation. 'Jeb,' Nesbitt said, 'all I know, when we played for a dance in Salisbury, I met a young fellow that they accepted.'

'You mean a colored?'

'Black as you and Hiram.'

'College boy, maybe?'

'Salisbury High School.'

'I doan' believe it.'

'Damn, man! I asked.'

This was Monday, and for two nights the Caters, none of them, could sleep. For Hiram to be a marine, with a uniform and self-respect and regular pay, was really too much to hope for, but the prospect was so dazzling that they had to hope. On Wednesday morning, when Will Nesbitt arrived to drive the boy to the recruiting office, Julia counseled him, 'Be relaxed. Before you go in the door, say to yourself, "I got all A's and B's and I was star catcher." ' Jeb wanted to give advice, but he was too excited to make sense, and when Nesbitt asked if he wanted to ride along, he cried, 'Good Lord, no!' And all that day he stayed in the shack, not actually praying, but thinking strong thoughts.

At seven that night he sensed what the result had been, for three blocks from the shack Will Nesbitt started blowing the horn and shouting, and when the three Caters ran to the fence, there sat Hiram looking straight ahead and trying not to betray his feelings. He was a marine.

'God A'mighty!' Nesbitt told the Neck, 'they said they didn't get anybody as good as Hiram once a month. I showed them the papers, told about his record and his respectable family—I didn't mention Luta Mae —and they grabbed him like he was made of silver.'

In the days that followed, girls came by the shack to admire the hero, and when the time came for him to report in Baltimore for his uniform and passage money to boot camp, his departure became a matter for wide celebration. Reverend Douglass, older now and no longer hoping for an important pulpit in Wilmington, came to the house to advise Hiram against certain pitfalls. 'You will be representing a whole community. You are more than just Hiram Cater. If you do well, other young boys may be able to follow in your steps.'

He did well. He had been in camp only a few days when the sergeants saw that in Hiram they had one of those powerful young men who were pliable not through weakness but because they relied upon a strong family inheritance. The young recruit absorbed abuse in drill, dismissed it, and reported next morning prepared for more. His long training in accepting orders from whites without surrendering his inner convictions made him an ideal marine, and no one in his class did better than he.

At a speed which bewildered him, he was sent to Korea, not with a formed unit but to a replacement depot, a repple depple he explained to his parents, and from there he was sent to a front-line company guarding a sector along the thirty-eighth parallel. There he discovered something that changed his life: in Asia the Koreans, he found, were much like blacks in America. They were second-class citizens, scorned by both the Chinese and the Japanese, who dismissed them as uncivilized, lacking in education and inclined toward criminal behavior. But the Koreans, as he saw them in action, bided their time, accepted insults, and in the end proved more reliable and clever than either the Chinese or the Japanese.

'Least, they survived for two thousand years,' he told black marines with whom he bunked. 'Damn, they look like us!'

He was right. The big, square Korean face, especially if it lacked a pronounced Mongolian fold about the eye, resembled the light-faced black. In personality, too, the similarity was pronounced, for the Korean was patient, long-suffering, explosive at the final outrage and terribly durable.

Corporal Cater went to the camp library to seek books about the Koreans and was entranced by the resolute manner in which this small nation, crushed between two behemoths, had survived. He then sought everything the librarian could find that gave an adverse report on the Koreans, and as he read Japanese critics, or Chinese, he often chuckled:

> The Korean is lazy, shiftless and untrustworthy, with a strong tendency toward criminal behavior. When young he does not do well in school, when old he cannot be relied upon to do steady work. He seems incapable of self-government and is probably happiest when some strong power occupies his land. If carefully and constantly supervised he can sometimes work productively, but it is best to restrict him to simple tasks.

And yet the Koreans had established and defended a tough little nation, beating back both the Chinese and the Japanese. In some centuries they had triumphed, in others they had gone under temporarily, but always they had struggled, and the condemnations cited against them were proofs of their durability.

'Damn, I like these people!' Hiram told his fellow marines, and he began catching rides into the village of Dok Sing, not to guzzle beer like the Army dogfaces, but to meet the people, and when a girl tending counter in a dry-goods store indicated that she might consider going to a base movie with him, he could hardly wait to walk her home for her parents' consent.

'This house is better than mine,' he told the girl, and she translated for her parents. It was the beginning of a fine relationship; Nak Lee was much like Luta Mae, a proud girl who could speak of politics and religion and the threat from the north, and as they talked she consistently wanted to bring her parents into the conversation, translating rapidly in two languages and sometimes explaining a subtle point in Japanese.

The older Lees made it clear that their daughter would never be permitted to marry an American, and certainly not a Japanese, and when this point was discussed, Hiram discovered the intense pride these Koreans had in their race, their willingness to combat the world in defense of their land, and he thought how different they were from his own parents, who had devised only a strategy for mean survival.

Nak Lee was obviously fond of her black American; she saw that he was superior to the other black marines and to most of the white ones, too, and she enjoyed accompanying him to dances. When she kissed him the first time, he heard his parents' thundering admonitions that he must never touch a white woman, or he might be slain, and damned if that very night a white Army man didn't try to make trouble over the fact that a nigger was dating a Korean girl!

It might have come to blows had not Nak Lee said quietly, 'Hey, Joe. Why you don't go back to the Ku Klux Klan?' The Army man was so startled that he stepped back, and the incident ended.

'You were very brave,' Hiram said as they kissed goodnight.

'We learned that against the Japanese,' Nak Lee said. And apparently she had been doing some reading too, for suddenly she took Hiram by two hands, and standing face to face, asked him, 'When you niggers start to fight back?'

On the morning of June 11, 1958, young Christopher Pflaum, aged thirteen, was about to encounter a major experience, although he could scarcely have suspected it. He was on his way to school with a certain lightness of heart, for this was the final day of the year, with a lazy vacation looming ahead, and Miss Paxmore—there seemed always to be a Miss Paxmore teaching somewhere—had promised her children that on closing day they would have no formal studies, which meant that lively boys like Chris approached the classroom in a state of euphoria.

'Hey, Chris!' one of the Steed boys whispered. 'Can you get your father's boat?' He thought he could, so three other boys wanted to know if they could join him on the Choptank for some rockfish. He thought this might be possible.

'If I may interrupt your consultations,' Miss Paxmore said, 'what I have in mind for today is a special treat. All year I've been assigning famous poems to be memorized. "Not a drum was heard, not a funeral note . . ." Some of you did well on that. "The breaking waves dashed high on a stern and rockbound coast." How did you like that?'

The boys around Chris groaned, and Miss Paxmore said, 'Years from now you'll recall those poems and be glad you learned them.' The boys groaned again, and Miss Paxmore smiled. 'Today you lazy fellows can sit back and let the words I read flow over you, because you don't have to memorize them. But if you listen carefully you may hear something important, for this poem is about the Choptank.'

Chris Pflaum sat up. 'It's not called the Choptank, of course,' Miss Paxmore continued. He slumped back in his seat. 'Nevertheless, it's about our river, believe me.' And she spoke with such conviction that even the boys who had been watching flies settle on the windowpanes looked casually at her. She held a smallish book in her hands and leaned forward over the desk as she opened it. 'Sidney Lanier was writing for us, but he named his poem after a part of the country he knew best— south of here, the marshes of Glynn.'

Chris Pflaum came to attention again; he loved marshes but had never imagined that anyone could write poetry about them. And then as Miss Paxmore read a poem she had loved ever since her days as a student at Earlham, he began to hear phrases which cut like sharp knives into the very heart of his existence:

'O braided dusks of the oak and woven shades of the vine,
While the riotous noon-day sun of June-day long did shine.
Ye held me fast in your heart and I held you fast in mine . . .

'. . . how ample, the marsh and the sea and the sky!
A league and a league of marsh-grass, waist-high, broad in the blade,
Green, and all of a height . . .

'Ye marshes, how candid and simple and nothing-withholding and free
Ye publish yourselves to the sky and offer yourselves to the sea!'

The poet, through Miss Paxmore's dignified reading, was uttering thoughts and conjuring images which young Chris himself had often attempted to verbalize. From his father he had caught something of the mystery of the river and how, at arbitrary intervals, it and the shore became one in marshland that was neither river nor shore. With his Turlock cousins he had penetrated the deepest of the Choptank marshes and had begun, in his simple way, to codify their secrets. He knew where the deer slept and the turtle hid. He saw duck feathers betraying where the birds nested and the minute tracks of the vole as it picked its way through insect-laden grasses.

But now he was hearing his deepest feelings externalized by a poet who had written about a marsh Chris would never see; yet it was his marsh and the man was uttering the most secret thoughts of the boy. It was remarkable, and he bent forward with great intensity to catch other fleeting images. He was certainly not prepared for what happened, a veritable explosion of ideas so potent that they tore his little world apart, allowing him to catch a glimpse of a total universe so splendid that a lifetime of study would never exhaust it. He was shown nothing less than the soul of the marsh, and he would never again be the same; from this moment on he would share the world's intricate grandeur:

'As the marsh-hen secretly builds on the watery sod,
Behold I will build me a nest in the greatness of God:
I will fly in the greatness of God as the marsh-hen flies
In the freedom that fills all the space 'twixt the marsh and the skies:
By so many roots as the marsh-grass sends in the sod
I will heartily lay me ahold on the greatness of God:
Oh, like to the greatness of God is the greatness within
The range of the marshes, the liberal marshes of Glynn.'

The theological implications of the poem escaped him, and he did not dedicate his life to either God or His greatness; he had before him the hell-raising years of education, and his initiation into the rough waterman's world of Amos Turlock and Martin Caveny, but he did learn, once and for all time, that a marsh, or a creek, or a river, or a great bay was a handiwork of nature so magnificent that it must not ever be abused.

Miss Paxmore's reading produced one aftermath that would have startled her. When Chris Pflaum reached home that afternoon he found his father cleaning his gun prior to patrolling the back streams to keep hunters obedient to the law, and he surprised the bull-necked warden by going to him impulsively and stammering, 'Pop . . . I like what you do.'

'What do I do?'

Chris would never be able to blurt out, 'Protect the marshes as God created them.' Instead he mumbled, 'Huntin' . . . and all that.'

In 1959 the Steed family was still divided into two branches: the Devon Steeds, who lived on what was left of the island; and the Refuge Steeds, who occupied a much more congenial series of estates on the mainland. The original strain had grown quite thin; after Judge Hathaway and Congressman Jefferson the Devon connection was quite barren, and after Lyman Steed the Refuge line was almost as bad. The family as a unit still owned the stores; their land was leaping ahead in value; and if the tomato canneries had proved a dead loss, the cornfields were replacing them. The prosaic condition of the once-dominant family could be summarized in one significant fact: no one was angry at them.

The Paxmores were equally quiescent. Woolman, their last luminary, was dead, and a set of routine artisans managed the boatyard from which daring schooners and swift skipjacks had once come; it was building motorboats from plans drafted in Boston. The moral fights in which these Quakers had once participated were settled now, and there was little vitality in their religion as they espoused it.

The Turlocks survived. During the Depression entire families of the clan had suffered years with no employment, but they had eaten off the land, and as long as the men could lay their hands on shotgun shells, theirs or other people's, they got their share of deer and ducks. The old hatreds against authority, and the Steeds, and the blacks had pretty well subsided, and through constant intermarriage with the Cavenys, even their bias against Catholics had diminished. A dozen Turlock men would experience three dozen different jobs over a four-year period, and some even became police officers, for brief periods. Their family genius was to produce beautiful girls now and then who married into new families like the Pflaums and a constant supply of thin, mean men who could fire a rifle with precision.

The Cavenys had become the backbone of the river towns. They were the policemen, the sheriffs, the minor court attendants, the wholesale merchants just below the Steeds, and the schoolteachers. With Father Patrick Caveny as titular head of the family, they prospered, both spiritually and socially. Real Catholics like the Steeds found this clarinet-playing priest a little hard to take, but he was so energetic and so easily wounded by defections from the faith that they supported him generously. It could be said with some accuracy that the Catholic church was one institution in Patamoke that was prospering, and as it grew, its acceptance among Protestants increased, mainly because of Father Patrick's common sense.

But it was the Caters who had made the most significant advances. Indeed, they were now almost a part of the establishment, for Julia Cater held three good jobs and sang in the choir of the A.M.E. Church; Jeb Cater had four jobs; and their daughter Helen had three. True, their second daughter, Luta Mae, was again in jail, in Boston, because of the street demonstration she had led of Harvard, Wellesley and M.I.T. undergraduates, but son Hiram had been made a sergeant in the Marines and was sending money home. The house carried no mortgage. The family had a Ford ten years old, which Jeb kept in good condition, and from time to time Will Nesbitt dropped by to play the banjo and ask how Hiram was doing.

Only one ominous note disturbed the Choptank as the 1950s drew to a close. Three families had produced children of extraordinary merit, and each of the three young people had felt it necessary to build their lives outside the local area; in the old days they would have made their contributions at home.

Owen Steed was the last of the Devon line, and he had really never lived on the Choptank after the age of twelve. He had then gone off to Lawrenceville, an excellent school that prepared for Princeton, and after graduation from college had gone west to become an officer in an oil company in Tulsa. Had he returned to Devon he might have led the family enterprises into bold new fields, for he proved to be a good administrator, rising to the presidency of his company in Oklahoma.

Pusey Paxmore had come home at first, but involvement with the family seaplane diverted him to Washington, and once he experienced the enticements of that city, he either could not or would not leave it. He had now held four different jobs of some distinction, and at each swearing-in the *Bugle* had run photographs showing him with either President Eisenhower or Vice-President Nixon. He always looked the same: the Harvard Law School graduate in the vested three-button dark suit. Had he stayed at home he might have taken the place of Woolman Paxmore as spiritual leader of the Quakers, for he had a strong theological predisposition, but now his life was cast in another mold and any possibility of preacherhood within the Quaker religion was lost. President Eisenhower once called him 'The conscience of the White House,' and he certainly looked the part, the cautious lawyer who hewed to the straight line which Paxmores had always followed when they laid down their keels.

Luta Mae Cater had also fled Patamoke to find her destiny, but her departure was somewhat more frenetic than that of her older male neighbors. One summer's day she had marched into the Blue and Gold Ice Cream Parlor, ordered her loganberry cone, and sat boldly down at one of the iron tables to consume it.

'You can't eat there, miss,' the proprietor said.

'And why not?' she demanded belligerently.

'Because we don't serve colored in here.'

'You just sold me this cone.'

'That's for buyin', not for eatin'.'

'Starting today, it's for eating, too.'

'Miss, I will give you fifteen seconds to leave that table.'

Insolently, a large dark girl with rumpled hair who sought a fight, she remained at the table, slowly nibbling away at the cone. The owner kept an eye on his watch, and when the fifteen seconds was up, grabbed a whistle that he had bought for just such a day and blew it madly. It made a hellish sound, and within two minutes a pair of white officers, who had also been briefed on how to handle such criminal acts, came quietly into the ice cream parlor and said respectfully, 'Miss, you can't eat in here.'

'Why not?' she snarled, as if daring them to strike her.

'Custom,' one of the officers said.

'Not no more,' Luta Mae said in her street language. 'We ain't gonna give this honky our money and eat outside.'

'Miss,' the officer said with quiet persuasion, 'we don't want trouble, do we?'

'I sure as hell do,' Luta Mae said, and this was used against her at the trial, where it was proved that she had resisted arrest, used harsh language against the proprietor and tried to bite the hand of the second officer who tugged at her arms.

'Aren't you ashamed?' the judge asked, 'to bring dishonor upon your fine father and mother, who this town respects as if they were white?'

Remorse was not what Luta Mae proposed to show that day, and when she abused the judge he dropped his attempts to conciliate her and gave her thirty days in jail. The charge was interesting: 'She did willfully disturb the peace.' The judge pointed out that over the centuries certain accepted rules had been fashioned for the happy relations between whites and blacks; these were understood, and when they were observed, the two races existed side by side in harmony.

'Ain't gonna be no more harmony,' she said as the two sheriffs dragged her away.

Jeb and Julia had been profoundly disturbed by this incident. As members of the black establishment, respected even more by whites than by fellow blacks, they deplored their daughter's behavior. They knew what a rash thing she had done, the terrible risk she had taken that her actions might stir the sleeping Turlocks and Cavenys. Her deportment before the judge merited a jail sentence, and they felt no resentment against the court.

But they were terribly against the judge's stated doctrine that ancient rules devised to keep blacks in a subservient position had somehow acquired moral sanction, forever preventing their amendment. They knew that Luta Mae was right, that it was no longer acceptable to give a white merchant money and accept fifth-class treatment in return. They knew that the old rules of Patamoke were about to be broken. But they did not want to get involved.

'Bes' thing can happen,' Jeb told Julia when they reached their cabin, 'Luta Mae serve her term and get out of here.'

'I think so too,' Julia said. 'Change gonna come, but doan' let it be on her shoulders.'

'Hiram, if'n he was here, he would of calmed her. Ain't nothin' I can do with that girl. She headstrong.'

'She's right,' Julia said stubbornly. 'But change ain't gonna happen as fast as she want. Like you say, Jeb. Bes' she get out of here.'

Luta Mae felt the same way, and when the judge released her ten days early, she kissed her mother goodbye and headed north.

When this disturbing element left town, Patamoke settled down to one of the finest years it had known since the peaceful 1890s. People had jobs. The oyster catch was far above average and crabs were plentiful, even the valuable soft shells. In October the geese returned in such numbers that any farmer who had waterfront to rent made a small fortune, and Christmas along the Choptank was like the gentlest week in September. In this way the somnolent 1950s drew to a close.

There was one man in Patamoke who rejoiced when the new bridge spanning the Chesapeake was opened. J. Ruthven Turlock had long realized that hordes of people from Baltimore and Washington, not to mention Pittsburgh and Harrisburg, would flood into the Eastern Shore on sightseeing expeditions—'And we will have the opportunity of catching our share of them as clients.' He enlarged his offices and ordered seven more signs for the highway.

But his genius manifested itself in a gesture which astounded the people of Patamoke. He conceived this plan one morning when visiting the Turlock cabin to pick up two geese his brother Amos had shot the night before; for such gifts Ruthven took care of Amos' paper work and whatever legal matters might arise. He was about to depart with the plucked geese hidden behind the spare tire in his trunk, when he chanced to see in a very favorable light the three hundred and ninety-eight acres of the Turlock marsh, and it occurred to him that he could convert this useless land to a constructive purpose that would make Amos and the family rich.

'What we could do,' he explained as he stood with the Turlocks at the door of their cabin, 'is palisade that whole front edge, throw some earth along the flanks and then announce that we're running a sanitary fill.'

'What would that accomplish?' Amos asked.

'Why, dump trucks from miles around would wheel in here, fill in the land behind the palisades, and before you could say Bob's-your-uncle, we have us four hundred acres of choice waterfront land. We call it Patamoke Gardens and we sell it to rich dudes from Chicago and Cleveland for so much money you'd never believe it.'

'Could we do that?' Amos asked.

'We sure could.'

'But won't it cost money to palisade?'

'I know ways of getting money,' Ruthven said, so a deal was arranged whereby he would fill in the marsh, subdivide it into two hundred lots and create the attractive new town of Patamoke Gardens. The beauty of his plan was that it was totally practical. He knew where to borrow the money at four percent; he knew builders eager to participate in such a gamble; and he knew scores of well-to-do doctors and dentists who were interested in either waterfront homes or real estate investments. Before the town planners of Patamoke could say Bob's-your-uncle, the plan was unleashed, the marsh was palisaded, and the waving grass in which deer and ducks and red-winged blackbirds had luxuriated was buried in waste so that new homesites could be formed.

When the project was well under way, Christopher Pflaum, home from college, heard of its magnitude and drove out to the cabin to see what his Uncle Ruthven was up to, and when he stood on the edge of what had once been a marsh, dodging the trucks as they hauled in garbage to fill the area, he was aghast. Looking about for someone in charge, he was frustrated; everything was happening automatically. The pile driver was finishing the last of the palisading as if it had a brain of its own: haul the weight up, center it, drop it on the head of the wooden piling, and close off another yard of marshland. The dump trucks rumbled in, backed up, raised their beds and automatically strewed the junk into hollows that would soon be filled. Other trucks hauled in earth to cover the garbage, and slowly, inevitably Patamoke Gardens took shape.

There was no one on the site to whom he could protest; the marsh was being erased and building lots were being created, with no one at the controls, no one evaluating the tremendous decisions being reached. He jumped into his car and sped back to town, where he banged his way into the Turlock Agency, demanding of his uncle, 'What in hell are you doing?'

'Creating taxable wealth,' Ruthven said, and with the aid of handsomely lettered maps and diagrams he showed young Chris how this operation was going to provide two hundred choice lots, which would house two hundred families, who for the rest of this century would spend on an average of eight thousand dollars . . . 'You add it up, Chris. This is the best thing ever happened to the Choptank. A new settlement. Strictly class.'

Only forty docks would be allowed to jut into the water, but there would be a marina partway up the creek at which everyone else could house a boat comfortably. 'School? We use the one already in existence . . . out beyond the cabin.' He put his arm about his nephew's shoulder. 'The beauty part is that all this land back here, it goes up in value too. That piece your father owns. Treble in one year. Your father wants to sell it for a handsome profit, I know a man from Baltimore . . .'

Numbed, Chris returned to the marsh; only a shred now remained, but he knelt in it and allowed the grass to twist through his fingers. This marsh had nurtured his Turlock ancestors for three centuries, and some of them would have died rather than surrender a blade of it. They had fought and endured and protected, and now in a flash it was gone.

'Jesus!' he cried, slapping at the grass, and based on his studies at the university, began to calculate what the building of this resort for outside doctors and dentists was costing in natural terms: Fifty deer lived here most of the year. Five hundred muskrats. Sixty otter. Thirty mink. Two hundred nutria. Two thousand geese, four thousand ducks, and so many birds you couldn't count them. Sixty turtles, five thousand crabs, a universe of oysters, rockfish and blue and enough perch to sink a skipjack.

He became quite angry, and splashed his feet in the water that oozed up from the dying marsh: And the worst loss is the stuff we can't see. The water grasses that feed the crabs, the tiny crabs that feed the fish, and the plankton that feeds us all. Gone! The whole shebang gone.

'Hey, you! Watch out!' A truckdriver, hauling in refuse from an abandoned tomato cannery—lengths of twisted steel and rusted corrugations—backed his vehicle close to where Chris had been standing, and mechanically the huge truck bed rose in the air, dropped its rear gate and threw its burden over the strangling grasses.

'Oh Jesus!' young Pflaum cried as the truck drove off to make way for another. 'What a bad bargain we made here.'

Despite Hiram Cater's enlightening experiences in the Marine Corps, his father might have succeeded in keeping the boy socially passive except for a genetic accident over which there was no control: Hiram was one of those fortunate men who take women seriously. This meant that his life gained an added dimension; unlike the moon, he did not move through the dark night with one hemisphere forever blank, for his association with women brightened it.

In Korea little Nak Lee had begun the dangerous task of educating him; she made him aware that he was as good as any white man, yet afraid of his own capacities. Now two women from his own family, one long in the grave, one in jail, rose to complete his education.

The first step occurred in 1965, when Reverend Jackson, the new minister, was cleaning out the attic of the A.M.E. manse, a pitiful shack, and came upon a document compiled by a black clergyman who had served Patamoke in the 1870s. This young cleric, overwhelmed by subterranean yarns about runaway slaves of previous generations, had listened with jaw agape as old men instructed him, and realized that he was hearing the epic of a race, which if not written down, might be forever lost. His interest began to center on an old black woman named Eden Cater, then in her seventies; her name surfaced in various accounts related by the old men, and in time he went to see her.

She lived in the Cater shack at the end of Frog's Neck, and she spoke with such fierce comprehension of what slavery meant and of how her Underground Railway had functioned that he knew immediately that it was her story he wanted to record. 'Miss Eden, you must write down your memories, so's your grandchildren can understand.' And when she replied, as he supposed she would, 'I cain't write,' he said, 'You tell me and I'll write.'

Two notebooks were filled with Eden's reconstructions of her expeditions into Pennsylvania, and on facing pages, wherever possible, the minister had written: 'This part of Eden's story was confirmed by John Goldsborough, now living in New Bedford, Massachusetts.' More than two thirds of her claimed exploits were thus substantiated, occasionally by white witnesses. Of course, when the escapes had been participated in by Bartley and Rachel Paxmore, those Quakers were available for detailed confirmation.

What evolved was a concise account, written in seminary English, of the dangers encountered by slaves who sought freedom and of the courage exhibited both by those who fled and those who helped them. When the narrative was completed, over a period of several months, the black minister gave it a title, *Fourteen Journeys North,* and noted Eden Cater as author. And it was this manuscript which Reverend Jackson handed to Eden's great-great-grandson one morning in July 1965.

Hiram carried the notebooks to a bench at the tip of the Neck, where he started to leaf through them casually, much less interested in the narrative than Reverend Jackson had supposed he might be. Hiram had often heard of Eden Cater, but all he actually knew about her was that she had intended buying her husband's freedom but had ended up providing money to buy a skipjack. She was remote, a slave ancestor whose history had been lost.

Therefore, the young marine could find no bond of association tying this shadowy woman to himself or to his problems. The situation today was so different that Eden could not possibly comprehend it, even if she were living through it, and for her to have any relevance was improbable. But toward the front of the second notebook he chanced upon two paragraphs that recalled his own boot training:

> We were now within six miles of Pennsylvania, and the freedom for which these fifteen had longed while working in the swamps of South Carolina was at hand and they began to grow careless, believing themselves to be shed of slavery. But I warned them that the greatest danger always arose in the last dash for the border, because there the enemy would concentrate his greatest power. To reach our goal we must use guile and not force, and I coached them how to do this.

> But as we were picking our way toward that land where others would be waiting to help us, two slave-catchers left the road and came through the fields, suspecting that we might have taken that route, and when it seemed that they must discover us, three strong men behind me vowed, 'If they find us, we got to kill them,' and I knew that no persuasion of mine would stay them. So I had our people lie flat in the grass, and the slave-catchers passed us by, and after a proper wait I gave the signal and we all ran for the border, but I could not restrain them from shouting as they ran.

Hiram kept a forefinger in the old booklet to mind his place, and as he stared out across the Choptank it became not merely the brown river he had always known but a dividing line between the Deep South, where slavery had flourished, and the modified slaveholding area from which escape had been possible, and the role played by Eden and her husband became clear: They were a lighthouse in the night. That lousy little cabin. If slaves could reach there, they were on their way.

He returned to the book, and in spite of the fact that this was a hot morning, with a strong sun blazing out of a cloudless sky, he kept reading, dipping into the manuscript at casual places, and generated a rage that would never be quenched. These were flesh-and-blood slaves risking their lives for freedom, and at one point he slammed the frail pages shut: Don't never tell me again that blacks submitted like tamed animals. These bastards fought every inch of the way.

Because of his desire to comprehend the relationship between whites and blacks, he was most interested in her assessments of the white men and women with whom she worked:

> The three whites from Patamoke on whom we could rely were Quakers, but each operated in a different way. Comly Starbuck frightened me, for he would venture anything. His sister, Rachel Starbuck Paxmore, had a warmth that touched every human being with whom she worked and a quiet courage which sometimes startled me. Bartley Paxmore, her husband, was like an oak tree, so reliable that we built our lives around him.
>
> But the white man I remember in my prayers and hope to see again in heaven was a modest farmer who lived near Bohemia. His name was Adam Ford, and since he was not a Quaker, he was under no compulsion to help us. He had no funds, no horses to spare and little surplus food. He offered only himself, but he offered all, for he was a widower and his children were gone. No matter when we crept up to his farm, or in what condition, he was ready to help, regardless of risk. I have watched him by candlelight as he washed the wounds of our children or carried water for old men. Twice the authorities in Wilmington threw him into jail for helping runaway slaves and once the sheriff took away what few belongings he had as a fine for aiding us, but he persevered. May God look kindly upon the soul of Adam Ford.

And just as Hiram was beginning to tire of this praise of white participants, Eden added the paragraph he sought:

> But on six of the fourteen escapes no white men or women helped. It was black freedmen like Cudjo Cater who took the risk. It was strong-minded slaves like Nundo who bore the heaviest burden. Even when we did travel with the noble Quakers we followed two different roads. If they were caught, they were fined or placed in jail

for a few months. If we were caught, we were hauled back to slavery, or hanged.

When Hiram finished reading this narrative he found himself with an understanding of the Choptank that would never dim: his ancestors had been slaves along this river and had endured tragedies he had not imagined. Eden Cater, especially, had combated the system, placing her life in jeopardy fourteen times, and in his veins ran her daring blood.

When he returned the booklets to Reverend Jackson he said, 'This ought to be in print. For everyone to read.'

'That's why I gave you the books. To get your opinion.'

'What could we do?'

'There's a history professor at Johns Hopkins. Says he thinks he could get a subvention . . .'

'What's that?'

'One of the big foundations would give him money . . . Hiram, many people in this country are eager to see the true stories of slavery unfold.'

'This should be one of the first.'

'I'm glad you feel so. Reinforces what I thought.'

So Hiram and Reverend Jackson drove to Baltimore to meet with the professor, a white man who said enthusiastically, 'I've approached the people in New York and I'm sure we can get the funds. What I have in mind is to publish Eden Cater's account, with full historical notes, tying her time and experience in with that of Frederick Douglass, who lived in the same area at about the same time.'

Hiram drew back. The black experience of his ancestors would be used to further the career of a white professor who looked at Eden's record not as a life-and-blood account of slavery but merely as a means of publishing a book. He was about to ask for return of the booklets when the professor said, 'I'm particularly desirous that the book be edited by some black scholar. After all, Mr. Cater, it is a black odyssey and I think we have in our department just the man you would want.'

A Professor Simmons was sent for, and as soon as Hiram saw his exaggerated Afro hairdo, he was satisfied. He was further assured when he learned that the young man was an activist, with a strong undergraduate degree from Howard University and a doctorate from Yale. Since he had grown up in one of the heavily black counties on Maryland's western shore, he could imagine the slave structure in which Eden and Cudjo Cater had lived.

The three blacks and the white senior professor had an exciting lunch, at the end of which the white professor called New York to advise the foundation secretary that all matters were settled: 'Professor Simmons will do the editing along the lines we suggested, and I'm pleased to assure you that Eden Cater's principal male descendant will cooperate.' A long pause followed, after which the professor slammed down the receiver and cried, 'We've got the money!'

Eden Cater's story would be told, *Fourteen Journeys North;* the long silence about black life on the Choptank would be broken; and henceforth it would be impossible for anyone to write a history of the river without taking into account the contribution of blacks.

But Eden Cater's triumph was fragmentary, so far as her descendant Hiram was concerned, for as he left the luncheon he felt himself torn away from the celebration, and he excused himself. 'Reverend Jackson, I won't be going back to Patamoke with you.'

'Why not?'

'I think I'd better go north . . . for a few days.'

'To Scanderville?' This was a daring question to which the minister did not expect a reply, but he did want to discuss the matter with Hiram if that was indeed his destination. The ex-marine said nothing, turned on his heel in military fashion and strode off.

But Reverend Jackson would not permit him to leave in this fashion. Running after him, he overtook him at the edge of the campus and said forcefully, 'Hiram, you're in an emotional state. The things Eden Cater reported. Don't rush off to Scanderville to find a lot of stupid conclusions.'

'Who's stupid?' Hiram demanded.

'Your sister Luta Mae. She is on the wrong—'

'Don't you say nothin' about Luta Mae.' The polished speech he had acquired in the Marine Corps vanished and he reverted to the double negatives of his childhood.

'Luta Mae is engaged in a private war that will end only in disaster. Don't become involved.'

'Luta Mae, she the same as Eden.'

'For the love of God, no! Don't be deceived by glib similarities.'

But Hiram stormed off, went to the edge of Baltimore and started hitchhiking north into Pennsylvania, and as one white traveler after another passed him by, the angrier he became. Finally a black salesman carried him as far as Harrisburg, where a white trucker, a brusque, heavy man in his fifties, invited him into his cab for the run to Scanderville.

'You got a friend in the prison there?' the trucker asked.

'My sister.'

'What she do?'

'Civil disobedience. Federal case.'

'Placards and stuff like that?'

'Yep.'

'I don't blame her. If I was black . . . How long she in for?'

'Two years. That is, two-to-six. She told the judge to go to hell. In open court.'

'She one of those with the big hairdos?'

'She goes the whole route.'

When they pulled up at a diner in Sunbury, the trucker said, 'Have supper on me,' and as they ate he said, 'You know, son, people like your sister . . . them god-awful hairdos . . . those loud-mouths . . . They make enemies they don't need to make.'

'Why did you pick me up?' Hiram asked. 'And offer to buy me supper? You got a guilty feeling, maybe?'

'I got a son in Vietnam. I got great respect for soldiers and I could see you'd been in service . . . the way you stood.'

'I was in the Marines.'

'I ain't surprised. And you came out willing to fight the world?'

'More or less.'

'Son, don't fight with me. Tell your sister to lay off, too. It ain't necessary, and it won't win you a goddamned thing. Play it cool and you'll get everything you want.'

The driver went out of his way to drop Hiram at the prison, then flashed the thumbs-up sign and cried, 'I'm on your side, buddy.' And for a moment, as Hiram watched the truck move down the highway, its red and green lights flashing in the darkness like beacons hailing a different day, he entertained a brief hope that the rough-and-ready accommodation proposed by the trucker might be possible, and he spent that night fashioning procedures which might lead to a juster America.

But in the morning, in the waiting room of the jail, he was electrified when he saw Luta Mae come slouching toward him, her sturdy body covered by prison garb, her insolence intended to infuriate her guards, and he surrendered any thought of conciliation. It was social warfare, and Luta Mae was in the vanguard.

She was implacable. From behind the wire mesh that separated them she growled, 'Hiram, it got to be all burned down.'

'You mean the old ways?'

'I mean everything. It all got to change.' She now preferred to use black speech, and she exaggerated its illiteracies.

He started to tell her about Eden Cater's book on slaves escaping north, but she interrupted. 'Why you tellin' me 'bout her?'

And he explained that he saw his sister as the inheritor of the fearless old slave woman. Luta Mae, with her flaming hairdo and her uncompromising manner was the Eden Cater of this generation, and as he watched the guard lead her back to her cell, her challenge echoed in his mind: 'It got to be all burned down.'

It was in the spring of 1965 that J. Ruthven Turlock had his final inspiration about the development at Patamoke Gardens. 'I was driving home from selling a lot to a doctor from Binghamton when it occurred to me that most of our buyers were elderly people . . . coming here to retire . . . comfort-filled final years. It was then I hit on the perfect name. Sunset Acres.'

Of course, when Ruthven implemented his design, the old Turlock cabin occupied by his brother Amos had to go—'It's an eyesore. You've made a bundle off the marsh, Amos, you can afford something decent.'

So this ancient center of incest, illiteracy, prejudice, lawbreaking, coon hunting and good living was burned off so that in its place could be wheeled a spanking new mobile home built in Sheboygan. Ruthven paid for the white picket fence that quarantined it from the more pretentious homes of Sunset Acres, but it was Amos who purchased the cement statuary that adorned the small lawn: Santa Claus with eight reindeer nicely disposed across the grass, a purple flamingo, a polar bear on his hind legs and a brown doe with two adorable gray fawns. When Chris Pflaum saw his uncle's concrete menagerie he had to compare it with the real birds and animals that once graced the site.

Chris was having his problems with the former marsh. At the community college he attended, his instructor in American Lit 107 was a bright young man from Brandeis University with a commitment to the best in American writing, and the concise manner in which he disposed of old myths that cluttered his pupils' minds impressed young Chris:

> 'There is no reason why any sane person should read Margaret Mitchell's *Gone With the Wind*. It is one of the worst books ever written by an American, shoddy, meretricious and without any redeeming social value.'

When Chris read the book, some years back, he had suspected that Miss Mitchell's depiction of blacks had been criminally unfair and her portrayal of whites sentimental and highly prejudiced; he was pleased to find his instructor confirming his youthful doubts. But in his next lecture the young man from Brandeis tore into all American poetry prior to Lowell —Robert Lowell, he explained—and his special scorn was reserved for Sidney Lanier:

> 'A sentimental, soggy, drum-beat rimester, representing all that was wrong with southern thinking of his time, he has become the litmus paper of American literature. If you like Lanier, you cannot like poetry.'

This time Chris was disposed to argue. 'I thought *The Marshes of Glynn* was rather good . . . the part about the bigness and the sky.'

The young scholar looked compassionately at Pflaum and said, 'I'm delighted to know that you studied Lanier. Not many bother, these days.

How old were you at the time? Yes, about thirteen? Well, Pflaum, "Little Miss Muffit" is ideally suited to the four-year-old and Felicia Hemans is just right for the nine-year-old. Sidney Lanier is the poet par excellence for the thirteen-year-old mentality, but now we're all growing up, aren't we?'

He then proceeded to demonstrate everything that was wrong with this long, painfully obvious old poem: its forced rhymes, its rhythms broken to order, the preposterous variations in line length and, above all, its religious sentimentality.

'Aren't some of the images good?' Chris asked.

'Yes, but they're terribly belabored. Take the marsh-hen building her nest in the greatness of God. Line after line, repetition after repetition. A real poet would have disposed of that goddamn bird in four well-chosen words.'

Chris would not let go. 'But wasn't Lanier way ahead of his time in dealing with an ecological problem?'

Now the young man from Brandeis could show some excitement. 'Indeed he was, Pflaum, and that's the only merit of this old war-horse. If Lanier had said simply, "Marshes are worth preserving," he'd have said it all.'

But it wouldn't have had the ring, Chris thought, and I'd never have remembered it the way I remember the real lines.

When he returned home he went to the public library and found that during the past four months thirty-one residents of a town that didn't read much had checked out *Gone With the Wind* and when he asked about it, the librarian said, 'We have to keep three copies. Local women like to make believe their ancestors lived on plantations.' And when he went out to Sunset Acres and stood where the Turlock marsh had once stretched, he could hear the rhythms of Lanier's poem, those words which had given his life its direction.

As he stood there, pondering these contradictions, he watched a pair of cardinals coming back to what had once been their home. They flew erratically, here and there, looking for vanished succulence, and Chris thought: Taking them both into consideration, they must be the handsomest pair of birds in any country. Sometimes I think the male is the most beautiful, that flaming scarlet. But at other times it's the female. Those muted colors, so perfect in combination. I wish I could put in words what I feel about those birds.

And then a tardy wedge of geese flew north, and as he watched their flight his world fell into place: I want to go to Canada . . . to see where the geese breed. If you live on the Choptank, you know only half the bird . . . October to March. Who wants to know half of anything? To the disappearing birds he cried aloud, 'I'm going to see the other half in Canada.'

The idea of this trip had been germinating for some time, in fact, ever since his English instructor had said in class, 'You may not know it, but your region has produced one masterpiece of American writing. Thomas Applegarth's *To the Ice Age*. I suggest you read it if you want to comprehend where you live.' The little book had been a revelation, and from it Chris deduced that every burgeoning mind ought to make some pilgrimage. His would be to the nesting place of the geese.

But his eyes kept coming back to the vanished marsh and his mind to the vanished poem, and he thought: So he takes away Lanier and gives me Applegarth. Fair trade, perhaps.

After Hiram Cater left his sister in Scanderville Prison he spent two years drifting through the major cities of the North, seeking viable solutions to the problem of blacks in American life, and in sharp discussions with young men and women from Harvard and the University of Chicago he could offer specific illustrations which summarized black experience much better than their philosophizing:

> 'My mom and pop have worked fourteen hours a day, six days a week for more than fifty years. Everybody says, "Best people in the community, white or black." And what's their reward? A two-room shack built in the 1840s which became a three-room shack in the 1940s. From birth to death they've been short-changed.'

In certain parts of the North conditions were slightly more promising, but in general, throughout the nation he found the cruel inequities of Frog's Neck endlessly repeated, and he spent most of his hours trying to construct some sensible explanation of why the United States seemed so determined to ignore and waste the human potential of so large a portion of its population. His experience in the Marines convinced him that he was positively as capable as any white man of comparable background, yet society was determined to prevent him from demonstrating his skills.

He listened attentively to the endless debates regarding basic policy— 'Shall we become spineless subservients like Booker T. Washington or leaders of the street rebellion?'—and he did not know where he stood. He could not erase his memory of the truckdriver who had argued that gradualism was the sensible path, nor could he forget Luta Mae's strident call to battle. The debates were fruitless, but he did make up his mind on one major aspect of black life, and for a public discussion on Boston television he prepared these notes:

> Moynihan and others argue that black family life is destructive because so many children are reared with no father in the home. When I first heard this argument I thought it stupid, because I grew

up in a family that had a father, and a very good one. But of the fourteen men who I meet with, eleven had no father at home. Bad consequences, etc.

However, when you look at the great nations of the world, the majors divide into two groups. In Germany, Japan, England and the United States the father is boss. Who ever heard on television of a 'kindly German mother.' To hell with Mom, Pop's boss and everyone knows it. These four societies are therefore harsh, militaristic, violent, cruel.

But look at Italy with its 'Mama mia!' and Jews with their 'typical Jewish mother, have a little more chicken soup.' It is not by accident that these societies are gentle, intellectual, artistic, philosophical and anti-militaristic. Mother influence predominates, the kids are humane, society also.

I can't speak about Africa, but if the blacks of America ever establish a nation, it will be like Italy or a Jewish country. Music, dance, theater, art, high philosophy will predominate. The blacks I know who grew up with mothers only are gentle people. Sometimes they have to riot in frustration, but they are basically good people, dedicated to music and dance and theater.

Close with a few words about my own mother. Spirit of the home. We had a father, but he might as well have been absent. Tell about oystering. Long absences. It was the mother . . . And no goddamned apologies about the black family.

His remarks were applauded, and after the cameras were turned off, the white moderator said, 'Cater, you ought to get a college degree,' but when he looked casually into the possibilities, he feared the barriers were too complex, and in frustration he came near to adopting Luta Mae's battle cry: 'It got to be all burned down.' But he had been so well received by white radicals, and by the white television people, that he clung to the hope that society could be modified peacefully. With such perplexities he returned to Patamoke, a handsome, well-disciplined marine, twenty-eight years old and as capable as any young man the Choptank had recently produced.

His parents were delighted to see him, for Luta Mae was once more in jail, this time in Michigan, and they had feared that he might fall into her revolutionary ways. 'How tall he is!' Julia cried, trying to restrain herself from embracing the self-conscious young man who stood before her, his dark skin glistening.

'You pretty much a real marine,' his father said admiringly. 'I bet you seen some adventures in Korea.' But Hiram thought: How old they've become. Seventy-one, their lives worn out with working, and he judged that he had been correct in citing them as epitomes of the black problem.

His two years of wandering had not improved his chances for employment, for he had mastered no trade nor improved his education in any specific field. His learning had consisted of long night sessions arguing radical philosophies, and weekend retreats with Black Muslims, listening to their theories. He had returned home prepared for only one job: to agitate the minds of blacks younger than he and to direct them in the analysis of their community.

In spite of his desire not to upset his parents, who had made their adjustment to the system, he could not refrain from raising questions which disturbed them. 'Pop, let's suppose you been slothful all your life. You'd be about as well off as you are now. Do you realize how you've been cheated? Not even a television after all these years of labor. Mom, I never knew a day you didn't work.'

When old Will Nesbitt, the bandleader, came by one night to warn them that their son was attracting unfavorable attention from the town authorities, Jeb and Julia nodded. 'From us, too.'

They asked Will what he thought they should do about Hiram, and the old man said, 'Get him out of here. Trouble is, he's growed faster than Patamoke.'

For a brief spell they dreamed that he would land a good position with Steed's or the boatyard, but neither of those establishments needed a philosophical young black who might have been contaminated by his unexplained residence in the North, and townspeople supposed that he would hang around for a while, then drift away, as his criminal sister Luta Mae had done.

But in the summer of 1967 Hiram Cater was still on hand, spending a few pennies now and then—no one could say where he acquired them —and arguing at night with other young blacks, also without jobs and no prospects of any. Patamoke now had two black policemen, and their reports on Hiram were ominous: 'Born troublemaker, probably in cahoots with his sister in Michigan.'

That guess was wrong. All the Caters were dismayed that Luta Mae had now been in jail four times, and despite the fact that they knew her to be one of the finest girls in Maryland, they were ashamed that she had so fallen athwart the law. It had not yet occurred to them that it was the system that was wrong, not Luta Mae, and in their familial shame they tried to forget her, even though her flaming words continued to reverberate in Hiram's consciousness.

He might have negotiated this long summer without incident had not Reverend Jackson and Will Nesbitt arranged for an August rally to replenish church funds. Signs went up in the Steed store, rope was found for cordoning off Frog's Neck, and Julia Cater began preparing for the crab cakes she would offer to the church she loved so well. It was these crab cakes that got Hiram into trouble.

On a hot, mosquito-ridden Friday afternoon he watched as his mother and Helen slaved in their kitchen so that the congregation could earn a few pennies, and the procedure seemed so ridiculous and unrewarding that he asked, 'Why you breakin' your backs for such foolishness?'

Old Julia, bent and heavy, explained, 'Because we likes to do God's will.'

'You sell a dollar crab cake to them whites for twenty-five cents, you call that God's will?'

'Many a time, Hiram, you wouldn't be alive 'ceptin' the church gave us the money.'

'I will not accept life on those terms,' he stormed. He would not remain in the kitchen, watching his mother pay such painful allegiance to outworn customs, and he stomped out of the house. Next night, when the rally flourished, with rich white families tiptoeing past the kiosks on their yearly condescension to the blacks of Frog's Neck, his fury rose.

At nine o'clock Will Nesbitt's creaking band uttered some ruffles, whereupon an avuncular Father Caveny produced his clarinet for a rendering of 'Bye Bye, Blackbird.' When the audience cheered not the music but the fact of the priest's having put in an appearance, Hiram muttered to a lanky young black named LeRoy, 'How contemptible!' When LeRoy asked what he meant, Hiram said harshly, 'The condescending priest. Selling our good crab cakes for pennies. And most of all, them lousy whites slidin' down here to see how us niggers live.'

Very softly LeRoy whispered, 'Why don't we run the whole lot out of here?'

The words were like the detonation of a dynamite cap, for without comprehending how he reached the top of a table, Hiram Cater found himself facing the crowd and shouting, 'Get out of here! The party's over!'

His mother, proudly selling her cakes, was one of the first to see her frenzied son, and from his behavior during the past week she knew that he was in some kind of torment. 'Hiram, no!' she cried, but her voice was weak and late.

The two black policemen had been watching Hiram and now moved briskly to drag him from the table, lest he wreck the rally, but before they could grab his knees, LeRoy and three other solemn-faced blacks blocked their way, and LeRoy shouted, 'Kick 'em out, Hiram!'

'We don't want your charity,' Hiram bellowed. 'Take your pennies and go home.'

Up to this point his commotion had produced no effect upon the rally, for only a few patrons had heard him, but one of the policemen, irritated and perhaps frightened by the actions of LeRoy and his gang, began blowing a whistle, and this penetrating, mournful sound produced confusion. Whites began running away from what they feared might be a riot, and as they left the scene Hiram remained atop his table, staring at the ancient, weather-worn school which the white authorities had utilized for half a century as an instrument of oppression and denied opportunity. All Hiram could see was the bleakness of this place, the abbreviated sessions, the ill-prepared teachers and the crowded classrooms in which he had rarely owned a book.

With no plan, no preparatory thought, he cried, 'That damned school!' And before the words died, LeRoy took them up, shouting belligerently, 'We ought to burn the damned thing down!' Hiram, hearing Luta Mae's words, and knowing from his own patient analysis that they would accomplish little, started to warn LeRoy, but the gang was already on its way to the schoolhouse, where fires were lit and wild cries uttered as dry timbers flamed upward in the night.

The effect was intoxicating, and many blacks rushed blazing fagots to ignite other buildings, but when LeRoy himself and two others took their brands to the old A.M.E. Church, Hiram leaped from the table and tried to intercept them. 'Not that! We need it!'

Someone knocked him down, and when he got to his feet he saw his mother and father among those trying vainly to quench the fire. They were powerless and had to withdraw, watching from a distance as the church they loved trembled in the scarlet glow and came crashing down.

Houses were burned, and the corner store which extended credit, and the police substation from which the two black cops operated.

In the hot night the flames roared upward, producing a wild excitement, and irresponsible children began throwing timbers already flaming, and it appeared that all of Frog's Neck might be destroyed.

The town fire engines clanged down the narrow road to the Neck, but rioting blacks held them off, so after two frustrated attempts the firemen departed with the threat: 'We'll let the whole damned place go up.' One of the first of the abandoned spots to go was the Cater cabin, built by the freedman Cudjo long before the Civil War. In one mighty gasp the raging fire consumed what might have become a black shrine, for it contained the room in which Eden Cater had recited *Fourteen Journeys North.* Hiram, watching the cabin disappear, muttered, 'Eden would understand.'

The burning of Patamoke was a curious affair, for the enraged blacks did not throw the torch at a single building occupied by whites; their fury was directed only at the intolerable conditions in which they were forced to live. They burned not because they wanted revenge on whites, but because they hoped that if they destroyed Frog's Neck, something better might take its place. In pursuit of this dream they were willing to sacrifice their homes, their church and their historical heritage.

But as the fire blazed, catching a pine tree now and then and flaming far into the sky, the wind carried sparks westward, and by ugly chance they fell upon the roof of the Paxmore Boatyard, lodging on the shingles and setting the desiccated old structure ablaze.

Now the firemen were free to operate their engines, for no blacks opposed them, but the boatyard was so inflammable, its boards soaked with a century of turpentine and oil, that salvage was impossible. Vast walls of flame swept along the sheds to burst through ceilings and explode roof coverings. Fire companies roared in from a dozen towns, the awed firemen whispering as they raced down country lanes, 'The niggers is burnin' Patamoke.'

Along the Choptank it had always been feared, since the arrival of slaves in 1667, that some night the niggers would rise in rebellion and set fire to white establishments, and now it was happening. Threescore of Turlocks congregated in terror to watch the burning, and untold Cavenys, and when the visiting fire companies were assembled, powerless to fight the blaze, grim Amos Turlock moved among them, issuing guns and one simple command: 'If the niggers try to burn the rest of the town, kill 'em.'

One citizen viewed the fire with numb horror. He was Pusey Paxmore, home from his duties in Washington, and he watched white-faced as his family business crumbled in smoking ash. From time to time he would try to speak, but his mouth would hang open, his eyes riveted on the desolation.

'Mr. Paxmore!' the mayor cried, running up in a night robe. 'We've got to get the National Guard here. You know the right people in Annapolis.' Pusey was unable to respond, and the mayor pleaded, 'Get the troops here, Pusey, or this whole town is gonna go up.'

Paxmore mumbled a name and the mayor ran off, but now a team of firemen grabbed Pusey by the arms and dragged him backward, just in time to escape the last wall as it came crashing with new bursts of flame.

All Pusey Paxmore could see was the death of an enterprise dating back to the 1660s. This boatyard had survived Indian raids, pirate attacks, the force of the British fleet in 1813, even assaults by Confederate freebooters in 1864. Now it was lost, a whole way of life destroyed in one foul night by neighbors. He could not believe that the blacks of Patamoke, to whom his family had been so considerate, could have done this evil thing.

'They did it,' a policeman assured him.

'Who?'

'Our black policemen say it was started by Hiram Cater. Brother to that girl in jail.'

'Arrest him!' And he raged off to telephone friends in the F.B.I.

Hiram was not arrested that night, for as soon as he saw that the fire had spread to the boatyard, he knew he must quit this town, and as he ran to find some car he might commandeer for a swift run to Pennsylvania, he was joined by LeRoy, who gloated over what he had accomplished.

'You shouldn't have burned the church,' Hiram said as they ran.

'It all had to go,' LeRoy replied.

'But not the boatyard. You can burn black homes and get away with it. But when you burn a white man's business . . .'

LeRoy spotted a Buick he thought he could start, and as he finagled with the wires, Hiram looked back on the blaze. 'We are in big trouble,' he said.

Voyage Thirteen: 1976

ON JULY 2, 1976, AMANDA PAXMORE SET FORTH TO recover a husband who had brought contumely upon himself, his wife, his children and his nation, and that was a burden which might have destroyed a lesser person.

She was equal to the task and never once did she try to avoid it. When news reached Peace Cliff that she could send someone, she controlled herself, coughed slightly and told the government prosecutor who had left Washington for the small town in Pennsylvania, 'Three tomorrow afternoon? I'll be there.'

'You're coming? Yourself?' he had asked.

'Who better?'

Replacing the phone, she had gone to the yard to call Martin Caveny, brother to the priest, who was mowing the grass so the place would look presentable on the Fourth. 'I'll need the motorboat. Seven tomorrow morning. To Annapolis.'

'Can I bring Amos Turlock?' Caveny asked quickly, for he liked to share excursions with his crony. 'Since we'll be crossing the bay, that is.'

'Isn't he rather old for such work?'

'With Amos it's never work.'

'Bring him along. He'll be a companion while you wait for me in Annapolis.'

When she reached the door to the house she looked back to see Caveny scurrying to put away the lawn mower, then rushing off to find his playfellow. She judged accurately that on the morrow, while she drove the rented car to Scanderville, they would be getting merrily drunk in some Annapolis bar.

'God bless them,' she said in a sudden wave of compassion. 'The sots.'

As soon as Caveny disposed of the mower, he jumped into his shattered Chevy and roared into Sunset Acres, yelling at each filling station, 'You seen Amos?' No one knew where the vagrant was, but finally a black boy said, 'He down at the river, fishin'.' And when Caveny ran out to the edge of the river, there was Amos, propped against a tussock, his hat well over his face.

'Amos!' Caveny shouted. 'We're goin' to Annapolis.'

Turlock half rolled sideways, propped himself on his arm and said, 'Now that's good news. Who's takin' us?'

'We got Mrs. Paxmore's motor launch.'

Amos looked at his accustomed partner suspiciously. 'How come she let you have it?'

'Because she's goin' along.'

'What's she to do in Annapolis?'

'I wondered myself. She told me, "You two can wait at the dock. We'll sail back at six." You know what I think?'

Amos rose from his hassock and reeled in his line. 'What's cookin'?' he asked gravely.

'I calculate that while you and me is at the dock, she'll be hirin' a car and drivin' to Scanderville.'

'Ain't been nothin' on television.'

'I'll bet that's what it is.'

The two men climbed into the Chevy and hurried back to Sunset Acres, stopping at the trailer which Amos now occupied with a woman who had deserted her husband in Crisfield. 'Midge,' he bellowed, 'you hear anything on the TV about Scanderville?'

'I ain't heard nothin'.'

Almost admiringly, Amos told Caveny, 'And she watches the tube all day.'

'Even so, that's my bet,' the Irishman said. 'Let's have some beer.' When the cans were opened, the partners sat on the trailer porch gazing at the statuary that crowded the lawn, and whenever a neighbor came by, Amos would shout, 'You hear any news about Scanderville?' No one had.

'If that's her target,' Caveny said, 'ain't no woman in Maryland could handle it better.'

'You like her, don't you?' Turlock asked as he pitched his beer can into the ditch beyond the picket fence.

'She's strong.'

'Don't she yell at you a lot?' Amos hated to be yelled at by people who hired him. 'They yell at me once, I'm off,' he said.

'She has her ways, but you don't have to listen,' Caveny said. 'But I'll tell you this, Amos, whenever my kids or the missus gets sick, it's Mrs. Paxmore who takes over.'

'Seems to me,' Amos said after getting another can of beer, 'that if she'd taken care of her husband a little bit, instead of your kids, ever'thing would of been better.'

Caveny pondered this, twisting his beer can in his palms and blowing into the triangular opening. Finally he said, 'On that I got no opinion. In a hunnerd years I'll never understand what happened to Pusey Paxmore.'

Turlock took a long swig on his beer, then placed the can judiciously on the bench beside him. 'Only person who does understand is Richard Nixon, and he ain't tellin'.'

'You're goddamn right he ain't. Would you, livin' like a king out there in San Clementime?'

Amos swilled deep and allowed as how it probably would remain a mystery. 'At least to me.'

In the morning the two men had the motorboat waiting at Peace Cliff when Amanda Paxmore came down the long walk in a summer dress, carrying two heavy sweaters, which she asked the men to stow. Caveny, noticing that she had brought two, looked knowingly at Amos, as if to say, 'I win the bet.'

'Shove off,' she said, and the men pushed the boat away from the dock. When the motor caught, Martin Caveny called out, 'I'm headin' due west to clear the point, then straight to Annapolis.'

She nodded, and thought how perverse it was that this day promised to be one of the most serene the bay had known in years. There to the right lay Oxford dreaming sleepily on the Tred Avon. Four early cars of tourists were riding the little ferry across to Bellevue, with at least a dozen children gaping and yelling directions to their parents.

When the ferry passed out of sight Amanda looked to the south, where the fragments of Devon Island could still be seen. There were the chimneys and the eastern walls of Rosalind's Revenge, fighting to stay erect, as if the indomitable will of that great woman still fortified them.

What a sad sight, Amanda said to herself. Almost an omen for a day like this. A ruin . . . The word came uneasily to her lips, but she repeated it: A ruin . . .

Caveny seeing her lips move, asked, 'What's that?'

'I was looking at the old house,' she replied.

'You won't be lookin' long,' he said.

They reached Annapolis at nine-thirty and pulled into the dock of a private marina, where two young men waited with a rented car and papers for Mrs. Paxmore to sign. As soon as she had done so, they handed her the keys and sped off in a second car, which they had brought with them.

'What'd I tell you?' Caveny asked. Turlock shrugged his shoulders. 'No big deal. She rented a car.'

'I should be back about six,' she told the men.

Caveny almost had to bite his tongue to keep from asking if she was headed for Scanderville. He refrained, nodded politely and said, 'We'll watch things for you.'

Mrs. Paxmore had not expected him to say this, and the charming way he did, as if he were a loyal retainer, disarmed her. Her voice caught and she almost burst into tears. Ripping open her purse, she produced a ten-dollar bill and jammed it into Caveny's hand. 'Have yourself a good time. Get some crabs and beer.' She grasped Turlock's hands and said, 'Enjoy yourselves. Damnit, if we enjoyed ourselves more . . .' She hurried to the car, wiped her eyes and drove north.

She found Route 2, which took her to Route 695, the superhighway circumnavigating Baltimore. From it she exited onto Route 83, which carried her into Pennsylvania, and when she was well north of Harrisburg she turned west for the small town of Scanderville, where the federal penitentiary stood.

It was a new type of prison, minimum security it was called, and it possessed no towering stone ramparts or twists of barbed wire. The main building looked much like the office of a prosperous motel, built in semi-Colonial style with white pillars, and there were green lawns. But it was a prison, nevertheless, and to it had been sent many of the distinguished and well-educated men who had participated, one way or another, in the great scandal of Watergate. All had originally been sentenced to three- or four-year terms, but because some had cooperated with government prosecutors, these had been diminished to six or eight months.

Pusey Paxmore, a minor figure in this attempt to subvert the government of the United States, was not one whose term had been shortened. He had refused to reveal the names of others, had refused to plead ignorance of what he had done, or to beg for mercy in any way. At both the Watergate hearings and his trial he had been a stubborn defender of the President.

Before the television cameras of the nation he had said, 'Unless you were in Washington in the summer of 1970 you cannot comprehend the dangers this nation faced.'

'Were they sufficient,' a young lawyer had asked, 'to warrant your breaking the basic laws of our land?'

'They were,' he had replied.

'You are testifying under oath that you knew what you were doing, and that you judged the temper of the times to justify those illegal, immoral and criminal acts?'

'You have asked two questions.'

'Then, please,' the young government lawyer said with extreme politeness, 'answer them one at a time.'

'I intend to. First you ask if I judged that the situation at the time was crucial. With rioting in the streets. With publications openly announcing the destruction of our system. With planned destruction of public institutions. Yes, the situation could have been fatal to our form of society and particularly to our form of government. Second, you ask if what I did was done with the knowledge that it was illegal and immoral . . . and some other word which I forget.'

'Criminal,' the young lawyer said helpfully.

'Yes, criminal. None of my acts were criminal.'

'Your assessment of your behavior is in sharp contrast to the way every well-intentioned man and woman in this nation sees it. They judge your acts to have been illegal, immoral and criminal.'

'That's the judgment now,' Paxmore had replied stubbornly.

'You suggest there will be a later judgment.'

'I certainly do.'

His refusal to bend had earned him a sentence of two years at Scanderville, and he had served it. Now he was being set free.

Some miles east of Scanderville, Amanda was flagged down by a mounted policeman, and before she could protest that she had been doing less than fifty—which was true, for she was apprehensive about entering the penitentiary town—he asked politely, 'Are you Mrs. Paxmore?'

'I am.'

'I've been sent to intercept you. There's press in town, and they might ask questions.'

'I would expect them to,' she said.

'Don't you want me to slip you in through the back?'

'Sooner or later I'll have to come out through the front.'

He felt rebuffed. 'That's your headache,' he said.

'It is indeed,' she said, throwing the car into gear and driving into the town.

As soon as her presence became known, a group of seven newsmen, some with cameras, descended upon her, pressing her to answer a veritable barrage of unassociated questions. In her neat summer dress, with her hair pulled back Quaker-fashion, she stood beside her car in the hot sun and responded briefly to every interrogation:

    . . .'I have no feelings about President Nixon. I voted for George McGovern.'

    . . .'My husband was honored when asked to serve at the White House. He respected the President, and from what I hear, did an excellent job.'

    . . .'No, my husband did not ask that I drive up here today. Nobody asked me. Whom better could I have sent?'

    . . .'Remorse? Every day of my life I experience remorse over something. Have you ever taken a faithful old dog to a veterinary to be put to death? That remorse lives with you for the rest of your life.'

. . .'Our nation has survived a score of disasters. If we elect Jimmy Carter this autumn, we'll have survived Watergate.'

. . .'I was never easy in the Nixon White House, but my husband worked for him and considered him one of the ablest administrators he knew.'

. . .'Naturally, I have often thought of President Nixon sitting free in San Clemente while my husband sat in this prison, and only because he did what Nixon directed. But long ago I learned that life does not dispense justice, and I do not expect it. I have absolutely no hard feelings, as you phrase it, against President Nixon.'

. . .'Yes, my husband is a Quaker, as I am. Yes, Nixon was a Quaker and so was Herbert Hoover. I think the lesson to be drawn is, "Don't send Quakers to Washington." '

. . .'I left home at seven this morning, crossed the Chesapeake Bay in a small boat, and will cross back tonight.'

. . .'Of course we intend to live where we live now. The Paxmores have lived there since 1664. The house was burned once and fired on three other times. Today is merely one more incident in a long, long history.'

. . .'You ask if I am as hard as my replies might indicate. No sensible answer can be given to that question. We live in an age when it is not customary for people to speak their minds. In an age when it is not usual for a man like my husband to refuse to crybaby and plead for mercy for wrongs he did not do. You call it hardness. You ought to get out in the countryside and find out how many hard people there are in this nation. People who give straightforward answers to devious questions. Now I must go in and fetch my husband.'

The motorcycle policeman who had wanted to smuggle Mrs. Paxmore in through the back door said to an associate, 'That cookie don't need no help from us,' and his friend replied, 'I wish Mabel could of heard her. She's always warnin' me not to speak up when Lieutenant Grabert is throwin' his weight around.' But the first man said, 'She'd be a tough one to be married to,' and the second said, 'I wish Mabel was a little tougher. She's like livin' with a panful of cookie dough.'

Refuge

WHENEVER A NEWCOMER SETTLED ON THE EAST-
ern Shore he was obligated to declare himself on three vital points: Are
you Protestant or Catholic? Republican or Democrat? And do you favor
Chesapeake retrievers or Labradors? The way in which he answered
these questions determined his status in society.

He was free to answer as he wished, for Catholics and Democrats were
tolerated, and a stranger could build a satisfactory life regardless of his
classification. Of course, the political question did present some difficulties, because definitions on the Eastern Shore were somewhat arbitrary
and many a newcomer found himself confused when arguing with a local
Democrat whose social opinions were far to the right of Genghis Khan.

For example, Jefferson Steed, who had served two terms in Congress,
was universally known as 'that radical,' and questions about the Russian
revolution or the spread of communism were customarily referred to him
on the grounds that 'Jeff would know about that, him bein' so radical.'

Steed was against labor unions, against women's rights, in favor of
child labor, strongly opposed to integration of schools, against ministers
who brought politics into their sermons, vigorously opposed to the federal income tax and distrustful of any foreign alliance. He believed in a
powerful army, the supremacy of the white race and the omnipotence of
J. Edgar Hoover. Yet the community classified him as radical because
in November 1944 he had voted for a fourth term for Franklin Roosevelt
on the theory that 'you shouldn't change horses in midstream.'

One confused emigrant from the biting winters of Minnesota said, 'I
love the Eastern Shore, its seventeenth-century architecture, eighteenth-
century charm and nineteenth-century congressman.' Steed considered
this a compliment.

As to the dogs, those city northerners who had always dreamed of a snarling beast protecting their rural demesnes, or who wanted to pursue honest hunting, chose the Chesapeake, while those who believed that a dog should be part of the family, a kind of perpetual five-year-old, forever young, forever loving, preferred the Labrador. Each encountered many neighbors of similar persuasion.

When the newcomer arrived he found an immediate friend in Washburn Turlock, head of the prestigious firm of realtors who seemed to control most of the good locations. Once inside the Turlock office, with its Colonial furniture, North Carolina hooked rugs and subdued light illuminating transparencies of beautiful waterfront homes, the prospective buyer was lost. His surrender became complete when Washburn himself appeared, all blandishment in his three-button vested suit, to nail down the deal.

'Prices are high,' he confessed, 'but where in America can you find comparable values? Our water, our sunsets? Crabs and oysters in your own stretch of river?' Land which Steeds and Turlocks had bought for ten cents an acre now sold at $55,600 for a two-acre plot, and such land had no road, no well, no house, no convenience, no virtue of any kind except one: it faced water.

In August 1976, when the real estate season was about to begin, Washburn Turlock convened his sales staff for a pep talk which would set the future course for his agency. As his fourteen salesmen finished their coffee, he startled them by distributing without comment his new advertising brochure. It was a shocker. From the cover leered a cartoon resemblance of Washburn dressed as a buccaneer, with sword, tricorn hat and pistol. Bold lettering proclaimed TURLOCK THE PIRATE, A MAN YOU CAN TRUST.

When the gasps had subsided, he informed his people that from here on, this was to be the sales pitch of the Turlock agency, and he directed their attention to the first inside page, which contained a brief, well-written account of selected Turlocks who had occupied Eastern Shore lands for more than three centuries:

> The original Timothy was no Virginia Cavalier. He appears to have been a petty thief who served his first years as a bonded servant, euphemism for slave.

This was too much for one of the women, who asked in a rather gray voice, 'Washburn, do you think that wise?'

'Read on,' he told her.

Much was made of General Washington's lauding of Teach Turlock, who was presented as a pirate devoting his energies to patriotic causes, while Matt Turlock was offered as a hero of the War of 1812. It was an exciting brochure, modern, witty, directed precisely to the kinds of clients the Turlock agency hoped to attract. But it was what Washburn said in his sales pitch that morning that set the pattern for the new era:

'The old days are gone, and if any of you are indissolubly linked to them, get out now. For new days are upon us. What are the characteristics, you ask. Well, I'll tell you.

'This agency no longer has any interest in properties selling for less than a hundred and fifty thousand dollars. Now, I know that some cheap clients will find their way to us. Can't escape them. But you can take a client only once to a ninety-thousand property. If he wants it, all right. If he doesn't make up his mind on that trip, drop him. Let someone else make that sale. We're not interested.

'The reason I say this is simple. Who buys the cheap property, the place at ninety thousand? Some young couple. They keep it for forty years, and what good does that do us? One commission and that's the end. But who buys the real property? The one for half a million? Some retired geezer in his late sixties. Lives in it five years and finds it too big to handle. Turns it back to us to sell. My father told me, "You get yourself four good properties at half a million each, you'll find one of them coming back on the market every year. You just keep selling those four year after year, you got yourself a good living."

'We are after the client who thinks of a quarter of a million as nothing . . . chicken feed. We are going to wine him and dine him and three years later sell him a new place for half a million. What we're really after is the million-dollar sale. On our lists right now we have eleven properties at more than a million each. Get out and sell them.

'The secret of such salesmanship is to think like a millionaire. What would you like? Who would you like to do business with? That's the reason for this new brochure . . . this new attack. Four billboards go up this week with the pirate theme. Why? Because a rich man is himself a pirate. That's why he's rich. He'll want to do business with me. He'll see me as a kindred spirit. You watch, this campaign will prove a gold mine.

'But the second part is also important. Turlock, a man you can trust. We emphasize that in everything we do. A client hands us a deposit, then changes his mind. We are happier to refund his money than we were to take it. He'll remember and come back. A young couple comes in here with forty thousand dollars. You bring them to me, and I'll explain that right now we don't happen to have anything in that price range. I give them coffee. I take them by the arm and lead them across the street to Gibbons, who does handle cheapies. I give them a brochure and ask them to let me know what they find. And later, when they have two hundred thousand to spend, they'll come back to us.

'When you get hold of a real client, provide what he expects—the history, the charm, the security, the gracious living. I was appalled when I found that Henry here had allowed that old shack on the Fortness place to be torn down. Henry! Didn't you realize you had a gold mine in that shack? Have the owner spend two thousand dollars propping it up, then tell the clients, "These were the slave quarters." Don't you know that every man who comes down here from up North wants to imagine himself as the master of a great plantation . . . cracking the whip . . . overseeing the cotton. A good slave quarters on a piece of land increases the price by fifty thou.'

His intuitions were correct, and Turlock the Pirate became not only the most prosperous agency on the shore, but also the most talked about. Its agents wore conservative suits, drove black cars, spoke in low voices about Rembrandt Peale's having lived in this house, or Francis Asbury's having stayed in that one during his famous revival. The firm concentrated upon those houses located on the best rivers, and Washburn instructed his agents:

'When clients ask you what the best locations are—how the various rivers rank socially, that is—you must tell them the story of the American military expert who went to Berlin to find out about the relative ranks in the German forces. An aide to the Kaiser explained, "First there's God. No, first there's God and the Kaiser. Then the cavalry officer. Then the cavalry officer's horse. Then absolutely nothing for a long, long way. And then the infantry officer."

'On the Eastern Shore there's the Tred Avon and its tributaries, Peachblossom and Trippe. Then there's nothing for a long, long way. Then there's Broad Creek but certainly not Harris. Then again there's nothing for a long way. Then we have the Miles and the Wye and the north bank of the Choptank. After that, there's absolutely nothing.

'If someone should ask about land south of the Choptank, you're to say, "It's rather attractive . . . if you like mosquitoes." But never take your car over that bridge. Turlock people are not seen on the other side.'

Washburn was in his office one September morning when what he judged to be an almost ideal client appeared. He was in his middle sixties, distinguished in appearance, had a gray mustache and was conservative in dress. He drove a Buick station wagon stylishly weatherbeaten, probably a '74. He moved as if he knew what he was about, and when his wife appeared, she wore expensive low shoes and soft tweeds. They both looked like hunters, but they had no dog.

'Hullo,' the visitor said deferentially to the girl at the reception desk. 'I'm Owen Steed.'

'Of the local Steeds?'

'Way back.'

Washburn came out of his office, smiled graciously at his receptionist and asked, 'Could I intrude, please?'

'This is Owen Steed,' she said.

'I thought I heard that name. I'm Washburn Turlock.'

'We've seen your signs. My wife said she thought . . .'

'I do a little genealogy,' Mrs. Steed said quietly. 'Weren't the Steeds and the Turlocks . . .'

'Intimately,' Turlock said. 'When my ancestors were pirates, yours were being ducked in the river for being witches. Unsavory lot, I'm afraid.'

'Ah, yes,' Mrs. Steed said. 'Rosalind's Revenge. Is it by chance still occupied . . .'

'A ruin,' Turlock replied, and without allowing the visitors to sit down, he suggested that he drive them to the wharf at Peace Cliff, where he was sure the Paxmores . . .

'Paxmore?' Mr. Steed asked.

'Yes, they're an old family. Quakers.'

'I'd rather not impose . . .'

'They wouldn't care, I'm sure.' He reached for the phone to see if he could utilize the Paxmore dock for a short trip to Devon Island, but Mr. Steed thrust his hand out so imperatively to prevent the call that Turlock dropped the idea. 'We'll go to a wharf closer in,' he suggested, and Mr. Steed quickly assented, 'That would be better.'

Washburn Turlock had discovered that in selling really large properties, there was no substitute for taking his clients to them by boat, and he maintained three or four powerboats at spots convenient for exploring the Tred Avon and what he termed 'the better rivers.' There was something about seeing the Eastern Shore from the water that was ravishing; it destroyed inhibitions and opened pocketbooks. In proposing to show the Steeds their ancestral home, he intended to assault their memories and soften them up for the real sale he intended making later, but since this subsequent property stood on water, he observed a fundamental rule of the Turlock agency: 'Never show an important property at low tide.

The client may be shocked at how shallow our water is.' So he stole a furtive glance at a special German wristwatch he wore; it showed not time but the condition of the tide—was it high or low? What he saw satisfied him; the tide was coming in. 'We're off to see one of the great mansions of the Eastern Shore,' he cried.

On the short trip across the Choptank he found that Owen Steed had gone to Princeton, like so many of his uncles, and from there had entered the oil business, in Tulsa, where he had risen to the rank of president of Western Oil. He had retired, apparently with what Washburn always referred to as a bundle, and was now seeking to renew his acquaintance with his past. He was a prime prospect for one of the million-dollar establishments.

'Did you grow up at Devon?' Turlock asked as the boat entered the creek.

'I was born there, but I grew up with the Refuge Steeds.'

No information could have excited Washburn more. He had on his list a plantation of two hundred acres at the Refuge that would excite any potential buyer, but would be irresistible to a returning Steed.

The visit to Rosalind's Revenge had precisely the effect Turlock sought. As the visitors landed at the crumbling wharf he said, 'From here the Steed ships sailed to England,' and as they climbed the disintegrating path he said, 'Some of these trees go back two hundred years.' At the mansion, its roof almost gone, he pointed out the two cannonballs lodged in the moldering wall and the great room in which Webster and Calhoun had dined. He was meticulous in his orchestration, allowing some grandeur to sink in but not enough to induce melancholy.

'Couldn't this be restored?' Mr. Steed asked.

'Of course,' Turlock said promptly. 'Except that the island's disintegrating.'

He showed them how the persistent northwest storms had eroded Devon to the point that many of the slave buildings had fallen into the bay, and the visitors were satisfied that any chance of salvaging the famous old mansion had vanished decades ago. Mrs. Steed started to utter regrets about the loss, but Turlock quickly diverted her to happier possibilities. 'While we have the boat,' he said in an offhand way, 'why don't we look at a little piece of land that's come on the market recently? One of the old Steed places. The Refuge.'

As they passed beneath Peace Cliff he observed Mr. Steed looking with some interest at the telescope house, then quickly looking away, but he attached no significance to the incident. Mrs. Steed, however, wanted to talk about the house, and Turlock told her that it represented the best seventeenth-century style. 'One of our architectural glories. That and the Patamoke meeting house.'

He was about to comment on the telescope construction, knowing that prospective clients enjoyed information about architecture, when he saw Mr. Steed staring back at the Paxmore house. Immediately he changed his tone, observing brightly, 'Now we're heading for Steed Creek.' He paused, tried to estimate the degree of interest these two had in a real purchase, then added, 'The creek invites you to look around . . . as a former resident.' Mrs. Steed smiled.

Then the boat slowed, and Turlock adeptly turned it so that his passengers could catch a glimpse of the peninsula on which the Choptank chieftain Pentaquod had built his refuge in 1605. A lawn of more than an acre swept down from a substantial house surrounded by oaks and loblollies; a solid wharf jutted out from the shore, inviting someone to tie his boat; small white buildings stood to one side; and all about the place reigned a quietness that calmed the spirit.

The silence was broken not by the chugging of the motor, which Turlock had prudently killed, but by a loud raucous cry from one of the streamlets that defined the peninsula. It was a kind of cry that Mrs. Steed had never heard before, and as she looked about in some consternation, she saw above her a gray-blue bird with a long projecting beak and very long trailing legs.

'Kraannk, kraannk!' it called. Then, seeing the boat, it veered away, to land a short distance up the creek.

'What is it?' she asked, and Turlock told her, 'Great blue heron. You'll have scores of them here.' It was a bold tactic, this speaking as if the client already owned the place, but sometimes it worked.

'We'll take it,' Mr. Steed said.

Washburn was not prepared for this and he started to say, 'But we haven't mentioned—'

Mr. Steed interrupted him, 'We'll take it.'

'But the price . . .'

'You can haggle with Mrs. Steed, and I warn you, she's damned good at haggling.'

Mrs. Steed said nothing. The peninsula was so magnificent, so infinitely better than she had imagined the Eastern Shore could be when contemplated from Oklahoma, that she felt no need to comment. Instead she leaned over and kissed her husband. Owen Steed had come home.

The Steeds never doubted that they had picked up a bargain. For $810,-000 they acquired not only the Refuge itself, two hundred and ten choice acres with 9,015 feet of waterfront and all the buildings pertaining to the old plantation, but also two adjacent farms providing an additional three hundred acres of cornfields and woodland. 'The beauty of the cornfields,' Washburn Turlock explained shortly after they moved in, 'is that when they're harvested you can leave generous amounts of corn, which ensures geese unlimited. You can have three different sets of blinds—in the water, on the shore and in pits throughout your fields. Mr. Steed, you can entertain half of Oklahoma, come next November.'

'That's hardly what I had in mind,' Steed replied.

'You could lease them out and earn back your taxes.'

'That won't be necessary.'

'What I mean, with the exposures you have, the geese are going to flock here. You could pick up six, seven thousand dollars a year for hunting permissions.'

Ethel Steed interrupted by wanting to know where she could find someone to drive four pilings into the creek bed, and her husband asked, 'Whatever for?' and she said cryptically, 'You'd never believe what the men at the store told me,' and when the pilings were driven she wanted to know where she could locate an ironworker to forge her some shallow steel baskets. This was too much, and Steed demanded to know what foolishness she was up to, and she teased, 'Wait till spring comes, and you'll see something striking . . . if the men at the store weren't pulling my leg.'

It was a long wait. December 1976 was fearfully cold, and even men in their eighties could recall no similar season when every expanse of water, from the merest creek to the great bay itself, froze solid. Winds howled down out of Canada with such heavy burdens of freezing air that thermometers dropped to historic lows, and the weather station at the mouth of the Choptank announced that this was the coldest winter ever recorded. Not even the remembered freezes of the 1670s surpassed this brutal year.

It was a trying time for the Steeds; Owen had promised his wife respite from the thundering winters of Oklahoma—'You'll find the Eastern Shore a gentle place . . . a little frost now and then.' This became their theme during the protracted freeze. Mrs. Steed would rise, see the unbroken snow, the creeks frozen so solid that trucks could cross them, and she would say, 'A little frost now and then.'

The long weeks of subfreezing weather—the whole month of January with the thermometer rarely above thirty-two—did not inconvenience the Steeds insofar as their own comfort was concerned. Their new home was snug; the fireplaces worked; the Turlock boy who cut wood from the forest kept a comforting stack beside the door; and it was rather fun to test oneself against the bitter cold. They walked together, bundled in ski suits, to all corners of their estate, and found delight in picking their way across frozen streams or pushing through marsh grass that crackled when they touched it. It was a challenging winter but one warm in associations, and they discovered that what they had hoped for back in Oklahoma was happening: they were growing closer to each other. They talked more; they watched television less; and certainly they spent more time together both indoors and out.

The difficult part of the winter came with the birds. One morning Ethel

Steed rose to look out her window at the familiar scene of snow and ice and saw to her horror that a whole congregation of ducks had gathered on the left fork of the creek, trying futilely to break the ice so that they could feed.

'Owen! Look at this!' He joined her and saw that these creatures were famished. For six weeks they had been cut off from grasses at the bottom of creeks and rivers; they had been able to dive for nothing; their feeding places were frozen solid.

The Steeds put in urgent phone calls to their neighbors, and the advice they got was concise and harsh: 'Mr. Steed, thousands of birds are perishing. Worst place of all is the creeks around your home. What to do? Feed them, damnit. Buy all the corn you can afford and scatter it along the edges of the ice.'

Without waiting for breakfast, they jumped into their station wagon, maneuvered it carefully down frozen roads and hurried out into the country east of Patamoke. They stopped at a dozen different farms, begging for corn, and when they had purchased a load which tested the springs of their Buick, they directed other farmers to the Refuge, buying from them as much corn as they could deliver.

They hurried home with their cargo, broke open the bags and began scattering the corn broadcast along the ice, and before they were half through with their work, great flocks of ducks and geese moved in, sometimes to within six feet of where they worked, and it was clear that the birds were starving.

For three days the Steeds bought corn, spending more than a thousand dollars, but when they saw how desperately the fowl needed it, how hungrily they waited for the Steeds to appear, they felt more than rewarded. Never before had they seen waterfowl at such close quarters, and when a flock of seventeen white swans flew in, emaciated and near death, Mrs. Steed broke into tears.

Her husband halted this in a hurry. 'Let's get the axes and break a hole in the ice. Those birds are dying for water.'

So in their fashionable hunting togs they worked until heavy sweat poured from their bodies, trying to hack an open space in ice two feet thick, and then Owen had an idea: 'I remember a Currier and Ives print in which they sawed the ice.' He fetched a long saw, and after making a hole in the ice, widened it out to an opening about ten feet on the side. Before he was done, more than three hundred birds had flown in to compete for the water.

For two days the Steeds did little but stay at the hole, watching the splendid birds as they ate and bathed. 'They'll explode!' Ethel Steed said, but the birds continued to gorge themselves. Then she began trying to identify them; with the aid of color plates she was able to spot the green-headed mallard and the copper-headed canvasback, but that was about all. There were at least twelve other breeds which her husband could rattle off: 'Black, gadwall, redhead, teal, scaup . . .' Once he had hunted ducks with a powerful gun and good eye; now he was content to feed them.

It was while endeavoring to explain the difference between a bufflehead and a baldpate that he had his bright idea. Running to the house, he telephoned Annapolis and after some delay got Admiral Stainback. 'Spunky, this is Owen Steed. Tulsa. Yes, good to hear you, too. Spunky, can you hire me a helicopter? I know you can't get hold of a Navy one. But there must be . . .'

The admiral, a crisp Oklahoma man who had done much business with Steed's company, wanted to know why his old friend should need a helicopter, and when Owen explained that it was a mission of mercy, saving a hundred thousand geese, he said, 'Hell, that would justify one of our choppers!' And he asked for specific landing instructions.

Within an hour a Navy helicopter landed at the Refuge, within fifteen feet of the barn, and was loaded with bags of corn. Admiral Stainback sat in back with Ethel, while Owen rode co-pilot to do the navigating. With graceful ease the chopper lifted into the air, tilted to starboard and swept at low altitude up one river after another, while the passengers in back ripped open bags of corn, scattering the golden kernels across the frozen rivers.

It was a trip that dazzled the Steeds: each pond of water, no matter how small, reflected from its icy surface the shimmering rays of the sun; each cove was a frozen diadem. Marvelously attractive were the thin strands of rivulets which in summer would go undetected; in frozen splendor they shone like veins of silver. The relationship of water to land was sharply defined; the mystery of the Eastern Shore lay revealed, this wedding of snow-covered land and bejeweled rivers.

Even when the bags were empty and their muscles tired, the Steeds did not want the flight to end, for they were seeing a wilderness of beauty that might never be repeated. Generations could pass before the shore would again be frozen as it was this day, so when Admiral Stainback asked on the intercom, 'Shall we head back now?' Owen said into his microphone, 'I'd like to see how the Choptank develops,' and Stainback said, 'Said and done. Pilot, fly to the headwaters.'

With lovely, falling, sideways motion the helicopter dipped low toward the mouth of the frozen river, then turned east and flew slowly up the river that Steeds had occupied for so long. There was the mansion, half eaten away by summer storms, its widow's walk collapsed. There was Peace Cliff and the red roofs of Sunset Acres, where the marsh had been. Here were the gaping, rusted girders of what had been the Paxmore Boatyard, and beyond it the new red-brick homes in Frog's Neck, replacing the burned-out wooden shacks. But it was east of Patamoke that the Choptank became most memorable, for here vast marshes spread along the shore, marked now and then by rotting piers to which the ancient steamboats had come, all white and silver and shot with romance; now the pilings were eaten to the waterline and silt filled the harbors where women in bombazine had once waited for their lovers returning from Baltimore. How noisy it had been then; how silent now.

There were the long stretches of river totally unoccupied, looking much as they had in 1700, and up toward the end the vast, rusting sheds at Denton where huge riverboats had once brought their cargos of guano from Peru. Beyond lay the flat fields of Delaware in which the river rose, and beyond them the vast Atlantic Ocean, whose waters salted the Chesapeake and all its estuaries.

As they flew at a few hundred feet above this frozen wonderland, Ethel saw from time to time some hole broken in the ice by mysterious forces; often the opening was no larger than a tennis court, but about it clustered thousands of birds, desperate for water, and often, at a distance from the opening, lay swans and geese and ducks whose feet had frozen to the ice, holding them prisoner till they died.

'We can go home now,' Owen said from his front seat, and like a homing pigeon the helicopter twirled, found its heading and crossed frozen fields to the Refuge.

There was one aspect of that fearful winter to which the Steeds would never refer; it was too painful.

One morning as Owen was shaving he heard the mournful cry of the heron—'*Kraannk, kraannk!*'—and he looked out to see two gaunt birds, whose habits he had studied with loving attention, land on the ice and walk in long awkward steps to those spots at which they had so often fed, hoping to find them free of ice, that they might fish.

Desperately they pecked at the unyielding surface. Then, with mounting terror, for they were starving, they hammered at the ice with their feet, a kind of death-dance. Accomplishing nothing, they pecked again, their long necks driving sharp bills with a force which would have broken normal ice. But this was different, and the poor birds moved from spot to spot, frustrated.

'Darling!' Steed called to Ethel in the bedroom. 'We've got to do something for the herons.'

'Are they back?'

'They were. Trying to find open water.'

'Why don't they eat the corn? Or go where the ducks are?'

The water at the big opening was too deep for them to fish; corn was a food they did not eat. What they required was some wading place in which they could feed in their accustomed manner, and across the entire Eastern Shore there were no such places.

The Steeds would make one. All morning they sweated at the onerous job of breaking ice along the shore, and by noon they had laid open a considerable waterway. They were eating a late lunch when they heard the familiar and now-loved cry, and they ran to the window to watch their friends feed.

But in those few minutes ice had formed again and the birds found nothing. In panic they tested all their feeding places, and all were barren.

'What will they do?' Mrs. Steed cried, tears in her eyes.

Owen, studying the birds with his glasses, saw how emaciated they were, but had not the courage to inform his wife of their certain doom. The herons, stepping along like ballerinas grown old, tried one last time to penetrate the ice, looked down in bewilderment and flew off to their frozen roosts. They were seen no more.

During the first five months of residence at the Refuge, Owen Steed followed one invariable rule. Whenever he left the plantation in his car, he turned right, even though an excellent road ran to the left toward various places he would normally have wished to visit. But that road also led past the Paxmore place, and he was not yet ready for such an excursion. But in February he relaxed, and one morning told his wife, 'I think it's about time I saw Pusey,' and she replied, 'I was wondering how long you could delay.'

He dressed carefully, as if for hunting, heavy shoes, rough tweed jacket, canvaslike trousers, a hound's-tooth cap. He wanted to appear casual, with no touch of the business administrator, but when he looked at himself in the hall mirror he felt disgusted: Totally fake. And he returned to his dressing room for khaki pants, plaid shirt and corduroy jacket: At least I look honest. He winced at the inappropriateness of this word.

He was not pleased with himself as he drove to the end of his drive, turned slowly left and headed for Peace Cliff. He had not seen Pusey Paxmore since that day in August 1972 when the prim Quaker had visited Tulsa. Who could forget that day—more than four years ago, almost five centuries away in moral significance? When he saw the plain entrance to the Paxmore lands, and the road leading up to the telescope house, he wanted to pass on, but realized that to do so would be craven. With no enthusiasm he turned into the lane, noticed favorably the crape myrtle trees which would be lovely in July, and parked by the front door.

After he knocked, it was some moments before anyone answered. Then he heard shuffling footsteps, a twisting of the old lock on the door and a creaking hinge. What happened next surprised him, for when the door finally opened he found neither Pusey nor his wife. Instead, a slatternly woman who seemed quite out of place in the neat telescope house growled, 'So you've come to take over?' And before he could respond, she slipped past him, jumped into a ramshackle pickup and spun her tires in the gravel.

'Who are you?' Steed shouted.

'Lily Turlock. You'll find him upstairs.' And she was gone.

When he turned back to the house he heard a fumbling at the door. 'Who's out there?' a tremulous voice inquired. Then plaintively: 'Oh, it's you, Owen. I wondered when you'd come. Do step in.'

The door opened slowly, as if the man inside had no spare strength, and then Steed saw the trembling figure. He was aghast. In the old days Pusey Paxmore had been a proper Quaker, erect, bright of eye and modest of manner; his principal characteristic had been his reserve and the heightened intellectuality he brought to any discussion. But now, his hair completely white and his cheeks sunken, he seemed almost a derelict. To compare this wasted figure with its trim predecessor was most painful. Steed, realizing that some greeting had to be offered, said quickly, 'How you doing, Pusey?'

'One adjusts.'

'I'm retired, too. Bought the Refuge.'

'So I heard. Come in.' Paxmore led the way into a living room whose large windows overlooked the Choptank; they had been a renovation in the 1960s when Pusey was earning considerable sums in government. 'I often wonder if we did right in breaking through the old walls,' he said querulously. 'One doesn't want to disturb old buildings, but one doesn't want to live cooped up, either.'

This was a most unfortunate metaphor, and each man backed away from it.

'Tell me, Owen, how was life in Oklahoma?' Pusey asked, quietly changing the subject.

'One thing, Pusey. You became an ardent football fan or you withered. I helped the university to three national championships.'

'What do you mean? You helped?'

'Scholarships. I gave scholarships to brutish young men who could neither read nor write. Did you happen to follow the case of the young fellow from Texas? They cooked his high-school grades.'

'What do you mean *cooked?*'

'Gave him A's when he earned F's. So he'd be eligible for my scholarship.'

'You were always generous,' Paxmore said, and this was so appallingly inappropriate that Steed thought: Jesus Christ, you can't say a word that doesn't have triple meanings. He was sorry he had come.

With an effort to get the conversation onto a less volatile track, he stood by the window and asked, 'Have you watched our island sinking back into the bay?'

'I have indeed! I went over there the other day and calculated that according to old maps . . . Did you know that Captain John Smith drew the first chart of Devon? He did, and since his day the land has been receding at a pretty constant rate.' Pusey had been good at mathematics and liked such problems. 'I figure the island has lost about thirty-five feet a year. Erosion coming at it from all sides. Sad.'

The two men looked at the faint outline of the island and a mournful silence prevailed, broken when Steed tried a new approach. 'How're your boys doing, Pusey?'

'Not well. They tried Harvard, but it must have been very difficult for them . . .'

'They didn't scuttle out?'

'As a matter of fact, they did. They'll find their sea legs. They're basically good boys.'

'Hardly boys.'

'I think of them as such. How are your children?'

'Clara's in Paris, I think. She did the Torremolinos bit.'

'Your son?'

'I'm worried about Logan. Divorced. Knocking around Boston, of all places. Damnit, Pusey! Why has this generation . . . You take my wife —one of the finest women Oklahoma ever produced. You'd think that with a mother like her the children . . .' Pause. 'We haven't seen either of them in three years.'

'We don't see ours much, either, although when I was in Scanderville, I'd have been satisfied for them to keep away. They came, though, that I must say.'

'Was it bad up there?'

'Jail is always bad. On some it has a worse effect than on others. At my age . . .'

This was the moment when Steed should have spoken openly of the tragedy that had overtaken them in their ardent support of the President, but in cowardly fashion he shied away. Instead of broaching the subject he had come to discuss, he said lamely, 'You must come over and meet Ethel. She's a fine person, breath of fresh air.'

'We could use that on the Eastern Shore.'

'We'll get together. One of these days I'll give you a call.'

'That'll be nice,' Paxmore said, and he walked his old friend to the car, watching as he drove down the lane between the myrtle trees.

When Steed reached home his wife said, 'You didn't stay very long,' and he said, 'We engaged in a few pleasantries,' and she raged, 'Owen, you didn't go all the way there to say nothing!'

He tried several times to explain, then fell into a chair and mumbled, 'I can be a real shit.'

'Yes, you can!' she cried. 'Owen, get out of that chair right now. We're going to the Paxmores'. . .'

'Ethel! I can't. We'll find the right time.'

'The right time was six months ago. Now, damnit, you get cracking, and I mean it.'

She thundered her way to the door, kicked it open and waited for her husband to follow.

When he walked to the left side of the car she pushed him aside and said, 'I'll drive. You might not get there.' And she roared down the driveway, scattering pebbles, and without slackening her speed went up the Paxmore hill, where Amanda was parking her car after a marketing trip to Patamoke.

'I'm Ethel Steed,' she said, extending her hand. 'We've come to apologize.'

With steel-like composure Amanda said, 'Not to me, to Pusey.'

'I mean to Pusey. He was a heroic man, Mrs. Paxmore, and we are most tardy.'

'It's difficult,' Amanda said. She led the way back into the house, called for her husband, and stood waiting with the Steeds until Pusey appeared, head down and shoulders bent. Steed's performance earlier in the day had distressed him, and he had been brooding in his room.

'Pusey,' his wife began, 'the Steeds have come back.'

'I haven't met Mrs. Steed,' he said, assuming that the evasions of the morning were to be repeated. They were not.

'We've come to apologize,' Ethel said, and she approached with hands extended. 'You were heroic,' she said, grasping him by his frail white fingers.

'I think we should sit down,' he said, going to a chair by the window, and there the four sat, quietly, without displayed emotion, as they reviewed in painful detail their misbehaviors.

'You bore the brunt for all of us,' Ethel said, 'and Owen should have been here six months ago to tell you how much we honor your sacrifices.'

'Rewards and punishment fall unevenly,' Paxmore said, and with this breaking of the dam he began the therapy of exploration, speaking without interruption, unleashing a veritable flood of memories and assessments:

'I was honored, any man would be, to have been taken into the White House, and at such a high level. To be close to power is not a trivial thing, and to influence both legislation and executive operations for good is something that any reasonable man could aspire to. During the first term I am not being immodest when I say that

I accomplished much. Take the water legislation, the study of Arab rights, the increased contributions for widowed mothers. I felt that I was continuing the work of Woolman Paxmore and Ruth Brinton. It was Christianity in action, and I am still proud of the things I attempted.

'But I was not an ordinary political agent in Washington. I was set apart. For I had seen my family's business go up in smoke during the civil riots. I had seen the hatred in the streets. I had lived close to real revolution. Better than anyone in the White House, I understood how close to disaster we were in 1969 and 1970.

'So when the '72 election approached, I saw it as my duty to reelect Mr. Nixon, to give him a chance to save this nation. I had seen the fires. I had tasted the revolution, and I was determined that it should not spread. When I talked with you in Tulsa in the summer of 1972, with the possibility staring us in the face that George McGovern might be President, with bombings and disruptions threatening from all sides, the danger was very clear and very present. Nothing less than the safety of our nation was at stake.

'I was most relieved, Owen, when you assured me that you would contrive some way to pass us two hundred thousand dollars of your corporate funds. This would enable me to support good men in New York and California and Texas, three states we thought we must win. Don't forget, it was reasonable for you to give the money, too, because your way of life was imperiled. All good principles were being corroded and only our victory could stay the drift.

'If there was one terrible error in the Watergate fiasco, it was that Mr. Nixon never found a platform from which he could state the true condition of this country in 1969 through 1972. We tottered on the brink of anarchy, and if we had not held fast, we would have lost this nation. You told me that day, Owen, that your own two children were making bombs, and devastating the university, and preaching rebellion. It was everywhere, and it was my conviction that if we had lost the election in November '72, revolution would have been upon us.

'Well, I did what I could to stem it. I collected the money. I arranged for its laundering in Mexico. And I lied to save my country's destiny. I have no regrets, except a foolish one. At the hearing they treated me like a sad old clown, made me laughable as the eyes of the nation looked on. Sam Dash, head of the interrogators, didn't even bother to question me. Turned the job over to a young fellow just out of law school. It was his big moment, and he played me like a trout. So I allowed myself to look the bumbling idiot, the serf loyal to his knight. And do you know why? Because then I didn't have to tell the whole truth. I was able to protect my President and my friends.'

He stopped. This last sentence brought the monologue into the present, and Ethel Steed looked meaningfully at her husband, who said, 'Pusey, those of us in debt to you will never forget the burden you bore.'

'Mr. Nixon forgot,' Amanda Paxmore said. 'All the time Pusey was in jail, not one word of condolence. Not to him, not to me.'

'We didn't do it for praise,' her husband said, his jaw tightening as it had before the television cameras. 'We did it because the nation was threatened.'

'And I appreciate it, Pusey.' Steed wanted to let his apology go at that, not through any meanness of spirit but because the memory of that dreadful summer when John Dean was testifying was too anguishing to relive. It was Ethel who conveyed the real apology, and like Paxmore, she spoke without pause:

'We sat paralyzed before the television, wondering when the vast bubble of make-believe would shatter, leaving us in headlines across the country. Greasy Thumb Polewicz brought no laughter in our family, because the money he lugged about in that paper bag came from us. When they traced the funds to Mexico City, it was our money they were talking about. And when we heard that you were going on the stand, Pusey, we shuddered. Because you knew the facts.

'On the night before you were to testify, Owen and I tried to make a brave face of it by going to the country club, as if we weren't living on the edge of a volcano. It was rather pleasant, as I recall. Mr. Nixon had a lot of support in Tulsa. I don't believe there could have been a single person there that night who had voted for McGovern, so we were among friends. I suppose that's what got to us, for we realized that if next day you told where the money had come from, illegal corporate funds from us, these very people would have to act shocked and fire Owen, and he might well have gone to jail. Suddenly—'

Owen Steed was not in the habit of allowing his wife to make excuses for his misconduct, and now he felt obligated to interrupt her narration regarding that summer of 1973:

'What happened was simple. I fainted. The realization that my world was collapsing and that I might go to jail overwhelmed me, and I fainted. Not flat on the floor. Just my head in my plate. Mayonnaise in my hair. Waiters explaining to the other tables that I had choked.

'Pusey, when you were on that stand we died with you. But damnit, even as we died we kept praying, "I hope he doesn't talk." And you didn't.'

No one spoke. The men looked out at the Choptank, and after a while Pusey surprised the Steeds by lapsing into the Quaker speech. 'Would thee like something to drink?'

'That's a charming phrase,' Ethel said.

'As I withdraw from the battle . . .' He did not like this imagery and changed it. 'I'm an old man now. I grow closer to my origins.'

'I came back for the same reason,' Owen said. 'To be closer to my origins . . . and because I was fired.'

'You were fired?'

'Well, eased out. I was so shaken by Watergate, I couldn't focus on the job. Six or seven members of the board had to know I gave you the money. Hell, they arranged it. And they knew that if you testified openly, I'd be the one they'd throw to the wolves. I wasn't happy with them and they weren't happy with me. So they paid me off and kicked me out.'

'But with thy name intact,' Amanda Paxmore said, not acidly but with a directness which could not be misconstrued.

Pusey did not wait for Steed to defend himself. 'No sensible man expects even-handed justice. But can thee guess what gives me my severest punishment?' He seemed driven to castigate himself. 'To sit in this room day after day and realize how far I strayed from what I was. Did thee ever know my father, Woolman Paxmore? A living saint. He used to tell us children in his wonderfully simple manner, "Thee has only one obligation to society, to bear witness." He warned me that before my life ended I would face every moral dilemma the Bible speaks of. And I did.'

Owen started to interrupt, but the flood continued. 'I wonder if young men attending their ethics classes in university realize that in later life every abstraction they discuss will become a reality. I was called upon to face every dilemma . . . save murder. And the other night as I was reviewing the White House days I even began wondering about that.'

He pondered this ugly possibility, then said with a half-chuckle, 'But the big lesson of my life I didn't learn in college or from my father. It came in high school from my Aunt Emily, the one who fought against the disfranchisement of the blacks. She was an old woman when I knew her, old and funny, and we paid her no attention. But she insisted on memorization, and the passage I speak of came in a play I've never seen. I doubt if anyone ever sees it, *King Henry the Eighth.* Cardinal Wolsey . . .' He stopped abruptly. 'Didn't thy family have dealings with Wolsey?'

'We did. Toadied to him while he was in power, turned against him when he was not.'

'Wolsey is departing, on his way to exile and perhaps to the scaffold, and as he leaves his White House, where he had exercised such power, he reflects:

'Had I but serv'd my God with half the zeal
I serv'd my king, He would not in mine age
Have left me naked to mine enemies.'

'Do you feel abandoned by the President?' Ethel Steed asked.

'We were all abandoned,' Pusey said, and suddenly the terrible weight of those years descended upon him, and it was more than he could bear. His shoulders sagged, his chin trembled and he became a very old man, although he was only sixty-four. He must have been aware of the dramatic alteration, for he apologized. 'I grow tired so quickly. Thee must excuse me.'

He started to leave the room, then turned to tell his guests, 'We lads from the Eastern Shore, we do poorly when we venture into the world. Much better we stay in our retreats and listen to the echoes coming across the bay.'

Because the good citizens of Patamoke, black and white, were determined that the burning of Frog's Neck not be used as an excuse for hardening racial animosities, and because Father Patrick was able to defuse his Turlock and Caveny relatives, life along the Choptank returned to normal much more rapidly than pessimists might have predicted. The National Guard was on duty for a few weeks, and some crosses were burned, but everyone was so tired of fire that passions subsided.

Hiram Cater was tracked down by the F.B.I. and sentenced to jail, but citizens from varied backgrounds petitioned the judge for leniency, so his sentence was not excessive. A new road was built around Frog's Neck and immediately dubbed the Congo Bypass, but black boys started playing on the football teams of Patamoke High, and after victories blacks and whites congregated in the Blue and Gold Ice Cream Parlor for celebrations.

But the tensions were not formally relaxed until early March of 1977, when the rowdy skipjack captains from Deal Island rolled into town with a proclamation that struck at the honor of the Choptank; blacks and whites rallied to defend their river, and old animosities were forgotten.

What the Deal Island men said was that they were the champions of the Eastern Shore and ready to prove it in a grand challenge race. To insult the Patamokes they added, 'Since you need every advantage to keep up with us, we'll hold the race in your backyard, Choptank River, first week in October.'

The Patamokes pledged themselves to enter seven skipjacks, five with white captains, two with black, but with the crews mixed three and three. The old craft were cleaned up and sailors began practicing the maneuvers required for victory, but the people organizing the race were unhappy over one deficiency.

'It would look better . . . by that we mean that the papers and television . . . Hell, you got to have the *Eden* in there. Oldest surviving skipjack, and all that.'

The Patamoke captains agreed that it would be a fine idea to have the side-assed skipjack participate in the race, but she had not sailed for some years and it was generally assumed that her days were done. When the experts went out to survey her, tied up behind the ruins of the Paxmore Boatyard, they confessed that she was not much.

But when Owen Steed heard of the problem, he said abruptly, 'I'll provide the funds to restore her. That is, if you can get Pusey Paxmore to supervise repairs.' The committee hastened to Peace Cliff, where Pusey told them firmly that he was too old and no longer knew enough, but he did direct them to a nephew who had once built a skipjack, and this Paxmore joined the effort.

When the refurbished boat stood on blocks beside the harbor, her mast raked and glistening in new spar finish, the question arose as to her crew. She was the property of the Cater family; a stoop-shouldered man named Absalom held title and he owned a fine reputation at oystering, bold in defending his location against competition.

But when Steed and the committee went to Absalom they found him a testy man, steeped in bitterness over the jailing of Hiram Cater. 'Ain't takin' her out.'

'But Captain Boggs at Deal Island . . .'

'To hell with him.' Absalom Cater was the rugged new-type black who would tolerate no affront to his personal dignity.

'Mr. Cater, we'd really like to have you—'

'Name's Absalom.'

'Goddamnit!' Steed snapped in oil-field anger. 'I spent thirty years in Oklahoma disciplining myself to call you sons-of-bitches Mister. Now you snarl at me for doing so. What do you want to be called? Negro, black, colored—you name it.'

Absalom laughed. 'My problem is to discipline myself to stop callin' you white-asses Mister. Now what in hell do you want, Steed?'

'I want you to assemble a crew that will win this race. We're providing you with a damned good boat.'

'There's a boy shucks arsters at Tilghman Island. He knows how to sail with me. And Curtis from Honga. That's three blacks. You pick three whites.'

This was an insolent challenge, and it excited the imagination of the white watermen. 'Turlocks used to own the *Eden,* so we'll ask Amos.'

'He's almost seventy.'

'He can cook. And in a fight he's very mean.'

'Cavenys always worked this skipjack, so we'll invite Martin. And the Pflaum family. Hugo's stupendous in water.'

It was a menacing crew that assembled to give the *Eden* her trials, and a Baltimore reporter wrote: 'They resemble pirates about to loot a burning plantation.' Lanky Amos Turlock had only a few teeth; Martin Caveny, round and sly, looked like some henchman guarding a castle keep; and Hugo Pflaum, past seventy, still had the thick, squashed neck of his Rhineland ancestors. The three blacks at least looked like sailors: Captain Absalom big and dangerous, his two helpers lean and ready for a brawl.

With such a crew the *Eden* caught the fancy of newspaper and television people; incidents in her history were resurrected: built in 1891; captained by that Jake Turlock who defeated the Virginians in the Battle of the Bay; captured single-handed by Otto Pflaum from five armed watermen; the boat of Big Jimbo Cater, first and best of the black captains. 'Besides which,' wrote the proud reporter from the *Bugle,* 'she is the only side-assed skipjack in history, but she is given slight chance in the race because she cannot perform well on the starboard tack.'

The reporter had it backward. Every ship, every boat that moves under sail goes better on one tack than the other. Some mysterious combination of forces resulting from the interrelationship of mast, boom, keel and curvature makes one boat perform best on the starboard tack while another of almost identical design excels on the port. Like twins who share identities but who develop differentiated skills, the skipjacks varied, and Captain Absalom knew that his advantage lay when the wind blew from the starboard side, for then the offset centerboard cooperated with the tilted keel to produce maximum speed.

'I think we got her tuned just right,' he assured Mr. Steed.

Once when the black-white crew was practicing on the Chesapeake, Amos Turlock, coming up from the galley, spotted a chance to pick up some easy money. An expensive yacht had gone aground on the unmarked mud flats that rested just under the surface of the water where the western end of Devon Island had once stood. It was a perilous spot, which had not yet been properly buoyed, and the yacht's crew could be forgiven for going aground there.

'Halloo!' Turlock shouted. 'You need help?'

'We need a tow,' came the cry.

'We haven't the power to get you off'n there.'

'Could you get us a tugboat? We've radioed the Coast Guard, but they have nothing.'

'I can get you off,' Turlock called as the *Eden* closed.

'Watch out!' the yacht captain cried. 'You'll ground.'

'We draw two feet, centerboard up.'

'That's a hell of an advantage.'

'In these waters, yes. Mister, I can get you off without scarrin' the paint. Fifty dollars.'

'Jump to it.'

'It's a deal?' Turlock asked suspiciously. When the yachtsman assented, Amos yelled, 'Caveny, break out the lines. You know what to do.'

The yacht had gone aground because its construction required a massive keel reaching eight feet below water line, and it was this bulbous steel projection which had imbedded itself in mud. No possible tow from the *Eden* would break this loose, and the people on the yacht could not imagine what the motley crew on the skipjack had in mind.

It was simple. Caveny climbed into the *Eden's* rowboat, brought one end of a long rope with him, pulled himself onto the deck of the yacht, where he immediately clawed his way as high up the mast as he could go. There he fastened the rope securely to the spreader and signaled to Turlock back on the *Eden* that all was ready.

Slowly the skipjack moved away from the yacht, and as it did so, the line tightened, but there was no possibility that the frail craft could break the heavy yacht free, and the grounded sailors shouted, 'Careful! You'll part the line!'

It was never Turlock's intention to exert much pulling power; what he wanted to do was maintain pressure until the line high on the mast pulled the yacht over on its port side. 'Watch out, stupid!' one of the yachtsmen shouted as the boat began to list. 'You'll capsize us!'

But Turlock maintained his gentle pulling, and slowly the yacht came down until its mast was almost parallel to the water; then the miracle on which he relied began to eventuate. What had been a massive yacht with an eight-foot keel was being converted into a bizarre craft with less than three inches of wood below the water line, and the huge bulbous keel stuck at an angle in the mud. The buoyancy of the new boat was so great that it began to suck the keel loose.

'Keep that line fast!' Turlock called, and everyone watched as the mast came down to touch the water, but as soon as it did, the yacht broke free, and with only a modest wind in her sails, the skipjack was able to pull the heavier craft out into deep water. Quickly she righted herself, and the yachtsmen cheered.

When it came time for the captain to hand over the fifty dollars, one of his crew complained, 'A lot of money for six minutes' work, and Turlock said, 'Five dollars for doin', forty-five for knowin'.'

Manifestations of nature along the Choptank exerted a therapeutic effect upon those humans who participated in them, and no example could be more typical than what occurred in late March 1977 after the prolonged winter. For while the Steeds were mourning the loss of their herons, an even more congenial bird was preparing to visit them.

If, as many assume, the last glacier to extend southward into regions drained by the Susquehanna collected its ice about seventy thousand years ago and finally dissolved some eleven thousand years back, the basic character of the Chesapeake must have taken form around 9000 B.C.

As soon as forests and fish appeared, osprey began to inhabit the area, and each year in the last days of winter they returned to the Choptank —that is, the males arrived. Large fishing hawks with white underpainting and jet-black joints in the sharply recurved wings, these handsome males were notable for their ability to hover, spot fish at great distances and dive for them with claws extended.

But each year on the day of their arrival after a long flight from the Amazon, the males were so exhausted that they did not fish, no matter how hungry, for a driving instinct compelled them to search for nesting sites, which they explored like any house-hunting husband. In 1977 those travel-weary males who elected the streams at the Refuge found much of their work done for them, because Martin Caveny, under the direction of Ethel Steed, had constructed four basketlike platforms from braided steel and had set them on tall pilings well out into the water.

'Watch what happens on St. Patrick's Day,' Caveny said with confidence. 'On that day, year after year, ospreys come back to this neck.'

'Preposterous!'

'The patron birds of Ireland,' he said reverently. 'St. Paddy's Day, they'll be here.'

In the week before the males arrived he instructed Ethel in how to spread on her lawn bits of cloth and dead branches from which the males would construct their nests, then said, 'You may not believe this, Mrs. Steed, but twelve days later, on March 29, the females will come flying in to inspect the nests.'

'Birds don't live by the calendar,' she protested.

'Other parts of the Choptank, they arrive at other times. But on your land, St. Patrick's Day.' And on the evening of March 16, when they surveyed the preparations, he assured her, 'If I was an osprey, here's where I'd come.'

She told her husband that night, 'I think Martin Caveny's teasing me,' but even so, next morning she was up early, just in case, and before the sun approached its zenith she heard from the sky a series of *cherk-cherks,* a whispery communication coming across the water, and she looked in its direction, to see lofty hawks hovering, darting, sweeping down with claws extended in a braking position, and within a few minutes of the birds' arrival, a handsome male was inspecting the first of her constructions, and before long three others had come to the creek; by nightfall much of the signaling cloth had disappeared from the shore.

Various attributes made Ethel Steed's braided platforms attractive to the opsrey: they were solidly constructed, set in water that promised to provide fish, and far enough from land to ensure protection from predators. And in recent years they had an added merit: farmers in the area were forbidden to use DDT, a splendid insecticide which unfortunately prevented birds who ingested it from depositing enough calcium in their eggshells to permit their young to hatch. In 1965 it had seemed that this noble bird must vanish from the earth; in 1977, thanks to concerned people like Ethel Steed, the birds seemed likely to survive.

'Do you believe me?' Caveny asked on the evening of the twenty-eighth, when the males had completed their nests in good form. 'Tomorrow morning the ladies arrive, and then we'll see something.'

This time she trusted the enthusiastic Irishman, and on the morning of the twenty-ninth, as they had for some ten thousand years, the female ospreys came back to the Refuge, and then began one of the spectacular sights of nature, for the males rose to meet them, and as they paired off they swept and darted and pirouetted through the sky, wing tip to wing tip, crying and reveling in the sun and the assurance of a summer's home, where the new generation would be born.

'Owen!' Mrs. Steed called as the osprey couples wheeled through the air. 'You must see this!' And he came from the house to stand with his wife as the wild courtship flight continued, now low above the water, now high in the heavens, and after a while one of the males led his partner to the nest closest to where the Steeds were standing, and as she inspected his work he flew up and down the creek until he spotted a small fish. Diving swiftly, he caught it, rose well into the heavens, then flew to his nest, where, standing on tiptoes, he fed the delicacy to his mate.

The watching humans joined hands, and Ethel said, 'We need nature for what it teaches us.'

'Or what it reminds us of,' Owen said.

In the days that followed, the females began to nest, and now the males had to fish with doubled tenacity.

When young Christopher Pflaum scandalized the citizens of Patamoke by establishing his home south of the Choptank—something no member of a major family had ever done—the men at the store had an easy explanation for his outrageous behavior: 'Think back! His grandmother was a Turlock. So was his mom, and with blood like that, you never know what to expect.' One village philosopher added, 'Come to think of it, them Turlocks always loved marshes. It was blood speakin', that's what it was.'

The reason was simpler and more beautiful. One dark night in 1967, as the lieutenant in charge of a bedraggled outfit struggling through the jungles of Vietnam, he had experienced a revelation. In Korea some years before, Hiram Cater had found the meaning of the Choptank; now Chris Pflaum was about to make his discovery in Vietnam, and that is the risk and reward which comes from sending generations of intelligent young men to duty in alien lands: when they return they see their homeland clearly.

Chris had already spent seven months in futile jungle fighting, and his unit had been so constantly engaged in destruction and pillage that he was sick of war, but he was even more sick of the manner in which some patrol mates complained of every aspect of their lives. Like his grandfather, Otto, and his rugged father, Hugo, he believed that men must tolerate what is unavoidable but strive to better it, yet he had to listen as the men bitched: the food, the gooks, the officers, the climate, the crud, the lack of ammunition, the absence of air cover, the failure of the corporal to locate a supply of fresh socks. The breaking point came when a soldier from New Hampshire slapped his arm and whined, 'These damned mosquitoes are killin' me.'

'Hell,' Chris snapped, 'they're gnats. Back home we got mosquitoes as big as pigeons.'

'You what?'

A brawl ensued, and when it ended, with no victors, Chris sat by himself in the growing darkness and tried honestly to evaluate his life: Happiest I've ever been was when I explored the marshes along the Choptank. And without further reflection, he wrote a letter to the only real estate dealer he knew, Washburn Turlock of Patamoke:

I have two thousand, eight hundred dollars saved and would be willing to obligate myself for double that amount on a mortgage. What I want you to do is go south of the Choptank and buy me the biggest area of marshland available. I don't want two acres or twenty. I want at least four hundred, but some of it can be fast land. I want a house in which a wife and kids can live, and I want some waterfront. This is a firm commission, and I am sending my check herewith. Don't bother to mail me complicated details. Just get me the land with lots of marsh.

Early next morning he posted the letter, and when it was gone he experienced such soaring euphoria that he knew he had done right; he had made his commitment to a way of life, to a specific quality of land and water and deer and muskrats. With each passing day in the jungle he was increasingly satisfied with his decision, and much sooner than he had expected, Washburn Turlock reported:

> Our office rarely handles property south of the Choptank, because the mosquitoes there are unbearable, but your instructions were so explicit and your father so firm in his belief that you knew what you were doing, that I felt obligated to explore the area on your behalf, especially since you are in service protecting our country. You will be pleased with what I found. On the attached map you will see that I have marked along the Little Choptank a stretch of land comprising an excellent blend of 160 acres of marshland and 50 acres of fast which can be cultivated if you desire. It contains a house, a barn, some outbuildings once used as slave quarters, and a magnificent stretch of riverfront with a dock leading to deep water. This is what is known as the Herman Cline place; he settled here before the Civil War and played a minor role in local history. It's all yours for the unbelievable price of $7,600 and I have already arranged a mortgage. You own it.

When the leave plane neared McGuire Air Force Base in 1968, Chris began to sweat, and on the speedy drive down to the Delmarva Peninsula his excitement grew. His wife reported, 'I haven't seen the land yet, but Mr. Turlock says it's exactly what you wanted.'

Chris stopped in Patamoke only long enough to embrace his mother, then sped over the bridge to the south shore. He drove west down one of the fingers reaching out toward the bay, then along a narrow road and finally down a long lane. 'These must be our loblollies,' he said as the stately trees closed in, and then before him stood the old Cline house, and the rotting slave quarters, and the solid pier stretching out into the Little Choptank, and all things were twice as appealing as he had imagined. But the best part lay off to the west, where the little estuary joined the bay, for there stood the marsh from which Herman Cline's rented slaves had chopped out fast land. It waited as it had in the time of Captain John Smith, unspoiled, trembling in the wind, crowded with living things and restless from the motion of the invading water. It seemed endless, many times larger than he had hoped for, and he could visualize himself leading his children into its heart and disclosing to them its secrets. He tried to speak, but his mind was filled with the drumbeat of the discredited poem:

Look how the grace of the sea doth go
About and about through the intricate channels that flow
Here and there,
Everywhere,
Till his waters have flooded the uttermost creeks and the
low-lying lanes,
And the marsh is meshed with a million veins . . .

In this twelve-month period four men—two old, two young—came back to the Choptank, impelled by sharply different motives. Pusey Paxmore had crept home to die at the end of a shattered life. Owen Steed had prudently fled Oklahoma with sufficient funds to repurchase his family plantation. And Chris Pflaum had retired from the Army as a bemedaled major, with a research job at the Chesapeake Center for the Study of Estuaries and a waiting home deep in the Choptank marshes.

Hiram Cater was difficult to categorize; the warden had granted him a compassionate leave so that he might attend the funeral of his parents. Jeb and Julia had been born in the same year, had struggled through decades of poverty enforced by their society, and had survived to see two of their children in federal penitentiaries. Often in their last years, as they sat in their antiseptic new brick cubicle, they castigated themselves for failures they could not explain, not realizing that it was Patamoke that had failed, not they. In 1977 they died within three days of each other, and their son Hiram was allowed home to bury them. At the grave he stood silent, and as soon as the brief ceremony ended he returned to prison, knowing that he could never again live in Patamoke.

Major Pflaum was different from the other three, for he returned with honor and a burgeoning desire to accomplish something; during his military service he had been assigned to many duty stations on four different continents and knew that few places on earth compared in physical beauty and spiritual ease with the Chesapeake.

But as he started his research at the estuarine center he found himself engaged in a furious running debate with his father, Hugo Pflaum, who had spent fifty-one years defending the rivers and the bay. He resented it when his son proclaimed, 'Nobody around here seems to give a damn about the future of this region.'

'In your omniscience,' Hugo growled, 'have you bothered to look at what we've accomplished? The laws that prevent men like Uncle Ruthven from palisading marshes and covering them with concrete? Our regulations protecting wetlands so that ducks will find something to eat? And the way we've confiscated those murderous long guns?'

'Uncle Amos's, too?'

'We'll get it, one of these days.'

'But the land, Pop. It's going to hell.'

'You talk like an idiot,' Hugo said. 'Our Eastern Shore's one of the best places left on earth.'

'Pop! Will you get in a car with me and take a look?'

'I sure will.' The old warden bristled, and he joined his son in a pickup for a survey of the roads leading out of Patamoke.

'Now all I want,' Chris said, 'is for you to look at the grassy shoulders . . . and the ditches.' And when Hugo did, he understood what his son was complaining about, for the roads were littered with empty beer cans and soda bottles. It seemed as if the law required each resident of Maryland to drink three cans of something every day and toss the proof along the highway.

Glumly the old man conceded, 'This is pretty bad, Chris.'

His son slammed on the brakes and said, 'I got a proposition for you, Pop. Let's walk a quarter of a mile, out and back. Just count the cans and bottles.' As they moved slowly down the road they counted eighty-seven. Crossing over and walking back to the pickup, they found another seventy-two. 'So on an average quarter mile of rural road we have a hundred fifty-nine—more than six hundred a mile. Schlitz, Miller, Budweiser, Michelob. The heraldry of modern America.'

'I think you stacked the deck on me,' Hugo objected. 'This is a lovers' lane and you know how young people like to mess up everything.' But when they found a lovely back road it, too, had its quota of empties, the aluminum cans and the bottles good for a thousand years.

Grudgingly Hugo said, 'It really is pretty bad, Chris,' and when his son launched a campaign in the *Bugle* to clean up the roadsides, he contributed a sharp article arguing that men and women who had done such a good job of saving ducks and geese ought also to stop desecrating their landscape. His letter drew scorn, but Chris's pressure goaded the authorities to appoint a commission to study the matter. Within a few weeks it reported:

> Two proposals have been made, that the government add five cents to the cost of every bottle or can to pay for clean-up service, or that disposable containers be outlawed. We reject the former because handling the deposit and the empties would place too great a burden on the merchant, and we reject the latter because Norman Turlock has spent a great deal of money building his canning factory for beer and soft drinks and to change the rules on him now would be unfair.
>
> This problem, which is not nearly so grave as certain agitators would want us to believe, can best be handled by having parents teach their children that cans and bottles should not be thrown in

public places. With a little attention, this minor irritation can be solved without governmental action.

Young persons, and some older too, expressed their displeasure at the Pflaum interference by initiating an interesting ritual: they accumulated empty beer cans in the backs of their cars and tossed them in large numbers into the Pflaum ditches. Some mornings on his way to work Chris would find two dozen beer cans at the end of his lane, but he realized that within a few weeks the animosity would be dissipated. What did disturb him was that wherever he looked in this marvelous bay region, the desecration was the same. It was this casual plundering of the landscape that infuriated him, this supine acceptance of despoliation. The government was powerless to protect the environment, because its citizens had become accustomed to drinking beverages from throw-away bottles and cans; Norman Turlock, having invested money in a process that deformed the landscape, was to be protected to infinity, and any system of picking up the refuse or preventing its deposit in the first place was forbidden because it would inconvenience someone.

'Hell!' he said one day as he drove along a road south of the Choptank. 'One fine morning we'll awaken to find the land smothered in beer cans.' But when he tried to reopen the question in the columns of the *Bugle,* he was told by the editor, 'No one's interested in that nonsense any more.'

It was Hugo who tried to temper his bitterness. 'Chris, you got to keep things in perspective. The beer cans are a disgrace, but there's a whole paradise here that's unsullied.' And he cranked up the boat he used to patrol the oyster beds. 'I want you to see for yourself how much we have left.' Mile after mile of the lesser rivers displayed banks carefully tended and expansive lawns free of contamination, but even so, Hugo said, 'You can't appreciate how well we've protected the Eastern Shore till you see the western.' So they roared out into the Chesapeake, crossing over to the rivers south of Annapolis, and there young Chris had a chance to see how lack of zoning and policing had encouraged this shoreline to become a marine slum. It was appalling, one little house after another crowded up against its neighbor, one wharf after another falling into disrepair. The shoreline was eroding and no attention was paid it; most developments had been haphazard and decrepit from the day of building.

'That's really something to worry about,' the older Pflaum said as they began their return trip. 'That's a lot more serious than beer cans.'

When they reached the broad mouth of the Choptank, Hugo steered toward that loveliest of the eastern rivers, the Tred Avon: a broad, quiet estuary, a group of exquisite tributaries and innumerable coves, each with its own superb view. The boat slowed as the Pflaums studied the shoreline, one well-preserved home after another, not ostentatious but most attractive, hiding among tall trees.

'You've heard what Turlock the Pirate tells his customers from up North? "If you don't live on the Tred Avon, you're camping out. And if you live south of the Choptank, you'll never be invited to the good parties." '

Chris, who preferred the wilderness of the Little Choptank, wanted to defend his choice, but Hugo raised both hands. 'Please, your mother and I are trying to hide your shame from the neighbors.'

The pre-race meeting of skipjack crews was held at the Patamoke Club, and the mood was established by Captain Boggs, a towering black from Deal Island, known to his men as the Black Bastard: 'The *Nelly Benson* observes on'y one rule. "Stand back, you sons-of-bitches." '

Another Deal Islander said, 'This here is a race of workin' boats. Each skipjack to carry two dredges, a pushboat aft on davits, two anchors and full gear.'

One of the Patamoke men suggested a triangular course, but the Deal Islanders protested, 'We're racin' in your water. We state the rules. If the southerly wind holds, a run up the river, turn and beat back.'

That was it, a clean-cut rugged race of up-and-back with no furbelows or fancy diagrams. When this was agreed, the drinking began and some of the crews did not get to bed till dawn. Owen Steed, who by now was totally immersed in the race, got his men home reasonably early and felt that the *Eden* had a good chance, unless Captain Boggs got an early edge, in which case he would be tough to beat.

Prizes for the race were not exorbitant: $75 to every boat that lined up for the start, and an additional $50 to each one that finished. The *Bugle* awarded a silver cup plus first prize of $100, second of $50 and third of $25, but most of the crews put together purses for wagers against boats of their class. The Deal Island men were especially eager to gamble, and Captain Boggs' *Nelly Benson* would go to the line with some $400 placed against various other boats.

The commodore for the race was a surprise, and a pleasant one. By acclamation, the watermen wanted Pusey Paxmore to serve as starter; in the old days he had been a man aloof, working at the White House and rather withdrawn from river life, but now that he had served time in jail he was more like them, and they insisted that since his family had built the oldest boats in the competition, the *Eden* and two others, his presence was obligatory. He had wanted to decline, but the Steeds would not permit it.

Since the race occurred in October, just before the start of the oystering season, the twenty-three skipjacks were in prime condition: all had been hauled out to have their bottoms painted, and all had been cleaned up on deck, their dredges neatly stacked, their lines coiled. Mr. Steed had purchased a complete new dress for the *Eden:* for halyards dacron rigging because of its inflexible strength; for docking lines and anchor cable nylon because it did yield. He had gone to Henry Brown down at the tip of Deal Island for new sails and he had specified canvas rather than dacron because the stitching in the latter chafed too easily. In its eighty-six years the *Eden* had rarely looked better.

The race was to start at the edge of the mud flats west of Devon Island, run up to Patamoke Light, turn it and tack back to a line between Devon and the mainland. A skipjack race started in a peculiar way: the boats jockeyed till they were in a straight line, then dropped anchors and lowered sails, waiting for the gun that would spring them loose.

It was a tense moment, for the honor of every settlement on the shore was at stake—the rough watermen of Deal Island against the dudes of the Choptank. Each boat had a crew of six experts, plus seven or eight casual hands to man the lines. The *Eden* had five extra Turlocks and two Caters, each with his own job to do. Little Sam Cater, aged nine, would perch as far aft as possible and stare at the water, prepared to utter his warning cry, 'Mud! Mud!'

'You can fire, Pusey,' one of the judges said, and what ensued made devotees of regular racing shudder. On each of the anchored skipjacks four men began hauling in the anchor while a team of two pulled heavily on the halyards that raised the huge mainsail. Since the crews worked at uneven speeds, some boats got under way quicker than others, which meant that they were free to cut across the path of the slow starters, impeding them further. But sometimes the early boats miscalculated, and the slow starters generated enough speed to ram their opponents and delay them. When this happened, crews from both boats cursed and threw things and tried to cut rigging.

One of the judges, a gentleman from a Long Island yacht club, said as the big boats slammed into one another, 'This isn't racing. This is marine suicide.' And when Pusey Paxmore said, with some relief, 'We got them off to a good start,' the visitor replied, 'Start? Good God, they're all disqualified.'

The first leg was a long run eastward with the wind directly aft, and Captain Boggs depended upon this to give him an early advantage; indeed, it looked as if he might outdistance the field, but the *Eden* and the old *H.M. Willing* from Tilghman lagged only a short distance behind. The latter was a memorable boat; it had been sunk twice, refitted three times: 'Cain't be more than seven percent of the original timbers left. All rebuilt, but she's still the *H.M. Willing,* because it ain't the timbers that determines a boat, it's the spirit.'

'We're in good shape,' Captain Cater assured his crew, 'because in ten minutes we swing onto a starboard run, and then we fly.'

He was right. Halfway to Patamoke the skipjacks had to veer to the southeast, which meant that the strong wind would blow from the starboard quarter, the exact advantage the *Eden* needed. How she leaped forward! Her great boom swung out to port; her bow cut deep; she heeled well over and rode on the chine.

'Stand back, you Black Bastard!' Captain Absalom shouted as his boat passed the *Nelly Benson* and headed for the turn at Patamoke Light.

A real yachtsman who had twice raced to Bermuda watched the turn in frozen amazement; when the *Eden* negotiated it this gentleman said to people near him, 'Why that man broke six rules! Doesn't anybody say anything?' A waterman who heard the question replied, 'They better not.'

When the turn was completed, it was traditional for the cook to break out a spread and for the first mate to open the portable refrigerators for beer. From here on, the race became a little looser, for emptied beer cans refilled with water began flying through the air, and men with long poles tried drunkenly to impede their competitors.

The food aboard the *Eden* was excellent: ham hocks and lima beans, *krees,* as the watermen pronounced the biting watercress, biscuits and honey with large slabs of yellow cheese. But as each plate was wiped clean, its owner began staring toward the cook's shack, and in due time Amos Turlock appeared with a wide grin, to announce, 'Gentlemen, we got pie-melon pie!' and the crew cheered. When he brought the first pies on deck he said, 'We got lemon on the sour side, vanilla on the sweet, and Sam gets first choice.' He carried two pies, brown-crusted and rich, aft to where the boy watched for mud, and the lad said, 'I takes lemon,' and a large chunk was cut.

A pie-melon was a kind of gourd raised along the edges of cornfields, and when properly peeled and stewed, it produced one of the world's great pies, succulent, tasty, chewy when burned a bit and unusually receptive to other flavors; the proportion was usually three lemon to two vanilla, and today that tradition held, but as the men ate, little Sam shouted, 'Mud! Mud!' and this meant that the centerboard had touched bottom. This did not imperil the skipjack, but if the drag continued, its racing speed would be impeded, so two men jumped to the pendant of the centerboard and raised it until the lad cried, 'No mud! No mud!' and this meant that the *Eden* was making maximum speed, and that its centerboard rode as deep as practical to ensure adequate protection against lateral drift.

It was now apparent that the race would be decided on the two final tacks, and although the *Nelly Benson* had picked up a slight lead on the port tack, the boats must soon switch to starboard, and there the advantage would move to the *Eden.* 'We're in strong position!' Captain Absalom cried encouragingly, but as he prepared to jibe, Captain Boggs ordered seven of his crewmen aft to launch a barrage of water-filled beer cans at the wheel of the *Eden,* and Captain Cater had to step back to avoid being maimed. In that moment the *Eden* lost headway; the sails flapped; and whatever advantage the Patamoke boat might have gained was dissipated.

But the *Eden* was not powerless. As soon as Absalom regained the wheel, he shipped his skipjack onto a course that would allow its bowsprit to rake the stern of the enemy, and when his tactic became evident the Deal Islanders cursed and threw more beer cans, but Absalom hunkered down, swung his wheel and watched with satisfaction as his long bowsprit swept the *Nelly Benson,* cutting a halyard and forcing the crew to quit their bombardment and try to put together a jury rig that would enable them to finish the race. They did this with such promptness that they entered the final tack only a few yards behind the *Eden* and well ahead of the others.

Captain Boggs now showed why his men called him the Black Bastard. Raising his sails to maximum height, keeping his keel as close to the wind as possible, he started to overtake the *Eden,* and when it appeared that he would succeed, he swung his bow sharply so that the bowsprit could sweep the stern of the Patamoke boat.

'Fend off, back there!' Captain Absalom shouted, but it was too late. The *Nelly Benson* crunched on, her bowsprit raking the *Eden,* and by some hellish luck it banged into a gasoline can carried in accordance with the rule that each boat must be in working dress. The can bumped along the deck, emptying some of its contents before it bounced overboard. The volatile liquid spread rapidly, with one long finger rushing into the galley where Amos Turlock was cleaning up.

A great flame filled the galley and flashed along the deck. Amos, finding himself ablaze, had the presence of mind to run topside and leap into the river. Hugo Pflaum, suspecting that his ancient enemy could not swim, as most watermen could not, grabbed a rope and jumped in after him, and so spontaneous was Pflaum's action that he was able to reach the struggling cook and hold him fast as men on deck pulled the heavy pair back to the *Eden.*

All hands turned to fighting fire, except Captain Absalom, who kept to the wheel, hoping that the starboard tack would allow his boat to pull ahead, but when confusion was its greatest, the boy aft began to shout, 'Mud!' and Absalom bellowed, 'Man the centerboard,' but there was none to hear, so he indicated that the boy should quit his post and try to haul up the dragging board.

A centerboard is a huge affair, often made of oak and a task for two grown men, so the boy accomplished nothing. 'Take the wheel!' Absalom shouted and the boy ran aft to steer the skipjack, while his father ran to the rope attached to the aft end of the centerboard and tugged on it mightily. It rose a few inches and the dragging ceased.

With the fire under control, the Patamoke crew turned to the job of bringing their damaged boat to the finish line. They had lost their lead, but they kept in mind that this was a starboard tack. With burned hands and sooty faces they began to cheer and throw beer cans and trim their sails, but they were impeded by a situation which had never before developed in a skipjack race: the intense heat of the gasoline fire had melted some of the dacron lines into blobs of expensive goo. But Patamoke men were ingenious, and the crew found ways to improvise substitutes and to pass their shortened lines through sheaves and thus keep their boat moving.

It was to be a photo finish, with the *Nelly Benson* slightly ahead, the *Eden* closing vigorously. Crews of the trailing skipjacks began to cheer and big Hugo Pflaum with two of the black crewmen stood forward to repel any new assaults.

'We can make it!' Amos Turlock bellowed, throwing beer cans like mad at Captain Boggs. But the Deal Island men knew how to handle their boat, and while the *Eden* crew was working on their sails they heard the cannon. The race was over and they were forty seconds from the line. The cup, the money, the honor—all were lost. The deck was scarred with flame, their fingers burned with gasoline.

'Damn,' Absalom growled as the *Eden* crossed.

'We almost made it,' his son said.

'Ain't nothin' in the world pays off on near-'ems 'ceptin horseshoes.'

'It was fun,' the boy said.

'Fun!' his father exploded. 'Goddamnit, we lost!'

That night, when the crews assembled to celebrate and collect their awards, Absalom had the graciousness to approach Captain Boggs, shake his hand and admit, 'You won fair and square.' Those standing nearby cheered and the Deal Islander said modestly, 'God was on our side. Ninety-nine times out of a hunnerd we wouldn't of hit that gasoline can.' And Absalom conceded, 'That's how the dice rolls.'

Mr. Steed, elated by the showing of the *Eden* and pleased to have been accepted into Choptank life so quickly, delivered the final judgment on the race: 'All things considered, we gained a moral victory.'

The Steeds had hoped that when Pusey Paxmore served as commodore the excitement would lure him out of the exile to which he had condemned himself. 'He came from this peninsula,' Owen told his wife, 'and returning to it should cure him.' When she replied that this was a curious doctrine, he said, 'It wasn't chance that the sovereign remedy, penicillin, was found in the earth. The Antaeus factor. When you're in trouble, scramble back to earth. Why do you think I scurried here when I was fired?'

Paxmore would not allow the cure to work for him. He believed that his humiliation in Washington barred him from normal life, and he continued to isolate himself, brooding over the misadventures which had brought him to this low estate.

This was regrettable, for he was now sixty-four and should have been entering that congenial stage of life when the orderly routine of the seasons, acting like a magnet, pulled him along from one anticipation to the next, whether his intellectual interests did so or not. In September on the Eastern Shore a man should be cleaning his guns and putting his dogs through performance trials. In October he should be out hunting doves, convening with friends, also retired, and comparing his Labrador to their Chesapeakes. Before November he hauls his boat out of the water, drains her fuel system and covers her with canvas. In the middle of that month he turns to the serious business of hunting geese. In late December he may ignore Christmas but not the ducks coming onto his property. In January he tends his loblollies, or marks his holly trees for pruning, and in March he spends a lot of time preparing his boat for the water, going to Annapolis for marine hardware and mending his crab pots. In June, when the first crabs come along, he ices his beer and sits on his screened porch, cracking the boiled claws and waiting for the perch to fry on the brazier. In July he runs his power mower, pushing his lawn back year by year until the day he shouts to his wife, 'We're going to sell this damned place and move into an apartment. Too much lawn to mow.' But in August, when the sun blazes down and a southwest breeze comes up the bay, cooling those on the eastern shores of the creeks but not on the western, he tells her, 'Best thing we ever did was find this southwest exposure. The Lathams over there on the wrong side are broiling.'

Thus the force of the earth, revolving in its passage through space, ought to carry an older man along, from year to year, making such honors as he may have earned seem even more delectable because of his reunion with primal agencies. Pusey Paxmore missed this experience; he remained oblivious of those changing faces of nature which had been the preoccupation of his family since their arrival on the cliff in 1664: the behavior of the Chesapeake, the altering salinity of the Choptank, the arrival and departure of the geese and, especially, the constant search for straight loblollies and oak knees. It was shameful to think that this man, whose blood ran with the tides, should have become so indifferent to his universe.

The Steeds, afraid that his rejection of his native earth might destroy him, did what they could to tempt him out of his closet, but the most they accomplished was a chain of October afternoons at Peace Cliff which he attended in a shabby sweater and frayed slippers. As he talked, certain themes began to unfold:

PAXMORE: Those of us who fought against the dissolution of this nation in the late 1960s did the right thing. We were in real peril, and enemies who abuse Nixon forget this.

STEED: I was thinking the other day about the songs of that period. The ones my children played incessantly. Did you ever listen to those songs, Pusey? The excitation to rebellion? The enticement to drugs. The glib assurance that all the old values had dissolved in the acid of recent truth? Especially the encouragement of war between the generations? I should think that as the Beatles grow older, they'd stand with signs about their necks in Trafalgar Square as penance for having corrupted a decade of young people.

PAXMORE: I keep thinking about the White House. Some very bright people there realized what was happening and they did their best to stem the rot. But their efforts were preempted by the so-called realists who were preoccupied with the 1972 election. The profoundest motives were perverted for the basest goals.

STEED: Would you concede that there had been a conspiracy?

PAXMORE: To do what?

STEED: To take over the government. What I mean, to subvert our form of government and ensure not only the election of Nixon but of Agnew in 1976 and then Haldeman in 1984. Was there such a conspiracy?

PAXMORE: No. What happened was, a group of California adventurers without political apprenticeship saw a chance to bend things their way. When they saw how easy it was to manipulate the system . . . Look, Owen, thee gave me two hundred thousand without even asking what it was for. It didn't come out at the hearings or the trial, but I myself collected over eight million dollars, and not one donor ever asked me what I intended doing with it. 'Honest Pusey Paxmore, the Maryland Quaker.' It was so easy, Owen, that the California mob slowly awakened to the fact that they had a stupefying opportunity. Plan? No. Opportunity? Yes.

STEED: How do you explain the corruption, the near-treason?

PAXMORE: Men without character slip from one position to the next. And never comprehend the awful downward course they're on.

STEED: Couldn't Nixon have stopped it?

PAXMORE: Woodrow Wilson could have. Or Teddy Roosevelt. And does thee know why? Because they had accumulated through years of apprenticeship a theory of government. A theory of democracy, if thee will. And they would have detected the rot the minute it started.

STEED: Why didn't the Californians?

PAXMORE: For a simple reason. They were deficient in education. They'd gone to those chrome-and-mirror schools where procedures are taught, not principles. I doubt if any one of them had ever contemplated a real moral problem, in the abstract where character is formed.

STEED: You did?

PAXMORE: Yes, and when the revelations began to unwind, long before John Dean, I knew what was wrong, and how very wrong it was.

STEED: Why didn't you quit, then?

PAXMORE: Because I stood so close to power, to the greatest power in the world, the presidency. It obliterated judgments. I knew, but I was powerless to react because I was poisoned by power.

STEED: What did you know?

PAXMORE: I knew that men like thee, across this country, had given our collectors more than seventy million dollars of unaccounted funds to keep the ball game going along lines thee preferred. I knew that this money was being laundered in Mexico, using channels established years before by Las Vegas gamblers. I knew that White House staffers were using Internal Revenue and the F.B.I. to punish leaders of the Democratic party. We'll teach those bastards to keep their noses clean, was the way they expressed it. I knew that high officials were ordering the bugging of their assistants' private phone calls. And I knew that everyone was lying to everyone else, in order to win an election, and to keep on winning them till the end of this century.

STEED: You don't call that a conspiracy?

PAXMORE: No, because it was not planned in advance from any intellectual base. We all just slipped downward, from one greasy step to the next. It was opportunism, Owen, a failure of moral intelligence.

STEED: Did Nixon know?

PAXMORE: Let me answer that most carefully. Of my own cognizance I never saw Richard Nixon do a single wrong thing. I was very close to him, in money matters, and I can avow that he never knew how the seventy million was collected, or how it was laundered, or how it was spent. He never once told me, 'Pusey, drop by Owen Steed's office. He owes us some favors.' So far as I know, he was clean. So when he went on television that night with the stack of transcripts and looked the American people in the eye, assuring them he was innocent, I believed him.

STEED: Did you begin to doubt when you read the transcripts?

PAXMORE: I was shocked by the sloppiness of thought in the world's most powerful office. They were incapable of keeping an idea in focus for three minutes. Instead of intelligence, we had rambling associations. The obscene language that bothered so many? I brushed it off as would-be manliness until I reached that dreadful description of me . . .

STEED: How did you react to the final disclosures? When he admitted his involvement?

PAXMORE: The only thing I could think of was his earlier performances, when he stared right at the television cameras and denied the existence of such evidence, and I wondered how any man could have the brazenness to do that—to stand there, knowing that the tapes were downstairs and that at least eight other persons knew what was on them. I've never been able to get that in focus.

STEED: Did you realize then that you would go to jail?

PAXMORE: Certainly. My world had collapsed, and not one of the men who had given me orders would extend a hand to help. So I braced myself and told Amanda, 'I'll take my share of the blame and say no more about it.'

STEED: You weren't tempted to drag men like me down with you? You could have, you know.

PAXMORE: Quite a few. A man doesn't collect eight million illegal dollars without knowing who gave them, and how.

STEED: Why didn't you?

PAXMORE: Because, having done everything possible to disgrace my family, I was determined that the least I could do was take my punishment and not whimper.

STEED: You ever waver?

PAXMORE: Yes. When the tapes were played at my trial, and I was forced to listen again to what the inner circle really thought of me: 'Tell that fucking Bible-spouting asshole to get the money and shut up.' These were words, Owen, that no Paxmore had ever dared use, even to his most inept workmen . . . Three centuries of Paxmores never used such words. But the leaders of the country felt free to use them against me. And why? Because I dared to raise questions of propriety.

STEED: You did?

PAXMORE: Of course! A dozen times I warned against lawbreaking.

STEED: Why didn't you quit? Throw the job in their faces?

PAXMORE: Because I refused to believe that criminal behavior could emanate from the White House. And vanity. I enjoyed being close to sources of power and wanted to remain there.

(At this point, one cold afternoon, he fell silent; obviously he was reconstructing the painful steps of his descent into Avernus, and Steed asked no more questions. Instead he launched upon his own reflective monologue.)

STEED: You could say the same about me. I was flattered that day a high official came to Tulsa and whispered, 'Steed, if you want to be a high-roller in the next administration . . . I mean, if you want real clout . . . say, our protection against the biggies in your business, you better give evidence of your support. You better give it early and you better give it big.' He took me by the arm, exactly the way the football captain had handled me during my freshman year at the university when he wanted me to join his fraternity, and he said, 'Steed, the committee—and these are people who're going to run this nation for the rest of this century—we put you down for three hundred thousand.' I told him I didn't begin to have that much, and he said in an even lower voice, 'But you can put your hands on it,' and when I said, 'But that would be corporate money,' he put his hand over my mouth and whispered, 'I'm going to assume you never said that. How you get the money is your affair, but I will tell you this. Whoever we select for Attorney General will be in our pocket, and you'll get no flap from him.' So, as you know, I devised a way to channel not the full three hundred thousand, but two hundred, and do you know why? Because I wanted to be a high-roller, throw my weight around when the unions got too tough, tell my secretary, 'Get me Washington, right now.' But beyond that . . .

(Steed paused to watch the return of geese from a foraging expedition, and as they wheeled over the Choptank he told Paxmore, 'You and me, we're going to get our share of those fellows.' He was disappointed when his withdrawn friend showed no excitement, and after a while he resumed.)

STEED: When Watergate broke I accepted it as minor, third-class, and assumed that no one would have bothered with the Democratic offices unless those goons were up to something illegal, which they usually are. When the President disclaimed any knowledge of the affair, I dropped it. Never occurred to me that my two hundred thousand could be involved, because I had never once thought of it as illegal. I was merely striving to save the good life of my nation and to keep its direction in proper hands. I listened to some of the Dean testimony, and when he couldn't even recall what hotel he'd been in, I classed him as a phony and dismissed his yarn as a concoction. And when the President came on television to proclaim his innocence, I thought that ended the affair. It should have, but the American press hates anyone who's successful. Reporters who didn't belong to fraternities in college or play football can't understand how a man with guts and brains can make thirty million dollars. They're inherent anarchists, and that's as clear as a bolt of lightning in August. They were out to destroy Nixon, and they did. But I was like you.

PAXMORE: How?

STEED: I could not believe it when the tapes proved that Nixon had been lying. It was inconceivable that a man could stand before those cameras, knowing that he had a time bomb ticking away at his heart, and utter the lies he did.

PAXMORE: What kept me believing was a silly article I read. Written by his older daughter, exculpating him from everything. It seemed so fresh and honest. So sincere.

STEED: My suspicions began when I heard the first tapes, the clean ones, and listened to those revelations of how these men conducted the business of this nation. The low quality of the thought. The inability to hold on to any subject consecutively. The frowzy language. The big enchilada. Pusey, I assure you, if a meeting I was conducting at Western

Oil had ever proceeded in such a sloppy manner, with my staff unable to keep to the main topic, I'd have fired the bunch.

PAXMORE: Thee falls into a common error, Owen. Thee expects a President to be presidential twenty-four hours a day. Thee must grant him license to be a human being, to speak from time to time like ordinary men, with all their vulgarities.

STEED: But in a presidential crisis I expect him to be presidential. And tell me this, Pusey. Didn't you ever have lawyers at those meetings?

PAXMORE: What does thee mean?

STEED: When we discussed something important, or even close to a moral problem, we always had at least one lawyer present. And after a while he might interrupt and say, 'But you can't do that. That's illegal.'

PAXMORE: Thee can't say no to a President. (Here he lost interest in the post-mortem, but after watching the geese for a while, he resumed.) Yesterday I was reading *The True History of Patamoke* and it says that in the old days men like Clay, Calhoun and Webster visited your family mansion. How would they have reacted to Watergate?

STEED: My Great-Grandfather Paul, who did the little book on slavery, defended it, if you remember. He left a group of memoranda on these men, and from them I conclude that if Daniel Webster had ever been elected President, he would probably have behaved exactly like Nixon, not because he was corrupt, but because he was so respectful of money and so personally vain. Henry Clay? Not a chance. He had a super-refined sense of honor which would have kept him honest in a nest of thieves. Calhoun? (Here the reverence in which the Steeds had always held this great man manifested itself.) It would have been unthinkable for him to behave poorly. He might have burned the nation down but he would never have stolen it.

PAXMORE: That's about my conclusion, Owen. Any man of flawed character would have stumbled into the Nixon errors.

STEED: But of one thing I can assure you. No one of those men, running the White House, would have tolerated the disgraceful thought processes displayed in the tapes. They'd have called the meeting to order sharply and reminded their associates, 'Let's get on with the main business.' Pusey, do you think the main business of your gang was installing a dictatorship?

PAXMORE: Thee must remember, Owen, how they characterized me. 'That Bible-quoting asshole.' I was never allowed to see their inner purposes. My job was to collect money, launder it, feed it into unknown hands. My job was to collect personal dishonor. (His voice trailed off, and Steed supposed that tears were choking him, but they were not. He was looking down at the Choptank, along whose banks the earlier Paxmores had gained so much honor in facing the routine tasks that arise on any river—the building of ships, the speaking in meeting, the teaching of others, the defending of the laws. He was dry and worn-out because of his faithlessness to those principles.)

STEED: We'll go hunting next month.

There was no answer.

The fact that Hugo Pflaum saved the life of Amos Turlock during the fire aboard the *Eden* did not mean that the stubborn old warden relaxed his determination to capture The Twombly. In semi-retirement, the thick-necked German reported to his office only three mornings a week, but whenever he saw the empty space on his wall of pictures, he resolved anew to find that gun.

His superiors in Annapolis were neither amused nor patient. 'For thirty-nine years you've been telling us, "I'll find that gun any day now." Where in hell is it?'

'We think it's hidden close to where the old marsh used to be. And we know he's using it because on some mornings when he comes to town we can smell powder on his clothes.'

'Sign out a warrant and search his trailer.'

'I been through that trailer four times when he was out. Found nothing.'

It was decided that since Amos used the gun as many as nine or ten times each season, he must keep it hidden somewhere close to the trailer, and Pflaum was directed to hold the place under surveillance, but this raised more difficulties than it solved, for the Turlock establishment had certain extraordinary features. From the enthusiastic potteries in North Carolina, Amos had enlarged his collection of lawn statuary to twenty-one major items, and casual passers-by were usually on hand to admire the art collection. Older people liked the white cement replica of an Italian marble; it showed a naked girl scrunched over from the waist, her hands in position to hide those parts deemed most vulnerable. But children preferred Santa Claus and his eight reindeer.

When Pflaum initiated his regular spying, things were complicated by the fact that Amos had imported an ensemble of eight fairly large pieces which gladdened his heart: Snow White accompanied by seven dwarfs, each carved with maximum cuteness. When trailed across the lawn, the sculptures captivated the public, and the local policeman said approvingly, 'Sort of rounds things out. More grass to trim by hand, but also more fun for ever'body.'

Hugo, seeing the eight additions for the first time, said, 'Place looks even junkier than when it was a shack,' and this was true, for in the old days the cabin, weathered and dilapidated though it was, had shared the dignity of the surrounding woods. But this chrome trailer with its little picket fence and lawn sculptures had been offensive at birth and got worse as it grew older.

What Pflaum particularly disliked was the stiff manner in which Amos had placed the three dwarfs Smiley, Bashful and Grumpy. 'He's got them lined up as if they were soldiers. The others, he at least has them strung out.' He was so offended by the awful aesthetic of this lawn, and so irritated by his failure to find the gun, that one morning he pushed open the low gate guarding the path to the trailer, then jumped back as a hidden spring triggered a set of automobile horns which sounded *Do ye ken John Peel?*

Alerted, Amos Turlock came to the Dutch door and opened the top half. 'Do you like the tune, Hugo? Me bein' a hunter and all that?'

The klaxon greeting had been the last straw, so without extending the amenities Hugo said, 'Amos, I want you to turn in the gun.'

'What gun?'

'The Twombly. I know you have it hidden, and I know you love it. But the time's come, Amos. I want it.'

'I haven't had my hands on that gun—'

'You fired it four nights ago.'

'How would you know?'

'Up and down the river, Turlocks eating geese.'

'We're good hunters, Hugo, all of us.'

'You are good, and you don't need that old cannon any longer.'

'Where could I hide a gun twelve feet long?' With a generous gesture he invited the warden to inspect the trailer, and even shouted, 'Midge, have we got a gun in there?'

'We sure have,' his toothless paramour called back, and forthwith she produced a shotgun. Amos laughed, and Pflaum said, 'I should of let you drown.' Then his irritation got the better of him, and he said, 'Those seven dwarfs look like hell,' and with that judgment he stomped off the premises.

Five nights later, when there was a strong frost in the air and no moon to betray the midnight hunter, Amos summoned Rafe, the grandson in whom he had most confidence. 'We ain't obliged to get ourselves some geese, because we ain't finished the ones we got last time, but a man oughta keep his hand in. We're goin' gunnin'.'

At eleven he and Rafe left the trailer, walked out into the yard, bent down and cautiously pulled on two rings hidden in the grass on which the three dwarfs stood: Smiley, Bashful, Grumpy. Slowly the dwarfs rose in the air, falling backward from a grave twelve feet long. It was a scene from a Dracula movie—even the hinge creaked—except that when the grave was opened, it revealed not a vampire but The Twombly.

With loving care Amos lifted it, stared at the moonless sky and told Rafe, 'Fetch the dog,' and as the Chesapeake bounded out of the trailer, Amos lowered the lid, checked the three dwarfs and led the way through the woods to where the skiffs lay hidden.

It was a perfect night for goose hunting, cold but not blustery, starry but with no moon. When they reached the spot where La Trappe River joined the Choptank they detected large numbers of fowl rafting at the proper distance, and as Amos primed his massive gun and checked the seating of its stock against the bags of pine needles, he whispered to his grandson, 'Best thing a man can do in this world is hunt, or fish, or go arsterin'. God put all these things down here for us to enjoy, but He hid 'em so's only a resolute man can catch 'em. It's our manly duty to try.'

As he sighted along the polished barrel of The Twombly, he saw the glimmer of Orion and he showed the boy how that constellation stalked through the heavens, a mighty hunter seeking game. 'It ain't by chance he comes out in winter. Stands up there to protect us . . . and the gun.' Softly he touched the brass cannon, and then asked, 'How old are you, Rafe?'

'Ten.'

'God A'mighty, boy, this here gun is fifteen times older'n you are. Think of it, fifteen different boys your age coulda' cared for this gun, and now it's your responsibility.'

The red Chesapeake, sensing the geese ahead, was growing restless; Amos hadn't even taken out the short paddles, and the dog feared something might spook those geese. He made soft noises to indicate his displeasure at the sloppy methods being pursued this night, but Amos growled at him to keep silent. He wanted to talk with the boy.

'Man's got only three obligations, really. Feed his fambly. Train his dog. Take care of his gun. You do them jobs properly, you ain't got no worries about such things as mortgages and cancer and the tax collector. You take care of the gun, God takes care of the mortgage.'

'Won't the law . . .'

'The law takes this gun away from us, Rafe, when it's smart enough to find it. I been guardin' this gun for fifty years. You're good for another fifty.'

'But Hugo Pflaum was practically standin' on it that other mornin'.'

'That's why us Turlocks will always have this gun.'

'Why?'

'Because we're smart, all of us, and game wardens is stupid, all of 'em.'

The dog whimpered, eager to get on with the hunt, but he was astonished at what happened. Amos Turlock was climbing gingerly out of the skiff that carried The Twombly and inviting his grandson to take his place with the short paddles.

'Time you learned, son,' he said when the delicate transfer was completed.

'You want me . . .'

'Two things to remember. Aim the skiff, not the gun. And for Christ's merry sake, stay clear of the stock, because it kicks like hell.' With a gentle and loving push he launched the skiff toward the rafted geese, then reached for his dog's head. Pulling the Chesapeake to him, he clutched him nervously as the boy disappeared into the darkness. The dog, sensing that this was an unusual night, stayed close to his master and waited for the great explosion that would project him into the water in search of geese.

It was a long wait, but neither the man nor the dog grew restless; Amos could remember nights when it had taken him an hour of working with short paddles before he had been satisfied with his position, and Rafe had been trained to be meticulous. In the blind, Amos remembered admiringly, Rafe had been the boy with guts to wait.

At last he began to tremble, hoping desperately that his grandson would handle the skiff properly, and the great gun, and the traditions of this river. 'It's a baptism,' he whispered to the tense animal, and the fingers of his right hand twined in the dog's hair so tightly that the Chesapeake whimpered and withdrew, going to his accustomed place in the bow, where he could stand with forefeet on the gunwales, peering into the darkness.

'Blessed God,' the old man prayed, 'let him do it right . . . so he gets the taste.'

Forty minutes passed, and Orion, failing as ever to catch his prey, roamed the heavens. But when the tension in Amos's skiff became intolerable, the night sky exploded, and geese cried, and the dog was gone.

Seven different homes called Hugo Pflaum's office next morning to report illegal gunning on the Choptank. 'I know they were out there, Mr. Pflaum, because two dead geese drifted to my shore. Besides, I was lookin' at the Late-Late Show and remarked to my wife, "That gunfire wasn't on TV." '

The reports were so circumstantial that Pflaum climbed into his pickup and roared out to the Turlock trailer, but as he had anticipated, Amos was absent. Distributing geese up and down the river, he supposed. Midge was gone too, doing her shopping at the Steed store in Sunset Acres. Only a boy, not more than eleven, stood at the corner of the lawn, watching suspiciously as the big, hulking warden moved among the seven dwarfs.

'Who are you, son?'

'Rafe.'

'You can't be Amos's son?'

'Grandson.'

'You wouldn't know where your grandfather is?' No response. 'You wouldn't know where he was last night?' No flicker in the pale-blue eyes.

Hugo was perplexed by the Turlocks, even though his mother and his wife came from that clan; always they seemed stupid, but always in a crisis they mustered just enough brains to outsmart their betters. Look at this boy! Blond hair almost in his eyes, cut in back with the aid of a bowl, vacant stare, heavy woolen pants held up by torn suspenders, didn't even seem to know that Pflaum was a relative of sorts and the game warden. Perhaps, Hugo thought in a misbegotten moment, I can trick this lad.

'Your gran'daddy out huntin' last night?'

'What?' The boy refused to leave his position at the corner of the lawn.

'Does he ever hunt with that big gun?'

'What?'

'Where's he keep it, Rafe?'

'Keep what?' the boy asked, a kind of stupid glaze over his face.

'You tell your father—'

'My father's in Baltimore.'

'I mean your grandfather,' Pflaum snapped.

'Tell him what?' the boy asked.

'That I was here.'

'Who are you?'

'You know damned well who I am. I'm Hugo Pflaum, your uncle more or less. You tell him I was here.'

'I'll tell him. Hugo Pflaum.'

With disgust, the game warden kicked at the sod, gingerly retraced his steps through the garden sculpture and drove back to town.

When he was gone, and well gone, with the pickup far around the bend, Rafe Turlock slumped against the trailer and would have fallen except that he caught hold of a coping. Keeping himself more or less erect, he began to vomit, not once or twice but seven times, until his stomach was empty and his body racked.

Midge found him there, still retching, and thought he might have whooping cough, for the boy would give no explanation for his spasms. She insisted that he go to bed, and he lay there with wet packs on his forehead, waiting for his grandfather's return.

Amos was absent for a long time distributing geese, but when he reached the kitchen and heard the rambling report of his grandson's seizure, he could guess what had caused it. Slipping into the sickroom, he asked, 'Hugo Pflaum here?'

'Yep. He was standin' right on the gun, askin' his questions.'

'About last night?'

'And the gun.'

'And what did you tell him?'

'Nothin', but when he kicked at one of the rings I almost vomited.'

'Midge says you did. All over the place.'

'That was after.'

Amos did not pat his grandson on the head, or congratulate him in any way. The boy had done only what was required, but he did want to let Rafe know that he was pleased, so he whistled for the Chesapeake, and to the dog's surprise, the door was opened and he was invited into the trailer. Quickly he sought out his young master, and realizing that the boy was ill, stayed by his bed, licking his limp fingers.

Amos, closing the door on the room, offered no explanation to Midge. He walked out onto the lawn to survey his twenty-one sets of sculpture: the deer were lined up behind Santa, the purple flamingo spread its concrete wings toward Sunset Acres, and the seven dwarfs trailed along behind their mistress in seven distinct styles of cuteness. Looking to where the three stood in line, Amos could visualize the great gun nesting at their feet.

'Safe for another fifty years,' he said.

One crisp November morning Owen Steed awoke to the sound of birds squabbling at the feeder outside his window, and he was so enchanted by their vitality that without dressing he went onto the lawn, where he could see the creeks from which the osprey had migrated. Standing reverently amidst a beauty he had discovered nowhere else on earth, he reflected that no one had successfully described the quiet splendor of the Eastern Shore. He was sixty-six that morning and aware that he could enjoy these estuaries for only a limited number of years, but he was grateful that misadventures in Oklahoma had forced him to come back to the drowsy glories of his youth.

When he returned to his bedroom he heard Ethel washing, and called, 'They refer to this as the land of pleasant living, but that's mere hedonism.'

'What are you talking about, Owen?'

'The lasting values of this place. Bright mornings like this. Cool nights.'

'They were cool last winter.'

'I'm trying to be serious. About a land worth preserving.' He hesitated. 'Are you joining me at the meeting?'

'What meeting?' And before he could reply, she cried enthusiastically, 'That chap from Annapolis. Going to advise us as to how we can end the plague of beer cans.' Indeed she was attending.

But as they entered the meeting hall Chris Pflaum dampened their enthusiasm. 'You're not going to like what he says. He's quite gloomy.' He certainly was, a tall angular man in his late fifties, worn down by bureaucratic haggling:

'I'm Dr. Paul Adamson, here to warn you that you're deluding yourselves if you think that reasoning or citing horrible examples will mend our defaced landscape. Seven states have conducted referenda within the past three years, and the voters have delivered a strong, clear message: "We like our clutter. We insist on the right to pitch our beer bottles wherever we damned well wish."

'It is counterproductive to argue that our citizens ought not to exhibit such destructive traits. Our problem is to uncover why they are so loyal to the empty beer can and why they insist upon using it to decorate our highways. Three disturbing factors operate. First, drinking from a can, whether it contains beer or soda pop, is a machismo thing, and in an age when we repress one machismo manifestation after another—old-style courtships, use of guns, certain speech patterns—young men are finding the beer can a last refuge. It is socially desirable to guzzle, and peer domination insists that when the can is emptied, it be thrown with arrogance wherever it will be most conspicuous.

'Second, in a period when the government restricts our actions in scores of new ways, and when it yearly sends out intrusive tax forms which not one person can understand, it is inevitable that the vigorous person must find some way to express his resentment, and what better way than with an empty beer bottle?

'Third, and this is much uglier than the first two reasons and also less susceptible to control, littering a lawn with empties is a form of social aggression used especially by those groups who feel they are disadvantaged by society. Do the responsible citizens of the community want to keep the ditches clear? The young rebel is opposed to everything the responsibles try to protect, and tossing empties into the very spots they cherish is satisfying revenge.

'Thus we have three powerful reasons urging us to deface the land, and almost none driving us to protect it. Good friends, you and I are engaged in a losing battle.'

Comments on this doleful litany were spirited. 'Can't we pass laws requiring deposits on cans and bottles?' Adamson replied that such plans had been rejected sharply by most voters on the grounds that they were an imposition on their freedom. 'Can't we appoint county officials with trucks to pick up the awful garbage?' Adamson pointed out eleven instances in which communities had rejected such proposals as unwarranted expense, the argument being that it penalized those who did not drink beer. 'Can we simply outlaw the damned things as socially destructive? We'd outlaw a plague of locusts quick enough.' Adamson did not have to go far afield for his answer to this; he referred to the commission's decision that since Norman Turlock had invested so much money in his canning plant, it would be unfair to him to change the rules now.

'What can we do?' Ethel Steed asked in some desperation.

'Nothing,' Adamson replied. 'I'm head of the agency that's supposed to prevent the plundering of Maryland's natural beauty, and there's not a damned thing I can do.' He paused to let this fact sink in, then added, 'There is, however, one thing you might try.' Everyone leaned forward, for the desire to end this nuisance was vigorous. 'Buy yourself a basket, and three days a week go out like me and pick the damned things up.'

The meeting ended on such a hopeless note that the Steeds did not want to go home, and they were relieved when Chris Pflaum suggested that they wait in the lobby and join Dr. Adamson for lunch. They found him in a reflective mood, wanting to talk about the problems of the Chesapeake. 'I was raised in Chestertown. Went to Washington College there. Didn't learn much calculus but I sure learned how to man a schooner. I lived on the bay in the good years, 1936 to the beginning of 1942. No bridge crossing the bay. No oil deposits on your hull. Crabs everywhere. The best oysters in America. And what I remember most fondly, you could jump overboard at any spot in the bay and swim. No jellyfish. It was then that my intense love for the bay was born.'

But he did not want to stress the old days at the expense of the present. 'This is still the world's most enchanting inland water. Chap in my office who loves to sail calculated that if a man owned a boat which drew less than four feet, he could cruise the Chesapeake for a thousand successive days, and drop anchor each night in a different cove.'

'Sounds improbable,' Steed said.

'Let's take the Tred Avon,' Adamson suggested, and from memory he rattled off eighteen contributory creeks. 'Now, let's take just one of them, Plaindealing, and recall only the coves we can name. Twelve of them. You could spend six months on the Tred Avon and each night anchor in some cove of heavenly beauty. And remember, we have forty rivers as good as the Tred Avon. My friend was conservative. There must be eight thousand coves along this bay—all of them in peril.'

He spoke of the dreadful burden humanity was throwing upon this inland sea: effluvia from the sewer systems, poisons from the plants, industrial waste from the entire Susquehanna Valley, the garbage of the small-boat fleet, the awful pressure of human beings, each year more insistent, less disciplined, more wasteful, less attentive.

'Ecologists in Germany and Japan and Russia are working on the theory that it is man himself who is the contaminant. Not his manufacturing plants, nor his chemicals, nor his oil spills. They're the conspicuous disasters, but the permanent one is the accumulation of men and women in great quantities and large clusters. Even if they do no single thing disastrous, it is they who create the great disaster. By their numbers alone shall ye know them.'

He dilated on this for nearly half an hour, developing the theme first enunciated by German scholars analyzing India. 'They found that numbers alone are determinant. Around the world, wherever six thousand people congregate they justify a city. Six thousand people merit having a shoemaker, and a barber, and a man who specializes in baking pastries, and a sewage engineer, however primitive. The outside specialist has no right to ask, "What is the justification for this city?" It is its own justification.

'Well, the same kind of limit probably operates negatively. If you have clustering on the shores of any body of water a large enough population, that water will be destroyed. You watch the Mediterranean two hundred years from now.'

A woman at the lunch made the obvious remark that she wasn't going to be on the Chesapeake two hundred years from now, and she doubted very much that any of the others would be there, either, to which Adamson replied, with no impatience, 'The individual witness disappears, yes, but the collective intelligence persists. Two hundred years from now, in 2177, someone like me, with every one of my apprehensions, will be lunching in Patamoke and weighing the future of the Chesapeake. We have to ensure that the bay still exists for him to worry about.'

'We were pessimistic over the possibility of controlling empty beer cans,' Steed said. 'How about the bay itself?'

'The numbers terrify me, Mr. Steed. All of central Pennsylvania contaminates our bay. Baltimore, Washington, Roanoke. Millions upon millions of people, all throwing their problems into the bay. How can it possibly survive?'

'We said that about the goose, forty years ago. Now look at the population.'

'Yes!' Adamson cried, his eyes brightening with that enthusiasm he had acquired as a boy. 'The hopeful factor is what we've discovered in various countries. Any body of water with a strong flow, no matter how contaminated, can flush itself out—renew itself completely—in three years. If it's protected. If it's allowed to regenerate in its own slow, sweet way.'

'Even Lake Erie?' a woman asked.

'Of course! Three years of total policing . . . no new contamination coming in from Huron . . . average rainfall. Even Lake Erie could cleanse itself. Now there would be some stubborn deposits on the bottom, but in time even they would be degraded and washed away. The Chesapeake Bay is like a beautiful woman. There's no humiliation from which she cannot recover.'

The room in which the ecologists were having their lunch overlooked the Choptank, and from this vantage point no one could have deduced that the river had altered much in the past three hundred and seventy years of the white man's occupancy: the width was the same; the color was still a chocolate-brown; the tides ebbed and flowed without creating much disturbance; and the geese were back. Land which had begun to perish under the weight of tomatoes was prospering when planted with corn—thousands upon thousands of acres—and out beyond Devon Island, what was left of it, the bay rested in the wintry sunlight.

'It's in dreadful shape now,' Adamson said. 'I suppose you know we had to close down three more creeks. Oysters all contaminated. Hepatitis factories, our doctors call them. You eat a plate of six, you're in bed for half a year. The bay's become a cesspool—a dumping ground for Baltimore . . . and the others. But it could be restored.'

He rose and walked nervously about the room, looking now at the Choptank, now at the forests of loblolly on the far shore. 'Our gamble has to be this. That at some point in the next two hundred years there will be a group of people like us able to convince society to give the bay three years of rest. It will revive. Oysters will be edible again. Fish will return. Grass will grow in the creeks and the ducks will be back, too. Millions of them.'

He was so excited by the endless possibilities of rejuvenation that his mind raced on. 'Of course, when the ducks return, the geese may leave. Then we'll change again and they'll come back. The entire bay can be revived, every one of its eight thousand coves . . .' He hesitated. His face grew somber. 'Unless, of course, we have so contaminated the oceans that they can no longer send fresh tides and fish into the bay.' He shrugged his shoulders. 'Mankind was destined to live on the edge of perpetual disaster. We are mankind because we survive. We do it in a half-assed way, but we do it. I suppose before the year ends we'll even see some blue heron wading back. Their struggle has lasted for eleven thousand years. Ours is just beginning.'

Not only were Commissioner Adamson's hesitant predictions depressing, but wherever the Steeds drove that afternoon they saw the necklace of empties littering the roadside to remind them that they were powerless to do anything about this relatively small contamination. Owen became so irritated that he could not sleep and thought of heading downstream to Peace Cliff to talk with Pusey Paxmore about the rise and fall of men's fortunes, but he felt that this would be an imposition.

Till well past midnight he listened to Beethoven's later quartets, and before dawn left the house to watch the geese feeding in the creek. As soon as the sun was up, he telephoned Chris Pflaum on the Little Choptank to ask if he could drop by. 'Nothing of importance. Yesterday depressed the hell out of me, and I thought you might like to run down to the old ferry at Whitehaven, see how they lived in the old days.' He was delighted when Pflaum said, 'Great idea. I'd like to visit the marshes.'

Without waking Ethel, he left the house, counted the empty cans on the quarter-mile stretch he used as his barometer, and crossed to the southern shore of the Choptank. He drove slowly westward, pausing to pay his respects at the house in which Governor Hicks had lived prior to the Civil War: Remarkable man. Slaveowner. Slave supporter to the death. Goes to Annapolis and by force of his courage alone holds Maryland in the Union. Dies in disgrace. Along the Choptank they spat on his grave. A lot like Pusey. He shook his head and muttered, 'That poor son-of-a-bitch,' but whether he meant the governor who had left the Choptank to find disgrace in Annapolis or the Quaker who had found his in the White House he could not have said.

Nor would he have admitted why he wanted to visit Chris Pflaum's residence; true, the Steeds had had some vague association with the old Herman Cline plantation now occupied by Pflaum, but no one was proud of it. And some interesting new houses were being built along the Little Choptank, but they held no fascination for a man who already owned his family plantation.

What Steed really wanted to see was how young Pflaum was living; he'd heard rumors and wished to satisfy himself as to their accuracy. He was rather relieved, therefore, to find that Chris was living alone in the rambling old house; his wife had left him—'Said she could stand either the mosquitoes or the loneliness, but not both.'

'You getting a divorce?'

'She is. Says she wants nothing from me. Ten years on the Little Choptank gave her memories enough for a lifetime.' The young naturalist spoke without rancor and suggested that Steed leave his Cadillac and travel in Pflaum's pickup. 'That's the proper way to cross the ferry.'

Each man was delighted with the trip south; it took them along the banks of those lesser rivers which wound through vast marshes where the true values of the Eastern Shore were being preserved. They drifted down to Deal Island and invited Captain Boggs for a drink. He showed them a shortcut to Whitehaven, where the ferry across the Wicomico could be reached.

'This is unbelievable,' Steed said in spiritual relaxation as he slumped back to watch a rural scene which had changed little in two hundred years. 'Only visible difference is those new chicken sheds producing birds for Frank Perdue.' On the incredibly ancient roads one expected to meet oxen dragging timbers for Her Majesty's ships—Elizabeth I, that is—and at the end of the road, where it dipped toward a small, muddy river, the ferry waited. It was on the wrong side, of course, but by pulling a rope the signal was raised, a grumpy black man moved aboard his rickety craft, the sidewheels engaged a cable, and slowly the little ferry came to fetch the pickup.

It was a crossing into another century; upstream stood the gaunt and rusting remnants of what had once been the proudest tomato cannery in the Steed chain; how many black men and women, recently in bondage, had toiled here in the 1870s; how many promising Steed lads had worked here to learn the business. The crossing required only a few minutes, but it was so restful, so far removed from the problems of today, that Steed was drawn back into the lost centuries when the Steeds governed, and he was tempted into a most baronial action.

Grasping Chris by the arm, he said almost imploringly, 'Don't remarry until you meet my daughter.'

'Sir?'

'I mean it. Damnit all, Ethel and I have this enormous place. The Steeds have always had plantations like it. My son's lost. Quite hopeless. But my daughter's worth saving. Chris, don't remarry till I get her home.'

'Mr. Steed, I don't even know her name.'

'Son, we're talking about the centuries, not a few lousy mixed-up years. Name's Clara. Have you any idea what Pusey Paxmore's gone through?'

The conversation was drowned out by a truck that began blowing its horn, not on the bank to which the ferry was heading but from the one it had left. 'Damn,' the black operator growled, 'you'd think just once they could fit together.' He looked ominously at Steed as if he had been at fault, and in some confusion the trip across the Wicomico ended, with Owen Steed staring at the ruined cannery and Chris Pflaum sadly bewildered.

'Let me put it simply,' Steed said as they headed back toward Herman Cline's plantation. 'My daughter Clara's a little younger than you. For three years she's been on one hell of a toboggan . . .' He fumbled, then said, 'You haven't done so damned well yourself. But the point is, Chris, you see land the way I do. You're authentic. I want you to marry Clara and take over our place when I die.'

'Mr. Steed, one day in the jungles of Vietnam, I discovered what was significant in my life. Marshes. Living with nature. And if I wouldn't give up marshes for Vera, whom I loved very much, I sure as hell won't give them up for a girl I've never met . . . and her fifty acres of mowed lawn.'

'You don't have to, damnit! You live in the marshes half the year, in a real house the other half.'

Chris drew back from the wheel, a husky young fellow who had already made the big decisions of his life, and as he studied the oilman he saw him as properly dressed, neatly trimmed and without a basic commitment in his body. 'You don't understand, Mr. Steed. North of the Choptank is for millionaires; south is for men.'

'That's bloody arrogant.'

'And true. I need the earth. I love the older ways down here. When I'm working in the marshes along the Little Choptank my soul expands. If I lived in a manicured place like yours, I'd die.'

He was stunned by Steed's response. 'Son, I want you to check with Washburn Turlock. Ask him about the time he showed me the Refuge from a boat. One minute he said, "It's got about two hundred acres," and within five seconds I said, "I'll buy it." I needed that land as much as you needed your marsh. Only difference between you and me is you're more primitive. If you're smart, you'll be at Patamoke Airport when Clara flies home from Paris. I think she's as hungry to get back to the land as either of us.'

Turlocks survived because they adjusted to their environment. From the moment Amos discovered what those newfangled tape recorders could do, he was satisfied that his goose problems were solved.

He had always been supreme with the goose call, luring birds when others failed, but even at his expert lips that stubby instrument was chancy, and on some days he accomplished nothing. So he drove across the bridge to De Soto Road in Baltimore, where radio shops proliferated, and there bought himself a pair of powerful loudspeakers and a rugged tape recorder built in Sweden.

When he reached home Midge bellowed from the kitchen, 'What in hell you gonna do with that crap?'

His intention was to record the calls of female geese as they came in heat, then to broadcast the calls to hordes of males as they flew overhead. 'We master this machine, Rafe, we'll have enough geese to stock every Turlock kitchen along the Choptank.'

He mastered it so well that hunters from distant counties assembled to observe his miracle. As the wildlife reporter for the *Baltimore Sun* explained: 'Forty minutes before sunrise Amos Turlock and his men move quietly to their blinds and hide themselves beneath pine branches. As dawn approaches and the big geese begin to fly, Amos turns on his Tandberg and through the sky float the sounds of a female goose signaling to the gentlemen aloft. The males, delighted to hear the mating call, wheel in the air and descend swiftly into the muzzles of the Turlock guns.'

Amos enjoyed his monopoly for only one season, then others began to copy it; but it was the legislature that delivered the deathblow. To it came game wardens like the Pflaums, complaining that the Turlocks were destroying the balance of nature: 'Give them three more years and we'll have the old days back. Not a goose along the Choptank.' The lawmakers, most of them hunters, responded with a tough edict—you can read it in the Maryland Statutes, Turlock's Law they call it: 'No hunter may seduce male geese by means of electronic devices.' And the tape recorders were confiscated.

But a Turlock never quits, and in September of 1977, just before hunting season began, Amos came up with the ultimate stratagem: he rented five cows.

When he fenced them in right beside the creek where geese assembled, he attracted more birds into his field than anyone on the Choptank had ever done before, and Chris Pflaum asked his father, 'What's the old man up to?'

'I don't know,' Hugo said, 'but we better find out.'

Together they drove out to Turlock's spread, and what they saw astounded them. There were the five cows. There were the geese. And on the ground lay more yellow grains of corn than the average outlaw would dare to scatter in four seasons. Whenever Turlock wanted a goose, two hundred would be waiting as they gorged on his illegal corn.

But was it illegal? As Amos explained to the judge, 'All I do is feed my cows extra generous.' By this he meant that he gorged them on whole corn sixteen, eighteen hours a day. His rented cows ate so much that a large percentage passed through their system untouched by stomach acids, and there it lay on the ground, an enticement to geese for miles around.

'I can't find this man guilty,' the judge said. 'He didn't scatter the corn. The cows did.' And when the season ended, with the Turlock iceboxes crammed, old Amos returned his rented cows.

For some time it had been understood that Owen Steed intended luring Pusey Paxmore from his exile in the telescope house; the tactic would be a morning's goose hunt over the cornfields at the Refuge, so on a brisk November morning, before the sun had even hinted that it would rise, he drove out to Peace Cliff and found Pusey and his wife waiting in the darkness.

'He insists on taking Brutus,' Amanda said as she held a black Labrador by his collar.

'Wouldn't have it any other way,' Steed said as he roughed the dog's head. 'In you go!' The dog leaped into the rear of the pickup, stiffened as Steed's Chesapeake snarled, then relaxed in the companionship of a good hunt.

The two men drove down the lane in darkness and back to the Refuge, where they parked the car and started walking in the faint haze of dawn. Soon they were in the middle of an extensive field, apparently barren but actually rich in stray kernels of corn skipped by the harvesting machines.

They were headed for a strange construction, a giant-sized coffin of wood, let down into the earth in such a way that a large flat lid, camouflaged with branches, could be pulled shut after they and their dogs had climbed in. Once secure inside the coffin, and hidden by branches, the men could stand erect and look out through long narrow slits parallel to the earth. Here they would wait for sunrise and the flight of geese.

It was a long wait. The area contained many geese, more than half a million if one considered all the estuaries and coves, but few were interested in the cornfield at the Refuge. Occasional groups of six or seven would veer in from the creek, stay far from the gunners, then fly on. Eight o'clock came, cold and windy, with never a goose. Ten o'clock and no geese. At eleven a bright sun burned off the haze, making what hunters called 'a blue-bird day,' and any hope of bagging a goose during the middle hours was lost; the hunters climbed out of their casket, replaced the lid and tramped back to the pickup, with the dogs almost as disappointed as they.

At the Refuge, Ethel Steed had two roasted ducks waiting, with beef bones for the dogs, and the midday hours passed almost somnolently. Ethel earnestly wanted to ask Pusey lingering questions about Watergate, but when she saw how relaxed he was she restrained herself, and the time was spent in the most casual conversation, each participant speaking gingerly, as if afraid to agitate painful nerve ends.

'I would like to add one comment to the talks we've had,' Pusey volunteered as he dressed for the field. 'Isn't it clear that either Eisenhower or Kennedy would have cleaned up that mess in one afternoon? Go on television, manfully confess error, fire everyone involved and promise never again to allow such a lapse. The American people would have accepted that.'

Ethel smiled mischievously and asked, 'When you speak of Kennedy's eagerness to make a clean breast of everything, I presume you're referring to Teddy at Chappaquiddick?' When she saw that her frivolity startled Paxmore, she threw her arm about his shoulder and said jokingly, 'You see, Pusey, Democrats can suffer paralysis of will as well as Republicans.'

'Sky's nicely overcast,' Owen interrupted, 'and about three-thirty the geese will start coming in. Let's go back for an hour.'

But Pusey, who had enjoyed this day, said hopefully, 'I'd like to stay two or three hours. They come flocking in at dusk.'

'You're right,' Owen said. 'But remember, I have to meet the airplane at five. Clara's flying in from Paris.'

'How fortunate thee is!' Paxmore said with obvious enthusiasm. 'Reuniting a family! Forget the geese. Take me home and be on thy way.'

'No. Those hours in the box were great, and I want you to try the new blind we've built in the creek.' And he was so insistent that they try at least an hour over the water that Pusey went to the phone and called his wife. 'Thee isn't to worry, dear. We shot nothing this morning but we're going to try the creek for an hour or so. Brutus won't let me come home till we get something.' He was about to hang up, when he added rapidly, 'Amanda, guess what! Clara Steed's flying home this afternoon. From Paris.' After he replaced the phone he told the Steeds, 'Amanda says how lucky thee is. We haven't seen our boys in ages.' This comment on families encouraged him to make his final observation on Watergate: 'In Georgia this afternoon many families must be boasting about their sons in Washington. Six years from now some of them may be in jail.'

The two men took their dogs to a spot near the confluence of the creeks, a place where Pentaquod had hunted nearly four hundred years ago. Out in the water, pilings had been sunk to support the kind of rude river house so often depicted when the *National Geographic* dealt with Malaysia or Borneo. Approach was made by small boat, into which the dogs leaped with enthusiasm and from which they sprang into the house. The two men climbed up after them, and the hunt resumed.

Steed had been right; with the sun blotted out, geese began to fly in search of one last meal, and before an hour had passed, one flight of nine came straight at the blind, and each man knocked one down. 'Get 'em!' Steed called to the dogs, but the admonition was unnecessary, for at the first flutter of a downward wing, the animals sprang into the water, swimming with abandon toward the fallen birds, and each retrieved perfectly, splashing back into the blind with the geese.

'We'd better call it a day,' Steed suggested, but Paxmore was so pleased with the hunting, and the performance of his dog, that he proposed they stay till dusk, and Steed had to remind him of the incoming plane.

'How thoughtless!' Paxmore cried. 'Of course thee must go. But I'd like to stay. Thee can pick me up when thee gets back.'

'I'll do better. I'll walk to the house, leave the pickup here for you. Drive home when you like.'

For the first time since his release from Scanderville Prison, Pusey Paxmore was alone, totally alone. Occasionally during the past months Amanda had driven into Patamoke without him, but because she knew how perilous his memories were, she had always notified someone that Pusey was by himself. Mysteriously, friends would drop by to talk of shipbuilding days, or Washburn Turlock would drive up the lane with clients who wanted to see a telescope house. He was never allowed to be alone.

In many ways it was a relief to be there in the blind, without prying questions or consoling assurances. This was the Chesapeake, timeless source of Paxmore vitality. It was to this creek that the first boatbuilders had come, seeking their oaks and the twisted knees from which their craft were built. A flock of geese flew overhead, but he did not bother to point his gun. Brutus, seeing the birds pass unmolested, began to whimper and tug at his master's sleeve.

Pusey paid no attention because he was again mouthing the platitudes which had recently sustained him: In 1969 America was in peril . . . Revolutionaries were burning our cities . . . The money I collected was for a good cause.

Even the sound of a flock of geese passing overhead did not break this rosary of shabby beads. The birds were too distant for a shot, but Brutus saw his master's inattention and grew uneasy; when five headed straight for the blind without awakening a response, he barked.

Paxmore did not hear, for he had reached a crisis in his self-examination: Perhaps I really was as pitiful as I appeared. When he attempted an excuse, he found himself trapped at the end of a long corridor from which there was no escape, so with cruel honesty he muttered the truth, 'I began service at the White House possessing the staunchest American virtues, and I sacrificed every one to expediency. Woolman Paxmore and Aunt Emily provided me with the strongest moral armor. Piece by piece I tossed it aside. And to what exalted purpose?'

The inescapable answer came harshly: To perpetuate in power men eager to destroy the bases of this nation.

He could not avoid assessing himself: They judged me to be of such trivial value that they could find no reason to defend me. Was their horrible summary correct? *That fucking Bible-spouting asshole.* Oh, Jesus! What have I done?

His disintegration was so complete that nothing could save him—not his faith, nor the love of his friends, nor even the cool waters of the Chesapeake. His horrible mistake had been to abandon the land which had nurtured him; men are not obligated to cling forever to the piece of land that bore them, but they had better pay attention to the principles they derived from it. To end one's life as Pusey Paxmore was finishing his was to end on a garbage heap.

End one's life! Was this the ignoble end, here in a goose blind on a cold afternoon?

There were reasons to think that an end to it all might be desirable: the shame that could not be erased; the jail sentence so justified in law; the rejection by those he had served; above all, the humiliation he had brought his family. These were punishments so terrible that mere death would be a release.

But there were also good reasons to reject the idea: the unfaltering love of his wife . . . He need enumerate no more. To his mind came the words of a hymn he had so often sung at Harvard:

The shadow of a mighty rock
Within a weary land.

No description could more perfectly summarize the character of his wife; she had warned him against Washington, had notified him of the dangers he faced in a White House lacking moral fiber, and had never said I told you so: If I had listened to her, it wouldn't have happened.

But this very acknowledgment of her strength excused him from basing his decision on what its effects might be on her: She'll survive. She isn't the shadow of a rock. She is the rock. And he dismissed her from his calculations.

It was the end of the day, the end of November, that tenuous and dangerous month. It was the end of a life spent in wrong directions and he could find no justification for its continuance.

Lowering his shotgun from the edge of the blind, where geese flew past with impunity, he wedged its stock on the floor between his booted feet. Bringing the muzzle up under his chin, he reached down with his right forefinger, located the trigger—and with neither regret nor hesitation, pulled it.

Voyage Fourteen: 1978

THE WORST STORMS TO STRIKE THE CHESAPEAKE are the hurricanes which generate in the Caribbean and seem to reach the bay about every twenty years. But there are also lesser storms which roar in from the Atlantic bearing vast quantities of water and winds of crushing power.

Such storms appear yearly, sweeping ashore at Norfolk in huge waves that engulf inattentive watermen. Within a space of five minutes a wind of more than eighty miles an hour will blow in, capable of capsizing even the largest craft. In 1977 one such storm destroyed a skipjack—six men drowned; a crabber—four lost; a rowboat out of Patamoke—two dead.

In November 1977 one of these storms roiled about the Atlantic for some days, hovering just south of Norfolk, and apprehensive watermen offered predictions as to whether it would ride high into Pennsylvania, inundating the valleys again, or remain low so that the Chesapeake would catch the brunt.

'Looks to stay aloft,' said Martin Caveny, brother to the priest.

'And if it does,' his friend Amos Turlock predicted, 'the bay gets flushed out again.'

'The bay recovers. Them crabs and arsters knows how to pertect themselves.'

'Did Mrs. Paxmore want us to supervise everything? I mean the barge and all?'

'She did,' Caveny said.

'You think the storm'll hold off till we get to Patamoke and back?'

Before volunteering an answer that might later be used against him, Caveny studied the heavy black sky. Moving his position so that he could see the jagged remnants of Devon Island, he watched the manner in which forerunners of the impending storm teased at the ruins of Rosalind's Revenge. 'Won't reach here before dusk.'

'We'll chance it,' Turlock said. 'Boats was Pusey's fambly business, and we wouldn't be buryin' him today if he'd stuck with 'em.'

'She'll insist on a boat,' Caveny said, 'barrin' a hurricane.'

'And a hurricane is what we'll be gettin',' Turlock said. 'Around midnight.' Hearing a noise, he turned to see the widow leave the telescope house. 'Here she comes, stern as ever.'

'Who has a better right? Television reviewing everything? Pictures of Scanderville and all that?'

'She don't give a damn about such stuff.'

'Everybody gives a damn. Wouldn't you?'

'I wouldn't of been in jail. Us Turlocks don't never overreach our position.'

'You think Pusey did?'

'If he'd of stayed home,' Turlock said, 'he wouldn't of landed in jail.'

Mrs. Paxmore came up to the watermen and studied the horizon. 'Do we get a howler?'

'We do,' Turlock said.

'How soon?'

'Not before sunset,' Amos said. 'In his opinion, that is.'

She turned to Caveny. 'Can we make it to Patamoke? I'm not worried about getting back.'

'I promise you we'll get there,' Caveny said. 'After the funeral we'll discuss about makin' it home.'

'Sounds sensible. We'll bring the coffin down at ten.'

She was about to leave when Caveny stopped her. 'Would you like us to wear black?'

Thinking that she was helping them to avoid embarrassment in case they had no black clothes, she said, 'I think not. A burial is an incident in living . . .'

'We have black suits, you know.'

'Oh! I would like it so much if thee wore black. It would be'—she found no satisfactory adjective and ended—'appropriate.'

At nine-thirty she called to the two men, now in their best, 'We'll bring the casket,' and they joined the two Paxmore boys, who had come home for the funeral. As they carried the casket to the barge the young men asked casually, 'Catches been good this year?'

'Never enough,' Turlock said.

'Is the Kepone from Virginia ruining the bay?'

'Ever'thing Virginia does ruins the bay,' Turlock said, reviving ancestral animosities.

'All your folks buried at Patamoke?' Caveny asked.

'They are.'

'Shame about your father.'

'It was. A damned shame, and nothing could have prevented it.'

'You think Nixon threw him to the wolves?'

'No, like all of us, we throw ourselves. But the wolves are waiting.'

When the casket was secure in the bottom of the barge, folding canvas chairs were provided for Mrs. Paxmore and the wives of the two sons. Turlock started the engine, and the long last voyage to the Quaker burying ground was begun, but as the barge drew away from the dock, three others fell in behind, and in the last one Amanda saw four members of the Cater family: Captain Absalom, his wife, a daughter and, to everyone's surprise, his cousin Hiram, dark and silent after his years in prison. The blacks said nothing, made no sign of recognition, simply clung to the cortege. It was an oral tradition in their family, revered like a passage from the Bible, that in hard times the Paxmores could be relied upon, and not even the fact that dead Pusey Paxmore had set the F.B.I. on Hiram's trail was enough to keep that young man from the funeral. When the barge reached Patamoke, he and Absalom stepped forward to help carry the casket to the graveyard; they would allow no taxi or truck to do that work.

Remarks at the grave would have been brief, in the Quaker manner, except that Father Patrick, an old man now, appeared unexpectedly to offer a short prayer which became a long one: 'He was never a Catholic, but he proved himself a friend to all who were. One of his ancestors built this meeting house, but Pusey gave us the money to rebuild our church. Blood will tell, and many's the time I was able to find help at his house when I could get but little among my own worshippers.' On and on he went, reviewing Pusey's life and uttering those relevant truths which others had been afraid to speak because of the tragic nature of his suicide.

'He was not only a generous man,' Father Caveny concluded, 'but a gallant one. When the nation needed him, he served. When his commander required a cover, he provided it. Little good it did him, little help he got from those he supported. We bury our friend Pusey with love and remembrance. No man or woman standing by this grave was ever poorer for what he did. Let those who loved him be the ones to place him in his final resting place.'

With that, he defiantly grabbed a shovel, even though he knew his own church looked sternly upon suicide, and tossed a meed of earth onto the coffin. With studied care he passed the spade along to Hiram Cater, to Martin Caveny, to Amos Turlock and, finally, to the Paxmore boys. So Pusey was buried among sea captains who had sailed to London and Barbados, among those unpretentious heroes who had resisted King George, and with the forgotten farmers and merchants who had made the Eastern Shore a place of dignity.

Following the funeral, a small reception was held at the home of a

Quaker family. There the Paxmores and the watermen discussed whether a boat trip back to Peace Cliff was feasible, and it became apparent that Mrs. Paxmore hoped to return by boat, even if a risk was involved—'Pusey loved this river.'

Her sons were dubious. 'This is bound to be a real storm, Mother. Thee shouldn't risk it.'

'Thee may be right. Take the girls back in the car. As for me, if Amos and Martin are willing . . .'

'He said the storm won't hit till dusk,' Turlock said. 'I'm game.' When Caveny said the same, the trio hurried to the barge, revved the motor and started home.

It was a sad and stately return. Waves were heavy and it took some minutes to clear the harbor and enter the river itself. But it was also a memorable voyage, for the skies were dark as if nature were lamenting the death of a son. The Turlock marshes were gone, of course, buried under a blanket of concrete, but in the woods behind, tall trees tested their crowns against the wind; small boats hurried to shore; geese moved in careful patterns.

During the final leg to Peace Cliff the waves became substantial, dousing the passengers, but when Mrs. Paxmore turned to wipe her face she discovered that the barge was not alone; trailing it came the smaller boat of the Cater family, on guard to see the Paxmores safely home before making the long run back to Patamoke.

It was late afternoon when Amos Turlock pulled the barge up to the Paxmore wharf, and when Amanda Paxmore was safely ashore, he said something which betrayed the anxiety he had felt during the last fifteen minutes of the trip: 'Caveny, let's hide this boat inland as far as we can get. This storm's risin' fast.'

'Is it to be a hurricane?' Amanda asked as she stamped her feet to squeeze out the water.

'Could be,' Turlock said briefly.

'Then we must bring the Caters in, too.' And she went to the end of the wharf, shouting and waving to the black people in their small boat, but they were determined to make it back to Patamoke; when they tried to enter the Choptank, however, great waves rolled toward them and it was futile to persist. Turning quickly, they scuttled back to the wharf, where Mrs. Paxmore helped them come ashore.

'This will be a blower,' Captain Absalom said, and he was right. Discharging no lightning or thunder, the clouds dropped so low they seemed to touch the waves they had created, and night fell a good hour earlier than normal, with enormous sheets of rain slanting down.

The five Paxmores, the two watermen and the four blacks gathered together in the front room at Peace Cliff, but it was so exposed to the fury of the storm that the large windows began to leak, and everyone had to find refuge in the kitchen; this provided little reassurance, for the lights went out, and in darkness the huddling figures could hear the wind ripping away the shutters, sending them crashing through the night.

'In the old days,' Amanda said, 'we'd have interpreted this as God's anger over the death of a great man. Tonight all we can say is what Mr. Caveny just said, "This is one hell of a storm." '

Through the bleak November night it continued, and toward four in the morning, when it reached a howling climax, one of the young wives, a Southern Baptist from Alabama, asked plaintively, 'Would it be all right if I prayed?' and Amanda said, 'I've been praying for some time.' This reminded the Baptist girl that Quakers prayed silently, and she asked, 'I mean . . . a real prayer . . . out loud?'

'Betsy,' Amanda said, 'we'll all pray with thee,' and she anticipated some tremendous religious statement, but the girl merely knelt beside her chair and in flickering candlelight said, 'Dear God, protect the men caught on the bay.'

'I'll say Amen to that,' Martin Caveny said, crossing himself.

'And so will I,' added one of the Paxmore boys.

At dawn the storm abated, and in full light they all went out to survey the wreckage and find what consolation they could: the barge thrown thirty feet into a field (but not smashed); the dock quite swept away (but the pilings still firmly in place); two of the large windows smashed (but they were insured); a substantial chunk of shoreline eaten away (but it could be rebuilt behind palisades); and many stately trees knocked so flat that no salvage was possible.

'We'd best see what's happened elsewhere,' one of the boys suggested, so Amos Turlock loaded a truck with ropes, crowbars, shovels and field glasses and led an expedition to Caveny's home, which had been roughed up but not destroyed. At the Turlock trailer he was aghast at the damage; of his twenty-one major statues, seven had been crushed by falling branches, but he found easement when he saw that the three dwarfs guarding the sunken gun remained at their post.

The truck could not enter Patamoke, trees barred the way, so they doubled back to Peace Cliff, where, from a height, they could survey the mouth of the Choptank and see the various boats driven inland by the storm. They were starting to inspect the opposite shore when Amos Turlock, using his binoculars, uttered a loud cry: 'Look at Devon!'

Everyone turned toward the island that guarded the river, and Caveny said, 'I don't see anything wrong.' He grabbed the glasses, stared westward and said in a low voice, 'Jee—sus!'

One of the Paxmore wives also looked toward the ruins she had sketched only two days ago. Saying nothing, she passed the binoculars to her husband.

He looked for a moment, lowered the glasses to check with his naked eye and said, 'It's gone. It's all gone.'

'What's gone?' his brother asked. And then, without need of assistance, he studied the turbulent waters and stood transfixed by what the storm had done.

The island had vanished. Above the crashing waves, where splendid fields had once prospered, there was nothing. On the spot where the finest mansion on the Eastern Shore had offered its stately silhouette, nothing was visible. The final storm which overtakes all existence had struck; that relentless erosion which wears down even mountains had completed its work. Devon Island and all that pertained to it was gone.

Incessant waves which eleven thousand years ago had delivered detritus to this spot, causing an island to be born, had come back to retrieve their loan. The soil they took would be moved to some other spot along the Chesapeake, there to be utilized in some new fashion for perhaps a thousand years, after which the waves would borrow it again, using and reusing until that predictable day when the great world-ocean would sweep in to reclaim this entire peninsula, where for a few centuries life had been so pleasant.

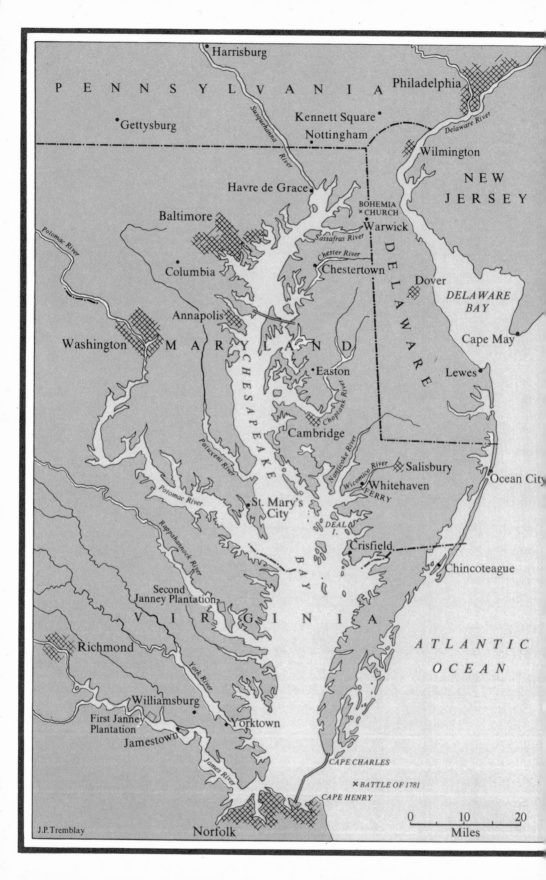

PENNSYLVANIA

• Harrisburg

• Philadelphia

• Gettysburg

• Kennett Square
Nottingham

Delaware River

Susquehanna River

• Wilmington

• Havre de Grace

NEW
JERSEY

BOHEMIA
× CHURCH

Warwick

Baltimore

Sassafras River

Chester River

• Chestertown

• Dover

DELAWARE
BAY

• Columbia

DELAWARE

Annapolis

M A R Y L A N D

• Cape May

Washington

• Easton

• Lewes

CHESAPEAKE

Choptank River

Patuxent River

Cambridge

Nanticoke River

Salisbury

Wicomico River

Ocean City

Potomac River

Whitehaven
FERRY

St. Mary's
City

*DEAL
I.*

Rappahannock River

BAY

Crisfield

Chincoteague

Second
Janney Plantation

V I R G I N I A

ATLANTIC

OCEAN

Richmond

York River

Williamsburg

• Yorktown

First Janney
Plantation
Jamestown

James River

CAPE CHARLES

× *BATTLE OF 1781*

CAPE HENRY

J.P. Tremblay

Norfolk

0   10   20
Miles